P9-DGH-839

Morris West

Morris West

The Devil's Advocate

The Second Victory
Backlash

Daughter of Silence

The Salamander

The Shoes of the Fisherman

Octopus / Heinemann

The Devil's Advocate was first published in the United States
by William Morrow & Co Inc in 1959; in Great Britain by William Heinemann Ltd in 1959.
The Second Victory was first published in the United States (as *Backlash*)
by William Morrow & Co Inc in 1958; in Great Britain by William Heinemann Ltd in 1958.
Daughter of Silence was first published in the United States
by William Morrow & Co Inc in 1961; in Great Britain by William Heinemann Ltd in 1961.
The Salamander was first published in the United States
by William Morrow & Co Inc in 1973; in Great Britain by William Heinemann Ltd in 1973.
The Shoes of the Fisherman was first published in the United States
by William Morrow & Co Inc in 1963; in Great Britain by William Heinemann Ltd in 1963.

This edition first published in the United States of America
in 1980 jointly by

William Heinemann Inc
450 Park Avenue, New York, NY 10022

and

Octopus Books Inc
747 Third Avenue, New York, NY 10017
ISBN 0 905712 17 X

This edition first published in Great Britain in 1977

Printed in the United States of America
by R. R. Donnelley and Sons Company.

The
Devil's Advocate

I

It was his profession to prepare other men for death; it shocked him to be so unready for his own.

He was a reasonable man and reason told him that a man's death sentence is written on his palm the day he is born; he was a cold man, little troubled by passion, irked not at all by discipline, yet his first impulse had been a wild clinging to the illusion of immortality.

It was part of the decency of Death that he should come unheralded with face covered and hands concealed, at the hour when he was least expected. He should come slowly, softly, like his brother Sleep–or swiftly and violently like the consummation of the act of love, so that the moment of surrender would be a stillness and a satiety instead of a wrenching separation of spirit and flesh.

The decency of Death. It was the thing men hoped for vaguely, prayed for if they were disposed to pray, regretted bitterly when they knew it would be denied them. Blaise Meredith was regretting it now, as he sat in the thin spring sunshine, watching the slow, processional swans on the Serpentine, the courting couples on the grass, the leashed poodles trotting fastidiously along the paths at the flirting skirts of their owners.

In the midst of all this life–the thrusting grass, the trees bursting with new sap, the nodding of crocus and daffodil, the languid love-play of youth, the vigour of the elderly strollers–he alone, it seemed, had been marked to die. There was no mistaking the urgency or the finality of the mandate. It was written, for all to read, not in the lines of his palm, but in the square sheet of photographic negative where a small grey blur spelt out his sentence.

'Carcinoma!' The blunt finger of the surgeon had lingered a moment on the centre of the grey blur, then moved outwards tracing the diffusion of the tumour. 'Slow-growing but well established. I've seen too many to be mistaken in this one.'

As he watched the small translucent screen, and the spatulate finger moving across it, Blaise Meredith had been struck by the irony of the situation. All his life had been spent confronting others with the truth about themselves, the guilts that harried them, the lusts that debased them, the follies that diminished them. Now he was looking into his own guts where a small malignancy was growing like a mandrake root towards the day when it would destroy him.

He asked calmly enough.

'Is it operable?'

The surgeon switched off the light behind the viewing screen so that the small grey death faded into opacity; then he sat down, adjusting the desk lamp so that his own face was in shadow and that of his patient was lit like a marble head in a museum.

Blaise Meredith noted the small contrivance and understood it. They were both professional. Each in his own calling dealt with human animals. Each must preserve a clinical detachment, lest he spend too much of himself and be left as weak and fearful as his patients.

The surgeon leaned back in his chair, picked up a paper-knife and held it poised as delicately as a scalpel. He waited a moment, gathering the words, choosing this one, discarding that, then laying them down in a pattern of meticulous accuracy.

'I can operate, yes. If I do, you'll be dead in three months.'

'If you don't?'

'You'll live a little longer and die a little more painfully.'

'How much longer?'

'Six months. Twelve at the outside.'

'It's a grim choice.'

'You must make it yourself.'

'I understand that.'

The surgeon relaxed in his chair. The worst was over now. He had not been mistaken in his man. He was intelligent, ascetic, self-contained. He would survive the shock and accommodate himself to the inevitable. When the agony began he would wear it with a certain dignity. His Church would guarantee him against want and bury him with honour when he died; and, if there were none to mourn him, this too might be counted the final reward for celibacy, to slip out of life without regret for its pleasures or fear of its unfulfilled obligations.

Blaise Meredith's calm, dry voice cut across his thought:

'I'll think about what you've told me. In case I should decide not to have an operation–go back to my work–would you be good enough to write me a report to my local doctor? A full prognosis, a prescription, perhaps?'

'With pleasure, Monsignor Meredith. You work in Rome, I believe? Unfortunately I don't write Italian.'

Blaise Meredith permitted himself a small wintry smile.

'I'll translate it myself. It should make an interesting exercise.'

'I admire your courage, Monsignor. I don't subscribe to the Roman faith, or to any faith for that matter, but I imagine you find it a great consolation at a time like this.'

'I hope I may, Doctor,' said Blaise Meredith simply, 'but I've been a priest too long to expect it.'

Now he was sitting on a park bench in the sun, with the air full of spring and the future a brief, empty prospect spilling over into eternity. Once, in his student days, he had heard an old missioner preach on the raising of Lazarus from the dead: how Christ had stood before the sealed vault and ordered it to be opened, so that the smell of corruption issued on the still, dry air of summer; how Lazarus at the summons had come out, stumbling in the cerecloths, to stand blinking in the sun. What had he felt at that moment, the old man asked? What price had he paid for this return to the world of the living? Did he go maimed ever afterwards, so that every rose smelled of decay and every golden girl was a shambling skeleton? Or did he walk in a dazzle of wonder at the newness of things, his heart tender with pity and love for the human family?

The speculation had interested Meredith for years. Once he had toyed with the idea of writing a novel about it. Now, at last, he had the answer. Nothing was so sweet to man as life; nothing was more precious than time; nothing more reassuring than the touch of earth and grass, the whisper of moving air, the smell of new blossoms, the sound of voices and traffic and high bird-songs.

This was the thing that troubled him. He had been twenty years a priest, vowed to the affirmation that life was a transient imperfection, the earth a pale symbol of its maker, the soul an immortal in mortal clay, beating itself weary for release into the ambient arms of the Almighty. Now that his own release was promised, the date of it set, why could he not accept it—if not with joy, at least with confidence?

What did he cling to that he had not long since rejected? A woman? A child? A family? There was no one living who belonged to him. Possessions? They were few enough—a small apartment near the Porta Angelica, a few ornaments, a roomful of books, a modest stipend from the Congregation of Rites, an annuity left to him by his mother. Nothing there to tempt a man back from the threshold of the great revelation. Career? Something in that maybe—Auditor to the Sacred Congregation of Rites, personal assistant to the Prefect himself, Eugenio Cardinal Marotta. It was a position of influence, of flattering confidence. One sat in the shadow of the Pontiff. One watched the intricate, subtle workings of a great theocracy. One lived in simple comfort. One had time to study, liberty to act freely within the limits of policy and discretion. Something in that . . . but not enough—not half enough for a man who hungered for the Perfect Union which he preached.

Perhaps that was the core of it. He had never been hungry for anything. He had always had everything he wanted, and he had never wanted more than was available to him. He had accepted the discipline of the Church, and the Church had given him security, comfort and scope for his talents. More than most men he had achieved contentment—and if he had never asked for happiness it was because he had never been unhappy. Until now . . . until this bleak moment in the sun, the first of spring, the last spring ever for Blaise Meredith.

The last spring, the last summer. The butt end of life chewed and sucked dry like a sugar stick, then tossed on to the rubbish heap. There was the bitterness, the sour taste of failure and disillusion. What of merit could he tally and take with him to the judgment? What would he leave behind for which men would want to remember him?

He had never fathered a child nor planted a tree, nor set one stone on another for house or monument. He had spent no anger, dispensed no charity. His work would moulder anonymously in the archives of the Vatican. Whatever virtue had flowered out of his ministry was sacramental and not personal. No poor would bless him for their bread, no sick for their courage, no sinners for their salvation. He had done everything that was demanded of him, yet he would die empty and within a month his name would be a blown dust on the desert of the centuries.

Suddenly he was terrified. A cold sweat broke out on his body. His hands began to tremble and a group of children bouncing a ball near a bench edged away from the gaunt, grey-faced cleric who sat staring with blind eyes across the shimmering water of the pond.

The rigors passed slowly. The terror abated and he was calm again. Reason took hold of him and he began to think how he should order his life for the time left to him.

When he had become ill in Rome, when the Italian physicians had made their first, tentative diagnosis, his instinctive decision had been to return to London. If he must be condemned, he preferred to have the sentence read in his own tongue. If his time must be shortened, then he wanted to spend the last of it in the soft air of England, to walk the downs and the beechwoods and hear the elegiac song of the nightingales in the shadow of old churches, where Death was more familiar and more friendly because the English had spent centuries teaching him politeness.

In Italy, death was harsh, dramatic–a grand-opera exit, with wailing chorus and tossing plumes and black baroque hearses trundling past stucco palaces to the marble vaults of the Campo Santo. Here in England it had a gentler aspect–the obits murmured discreetly in a Norman nave, the grave opened in mown grass among weathered headstones, the libations poured in the oak-beamed pub which stood opposite the lych-gate.

Now this, too, was proved an illusion, a pathetic fallacy, no armour at all against the grey insidious enemy entrenched in his own belly. He could not escape it, any more than he could flee the conviction of his own failure as a priest and as a man.

What then? Submit to the knife? Cut short the agony, truncate the fear and the loneliness to a manageable limit? Would not this be a new failure, a kind of suicide that the moralists might justify, but conscience could never quite condone? He had enough debts already to bring to the reckoning; this last might make him altogether bankrupt.

Go back to work? Sit at the old desk under the coffered ceiling in the Palace of Congregations in Rome. Open up the vast folios where the lives and works and writings of long-dead candidates for canonisation were recorded in the script of a thousand clerks. Examine them, dissect them, analyse and notate. Call their virtues in question and cast new doubts on the wonders attributed to them. Make new notes in a new script. To what end? That one more candidate for canonical honours might be rejected because he had been less than heroic, or less than wise in his virtues; or that half a century hence, two centuries maybe, a new Pope might proclaim in St Peter's that a new saint had been added to the Calendar.

Did they care, these dead ones, what he wrote of them? Did they care whether a new statue were permitted to wear an aureole, or whether the printers circulated a million little cards with their faces on the front and their virtues listed on the back? Did they smile on their bland biographers or frown on their official detractors? They had died and been judged long since, as he must die and soon be judged. The rest was all addendum, postscript and dispensable. A new cultus, a new pilgrimage, a new mass in the liturgy would touch them not at all. Blaise Meredith, priest, philosopher, canonist, might work twelve months or twelve years on their records without adding a jot to their felicity, or a single pain to their damnation.

Yet this was his work and he must do it, because it lay ready to his hand–and because he was too tired and too ill to begin any other. He would say Mass each day, work out his daily stint at the Palace of Congregations, preach occasionally in the English Church, hear confessions for a colleague on vacation, go back each night to his small apartment at the Porta Angelica, read a little, say his office, then struggle through the restless nights to the sour morning. For twelve months. Then he would be dead. For a week they would name him in the Masses . . . 'our brother Blaise Meredith': then he would join the anonymous and the forgotten in the general remembrance . . . 'all the faithful departed.'

It was cold in the park now. The lovers were brushing the grass off their coats and the girls were smoothing down their skirts. The children were dragging listlessly down the paths in the wake of scolding parents. The swans were ruffling back to the shelter of the islets, to the peak-hour drone of London traffic.

Time to go. Time for Monsignor Blaise Meredith to pack his troubled thoughts and compose his thin features into a courteous smile for the Administrator's tea at Westminster. The English were a civil and tolerant people. They expected a man to work out his salvation soberly or damn himself with discretion, to hold his liquor like a gentleman and keep his troubles to himself. They were suspicious of saints and chary of mystics, and they more than half-believed that God Almighty felt the same way. Even in the hour of his private Gethsemane, Meredith was glad of the convention that would force him to forget himself and attend to the chatter of his colleagues.

He got up stiffly from the bench, stood a long moment as if unsure of his own tenancy in the body, then walked steadily down towards Brompton Road.

Doctor Aldo Meyer had his own preoccupations this mild Mediterranean evening. He was trying to get drunk—as quickly and painlessly as possible.

All the odds were against him. The place where he drank was a low stone room with an earthen floor that stank of stale wine. His company was a brutish peasant proprietor and a stocky mountain girl with the neck and buttocks of an ox and melon breasts straining out of a greasy black dress. The drink was a fiery *grappa*, guaranteed to drown the stubbornest sorrow—but Aldo Meyer was too temperate and too intelligent to enjoy it.

He sat hunched forward over the rough bench, with a guttering candle beside him, staring into his cup and tracing monotonous patterns in the spilt liquor that flowed sluggishly in the wake of his finger. The *padrone* leaned on the bar, picking his teeth with a twig and sucking the remnants of his supper noisily through the gaps. The girl sat in the shadows waiting to fill the cup as soon as the doctor had emptied it. He had drunk swiftly at first, gulping on each mouthful, then more slowly as the raw spirit took hold of him. For the last ten minutes he had not drunk at all. It was as if he were waiting for something to happen before making the final surrender to forgetfulness.

He was a year short of fifty, but he looked like an old man. His hair was white, the skin of his fine Jewish face was drawn tight and spare over the bones. His hands were long and supple, but horned like a labourer's. He wore a townsman's suit of unfashionable cut, with frayed cuffs and shiny lapels, but his shoes were polished and his linen clean, save for the fresh stains where the *grappa* had splashed. There was an air of faded distinction about him which matched oddly with the crudeness of his surroundings and the coarse vitality of the girl and the *padrone*.

Gemello Minore was a long way from Rome, longer still from London. The dingy wine-shop bore no resemblance at all to the Palace of Congregations. Yet Doctor Aldo Meyer was concerned with death like Blaise Meredith, and, sceptic though he was, he too found himself embroiled with Beatitude.

Late in the afternoon he had been called to the house of Pietro Rossi, whose wife had been in labour for ten hours. The midwife was in despair and the room was full of women chattering like hens, while Maria Rossi groaned and writhed in her spasms, then relapsed into weak moaning when they left her. Outside the hovel the men were grouped, talking in low voices and passing a wine bottle from hand to hand.

When he came they fell silent, watching him with oblique, speculative eyes, while Pietro Rossi led him inside. He had lived among them for twenty years, yet he was still a foreigner; in these moments of their tribal life he might be necessary to them, but he was never welcome.

In the room with the women, it was the same story: silence, suspicion, hostility. When he bent over the great brass bed, palpating and probing the swollen body, the midwife and the girl's mother stood close beside him, and when a new spasm came, there was a shocked murmur, as if he were the cause of it.

Within three minutes he knew there was no hope of normal birth. He would have to do a Caesarean. He was not unduly perturbed at the prospect. He had done them before, by candlelight and lamplight, on kitchen tables and plank benches. Given boiling water and anaesthetic and the tough bodies of the mountain women, the odds were loaded in the patient's favour.

He expected protests. These people were thick-headed as mules and twice as panicky—but he was unprepared for an outburst. It was the girl's mother who began it—a stout, muscular shrew, with lank hair and gapped teeth and black snake eyes. She rounded on him, yelling in thick dialect:

'I'll have no knives in my girl's belly. I want live grandchildren, not dead ones! You doctors are all the same. If you can't cure people you cut 'em up and bury 'em. Not my daughter! Give her time and she'll pop this one out like a pea. I've had twelve of 'em. I ought to know. Not all of 'em were easy, but I had 'em—and I didn't need a horse-butcher to gouge 'em out either!'

A burst of shrill laughter drowned the moaning of the girl. Aldo Meyer stood watching her, ignoring the women. He said simply:

'If I don't operate, she'll be dead by midnight.'

It had worked before—the bald professional pronouncement, the contempt for their ignorance—but this time it failed utterly. The woman laughed in his face.

'Not this time, Jew-man! Do you know why?' She plunged her hand inside her dress and brought up a small object wrapped in faded red silk. Her fingers closed over it and she thrust it under his nose. 'You know what that is? You wouldn't of course—you being an infidel and Christ-killer. We've got a saint of our own now. A real one! They're fixing to have him canonised in Rome any minute. That's a piece of his shirt. A real live relic, stained with his blood. He's worked miracles too. Real ones. They're all written down. They've been sent on to the Pope. Do you think you can do more than he can? Do you? Which do we choose, folks? Our own Saint Giacomo Nerone—or this fellow!'

The girl on the bed screamed in sudden agony and the women fell silent, while the mother bent over the bed making little soothing noises and rubbing the dingy relic round and round on the swollen belly under the coverlets. Aldo Meyer waited a moment, searching for the right words. Then, when the girl was quiet again, he told them soberly:

'Even an infidel knows that to expect miracles without trying to help ourselves is a sin. You can't throw away medicines and expect the saints to cure you. Besides, this Giacomo Nerone isn't a saint yet. It will be a long time before they even start to discuss his case in Rome. Pray to him if you want, but ask him to give me a steady hand, and the girl a strong heart. Now stop being silly and get me boiling water and clean linen. I haven't much time.'

No one moved. The mother barred his way to the bed. The women stood ranged in a tight semicircle, shepherding him in the direction of the door, where Pietro Rossi stood, blank-faced, watching the drama. Meyer swung round to challenge him.

'You, Pietro! Do you want a child? Do you want your wife? Then for God's sake listen to me. Unless I operate quickly, she will die and the child will die with her. You know what I can do—there are twenty people in the village to tell you. But you don't know what this Giacomo Nerone can do—even if he is a saint . . . which I very much doubt.'

Pietro Rossi shook his head stubbornly.

''Tisn't natural to rip out a child like a sheep's gut. Besides, this isn't an ordinary saint. He's ours. He belongs to us. He'll look after us. You'd better go, Doctor.'

'If I do, your wife won't see out the night.'

The matt peasant face was blank as a wall. Meyer looked round at them, the dark secret people of the South, and thought despairingly how little he knew of them, how little power he had over them. He made a shrugging gesture of resignation, picked up his bag and walked towards the door. At the threshold he stopped and turned to face them.

'You'd better call Father Anselmo. She hasn't much time.'

The mother spat contemptuously on the floor, then bent down again to rub the little silk bundle on the twitching belly of the girl, mumbling prayers in dialect. The other women watched him, stony-faced and silent. When he walked out and down the cobbled road, he felt the eyes of the men like knives at his back. It was then that he decided to get drunk.

For Aldo Meyer, the old liberal, the man who believed in man, it was the final gesture of defeat. There was no hope for these people. They were rapacious as hawks. They would eat your heart out and let you rot in a ditch. He had suffered for them, fought for them, lived with them and tried to educate them, but they took everything and learned nothing. They made a mockery of the most elementary knowledge, yet lapped up legends and superstitions as greedily as children.

Only the Church could control them, though it could not better them. It plagued them with demons, obsessed them with saints, cajoled them with weeping madonnas and fat-bottomed bambini. It could bleed them white for a new candelabrum, but it could not—or would not—bring them to a clinic for typhoid injections. Their mothers wasted away with TB and their bambini had swollen spleens from recurrent malaria. Yet they would as soon put a devil in their mouths as an Atabrine tablet—even though the doctor paid for it himself.

They lived in hovels where a good farmer would not house his cattle. They ate olives and pasta and bread dipped in oil, and goat meat on feast days, if they could get it. Their hills were bare of trees and their terraces held a niggardly soil, from which the nourishment leached out with the first rains and was lost on the stony slopes. Their wine was thin and their corn was meagre and they moved with the sluggish gait of folk who eat too little and work too hard.

Their landlords exploited them, yet they clung to their coat-tails like children. Their priests lapsed often into liquor and concubinage, yet they fed them out of their poverty and treated them with tolerant contempt. If the summer was late or the winter was harsh, the frost burned the olives and there was hunger in the hills. They had no schools for their children, and what the State would not supply they would not make for themselves. They would not sacrifice their idle hours to build a school-house. They could not pay a teacher, yet they would dig into their tiny hoards of lire to finance the canonisation of a new saint for a Calendar that was already overloaded with them.

Aldo Meyer stared into the dark lees, of his *grappa* to read futility, disillusion and despair. He lifted the cup and tossed off the dregs at a gulp. They were bitter as wormwood and there was no warmth in them at all.

He had come here first as an exile, when the Fascisti had rounded up the Semites and the left-wing intellectuals and the too vocal liberals, and presented them the curt alternative of rustication in Calabria or hard labour on Lipari. They had given him the ironic title of Medical Officer, but no salary, no drugs, and no anaesthetics. He had arrived with the clothes he stood up in, a bag of instruments, a bottle of aspirin tablets and a medical compendium. For six years he battled and intrigued, cajoled and blackmailed to build up a sketchy medical service in an area of constant malnutrition, endemic malaria and epidemic typhoid.

He lived in a crumbling farmhouse which he restored with his own hands. He farmed a stony two acres, with the help of a cretinous labourer. His hospital was one room in his house. His theatre was his kitchen. The peasants paid him in kind, when they paid at all, and he exacted from the local officials a tribute in drugs and surgical instruments, and protection from a hostile Government. It had been a bitter servitude, but there had been moments of triumph, days when he seemed at last to be entering into the closed circle of the primitive mountain life.

When the Allies straddled the Strait of Messina and began their slow bloody progress up the peninsula, he had fled and joined the Partisans, and after the armistice he had spent a brief while in Rome. But he had been away too long. Old friends were dead. New ones were hard to make, and the small triumphs of the locust years challenged him to greater ones. With freedom and money, and the impetus to reform, a man of good will might work miracles in the South.

So he had come back—to the old house, in the old town, with a new dream and a sense of renewed youth in himself. He would become a teacher as well as a doctor. He would lay down a prototype organisation for co-operative effort, an organisation that would attract development money from Rome and aid money from overseas foundations. He would teach them hygiene and the conservation of soil and water. He would train young men who would carry his message to outlying districts. He would be a missioner of progress in a land where progress had stopped three centuries before.

It had been a fine, fresh dream twelve years ago. He knew it now for a bleak illusion. He had fallen into the error of all liberals: the belief that men are prepared to reform themselves, that good will attracts good will, that truth has a leavening virtue of its own. His plans had made shipwreck on the venality of officials, the conservatism of a feudal Church, the rapacity and mistrust of a primitive, ignorant people.

Even through the thick fumes of the liquor he saw all too clearly. They had beaten him. He had beaten himself. And now it was too late to mend.

From the dusk outside came a long, wailing cry of women's voices. The girl and the *padrone* looked at each other and crossed themselves. The doctor stood up and and walked unsteadily to the door to stand looking out into the cool spring twilight.

'She's dead,' said the *padrone* in his thick, husky voice.

'Tell the saint about it,' said Aldo Meyer. 'I'm going to bed.'

As he lurched out into the roadway the girl put out her tongue at him and made the sign against the evil eye.

The dirge-cry rose and fell, whining like a wind over the sleeping mountain. It followed him down the cobbled street and into his house. It battered on his door and searched at his shutters and haunted him through the night of restless, muttering sleep.

In the fall of the same spring dusk, Eugenio Cardinal Marotta walked in the garden of his villa on Parioli. Far below him the city was wakening from the torpor of afternoon and settling back to business with screaming horns and clattering motor-scooters and chaffering shopkeepers. The tourists were trudging remorsefully back from St Peter's and St John Lateran and the Colosseum. The flower sellers were spraying their blooms for the last assault on the lovers of the Spanish Steps. The sunset spilled over the hills and down on to the roof-tops, but down in the alleys the dust-haze hung thickly, and the walls of the buildings were grey and tired.

Up on Parioli, however, the air was clear and the avenues were quiet, and His Eminence walked under drooping palms to the scent of jasmine flowers. There were high walls about him and grilled gates to keep him private, and armorial bronzes on the lintels to remind the visitor of the rank and titles of Eugenio Cardinal Marotta, Archbishop of Acropolis, Titular of St Clement, Prefect of the Sacred Congregation of Rites, Proprefect of the Supreme Tribunal of the Apostolic Signature, Commissioner for the Interpretation of Canon Law, Protector of the Sons of St Joseph and the Daughters of Mary Immaculate and twenty other religious bodies great and small in the Holy Roman Church.

The titles were ample, the power that lay behind them was ample too; but His Eminence wore it with a bland good-humour that masked a subtle intelligence and a dominating will.

He was a short, round man, with small hands and feet and a dewlapped face, and a high domed head, bald as an egg under the scarlet skullcap. His grey eyes twinkled with benevolence and his mouth was small and scarlet as a woman's against the matt olive of his complexion. He was sixty-three years of age, which is young for a man to reach the red hat. He worked hard, though without apparent effort, and still had energy left for the devious diplomacies and manipulations of power inside the closed City of the Vatican.

There were those who favoured him for election to the papacy itself, but there were others, more numerous, who held that the next Pontiff should be a more saintly man, less concerned with diplomacy than with the reform of morals among clergy and laity alike. Eugenio Marotta was content to wait on the outcome, knowing that he who goes into the conclave a Pope is likely to leave it a Cardinal. Besides, the Pontiff might be old, but he was still a long way from dead, and he looked with small favour on those who coveted his shoes.

So His Eminence walked in his villa garden on Parioli, watching the sun decline over the Alban hills and pondering the day's questions in the relaxed attitude of a man who knew he would answer them all in the end.

He could afford to relax. He had come by steady progression to the high plateau of preferment from which neither malice nor disfavour could unseat him. He would remain a Cardinal till the day he died, a Prince by protocol, a Bishop by irrevocable consecration, citizen of the smallest and least vulnerable State in the world. It was much for a man in his vigorous sixties. It was much more, because he was untramelled by a wife, unplagued by sons and daughters, set far beyond the pricks of passion. He had come as far as talent and ambition could drive him.

The next step was the Chair of Peter; but this was a high leap, halfway out of the world and into a vestibule of divinity. The man who wore the Fisherman's ring and the triple tiara carried also the sins of the world like a leaden cope on his shoulders. He stood on a windy pinnacle, alone, with the spread carpet of the nations below him, and above, the naked face of the Almighty. Only a fool would envy him the power and the glory and the terror of such a principality. And Eugenio Cardinal Marotta was very far from being a fool.

In this hour of dusk and jasmine he had problems enough of his own.

Two days before, a letter had been laid on his desk from the Bishop of Valenta, a small diocese in a run-down area of Calabria. The Bishop was known to him vaguely as a rigid reformer with a taste for politics. He had caused a stir two years previously by unfrocking a couple of country curates for concubinage and pensioning off some of his elderly pastors on the grounds of incompetence. The election figures from his diocese had shown a marked swing towards the Christian Democrats, and this had earned him a Pontifical letter of commendation. It was only the more subtle observers like Marotta who had noted that the increase had come from the Monarchist Party and not from the Communists, who had also registered a slight gain. The Bishop's letter was simple and explicit–too simple to be guileless and too explicit not to rouse suspicion in a seasoned campaigner like Eugenio Cardinal Marotta.

It began with salutations, florid and deferential, from a humble bishop to a princely one. It went on to say that a petition had been received from the parish priest and the faithful of the villages of Gemelli dei Monti for the introduction of the Cause for Beatification of the Servant of God, Giacomo Nerone.

This Giacomo Nerone had been murdered by Communist Partisans in circumstances which might well be called martyrdom. Since his death, spontaneous veneration had been paid to him in the villages and the surrounding countryside, and several cures of a miraculous nature were attributed to his influence. Preliminary investigations had confirmed the reputation for sanctity and the apparently miraculous nature of the cures, and the Bishop was disposed to grant the petition and admit the case to juridical investigation. Before doing so, however, he sought counsel of His Eminence, as Prefect of the Congregation of Rites, and his assistance in appointing, from Rome itself, two wise and godly men–one as the Postulator of the Cause, to organise the investigation and carry it forward, the other as the Promoter of the Faith, or Devil's Advocate, to submit the evidence and the witnesses to the severest scrutiny in accordance with the appropriate provisions of canon law.

There was more, much more, but this was the core of the apple. The Bishop might have a saint in his territory–a convenient saint, too, martyred by the Communists. The only way he could prove the sanctity was by a judicial investigation, first in his own diocese and then in Rome, under the authority of the Congregation of Rites. But the first investigation would be made in his own See and under his own authority, with officials appointed by himself. Local bishops were normally jealous of their autonomy. Why then this deferential appeal to Rome?

Eugenio Cardinal Marotta walked the trim lawns of his villa garden and pondered the proposition.

Gemelli dei Monti lay deep in Midday Italy, where cults proliferate and die as quickly, where the Faith is overlaid with a thick patina of superstition, where the peasants make with the same hand the sign of the Cross and the sign against the evil eye, where the picture of the Bambino is hung over the bed and the pagan horns are nailed over the barn door. The Bishop was a canny man who wanted a saint for the good of his diocese, but declined to put his own reputation on trial with that of the Servant of God.

If the investigation went well, he would have not only a *beato*, but a rod to beat the Communists. If it went ill, the wise and godly men from Rome could bear some of the blame. His Eminence chuckled at the subtlety of it. Scratch a Southerner and you found a fox, who smelled out traps a mile away, and trotted around them to the chicken-run.

But there was more at stake than the reputation of a provincial bishop. There was politics involved, and Italian elections were only twelve months away. Public opinion was sensitive to the influence of the Vatican in civil affairs. The anti-clericals would welcome a chance to discredit the Church, and they had enough weapons without putting another into their hands.

There were deeper issues yet, matters less relevant to time than to eternity. To name a man Blessed was to declare him a heroic servant of God, to hold him up as an exemplar and an intercessor for the faithful. To accept his miracles was to admit beyond all doubt the divine power working through him to suspend or cancel the laws of nature. Error in such a matter was unthinkable. The whole massive machinery of the Congregation of Rites was designed to prevent it. But premature action, a botched investigation, could cause grave scandal and weaken the faith of millions in an infallible Church which claimed the direct guidance of the Holy Ghost.

His Eminence shivered as the first chill darkness came down on Parioli. He was a man hardened by power and sceptical of devotion, but he too carried on his shoulders the burden of belief and in his heart the fear of the noonday devil.

He could afford less than others the luxury of error. Much more depended on him. The penalty of failure would be so much more rigorous. In spite of the pomp of his title and the secular dignity which attended it, his prime mission was spiritual. It related to souls—their salvation and damnation. The curse of the millstones could fall equally upon an erring Cardinal and a faithless curate. So he walked and pondered soberly while the faint harmony of bells drifted up from the city and the crickets in the garden began their shrill chorus.

He would grant the Bishop of Valenta his small triumph. He would find the men for him—a Postulator to build the case and present it, a Devil's Advocate to destroy it if he could. Of the two, the Devil's Advocate was the more important. His official title described him accurately: Promoter of the Faith. The man who kept the Faith pure at any cost of broken lives and broken hearts. He must be learned, meticulous, passionless. He must be cold in judgment, ruthless in condemnation. He might lack charity or piety, but he could not lack precision. Such men were rare, and those at his disposal were already occupied on other causes.

Then he remembered Blaise Meredith, the spare, sober man with the greyness of death on him. He had the qualities. He was English, which would remove the taint of political involvement. But whether he had the will or the time left to him was another matter. If the medical verdict were unfavourable he might not feel disposed to accept so heavy an assignment.

Still, it was the beginning of an answer. His Eminence was not unsatisfied. He made one more leisurely circuit of the darkened garden, then walked back to the villa to say vespers with his household.

2

Two days later Eugenio Cardinal Marotta sat in his study chair behind the great buhl desk and talked with Monsignor Blaise Meredith. His Eminence had slept well and breakfasted lightly and his round, good-humoured face was fresh and shining from the razor. In the lofty room, with its coffered ceiling and its Aubusson carpets and its noble portraits in gilded frames, he was invested with the unconscious dignity of possession.

By contrast, the Englishman seemed small and grey and shrunken. His soutane hung loosely on his thin body and the scarlet piping only emphasised the unhealthy pallor of his face. His eyes were clouded with fatigue and there were deep furrows of pain at the corners of his mouth. Even in the brisk, Romanesque Italian his voice was flat and expressionless.

'There it is, Eminence. I have at best, twelve months. Half of that, perhaps, for active work.'

The Cardinal waited a few moments, watching him with detached pity. Then he said gently:

'I grieve for you, my friend. It comes to all of us, of course; but it is always a shock.'

'Yet we of all people should be prepared for it.' The drooping mouth twitched upward into a wry smile.

'No!' Marotta's small hands fluttered in deprecation. 'We mustn't overrate ourselves. We are men like all the others. We are priests by choice and calling. We are celibates by canonical legislation. It is a career, a profession. The powers we exercise, the grace we dispense, are independent of our own worthiness. It is better for us to be saints than sinners–but like our brothers outside the ministry we are generally something in-between.'

'Small comfort, Eminence, when one stands in the shadow of the judgment seat.'

'It is still the truth.' The Cardinal reminded him coolly, 'I've been in the Church a long time, my friend. The higher one climbs the more one sees–and the more clearly. It's a pious legend that the priesthood sanctifies a man, or that celibacy ennobles him. If a priest can keep his hands out of his pockets and his legs out of a woman's bed till he's forty-five, he stands a reasonable chance of doing it till he dies. There are plenty of professional bachelors in the world too. But we are all still subject to pride, ambition, sloth, negligence, avarice. Often it's harder for us to save our souls than it is for others. A man with a family must make sacrifices, impose a discipline on his desires, practise love and patience. We may sin less, yet have less merit in us at the end.'

'I am very empty,' said Blaise Meredith. 'There is no evil that I repent and no good that I count. I have had nothing to fight. I cannot show even scars.'

The Cardinal leaned back in his chair, toying with the big yellow stone on his episcopal ring. The only sound in the room was the soft ticking of an ormolu clock on the marble mantel. After a while he said thoughtfully:

'I can release you now if you wish, I can provide you with a pension from the funds of the Congregation. You could live quietly. . . .'

Blaise Meredith shook his head.

'It's a great kindness, Eminence, but I have no talent for contemplation. I should prefer to go on working.'

'You will have to stop one day. After that?'

'I shall go into hospital. I understand I shall suffer a good deal. Then . . .' He spread his hands in a gesture of defeat. '*Finita la commedia.* If it were not too much to ask, I should like to be buried in Your Eminence's church.'

In spite of himself Marotta was touched by the bleak courage of the man. He was tired and sick. The worst of his Calvary was yet to come, yet he was walking towards it with a desolate dignity that was typically English. Before the Cardinal had time to comment, Meredith went on.

'In all this, of course, I assume that Your Eminence wants to use me. I . . . I'm afraid I can't guarantee the best of service.'

'You have always done better than you knew, my friend,' said Marotta gently, 'you have always given more than you promised. Besides there is a matter in which you can help me greatly–and perhaps–' he paused as if struck by an odd afterthought–'perhaps help yourself too.'

Then, without waiting for an answer, he told him of the petition of the Bishop of Valenta, and his need of a Devil's Advocate in the cause of Giacomo Nerone.

Meredith listened, intent as a lawyer on the details of a new brief. A new life seemed to take possession of him. His eyes brightened, he straightened in his chair and a small tinge of colour crept into his faded cheeks. Eugenio Marotta noted it but made no comment. When he had finished his outline of the situation he asked:

'Well, what do you think of it?'

'An indiscretion,' said Meredith precisely. 'It's a political move and I distrust it.'

'Everything in the Church is political,' Marotta reminded him mildly. 'Man is a political animal who has an immortal soul. You cannot divide him–any more than you can divide the Church into separate and unrelated functions. Everything the Church does is designed to give a spiritual character to a material development. We name a saint as patron of television. What does it mean? A new symbol of an old truth: that every lawful activity is conducive to good or can be perverted to evil.'

'Too many symbols can cloud the face of reality,' said Blaise Meredith dryly. 'Too many saints can bring sanctity into disrepute. I've always thought that was our function at the Congregation of Rites–not to put them into the Calendar, but to keep them out of it.'

The Cardinal nodded soberly.

'In a sense that's true. But, in this as in all cases, the first motion doesn't come from us. The Bishop begins it in his own diocese. Only afterwards the papers are forwarded to us. We have no direct authority to forbid the investigation.'

'We might counsel against it.'

'On what grounds?'

'Discretion. The timing is bad. We are on the eve of elections. Giacomo Nerone was murdered by Communist Partisans in the last year of the war. What do we want to do? Use him to win a provincial seat—or as an example of heroic charity?'

The Cardinal's red lips twitched into a small ironic smile.

'I imagine our brother Bishop would like to have it both ways. And up to a point he's likely to get it. Miracles have been claimed. An apparently spontaneous cult has sprung up among the people. Both must be judicially investigated. The first investigation has been made and the verdict leans towards approval. The next stage follows almost automatically ... the introduction of the Cause for Beatification to the Bishop's own court.'

'Once that happens, every newspaper in Italy will run the story. The travel agencies will start organising unofficial tours. The local merchants will start shouting from the housetops. You can't avoid it.'

'But we may be able to control it. That's why I've decided to give His Lordship what he wants. That's why I'd like you to become the Devil's Advocate.'

Blaise Meredith pursed his thin, bloodless lips, considering the offer. Then after a moment he shook his head.

'I'm a sick man, Eminence. I could not do you justice.'

'You must let me judge that.' Marotta reproved him coolly. 'Besides, as I said, I believe it may help you too.'

'I don't understand.'

The Cardinal pushed back his high, carved chair and stood up. He walked across the room to the window and drew back the thick curtains so that the morning sun flooded into the room, lighting the scarlet and the gilt, making the rich patterns on the carpet leap into life like flowers. Blaise Meredith blinked at the raw brilliance and shaded his eyes with his hand. The Cardinal stood looking out into the garden. His face was hidden from Meredith, but when he spoke his voice was touched with a rare compassion.

'What I have to say to you, Monsignor, is probably a presumption. I am not your confessor. I cannot look into your conscience; but I believe you have reached a crisis. You, like many of us here in Rome, are a professional priest—a career churchman. There is no stigma in that. It is much already to be a good professional. There are many who fall far short even of this limited perfection. Suddenly you have discovered it is not enough. You are puzzled, afraid. Yet you do not know what you should do to restore the lack. Part of the problem is that you and I and others like us have been removed too long from pastoral duty. We have lost touch with the people who keep us in touch with God. We have reduced the Faith to an intellectual conception, an arid assent of the will, because we have not seen it working in the lives of common folk. We have lost pity and fear and love. We are the guardians of mysteries, but we have lost the awe of them. We work by canon, not by charity. Like all administrators we believe that the world would topple into chaos without us, that we carry even the Church of God on our backs. It is not true, but some of us believe it till the day we die. You are fortunate that even at this late hour you have been touched with dissatisfaction . . . yes, even doubt, because I believe that you are now in the desert of temptation. . . . That is why I believe this investigation may help you. It will take you out of Rome, to one of the most depressed areas of Italy. You will rebuild the life of a dead man from the evidence of those who lived with him—the poor, the ignorant, the dispossessed. Be he sinner or saint, it makes no difference in the end. You will live and talk with simple people. Among them perhaps you will find the cure for your own sickness of spirit.'

'What is my sickness, Eminence?' The pathetic weariness of the voice, the desolate puzzlement of the question, touched the old churchman to pity. He turned back from the window to see Meredith slumped forward in his chair, his face buried in his hands. He waited a moment, weighing his answer; then he gave it, gravely.

'There is no passion in your life, my son. You have never loved a woman, nor hated a man, nor pitied a child. You have withdrawn yourself too long and you are a stranger in the human family. You have asked nothing and given nothing. You have never known the dignity of need nor gratitude for a suffering shared. This is your sickness. This is the cross you have fashioned for your own shoulders. This is where your doubts begin and your fears too—because a man who cannot love his fellows cannot love God either.'

'How does one begin to love?'

'From need,' said Marotta firmly. 'From the need of the flesh and the need of the spirit. A man hungers for his first kiss, and his first real prayer is made when he hungers for the lost Paradise.'

'I am so very tired,' said Blaise Meredith.

'Go home and rest,' said the Cardinal briskly. 'In the morning you can leave for Calabria. Present your credentials to the Bishop of Valenta and begin work.'

'You are a hard man, Eminence.'

'Men die every day,' Eugenio Marotta told him bluntly. 'Some are damned, some achieve salvation; but the work of the Church continues. Go, my son—in peace and in the name of God!'

At eleven o'clock the following morning Blaise Meredith left Rome for Calabria. His luggage was one small suitcase of clothes, a brief-case containing his breviary and his notebooks, and a letter of authority from the Prefect of the Congregation of Rites to His Lordship the Bishop of Valenta. There was a ten-hour journey ahead of him and the *rapido* was hot, dusty and crowded with Calabresi returning from an organised pilgrimage to the Holy City.

The poorer folk were herded like cattle into the second-class coaches, while their betters spilled over into first-class and spread themselves and their belongings over the seats and the luggage-racks. Meredith found himself anchored firmly between a stout matron in a silk frock and a swarthy-faced cleric chewing noisily through a packet of peppermints. The seat opposite was occupied by a country man and his wife and four children who squalled like cicadas and tangled themselves in everyone's feet. All the windows were closed and the air was sour and stifling.

He took out his breviary and settled down with grim concentration to read his office. Ten minutes out of Rome Central he gave up in disgust. The foul air nauseated him and his head throbbed with the chatter of the train and the shrilling of the children. He tried to doze, but the stout woman shifted uneasily in her tight dress and the noisy mastications of the priest fretted him to screaming point. Defeated and dyspeptic, he struggled out of the seat and into the corridor, where he stood, propped against the panelling, looking out on the countryside.

It was green now, with the first flush of spring. The scars of erosion and tillage were covered with new grass, the stucco of the house-fronts had been washed clean by the rains and bleached by the sun, and even the ruins of the aqueducts and the old Roman villas were flecked with fresh moss and weeds that sprouted out of their weathered stones. The cyclic miracle of rebirth was more vivid here than in any other country of the world. Here was a tired land, raped ruinously for centuries, its hills eroded, its trees cut down, its rivers dry, its soil bled into dust; yet somehow every year it made this brief, brave show of leaf and grass and flower. Even in the mountains, on the ragged tufa slopes, too poor for goat-cropping, there was still a faint dapple of green for a reminder of past fruitfulness.

If one could leave the land a while, thought Meredith, if one could empty it of its proliferating tribes for half a century, it might come into heart again. But it would never happen. They would breed while the land died under their feet–slowly indeed, yet too fast for the technicians and agronomists to restore it.

The moving sunlit vistas began to weary his eyes, and he looked up and down the corridor at the others who had been driven out of the compartments by cigar smoke and stale salami and garlic and the smell of unbathed bodies. There was a Neapolitan business man with stovepipe trousers and short-tailed coat and a flashing zircon on one pudgy finger, a German tourist with thick shoes and an expensive Leica, a pair of flat-chested Frenchwomen, an American student with cropped hair and a freckled face, and a pair of provincial lovers holding hands near the toilet.

It was the lovers who held Meredith's attention. The youth was a nuggety peasant from the South, dark as an Arab, with flashing eyes and voluble hands. His thin cotton trousers were moulded over his flanks and his sweat-shirt clung to his chest so that the whole, compact maleness of him was suggestively visible. The girl was short and dark as he was, thick of waist and ankle, but her breasts were full and firm and they strained against the low-cut bodice of her dress. They stood facing one another across the narrow corridor, their locked hands a barrier against intrusion, their eyes blind to all but themselves, their bodies relaxed and swaying to the rhythm of the train. Their passion was plain, yet it gave no impression of urgency. The boy was preened like a cock, yet confident of his possession. The girl was content with him and with herself, in the small private eternity of new love.

Looking at them, Blaise Meredith was touched with a vague nostalgia for a past that had never belonged to him. What did he know of love but a theological definition and a muttered guilt in the confessional? What meaning had his counsel in the face of this frank, erotic communion, which by divine dispensation was the beginning of life and the guarantee of the human continuum? Soon, this very night perhaps, these two would lie together in the little death out of which a new life would spring–a new body, a new soul. But Blaise Meredith would sleep solitary, with all the mysteries of the universe reduced to a scholastic syllogism inside his skull-case. Who was right–he or they? Who came nearer to the perfection of the divine design? There was only one answer. Eugenio Marotta was right. He had withdrawn himself from the human family. These two were thrusting forward to renew it and perpetuate it.

His feet began to burn. His back ached. The small nagging pain started again in the pit of his belly. He would have to sit down and rest awhile. As he made his way back to his seat he found the Calabrian cleric launched on a full-scale sermon:

'. . . A wonderful man, the Holy Father. A saint in his own right. I was very near him in St Peter's. I could have stretched out my hand to touch him. One could feel the power going out from him. Wonderful . . . wonderful. . . ! We should thank God all the days of our lives for the privilege we have enjoyed on this pilgrimage.'

A wave of peppermint wafted through the compartment. Blaise Meredith closed his eyes and prayed for a respite, but the thick Calabrese voice droned on and on:

'. . . To have come to Rome, to have trodden in the footprints of the martyrs and knelt at the tomb of Peter, what other experience could match this? Here one sees the Church as it really is–an army of priests and monks and nuns preparing themselves to conquer the world for Christ. . . .'

If this is the way we conquer it, thought Blaise Meredith irritably, God help the world. This sort of mummery never did anyone any good. The fellow talks like a travelling salesman. If only he would shut up and think a little.

But the Calabrese was well launched now and the presence of a brother cleric only urged him to greater efforts.

'They are right when they call Rome the Holy City. The spirit of the great Pontiff broods over it night and day. Mind you, not all the saints of the Church are in Rome. Oh no! Even in our own small province we have a saint–not an official one yet–but real. Ah yes! Very real!'

Blaise Meredith was instantly alert. His irritation vanished, and he waited intently for the rest of it.

'Already the Cause of his Beatification has been opened. Giacomo Nerone. You have heard of him perhaps? No? A strange and wonderful story. No one knows where he came from, but he appeared one day in the village, like a man sent by God. He built a little hermitage with his own hands and gave himself over to prayer and good works. When the Communists moved in to take over the village after the war they murdered him. He died a martyr in defence of the Faith. And since his death miracle after miracle has been performed at his tomb. The sick have been cured; sinners brought to penance: sure marks of the favour of the Almighty.'

Blaise Meredith opened his eyes and asked innocently:

'Did you know him, Father?'

The Calabrese shot him a swift, suspicious glance.

'Know him? Er, well, not personally. Though, of course, I know a lot about him. I'm from Cosenza myself. The next diocese.'

'Thank you,' said Blaise Meredith politely, and closed his eyes again. The Calabrian shifted uncomfortably in his seat and then got up to relieve himself in the toilet. Meredith took advantage of his absence to stretch his legs and ease his aching head against the padded back-rest. He felt no compunction for what he had done. More than ever now, this sort of claptrap was distasteful to him. It was a kind of ecclesiastical jargon, a debased rhetoric that explained nothing but brought the truth into disrepute. It begged all the questions and answered none. The massive structure of reason and revelation on which the Church was founded was reduced to a ritual incantation, formless, fruitless and essentially false. Peppermint piety. It deceived no one but the man who peddled it. It satisfied no one but the old ladies and girls in green-sickness; yet it flourished most rankly where the Church was most firmly entrenched in the established order. It was the mark of accommodation, compromise, laxity among the clergy, who found it easier to preach devotion than to affront the moral and social problems of their time. It covered fatuity and lack of education. It left the people naked and unarmed in the face of terrifying mysteries: pain, passion, death, the great 'perhaps' of the hereafter.

The swarthy Calabrian came back, fumbling with the buttons of his cassock, and determined to re-establish himself with his audience and with his lean-jowled Monsignor. He sat down, blew his nose noisily and then tapped Meredith confidentially on the knee.

'You are from Rome, Monsignor?'

'From Rome, yes.' He was nettled by this intrusion on his rest, and his tone was terse; but the Calabrese was a hardhead, blind to all obstacles.

'But you are not Italian?'

'No. I'm English.'

'Ah, a visitor to the Vatican? A pilgrim?'

'I work there,' said Meredith coldly.

The Calabrese gave him a fraternal smile that showed a mouth full of carious teeth.

'You are fortunate, Monsignor. You have opportunities denied to us poor country folk. We work the stony acres while you till the lush pastures of the City of Saints.'

'I don't till anything,' Meredith told him baldly. 'I'm an official of the Congregation of Rites, and Rome isn't the City of Saints any more than Paris or Berlin. It's a place that's kept fairly orderly because the Pope insists on his rights under the Concordat to preserve its sacred character as the centre of Christendom. That's all.'

The Calabrese was as canny as a badger. He sidestepped the snub and seized swiftly on the new topic presented to him.

'You interest me very much, Monsignor. You live of course in a bigger world than I. You have much more experience of affairs. But I have always said that the simple country life is much more conducive to sanctity than the worldly bustle of a great city. You work with the Congregation of Rites. You deal possibly, with the causes of saints and *beati*. Wouldn't you agree?'

He was trapped and he knew it. He would be plagued into conversation in the end. It would save time and energy to submit now—and try to change his seat at Formio or Naples. He answered dryly:

'All my experience is that saints are found in the most unlikely places—at the most unpromising times.'

'Exactly! This is what has interested me so much about our own Servant of God, Giacomo Nerone. You know the place where he lived, Gemelli dei Monti?'

'I've never been there.'

'But you know what the name means?'

'What it says, I imagine . . . the mountain twins.'

'Precisely. Twin villages set on the horns of a hill in some of the most desolate country in Calabria. Gemello Minore the little town. Gemello Maggiore the greater. They're about sixty kilometres from Valenta, and the road is a nightmare. The villagers are as poor and depressed as any in our province. At least they were, until the fame of the servant of God began to spread.'

'And then?' In spite of himself, Meredith found his interest quickening.

'Ah, then!' One stubby hand was raised in a preacher's gesture. 'Then a strange thing happened. Giacomo Nerone had lived and worked in Gemello Minore. It was in this village that he was betrayed and murdered. His body was taken secretly to a grotto near Gemello Maggiore and buried there. Since that time Gemello Minore has sunk deeper and deeper into ruin and poverty, while Gemello Maggiore grows more prosperous every day. There is a new church, a hospital, an inn for tourists and pilgrims. It is as if God were visiting punishment on the betrayers and reward on those who sheltered the body of the Servant of God. Don't you agree?'

'It's a dubious proposition,' Meredith told him, with thin irony. 'Prosperity isn't always a mark of divine favour. It could be the result of some shrewd promotion by the Mayor and the citizens—even the parish priest. These things have happened.'

The Calabrese flushed angrily at the imputation and burst into an impassioned rebuttal.

'You presume too much, Monsignor. Wise and godly men have looked into this matter—men who understand our people. Do you set yourself in opposition to them?'

'I'm not in opposition to anyone,' said Meredith mildly. 'I simply disapprove of rash judgment and doubtful doctrine. Saints are not made by popular verdict but by canonical decision. That's why I'm going to Calabria now, to act as Promoter of the Faith in the cause of Giacomo Nerone. If you have any firsthand evidence to offer, I'll be happy to receive it, in the proper form.'

The priest gaped at him a moment; then his confidence collapsed in mumbled apologies, cut mercifully short by their arrival at Formio.

They had twenty minutes to wait for the north-bound train, which gave Blaise Meredith the opportunity to stretch his legs—and the grace to be ashamed of himself.

What had he gained by this cheap, dialectic victory over a country cleric? The Calabrese was a bore—and, worse, a pious bore—but Blaise Meredith was a dyspeptic intellectual with no charity in him at all. He had gained nothing and given nothing—and he had missed the first opportunity of learning a little about the man whose life he was charged to investigate.

As he paced the sunlit platform, watching the peasant travellers pressing about the drink vendor, he asked himself for the hundredth time what was the lack that cut him off from free communication with his fellows. Other priests, he knew, found an intense pleasure in the raw, salty dialect of peasant conversation. They picked up pearls of wisdom and experience over a farmhouse table or a cup of wine in a workman's kitchen. They talked with equal familiarity to the rough-tongued whores of Trastevere and the polished *signori* of Parioli. They enjoyed the ribald humour of the fish market as much as the wit of a Cardinal's dinner table. They were good priests, too, and they did much for their people, with a singular satisfaction to themselves.

What was the difference between him and them? Passion, Marotta had told him. The capacity to love and to desire, to feel with another's pain, to share another's joy. Christ ate and drank wine with touts and tavern-girls, but Monsignor Meredith, his professional follower, had lived alone amid dusty tomes in the library of the Palace of Congregations. And now, in this last year of his life, he was still alone, with a small grey death growing in his belly–and no soul in the world to bear him company.

The guard blew his whistle and Meredith climbed aboard again, to sweat out the long, humid voyage–Naples, Nocera, Salerno, Eboli, Cassano, Cosenza and, in the late evening, Valenta, where the Bishop was waiting to welcome him.

Aurelio, Bishop of Valenta, was a surprise, in more ways than one. He was a tall, spare man, still in his vigorous forties.

His iron-grey hair was meticulously brushed and his fine aquiline features were bright with intelligence and humour. He was a Trentino, which seemed an odd choice for a Southern diocese, and before his translation he had been an auxiliary in the Patriarchate of Venice. He was waiting at the station with his own car and instead of driving into the town he took Meredith a dozen kilometres into the country to a handsome villa, set in acres of oranges and olives, and looking down into a valley where a narrow stream glowed faintly under the moon.

'An experiment,' he explained in clear metallic English. 'An experiment in practical education. These people imagine that the clergy are born in cassocks, and that their only talent is for Paters and Aves and swinging censers in the cathedral. I was born in the North. My people were mountain farmers–good ones. I bought this place from a local landowner who was up to his eyes in debt, and I'm farming it with half a dozen lads, to whom I'm trying to teach the rudiments of modern agriculture. It's a battle; but I think I'm winning. I've also made it my official residence. The old one was hopelessly antiquated . . . right in the middle of the town, next to the cathedral. I've handed it over to my Vicar General. He's one of the old school–loves it!'

Meredith chuckled, caught by the infectious good-humour of the man. The Bishop shot him a quick, shrewd look.

'You are surprised, Monsignor?'

'Pleasantly,' said Blaise Meredith. 'I expected something quite different.'

'Bourbon baroque? Velvet and brocade and gilt cherubs with the paint peeling off their backsides?'

'Something like that, yes.'

The Bishop brought the car to a stop in front of the stuccoed portico of the villa and sat a moment behind the wheel, looking over the fall of the land, where the moonlight touched the treetops with silver. He said quietly:

'You will find more than enough of it here in the South . . . formalism, feudalism reaction, old men following old ways because the old ways seem safer, and they are unprepared for the new. They see poverty and ignorance as crosses to be borne and not injustices to be remedied. They believe that the more priests and monks and nuns there are, the better for the world. I'd like to see fewer and better ones. I'd prefer to have fewer churches and more people going to them.'

'Fewer saints too?' asked Meredith blandly.

The Bishop looked up sharply, then burst out laughing.

'Thank God for the English! A little tramontane scepticism would do us all a lot of good at this moment. You wonder why a man like me should take up the cause of Giacomo Nerone?'

'Frankly, yes.'

'Let's keep it for the fruit and the cheese,' said His Lordship without malice.

A servant in a white coat opened the car door and ushered them into the house.

'Dinner in thirty minutes,' said His Lordship. 'I hope you'll find your room comfortable. In the morning you can look right down over the valley and see what we've done.'

He took his leave, and the servant led Meredith upstairs to a large guest-room with french doors that opened on to a narrow balcony. Meredith was struck by the clean, modern lines of the furniture, the ascetic strength of the wooden crucifix over the prie-dieu in the corner. There was a shelf of new books in French, Italian and English, and a copy of the *Imitation of Christ* on the bedside table. A door opened from the bedroom into a freshly tiled bathroom, with a toilet and a shower recess. His Lordship had the instincts of a builder and the good taste of an artist. He also had a sense of humour, a virtue all too rare in the Italian Church.

As he bathed and changed, Meredith felt the weariness and frustration of the journey falling away from him like a sloughed skin. Even the nagging pain of his illness seemed to subside, and he found himself looking forward with pleasure and curiosity to dinner with His Lordship. It was a simple meal—*antipasto, zuppa di verdura*, a roast of chicken, local fruit and a sharp country cheese—but it was cooked with distinction and meticulously served, and the wine was a full-bodied Barolo from the vineyards of the North. The talk that went with it was much more subtle; a fencing match between experts, with the Bishop making the first probing thrusts.

'Until you came, my dear Meredith, I was beginning to feel I had made a mistake.'

'A mistake?'

'In appealing to Rome for assistance. It involved a concession, you see—a certain sacrifice of my autonomy.'

'Did it cost Your Lordship so much?'

The Bishop nodded gravely.

'It could have, yes. Modernisers and reformers are always suspect, especially here in the South. If they succeed they become a reproach to their more conservative colleagues. If they fail, they become an example. They have tried to do too much, too fast. So I've always found it wiser to go my own way and keep my affairs to myself—and leave the critics to make the first move.'

'Do you have many critics?'

'Some, yes. The landowners don't like me—and they have strong voices in Rome. The clergy find me too rigid in matters of morals, and too indifferent to local ritual and tradition. My metropolitan is a Monarchist. I'm a moderate socialiser. The politicos mistrust me, because I preach that the party is less important than the individual who represents it. They make promises. I like to see that they are kept. When they're not, I protest.'

'Do you find support in Rome?'

His Lordship's thin mouth relaxed into a smile.

'You know Rome better than I do, my friend. They wait for the results—and the results of a policy like mine in an area like this may not be seen for ten years. If I succeed, well and good. If I fail—or make the wrong mistake at the wrong time—they'll nod their heads wisely and say they've been expecting it for years. So I prefer to keep them guessing. The less they know, the freer I am.'

'Then why did you write to Cardinal Marotta? Why did you ask for Roman priests as Postulator and Promoter of the Faith?'

His Lordship toyed with his wineglass, twirling the stem between his long, sensitive fingers, watching the light refract through the red liquid on to the snowy tablecloth. He said carefully:

'Because this is new ground to me. I understand goodness, but I am unfamiliar with sanctity. I believe in mysticism, but I've had no experience of mystics. I'm a northerner, a pragmatist by nature and education. I believe in miracles, but I've never expected to find them performed on my own doorstep. That's why I applied to the Congregation of Rites.' He smiled disarmingly. 'You are the experts in these matters.'

'Was this the only reason?'

'You talk like an inquisitor,' said His Lordship, with wry good-humour. 'What other reason should there be?'

'Politics,' said Meredith flatly. 'Election politics.'

To his surprise, the Bishop threw back his head and laughed heartily.

'So that's it. I wondered why His Eminence was so co-operative. I wondered why he'd sent an Englishman instead of an Italian–and a secular priest instead of a long-faced Barnabite. Clever of him! But I'm afraid he's wrong.' The laugh died suddenly on his lips and he was as serious again. He set down his wineglass and spread his hands in an eloquent gesture of explanation. 'He's quite wrong, Meredith. That's what happens in Rome. The stupid get stupider still and the clever fellows like Marotta get too clever for everyone else's good. There are two reasons why I'm interested in this case. The first is simple and official. It's an unauthorised cultus. I have to investigate it, for approval or condemnation. The second isn't half so simple–and the officials wouldn't understand it.'

'Marotta might,' said Meredith quietly. 'I might too.'

'Why should you two be different?'

'Because Marotta's a wise old humanist–and because I'm due to die of a carcinoma in twelve months.'

Aurelio, Bishop of Valenta, leaned back in his chair and studied the pale, drawn face of his visitor. After a long moment he said softly:

'I've been wondering about you. Now I begin to understand. Very well, I'll try to explain. A man in the shadow of death should be beyond scandal, even from a bishop. I believe that the Church in this country is in drastic need of reform. I think we have too many saints and not enough sanctity, too many cults and not enough catechism, too many medals and not enough medicine, too many churches and not enough schools. We have three million workless men and three million women living by prostitution. We control the State through the Christian Democratic Party and the Vatican Bank; yet we countenance a dichotomy which gives prosperity to half the country and lets the other half rot in penury. Our clergy are under-educated and insecure and yet we rail against anti-clericals and Communists. A tree is known by its fruits–and I believe that it's better to proclaim a new deal in social justice than a new attribute of the Blessed Virgin. The first is a necessary application of a moral principle, the second is simply a definition of a traditional belief. We clergy are more jealous of our rights under the Concordat than the rights of our people under the natural and divine law. . . . Do I shock you, Monsignor?'

'You encourage me,' said Blaise Meredith. 'But why do you want a new saint?'

'I don't,' said the Bishop, with surprising emphasis. 'I'm committed to the case, but I hope, with all my heart, it fails. The Mayor of Gemello Maggiore has collected fifteen million lire to advance the cause, but I can't get a thousand out of him for a diocesan orphanage. If Giacomo Nerone is beatified, they'll want a new church to house him—and I want nursing nuns and an agricultural adviser and twenty thousand fruit trees from California.'

'Then why did you ask His Eminence for help?'

'It's a principle in Rome, my dear Meredith. You always get the opposite of what you ask for.'

Blaise Meredith did not smile. A new and disturbing thought was shaping itself in his mind. He paused a little, trying to find words to frame it.

'But if the case is proved? If Giacomo Nerone is really a saint and a wonder-worker?'

'I'm a pragmatist, as I told you,' said His Lordship with side-long humour. 'I'll wait on the facts. When would you like to begin work?'

'Immediately,' said Meredith. 'I'm living on borrowed time. I'd like to spend a few days studying the documents. Then I'll move out to Gemelli dei Monti to begin taking depositions.'

'I'll have the records delivered to your room in the morning. I hope you will regard this house as your home and myself as your friend.'

'I am grateful to Your Lordship, more grateful than I can say.'

'There is nothing to be grateful for.' The Bishop smiled in deprecation. 'I shall be glad of your company. I feel we have much in common. Oh . . . there is a small counsel I would give you.'

'Yes?'

'It's my private opinion that you will not find the truth about Giacomo Nerone in Gemello Maggiore. They venerate him there. They make profit from his memory. In Gemello Minore, it's quite another story—provided you can get them to tell it. So far none of my people has succeeded.'

'Is there any reason?'

'Better you ask the reasons for yourself, my friend. As you see, I'm rather prejudiced.' He pushed back his chair and stood up. 'It's late and you must be tired. I suggest you rest late in the morning. I'll have breakfast sent to your room.'

Blaise Meredith was touched by the patrician politeness of the man. He was chary of confidences, jealous of his own privacy, but he said very humbly:

'I am a sick man, Your Lordship. I am suddenly very lonely. You have made me feel at home. Thank you.'

'We are brothers in a big family,' said the Bishop gently. 'But being bachelors we grow selfish and singular. I'm glad to be of service. Good-night—and golden dreams.'

Alone in the big guest-room with the moonlight streaming through the open casements, Blaise Meredith prepared himself for another night. Its course was familiar to him now, but none the less frightening. He would lie wakeful till midnight, then sleep would come, shallow and restless. Before the cocks began to screech at the false dawn he would start up, his belly cramped with pain, his mouth full of the sour taste of bile and blood. He would struggle to the toilet, weak and retching, then cram himself with opiate and go back to bed. Just before sunrise he would sleep again—one hour, two at most—not enough to refresh him, but enough to keep the sluggish, diminishing life-stream flowing in his arteries.

It was a strange compound of terrors: the fear of death, the shame of slow dissolution, the eerie solitude of the believer in the presence of a faceless God whom he acknowledged unseen but must soon meet unveiled and splendid in judgment. He could not escape them into sleep and he could not exorcise them by prayer, since prayer had become an arid act of the will which could neither stifle pain nor set a balm to it.

So tonight, in spite of his fatigue, he tried to defer the purgatory. He undressed, put on pyjamas, slippers and dressing-gown and walked out on the balcony.

The moon was high over the valley—a ship of antique silver, placid on a luminous sea. The orange groves glowed coldly and the olive leaves were bright as dagger-tips out of a twisted mass of shadows. Below them the water lay flat and full of stars, behind a barricade of logs and piled rubble, while the arms of the mountains encircled it all like ramparts, shutting out the chaos of the centuries.

Blaise Meredith looked at it and found it good. Good in itself, good in the man who had made it. Man did not live by bread alone—but he could not live without it. The old monks had had the same idea. They planted the Cross in the middle of a desert—and then planted corn and fruit trees, so that the barren symbol flowered into a green reality. They knew, better than most, that man was a creature of flesh and spirit; but that the spirit could not function except in and through the flesh. When the body was sick, the moral responsibility of man was reduced. Man was a thinking reed, but the reed must be anchored firmly in black earth, watered at the roots, warmed by the sun.

Aurelio, Bishop of Valenta, was a pragmatist, but a Christian pragmatist. He was the inheritor of the oldest and most orthodox tradition in the Church: that earth and grass and tree and animal were the issue of the same creative act that produced a man. They were good in themselves, perfect in their nature and in the laws that governed their growth and decay. Only Man's misuse could debase them to instruments of evil. To plant a tree was therefore a godly act. To make barren earth flourish was to share in the act of creation. To teach other men these things was to make them, too, participate in a divine plan. . . . Yet Aurelio, Bishop of Valenta, was suspect to many of his own colleagues.

This was the mystery of the Church: that it should hold in organic unity humanists like Marotta and formalists like Blaise Meredith and fools like the Calabrian, reformers, rebels and puritan conformists, political Popes, and nursing nuns, worldly priests and devout anti-clericals. It demanded an unwavering assent to defined doctrine and permitted an extraordinary divergence of discipline.

It imposed poverty on its religious, yet played the stock markets of the world through the Vatican Bank. It preached detachment from the world, yet collected real estate like any public company. It forgave adulterers and excommunicated heretics. It was harsh with its own reformers, yet signed concordats with those who wanted to destroy it. It was the hardest community in the world to live in—yet all its members wanted to die in it, the Pope, Cardinal or washerwoman, they would take their viaticum with gratitude from the lowest country priest.

It was a mystery and a paradox, yet Blaise Meredith was further from understanding it, further from accepting it than he had been for twenty years. This was what troubled him. When he had been well, his mind had bent naturally to accept the idea of a divine intervention in human affairs. Now that the life was bleeding out of him, slowly, he found himself clinging desperately to the simplest manifestation of physical continuity—a tree, a flower, lake water quiet under an eternal moonlight.

A faint breeze stirred along the valley, rattling the crisp leaves, ruffling the stars in the water. Meredith shivered in the sudden chill and went inside, closing the french door behind him. He knelt down on the prie-dieu under the wooden figure of the Christus and began to pray . . .

'*Pater Noster qui es in Coelis . . .*'

But heaven, if heaven there were, was shut blank against him, and there was no answer from the faceless Father to his dying son.

3

Doctor Aldo Meyer stood at the doorway of his house and watched the village wake sluggishly to a new day.

First, old Nonna Patucci opened her door, peered up and down the cobbled street, then tottered across the road and emptied her chamber-pot over the wall and on to the vine-terrace below. Then she went inside, furtive as a witch, and closed the door with a resounding slam. As if at a signal, Felici the cobbler came out, in singlet and trousers and wooden pattens, to stand yawning and scratching his armpits and watch the sun light up the roof of the new hospital in Gemello Maggiore, two miles across the valley. After a minute of contemplation, he hawked noisily, spat on the ground and proceeded to unbolt his shutters.

Then the door of the priest's house opened and Rosa Benzoni waddled out, fat and shapeless in a black dress, to draw water from the cistern. As soon as she had gone the upstairs window opened and Father Anselmo's tousled grey head appeared, tentative as a tortoise making its first cautious exploration of the day.

Martino the smith came next, squat, barrel-chested, brown as a nut, to open the door of his shed and start the bellows working. By the time the first strokes of his hammer began to sound on the anvil, the whole village was stirring—women emptying slop-pails, barelegged girls wandering down to the cistern with great green bottles on their heads, half-naked children piddling against the road-wall, the first labourers moving off to the terraces and the garden patches, with ragged coats slung over their shoulders and their bread and olives wrapped in cotton handkerchiefs.

Aldo Meyer watched it all, without curiosity, without resentment, even when they passed him with averted heads or made the sign of the evil eye in the direction of his door. It was the measure of his disillusionment that he could ignore their hostility and yet cling like an animal to familiar sights and sounds: the rhythmic clang of the hammer, the trundle of a donkey cart on the stones, the shrill cries of children, the scolding of housewives; the vines and the olive groves, climbing down the hillside towards the valley fields, the straggle of crumbling houses up the road towards the big villa that crowned the hill-top, the gleam of sunrise on the prosperous town on the farther hill where the saint worked wonders for the tourists while Maria Rossi died in child-bed with his relic on her swollen body.

Each day he promised himself that tomorrow he would pack and go–to a new place with a new future–and leave this graceless tribe to its folly. But each night the resolution drained out of him and he sat down to drink himself into bed. The comfortless truth was that he had no place to go and no future to build. The best of himself was here–faith, hope and charity poured out to exhaustion, sucked up and wasted in a barren earth, trodden by a thankless, ignorant people.

From far down in the valley he heard the muted clatter of a motor-cycle and, when he turned towards it, he saw a small Vespa with a pillion passenger jolting up the track in a cloud of grey dust. The spectacle was banal enough but it moved Aldo Meyer to wintry amusement. The Vespa and the Contessa's automobile were the only motor vehicles in Gemello Minore. The Vespa had caused a minor riot and a gaping wonder that went on for weeks. Its rider was an oddity, too–an English painter, house-guest of the Contessa who lived in the villa on the hill-top and who owned all of the farmland and most of Gemello Minore as well. The painter's name was Nicholas Black, his pillion passenger was a local youth, Paolo Sanduzzi, who had attached himself to Black as guide, baggage animal and instructor in local dialect and customs.

To the villagers, the Englishman was *matto*–a crazy fellow who ambled about with a sketch book or sat for hours in the sun painting olive trees and tumbled rocks and angles of ruinous buildings. His dress was as crazy as his habits, a bright red shirt, faded denims, rope sandals, and a battered straw hat, under whose brim a faun-like face grinned crookedly at the world about him. He had not even the excuse of youth–he was past thirty–and when the girls gave up sighing after him, the elders began to make crude gossip about his association with the Contessa, who lived in solitary splendour behind the grilled gates of the villa.

Aldo Meyer heard the rumours and discounted them. He knew too much about the Contessa, and in his Roman days he had met too many artists, and quite enough Englishmen like Nicholas Black. He wondered more about Paolo Sanduzzi, with his slim, Arab body and his smooth face and his bright, shrewd eyes and his tyranny over his eccentric master. He wondered the more because he had seen the boy into the world and he knew that his father was Giacomo Nerone, whom folk were beginning to call the Saint . . .

At the lower end of the village the Vespa stopped, the youth got off and Meyer watched him scrambling down the hill-side towards his mother's house, a rough stone hut set in the middle of a small garden patch and sheltered by a clump of ilex. The Vespa started off again with a clatter and a few moments later came to a halt outside Meyer's cottage. The painter eased himself stiffly out of the saddle and threw out his arm in a theatrical salutation:

'*Coméva, Dottore?* How goes it this morning? I'd like some coffee if you've got any.'

'There's always coffee,' said Meyer, with a grin. 'How else would I face the sunrise?'

'Hangover?' asked the painter with malicious innocence.

Meyer shrugged wryly and led the way through the house and out into a small walled garden, where an old grey fig tree made a canopy against the sun. A rough table was covered with a checked cloth and set with cups and dishes of Calabrese pottery. A woman was bending over it, laying out new bread, a cut of white cheese, and a bowl of the small local fruit.

Her legs and feet were bare in the peasant fashion, and she wore a black cotton dress and a black head-scarf, both meticulously clean. Her back was straight, her breasts deep and firm, and her face was pure Greek, as if some ancient colonist from the coast had wandered into the mountains and mated with a woman of the tribes, to begin this new hybrid strain. She was perhaps thirty-six years of age. She had borne a child, yet she had not coarsened like the mountain women, and her mouth and eyes were curiously serene. When she saw the visitor, she gave a small start of surprise and looked inquiringly at Meyer. He said nothing, but made a cautionary gesture of dismissal. As she walked back into the house the painter's eyes followed her and he grinned like a knowing goat.

'You surprise me, Doctor. Where did you find her? I've never seen her before.'

'She belongs here,' said Meyer coolly. 'She has a house of her own and she keeps pretty much to herself. She comes up each day to clean and cook for me.'

'I'd like to paint her.'

'I don't advise it,' Meyer told him curtly.

'Why not?'

'She's the mother of Paolo Sanduzzi.'

'Oh.' Black flushed and let the subject drop. They sat down at the table and Meyer poured the coffee. There was silence for a few moments; then Black began to talk, volubly and dramatically.

'Big news from Valenta, Dottore! I was down there yesterday to pick up canvases and paints. The place is humming with it.'

'What sort of news?'

'This saint of yours, Giacomo Nerone. They're going to beatify him, it seems.'

Meyer shrugged indifferently and sipped his coffee.

'That's not news. They've been talking about it for twelve months.'

'Ah, but it is!' The sharp faun's face lit up with sardonic amusement. 'They've stopped talking and started an official process. They're circulating the notices now—tacking them up in all the churches, and calling for any person who has evidence to give. The Bishop's got a house-guest, a Monsignor from Rome who has been appointed to open the case. He'll be coming up here within a few days.'

'The devil he will!' Meyer set down his cup with a clatter. 'Are you sure of that?'

'Certain of it. It's all over town. I saw the fellow myself driving in His Lordship's car—grey and pinched like a Vatican mouse. He's English, it seems, so I took it on myself to offer an invitation from the Contessa to lodge him. She's a godly woman and lonely, as you know.' He chuckled and reached out to pour himself another cup of coffee. 'This place will be famous, Dottore. You'll be famous too.'

'That's what I'm afraid of,' said Meyer sombrely.

'Afraid?' The painter's eyes brightened with interest. 'Why should you be afraid? You're not even a Catholic. It's no concern of yours.'

'You don't understand,' Meyer told him irritably. 'You don't understand anything.'

'On the contrary, my dear fellow!' The long artist's hands gestured emphatically. 'On the contrary I understand everything. I understand what you have tried to do here and why you have failed. I know what the Church is trying to do, and why it will succeeed, at least for a while. What I don't know—and what I'm dying to see—is what will happen when they start digging up the real truth about Giacomo Nerone. I'd intended to leave next week; but now I think I'll stay. It should be quite a comedy.'

'Why did you come here in the first place?' There was an edge of anger in Meyer's voice and Nicholas Black was quick to notice it. He grinned and fluttered an airy hand.

'It's very simple. I had an exhibition in Rome—quite successful, too, even though it was on the fringe of the season. The Contessa was one of my clients. She bought three canvases. Then she invited me to come down here and paint for a while. I'm hoping she'll finance another show in the near future. It's as simple as that.'

'Nothing is ever as simple as that,' said the doctor mildly. 'And the Contessa is not a simple person. Neither are you. What you see as a provincial comedy may well turn into a grand tragedy. I advise you not to become involved in it.'

The Englishman threw back his head and laughed.

'But I am involved, my dear Doctor. I'm an artist, an observer and recorder of the beauty and the folly of mankind. Imagine what Goya could have made out of a situation like this one. Fortunately he's been dead a long time, so now it's my turn. There's a whole gallery of pictures here—and the title's ready made: "Beatification", by Nicolas Black! A one-man show on a single theme. A village saint, the village sinners, and all the clergy, right up to the Bishop himself. What do you think of that?'

Aldo Meyer looked down at the backs of his hands, studying the brown liver spots and the rough slack skin that told him more clearly than words how old he was getting. Without lifting his eyes, he said quietly:

'I think you are a very unhappy man, Nicholas Black. You are looking for something you will never find. I think you should go away immediately. Leave the Contessa. Leave Paolo Sanduzzi. Leave us all to deal with our problems in our own way. You don't belong here. You speak our language, but you don't understand us.'

'But I do, Doctor!' The handsome, epicene face was lit with malice. 'I do indeed. I know that you've all been hiding something for fifteen years, and now it's going to be dug up. The Church wants a saint and you want to keep a secret that discredits you. That's true, isn't it?'

'It's half a truth; which is always more than half a lie.'

'You knew Giacomo Nerone, didn't you?'

'I knew him, yes.'

'Was he a saint?'

'I know nothing about saints,' said Aldo Meyer gravely. 'I only know men.'

'And Nerone . . . ?'

'. . . was a man.'

'What about his miracles?'

'I have never seen a miracle.'

'Do you believe in them?'

'No.'

The bright sardonic eyes were fixed on his drawn face.

'Then why, my dear Doctor, are you afraid of this investigation?'

Aldo Meyer pushed back his chair and stood up. The shadow of the fig tree fell across his face, deepening the hollows of his cheeks, hiding the stark pain in his eyes. After a moment he answered:

'Have you ever been ashamed of yourself, my friend?'

'Never,' said the painter cheerfully. 'Never in my life.'

'That's what I mean,' said the doctor softly. 'You will never understand. But I tell you again, you should go—and go quickly.'

His only answer was a smile of rueful mockery as Black stood up to take his leave. They did not shake hands and Meyer made no attempt to accompany him out of the garden. Halfway to the house, the painter stopped and turned back.

'I'd almost forgotten. There's a message for you from the Contessa. She would like you to dine with her tomorrow evening.'

'My thanks to the Contessa,' said Meyer dryly. 'I'll be happy to come. Good day, my friend.'

'*Ci vedremo*,' said Nicholas Black casually. 'We'll see each other again—quite soon.'

Then he was gone, a slim, faintly clownish figure, too jaunty for the years that were beginning to show themselves in his intelligent, unhappy face. Aldo Meyer sat down again at the table and stared unseeingly at the broken crusts and the brown, muddy dregs in the coffee cups. After a while the woman came out of the house and stood looking down at him, with gentleness and pity in her calm eyes. When he looked up and saw her standing there, he said curtly:

'You can clear the table, Nina.'

She made no move to obey him, but asked:

'What did he want, that one who looks like a goat?'

'He brought me news,' said Meyer, lapsing into dialect to match the woman's. 'They are starting a new investigation into the life of Giacomo Nerone. A priest has come down from Rome to assist the Bishop's court. He will be coming here shortly.'

'He will ask questions, like the others?'

'More than the others, Nina.'

'Then he will get the same answer—nothing!'

Meyer shook his head slowly

'Not this time, Nina. It has gone too far. Rome is interested. The press will be interested. Better they get the truth this time.'

She stared at him in shocked surprise.

'You say that? You!'

Meyer shrugged defeatedly and quoted an old country proverb.

'Who can fight the wind? Who can drown the shouting they make on the other side of the valley? Even in Rome they have heard it—and this is the result. Let's tell them what they want and be done with it. Maybe then they will leave us in peace.'

'But why do they want it?' There was anger now in her eyes and in her voice. 'What difference does it make? They called him all sorts of names in his life—now they want to call him a *beato*. It's just another name. It doesn't change what he was—a good man, my man.'

'They don't want a man, Nina,' said Meyer wearily. 'They want a plaster saint with a gold plate on top of his head. The Church wants it because it gives them another hold on the people—a new cult, a new promise of miracles to make them forget their belly-aches. The people want it because they can get down on their knees and beg for favours instead of rolling up their sleeves and working for them—or fighting for them. It's the way of the Church—sugar for old sour wine.'

'Then why do you want me to help them?'

'Because if we tell them the truth, they'll drop the case. They'll have to. Giacomo was a remarkable man, but he was no more a saint than I am.'

'Is that what you believe?'

'Don't you, Nina?'

Her answer shocked him like a blow in the face.

'I know he was a saint,' she told him softly. 'I know he did miracles, because I saw them.'

Meyer gaped at her; then he shouted.

'God Almighty, woman! Even you? He slept in your bed. He gave you a bastard child, but never married you. And you can stand there and tell me he was a saint who did miracles. Why didn't you tell the priests that the first time? Why didn't you join our friend across the way and go shouting to have him beatified?'

'Because he would never have wanted it,' said Nina Sanduzzi calmly. 'Because it was the one thing he asked—that I should never tell what I knew about him.'

He was beaten and he knew it, but there was one more weapon left and he struck with it viciously.

'What will you answer, Nina, when they point to your boy and say, "There is a saint's son, and he makes himself a *feminella* for the Englishman?"'

There was no hint of shame in the calm, classic face as she replied:

'What do I say when they point to me in the street and whisper: "There is the one who was a saint's whore?" Nothing, nothing at all! Do you know why, Dottore? Because before Giacomo died, he made me a promise, in return for mine. "No matter what happens, *cara*, I shall look after you and the boy. They can kill me, but they can't stop me caring for you from now to eternity!" I believed him then, I believe him now. The boy is foolish but he is not lost yet.'

'Then he damned soon will be,' said Meyer brutally. 'Go home now, for God's sake, and leave me in peace.'

But even after she was gone there was no peace; and he knew there never would be until the inquisitors came and dragged the truth out into the daylight.

No hint of morning had yet entered the high, baroque room in the villa where the Countess Anne Louise de Sanctis slept behind velvet curtains. No premonition of trouble could penetrate the barbituric haze beyond which she dreamed.

Later, much later, a servant would come in and open the curtains to let the sun flow over the worn carpet and the rusted velvet and the dull patina of the carved walnut. It would not reach as far as the bed, which was a kindness, because the Contessa in the morning was an unpleasing spectacle.

Later still, she would wake, dry-mouthed, grey, puffy-eyed and discontented with the advent of a new day exactly like the old. She would wake, and doze, then wake again and thrust the first cigarette of the day into her pale, down-drawn lips. The cigarette finished, she would pull the bell-cord and the servant would return, smiling in anxious good-humour and carrying a breakfast tray. Since the Contessa disliked eating alone at any time, the servant would remain in the room, folding the scattered clothes, laying out fresh ones, bustling back and forth to the bathroom, while her mistress kept up a flow of waspish comment on the household and its shortcomings.

Breakfast finished, the servant would take away the tray, the Contessa would smoke one more cigarette before beginning the small intimate ritual of the toilet. It was the one important ceremony of her unimportant day, and she performed it in rigid secrecy.

She stubbed out her cigarette in the silver ashtray, then got out of bed, walked to the door and locked it. Next she made a circuit of the room, standing at each of the windows and looking out on the terraces and over the gardens to make sure no one was near. Once an inquisitive gardener had stood staring through the casements, and he had been instantly dismissed for this sacrilegious intrusion into the mysteries.

Assured at last of her privacy the Contessa went to the bathroom, undressed and stepped into the great marble bath with its gilt taps and its array of soaps and sponges and bottles of bath-salts. There was no pleasure now to be compared with this first solitary immersion in steaming water that soaked away the effusions of a drugged sleep and brought back the illusion of youth to an ageing body. Unlike other pleasures this one could be renewed at will, prolonged to satiation. It demanded no partner, involved neither dependence nor surrender; and the Contessa clung to it with the passion of a devotee.

As she lay back in the steaming water, she surveyed herself: the lines of the flanks, still slim and youthful, the belly flat and unmarked by childbearing, the waist, thickening a little, but not too much, the breasts massaged to firmness, small but round and still youthful. If there were lines about her neck, there was no mirror yet to tell her, and the tell-tale creases at mouth and eyes could still be massaged into subjection. Youth had not yet dried out of her and age could be held a little longer at bay with a weekly consignment of compounds from a discreet salon on the Via Veneto.

But the bath was only the beginning. There was the drying with soft warm towels, the rubbing with rough ones, the perfuming with sharp, astringent lotion, the powder dusted on and whisked gently away, the first combing of the hair—no grey in it yet, though the gold was fading—the ribbon to tie it back from the scrubbed and shining cheeks. Finally, she was ready for the processional climax of the ritual.

Naked and glowing from the new illusion, she walked back into the bedroom, crossed to the dressing table and took from the top drawer the photograph of a man in the uniform of a colonel of Alpini and set it up facing the room. Then, self-conscious as a mannequin, she began to dress herself in front of it, carefully, coquettishly, as if to charm him out of the frame and into her expectant arms.

When she was clothed, she laid the photograph back in the drawer, closed it, locked it, then, quite calmly, sat down in front of the mirror and began to make up her face.

Twenty minutes later, dressed in a modish summer frock, she walked out of the bedroom, down the stairs and into the bright garden, where Nicholas

Black, stripped to the waist, was working on a new canvas.

He turned at her footfall and came to greet her with theatrical pleasure, kissing her hands and then spinning her round to display her frock, while he chattered like a happy parrot:

'Magnificent, *cara*! I don't know how you do it! Every morning is like a new revelation. In Rome you were beautiful but rather terrifying. Here you're a country beauty reserved for my private admiration. I must paint you in that frock. Here, sit down and let me look at you.'

She bridled happily at the compliments and let him lead her to a small stone seat shaded by a blossoming almond tree. He made a great show of settling her to his satisfaction, fanning out her frock along the bench, tilting her head upward to the flowers and settling her hands in her lap. Then he snatched up a sketch-block and, with swift, bravura strokes, began to draw, talking all the time.

'I had coffee with our doctor friend this morning. He had his usual hangover, but he brightened up when I told him of your invitation to dinner. I had the idea he's more than half in love with you. . . . No, no! don't talk, you'll spoil the pose. I don't suppose the poor fellow can help it. He's lived so long among the peasants, you must seem like the fairy princess up here in your castle. . . . Oh, and another thing: the Bishop of Valenta is starting a full-scale investigation into the life and virtues of Giacomo Nerone. He's imported an English Monsignor from Rome to act as Devil's Advocate. He'll be coming up here in a few days. I took the liberty of telling His Lordship you'd be happy to have him as a guest.'

'No!' It was a panic cry. All her composure fell away and she stared at him, angry and afraid.

'But, *cara*!' He was instantly penitent. He put down the sketch-block and went to her, with solicitous hands and voice. 'I thought that's what you'd want me to do. I couldn't consult you, but I knew you were friendly with the Bishop and I knew there was really no other place for the visitor to lodge. He couldn't sleep with the peasants, now could he? Or under the counter in the wine-shop? Besides, he's a countryman of yours–and mine. I thought it would give you pleasure. If I've offended you, I'll never forgive myself.'

He went down on his knees beside her and buried his face in her lap, like a penitent child.

It was an old, old trick to charm the dowagers, and it worked again. She ran her fingers caressingly through his hair and said gently:

'Of course you haven't offended me, Nicki. It was surprise, that's all. I . . . I'm not prepared for them now as I used to be. Of course you did right. I'll be happy to have this Monsignor.'

'I knew you would be!' Instantly he was gay again. 'His Lordship was grateful–and I don't think our visitor will be too stuffy. Besides . . .' A small smiling malice shone again in his eyes. 'We'll be able to follow the investigation from the inside, won't we?'

'I suppose so.' Her face clouded again and she began to pluck nervously at the folds of her frock. 'But what will he do here?'

Nicholas Black gestured airily.

'What they all do. Ask questions, take notes, examine witnesses. Come to think of it, you'll probably be one yourself. You knew Nerone, didn't you?'

She shifted uneasily and refused to meet his eyes.

'Only slightly. I . . . I couldn't tell anything worth knowing.'

'Then what are you worrying about, *cara*? You'll have a box seat at the village comedy–and some Roman gossip as well. Come on now, settle yourself again and let me get this sketch done.'

But for all his care, he could not charm the fear out of her, and when he came to draw her face, every stroke was a lie. But all women were fools. They saw only what they wanted to see–and Nicholas Black had been making a profit from their follies for the best part of his life.

When the sketch was done, he handed it to her with a flourish and grinned inwardly at her expression of relief and pleasure. Then with calculated casualness he kissed her hand and dismissed her:

'You disturb me, darling. You're a beautiful nuisance. Go and pick me some flowers for the bedroom and let me finish my picture.'

As he watched her walking uncertainly across the lawn he chuckled to himself. She had been kind to him, and he bore her no personal malice. But he too had his secret pleasures, and the most subtle of all was to humble by intrigue what he could never subdue by possession–the hungry, hateful flesh of womankind.

For Anne Louise de Sanctis the moment had far other meanings. She was neither stupid nor vicious, though she consented equally to the follies of middle age and the vices that a still lively body imposed on her. When she submitted herself to the small tyrannies of the painter, it was because they piqued her vanity, and because she knew that she still held the balance of power. He wanted her to finance a new exhibition in Rome. She could do it–or she could send him packing tomorrow, back to the catch-penny life of a mediocre artist, and the sedulous pursuit of complaisant dowagers.

It pleased her to see that he, too, was getting old, and that each new conquest was a little more difficult. His malice was like the malice of a child, hurtful sometimes, but always joined with an unacknowledged need of her. And it was a long time since she had been needed by anyone. She had her own needs, too, but though he understood them and played on them, he was powerless to use them against her. He played on her fears and her loneliness, but the real terror he had not yet discovered.

It was this terror that walked with her now in the dappled garden on the hill-top, where wealth and cheap labour had planted an oasis in the raw, parched land of Calabria. The earth for the lawns and flower-beds had been brought up the hill in baskets on the shoulders of village women. The stone had been hacked out of the hill-side by local masons, the olives and the pines and the orange groves planted by tenant farmers as their tribute to the family that had held them in fee for centuries. Neapolitan artists had painted the walls and the coffered ceilings, and a dozen connoisseurs had bid for the pictures and the statuary and the porcelain demanded by Count Gabriele de Sanctis for his English bride.

The circling wall had been built, and the crested gates forged, to give her privacy. The staff had been chosen by the Count himself to serve her solicitously. The house and the land and everything in it were his wedding gift to her; a provincial retreat after the hectic season of Rome, where Gabriele de Sanctis was rising high in the service of the Duce. For the daughter of a minor diplomat, fresh from her first season in London, it was like an Arabian night's enchantment, but the terror had come in with her at the gates and it had stayed with her all the years since.

Gabriele de Sanctis had begun it–but he was dead long ago, a discredited suicide in the Libyan desert. A dozen other men had come and gone in the intervening years, but none of them had been able to rid her of it.

Then there was Giacomo Nerone. In this same garden, on a morning such as this, she had humbled herself and begged him to exorcise her, but he had refused. She had revenged herself in the end, but the revenge had brought new furies to torment her—nightmares in the big baroque bed, ghosts haunting the olive groves and grinning like satyrs through the orange-blossom. Lately they had plagued her less. There were drugs to bring sleep, and Nicholas Black to divert her in the daytime.

But now a man was coming: a grey-faced cleric from Rome commissioned to dig into the past, to tally old debts and record buried guilts, no matter what pain might follow the revelation. He would lodge in her house and eat at her table. He would pry and probe and even the locked door of her bedroom would keep no secrets from him.

Suddenly the life she had drawn in from the morning bath seemed to drain out of her, leaving her slack and tired. She made her way with slow, dragging steps to a small arbour on the fringe of the olive plantation where a small statue of a dancing faun was poised on a weathered stone pedestal. In front of the faun was a rustic bench over which honeysuckle drooped, languid and cloying. She sat down, lit a cigarette and inhaled greedily, drawing the smoke down into her lungs and feeling the tension in her relax slowly.

She understood now. She had been running too long. There was no escape from the fear which she carried like a tenant in her own body. There must be an end to it, else she would topple over into the black madness that threatens all women who come to the climacteric unhappy and unprepared. But how to end it? Break down all doors, humble herself to the inquisitors, submit to a confessional purging? She had tried it before, and it had failed utterly.

There was one alternative, bleak, perhaps, but sure: the small bottle full of gelatine capsules that seduced her nightly into sleep. The little more—and so little more—and it would be finished, once for all. In a sense it would be the completion of her revenge on Giacomo Nerone, and a revenge on the body which had betrayed her to him, and him to her.

But not yet. There was still a little time. Let the priest come, and if he did not press her too hard it would be a favourable omen—a promise of other solutions. If he did . . . why, then it would be simple, ironic and final; and when they found her she would still be beautiful as she was each morning from the perfumed bath.

4

For Blaise Meredith, the days he spent in the Bishop's house were the happiest of his life. A cold man by nature, he had begun to understand the meaning of fellowship. Withdrawn and self-sufficient, he saw, for the first time, the dignity of dependence, the grace of a shared confidence. Aurelio, Bishop of Valenta, was a man with a gift of understanding and a rare talent for friendship. The loneliness and the wintry courage of his guest had touched him deeply, and with tact and sympathy he set about establishing an intimacy between them.

Early the first morning he came to Meredith's room carrying the bulky volume of records on the first investigation of Giacomo Nerone. He found the priest, pale and fatigued, sitting in bed with the breakfast tray on his knees. He put the volume down on the table and then came, solicitously, to sit on the edge of the bed.

'A bad night, my friend?'

Meredith nodded wanly.

'A little worse than usual. The travel perhaps, and the excitement. I must apologise. I had hoped to serve Your Lordship's mass.'

The Bishop shook his head, smiling.

'No, Monsignor. Now you are under my jurisdiction. You are forbidden all but the Sunday Mass. You will sleep late and retire early, and if I find you working too hard, I may have to withdraw you from the case. You're in the country now. Take time for yourself. Smell the earth and the orange-blossom. Get the dust of the libraries out of your lungs.'

'Your Lordship is kind,' said Meredith gravely. 'But there is all too little time.'

'All the more reason to spend some of it on yourself,' the Bishop told him. 'And a little on me as well. I'm a stranger here too, remember. My colleagues are good men, most of them, but very dull company. There are things I should like to show you, talk I should like to hear from you. As for this—' he pointed to the bulky, leather-bound volume–'you can read it in the garden. Half of it is repetition and rhetoric. The rest you can digest in a couple of days. The people you want to see are only an hour away by car . . . and mine is at your disposal at any time, with a driver to look after you!'

A slow, puzzled smile dawned on Meredith's pallid face.

'You are kind to me and I find it strange. I wonder why?'

A youthful grin brightened the face of the Bishop.

'You have lived too long in Rome, my friend. You have forgotten that the Church is a family of the faithful, not simply a bureaucracy of believers. It's a sign of the times–one of the less hopeful signs. This is the century of the machine and the Church has conceded too much to it. They have time-clocks in the Vatican now and adding machines and ticker tape to tally the stock market.'

In spite of his weariness, Meredith threw back his head and laughed heartily. The Bishop nodded approvingly.

'That's better. A little honest laughter would do us all good. We need a satirist or two to give us back a sense of proportion.'

'We'd probably prosecute them for libel,' said Meredith wryly, 'or indict them for heresy.'

'*Inter faeces et urinam nascimur,*' the Bishop quoted quietly. 'It was a Saint who said it–and it applies equally to Popes and priests and the prostitutes of Reggio di Calabria. A little more laughter at our comic estate, a few honest tears for the pity of things–and we'd all be better Christians. Now finish your breakfast and then take a walk in the garden. I've spent a lot of time on it; and I'd hate an Englishman to ignore it!'

An hour later, bathed, shaved and refreshed, he walked out into the garden, taking with him the volume of depositions of Giacomo Nerone. It had rained during the night and the sky was clear, while the air was full of the smell of damp earth and washed leaves and new blossom. The bees were bumbling round the orange-flowers and the scarlet hibiscus, and the yellow gillyflowers stood straight and strident round the stone borders of the paths. Again Meredith was touched with hunger for a permanence on this thrusting earth whose beauty he was seeing for the first time. If only he could stay with it longer, root himself like a tree, to be weathered and blown, but still survive for the rain and the sun and the renewal of spring. But no. He had lived in the dust of the libraries too long and when the time came they would bury him in it. No flowers would grow out of his mouth as they did from the mouths of humbler men, no roots would twine themselves round the moult of his heart and his loins. They would screw him down in a leaden box and carry him to a vault in the Cardinal's church, where he would moulder, barren as he had lived, until Judgment Day.

Round the trunks of the olive trees the grass was green and the air was warm and still. He took off his cassock and his stock and opened his shirt to let the warmth fall on his thin chest: then he sat down, leaning against the bole of a tree, opened the big leather volume, and began to read:

'Preliminary depositions on the life, virtues and alleged miracles of the Servant of God, Giacomo Nerone. Collected at the instance and under the authority of His Lordship, Aurelio, Titular of Valenta in the Province of Calabria, by Geronimo Battista and Luigi Saltarello, priests of the same Diocese.'

Then followed the careful disclaimer:

'The following depositions and information are of a non-judicial character, since to this date no court has been set up and no authorities promulgated to examine officially the cause of the Servant of God. Though every effort has been made to arrive at the truth, witnesses were not sworn, nor placed under canonical sanction to reveal any matters known to them. None of the processes of a diocesan court have been observed either as to secrecy or the method of recording. Witnesses have, however, been warned that they may be called to give evidence under oath at such a court, when and if constituted.'

Blaise Meredith nodded and pursed his thin lips with satisfaction. So far so good. This was the bureaucracy of the Church in action–Roman legality applied to the affairs of the spirit. The sceptics might sneer at it, believers might chuckle at its excess, but in essence it was sound. It was the same genius that had given to the West the civilising code under which, in part at least, it still lived. He turned the page and read on:

'De non cultu. (Decree of Urban VIII, 1634)

'In view of the reports about the visits of pilgrims and the veneration paid by certain members of the faithful at the resting place of the Servant of God, we deemed it our first duty to inquire whether the decrees of the Pontiff Urban VIII prohibiting public cultus have been observed. We found that many members of the faithful, both visitors and local people, do visit the tomb of Giacomo Nerone and pray there. Some of them claim spiritual and temporal favours through his intercession. The civil authorities and, in particular, the Mayor of Gemello Maggiore have organised certain press publicity and improved transport facilities to encourage the flow of visitors. While this may constitute an indiscretion, it does not contravene the canons. No public worship is permitted in the canonical sense. The Servant of God is not invoked in liturgical ceremonies. No pictures or images are exposed for public veneration and, apart from garbled press accounts, no books or leaflets containing accounts of miracles have so far been circulated. Certain relics of the Servant of God are in private circulation among the faithful but no public veneration has been permitted to be paid to them. It is our view therefore that the canons prohibiting public cultus have been observed. . . .'

Blaise Meredith drowsed lightly over the formal phrases. This was old ground to him—familiar but reassuring. It was the function of the Church not merely to impose belief, but to limit it as well, to encourage piety but discourage pietists. The laws were there, however much they were obscured by ignorance, and their cool reason was a curb on the excesses of devotees and the harsh demands of the puritans. But he was still a long way from the heart of the problem—the life and virtues and alleged miracles of Giacomo Nerone. The next paragraph brought him no closer. It was headed:

'De scriptis

'No writings of any kind attributable to the Servant of God have been found. Certain references, noted later in the depositions, point to the possible existence of a body of manuscript which has been either lost, destroyed or is being deliberately concealed by interested persons. Until a judicial process has begun and it is possible to bring moral pressure to bear on witnesses, we are unlikely to get further information on this important point.'

Blaise Meredith frowned with dissatisfaction. No writings. A pity. From a judicial point of view the things a man wrote were the only sure indication of his beliefs and intentions, and, in the rigorous logic of Rome, these were even more important than his acts. A man might murder his wife or seduce his daughter and still remain a member of the Church; but let him reject one jot of defined truth and he set himself immediately outside it. He might spend himself in lifelong charities, yet have no merit in him at the end. The moral value of an act depended on the intention with which it was performed. But when a man was dead, who was to speak the secrets of his heart?

It was a discouraging beginning and what followed was even less reassuring:

'Biographical Summary

'Name: Giacomo Nerone. There is reason—noted later in the depositions—to assume that this was a pseudonym.

'Date of Birth: Unknown. Physical descriptions by witnesses vary considerably, but there is general agreement that he was from 30 to 35 years of age.

'Place of Birth: Unknown.

'*Nationality:* Unknown. There is evidence that Giacomo Nerone was at first accepted as an Italian, but that, later, doubts were cast on his identity. He was described as tall, dark and brown-skinned. He spoke Italian fluently and correctly though with a Northern accent. He did not at first speak dialect, but later learned it and spoke it constantly. During the period covered by his life in Gemelli dei Monti, there were units of German, American, British and Canadian troops operating in the province of Calabria. Various guesses have been made at his nationality, but the evidence advanced in support of them is, in our view, inconclusive.

'We are of the opinion, however, for reasons not yet clear that he did make a deliberate effort to conceal his true identity. We are also of the opinion that certain persons knew his identity and are still attempting to hide it.

'*Date of Arrival in Gemelli dei Monti:* The exact date is uncertain, but there is general agreement that it was towards the end of August, 1943. This date corresponds roughly with the Allied conquest of Sicily and the operations of the British Eighth Army in the Calabrian province.

'*Period of Residence in Gemelli dei Monti:* August, 1943, to 30th June, 1944. The whole of the testimony refers to this period of less than twelve months and any claims to heroic sanctity must be judged on the available records of this unusually short time.

'*Date of Death:* June 30th, 1944. 3 p.m. Giacomo Nerone was executed by a firing squad of Partisans under the leadership of a man known as Il Lupo, the Wolf. Both the date and the time are specific and confirmed by eye-witnesses. The circumstances are also confirmed by unanimous testimony.

'*Burial:* The burial took place at 10.30 p.m. on June 30th. The body of Giacomo Nerone was removed from the place of execution by six persons and buried in the place known as Grotta del Fauno, where it now lies. Both the identification of the body and the circumstances of the burial are confirmed by the unanimous testimony of those who took part in the interment.'

Blaise Meredith closed the thick volume and laid it down on the grass beside him. He leaned his head back against the rough bole of the olive tree and thought about what he had just read. True, it was only a beginning, but from the point of view of the Devil's Advocate it was a dubious one.

There were too many unknowns and the imputation of deliberate secrecy was disturbing. All that was known and covered by testimony was a period of eleven months, out of a lifetime of thirty to thirty-five years. There were no writings available for scrutiny. None of these things precluded sanctity, but they might well preclude proven sanctity, which was the matter of Meredith's investigation and the judicial process of the Bishop's court.

Always, in cases like this, one was forced back to the cool logic of the theologians.

It began with the premise of a personal God, self-continuing, self-sufficient, omnipotent. Man was the issue of a creative act of the divine will. The relationship between the Creator and His creature was defined first by the natural law, whose workings were visible and apprehensible by human reason, then by a series of divine relations, culminating in the Incarnation, the Teaching, Death and Resurrection of God-made-Man, Jesus Christ.

The perfection of man and his ultimate union with the Creator depended on his conformity to the relationship between them, his salvation depended on his being in a state of conformity at the moment of death. He was aided to this conformity by divine help, called grace, which was always available to him in sufficient measure to guarantee salvation, provided he co-operated with it by the use of free will. Salvation implied perfection, but a limited perfection.

But sanctity, heroic sanctity, implied a special call to a greater perfection, through the use of special graces—to none of which a man could attain by his own power. Every age has produced its crop of saints, not all of them were known, and not all known were officially proclaimed.

Official proclamation involved something else again: the implication that the Divinity wished to make known the virtues of the saint by calling attention to them through miracles—acts beyond human power—divine suspensions of the law of nature.

It was this implication that troubled Meredith at the outset of the case of Giacomo Nerone. It was a simple axiom of every theologian that an omnipotent Being could not, of his nature, lend himself either to triviality or to trivial secrecy.

There was nothing trivial in the birth of a man, since it involved the projection of a new soul into the dimensions of the flesh. There was nothing trivial in the progression of his life, since every act conditioned him for the last moment of it. And his death was the moment when the spirit was thrust out of the body in the irrevocable attitude of conformity or rejection.

So, whatever the gaps in the personal history of Giacomo Nerone, they must be filled. If facts were concealed, Blaise Meredith must ferret them out, because he, too, must soon be called to judgment.

But what a man must do and what his strength permits him are often two different things. The air was warm, the bourdon of the insects were deceptively soothing and the weariness of a sleepless night crept back insidiously. Blaise Meredith surrendered himself to it and slept on the soft grass until lunch-time.

His lordship chuckled delightedly when Meredith made rueful confession of his morning's slackness.

'Good! Good! We'll make a countryman of you yet. Did you dream pleasantly?'

'I didn't dream,' said Meredith with dry good-humour. 'And that was as big a mercy as sleep. But I didn't get much work done. I glanced through a few of the testimonies just before lunch, but I'm afraid I find them rather unsatisfactory.'

'How?'

'It's hard to define. They're in the normal form. They're obviously the result of careful cross-examination. But—how shall I put it?—they give no clear picture either of Giacomo Nerone, or of the witnesses themselves. And for our purposes both are important. The picture may grow, of course, as I go further, but just now there are no clear outlines.'

The Bishop nodded agreement.

'It was my own impression, too. It is one of the reasons for my doubts about the matter. The depositions are all of one piece. There are no elements of conflict or controversy. And saints are generally very controversial people.'

'But there are elements of secrecy.' Meredith put it to him quietly.

'Precisely.' The Bishop sipped his wine and considered his explanation. 'It is almost as if one section of the population had convinced itself that this man was a saint and wanted to prove it at all costs.

'And the other section?'

'Was determined to have nothing to say—either for or against.'

'It's too early for me to judge that,' said Meredith carefully. 'I haven't read enough or studied enough. But the tone of the statements I have read so far is stilted and strangely unreal, as if the witnesses were speaking a new language.'

'They are!' said the Bishop with sharp interest. 'Oddly enough, my friend, you have put your finger on a problem that has exercised me for a long time: the difficulty of accurate communication between the clergy and the laity. It is a difficulty which grows greater, instead of less, and which inhibits even the healing intimacy of the confessional. The root of it, I think, is this: the Church is a theocracy, ruled by a priestly caste, of which you and I are members. We have a language of our own—a hieratic language if you like—formal, stylised, admirably adapted to legal and theological definition. Unfortunately we have also a rhetoric of our own, which, like the rhetoric of the politician, says much and conveys little. But we are not politicians. We are teachers—teachers of a truth which we claim to be essential to man's salvation. Yet how do we preach it? We talk roundly of faith and hope as if we were making a fetishist's incantation. What is faith? A blind leap into the hands of God. An inspired act of will which is our only answer to the terrible mystery of where we came from and where we are going. What is hope? A child's trust in the hand that will lead it out of the terrors that reach from the dark. We preach love and fidelity, as if these were teacup tales—and not bodies writhing on a bed and hot words in dark places, and souls tormented by loneliness and driven to the momentary communion of a kiss. We preach charity and compassion but rarely say what they mean—hands dabbling in sick-room messes, wiping infection from syphilitic sores. We talk to the people every Sunday, but our words do not reach them, because we have forgotten our mother tongue. It wasn't always like this. The sermons of St Bernardine of Siena are almost unprintable today, but they reached hearts, because the truth in them was sharp as a sword, and as painful. . . .' He broke off and smiled, as if in deprecation of his own intensity. Then, after a moment, he said gently, 'That's the trouble with our witnesses, Monsignor. We don't understand them because they are talking to us as we talk to them. And it means as little either way.'

'Then how do I, of all people, come near them?' asked Meredith, with wry humility.

'The mother tongue,' said Aurelio, Bishop of Valenta. 'You were born, like them, *inter faeces et urinam,* and they will be surprised to know that you have not forgotten it—surprised enough, maybe, to tell you the truth.'

Later that afternoon, while the sun blazed outside the closed shutters and the wise folk of the South dozed away the heat, Blaise Meredith lay on his bed and pondered the words of the Bishop. They were true and he knew it. But the habit of years was strong on him; the careful euphemism, the priestly prudery, as though his tongue should be shamed by mention of the body that bore him and the sublime act that gave him being.

And yet Christ himself had dealt in such common coinage. He had talked in the vulgar tongue of vulgar symbols: a woman screaming in labour, the fat eunuchs waddling through the bazaars, the woman whom many husbands could not satisfy and who turned to a man who was not her husband. He had invoked no convention to shield himself from the men He had himself created. He ate with tax-farmers and drank with public women, and He did not shrink from the anointing hands that had caressed the bodies of men in the passion of a thousand nights.

And Giacomo Nerone? If he were a saint, he would be like his Master. If he were not, he would still be a man and the truth about him would be told in the simple language of the bedroom and the wine-shop.

As the afternoon wore on and the first chill of evening filtered into the room, Blaise Meredith began, slowly, to understand the task that lay ahead of him.

His first problem was a tactical one. Although the notices had been published, and the two major officials appointed, the court itself had not yet been constituted. Since all court testimony would be sworn and secret—and since there was no point in wasting its time with frivolous or unco-operative people—it was necessary to test them first in private and unsworn interviews, in the same fashion as a civil lawyer tests his witnesses before presenting them.

They had already been interviewed once by Battista and Saltarello, whose records were in his hands. But these were local priests, and by presumption impartial—if not actually in favour of the candidate. His own position was vastly different. He was a foreigner, a Vatican official, the crown prosecutor. He was suspect by the very nature of his office, and if worldly interests were involved—as they undoubtedly were—he could count on active and powerful opposition.

Those who were promoting the Cause of the Saint would be careful to steer him clear of any contentious information. If they had given testimony in favour of Giacomo Nerone, they would not change it for the Devil's Advocate—though they might break down if he could find grounds on which to challenge them. It was folly, of course, to make intrigues about the Almighty, but there was as much folly and intrigue inside the Church as there was outside. The Church was a family of men and women, none of them guaranteed impeccable even by the Holy Ghost.

His best chance therefore seemed to lie with those who had refused to give evidence at all. It might not be easy to find out why some people didn't believe in saints and regarded their cults as a noxious superstition. These might well be willing to reveal anything that pointed to clay feet on a popular idol. Some folk believed in saints but wanted no truck with them at all. They found them uncomfortable company, their virtues a perpetual reproach. There was no one so stubborn as a Catholic at odds with his conscience. Finally there might be those who hesitated to reveal facts creditable to the candidate because they were discreditable to themselves.

The next problem was where to find such people. According to the records of Battista and Saltarello, all the positive information came from Gemello Maggiore, the prosperous village, and all the refusals from the depressed twin across the valley. The distinction was too obvious to be ignored and too artificial to be accepted without question. Meredith decided to discuss it with the Bishop at their next meal together.

His Lordship approached the question with more than usual caution.

'For me, too, this has been one of the most puzzling features of the situation. Let me try to put it into perspective for you. Here are two villages, twins by name and twins by nature, perched on the horns of the same mountain. Before the war, what were they? Typical Calabrian hamlets—small depressed places, inhabited by tenant farmers of absentee landlords. In their outward aspect and in their standard of living there was no perceptible difference between them; except that in Gemello Minore there was a resident *padrona*, the Contessa de Sanctis. . . .' The Bishop leaned ironically on the parenthesis. 'An interesting woman, the Contessa. I'll be curious to know what you think of her. You'll be her house-guest when you go to Gemello Minore. However, her presence, then as now, made no difference to the state of the local population. . . . Then came the war. The young men were taken for the Army, the old ones and the women were left to farm the land. It is poor land at best, as you will see, and it got poorer and poorer as the years went on. There was a State levy on the crops, and by the time the landlords had taken their share, there was little enough left for the peasants, and often there was real starvation in the mountains. Now . . .' His Lordship's long, sensitive hands gestured emphatically. 'Into this situation comes a man, a stranger, who calls himself Giacomo Nerone. What do we know about him?'

'Little enough,' said Blaise Meredith. 'He arrives from nowhere dressed in peasant rags. He is wounded and sick with malaria. He claims to be a deserter from the fighting in the South. The villagers accept him at face value. They have sons of their own who are far away. They have no sympathy with a lost cause. A young widow named Nina Sanduzzi takes him into her house and cares for him. He enters into a liaison with her which is later broken off . . . right in the middle of her pregnancy.'

'And then?' The Bishop prompted him shrewdly.

Blaise Meredith shrugged in puzzled fashion.

'Then I find myself at a loss. The record is unclear. The witnesses are vague. There is talk of a conversion, a turning to God. Nerone leaves the house of Nina Sanduzzi and builds himself a small hut in the most desolate corner of the valley. He plants a garden. He spends hours in solitude and contemplation. He appears in church on Sundays and takes the Sacraments. At the same time—the same time, mark you—he appears to have taken over the leadership of the villages.'

'How does he lead them, and to what? I'm quizzing you, Meredith, because I want to see what you, the newcomer, have made of this story. I myself know it by heart, but I am still puzzled by it.'

'As I read the evidence,' said Meredith carefully, 'he began by going from house to house offering his services to anyone who needed them—an old man whose land was getting away from him, a grandmother, feeble and alone, a sick farmer who wanted someone to hoe his tomato patch. From those who could afford it he demanded a payment in kind—goat milk, olives, wine, cheese—which he passed on to those who were in need of these things. Later, when winter came, he organised a pooling of labour and resources, and enforced it rigorously, sometimes violently.'

'An unsaintly proceeding, surely?' suggested the Bishop, with a thin smile.

'That was my own feeling,' admitted Meredith.

'But even Christ whipped the money-changers out of the Temple, did he not? And when you know our Calabresi, you'll agree that they have the hardest heads and the tightest fists in Italy.'

Meredith was forced to smile at the trap the Bishop had set for him.

He conceded the point, smiling:

'We mark it then to the credit of Giacomo Nerone. The next thing is in his favour too. He nurses the sick and appears to have given some kind of rough medical service in collaboration with a certain doctor, Aldo Meyer, a political exile, who curiously enough refused to give any testimony in the case.'

'That point, too, has been much in my mind,' the Bishop told him. 'It is the more interesting since, before and after the war, Meyer himself had tried to organise these people for their own benefit, but failed completely. He's a man of singular humanity, but handicapped by being a Jew in a Catholic country–perhaps by other things too. You should try to get close to him. You may be surprised. . . . Go on, please.'

'Next we find evidence of more religious activity. Nerone prays with the sick, comforts the dying. He makes journeys in the snow to bring the priest with the Last Sacrament. When there is no priest he himself waits out the death-watch. Now there's an odd thing . . .' Meredith paused for an uncertain moment. 'Two of the witnesses say: "When Father Anselmo refused to come . . ." What would that mean?'

'What it says, I imagine,' His Lordship told him coolly. 'There has been much scandal about this man. I have thought often of removing him, but so far I have decided against it.'

'You have a reputation for rigid discipline. You have removed others. Why not this one?'

'He is an old man,' said the Bishop softly. 'Old and, I think, very near to despair, I should hate to think I was the one who drove him into it.'

'I'm sorry.' Meredith was instantly apologetic.

'Not at all. We're friends. You have a right to ask. But I'm a Bishop, not a bureaucrat. I carry the shepherd's crook and the stray sheep are mine, too. Go on. Read me more of Giacomo Nerone.'

Meredith ran a hand through his thinning hair. He was getting tired. It was an effort to keep his thoughts in order.

'Somewhere about March, 1944, the Germans came–a small detachment at first, then a larger one–garrison reinforcements for those fighting against the British Eighth Army, which had crossed the Strait of Messina and was fighting its way up the toe of Calabria. Giacomo Nerone is the one who negotiates with them, successfully, it seems. The peasants will supply a guaranteed minimum of fresh food in return for medicines and winter clothing. The garrison commander will discipline his troops and protect the women whose husbands and brothers are away. The bargain is kept reasonably well, and Nerone establishes himself as a respected mediator. This association with the Germans was later alleged as a reason for his execution by the Partisans. When the Allies broke through and began pushing up towards Naples, they bypassed the villages and left the local Partisans to deal with the scattered and retreating German forces. Giacomo Nerone stayed on . . .'

The Bishop checked him with a slim, upraised hand.

'Stop there a moment. What do you see, so far?'

'Ignotus!' said Meredith calmly. 'The unknown. The man from nowhere. The lost one, who suddenly becomes the godly one. He has a sense of gratitude, a touch of compassion, a talent, and perhaps a taste, for leadership. But who is he? Where does he come from, or why does he act as he does?'

'You see no saint in him?'

Meredith shook his head.

'Not yet. Godliness perhaps, but not sanctity. I have not yet examined the evidence for the alleged miracles, so I leave this out of consideration. But I make one point. There is a pattern in sanctity, a great reasonableness. As yet I see no reason here, only secrecy and mystery.'

'Perhaps there is no mystery—just ignorance and misunderstanding. Tell me, my friend, what do you know of conditions here in the South at that time?'

'Little enough,' Meredith admitted frankly. 'For all of the war I was locked inside Vatican City. I only knew what I heard and read—and that was garbled enough, God knows.'

'Then let me explain them to you.' He got up and walked to the window, to stand looking out on the garden, where the wind stirred faintly through the shrubbery and the shadows were deep because there was still no moon over the hill-tops. When he spoke his voice was tinged with an old sadness. 'I am an Italian, and I understand this story better than most though I do not yet understand the people in it. First you must realise that a defeated people has no loyalties. Their leaders have failed them. Their sons have died in a lost cause. They believe in no one—not even in themselves. When our conquerors came in, shouting democracy and freedom we did not believe them either. We looked only at the loaf of bread in their hands and calculated exactly the price they would ask us to pay for it. Hungry people don't even believe in the loaf until it is safely swallowed and they can feel it aching in their unaccustomed stomachs. That's the way it was here in the South. The people were defeated, leaderless, hungry. Worse than that, they were forgotten; and they knew it.'

'But Nerone hadn't forgotten them,' Meredith objected. 'He was still with them. He was still a leader.'

'Not any more. There were new barons in the land. Men with new guns and full bandoliers and a rough rescript of authority from the conquerors to clean out the mountains and hold them tidy until a new and amenable Government was established. Their names and their faces were familiar—Michele, Gabriele, Luigi, Beppi. They had bread to bargain with and meat in tin cans and bars of chocolate, and old scores to settle as well: political scores and personal ones. They saluted with the clenched fist of comradeship, and with the same fist beat the faces of those who dared to differ from them. They were many and they were strong, because your Mr Churchill had said that he would do business with anybody who could help him to clean up the mess in Italy and let him get on with the invasion of France. What could Giacomo Nerone do against them—your Ignotus from nowhere?'

'What did he try to do? That's what interests me. Why did some folk cling to him as the holy one and others reject him and betray him to the executioners? Why were the Partisans against him in the first place?'

'It's in the record,' said His Lordship with a tired smile.

'They called him a collaborator. They accused him of profitable commerce with the Germans.'

Meredith rejected the suggestion emphatically.

'It's not enough! It's not enough to explain the hate and the violence and the division and why one village prospers and the other lapses deeper into depression. It's not enough for us either. The people claim a martyrdom–death in defence of the Faith and moral principles. All you've shown me is a political execution–unjust and cruel maybe–but still only that. We're not concerned with politics, but with sanctity, the direct relationship of a man with the God who made him.'

'Perhaps that's all it was–a good man caught up in politics.'

'Does Your Lordship believe that?'

'Does it matter what I believe, Monsignor?'

The shrewd patrician face was turned towards him. The thin lips smiled in irony.

Then, quite suddenly, the truth hit him, cold water in the face. This man too had a cross to bear. Bishop he might be, but there were still doubts to plague him and fears to harry him on the high peak of temptation. A rare compassion stirred in the dry heart of Blaise Meredith and he answered quietly:

'Does it matter? I think it matters much.'

'Why, Monsignor?' The deep, wise eyes challenged him.

'Because I think that you, like me, are afraid of the finger of God.'

5

Nicholas Black, the painter, was making a new picture.

It was a simple composition but oddly dramatic: a tumble of bare rocks, pitted and weathered, stained by fungus and mottled like the sloughed skin of a snake; out of the rocks grew a solitary olive tree, dead and bare of leaves, whose naked arms were outflung like a cross against the clear blue of the sky.

He had been working on it for an hour now, in the bright solitude of a small plateau behind the shoulder of the hill, with the chequer-board valley below him, and above, the heave of the tufted mountain, splashed with noon sun.

The sun was warm on his brown, stringy torso. The air was languid and dry but noisy with cicadas, and Paolo Sanduzzi dozed a yard from his feet, relaxed as a lizard on a grey rock.

Nicholas Black was a stranger to contentment, and full satisfaction came to him rarely; but in this quiet place and hour, in the company of the sleeping boy, with a picture growing strongly under his hand, he was as close to it as he had ever been.

He painted steadily, contentedly, his thoughts turned outwards on the canvas and on the grey, writhing tree, which was like a gallows on a miniature Golgotha. There was a strength in it that appealed to him–a sinew in the wood, muscle and bone under the rough, grey bark, as if one day it might split asunder and a man emerge shining and new to a kind of resurrection in the dawn.

He admired strength–the more because there was so little in himself–yet he was rarely able to translate it into works. The critics had noted the lack long ago. They admired the charm of his pictures, the bravura, the dramatic brilliance, but deplored the soft bone and the pale blood beneath their sleek skin. Later they called him *raté*–the man who would never quite make it, because of some fundamental weakness in his own personality. After that, of course, they were kind to him, in the condescending style they reserve for amiable mediocrities and hardy perennials. They always noticed his shows. They gave him praise enough to keep the dowagers buying and the smaller dealers mildly interesed. But they never took him seriously.

Now and again one of the young bloods sharpened his teeth on a Nicholas Black exhibition, and it was one of these who had written the brutal epitaph that set London laughing for a week and drove Black across the Channel to Rome and Anne Louise de Sanctis.

'One of the eunuchs of the profession,' said the clever young critic. 'Doomed to live forever in the contemplation of beauty, but never, never to possess it.'

In the Bag O' Nails and the Stag and the B.B.C. Club they chuckled into their beer. In the Georgian sitting-rooms of Knightsbridge they giggled over the cocktails. Under the mansards of Chelsea they made a bawdy lyric about it; and the one who shared his flat and more than half his love chanted it to his face at the end of a quarrelsome evening.

It was the bitterest moment in his life, and even now, two thousand miles and six months away from it, the memory was vivid and shameful. It was a special terror, this one; a very particular hell reserved for those poor devils who, by oversight or irony of the Creator, come into the world defective in those attributes which define a man. Their more normal fellows disdain them, as poetasters disdain a parody which points to the pomposities of their own work, as honest wives disdain a prostitute who sells for money what they refuse for love. So they make a kingdom among themselves, a half-world of lost lovers, of furtive encounters and strange marriages. There is loyalty in the half-world, but not enough of it for armour against the intriguers inside and the mockers at the flimsy gates. And when a man like Nicholas Black leaves it he becomes the lone pilgrim of a secret cult, whose symbols are the *graffiti* on toilet walls, the phallic gesture and the brushing touch in an assembly of strangers.

But now he had come to an oasis on the pilgrim road. He was painting a tree as strong and alive as a man. And a boy, berry-brown and languid, was sleeping at his feet in the sun. He made one last careful stroke, then laid down his brush and palette and stood looking down at Paolo Sanduzzi.

He was lying on his back, one knee drawn up, one arm pillowed under his head, the other lying slack on the warm grey rock. His only clothing was a pair of stained shorts and worn leather sandals. In the dry, warm air his skin shone like oiled wood and his smooth boyish face wore, in repose, an air of curious innocence.

Nicholas Black had long been a stranger to innocence. He had joined too often in the mockery and seduction of it. But he could still recognise it, still be jealous of it—and here, remote from the mockery, he could still regret the loss of it.

He sat down on the warm rock a few paces from the boy and smoked a pensive cigarette, caught in the rare syncope of contentment between the accusing past and the dubious future.

Suddenly the boy sat up and looked at him with shrewd, speculative eyes.

'Why do you always look at me like that?'

Black smiled calmly and said:

'You are beautiful, Paolino. Like the Young David whom Michelangelo carved out of a piece of marble. I am an artist—a lover of beauty. So I like to look at you.'

'I want to piss,' said the boy, grinning.

He leapt up and walked to the edge of the plateau and stood straddle-legged, easing himself in full view of Nicholas Black, who saw the mockery in it but made no protest. The boy came lounging back and squatted down beside him. He was still smiling, but there was a sidelong calculation in his dark eyes. He asked bluntly:

'Will you take me to Rome when you go?'

Black shrugged in the manner of the South.

'Who knows? Rome is a long way and expensive. I can get plenty of servants here. But a friend–that might be different.'

'But you told me I was your friend!' The eagerness was so bright and childish that it might have deceived him, but the truth was in the boy's eyes, dark as onyx.

'A friend must prove himself,' said the painter, with careful indifference. 'There's time yet. We'll see.'

'But I'm a good friend. A true one,' Paolo pleaded childishly. 'Look, I'll show you!'

He flung his arms round Black's neck, embraced him quickly, and then leapt away, shy as an animal, out of reach. The painter wiped his mouth with the back of his hand and then got up slowly, with the salt taste of disillusion on his tongue. He did not look at the boy who stood, arms akimbo, on a rock ledge ten feet away. He walked to the easel, picked up his brush and palette and said over his shoulder:

'Take off your clothes!' The boy stared at him.

Black yelled at him harshly.

'Go on! Take them off. I want to use you as a model. That's what you're paid for, among other things.'

After a moment's uneasy pause, the boy obeyed, and Black smiled with sardonic satisfaction when he saw how the boldness and the challenge was stripped from him with the tattered breeches. He was just a child now–scared, uncertain, in the presence of a temperamental employer.

'Stretch out your arms. Like this.'

The boy raised his arms slowly to the level of his shoulders.

'Now hold them there.'

With swift sure strokes Nicholas Black began to paint a crucified figure on the writhing shape of the olive tree: no tormented Christus, but a youth in full puberty with the face and body of Paolo Sanduzzi, nailed to the tree bark through hands and feet, with the red spear thrust in his breast, but smiling even while the life bled out of him.

The boy was weary long before it was finished, but he kept him standing there and cursed him whenever he dropped his arms. Then when it was done he called him over and showed him the picture. The effect was startling. The boy's face crumpled into a mask of terror, his mouth dropped open and he stood shivering and gibbering and pointing at the canvas.

'What's the matter? What are you trying to tell me?'

Black's voice was high and harsh but it made no impression on Paolo Sanduzzi. He was like someone at the beginning of an epileptic fit. Black walked up to him and slapped him sharply on both cheeks. The boy cried out in pain and then began to weep, squatting on the ground and covering his face with his hands, while Black knelt beside him trying to soothe him. After a while he asked him again:

'What's the matter? What frightened you?'

The Devil's Advocate

The boy's voice was almost a whisper.

'The picture!'

'What's the matter with it?'

'That's my father's tree!'

The painter gaped at him.

'What do you mean?'

'That's how they killed my father. On that same tree. They stretched him out on it, like on a cross, tied him up—and then shot him.'

'O God!' Nicholas Black swore softly. 'Sweet angels, what a story! What a sweet, sweet story.'

Then after a while he began to laugh, and the boy slunk away, frightened and subdued, carrying his trousers and sandals in his hand.

The same noontide saw Doctor Aldo Meyer restored to temporary favour in Gemello Minore.

Martino the smith had suffered a stroke while working at the anvil. He had fallen against the forge and been badly burned on the breast and face. They had carried him down the road to Meyer's cottage and the doctor was working on him now, assisted by Nina Sanduzzi, while Martino's wife watched nervously from the corner of the room and the villagers crowded outside the cottage chattering like starlings over this crumb of drama.

The thick barrel body of the smith was wrapped in blankets and laid on the plank table in Meyer's kitchen. One side of him was completely paralysed—the leg and arm useless, the face wrenched sideways into a rictus of surprise and fear. His eyes were closed and his breathing was shallow and noisy. As Meyer probed and swabbed the burns on his cheeks, a low, mumbling cry issued from his twisted mouth. When they had finished dressing the face, they unrolled the blankets and Meyer gave a low, thoughtful whistle as he saw the extent and the depth of the body burns. Nina Sanduzzi stood impassive as a statue, holding the bowl of boiling water and the swabs. When Martino's wife started forward, she laid down the bowl quite calmly and led her back to the corner, soothing and chiding her in a low confident voice. Then she came back to Meyer and, attentive as any nurse, helped him to pick the charcoal from the burns, cleanse them and dab them with gentian violet and the last small stock of Merthiolate.

When the dressings were done, Meyer made another auscultation and a pulse count, wrapped the blankets back again, and turned to talk to the weeping woman in the corner. He told her gently:

'You'd better leave him here for a couple of hours. Then I'll have him taken home to you.'

She pleaded with him, plaintive as an animal.

'He won't die, will he, Doctor? You won't let him die?'

'He's as strong as an ox,' said Meyer calmly. 'He won't die.'

She caught at his hands, kissing them and calling on the saints to bless the good doctor. Meyer disengaged himself brusquely.

'Go home now, like a good woman, and get your children fed. I'll send for you, if I want you—and later you'll get your husband home.'

Nina Sanduzzi took her by the arm and led her out of the room, and when he turned back to his patient he heard her at the door, shouting at the bystanders and urging them off about their business. When she came back she asked bluntly:

'Did you mean what you told her? He will live?'

'He'll live,' Meyer told her, shrugging. 'But he'll never be any good to himself or to her.'

'He's got six children.'

'Too many,' said Meyer with thin humour.

'But he has them,' she persisted stubbornly. 'Who is to feed them now that he cannot work?'

Meyer shrugged.

'There's public relief. They won't starve.'

'Public relief!' She flung it back at him scornfully. 'A dozen interviews and a hundred printed forms for a kilo of pasta! What sort of answer is that?'

'It's the only one I know these days,' Meyer told her with cool bitterness. 'I used to have lots of others, but no one would listen. They wanted to go on in the old way. Well . . . this is the old way!'

Nina Sanduzzi stared at him. There were pity and contempt in her dark, intelligent eyes.

'You know what Giacomo would have done, don't you? He'd have gone into the forge himself and worked. He'd have knocked on every door and begged or bullied people into helping. He'd have gone up to the villa and talked to the Contessa for money and work for Martino's wife. He'd have prised some poor-box money out of Father Anselmo. He understood this sort of thing. He knew how scared people get. He could never bear to hear a child crying . . .'

'He was a remarkable man, your Giacomo,' said Meyer tersely. 'That's why they killed him. Martino, as I remember, was one of those who fired the volley.'

'And you signed a paper saying that he had been legally executed after a proper trial.' There was no anger in her voice, only a quiet recollection of familiar facts. 'But none of you ever told the true reason why he was killed.'

'What was it, then?' he challenged her harshly.

'There was not one reason. There were twenty. There was Martino's reason and the Contessa's and Father Anselmo's and Battista's and Lupo's and yours, too, *dottore mio*. But you couldn't admit them, even to one another, so you found one that suited you all – Giacomo was a collaborator, a lover of Fascists and Germans! You were the liberators, the friends of freedom, the little brothers of all the world. You brought us democracy. All Giacomo ever brought was a crust of bread and a bowl of soup and a pair of hands to work when the man of the house was sick.'

Her calm indictment goaded him and he blazed back:

'That's the whole damn trouble with this country. That's why we're still fifty years behind the rest of Europe. We won't organise, we won't discipline ourselves. We won't co-operate. You can't build a better world on a bowl of pasta and a bucket of holy water.'

'You can't build it on bullets, either, Dottore. You got what you wanted. You killed Giacomo. Now what's to show for it? Martino can't work any more. Who's to feed his wife and six children?'

There was no answer to this brutal logic and he turned away, shamed and impotent, and walked to the door that gave on to the hot, bright garden. After a moment Nina Sanduzzi followed him and laid a tentative hand on his sleeve.

'You think I hate you, Dottore. I don't. Giacomo didn't hate you either. Before he died, he came to see me. He knew what was going to happen. He knew you were concerned in it. But do you know what he said to me? "This is a good man, Nina. He has tried to do too much, but he is unhappy because he has never really understood what it is to love and to be loved. He wants to organise and reform, but he does not see that these are barren things without loving. I'm lucky, because I had you to teach me in the beginning. He has been alone too long. When I am dead, go to him and he will be kind to you. If a time should come when you find that a man is necessary to you again–this would be one who would be good to you and to the boy." He wrote a letter to you and put it among his papers. I was to deliver it to you, after he died.'

Meyer swung round to stare at her.

'A letter! Where is it, woman? Where, for God's sake?'

Nina Sanduzzi spread her hands in despair.

'I had all his papers in my cupboard. When Paolo was little, one day he got to them and jumbled them together. Some he tore, others he crumpled, and when I gathered them up again, I could not tell one from the other. . . .' She blushed as if at a shameful revelation. 'I–I've never learned to read!'

His hands reached out and grasped her roughly by the shoulders.

'I must see the papers, Nina. I must see them. You don't know how important it is.'

'Six children are important,' said Nina Sanduzzi quietly. 'And a woman whose man cannot work any more.'

'If I help them, you'll show me the papers?'

She shook her head in outright refusal.

'That was something else Giacomo said: "One should never bargain with people's bodies." If you want to help them you will do it, without asking to be paid. Later we can talk about the papers.'

He was beaten and he knew it. There was a granite strength in this woman who could not read, an inviolable reserve of wisdom which he, the lifetime student, could not match. What puzzled him was that there were no roots for it in her peasant origins and he would not admit she had acquired it from Giacomo Nerone. Yet she, like Nerone, held the key to a mystery that had eluded Aldo Meyer for twenty years: why some men with talent, good will and compassion never achieve full human contact and raise only contention and ridicule among those they try to help; and why others, with no apparent effort, walk straight into intimacy and are remembered with love long after their death.

In Nerone's papers he might read the answer which he lacked the courage to ask from Nina Sanduzzi. But he could not get them on her terms. So he shrugged in resignation and told her:

'I'm dining tonight with the Contessa. I'll tell her about Martino and see what we can do.'

A smile lightened her calm, classic face. With an impulsive gesture, she caught up his hand and kissed it.

'You are a good man, Dottore. I'll tell Martino's wife. No one should be left afraid too long.'

'You can tell me something too, Nina.'

'Yes, Dottore?'

'What would you say if I asked you to marry me?'

Her dark, deep eyes showed neither surprise nor pleasure.

'I would tell you what I told you the first time, Dottore. Better you didn't ask.'

The she left him quickly and Aldo Meyer returned to his patient to feel the fluttering, uncertain pulse and hear the hardy peasant heart battling for life inside the scarred breast.

Paolo Sanduzzi stood on the edge of the stream, bouncing pebbles off the water and watching them skip into the bushes on the opposite side. The stream had one name and three faces. Its name was Torrente del Fauno–the torrent of the faun–because in the old days, long before Christ came down from Rome with St Peter, the fauns used to play here, chuckling goat boys, chasing the tree girls who were called dryads. After the church was built, they all went away; which was rather a pity, because the valley was dull without them. But the name persisted and sometimes the boys and girls of the village met here secretly to play the old pagan games.

The face of the stream changed with the seasons. In winter it was dark, cold and sinister, fringed sometimes with the white rime of frost and piled snow. In spring it was brown and boisterous, roaring so loud with thaw water that one could hear it right up in the village. By summer it had dwindled to a thin, clear runnel singing softly over the stones, lying in quiet pools under the overhang of the banks. Before autumn came, it was dry again–a parched bed full of bleached stones. Now it wore its gentle face, and Paolo Sanduzzi, who was like a faun himself, was glad to be here away from the dead gallows-tree and the Englishman whose laughter was like water bubbling in a black pot.

He had never been so frightened in his life; and he was still frightened. It was as if the painter held the key to his life: to the past which shamed him and to the future which he could see only dimly as a vision of Rome with its churches and palaces, its streets full of shiny automobiles and its pavements crowded with girls who dressed like princesses.

The vision laid a spell on him–half-pleasant, half-sinister–like the charms old Nonna Patucci gave to the girls to draw their lover to them. He could feel it working now, an itch under his skin, an oppressive image behind his eyeballs. Sooner or later it would draw him back to the Englishman, whose mocking smile sometimes made him feel awkward as a child and sometimes woke strange, disturbing passions in him, without even a word or a hand's touch.

He tossed a last negligent stone into the water, thrust his hands into his pockets and began to walk downstream. As he rounded a bend in the bank, a shrill voice hailed him.

'Eh, Paoluccio!'

He looked up and saw Rosetta, the daughter of Martino the smith, sitting on a rock and dangling her legs in the water. She was a thin, elfin child, a year younger than himself, with lank hair and a small, pert face and budding breasts under the faded cotton shift which was her only clothing. In the village he ignored her studiously, but now he was glad to see her. He waved an indifferent hand.

'Eh, Rosetta!'

Then he went and sat beside her on the rock.

'My father's sick. He fell down in a fit and burned himself on the forge. He's in the doctor's house.'

'Is he dying?'

'No. The doctor says he'll live. Mother's crying. She gave us all bread and cheese and sent us out to play. Want some?'

She held up a hunk of rough bread and a cut of goat cheese.

'I'm hungry,' said Paolo.

She broke the bread and the cheese carefully into equal pieces and handed him his share. They sat there munching silently in the sun, cooling their feet in the water. After a while she asked him:

'Where have you been, Paoluccio?'

'With the Englishman.'

'What doing?'

He shrugged indifferently, as a man does with inquisitive women.

'Working.'

'What sort of work?'

'I carry his things. When he paints, I watch. Sometimes he asks me to model for him.'

'What's model?'

'I just stand there and he paints me.'

'Teresina says there are girls in Naples who take off their clothes for men to paint them.'

'I know,' he nodded wisely.

'Do you take your clothes off, too?'

The question caught him unawares and he answered it roughly.

'That's my business.'

'But you do, don't you? If you're a model, that is.'

'It's a secret, Rosetta,' he told her seriously. 'Don't tell anyone; they wouldn't understand.'

'I won't tell. I promise.' She put her thin arm round him and leaned her head on his bare shoulder. The gesture embarrassed him, but pleased him, too. He let her stay there and because he was pleased, he said:

'The Englishman says I'm beautiful, like the statue that Michelangelo carved out of marble.'

'That's silly. Only women are beautiful. Boys are nice or nasty. Not beautiful.'

'That's what he said anyway,' he answered defensively. 'He said I was beautiful and he loved beauty and liked to look at me!'

In her odd elfin way she was angry with him. She took her arm away from him and slewed around to face him.

'Now I know you're making it up. Men don't say things like that. Only women!'

She put her arms round his neck and pressed her lips on his, and when he tried to resist, she held him more tightly; and when he felt her breasts against him through the shirt, he decided that it was pleasant after all. And he began to kiss her, too.

Later she took his face in her small hands and said gravely:

'I love you, Paoluccio. I love you really. Not like a statue.'

'I love you, too, Rosetta!'

'I'm glad.' She leaped up and stood holding her hand out to him. 'Now take me for a walk!'

'Why?'

'Because we love each other, silly, and that's what lovers do. Besides, I've got a secret.'

'What secret?'

'Take me for a walk and I'll show you.'

In spite of himself, he reached up his hand to her. She caught it and dragged him to his feet, and they walked upstream, through the clear water and under the green bushes, to share the old secrets that the dryads told to the dancing fauns.

From his high, plateau eyrie behind the shoulder of the mountain, Nicholas Black looked down on the spread pattern of his past. For the first time in his life, its form was clear to him—and how the future grew out of it, inevitable and identical, as the new shoots on a tree.

From the beginning, he had been cheated: the hidden foetal beginning when the determinant elements were doled out by whatever power decided that, out of the blind coupling of man and wife, there should grow a parody of a man.

He had been born a twin—identical in face and form with the brother who preceded him by an hour out of the womb. He had been born a Catholic, to one of the old Fenland families who had kept the Faith whole from the time of the first Elizabeth to that of the last George. He had been baptized with his brother and blessed with the same blessing, in the manor chapel from whose steps the lawns flowed down broad and green to the reed fringe and the grey fen-water.

But here the identity ended and the slow division began. The first-born grew swart and strong, the second was wan and sickly. They were like Esau and Jacob—but Esau enjoyed the birthright: the field sports, the fishing, the long rides in the dappled summer; while Jacob clung to the shelter of the house and the safe harbour of the sewing-room and the library. At school he lagged behind, was a year late at Oxford; and while his twin went off with a gunnery commission in the Western Desert, he was confined to a hospital bed with rheumatic fever. All the strength was in the one; all the weakness in the other. All the maleness belonged to the first-born, and in Nicholas Black there was only an epicene beauty, the soft subtlety of a mind turned back too long upon itself.

While his brother lived, there was a hope for him that he might borrow strength and find dignity in affection. Afterwards, when the word came through, 'Missing, believed killed', the last hope died and the hidden bitterness began to grow. He had been cheated: by God, by life, by his dead twin, by his father, who after a hushed scandal in London had warned him out of the house and given him a small annuity to keep him away from it.

He had been solitary ever since. His belief had been shipwrecked on the most difficult mystery of all: that a just God can make monsters and still expect them to live like men. His heart had been hardened by the brief loves of the half-world. And now, suddenly, power was put in his hands—power to make another what he had failed to make himself: a man, noble in nature, talent and execution. In the making he might reframe his own life—to dignity, to understanding, to a purer love than any he had yet experienced.

He was getting old. Passion woke more slowly and was easier to control, except when it was piqued by vanity and competition. With the boy as his ward, he would achieve a kind of paternity, which would give to his own life a discipline and a direction it had always lacked.

It was a dizzy moment, a god-like elevation.

This youth was the son of a reputed saint, begotten on the body of a village whore. His life was as predictable as that of a million others in the workless villages of Midday Italy. He would mature in idleness, marry too young and breed too often and live aimlessly on the extreme margin of poverty. Whatever talent he had would be stifled by the brute struggle for existence. The Church would censure him while he lived and absolve him before he died. The State would be saddled with a dozen reproductions of him, fecund and hungry as rabbits, eating out the last green of an impoverished land.

But take him out of the village, give him opportunity and education, and he might well grow to greatness, justifying himself and his teacher as well. Where his father had failed, and the Church had failed, Nicholas Black might yet succeed–and his success would be a splendid negation of the beliefs he had long rejected.

To the critics, Nicholas Black was a mediocre artist. If out of this peasant clay he could mould a perfect man, it would be a triumph beyond cavil, a masterwork beyond the reach of malice.

It was a strange ambition, and yet, in its own idiom, no stranger than the triumphs and revenges that other men dreamed for themselves–financial empires strong enough to crush all opposition, power in the press to make men or bury them in obscurity, woman dreams and opium dreams and the dream of standing one day at the dispatch box to hear one's enemies say . . . 'The Right Honourable the Prime Minister . . .'

Each man to his own damnation, and nobler men have dreamed more basely in their nightshirts than Nicholas Black on his sunlit plateau in Calabria.

It was late and he had not eaten, but he was drunk on the heady wine of anticipation and he did not care. The village would be settling down to siesta. The Contessa would be locked in her baroque room and he could bring his picture into the villa without exciting too much attention.

He was counting much on this canvas. He wondered how Anne Louise de Sanctis would react to it–and Aldo Meyer, and the grey cleric who was coming to research into the past of Giacomo Nerone. He smiled as he pictured them gaping at it for the first time, their secrets written in their eyes and on their faces.

He cast about for a title, and found one almost immediately–'The Sign of Contradiction'. The more he thought of it, the more he liked it. It reminded him of the old *graffito* in which an ass is crucified to represent the Christus, a bawdy joke by a bumpkin comedian. But for Nicholas Black the symbol had a new significance: youth nailed to the cross of ignorance, superstition and poverty, half-dead and damned already, but smiling still, a drugged, ecstatic victim of time and its tyrannies.

6

Monsignor Blaise Meredith and Aurelio, Bishop of Valenta, were concerned with another contradiction: the alleged miracles of Giacomo Nerone.

They were standing on the broad, flagged terrace of the villa looking down into the valley, where workmen were moving slowly up and down the plantation, spraying the young trees from new shoulder-packs of American pattern. On the wall of the small dam others were working to instal new sluice-gates that would control the flow of water to farms outside the

Bishop's domain. Beyond the spillway, on a grey, untilled hill-side, women with baskets on their backs were carrying stones to build new vine-terraces, and earth to pack behind them.

They were like ants, small and industrious, and Meredith was moved to the ironic reflection that this was as great a miracle as any in his leather folio: barren land being built back slowly to fruitfulness by the creative will of one man. He said as much to the Bishop, whose lean, intelligent face puckered into a smile.

'It's bad theology, my friend; but a pleasant compliment. To these people, it is a kind of miracle. Suddenly there is work and bread on the table and an extra litre of oil for the cook-pot. They cannot understand how it has happened, and, even now, they have a shrewd suspicion that there's a catch in it somewhere. Those sprays for instance . . .' He pointed to the humped figures threading their way between the orange trees. 'I had to buy them with my own money, but they were worth every lira. It is only a year or two since these people were washing their trees from a spit bucket—a pail of water set in the middle of the floor, into which the men of the house spat tobacco juice as they smoked or chewed. Some of the old ones still refuse to see that my method is better than theirs. The only thing that will convince them is when I get three oranges to their one, and sell them for twice the price because they are full of juice. But we'll show them in the end.'

'You puzzle me,' said Meredith frankly.

'Why?'

'What have oranges got to do with the human soul?'

'Everything,' said the Bishop flatly. 'You can't cut a man in two and polish up his soul while you throw his body on the rubbish heap. If the Almighty had designed him in that way, he would have made him a biped who carried his soul in a bag round his neck. If reason and revelation mean anything they mean that a man works out his salvation in the body by the use of material things. A neglected tree, a second-rate fruit, are defects in the divine scheme of things. Unnecessary misery is an even greater defect because it is an impediment to salvation. When you don't know where your next meal is coming from, how can you think or care about the state of your soul? Hunger has no morals, my friend.'

Meredith nodded thoughtfully.

'I've often wondered why missionaries are usually better priests than their brothers in the centres of Christendom.'

His Lordship shrugged and gestured with expressive hands.

'Paul was a tentmaker and he worked at his trade so as not to be a burden on his people. Christ himself was a carpenter in Galilee of the Gentiles—I imagine he was a good one. When I am dead, I should like to be remembered as a good priest and a good farmer.'

'It is enough,' said Meredith gravely. 'Enough for you, enough for me. I imagine the Almighty Himself would hardly quarrel with it. But is it enough for everybody?'

'What do you mean?'

'There are miracles all around us: the miracle of an orange tree, the miracle of design that holds the fidget wheels of the universe spinning on their axes. But still people want a sign—a new sign. If they don't get it from the Almighty they turn to palmists and astrologers and table-rappers. What does all this mean—' he tapped the heavy volume of depositions—'But that folk demand wonders in the sky and miracles on earth?'

'And get them sometimes,' the Bishop reminded him tartly.

'And sometimes make them for themselves,' said Blaise Meredith.

'You're not satisfied with the miracles of Giacomo Nerone?'

'I'm the Devil's Advocate. It's my business to be dissatisfied.' He smiled ruefully. 'It's a curious assignment, when you come to think of it. To test by reason the alleged operations of Omnipotence, to apply the code of canon law to the Lawgiver who framed the universe.'

His Lordship nodded a grave assent and said quietly:

'It may be less disturbing to think about Giacomo Nerone.' Blaise Meredith put on again his prim, pedant's manner.

'It's the problem with all new Causes—to apply to alleged miracles the medico-legal methods of the twentieth century. In the case of Lourdes, for example, it's fairly easy. A medical bureau has been established and a series of tests laid down which conform to both medical knowledge and the rigid demands of the Church. A sufferer arrives with a complete medical history. The bureau examines the patient in the approved fashion—X-rays, clinical and pathological tests. All diseases of neurological or hysterical origin are discounted as grounds for a miraculous claim. Only deep-seated organic disorders whose prognoses are familiar are accepted. If a cure is claimed, the bureau examines the patient again and makes an interim certification of the cure. But it is not finally certified until two years afterwards, and then on new medical evidence.

'So far as it goes, it is a sound method. It enables us to say that, in the present state of medical knowledge, this cure has taken place in defiance of, or by a suspension of, the known laws of nature. Now . . . in the case of a new thaumaturge, in a new place, these tests cannot be applied. At best we have eye-witness accounts, a garbled medical history, with perhaps a certification from a local doctor. It may well be a miracle. But in the legal sense, demanded by canon law, we find it very hard to prove. We may accept it on the sheer weight of non-expert evidence, but generally we don't.'

'And the evidence in the case of Giacomo Nerone?'

'Of the forty-three depositions I have read, only three show any conformity to the canonical demands. One is the cure of an elderly woman certified as suffering from multiple sclerosis, the second is that of the Mayor of Gemello Maggiore, who claims to have been cured of a spinal injury incurred during the war, and the third is that of a child in the last stages of meningitis who recovered after an application of a relic of Giacomo Nerone. But even these . . .' He paused and went on in his emphatic advocate's voice. 'Even these will require a much more rigid examination before we go half-way to accepting them.'

To his surprise the Bishop smiled, as if at some private joke. Meredith was nettled.

'Have I said something amusing to Your Lordship?'

'I was asking myself what happened in the old days when medical knowledge was limited and the rules of evidence were less stringent. Is it not possible that many miracles then accepted were not miracles at all?'

'Very probable, I should say.'

'And that certain saints are venerated whose records are so obscure that their very existence is doubtful?'

'That's true. But I don't see where Your Lordship is leading me.'

'I've been reading recently,' said His Lordship coolly, 'that certain theologians are again advancing the opinion that the canonisation of a saint constitutes an infallible declaration by the Pope, binding on all the faithful. In my view it's a dubious proposition. Canonisation is generally based on biography and the historical record of miracles. Both are open to error—and the Pope is only infallible in the interpretation of the deposit of Faith. He can't add to it. And every new saint is an addition to the Calendar.'

'I agree with Your Lordship,' said Meredith with a puzzled frown. 'But I don't see that a minority theological opinion matters very much.'

'It's not the opinion that worries me, Meredith. It's the tendency: the tendency to elaborate so much by commentary, glossary and hypothesis that the rigid simplicity of the essential Faith is obscured, not only for the faithful but for honest inquirers outside it. I deplore this. I deplore it greatly because I find it raises barriers between the pastor and the souls he is trying to reach.'

'Do you believe in saints, Your Lordship?'

'I believe in saints as I believe in sanctity. I believe in miracles as I believe in God, who can suspend the laws of His own making. But I believe, too, that the hand of God writes plainly and simply, for all men of good will to read. I am doubtful of His presence in confusion and conflicting voices.'

'As I am doubtful of the miracles of Giacomo Nerone?'

The Bishop did not answer him immediately, but walked away from him to stand looking out across the peace of the valley, at the grey olives and the green orange trees and the flat water where the men were working on the sluices, stripped to the waist in the sun. His face was clouded as if he were absorbed in an inner struggle. Meredith watched him with puzzlement and anxiety, afraid of having offended him. After a while the Bishop came back. His face was still sombre, but his eyes were full of a grave gentleness. He said slowly:

'I have thought much these last days, Meredith. I have prayed too. You have come into my life at a moment of crisis. I am a Bishop of the Church, yet I find myself in opposition to much that is currently being said and done by my colleagues in Rome, not in matters of faith, but in discipline, policy, attitude. I believe that I am right, but I know there is danger that in following my own path I may tumble into pride and ruin all I hope to do. You were right when you told me that I am afraid of the finger of God. I am ... I sit on a high pinnacle. I am subject only to the Pontiff. I am lonely and often puzzled ... as I am by this matter of Giacomo Nerone. I told you I do not want a saint. But what if God wants him? This is only one thing. There are many others. Now you come, a man in the shadow of death. You too are puzzled and afraid of the finger of God. I find in you a brother, whom I have come to love and trust with my heart. Both of us at this moment are looking for a sign ... a light in the darkness that besets us.'

'I lie awake at night,' said Meredith. 'I feel the life slipping out of me. When the pain comes, I cry out, but there is no prayer in it, only fear. I kneel and recite my Office and the Rosary but the words are empty—dry gourds rattling in the silence. The dark is terrible and I feel so alone. I see no signs but the symbols of contradiction. I try to dispose myself to faith, hope and charity, but my will is a blown reed in the winds of despair ... I am glad that Your Lordship prays for me.'

'I pray for both of us,' said Aurelio, Bishop of Valenta. 'And, out of the prayer, I have come to a decision. We should ask for a sign.'

'What sign?'

The Bishop paused, and then, very solemnly, he told him.

'We should make this prayer, both of us. "If it is your will, O God, to show the virtue of your servant Giacomo Nerone, show it in the body of Blaise Meredith. Restore him to health and hold him longer from the hands of death, through Jesus Christ our Lord!'

'No!' The word was wrung from Meredith like a cry. 'I can't do it! I daren't!'

'If not for yourself, then for me!'

'No! No! No!' The desperation of the man was pitiful, but the Bishop pressed him brutally.

'Why not? Do you deny omnipotence?'

'I believe in it!'

'And mercy?'

'That too!'

'But none for yourself?'

'I've done nothing to earn it.'

'Mercy is given, not earned! Bestowed on beggars, not bought with virtue!'

'I dare not ask for it.' His voice rose higher in fear. 'I dare not!'

'You will ask for it,' the Bishop told him gently. 'Not for yourself, but for me and all poor devils like me. You will say the words even if they mean nothing, because I, your friend, ask you.'

'And if they fail. . . .' Meredith lifted a ravaged face at last. 'If they fail, I am in greater darkness yet, not knowing whether I have presumed too much or believed too little. Your Lordship lays a new cross on my back.'

'It is a strong back, my friend—stronger than you know. And you may yet carry Christ on it across the river.'

But Meredith stood like a stone man, staring out across the sunlit land, and after a while the Bishop left him, to talk with the gardeners who were spraying the orange trees.

It was the moment he had long dreaded, but never quite understood: the moment when the harsh consequences of belief became finally clear.

For a man born into the Church there is a singular comfort in the close-knit logic of the Faith. Its axioms are easy of acceptance. Its syllogisms are piled one on top of the other, firm as the bricks in a well-built house. Its disciplines are rigid, but one moves freely inside them, as one does in the confines of a well-bred family. Its promises are reassuring: that if one submits to the logic and the discipline, one walks naturally in the way of salvation. The complex, terrifying relationship of Creator and Creature is reduced to a formula of faith and a code of manners.

For priests and monks and nuns, the logic is more meticulous, the disciplines more rigid, but the security of body and spirit is commensurately greater. So that if a man can surrender himself completely to the Will of the Creator, as expressed by the Will of the Church, he can live and die in peace—either a cabbage or a saint!

Blaise Meredith was by temperament a conformist. He had kept the rules all his life; all the rules—except one: that sooner or later he must step beyond the forms and the conventions and enter into a direct, personal relationship with his fellows and with his God. A relationship of charity—which is a debased Latin word for love. And love in all its forms and degrees is a surrender of bodies in the small death of the bed, the surrender of the spirit in the great death which is the moment of union between God and Man.

Never in his life had Blaise Meredith surrendered himself to anyone. He had asked favours of none—because to ask a favour is to surrender one's pride and independence. Now, no matter what name he put to it, he could not bring himself to ask a favour of the Almighty, in whom he professed belief, to whom, according to the same belief, he stood in the relationship of son and father.

And this was the reason for his terror. If he did not come to submission he would remain for ever what he was now: lonely, barren, friendless, to eternity.

Aurelio, the Bishop, sat in his cool, austere study, writing letters. It was an activity he distrusted, even when his office forced it upon him. He had been bred a farmer, and he would rather watch a tree grow than write a treatise on it. He had been trained to diplomacy and he knew that a thing, once written, is beyond recantation. Many a hapless fellow has been damned for heresy simply because he was weak in grammar or discretion.

So, when he wrote officially, over the seal of his bishopric, he kept to the conventions for his clergy, a blunt message thinly coated with Southern rhetoric; for Rome, a studied circumlocution, a careful qualification, a slightly florid style. Those who knew him well chuckled at his shrewdness. Those who knew him little—even acute fellows like Marotta—were apt to be misled by it. They regarded him as a somewhat stuffy provincial who would be very good for the locals, but a bumbling nuisance in Rome. Which was precisely the Bishop's intention. Too many new men had been abruptly translated to Rome, just when they were getting things done in their own diocese. It was the Vatican's way of kicking them upstairs: a bishop in his own See is a power to be reckoned with; in the city of the popes he is very small beer indeed.

But this afternoon's letters were private ones, and His Lordship composed them with more than usual care. To Anne Louise de Sanctis he wrote:

> ... I am more grateful than I can say for your offer to receive Monsignor Meredith as a house-guest during his stay in Gemello Minore. We clerics are often a burden to our flock—and sometimes an embarrassment; but I am sure you will find in Monsignor Meredith an agreeable and witty compatriot. He is a sick man who is marked, unfortunately, for an early death; and whatever you can do for him I shall count as a personal favour.
>
> You are much in my mind these days. I am not unaware of the loneliness which afflicts you as the châtelaine of a poor and primitive community. It is my hope that you will find in Monsignor Meredith a confidant for your problems and a counsellor in the affairs of your conscience.
>
> > Believe me, my dear Contessa,
> > Yours affectionately in Christ Jesus
> >
> > > Aurelio+
> > > Bishop of Valenta

He signed his name with a flourish and sat awhile scanning the letter, wondering whether he should have said less or more—and whether there were words to touch the heart of a woman like this one.

Women were the perennial problem of the priesthood. More women than men knelt at the Judas-window of the confessional. Their outpourings were franker and more disturbing to the celibate who sat behind it. Often they tried to use him as the replacement for an unresponsive husband and what they dared not whisper in the marriage-bed they talked freely and often grossly in the coffin-box at the side of the church. The men could be reached through the women–the children too. But often the old Adam who slept under the cassock was wakened dangerously by the murmured confidences of an adolescent girl or a dissatisfied matron.

Aurelio, Bishop of Valenta, was very much a man, and he was quick to see the passion that stirred behind the polished gentility of the Contessa de Sanctis. She, too, was one of his sheep, but discretion put her beyond the reach of his shepherd's crook and he asked himself whether Blaise Meredith, the cold, suffering man, might come any closer to her.

To Doctor Aldo Meyer he wrote in far different terms:

> . . . Monsignor Blaise Meredith is a sensitive and liberal man whom I have come to cherish as a brother.
>
> His commission to investigate the life of Giacomo Nerone is a difficult one, and I have hopes that you may be willing to place your considerable local knowledge at his disposal. You may feel, however, that, as a non-Catholic, you prefer not to embroil yourself in this delicate affair. Let me assure you then that neither Monsignor Meredith nor I would wish to embarrass you with inquiries.
>
> I have, however, a personal favour to ask you. Monsignor Meredith is a very ill man. He is suffering from carcinoma of the stomach and, in the normal course of events, will die very soon. He is reserved, as the English are, but he has considerable courage, and I am concerned lest he overwork himself and endure more pain than is necessary.
>
> It would please me greatly, therefore, if you would consent to act as his medical adviser during his stay in Gemello Minore, and do your best to look after him. I shall make it my business to procure for you whatever drugs you may need and I shall be personally responsible for all the expenses of consultation and treatment.
>
> I commend him most warmly to your charity and your professional care. . . .

Basta! thought His Lordship. Enough. One does not make homilies to the Sephardim. They understand us as well as we understand them. They are theocrats as we are–absolutists as we are. They know the meaning of charity and fraternity; and often they practise them better than we do. They have been persecuted as we have. They have had their Pharisees as we–God help us–have ours, even in the highest places. Meredith my brother will be in good hands.

The third letter was the most difficult of all, and His Lordship pondered it a long time before he wrote, in a fine cursive hand, the superscription:

> The Very Reverend Don Anselmo Benincasa,
> Pastor of the Church of the Madonna of the Seven Dolours,
> Gemello Minore, Diocese of Valenta.

> Dear Reverend Father,
>
> We write to inform you of the arrival in your Parish of the Right Reverend Monsignor Blaise Meredith, Auditor of the Sacred Congregation of Rites, who has been appointed Promoter of the Faith in the Ordinary Cause for the Beatification of the Servant of God, Giacomo Nerone. We beg that you will extend to him a fraternal hospitality and render him every assistance to carry out his canonical commission.
>
> We are aware of your poverty and the straitness of your accommodation and we have, therefore, accepted an invitation from the Contessa de Sanctis to lodge him during his stay in the parish. We know, however, that you will not deem

yourself dispensed on this account from the courtesies owed to a brother priest, who is also a commissioner of the Diocesan Court.

We have been long exercised, Reverend Father, by reports reaching us of the low state of spiritual affairs in your parish, and of certain scandals touching your own private life. Not the least of these scandals is your long association with the widow Rosa Benzoni, who acts as your housekeeper.

Normally such an association would have caused us to institute a canonical process against you, but we have refrained from this drastic step in the hope that God may give you grace to see your error and reform it, so that the last years of your priesthood may be spent in penitence and dignity and the proper service of your flock.

It may well be—God grant it so!—that because of your advanced years, this association may have lost its carnal character and that we may be disposed to permit you to retain this woman in your employment in discharge of the debts you have contracted towards her. But such lenience on our part would not dispense you from the moral duty of repairing the scandal and of devoting yourself with renewed vigour to the interests of your people.

We suggest that the presence of a visiting priest in your parish may give you the opportunity of taking counsel with him and setting your conscience in order without too much embarrassment.

Our patience has been long and we have great care for you as our son in Christ, but we cannot ignore the sorry state of the souls in your charge. One cannot tempt God too long. You are already old and time grows dangerously short.

We remember you daily in our prayers and we commend you to the patron of your church, the Madonna of the Dolours.

Yours fraternally in Christ,
Aurelio+
Bishop of Valenta

He laid down the pen and sat a long time staring at the thick crested note-paper and the script that flowed across it in urgent disciplined lines.

The case of Father Anselmo was a symbol of all the ills of the Mediterranean Church. It was not an isolated case. It was common enough to have become a cliché in the depressed area of the South—and it was none too rare in the North either. In its local context, it was a small scandal—the Church was founded on the idea of sin, and its oldest maxim was that the habit did not make a monk, nor the tonsure a religious man. But in the context of a national Church, of a country in which Catholicism was the dominating influence, it pointed to grave defects, to a singular need of reform.

A man like Anselmo Benincasa was the product of a seminary ill-staffed and dispensing an outdated system of education. He came to ordination half-educated, half-disciplined, and with his vocation wholly untested. He emerged another priest in a country where there were too many priests and, not enough priestliness—and immediately he became a charge on another depressed community. His stipend from the diocese was purely nominal. With the swift debasement of modern currency, it would not buy him a loaf of bread. And the Hierarchy still clung to the comfortable fiction that those who preached the gospel should live by the gospel—without caring to define too clearly how they were to do it. He had no pension, and there was no institution to receive him when he lapsed into senility: so that he was plagued by the constant fear of age, and the constant temptation of avarice.

When he came to a village like Gemello Minore, he represented another mouth to feed. And if he opened his mouth too wide, he was liable to go hungry. So he was forced to accommodate himself: to submit to the patronage of the local landowner, or make an unhappy compromise with his depressed flock. In many Calabrian communities there was a shortage of men. Pre-war emigration and war-time levies had denuded them, and women lived for years separated from their husbands, while marriageable girls were forced to take temporary lovers, or husbands years older than themselves. But the priest was there. The priest was poor and dependent on the poor to get his washing done and his food cooked and his house cleaned and his collection plate full enough to buy next week's pasta.

Small wonder that he lapsed often and that his bishop preferred to deplore the lapse as fornication, rather than haul him to court for the canonical scandal of public concubinage.

It was the system that was to blame as much as the man, and reformers like Aurelio, Bishop of Valenta, were hard put to change it, saddled as they were with the historic sins of a feudal Church. The answer was fewer priests and better ones, money to provide at least a basic living independent of the contributions of the faithful, pensions for old age and sickness, better seminary training, more rigid screening of aspirants to Holy Orders. But money was short and prejudice was strong and men like Anselmo Benincasa took a long time to die, and the youths who grew up in the villages were uneducated and unsuitable.

A bishopric like Valenta was poor and obscure. Rome was rich, remote and preoccupied—and requests for special funds to make tendentious reforms were greeted coldly by the Cardinals who were the stewards of the Patrimony of Peter.

So Anselmo Benincasa stayed on in Gemello Minore and His Lordship of Valenta was left with the problem of what to do with him, and how, at least, to salvage his immortal soul.

He folded the letters, put them in envelopes, sealed them with red wax and the arms of his bishopric, then rang for a messenger to arrange their immediate delivery, by motor-cycle to Gemello Minore. He had no illusions about their importance. He had been a long time in the priesthood and he understood that the truth can lie barren for a hundred years until it strikes root in the heart of a man.

On the eve of his departure for Gemello Minore, Blaise Meredith was lonelier than he had ever been in his life.

The brief, brotherly communion between himself and the Bishop was about to be broken. He must go out among strangers, a sedulous inquisitor digging up unpopular facts. His night-time terrors he must bear alone. He could give no more confidences, only try to worm them out of others. He must exchange the trim privacy of the Bishop's domain for the poverty and depression of a mountain village, where there was little privacy even for birth, death and the act of love.

He would be the house-guest of a woman—and, unlike many of his colleagues, he had small talent for dealing with the opposite sex. He was a celibate by profession and a bachelor by disposition; and he resented the effort he would have to make for small-talk over the coffee cups. His strength was running out swiftly and he could not bear to waste it on the trivia of domestic intercourse.

So, while the labourers slept under the olive trees and His Lordship wrote in his study, he surrendered himself to the final indulgence of a walk round the plantations. He took off his cassock and stock, rolled up his sleeves to let the sun shine on his thin, pale arms, and then headed down the narrow path that led to the dam and the outer fringe of the domain.

Under the trees the air was cool and the path was dappled with sunshine, but when he broke out into the valley, where the dam lay shining between the grey walls of the hill, the heat hit him like an oven-blast. When he looked about him he could see it rising in shimmering waves from the tufa rock. He hesitated a moment, regretting the shelter of the plantations, but then, ashamed of his weakness, walked steadily forward round the fringe of the dam and towards the retaining wall.

On the slope above the path the labourers were sleeping, heads pillowed on their jackets, in the shadow of jutting rocks. Their short brown bodies were sprawled, slack as rag dolls, and Meredith, who had long been a stranger to sleep, was moved to envy of their good fortune.

They were poor, but not so poor as many. They had work with a benevolent master. Their clothes were stained and dusty and they wore wooden sandals instead of shoes, but they could sleep quietly and walk home with dignity, because they had work, and pasta for the table and wine and oil to go with it. In a poor land with three million workless it was very much indeed.

At the edge of the spillway the path forked into two goat tracks, one leading down to the bed of the stream, the other heading up towards the saddle of the hill. Meredith chose the upward path, hoping vaguely that from the top he might get a view of the surrounding countryside. The track was rough and covered with sharp stones, but he trudged on with dull determination, as if to defy the weakness of his wasting body and affirm that he was still a man.

Halfway up, he found himself on a small plateau, invisible from the valley, where the rock walls folded back into a shallow re-entrant like a cave. There was a shadow here and he sat down gratefully to rest a few moments. As his eyes rested themselves from the glare, he saw near the base of the wall a few courses of rough stonework, reticulated in the old Roman manner, and above them the toolmarks on the walls where other courses had once been keyed to the natural stone. He stood up and began to examine them more closely, and followed the lines of the stonework back towards the rear of the re-entrant.

The shadows were deeper here, and it was a moment or two before he noticed a small shelf cut back into the rock on which lay a few withered marigolds and crumbling vine leaves. Behind the offerings was a piece of marble, so old and weathered and stained that at first he could not make out what it was. Then he saw that it was part of the base of an old statue, roughly cubic in shape, out of which jutted the crude shape of a phallus.

In antique days, when the hills were covered with forests before the hungry tribes had denuded them for fuel and building, this cave must have been the shrine of a wood god. Now all that was left of him was the symbol of fertility; but the flowers were of the twentieth century–the first offering of spring to an old discredited god.

Meredith had heard, often enough, of the superstitions that still persisted among the mountain people–of charms and spells and love philtres and odd rites–but this was the first time he had seen the evidence with his own eyes. The marble block was stained and discoloured, but the phallus was white and polished as if by frequent contact. Did the women come here, as they used to in old times, for an assurance against barrenness? Did the males still worship the symbol of their dominance? Was there yet in these mountain folk a half-conscious hope that Pan might do what the new god had not done: make the raped land virgin again and fruitful with grass and trees?

The worship of the male principle was rooted deep among these people. The young men stood arrogant as preened cockerels while the girls came in at least putative virginity to present themselves for inspection and admiration. When they were married they bred their women into exhaustion and coddled their sons to precocious maleness while they beat their daughters into chastity. In a barren land they were the last symbols of fruitfulness and the first symbols of joy to a woman whose end would be a joyless servitude in a tumbling hovel in the hills.

Perhaps this was why the correlative Christian symbol was not the agonised Christus, but the fruitful Madonna with the Bambino suckling at her peasant breast.

Blaise Meredith found himself curiously fascinated by the crude stone symbol and its active survival not half a mile from the Bishop's domain. Perhaps this was the explanation of much of the anomaly of the Mediterranean Church: the strong belief in the supernatural, the thick overlay of superstition, the fierce zeal of the Latin saints and the equally fierce rejection of the Communists and the anti-clericals. Perhaps this was the reason why cool liberals and urbane sceptics made so little impact on these people; why an exalted mysticism was the only answer to the Bacchic frenzy that woke in their brown, undernourished bodies. Was this the real explanation of the death of Giacomo Nerone, that he had been trampled under the hoofs of the goat-god?

And how could.Blaise Meredith, the legalist from Rome, enter into the mind of this secret people who were old when Rome was young, and who had once made alliance with the black, fiery god of Hannibal's Carthage?

In spite of the heat he felt suddenly cold. He turned away from the obscene little image and walked out into the sunlight.

An old woman, bent almost in two under a load of twigs and driftwood from the stream, was struggling up the path, towards the saddle. When she came abreast of him he raised his hand and called a greeting in his precise Roman Italian. She turned her head and stared at him with blank rheumy eyes, then passed by without a word.

Blaise Meredith stood a moment looking after her, then turned his face towards the valley. He felt old and tired and strangely afraid of going to Gemello Minore.

7

Anne Louise de Sanctis woke from her siesta in a mood of black depression. When she remembered that Aldo Meyer was coming to dinner her mood became blacker still; and when His Lordship's letter was delivered into her hands by the messenger, her temper was frayed to screaming point. It was all too much. She could not cope with these intrusions on her privacy. Even boredom was preferable to the effort she would have to make to be agreeable.

When they met for tea in the afternoon, Nicholas Black was quick to notice her ill-temper, and subtle enough to suggest an immediate remedy.

'You're tired, *cara*,' he told her solicitously. 'It's the heat–spring fever. Why not let me charm it out of you?'

'I wish you could, Nicki.'

'Will you let me?'

'How? I still have to cope with Meyer. And tomorrow this cleric arrives.' Her voice took on the petulant tone of a child's. 'I wish they'd leave me alone.'

'You have me, *cara*,' he said gently. 'I'll keep them amused. I shan't let them bother you. Now, why don't you let me give you a face massage and do your hair for dinner?'

She brightened immediately.

'I'd love that, Nicki. It's the thing I miss most here. I feel I'm getting to be an old hag.'

'Never, *cara*! But a new hat and a new hair-do are the best cures for the megrims. Where shall we do it?'

She hesitated a moment, then answered with affected casualness:

'I suppose the bedroom's the place. I've got everything there.'

'Come on, then! Let's start. Give me an hour and I'll have you ravishing as any Roman beauty.'

He took her hand with stagey gallantry and led her upstairs to the baroque bedroom, chuckling inwardly at the easy victory. If there were secrets to be learned about the Contessa he would find them here, given time, patience and the sedulous skill of his own soft hands.

When the door closed behind them he made a sexless little ceremony of helping her off with her dress and wrapping the negligée about her and settling her in a brocaded chair opposite the dressing-table with its rows of toiletries in crystal jars. She bridled dutifully and made coquettish remarks intended to underline the intimacy of the occasion. The painter smiled and flourished his towels and let her prattle contentedly. He had a chameleon talent for identifying himself with every situation even while his thoughts and plans ran contrariwise. Now he was the *parrucchiere*–my lady's confidant, witness of things denied even to lovers, teller of scabrous little tales for which my lady had no need to blush, since valets are impervious to the best pretended virtue.

He laid her head back, cleansed the face of make-up, creamed it carefully and then began to massage with firm but gentle fingers, upward from the slack throat and the corners of the discontented mouth. She was stiff and cautious with him at first, but she surrendered quickly to the rhythmic, hypnotic touch and after a while he could feel the slow sensuality waking in her. It gave him a special satisfaction to coax her while he himself remained unmoved; and, while he worked, he began to talk in the devious idiom of the salon:

'You have beautiful skin, *cara*; supple as a girl's. Some women lose that very quickly. You're one of the fortunate ones . . . like Ninon de L'Enclos, who kept the secret of eternal youth . . . That was a strange story. When she was still the rage of Paris, at sixty, her own son came to pay court to her without knowing who she was. He fell in love with her, and committed suicide when he found out the truth . . .' He chuckled lightly. '. . . You're lucky you have no sons!'

She gave a small complacent sigh.

'I've always wanted children, Nicki. But ... perhaps it's just as well I didn't have them.'

'You could still have them, couldn't you?'

She giggled girlishly.

'I'd need some help, wouldn't I?'

'I've often wondered why you never married again; why an attractive woman chose to bury herself in the wilds of Calabria. You're not poor. You could live anywhere you liked–London, Rome, Paris . . .'

'I've been there, Nicki. I still go regularly to Rome, as you know. But this is my home. I always come back.'

'You haven't answered my question, *cara*.' His deft hands covered the malice in the query. As he massaged her cheeks and the fine network of lines about her eyes, he could feel the tension gathering in her as she fumbled for an answer.

'I've been married, Nicki. I've been in love. I've had affairs too and I've had proposals. None of them really satisfied me. It's as simple as that.'

But it wasn't simple, and he knew it; she was more complex than any other woman he had known–and she was shrewd enough to turn the tables on him immediately.

'You've never married either, darling. Why?'

'I've never needed marriage,' he told her lightly. 'I've always managed to get what I want outside it.'

'You gay bachelors!'

'If there weren't gay bachelors, *cara*, there wouldn't be merry widows–only frustrated dowagers.'

'Do you ever get frustrated, Nicki?'

He smiled secretly at the new plaintive note in her voice. Odd, he thought, how the word brings them every time; how they use the Freudian jargon as if it were the answer to the ultimate riddle of the universe. They're never spoilt. They're never hot for a man they can't have. They're never scared of getting too old for a tumble in the hay. They're frustrated. I am too, for that matter, but I'm damned if I'll let her know it.

'With you, *cara*, how could any man be frustrated?'

As if in gratitude for the compliment she reached up and took his hand, still greasy from the cream, and pressed it to her lips. Then, without warning, she drew it down and laid it on the naked curve of her breast under the negligée. The action took him by surprise and he reacted sharply.

'Don't do that!'

Then, surprisingly, she laughed.

'Poor Nicki! Didn't you think I knew?'

'I don't know what you're talking about!' His voice was high with irritation, but Anne Louise de Sanctis was still laughing.

'That you're different, darling. That you don't really care for women at all. That you're head over heels and gone for young Paolo Sanduzzi. It's true, isn't it?'

He was almost weeping with anger as he stood there with the towel in his hands, staring over her head at the gilt *amorini* on the ceiling. Her hand reached out for him again and held him. She stopped laughing and her voice was low, almost caressing.

'You don't have to be angry, Nicki. You don't have to have secrets from me!'

He wrenched away from her fiercely.

'There's no secret, Anne. I like the boy. I think I could do a great deal for him. I'd like to get him out of the village and have him educated and give him a decent start in life. I haven't much money, God knows, but I'd be willing to lay out every penny on that.'

'And what would you want in return?' Her voice was still soft, but edged with irony.

He gave the answer with an odd pathetic dignity.

'Nothing. Nothing at all. But I don't expect you to believe that.'

For a long moment she stared at him with bright, speculative eyes. Then she told him:

'I do believe you, Nicki. And I think I might help you to get him.'

Wondering, he raised his head and looked at her, trying vainly to decipher the thoughts behind her subtle, smiling lips.

'I have my own reasons, Nicki. But I mean what I say. You help me handle this priest and I'll help you with Paolo Sanduzzi. Is that a bargain?'

He bent and kissed her hand in abject gratitude, and she rumpled his hair with the half-maternal, half-contemptuous gesture she used towards him.

It was an alliance of interest, and each of them knew it. But even enemies smile at one another across the treaty table. So, when Doctor Aldo Meyer arrived for dinner, the Contessa was radiant and Nicholas Black was as deferential as a page in the service of a beloved mistress.

Meyer himself was tired and ill-disposed for society. He had spent the whole afternoon with Martino the smith, waiting for the second, and possibly fatal, seizure which might well follow the first one. It was nearly dark when he decided it was safe to move the patient to his own house, and then he had been forced to listen to the lamentations of the wife who had just become aware of the precarious situation of her family. He had had to give assurances that he was unconfident of fulfilling: that the illness would not last too long, that someone–the Countess perhaps–would see the family fed, that he himself would make arrangements for assistance from the commune, that he would try to find someone who would keep the smithy working and not charge too much.

By the time he made his escape he had mortgaged his soul and his reputation twenty times over, and was more convinced than ever of the hopelessness of reform among this ignorant people, bred for centuries to feudalism, who would kiss the hand of the meanest baron provided it held a loaf of bread and offered them an illusion of safety against acts of God and the politicians.

When he reached his house, he found the Bishop's letter waiting for him, and this was another straw added to the burden of the day's irritations. His Lordship asked nothing but a medical service, better paid than that which he normally performed, but he suggested much more: a courtesy that might grow into a heavy commitment. Aldo Meyer the liberal Jew had a healthy mistrust of the absolutist churchman whose predecessors had harried his people out of Spain and then given them uneasy refuge in the ghettos of the Trastevere. But willy-nilly, the Englishman would come, and under his Æsculapian oath Meyer would be bound to serve him. He hoped perversely that he would not be seduced into friendship.

There was no friendship in his relations with Anne Louise de Sanctis. He was her physician for want of a better one. He was her guest for want of other educated company to divert her dinner table. Occasionally he was the mouthpiece of the villagers in their pleas to the *padrona*. But beyond these narrow definitions, there was an area of unspoken mistrust and concealed animosity.

Both had known Giacomo Nerone. Each, for an opposite reason, had been involved in his death. Meyer knew only too well the nature of his patient's illness though he never put the diagnosis into words. Anne Louise de Sanctis knew her doctor's failures and she goaded him with them because he knew too much about her own. But, because they saw each other rarely, they rubbed along in reasonable politeness, and in a cross-grained fashion were grateful to each other—Meyer for good wine and a well-cooked meal, the Contessa for the chance to dress and dine with a man who was neither a clod nor a cleric.

But tonight there was something else in the wind. The presence of Nicholas Black and the coming of the Roman emissary lent a new and faintly sinister character to the occasion. As he shaved and dressed by the yellow light of a paraffin lamp, he prepared himself for a disagreeable evening.

At first meeting his fears seemed groundless. The Contessa was well groomed, relaxed and charming. She seemed genuinely glad to see him. The painter's smile was free of sardonic subtleties, and he talked well and amiably on whatever subject was started.

With the aperitif they talked weather and local customs and the decline of the Neapolitan school of painters. By the soup they were up to Rome, and Black was retailing the pleasanter scandals of the Via Margutta and the price the critics were charging for a favourable notice. When the fish was brought they were through the Vatican and out among the politicos, discussing the prospects for the forthcoming election. The wine had loosened the doctor's tongue and he was launched on a lively dissertation:

'. . . last time the Christian Democrats came in through the confessional box and the American dollar aid. The Church held damnation over the head of every Catholic who voted Communist, and Washington waved a bundle of dollar bills on the sideline. The people wanted peace and bread at any price, and the Vatican was still the only institution in Italy with stability and moral credit. So between them they carried the polls. But we still have the strongest Communist party outside of Russia, and a singular disunity of aim even among those who voted under the Vatican banner. What's going to happen this time? The Democrats will hold on, of course, but they'll lose votes in a general swing to the left. The Monarchists will gain somewhat in the South, and the Communists will stay about where they are—a hard core of discontent.'

'What will cause the losses in the Christian Democrats?' Nicholas Black put the question with sharp interest.

Meyer shrugged expressively.

'The record first. There are no spectacular reforms, no perceptible diminution in the pool of unemployed. There is an equilibrium in industry, held by the infusion of American money and aid from the Vatican Bank. There is a rise in the national income, which is reflected hardly at all in the living standards of vast numbers of the population. But it's enough to keep the financiers reasonably happy and the votes stable for another term. The second reason is that the Vatican itself has lost credit through its identification with a party. It's the trouble with a political Pope. He always wants it both ways—the kingdom of Heaven and the majority in the earthly parliament as well. In Italy he can get it–at a price, and the price is anti-clericalism among his own flock.'

'It interests me.' Black caught at the tag of the statement. 'All over Italy you meet women who communicate every day and men who wear the badges of half a dozen confraternities and they still quote the old phrase: *Tutti i preti sono falsi*–All priests are cheats. It's amusing, but damned illogical.'

Meyer laughed and spread his hands in mock despair.

'My dear fellow, it's the most logical thing in the world. The more priests you get, the more their faults show up. Clerical government is like petticoat government–bad for both sides. I don't believe all priests are liars. I've met some damned good ones in my time. But I'm an anti-clerical for all that. The Latin is a logician at heart. He's prepared to admit that the Holy Ghost guides the Pope on matters of faith and morals; but he chokes on the proposition that he fixes the bank rate as well.'

'Talking of priests,' said Anne Louise de Sanctis, 'I wonder what Monsignor Meredith will be like.'

It was as bland as butter, but Aldo Meyer understood the malice of it. They had herded him like a sheep from one topic to another–and now they had him penned and they watched him, grinning with subtle mockery, to see what he would do to escape. To hell with them, then. He wouldn't give them any satisfaction. He shrugged off the question.

'You mean our Roman inquisitor? He's no concern of mine. He comes and goes away. That's all. Just now I have problems of my own–which I wanted to discuss with the *padrona*.'

'What sort of problems?' the Contessa frowned at this check to her mockery.

'Martino, the smith, had a stroke today. He's paralysed and incapacitated. The family's going to need help. I wondered if you'd make some money available–and also take a couple of the girls into service here. Teresina and young Rosetta are old enough to begin work.'

To his surprise the Contessa took it quite casually.

'Of course. It's the least I can do. I've been thinking quite a lot lately about the young people. There's nothing for them here–and even if they try to migrate, they end up on the streets in Reggio or Naples. I thought we should begin to revive some of your plans, Doctor, and create work for them here.'

'A good idea,' said Meyer cautiously; and wondered where the devil she was leading him. Her next words showed him all too plainly.

'Paolo Sanduzzi, for instance. Nicki tells me the boy is intelligent and willing. It seems such a waste to have him lounging about so much. I'll bring him here and set him to work with the gardeners. No doubt his mother could use some extra money.'

Now he was really trapped. He had accepted a favour and he must take the sour portion that went with it. They sat there, smiling at him over the rims of their glasses, challenging him to protest and make a fool of himself. Instead he nodded and said indifferently:

'If you can use him, why not? You'd have to discuss it with his mother, of course.'

'Why?' asked Nicholas Black.

'Because he's under age,' said Meyer pointedly. 'His mother is still his legal guardian.'

The painter flushed and buried his nose in his glass, and Anne Louise permitted herself a small, secret smile at his discomfiture. She said simply:

'You might ask Nina Sanduzzi to call and see me tomorrow, Doctor.'

'I'll ask her, certainly. She may not care to come.'

'For barefoot peasants, we ride damned high!' Black commented sourly.

'We're an odd people,' Meyer told him mildly. 'It takes time to understand us.'

Anne Louise said nothing, but signalled to the servant to pour more wine and serve the roast. She had made her point. Meyer had taken it—and if Nicki cared to cross swords with the Jew, she might be amused, but she would not be embroiled. Meyer's next words drew her back into the argument.

'I had a letter from the Bishop today. He asks me to act as medical adviser to Monsignor Meredith. Apparently he's dying of carcinoma.'

'My God!' Nicholas Black swore softly. 'That's a damned nuisance.'

'You invited him, Nicki,' said the Contessa irritably. 'I don't see what you have to complain about.'

'I was thinking of you, *cara*. A sick man in the house is a big burden.'

'There's a room in my place,' said Meyer amiably. 'It's none too comfortable, but it's adequate.'

'I wouldn't hear of it.' She reacted sharply. 'He'll stay here. There are servants to look after him and you can visit him whenever he needs you.'

'I thought you'd say that,' said Meyer calmly and there was no hint of irony in his eyes.

The roast was brought and the wine was served and they ate for a while in silence, each totting up the score in the battle of interests that had gone on under the thin politeness of the talk. After a while the Contessa put down her fork and said:

'I've been thinking that, as a courtesy to His Lordship, we should arrange a welcome for this man.'

Nicholas Black choked suddenly over the chicken.

'What sort of welcome, *cara*? A procession of the Confraternity of the Dead and the Children of Mary and the Society of the Holy Name? Banners and candles and acolytes, and Father Anselmo trotting behind in a dirty surplice?'

'Nothing of the sort, Nicki!' Her tone was harsh and peremptory. 'A quiet dinner party, tomorrow night, with ourselves and the doctor and Father Anselmo. Nothing elaborate, but a simple occasion to meet the people in the village who are best able to help him.'

Aldo Meyer kept his eyes studiously fixed on his plate. How could you match a woman like this one? A simple dinner party!—with the *padrona* playing gracious lady to a country doctor and a cloddish priest who would fumble the cutlery and slop his wine and probably fall asleep over the fruit bowl while the Roman Monsignor looked on with tolerant good-humour. And when he came to take evidence, whom would he lean on, but this same gracious lady, who gave him such courteous house room? A simple party—how very, very simple!

'Well, Doctor, what do you think?'

He looked up, cool and unsmiling.

'It's your house, he's your guest.'

'But you'll come?'

'Certainly.'

He could see her relax, and he caught the furtive triumph dawning in her eyes. When he looked at Nicholas Black, he too was smiling and Aldo Meyer felt suddenly naked to the daggers of this oddly matched pair of intriguers.

'I wonder what he'll be like?' Black asked the question of no one in particular.

'Who?' queried the Contessa.

'Our Monsignor from Rome. When I saw him in Valenta he looked pinched and grey and rather like a mole.'

'He's dying,' said Meyer bluntly. 'That tends to spoil a man's complexion.

The painter laughed.

'But not his temper, I hope. I hate people who are crotchety at meals. He's English, of course, which should make a difference. Probably dry and brilliant and dull as ditch-water in conversation. I wonder if he'll be stuffy. Some of the Roman clergy are very liberal. Others would like to see creation rearranged to have universal autogenesis. I'm anxious to see what this one makes of the love affair of Giacomo Nerone.'

Aldo Meyer turned sharply to face him.

'What do you know about it?'

The painter's smile was a bland insult.

'Not quite as much as you perhaps. But I do employ his son and you've got his mistress doing your housework. Of course that could be useful, too. The recent lists are full of virgins and confessors and beardless boys just out of novitiate. They could use a good penitent like Augustine or Margaret of Cortona. It helps them to cope with the sinners. You know . . . "There's always a way to come back to God!" They're great opportunists, these clerics. Don't you agree, Doctor?'

'I'm a Jew,' said Meyer with tart finality. 'I have small taste for Catholicism, but even less for blasphemy. I'd like to change the subject.'

The Contessa added her own abrupt warning:

'You're drinking too much, Nicki!'

The painter flushed angrily, pushed back his chair and marched out of the room. At a sign from the Contessa the servant left too, and Anne Louise de Sanctis was alone with her medical adviser.

She took a cigarette, pushed the box across the table to Meyer and waited while he lit up for both of them. Then she leaned forward and blew a cloud of smoke full in his face.

'Now then, *dottore mio*, stop fencing and say what you have to say.'

Meyer shook his head.

'You wouldn't thank me, Anne. And you wouldn't believe me.'

'Try me. I'm in a receptive mood tonight.' She laughed lightly and held out her hand to him across the table. 'You're an obstinate fellow, Aldo *mio*, and when you look down that damn Jewish nose at me, you make me obstinate too. Come on now, tell me, and tell me nicely–what's wrong with me, and what's your prescription?'

For a moment he sat silent, staring at the face which had once been beautiful–the fine bones of it, the slack sagging muscles, the crowsfeet round the eyes, the dragging lines of discontent, the tired skin under the careful make-up. Then with clinical bluntness he answered her.

'I'll give you the prescription first. Stop stuffing yourself with barbiturates. Stop collecting oddities like Black who fill you up with dirty stories and give you no joy at the end of it. Sell up this place–or put a steward in—and get yourself a flat in Rome. Then get yourself married to a man who'll keep you happy in bed and make you keep him happy afterwards.'

'You've got a dirty mind, Doctor,' she told him with a smile.

Aldo Meyer went on, unsmiling:

'It gets dirtier yet. You missed satisfaction in marriage because you were too young and your husband too careless to worry. You've never had it since because, every time you tried, you failed yourself and the man. It's common enough and curable enough, provided you face up to what you want and what you need to prepare yourself to get it. But you've never done that. You've retired into your own private little world, and filled it with a kind of mental pornography that drives you crazy with desire and leaves you still unsatisfied. You're the wrong age for that, my dear. It's dangerous. You end up with gigolos and fellows like Nicholas Black and an overdose of sedatives at the end of it. You can still be a lover. But you may make yourself a bawd—as you're doing with Paolo Sanduzzi.'

She ignored that last thrust, and asked him, smiling:

'And how do I get myself a husband, Doctor? Buy one?'

'You might do worse,' said Aldo Meyer soberly. 'Given the elements, you'll probably do better with an honest bargain than a dishonest love. That's why you like to tyrannise over your painter, because you're under the tyranny of an unsatisfied body.'

'Anything else, Doctor?'

'Only one thing,' said Meyer calmly. 'Get Giacomo Nerone off your mind. Stop trying to strike at him through Nina and the boy. You aren't the first woman who destroyed a man because he rejected her. But if you can't look that one in the face, you'll end by destroying yourself.'

'You've forgotten the most important thing, Doctor.'

Meyer looked at her with sharp interest.

'What's that?'

'I've always wanted a child, needed one more than you know. My husband couldn't give me one. Giacomo Nerone refused me and bred himself a boy out of a barefoot peasant. I hated him for that. But I don't hate him any more. If you didn't stand between me and his mother, I could do something for the boy ... give him a good start in life, save him from running to seed like the rest of the lads in the village.'

'What would you do with him, Anne?' asked Meyer coldly. 'Hand him to your painter?'

Without a word, she picked up a half-empty wineglass and dashed the contents in his face. Then she laid her head down on her arms and sobbed convulsively. Aldo Meyer wiped the wine from his thin cheeks, got up from the table and rang for a servant to show him out.

When he reached his house, he was surprised to find the lamp lit and Nina Sanduzzi sitting at the table with a pile of mending in front of her. Her presence at this late hour was sufficiently rare to make him comment on it. Her answer was quite simple.

'I spent the evening with Martino's wife. She's a fool, but kind, and she just begins to see what trouble she is in. When I got the family bedded down and made Martino comfortable, I thought I would wait here and see what news you had from the Contessa.'

For a moment he was tempted to vent his feelings in an ironic outburst; then he remembered that she did not understand irony and would only be troubled by it. So he answered her baldly:

'It's good news for Martino. The Contessa will make a gift of money and also take Teresina and Rosetta into service with her. With their wages and the bit of help from public assistance, they won't be too badly off.'

'Good!' She gave him one of her rare, calm smiles. 'It's a beginning. Later, perhaps, we can improve it. Would you like coffee?'

'Yes, please.' Meyer slumped heavily into a chair and began unlacing his shoes. Instantly she was at his feet, helping him. This, too, was new; she had never before assumed the functions of a body servant. Meyer said nothing, but sat watching her thoughtfully as she crossed the room to light the small primus under the coffee-pot. He said, without emphasis:

'The Contessa would like to see you tomorrow, too.'

'Why would she want to see me?'

'She wants to offer Paolo a job helping the gardeners.'

'Is that the only reason?' She was still bending over the primus.

'For you, yes. For Paolo, there could be other reasons!'

Slowly she turned to face him across the shadowy room. She asked:

'What sort of reasons?'

'The English painter has a fondness for him. The Contessa wishes to use him in a way that is not yet clear. Also I think she wants the boy to be there when this priest comes from Valenta to inquire about Giacomo.'

'They are like dogs rutting on a dung heap,' said Nina Sanduzzi softly. 'There is no love in anything they do. I won't go. The boy won't go, either.'

Meyer nodded agreement.

'I promised only that I would tell you. For the rest, I think you're wise. It's a house with a touch of madness in it.'

'They practise on us, as if we were animals.' She threw out her arms in an angry gesture. 'This is a child—a boy with his first manhood stirring in him—and they want to use him like that.'

'I warned you,' he reminded her soberly.

'I know.' She began to lay out the coffee cups on the table, talking as she moved. 'And this is another reason I came here tonight. Paolo told me he had been walking by the Torrente del Fauno, with young Rosetta. I was glad of it. They are both young, and this is a good time for love to begin, provided it begins the right way. I think Paolo was glad too. I know he wanted to talk, but he did not know how to put it into words. I wanted to help, but . . . you understand how it is with a boy. He would never believe his mother might know the words, too. It's hard when there's no man in the house, and I wondered whether—whether you might help him a little.'

The coffee-pot boiled over, and as she hurried to rescue it Meyer had time to consider his answer. He gave it to her gently and haltingly.

'A boy in his first waking is like a strange country, Nina. There are no maps, no signposts. Even the language is different. I could make mistakes and do him harm. What he feels for the Englishman I don't know. What has happened between them I don't know. But whatever it is there will be shame in it for the boy; just as there is a shame in his first want for a girl. This is what makes him furtive like a fox, timid like a bird. You understand?'

'I understand, surely. But I understand his need too. It is a strange world for him. His father was someone they call a saint. His mother is someone they call a whore. I will not justify myself or his father to him. But how do I explain the wonderful thing there was between us? And how it should be wonderful for him too?'

'How can I explain it—' Meyer grinned ruefully–'when I didn't understand it myself?'

Her next question shocked him out of his weariness.

'Do you hate the boy?'

'God Almighty, no! What makes you say that?'

'He might have been yours–before Giacomo came.'

Meyer's face clouded with old memories.

'That's true. But I never hated the child.'

'Do you hate me?'

'No. There was a time when I hated Giacomo and when he died I was glad–but only for a while. Now I am sorry.'

'Enough to help his son?'

'And you, too, if I could. Send him to me and I'll try to talk to him.'

'I've always known you were a good man.'

And that for the moment was all the thanks she gave him. She went to the stove, picked up the coffee-pot and brought it back to the table. She poured a cup for him and one for herself, and stood watching him while he sipped tentatively at the bitter scalding liquid. Her own cup she tossed off at a gulp and then crossed to the corner of the room to gather up her wooden sandals and the battered basket which held her day's purchases: a bundle of charcoal, pasta and a few vegetables.

Then she came back to the table and held out to him a thick parcel wrapped in cotton cloth and tied with a faded ribbon.

'Take it,' she told him firmly. 'I don't want it any more.'

'What is it?' His eyes searched her calm face.

'Giacomo's papers. Somewhere in there is his letter to you. They may help you to understand him and me. They may help you to help the boy.'

Wondering, he took the soiled package and held it between his hands as he had once held the lolling, lifeless head of Giacomo Nerone. Memories flooded back, vivid and oppressive–old fears, old hates, old loves, small triumphs and monstrous failures. His eyes misted and he felt his stomach knot up and a small nerve begin twitching at the corner of his mouth.

When he raised his eyes at last he saw that Nina Sanduzzi was gone and that he was left alone in the lamplight with the soul of a dead man, held between his own trembling fingers.

Nina Sanduzzi walked back to her house in the peace of spring moonlight. The harsh outlines of the hills were soft, under the stars; the crumbling village was no longer drab but silvered to an antique beauty and down in the valley the torrent ran, a ribbon of grey light through the shadows. The air was crisp and clean and her wooden sandals clattered sharply on the stones above the intermittent voices of the crickets and the distant muted sound of the water.

But Nina Sanduzzi was blind to the beauty and deaf to the night-music. She was a peasant, rooted in the countryside as a tree is rooted, tough, persistent, insentient to the pathetic fallacy which is at best a sentimental diversion for the literate. The landscape was a place in which she lived.

Only the figures in it were important. The beauty she saw–and she saw much of it–was in faces and hands and eyes, smiles and tears and the laughter of children, and the memories treasured like water in a cistern. Spring was a sensation in her own strong body. Summer was a warmth on the skin and dust under her bare feet, and winter was a cold hibernation and a careful husbanding of twigs and charcoal.

She could neither read nor write, yet she understood peace, because she had known conflict, and she was receptive to harmony, because it built slowly but perceptibly out of the dissonances of the life about her.

Tonight she was at peace. She could see the beginning of fulfilment to the promise of Giacomo Nerone, that even after his death there would be care of herself and the boy. They were poor, but poverty was their natural state and Giacomo had never let them want too much or too long. Now in their greater need there was Aldo Meyer, ready to pay, out of his own need, a debt to a dead man.

There was harmony in her life, too—a slow concordance building between her and the villagers. They needed her. They were grateful, like Martino's wife, for her help in their troubles; and, when they called her the old crude names—'the whore', 'the woman who slept with a saint'—there was no longer much malice in it; only a dim memory of old jealousies. They were a harsh people and they used harsh words, because they had few others. Their symbols were vulgar, because their life was brutish—and belly hunger cannot be satisfied with dreams.

So tonight as she walked home to the small hut among the ilex trees she was grateful, and all her gratitude centred on Giacomo Nerone, dead long since and buried in the Grotto of the Faun, where folk came to pray and went away cured of their infirmities of body and spirit.

Everything else in her life was blotted out by the memory of this man: her parents, who had died of malaria when she was sixteen and left her the hut, a few sticks of furniture and a small dowry chest; her husband, a brown, turbulent boy who had married her in the Church and slept with her for a month and then been taken by the Army to die in the first Libyan campaign. After his death she had lived, as the other women did, alone in her small hut, hiring herself out for farm labour and occasional house service when one of the maids fell sick in the Contessa's villa.

Then, Giacomo Nerone had come . . .

It was a summer's night, hot and heavy with thunder. She was lying naked on the big brass bed, tossing restlessly with the heat and the mosquitoes and the need that woke often in her strong body for a man's arms and the feel of him in the bed beside her. It was long past midnight, and even after a gruelling day on the vine-terraces sleep would not come.

Then she heard the knocking—weak and furtive on the barred door. She sat up in sudden terror, drawing the bedclothes about her breasts. The knocking came again, and she called out:

'Who is it?'

A man's voice answered her in Italian.

'A friend. I'm sick. Let me in, for the love of God!'

The weak urgency of the voice touched her. She got out of bed, pulled on her dress and went to the door. When she unbarred it and opened it cautiously, he tumbled forward on to the earthen floor—a big, dark man with blood on his face and a glutinous stain seeping into the shoulder of his ragged shirt. His hands were bramble-scratched and his boots were broken and gaping, and when he tried to get up, he crawled two paces and then pitched forward on his face.

It took all her peasant strength to drag him and lever him on to the bed. While he was still unconscious, she bathed the cuts on his face and cut his shirt away from the wound in his shoulder and washed that too. Then she took off his boots and drew the bedclothes over him and let him sleep until the first dawn brightened the eastern sky. He woke in the sudden panic of the hunted, staring about him with wide, scared eyes; but when he saw her he smiled and relaxed again, grimacing ruefully at the pain of his shoulder wound.

She brought him wine and black bread and cheese, and marvelled that he wolfed it so greedily. He drank three cups of wine, but would take no more food because, he said, folk were hungry and he had a right only to the traveller's share. He smiled again, as he said it, a wide, boyish smile that charmed the last fears out of her and brought her to sit on the edge of the bed and ask who he was and what had brought him to Gemello Minore and how he had come by the wound in his shoulder.

His accent was strange to her and he had difficulty in understanding her thick Calabrese dialect, but the lines of his story were clear enough. He was a soldier, he said, a garrison gunner based at Reggio at the tip of the boot of Italy. The Allies had taken Sicily and the British Army had crossed the Strait of Messina and was working its way up the peninsula. Reggio had fallen. His unit had broken and he was on the run. If he rejoined his own army they would patch him up and send him back into the line. If the British got him they would make him a prisoner of war. So he was trying to make his way back to Rome, to his own family. He had been hiding by day and travelling by night, living on what he could steal. Last night he had been flushed by a British patrol and they had fired at him. The bullet was still in his shoulder. It would have to be taken out, or he would die.

Because she was a simple peasant, she accepted his story at face value. Because she liked him and because she was lonely for a man, she was willing to hide him and care for him until his wound was better. Her hut was away from the village and no one ever came there. That was the beginning of it: simple and unimportant as a hundred other war-time tales of lonely widows and soldiers on the run. But the richness that grew out of it and the tragedy that ended it, and the peace that followed it, were her daily wonder and her nightly remembrance . . .

When she reached the house, she found the lamp burning low, and Paolo curled up, apparently asleep, on the rough truckle bed on the opposite side of the room from the big brass *letto matrimonio* in which he had been begotten and born. Until the onset of puberty he had slept with her, in the custom of the South, where whole families sleep in the one great bed, husbands and wives and babes and maturing boys and girls growing into womanhood. But for a lone woman and her son it was a bad thing, so she had bought another bed and each of them slept alone.

She closed the door, barred and bolted it, then put down her basket and kicked off her sandals. The boy on the bed watched her through veiled eyes, feigning sleep. Every detail of the ritual that followed was familiar to him though, for a long time now, he had refused to take part in it.

Nina Sanduzzi crossed the room to the rough dower chest that stood at the head of her bed. From the inside of her dress she unpinned a small key with which she unlocked it. Then she took out a flat parcel wrapped in white paper. She unwrapped it carefully and took out a man's shirt, old and tattered and stained in many places as if with rust. She held it a moment to her lips and then unfolded it and spread it over the back of a chair so that the tatters were seen as old bullet holes and the stains were the marks of blood. Then she knelt down awkwardly, buried her face in her hands on the seat of the chair and began to pray in a low muttering voice.

Try as he might the boy had never been able to catch the words. When he had knelt there with his mother she had told him simply to say Paters and Aves as he did in church, because his father was a saint who had great power with God—like San Giuseppe, who was the foster-father of the Bambino. But she would never admit him to the privacy of her own communion with his father and, in an odd way, he was jealous of it. Now he looked on the whole thing as a piece of woman's nonsense.

Her prayers over, Nina Sanduzzi re-wrapped the parcel and locked it away in the dower chest. Then she came over to her son's bed, bent to kiss him and turned away. Paolo Sanduzzi kept his eyes closed and breathed steadily because, although he wanted often to kiss her and have her hold him as she did in the old days, there was now a revulsion in him that he could not explain. It was the same thing that made him close his eyes and turn away his head when she undressed her thickening body or got up to relieve herself in the night. He was ashamed of her and he was ashamed of himself.

So he lay still until his mother blew out the lamp and climbed into the creaking brass bed. Then he too settled himself and lapsed slowly into sleep. While he slept, he dreamed—of Rosetta standing on the rock ledge by the torrent and calling him to her. He went to her running and scrambling, seeing her lips parted and her eyes laughing and her arms outflung to welcome him. But before the arms closed round him, they changed to the arms of Nicholas Black, and instead of the girl's face there was the pale goat visage of the painter.

Paolo Sanduzzi stirred and groaned and opened his eyes in the half-sweet, half-shameful moment when the sap of youth runs over, and a boy is not sure whether he sleeps or wakes.

8

It was Blaise Meredith's last night in Valenta: his last in the company of Aurelio the Bishop. They dined, as they always did, comfortably and well. They talked without nostalgia of a variety of subjects, and, when the meal was over, His Lordship suggested that they take coffee in his study.

It was a big, airy room, lined from floor to ceiling with books but sparsely finished with a desk, a prie-dieu, a set of steel cabinets and a grouping of leather chairs near a big majolica stove. Yet somehow it reflected accurately the character of the man who worked in it: learned, ascetic, practical, with a taste for modest comfort.

The coffee was brought and with it a bottle of old brandy, dusty from the cellar, with the seals still intact. His Lordship insisted on opening it and pouring it himself.

'A libation,' he told Meredith, smiling. 'The last cup of the *agape*.' He raised his glass. 'To friendship! And to you, my friend!'

'To friendship,' said Blaise Meredith. 'I'm sorry I've come to it so late.'

They drank, as good men should, of an old and precious liquor, slowly and with savour.

'I shall miss you, Monsignor,' said the Bishop gently. 'But you will come back. If you're ill, send me word immediately and I'll have you brought back here.'

'I'll do that.' Meredith's eyes were fixed studiously on his glass to hide the pain in them. 'I hope I may do well for Your Lordship.'

'I have a small gift for you, my friend.' The Bishop put his hand into his breast pocket and brought out a small box of tooled Florentine leather, which he handed to Meredith.

'Go on, open it!'

Meredith pressed the catch and the lid flew open to reveal, bedded in satin, a small *bulla*, a bubble of antique gold, about the size of his thumb-pad, attached to a fine gold chain. He took it out and held it in the palm of his hand.

'Open the *bulla*,' said His Lordship.

But Meredith's fingers trembled and the Bishop took the ornament from him, opened the bubble, and held it out to him. Meredith gave a small gasp of surprise and pleasure.

Set inside the curve of the gold was a large amethyst, carved with the most ancient symbol of the Christian Church, the fish, with the loaves on its back, whose name was the anagram of the Christus.

'It is very old,' said His Lordship. 'Probably early second century. It was found during the excavations in the catacomb of San Callisto and presented to me on the occasion of my consecration. The *bulla* was a common Roman ornament, as you know, and this must have belonged to one of the very early Christians–possibly a martyr, I don't know. I'd like you to have it–for friendship's sake.'

Blaise Meredith, the cold man, was moved as he had not been moved for twenty years. Tears pricked at his eyelids and his voice was unsteady.

'What can I say, but "Thank you." I shall keep it till I die.'

'There's a price on it, I'm afraid. You'll have to listen to a final sermon.'

'This will be my charm against boredom,' Meredith told him with wry humour.

The Bishop leaned back in his chair and sipped his brandy. His opening gambit seemed curiously irrelevant.

'I've been thinking, Meredith, about the little phallic shrine. What do you think I should do about it?'

'I don't know. . . . Destroy it, I suppose.'

'Why?'

Meredith shrugged.

'We-ell . . . it's a link with paganism, a symbol of idolatry, an obscene one at that. Someone obviously pays some sort of homage to it.'

'I wonder if that's right,' His Lordship queried thoughtfully. 'Or is it something very much simpler?'

'What, for instance?'

'A good-humoured piece of vulgarity–a genial superstition like throwing coins in the Trevi fountain.'

'I'd hardly have thought genial was the word,' said Meredith. 'Bawdy perhaps. Even sinister.'

'All primitive peoples are bawdy, my dear Meredith. They live so familiarly with the grosser natural functions that their humour becomes very earthy indeed. Listen to the chatter and the songs at a village wedding and–if you can translate the dialect and the allusions–you'll blush to your reverend ears. But such people have their own modesties too, which, if they seem less logical, are often more sincere than the false modesties of evolved communities.... As for "sinister"–yes, it could be sinister. Vestigial paganism does exist here. You'll find a woman selling charms and love philtres in Gemello Minore.... But what do I do about it? Make a big song and ceremony? Hold an exorcism and break the marble to bits? They can draw a dirty picture on any wall in town if they really want to–and they would probably put my face on top of it. You see?'

In spite of himself, Meredith laughed heartily and the Bishop smiled approvingly.

'My sermon goes well, Meredith. And you've got the text of it already–*"Piano, Piano!"*–walk softly and talk gently. You're an official, remember, and they mistrust officials–Church officials most of all. You've also got the official point of view. Which is a handicap. Look!' He waved an expressive hand at the book-lined walls. 'All the Fathers from Augustine to Aquinas.. All the great historians, all the great commentators. All the encyclicals of the last five pontiffs–and a selection of the more important mystics as well. The mind of the Church, inside these four walls. The man who wore that *bulla* had never heard of one of them–yet he was as much a Catholic as you or I. He had the same faith, though much of it was implicit and not explicit as it is now. He was close to the Apostles, who taught what they had learned from the lips of Christ and what they had received from the infusion of the Holy Ghost at Pentecost. The mind of the Church is like the mind of a man, expanding itself to new consequences of old beliefs, to new knowledge flowering out of the old, as leaves spring from a tree.... Who among my flock can digest all this? Can you or I? This is the mind of the Church, complex and subtle. But the heart of it is simple, as these people are simple. So when you go to them, you must work with your heart and not your head.'

'I know,' said Blaise Meredith; and the words sounded very like a sigh. 'The trouble is I don't know how to work that way. I confess it frankly, it is only with Your Lordship that I have come to any warmth at all. I'm defective in sympathy, I suppose. I regret it, but I don't see how I can mend it. I don't know the words. The gestures are awkward and theatrical.'

'It's a matter of attitude, my friend. If you feel pity and compassion you are not far from love. These things communicate themselves even through the most stumbling words. The way to these people is through their needs and through their children. Try filling your pockets with sweets and strolling down the street. Try taking a gift of oil or a kilo of pasta when you go into the houses of the poor. Find out where the sick are and visit them with a flask of *grappa* on your hip.... And that, my friend, is the end of my sermon!'

He leaned forward and poured another dram of brandy into their glasses. Meredith sipped the smooth, fragrant liquor and looked down at the small golden *bulla* in its satin bed. Aurelio the Bishop was a good pastor. Everything he preached he practised himself. And Blaise Meredith had not yet performed the one thing asked of him in friendship. He confessed it gravely:

'I've tried several times to bring myself to pray for this miracle, but I can't do it. I'm sorry.'

His Lordship shrugged as if the delay were of no consequence.

'You will come to it in the end. *Piano . . . Piano . . .*! Now I think you should go to bed. Tomorrow will be a long day, and possibly a troubling one for you.'

He stood up, and, moved by a sudden impulse, Blaise Meredith knelt to kiss the big Episcopal ring on his finger.

'Will Your Lordship bless me for the journey?'

Aurelio, Bishop of Valenta, raised a slim hand in the ritual gesture.

Benedicat te Omnipotens Deus. . . . May God bless you, my son, and keep you from the noonday devil—and from the terror of the long night . . . in the name of the Father and of the Son and of the Holy Ghost . . .'

'Amen,' said Blaise Meredith.

But the blessing had no virtue against the pain which took him that night: the worst of his illness, a retching agony that drained him of all strength, so that when he left in the morning he looked like a man riding to his own funeral.

From Valenta to Gemello Minore the survey distance is sixty kilometres, but the road is so winding, the surface so poor and rutted, the climb so steep, that it takes two full hours by car.

Immediately after he left the town, Meredith lapsed into an uneasy doze, but soon the jolting and wrenching wakened him, and he began to take a forced interest in the landscape. The hills were not high by alpine standards, but they were steep and scarped and folded one upon the other so that the road seemed to cling precariously to their flanks, now crawling upwards, now plunging downwards out of a hair-pin bend towards a rickety bridge that looked as if it would hardly support a mule-cart.

The valleys were green where the peasants farmed the silt-wash, but the hills were sparsely grown, hardly fit for goat pasture. It was hard to believe that in the old days the Romans had cut pines here to build their galleys and burned charcoal for the armourers' forges. All that was left now was a rare plantation encircling a villa whose owner or steward was a better farmer than his fellows.

Some of the villages were built on the saddles of the hills, a huddle of rusty buildings round a crumbling church, built perhaps by some old Angevin mercenary who had trailed his pike and his petty title round this roistering, southern kingdom. Others were simply a line of peasant huts lower down in the valleys, where the water was nearer and the soil less sparse. But all of them were poor, shambling and depressed. Their inhabitants had the weathered, used-up look of the mountains themselves. Their children were draggled and spindly as their goats and chickens and cage-ribbed cows.

This was poverty as Meredith had not seen it, even in the baser alleys of Rome. This was what Aurelio the Bishop had meant when he pointed out the folly of coming here with a textbook in one hand and a missioner's cross in the other. These people understood the Cross . . . they had endured their own crucifixion for a long time; but they could not eat ideas, and the Christ of Calabria would need to announce himself with a new miracle of the loaves and fishes, and the old compassion for the maimed and the unclean.

They lived in houses that were no better than cow byres. Some of them were still troglodytes, inhabiting caverns in the rocks, where the damp festered on the walls. They had no gas, no electricity, no sewage, no safe water supply. Their children died of malaria and tubercular infections and pneumonia. Their women died of septicaemia and puerperal fever. Their men were twisted with arthritis before they were forty. Typhoid could wipe out a whole community in a month. Yet somehow they survived. Somehow they clung to a belief in God and the hereafter, in prayer and the ministrations of the Church–clung to it with a fierce logic because in this belief were the roots of human dignity. Without it they would become what they seemed to most of the world, animals in form and habit.

Blaise Meredith's heart sank as they drove farther and farther into the mountain reaches. A deep depression had settled on him after his night's ordeal, and he pictured himself wasting helplessly among these people and begging for death to release him from their company. If he must die out of due time, then at least let him die in dignity, with clean sheets and a clean smell and sunlight coming through the windows. It was a childish thought and he tried to put it away, but the depression stayed with him, until, suddenly, at the top of a steep rise, the driver halted and pointed across the valley:

'*Ecco, Monsignore!* Look! There they are, *Gemelli dei Monti*–the Mountain Twins!'

Meredith got out of the car and walked to the edge of the road to get a better view. Below him the road ran steeply into a valley on the other side of which a single mountain reared itself up against the clear sky. For more than half its height it was a solid mass; then it parted into twin peaks, separated by a broad cleft, about two miles across. On each peak was a village, girt by a crumbling wall, below which the cultivation began and spread itself into the hollow between them. Out of this hollow a stream flowed, tumbling down the solid flank of the mountain into the valley at Meredith's feet.

What struck him most sharply was the difference between the two peaks. One of them was in full sunlight; the other shadowed darkly by its twin. The sunlit village seemed larger, less ruinous; and right in the centre of it, under the campanile of the church, a large white building shone in bright contrast to the burned tiles of the surrounding roofs. The road which forked up to it was black and shining with new bitumen and at the top of it, just outside the walls, a large flat parking space had been made, on which half a dozen cars were standing, their windscreens gleaming in the sun.

'Gemello Maggiore,' said the driver at his shoulder. 'You see what the saint has done for it. The new building is the hospital for pilgrims.'

'He's not a saint yet,' said Meredith coolly.

The driver spread his hands in disgust and moved away. One could not reason with a priest who had a belly-ache. Blaise Meredith frowned and turned to took at the darker twin, Gemello Minore.

There were no cars on the dusty goat track that led up to it, only a tiny donkey-cart with an old peasant padding beside its wheels. The walls were breached in many places, and on some of the taller buildings he could see the naked roof-trees where the tiles had been blown off and never been replaced. The roof line was gapped and ragged in contrast to the compact security of Gemello Maggiore. Meredith knew only too well what it would be like inside the walls–a single main street, a tiny piazza in front of the church, a warren of narrow lanes with washing strung between the walls and filth running over the cobbles and ragged children squalling among the refuse. For a moment his heart failed him and he was half-inclined to head for Gemello Maggiore and make his headquarters there, in the new hostel or even with the Mayor, who would be happy to welcome an official of the Bishop's court. But he knew that he would never outlive the shame of such a surrender, so he got back into the car and told the driver:

'Gemello Minore. *Subito!*'

The labourers in the lower fields saw him first, as the car lurched over the pot-holes and skidded in patches of loose gravel. The leaned on their hoes and watched it pass, and some of the younger ones waved derisively, but the old ones simply wiped the sweat from their faces and rubbed their hands on their breeches and began work again. A car or a coach-and-four—or a rocket from the moon—it was all one. You weeded one line and you began another. The women piled the weeds for compost and gleaned the twigs for fuel. And when the last row was weeded there was water to be hauled from the stream and poured avariciously at the roots of the plants. There were stones to be carried too for the storm-breaches in the terraces, and sods to be turned in the fallow. . . . You couldn't make pasta from engine oil, nor get milk from a priest's tit. So to hell with them both—and back to the hoeing!

Paolo and Rosetta saw him as they squatted under a clump of bushes where Paolo swore he had seen quail, and where there was nothing but the droppings of the hare which nibbled the cabbage plants, and an old grey lizard dozing in a patch of sun. Rosetta clapped and shouted and hopped from one leg to another—a brown elf in a ragged frock; but Paolo stood, arms akimbo, staring after the car. The time would come when this fellow would want to talk to him about his father, and he was determined to meet him as a man, not a snot-nosed urchin to be coaxed first and beaten afterwards. Besides, the affair was important to him and if Rosetta was to be his girl she must understand that. And if he was a little afraid of a black ferret rooting into his mother's life and his own, nuzzling the village into an ants' nest of curiosity, this, after all, was his own business, and his girl should be the last one to know it. So, after the car had passed, he took her by the hand and, in spite of all her protests, hurried her through the bushes and down to the secret stretch of the torrent where no one ever came in the daytime.

Aldo Meyer saw him when the car slowed just outside his doorway and began nosing its way slowly through a mob of yelling children. He saw the grey, pinched face and the lips drawn back in a painful smile, and the hand up-raised in a half-hearted greeting to the children. Here, if ever he knew one, was a man with the sign of death on him. He wondered what tortuous reasoning had induced the Bishop to accept an official like this and send him to be harried and badgered by all the conflicting interests in the affair of Giacomo Nerone. He wondered what manner of man he was and what the pain and the daily familiarity with death were making of him: what he would make of the Contessa and her dinner guests and how he would react to the tangled stories he must hear. Then he remembered that he would be taking the butt end of this life into his own hands, and he was ashamed that he had not even saluted the visitor as he passed.

By the time the car had reached the piazza the whole village was out. Even old Father Anselmo had stood peering furtively through his shutters, with the Contessa's summons in his hand, wondering vaguely how he was to show the 'courtesies to a brother priest' which the Bishop demanded of him. His most urgent problem, however, was what to wear to dinner at the villa; and, as soon as the car had passed, he waddled into the kitchen, shouting for old Rosa Benzoni to wash him a collar and sponge the sauce stains off his best soutane.

Only Nina Sanduzzi refused to make herself a spectator of this inauspicious arrival. She was sitting on the bed in the house of Martino the smith, spooning broth into the big man's twisted mouth, and when they beckoned her to the door she would not come. She had her own dignity, and if the priest wanted to see her he would come and she would know what to answer him.

As for Blaise Meredith, he saw them all, yet saw none of them. They were a blur of faces and a clamour of alien voices and a pervasive smell of dust and bodies and refuse rotting in the sun. He was glad when the car pulled out of the village and roared up the last steep incline to the villa, where the porter stood at the great iron gates to let him in and the Contessa was waiting to greet him, fresh as a flower on the cropped lawn.

'My dear Monsignor Meredith! So nice to see you!'

The smile was warm; the eyes unclouded; the hand soft but firm in greeting. After the clatter of village dialect, Meredith was comforted by the sound of an English voice. His pinched face brightened into a smile.

'My dear Contessa! Thank you for having me here!'

'Did you have a good journey?'

'Fair enough. The roads are rough and I'm not a good traveller these days. But I'm here in one piece.'

'You poor man! You must be quite exhausted. I'll have Pietro show you your room, then you can wash and rest a little before lunch.'

'I'd like that,' said Meredith. And he thought gratefully: Thank God for the English. They understand these things better than anyone else in the world! They don't fuss and they know that when a man is tired his first need is privacy and hot water!

At a sign from the Contessa the servant picked up the bags and led Meredith into the house. The Contessa stood on the edge of the lawn watching his stooped, retreating back until the shadow of the doorway swallowed him up.

A moment later, Nicholas Black walked out from the shrubbery and joined her. He was grinning all over his lean satyr's face.

'Well, well, well! So that's what we're in for! He looks like a seedy edition of John Henry Newman. Oxford, I'd say. Magdalen probably, with a dash of the English College–and a Vatican veneer to top it off. . . . You did it beautifully, *cara*. Not too little, not too much. The charming châtelaine welcoming the Church, the expatriate *Inglesa* doing the honours to a fellow countryman. You're quite an actress!'

She ignored his irony and said thoughtfully:

'He looks very ill.'

'Prayer and fasting will do that too, darling. I wonder if he wears a hair shirt.'

'Oh, for God's sake, Nicki!'

He shrugged irritably and demanded:

'What do you expect me to do? Kiss his clerical backside and ask him to bless my medals? What's happening to you, anyway? Don't tell me you're in the full flush of conversion!'

She rounded on him with low, fierce invective.

'Listen, Nicki! You're a nice enough little man and a middling good painter. You're doing very well out of me and I'm helping you to get some things you want very badly. But I've got my own problems with this priest and I'm not having you make bigger ones just to show how clever you are. If you're not prepared to behave, you can pack your bags and I'll have Pietro drive you down to Valenta to catch the next train to Rome! I hope that's clear.'

He wanted to scream at her and strike her in the face and call her all the bawdy names he could think of; but, as always, he was afraid. So he caught at her hand and kissed it and said in his penitent boyish fashion:

'I always do it, *cara*, don't I? I'm sorry. I don't know what gets into me. I'll behave. I promise! Please, please forgive me.' Anne Louise de Sanctis smiled. She had made her point. She had tasted again the sour pleasure of flagellation and she could afford to be generous. She rumpled his thin hair and patted his cheek and said:

'All right, darling. We'll forget it this time. But be a good boy in future.'

Then she made him take her arm and walk her around the garden, gossiping about Roman scandals. But, clever as she was, she never quite understood how much he hated her.

Alone in his high room, with the shutters drawn against the noonday heat, Blaise Meredith washed and changed and lay down on the big walnut bed.

Once again, it seemed, he had reason for gratitude. His lodging was comfortable; his hostess was charming; the servants were attentive. Whatever the squalor of the village he could come back here and forget it. Whatever his problems, he could count on the good will of the Contessa to help him unravel them. When he was ill he would not be alone, and, with a full staff, he would not be too much of a burden.

He reminded himself that he should write to the Bishop and tell him of his satisfaction with the arrangements made for him. Then, relaxed and resting, he thought about his work and how he should go about it.

A talk with the Contessa first, he decided: a survey of the village and its characters, an indication of the most likely sources of information on Giacomo Nerone. She would know much. She would have a certain valuable authority. As a feudal châtelaine she would stand *in loco parentis* with the peasants, and a word from her might loosen many tongues.

Then he should call on the parish priest to present his letter of authority and request his official co-operation. Whatever the reputation of the pastor, he still had canonical status in the matter. He had also a long and apparently contentious acquaintance with Nerone. There was a problem here, of course. If he had been, even for a while, Nerone's confessor, he could not be called on for evidence. Even if his penitent had released him from the seal, his evidence could not be admitted in the court. It was a wise provision of the law; but it was also a useful bolt-hole for a man who had something to conceal. He could sit pat and refuse even to indicate sources of information and the canonists would uphold his discretion. On all counts it looked as if Father Anselmo might prove a problem to the Devil's Advocate.

Who next? The doctor, perhaps, Aldo Meyer, who was a Jew and a disappointed liberal. There were problems here too. He would know too much. His evidence was admissible, since even infidels and heretics might give testimony for or against the Cause. But he could not be forced to give it, as a Catholic could, by moral sanctions. One could only depend on his good will. For the present, at least, Doctor Aldo Meyer must be put down as doubtful.

Then there was Nina Sanduzzi, who had been the mistress of Giacomo Nerone and had borne his child. According to the records of Battista and

Saltarello, she had refused to give any information at all. It seemed unlikely that a foreign priest would have any greater success with her. But even if he had, the inquiry promised to be most distasteful of all. It would entail a confessional probing into the deepest intimacies of their relationship: their mutual confidences, their moral attitudes, the reasons for their separation, even the nature of their sexual commerce. And all this between a priest who spoke only Roman Italian and a woman whose tongue was the bastard dialect of Calabria with its polyglot elements of Greek, Phoenician, Levantine Arab and Angevin French. . . .

Blaise Meredith was still wrestling with this problem when a servant entered and announced that luncheon was served and that the Contessa was waiting for him downstairs.

Luncheon began well: a pleasant conversation piece between people of taste and breeding, oddly met in a strange land. The Contessa steered the talk carefully. Nicholas Black seemed to enjoy his role as the urbane cosmopolite, and Blaise Meredith, relaxed after his rest, talked with a rare charm and considerable knowledge of books and music and the politics of Europe and the Church.

By the time they came to the cheese and the fruit, the Contessa had begun to feel comfortable again. This was a man she could understand. She had met many like him, in the old days in London and Rome. He had polish and discretion and, what was more important, he understood the English idiom of allusion and understatement. With a little care she could bring him to lean on her to interpret the provincial crudities. Provided Nicki continued to behave himself, there would be no trouble at all. She felt confident enough to put the first probing questions to Meredith.

'You must forgive my ignorance, Monsignor; but how do you usually begin work in a case like this?'

Meredith made a small, rueful gesture.

'I'm afraid there aren't any rules at all. It's a question of talking to as many people as possible and then collating and comparing their information. Later, when the Bishop's court is set up, one can question and cross-examine them under oath–and in secrecy, of course.'

'And where do you think you'll start now?'

'I had hoped that you might be able to help me first. You've lived here a long time. You're the *padrona*. Your knowledge of local conditions would be a very good preparation for me.'

Nicholas Black shot a swift, ironic glance at the Contessa, but she was smiling calmly.

'I'm happy to do anything I can of course, but I think there's a danger in referring to me. I'm the *padrona*, as you say, and I'm English as well. I live a different life. I think differently from these people. I could be quite wrong in my ideas. I've been proved so many times. But I do want to help, for your sake and for the Bishop's. He's an old friend of mine, as you know.'

'Of course.' Meredith nodded and did not press the point.

The Contessa went on:

'After His Lordship wrote to me, I thought that the most helpful thing would be to have you meet the doctor and the parish priest. They both know much more about the village than I do. I've asked them both to come to dinner tonight. Then we can all four of us exchange views. I'll feel more confident then, that you are getting a balanced opinion. Nicki agrees with me, don't you, Nicki?'

'Of course, *cara*. This is a strange country. Quite different from Rome. I'm sure your idea is the right one. Don't you agree, Monsignor?'

'You're the experts,' said Meredith deprecatingly. 'I appreciate the trouble you're taking for me.'

The Contessa pushed back her chair.

'I don't usually take coffee in the afternoon. I find it spoils my siesta. Pietro will serve yours on the terrace, and afterwards Nicki will show you the gardens. Will you excuse me, Monsignor? A woman's beauty sleep, you know. . . .'

The two men stood up as she left the table, and when she was gone, Nicholas Black led the way out on to the terrace, where the coffee service was laid under the shade of a striped awning. The painter offered Meredith a cigarette from a slim gold case.

'Smoke?'

'No, thank you. It's a luxury I've had to give up since my illness.'

'The Contessa tells me you've been very ill.'

'Very,' said Meredith flatly. He was feeling warm and at ease and he did not want to be reminded of death.

The servant came out and poured the coffee and Black smoked a few moments in silence, pondering his next gambit. For all his charm, this fellow was acute and intelligent. A mistake with him might be irreparable. After a while he said, casually:

'While you are here, Monsignor, I hope you will let me paint you. You have an interesting face and expressive hands.'

Meredith shrugged disarmingly.

'You must have twenty better subjects than I, Mr Black.'

'Let's say you provide the contrast,' said the painter with a grin. 'The courtly Roman among the provincials. Besides, I'm hoping to make a pictorial record of the whole case of Giacomo Nerone. It could be a wonderful basis for a one-man show. I've thought of calling it "Beatification".'

'It may never come to beatification,' said Meredith carefully. 'Even if it does, it may take years.'

'From an artistic point of view that hardly matters. It's the characters that count—and there's a fantastic gallery of them here. I'm wondering what you'll make of them, Monsignor.'

'I'm wondering, too,' Meredith told him frankly.

'The thing that interests me, of course, is the love affair. I don't really understand how one could possibly consider beatifying a man who seduces a village girl, gives her a bastard boy and then leaves her. He was here long enough to marry her.'

Meredith nodded thoughtfully.

'It raises problems, of course—problems of fact and motive. But it doesn't necessarily put the case out of court. There's the classic example of Augustine of Hippo, who lived with many women and had, himself, an illegitimate son. Yet he became in the end a great Servant of God.'

'After a much longer life than Nerone's.'

'That's true, too. I'll admit candidly the circumstances are puzzling. I'm hoping to find out the full story while I'm here. But, in strict theology, one cannot ignore the possibility of sudden and miraculous conversion.'

'If one believes in miracles, of course,' said the painter dryly.

'If one believes in God, one believes necessarily in miracles.'

'I don't believe in God,' said Nicholas Black.

'It's a pointless world without Him,' said Blaise Meredith. 'And it's rough enough with Him. But . . . one can't argue a man into faith. So let's agree to differ, shall we?'

But the painter was not to be put off so easily. He was too anxious to see what sort of man lay under the black soutane. He returned to the argument.

'I'd like to believe. But there's so much professional mumbo-jumbo. So many mysteries.'

'There are always mysteries, my dear fellow. If there were none, there would be no need of faith.'

'But you're not taking Giacomo Nerone on faith,' said Black pointedly. 'You're investigating him legally.'

'That's a matter of fact and not of faith,' said Meredith.

The painter chuckled happily.

'But you'll still find lots of mysteries, Monsignor. More than you bargain for, I think. And the biggest mystery of all is why nobody in Gemello Minore wants to talk about him . . . not even the Contessa.'

'Did she know him, then?' A new interest quickened in Meredith's voice.

'Of course she knew him. She's trying to get his son to come and work for her. She was here when he was alive. She was here when he died. All the others were too. They're not all amnesiacs. But they're as close as oysters just the same. You'll see, at dinner tonight.'

'And what's your interest in the case?' There was an undertone of irritation in the question.

'A village comedy,' said Black blandly. 'And a one-man show growing out of it. It's really quite simple. Anyway, you're involved in the case. I'm not. I'm just giving you a friendly tip. . . . If you're finished with your coffee, I'll show you the garden.'

'I'll sit awhile if you don't mind. Then I may take a siesta.'

'Just as you like. I'm a painter. I don't like wasting light. I'll see you at dinner, Monsignor.'

Meredith sat and watched him go, a tall, slim figure lounging across the lawn and into the shrubbery. He had met men like this before, some few of them, even in the cloth. He wondered what was the root of the malice he bore towards the Contessa and why she continued to give him house room. He wondered also why the Contessa had fobbed off his own request for help with the promise of a country dinner party.

Doctor Aldo Meyer sat in his kitchen and watched while Nina Sanduzzi polished his shoes and pressed his shirt and sponged the lapels of his last respectable suit. He, too, was preoccupied with the Contessa's dinner party. After the scene of the night before, he had been tempted to cut it altogether, but the more he thought, the more sure he was that he should go. It was as if a battle had been joined, and he could not afford to surrender a single advantage to the Contessa and her intriguing cavalier, Nicholas Black.

The real difficulty was that he could not be sure what he was fighting for—unless it were the interests of Nina and Paolo Sanduzzi. But this was too limited a goal to explain his anxiety to meet the English priest, and his complete involvement in the affair of Giacomo Nerone.

He was looking for a key to the mystery of his own failure, and for a signpost in the waste of his future. He had the curious conviction that Blaise Meredith might supply him with both. Part of his answer lay in the papers of Giacomo Nerone, which were still in the drawer of his bureau, but so far he had not found courage to open them.

Several times he had held them in his hands and fumbled with the wrappings; but each time he had drawn back, afraid of the hurt and shame they might hold for him. They were like the letters of a rejected lover, which, once reopened, would remind him of the times when he had been less than a man. Sooner or later he would have to face the revelation: but not now, not yet.

Nina Sanduzzi looked up from her ironing and said calmly:

'I've been thinking about Paolo. I've decided he should work for the Contessa after all.'

Meyer stared at her open-mouthed.

'Good God, woman! Why?'

'First, because Rosetta will be there, and I think she is good for him. She is near to being a woman, and she will fight for what she wants. Also she will talk and I will know what is going on at the villa. Once she starts to work, Paolo will have nothing to do but idle and wander the hills—and the painter will get him anyway.'

'The Contessa will be there, too,' Meyer cautioned her gravely. 'And she is a woman also—older and cleverer than Rosetta.'

'I've thought of that,' she admitted quietly. 'But I have thought also that there will be the priest in the house. He will come to see me, like the others did, and I will tell him what goes on there. I will ask him to look after Paolo.'

'He might not believe you.'

'If I tell him all the others things—about Giacomo—I think he will believe me.'

Meyer looked at her with puzzled, brooding eyes.

'Yesterday you were decided to tell him nothing at all. What made you change your mind? What about your promise to Giacomo?'

'The boy is more important than a promise. And besides—' there was a strange conviction in her voice—'I prayed last night as I always do, to Giacomo. I don't see him, I don't hear him—there is just the shirt he wore when he was killed, with the bullet holes round his heart. But I know what he wants, and this is what I shall do.'

'I didn't think people changed their minds when they were dead,' said Meyer with wintry humour, but there was no answering smile on the calm face of the woman. She said simply:

'It is not changing his mind. It is just that the time was not right before—and now it is right. The priest will come to me when he is ready. Then I shall tell him.'

Meyer shrugged and spread his arms in a small despair.

'Whatever I say, you will do what you want. But before the boy goes to the villa have him talk with me.'

'I'll do that. Have you read Giacomo's papers yet?'

'Not yet.'

'You should not be afraid,' she told him, with singular gentleness. 'He did not hate you, even at the end. Why should he shame you now?'

'I'm ashamed of myself,' said Aldo Meyer curtly, and he walked out into the garden, where the cicadas were shrilling in the blaze of the afternoon, and the dust clung to the green leaves of the fig trees.

9

When Meredith came down to dinner that night, he found the Contessa and her guests already assembled, taking drinks in the salon.

The contrast between them was startling. The Contessa was groomed as if for a Roman evening and Nicholas Black was immaculate in a black dinner jacket. Meyer was dressed in a shabby lounge suit, much cleaned and shiny with long wear. His shirt was clean and newly pressed, but the collar and the cuffs were beginning to fray, and his tie was faded and old-fashioned. Yet he carried himself with dignity and his worn, intelligent face was calm. Meredith was drawn to him immediately and his greeting was less reserved than usual.

'I'm happy to meet my medical adviser. I'm going to be in good hands.'

'Better reserve judgment, Monsignor,' said Meyer, with cool humour. 'I have a bad reputation.'

And there they left it, while the Contessa drew Father Anselmo out of his corner and presented him to his Roman colleague.

He was a short man, on the wrong side of sixty. His face was lined and weathered like that of a peasant and his lank grey hair was long and brushed down over his collar. The shoulders of his soutane were speckled with dandruff and the front of it was spotted with old wine stains and sauce droppings. His hands were knotted with arthritis and he kept twining and untwining them as he talked. When he greeted Meredith his Italian had the thick, coarse accent of the province.

'I'm glad to see you, Monsignor. We don't get many Romans down this way. Too far and too rough for 'em, I suppose.'

Meredith smiled uneasily and murmured a banal remark, but the old man was garrulous and would not be put off.

'That's a trouble we have in this part of the world. The Vatican doesn't even know what's going on. They've got more money than you could poke a stick at, but we never get a smell of it. I remember when I was in Rome . . .'

He would have gone on talking for an hour, had not the Contessa signalled to the servant, who put a glass of sherry into his hands and edged him gently away from the visitor. Meredith was embarrassed. Seedy clerics were distasteful to him at the best of times, but the prospect of a longish association with this one was daunting in the extreme. Then he remembered Aurelio, Bishop of Valenta, and his care for the lost one of his flock, and he was instantly ashamed of himself. Ignoring the shepherding servant, he moved back to the old man and said in a friendly fashion:

'His Lordship sends you his greeting and hopes that I won't be too much trouble to you. But I'm afraid I'll have to lean on your judgment a good deal.'

Father Anselmo took a long swallow of sherry and fixed him with a rheumy eye. He shook his head and said querulously:

'His Lordship sends his greetings! Nice of him! I'm a flea in his ear and he'd like to get rid of me. But he can't do it without a court case. That's the way it is. We might as well understand each other.'

Like most polite people, Meredith had no armour against the grossness of others. It pained him, but he lacked the brutality to administer a frank snub. He said, genially enough:

'I'm the visitor, I'm not up on local politics. There's no reason why we shouldn't get along.'

Then he turned back to make small talk with Anne Louise de Sanctis.

Aldo Meyer had been quick to notice the brusque little exchange and mark it as a credit to Blaise Meredith. The man had breeding and discretion. There was hope that later he might reveal a heart as well.

Nicholas Black had noticed it too, and he grinned slyly at the Contessa, whose answering eyebrow lift told him plainer than words: This goes as I planned it—crookedly and well. And because his interest was common with hers in this moment, he was prepared to co-operate and forget his hatred of her. While Meredith talked with his hostess and Father Anselmo stood a little apart, with one eye on the sherry and one ear on the talk, he drew Meyer aside and said, grinning:

'Well, *dottore mio*, what do you think of our Devil's Advocate?'

'I'm sorry for him. He has the mark of death on him. Already he must be suffering a good deal.'

The painter shivered involuntarily, as if a goose had walked over his grave. He answered plaintively:

'Let's not have death at the dinner table, my dear chap. I was thinking of something else. How do you think he'll work? Pleasantly or . . .?'

He let the question hang, a suspended chord of irony; but Meyer made no move to resolve it.

'Why should we care, you and I?'

'Why indeed,' said Nicholas Black tartly, and dropped the subject.

Meyer sipped his sherry and watched Meredith's face as he talked to the Contessa and Father Anselmo. He noted the leanness of it, the sallow transparency of the skin, the lines of pain etched deeper and deeper round the mouth, the tired, injected eyes that slept too little and saw too much of the tears of things. Men reacted variously to pain and fear. This one seemed to be bearing both with courage, but it was too early to see what else was happening to him.

A few moments later dinner was announced and they filed into the dining-room. The Contessa took the head of the table, with Meredith on her right, Meyer on her left and Father Anselmo and Nicholas Black in the lower places. Before they were seated, she turned to Meredith.

'Will you give us a grace, please, Monsignor?'

As he stood with bowed head through the brief Latin formula, the painter chuckled to himself. What an actress the woman was! Not one piece of business forgotten! He was so absorbed in his amusement that, without thinking, he made the Sign of the Cross after the grace and spent an uncomfortable five minutes wondering whether Meredith had noticed it. As a confirmed atheist, the priest would leave him to the mercy of God; but as a lapsed Catholic he would probably come fishing for his soul, which could be an embarrassment in his plans for Paolo Sanduzzi.

As if on cue, the Contessa repeated the name to Aldo Meyer.

'About young Paolo, Doctor? Is he coming to work for me?'

'I believe so,' said Meyer cautiously. 'His mother will probably come to see you tomorrow.'

'I'm glad.' She bent to explain it to Meredith. 'This will probably interest you, Monsignor. Young Paolo Sanduzzi is, of course, the son of Giacomo Nerone. He was baptised with his mother's name. He's rather wild, but we—that is, Doctor Meyer and I—thought it would do him good to begin work. I've offered him a job as assistant gardener.'

'That seems a kind thought,' said Meredith casually. 'How does his mother live?'

'She works for me,' Meyer told him.

'Oh.'

'She used to be a very pretty woman,' said Father Anselmo, with his mouth full of fish. 'She's thickened up now, of course. I remember her when she made her First Communion. Lovely child!'

He washed the fish down with a draught of wine and wiped his lips with a crumpled napkin. Then, as nobody answered, he bent over his plate again. Meredith turned to Meyer.

'You knew Giacomo Nerone, I believe, Doctor?'

'Yes, I knew him,' Meyer answered with easy frankness. 'I was the first person who saw him after Nina Sanduzzi. She called me in to pick a bullet out of his shoulder.'

'She must have trusted you, Doctor,' said Nicholas Black blandly.

Meyer shrugged the thrust aside.

'There was no reason why she shouldn't. I was a political exile. My sympathies were known to be against the Administration.'

The painter grinned and waited for the next question. His face clouded with disappointment when Meredith said simply:

'You're probably aware, Doctor, that in a Cause for Beatification even the evidence of non-Catholics is admitted, provided they're willing to give. I'd like to talk to you about that, at your convenience.'

'Any time, Monsignor.'

And he thought gratefully: He measures bigger than I thought. They won't snare him too easily.

Anne Louise de Sanctis cut quickly into the small following silence.

'Father Anselmo can probably help you a good deal too, Monsignor. He's very close to all our people. You knew Nerone too, didn't you, Father?'

Anselmo put down his fork with a clatter and took another draught of wine. His voice was thickening noticeably and his accent was broader than ever.

'I never thought much of the man. He interfered too much. Anyone would have thought he was a priest himself. Used to come battering on my door as soon as anyone had a belly-ache. Wanted me to come racing out with the Sacraments. One night he nearly had me shot by the Germans. After that I wouldn't go out after curfew.'

'I'd forgotten,' said Meredith easily. 'You had the Germans here, of course. That must have been uncomfortable.'

'They took over the villa,' said the Contessa quickly. 'I was under open arrest most of the time. It was terrible. I've never been so afraid in my life.'

Nicholas Black wiped his thin lips and smiled behind the napkin. He pictured her walking the lawns with the conquerors, making her coquetries on the arm of a blond captain, bedding with him in the big baroque room behind the velvet curtains, while the peasantry starved outside the iron gates and the stone wall. House arrest? There might be other names for it. A little patience and he would have the whole story of Anne Louise de Sanctis.

Blaise Meredith seemed unconscious of the irony and went on:

'The first evidence seemed to indicate that Giacomo Nerone acted as a kind of mediator between the peasants and the occupying troops. What would you think of that, Contessa?'

'I think that's probably an exaggeration. Most if not all of the mediation was done by myself. When relations became strained in the village my servants would tell me, and I would approach the commander. . . . On a very official basis, of course. Usually he was co-operative. I think perhaps Nerone exaggerated his influence to build up his credit with the people.'

At that moment the servants began moving round the table clearing the dishes and laying out the next course. Meredith seemed in no hurry to pursue the question. Nicholas Black took advantage of the lull to pose his own barbed query:

'Has anyone ever established definitely who this man was and where he came from?'

Anne Louise de Sanctis was busy with the manservant. Meyer was quizzically silent. Father Anselmo was busy with another glass of wine and, after a moment's awkward pause, Meredith answered him:

'It's never been clearly established. At first he was accepted as an Italian. Later, it seemed, there was an opinion that he might have been a member of one of the Allied units in the South–English, perhaps, or Canadian.'

'Interesting,' said the painter dryly. 'There were quite a few thousand deserters in the Italian theatre.'

'That's possible too,' said Meredith. 'It's something I hope to find out more definitely.'

'If he were a deserter, he couldn't be a saint, could he?'

'Why not?' asked Meyer with sudden interest.

The painter spread his hands in mock humility.

'I'm no theologian, of course; but every soldier takes an oath of service. To break a lawful oath would be a sin, wouldn't it? And a deserter would be living in a constant state of sin.'

'For a non-believer you have a very Christian logic,' said Meredith, with mild humour. A small chuckle went round the table and the painter flushed uncomfortably.

'It seems a logical proposition.'

'Perfectly logical,' said Meredith. 'But there may be other facts. A man cannot bind himself by oath to commit sin. If a sin is required of him under an oath of service, he is obliged to refuse it.'

'How do you establish the fact, Monsignor? And the motive?'

'We must rely on the sworn testimony of those who knew him intimately. Then the court must examine the value of the testimony.' He smiled disarmingly. 'It's a long job.'

'Trouble with you Romans,' said Father Anselmo suddenly, 'you don't see the simplest things–even when they stick up under your noses . . .' His voice was so blurred and unsteady that the guests looked at one another in sharp uneasiness and then at the Contessa, sitting rigid at the head of the table. The old man stumbled on . . . 'Everybody's talking as though they knew nothing. We all knew who he was. I knew. The doctor knew. The . . .'

'He's drunk,' said the Contessa, in a clear hard voice. 'I'm sorry for this exhibition, Monsignor, but he should be got home immediately.'

'He's old,' said Meyer quietly. 'His liver's packing up and it takes very little to put him under the table. I'll get him home.'

The old man stared hazily round the table, fumbling for the thread of his thought. His grey head nodded and a small runnel of wine dribbled down from his slack lips.

'Pietro can go with you,' said the Contessa curtly.

'I'll go,' said Nicholas Black.

Meredith pushed back his chair and stood up. There was a new ring in his flat precise voice.

'He's a brother priest. I'll get him home, with the doctor.'

'Take my car,' said Anne Louise de Sanctis.

'Better he walks,' Aldo Meyer told her quietly. 'The air will sober him up a little. It isn't far. Give me a hand with him, Monsignor.'

Together they got him out of the chair and manoeuvred him past the servant at the door and out on to the gravelled drive.

Nicholas Black and the Contessa sat still at the table, staring at one another. After a while the painter said softly:

'A near thing, *cara,* a very near thing, wasn't it?'

'Go to hell!' said the Contessa and left him alone, grinning like a satyr at the wreckage of my lady's dinner party.

As they walked down the rough road towards the village with Father Anselmo hanging from their shoulders, his feet trotting aimlessly in rhythm with their own, Meredith was astonished to feel how light he was. In the salon and at the dinner table he had seemed bloated and gross; now he was just a frail old man with a pot-belly and a lolling, greasy head, who mumbled and dribbled and clung to them, helpless as a sick child.

Meredith, who had rarely come near a drunk and had never seen a drunken priest, was at first disgusted and then touched with a sharp compassion. This was what happened to some men when the terror of life caught up with them. This was what they became when age weakened the faculties and decay crept in among the tissues and the will faltered under the burden of time and memory. Who could love this shambling old wreck? Who now could care whether he lived or died and whether his soul was damned to eternity–if indeed a soul was left after the long wasting of the years?

Meyer cared–enough at least to whisk him quickly away from further indignities, to make dignified apology for him, to lend him a shoulder and walk him home on his two feet. Meyer cared: the shabby Semite with the tarnished reputation, who understood what happens when a man's liver packs up and his prostate fails him and he can't hold his spoon straight because of the arthritis in his joints. And Blaise Meredith? Did he care too? Or was he so preoccupied with his own belly-ache that he could not see that there were meaner ways of dying, and sharper torments than his own?

He was still chewing on this tasteless cud when they came to the door of the priest's house. They eased him off their shoulders and propped him against the wall, and Meyer hammered loudly on the front door. A few moments later they heard shuffling footsteps inside, and then the door was opened by a fat old woman in a shapeless black shift with a soiled nightcap askew on her tousled hair. She peered at them sleepily.

'Well! What's the matter? Can't you let a body sleep? If you want the priest, he's not here, he's . . .'

'He's drunk,' said Meyer amiably. 'We brought him home. You'd better get him to bed, Rosa.'

She turned on him angrily.

'I knew it would happen. I warned him. Why can't they leave him alone?
He's not made for hobnobbing with the quality. He's just an old man—and a
big baby who doesn't know how to look after himself.' She took Anselmo's
hand and tried to lead him into the house. 'Come on, crazy one. Rosa will
get you to bed and look after you . . .'

But the old man lurched and stumbled and would have fallen unless
Meyer had caught him. He said curtly:

'Come on, Monsignor. We'd better carry him to bed. The woman's
almost as old as he is.'

They lifted him head and feet and carried him into the house and up a
flight of rickety stairs, with Rosa Benzoni lighting the way ahead with a
tallow candle. The house smelt stale and musty as a mouse-hole, and when
they came to the bedroom Meredith saw that it held a large double bed
covered with greasy blankets, and that one side of it was already in disorder.
They carried the old man over to it and laid him down. Meyer began to
loosen his collar and his shoes.

The old woman bustled him away, grumbling.

'Leave him! Leave him for pity's sake! You've done enough damage
tonight. I can look after him. I've been doing it long enough.'

After a moment's hesitation, Meyer shrugged and walked out of the
room. Meredith followed him, feeling his way down the creaking stairs,
through the fusty air, and out into the grateful freshness of the moonlight.

Meyer put a cigar between his thin lips, lit it and inhaled deeply. Then he
gave Meredith a sidelong speculative look and said coolly:

'Are you shocked, Monsignor?'

'I'm sorry for him,' Meredith answered in a low voice. 'Deeply sorry.'

Meyer shrugged.

'The Church is to blame for half of it, my friend. They send a poor devil
like Anselmo out to a place like this, with half an education and no stipend
and no security at all—and expect him to stay celibate for forty years. He's
just a peasant and not very intelligent at that. He's damned lucky to have
found a woman like Rosa Benzoni, to bully him and keep his socks clean.'

'I know,' said Meredith absently. 'That's what touched me most of all.
She was like a wife to him. She—she loves him.'

'Does that surprise you, Monsignor?'

'It shames me . . .' He shook his head as if to chase away a haunting
nightmare. 'I've spent all my life in the priesthood and I think . . . I think
I've wasted it.'

'That makes two of us,' said Aldo Meyer softly. 'Come down to my place
and I'll make you a cup of coffee.'

In the low, dimly lit room of Meyer's cottage, with its peasant furniture and
its rows of copper vessels, polished by the careful hands of Nina Sanduzzi,
Meredith felt the same relaxation and intimacy that he had experienced in
the house of Aurelio the Bishop. He was grateful for it, as he had been
before, but this time he warmed to it more quickly and less consciously. He
knew now how much he needed friendship, and he was prepared to go more
than halfway to the making of it. As Meyer moved about the room laying
out the cups, spooning out coffee, and slicing the last of a loaf to go with the
cheese, he asked him bluntly:

'What was the meaning of the dinner party tonight? Everything seemed very pointed; but I couldn't see what it was pointing at.'

'It's a long story,' Meyer told him. 'It will take some time to put it in order for you. The party was the Contessa's idea. She wanted to show you the type of people you'd be dealing with—and how much better it would be to lean on her, not on a couple of country bumpkins like Anselmo and me.'

'I had the idea she was afraid of what might be said.'

'That too.' Meyer nodded. 'We've all been afraid, for a long time.'

'Of me?' Meredith looked at him in surprise.

'Of ourselves,' said Meyer with a crooked grin. 'All of us there tonight were involved one way and another with the life and death of Giacomo Nerone. None of us came out of it very creditably.'

'Does that include the Englishman—the painter fellow?'

'He's a late involvement. He's an odd one—and he's taken a fancy to young Paolo Sanduzzi. He's enlisted the Contessa's help to seduce him.'

Meredith was shocked.

'But that's monstrous!'

'It's human,' Meyer told him quietly. 'It sounds better if it's a girl and not a boy. But the idea's the same.'

'But the Contessa said you had agreed the boy should work at the villa.'

'She was lying. She's a very accomplished liar. Which makes it difficult to help her.'

He brought the coffee-pot to the table and poured the steaming contents into the earthenware cups. Then he sat down opposite Meredith, who looked at him with puzzlement in his eyes.

'You're very frank, Doctor—why?'

'I've learned something, very late in life,' said Meyer firmly. 'You can never bury the truth so deep that it can't be dug up. We've been trying to bury the truth about Giacomo Nerone, and now it's festering round our feet. You'll get it sooner or later—and it's my view you ought to get it now. Then you can go back to Rome and leave us in peace.'

'Does this mean you're prepared to give evidence as well?'

'It does.'

'And this is your only motive—truth?'

Meyer looked up quickly and saw, for the first time, the inquisitor who lived in the skin of Blaise Meredith. He said cautiously:

'Does my motive matter, Monsignor?'

'It colours the evidence,' Meredith told him. 'It may obscure the truth—which is the truth about a man's soul.'

Meyer nodded gravely. He saw the point. He respected the man who made it. After a pause he answered:

'So far as any man can be honest about his motives, this is mine. I've made a mess of my life. I'm not quite sure why. I had a part, too, in the death of Giacomo Nerone. I was wrong in that. But I don't believe I was wrong in my other estimates of him. I want to talk all this out; have another set it in perspective for me. Otherwise I'm going to end like old Anselmo giving myself cirrhosis of the liver because I can't face my nightmares. . . . That's why I was afraid of you, like the others. If I couldn't trust you I couldn't talk to you.'

A gleam of amusement showed in Meredith's eyes. He asked quizzically:

'And what makes you think you can trust me, Doctor?'

'Because you have the grace to be ashamed of yourself,' said Meyer baldly. 'And that's rare enough in the Church or out of it. . . . Now drink your coffee and we'll talk awhile before I send you to bed!'

But there was no more talk for Meredith that night. The first mouthful of coffee choked him; the pain in his stomach took him again and Meyer led him stumbling out into the garden to void the bile and the blood that choked him. Then, when the spasm had passed, he laid him down on his own bed and began palpating the shrunken belly, pressing down to the hard, deadly mass growing against the wall of it.

'Is it like this often, Monsignor?'

'It's getting more frequent,' Meredith told him painfully. 'The nights are the worst.'

'How long did they give you?'

'Twelve months, possibly less.'

'Halve it!' Meyer told him flatly. 'Halve it again and you'll be nearer to the truth.'

'As soon as that?'

Meyer nodded.

'By rights you should be in hospital now.'

'I want to stay on my feet as long as I can.'

'I'll try to keep you there,' said Meyer with grudging admiration. 'But too much of this, and it'll take a miracle!'

'That's what the Bishop wanted me to ask for—a miracle.' He said it humorously to make a joke out of the new pain that was coming on him. But Meyer seized on the tag like a terrier.

'Say that again!'

'The Bishop wanted me to ask for a sign—a tangible proof of the sanctity of Giacomo Nerone. Some of the reported cures could be miracles, but I doubt we'll prove any of them judicially . . . so I could be the one provable one.'

'And you, Monsignor? What did you say to that?'

'I didn't have the courage to agree.'

'You would rather bear the pain you have now—and what is still to come?'

Meredith nodded.

'Are you so afraid of your God, my friend?'

'I'm not sure what I'm afraid of. . . . It's—it's as if I were being asked to make a leap through a paper hoop, on the other side of which is either darkness or a shattering revelation. The only way I can find out, is to leap. And I . . . I haven't the courage to do it. Does that sound strange to you, Doctor?'

'Strange—and yet not so strange,' Meyer said thoughtfully. 'Strange from a man like you; but for me, easy enough to understand.'

He was thinking of the papers of Giacomo Nerone that still lay untouched in his bureau: and he was thinking of the fear that came on him every time he tried to open them.

But Meredith did not ask for explanations. He closed his eyes and lay back, pale and exhausted, on the pillow. Meyer let him doze till midnight and, when he woke again, walked him back to the villa and had the gatekeeper take him up to his bedroom.

At midnight Nicholas Black was wakeful, too. He was sitting up in bed, smoking a cigarette and contemplating with deep satisfaction the picture of Paolo Sanduzzi, which was propped on the easel in front of the drawn curtains. He had chosen the position with some care, so that the light fell on it from the correct angle and the white figure of the boy seemed to thrust itself forward from the dark wood of the gallows tree. The scarlet lips smiled at the man who had painted them, and the eyes were bright in contemplation of the veiled, deceptive future.

Narcissus in his pool saw himself no more beautiful than Nicholas Black in his solitary contemplation of his own creation. Yet even this pleasure could not blind him to the pity of his situation: that this was the nearest he could come to what other men had by natural right—sons of their own to love, cherish and train towards the maturity of manhood. Would there never be an end to the pursuit, the panic grasping, the sour humiliation of defeat?

Sometime, with someone, there must be a term to it. Other rakes married their virgins who bred them children and warmed their slippers, while they repented happily in their Indian summer. Soon, soon, he must come to his own harbour, before the winter winds began to blow and the dead leaves rattle around the garden walks.

Then he remembered the dinner talk and hope began to wake again. Tomorrow, Meyer had said, the boy would come. His mother would speak with Anne Louise de Sanctis and he would be signed into service with the gardeners. Morning and afternoon he would be there—a raw peasant to be drawn towards gentility, a servant to be attracted into sonship. It would need tact and gentleness, firmness, too, sometimes, so that from the first the nature of the relationship should be clearly established. Nicholas Black was shrewdly aware of the attraction he had for the boy, equally aware of the boy's capacity to attract him, to their mutual ruin. The boy must be brought to see that all his hopes lay in a disciplined association, and that any attempt to exploit his patron would wreck them utterly. Still, given time and the casual intimacy of the villa, he felt confident that he could do it.

What troubled him still was that he could see only half the motive of the Contessa in helping him to the conquest. The half he saw was simple enough. She wanted his co-operation in handling the priest. She needed an understanding ally to bolster her courage. But the reasons which she still held back were of much deeper concern to him.

The world of lost lovers is a jungle where it is rutting season all the time. There is no mercy in the desperate, headlong flight from loneliness.

The race is to the swift, possession is for the strong. The wild urge to couple and forget colours the most civilised gestures. The simplest words take on a colour of passion and intrigue.

Nicholas Black had lived a long time in the jungle, and he had no illusions left. If Anne de Sanctis helped him, it would be to compass her own designs in the end. What were they? Passion, perhaps? Every season brought its crop of dowagers who hoisted their skirts and played hot cockles with the boys in the Mediterranean spring. The dowagers paid and the boys acted out the cold comedy with Latin cynicism and went back to marry their girls on the profits. But the Contessa was too experienced to make a fool of herself in her own village. Capri was just round the corner. Rome was distant and more discreet. She had money and freedom to pleasure herself where she chose.

So there must be another reason. Her fear of Meredith pointed to a personal involvement with Giacomo Nerone. Potiphar's wife, perhaps? My lady bountiful turned bitch when Joseph fled from her, leaving his cloak in her hands—and taking his fun with a peasant wench instead of the *padrona* of the villa.

Jealousy took freakish forms at times. Paolo Sanduzzi, the stripling boy, would be a perpetual reproach to her failure as a woman and a lover. To seduce him from his mother would be an oblique revenge on his father . . . and a consummate insult to Nicholas Black.

A slow heat of anger grew in him and he lay back on the pillows staring at the picture of Paolo Sanduzzi, loathing the woman who for house room and the promise of an exhibition had thought to buy him into so brutal a bondage.

Anne Louise de Sanctis lay back in her marble bath and felt the soft water move over her skin like a symbol of absolution. The perfumed steam rose gratefully, blurring the harsh edges of reality and blending with the euphoric haze of the barbiturates which would soon coax her downwards into forgetfulness.

This narrow room, with its crystal bottles and its misted mirror, was the womb from which she issued, new, each morning, into which she retreated each night from the howling confusion of loneliness. Suspended in the foetal fluid, within the warm, veined walls of marble, she could float self-absorbed, self-justified, irresponsible, lapped in an illusion of eternity.

But the illusion became more tenuous each night. The impact of each morning became more brutal. Invading hands reached forward into her privacy: voices challenged her out of the twilight into the bitter day and she knew she could not shut them out much longer.

Meyer was the first of her adversaries: the down-at-heel doctor with the disappointed face and the frayed cuffs, the shoe-string reformer, the penny philosopher, the man who knew everything and did nothing, who was the enemy of illusions because he had none himself. Once she might have commanded his alliance against Giacomo Nerone, but now all his care was for Nina Sanduzzi, who had borne Nerone's child. He had refused even the pity she had pleaded from him, and with one brutal sentence had laid bare her self-deceit.

She wanted a child. There was truth in that. She wanted Paolo Sanduzzi. There was truth in that, too. But she wanted him for herself. He was Nerone's boy, flesh of his flesh, bone of his bone. She had love to spend on him—money, too. Love that Nerone had tossed back in her face. Money to ransom him out of the sordid life to which his father had condemned him. But Meyer stood in her way. Meyer and Nina Sanduzzi, and even the grey cleric from Rome.

She had lived a long time in Italy and she understood the subtle workings of the Church in its southern vineyard. Its princes played politics with Machiavellian skill, but they were rigid in the enforcement of the public moralities, through which they ruled a passionate and recalcitrant people. They did not hesitate to invoke the civil statute as a sanction for the ten commandments. As an ally, Meredith could help her greatly; as an enemy he would be implacable and unconquerable.

So, by twisting roads, she came back to Nicholas Black. She had small faith in his stability; but she needed an ally, and this one was already bought and easy to manage. She did not for a moment believe his protestation of pure affection for the boy. She saw it simply as a calculated gambit of seduction; and her promise of help was equally calculated.

She would give the painter time and opportunity to work on Paolo, tempting him with friendship and the promise of a gentleman's life in Rome. The boy would respond quickly, being touched already with the discontents of adolescence. The small scandal of their association would grow to a larger one. Nina Sanduzzi's maternal control would be called in question. Then . . . then the Contessa would step in, the solicitous *padrona*, the châtelaine careful of the interests of her people. She would offer to remove the boy from an occasion of corruption, to educate him, in Rome first and later in England.

Even the Church would see merit in such a course. If Giacomo Nerone were to be raised to the altars, they would not want his son whoring round the villages like so many other country youths. Let Nicholas Black play to his heart's content the role of petty intriguer, she would still win the game in the end. She would walk down the Via Veneto with Paolo Sanduzzi, proud and complete, as though Nerone had fathered him on her own barren body.

She got out of the bath, dried and perfumed herself and dressed for bed. Then she lay down under the great brocaded canopy and let herself drift into a drugged sleep, dreaming of a dark smiling youth whose hand was clasped firmly in her own. And when he changed from youth to man, from son to passionate lover, this was, after all, a delusion of the night, with no guilt in it at all. . . .

10

Early the following morning, while Nina Sanduzzi swept and polished his cottage, Aldo Meyer sat under the fig tree and talked with Paolo.

The interview began awkwardly. The boy was sullen and withdrawn and Meyer's first fumbling queries did nothing to gain his confidence. He kept his eyes fixed on the tabletop, chewed nervously at a twig and gave his answers in a mumbling undertone, so that Meyer was forced to fight down his irritation and keep a proper friendliness in his voice.

'Your mother has spoken to you about working for the Contessa?'

'Yes.'

'You know young Rosetta's going to the villa too?'

'Yes.'

'How do you feel about it?'

'I s'pose it's all right.'

'Do you want to go, or not?'

'I don't mind.'

'The pay's not bad. You'll be able to help your mother and still have something for yourself.'

'Yes, I know.'

'This means you're getting to be a man, Paolo.'

The boy shrugged and picked his teeth with the twig. Meyer took a sip of coffee and lit a cigarette. The next gambit was the important one. He hoped he would not spoil it. After a moment he said, as gently as he could:

'The beginning of a man's life is the most important part of it. It's usually a father's job to set his son on the right road. You haven't a father, so . . . I'd like to help instead.'

For the first time the boy raised his eyes and looked at him squarely. There was a challenge in the look and a faint hostility. His question was blunt and unfriendly.

'Why should you care?'

'I'll try to tell you,' said Meyer equably. 'If I don't satisfy you, ask me anything you like. The first thing is that I haven't a son of my own. I'd like to have one. You could have been my son, because once upon a time I was in love with your mother. I'm still very fond of her. However, she chose your father—and that was that. I knew your father. For a while we were friends, then . . . we were enemies. I had a hand in his death. I'm sorry for that now. If I can help you, I'll be paying a debt to him.'

'I don't need your help,' the boy told him roughly.

'We all need help,' said Meyer quietly. 'You need it because you're involved with the Englishman and you don't quite know what to do about it.'

Paolo Sanduzzi was silent, staring down at the mangled twig in his fingers. Meyer went on:

'I want to explain something to you, Paolo. You know what men are, and women. You know how they come to kiss and caress and what passes between them when they make love. You know what you feel when you look at a girl whose breasts are grown and who begins to walk like a woman. But what you don't understand is how you can feel this for Rosetta, and at the same time feel it when the Englishman touches you.'

Again the boy's head jerked up, defensively.

'There is nothing between me and the Englishman. He has never touched me!'

'Good!' said Meyer calmly. 'Then there is nothing to shame you. Still, you should know that when a man's heart wakes and his body, too, they can be bent this way or that, as the wind bends a sapling. But after a while the sapling stiffens and grows hard as a tree. Then it cannot be bent any more, but grows to its own shape. The proper way for a man to grow is towards a woman—not towards a *feminella*. That is why you cannot stay with the painter. You see that, don't you?'

'Then why are you sending me to work at the villa? He'll be there all the time. He frightens me. He makes me feel that I don't know what I want.'

'Which do you want—him or Rosetta?'

'I want to get out of Gemello!' said the boy savagely. 'I want to go somewhere else, where people don't know about me or my mother or my father. Do you think I like to be called a saint's bastard—the son of a whore? That's why I want to stay with the Englishman. He can do that much for me. He can take me to Rome, give me a new start. . . .'

'And in Rome they'll put a dirtier label on you—and you'll never shake it off wherever you go! Listen, boy . . .' He pleaded with him in a low, passionate voice. 'Try to be patient with me. Try to understand what I'm going to tell you. Your mother is a good woman—ten times better than those who put this name on her. Whatever she did, she did for love—and a whore is one who sells herself for money. Your father was one with a touch of greatness in him . . . and I say that—the man who helped to kill him.'

'Then why didn't he marry my mother and give me his name? Was he ashamed of it? Or of us?'

'Have you ever asked your mother that?'

'No–how could I?'

'Then I think we should ask her now,' said Aldo Meyer. Without waiting for an answer, he called loudly: 'Nina! Come here a moment, please.'

Nina Sanduzzi came out of the house and the boy watched her approach with frightened eyes.

'Sit down, Nina.'

She sat down between them, looking from one to the other with grave, questioning eyes. Meyer told her soberly:

'There is a question the boy has asked, Nina. I think he has a right to the answer. You are the only one to give it. He wants to know why his father didn't marry you.'

'Will you believe me if I tell you, son?'

The boy looked up, troubled and ashamed, and nodded dumbly. Nina Sanduzzi waited a moment, gathering her strength and her words; then, in a steady voice, she told him.

Blaise Meredith too was stirring early on this fine spring morning. After his attack in the doctor's house, he had slept less restlessly than usual, and when the servant came to bring his coffee and draw back the curtains on the new day, he decided to get up and begin work.

He drank his coffee, ate a little of the new bread and the salt country butter, bathed and shaved, and went downstairs to read his Office in the sunshine. With this liturgical duty behind him, he would be free to begin his interviews with the witnesses. Meyer's warning was still vivid in his mind. His time was running out faster than he had hoped and he could not afford to waste a minute of it. He was glad that the Contessa and Black were still in bed so that he would be spared the rituals of greeting and breakfast small talk.

He had finished Matins and was halfway through Lauds when he heard the sounds of footsteps on the gravel path and looked up. A woman and a boy were walking towards the rear of the house. The woman was dressed peasant-fashion in shapeless black, with a bandanna tied round her head. The boy had on a striped shirt and a pair of patched trousers, and his feet were thrust into worn leather sandals.

He walked uncertainly, looking this way and that, as if overcome by the splendour of his surroundings after the barren harshness of the village. The woman walked proudly, head erect, eyes straight ahead of her, as if determined to discharge an uncomfortable duty with dignity. Meredith was struck by the classic serenity of her face, rounding with middle age, but still touched with a youthful beauty.

This would be Nina Sanduzzi, he decided. The boy would be the son of Giacomo Nerone, who, Meyer had told him, was the subject of the conspiracy of seduction between the Contessa and Nicholas Black. They would have a long time to wait before the Contessa was up and ready to see them.

Moved by a sudden impulse, he put down his book and called:

'Signora Sanduzzi!'

They stopped in their tracks and turned to look at him. He called again:

'Can you come here a moment, please?'

They looked at one another uncertainly; then the woman walked across the lawn with the boy a couple of paces behind her. Meredith stood up to greet her.

'I'm Monsignor Meredith, from Rome!'

'I know,' said the woman calmly. 'You came yesterday. This is my son, Paolo.'

'I'm happy to know you, Paolo.'

Meredith held out his hand, and after a nudge from his mother the boy took it, limply.

'You know why I'm here, signora?'

'Yes, I know.'

'I'd like to have a talk with you as soon as possible.'

'You'll find me at the doctor's place—or at home.'

'I thought perhaps we could talk a little now.'

Nina Sanduzzi shook her head.

'We have to see the Contessa. Paolo begins work today.'

Meredith smiled.

'You'll have a long wait. The Contessa isn't up yet.'

'We're used to waiting,' she told him gravely. 'Besides, I will not talk to you here.'

'Just as you like.'

'But when Paolo is working here you can talk to him. That would be different.'

'Of course. May I come and see you today?'

'If you want. In the afternoon I'm at home. Now we must go. Come, Paolo.'

Without another word she turned away. The boy followed her, and Meredith watched their retreating backs until they disappeared round the rear corner of the villa.

Brief as their encounter had been, the woman had impressed him deeply. There was an air about her—an air of serenity, containment, wisdom perhaps. She walked and talked like one who knew where she was going and how she intended to get there. She had neither the thrusting impudence of some peasant women, nor the practised humility which centuries of dependence had imposed on others. Her tongue was the roughest dialect in Italy, yet her voice was soft and strangely gentle even in her blunt refusal. If Giacomo Nerone had taught her these things, then he, in his time, must have been a greater man than most.

Meredith found his attention wandering from the Latin cadences of the Psalms to the consideration of two important elements in the sketchy life of Giacomo Nerone.

The first was the element of conflict. It was an axiom in the Church that one of the first marks of sanctity was the opposition it raised, even among good people. Christ himself had been the sign of contradiction. His promise was not peace, but the sword. No saint in the Calendar had ever done good unopposed. None had ever been without detractors and calumniators. The absence of this element from the records of Battista and Saltarello had troubled him. Now he was beginning to be aware of its existence and of its strength and complexity.

The second element was equally important: the tangible good or evil that sprang from the life, works and wonders of a candidate for saintly honours. There was an axiom here too: the Biblical axiom that a tree is known by its fruits. Sanctity in one man leaves its imprint like a seal on the hearts of others. A good work reproduces itself as the seed of one fruit grows into another. A miracle that produces no good in a human heart is a pointless conjuring trick unworthy of omnipotence.

If there was good in Nina Sanduzzi, and if this good had sprung from her association with Giacomo Nerone, then it must be weighed in the meticulous reckoning of the Devil's Advocate.

He bent again to his breviary, his lips moving in the familiar strophes of the poet-king. Then, when he had finished, he closed the book, thrust it into the pocket of his cassock and walked out of the villa to talk with Father Anselmo.

Old Rosa Benzoni met him at the door and, after a grumbling parley, let him into the house, where he found the old priest, in shirt-sleeves and braces, shaving awkwardly in front of a cracked mirror tacked to the wall of the kitchen. His eyes were blearier than usual and his knotted hands trembled as he scraped at his stubbled chin. He was using an old blade razor and Meredith marvelled that he had not yet cut his throat with it. His greeting was less than cordial.

'Hullo! What do you want?'

'I'd like to talk to you,' said Meredith mildly.

'I'll listen. I don't promise to answer, though.'

'Better we were private, don't you think?' suggested Meredith.

The old man chuckled and then swore as he nicked himself.

'You mean Rosa? She's half-deaf and I doubt she'd understand a word when you talk with a Roman grape in your mouth. Besides, she's got a bad temper—and I've got to live with her. Go ahead, man, and say what you've got to say.'

Meredith shrugged and went on.

'It's about Giacomo Nerone. I notice from the first reports that you refused to give any evidence about him. Is that because you were his confessor?'

'No. I didn't like the fellows they sent round. Long-nosed humbugs the pair of 'em. Read me a long lecture about doomsday and damnation. I sent 'em off with a flea in the ear. Besides, who the hell cares what I say? I'm the scandal of the diocese.'

'I'm not interested in scandals,' said Meredith coolly.

The old man put down the razor and daubed at his face with a soiled towel. He said roughly:

'Then you're the first one I've met who isn't. God, how they love 'em! Give 'em a piece of dirt and they'll chew on it like dogs on a ham-bone. I had a letter from the Bishop hoping my association with Rosa had lost its carnal character. . . .' He gave a high, harsh laugh. 'How long does he think a man keeps going at that sort of thing? At my age the best you can hope for is to keep warm at night.'

'At your age,' suggested Meredith gently, 'most married couples sleep in separate beds.'

'In Rome, maybe,' growled Father Anselmo. 'But down here we haven't enough money to buy a new bed—let alone two sets of blankets. Look . . .' He flung down the towel with a gesture of impatience. 'We're not children, Monsignor. I don't like the position I'm in, any more than the Bishop. But at my age, how do I get out of it? I can't toss Rosa out into the street. She's an old woman. She's been good to me—when a lot of my damned brothers in the cloth couldn't have cared whether I lived or died. I've got little enough, God knows, but she's entitled to half of it. Does His Lordship have any answer to that one?'

Meredith was moved. The naked dilemma of the man was frightening. For the first time in his priestly life he began to understand the real problem of repentance, which is not the sin itself, but the consequences which proliferate from it, like parasites on a tree. The tree has no remedy but must go on lending its life to the parasite, borrowing beauty from it, but dying slowly all the time, for want of a knowledgeable gardener. It was a stark thought that a man might lapse into despair and damnation because he couldn't afford a pair of blankets. Suddenly the case of Giacomo Nerone seemed small and insignificant beside the case of Father Anselmo. If Giacomo was a saint he was lucky–he had finished with the long fight. All else was glossary and of little moment. A sudden thought struck Meredith but he hesitated to give it voice. After a moment he said carefully:

'His Lordship's a surprising man. He'd like to help you. I think–I'm sure–if you were to move Rosa to another bed in another room, he'd accept that and let the rest of it drop.'

The old man shook his head stubbornly.

'Who pays for the bed and bedclothes? You don't seem to understand. We live down to the knuckle-bone here. It's a matter of eating.'

'I'll tell you something,' said Meredith with a wry smile. 'I'll pay for them. I'll give you and Rosa enough to set yourselves up with some new clothes and I'll put a hundred thousand lire in the Banco di Calabria for you. Would that help?'

Father Anselmo shot him a swift suspicious glance.

'And why should you care so much, Monsignor?'

Meredith shrugged.

'I'm due to die in three months. I can't take it with me.'

The rheumy eyes stared at him in unbelief. The rough peasant voice questioned him again.

'What else do I have to do?'

'Nothing. If you want me to confess you, I'll do it gladly. You can't tell me much I don't know already, so it shouldn't be too hard. There's no point in going halfway. You've got to set your conscience in order some time.'

'The Bishop talked about repairing the scandal.' There was still doubt in his voice, but the stubborn harshness had gone out of it.

Meredith gave him one of his rare, humorous smiles.

'The Bishop's a character in his own right. I think he knows that most people make their own scandals. Good Christians keep their mouths shut and pray for their brothers in distress. It'll soon get around the village that you're sleeping apart. The rest will grow out of what you do from then on. . . . Well, what do you say?'

Anselmo rubbed a knotted hand across his badly shaven chin. His slack mouth twisted into a grin.

'I–I suppose it's a way out. I've been worried a long time, but I love the old girl in a way and I'd hate to hurt her.'

'I don't think the loving does any harm. I could use some of it myself just now.' The voice seemed to belong to another man, not Blaise Meredith, the cold fellow from the Congregation of Rites.

'All right!' said the old man brusquely. 'I'll think about it. I'll talk to Rosa and explain things to her. But you can't do things like that in a rush. Women are sensitive–and when they're old they get stupid as well. . . .' His old eyes gleamed shrewdly. 'And when do we see the colour of *your* money, Monsignor?'

Meredith took out his wallet and laid thirty one-thousand lire notes on the table.

'That's the beginning of it. You can buy the blankets and the bed. The rest I'll have to fix in Valenta. Will that do?'

'It'll have to,' the old man told him grudgingly. 'We'd like something fixed before you die. Once the lawyers get their hands on an estate—finish! All that's left is birdseed! Now, what else did you want?'

'Giacomo Nerone. . . . What can you tell me about him?'

'What happens if I do tell you?'

'I'll make notes and then you'll be examined under oath at the Bishop's court.'

'Tell you what, Monsignor. Wait till you hear my confession. Then I'll give you the full story. Will that do?'

'A confessional secret is no good for the court record.'

The old man threw back his head and laughed in his high harsh fashion.

'That's what I mean, friend! They've had enough scandals out of me already. Damned if I'm going to give 'em another one.'

'Just as you say,' said Meredith wearily. 'I'll call and see you in a few days.'

'And don't forget what you have to do in Valenta.'

'I won't forget.'

He got up and walked to the door. There was no farewell, no word of thanks, and as he walked down the hill towards the doctor's cottage, he had the uncomfortable feeling that he had made a fool of himself.

Meyer greeted him good-humouredly, led him into the garden and poured him a cup of country wine from an earthenware pitcher, cooling in the sun. Meredith was quick to notice the change in him: his eyes were clear, his drawn face was relaxed, and he had the comfortable air of a man who has come to terms with himself and his situation. Meredith commented on it quizzically.

'You look better this morning, Doctor.'

Meyer grinned into his wine-cup.

'A good beginning to my day, Monsignor. I've talked to a boy like a father; and heard wise things from his mother.'

'Nina Sanduzzi?'

'Yes. Between us I hope we have done something for the boy.'

'I saw them at the villa—spoke to them for a few moments. I'm calling on Nina Sanduzzi this afternoon. She's prepared to talk.'

'Good.' Meyer nodded with satisfaction. 'I'll give you a tip, my friend. Walk gently and you will go a long way with her. She is disposed now to be frank. And she wants you to keep an eye on the boy while he's at the villa.'

'I'll do my best. She impressed me deeply.'

'And Paolo?'

'Is like any other adolescent.'

'Not quite like . . .' Meyer cautioned him. 'He is in the dangerous years. He is attracted to the Englishman and he is afraid of him as well. Also he is curious about his mother and father. Not quite so curious now that Nina and I have spoken to him. But when you're old, you never know how much a young man understands—or what bees he has buzzing in his bonnet. And what now, Monsignor?'

'I'd like to talk with you, Doctor.'

'About Nerone?'

'Yes.'

Aldo Meyer took a long draught of wine and then wiped his thin lips with the back of his hand. He said with bleak humour:

'Isn't it usual to put on a stole when you hear confessions?'

'I'll take off my shoes instead,' said Blaise Meredith.

'It's a long story, Monsignor. When it gets dry, you help yourself to a drink. . . .

. . . It was full summer in a world without men. Hot mornings and blazing noons, and nights when the clouds rolled in, sweating, over the valley and then moved on unspent of rain. Tempers were high, and vitality was low, because the armies were like locusts, eating out the land, and there were no men in the beds–except the old ones, who were a nuisance, and occasional visitors, like the *polizia* and the *carabinieri* and the agricultural inspector and the requisitioning officers from the Army. These were a nuisance, too, because when they were gone there were quarrels in the houses and bloody faces and torn skirts in the fields.

The valley was like a nest of cats, musky and hot and languid for coupling, then breaking suddenly into screams and violence. Meyer lived in it, because he was a Jew and an exile and every second day he must tramp across the valley to Gemello Maggiore to assure the *quaestura* that he was neither sick nor dead. They were indifferent either way, but they cursed him when he came and threatened him if he missed a day–and then gave him wine and cheese and cigarettes if their children were sick or their girls pregnant or they themselves went down with malaria. They made coarse jokes about his being a Jew and circumcised and warned him about polluting the pure blood of the women, who, being good Calabrese, were part Greek, part Phoenician, part French and Spanish and Italian and Levantine Arab–anything and everything but Jew.

Meyer swallowed it all, and digested it in secret and kept his ears open to the rumours that bumbled like bees in and out of the valley. The Allies were in Sicily, there were beach-heads in other places. Partisans were arming in the hills, deserters were holing up in caves and friendly beds. The Germans were rushing reinforcements south. Sooner or later the end would come and he wanted to be alive to see it.

He worked his rough acres, made his rounds of the sick, dozed at siesta time and in the night sat late over his books and his bottle.

If he kept himself free of the village women, it was because he was a fastidious man, and also because he did not want to face the dawning future with a village shrew at his coat-tails. He had waited a long time. He could afford to wait a little longer.

It was in the night time, late, that Nina Sanduzzi came to see him. She came barefooted lest the sound of her wooden sandals be heard in the sleeping village; and she climbed the garden wall from the valley side, in case some late busybody saw her knocking on the doctor's door. She was right inside the pool of lamplight before he woke from his reverie and saw her. He was startled and angry.

'Nina! What the devil are you doing here?'

She put her finger to her lips to silence him and then explained in low, rattling dialect:

'There's a man in my house. He's a deserter and wounded. There's a bullet hole in his shoulder all red and swollen, and he tosses and mutters as if he had the fever. Will you come and see him, please? I've brought money.'

She fished into the neck of her dress and brought up a small bundle of greasy notes. Meyer waved it away impatiently.

'Keep it, for God's sake! Does anyone else know he's there?'

'No one. He came last night. I gave him breakfast and he stayed inside all day. When I got back from work he was like this.'

'All right, I'll come.'

He closed his book, turned down the lamp and gathered up his bag of instruments and his small stock of antiseptic, and followed her out from the back of the house, over the wall and down to the small hut hidden in the ilexes.

He found his patient delirious on the big brass bed, a long dark fellow with days of stubble on his shrunken cheeks, and staring eyes and a drooling, muttering mouth, from which issued broken words and phrases that he recognised as English. A pretty situation! Deserters were bad enough, but an English soldier was sudden death. He made no comment to the girl, but bent over the bed and began cutting the sodden bandages from the shoulder wound.

When he saw it, he gave a low whistle of surprise. It was pulpy and swollen, and a slow yellow suppuration had already begun. An awkward job and a dirty one. It would hurt like hell without an anaesthetic and the fellow might well die in a matter of days.

He turned back to Nina Sanduzzi.

'Get the fire going. Boil me a pot of hot water. Then you'll have to hold him down for me.'

The girl's white teeth showed in a smile.

'It's a long time since I've had a man in my arms, Dottore. It'll be a pleasure.'

But the pleasure soon went out of it, even for her. The bullet had struck the shoulder blade and slanted downward against the bone, and Meyer had to probe for it for twenty minutes, while the sick man shouted vainly against the gag they thrust in his mouth, and Nina Sanduzzi had to use all her strength to hold him.

Then when it was over and the worst of the pain was finished they tucked him into the bed, and Nina and Meyer sat down to drink wine and break a crust together.

'You can't keep him here. You know that, Nina. If anyone finds out, you're as good as dead.'

She stared at him in astonishment.

'You want me to throw him out. A sick man like that?'

'Afterwards,' said Meyer wearily. 'When he's better.'

'Let's wait for afterwards, then,' said Nina Sanduzzi with a smile.

Looking at her then by lamplight in the low room, he had felt his first real temptation in years. Her face was pure Greek. Her body was slimmer than those of her peasant fellows. Her breasts were full and firm and there was a thrusting animal vitality under her olive skin. She had intelligence, too, and courage. She did not wait and scream like the others. She knew what was needed and she did it, calmly and competently. It amazed him that he had passed her a hundred times and never noticed her.

But he was a cautious fellow and accustomed to continence, so he finished his wine quickly and made to go.

'Understand something, Nina. He's very sick and he could die. Make some soup and see if he can hold it down. When you go to work, lock the door and leave him wine and food. I daren't come here in the daytime, but I'll come again in the night after the village has settled down.'

'You're a good one,' said Nina Sanduzzi softly. 'In a place full of pigs you stand up like a man.' She snatched up his hand and kissed it quickly. 'Now go, *dottore mio*! I'm not used to men around the place!'

As he trudged up the rocky slope, avoiding the roadway, he wondered whether continence was not, like all his other sacrifices, a pointless waste—and whether this might be a woman with whom he could be happy. It was the thing he had been afraid of all his exile—the thing his enemies wanted him to do—go slack, go native, hit the bottle and the country whores, and forget to wash his shirts and use a knife and fork with his dinner. So far he had managed to avoid it. With Nina Sanduzzi he might still avoid it. . . . But the risk was there—and there were faint trumpets sounding in the hills. Better forget it and go home to sleep.

It took him more than a week to nurse the patient out of danger. The wound was deep and new infections broke out, and he had to keep draining the wound with the primitive means at his disposal. More than one night he sat up, with Nina, watching the fever rise and break, until the false dawn lightened in the east and it was time to go home before the village was astir.

Each night he came, he felt the need of her. Each time he left, he felt a pang of jealousy at leaving her alone with the sick man, who now had begun to eat and talk a little between the fever bouts and the long intervals of restless sleep.

At first he was cautious with them; but when he understood Meyer's position as a political exile, and the risks the girl was taking for him, he relaxed a little, but still refused to tell them anything but the story he had first told Nina Sanduzzi.

'Better you don't know any more than that. If you're questioned, you can answer truthfully. Though I hope to God you won't be. I'm Giacomo Nerone, a gunner from Reggio. I'm trying to get back to Rome to my family. When do you think I'll be strong enough to travel, Doctor?'

Meyer shrugged.

'A fortnight, three weeks, maybe—unless you get another infection. But where do you aim to go? There's talk that the Allies have landed north of here, and that they're advancing up the toe from Reggio. But this place is a pocket in the hills. With our chaps pulling back and the Germans moving down, you'll have trouble getting very far. Your accent doesn't belong to Calabria. Sooner or later someone's going to ask questions . . . unless you're going into hiding again—and then how do you eat?'

Nerone smiled ruefully and they saw how the humour transfigured him, into a boy again.

'What else do you expect? I can't stay here.'

'Why not? demanded Nina Sanduzzi. 'There's a house and a bed and food. It's not much, but it's better than dying in a ditch with another bullet in you.'

The two men looked at each other. After a pause Meyer nodded dubiously.

'She could be right. Besides . . .' He made the point cautiously. 'When things change here, you might be in a position to help.'

The dark fellow shook his head.

'Not in the way you think, Doctor.'

Meyer frowned, then said bluntly:

'You don't understand me. I heard you talking in your sleep. You have other loyalties, it seems. These might be useful to us later.'

Now it was the girl's turn to stare. She demanded sharply:

'What do you mean, other loyalties?'

'I'm English,' said Nerone. 'And now that it's said, forget it.'

'English!' Nina Sanduzzi's eyes widened.

'Forget it!' said Meyer harshly.

'It's forgotten.' But she smiled as she said it and then put another proposition which left them momentarily speechless. 'If you stay here, there's no reason why you can't work for your living. . . . Don't look so surprised! There are half a dozen lads doing it this very minute. They've given the war away too. Two of them are locals and the others come from God knows where. But we're short of men, and there's a lot to be done before winter–and nobody wants to make a fuss about it. If there's anybody suspicious hanging around, the boys go to cover, but most of the time they work out in the open. . . .' She laughed cheerfully. 'And they're never short of a bed! I could get you a job with old Enzo Gozzoli. He's the foreman of my crowd. He's lost two sons in the war and he hates the Fascisti like poison. When you're better, I'll talk to him. . . . If you want to, that is.'

'I'll think about it,' said Giacomo Nerone. 'I'm very grateful but I'll have to think about it.'

He lay back on the pillow and closed his eyes, and a few moments later he lapsed into sleep.

The girl poured Meyer another cup of wine, and he drank it, thoughtfully, watching her as she bent over the bed, settling the dark head on the pillow, drawing the bedclothes carefully round the wounded shoulder, standing a moment in silent comtemplation of the sleeping guest.

When she came back, Meyer stood up, took her in his arms, and tried to kiss her. She pushed him away, gently.

'No, *dottore mio*. Not now.'

'I want you, Nina!'

'You don't want me really, *cara*,' she told him softly. 'Otherwise you'd have taken me long before now–and I'd have been glad of it. It's summer and you're lonely, and we've spent some evenings together. But I'm not for you and you know it. . . . Afterwards you would hate me. I want a man, God knows! But I want all of him.'

Meyer turned away and picked up his bag. He made a quick gesture towards the bed.

'Maybe you've got him!' he said dryly.

'Maybe,' said Nina Sanduzzi. Then she walked to the door and held it open for him, and as he walked up the hillside he heard it shut–a dry, sharp sound in the languid air.

. . . 'And that was the beginning of it?' asked Blaise Meredith.

'The beginning.' Meyer reached for the pitcher of wine. 'In three weeks he was out and about, working for Enzo Gozzoli. At night he went back to Nina's house and they were lovers.'

'And, beyond the fact that he was English, you still had no idea who he was?'

'No.' Meyer took a long swallow of wine and wiped his lips with a soiled handkerchief. 'There were three things he might have been: an escaped prisoner, a British agent sent to make contact with the first Partisan groups, a deserter.'

'And which did he look like to you?'

'I took them in turn and tried to fit him into the mould. An escaped prisoner? Yes. Except that he showed no inclination to do what such a man should do–try to rejoin his unit. An agent? This too. He spoke good Italian–not the *argot* of the cookhouse and the military brothel. He was an educated man. He was alive to the local colour. But when I threw out hints about joining me in an attempt to contact the Partisans, he refused.'

'Did he give any reason?'

'No. He refused politely, but quite definitely.'

'A deserter, then?'

Meyer pursed his thin lips thoughtfully.

'It seemed the most likely category. But a deserter is a man who is afraid. He has the fugitive look. He lives with the conviction that one day he must be caught. Nerone had none of that. Once he was well, he walked and talked and laughed like a free man.'

'Was he an officer?'

'I thought so. As I say, he was a cultivated man. He had the habit of decision, a talent for getting things done. But he carried no identification at all. I pointed out that if he were caught like this by the Germans or the Italians, he could be shot as a spy. He just laughed and said Giacomo Nerone was a good Italian who saw no reason in the war. . . . More wine, Monsignor?'

Meredith nodded vaguely, and as Meyer filled his glass he asked:

'What estimate did you form of his character at this first period?'

'Part of it, I've already given you,' said Meyer. 'Courage, good-humour, a capacity for getting things done. The rest? I wasn't quite sure. I was jealous of him, you see.'

'Because of Nina Sanduzzi?'

'That and other things. I had lived among these people, served them, too, for years. I had never arrived at intimacy with them. Nerone was at home in a week. The men trusted him. The women loved him. He could make them laugh by twitching his black eyebrows. They told him all the scandals and taught him dialect and shared their wine with him. I was still the outsider–the Jew from Rome.'

'I know how you felt,' said Meredith gently. 'I've been like that all my life. Except that I've never served anyone.'

Aldo Meyer shot him a quick appraising glance, but Meredith was staring absently at the dark wine in his cup. He went on.

'The thing that irritated me about him was that he seemed to take everything for granted and for permanent. As if the present were the only thing that mattered. For him it was natural enough, I suppose. He had had his war. He was content with the day. I had been waiting so long that I cried for action and for change.'

'So you were at odds with each other?'

Meyer shook his head.

'That's the queer part. When I didn't see him, I disliked him. But when we met in passing–or when, later, he used to come to my place in the evening to talk or borrow a book, he charmed me. There was a calm about him–a gentleness. The same sort of thing you find now in Nina Sanduzzi.'

'What did you talk about?'

'Everything—except Nerone. He refused any topic that might give me a clue to his identity. What interested him most was the place itself, the people, their history, their customs, their relationships with one another. It was as if he were trying to forget all that had belonged to him and absorb himself into the life of the mountains.'

'Was he concerned for them?'

'At first, no. He seemed to regard himself as one of them. But he had no plans as I had. No schemes for their betterment.'

'What were his relations with Nina Sanduzzi?'

Meyer grinned wryly and spread his hands in deprecation.

'They were happy together. One saw it in their faces. That was all I knew. More than I wanted to know. For the rest you'll have to talk to Nina.'

Meredith nodded.

'I'm sorry to press you like this, Doctor. But you understand what I am commissioned to do.'

'I understand. I'm not hedging. I'm trying to keep my evidence first-hand.'

'Please go on.'

'The next stage begins about the end of October ... the middle of autumn. Nerone called me in to examine Nina. She was two months' pregnant.'

'What was his reaction to that?'

'He was glad of it. They both were. I think I was never more jealous of him than at that moment. He had come from nowhere and he had achieved what had eluded me all my life: acceptance, love, a promise of purpose and continuity.'

'Yet he made no move to marry Nina?'

'No.'

'Did she want it?'

'I put it to them both,' said Meyer carefully, 'not because I was concerned—in a country without men, there is no shame in a fatherless child—but because I wanted to see what sort of man this was.'

'What did he say?'

'Nothing. It was Nina who answered. She said: "Time enough for wedding bells, Dottore, when we know what is going to happen."'

'And Nerone?'

Meyer looked down at the backs of his hands, spread like spiders on the warm wood of the table. He hesitated a moment, then said:

'I remember the next part very well. Just when it seemed I had measured Nerone for what he was—a fly-by-night who would be on his way before the dawn showed—he surprised me again.'

'How?'

'He said, quite simply, apropos of nothing at all: "It's going to be a bad winter, Doctor. You and I had better start preparing for it now!"'

... In the old days, before the men were taken, before the war had started to go wrong, when there was still an authority and a purpose in the land, the winter had been bearable—if never a happy time.

There was charcoal in store and wine laid down and oil in the big green bottles. The onions hung in strings from the rafters and the corncobs were piled in the corner and there were potatoes buried in straw. There was cheese to be bought, and salami and smoked ham and lentils, and the millers had flour to sell for the pasta. The food was there, even if you had to scratch a hole in your breeches to find the money to buy it. Before the snows closed in, there was always a traffic of barter between the villages; and when work in the fields slowed down to a dead stop, the commune paid out a small dole to have the roads cleared and gravel spread on the ice patches.

It was a life–not much of a life, to be sure–but if you hung on to it long enough, you would hear the torrent roaring and smell the first warm winds from the south and feel the ice thawing out of your bones with the coming of spring.

But now there were no men and the crops were poor and the Quartermaster's levies took the best of them. The barter was a nothing, because who would take his donkey-cart to market and risk the thieves and deserters and patrols on the way? Better to stay at home and live on your own fat as long as you could. Besides, the boys were straggling back, leaderless, disillusioned and belly-hungry–new mouths to feed out of the diminished stores.

There was no government any more. Those officials who had been reasonable fellows stayed on, hoping their pay packets might arrive and, if they didn't, hoping for a small return for their kindness. Those who had been bastards were moving out, tagging themselves on to still active units, or selling themselves and their local knowledge to the German detachments moving south to engage the Allied Eighth Army.

And in Gemelli dei Monti they smelt the wind, and felt the first rain squalls, and counted the first frosts, and said: 'It's going to be a bad winter.'

Giacomo Nerone said it too, coolly and emphatically. But he added a rider or two of his own.

'You and I are the only people round here with any brains or any influence. We'll have to run the organisation.'

Meyer gaped at him, thunderstruck.

'For God's sake, man! You don't know what you're talking about. You're on the run! I'm a political exile. The moment we stick out our necks, they'll drop the axe on them.'

'Who's they, Doctor?' Nerone grinned at him.

'The authorities. The police. The *carabinieri*. The Mayor of Gemello Maggiore.'

Nerone threw back his head and laughed as heartily as if it were a washerwoman's joke down by the torrent.

'My dear doctor! These fellows are so scared just now, they're only interested in saving their own hides. We haven't seen any of 'em round here for weeks. Besides, this is our business, not theirs. We handle it ourselves.'

'Handle what, for God's sake?'

'The elementary problem of survival for three months. We've got to see that everyone gets enough food and fuel to keep alive during the winter. We've got to get you some more medicines and try to find some more blankets. We've got to set up a central store and see that rations are doled out fairly. . .'

'You're mad!' Meyer told him flatly. 'You don't understand these people. They're close-fisted at the best of times, but in famine they're like carrion birds. They'll eat out one another's livers before they'll let a crust of bread pass from one house to another. The family's the only thing that counts. The rest can rot in a ditch.'

'Then we'll teach 'em the next step,' said Nerone calmly. 'We'll make 'em a tribe.'

'You can't do it.'

'I've already started.'

'The hell you have!'

'I've got ten families to agree to put a quarter of their food stocks into a common store for the winter. Each of these families is going to try to bring in one more. Then you and I will go round and try to beat some sense into those who are still standing out.'

'I don't understand how you did it.'

Giacomo Nerone smiled and shrugged.

'I talked to them. I pointed out that there are still more levies to come: Italian, German, Allied. When things get tough–as they will in the winter–there'll be house searches for hoarded stocks. No, while the going's good, we'd better co-operate and build up a common store in a secret place. I told them Nina and I would make our own contribution first, as evidence of good faith; and then we'd set up a committee to administer it. You, me, and three others. Two men and a woman. It took a little time, but they agreed in the end.'

'I've been here all this time,' said Meyer sombrely, 'and I've never been able to do anything like that.'

'You have to pay a price for it, of course.'

Meyer stared at him puzzled.

'What sort of price?'

'I don't know yet,' said Nerone thoughtfully, 'but I think it will come very high in the end.....'

... 'Did he explain what he meant?' asked Blaise Meredith.

'No.'

'Did you ask him to explain it?'

'Yes.' Meyer made a rueful mouth. 'But once again it was Nina who answered for him. She was standing behind him, I remember, and she bent down and kissed his hair and then held his face between her hands. Then she said: "I love this man, *dottore mio*. He's afraid of nothing–and he always pays his debts!"'

'Did that satisfy you?'

Meyer chuckled and thrust himself back in his chair to reach for the wine.

'You miss the point, Monsignor. When you see a man and a woman like that–and when you are in love with the woman yourself–there's only one satisfaction. And you can't have it. I got up and went home. Next day Nerone and I met again and began to prepare for winter.'

'And you succeeded?'

'Yes. Before the first snows came, everybody in Gemello Minore had agreed, and we had nearly three tons of supplies sealed up in the Grotta del Fauno.'

Recollections stirred sharply behind the thoughtful eyes of Blaise Meredith.

'The Grotto of the Faun. .... That's where they buried him, wasn't it?'

'That's where they buried him,' said Aldo Meyer.

I I

While Blaise Meredith talked under the fig tree with Doctor Aldo Meyer, Anne Louise de Sanctis sat in the ornate salon at the villa and interviewed Nina Sanduzzi.

She had risen late, but less ill-tempered than usual, and when the servant informed her that Nina Sanduzzi was waiting to see her with the boy, she had taken a little longer with her breakfast and her toilet. She had chatted for ten minutes with Nicholas Black, who was off to the garden with his paint-box; she had looked over the household accounts and the menu for the evening meal; then she had settled herself in the salon and sent a servant to fetch Nina Sanduzzi.

Now they were alone while Paolo scuffed his feet on the path outside and watched the gardeners moving up and down the flower-beds and the flight of a yellow butterfly, lazy among the shrubbery.

The Contessa was seated in a high-backed chair, freshly groomed, faintly triumphant, her hands placid in her lap, her eyes searching the blank face of the peasant who stood before her, dusty from the road, feet bare in wooden sandals, but straight and proud as a tree waiting for the wind to blow.

'You understand,' said Anne Louise de Sanctis, 'this is a great opportunity for the boy.' She used the familiar *thou* to indicate the vast gulf that lay between the châtelaine and the servant.

'It is work,' said Nina Sanduzzi calmly. 'That is good for the boy. If he works well, it is good for you, too.'

'How does he feel about it? Is he glad to come?'

'Who can say how a boy feels? He is here. He is ready to start work.'

'We haven't yet discussed payment.'

Nina Sanduzzi shrugged indifferently.

'The *dottore* said you would pay what was usual.'

Anne Louise de Sanctis smiled benevolently.

'We'll do better than that. Signore Black tells me he is intelligent and willing. We'll pay him a man's wage.'

'For a man's work—good! So long as it is a man's work!'

The reply was barbed, but the Contessa, being weak in dialect, missed the sharpness of it. She went on, genial and condescending.

'If the boy works well and shows promise, we may be able to do much for him—give him an education, help him to make a career—send him to Rome, perhaps.'

Nina Sanduzzi nodded thoughtfully, but her eyes were veiled and expressionless as a bird's. She said simply:

'His father was an educated man. He used to say, one should educate the heart first and the head later.'

'Of course,' said the Contessa with unnatural brightness. 'His father! Giacomo Nerone was your lover, wasn't he?'

'He was the man I loved,' said Nina Sanduzzi. 'He loved me and he loved the boy.'

'Strange that he never married you.'

There was no flicker of emotion in the blank eyes and the calm face. The sentence hung suspended in the silence between them. Anne Louise de Sanctis was irritated. She wanted to strike out and see the marks of her fingers rise in weals on the other's olive cheeks. But this was an indulgence she could not afford, being committed to diplomacy and an alliance of smiles and concealment. She said briskly:

'The boy will lodge here, of course. He'll be well fed and comfortable. You can have him home with you on Sundays.'

'I've spoken to the Monsignor from Rome,' said Nina Sanduzzi quietly. 'I've asked him to talk with the boy and help him. These are awkward years in his life.'

'You shouldn't have bothered Monsignor Meredith,' the Contessa snapped at her. 'He's a sick man and busy with important affairs!'

'He is busy with my Giacomo, Signora. And what could be more important than Giacomo's son? Besides, the Monsignor said he would be happy to help.'

'You may go,' said the Contessa. 'Leave the boy here and the gardener will set him to work.'

Nina Sanduzzi made no move to go. Instead she stooped and picked up the straw bag she always carried. She fumbled inside it, brought up a small package neatly wrapped in paper and held it out to the Contessa.

'What's this?'

'My boy is coming into your house. He should not come empty-handed. It's a gift.'

The simple grace of the gesture embarrassed her. She took the package in her hands and said awkwardly:

'Thank you. May I ask what it is?'

'We are poor people,' said Nina Sanduzzi carefully. 'We give from our hearts and not from our wealth. One day Giacomo may be made a *beato*, and then this will be precious to you. It is part of what he wore when they killed him. His blood is on it. I would like you to have it—from his son!'

Anne Louise de Sanctis said nothing, but sat there, staring like a hypnotic at the package, her face dead white, her lips moving in a soundless murmur. When, after a long time, she looked up, Nina Sanduzzi was gone, and there was only the sunlight slanting in through dust motes, and a vista of green lawn where a boy walked side by side with a gardener—a boy who might have been her own son.

Aldo Meyer and Monsignor Blaise Meredith had got up from the table and were walking, side by side, up and down the flagged path that ran the full width of the garden. They passed alternately from sunlight into shadow and their shoes made a dry, crisp sound on the stones.

'To this point,' said Meredith, in his precise, legal fashion, 'what have we? A man in flight, a man in love, a man assuming leadership and responsibility in the community which has given him refuge. His past is a mystery. His future, a doubt in his own mind. His present . . . what you have told me. We have no indication of his religious belief or his moral attitude. On the face of it, he is living in sin. His acts, good in themselves, have no spiritual value. Now . . .' He kicked at a small pebble and watched it bound away towards the rough stone wall. 'Now, according to my records, he comes to a crisis, a moment of conversion, in which, or as a result of which, he turns away from this woman and surrenders himself to God. What do you know about this?'

'Less than I should, perhaps,' said Meyer deliberately. 'Certainly much less than Nina, to whom you will be talking this afternoon. But I do know something. I give it to you for what it's worth. . . .'

. . . The winter was harder than they had ever dreamed possible. The snows came down in blinding blizzards from the high peaks to the west; they piled in drifts along the roads and in the hollows. They choked the mountain tracks and broke the olive branches and heaped themselves against the doors of the houses. They froze hard, and the winds whipped the powder off them, leaving exposed ridges of ice like ripples on a dead white sea. Then came new calms and new downfalls so that a soft layer was laid on the hard rime underneath.

In the south the engaged armies dug themselves in and waited for the thaw. The patrols bivouacking in the hills lost men from exposure and frostbite. The stragglers and deserters hammered on barred doors in the night and, if they were not opened, died in the snow before morning.

Inside the houses, the families clung together for warmth in the big brass beds, rising only to relieve themselves or to seek food and brew coffee, because charcoal stock had to be conserved, and the earthen floors were frozen and the wind searched keenly through the cracked doors and the crazy window frames stuffed with mud and old newspapers. The old ones coughed and grumbled with the rheumatic cold in their joints; the young ones fretted with flushed cheeks and sore throats and congested chests; and when any of them died, as many did, they were carried out into the snow and buried there until the thaw—because who would make coffins in this bleak weather and who could turn a sod in the Campo Santo when the ground was frozen hard as granite?

They lived like hibernating animals, each litter an island in a sea of snow, drawing warmth from each other's bodies, familiar with each other's stench, munching blindly on the common crust, wondering bleakly how long they would last and whether there would ever be another spring.

If a knock came on the door, they ignored it. Who but thieves or crazy men or starving ones would be abroad at this time? If the knock was persistent, they cursed in chorus, until finally it stopped and they heard the crackling footsteps retreat across the frozen snow. There was only one knock they knew and one voice to which they answered—Giacomo Nerone's.

Every day and all day he was about, making the rounds of the houses—a black-jowled, smiling giant, with his boots wrapped in sacking and his body padded in layers of scarecrow garments and his head muffled in a cap made of one of Nina's stockings. On his back he carried an old army knapsack, filled with rations, and his pockets were stuffed with aspirin tablets and a bottle of cod-liver oil and odds and ends of medicine.

When he came into a house, he stayed as long as they needed him and no longer. He checked their food stocks, looked at the sick, dosed them when he could, cooked a broth for those who were incapable, cleaned up the accumulated messes and then moved on. But before he went there were always five minutes for news and greetings, and a couple of minutes for a joke to leave them laughing when he trudged out again into the waste. If they needed Meyer, he would bring him back. If they were ready for a priest, he tried to get one—though this was a rather more chancy proceeding since Father Anselmo was old and cold, and disinclined to stir, and the young curate from Gemello Maggiore often had his hands too full with his own dying.

Always his last call of the day was on Aldo Meyer. They would drink a thimbleful of *grappa*, exchange notes, and then Nerone would plunge off down the hill to Nina's hut.

At first he was cheerful, exulting in the challenge to his strength and vitality. Then, as December wore on into January and there was still no break in the weather, he began to get edgy, preoccupied, like a man who slept too little and thought too much. Meyer urged him to rest, give himself a couple of days at home with Nina, but he refused curtly, and afterwards seemed to drive himself even harder.

Then one evening when it was late and bitter with a new wind, he came in, dumped his pack on Meyer's floor, tossed off the *grappa* at one gulp and said abruptly:

'Meyer! I want to talk to you!'

'You always do,' said Meyer mildly. 'What's so different about tonight?'

Nerone ignored the irony and plunged on.

'I never told you why I came here, did I?'

'It's your own business. You didn't have to tell me.'

'I'd like to tell you now.'

'Why?'

'I need to.'

'It's a good reason,' said Meyer with a grin.

'Tell me . . . do you believe in God, Meyer?'

'I was brought up to believe in Him,' said Meyer guardedly. 'My friends the Fascisti have done their best to persuade me otherwise. Let's say I have an open mind in the matter. Why do you ask?'

'I could be talking nonsense to you.'

'It's a man's right to talk nonsense when he has a need.'

'All right. You make what you like of it. I'm English, you know that. I'm an officer, which you didn't know.'

'I guessed it.'

'I'm also a deserter.'

'What do you want me to say?' asked Meyer with dry humour. 'How much I despise you?'

'Say nothing, for God's sake. Just listen. I was in the advance guard for the assault on Messina. It was the last toe-hold in Sicily. For us, nothing to it. Your people were beaten. The Germans were pulling out fast. Just a mopping-up operation. My company was assigned to clean out a half-mile square of tenements leading down to the docks. Scattered snipers, a couple of machine-gun posts . . . nothing. There was a blind alley, with windows facing down towards us and a sniper in the top window. He had us pinned down for ten minutes at the mouth of the alley. Then, we thought we might have got him. We moved in. When we got to the house, I followed the usual routine, and shouted a surrender warning. There was another shot—from the lower window this time. It got one of my boys. I pitched a grenade through the window, waited for the burst and then went in. I found the sniper—an old fisherman, with a woman and a nursing child. All dead. The baby had taken the full burst. . . .'

'It happens in war,' said Meyer coolly. 'It's the human element. It has nothing to do with God.'

'I know,' said Giacomo Nerone. 'But I was the human element. Can you understand that?'

'Yes, I can understand it. So you decided this was the end for you. You had done what you'd been paid to do. You were dispensed from all the rest. Your war was over. Is that right?'

'More or less.'

'You went on the run. But where did you expect to go?'

'I didn't know.'

'Why did you come here?'

'I don't know that either. Call it an accident if you want.'

'Do *you* believe in God, Nerone?'

'I used to. Then for a long time I didn't.'

'And now?'

'Don't press me, man! Let me talk it out!'

Meyer shrugged and poured an extravagant measure of *grappa* into Nerone's glass. When Nerone protested, he said with wintry humour:

'*In vino veritas.* Drink it.'

Nerone held the glass with two shaky hands and drank it greedily, then wiped his chapped mouth with the back of his hand. He said moodily:

'When I met Nina, she was a refuge. When we fell in love it was more–a kind of absolution. When she became pregnant, I felt as if I was undoing what had been done; putting a new life back in the place of the one I'd destroyed. When we started to do something for these people, it was my kind of reparation to the old fisherman and the dead woman. . . . It wasn't enough. It still isn't enough.'

'It never is,' said Aldo Meyer. 'But where does God come in?'

'If He doesn't, it's all a monstrous folly. The death means nothing, the reparation means less. We're ants on the carcass of the world, spawned out of nothing, going busily nowhere. One of us dies, the others crawl over us to the pickings. This whole valley could freeze to death and it would mean nothing–nothing at all. . . . But if there is a God . . . everything becomes enormously important . . . every life, every death. . . .'

'And the reparation?'

'Means nothing at all,' said Nerone sombrely, 'unless you give yourself as part of it.'

'You're in deep water, my friend,' said Aldo Meyer gently.

'I know,' Nerone told him in a dead voice. 'I'm damn near drowning in it.'

He leaned his head on his hands and began running his fingers through his hair. Meyer came and sat on the edge of the table and said good-humouredly:

'Let me give a piece of advice, my friend–medical advice. You're running yourself ragged with fatigue and undernourishment. You've never been quite sure whether you were right or wrong to walk away from your war; and, because you're fatigued, you're beginning to worry about it. You've done a good job for all of us here and you're still doing it. Now, all of a sudden, you're preoccupied with God. If you'll forgive my saying so–half the shoddy mysticism in the world comes from bad digestion, overwork, lack of sleep or lack of sexual satisfaction. If you want a doctor's advice, stay at home and play honeymooners with Nina for a few days. Vote yourselves an extra day's ration and give yourselves a *festa*.'

Nerone looked up and his dark, stubbled face relaxed into a grin.

'You know, Meyer, that's where all you liberals make your mistake. That's why there's no place for you any more in the twentieth century. There are only two things you can do about God: affirm Him like the Catholics or deny Him like the Communists. You want to reduce Him to a belly-ache or a hot flush, or a comforting speculation for the coffee and cigars. You're a Jew. You should know better.'

'And what are you?' Meyer was nettled.

'I used to be a Catholic.'

'That's your trouble,' said Meyer definitely. 'You might make a good Communist, but you'll never make a good liberal. You're an absolutist at heart. You've got religion like an itch in the crutch, and you'll carry it till the day you die. . . . But my prescription still stands.'

'I'll think about it, Doctor. I've got to think about it—very carefully.'

. . . Meredith stopped walking and stood a moment in the shade of the fig tree, absently shredding one of the thick, tough leaves and feeling the white sap glutinous on his fingers. After a while, he said:

'This is the first glimmer I've seen of the thing one looks for in every case history: the entry of God into a man's calculations, the beginning of acceptance of the consequence of belief, the start of a personal relationship between Creator and Creature. If this theme continues. . .'

'It recurs,' said Meyer slowly. 'But there are gaps in my story. You'll have to fill them in from other witnesses, like Nina Sanduzzi.'

'If there were writings,' said Meredith thoughtfully, 'they would help immensely. One might be able to follow a personal attitude that would explain the external relationships.'

'There are writings, Monsignor. I have them.'

Meredith stared at him in surprise.

'Is there much of them?'

'There's a large packet. I haven't opened it yet. Nina gave them to me.'

'Could I see them?'

'If you don't mind waiting a while,' Meyer agreed awkwardly. 'I haven't read them myself yet. I've been afraid of them—in much the same way as you have been afraid of your request for a miracle. Somewhere in them may be the answer to a lot of questions that have plagued me for a long time. Till now I haven't been sure I wanted the answer. I'd like to read them this afternoon while you're talking to Nina. Then tomorrow I'll hand them over—with the rest of my own evidence. Would that satisfy you?'

'Certainly. Take longer if you want.'

'It's enough,' said Meyer with a wry smile. 'You're a good confessor, Meredith. I'm glad to talk with you.'

A grave pleasure dawned in the eyes of Blaise Meredith. He said:

'If only you knew how glad I am to hear that.'

Meyer looked at him quizzically.

'Why, Monsignor?'

'For the first time in my life, I think, I am beginning to be close to people. It terrifies me to think how much time I've wasted—and how little there is left.'

'Afterwards,' said Meyer soberly. 'You will be close to God.'

'That terrifies me most of all,' said Blaise Meredith.

In a far corner of the villa grounds, Paolo Sanduzzi was at work, sawing a fallen olive tree into firewood. The head gardener, a taciturn fellow, himself gnarled and dark as a tree, had left him there with a curt direction to keep his hands out of his pockets and work off his puppy fat, and have the whole tree cut and corded by sundown.

He was glad to be alone. The place was new and strange. This was his first man's work and his hands were clumsy and inexpert. To be laughed at would be an agony, and he needed time to learn the rhythm of the tool he was using, and the idioms of this life among the *signori*.

He had stripped off his shirt because the sun was hot, and after lopping away the twigs with a hatchet, had set to work sawing off the main branches. The wood was dry and easy enough to cut, but he was too eager and the saw jammed and twanged in his hand until, little by little, he fell into the knack of it, and the teeth bit cleanly into the wood while the sawdust spilled on to the leaves at his feet. He liked the sound of it and the smell of it and the salt taste of the sweat trickling down his face to the corners of his mouth.

It would have been pleasant to have Rosetta here to sit and talk with him and admire his skill, but she was not coming till tomorrow and then she would be in the kitchen with the cook, or dusting and polishing about the villa with the other maids. She would sleep in the women's quarters, sharing a bed with one of the young girls, while he would have his own place—a narrow cubbyhole next to the tool shed, with a straw mattress and a chair and a box with a candle on it. But they would meet at meals and walk out on Sundays, and perhaps at siesta time they might steal an hour together. He would feel better when she was there; less raw and less afraid of the Contessa, whom he had not met, and of the Englishman, whom he had met all too often.

Now that his secret was out and shared with the doctor, now that he knew more of his father, he felt safer, more his own man. To be a bastard was no longer a terrifying mystery, and to be attracted by the Englishman was not, it seemed, so strange a thing at all.

Perhaps even a way might be found to do the thing he wanted most of all: shake the dust of the village off his sandals and go to Rome, where the Pope lived and the President, and the streets were full of fountains and everyone had a car and the girls wore smart clothes and shoes and every house had running water and, sometimes, even a bath and a toilet. These were wonders about which the painter had spoken to him often, and their magic was still strong on him. He had made the first step. He had left the village and entered the green, enclosed world of the villa. Rome was so much nearer, so much more possible.

Thinking of Rome, he thought naturally of Nicholas Black, with his mocking eyes and his mouth twisted up in the smile that could make you feel either a man or a child, and could promise all kinds of revelations without a word spoken. The impression was so vivid that when a dry twig cracked behind him, he spun round, startled, expecting to see the Englishman behind him.

Instead it was the Contessa who stood there, bright as a butterfly, in a new spring frock, with a scarlet beach hat shading her face from the sun.

Not knowing what to do or say, he stood gape-mouthed, arms hanging slackly at his sides, feeling the sweat running down his face and chest, yet not daring to move and brush it away. Then she smiled at him and the smile was in her eyes, too.

'Did I startle you, Paolo?'

'A little,' he mumbled awkwardly.

The Contessa came closer and looked around at the sawn wood.

'You've been working hard, I see. That's good. If you work well for me, Paolo, you'll never be sorry.'

'I'll try, signora.'

Her smile gave him confidence, and when she drew her skirts aside to sit down on the fallen trunk of the olive, he acted on a sudden impulse and spread his shirt on the rough bark.

'The tree's dirty, signora. You'd spoil your dress.'

'Charming boy!' murmured Anne Louise de Sanctis. 'That was the sort of thing your father would do. Did you know I knew your father?'

'Did my father work for you, too, signora?'

'Dear me, no!' She gave a high, tinkling laugh. 'Your father was a friend of mine. He used to come here sometimes to visit me. He was a *signore—a gran' signore!*'

He felt a sudden pang of shame that he should be standing here, a servant, where his father had once walked as a guest of the house. Before he had time to answer, the Contessa went on.

'That's why I brought you here, for your father's sake. Mr Black tells me you're bright and learn things quickly. If that's true, we may be able to make you into a gentleman like your father.'

There was no mention of his mother, he noticed, and once again he was ashamed of her, with her rough dialect and her coarse clothes and her bare dusty feet. He said quickly:

'I'd like that, signora. I'll work well, I promise.' Then, made bold by her approving smile, he told her: 'I don't know very much about my father. What was he like?'

'He was English,' said the Contessa. 'Like me, like Signor Black and the Monsignor from Rome.'

'English!' He seemed not to believe the sound of his own voice. 'That means I'm half-English too!'

'That's right, Paolo. Didn't your mother ever tell you?'

He shook his head.

'Didn't she ever say how much you were like him?'

'Sometimes. But not very often.'

'That's another reason why I want you to do well here. I'll see that you go to school at Valenta, learn to read and write and speak properly, wear the right clothes. Then, perhaps, you can be my friend, too. Would you like that?'

'And could I go to Rome?'

'Of course!' She smiled at him. 'You want that very much, don't you?'

'So much, signora!'

'I might ask Signor Black to take you there for a visit.' She was still smiling at him but there was an odd warning in her eyes. Without quite knowing why, Paolo said quickly:

'I'd much rather go with you.'

As he flung out his arms in the Southern gesture of appeal, she caught his hands and drew him down so that he was half-kneeling, half-squatting, at her feet. Her perfume was all about him and he could see her breasts rising and falling under the thin frock. She took his face in her hands and tilted it up towards her and said softly:

'Before I could do that, Paolo, I'd have to trust you. You'd have to know how to keep secrets. Not to gossip to the village people—not even to the Monsignor or Signor Black.'

'I would, signora. I promise.'

'Then we'll think about it, Paolo. But not a word—even to your mother.'

'Not a word.'

Her hands were soft and perfumed on his cheeks and he had the odd feeling that she wanted to bend down and kiss him; but at the same moment there was the sound of a footfall behind them and the bland voice of Nicholas Black said:

'Really, *cara*! You're quite shameless. The boy hasn't lost his milk teeth and you're trying to seduce him already.'

'You're a fine one to talk about seduction, Nicki!'

The words were English and Paolo did not understand them; but when he looked up at the thin satyr's face of the painter and the flushed angry one of the Contessa, he felt trapped—like a mouse in a corner with two cats ready to pounce.

Shortly after noon, Blaise Meredith returned to the villa to wash and rest awhile before luncheon. He was not unpleased with his morning's work. Meyer was a good witness and his recollections were dispassionate but vivid; so that, for the first time since his assignment began, Meredith was beginning to see Giacomo Nerone as a man and not a legend.

He would have preferred to lunch with Meyer, to have gone on talking about the next critical period in Nerone's life. But Meyer had not invited him, and Meredith sensed that he needed time to recover himself and privacy to begin his reading of the papers of the dead man.

As he lay back, resting on the bed, feeling the familiar ache in the pit of his belly, he wondered how he should comport himself at the meal with the Contessa and Nicholas Black. Now that he knew the Contessa for a liar and the pair of them for conspirators, his position was vastly distasteful to him. As a house-guest he was bound by discretion and courtesy. As a priest, he could not make himself, even by silence, a partner in the corruption of a child. As Devil's Advocate he came in search of evidence and he needed co-operation from his witnesses.

Once again, as it had done in the house of Father Anselmo, the case of Giacomo Nerone faded into unimportance. There were souls at stake, and if priesthood meant anything it meant the care of souls. A simple statement but a complex proposition. One solved nothing by waving the commandments like a bludgeon at people's heads. There was no point in shouting damnation at a man who was already walking himself to hell on his own two feet. One had to pray for the Grace of God and then go probing like a good psychologist for the fear that might condition him to repentance or the love that might draw him towards it. Even then one had to wait for the place and the propitious moment—and one could still fail in the end. When one's own body was sick and one's mind preoccupied, the difficulty doubled itself.

When lunch-time came, he got up, combed his hair, put on a light summer cassock and walked down to the terrace under the striped awning. Nicholas Black was already seated alone at the table. He waved an airy greeting and said:

'The Contessa sends her apologies. She has a migraine. She'll lunch in her room. She hopes to see us both at dinner.'

Meredith nodded and sat down, and immediately a servant spread his napkin and poured wine and iced water into the glasses before him.

'A good morning, Monsignor?' asked the painter.

'Very good. Very informative. Doctor Meyer's an excellent witness.'

'A clever fellow. I'm amazed he hasn't done better for himself.'

Meredith shrugged off the insinuation. He had no wish to be drawn into an argument with the *antipasto*. Black dug into his plate and sipped his wine and they ate in silence for a while. Then the painter asked again:

'How is your health, Monsignor?'

'Indifferent, I'm afraid. Meyer gives me a worse prognosis than I expected. Three months, he says.'

'Do you have much pain?'

'Quite a lot.'

'In three months,' said the painter, 'you'll hardly finish your case.'

Meredith smiled ruefully.

'I'm afraid not. Fortunately the Church doesn't care to hurry these things. A century or two is neither here nor there.'

'And yet I have the impression that you are anxious to get through with it.'

'The witnesses are available,' Meredith told him coolly. 'Some of them are co-operative. The more testimony I can collect now the better for everybody. Besides ...' He wiped a crumb from the corner of his pale mouth. 'When your term has been set, you suddenly become aware of the shortness of it. "The night comes, when no man can work."'

'Are you afraid of death, Monsignor?'

'Who isn't?'

'At least you're frank about it. Many of your colleagues aren't, you know.'

'Many of them haven't yet had to face the reality,' said Meredith tartly. 'Have you?'

Black chuckled and took a long swallow of wine, then leaned back in his chair while the servant changed the dishes in front of him. He said in mock apology:

'I'm teasing you, Monsignor. Forgive me.'

Meredith bent over his fish and said nothing. A few moments later, Paolo Sanduzzi came out of the shrubbery and walked across the lawn in the direction of the kitchen. The painter watched him, and Meredith watched the painter with a sidelong speculative eye. When the boy had disappeared round the angle of the house, Black turned back to the table and said casually:

'Charming boy. A classic David. Pity to think he'll go to seed in a village like this. I wonder the Church doesn't do something for him. You can't have the son of a *beato* chasing the girls and getting into trouble with the police like any other youth, can you?'

The bland effrontery of the man was too much for Meredith. He put down his knife and fork with a clatter, and said, with cold precision:

'If the boy is corrupted, Mr Black, you will be the one to do it. Why don't you go away and leave him alone?'

To his surprise the painter threw back his head and laughed.

'Meyer must have been a very good witness indeed, Monsignor. What else did he tell you about me?'

'Isn't that enough?' asked Meredith quietly. 'You are doing a detestable thing. Your private vices are a matter between you and the Almighty. But when you are set out to corrupt this boy, you are committing a crime against nature.. . .'

The words were hardly out of his mouth before Black cut him short.

'You've judged me already, haven't you, Meredith? You've picked up every shred of filthy gossip round the village and damned me with it, before you've heard a word in my defence.'

Meredith flushed. The accusation was uncomfortably close to the truth. He said quietly:

'If I've misjudged you, Mr Black, I'm deeply sorry. I'd be more than happy to hear you deny these—these rumours.'

The painter laughed bitterly.

'You want me to defend myself to you? Damned if I'll do it, Monsignor. I'll take you on your own ground instead. Let's say I am what everybody calls me—an unnatural man, a corrupter of youth. What does the Church offer me by way of faith, hope or charity?' He stabbed a lean, accusing finger at the priest. 'Let's understand each other, Meredith. You can bluff your penitents and charm your Sunday congregations, but you can't fool me! I've been a Catholic myself and I know the whole shoddy routine. You know why I left the Church? Because it answers every damn question in the book—except the one you need answering. . . . "Why?" You tell me I'm committing a sin against nature because you think I'm fond of this boy and intend to get him. Let's examine that. If you can give me a satisfactory answer, I'll make you a promise. I'll pack my bags and leave here on the first available transport. Do you agree to that?'

'I can't bargain with you,' said Meredith sharply. 'I'll listen and I'll try to answer. That's all.'

Nicholas Black laughed harshly.

'You're hedging already, you see. But I'll take you all the same. I know your whole argument on the question of the use and misuse of the body. God made it first for the procreation of children and then for the commerce of love between man and woman. That's the end. All its acts must conform to the end and all else is sin. The sin according to nature is an act in excess of the natural instinct . . . like sleeping with a girl before you marry her, or lusting after another man's wife. To want a boy, in the same fashion, is a sin against nature. . . .' He grinned sardonically at the pale, intent face of the priest. 'Do I surprise you, Meredith? I was stuffed full of Aquinas, too. But there's a catch, and here's what I want you to tell me. What about my nature? I was born the way I am. I was a twin. See my brother before he died and you'd have seen the perfect male—the excessive male, if you want. Me? . . . It wasn't quite clear what I was to be. But I knew soon enough. It was my nature to be drawn more to men than to women. I wasn't seduced in the shower-room or blackmailed in the bar. This is what I am. I can't change it. I didn't ask to be born. I didn't ask to be born like this—God knows I've suffered enough because of it. But who made me? According to you—God! What I want and what I do is according to the nature He gave me. . . .'

In the passion of the argument his attitude had changed from a sardonic insult to a plea for understanding. He himself was unconscious of it, but Meredith was quick to see it, and he was again ashamed of his own obtuseness. Here was the place and the moment made ready for him, but again, it seemed, for lack of wisdom and sympathy he had misused them. The painter plunged on, the words tumbling out of him in a bitter spate.

'. . . Look at yourself! You're a priest. You know damn well that if I were setting out to seduce a girl at this moment instead of young Paolo, you'd take an entirely different view. You'd disapprove, certainly! You'd read me a lecture on fornication and all the rest. But you wouldn't be too unhappy. I'd be normal . . . according to nature! But I am not made like that. God didn't make me like that. But do I need love the less? Do I need satisfaction less? Have I less right to live in contentment because somewhere along the line the Almighty slipped a cog in creation? . . . What's your answer to that, Meredith? What's your answer for *me*? Tie a knot in myself and take up badminton and wait till they make me an angel in Heaven, where they don't need this sort of thing anymore? . . . I'm lonely! I need love like the next man! My sort of love! Do I live in a padded cell till I die? You're the Church and the Church has all the answers! Give me this one!'

He broke off and sat, waiting, his silence a greater challenge to Meredith than the rush of his invective. Meredith stared down at the small chaos of crumbs on his plate and picked over the words to frame his answer. He tried to make a silent prayer for this soul, naked in front of him—but the prayer, like the argument he gave, seemed strangely arid and impotent. After a moment, he answered gravely:

'You tell me you've been a Catholic. Even if you weren't you'd understand the words and what they mean. To your problem—and to lots of others—there's no answer that doesn't involve a mystery and an Act of Faith. I can't tell you why God made you the way you are any more than I can tell you why he's planted a carcinoma in my stomach to make me die painfully while other men die peacefully in their sleep. The cogs of creation seem to slip all the time. Babies are born with two heads, mothers of families run crazy with carving knives, men die in plague, famine and thunderstorms. Why? Only God knows.'

'If there is a God.'

'I'll accept the "if",' said Meredith, with quiet concern. 'If there is no God, then the universe is a chaos with no meaning. You live in it as long and as pleasantly as you can, for the best you can get out of it. You take your Paolo and enjoy him—the police and social custom permitting. I can't quarrel with you. But if there is a God—and I believe there is—then. . .'

'Don't tell me the rest of it, Monsignor,' said the painter bitterly. 'I know it by heart. No matter what a bloody mess Creation gets into, you take it and like it; because that's a cross God lays on your back. If you take it long enough, they'll make you a saint like Giacomo Nerone. That's no answer, Meredith.'

'Have you got a better one, Mr Black?'

'I have indeed. You keep your cross and your hair-shirt, Meredith. I'll take the cash in hand and waive the rest!'

He pushed back his chair, got up from the table, and without another word walked into the house. Blaise Meredith wiped his clammy hands on his napkin and took a sip of wine to moisten his dry lips. He was surprised to find it suddenly sour, like vinegar on a sponge.

12

Early the same afternoon, in the small hut between the ilexes, Nina Sanduzzi talked with the Monsignor from Rome. They sat, one on either side of the rough scrubbed table, halfway between the open door and the big brass bed where Giacomo Nerone had slept and where his son had been born. After the blaze outside, the room was cool and shadowy and even the chatter of the cicadas was muted to a half-heard monotone.

The tramp down the hill had tired Meredith quickly; his face was grey and his lips bloodless, and a small knot of pain tightened in the pit of his stomach. Nina Sanduzzi looked at him with faint pity. She had small experience of priests and those she knew, like Father Anselmo, had little to recommend them. But this one was different; he would have understanding and delicacy. He would not trespass too roughly on the privacy of her past with Giacomo. Still, she was cautious, and when he began to question her she answered briefly and without embellishment. Meredith for his own part was sedulously delicate.

'I want you to understand something first: there are questions that must be asked. Some of them may seem strange—even brutal. I ask them, not because I think ill of Giacomo Nerone, but because we must try to know everything, good and bad, about this man. Do you understand that, signora?'

She nodded calmly.

'Better you should call me by my name, Nina. The doctor does and you are a friend of his.'

'Thank you. Now, Nina, my information is that shortly after his arrival in Gemello you and Giacomo Nerone began to live together.'

'We were lovers,' said Nina Sanduzzi. 'It's not quite the same thing.'

Meredith, the legalist, smiled, where once he might have frowned. He went on.

'You were a Catholic, Nina. So was Giacomo. Didn't you think this was a sin against God?'

'When you are lonely, Monsignor, when there is fear just outside the door, and the winter is coming and tomorrow you may not be alive, you think of these things and you forget about sin.'

'You can never quite forget.'

'Not quite. But when these things happen so often—even to priests—they do not look so bad.'

Meredith nodded. A week ago, he might have understood less and said more. Now he knew that the heart had deeper reasons than most preachers ever knew. He asked again:

'Your relations with this man—your physical relations—were they normal? Did he ever ask you for what should not be done between men and women?'

She stared at him in momentary puzzlement. Then her head went up proudly.

'We loved each other, Monsignor. We did what lovers do and were glad of each other. What else could there be?'

'Nothing,' said Meredith hastily. 'But if you loved each other so much, why didn't you marry? You were having a child. Did you owe nothing to him? What did Giacomo think?'

For the first time since he had known her, he saw a smile brighten on her lips and in her eyes. It was like an echo of the old Nina—the one who had wanted a man to hold in her arms and was prepared to face the executioner to get him. She told him in vivid, slangy dialect:

'You all ask the same question—as if it were big and important instead of a wart on a green melon. You don't understand how it was in those days. Only today was certain. Tomorrow the police might come or the Germans or the English. We could all die of the *tifo* or of malaria. A ring on your finger meant nothing. I had a ring, but I had no man to go with it.'

'Did Giacomo refuse to marry you?'

'I never asked him. More than once he told me he would marry me if I wanted it.'

'And you didn't want it?'

Once again the old fire flickered in her eyes, and the proud Greek smile twitched at the corners of her mouth.

'You still don't see it, Monsignor. I had a husband once. I wanted to hold him and the Army took him away to be killed. Now I had a man. If he wanted to go—he would go and no ring would keep him. If the police took him or the soldiers, he would still be lost to me. Marriage might come later, if ever it were important enough. Besides, there was another thing Giacomo talked about often. . . .'

'What was that?'

'He had it fixed in his head that one day, soon, something would happen to him. He was a deserter and if the English won the war they would take him. The Fascisti were active still and they might take him. Or the Germans. If they did, I would never know whether he was alive or dead. He wanted me to be free to marry again. Free to disown him so that they could not punish me and the child.'

'Was that important to you, Nina?'

'To me, no. But to him, yes. If it made him happy to feel that, I was happy too. Nothing else mattered. Have you never been in love, Monsignor?'

'Never, I'm afraid.' Meredith's thin lips puckered into a smile. 'You'll have to be patient with me. . . . Tell me, when you were living together, what sort of a man was Giacomo? Was he good to you?'

It was almost eerie to see how memory flooded back on her and how her whole body seemed to come alive like a flower in the rain. Even in her voice there was a kind of splendour.

'What sort of man? . . . How do you expect me to answer that, Monsignor? Everything a woman wants was in this man. He was strong in bed and yet gentle as a babe. He could be angry so that you trembled at the silence of him and yet he never lifted his hand or raised his voice. When I served him, he was grateful and thanked me as if I were a princess. When I was afraid, he would make me laugh and when he laughed it was like the sun coming up in the morning. He was afraid of nobody and nothing except that I should be hurt. . . .'

'And yet,' said Meredith, with calculated bluntness, 'he left you in your pregnancy and never lived with you again.'

Her head came up, proud as a marble goddess in the sun.

'We lived in love and we parted in love—and there was never a day afterwards that I did not love him....'

... Winter fretted itself out in a long alternation of storms and frozen calms. In the village and in the mountains there was much sickness. Some died and some recovered—but slowly, because of the damp and the foulness of the closed hovels and because food was getting scarcer every day.

Once there was an epidemic in which people came out in spots and had sore eyes and fever. Nina herself fell sick of it, and she remembered the doctor and Giacomo talking gravely in the corner about something they called *rubella*. But she got better soon and thought no more of it.

Even Giacomo Nerone was showing the strain of the long, cold time. The flesh was being honed off his big frame; his dark, stubbled cheeks were hollow and his eyes were sunken and burning when he trudged home from a day in the hills.

Nina, with the constant nausea and tiredness that comes to some women in early pregnancy, found the monotony of the food revolted her, and as her body thickened slowly, she was even disinclined for the love-making in which formerly she had taken so much and such frank delight. Both these things troubled her. A man was a man and he demanded to be soothed and satisfied, however his woman felt. But Giacomo was different from the men of her own people. He was gentle with her when she was sick. He made, with his own hands, food to tempt her. If she was unready for him, he would not force himself on her, and in the long mourning nights of the storm he would distract her with stories of strange places and people and cities piled like blocks almost to the sky.

She loved him the more for his attentions because she knew he had his own troubles: problems that kept him wakeful at night and preoccupied in the daytime. Sometimes he would talk them out with her, fumbling for the right phrase in dialect to explain his meaning. In this, too, he was different from her own menfolk, who took their counsel in the wineshop and not from their wives, because a woman was supposed to know nothing but the house and the bed and the simpler aspects of religion. But Giacomo talked freely, so that she felt strong and wise with him.

'Listen, Nina *mia*, you know how it is sometimes, that a man does a thing and his woman hates him, because she doesn't understand why?'

'I know, *caro mio*, but I understand you. So why should you worry?'

'Whatever I did, you would still love me?'

'Always.'

'Then listen now, Nina. Don't stop me talking, because this is hard to say. When I'm finished tell me if you don't understand. For a long time now I've been a lost man. I've been like a Calabrese standing in the middle of Rome and asking everyone: "Who am I? Where did I come from? Where am I going?" No one answers him, of course, because they don't understand him. ... And even if they did, he wouldn't understand because he doesn't speak with a Roman tongue. It wasn't always like this. There was a time when I was like you. I knew that I came from God and would go back to Him in the end, that I could talk to Him in the Church and take Him to myself in Communion. I could do wrong and still be forgiven. I could stray a little and still come back to the straight road. ... Then, suddenly, there was no road. There was darkness and voices shouting at me: This way! That way! I followed the voices into a deeper darkness and then there were other voices. But no road–I was lost. There was no God, no Church, no place to go in the end. I was your Calabrese shouting in a city of strangers. . . . When this thing happened to me in Messina I could not be like other men and say: "This is war! This is the price of peace! I will forget about it and go on fighting for what I believe." I didn't believe in anything–in war, in peace, in anything at all! There was just a child, a woman and an old man whom I had killed for no good reason at all. . . . Then I began to run, and suddenly, without knowing why or how, I am here with you–home again. But nothing is quite the same. I am changed. It is not dark any more but misty, like the valley in the first grey of morning. I see you and I know you and love you, because you are near and you love me, too. But outside the door there is the mist and the strangeness. Even the people are different. They look at me with wondering eyes. For no reason that I know, I am a big fellow to them. They depend on me. I am their Calabrese who has been to the big city and seen it all, who knows the Pope and the President and the way to get things done. I am their man of confidence. I should be proud of this, but I am not, because I am walking in the mist, still uncertain where I came from and where I am going and what I should do. . . . Can you understand me, Nina? Or am I talking like a crazy man?'

'You are talking to me with love, *caro mio*, and my heart understands.'

'Will you understand what I am going to ask you?'

'When you hold me like this and I can feel the love in your hands and in your voice, nothing is hard.'

'It is hard for me to tell you. . . . When the spring comes and life is easier, I want to leave you–go away for a while.'

'No, *caro mio!*'

'Not from the valley. From this house.'

'But why, *caro mio*? Why?'

'There are two reasons and the first is mine. I want to find myself a small secret place–build it, if I must, with my own two hands. I want to live there alone with this God whose face I cannot see any more. I want to say to him: Look, I am lost. It's my own fault, but I am lost. If You are there, speak to me clearly. Show me who I am, where I come from, where I am going. These people of Yours who know You–why do they turn to me and not to You to help them? Is there a mark on my forehead I cannot read? If there is, tell me what it means. . . .' I must do this, *cara*.'

'And what about me and your child?'

'I will be here all the time. I will see you often and if God speaks to me, I will speak to Him for you–because if He knows anything at all, He knows I love you.'

'And yet you go away?'

'There is love in this, too, Nina–more love than you know. And there is great reason in it, too. When spring comes the armies will be on the move again. The Germans will come first and there will be fighting south of here. The Partisans will move in to harry the Germans, and the Allies must in the end push them back. Some of these or all of them will come, in their turns, to Gemello. I will come under their notice because of what I am–Giacomo Nerone, the man of confidence, the big, black one. If I am lucky, they will accept me and I can help the people. If I am not, one or other of them will take me–and possibly kill me.'

'*Dio!* No!'

'It may happen, Nina. It may be this is what lies behind the mists and that I will see at the one time the face of God and the face of the executioner. I don't know. But, whatever happens, when spring comes we must be separate. You cannot be involved with me, because there is the child. If I am taken, Meyer will look after you. If not, I shall be here to look after you. And if it falls well, I shall marry you and give the boy my name. You are both mine and I love you and I will not let you suffer for me or the people.'

'I will suffer anyway, when you are not here.'

'Less that way than the other, Nina. There will be so much hate, you will not believe it possible. I've seen it all before and it is very terrible.'

'Hold me, *caro mio*! Hold me, I'm afraid.'

'Lie on my arm, *carissima*, and hear my heart beating. I'm your man of confidence, too, and you can sleep safe.'

'Now, perhaps–but when you are gone?'

'I shall never be wholly gone, Nina *mia*. Never, till eternity.... '

... The Biblical simplicity of her narrative was more compelling than any rhetoric, and Blaise Meredith, the dry man from the Congregations, found himself hurried along by it like a twig in a torrent. Even through the harsh dialect the dialogue rang like a poet's lines in the mouth of a lover–long cherished and long remembered. Behind them the face of Giacomo Nerone took shape and hardened into reality–a lean, dark, suffering face, with a tender mouth and deep eyes suffused with gentleness. The face of a searcher–one of those on whom is laid the burden of mysteries and who come sometimes to a great holiness.

But this was not enough for the grey lawyers at the Congregation of Rites, the inquisitors at the Holy Office. They must see more than this, and Blaise Meredith must give it to them. So, more gently, but no less persistently, he questioned Nina Sanduzzi again:

'When did he leave you?'

'After the thaw, when the spring was breaking.'

'And up till the time he left, he slept with you–made love to you?'

'Yes. Why?'

'Nothing. It is a question that must be asked.' But what he did not say to her was what it proved to him. This was still a man in the dark, a searcher, perhaps, but one who had not yet found his God, nor made the act of abandonment to His will. There was love in him, but it was yet a defaced symbol of the love which is the beginning of sanctity.

'And when he left, what then?'

'He went up into the neck of the valley where the caves are and began to build his hut. While it was building, he slept in a cave and cooked his own food and in the daytime did what he had done in the winter–travelled the valley, working for those who could not work, looking after the sick, bringing food to those who needed it.'

'Did you see him during this time?'

'He came every day, as he promised.'

'Was he changed at all?'

'To me? No. Except that he was more gentle and more careful of me.'

'Did he make love to you?'

Once again she smiled at him with that faint pity for his clerical ignorance.

'I was big with the child, Monsignor. I was calm and content . . . and he did not ask it.'

'Had he changed in himself?'

'Yes. He was thinner than I had ever seen him. His eyes were sunk right back in his head and his skin was stretched tight over the bones of his face. But he was always smiling and much happier than I had known him.'

'Did he say why?'

'At first, no. Then one day he took my hands in his and said: 'I'm home, Nina. I'm home again.' He had been over to Gemello Maggiore to make his confession to young Father Mario and on the Sunday he told me he was going to Communion. He asked if I would go to church the same day.'

'And did you?'

'No. On the Saturday the Germans arrived and made their headquarters in the villa. . . .'

. . . They came, early in the morning, while the village was still rubbing the sleep out of its eyes. There was an armoured car, with a sergeant driver and a worried-looking captain sitting in the back. There were two truckloads of troops and a fourth vehicle loaded with ammunition and supplies. They churned up the dusty road with engines roaring, checked a little in the narrow street of the village with a clatter of gears and some strange cursing, then headed straight up the last hill to the villa of the Contessa de Sanctis.

Nina Sanduzzi heard them come, but paid small attention. She was still heavy with sleep, wrapped in the remote contemplation of a woman who feels the first life stirring inside her. She did not wake fully until she heard the urgent knocking on the door and Aldo Meyer's voice calling her to open it.

When she let him in, she was surprised to see him dressed for the road, with heavy boots and a sheepskin jacket and a pack hitched on to his shoulders. First he asked her to feed him, and while she bustled to do it he talked to her in swift, terse sentences—half-fearful, half-elated.

'When you see Giacomo tell him I've pulled out. The Germans are here and it won't be long before they hear there's a Jew in the valley. If they catch me, I'll be shipped north to the concentration camps. I'm taking my instruments and some medicines, but I've left a stock for Giacomo in the big box under my bed.'

'But where are you going, Dottore?'

'Farther east, into the hills, towards San Bernardino. It's a Partisan hide-out and I've been in contact with them for some time. Their leader's a man who calls himself Il Lupo. I think he came from the North especially for this job. He has the look of a trained man. He has guns and ammunition and a good system of communication. If Giacomo wants to get in touch with me, tell him to go out along the San Bernardino road for about ten kilometres, then turn off at the place they call Satan's Rock. That's where the first Partisan sentries are. He's to climb to the top of the rock, sit down and light a cigarette—then take his handkerchief and knot it round his neck. Someone will come out to make contact with him. Have you got that? It's important. If he forgets, he's liable to get shot.'

'I won't forget.'

She laid coffee and bread and cheese in front of him, and while he ate she made a parcel of food and stuffed it into his knapsack. It was only when she saw the pistol and felt the hard shapes of the ammunition clips that she understood what Giacomo had told her. The war was coming to Gemello Minore and all the hate and killing, too.

With his mouth full of bread and cheese, Meyer said to her:

'I tried to get Giacomo to come with me and bring you too. The Germans won't be much kinder to him than to me. He could be shot as a spy.'

'What did Giacomo say to that?'

'Just laughed and told me he knew the Germans better than I did. I hope he's right. What time do you usually see him?'

She shrugged and made a vague gesture with her hands.

'It changes. Sometimes early in the day, sometimes late. But he always comes.'

Meyer looked at her quizzically over the rim of his cup.

'Are you happy with this arrangement, Nina?'

'I'm happy with Giacomo. There was never another man like this.'

Meyer smiled sourly.

'You could be right at that. Do you know what he does up there in his hut?'

'He prays. He thinks. He works in his garden . . . when he isn't working for someone else or out among the hills. Why do you ask?'

'I went up there the other night to look for him and talk about this thing. I called to him, but there was no answer although his lamp was burning. I went inside and found him kneeling in the middle of the floor with his arms stretched out. His eyes were closed and his head was thrown back and his lips were moving. I spoke to him and he didn't hear me. I went up and shook him, but his body was quite rigid. I couldn't budge him. After a while I went away.'

There was no surprise in her dark eyes. She nodded and answered quite casually:

'He told me he prays a lot.'

'And doesn't eat very much either,' said Meyer with faint irritation.

'That, too. He's got very thin. But he says the praying gives him what strength he needs.'

'He should take more care of himself. Lots of people depend on him. They're going to depend more now that the Germans are here. This prayer business is all right in its way–but men go crazy with too much of it.'

'Do you think Giacomo's crazy?'

'I didn't say that. He's strange, that's all.'

'Perhaps it's because there aren't so many good men around. We've forgotten what they look like.'

Meyer chuckled and wiped his lips with the back of his hand.

'You could be right, Nina *mia*.' He stood up and hoisted his pack on to his shoulders. 'Well, I must be moving. Thanks for the breakfast and the other stuff. Tell Giacomo what I said.'

'I'll tell him.'

He put his hands on her shoulders and kissed her on the lips. She did not resist because she liked him and he was a man going off to his own private war.

'Good luck, Dottore!'

'Good luck, Nina *mia*. You deserve it!'

She stood at the door and watched him scrambling down the valley. She thought he had never looked so young nor so alive, and she wondered idly what would have happened if Giacomo had not come to Gemello Minore.

But Giacomo was there and his presence filled all her life, and when he came just before lunch-time she clung to him desperately, crying on his shoulder. He held her there until the strain went out of her; then he disengaged her gently and listened while she told him about Aldo Meyer and his message. He listened gravely and then said:

'I tried to talk him out of it. These Germans are nothing—a patrol detachment, nothing more. They won't bother anyone very much. But Meyer's been waiting so long for his own war he can't see what he's in for.'

'It will probably be good for him, *caro mia*. I saw him go and he was happy as a boy going to hunt.'

Nerone shook his head gravely and his face clouded.

'Meyer is the wrong man for this company. I've heard about Il Lupo and I can guess where he comes from. He's a professional and he's been trained in Russia. He wants more than a victory. He wants a Communist State in Italy. When the Germans are pushed out and the Allies move in, he'll bid for control of the civil administration. On their record, he'll probably get it. Meyer's in the wrong boat. He thinks Il Lupo wants another gun. What he wants is a man to use afterwards. I wonder what will happen when Meyer finds out.' He shrugged and smiled and spread his hands palm-downwards on the table. 'Anyway, it's done now. We've got our own work to do here.'

She brought a big bowl of pasta to the table and stood over him while he ate it, noting how sparing he was, and how little relish he took in the spicy sauce.

'And what are you going to do, Giacomo?'

'What I'm doing now—except that I've had to bring the Germans into my calculations. I went up to see the Contessa a couple of days ago.'

It was something he had not told her and she felt a sharp pang of jealousy. It was as if she saw him stepping back into a world he had left—a world where he had been lost and where she could never reach him. But she said nothing and waited for him to tell her the rest of it.

'I told her I was English. I didn't tell her but I let her think I was an agent, moved in here to prepare the way for the Allies. She was glad to see me. She's in an awkward position. I suggested she nominate me steward of her estate so that I can talk on fairly equal terms with the German commander. She's given me a room in the servants' quarters.'

'You're going to live at the villa?'

'I have a room there. I'll sleep there when I must. But I'll get a pass from the commander and I'll be free to come and go. I'll need that. The whole villa has been turned into an armed camp.'

'Nice for the Contessa!' she told him with sudden viciousness. 'She'll be able to have a new man every night.'

Nerone's face clouded. He reached out and took her hands and drew her gently towards him.

'Let's not say that, *carissima*. She's a strange, lonely woman, with a fire in the blood that no man has yet been able to put out. That's a torment and not a joke. Why should we cock our fingers at her when we have so much?'

'She eats men, *caro mio*. And I don't want her to eat you.'

'She'll get indigestion if she tries it,' he told her with a smile.

But when he was gone the fear was still with her, and often she would wake in the night, dreaming that Giacomo had left her and was married to the woman on top of the hill with her flat childless belly and her pinched mouth and her predatory eyes....

... 'There is another thing I must ask,' said Blaise Meredith, in his dry voice. 'During this time, did Giacomo perform any religious duties? Did he go to Mass and the Sacraments?'

Nina Sanduzzi nodded.

'Whenever he could—except when there were sick in the mountains, or lost men to be hidden away from the Germans. He used to go to the Mass here on Sundays and I would see him, though it was an arrangement that we would not sit together nor greet each other, because some of the Germans were there. They came it seems, from a part of Germany where there are many Catholics. When he wanted to go to confession he would walk across the valley to young Father Mario.'

'But not Father Anselmo.'

She shook her head.

'Father Anselmo didn't like him. Sometimes there were angry words between them, when Father Anselmo refused to go out to the sick, after curfew.'

'And what did Giacomo say about Father Anselmo?'

'That he was to be pitied and prayed for—but that the men who sent him here would have a heavy judgment. He used to say that *Gesù* had built the Church like a house for his family to live in, but that some men—even priests—used it like a market and a wineshop. He said they made trade out of it and filled it with quarrels and shouting and even fouled the floor like drunken men do. He said if it were not for the love of *Gesù* and the care of the Holy Spirit, it would fall into ruin in a generation. He said that was what every house needed—much love and little argument. And he was right.'

'I know he was,' said Meredith. And wondered that his voice sounded so vehement. 'Now tell me, what did Giacomo say and feel about the Germans?'

For the first time, the question seemed to give her pause. She thought about it a long moment and then she said:

'This was a thing he talked about often, and sometimes I found it hard to understand him. He would say that countries are like men and women and that people take the character of the country they live in. Each country has its own special sin and its special virtue. The English were a sentimental people, but tough and selfish with it, because they lived on an island and wanted to keep it for themselves as they had always done. They were polite. They had much justice, but little charity. When they fought, they fought stubbornly and bravely, but they always forgot that many of their wars had sprung from their own selfishness and indifference. The Americans were different. They were sentimental and tough, too, but they were simpler than the English, because they were younger and richer. They liked to possess things, even though they often did not know how to enjoy them. They were, like all young men, inclined to violence. They could easily be deceived by loud voices and magnificence. And they often deceived themselves, because they like the sound of words, even if they did not understand their meaning. The Germans were something else again. They were hard workers, lovers of order and efficiency and very proud. But there was a grossness in them and a violence that was released by liquor and big speeches and the need to assert themselves. Giacomo used to laugh and say that they liked to feel God rumbling in their bellies when a big music played....'

'Was that all?'

'No. Giacomo liked to talk like that. He said you had to skim the grease off the soup or it would go sour. But he always came back to the same thing: no matter what people were like–or countries–they had to live together like a family. This was how God made them; and if a brother waved a gun at his brother, they would end by destroying each other. There were times when each had to swallow his pride and give way–be polite when he felt like spitting in someone's eye. And that was how he tried to live with the Germans here.'

'Did he succeed?'

'I think so. We lived in peace. We were not robbed. A girl could walk safely to the cistern and home again. Sometimes there were killings when the Partisans met a German patrol–but that was always away from Gemello. There was a curfew and we stayed inside at night. If there were quarrels, Giacomo talked to the commander and the thing was worked out. After a while, the Germans went away, moving down to the south, and the Partisans followed them, as wolves follow the sheep in the Abruzzi.'

'And afterwards?'

'In May we heard the news that Rome had fallen to the Allies, and early in June Paolo was born–and he was born blind. . . .'

. . . The first warnings came late one morning while Giacomo was with her. They were light and uncertain, but Giacomo was so concerned that he insisted on calling Carla Carese, the midwife, and Serafina Gambinelli and Linda Tesoriero. They came running and clamouring because he was so urgent with them; but when they saw that she was still on her feet and in no trouble at all, they all stood around with their hands on their hips and laughed at him. Nina laughed too, and was surprised to see the cloud of anger that darkened his face. His voice was angry too and he snapped at them.

'You're fools–all of you! Stay with her and don't leave her. I'm going to get Doctor Meyer.'

They gaped at him then, and even Nina was amazed, because this business of bearing a child was a woman's affair. Doctors were for sick people and they knew that, if everything went well, childbirth was a simple if noisy business, with a lot of joy to follow it. But before they had time to tell him all this, Giacomo was gone, a lean, ominous figure, thrusting up the track towards the San Bernardino road.

Nina was concerned for him because of the long distance; but the women soon laughed her out of it. The child would arrive before he got back, they told her; and he and the doctor could get drunk together as good friends should when one of them has fathered a bouncing *bambino*.

They were half-right at least. The babe was born and washed, wrapped and laid in her arms an hour before Giacomo arrived with Aldo Meyer. But they did not act like other men at a birth. Giacomo kissed her and held her in his arms for a long time. Aldo Meyer kissed her, too, lightly, like a brother. Then Giacomo lifted the child from her arms and carried him over to the table and held the lamp while Meyer sounded the heart and peered into the ears and lifted the tiny eyelids and bent closer and closer to examine them.

The midwife and the women stood in a small group by the bed, and Nina hoisted herself up on to the pillows to ask fearfully:

'What's the matter with him? What are you looking for?'

'Tell her,' said Aldo Meyer.

'He's blind, *cara*,' said Giacomo Nerone gently. 'He was born with cataracts growing on his eyes. It was the fever you had, the illness with the spots, which is called *rubella*. A woman who gets it the second or third month sometimes bears a blind child or a deaf one.'

It was perhaps half a minute before his meaning reached her. Then she screamed like an animal and buried her face in the pillow while the women huddled about her like hens, clucking to comfort her. After a time, Giacomo came to her and put the child in her arms and tried to talk to her, but she turned her face away from him, because she was ashamed to have given a maimed child to the man she loved so much.

Then a long while later the women went away and Giacomo came back to her with Aldo Meyer. She was calmer now and Meyer talked to her soberly.

'This is a sad thing, Nina; but it has happened and, for the present, it cannot be altered. If things were different, I could take you down to the hospital at Valenta and then, maybe, to Naples to see a specialist and find out if anything can be done. But the war is not over yet. There is still fighting and the roads are cluttered with refugees. Broken German units are fighting their way home and the Partisans are out after them. Naples is a shambles and you would be just another peasant with no one to help her. Giacomo is a wanted man and I am committed to my band in the mountains. So, for the present, there is nothing to do but wait. When there is peace again, we shall see what can be done.'

'But the boy is blind!' It was all she could think or say.

'The maimed ones need much love,' said Aldo Meyer.

Giacomo Nerone said nothing at all; but her heart almost broke at the grief and the pity in his eyes. Meyer went on talking to her in his gentle, professional fashion, showing her the growths on the child's eyes, making some kind of reason out of the first terror. Giacomo poured wine for them all and then set about preparing a meal. The two men ate it at the table, while Nina held the bowl on her lap and talked to them from the bed. When the child whimpered, she put it to the breast, and when the small, blind bundle nuzzled against her, she found herself weeping silently.

Meyer left before midnight to sleep in his own house, safe at last from the threat of the concentration camp. When Giacomo took him to the door, Nina was dozing, but she heard Giacomo's voice say sharply:

'You're a friend of mine, Meyer, and I understand, even if I don't agree. But keep Lupo away from the village. Keep him away from me.'

And Meyer's voice in the terse reply:

'This is history, man! You can't stop it. I can't either! Someone's got to start organising. . .'

The rest of it was lost as they moved to the door and into the clear night. A few minutes later Giacomo came back and bolted the door behind him. He said quietly:

'You can't be alone tonight, *cara*. I'll stay with you.'

Then all the disappointment welled up like a spring inside her and she clung to him, sobbing as if her heart were broken, as indeed it nearly was.

Then, when she was calm again, Giacomo settled her on the pillows and turned the lamp low, and through half-closed eyes she saw him do a strange thing. Quite unselfconsciously, he knelt down on the earthen floor, closed his eyes and stretched out his arms like the arms of *Gesù* on the cross, while his lips moved in soundless prayer. There was a moment when his whole body seemed to become rigid, like a tree, and when she called out in fright he did not hear her. She lay back watching him until exhaustion overcame her, and she slid into sleep.

When she woke, the room was full of sunlight and the baby was bawling lustily and Giacomo was boiling the coffee-pot for breakfast. He came and kissed her and lifted the child in his arms and said gravely:

'I want to tell you something, Nina *mia*.'

'Tell me.'

'We will name the boy Paolo.'

'He's your son, Giacomo. You must name him–but why Paolo?'

'Because Paolo, the Apostle, was a stranger to God, and, like me, found Him on the road to Damascus. Because, like this boy, Paolo was blind but saw again, through the mercy of God.'

She stared at him in disbelief.

'But the doctor said. . .'

'I am telling you, *cara*.' His voice was strong and deep as a bell. 'The boy will see. The cataracts will disappear in three weeks; when a baby should begin to see the light, our Paolo will see too. You will hold the lamp in front of his eyes and watch how he blinks and begins to follow it. I promise you, in the name of God.'

'Don't tell me that just to comfort me, *cara*. I could not bear to hope and be cheated at the end.' There was agony in her voice, but he only smiled at her.

'It's not a hope, Nina *mia*. It's a promise. Believe it.'

'But how do you know? How can you be sure?'

All he said was:

'When it happens, Nina, let it appear like news to you, too. Tell nobody about this morning. Will you promise me?'

She nodded dumbly, wondering how she could bear the waiting and hide the doubt she felt.

Three weeks later, to the day and the hour, she took the child from his cradle and wakened him. When he opened his eyes, they were clear and shining like his father's, and when she held him to the light he blinked. She shaded it with her hand and his eyes stared steadily, then blinked again when she took her hand away.

The wonder of the moment was like a revelation. She wanted to shout and sing and go calling down the village street to tell them all that Giacomo's promise had come true.

But Giacomo was already dead and buried. The village folk turned away in shame as she passed. Even Aldo Meyer had gone to Rome, and she thought he would never come back. . . .

. . . 'I should go home now,' said Monsignor Blaise Meredith. 'It's late and you've given me a lot to think about.'

'Do you believe what I have told you, Monsignor?'

Her voice and her eyes challenged him, calmly. He looked at her for a long moment, and then he said, with a curious finality:

'Yes, Nina. I don't know what it means yet. But I do believe you.'

'Then you will look after Giacomo's boy, and keep him safe?'

'I'll look after him.' But even as he said it, his conscience challenged him: How? In God's name, how?

13

For Doctor Aldo Meyer, evening was closing in on an afternoon of strange calm.

Immediately after luncheon he had sat down to read the papers of Giacomo Nerone. He had come to them hesitant and afraid, as if to a moment of crisis or revelation. But when he opened them and set them in order and began to read the bold cursive hand, it was like hearing the old challenging arguments of Giacomo himself.

There were moments of shame at his own failures, moments of poignant recollection, of nostalgia for a relationship that had begun in conflict, had come at times close to friendship and was soon to end in tragedy. But there was no bitterness in the record—as there had never been bitterness in Giacomo himself. There were passages of child-like simplicity that touched Meyer almost to tears, and phrases of mystical exaltation that left him groping, as Giacomo had often done, for the explanation of his own bankruptcy.

But at the end there was peace and calm and certainty, which communicated itself to the reader even after the lapse of years. And in the last writing of all, the letter to Aldo Meyer, there was a great gentleness and a singular grace of forgiveness. The rest of the papers were in English, but the letter was in Italian and this, too, was a delicacy not to be lightly forgotten:

My dear Aldo,

I am at home and it is late. Nina is asleep at last and the boy is sleeping, too. Before I go in the morning, I shall leave this note with her, among my other papers, and, when it is all over and the first grief has passed, perhaps it will come safely into your hands.

We shall be meeting tomorrow, you and I, but as strangers, each committed to an opposite belief and an opposite practice. You will sit with my judges and walk with my executioners, and sign the certificate of my death, when it is all done.

I blame you for none of this. Each of us can walk only the path he sees at his own feet. Each of us is subject to the consequences of his own belief—though I think one day you will come to believe differently. If you do, you will hate what has been done, and you may be tempted to hate yourself for your part in it, the more because there will be no one to whom you can say you are sorry.

So I want to tell you now I do not hate you. You have been my friend and a friend of Nina and the child. I hope you will always lean to them and care for them. I know you have loved Nina. I think you still do. And this will be another cross on your back, because you will never be sure whether, in joining yourself to my condemnation, you have done it from belief or jealousy. But I know and I tell you now that I shall die still counting you my friend.

Now there is a service I want to lay on you. When you get this letter, will you go to Father Anselmo and to Anne de Sanctis and tell each of them that I bear them no grudge for what they have done and that, when I come to God, as I hope I may, I shall remember them both.

So, *dottore mio*, I leave you. It is not long till the dawn and I am cold and afraid. I know what must happen and my flesh crawls with terror at the thought of it. I have no strength left and I must pray awhile. It is a thing I have always desired, the grace to die with dignity, but never, till now, have I understood how hard it is.

Good-bye, my friend. God keep us both in the dark time.

Giacomo Nerone

When Meyer read the letter for the third time, he had been moved to rare tears, but when he had walked awhile and pondered it and read it again, the charity of it lay on him like an absolution. If he had failed in all else—and his failures were written large on the calendar of fifteen years—he would not die unloved or unforgiven. And this was the answer to the question that had plagued him so long: why great men die and drop out of creation without a ripple of care for them, and the memory of others is cherished in the secret hearts of the humble.

The thought lingered with him through the fall of the afternoon, and it was still expanding itself when the knock came at the door and he opened it to find Blaise Meredith standing outside.

The priest's appearance shocked him. His face was ashen, his lips bloodless, and small beads of sweat stood out on his forehead and on his upper lip. His hands were shaky and his voice husky and trembling.

'I'm sorry to bother you, Doctor. I wonder if I could rest awhile with you.'

'Of course, man! Come in, for God's sake! What's happened to you?'

Meredith smiled wanly.

'Nothing's happened. I'm on my way back from Nina's place. But it's a long scramble before you get to the road, and it was just a little too much. I'll be all right in a minute!'

Meyer led him into the house, made him lie down on the bed and then brought him a stiff tot of *grappa*.

'Drink that. It's foul stuff, but it will put some life into you.'

Meredith choked on the raw spirit, but he got it down and after a few moments he began to feel the warmth spreading out and the strength returning to his limbs. Meyer stood looking down at him with grave eyes.

'You worry me, Meredith. This sort of thing can't go on. I'm half-inclined to get in touch with the Bishop and have you sent to hospital.'

'Give me a few more days, Doctor. After that, it won't matter so much.'

'You're a very sick man. Why drive yourself like this?'

'I'll be a long time dead. Better to burn out than rust out.'

Meyer shrugged despairingly.

'It's your life, Monsignor. Tell me—how did you get on with Nina?'

'Very well. I'm deeply impressed by what she's told me. But there are a couple of questions I'd like to clear up with you—if you don't mind, that is.'

'Ask what you like, my friend. I've gone too far to draw back now.'

'Thank you. Here's the first one. Was there an outbreak of German measles here in the winter of 1943? And was Paolo Sanduzzi born blind because of it?'

'Yes.'

'How long was it before you saw the child again?'

'Three years—no, nearer to four. I went away to Rome, you see.'

'When you came back, the boy could see?'

'Yes. The cataracts had disappeared.'

'Medically speaking, was this strange?'

'Quite abnormal. I'd never know another case.'

'Did you remark on it to Nina Sanduzzi?'

'Yes. I asked her how and when it had happened.'

'What did she say?'

'She just shrugged and said, the way the peasants do ... "It just happened." Our relations then weren't as good as they are now. I didn't press the point. But it puzzled me. It still does. Why do you ask, Monsignor?'

'Nina told me that, on the day of the birth, after you had left, Giacomo had prayed all night—and that, in the morning, he had promised her that the baby would see normally, when other children did—three weeks later. According to her that's just what happened. The cataracts were gone. The child could distinguish light and shadow. And afterwards the sight developed as it did in other children. What would be your opinion of that, Doctor?'

But Meyer did not answer him immediately. He seemed lost in a new thought of his own. When he spoke it was as if to himself:

'So that's what she meant when she said Giacomo had done miracles and that she had seen them.'

'When did she say that?' Meredith prompted him sharply.

'When we were discussing your arrival, and I was trying to persuade her to talk to you.'

'Would you say she was telling the truth?'

'If she said it,' Meyer answered him sombrely, 'it was the truth. She would not lie to save her life.'

'What would be your medical opinion?'

'At first blush I would say it couldn't happen.'

'But it did. The boy is seeing today.'

Meyer gave him a long, searching look; then smiled and shook his head.

'I know what you want me to say, Meredith, but I can't say it. I don't believe in miracles, only in unexplained facts. All I can admit is that this doesn't normally happen. I might go further and say I've never heard of another case like it, that I don't know of any medical explanation for it. But I'm not prepared to make a leap in the dark and tell you this is a miracle caused by divine intervention.'

'I'm not asking you to say that,' said Meredith good-humouredly. 'I'm asking you whether you can explain it medically.'

'I can't. Others might.'

'If they could, could they explain Giacomo Nerone's foreknowledge of the cure?'

'Clairvoyance is an established, if unexplained, phenomenon. But you can't ask anyone to judge a second-hand report of something that happened fifteen years ago.'

'But you accept the truth of the report?'

'Yes.'

'You would record it as unexplained and, possibly, unexplainable in the present state of medical knowledge?'

'. . . Of my medical knowledge,' Meyer corrected him, smiling.

'And you would testify in these terms at the Bishop's court?'

'I would.'

'That's all,' said Meredith with gentle irony. 'I'll put it on record in my notes.'

'What's your own opinion, Monsignor?' Meyer quizzed him pointedly.

'I've an open mind,' said Meredith precisely. 'I shall try, and so will my successor, to prove by every possible means that this is not a miracle, but simply a rare physical phenomenon. As it rests only on one witness and your later testimony, we shall probably end by refusing to accept it as a miracle–though in fact it may be one. Where you and I differ, my dear Doctor, is that you reject the possibility of miracles and I accept it. It's a long argument but I suggest my position is rather more tenable than yours.'

'You'd have made a good lawyer, Monsignor.' Meyer tacked away from the supposition. 'What's your next question?'

Meredith gave it to him baldly.

'Who was Il Lupo? And why did Nerone tell you to keep him away from the village?'

Meyer looked at him in swift surprise.

'Who told you that?'

'Nina. She was half-asleep but she heard you and Nerone talking at the door.'

'What else did she hear?'

'You said ... "This is history! You can't stop it. Neither can I. Someone's got to start organising..."'

'That was all?'

'Yes. I thought you could tell me what it meant.'

'It had many meanings, Monsignor. I can only try to give its meaning for me....'

... Their camp was a shallow basin, high up in the spine of eastern hills. Æons ago it might have been the crater of a volcano. The lip of it was jagged as a saw, and the outer slopes were barren and scree-covered; but inside there was a small lake into which the water drained, and beside it there were copses and a stretch of tough, wiry grass. Their tents were hidden under the bushes, and the goats and the cow they had levied from the local peasants cropped safely on the inside of the saucer, while their look-outs swept the countryside from the shelter of the high sawteeth.

There was only one way in–the goat track that began at Satan's Rock, where the first sentry was posted. The watchers on the rim could see him all day–and if a visitor were admitted they could keep him in their sights every step of the way. When he reached the lip of the crater he would be met and searched and two men would walk him down through the tussocks to the tent of Il Lupo, who was their leader.

Meyer remembered him vividly–a short, fair man, with clear eyes and a chubby face and a smiling mouth, from which a placid voice spoke, now in the purest Tuscan, now in the roughest provincial dialect. His dress was rough like that of his men, but his hands and teeth were immaculate and he shaved, carefully, every day. He talked little about his past, but Meyer gathered that he had fought in Spain and then gone to Russia and then returned to Italy before the outbreak of war. He had worked in Milan and Turin and later still in Rome, though how or at what was never quite clear. He had admitted to being a party man, and he discussed policy with authority and expertness.

The day Giacomo Nerone was brought in from Satan's Rock, Meyer was in Il Lupo's tent discussing a new patrol operation. The guards gave his name and his business and Il Lupo stood up and held out his hand.

'So you're Nerone! I'm happy to know you. I've heard a great deal about you. I'd like to talk with you.'

Nerone returned the greeting but said briskly:

'Could we leave it? My wife's in labour. I'd like the doctor to see her as soon as possible. It's a long walk back.'

'She's had *rubella*,' Meyer explained hastily. 'We're afraid of complications.'

The clear eyes clouded with immediate concern. Il Lupo clucked sympathetically.

'A pity. A great pity. That's where a State Medical Service is such a help. One can start inoculations at the first hint of an outbreak. You had no serum, Meyer, of course.'

'No. We can only wait and see how the child is born.'

'The midwives are with her?'

Nerone nodded.

'Then she's being looked after, at least. Ten minutes won't make any difference one way or the other. Let's have a cup of coffee and talk a while.'

'Relax, Giacomo,' Meyer told him genially. 'Nina's as strong as an ox. We'll make up the time on the downhill walk.'

'Very well.'

They sat down on torn canvas chairs. Il Lupo offered cigarettes and shouted for coffee, and after a few moments of polite fencing he came to the point.

'Meyer's told me about you, Nerone. I understand you're an English officer.'

'That's right.'

'And a deserter.'

'That's right, too.'

Il Lupo shrugged and blew a cloud of smoke up towards the canvas roof.

'It's immaterial to us, of course. The capitalist armies have served their purpose in winning the war. It's our job to establish the peace we want. So your personal history is no disadvantage. On the contrary, it could even help you–with us.'

Nerone said nothing, but sat waiting calmly.

Il Lupo went on in his quiet, educated voice.

'Meyer's also told me of the work you've done in Gemello. The confidence you've built up with the people. That's excellent ... as a temporary measure.'

'Why temporary?' asked Nerone quietly.

'Because your own position is temporary–and equivocal. Because when the war ends–as it soon must–this country will need a strong and united Government to organise it and run it.'

'That means a Communist Government?'

'Yes. We're the only people who have a clear platform and the strength to carry it into practice.'

'You need a charter too, don't you? A mandate?'

Il Lupo nodded amiably.

'We've got it now. The British have made it clear that they'll play ball with anyone who can help them run the country. They've armed us and given us at least a reasonable scope for military operations. The Americans have other ideas, but they're politically immature and we can discount them for a while. That's the first half of the mandate. The second we must win for ourselves.'

'How?'

'How does any party win confidence? By showing results. By establishing order out of chaos. By getting rid of dissenting elements and building unity on strength.'

'That's what the Fascisti tried to do,' Nerone told him evenly.

'Their mistake was to build their dictatorship on one man. Ours will be the dictatorship of the proletariat.'

'And you'd like me to join you in that?'

'As Meyer has done,' Il Lupo pointed out calmly. 'He's a liberal by nature but he's seen the failure of liberalism. It's not enough to hold out promises of work and education and prosperity as the rewards of co-operation. People aren't built like that. They're naturally stupid, naturally selfish. They need the disciplines of strength and fear. Take yourself, for instance. You've done a good job, but where has it led you? You'll be running round with a basket of eggs on your arm playing Lady Bountiful till the day you die. . . . And they'll let you do it. What's the future in that?'

For the first time since his coming, Meyer saw Nerone relax. His lean, dark face split into a grin of genuine amusement.

'There's no future at all. I know that.'

'Why do it, then?'

'The world's a grim place without it,' said Nerone lightly.

'Agreed,' said Il Lupo. 'But in the world we build there won't be any need of it.'

'That's what I'm afraid of,' said Giacomo Nerone. He stood up. 'We understand each other, I think.'

'I understand you very well,' said Il Lupo, without resentment. 'I'm not sure if you understand me. We're moving into the villages one by one and setting up our own administration. Gemello is next on the list. What do you propose to do about it?'

Nerone smiled, denying the proposition before he uttered it.

'I could rally the people and fight you.'

Il Lupo shook his head.

'You're too good a soldier for that. We have the guns, the bullets and the training to use them. We'd cut you up in an afternoon. What's the profit in that?'

'None,' Nerone told him calmly. 'So I'll pass the word around to the people to wait it out without violence until the first free elections.'

A ghost of a grin twitched Il Lupo's thin lips.

'By that time they'll have forgotten the guns. They'll remember only the bread and the pasta and the bars of American chocolate.'

'And the boys you've shot in the ditches!' Sudden anger rang in Nerone's voice. 'The old men beaten, and the girls with shaven heads! The new tyranny built on the old—the liberty pawned again for an illusion of peace. They'll submit now, because they're lost and afraid. Later they'll rise in judgment and throw you out!'

'Give a man a day's work, a full belly at night and a woman in his bed, and he'll never think of Judgment Day.' Il Lupo stood up. His lean figure seemed to grow in stature, filling the tent. 'Another thing, Nerone. . .'

'Yes?'

'There's no room for two of us in Gemello. You'll have to get out.'

Surprisingly, Nerone threw back his head and laughed heartily.

'You want the meat without the mustard. You want me discredited and running like a rabbit while you march in as the Saviour of Italy. You're too greedy, man!'

'If you stay,' said Il Lupo with cool deliberation, 'I'll have to kill you.'

'I know,' said Giacomo Nerone.

'You want to make yourself a martyr, is that it?'

'That would be a folly and a presumption,' Nerone told him simply. 'I don't want to die any more than the next man. But I stand on land that I've tilled with my own hands, in a place where I've found love and hope and belief. I refuse to be hunted out of it to give you a cheap victory.'

'Very well,' said Il Lupo without resentment. 'We know where we stand.'

'Do you mind if Meyer comes now?'

'Not at all. If you'll wait outside a second, we'll just tidy up our business.'

When he had gone, Il Lupo said, without emphasis:

'He's a zealot. He'll have to go.'

Meyer shrugged uneasily.

'He's a good fellow. He does a lot of good and no harm at all. Why not let him be?'

'You're soft, Meyer,' said Il Lupo genially. 'We'll be taking over Gemello in ten days. You've got that long to talk some sense into him.'

'I wash my hands of it,' said Meyer tersely.

'That's Pilate's line, my dear doctor. The Jews have another one–"It is expedient that one man should die for the people."'

He was still smiling when Meyer turned and went out to join Giacomo Nerone....

...Blaise Meredith lay back on the bed, relaxed in body but active in mind, listening to the cool, clinical narration of the doctor. When Meyer paused awhile, he asked:

'It's a personal question, Doctor. Did you actually join the Communist Party?'

'I never held a party ticket. But that's irrelevant. There weren't any tickets in the mountains. The important thing was that I had committed myself to Il Lupo and to what he stood for: the dictatorship of the proletariat, order imposed by strength.'

'May I ask why?'

'It's quite simple.' Meyer's hands gestured eloquently in exposition. 'For me it was the most natural development. I'd seen the breakdown of liberalism. I'd seen the drawbacks of clericalism. I'd been the victim of a one-man dictatorship. I understood the need for equality and order and a redistribution of capital. I'd also seen the stupidity and stubbornness of depressed people. Il Lupo's answer seemed to me the only one.'

'And his threat to Giacomo Nerone?'

'Was also logical.'

'But you disagreed with it?'

'I disliked it. I didn't disagree.'

'Did you talk to Giacomo about it?'

'Yes.'

'What did he say?'

'Surprisingly enough, Monsignor, he agreed with Il Lupo.' Meyer's face clouded at the recollection of it. 'He said quite plainly: "You can't believe one way and act another. Il Lupo's right. If you want to build a perfect political mechanism, you must toss out the parts that don't work. Il Lupo doesn't believe in God. He believes in man only as a political entity, so he's quite logical. You're the illogical one, Meyer. You want omelettes for breakfast, but you don't want to crack the eggs."'

'Did you have any answer to that?'

'Not a very good one, I'm afraid. It was too close to the truth. But I did ask him how he squared up his own admission that there was no future in the work with the fact that he was prepared to die for it.'

'What did he say?'

'He pointed out that he, too, had his own logic. He believed that God was perfect and man, since the fall, was imperfect, and that there would always be disorder and evil and injustice in the world. You couldn't create a system that would destroy these things, because the men who ran it would be imperfect, too. The only thing that dignified man and held him back from self-destruction was his sonship with God and his brotherhood in the human family. Giacomo's own service was an expression of this relationship. Between him and Il Lupo conflict was inevitable, because their beliefs were opposed and contradictory.'

'And Il Lupo, being the man with the guns, must destroy him?'

'That's right.'

'Why didn't he go away?'

'I put that to him, too,' said Meyer wearily. 'I suggested he take Nina and the boy and move out to another place. He refused. He said Nina would come to no harm—and he himself had stopped running long ago.'

'So he stayed in Gemello?'

'Yes. I returned to the mountains. The day before Il Lupo was due to move in and set up his administration, I came back. They were going to use my house as headquarters and I had to get it ready. Also, I had been told to have a last talk with Giacomo Nerone to get him to change his mind....'

... It was early afternoon, warm with the late spring, noisy with the first cicadas. They walked together in the garden under the fig tree, and talked as soberly as lawyer and client about what would happen when Il Lupo came down with his men. There was no argument between them. Nerone was firm in his refusal to quit, and Meyer's words were a flat recitation of the inevitable.

'Il Lupo's quite clear on what will be done. You're to be discredited first and then executed.'

'How does he propose to discredit me?'

'Their arrival is timed for sunrise. You'll be arrested round about nine and brought here for summary trial.'

'On what charges?'

'Desertion from the Allied cause and co-operation with the Germans.'

Nerone smiled thinly.

'He shouldn't have much difficulty proving those. What then?'

'You'll be sentenced and taken out for immediate and public execution.'

'How?'

'The firing squad. This will be a military court. Il Lupo is careful about the formalities.'

'And Nina and the boy?'

'Nothing will be done to them at all. Lupo was quite definite on that. He sees no benefit in raising sympathy by punishing a woman and a child.'

'He's a clever man. I admire him.'

'He asks me to point out that this leaves you nearly eighteen hours to clear out, if you want to. I'm carrying enough money to keep you and Nina and the baby for two months. I'm authorised to give it to you on your assurance that you'll be clear of the area by sunrise.'

'I'm staying. Nothing will change that.'

'Then there's nothing more to be said, is there?'

'Nothing. I'm grateful to you for trying. Meyer. We've been good friends. I appreciate it.'

'There's one thing—I'd almost forgotten it.'

'What's that?'

'Where will you be at nine in the morning?'

'I'll save Il Lupo the trouble. I'll come here.'

'That wouldn't do. I'm afraid. He wants a public arrest.'

'He can't have everything. I'll walk here on my own two feet at nine o'clock.'

'I'll tell him what you say.'

'Thank you.'

Then, because everything was said that needed to be put into words and because neither quite knew how to say good-bye, they walked in silence up and down the flagged path under the fig tree until Meyer said, awkwardly:

'I'm sorry it's ending like this. It's not my business any more, but what are you going to do now?'

Nerone answered him quietly and frankly:

'I'm going down to have Father Anselmo hear my confession. I'll call at the hut to collect a few things and hand them to Nina. Then, I'll walk up to the villa to ask the Contessa if she'll have Nina and the boy there till it's all over. She's British by birth and Il Lupo's too clever to fall foul of the people who are giving him his guns. Then . . .' His dark, hollow face broke into a smile. 'Then I'm going to say my prayers. I'm lucky to have time to prepare. It isn't every man who knows the time and place of his death.' He stopped pacing and held out his hand. 'Good-bye, Meyer. Don't blame yourself too much. I'll remember you in eternity.'

'Good-bye, Nerone. I'll have a care for Nina and the boy.'

He wanted to use the old, familiar formula and say 'God keep you'. But he remembered in time that, in Il Lupo's new world, which was now his own, there would be no God any more. The farewell was therefore pointless, and he did not say it. . . .

. . . Blaise Meredith asked:

'What happened with Father Anselmo?'

Meyer made a gesture of indifference.

'Nothing much. The old man didn't like him. They'd quarrelled often, as you know. He refused to hear his confession. I heard about it later in the village.'

'And the Contessa?'

'This isn't first-hand. I gathered it from Pietro, the manservant, who's a patient of mine. Giacomo went up to the villa to ask a refuge for Nina and the boy. Also, I gathered, he wanted to sleep there the night, so that Il Lupo would not know where he was and would have to forgo the value of a public arrest. Anne de Sanctis was willing enough, it seems, but she wanted a price for it.'

'What price?'

'She's a strange woman,' said Meyer, obliquely. 'I've known her a long time, but I would not claim to understand her fully. She is passionate by nature and she has great need of a man—a greater one now that she faces the terror of the middle years. Her husband disappointed her. Her other lovers came and went away as soldiers do in war-time. She was always too proud to satisfy herself with a man from the village. Nerone might have matched her, but he was already in love with Nina Sanduzzi. From the beginning she was jealous of that. So her whole emotional life has taken on a colour of perversion. Her price was that Nina sign over the boy as her ward and Giacomo Nerone sleep with her that night.'

'A man on the eve of execution?' Meredith was shocked.

'I told you,' said Meyer evenly, 'everything is coloured for her. That's why this painter fellow has so much influence at the villa. He panders to her. Anyway, as you might expect, Giacomo refused. Apparently she was shrewd enough to guess that he would spend the night at Nina's place. She sent a man down with the message to Il Lupo. Giacomo was arrested two hours after sunrise.'

'So that's why she hates his son.'

'I don't think she hates the boy,' said Meyer, with grim humour. 'If anything, she's probably attracted to him. But she is still jealous of Nina and she hates herself, but doesn't know it.'

Blaise Meredith swung his legs off the bed and sat up, running his fingers through his thin hair in a pathetic gesture of weariness and puzzlement. In a voice that was very like a sigh, he said:

'It's late. I'd better get back for dinner. Though, God knows, I don't feel like facing them both tonight.'

'Why not dine here?' said Meyer impulsively. 'You'll eat worse, but at least you won't have to be polite. I'm nearly at the end of my evidence and you might as well get the rest of it tonight. I'll send a lad up to the villa to make your apologies.'

'I'd be grateful, I assure you.'

'I'm grateful to you,' said Meyer with a grin. 'And from a Jew to an inquisitor, that's a big compliment.'

In the ornate room at the villa, the Contessa and Nicholas Black dined by candlelight, in the uneasy intimacy of conspirators. The Contessa was irritable and snappish. She was beginning to understand how far the situation had passed out of her control—with Nicholas Black holding her to ransom and Meredith picking up God knows what information from Meyer and Nina Sanduzzi and old Anselmo. Very soon now he must come to her with his dry, pedantic questions and his sunken, probing eyes. Whether she answered or remained silent, she stood to be discredited while the painter walked off, grinning, with the prize.

Nicholas Black was edgy, too. Meredith had forced his hand at lunch-time and things had been said which could never be recalled. Now they were in open opposition and, for all his mockery, Black had a healthy respect for the temporal influence of the Church in a Latin country. If Meredith took it into his head to invoke the help of the Bishop, all sorts of influences might

be set in motion—influences reaching back to Rome itself—and the end
might be a discreet call from the police and the revocation of his sojourn
permit. It had happened before. The Christian Democrats were in power
and behind them was the Vatican, old and subtle and ruthless.

So he was quick to seize on the Contessa's fear and exploit it to his own
advantage.

'The priest's a damn nuisance, I agree, *cara*. I feel it's my fault for
bringing him here. You're in a mess. I'd like to help you get out of it.'

Her face brightened immediately.

'If you can do that, Nicki. . .'

'I'm sure we can, *cara*.' He leaned over and patted her hand in
encouragement. 'Now listen! The priest is here. We're stuck with him. We
can't get rid of him without a discourtesy, and you don't want that.'

'I know.' She nodded miserably. 'There's the Bishop, you see, and. . .'

Black cut in briskly:

'I know about the Bishop, too, *cara*. You've got to live here, so it pays to
be friendly. Meredith must stay. We're agreed on that. But there's nothing
to stop you going away, is there?'

'I–I don't understand.'

'It's simple, *cara*.' He waved an eloquent hand. 'You haven't been feeling
well at all. Meredith himself knows you've been suffering with migraine and
God knows what other feminine ills. You need to consult your doctor
immediately. So you go to Rome. You've got an apartment there. You need
staff to run it. You take your maid, and Pietro—and, as a special favour to
Nina Sanduzzi, you take the boy. You want to buy him new clothes. You
want him to be trained to service in polite society. You may even want to
thinking about having him educated by the Jesuits. . . .' He chuckled
sardonically. 'What mother could refuse an opportunity like that? And if
she did? The boy's under a contract of service to you. Italian law is such a
confounded muddle, I think you'd get away with it, provided the boy
consents. The onus would be on his mother to show why she wanted him
here and what work she could find for him. You'd cover that, too, by
providing a weekly remittance of part of his wages through your major-
domo here.'

Her eyes lit up at the new, encouraging thought, but immediately clouded
again.

'It's a wonderful idea, Nicki. But what about you? Meredith knows what
you want. He'd do his best to make trouble.'

'I've thought of that, too,' said the painter, with his satiric grin. 'I stay
here—at least for a week. If Meredith asks any questions, you can tell him
quite frankly you think I'm a bad influence on the boy. You want to act like a
good Christian and get him away from me. Simple, isn't it?'

'Wonderful, Nicki! Wonderful!' Her eyes sparkled and she clapped her
hands in delight. 'I'll make all the arrangements tomorrow and we'll leave
the day after.'

'Why not tomorrow?'

'We can't, Nicki. The train for Rome leaves Valenta in the morning.
There wouldn't be time to get everything done.'

'A pity,' said Black irritably. 'Still, it's only a day. I think we can keep our
Monsignor at bay for that long. You'd better talk to the boy yourself. I
mustn't seem to be involved.'

'I'll talk to him in the morning.' She reached out and filled his wineglass.

'Let's drink, darling! Then we'll open another bottle and make a celebration of it. What shall we drink to?'

He raised his glass and smiled at her over the rim.

'To love, *cara!*'

'To love!' said Anne Louise de Sanctis—then choked suddenly on the thought: But who loves me? And who will ever love me?

'I'll be frank with you, Doctor,' said Meredith, picking moodily at the last of his dinner. 'At this moment, I'm less concerned with Giacomo Nerone than with his son. Nerone's dead; and, we hope, among the blessed. His boy is in a grave moral crisis, in daily danger of seduction. I feel responsible for him. But how do I discharge the responsibility?'

'It's a problem,' said Meyer, with sober concern. 'The boy's more than half a man. He has free will and he's morally responsible—if inexperienced. He's certainly not ignorant of what's involved. Children mature early in the matrimonial beds. I think he's a sound lad; but Black's a very persuasive character.'

Meredith was toying absently with a broken crust, crumbling it on his plate and making small patterns of the grey particles.

'Even in the confessional it's hard to reach an adolescent. They're shy as rabbits and much more complex than adults. If I could get at either the Contessa or Black himself I might stand some chance.'

'Have you tried?'

'With Black, yes. But the man is fixed in bitterness and resentment. I couldn't find a common term of agreement. I haven't tried the Contessa yet.'

Meyer gave him a wintry smile.

'You may find that even harder, Monsignor. There's no logic in women at the best of times and this one has a sickness on her: the sickness of the middle years and an old love turned sour and shameful. There's a cure for one, but the other . . .' He paused a moment, frowning dubiously. '. . . One thing I'm sure of, Meredith. No priest can cure it.'

'How will she end, then?'

'Drugs, drink or suicide,' said Meyer flatly. 'Three words for the same thing.'

'And that's the only answer?'

'If you want me to say that God is the answer, Monsignor, I can't do it. There is another one, but it's a dirty word and you mightn't like it.'

To his surprise, Meredith lifted his grey face and smiled at him good-humouredly.

'You know, Meyer, that's the dilemma of the materialists. I wondered so few of them see it. They cut God out of the dictionary and their only answer to the riddle of the universe is a dirty word.'

'Damn you!' said Meyer, with a crooked grin. 'Damn you for a long-nosed inquisitor. Let's have some coffee and talk about Giacomo Nerone. . . .'

. . . At eight o'clock in the morning they arrested Nerone in Nina's house. They were not too rough with him, but they bloodied his face and tore his shirt, so that it would seem that he had put up a struggle. In fact he did not struggle at all, but stood there, silent, while two of them held his arms and a third battered him, and the others held Nina, who screamed and struggled like a wild thing—and, when they took him away, collapsed moaning on the bed. The child did not scream, but lay quietly in its cot, groping with tiny bunched hands at the folds of the pillow.

They then marched him up the hill and on to the road, and, to make a better spectacle, they twisted his arms behind his back and bent him almost double to walk through the village. The people stood at their doors, silent and staring, and even the children were hushed as he passed. No voice was raised in protest, no hand raised to help him. Il Lupo had calculated exactly. Hunger had no loyalties. These folk had seen too many conquerors come and go. Their allegiance was to the strong and not to the gentle. This was a harsh land with a harsh history. It was not the inheritance of the meek.

When they came to Meyer's house, they thrust him roughly inside and shut the door. The people came running like ants to stand outside, but the guards drove them back, cursing them into their houses. Il Lupo wanted an orderly trial, and no riots to disturb it.

Inside the room, Giacomo Nerone stood a moment flexing his cramped arms and wiping the blood from his face. Then he looked around him. The room was set like a court. Il Lupo and Meyer and three other men sat at the table, and behind them the guards were ranged—dark, stubble-faced men, in leather jackets and cocked berets, with pistols in their belts and automatic rifles held loosely in their hands. Two other guards stood between Nerone and the door, and between him and the table there was a clear space with a single chair.

All the faces were set and serious, as was becoming to men witnessing a historic act. Only Il Lupo was smiling, clear eyed and polite as a host at a dinner party. He said in his cool voice:

'I'm sorry we had to be rough with you, Nerone. You shouldn't have resisted arrest.'

Nerone said nothing.

'You have a right, of course, to know the charges against you.' He picked up a paper from the table and read from it in careful Tuscan: 'Giacomo Nerone, you are charged before this military court with desertion from the British Army and with active collaboration with German units operating in the area of Gemelli dei Monti.' He laid the paper down on the table and went on: 'Before you are brought to trial on these charges, you are at liberty to say anything you wish.'

Nerone looked at him with calm eyes.

'Will you put my remarks in the record?'

'Certainly.'

'On the charge of desertion, this court has no jurisdiction. Only a British Army court martial can try me for that. Your proper procedure is to hold me in custody and hand me over to the nearest British command.'

Il Lupo nodded placidly.

'We will note your objection, which seems to me well founded, in spite of the fact that you have no proof of your identity as a British soldier. You will, however, be brought to trial on the second charge.'

'I challenge your jurisdiction on that, too.'

'On what grounds?'

'This is not a proper court. Its officials hold no legal commission.'

'I disagree with you,' said Il Lupo placidly. 'Partisan groups are guerrillas operating in support of the Allies. They have a *de facto* identity as military units and a summary jurisdiction in local theatres of war. Their authority derives ultimately from the Allied High Command and from the Occupation Authority in Italy.'

'In that case, I have nothing to say.'

Il Lupo nodded politely.

'Good. We're anxious, of course, to see that justice is done. You will be given some time to prepare your defence. I propose to clear the room. You will be given coffee and something to eat. Doctor Meyer here is prepared to act as your defence counsel. As president of the court I am prepared to give full weight to any points you may care to raise with me. Is that clear?'

For the first time since his arrival, Nerone smiled.

'Quite clear. I'd enjoy the coffee.'

At a sign from Il Lupo, the guards went out into the garden and the three men were left alone. Meyer said nothing, but went to the stove and began making the coffee. Nerone sat down and Il Lupo offered him a cigarette and lit it for him. Then he sat on the edge of the table and said pleasantly:

'You were foolish to stay, you know.'

'It's done,' Nerone told him briefly. 'Why discuss it?'

'You interest me, that's why. I have a good deal of admiration for you. But I can't see you in the role of a martyr.'

'You cast me for it.'

'And you accepted it.'

'Yes.'

'Why?'

'I like the lines,' said Nerone, with grave humour. 'The last one most of all: *"Consummatum est."*'

'You–and the work,' said Il Lupo.

Nerone shrugged.

'The work isn't important. A million men can do it better. You will probably do it better yourself. The work dies. How many men did Christ cure? And how many of them are alive today? The work is an expression of what a man is, what he feels, what he believes. If it lasts, if it develops, it's not because of the man who began it, but because other men think and feel and believe the same way. Your own party's an example of it. You'll die too, you know. What then?'

'The work will go on,' said Il Lupo. The clear eyes lit suddenly as if at a great revelation. 'The work will go on. The old systems will perish of their own corruption, and the people will come into their own. It's happened in Russia. It will happen in Asia. America will be isolated. Europe will be forced into line. It will happen. Nerone, I may not be here to see it, but I'm not important.'

'That's the difference between us,' said Giacomo Nerone softly. 'You say you're not important. I say I am. . . . What happens to me is eternally important, because I was from eternity in the mind of God . . . me! The blind, the futile, the fumbling, the failed. I was, I am, I shall be!'

'You believe that, really?' Il Lupo's eyes probed him like a scalpel.

'I do.'

'You'll die for it?'

'It seems so.'

Il Lupo stubbed out his cigarette and stood up. He said with flat conviction:

'It's a monstrous folly.'

'I know,' said Giacomo Nerone. 'And it's gone on for two thousand years.

I wonder whether yours will last so long.'

Il Lupo made no answer. He looked at his watch and then said briskly: 'We'll have coffee and then you can rest for the morning. We'll bring the trial on at one o'clock. How do you propose to plead?'

'Does it matter?'

'Not really. The finding's a matter of course. The execution is fixed for three o'clock.'

Nerone's face clouded momentarily and he said:

'Why so late? I'd like to get it over.'

'I'm sorry,' said Il Lupo politely. 'I'm not being cruel. It's just a matter of policy. There'll be less time for riots or demonstrations. By the time they get the gossip over and begin to think about it, they'll be ready for supper. You understand, I hope?'

'Perfectly,' said Giacomo Nerone.

Meyer brought the coffee and the breakfast things and they sat together at the table eating in silence, like a family. When they had finished, Il Lupo asked him:

'By the way, do you intend to make any speeches before the execution?' Nerone shook his head.

'I've never made a speech in my life. Why?'

'I'm glad,' Il Lupo told him genially. 'Otherwise I'd have to have you beaten before you went out. The one thing I can't afford is heroics.'

'I'm no hero,' said Giacomo Nerone.

For the first time since his arrival, Meyer spoke to him. Without raising his eyes from the table-top, he said gruffly:

'If you want to be private for a while, use the other room. No one will disturb you. I'll call you when we're ready to begin.'

Nerone looked at him with gratitude in his sombre eyes.

'Thank you, Meyer. You've been a good friend. I'll remember you.'

He got up from the table and walked into the other room, closing the door behind him. The two men looked at each other. After a moment, Il Lupo said, not ungently:

'I'll release you from service after the execution, Meyer. If you take my advice you'll cut loose and go away for a while. You're not made for this sort of thing.'

'I know,' said Aldo Meyer in a dead voice. 'I don't believe enough—either way....'

... 'And the rest of it' asked Blaise Meredith.

Meyer's long hands made a gesture of finality.

'It was quite simple. He was tried and found guilty. They took him up the hill to the old olive tree, tied him to it, and shot him. Everyone was there, even the children.'

'And Nina?'

'She, too. She went up to him and kissed him and then stood back. Even when they shot him, she didn't say a word: but when all the others left, she stayed there. She was still there when the burial party came that night to take him away.'

'Who buried him?'

'Anselmo, the Contessa, two men from the villa, Nina—and myself.'

Blaise Meredith frowned in puzzlement.

'I don't understand that.'

'Simple enough. All three of us wanted to hate him—but at the end he shamed us into loving him.'

'And yet,' persisted Meredith, 'when I came you were all afraid of him.'

'I know,' said Meyer gruffly. 'Love is the most terrible thing in the world.'

It was after eleven when Blaise Meredith left the doctor's house to walk back to the villa. Before he went, Meyer showed him Nerone's last letter and handed him the package containing the rest of the papers. They said good-night to each other and Meredith began to stroll up the cobbled street in the grey moonlight.

A sense of remoteness and separation took hold of him, as if he were walking out of his own body, in a strange place and another time. There were no doubts any more, no storms, only a great tranquillity. The storms were all about him, roaring and restless, but he lay becalmed in the eye of the cyclone, in a wonder of silence and flat water.

Like Giacomo Nerone, he was near the end of his search. Like Nerone, he saw how his death must come in a flurry of violence, inevitable but brief as sunset. He was afraid of it, yet he walked towards it, on his own two feet, enveloped in the peace of a final decision.

He came to the iron gates of the villa and passed them, pressing onwards up the last steep incline to the place of Nerone's execution—the small plateau where the olive tree stood like a cross, black against the white moon. When he reached it, he laid down the package and leaned against the tree, feeling his heart pounding and the rough touch of the bark against his skin. He raised his arms slowly, so that they lay along the knotted branches and the dead twigs pricked the skin of his hands.

Giacomo Nerone had stood like this, with wrists and ankles bound and eyes covered, in the moment of final surrender. Now it was his turn—Blaise Meredith, the cold priest from the Palace of the Congregations. His body stiffened, his face knotted in the agony of decision as he struggled to gather his will to the act of submission. It seemed an age before the words wrenched themselves out of him, low and agonised:

'... Take me, O God! Make me what you want ... a wonder or a mockery! But give me the boy—for his father's sake!'

It was over—done, finished! A man sold under the hammer to his Maker. Time to go home. To bed, but not to sleep. Time was running out. Before morning came, there were Giacomo Nerone's papers to be read, and a letter to be written to Aurelio, Bishop of Valenta.

14

To Blaise Meredith, the legalist—and even in this time of climax he could not lay aside the mental habit of a lifetime—the writings of Giacomo Nerone were, in many respects, a disappointment. They added nothing, except by inference, to the biography of his past, and little but glossary to the known details of his life, works and death in Gemello Minore.

What Aldo Meyer had found in them—a poignant recollection, a glimpse into the mind of a man once known, once hated, finally loved–presented itself under another aspect to the Devil's Advocate. Blaise Meredith had read the writing of a hundred saints, and all their agonies, all their revelations, all their passionate outpourings had for him the familiarity of old acquaintance.

They conformed to the same belief, to a basic pattern of penance and devotion, to the same progression from purgation to illumination, from illumination to a direct union with the Almighty in the act of prayer. It was the conformity he was looking for now, as each of the examiners and assessors would look for it, in each of the processes that must follow the first presentation of evidence in the Bishop's court.

To the biographer, to the dramatist, to the preacher, the personality of the man was important. His quirks and oddities and individual genius were the things that linked him to the commonalty of men and made them lean to him as patron and exemplar. But to the Church itself, to the delving theologians and inquisitors who represented it, the importance lay in his character as a Christian–his conformity to the prototype which was Christ.

So, in the slow hours of the night, Blaise Meredith bent himself to the scrutiny, coolly and analytically. But even he could not escape the personal impact–the living man thrusting himself out from the yellowed leaves and the strong, masculine hand-writing.

The writing was disjointed: the jottings of a man torn between contemplation and action, who still felt the need to clarify his thoughts and make his affirmations clear to himself. Meredith pictured him, sitting late at night in the small stone hut, cold, pinch-bellied, yet oddly content, writing a page or two before the time came to begin the long prayerful vigil which, more and more, became his substitute for sleep.

Yet, in spite of their random character, the writings had a rhythm and a unity of their own. They grew as the man grew. They ended as the man ended, in dignity and calm and a strange content.

. . . I write because of the common need of man to communicate himself, if only to a blank sheet of paper; because the knowledge of myself is a weight on me and I have no right to lay it all on the woman I love. She is simple and generous. She would bear it all and still be ready for more, but concealment is as much a part of love as surrender. A man must pay for his own sins and he cannot borrow another's absolution. . . .

. . . To be born into the Church–and I can only speak of my own Church, knowing no other–is at once a burden and a comfort. The burden is felt first. The burden of ordinance and prohibition and, later of belief. The comfort comes afterwards, when one begins to ask questions; and when one is presented with a key to every problem of existence. Make the first conscious act of faith, accept the first premise, and the whole logic falls into place. One may sin, but one sins inside a cosmos. One is constrained to repentance by the sheer order of it. One is free within a system, and the system is secure and consoling, so long as the will is fixed in the first act of faith. . . .

. . . When Catholics become jealous of unbelievers, as they often do, it is because the burden of belief lies heavy and the constraints of the cosmos begin to chafe. They begin to feel cheated, as I did. They ask why an accident of birth should make fornication a sin for one, and a week-end recreation for another. Faced with the consequences of belief, they begin to regret the belief itself. Some of them end by rejecting it, as I did when I came down from Oxford. . . .

. . . To be a Catholic in England is to submit to a narrow conformity instead of a loose, but no less rigid, one. If one belongs to the old families as I did, to the last Elizabethans, the last Stuarts, it is possible to wear the Faith like a historic eccentricity—as some families sport the bar sinister, or a Regency rakehell, or a gambling dowager. But in the clash of conformities this is not enough. Sooner or later one is forced back on the first act of faith. If one rejects this, one is lost. . . .

. . . I was lost a long time, without knowing it. Without the Faith, one is free, and that is a pleasant feeling at first. There are no questions of conscience, no constraints, except the constraints of custom, convention and the law, and these are flexible enough for most purposes. It is only later that the terror comes. One is free—but free in chaos, in an unexplained and unexplainable world. One is free in a desert, from which there is no retreat but inward, towards the hollow core of oneself. There is nothing to build on but the small rock of one's own pride, and this is a nothing, based on nothing . . . I think, therefore I am. But what am I? An accident of disorder, going nowhere. . . .

. . . I have examined myself a long time on the nature of my act of desertion. At the time, it had no moral significance. The oath of service ends with invocation of the Deity. But for me there was no Deity. If I chose to risk liberty and reputation and suffer the sanctions of the State, this was my business. If I escaped the sanctions, so much the better. But I did not reason like this at the time. My action was instinctive—an unreasoning reaction from something that did violence to my nature. But, by what I then believed, I had nothing that could be called a nature. I was cast in a common form, like a spark out of a furnace, but if one spark sputtered out, what did it matter? I was lost already . . . I could only plunge a little deeper into darkness. . . .

. . . Then there was Nina. I woke to her as one wakes to the first light of morning. The act of love is, like the act of faith, a surrender; and I believe that the one conditions the other. In my case, at least, it has done so. I cannot regret that I loved her, because love is independent of its expression—and it was only my expression of it that was contrary to the moral law. This I regret and have confessed and prayed to be forgiven. But even in sin the act of love—done with love—is shadowed with divinity. Its conformity may be at fault, but its nature is not altered, and its nature is creative, communicative, splendid in surrender. . . .

. . . It was in the splendour of my surrender to Nina, and hers to me, that I first understood how a man might surrender himself to God—if a God existed. The moment of love is a moment of union—of body and spirit—and the act of faith is mutual and implicit. . . .

. . . Nina has a God, but I had none. She was in sin, but within the cosmos. I was beyond in sin, in chaos. . . . But in her I saw all that I had rejected, all that I needed, and yet had thrown away. Our union was flawed because of it, and one day she would understand and might come to hate me. . . .

. . . How does one come back to belief, out of unbelief? Out of sin, it is easy; an act of repentance. An errant child returns to a Father because the Father is still there, the relationship is unbroken. But in unbelief there is no Father, no relationship. One comes from nowhere, goes nowhere. One's noblest acts are robbed of meaning. I tried to serve the people. I did serve them. But who were the people? Who was I? . . .

. . . I tried to reason myself back to a first cause and first motion, as a foundling might reason himself back to the existence of his father. He must have existed, all children have fathers. But who was he? What was his name? What did he look like? Did he love me–or had he forgotten me for ever? This was the real terror, and, as I look back on it now, from the security I have reached, I tremble and sweat and pray desperately: 'Hold me close. Never let me go again. Never hide Your face from me. It is terrible in the dark!' . . .

. . . How did I come to Him? He alone knows. I groped for Him and could not find Him. I prayed to Him unknown and He did not answer. I wept at night for the loss of Him. Lost tears and fruitless grief. Then, one day, He was there again. . . .

. . . It should be an occasion, I knew. One should be able to say: 'This was the time, the place, the manner of it. This was my conversion to religion. A good man spoke to me and I became good. I saw creation in the face of a child and I believed.' It was not like that at all. He was there. I knew He was there, and that He made me and that He still loved me. There are no words to record, no stones scored with a fiery finger, no thunders on Tabor. I had a Father and He knew me and the world was a house He had built for me. I was born a Catholic, but I had never understood till this moment the meaning of the words 'The gift of faith'. After that, what else could I do, but say: 'Here am I, lead me, do what you want with me. But please stay with me, always. . . .'

. . . I am afraid for Aldo. There is much merit in his sceptic honesty, but when the others get hold of him, I do not know what will happen. This is the difference between the two absolutes–the Church and Communism. The Church understands doubt and teaches that faith is a gift, not to be acquired by either reason or merit. Communism permits no doubt and says that belief can be implanted like a conditioned reflex. . . . To a point, it is right, but the conditioned reflex answers no questions–and the questions are always there–Whence? Where? Why? . . .

. . . The question of reparation worries me greatly at times. I am changed. I have changed. But I cannot change any of the things I have done. The hurts, the injustices, the lies, the fornications, the loves taken and tossed away. These things have changed and are still changing other people's lives. I am sorry for them now, but sorrow is not enough. I am bound to repair them as far as I can. But how? It is winter. The paths are closed before me and behind. I am a prisoner in this small world I have found. I can only say: When the way is clear, I will do what is asked of me. But the way is never clear. There is only the present moment in which one can live with certainty. Why do I fear so much? Because repentance is only the beginning. There is still a debt to pay. I ask for light, pray for submission, but the answer is unclear. I can only go on in the present. . . .

. . . Meyer laughs at me about good works. He points out that they have no continuity. The sick die and the hungry are hungry tomorrow. Yet Meyer himself does the same things instinctively. Why? Men like Meyer doubt the existence of God and therefore doubt any but a pragmatic relationship between man and man. Yet I have seen Meyer spend himself more freely than I have ever done. The man who does good in doubt must have so much more merit than one who does it in the bright certainty of belief. 'Other sheep I have which are not of this fold. . . .' A warning against the smugness of inherited Faith. . . .

. . . Nina tells me I am getting thin. I don't eat enough or sleep enough and pray too long at night. I try to explain how the need for food and sleep seems to get less, when one is absorbed in this new wonder of God. She seems to understand it better when I point out that she does not feel the need of me, physically, because of the child filling her womb. . . . I ask myself what must be done about this question of marriage. We are apart in body now, but close in heart and spirit. I have the feeling that things are being prepared for me over which I have no control and that, for this reason, marriage might be a greater injustice than those I have already done. I am ready to do what seems right. I have told her that she has the first claim to decide, but that I believe it wise to wait. . . . I have had so much these last months–of love, of happiness, of spiritual consolation. I must pay for it sometime. I do not know how the payment will be asked. I pray and try to make myself ready. . . .

. . . Father Anselmo worries me. I have quarrelled with him and I regret it. There is nothing solved by anger. I must understand that a priest is just a man with sacramental faculties. The faculties are independent of his personal worth. Anselmo is carrying his own cross, the load of one lapse, multiplied by its consequences. But even in the sin there is an element of love, and this, I know, is a goodness not to be despised. Celibacy of the clergy is an ancient discipline, but not an article of faith. One sees its value, but one must not judge too harshly when men stumble under the weight of it. Poverty is a state which some men accept to make themselves holy. It can be for others conducive to damnation. If there were a way to talk to Anselmo, as a friend . . . but this is another problem for a priest. He is trained to direct the faithful, but never to accept counsel from them. This is a defect in the system. . . .

. . . Today I met the man who calls himself Il Lupo. Strange how quickly and easily we understood each other. I believe in God. He believes in no-God. Yet the consequences of each belief are equally rigid and inescapable. He is honest in what he believes. He does not expect me to be less honest in my own faith. He knows that there can be no coexistence between us. One must destroy the other. He is the prince of this world and he has the power of life and death. What power have I against him? 'My kingdom is not of this world.' I could rally the people. I could make them follow me to resist Il Lupo's band. But to what end? Fratricide is not Christianity. Bullets breed no love. . . . Il Lupo would like me to argue and act. I must not argue. I must only accept. But I fear for Meyer. He is too gentle a man for this embroilment. I must try to make him see that I understand. Later, he will have much to suffer. The weight of doubt is heavy on honest men. . . .

. . . I have a son and the boy is blind. Nina's grief is harsh on me. I understand now how faith can stagger on the mystery of pain. I understand how the old Manichees could fall easily into their heresy–since it is hard to see how pain and evil come into a creation of which an omnipotent Goodness is the sole author. A black time for me. It seems I am back in darkness and I pray desperately and cling to the first act of faith and say: 'I cannot understand; but I believe. Help me to hold to it!' . . .

. . . If faith can move mountains, faith can open blind eyes. If God wills it. How do I know what He wills? Speak to me, O God, for Your Son's sake. . . . Amen. . . .

There was more, much more, and Blaise Meredith scanned it meticulously as a good advocate should, but he had found the core of it, and the core was sound and solid. The conformity was there, the conformity of mind and heart and will. And the surrender had been made by which a man cuts loose from every material support to rest in faith, hope and charity, in the hands that framed him.

On the last page of all, Giacomo Nerone had written his own *obit*.

... If there be any, after my death, to read what I have written let them know this of me:

I was born in the Faith; I lost it; I was led back to it by the hand of God.

What service I have done was prompted by Him. There is no merit in it of my own.

I have loved a woman and begotten a son, and I love them still in God and to all eternity.

Those I have injured, I beg to forgive me.

Those who will kill me, I commend to God, as brothers whom I love.

Those who forget me will do well. Those who remember me, I beg to pray for the soul of

Giacomo Nerone,
Who died in the Faith.

Blaise Meredith laid down the yellowed sheet on the counterpane, leaned back on the pillows and closed his eyes. He knew now with certainty that he had come to the end of his search. He had looked into the life of a man and seen the pattern of it—a long river winding slowly, but with certainty, homeward to the sea. He had looked into the soul of a man and seen it grow, like a tree, from the darkness of the earth, upward into the sun.

He had seen the fruit of the tree: the wisdom and the love of Nina Sanduzzi, the struggling humanity of Aldo Meyer, the reluctant repentance of Father Anselmo. It was good fruit, and in the bloom of it he saw the mark of the nurturing finger of God. But all the fruits was not yet mature. Some of it might wither on the branch, some of it might fall unripe and rot into extinction, because the gardener was careless. And he, Blaise Meredith, was the gardener.

He began to pray, slowly and desperately, for Anne de Sanctis and Paolo Sanduzzi and Nicholas Black, who had chosen the same desert to walk in as Giacomo Nerone. But before the prayer was finished, the old sickness took him, griping and wrenching so that he cried out in the agony of it, till the blood welled up, hot and choking in his throat.

A long time later, weak and dizzy, he dragged himself to the writing desk and, in a shaky hand, began to write. . . .

My Lord Bishop,

I am very ill, and I believe that I may die before I have time to record fully the results of my investigations here. In spite of all the medical predictions, I feel that I am being hurried out of life and I am oppressed by the thought of the little time left to me. I want Your Lordship to know, however, that I have made my surrender, as you promised I would, and that I rest content, if not courageous, in the outcome.

First, let me tell you what I have found. I believe most firmly, on the evidence of those who knew him and on the writings which I have found, that Giacomo Nerone was a man of God, who died in the Faith and in the attitude of martyrdom. What the Court will decide is another matter—a legality, based on the canonical rules of evidence, and irrelevant, it seems to me, to the fundamental facts, that the finger of God is here and that the leaven of goodness in this man is still working in the lives of his people.

Your Lordship's best witnesses will be Doctor Aldo Meyer and Nina Sanduzzi. This latter has produced evidence of a cure that may well be miraculous, though I doubt seriously whether it will pass the assessors. The writings of Nerone which I shall send you with this letter are authentic and definitive, and, in my view, sound corroboration of his claim to heroic sanctity.

I confess to you, My Lord, in friendship, that I am less concerned at this moment for the Cause of Beatification than for the welfare of certain souls here in Gemello Minore. I have spoken to Father Anselmo and presumed to suggest that if he separates physically from Rosa Benzoni, even while lodging her still in his house, and if he makes a sincere confession, Your Lordship will accept these as evidence of reform. I'm sorry for him. It is a question of money and security for a poverty-stricken and rather ignorant man. I have promised him a lump sum of a hundred thousand lire from my estate as well as money enough to buy bedding and other needs for a separate sleeping room for Rosa Benzoni. It seems now that I may not have time to arrange these things. May I count on Your Lordship to do them for me, and use this letter for a claim on my executors? To fail Anselmo now would be an intolerable thought.

The other matter touches the Contessa de Sanctis, Paolo Sanduzzi, who is the son of Giacomo Nerone, and an English painter, who is house-guest at the villa. It is too sordid to detail in this letter; and I fear there is little Your Lordship could do about it. I have commended them all to God and asked Him to accept my surrender as the price of their salvation. I hope tomorrow to be able to plan more active measures; but I am so weak and ill, I dare not count on anything.

I have two favours to ask, which I trust Your Lordship will not find burdensome. The first is that you write to His Eminence, Cardinal Marotta, explaining my position and making my apologies for what I count as a failure in my mission. Give him my greetings and beg him to remember me in his Mass. The second is that you will permit me to be buried here in Gemello Minore. I had once asked to be buried in His Eminences's church, but Rome is very far—and here, for the first time, I have found myself as a man and a priest.

It is very late, my Lord, and I am tired. I can write no more. Forgive me and, in your charity, pray for me.

I am Your Lordship's most obedient servant in Christ,

Blaise Meredith

He folded the letter, sealed it in an envelope and tossed it on the desk. Then he crawled back to bed and slept till the sun was high over the green lawns of the villa.

Paolo Sanduzzi was working on the rock garden at the back of the villa. The terraces had been breached in places where the mortar had weathered out, and the soil was spilling. When it rained, the soil would be lost and, in this rocky land, it was too precious for that. The old gardener had shown him how to mix lime with the black volcanic sand from the river, and how to work it into the crevices with a trowel, then trim and surface it.

It was a new thing learned, a new skill to be proud of, and he knelt there with the sun shining on his back, whistling contentedly. The lime burned his fingers and made his hands feel rough and sandy, but this was another small pride—his hands were hardening like a man's. The gardener was pleased with him, too. Sometimes he would stop and talk in his gruff chewing fashion, and tell him the names of the plants, and how they grew and why the grubs would eat one and not another.

At mealtimes, in the long flagged kitchen, the old man would protect him from the chaffing of the women, who made jokes about his young maleness and what the girls would do to him when they got hold of him. The only one who did not laugh at him was Agnese the cook, a waddling mountain of a woman, who fed him double portions of pasta and always had a lump of cheese or a piece of fruit to tuck in the pocket of his breeches.

He had no name to put to all this, but he understood that it was a good way to be. He had a place and work to do, and friendly people about him—and at the end of the month there would be lire to rustle in his pocket and take home to his mother. Even Rome was beginning to recede into a dimmer distance. The Contessa had not spoken to him again, and the painter had left him alone, except for a genial word or two in passing. His fear of them had begun to diminish and they wove themselves pleasantly into his daydream of fountains and girls with shoes, and streets full of shining automobiles.

He was dreaming now, to the rhythm of his own whistling and the scrape of his trowel on the grey stone, when suddenly the dream became a reality. The Contessa was standing behind him and saying in her gentlest voice:

'Paolo! I want to talk to you.'

He straightened immediately, dropped his trowel and scrambled down from the rockery to stand before her, acutely conscious of his sweating, naked torso and his grimy hands.

'Yes, signora. At your service.'

She looked around quickly as if to make sure they were alone. Then she told him:

'Tomorrow, Paolo, I'm going away to Rome. I'm not very well and I must see my doctor. I'm taking Zita and Pietro to look after my apartment and I thought of taking you, too.'

He gaped and stammered at the sudden wonder of it and the Contessa gave her high, tinkling laugh.

'Why are you so surprised? I promised you, didn't I? And you have worked well.'

'But . . . but . . .'

'But you didn't believe me? Well, it's true. The only thing is, you'll have to ask your mother. You'll tell her that you'll be away for a couple of months and that part of your money will be paid to her here each month. Is that clear?'

'Yes, signora!' It was clear and bright as summer.

'You will tell her that Pietro is going and Zita, too, and that Pietro will be training you all the time.'

'Yes, signora. But . . .'

'But what, Paolo?'

He did not know how to say it, but finally he got it out in a swift stumble of words.

'My . . . my mother doesn't like the Englishman, Signor Black. She may not let me go.'

Again she laughed and charmed all the fears out of him.

'You tell your mother, Paolo, that Signor Black is staying here to work. And that this is why I am taking you away, because it is better for you not to see him.'

'When—when can I tell her?'

'Now, if you like. Then come back and let me know what she says.'
'Thanks, signora. Thanks a thousand, thousand times.'

He snatched up his shirt, struggled into it so roughly that he tore it, and then went racing away down the gravelled path towards the iron gates. Anne Louise de Sanctis watched him go, smiling at the boyish eagerness of him. It was a good thing to see, a pleasantness to have near one in the house. This must be what other women found in their sons, in the autumn of marriage, when the sap of passion was drying out, and a husband was a companion perhaps, but no longer a youthful lover.

Suddenly, and quite clearly, she understood what she had done—the malice of it, the dirt of it, the stark damnation into which she had walked herself on the arm of Nicholas Black. Her blood ran cold at the thought. She shivered and turned away; and as she rounded the corner of the house, she walked almost into the arms of Blaise Meredith, who was stepping on to the lawn with a folder of papers in his hand.

When he greeted her, quietly, she was shocked by the look of him. His face seemed to have shrunken overnight. His eyes were like red coals set deep in his skull. His skin was the colour of old parchment and his lips were bloodless. His back was stooped as if he walked under a heavy load and his long hands were tremulous against the black fabric of his soutane.

For a moment she forgot her own thought and said:
'Monsignor! You're ill!'
'Very ill, I'm afraid,' he told her. 'I don't think I have much more time. Would you walk with me a little?'

She wanted to refuse outright, to run from him and hide herself in her bedroom within reach of the small bottle of oblivion, but he took her arm gently and she found herself falling into step beside him, listening to his voice and answering him in a voice that seemed not to belong to her.

'I saw young Paolo running down the path. He seemed to be excited about something.'
'He was—very excited. I'm taking him to Rome with me tomorrow, if his mother will let him come.'
'Is Mr Black going, too?'
'No. He's staying on here.'
'But joining you later, is that it?'
'I—I don't know what his plans are.'
'You do.' The voice was tired but gentle and it held her, hypnotically.
'You do, my dear Contessa, because you made the plans with him. Terrible plans. Terrible for you and him—and the boy. Why did you do it?'
Her feet were fixed to the treadmill rhythm of their pacing. In spite of herself, the words came out:
'I—I don't know.'
'Did you still want revenge on Giacomo Nerone?'
'So you know that, too?'
'Yes. I know.'

It didn't matter now. Nothing mattered. He could ask what he liked and she would answer, and when it was finished she would go upstairs and take a bath, and lie down to sleep and never wake again. This was the last terror. It would soon be over.

His next words shocked her back into reality. Meyer might have said them but not this priest with the mark of death on him. In Meyer's mouth, they would have lacked something—an intimacy, a gentleness, a love, perhaps? It was hard to say.

'You know, my dear Contessa, Italy is a bad country for a woman like you. It is a country of the sun, aggressive in its worship of the processes of generation. It is primitive and passionate. The male symbol is paramount. The woman unloved, unbedded, childless, is a sign of mockery to others and of torment to herself. You're a passionate woman. You have a great need of love—a need, too, of the sexual commerce that goes with it. The need has become a frenzy with you—and the frenzy betrays you into viciousness while it inhibits your own satisfaction. You're ashamed of it and you do worse things, because you don't know how to do better. . . . Is that right?'

'Yes.'

It was all she said—but she wanted to add: I know all this, know it more terribly than you. But knowing isn't enough. Where do I go? What do I do? How do I find what I need?

Meredith went on, his dry voice warming as he talked.

'I could tell you to pray about this—and that wouldn't be a bad thing, because the hand of God reaches down even into the private hells we make for ourselves. I could tell you to make a general confession—and that would be a better thing, because it would give you a free conscience, and set you in peace with your God and yourself. But it wouldn't be the whole answer. You would still be afraid, still unsatisfied, still lonely.'

'What do I do then? Tell me! For God's sake, tell me!'

The plea was wrung out of her at last. Meredith answered her, calmly.

'Leave this place for a while. Go away. Not to Rome, which is a small city and can be a vicious one. Go back to London and establish yourself there for a while. I'll give you a note to a friend of mine at Westminster, who will put you in touch with a specialist who deals with problems like yours—problems of the body and of the mind. Put yourself in his care. Don't expect too much too soon. Go to theatres, make some new friends, find yourself a charity that interests you. . . . Maybe, too, you will find a man, not to sleep with only, but to marry you and love you. You're still attractive—particularly when you smile.'

'But if I don't find him?' There was a note of panic in her voice.

'Let me tell you something very important,' said Meredith patiently. 'It is no new thing to be lonely. It comes to all of us sooner or later. Friends die, families die. Lovers and husbands, too. We get old, we get sick. And the last and greatest loneliness is death, which I am facing now. There are no pills to cure that. No formulas to charm it away. It's a condition of men that we can't escape. If we try to retreat from it, we end in a darker hell—ourselves. But if we face it, if we remember that there are a million others like us, if we try to reach out to comfort them and not ourselves, we find in the end that we are lonely no longer. We are in a new family, the family of man, whose Father is God Almighty. . . . Do you mind if we sit down now? I'm—I'm very tired.'

Now it was her turn to take his arm and help him to the small stone seat under the honeysuckle. Meredith sat down but she remained standing, looking down at him with slow wonder and a pity she had never felt for any but herself. After a moment, she asked him:

'How do you understand all this? I've never heard a priest talk like that before.'

His bloodless mouth twitched into a tired smile.

'People ask too much of us, my dear Contessa. We're human too. Some of us are very stupid, and it takes us a lifetime to learn the simplest lessons.'

'You're the first man in my life who's ever helped me.'

'You've been meeting the wrong men,' said Meredith, with dry irony.

She smiled at him then, and he saw, as if for the first time, how beautiful she had been.

'Would you–would you hear my confession, Father?'

Meredith shook his head.

'Not yet. I don't think you're ready for it.'

She stared at him, frowning, more than a little afraid. He went on, gravely:

'Confession is not the psychiatrist's couch, a device to encourage self-revelation, to promote well-being by a purge of memory. It is a judicial sacrament, in which pardon is given on an admission of guilt and a promise of repentance and reform. For you the first part is easy–it is already half-done. For the second, you must prepare yourself, by prayer and self-discipline–and by beginning to repair the evil you have already done.'

She looked at him with troubled eyes.

'You mean Nicki–Mr Black?'

'I mean you, my dear Contessa–your own desires, your jealousy of Nina Sanduzzi and her son. As for Mr Black . . .' He hesitated a moment; then his eyes clouded and his mouth set into a grim line. 'I'll talk to him myself. But I'm very much afraid he won't listen.'

15

Halfway through the village, Paolo Sanduzzi ran, full tilt, into his mother. She was standing outside the smithy, talking to Martino's wife. Rosetta was with them, dressed in her Sunday finery, ready to be taken to the villa for the first time. Nina stared at him in amazement.

'Where do you think you're going? You're supposed to be working. What's all the hurry?'

The words tumbled out of him in a torrent.

'I don't have to work today. The Contessa told me. I'm going to Rome. She said I was to ask you and tell you that Pietro's going and Zita and I'm going to be trained . . .'

'Wait a minute!' Nina Sanduzzi's voice was harsh. 'Start again! Who said you're going to Rome?'

'The Contessa. She's going up there to see her doctor. She'll be there for two months.'

'And she wants to take you?'

'Yes.'

'Why?'

'She needs servants, doesn't she?'

'You're a gardener, son. There are no gardens in Rome.'

The boy's mouth dropped sullenly.

'She wants me, anyway. She sent me down to ask you.'

The two women looked at each other significantly. Nina Sanduzzi said bluntly:

'Then you can go straight back and tell her you're not going. I know who wants you in Rome and it's not the Contessa.'

'But it isn't like that at all! She told me to tell you. The Englishman is staying on here.'

'For how long?' Slow anger began to build behind the classic face. 'A week–ten days, maybe! And then he'll be packing his bags for the big city–and for you, Paolo *mio*. That trick wouldn't fool a baby.' She caught at his arm roughly. 'You're not going and that's flat. I'm your mother and I won't allow it.'

'Then I'll go anyway.'

She lifted her hand and slapped him hard on the face.

'When you're a man and can pay your own fare, and find your own work–then you can talk like that. If the Contessa asks me, I'll tell her to her face. And if there's any nonsense I'll have the doctor get in touch with the police at Gemello Maggiore. That'll keep your Englishman quiet for a while. Now forget about it, like a good boy!'

'I won't forget about it! I won't! She asked me and I want to go. She's the *padrona* and you're nobody! You're just–just a saint's whore!'

Then he wrenched away from her and went running down the street, with his shirt-tails flapping over his rump. Nina Sanduzzi stared after him, her face a marble mask. Martino's wife scuffed the ground with her bare feet and said awkwardly:

'He didn't mean it. He's just a boy. They hear things. . . .'

'His father was a saint,' said Nina Sanduzzi bitterly. 'And his son wants to make himself a *feminella*.'

'He doesn't at all,' said Rosetta, in her high clear voice. 'He's just a baby. He doesn't know what he wants. I'll bring him back and make him say sorry.'

Before her mother could protest, she had started away, running swiftly in her Sunday shoes, and the last they saw of her was a flurry of skirts and a pair of brown legs up-ended over the wall that screened the torrent from the road.

In a sunlit corner of the garden, Nicholas Black was putting the final varnish on the picture of Paolo Sanduzzi crucified on the olive tree. At the sound of Meredith's footfall, he looked up and called ironic greeting.

'Good morning, Meredith. I trust you slept well.'

'Indifferently, I'm afraid. I hope I'm not disturbing you?'

'Not at all. I'm just finishing. Would you like to see it? I think it's my best work so far.'

'Thank you.'

Meredith walked round to the front of the easel and looked at the picture. The painter grinned when he saw the expression on his face.

'Do you like it, Meredith?'

'It's a blasphemy, Mr Black.' The priest's voice was cold.

'That depends on the point of view, of course. To me it's a symbol. I've called it "The Sign of Contradiction". An apt title, don't you think?'

'Very.' Meredith walked a pace or two away from the picture and then said, 'I've come to tell you, Mr Black, that neither the Contessa nor Paolo Sanduzzi will be going to Rome. The Contessa would be pleased if you would leave the villa as soon as possible.'

The painter flushed angrily.

'She might have had the politeness to tell me herself.'

'I offered to do it for her,' Meredith told him quietly. 'She's an unhappy woman who needs a great deal of help.'

'Which the Church is only too ready to give her. She's quite rich, I believe.'

'The Church would like to help you, too, Mr Black—and you are very poor indeed.'

'To hell with your help, Meredith. I want nothing from you. Now do you mind going? I'm busy.'

'I've brought you something that might interest you.'

'What is it—a tract from the Catholic Truth Society?'

'Not quite. They're the personal papers of Giacomo Nerone. Would you care to look at them?'

In spite of himself, the painter was interested. He wiped his hands on a scrap of cloth and, without a word, took the folder from Meredith. He turned back the manila cover and scanned a few pages in silence. Then he closed the folder and asked in an odd, strained voice:

'Why do you show me this?'

Meredith was puzzled by the strangeness of him, but he answered simply:

'They make a very moving document—the spiritual record of a man who had lost the Faith, as you have, and then came back to it. I felt they might help you.'

Nicholas Black stared at him a moment; then his lips drew back in a smile that looked more like a grimace of agony.

'Help me! You have a wonderful sense of humour, Meredith! You know what you've done, don't you? You've had me thrown out of the house. You've robbed me of the last chance to finance an exhibition that might have re-established my reputation as an artist. And you've dirtied the one decent thing I've ever tried to do in my life.'

Meredith gaped at him blankly.

'I don't understand you, Mr Black.'

'Then I'll explain it to you, Monsignor,' said the painter, in the same taut voice. 'Like everyone else in this damned village, you've convinced yourself that my only interest in Paolo Sanduzzi is to seduce him. That's true, isn't it?'

Meredith nodded but did not speak. The painter turned away and stood for a long time looking out across the sun-dappled lawns towards the villa. When he spoke at last, it was with a strange, remote gentleness.

'The irony is, Meredith, that any time in the last fifteen years you might have been right. But not now. I'm fond of this boy—yes. But not in the way you think. I've seen in him everything that's been lacking in my own nature. I wanted to take him and educate him and make him what I could never be—a full man, in body, intellect and spirit. If it meant denying every impulse to passion and every need I have for love and affection, I was prepared to do it. But you'd never believe that, would you?'

Then, without thinking, Meredith made the most brutal remark of his life. He said gravely:

'I might believe you, Mr Black, but you could never do it—not without a singular grace from God. And how could you ask it, not believing?'

Nicholas Black said nothing. He was staring at the picture of Paolo Sanduzzi, nailed to the dark olive tree. After a while he turned to Meredith and said, with bleak politeness:

'Will you please go, Monsignor? There is nothing you can do for me.'

Blaise Meredith walked slowly back to the house, sick with the consciousness of his own failure.

Luncheon was a dismal meal for him. His head buzzed, his hands were clammy and whenever he breathed deeply he could feel a sharp pain in the region of his ribs. His food had no taste, the wine had a sour edge to it. But he was forced to smile and make conversation with the Contessa, who, now that her fear of him was gone, was disposed to be talkative.

Nicholas Black did not appear at all. He sent a message by the manservant excusing himself and asking that a collation be sent to his room. The Contessa was curious to know what had passed between them, and Meredith was forced to fob her off with the courteous fiction that they had exchanged a few bad-tempered words and that Black was ‚probably too embarrassed to join them.

When the meal was over, he went upstairs to rest through the hot hours. The climb up the stairs told him, more plainly than a doctor, how ill he was. Each step was an effort. Perspiration broke out on his face and his body, and the pain in his ribs was like a knife whenever he breathed deeply. He knew enough of medicine to understand that this was what happened to cancer patients. The growth and the haemorrhages weakened them so much that they lapsed into pneumonia, which killed them quickly. But, by all the norms, he was still a long way from this stage. He was still on his feet and he wanted to stay there as long as he could.

When he reached the landing at the top of the stairs, he did not go straight to his own room, but turned down the corridor to the one occupied by Nicholas Black. He could hear the painter moving about inside; but when he knocked there was no reply, and when he tried the handle he found that the door was locked. He knocked again, waited a moment and then went back to his own room.

Alone in his high room, with the sun slanting through the lattices on to the picture of Paolo Sanduzzi, Nicholas Black lapsed quietly into the final blankness of despair. There was no madness in the act, no wild ruin of reason under the impact of unexplainable terrors. It was a simple, final admission that life was a riddle without an answer, a game not worth the candle that guttered over its last, profitless gambits.

Those who won might surrender themselves a little longer to the gambler's illusion; but those who lost, as he had lost, had no recourse but to walk away with as much dignity as possible from the scattered cards and the spilt liquor, and the staling smoke of the last cigars.

He had staked everything on this last play—money, the patronage of the Contessa, the opportunity to re-establish his reputation as an artist, the hope to justify even the maimed and incomplete manhood with which nature had endowed him. But now he knew that he had been playing, as always, against marked cards and with every pack stacked against him. His own nature, society, the law, the Church, all conspired to shut him out from the simplest and most necessary satisfactions of existence. He was stripped clean—bankrupt even of hope. There was no place for him to go but back to the half-world, which had already laughed him out.

The Church would take him back, but it would exact a brutal price:

submission of intellect and will, repentance, and a lifelong bitter denial. The grey inquisitors like Meredith would purge him relentlessly, then coax him forward with the stale carrots of eternity. He could not face it and he would not. No man should be asked to pay for the freaks and whims of a sardonic Creator.

He got up, walked to the writing desk, pulled a sheet of notepaper towards him, scribbled three hasty lines and signed them. Then he picked up a palette knife, walked to the picture on the easel and began coolly and methodically, to cut the canvas to pieces.

Never in his life had Meredith felt so ashamed of himself. Whatever the past sins of Nicholas Black, whatever the follies of his thwarted nature, he had still been the subject of calumny, and he had revealed in himself a deep and not unnoble impulse to good. Kindness might have nurtured it, gentleness might have bent it to better purpose. Yet his only comment, his only offering as a priest, had been a cloddish and brutal indiscretion. There was no excuse for it. To invent one would be a hypocrisy. The charity he thought to have acquired through Giacomo Nerone was a monstrous sham, which had failed him when he needed it most. He was what he had been at the beginning: an empty man, devoid of humanity and godliness.

The thought haunted his shallow sleep and when he woke in the late cool, it was still with him. There was only one thing to do. He must make an apology for his grossness and try again to make a humane contact with Black, who must be suffering greatly.

He got up, washed and tidied himself and walked back along the corridor to the painter's room. The door was ajar this time, but when he knocked there was no answer. He pushed it open and looked in. There was no one there. The bed was unruffled. But the picture of Paolo Sanduzzi stood on its easel by the window, slashed to ribbons.

Meredith stepped into the room and walked over to look at it. As he passed the writing desk his eye was caught by a single sheet of paper lying on the green baize top. The superscription bore his own name:

My dear Meredith,
 I've taken the Almighty's jokes all my life. Yours is one too many. You'll be able to make the old sermon on me—Galilean, thou hast conquered. All the best preachers use it.

Yours,
Nicholas Black

Seconds ticked past unnoticed as he stood there, staring down at the paper in his pale hand. Then the full horror of it burst on him and he hurried from the room, down the stairs, along the gravelled path, shouting for the gatekeeper to open for him. The old man opened the grille, rubbed the sleep out of his eyes and then trotted out into the roadway to watch the crazy Monsignor pounding up the hill with his cassock flapping about his heels.

It was quite late when they were missed and later still when they were found—Nicholas Black swinging aimlessly from a branch of the olive tree and Blaise Meredith prone at the roots of it. At first it seemed they were both dead, but Aldo Meyer heard the faint beating of Meredith's heart and sent for Father Anselmo, while Pietro drove the Contessa's car like a madman to the Bishop's Palace in Valenta.

Now the thing he had feared most of all was come to pass. He was trying to explain himself–not to justify, because he knew that justification was impossible–but just to explain to God how it had happened, and how he had lapsed, without any intention of malice.

But there was no God, there was only a mist and silence and, out of the silence, the echo of his own voice.

'. . . I was sleeping, you see. I didn't know he was gone. I ran to find him and he was already hanging there. I couldn't get him down; I wasn't strong enough. I thought he might be alive and I tried to pray with him. I said the Acts of Contrition and of Love–of Faith and Charity, hoping he would hear and join me in them. But he didn't hear. After that I don't remember. . . .'

'But God would hear and God would remember.'

The voice came to him out of the mist, familiar, but far away.

'I failed him. I wanted to help, but I failed.'

'No one can judge failure but the Almighty.'

'A man must judge himself first.'

'And then commit himself to mercy.'

The mists cleared slowly and the voice came nearer; then he saw bending over him the face of Aurelio, Bishop of Valenta. He stretched out one emaciated hand and the Bishop held it between his own.

'I am dying, My Lord.'

Aurelio, the Bishop, smiled at him, the old, brotherly ironic smile.

'As a man should, my son. With dignity and among friends.'

He looked beyond the Bishop and saw them grouped at the foot of his bed. Anne de Sanctis, Aldo Meyer, Nina Sanduzzi, old Anselmo in his stained cassock with the sacramental stole round his neck. He asked weakly:

'Where is the boy?'

'With Rosetta,' said Nina in dialect. 'They are friends.'

'I'm glad of that,' said Blaise Meredith.

'You shouldn't talk too much,' said Meyer.

'It's my last chance, Doctor.' He rolled his head on the pillow and turned back to the Bishop. 'Nicholas Black . . . you'll give him a Christian burial?'

'Who am I to deny him?' said Aurelio, the Bishop.

'I . . . I wrote a letter to Your Lordship.'

'I have it. Everything will be done.'

'How are the oranges?'

'Ripening well.'

'You should . . . send some to His Eminence. . . . They might help him to understand. A present from me.'

'I'll do that.'

'Will Your Lordship confess me, please? I'm very tired.'

Aurelio, the Bishop, took the grubby stole from the neck of Father Anselmo and laid it on his own shoulders; and when the others had gone from the room, he bent forward to hear the last tally of the last sins of Monsignor Blaise Meredith. When he had absolved him, he called the others back and they knelt around the bed holding lighted tapers while old Anselmo gave him the Viaticum, which is the only food for the longest journey in the world.

When he received it, he lay back with closed eyes and folded hands, while the room filled slowly with the murmur of the old prayers for the departing spirit. A long time after, after they were finished, Meredith opened his eyes and said, quite clearly:

'I was afraid so long. Now, it's so very easy.'

A faint rigor shook him and his head lolled slackly on to the white pillow.

'He's dead,' said Aldo Meyer.

'He is with God,' said Aurelio, the Bishop.

Eugenio Cardinal Marotta sat in his high-backed chair, behind the buhl desk on which his secretary had just laid the day's papers. Beside him was a small box of polished wood, in which were six golden oranges, each nestling in a bed of cotton-wool. In his hands was a letter from His Lordship, the Bishop of Valenta. He was reading it, slowly, for the third time:

> ... I regret to inform Your Eminence that Monsignor Blaise Meredith died yesterday morning at nine o'clock in the full possession of his faculties and after receiving the full rites of our Holy Mother the Church.
>
> I regret him, as I regret few men. I mourn him as the brother he had become to me. He had great courage, a singular honesty of mind and a humanity of whose richness he was never fully aware. I know he will be a great loss to Your Eminence and to the Church.
>
> Before he died, he charged me to apologise to Your Eminence for what he termed the failure of his mission. It was not a failure. His researches have thrown great light on the life and character of the Servant of God, Giacomo Nerone, and have proved him, in the moral if not the canonical sense, a man of great sanctity. I am still doubtful whether any good will be served by advancing this Cause even as far as the Ordinary Court, but I have no doubt at all of the good that has already been done through the influence of Giacomo Nerone and the late Monsignor Meredith. An erring priest has returned to God, a child has been kept from great moral harm and a lost and unhappy woman has been given light enough to seek remedies for her condition.
>
> In the worldly sense, these are small and insignificant things. In the true sense of our Faith they are very great ones, and in them I, who am normally sceptical, have seen clearly the finger of God.
>
> The oranges which I send you are a last gift from Monsignor Meredith. They are from my own plantation—first fruits of a new strain which we have imported from California. Next year, God willing, we hope to have more of these trees to distribute on a co-operative basis to local growers. Monsignor Meredith was much interested in this work; and, had he lived, I think he would have liked to take part in it. His request to send this gift was made on his deathbed. He said—and I quote exactly: 'They might help him to understand.' Your Eminence will no doubt understand the allusion.
>
> The body of Monsignor Meredith is now lying in the Church of the Madonna at the Dolours in Gemello Minore, from whence it will be buried tomorrow, in newly consecrated ground, close to the tomb of Giacomo Nerone. I shall myself officiate at the Mass and the interment.
>
> The usual Masses will, of course, be said, and I myself shall make special, permanent remembrance in my own Masses—as Your Eminence will no doubt wish to do in yours.
>
> I understand that Monsignor Meredith once made a request to be buried in Your Eminence's church in Rome. The reason for his change of heart may be of some final interest. In his last letter to me written on the eve of his death, he says: 'Rome is very far—and here, for the first time, I have found myself as a man and a priest.'
>
> I am humbled by the thought that many of us have lived longer and done much less.
>
> Yours fraternally in Christ Jesus,
> Aurelio+
> Bishop of Valenta

His Eminence laid the letter down on his desk and leaned back in his chair, thinking about it. He was getting old, it seemed. Or perhaps he had lived too long in Rome. He could neither read a letter nor judge a man.

The man who had died was not the man he had sent away—a desiccated pedant with the dust of the libraries thick on his heart.

The Bishop who had written the first request for a Devil's Advocate was not this Aurelio, with his trenchant mind and his more than a hint of irony.

Or perhaps they were the same men, and only he was changed—another victim to the insidious temptations of princes: pride, power, blindness and coldness of heart. Christ had made bishops and a Pope—but never a cardinal. Even the name held more than a hint of illusion—*cardo*, a hinge—as if they were the hinges on which the gates of Heaven were hung. Hinges they might be, but the hinges were useless metal, unless anchored firmly into the living fabric of the Church, whose stones were the poor, the humble, the ignorant, the sinning and the loving, the forgotten of the princes, but never the forgotten of God.

It was a disturbing thought and he promised himself to return to it at the time of his evening examination of conscience. He was a methodical man and now he had other things to attend to. He took out of his pocket a small leather notebook and wrote, under the date for the following day, 'Remembrance in Mass . . . Meredith.'

Then he put the notebook back in his pocket, glanced quickly through his correspondence, and rang to have his car brought round to the entrance. The time was a quarter to eleven. It was the second Friday of the month, the day when the Prefect of the Sacred Congregation of Rites waited on His Holiness the Pope to discuss, among other things, the beatification and canonisation of Servants of God.

The Second Victory
Backlash

THE SECOND VICTORY

For
Paul Buckhill

Any man's death diminishes me, because I am
involved in Mankinde.

JOHN DONNE: *Devotions*

I

They had left the lowlands and were climbing steadily on the narrow road that wound dangerously round the high flank of the mountain. Below them was the steep fall to the river rushing loud and boisterous under the overhang of ice and the bare branches of the alders. Above was the heave of the mountainside with its swathes of black pines, beyond which the snow ran clear to the summit and the blue of the midday sky.

The jeep skidded perilously on the icy surface and Sergeant Willis wrestled it away from the drop. They stopped, got out and jacked up the wheels to put on the chains. While Willis was fitting them, grunting and cursing at the cold, Major Mark Hanlon stepped out in the middle of the road and looked up at the mountain.

Straight ahead of him was a broad gap in the pines. On either side the dark trunks rose like pillars in an ancient nave and their diminishing perspective drew his eyes onward and upward to the sharp line where the sky and the saddle met. Under the trees, the snow was stained brown with fallen needles, but beyond, it was a white dazzle broken only by the grey of rocky outcrops and the organ-pipes of the distant Grauglockner.

Then he saw the skier.

He was right on top of the ridge, a tiny black puppet, with his head in the blue sky and his feet in the white snow. Hanlon took the field-glasses from the case round his neck and trained them on the motionless figure.

A moment later the puppet began to move, slowly at first, thrusting himself forward with his stocks, then gathering speed as he hit the steeper fall. At the first outcrop he checked and made a tight stem turn that brought a whistle of admiration to Hanlon's lips. The glasses showed the wild flurry of snow and the precarious angle of the skier's body. Then he righted himself again and headed downhill in a long, diagonal *schuss*, straight for the opening in the pines. When he reached them, he would be doing seventy miles an hour.

Hanlon's shout of surprise brought Willis racing to his side and together they stood and watched the wild, suicidal plunge down the dazzling hillside. He did not check or turn at the humps, but took them, flying like a skeleton bird, his stocks trailing like wing-tips to balance his landing.

The two men watched him, breathless, waiting for the fall that would send him tumbling and broken down the slope. But he did not fall. He came onward, faster and faster, until they could see the grey of his uniform and the green flashes of the Alpenjäger regiment and the rifle slung between his shoulder-blades and the gleam of his polished pistol-belt.

Hanlon lowered the glasses for a moment and looked at Willis in surprise. The war was over, months now. All Austrian units were reported to be disarmed and disbanded. The Occupying Powers were spreading their authority into all the corners of the land. What was this one doing, armed and in battledress, in wild career down the mountain?

Hanlon raised the glasses again. The skier was nearing the end of his run. He was going like the wind and they saw that he would overshoot the clearing and end up behind the barrier of pines. A moment later they lost him and they stood, staring up through the colonnade of trees, waiting for the crash and the cries. But there was no sound, except the thunder of the river and the faint whisper of the wind in the branches.

It was perhaps thirty seconds before the skier came into view again, sliding easily down the transverse slope behind the grove. He was carrying his two stocks in one hand while the other held his rifle at the trail. At the focal point of the long perspective of trees he stopped, dug his stocks into the ground and stood watching them. A shaft of sunlight fell on his face and they saw the lean sunken jaws darkened by stubble and the red weal of a freshly healed scar running from eye to chin down his right cheek.

Hanlon raised his hand and shouted in German:

'*Grüss Gott!* Come down here a minute! We'd like to talk to you.'

Before the words were out of his mouth he saw the rifle thrown up—as a trapshooter throws it—fast, sighting and swinging in the same movement. He yelled and threw himself against Willis to drive him off balance, but before they hit the ground the shot rang out, and as Hanlon rolled spinning towards the shelter of the jeep he saw more bullets chipping up the ice by his face and heard the wild echoes thundering round the valley.

He wrenched his pistol out of its holster and eased himself cautiously back in the shelter of the body-work. The echoes were still shouting from hill to hill, but the clearing was deserted and Sergeant Willis lay on the road with a bullet in his head. When Hanlon bent over him he saw that he was dead and that the blood was frozen already on his cheek and on the ice beneath him.

After a while he stood up, finished putting on the chains, let down the jack and hoisted Willis's body into the jeep. Then he climbed into the driver's seat, started the engine and drove, very slowly, up the mountain road towards Bad Quellenberg.

Bad Quellenberg—so the legend says—was founded by a holy hermit named St Julian, who lived in the mountains with the deer and the bears and the eagles and the golden pheasants for company. He was a gentle man, it seems, a kind of Gothic St Francis, whose life was a protest against the violence of his times. When a stag was torn by a wolf, Julian struck the rock and a stream of warm, healing water gushed out, a perennial medicine for man and beast.

The legend suffers a little from the historians. There were men here in the Bronze Age. The Romans traded salt over the mountain roads from Salzburg and mined gold in the high passes of Naasfeld. The Goths were here and the Vandals and the Avars, and all of them, for health or comfort or cleanliness, bathed in the warm waters from which the town takes its name—Mountain of Springs.

Martin Luther came here too, but there is no record that he bathed. He seems to have spent most of his time hiding in log farmhouses high up on the slopes where the chamois came to graze in the bitter winter weather.

An enterprising peasant built an inn and a post-house at the neck of the pass, where travellers from Carinthia might change their horses and eat venison steaks and pinch the bottoms of the peasant girls before crossing into the troubled land of Salzburg, where Wolf Dietrich sat in his stone fortress with a crozier in one hand and a naked sword in the other.

Later, much later, a church was built and a monastery school, and a straggling town began to line itself down the banks of the torrent that gushed out of the mountain and went tumbling through the widening gorge into the lowlands. The inn became a hotel and canny Viennese and Salzburgers moved in to build guest-houses and shops and terraced gardens and bath-huts fed from the hot mineral springs in the heart of the mountain.

The buildings spread themselves in a huge terraced amphitheatre round the throat of the valley, dwarfed by the peaks of the Grauglockner and the Gamsberg.

Later still they drove a tunnel through the mountain to make a railway link with Klagenfurt and Villach and Trieste and Belgrade and Athens. With the railway came Baedeker and Thomas Cook, so that soon Bad Quellenberg blossomed like a gentian patch under the golden rain of tourism.

They came in the summer to take the waters, to sit on the terrace for *Kaffeeklatsch,* to walk under the pines on the promenades, to flirt in the evening while the orchestras played Strauss waltzes and the peasant troupes came in to dance the *Schuhplattler* and play the zither for local colour. They came in the winter for the ski-ing and, in between, for the shooting, so that the hoteliers grew fat and the peasants rich and the woodcutters were hard put to it to feed enough pine-logs into the mills to keep pace with the building.

High up in the mountains they built a power station to light the town and electrify the railway. When Austria was annexed to become a part of Greater Germany, the Party pundits came here for holidays and the youth groups marched singing through the valleys and Reichsmarschall Göring arrived, resplendent as a peacock, to sun himself and take the baths.

Then came the war, with England first and later with Russia, and the youth of Quellenberg were enlisted into Alpenjäger regiments and sent off to the Eastern front. As the years went on, the little forest of headboards grew and grew in the churchyard of St Julian. The hotels were turned into *Lazaretts* for the wounded and the shops closed one by one because there was nothing to sell and nobody with money to buy.

The trains ran erratically because Villach was bombed and Klagenfurt and the junctions at Salzburg and Schwarzach. When they did run the compartments were full of haggard, bitter men pulled back from the Udine and from Greece. The trucks were loaded with battered vehicles and guns that were useless because there was no fuel to run them and no ammunition left for the breeches.

Finally, there came a day when they heard on the radio that Germany had surrendered. The Quellenbergers gathered in the streets and the wounded sat up in their beds in the big hotels and on the lips of each one was the same frightened question: What now?

No one was in a hurry to answer them because Bad Quellenberg was a small place, a bath town, a cure resort, of no military or economic importance. So they waited, stunned and fearful, for a month, two months, until a company of troops arrived from Occupation Headquarters at Klagenfurt. The captain was a tow-headed youth with a wispy moustache and cold eyes. He presented himself and his orders to the Bürgermeister.

The Sonnblick Hotel, largest in Quellenberg, would be evacuated immediately and prepared as a headquarters for the Commander, Occupation Forces, Quellenberg Area. The commander himself would arrive in forty-eight hours. The Bürgermeister would see to it that all preparations were complete by that time.

The last maids were being hustled out of the corridors, the first guard was being mounted outside the entrance, as Major Mark Hanlon drove up the mountain pass with a dead man at his side.

Bürgermeister Max Holzinger stood at the big picture-window of his lounge and looked down over the pine-tops to the snow-bound valley.

It was a prospect that had rarely failed to please him: the broad meadow-reaches with the river winding like a black snake between the stripped alders, the log barns crouching under their snowy roofs, the thin lines of the fences, the peasant village huddled round the spire of the old church, the pines marching like spearmen along the mountainsides, the high saddles rising for ramparts against the world outside, the defiles with their treacherous mists and down-draughts. No gunfire had startled the eagles nesting on the crags. Men had died, to be sure, in Russia, in Rumania, in Hungary, in Crete. His own son had died with them. But their dying had been a distant thing. Its tragedy had been dwarfed by the towering majesty of the mountains.

The Party leaders had come here to relax and play. The wounded had been sent here to recover—and forget if they could. Right to the end, Reichsminister Göbbels had controlled the press and the radio, so that the pogroms and torture chambers and concentration camps became musty legends, and the tally of death, defeats and ruined cities reached them only as travellers' tales, fearful but far away.

Life in the valley had followed the old, old pattern. Winter passed and the meadows were green again and the sleek cattle grazed halfway to the peaks. The peasants came still to the market with milk and meat and eggs. The convalescents walked in the dappled sunlight of the promenades, and made love to the hungry girls in the grass. The sound of the axes rang cheerily enough from the timber-slides, beating out the time for the melody of the running waters. At summer's end there was the mowing, when the women in bright dirndls tossed the grass into sheaves and hung it on the drying poles, fragrant as apples. And when the first chill returned to the hills the cattle were brought down, garlanded with the last flowers, the best milker crowned with a head-dress of blooms and tinkling her bells in triumph.

Bells! They too were part of the life of the valley—part of its peace: cow-bells clapping dull yet musical from the high meadows, sleigh-bells in winter, the Angelus floating out from the church-tower, morning, noon and evening, small silver bells when Father Albertus carried out the body of Christ for the blessing of the crops, the ominous slow tolling of the passing knell, more and more frequent as the end of the war drew near.

The mountains caught at their chimes and shuttled them back and forth, weaving a pattern of sound which was like the pattern of the old faith, familiar, repetitive, threatening and cajoling by turns, often ignored but never quite forgotten.

There had been a time when orders had come from the Party to silence the bells and send them as a gift to the gunsmiths, but he had set his face against it as he had set his face against so many other demands, and in the end he had won. It was a small victory when you laid it against the great compromise to which he and others had committed themselves. But he was glad that he had won it, because the bells had helped to maintain, almost to the end, the small illusion of peace in the valley.

Now there were no illusions left. The ramparts had been breached, the conquerors were coming in. A blond boy with a handful of troops sat in the hotel where Reichsmarschall Göring had lodged and a nameless man with an ominous title was driving up the road to become the new ruler in the mountains.

Bürgermeister Max Holzinger wondered how he should greet him and how he would be answered. One thing he knew with certainty: he must preserve his dignity, because dignity is the last possession of the conquered.

He had been conquered before and he understood how important it was.

In the first war he had fought in a Carinthian cavalry regiment and he still walked stiffly from the bullet that had smashed his knee. He knew what it meant when a man could talk only of the battles he had lost and of the inglorious survivals of defeat. *Vae victis!* It is only the victors who are absolved by history.

Better than any, he knew that this time would be worse than the last. The ghosts were rising now in accusation. The living were crawling out of the cellars and the concentration camps. The judges were assembling already, lean and pitiless. Men like himself who had closed their eyes hopefully and too long were to be joined as accessories in the indictment. They had eaten the fruits of conquest, now they must be crammed with the dust of defeat.

He stared out across the white valley and wished the day were over.

He was a man of middle height, black-haired in spite of his fifty years, with a lean, intelligent, Magyar face inherited from his mother, who was a Harsanyi from Buda before she married Gerhardt Holzinger from St Veit on the Glan. He himself had married a girl from Hamburg, tall, blonde, deep-bosomed, and the son she had given him had died in the first descent on Crete. She had given him a daughter too, dark, slim and vital. They had named her Irmtraud, because Valkyries were in fashion then, but the name matched oddly with her restless gipsy beauty. She was twenty-six years old, ripe to be married, but all the men she might have wed were dead or prisoners, or wandering lost and leaderless about the country.

He turned back from the window and saw them both sitting in their chairs, watching him.

His wife was working placidly over a piece of embroidery, but her hands were unsteady and her troubled eyes flickered back and forth from the work to himself. Her hair was greying now, and her waist thickening, but she was still strong-boned and firm-bodied, for all the years and the griefs. A vague regretful desire stirred in him as he remembered their youth together and wondered about their future.

Irmtraud sat sprawled in a deep armchair smoking a cigarette. She was dressed in a ski-costume that emphasised her long, slim legs and her flat belly, and the thrust of her youthful breasts. Her full mouth quirked into a malicious smile and the expression in her dark eyes was half hostile, half amused.

Holzinger wondered how one explained these things to the young—defeat, despair, betrayal and disillusion!

He faced them squarely, straddling a little to ease the weight of his stiff leg. He spoke quietly, piecing out the phrases with care, as if afraid they might mistake his meaning.

'I think you should both understand our situation.'

'I'm sure we do, Max.' His wife's deep, placid voice reassured him.

He shook his head.

'I'm afraid it's worse than you think, Liesl.'

'How much worse?' His daughter sat up suddenly and her voice was sharp with curiosity.

'As a Party member I shall most certainly lose my job. Our money and property are liable to confiscation.'

'*Du lieber Gott!*' Liesl's lips trembled and she bent quickly over the embroidery to hide her tears.

'But they can't do that!' Traudl's voice was firm but angry.

'They can do anytning they wish, child,' he told her soberly. 'We should thank God we have the British and not the Russians. They have a respect for law and for the rights of the subject. More than we, I think. However . . .' he shifted uneasily, 'I've tried to take precautions. I had Kunzli draw a deed of gift making you, Liesl, the owner of this house. It is pre-dated to 1938. I have hoped that it may survive an investigation–unless Kunzli decides to blackmail me, as he well may do. The rest I'm afraid we'll have to let go if they claim it.'

'What's going to happen to us then?' She put the question coolly, as if it were a simple household matter.

'We'll survive, my dear.' He smiled at her with thin irony. 'Whatever happens, we shan't starve. I can still get a job sweeping the snow outside the hotels or spreading gravel on the promenades. We'll pocket our pride and . . .'

Sharp and sudden the telephone rang and Holzinger hurried to the table and lifted the receiver. The women watched him, wide-eyed and tense.

'This is Holzinger. . . . Yes?'

They saw his face blench as the voice crackled through the receiver and they strained forward to catch the words, but could not hear them.

'When? . . . Where? . . . God in Heaven! Yes, yes, I'll come immediately. . . . *Auf Wiedersehn.*'

He put down the receiver and turned to face them. His face was grey and little beads of perspiration broke out in his temples. His wife started out of her chair towards him but he thrust her back with a gesture.

'What is it, Max? What's happened?'

'The worst, Liesl, the very worst.' He passed a weary hand over his forehead. 'The Occupation Commander has arrived. On the way up his driver was shot dead by a skier in Austrian uniform. I am ordered to wait on him immediately.'

Without another word he turned on his heel and walked from the room. The two women followed him with wide, frightened eyes. When the door closed they looked at each other and Liesl Holzinger buried her face in her hands and wept. Her daughter came and knelt in front of her, stroking her hair and soothing her with little gentle words out of a forgotten childhood.

After a while she stopped weeping and raised her head. The girl wiped the tears from her face with a lace handkerchief; then her mother reached out and gripped her shoulders with urgent hands. Her voice was low and bitter and her eyes were strange:

'Twice in my life I have seen this happen, Traudl. Twice the men of this country and mine have made wars and lost them. They took our husbands and our brothers and our sons and left them to die on the beaches and on the steppes. Those who were left came limping home, like your father, to lie with us again and breed again—new sons for a new sacrifice. They built us homes, only to destroy them again. We planted gardens, to find them trampled by new armies. Now we're too old to breed and too tired, I think. to build any more.'

'No, *Mutti*!'

She disengaged herself from the urgent hands and stepped back.

'Yes!' Liesl was passionate and insistent. 'Yes! They make the messes and they expect us to clean them up. They make the ruins and expect us to patch them up. But they give us no voice in the decisions. It is a man's world, so long as there are victories. But in defeat it is a woman's, because the best of the men are dead.

'The lips you might have kissed are cold. The arms that might have held you are buried under the snow. The bodies that might have warmed you are eaten by the wolves. Only the maimed are left, and the old, to give you children you will never love—because there will be no passion in their begetting. The strong ones are gone, who might have treated with the conquerors. The good ones are lost, who might have established a new faith with them. There is only you and the millions of women like you. . . . Do I frighten you, Traudl?'

'No.' The girl's full lips curved into an ironic smile. 'You don't frighten me. All men want the same thing. It's up to the woman to get the best price she can. I'll do as well as most.'

Liesl Hozinger stared at her in momentary surprise. Then she too smiled and nodded slowly.

'I'm glad. That makes it easier for you—for all of us.' With an odd, shy, sensual gesture, she reached out and let her hands rest for a moment on the thrusting breasts of the girl, then slide down slowly over the flat belly and the slim, boyish flanks. 'In the end, it is the women who win, because they have the strongest weapon of all. The conquerors come like kings and end like children, naked in your arms, with their lips against your breast. They are young and they are lonely and they are afraid because they are strangers far from home. The life they bring you is robbed from their own women, and that is your revenge on them for all you have lost, on the folly of your own men who followed the trumpets while you were crying in a cold bed, all alone. Can you understand that?'

Wide-eyed, wondering at the unfamiliar eloquence of her mother, vaguely stirred by the touch of her hands, the girl nodded slowly.

'Yes, I understand. But . . . but . . .'

'But what, child?'

'How do you know all this? How do you feel it?'

The ghost of a smile lightened the drawn face of Liesl Holzinger. Her eyes seemed to look beyond her daughter, beyond the valley and ridges, backward to a distant time, a distant country. She drew her girl close to her, pillowing the dark head on her breast.

Then, simply and flatly, she gave her the answer.

When Holzinger walked up the steps to the entrance of the Sonnblick Hotel, two guards stepped forward and barred his way with crossed bayonets. They were muffled to the ears in greatcoats and gloves and balaclavas, but their faces were pinched with cold and their eyes were blank. Even when he had identified himself in terse but halting English, they kept him standing in the wind while one of them went to fetch the sergeant of the guard.

The sergeant put him through a leisurely interrogation and finally admitted him. As they walked across the foyer to the lift, he saw Franz Mayer, the manager, and old Wilhelm, the porter, peering at him from behind the potted palms. He nodded a greeting, and saw them pop back into shelter like rabbits. He smiled bleakly at their retreating backs.

Helmut, the little lift-boy, gave him a shy '*Grüss Gott*', and Holzinger rumpled his hair affectionately as they rode upwards to the fifth floor, where the suites, he remembered wryly, had always been reserved for visiting dignitaries.

In spite of the fuel shortage, the central heating was turned up full and the big stone urns were full of hot-house flowers. Mayer was a good hotelier. He understood the refinements of service.

The sergeant led him briskly along the carpeted corridor and stopped outside the suite which Reichsmarschall Göring had occupied not twelve months before. He pressed the buzzer and a muffled voice said 'Come in!' The sergeant opened the door and stood aside to let him enter. Then he closed the door, snapped to attention and announced the visitor.

'This is the Mayor, sir. He says he has an appointment with you.'

'Thanks, Jennings. You may go.'

'Very good, sir.'

Another salute, the door opening and closing again, and Bürgermeister Max Holzinger stood in the presence of the Occupying Power.

He was seated at a big buhl desk, his back to the window, so that the shadows deepened the network of lines about his brown eyes, and the creases at the corners of his wide, quirky mouth. He had a high forehead and strong nose and there were small flecks of grey in his unruly hair. In spite of the grey hair and the lines, Holzinger put him at no more than thirty.

He wore fresh battledress and a starched shirt and his face had been newly shaven. The major's crowns on his shoulders were brightly polished and his long expressive hands were relaxed on the manila folder in front of him.

At his side stood the tow-headed captain who had come in with the advance party. Holzinger clicked his heels and bowed stiffly and waited for the opening gambit.

'My name is Hanlon, Occupation Commander for this area. You, I understand, are Bürgermeister Max Holzinger. Please sit down.'

The voice was crisp and authoritative. The German flowed out, easy and pure, with a Viennese lilt to it. Holzinger was surprised, but he kept his face studiously blank and sat down. He put his gloves and his hat on the corner of the desk and waited. Hanlon opened the manila folder and spread the pages in front of him. He asked formally:

'You understand the terms of the Armistice and the status of the Occupying Forces?'

'I have not yet been informed of them.'

'Very well. First, Austria is occupied by units of four Allied Armies: British, French, American and Russian. Bad Quellenberg is in the British Occupation Zone.'

'Fortunately for us,' murmured Holzinger dryly.

Hanlon ignored the comment and went on in the same detached tone.

'Occupation forces, their billeting, messing, transport and general maintenance, are a charge on the Austrian Government, through local authorities. The representative of the Occupying Power has the right to requisition such property or supplies as he may deem fit or necessary from time to time. He may recruit local labour and fix equitable wages. Local administrations and local police units are required to co-operate with him in the maintenance of order and in investigation or pursuit of suspected war criminals. Am I making all this clear?'

'Perfectly. You speak excellent German '

'Thank you.' Hanlon did not smile. His eyes were cool and his tone impersonal. 'The representative of the Occupying Power will, on his part, do everything possible to restore and maintain order, to assist in the reconstruction of local industries and in the repatriation and re-employment of discharged troops, other than suspected war criminals–subject to such directives as may be received from time to time from the General Officer Commanding Occupation Area. . . .' He closed the folder and leaned forward across the desk, his brown eyes searching the impassive face of the Bürgermeister. 'I'll send you a copy of the documents. There's a couple of hours' solid reading in 'em. But they all boil down to this: it's a two-way deal. The Allies are sympathetic to Austria. Play ball with us and you'll benefit. Obstruct us and you'll land in bother.'

'There's something you've forgotten, Major.' Holzinger spoke quietly but distinctly, mindful of his own dignity and of the respect due to the new masters in the land.

'What's that?'

'I am told that former members of the Party are ineligible for public office and are to be dismissed forthwith and replaced by non-Nazi personnel. I've been a member of the Party for a long time. I think I should hand you my resignation.'

A wintry smile twitched up the corners of Hanlon's mouth and a twinkle showed in his brown eyes. He said blandly:

'The local commander has a temporary discretion in these matters. I propose to exercise it and ask you to continue in office for the time being.'

'And if I should decline?'

'You would be doing yourself and your people a disservice.'

'In that case, you leave me no alternative but to accept.'

'I was sure you'd understand that,' said Mark Hanlon softly. 'Now . . .' He closed the manila folder and sat back in his chair. His eyes were grim again and his mouth was tight as a trap. There was anger in his voice and cold bitterness. 'We begin our association with a murder. . . .'

Holzinger nodded gravely.

'I've been told about it. I–I ask you to believe me when I say that I am ashamed and deeply sorry.'

'I believe you,' said Hanlon curtly. 'I take it I can count on your full co-operation in hunting down this man and bringing him to justice.'

'You may count on it, yes. If you will give me a full description of the man, the exact location of the crime, I'll speak immediately with the police and arrange searches of the town, the hamlets and the mountain farms.'

'Good!' Hanlon nodded briskly and hurried on. 'Captain Johnson here will supply you with a full description, which I have just dictated to him. The road point is clearly marked on the map which he will also give you. I've already telephoned the police from here and asked for an immediate search of the area. There has been no snow. The ski-tracks will be clearly marked. The man is a Quellenberger, so it shouldn't be too difficult to smoke him out. His face is badly scarred. He'll be quite conspicuous.'

'How do you know he's a Quellenberger?' Holzinger looked up in sharp surprise.

'I saw his flashes. They tally with those of the Quellenberg regiment, which according to the order of battle was almost totally destroyed in the Ukraine. He's an excellent skier and he took that run as if he'd known it since childhood. He belongs here—no doubt of it.'

'You're a very efficient officer,' said Max Holzinger with sour admiration.

'I'm glad you understand it. I hope you'll make your police understand it too. I'll want reports twice daily, with full map references. If necessary local huntsmen and woodcutters are to be recruited to assist in the search. I want this man found and I'll give you forty-eight hours.'

'I'll do my best.'

'You yourself will report to me each morning at 0930 hours for discussion of town business and the planning of reconstruction operations.'

'Anything else?'

'Yes. I want the parish priest to call on me at his convenience this afternoon.'

'The—the priest?' Try as he might to subdue his curiosity, he could not avoid the question. Hanlon nodded.

'Yes. Sergeant Willis was a Catholic. We have no chaplain. I should like to arrange for his burial according to the rites of the Church . . . and another thing . . .' He broke off and seemed to hesitate over the next order. Holzinger prompted him gently:

'I'm at your service, Major.'

'We need a coffin,' said Hanlon with cold deliberation. 'We need it delivered to the hotel by 2000 hours this evening. We need coffin-bearers, six of them, who will be the principal citizens of Quellenberg. All shops and businesses will be closed tomorrow and all citizens will be required to line the streets from this hotel to the church. The procession will leave the hotel at 0900 hours and the coffin will be carried to the church for the Requiem Mass. After which the burial will take place in the churchyard of St Julian. You will see that a gravedigger is in readiness for the final ceremonies. That is all for the present.'

Every word was a slap in the face and the dismissal was a final contempt. Holzinger stood up and faced the Occupying Power. Try as he might, he could not control the tremor of his voice:

'We shall be there, Major, as you ask. We should have been there anyway without asking. You're new here. You can't be expected to understand that a soldier's funeral is an occasion for us. Most of our boys died a long way away and we don't know where they are buried—or whether they were buried at all. We—we have a sympathy for soldiers—all of them, poor devils—and we like to think they will lie in friendly earth and under the sound of the bells. We'll be there, Major. All of us!'

He bowed and turned away, and Mark Hanlon watched him limping, stiff and straight-backed, to the door. Then he slammed his fist on the table and swore bitterly:

'God damn him! God damn and blast them all!'

The blond captain watched him with faint amusement. He was twenty-three years old—too young for hate, and not yet ripe for pity or for tears.

2

Karl Adalbert Fischer was Chief of Police in Baa Quellenberg. He was a stubby man, with a small head that sat incongruously on his round barrel-body. He had short legs and a long neck and bright, unwinking eyes like a bird's. When he walked the streets in his long cloak and his square peaked cap he looked like an amiable duck.

He was a good-humoured fellow with a taste for schnapps and bouncing peasant girls. He ran his command with a genial inefficiency that had endeared him to the Quellenbergers and kept him comfortably in office for fifteen years. He had survived a dozen purges under the Greater German administration and he had counted on his shrewdness and experience to keep him safe until his retirement. Now he wasn't so sure.

When Max Holzinger came into his office he was warming his bottom against the stove, drinking schnapps and munching a butter-cake. He waved a vague hand and murmured:

'*Grüss Gott*, Herr Bürgermeister. Pour yourself a drink. Come and warm yourself.'

Holzinger tossed his hat on the littered table and peeled off his gloves. He poured a glass of the white fiery liquor and tossed it off at a gulp. The little policeman watched him with canny, appraising eyes. He grinned and said:

'You're upset, my friend. I take it you've met the Englishman?'

'I've met him,' said Holzinger curtly. 'He told me he'd been in touch with you.'

'Oh yes! He's been in touch.' He chuckled and choked on his liquor. 'I thought it was a joke at first. He talks like a Viennese.'

'It's no joke. He means business.'

'I know. I assured him of our full co-operation and our earnest desire to assist him.'

Holzinger looked up sharply.

'Don't underrate him, Karl. He's shrewd and efficient. He knows what he wants and he'll stop at nothing to get it. This—this killing is a bad start for us.'

'Very bad.' Fischer put down his glass and wiped his mouth with the back of his hand. 'I've sent my boys up to look at the tracks. I hope they get there before dark.'

'Before dark?' Holzinger stared at him, puzzled. 'It's barely midday. The place is not ten miles out.'

'The car is old,' said Fischer thoughtfully. 'The tyres are worn. The steering-rod is defective. The roads are icy. If there were an accident the boys would have to walk—and the Occupying Power would have to supply us with a new car. We could use one! Besides,' he tilted his comical head and sniffed the air, 'it should snow this afternoon. If it comes early enough, there'll be no tracks left.'

'No!' Holzinger gaped at him, half angry, half amused. 'This is serious,

Karl. We can't play games.'

'I'm not playing,' said Karl Adalbert Fischer.

'What then? This is murder. We're responsible–both of us–to the Occupation Commander.'

Fischer took a cigarette out of a leather case and tapped it reflectively on his thumb-nail. His eyes were blank and hooded. He said soberly: 'There have been a lot of murders in the past ten years, Max. In a way we've been responsible for those too. I don't see why one poor, crazy devil should be hanged for all of them.'

'He killed a Britisher.'

'Until two months ago he was paid to do just that–and would have been shot himself if he hadn't. Maybe he didn't know the war was over. . . .'

'The court would accept that as . . .'

'What court!' The little head jerked up, wagging angrily on its long neck. 'The drum-head! Where the judges sit with the stink of the concentration camps and the smell of the crematorium in their nostrils and lump us all together as torturers and sadists. I don't blame them for that either. But I'm not going to hand them this boy's head on a dish. Look. . . .' He turned away to the farther wall, on which still hung a map of the battle areas of Europe, stuck with little coloured flags. The flags were drooping and the map was stained with flung wine and coffee-slops from the last despairing party before the Armistice.

It was typical of Fischer that he hadn't thought of tearing it down. Now he stood beside it, tracing the lines with his blunt finger, while the Bürgermeister watched him with growing wonderment.

'I'll show you where he came from and what happened to him on the way. He started here in the Ukraine at Mukachevo, which was the regimental hospital for our Quellenberg boys. He was a doctor, you see, young, not very experienced. But then none of our boys were old, were they? He soon got all the experience he wanted, what with amputations, belly-wounds, frost-bite and typhus, and all the other damn things that came when the Russkis started to roll us back all along the line. When the regiment was cut off he kept working night and day, with no drugs, no anaesthetics, until he dropped on his face in a dead man's blood. That probably saved his life, because when the Cossacks broke through, they went through the *Lazarett* with bayonets, shouting and singing. That's how he got the scar on his face. Had he been awake, he'd have got it in the guts. When he woke, he was lying with the dead and even when he screamed there was no one to hear him because the Cossacks were a long way forward now and the snow was falling and the wind driving it across the steppes. His face was hanging open, but the cold had stopped the bleeding and he rummaged through the wreckage to find a hand mirror and sutures so that he could sew it up. Then he went through the pockets of the dead to find food scraps and cigarettes. He stripped the woollen clothes off those who had them and padded himself with bloody underclothing. Then he picked up a rifle and a bayonet and a dead man's pistol and set out to fight his way home. You know how long it took him?' Fischer's hand stabbed accusingly at his friend. 'Twelve months! Twice he was taken, and twice he escaped. He walked from Mukachevo to Budapest, which is halfway across Hungary. The Russkis were round the city in a week, so he turned back east and came to Salonta in Rumania. Then he went south into Yugoslavia and headed north again towards Carinthia. He killed three men. He hunted like an animal for his food. He slept with prostitutes and seduced peasant girls so that they would feed him and hide him. In Yugoslavia the Chetniks took him and tortured him, so that he would never be good to a woman again. Then they laughed in his face and turned him out to die. By some miracle he survived. His wounds healed but his face was scarred into a Krampus mask. And, like all hunted, hungry men, he became a little mad. He saw enemies behind every tree. All his dreams were full of monsters . . . they still are, though he has been home a month. He wakes in the night screaming. The house seems like a prison to him and sometimes he goes out, with his gun and his pistol, ranging the mountains. They've tried to disarm him but he snarls like a cornered wolf. Lately they thought he was getting better. The nightmares didn't come so often. The wanderings were not so frequent. . . . Then, this happens. . . .'

'You talk . . .' said Holzinger, slowly, 'as if you know him well.'

'I do,' said Karl Adalbert Fischer, 'he's my sister's son.'

'God in Heaven!'

'You—you see now why I can't let them have him?'

'I see it, yes. But I don't see how you can hold him safely. The Occupation may last for years.'

The comical head nodded grimly.

'I'll hold him. I'll shift him from valley to valley, from farm to farm, and I'll have the English scouring every mountain but the right one. I'll keep him for ten years if I have to—and Hanlon will never come within a shot of him.'

'You'll never keep a secret like that, Karl. People talk—our people more than most. Hanlon will come to hear of it, then you'll be the one he'll take.'

The face of the little policeman relaxed again into a good-humoured smile. He poured himself another schnapps and savoured it slowly. Then he crossed to a steel cabinet in the corner of the room, unlocked it and took out a large folio bound in leather. When he spread it on the table, Holzinger saw that every page was covered with small Gothic script.

'What's that?'

'This?' said Fischer with a grin. 'This is why a no-good fellow like me has held a job like this for fifteen years—and never a black mark against him. My office records are six months behind, but this has been written up every evening for all that time.'

'What is it?' Holzinger looked puzzled.

'Dossiers, Herr Bürgermeister! My personal record on every man, woman and child in Quellenberg and the valley. Fact, gossip, suspicion, guesswork. Things I've heard in bed. Whispers I've picked up at funerals. All there. All mine. Most of it I've never used. But it's there when I want it.'

'Have you got me there too?' Holzinger laughed uneasily.

Fischer nodded. 'You and your wife and your daughter—and your son, God rest him. You're in good company. You have the page next to Father Albertus.'

'Have you got Kunzli too?'

'Kunzli!' He spat contemptuously into the waste-paper-basket. 'I've got a long chapter on that one. Why do you ask?'

'I might want you to use it one day,' said Holzinger softly.

Fischer made an emphatic gesture of refusal.

'Not even for you, Herr Bürgermeister. There's a lifetime of work in that book. I've never used it for blackmail, and I hope I never shall. But I intend to make a profit out of it—one way or another.'

'You're making a profit out of it now, Karl.'

'I am?' He cocked his head like a restless bird, ready to fly off at the slightest stir of danger.

'Yes. You see, I've forgotten all about your sister's son. So far as I know he died in Russland.'

'Good!' The word came out on a long breath of satisfaction as Fischer bent over the table to pour two glasses of schnapps. 'I was sure you'd understand, Max ... And if you have any trouble with Kunzli, let me know.'

'I'll do that,' said Max Holzinger calmly. '*Prost!*'

'*Prost!*'

They raised their glasses and drank, standing in front of the fly-blown map where the wine was like spilt blood and the little flags drooped in drunken defeat.

'We deserve it,' thought Holzinger bitterly. 'We deserve everything that happens to us—the rulers we get, the sons we lose, the woman who betrays us. We've lost the war. The yoke is on our necks again—and we're still conspiring one against the other. God damn our miserable souls.'

He drained his glass, picked up his hat and gloves and walked out to discuss funeral arrangements with Father Albertus.

The door of the Pfarrhaus was opened by an apple-cheeked widow with an acid tongue. The Father wasn't there, she told him. He was down in the churchyard, shovelling snow like any labourer. Before he could check her she was launched into a clatter of dialect mourning the follies of the clergy and the burdens they laid on her own broad shoulders:

'He'll kill himself, that's what! And him old enough to know better. If he goes down with pneumonia, who has to nurse him? Me! He's hard enough to handle when he's well—God knows. Eats enough for a sparrow, waters his wine till it tastes like dish-slops, sleeps maybe two hours a night. I wouldn't mind that if he'd let me sleep too. I'm two floors down but I hear him pacing up and down, muttering and praying. Sometimes he beats himself so that his shirts are bloody. Then it's me that has to wash them. You've only got to look at him to ...'

'All right! All right! It's none of my business.' Holzinger's patience was fraying thin. He had troubles enough of his own without peasant gossip on the ascetic oddities of an old priest. He turned away brusquely and the housekeeper shut the door with a bang and went back to her kitchen, mumbling unhappily about officials who got too big for their boots and whose womenfolk were no better than they should be anyway.

The Quellenbergers had never approved of the deep-voiced blonde from Hamburg and the escapades of the daughter had made meaty gossip round the farmhouse stoves.

Holzinger thrust his hands into his pockets, twitched his fur collar up round his ears, and walked with head thrust forward and eyes downcast to the solid ice of the roadway. Idling townsfolk raised their hats and '*Grüssed*' him, but he neither saw nor heard them, and they turned away troubled, because normally he was a polite man who never failed to acknowledge a salute.

When he came to the high wall that hid the churchyard of St Julian from the roadway, a tiny blonde girl stepped out and held up a bunch of snow roses, begging in her piping voice:

'*Schneerosen*, Herr Bürgermeister! For the poor?'

Her sudden presence startled him, but there was so much innocence in her small, glowing face that he forced a smile and fumbled in his pocket for change to give her.

She curtsied and thanked him prettily, then thrust the roses into his hand and went skipping off towards the valley. Holzinger looked at the tiny white blooms with their waxy leaves, and wondered what the devil to do with them.

As he walked into the churchyard he saw the old wooden crucifix rearing itself among the forest of headboards. Acting on a sudden impulse he laid the flowers at the feet of the Christus, crossed himself awkwardly and turned away, feeling faintly guilty, like a boy caught at the jam-jar.

Then he saw Father Albertus.

He was chipping the ice away from the grey stone steps of the entrance and shovelling it into a heap behind one of the buttresses. With his mane of white hair and his stooped shoulders, his threadbare cloak and his heavy boots, he looked like any aged peasant from the hills. But when he straightened at the sound of the footfall and turned to greet Holzinger, he was another man entirely.

The first thing one noticed was the extraordinary transparency of his face. It was as though a lamp burned behind it—a fire slowly consuming the flesh, so that there were only the fine aquiline bones and the old, translucent skin stretched over them.

Then one saw his eyes, cornflower-blue, limpid as a child's, lit with an eager tenderness as a child's are lit when it has a secret to share with someone beloved. The mouth was firm but quirked upwards into a smile that belied the lines of suffering cut deep into the cheeks. The voice that issued from it was deep as a bell.

It was only afterwards that you remembered his hands.

They were gnarled and crooked like the talons of a hawk, the joints enlarged and anchylotic, so that the only movement left was in the thumbs and the forefingers.

Early, after the Anschluss, when he had been Rector of the Jesuit Novitiate at Graz, he had been taken to Mauthausen, for a course of 'corrective treatment'. One of his gaolers was a former pupil who had conceived the gentle revenge of breaking one of his fingers each week, and tormenting him with the thought that in the end the consecrated fingers would go too, so that he would never again be able to say Mass.

Father Albertus was a man who believed in prayer—and in Mauthausen there was nothing left to do but pray. Before six weeks were out, the Cardinal in Vienna had had him released and prudently offered him, through his superiors, the choice of expulsion from Austria or a parish appointment in the mountains.

So now he was in the churchyard of St Julian, leaning on his shovel like a peasant and listening to Holzinger's querulous report of his interview with Mark Hanlon. He heard him out in silence, then his eyes clouded with gentle regret and he said slowly:

'You must understand, Max, it's hard for any of us to behave well in a situation like this.'

That was another characteristic of the old man. He never said the expected thing. He never wasted words on courteous preludes. He had no time now for anything but the truth.

'Harder for us than for him,' said Holzinger sourly.

'No. Power is like the king's new clothes: an illusion that leaves a man naked to the laughter and the swords.'

'You'll go to see him?'

'Yes.'

'Try to explain to him that while I can direct the people to come to the funeral, I can't guarantee a full attendance. I can't force my colleagues to act as pall-bearers.'

'Forget your vanity, Herr Bürgermeister.' There was a gentle irony in the old man's smile. 'Forget that this is an order from the Occupying Power. Make it a personal request from yourself, a suggestion that courtesy and charity are involved. Our people understand these things—most of the time.'

'It gives Hanlon an easy victory.'

'Hanlon . . .?' He seized on the name suddenly. 'That's not an English name, is it?'

'I don't know. I'm not so familiar with the language. Why?'

Father Albertus shrugged.

'A passing thought. A tag of memory. It doesn't matter.'

'By the way,' Holzinger glanced around the churchyard, at the old headstones in the family plots, at the small forest of pine-slabs that were the memorials of the unburied regiment, 'where do we bury this man?'

'Over there.' Father Albertus pointed to the big crucifix standing among the headboards. 'At the feet of the Christus.'

'In the middle of our boys?' Holzinger was alarmed. 'The people won't like that.'

'We are all one family in the womb and in the tomb,' the old man admonished him gravely. 'We are all brothers in Christ. The sooner the people understand that, the sooner they will come to peace.'

Holzinger looked down at the gnarled and broken hands of the priest and knew that he could not gainsay him.

Major Mark Hanlon sat in his big lounge at the top of the Sonnblick Hotel and discussed the future with Captain Johnson. A white-coated waiter had just taken away the remains of their lunch and they sat sprawled in the big armchairs, drinking coffee and sipping a strong, sweet Austrian liqueur. The meal and the wine had relaxed them, the first strangeness of the place had worn off and they were beginning to be at ease with each other.

Johnson took out his cigarette-case, offered it to Hanlon, then lit up for both of them. They smoked a few moments in silence, watching the blue spirals drift drowsily upward to the coffered ceiling. Johnson grinned boyishly and murmured:

'This is the life, Mark; I can take lots of it.'

'You'll get it, Johnny,' said Hanlon with cool good-humour. 'We're going to be here a long time. Are the boys settled in?'

'Yes. I've bedded them on the first and second floors, N.C.O.s on the ground level. They'll eat in the main dining-room and use the *Stüberl* as a canteen. The N.C.C.s can use the cocktail bar. The ball-room we'll turn into a theatre, the lounge and writing-room will do as they are. I thought you'd be happy with what we've got up here—there's room enough for a regiment.'

Hanlon nodded reflectively and drew on his cigarette.

'They'll start getting bored in a week. We'll need some entertainment. See if Mayer can rake up some musicians for us. I'll write to Klagenfurt and ask 'em for a projector and a regular supply of films. You can probably find a ski-instructor for those who want to learn. We'd better close the bars at eleven. Lights out at midnight. All troops to be back in quarters by then.'

'What about the non-fraternisation order?'

'It can't work, Johnny. They'll have to cancel it sooner or later. Probably sooner. Meantime . . .'

He broke off and stared up at the gold traceries of the ceiling. Johnson prompted him curiously.

'Meantime?'

'We don't want a bunch of pregnant servants in the hotel. So we'll make our own rules. All bars and *Stüberls* in the town are out of bounds to troops. If they want to take the girls walking or ski-ing, that's fine. If they're entertained in private houses, that's fine too. But no public fraternisation and no women on the premises here, unless we organise an official entertainment—which won't be for a while yet.'

'Aren't you sticking your neck out, Mark? Don't misunderstand me,' he amended hastily. 'I think you're right. But what will Headquarters have to say about it?'

'I don't propose to tell 'em,' said Hanlon bluntly. 'I'm leaving it to you and the N.C.O.s to talk sense into the troops and see they don't abuse the privilege—or the girls. If there's trouble I'll use the chopper, without mercy.'

'Fair enough.' Johnson nodded agreement. 'I'll ride 'em on a tight bit for a week or two, then gradually relax. I think it's better that way.'

'It's up to you, Johnny. I've got my hands full already.'

His eyes clouded and his mouth set into a grim line. Johnson looked at him with vague uneasiness.

'Something on your mind, Mark?'

Abruptly Hanlon heaved himself out of the chair and walked to the window, where he stood watching the grey clouds roll in from the defile and over the white shoulders of the Grauglockner. He said absently:

'It'll be snowing soon.'

'That doesn't answer the question.'

'It does, you know.' Hanlon swung round to face him. 'All tracks will be blotted out in twenty minutes. The police will come back and say they couldn't find any trace of the man who killed Willis.'

'You expected that, didn't you?'

'I expected it. I don't have to be happy about it.'

'He's dead,' said Johnson with the unconscious cruelty of youth. 'You can't bring him back. He was killed after the whistle blew—which turns an act of war into a crime. You've set the machinery in motion to catch the criminal. I don't see why you have to tear your tripes out. It's part of the job. We bury Willis decently and forget him—because we can't remember him any more than the millions of others who've died in the past few years. Here, have another drink.'

He slid the bottle and the glass along the polished table towards Hanlon. It surprised him a little when Hanlon stepped back from the window, picked them up and poured himself a double measure. He cocked a sardonic eye at his junior, raised the glass and gave the toast.

'To the New Order! *Prost!*'

'There's no new order,' said Johnson cheerily, 'because men are always the same and girls are always different. But that's no reason to waste the liquor. *Prost!*'

Then the telephone rang, and when Halon picked it up the sergeant of the guard told him that Father Albertus was waiting to see him.

'Keep him three minutes, then bring him up.'

'Yessir.'

He put down the receiver and turned briskly to Johnson.

'Visitor, Johnny! The vicar's calling. Let's clean up the mess and make ourselves look respectable.'

'Don't the customers ever see through it?' Johnson was full of food and wine, and he was feeling a little larger than life. Hanlon shot him a quick glance and answered sourly.

'If they do, it's our own damn fault! Jump to it, Johnny! Empty the ashtrays and get that liquor out of sight.'

They bustled about the room like a pair of housemaids, and when Father Albertus was ushered in a few minutes later Hanlon was sitting behind the buhl desk and Johnson was standing beside him, the proper symbols of the Occupying Power.

The sergeant stood aside and the old priest walked slowly across the wide carpet till he stood in front of the desk. He held out his hand and said: '*Grüss Gott*, Major!'

Johnson jumped at the sound of his deep bell-toned voice. Hanlon stared at him, wide-eyed and gaping, as if he were a ghost. He made no move to touch the outstretched hand, but raised himself slowly from the chair, his eyes fixed on the spare, luminous face and the white silken hair that framed it. His voice was a whisper of wonderment.

'God Almighty! No!'

Johnson and the sergeant stared at him, and he turned to them with an imperative gesture.

'Leave us please. Both of you!'

They hesitated a moment, then saluted smartly and walked from the room. Only when the door had closed on them, did he take the old man's hand. When he felt the stiff, broken fingers he looked down at them in shocked surprise, then back again at the smiling eyes.

'The name meant nothing when I heard it, Father. I still can't believe it's you!'

'Brother Mark! The restless lion. I remembered the name when Holzinger told me. You've changed, my son.'

'You too, Father. Won't you sit down?'

He came out from behind his desk and brought up a chair for the old man. He offered a cigarette and a drink, but Father Albertus refused them both. Hanlon pulled up another chair and sat facing him, as if ashamed to occupy the seats of the mighty in the presence of the worn old scholar.

'God leads us on strange roads, my son.' The mild eyes were studying every line of his face. 'I come to bend the knee to Caesar and I find my old novice sitting under the eagles.'

'I was more comfortable in your lecture-room,' said Hanlon dryly.

The old priest smiled and shook his head.

'You were restless then, too. The habit of religion sat uneasily on your shoulders.' He glanced up at the shining crowns on the epaulettes. 'Does this one chafe you less?'

'It suits me better, Father. I was never made for a monk.'

'I often wondered. You were unhappy when you left us. Are you happy now?'

'I'm older.' Hanlon skirted the answer carefully. 'I'm not unhappy now.' He looked down at the twisted hands clamped like talons on the arms of the chair. 'Tell me about yourself, Father. What happened to your hands?'

'Mauthausen,' said Father Albertus briefly. 'An unhappy man who thought that by tormenting me he could ease the torment of his own conscience. He had been a student of mine, before I was made Novice-Master. I must have failed him very badly. This, I feel, is a kind of penance for it.'

'It's a madhouse!' Hanlon's voice was soft and surprisingly bitter. 'What's happened to these people that they can do things like this—slow torture, sudden murder? In the old days, when I was at Graz with you, they weren't like that. They were gentle, *gemütlich*, full of *Schmalz* as a suet-pudding. What's happened?'

'Nothing,' said Father Albertus gravely. 'Nothing but the flowering of the evil that was already in our hearts. Nothing that could not happen to you also, my son.'

'I don't understand you.' Hanlon's head jerked up resentfully.

'I think you do. You lived among us a long time. You loved us enough to learn the language like our own children. Unless I'm mistaken, that's why you came back—because you wanted to see us again, help us perhaps. Is that true?'

'Truer than you know. It took me six months to prepare the ground for this appointment, Father. After all the bloody mess of the war, it seemed a chance to build instead of destroy.' He smiled and spread his hands in ironic deprecation. 'You taught me better than you know, Father Novice-Master. You took the taste out of a lot of kisses and the savour out of the best wine. You left me with this itch to mend the world—but never taught me the art of living in it comfortably. That, I had to learn myself. But . . . you're right enough. I wanted to come back. I did want to help. I did love these people.'

'Until one of them murdered your friend.'

'That's right.'

'One is not all.'

'But all of them will hide the one, won't they?'

'Don't blame them too much for that. They've lost nearly all their young men. There will be many girls in the valley who will never have a husband. Can you chide them for wanting to save even this maimed one?'

'They won't save him this way. Don't they understand? There's the law . . .'

'The law has been a mockery in Europe for a long time, Mark. You should understand that.'

'There's a new law now.'

The old man smiled with gentle irony and shook his head.

'The law of the conqueror. That is suspect from the beginning.'

'I know that as well as you do. But don't you see they've got to give it a trial? Otherwise there's no hope of a new start. You, of all people, should have respect for the law, Father.'

'I do, my son, but I've never believed the hangman was its best interpreter.'

'For God's sake! I'm no hangman.' Hanlon's voice was harsh with anger.

'I'm here to see justice is done. And I remember enough of my life in Austria to temper it with mercy.'

'You can't guarantee either justice or mercy,' said Father Albertus bluntly. 'You're a man subject to authority–like the centurion. You may arrest this fellow. You may arraign him. But you can neither plead his cause or change the code by which he will be judged.'

'Spare me the dialectics, Father!' Hanlon exploded impatiently. 'It's a practical problem. A murder has been committed. If the people don't co-operate in bringing the murderer to trial they'll be joined as accessories in the act. They'll find themselves in opposition to the only authority which can help them back to a normal life. There'll be no peace for them until this man is found.'

'And this love you bring, Mark? Where does that show itself?'

'We dispense with it,' said Hanlon flatly. 'Because a one-sided love is barren and bitter. We administer justice. We rule according to the statute books. It's probably wiser in the long run.'

'Are you sure that you can dispense with it?'

'I'm sure of it, Father. I have to be.'

The old priest stood up and gathered his cloak about him. His eyes were sombre now and the fire seemed to have died a little behind his drawn face. He said quietly:

'The Bürgermeister told me what you wanted. I've made arrangements for the requiem and the funeral. I wondered, perhaps, if you'd care to serve my Mass. It–it would be like old times.'

Some of the coldness melted out of the eyes of Mark Hanlon as he looked at his white-haired mentor and saw how old and tired and frail he was. He hesitated a moment, then he told him, kindly enough:

'Better not, Father. I haven't been to the Sacraments for a long time. And, besides, there's a political aspect as well. There are Lutherans as well as Catholics in Bad Quellenberg. The Occupying Power cannot afford to identify itself too closely with either. I'll be at the Mass and the funeral. That's the best I can do.'

The old priest looked at him steadily for a long moment, then he drew himself up and said in his deep, firm voice:

'You asked me what made this a madhouse, my son. You yourself have given me the answer. Too much politics and too little love.'

He did not offer his hand this time but bowed stiffly and turned to go.

'*Servus*, Major.'

'*Auf Wiedersehn*, Father,' said Mark Hanlon coolly.

3

At the highest point on the scenic promenade which encircled Bad Quellenberg, a house had been built. An acre of pines had been cleared and milled for timber, the clearing had been levelled behind a retaining wall of mountain rock, and on the broad, artificial plateau the building had been reared, three storeys of stone and timber, whose windows stared out across the town and the fall of the valley.

A fringe of pines screened it from the road and a grilled gate with an electric lock kept it private from casual visitors. Behind the pines there was a wide expanse of lawn, which in spring-time blazed with flowers and blossoming bushes. There was a paved terrace which took the sun, summer and winter, and the mountains screened it from the winds that came searching down the defiles.

The place was called, conventionally enough, Valhalla; but the locals had another name for it—*das Spinnenhaus*, the Spider-house. A brass plate on the gate-post named its owner: Doctor Sepp Kunzli, Solicitor.

No one, at first sight, looked less like a spider than this trim, dapper advocate. His sleek dark hair and his olive skin recalled the Romans who had garrisoned the Danube centuries ago. The disciplined grace of his movements made him look younger than his forty-five years.

It was his eyes that gave him away. They were dark and dead like an insect's. They saw at all angles, from a multitude of facets. But there was no light in them—no faintest hint of the thoughts that went on behind them. They were a spider's eyes, calculating, predatory, pitiless.

The truth about Sepp Kunzli was simple but startling: he had been dead for a long time.

Most men die slowly, under the small, daily crucifixions of living. They submit, gratefully enough, to the last drugged decline into old age and forgetfulness. Some, the fortunate, achieve a fuller flowering of the spirit, as their physical life is pruned away.

Sepp Kunzli had died, suddenly and despairingly, one bright summer's day; and the man who walked thereafter, in his shoes, was a cold spectre with a first-class brain—and a splinter of ice where his heart should have been.

In the mid-'thirties he had been a rising young lawyer in Vienna. He had stepped straight from university into his father's practice, an old family firm, with connections in Bavaria and Hungary and Switzerland and all the provinces of Austria. Land was changing hands quickly, long-headed folk were liquidating their holdings and building up foreign funds, so that more and more clients came to the sober, baroque office near the Ringstrasse.

He met and married a young Jewess, daughter of one of the minor merchant bankers, who brought him a handsome dowry. They had no children, but they had been singularly happy, in the last spring-time before the Anschluss.

A week after the first German units had rolled into Vienna, Sepp Kunzli came home to find his wife with her head in the gas oven and a pathetic little note clasped in her hand:

'I have loved you too much to be a burden to you now. Forgive me.'

Another man might have shot himself or run crazy, or embarked on a despairing campaign of hate and vengeance. Kunzli did none of these things. He buried his wife quietly, sold his house, settled into bachelor lodgings in another quarter and went about his business with a cold concentration that shocked his family and alienated his friends.

He closed the accounts of old clients and began to build new ones—senior Party officials, members of the new administration, investors from Germany.

He bought property and sold it for them. He advised them on their investments at home and found loopholes for their dealings abroad. He became the confidant of their marriage secrets and the negotiator of their diplomatic divorces. When they pressed him to join the Party he pointed out that he could serve them better by remaining out of it. But he made substantial donations to its funds and travelled freely abroad on a special endorsed passport.

Finally, he broke with his father's firm and took all his clients with him. He left Vienna and came to Bad Quellenberg–and his clients came too, after he had showed them the advantages of representation so near to the borders of Italy, Yugoslavia and Switzerland, so far from the muddy intrigues of the capital.

What he did not tell them was that this was the final step out of a world he hated, the first move in a cool campaign to exploit the men who had killed his wife and quenched the last spark of love in himself.

He found no joy in it. He was incapable of joy. All that was left was the icy passion of the chess-player, toppling the pawns from the board, moving relentlessly forward to the final, savourless checkmate.

When he traded for his clients in Switzerland, he charged them exorbitant commissions. When Berlin issued new regulations against foreign trading, he opened cover accounts for them in his own name, using their securities to bolster his private trading, invoking the influence of senior officals to preserve his own immunity. The timid he blackmailed, subtly. The bold he encouraged to excesses that put them further and further in his debt. He was always ready to guarantee a mortgage or pick up a promissory note. A spendthrift wife could always count on him for a loan–and he was never too anxious to collect it.

When the big men came to Bad Quellenberg he entertained them lavishly. When they were recalled to duty he seduced their wives and their daughters and their mistresses with a calculated passion that left them gasping at first–and afterwards strangely afraid.

In Bad Quellenberg itself he played the same game, easily and with discretion. He held liens on the best building land, notes against the biggest hotels. The contractors were in his pocket and the councillors followed the policies he drew for them.

The web that was spun in the Spider-house spread more widely and intricately as the years went on and its threads were anchored in the most unlikely places. There was a man in Zürich named John Winter to whom he had sought an introduction through a close-mouthed Swiss banker. Whenever he came to Switzerland they met by appointment in the banker's private office and Kunzli passed on to him information that ranged from troop movements on the Tauern line, to the latest indiscretions of a Reichsminister's wife. He always refused payments for this information, presenting himself as a patriot who had the interests of his country at heart. The closest scrutiny in London had failed to find any flaws in the information or any suggestion of double-dealing by the donor. Kunzli was written down as a safe agent, a man to be remembered in later days.

It was the biggest of his gambles, but without it there could be no triumph. There was no point in ruining an enemy if you too were involved in his downfall. Now the gamble seemed to have paid off. The Allies had won the war. The men who had killed his wife were coming, each in his turn, to their proper end. Out of their fear and greed he had made a fortune. At last the flies were struggling in the web and the spider could sit and smile and eat them at his leisure. . . .

So, on this winter afternoon, while the first snow-fall settled on the hills and on the black pines, he sat in his study and pondered his diplomatic approaches to the Occupying Power.

He smiled bleakly when he thought of Holzinger called in like a messenger, and Fischer trounced into activity, and even the Church hauled up for discipline.

Mayer had telephoned him from the Sonnblick with a series of commentaries on their comings and goings. A useful man, Mayer, admirably placed for inside tips on the market. Mayer had been his personal appointee and had covered his salary ten times over with bedroom gossip and indiscretions from the conference room.

The new commander was something of an enigma. He talked perfect German. He acted like a man who knew his own mind. He would need to be approached carefully. Co-operation, on equal terms: that should be the keynote. The occasion would present itself soon enough.

The murder was already the talk of the town. Holzinger and Fischer were in a neat dilemma. If they caught the boy the whole population would be at their throats. If they didn't, they fell foul of the new authority. It would be interesting to know whether the English wanted him caught or whether they would prefer to forget the business after a decent interval. They were a subtle people, with a great respect for law and a singular talent for interpreting it to suit themselves.

He wondered if the killer had been named yet, and whether he came from the hills or from the town. These things were important too. If he belonged to one of the old families, the peasants would hide him for years, fending off all investigations with a blank, animal stubbornness. If he were from the town, one of the immigrant stock from Salzburg or Vienna or Graz, they might be happier to let him go to save themselves trouble. The tribal instinct was still strong in the upland valleys.

One thing was certain. Whatever happened, Sepp Kunzli would make a profit. Both sides would need a mediator. Both would pay, in their own coin, for his skilled services.

He was still chewing on this sweet thought, when the door opened and his niece came into the room.

She was dressed, mountain-fashion, in ski-trousers and walking boots and a long greatcoat with a fur collar. Her blonde hair was braided and wound into a coronet, and her green Tyrolean hat was tipped at a jaunty angle over a face bright as a porcelain doll's.

She crossed the room quickly and kissed her uncle lightly on the forehead. He made no response to the gesture but asked her calmly:

'Are you going out?'

'Yes. To the hospital first. There's an hour's therapy with the amputees.'

'How are they getting along?'

He had no interest in the answer, but he asked the question with that cool impersonal courtesy which seemed necessary to maintain a comfortable relationship.

'Some of them are doing very well. Young Dietrich starts with his sticks today. And Heinzi Reitlinger can light a cigarette with his artificial hand. I'm quite proud of them.'

'I'm glad.'

'I–I was wondering. Uncle . . .' She faltered and broke off.

'What were you wondering, Anna?'

'Whether you'd mind if I invited a few of them to the house one evening. The ambulance would bring them and . . .'

'I'm sorry, my dear. I've spent a good deal of money to provide recreation facilities in the town. I see no reason why my privacy should be invaded.'

'Just as you say, Uncle.' If she was disappointed, she gave no sign of it. Her voice was as calm as his own, but warm still and friendly. 'By the way, I shan't be back to tea.'

'Why not?'

'Father Albertus telephoned. He's asked for choir practice this evening. The English soldier is to be buried tomorrow. We're to sing the requiem.'

For the first time a flicker of interest showed in Kunzli's dark, dead eyes. He said, with mild sarcasm: 'We don't have requiems sung for our own boys. I wonder why.'

'Perhaps because there are too many of them.'

He looked up sharply, but there was nothing in her face but that frank, bewildering innocence which she had brought with her into his house and against which all his ironies blunted themselves. At first it had annoyed him. He thought it the kind of careful insolence which children use on people they dislike. He had tried to goad her out of it, until one day she faced him, a leggy, gangling schoolgirl, and said quite gently: 'You mustn't be cruel to me, Uncle; you will only hurt yourself more and make me unhappy. Then we couldn't live together, could we?'

It was then he had made his first surrender to an innocence he didn't believe in. He made it again now. He shrugged and said: 'Don't be late for dinner.'

'I won't; *Auf Wiedersehn*, Uncle.'

'*Wiedersehn*, Anna.'

She brushed her hand lightly across his hair and was gone. Sepp Kunzli wondered, for the thousandth time, what folly had made him admit her into his life.

She was his brother's child, but after his departure from Vienna he had neither seen nor heard of her until one day she turned up on his doorstep, scared and red-eyed, accompanied by a brawny peasant woman from the Burgenland.

The Burgenländerin came with a poor opinion of Sepp and a determination to see justice done to her chick.

In her thick, raw dialect she told him that Anna's father was dead–shot down over England–and that the mother was coughing her heart out in a Vienna sanatorium and likely to die in weeks. The old people were dead and Sepp was the last surviving relative. Was he going to do his duty or wasn't he? How in the name of the seven saints could he live in this big barn of a place while his own kin were left lonely? It didn't matter to her, she'd take the child happily and bring her up in the Burgenland. Come to that, she'd probably be better off with a good God-fearing family. But she had rights didn't she? And if the *seine Mann* didn't want to look after her, he should be ashamed of himself.

Ten minutes of this and Sepp Kunzli was beaten. He took the girl–an awkward fifteen-year-old–into the house and consigned her to the care of his housekeeper and tried to forget her. Both the housekeeper and Anna herself seemed happy to help him do it. When her mother died it was the housekeeper who soothed her out of her grief, while Kunzli took himself off to Switzerland, oblivious of a lonely teenager moping through the big house.

It was the housekeeper who bought her clothes and encouraged her to meet other girls and had Father Albertus introduce her into the choir and the Church Guilds and the Hospital Auxiliary.

One day, with a shock of surprise, Kunzli realised that he had a woman in the house, a young and beautiful woman, with a curious, tolerant affection for him and a critical eye for his calculated follies. He couldn't ignore her any more—nor did he want any longer to dispense with her. She was as familiar as an article of furniture, and as comforting.

When she suggested, quite simply, that he should make her a small allowance to save repeated demands for clothing and feminine necessaries, he agreed without question and doubled what she asked. He was even prepared to commend her common sense. She bought him small, useless gifts for his birthday and for the feasts; and he was forced to return the courtesy. He had never once kissed her, nor taken her in his arms, but she showed no resentment at his lack of love. His barbed humour left her untouched. If she disapproved of his seductions, she said nothing, and she was impervious to the strugging gallantries of his male guests. In a world gone mad she seemed to carry with her the spring-time sanity of Eden. But Sepp Kunzli's Eden was so long lost, he lacked the wit to recognise it.

The girl was there. She would probably stay there until some man asked her to marry him—and the sooner one did, the better. Meanwhile she was an uncomfortable reminder that little girls grow up and rich men grow old, and that revenge and money are the dustiest triumphs of all.

The sudden shrilling of the desk phone cut across his reverie. He lifted the receiver and heard an unfamiliar Viennese voice:

'Doktor Kunzli?'

'This is Kunzli. Yes?'

'This is Mark Hanlon, Occupation Commander.'

Kunzli was instantly cordial.

'My dear Major Hanlon! Nice of you to ring. I was waiting until you'd settled in before coming to pay respects. I knew you would have much to do and . . .'

'I've had word about you from Klagenfurt,' Hanlon cut in crisply. 'I'd like to see you as soon as possible.'

'Certainly, Major. Perhaps you would care to dine with me tonight; I could send a car . . .'

'I'm sorry. That's not possible. I'd like to see you in my office about five this afternoon. Can you manage that?'

'Well . . . it's somewhat short notice, but . . .'

'Thank you, Doktor. I'll expect you. *Auf Wiedersehn.*'

'*Auf Wiedersehn*, Major,' said Sepp Kunzli, but the line was already dead. He replaced the receiver slowly on its cradle and sat back in his chair, cupping his chin on his hand and staring out at the noiseless, tumbling snowflakes and the grey mist gathering in the valley.

As the first day of his command wore itself out, Hanlon lapsed deeper and deeper into a black temper. The visit of Father Albertus had revived memories he preferred to leave buried, and had raised issues, personal and public, which promised new problems in his already complex task. The attitude of the local authority was already defining itself as one of passive resistance and Captain Johnson was showing himself an amiable cynic apt enough for militiary command but too young to lend either moral support or useful counsel to his senior officer.

Quicker than he had dreamed, Mark Hanlon was coming to the conclusion that sentimental journeys were always a mistake, and that old loves, like old kisses, should be left to fade gracefully in the memory chest. Love was a shared thing. It demanded an equality, a confession of mutual need. When there was one who kissed and another who turned the cheek, love died of quick starvation. He had found that in his private life. It was being thrust upon him now in his public one. If he wanted to lie comfortably in his bed, he must sleep alone, with bayonets at the door and the sword of office always at his hand. And if there came those who talked the language of love and offered a little more than the cold coin of tribute, he must mistrust them. If he made commerce with them it must be the commerce of the bawdy house—money paid for value received. And a pox on the careless who picked the wrong bedfellow!

Which explains why Karl Adalbert Fischer got a poor welcome and the rough edge of the Major's tongue when he came to make his first report. Hanlon kept him standing, like a junior, in front of the desk and questioned him with cool precision.

'The car is wrecked you say?'

'That's right, Major. The roads are icy, as you know. The tyres were worn and the steering has always been slightly defective. A tyre burst and the car skidded off the road and down the embankment. It was lucky my men were not killed.'

'Odd that this should have happened only five miles from town.'

Fischer shrugged and spread his hands helplessly.

'Who can say where an accident will happen? My men's behaviour was quite exemplary. One of them came back to report to me. The other two went forward on foot to the scene of the crime. By the time they got there, the snow was falling heavily. All tracks had been obliterated. Questions at the nearest farmhouses revealed nothing.'

'Very convenient.'

'If the Major insinuates . . .' Fischer flushed and wagged his head in comical indignation.

'Save it!' Hanlon cut him off curtly. 'How do you propose to function without a car?

'We can't.'

'Then use your private vehicle. Pay yourself petrol and maintenance, and I'll give you one of my men to drive it. He speaks German and will be able to assist you in your investigations.'

Fischer gulped and stammered uneasily. 'We—we will welcome any assistance you can give us.'

'I'm sure you will. You'll be sending out ski-parties daily to question the outlying farmers. I have four good skiers among my troops. I'll appoint one to each party.'

'Ski-parties!' Fischer's eyes widened in surprise. 'Does the Major know how many men I have? Six! I still have to maintain order in the town—and you ask me to search the mountains and the valleys with ski-parties!'

'There are four Alpine guides and at least ten foresters who are out of work in the winter. Use them to make up your parties. They'll report here each morning for their orders. I'd hate to think that advance information was circulated in the search areas.'

'Major, I did not come here to be insulted! I must ask you to . . .'

Hanlon went on with the same unhurried irony: 'You will have in the town records a nominal roll of the members of the Quellenberg Regiment. You will also have a casualty list showing those dead and missing, and those already repatriated. We take out the dead—who are the majority—and we have a first list of families who may know something about the soldier with the scar. Does that make sense to you, Fischer?'

'No!' said the little policeman, with sudden anger. 'I cannot work with a man who mistrusts me.'

Hanlon leaned back in his chair and looked at him with sardonic amusement.

'You're mistaken, my friend, I do trust you—to hold up this search in every way possible! I'm not sure that I blame you either. In your place I'd probably do the same. I hope to convince you you'll be making a mistake.' He straightened again and opened the folder that lay in front of him. His tone was deceptively mild. 'It's in my competence to dismiss you, Fischer; the grounds are: Party associations, incompetence, or unwillingness to co-operate. I could even trump up a case to have you detained for investigation by the War Crimes people. Your salary would stop. You'd lose all pension rights. Your name would be circulated on a black-list to other Occupation areas. You'd find it very hard to get another job even as a snow-sweeper.'

'Why do you want to keep me, then?'

'I'm a practical fellow.' Hanlon smiled at him blandly. 'I think a town functions better under its normal administrators. This place has a fairly clean record. If it were kept clean, everyone would profit. There'd be a better chance of getting food and coal rations and penicillin for the hospital. There'd be a good case to put up to Klagenfurt for turning it into a rest area for Occupation troops—which would bring revenue into the town and make a beginning for the old tourist trade. We could make a show-piece of it, Fischer, a model for the rest of Austria—if we could co-operate.'

'You mean, if I hand you an Austrian soldier for hanging.'

'Put it that way if you like.'

'How else should I put it, Major?'

'There are two ways,' said Hanlon deliberately. 'You can call it a recognition of common law, a recognition that murder is crime and deserves punishment to protect the community. You can't change that principle because the victim happens to wear a British uniform. If you don't like the taste of that, try this one.' He quoted in the old German of the Bible—'It is expedient that one man should die for the people.'

'Too many men have died already "for the people",' said Fischer with surprising bitterness. 'The people! The nation! Greater Germany! Millions died for them. And you demand yet another victim.'

'I don't want victims,' said Hanlon quietly. 'I'm trying to point out that you can't live in two worlds. If you want to live by law you've got to accept the codes. If you want to live in the jungle you can do that too, at a price. It's up to you.'

'Have you ever killed a man, Major?'

The question took him by surprise. He stared at the little policeman, who stood, stiff and impassive, clothed with a new, curious dignity. He hesitated a moment, then gave him the answer.

'Yes. I've killed several in five years of war.'

'Then why do you talk like God Almighty on Judgment Day?'

Hanlon crashed his fist on the desk so that the inkstand jumped and the papers fluttered wildly to the floor.

'Because I've got to! Because somebody's got to play God and bring order in this bloody chaos!'

'Give us a chance and we'd do it ourselves.'

A slow smile dawned on the bird-like face of the little policeman. The Major was human after all. There was a fund of anger in him and angry men were apt to indiscretion. It surprised him therefore when Hanlon returned his smile and tossed the argument back to him.

'I'm sure you could organise yourselves, Fischer, but I can't put my head on the block for your mistakes. So either we work together, or you go under guard to Klagenfurt on tonight's train. Which is it?'

'I'll co-operate,' said Karl Adalbert Fischer. His long neck drooped, his shoulders sagged and he stood with downcast eyes like a man who has just thrown away the last shreds of honour. In reality he was bubbling with satisfaction. The Englishman was scared, the job was too big for him. He would accept a compromise, even if he wasn't prepared to admit it. Hanlon's next blunt words shattered the brief illusion.

'Good! Now tell me—what's the man's name? And where does he live?'

The comical head snapped back and his mouth gaped open. 'I—I don't understand you.'

'I think you do. You wouldn't have risked your job for someone you didn't know. Let's have it, Fischer. What's his name?'

'You're mistaken, Major,' said Fischer with stiff dignity. 'I don't know the man. If I did you'd have had him by now.'

'I'll accept your word for it,' said Hanlon genially. 'But I'll charge you as an accessory if I find you're lying. Now let's get down to business.'

For the next thirty minutes he rehearsed the policeman in the strategic details of a man-hunt in the mountains. By the time he had finished, Fischer was sweating under his collar and wondering whether his nephew's neck or his own was more in danger.

Then Hanlon dismissed him and telephoned the Spider-house to summon Sepp Kunzli.

He came, like a man of substance, in his own car, driven by a uniformed chauffeur. His entrance to Headquarters was managed with some care. The chauffeur got out and parleyed with the guard, so that when the Herr Doktor descended he was not kept waiting in the cold like the others but ushered in with ceremony and taken immediately upstairs.

The lounging soldiers looked curiously at his dapper figure, the sober black hat, the coat with the high astrakhan collar, the pigskin gloves, the elegant cane. Mayer and the porter bowed ceremoniously as he passed, but he gave them no more than a cursory nod.

To the surprise of Johnson and the sergeant, Hanlon stood to greet him, shook hands, seated him comfortably and offered cigarettes.

Kunzli accepted the courtesies with grace and a warm inward content. His first fears were groundless, it seemed. The peremptory telephone call meant no more than the brusqueness of a busy man. Hanlon had charm and intelligence. It shouldn't be too difficult to establish an understanding.

The opening gambit was encouraging. Hanlon opened his folder and took out a letter which he unfolded and laid on the desk in front of him. He said cordially:

'Klagenfurt have sent me a letter, Herr Doktor. It came from Zürich via London.'

'I'd be interested to hear the contents.'

'It's quite short. It says: "Doktor Sepp Kunzli of Bad Quellenberg has been known to us as a reliable agent since 1943. We recommend that you extend to him the immunities usual in such cases and we suggest that his services may be of some value to your local commander.' It's signed John Winter, Lieutenant-Colonel, British Military Attaché, Geneva, Switzerland.'

'I'm flattered. Also I am grateful. The English are men of their word.'

'We like to remember our friends,' said Hanlon casually. 'We need some help at this moment. I'd like to know whether you're interested in co-operating.'

'Naturally, Herr Major. Anything in my power. These are difficult times–for all of us.'

The lips smiled, but the slate-grey eyes were void of expression. The hands were slack and expressionless on the arm-rests of the chair.

'Good. Tell me, Herr Doktor–how would you assess the strength and political importance of the Nazi Party in Bad Quellenberg?'

'Numerically strong, but of no importance whatsoever, then or now.' The answer came out readily and with conviction. 'Important people came here, important issues were discussed here, but the local membership was made up of petty functionaries, gauleiters, policemen, school-teachers whose promotion depended on a good Party record. For the rest...' Kunzli shrugged expressively, 'you know what these mountain people are–irredentist, isolationist, intolerant of foreigners and officials alike. The Party never penetrated below the surface of their lives.'

Hanlon nodded appreciatively. The answer was concise and intelligent. It squared with the information at his disposal, with his own younger experience.

'Was there any sort of persecution of Jews or opposition elements?'

Kunzli shook his head. 'None that would come within the scope of your inquiry, Major. There were no crimes of violence. There were no midnight arrests. This province is predominantly Catholic and the Party handled it with more than usual discretion. There was discrimination. There was an exodus of Jews in the early days. But the violence and the terror were no more than a legend in the valley.'

'For a man with a tragic history, you're being very fair, Herr Doktor.'

Kunzli shrugged and made a small rueful mouth. 'New lies will not bring back the dead. New persecutions will not wipe out the memory of the old. These people here–what are they? A small country folk wrapped up in themselves and their tiny problems. We can afford to be generous with them, Major.'

The 'we' was carefully placed, neatly timed. It suggested identity of interest without presuming to state it. The English had a taste and a talent for subtleties like that. Hanlon smiled absently and passed on to the next question.

'You, of course, were never a Party member.'

'Never.'

'But you did considerable business with its members–and on their behalf?'

Kunzli felt a faint uneasy fear, like a knife pricking round his heart, but his eyes were blank and his face composed as he gave the offhand answer:

'I'm a professional man, Major. If I made religion or politics a condition of service I'd have starved long ago; as would every business man in the world.'

'I was making another point,' murmured Hanlon apologetically. 'Attached to the letter from Switzerland was a memorandum pointing to the scope of your interests, particularly in negotiating property and bonds on behalf of prominent Party members.'

'That's every solicitor's bread and butter.'

'It is suggested there was jam too–lots of it.'

'I made considerable profit, yes. I would have made more if I could. It was part of my revenge on these people for what they had done to my life.'

'We're happy in the success of our friends.' Hanlon grinned disarmingly. 'But a question does arise: how much of this property was originally expropriated–say, from concentration camp victims–and how much of it can be traced and restored to them, or to their heirs?'

So that was it! The blades were pricking closer now. And behind the spider's eyes a careful brain ticked like an adding machine, balancing the odds, weighing the risks against the profits. He hesitated a moment, then answered with easy frankness:

'I can tell you now that a good many expropriated estates passed through my hands at one stage or another. How many, I couldn't guess. Many reached me at third or fourth hand. To make an accurate list would require months of search–years, possibly.'

'But you would be prepared to assist us in such a search.'

'Naturally.'

'You would make available your personal records?'

'Of course.'

'Including those held in Swiss banks?'

'Certainly. But I should have to go there myself and withdraw them from the various safe deposits. They are in different names, the procedure is a little too complicated to be dealt with by post.'

'I'll arrange your exit papers,' said Hanlon with gentle gratitude. 'And while you're away no doubt our assessors could begin working on your papers here?'

'I doubt they'd make any sense of them.' A faint irritation coloured his tone. 'You must remember, Major, I was running a risky business and like your diverting Mr Pepys I kept many of my records in a code decipherable only by myself.'

'In that case I'll make your exit papers valid for seven days only. Naturally you'll want to get back as soon as possible.'

'Of course.'

'How soon can you leave?'

'That depends on you, Major,' said Kunzli tartly. 'Naturally I shall need a specific list of instructions. Then I shall have to check this list against my files here, to see what additional material is required from Switzerland. . . .'

'I'll send you the instructions tomorrow,' said Hanlon. 'Might we say a week from then?'

He flipped over the pages of his date pad, and waited, pencil poised for the confirmation.

'A week will be enough.'

'Good.' He made a swift notation on the pad. 'Your exit papers will be ready the day before you leave. I'll have them sent round to you.'

'As you wish, Major.'

'Then I don't need to detain you any longer, Herr Doktor. Thank you so much for coming. *Auf Wiedersehn.*'

He stood up and offered his hand. Kunzli took it limply and turned away. His back was straight and his face was composed, but behind the metallic eyes a bitter thought was framing itself. For the first time in many long years, he had misjudged the market. It was only a matter of time before the bottom dropped out of it completely. He'd better start selling, and selling fast!

4

When Sepp Kunzli had left, Hanlon changed into ski-clothes and walked out alone to look at the town. His first day in Bad Quellenberg was nearly over and he needed time and privacy to ponder the experience.

The snow was still falling heavily, filling the air like blown feathers, softening the harsh contours, icing the bleak trees, coating the town from road to roof-top, deadening the footfalls of the homing burghers. The mountains were hidden by a mist that swirled in from the southern defiles and drooped in ragged streamers over the pines. Yellow lights pricked out round the amphitheatre of buildings, and already the dusk was darkening into night.

From the entrance to the Sonnblick, the road wound downwards through buildings of diminishing importance, towards the centre of the old town, where the waterfall ran under the roadway, a silent ice-bound torrent, writhing fantastically from the steep crags to the valley floor.

When Hanlon moved out from the lighted doorway, the cold hit him like a knife and he twitched the hood of his parka up over his head and walked briskly down the slope. Behind him he heard the frosty tinkle of bells and he stepped aside to watch the passing of a peasant sleigh piled high with firewood and driven by an old man with Bismarck whiskers and a high green hat. The horse stepped awkwardly on its high-toed shoes and its breath made little cloud-puffs among the fluttering snowflakes. Hanlon followed the silver music of the harness down the road.

The first buildings he passed were high and dark, their windows were shuttered and their balconies covered with board frames to protect them from the snow. Their doors were locked and the snow was piled high on the deserted steps.

These were the big hotels, pride of the town, source of its boom-time revenue. Now they were white elephants, eating their heads off, the interest piling up on their mortgages, the snow ruining the roof-covers, the water freezing in the pipes, the dank cold of winter seeping through their corridors.

'This,' thought Hanlon moodily, 'is the way towns die, and empires too. Not by the sporadic cataclysms—war, earthquake, fire and flood—but by the slow recession of life from the members towards the small pumping heart, whose ventricles are the market, the shops, the beer-house, the church.

After a while the heart stops too, because when the members are dead the body is inert and useless, and life is a fruitless repetition of pulse-beats–lost energy, motion that leads nowhere!'

Then he remembered that this was the purpose of his own coming: to jolt new life into the fading heart, to set the blood moving outwards again to the cold extremities, to give them warmth and articulation and a new direction. Instead he had wasted a whole day on a cynical display of power, as if one frightened a dying man back to life, instead of coaxing him slowly to desire it first, then fight for it.

Thinking of death, he remembered Sergeant Willis, who was now being laid in his little pine box and who tomorrow would be buried in the churchyard of St Julian. A man of no importance during his life, his death had made him important to many people. A bachelor, without relatives, he might have died of a coronary occlusion and dropped out of time without a ripple of significance. But because he had been killed a little after the legal season, a whole town lay under the threat of an interdict as fearful as that which the old Popes visited on faithless cities. And he, Mark Hanlon, who had sat, a stripling novice, at the feet of Father Albertus, was the sinister Eminence who could nail the damnation on the locked doors of the church and mete out a rigorous justice instead of a life-giving mercy.

But interdicts were out of fashion. Even the Church had dropped them long since. No matter how many sacks of ashes you tipped on a man's head, you couldn't bend his will to repentance. The folk of Bad Quellenberg regretted the crime–there was no doubt of that. The rub was that they would not assume the guilt of the murderer or the responsibility for hunting him down. Morally–and Mark Hanlon had a nice moral judgment–they were right. A man was answerable for his own sins, but not for those of his neighbour.

Which brought him to the core of a very sour apple. He had put off the cassock long ago. His hands had never been anointed for shriving in the tribunal of the spirit. He wore a new uniform now. He carried a commission to administer a new and sinister legality: collective guilt.

'There is not one criminal,' said the jurists of the New Order, 'there are many. There is not only the man behind the gun, but all the others before him and after him: the father who begot him, the mother who suckled him, the woman who married him, and the priest who baptised him. All of them had a part in his making, all of them must share his guilt and his punishment.'

So Major Hanlon came at one stride to a blank wall of frustration, and to the lighted entrance of the last big hotel on the promenade.

Unlike its neighbours on the high ground, this one was set back from the road and reached by a gravelled arc of driveway. It was flanked by a parking apron where three battered ambulances stood, grey and forlorn, with the snow piling up on the radiators and canopies, and making small drifts around the hub-caps.

The stucco was peeling off the pediment and the proud Gothic 'Hotel Kaiserhof' was half-hidden by a white pine board with the inscription '121. Allgemeines Feldlazarett'. A pale yellow light shone behind the glass doors, and Hanlow saw an elderly corporal, with his jacket unbuttoned, picking his teeth behind the reception desk.

Beyond him was a sparse passage of people–an orderly wheeling a trolley of food, a nurse in a drab uniform, a shuffling convalescent with a military tunic over a pair of striped pyjama trousers, a lumpish woman in a long green coat with a pigtailed child at her side.

It came to him with a faint shock of surprise that this place too, and its inmates, were part of his charge. The charge, like the name, had a sinister sound to it. Lazarett–the house of the beggars, the dwelling of the maimed, the defeated, the abode of all poor devils who fought for lost causes and hopeless creeds, and who must now lick their sores at the gates of the New Princes.

He must come to see them, inspect their quarters, examine the problems of restoring them to normal life. His skin crawled at the thought of the shame to them and to himself, when he walked down the rows of beds in the uniform of the victor. What would they think? How would they feel? What words could he find to mend their broken dignity?

Every fighting man had that right at least–they stripped him of all others when he put on his uniform, even the right to question the cause for which he died. But how did you make him feel you understood and respected him, when you walked by with crowns up and polished buttons, while he sat on a bed-pan or lay with tubes in his belly or a raw stump where his hand should be?

Then he remembered he wasn't in uniform. He was dressed like any mountain man, in ski-clothes and hooded parka. Now was the time to get it over and done with. He pushed open the door and walked into the foyer.

The elderly corporal looked up and questioned him with hostile indifference.

'Well? Who are you? What do you want?'

Hanlon fought down his irritation and answered, mildly enough: 'I'd like to see the Chief Medical Officer.'

'Got an appointment?'

'I don't need one.'

'What's your name?'

'You wouldn't be able to spell it if I told you.' Hanlon grinned at him with sour humour. 'Now be a good chap and tell me where I can find him.'

The corporal shook his head stubbornly.

'Regulations, friend. We sign all visitors in and sign 'em out. We don't disturb the medical staff unless it's urgent. They're overworked, they say. Now let's have your name, eh?'

'Hanlon, H-A-N-L-O-N,' he spelt it out slowly, German fashion, while the orderly licked his pencil stub and copied it slowly on a printed form.

'Business?'

'Personal.'

The pencil stayed poised in mid-air and the corporal grumbled impatiently.

'Oh no! Not again! We get 'em all shapes and at all hours. They want to know how their Heinzi's getting on with his belly-ache or whether Gerhardt's going to be any good to his wife when he comes out. You'll have to do better than that. Now, why do you want to see the Chief?'

'To hell with you!' thought Hanlon irritably. 'I try to do you a kindness and you want to put me through the hoops like a performing monkey!'

Aloud he said: 'My business is personal with the Chief Medical Officer. It has nothing to do with any individual patient. Please telephone my name and ask him to see me.'

'Sorry, friend. That's the regulation; I'm here to see it's carried out. You tell me your business and I'll see what I can do.'

'You've got my name,' snapped Hanlon. 'My rank is Major. I'm the British Occupation Commander for the Quellenberg Area. Now, do I see the Chief Medical Officer or not?'

The corporal leapt up as though he had been stuck with a pin. He stood rigidly at attention and stammered apologies. Hanlon cut him off in mid-period.

'Where do I find him?'

'Upstairs, Major. First floor, room twenty. I–I'll take you up.' He buttoned his tunic hastily and came out from behind his desk. Hanlon followed him up the carpetless stairs to room twenty.

The man who stood to greet him was something of a surprise. He was more than six feet tall, broad as a tree-trunk, with blond hair and ruddy cheeks and ice-blue eyes and fists like small hams. He had a ready smile and a deep voice that still retained a trace of the Tyrolese burr. His name, he told Hanlon, was Reinhardt Huber. He carried Colonel's rank and Doctorates from Vienna and Padua.

His blunt good-humour and his shrewd peasant wit were a tonic to Hanlon's flagging spirits. The first courtesies over, he plunged straight into discussion.

'So we both have problems, Major. You help me to solve mine; maybe I can show you some answers in return.'

'Let's hear yours first, Herr Doktor.'

'I give them to you in one packet, my friend. I have four hundred men in this place, two hundred serious cases–everything from amputations to paraplegia. How do I cure them with starvation rations, poor equipment, no drugs and the last litres of anaesthetics? Faith healing? But even that's no good when they have lost faith in the past and can see no hope for the future.'

'I can improve the rations, I think,' said Hanlon calmly. 'We can co-ordinate local supplies and shipments from other provinces. We can organise the market so that you get a better share for the sick. Drugs? I doubt it. All available supplies are being rushed to concentration-camp victims. I can't get any of these. We might do better with surgical anaesthetics. I'll try anyway.'

Huber's face clouded. He looked down at the backs of his large, spatulate hands.

'The time of the hecatombs! The day of the genocides! The world will remember them for a thousand years.'

'I doubt it,' said Hanlon dryly. 'One dead man makes a tragedy, a million make a compost heap. Plant the graveyards with pines and they'll disappear in twenty years. Give the journalists their heads for the same time–and they'll bury the truth under a mountain of newsprint. That's why nobody learns the lessons of history. There's no history left–only broken pillars and scattered shards. The rest is commentary and partisan opinion.'

Huber looked up sharply, scanning the quirky Celtic face for any sign of mockery. Then, surprisingly, he chuckled softly.

'My God! Maybe we have one at last–an honest man with a sense of proportion. We can use both. So, no drugs, possibly some anaesthetics, better food. It's a beginning.'

'What else do you need?'

'Clothing, new bedding and surgical instruments.'

Hanlon shook his head. 'All hopeless until the priorities have been met—which won't be for a long time yet. What else?'

'Information. What happens to the boys when I discharge them?'

'You clear them with me and I'll arrange a rail warrant, inter-zone passes and enough rations to see them back to their home towns. After that they come under the jurisdiction of local authorities. If there are cases of special hardship, let me know and I'll deal with them as best I can.'

The big Tyrolean nodded. He leaned back in his chair, stretched his long legs and clasped his hands behind his head.

'We are better off than I expected, Major. I'm grateful. Now tell me—is there anything I can do for you?'

'You can give me some advice,' said Hanlon quietly.

Huber threw back his head and laughed gustily. Hanlon looked at him with faint irritation.

'Something amusing, Herr Doktor?'

'No, no! Something unexpected and rather wonderful. A man who sits where you sit and asks advice of the defeated. The best I can promise you is an honest answer.'

'It's all I want.'

Then, without quite knowing why—unless it were by that sudden act of faith that makes one man sometimes trust another—he told him all that had happened since his coming to Quellenberg, and all the questions it had raised in his own mind. Huber heard him out with growing seriousness, and when the story was done he leaned forward across the desk, gesturing with his large, strong hands.

'First, there is yourself. I do not see that you can take any other view, or any other action than you have done. This is a crime—it demands pursuit and legal process. You have a right to insist on the co-operation of the local authorities. If they don't give it to you, they must take the consequences. But there are other things you should remember. Understand me!' He waved a deprecating hand. 'I have no local loyalties. I do not belong here. I am a surgeon, which gives a man a certain detachment and a respect for the scalpel. First, you should think of the killer himself—and the reason for this motiveless murder.'

'That's the point.' Hanlon leaned forward earnestly. 'Why? Why?'

'I'm guessing,' said Huber in his deep, grave voice. 'But it is a guess based on my daily experience in this place. There is a limit to what the human body and the human mind can bear. A man may die of surgical shock. A man may go mad with terror or grief or the sudden impact of the evil of the world. These are the extremes. But there are a thousand steps downward to the valley of death or the caverns of insanity. The smallest wound leaves a scar in the tissue. The smallest shock makes a striation in the memory. Sometimes the faculties are permanently impaired. I can patch up a cripple, but I cannot make him walk straight. Still less can I make a crippled mind think straight. You have been a soldier. You know what war can do to the most normal man. How one will run screaming at the thunder of the barrage, and another will sit drooling and dumb as a cataleptic. How one goes into a rut like a beast at the smell of blood and another sweats with terror in a closed carriage. . . .'

Hanlon nodded thoughtfully. It was a new thought and vaguely comforting. Huber went on:

'From what you tell me of this killing, its suddenness, its blank unreason,

I guess that it was done by a man who is temporarily or permanently deranged.'

'All the more reason for bringing him in,' said Hanlon sharply, 'before it happens again.'

'I agree.'

'Then why this closing of the ranks? Why this attempt to turn me into a hangman, and the other fellow into a hunted hero?'

'That's a different matter altogether.' Huber grinned and relaxed again. 'If—if you were to offer me a cigarette, Major, I wouldn't refuse it.'

'Of course. I'm sorry.' He took out his cigarette-case and then lit up for both of them. The Doktor leaned back and inhaled long and gratefully. Then he took up the thread of his argument.

'First you must try to understand these people—the way they live, the way they think.'

'I thought I did understand them,' said Hanlon wryly. 'I lived among them long enough.'

'Where? When?'

'Years ago—before the war. I was a Jesuit novice in Graz. Four years.'

'That explains it.'

'What?'

'The perfect accent. The—the fact that you are *sympathisch,* and more liberal than I expected.'

'To you perhaps, but not to them.'

'Give them time, my friend, give them time. They too are suffering from shock.' He heaved his big frame out of the chair and began to pace the floor, piecing out his thoughts slowly at first, then with more emphatic eloquence. 'These people—my own folk in the Tyrol—are centuries away from the plainsmen and from the city-dwellers. It is the mountains, you see. They make a barrier to change, a frontier behind which retreat the best and the worst of the old customs. Cross one ridge and you must learn a new language. Push into the farther valleys, and you are back with the tribes—Celts, Alemanni, Cimbrians, Goths and Vandals. Examine their beliefs and you find that they worship the Christus in the shadow of the old gods. They are moody and suspicious. A man from the next valley is a stranger. An Ausländer like yourself is a man from another planet. I might stay in Quellenberg till the end of my days but they would still call me an immigrant—as they do these hoteliers and shopkeepers. Look at their land and you will learn something more about them, perhaps the most important thing of all. The meadows cling precariously to the hillsides, small and sparse for all their summer green. The last mowing must feed their stock all through the winter. So there are few beasts and each one is precious. If they cut down too many pines the avalanches come and sweep everything down into the valley. When they kill a pig, it is a big event, and they live on black bread and salted pork and the milk from one cow. If they fish out the streams there is no food for Fridays. When a son dies it is one hand less to the axes and the mowing. When a child is born it is one more mouth to feed, but one more assurance of continuity. Their life is harsh, you see, and their hold on it is insecure, so they treasure it, in all its forms—the strong son, the weanling heifer, the woman who breeds well and makes good milk. In Carinthia and in the Tyrol it is an old joke that the girls can't say no and that half the babes are begotten on the wrong side of the blanket. Yet even this is a sort of homage to life. A barren girl is a burden to her husband. A couple

without children go hungry in their old age. Better then that they begin to
breed before they marry.' He broke off and faced Hanlon with a wry,
apologetic smile. 'I don't know how much sense this makes to you, but . . .'
'It makes sense. But it doesn't make my job any easier.'
'Agreed. But it might save some wear on your temper.'
Hanlon stood up and held out his hand.
'I'll remember that, Doktor. And thank you.'
Huber's big fist closed over his own.
'It was nothing. I hope it helps a little. You are already helping me a great
deal. Would you like to see the rest of the place?'
'No, thanks. Another time. I've had a big day.'
'Let me walk down with you.'
As they walked out of the door, Hanlon cannoned against the girl who was
hurrying down the corridor. He murmured an apology and stepped aside,
but Huber caught the girl by the arm and brought her back.
'Not so fast, Fräulein. This is someone you should meet.' He made the
introduction with a humorous flourish: 'Fräulein Anna Kunzli, Major
Hanlon, British Occupation Commander. Fräulein Kunzli is one of our
voluntary aides. She helps to exercise the amputees with their new limbs.'
'Happy to meet you, Fräulein. Er–you did say Kunzli?'
'That's right.' Huber gave him a quick, shrewd glance. 'Herr Doktor
Kunzli is one of our prominent citizens.'
'I met him this afternoon,' said Hanlon carefully.
'This young lady is his niece.'
'Oh.'
Huber was quick to cover the awkward hiatus.
'How were your patients this afternoon, Anna?'
'Good–very good. They only need some encouragement and they try
very hard. But they get tired so quickly.'
'Thanks to Major Hanlon, we may soon be able to feed them better. Then
they won't tire so easily.'
'That would be wonderful, truly wonderful.' Her pleasure was so
genuine, her smile so frank, that Hanlon looked at her with faint surprise.
He was old enough to have a salutary cynicism about women, and the fresh
innocence of this one was all the more startling. He smiled gently and
said:
'It will take a little time, but we'll get something moving.'
'Where are you going now, Anna?' asked Huber.
'Down to the church. We're practising for the requiem tomorrow.
That–that was a terrible thing, Major. We're all very upset about it. That's
why we're making a special effort. The whole choir will be there, and . . .'
'Perhaps I could walk down with you. I'm going that way.' The words
came out unbidden, and hastily, as if he were faintly ashamed of them, but
the girl accepted simply.
'Thank you. I'd like that.'
They made their farewells, and Huber stood at his door watching them
walk side by side down the corridor. He wondered idly what was the
connection between Hanlon and Sepp Kunzli, and what might come of this
chance meeting with Kunzli's niece. The girl wore her innocence like an
armour and Hanlon was preoccupied with the devious manipulation of
power. But given time they would both come to bed, together or with
others, it made small matter, so long as new blood came into this old land

whose young sires had been killed off, or were lying, restless and impotent, in every room of the 121. Allgemeines Feldlazarett.

Hanlon's own thoughts were never further from bed or the breeding of new Quellenbergers.

As he stepped out of the hospital with the girl at his side he was suddenly angry with himself. His small, eager courtesy was a diplomatic error. It established a personal element in a relationship which, to be successful, must remain impersonal.

The girl was a link, however tenuous, between himself and Sepp Kunzli. Through her he could be subjected to the small demands of politeness. Her innocence might set a limit to his dealing with a man who, like himself, was far from innocent. He could ignore politeness, of course, and break down the barriers, but that would entail a certain blame, and this too he was unwilling to shoulder.

He pulled his hood farther round his face and hoped that no one would recognise him as they passed the lighted shop-fronts farther down the road. That would make a gossip in the town. It would range him with the immigrant and the exploiter, a thing he could ill afford.

Unconsciously he began to hurry and the girl had to double her step to keep pace with him. She made no complaint, but after a few moments she slid on a patch of loose snow and would have fallen had he not thrown out an arm to steady her. In the brief moment when he held her to him and felt the young warmth of her, he realised that he was making a fool of himself. He was a man doing a courtesy to a girl ten years his junior. To hell with the gossip. To hell with the diplomacies. He apologised warmly.

'I'm sorry. I didn't realise I was walking so fast. Will you take my arm?'

'Thank you.'

They fell into step and walked leisurely along the arched colonnade with its quaint shop-signs and its shabby naked windows. No new goods had come into Quellenberg for a long time now and the merchants were hoarding their last stocks under the counter. They passed one man putting up his shutters, a grey stooping woman trotting a dachshund on a frayed leash, a pair of peasants talking in a dark alcove. No one paid any attention to them. After a moment the girl said in her clear, untroubled voice:

'This is a sad town now.'

'War is a sad business,' said Mark Hanlon.

'It's not the war. It's the end of it. Everything seems suddenly pointless.'

'To you too?'

'Oh no, not to me.'

'What's the difference?' Her frankness disarmed him and piqued his curiosity.

'I suppose because I've got nothing to lose.' She said it so simply that it took his breath away. 'My father was killed–flying a plane over England. My mother died in Vienna. So I came to live with Uncle Sepp. I love him, but he's not very fond of me. So I'm not afraid of losing him. I'm young and I don't seem to want very much–so I'm lucky, I suppose.'

'Luckier than you know.' But privately he wondered how long that luck would last, and what would happen when desire awoke and the hunger for the unattainable.

Her next question left him momentarily speechless.

'Are you a Catholic, Major?'

'Well . . . yes. Why do you ask?'

'Father Albertus said we'd be lucky if we got a Catholic here. He said Catholics all over the world have the same belief, so they are better able to understand one another–and be kind to each other.'

He was glad that his face was hooded so that she could not see the irony in his smile. He told her gently:

'It doesn't always follow, my dear. It's one thing to believe. It's quite another to put your belief into practice. Catholics can be just as brutal to one another as Buddhists or Lutherans. They can lie and cheat just as well as those of other faiths. It was a Catholic who broke Father Albertus's hands for him.'

'I've never been able to understand that.'

'It takes a long time,' said Hanlon softly.

They walked the rest of the way in silence, and when they came to the churchyard gate he stopped. The girl hesitated a moment, then thanked him and held out her hand.

'I–I hope you'll come to visit us some time, Major. I know my uncle will be glad to see you.'

'Later perhaps. When we're all more settled.'

'*Auf Wiedersehn*, Major.'

'*Auf Wiedersehn*, Fräulein.'

He watched her walk down the path through the silent forest of headboards, and a few moments later he heard the first plangent notes of the organ, and the sound of young voices, clear as bells in the mountain air. He stood a long time, listening, while the snowflakes settled on his head and on his shoulders, and the cold crept into his blood like a slow death.

5

When the *Mädchen* had cleared away the last of the dinner dishes, Bürgermeister Max Holzinger exploded into dyspeptic anger.

'The man is a cold intriguer–the worst possible choice for us here! He has a charm that might beguile you into trusting him. Then at the last moment he is smiling coldly and twisting the knife in your ribs. I have never been so disappointed, or so humiliated!'

His wife and daughter watched him as he strode unevenly up and down the carpet, pouring out on them the shame and puzzlement of his first encounter with the Occupying Power. He had come home silent and depressed. He had picked sourly at his dinner and drunk twice as much wine as usual. He had snapped at the maid and hustled her weeping from the room as soon as the meal was done. Then, private at last and a little drunk, he had given full vent to his helpless fury.

'. . . His attitude to the funeral ceremony was quite cold-blooded, a show-piece not to honour the dead but to shame the people and let them feel the new power in the land. He's organising a man-hunt. As if we had not had enough of them all these years! I wonder he doesn't call for bloodhounds as well. I had a long talk with Fischer and we're both quite decided he'll get no co-operation from us. We'll teach him a . . .'

'You're a fool, Max!' said Liesl Holzinger, and the venom in her voice stopped him like a bullet. He gaped at her.

'Wha–what did you say?'

'You're a fool to join yourself with Fischer–and a bigger one to set yourself in opposition to the *Engländer*! He can crush you at one blow!'

He was vaguely afraid of the new woman looking out from her eyes and speaking with her lips. Like all his countrymen he was accustomed to submission from his women and a soothing audience for his outbursts. He answered her tartly:

'You don't understand, Liesl. This is politics–men's business. Unless we begin with strength we shall end with a heavier yoke round our necks. I tell you, Liesl . . .'

'I tell you, Max!' She stood up, eyes blazing, mouth tight and angry, facing him. Her daughter saw with some surprise how her big, full figure dwarfed her husband, and how uncertain he seemed in the face of her attack. 'Once you could tell me what was my business, and what wasn't. Now it's changed. I tell you! Why? Because my life is at stake, and Traudl's and the lives of all women like us. If you fight this man he will destroy you–and us with you. You've done it before–you and your dreamers. You killed my son . . .'

'Liesl, I beg of you . . .'

'No, Max! It's too late now. The war's finished. You lost it. We've got peace now–and we're not going to let you lose that too.'

'Liesl, you don't understand what he wants. He wants us to hand a boy over to him–like common informers, like–like—'

'Then hand him over!' she blazed at him. 'Hand him over and let us have some quiet in our lives. You handed over our son, didn't you? You didn't plot with Fischer to keep him from the Army. Why this one?'

'Because . . .' he stumbled and stammered, knowing how much of it was hurt pride, and how little was reasoned argument. 'It's hard to explain, but . . .'

'Then let me explain something, Max.' Her voice was quiet now, but cold and loveless. 'If you persist in this, I leave you. We both do. We go to the *Engländer* and explain our position. We tell him what you've done about the house. We tell him we want no part of plots and politics–only to be left quiet to remake our lives. I think he will listen. I don't think he'd let us starve.'

'You wouldn't dare!'

'I would–and so would Traudl.'

Holzinger looked at his daughter, lounging as she always did in the chair, smoking placidly, watching them both with the cool irony of disappointed youth.

'Is this true, Traudl?'

'Quite true, Father.' And she smiled as she said it. 'Life's been a one-sided bargain for a long time. I agree with Mother. It's time we changed it.'

He was beaten and he knew it. A man can fight all enemies but those of his own household. For a long moment he looked from one to the other, then his face sagged and his shoulders drooped so that he looked like a man become suddenly old. Then he turned away and walked to the window and stood there, hands clasped behind his back, his fingers lacing and unlacing nervously. When he spoke again his voice was low and hesitant:

'I . . . I don't know what you expect me to do.'

It shocked him to hear his daughter's voice answer him, deliberate and merciless:

'Make friends with him, Father. Co-operate. Play games with Fischer if you want, but remember always where the real power lies. After a while the Englishman will be lonely. All men get lonely away from their own countries and their own women. Pay him courtesies. When a moment offers, invite him here.'

'And then?'

'Mother and I will do the rest.'

For a good half-minute he did not answer, then the full import of her words seemed to strike him. He swung round and faced them again. His voice was almost a whisper.

'Do you know what you're saying? It's . . . it's almost obscene.'

'Is it, Father?' Her full lips twisted into a small bitter smile. 'It seems to me all life is a sort of obscenity—the way children are bred and born, the way they die, spilling their brains out on the ground, their bellies bursting open with bullets, the way women breed them again, because their husbands come home and want to be warmed and feel like men. It's the way the world rolls. I don't see what you have to complain about.'

'I won't have my daughter made a harlot.'

'It's a risk you take—with wives and daughters,' said Liesl Holzinger coldly. 'But, with any luck, we might get her married to the Englishman.'

As he looked from one to the other—at the blonde Teuton strength of the mother and the dark changeling beauty of the daughter—an old doubt began to stir like an aching tooth. And Max Holzinger asked himself whether history might not be repeating itself in the mountain house of Bad Quellenberg.

Karl Adalbert Fischer had troubles of a different kind.

The sagging telephone lines that led from Quellenberg to the high villages were coated with ice and conversation was carried on through a constant sizzle of static that sounded like frying bacon. So he was obliged to shout to make any sense at all—and his brother-in-law Franz Wikivill was an obstinate fellow who needed constant repetition to beat sense into his head.

'Listen, Franz, for God's sake! I don't want arguments, I want facts. Is the boy home yet?'

'He's home, yes. But . . .'

'How is he? Does he know what he's done?'

'I can't get any sense out of him at all. He was raving when he came in. Now he just lies on the bed staring at the ceiling.'

'Did you get his guns?'

'What's that?'

'I said, did you get his guns?'

'How can I? He won't let them out of his reach.'

'*Gott im Himmel!* What sort of children do I deal with? All right. Now listen carefully. I want you to get him out of the house now and take him up to the ski-hut on the Gamsfeld.'

'It's late, Max. It's still snowing. You know that's a bad trip even in daylight.'

'Get him up there tonight if you don't want him in gaol tomorrow!' Fischer was almost sobbing with anger and frustration. 'The English will be combing the hills, and the Gamsfeld is the safest place for a while. I'll try to get up to see him myself tomorrow.'

'But you don't understand, Karl. He won't stay there. He won't stay anywhere. For a while he's quite normal, then this black mood comes on him and we can do nothing with him. The only one who can reach him at all is his sister. Even she . . .'

'Then for God's sake send her up to the hut with him. She's young and healthy. She can make the trip. Have them take food and wine. There's fuel enough to keep them going.'

'We can't go on like this, Karl.' Even with the distance and the static his brother-in-law's voice was fretful and panicky. 'Can't you get him out into another zone?'

'What zone, for God's sake? The French and Americans will be notified that he's wanted. If they take him they'll send him back under guard. If the Russians get him they'll send him to Siberia–if they don't shoot him out of hand. Our only hope is to keep him moving about the hills.'

'But can't you give him new papers?'

'Yes. But I can't give him a new face! If I could, everything would be . . .' He broke off and stood staring at the receiver. A new and startling idea had come to him. He watched it flower, swiftly and suddenly like a conjuror's tree. If he could bring it to fruit it would be the sweetest triumph of all. The faint voice crackled petulantly in his ear.

'Karl! . . . Karl! . . . Are you still there?'

'Yes. But I'm going now. I've just got a thought.'

'I can't hear you!'

'It doesn't matter. Get the boy up to the Gamsfeld tonight. Without fail.'

'I tell you, Karl . . .'

'Get him there! If you don't I wash my hands of the whole business and the boy will hang. *Auf Wiedersehn*, Franz.'

He slammed down the receiver and stood there, a small triumphant smile playing about his lips.

A new face! Give the boy a new face and you had a new man, safe from pursuit and punishment. Hanlon's description of the murderer was now a matter of record–a lean, vulpine fellow with a scar on his right cheek. Remove the scar, let a plastic surgeon rebuild the face and the case broke down on the first process–identification.

With a new face and new papers he could move his nephew quietly into the American zone and let him fend for himself. There were friends in Salzburg who would be happy to give him a start. The more he thought about it, the more he liked it.

He crossed to the filing cabinet, unlocked it and took out the leather-bound folio. He carried it to the table, laid it open and began to leaf carefully through the last pages until he came to the name he wanted. Then slowly, but with deepening satisfaction, he began to read the very private history of Rudi Winkler.

In the palmy days of the town he had been a frequent visitor–a little roly-poly Bavarian with a dimpling face and soft hands and a gossipy humour. He had bought a small building plot on one of the less favoured promenades and built himself a log chalet which he had decorated in rustic fashion and which was kept for him by a bony widow with a trap mouth and a bitter tongue.

During the summer holidays he filled the place with blond young men who did the less arduous climbs, swam naked in the mountain pools and drank wine and sang sentimental *Lieder* till the small hours of the morning.

The upper circles of visiting society knew nothing about him and the locals knew little more, because he was an amiable fellow who took his pleasures with discretion and because his housekeeper kept her knowledge and her disapproval to herself. His documents gave small information. He was a doctor, it seemed, medical officer to an obscure S.S. unit in Bavaria. For a transient record it was enough, but, once Winkler became a property-owner in Quellenberg, Fischer could not be content until he had burrowed deeper into his past and built up a more satisfactory dossier.

It took time and patience, but in the end he got it.

Winkler had been a surgeon in Munich, a rising man with a fashionable practice in the new plastic surgery: women wanted their breasts lifted and their wrinkles smoothed out and their noses trimmed to the new Nordic fashion of beauty. There had been a scandal—one of Winkler's boys and the son of a Party official. The boy had been beaten up after a drinking party and had died of his injuries. The scandal had been hushed up quickly and Winkler had found it convenient to close his practice and find a new job. The S.S. unit turned out to be a concentration camp where Winkler was engaged on plastic experiments with the inmates.

All of it—names, dates, places—was studiously entered in the leather-bound folio.

Just after the Allied breakthrough, Winkler had turned up again, for good. Austria was still the Third Reich, he was living in his own house, he carried a valid-looking discharge paper: his legal status was beyond question. Fischer had been happy to let him keep it. He was happier still now that he saw some profit forthcoming.

He closed the big folio, wrapped it carefully in brown paper, stowed it in his battered brief-case and locked the catch. He took a last look round the dusty, disordered office, then switched off the lights and walked out, closing the door behind him.

It was late and he had not eaten, but he was confident that Rudi Winkler would be only too happy to feed him.

He was surprised to find the little Bavarian a genial host and his trap-faced housekeeper an excellent cook. They dined in comradely fashion on buttered trout and a well-mixed salad. They approached the proposition as coolly as if it were a business contract, as indeed it was.

They drank a litre of *Gumpoldskirchner* and finished with an *Apfelstrudel*, light as an angel's wing. Fischer was wiping the last crumbs of it from his mouth when Winkler smiled happily and said in his amiable voice:

'You know my friend, I like the idea very much.'

Fischer stared at him, incredulous. The roly-poly fellow wasn't frightened at all. He was treating the matter as a joke; which from one point of view was encouraging, and from another strange and slightly sinister. Fischer challenged him curtly:

'It's no joke, Winkler, believe me. If you make a slip, it's the end for you.' He slashed the edge of his hand across his throat in the hangman gesture. '*Kaputt!* Just like that.'

'*Kaputt* for both of us,' chuckled Rudi Winkler.

'Don't be so sure of that,' growled Fischer. 'I've got mitigating circumstances. The boy's my relative. You've got none—and a dirty history besides.'

Winkler was still laughing. His eyes had the vacant innocence of a child's.

His light girlish voice might have been retailing boudoir gossip.

'We're going to bury my past tonight. We're never going to think of it or refer to it again. You're going to tear my record from your dossier. You're going to give me new papers and a new past and a new future. And I'm going to give your nephew a new face.'

'Do you think you can do it?'

'Sure of it, my dear man. Whether it will be better or worse than the old one is a moot point, depending on my nerves, and how creative I feel. But it will be a new one. Oh yes.'

'Where will you do the job?'

'Here of course, private and comfortable. I hope your nephew is an agreeable fellow. I'm lonely. I crave company.'

'He's all right when he's normal,' said Fischer irritably. 'He's a doctor, like you. Very intelligent—which is a wonder, considering the damn fool my sister married. But when he gets these violent spells . . .' A new thought struck him and sent him off at a tangent. 'How will you be able to handle him?'

'Sedatives,' said Winkler cheerfully, 'which of course you'll have to rake up for me. I'll be giving you a list of the anaesthetics, drugs and other stuff I'll need. God knows where you'll get them, but we can't start until they're available.'

'I'll get 'em. Anything else?'

'I'll need an assistant for the operations. A trained nurse or medical orderly would be ideal. If not, then someone intelligent and trustworthy.'

'I'll think about it. I don't like trusting anybody these days.'

'You're scared, aren't you?' Winkler giggled with girlish malice.

'I am,' said Fischer bluntly. 'I find it keeps me careful.'

'I'm not.'

'I've been wondering why.'

The dumpling face creased into a good-humoured smile. His childish eyes sparkled. The soft hands fluttered like white moths in delicate gesture.

'I'm an epicure, my dear Fischer. I have tasted all the pleasures—even the subtlest, which is that of watching a man die, slowly, under my own meticulous hands. Thanks to you, I hope to prolong my enjoyment in modest comfort. If, however, it is necessary to curtail it, I shall not be too unhappy, because the term will be set not by another but by myself.' He put a hand into his breast pocket and brought out a small gelatine capsule which he held up to the light. 'There it is, my friend. Death in my own fingers. I can accept or reject it at a whim. Why should I be afraid—of you or of anyone else? I am beyond the reach of any man, and even my going will be a kind of pleasure. Does that answer your question?'

Fischer nodded but did not answer. He shivered, involuntarily, as if a goose had walked over his gravestone. He had heard his quota of tales about the concentration camps, and had shrugged them off as an Englishman might shrug off some story of provincial bedlam, or an American might dismiss a rumour of third degree in the precinct cellars.

There were trash in every country and you had to make places to dump them. It was the system. You had to administer it. You couldn't argue with it. In a place like Quellenberg you were able to forget it. Now for the first time he saw the kind of fellow who flourished on the rubbish heap and how little like a man he really was. With a shock of horror he realised that he had just made a partner of him.

In the warm comfort of the Spider-house, Sepp Kunzli savoured his brandy and listened with careful disinterest to his niece's story of her meeting with Mark Hanlon. The narrative excited her–a new man, an *Ausländer*, an officer of the Occupation forces, had walked unbidden into the small ambit of her life. She remembered all the details: his dress, his voice, his face. She gave a literal transcript of his few, laconic remarks.

Kunzli nodded and smiled in his distant fashion, but behind the dead, metallic eyes every item was shuffled and indexed and filed for future reference; the sum of trivial facts was added to his own experience. The final tally was disturbing. A subtle man himself, Kunzli was quick to sense the talent in others, quicker still to see the danger of it.

He questioned the girl with elaborate unconcern:

'I wonder what he was doing at the hospital.'

'I told you, Uncle. He was seeing Doktor Huber. He's promised to arrange better food for the patients.'

'Rash of him,' said Kunzli mildly, 'considering it's winter and food stocks are low, and the black market gets most of it before it leaves the cities.'

'But he would know, wouldn't he? He wouldn't promise if he couldn't do it.'

'Probably not. He struck me as a careful man. You left him at the church, you say?'

'Yes, why?'

'I wondered why he didn't go on. You tell me he's a Catholic. It seems strange.'

'I–I was going to ask him in–to hear the singing. Then I didn't like to.' And she added the innocent rider, 'Men aren't usually very interested in such things, are they?'

'Not usually,' said her uncle dryly. 'By the way . . .'

'Yes, Uncle?'

'I haven't told you, but Major Hanlon has asked me to make a visit to Switzerland.'

'That's wonderful. Why?'

'He wants me to dig up some information on the estates of concentration-camp victims–and other persons. I'll be gone about a week. If you cared to invite the Major to the house during that time I'm sure he'd appreciate it.'

'Do you think so, Uncle? Do you think I should–with you away?'

'Why not? You have Martha to chaperone you, and prepare the place. The Major himself would certainly be grateful. A new man in a foreign town–it would be only courteous.'

'How . . . how should I ask him?'

'A note, of course. Quite short and formal. Fräulein Anna Kunzli requests the pleasure of Major Hanlon and his officers–don't forget that, ask his officers as well. It's only politeness. Dinner is the best invitation. Gives you time to relax and know one another.'

'Yes, Uncle. Tell me . . .' She stumbled a little and flushed as she put the question. 'What do you think of the Major, Uncle?'

'Charming,' said Sepp Kunzli softly. 'An exceptionally clever man.'

'He must think very highly of you too, Uncle. Otherwise he wouldn't ask you to go to Switzerland.'

'He hasn't told me what he thinks, my dear. I'd give a great deal to know.'

He smiled as he said it, knowing that the irony would be lost on her. But the smile died quickly when he looked down and saw in her eyes a light he had never thought to find there.

Green-sickness, he told himself. The first late flowering of interest in a man. It should bloom briefly and die as soon. But if it did not? A new doubt pricked at him, a new irony of which he himself was the butt. He shrugged it away hastily. What could possibly grow between this innocent and a man twice her age who sat in the shadow of the eagles and the victor's axe?

In the ornate suite at the Sonnblick, which once housed the ornate bulk of Reichsmarschall Göring, Major Mark Hanlon was preparing himself for bed. He had dined late with Captain Johnson and over the wine and the brandy they had rehearsed the day's doings, the programme of the funeral, the lines of the policy they would follow for the first weeks of the Occupation.

Then, at one stride, fatigue had overtaken him. His eyes burned, his head felt as though it were stuffed with cotton-wool, his limbs were heavy and languid.

He had hustled Johnson off to finish his drinking with the sergeants, and had rung for the maid to draw a bath and lay out his night things.

Now he lay steaming in the big marble tub, feeling his tiredness soak out of his bones, while the sharp mountain water toned his skin and relaxed his muscles. It was a historic luxury, this of the bath, and years of campaign living had given it a new edge of pleasure for him.

A daily baptism in hot water gave a man the illusion, if not of renewed innocence, at least of renewed competence in his traffic with the world. Scrubby genius was always at a discount. The biggest killings were made by men with fresh collars and clean hands.

Soap and water worked miracles for a man's self-esteem, and the perfumed vapour clouds softened the harsh outlines of reality. Which was probably the reason why the old patricians had sat comfortably in the steam room while the Huns were battering on the gates of the Empire, and why Mark Hanlon forgot for a while the dead man being screwed into his coffin in the basement, and the scar-faced killer skulking somewhere between the pines and the white peaks.

He smiled wryly at the tag end of the thought and hoisted himself reluctantly from the water. His towel lay warm and crisp on the heated rail and as he rubbed himself briskly a new thought came to him.

All this profusion of wine and food and service was the perquisite of the conqueror. Children were whimpering with hunger in the cellars of Berlin. Girls were selling themselves in Vienna for a tin of American coffee. Families were shivering over a dish of smouldering twigs in a hundred ruins. And all over Europe men like himself were sitting like Caesars, with full bellies and warm bodies and stewards to serve them and women to solace them at a finger-click.

Some would grasp the luxury avidly and gorge themselves into a sickness of body and soul. Some would accept it with thoughtless arrogance as the natural coin of tribute. Others, like himself, would have the grace to be ashamed of themselves. But they would all enjoy it and none of them would have the courage to deny themselves in order to keep their dignity among the dispossessed. It was the beginning of the slow corruption of conquest which would end with victor and vanquished lying together in the stink of common defeat, in the despairing repetition of ancient sins.

He finished his toilet, put on his pyjamas and climbed into the huge bed under the billowing mountain of eiderdown.

It was the time he always dreaded, this last lonely hour of the day, when memory stirred and conscience itched and desire woke, warm and fruitless in his loins. There was much to remember, much that he wished forgotten, more that he wanted but knew that he could never have.

The thing that plagued him was the inevitability of it all.

There was the illusion of choice, the illusion of determining one's road. But the lines were cast by others and when you came to the crossroads the decision was already made for you. You looked back and thought, 'If I had done this . . . if I had chosen thus and thus . . .' But this was hindsight and historic fallacy. In spite of the signposts there was only one road—and you were already predisposed to walk it.

Father Albertus preached that there was a grace sufficient to every moment. But even he added the rider that some moments needed an extraordinary grace and this a man must petition with prayer and fasting, if it were not to pass him by.

'Drop it, man! Drop it! For this one night forget that you're a spoiled priest and a husband whose wife doesn't love him and a celibate by temporary circumstance and not by choice.

'You're the Occupying Power, the consul on his couch with guards at the door and servants within call. Tomorrow you bury the dead and begin to rule the living. Who knows? History tells strange stories. Kings have coupled happily with serving maids. Prefects have been known to enjoy their wine. And some Caesars have slept quietly—if only for a little while.'

He reached out, switched off the light and turned over on his side. Five minutes later he was asleep and that night he did not dream at all.

6

The funeral is man's oldest theatre. The only time he looks larger than life is when he is dead. All his debts are paid. He has no detractors, only friends. Even for the least loved, there is the pantomine of graveside affection. The humblest oaf commands respect when he lies under the pall.

The funeral of Sergeant Willis was a beautifully mounted performance.

At eight in the morning the coffin was brought up from the cellars and laid on trestles in the foyer of the Sonnblick. A Union Jack was draped over it and a sergeant and four men mounted the death watch.

At eight-thirty the Bürgermeister arrived with the five senior councillors of Bad Quellenberg. They were dressed in the costume of the province: light grey trousers and jackets, faced and piped with mountain green, their lapels decorated with carved bone ornaments—stags' heads, edelweiss, wolf-jowls. They wore long cloaks and green hats, each crested with a tuft of chamois hair.

After them came Father Albertus, in stole and surplice, accompanied by a cross-bearer and acolytes with wax tapers.

They stood talking and shuffling uneasily for nearly half an hour, because Major Hanlon was busy giving the final briefing to the ski-patrols who were to make the first search of the mountain farms. They watched Captain

Johnson assembling the cortège guard and those who understood English gathered that he was telling them how to keep step and formation on the steep, icy roadway.

At nine o'clock Hanlon himself came down, in battledress and greatcoat, carrying his gloves and his swagger-stick like a symbol of office. He greeted them coolly and gave the order for the procession to begin.

The troops formed up in the roadway, the acolytes paired off with the cross-bearer in front and Father Albertus behind, the councillors hoisted the coffin on to their ageing shoulders, and, at a command from Captain Johnson, the cortège moved off, with Johnson and Hanlon bringing up the rear.

It had stopped snowing, but the sky was still overcast and the flames of the tapers wavered uncertainly in the chill air. The only sounds were the muffled tread of the marchers and the deep voice of Father Albertus reciting the antiphon and the shrill boy-chorus answering him.

The familiar Latin cadences brought back a rush of memories to Hanlon and for a moment he thought that he was back in the monastic serenity of Graz, taking part in the comforting ceremonies of dismissal when one of the older brethren had died. The sight of Johnson, pacing it out self-consciously beside him, recalled him to reality.

Then he saw that the street was lined with people.

They were all there, ankle-deep in the snow—the very young, the very old, the walking cripples from the Lazarett, the gnarled grey foresters with the dignity of the mountain still on their bent shoulders. Peasant mothers with scrubbed shiny faces held firmly to the shoulders of their children who stood huddling back against their skirts. The shopkeepers stood stiffly outside their shuttered windows. The nurses and medical staff were lined outside the portico of the hospital, whose upper windows were crowded with patients wiping the mist from the glass to get a better view.

They were silent and stony-faced, but, as the cortège passed, some of the women bent their heads and wept silently, remembering their own dead ones. Husbands put their arms protectively round the shoulders of their wives. Fathers patted their daughters' arms in self-conscious sympathy. After his first hurried glance, Hanlon stared straight ahead, marching slowly and carefully on the treacherous surface.

When they reached the flat ground which was the last approach to the church, the bells began to toll, slowly and mournfully. The mountains took up the sound and soon the valley and the town were full of the echoing threnody.

As if by common instinct, the townsfolk stepped out into the roadway and formed into a long straggling procession behind the coffin. Hanlon could hear their shuffling tread like a counterpoint to the melody of the bells.

At the lych-gate the procession halted. The troops re-formed themselves into a guard of honour so that the acolytes and the priest and the following townsfolk could pass between them into the building. Johnson remained outside, but Hanlon went into the church, where a verger led him to a pew in the front row. He saw the bearers lay the coffin on the big brass stand in front of the sanctuary, then to his amazement the vergers came and stacked it about with wreathes of pine and holly and snow flowers and hot-house blooms that must have come from a dozen private homes—cyclamen, orchids, liliums and azaleas.

A lump came into his throat and he buried his face in an attitude of prayer. When he raised his head the church was full of the rustle of people, the guard was mounted on the coffin and Father Albertus was robing himself in the back chasuble to begin the Mass. When he came to the foot of the altar the first notes of the organ pealed sombrely under the lofty groining of the roof.

'*Requiem aeternam dona eis, Domini.*' The young voices of the choir rose in urgent supplication. '*Et lux perpetua luceat eis.*'

'A hymn is due to Thee, O God, in Sion. A vow shall be paid to Thee in Jerusalem. Hear my prayer. All flesh shall come to Thee . . .'

The chant swept over him in plangent waves as he watched the frail figure of the priest moving stiffly in the heavy Catholic vestments through the preparatory rituals of the sacrifice.

The prayer for the departed: 'O God, whose property is mercy and forgiveness, we pray Thee on behalf of the soul of Thy servant . . .'

The letter of Paul to the Corinthians: 'Behold, I show you a mystery . . . We shall all be changed. . . . This corruptible must put on incorruption, and this mortal must put on immortality . . .'

Then the choir again, the long minatory chant of the *Dies Irae*. It was sung as he had not heard it before, the first line of each verse taken solo, the following couplet sung with full voice by the choir:

> *Dies Irae, dies illa,*
> *Solvet saeclum in favilla,*
> *Teste David cum Sybilla . . .*

The clear impassioned voice of the singer was familiar to him—Anna Kunzli, the girl who lived without love in the Spider-house.

When the hymn was finished Father Albertus crossed the altar and after the ritual responses began to read in his deep, throbbing voice the Gospel for the day of decease:

'. . . I am the resurrection and the life. He that believeth in me, though he were dead, yet shall he live: and whosoever liveth and believeth in me shall never die . . .'

Every line and every cadence was familiar to Hanlon, yet in spite of himself he was caught by its perennial majesty and swept backward to a vision of the lost paradise, before he had eaten the fruit of the tree of knowledge and began his long progress as a citizen of the world.

He belonged here, as did all the others. He had been born into the Church as into a family. He needed it, as a plant needs contact with the soil from which it sprang, as a branch needs sap from its own tap-root. Yet by a series of decisions, by repeated concessions to circumstance, he had withdrawn himself from it, so that the life-spring was cut off and the sap no longer flowed. The hunger was deep in him, but he could not yet bend himself to confess it. He was still the prodigal, welcome whenever he cared to come, but no longer a sharer in the intimate strengthening life around the hearthstone.

This was what the theologians meant when they talked of sin as a truncation and a kind of death. This was the meaning of mercy and man's need of it . . . a light in the darkness, a hand stretched out to lead the wanderer on new paths, unguessed, undreamed of, in so much perplexity.

The silver bells sounded for the Consecration and the Elevation and he bent his head, though he could not bend his will.

When, at long last, the Mass was over, Father Albertus took off his chasuble and with only the black stole around his neck came down to bless the coffin. The acolytes formed up, the bearers came forward again and they carried Sergeant Willis out into the churchyard, to the black hole that gaped in the snow at the foot of the Christus.

The troops were drawn up in front of the grave, their arms and battledress incongruous among the bleak headboards and the limp figure of the Crucified. The flag was stripped off the coffin and it was lowered slowly into the hole while Father Albertus recited the prayers of dismissal and the responses ran like a small ripple of wind through the crowd.

When the prayers were finished the grave-digger handed Hanlon a clod of earth, frozen and hard as stone. He took it gingerly, and tossed it into the open grave and heard it thud hollowly on the coffin lid. Somewhere in the crowd a woman sobbed and a rustle of pity stirred them all.

As the grave-digger began shovelling the earth, Father Albertus's strong voice led them into the recitation of the Rosary and Hanlon heard his own voice making the repetitive response: 'Holy Mary, Mother of God, pray for us sinners now and at the hour of our death. Amen.'

When the earth was piled into a little mound, the digger covered it with clean snow and the men came forward to pile the wreaths and the flowers on top of it. The sergeant gave a series of sharp commands and the volley rang out, clattering from hill to hill.

It was over. Sergeant Willis was committed to an alien earth. The troops marched away and the people stood aside to let them pass, then they too began to drift away, silent and constrained, while Hanlon still stood, bowed and numb beside the wooden Christus.

An old grandmother pushed a tiny child towards him. She held up a bunch of snow-roses and said in her piping voice:

'*Für den Toten*. For the dead one.'

Hanlon took the flowers, and bent to lay them with the others. Then the pity and the shame of it took hold of him and for the first time in many years he found himself weeping. The last townsfolk turned away discreetly, and after a while he felt Father Albertus's hand on his shoulder and heard his voice, soft and strangely comforting:

'When a man can weep, there is still hope for him. Go home, my son, and I will pray for you.'

As he walked out of the churchyard he saw Anna Kunzli standing under the pines and feeding the birds that came fluttering down to take the crumbs from her hands. He passed her by without a word, but her eyes followed him, full of the soft pity of youth and innocence.

7

One of the few Quellenbergers who did not attend the funeral was Karl Adalbert Fischer.

This morning he had his own fish to fry and, with the town closed and the citizens involved in a longish ceremony, he counted on being private for the cookery.

He rose early, shaved and dressed himself in ski-clothes, over which he put his long cloak in case any of the citizens should remark on the curious appearance of their police chief. When his housekeeper offered him coffee, he refused curtly and told her he would breakfast later in the office. Then he went out, hurrying to reach the town before the citizens were astir.

His first call was Frau Greti Metzger, the plump young matron with a breast like a pouter pigeon, who kept the tobacco shop. Long ago he had had a placid but pleasant affair with her, which had ended, with mutual goodwill, when he had found a younger girl friend. She married a works-foreman on one of the building projects—a vacuous youth who talked too much and drank more than he earned. When he had been called to the colours, Gretl came to Fischer for advice and he had recommended her for a tobacco licence under the state monopoly. Since then he had always been sure of a smoke—and a bed during the intermissions of his love life.

But this morning's visit had nothing to do with love. Gretl's husband was home again—halfway home, at least. He was a patient in the Feldlazarett. On the retreat from Russia he had walked into a grenade blast. They had brought him back, wretched but alive, to the pointless purgatory of the Lazarett. Gretl visited him dutifully every evening, and every second evening she walked back home with a strapping young orderly from the hospital. This fact, like all others, had been entered in Fischer's big folio. Now he intended to make use of it.

Gretl met him at the door with her hair in curlers and her plump body wrapped in a loose dressing-gown that gaped a little wider when she greeted him. Fischer grinned with satisfaction and patted the nearer curves as he moved past her into the apartment.

She giggled with pleasure, kissed him roundly and drew him into the small sitting-room, where she sat beside him on the settee.

'Karl! This is a nice surprise. What brings you here so early?' She bridled girlishly. 'Don't tell me you . . .'

'No, *Liebchen*,' he assured her genially. 'Much as I'd like to, I'm a busy man and I've got a hard day ahead of me. I'll have to save my strength. I want you to do something for me.'

'Anything you want, Karl, you know that.' She drew the dressing-gown over her plump chest. There was no point in getting cold if there was no pleasure at the end of it.

'Good. This boy-friend of yours, Gretl . . .'

She pouted prettily and tossed her curl papers.

'That one! He's nothing. He talks too much and does too little. Sometimes I think he's half a you-know-what. But what's a girl to do? All the good ones are dead or damaged.'

'It's a hard world,' agreed Karl Adalbert Fischer. 'Is he fond of you?'

'Raves about me,' said Gretl emphatically. 'There's never been a woman like me. If my husband were dead he'd marry me. Probably because I remind him of his mother.'

'That's good too. I want you to get him to do something for me, privately, you understand. No names, no questions.'

'What is it, Karl?'

He handed her the list of drugs that Rudi Winkler had written for him.

'This lot—all of them should be available in the hospital. Your boy-friend should be able to lay his hands on them easily enough. Get him to bring them to you, a little at a time if he has to. But I must have them quickly.'

She stared at him in surprise.

'You mean, steal them?'

'Acquire them,' said Fischer with a gentle smile. 'If he asks questions tell him there's money in it. I'll pay for them.'

'But if he refuses?'

'You told me he was crazy about you, *Liebchen*. If he did refuse . . .' He shrugged away the threat. 'It might be hard to recommend your tobacco licence when it comes up for review.'

'You wouldn't do it, Karl!'

He patted her breast with a reassuring hand.

'Of course I wouldn't, Gretl. I just want you to understand that's it's important. That's all.'

'I–I understand, Karl.' She bent towards him, so that the gown fell open again. 'Couldn't you stay a while . . . a little while?'

'Long enough for a cup of coffee,' said Fischer briskly. 'Then I must go. Another time, eh?'

Half an hour later he was knocking on the door of the small cabin that stood at the foot of the Gondelbahn, the long aerial cable that swung the shining gondolas up the slope to the summit of the Grauglockner. The man who opened it to him was the engineer who ran the machinery and maintained it in the off-season. Fischer gave him his instructions bluntly and briefly.

'This is police business. No one must know that I've been here. Fit me with skis and a pair of sticks. Then start the engine and hoist me to the top. If anybody wants to know why the *Gondel* is running, tell them you're testing the motors. I'll be gone a couple of hours. When I'm ready to come down I'll telephone you from the peak. You'll tell me whether the coast is clear before you bring me down. Is that clear?'

It was clear. The engineer was a canny fellow who knew when weather was blowing up. He brought out his own skis and shifted the clamps with a screwdriver so that they fitted snugly on the small feet of the policeman. He gave him a pair of women's sticks, because he was a small man. Then he led him over to one of the small aluminium gondolas and closed him inside.

Three minutes later, Fischer was swaying out over the pine-tops on the first stage of his journey to the Gamsfeld hut.

When he got out of the gondola, lugging the skis and sticks after him, an icy wind struck him, whipping at his cloak, searing his eyes and his nostrils. He cursed savagely and struggled into the shelter of the small log hut. He should have known better. He was too old for this sort of thing. He shed his cloak, folded it neatly on the wooden bench and laid his uniform cap on top of it.

He pulled on a skier's cap, laced it under his chin and pulled up the hood of his jacket. Then he bent down to lock his boots into the skis and shuffled out into the snow, keeping in the shelter of the log walls. Then he looked about him.

He was ringed by mountains–a tumult of waves in a petrified sea. Their troughs were dark with pine-belts and the nestling of villages. Their peaks were bright with snow-spume, spilling downward in a continuous flow broken only by black tors and knife-edge spurs, jagged and sinister. The desolation dwarfed him. The cold wind shook the props of his small courage. He had to make an effort of will to thrust out from the shelter of the wall for the long, transverse run down to the Gamsfeld.

His goal was a small log hut, about five hundred feet from the saddle on the opposite side of the range from Bad Quellenberg. In the old days it had been the first stage of a half-day run for the novices–down to the Gamsfeld, two miles more down to the Hunge valley, up by the chair-lift and then a long, steady run home to Quellenberg. Fischer had done it a hundred times in his youth–now it was a middle-aged folly, forced on him by the ties of blood and family. Besides, he couldn't afford time for the Hungetal run. He would have to climb back to the saddle and take the *Gondel*.

He could see the hut clearly from his take-off point–a low stone building crouching like a big animal under its snowy roof. A thin spiral of smoke rose from the squat chimney and was blown away down the valley by the driving wind. They were there, then. His journey had not been in vain. He pushed himself off, uncertainly at first, but when he felt the blades bite in for purchase and the wind whipping his cheeks, he began to relax. His slack muscles responded to old memories, and for the first time in years Karl Fischer began to enjoy himself.

Like most pleasures, this one ended all to quickly.

The door of the hut faced downward over the valley. His approach brought him to the blind side of the building. He slipped off his skis and walked carefully round it, bending low as he passed under the window. If his nephew were in one of his crazy fits, there was no knowing how he might be welcomed.

When he reached the door he stood to one side of it, flattening himself against the wall. Then he reached over and knocked firmly. There was no answer, but he heard a small rustle of movement inside the hut. He called loudly:

'Martha! Johann! It's me, Uncle Karl. Open up!'

There was a pause, then a man's voice, harsh and strained, challenged him:

'If you're not, I'll blow your head off.'

'Nonsense boy! Look, I'll step back so that you can see me from the window. For God's sake try to talk sense to him, Martha.'

He heard her chiding her brother angrily:

'Don't be silly, Johann. I'll go. Nobody will harm me; besides, that's Uncle's voice.'

Fischer stepped back into the snow and, a moment later, the curtain was drawn aside from the window and his niece's face looked out at him. Then the door opened and, half laughing, half crying, she drew him into the hut.

The first thing he saw was his nephew crouched in a corner of the bunk, his pistol aimed at the doorway. Fischer grinned at him cheerfully. 'Put it away, lad, for God's sake! You'll hurt someone.'

Johann stared at him for a moment with sullen mistrust, then slowly lowered the pistol and put it down on the bunk, still within reach. Fischer peeled off gloves and cap and moved over to the old round-bellied stove to warm himself. The girl followed, questioning him anxiously:

'What is it, Uncle? What's going on! What will happen to Johann–all of us?'

'Nothing,' he told them breezily. 'Nothing at all. Uncle Karl has fixed everything. I'll tell you about it later. Now I'm cold and hungry. Can you fix me something?'

'Of course. Oh, Uncle, that's the best news we could have.'

She threw her arms round his neck and kissed him, then bustled away, rummaging in the knapsacks for bread and cheese, spooning black ersatz coffee into a saucepan of snow-water. Fischer took out his cigarette case and held it out to his nephew.

'Like one?'

'Throw it to me.'

'Just as you like.'

He took out a cigarette for himself, lit it, then tossed the case and the lighter to his nephew, who took out three cigarettes. One he put in his mouth, the other two he laid down on the shelf at the side of the bunk. He lit up and began to smoke avidly.

'You can have the lot, if you like,' said Fischer mildly.

'Thanks.'

He emptied the case and tossed it back to Fischer with the lighter. The lighter fell short and Fischer moved across the floor to pick it up. Johann raised the gun and kept it trained on him until he had retrieved the lighter and moved back to his place beside the stove. Fischer said nothing, but smoked placidly, watching him through the smoke-drift.

'Like a wolf,' he thought. 'Scarred, hungry, run down to the rib-case, but he'd snap your throat out before you could say God's mercy. Not so long ago he was a child, with a bright pink face and his mother's eyes. I used to dandle him on my knee and feed him with sugar-plums. Then he was a student, feckless as most, but with a charm to him. And afterwards the big thing–Universität–when he'd come home sober and serious at term's end, with his mouth full of big words and his head full of dreams about saving the world with a scalpel and a bottle of dill-water. Now look at him. What did the war do to him that he hasn't told us? Or is it simply that if you hunt a man long enough and keep him running far enough, you turn him into a wolf? And what do we do with you now, boy? How do we coax you out of your corner and begin to make you a man again?

Suddenly his nephew began to speak, and Fischer felt the hairs bristling on his nape. The voice had changed completely, although the man himself still sat tense and crouching, with staring bloodshot eyes, the fingers of his free hand still lying on the gun-butt. It was a calm voice, measured, mild, almost academic in its dryness, as if another man were speaking out of the distorted wolf's face. It said:

'I'm sorry to be a worry to you, but you must try to understand. There's a name for this trouble of mine–a doctor would know it–trauma. It's as if I were cut in two, with the best part of me on one side and the worst on the other, and the good beyond my reach. If you tried to take my gun now I'd shoot you, I know that. I'd know I shouldn't, but I couldn't help myself. Instinct, instead of reason. The control mechanism doesn't function. The family told me I killed a man. I–I remember it vaguely. I saw them driving up the road. I thought they were Russkis coming after me again. I was tired of running. I wanted to get down and fight it out, once for all. I know I should give myself up. But I can't. I'd go screaming crazy, without hope of recovery. I'm a good enough doctor to know that. Maybe if I could rest a while, stop running, have a good doctor to help me, I could get better. But that's not possible now, is it?'

As he spoke the wild look died slowly from his eyes, which became glazed and dead, and when he had finished, two large tears squeezed themselves out of the inflamed ducts and rolled slowly down his lean, stubbled cheeks.

His sister watched him spell-bound, the saucepan suspended in mid-air, but Fischer went on smoking casually. After a while he said, very quietly:

'That's what I came to talk to you about. I've found a doctor for you, and a place where you can be treated in quiet and safety.'

'I won't go. I can't.' The wild light came back into his eyes. His fingers closed convulsively round the pistol.

'It's up to you,' said the policeman calmly. 'The English have patrols out, searching the valleys and the heights. They'll do it for months if they have to. Which means I'll have to keep shifting you round from hut to hut. A few weeks of that and you'll be dead. The only other alternative is the one I've given you. Take your pick.'

'Where is this place? Who's the doctor?'

'His name is Winkler. He's on the run like yourself. I've offered him new identity papers if he'll take you in, nurse you a while, then do a plastic on your face so that we can get you out into the American zone when you're well again.'

'Where does he live?'

'Quellenberg. He's got a chalet tucked away in the trees at the wrong end of the Mozart promenade.' He chuckled amiably. 'His housekeeper's got a face like an axe, but she cooks like an angel. I dined with them last night. Winkler's got a good cellar too. You could live like a king—and thumb your nose at the world. Think it over anyway, while we have some coffee.'

The girl took the hint and turned back to her preparations. Fischer sat down on the opposite bunk and began leafing throught a four-year-old copy of the *Wiener Zeitung* full of smiling Party men and marching heroes. He felt like tossing it into the stove, but it gave him something to do and left the boy free to sort out his tangled thoughts. After a while he spoke again, and for the first time a note of uncertainty made itself heard:

'How—how would you get me down to town without being seen?'

His uncle looked up from his newspaper and answered easily:

'That one worried me at first, but I think I've got the answer.'

'What?'

'It means staying up here for another day or two, of course. But that's nothing, so long as we can steer the Englishmen away. I might start a rumour or two to take them to the other side of the valley. Toss me another cigarette, will you?' Without thinking, his nephew reached out and threw one of the cigarettes from the pile at his elbow. Fischer felt a small flutter of hope. He lit the cigarette and went on: 'December the sixth is St Nicholas's Day. The saint visits all the houses with his page and with the Krampus following behind to scare the naughty children. They'll be twenty or thirty Krampuses coming into town on that night; if we dress you in goatskins and put a Krampus mask on your head, who's to tell what you are?'

'Uncle!' The girl swung round excitedly, almost overturning the coffee-pot. 'That's brilliant. It couldn't fail. You know yourself, Johann, you've never been able to guess who it was under the goat masks. Say you'll agree, say it, please!'

She went to him swiftly and sat in the bunk beside him, and for the first time his hands reached not for the gun but for her. He buried his face in her shoulder and said wearily: 'I wish I could believe it, Martha.'

Fischer turned studiously back to his paper, while she coaxed and pleaded with him until the coffee boiled over on the stove and she had to leap up to rescue. There were only two cups, so she gave one to each of the men together with a round of black bread and a large slice of cheese. It was rough fare and Fischer felt himself choking on it, but his nephew ate and drank ravenously as if afraid it might be snatched from him.

When it was all gone he put down the cup and wiped his mouth with the back of his hand. Then he lit a cigarette and stretched out on the bunk, smoking and staring up at the timbers of the roof. Without turning his head he asked cautiously:

'Are you sure we can do this, Uncle?'

'I'm risking my own neck,' said Fischer with a show of irritation. 'If I'm caught, I'll have a harder time than you. Any lawyer could get you mitigation—a good one might save you altogether. For me there's no defence. You're not even my son!'

'I'll do it, then.' He said it in a voice so near to normal that they both stared at him. Then Fischer told him bluntly:

'There's a condition.'

'What?'

His nephew slewed round sharply to face him.

'I want you to give me your guns.'

'No!' Instantly, he was an animal again, tense, staring, his lips drawn back in a rictus of fear.

'When you go into town,' said Fischer calmly, 'you will be afraid. If you carry your guns, you will kill someone else as you killed the Englishman. You must know that. If you don't give them to me now, I wash my hands of you. You can go your own way, running and running till you die in your tracks or somebody puts a bullet in your head. I'm risking my whole career on you, lad. The one thing I won't risk is another killing. That's final.'

There was a long silence. The girl and her uncle looked warily at the haggard face and the wild eyes, hoping for some sign that reason had penetrated to the still functioning intelligence. They could see the eyes glaring again, the mouth slackening, after the first impact of panic. Then a new question was tossed at them:

'I—I trust you, Uncle. But what about the others? You know what the town is like for talk. Sooner or later they'll know where I am, and who I am. What then?'

'It's a fair question, boy. I'll give you a straight answer.' Fischer stuck his thumbs in his belt and rocked gently back and forth on his heels, grinning cheerfully. 'I know the people better than you do. First, they've got too many worries of their own to stick their noses into my business. Second, they know that there'd be no profit if they did, I know too much about 'em. Third—and this may surprise you, but it's true—they don't want you caught. They need you safe and well. So many of the boys are gone, the ones that are left are doubly precious. Once we've patched you up you'll have so many offers of marriage you'll have to beat 'em off with sticks.'

'Marriage!' The word burst out of him in a wild shout of laughter. 'Marriage! That's a good one! That's the funniest joke I've heard in years. Laugh, why don't you, laugh!'

'It isn't funny,' said Fischer.

'Isn't it?' He was halfway off the bunk, shouting wildly. 'Then try this, Uncle! Twice the Russkis took me, and twice I escaped. The Chetniks got me too in Yugoslavia, but they let me go. You know why? Because they said I was no good to them any more. I was no good to anyone any more . . .'

His voice rose to a high scream that cut off suddenly as he pitched to the floor in a dead faint. The girl ran to him and knelt down, cradling his head on her lap, crooning to him in a low desperate voice. Fischer stood looking down at him like a man turned to stone.

'You poor bastard,' he said softly, 'you poor, poor bastard.'

He walked back to the bunk, picked up the pistol and the rifle and turned towards the door. The girl's voice stopped him:

'You're not leaving us, Uncle?'

'Better I do,' said Fischer sombrely. 'When he comes round put him to bed and keep him warm. Tomorrow I'll send your father up with the costume and instructions for getting him down to the town. Can you control him till then?'

The girl looked down at the shabby, shrunken figure on the floor, then up again at her uncle.

'There's not much left to control, is there?'

'Nothing at all,' said Karl Adalbert Fischer.

Then he went out, closing the door softly behind him.

8

Half an hour after the funeral, Mark Hanlon was back at his desk in the Sonnblick. The crisis of emotion had passed quickly, leaving him, as tears and passion do, purged for a while of anger, regret and indecision, and ready for the work in hand.

There was a mountain of it waiting for him: supply arrangements for his troops and for the town, a survey of local economic resources, a security check to screen war criminals and Party fanatics, an examination of the town records and the impounding of relevant documents, a search for expropriate estates, the repatriation of Austrian troops, border liaison with the American zone, road and rail traffic control, democratic reform of local education, a search for arms dumps and privately held weapons . . .

Johnson and he worked through the stacks of memoranda till their heads were buzzing and the mimeographed type danced crazily in front of their eyes. Their lunch was a plate of sandwiches and a pot of coffee and at three in the afternoon they were still wrestling with the primary problem: how to set up a complete system of local government with a handful of tired troops and a set of officials all of whom were suspect on one count or another.

'It can't be done,' said Johnson wearily. He canted his chair at a perilous angle, put his feet on the table and lit a cigarette. 'Ten into one won't go. That's all there is to it.'

'Try telling that to Klagenfurt, laddy. You'll get a flea in your ear and a quick discharge . . . services no longer required.'

'Not such a bad idea. It's been a damn long war.'

'All wasted if we ball-up the peace.'

'It's balled-up already,' said Johnson with youthful wisdom. 'Always has been. Always will be. The minute the guns stop, the politicians are in, carving up the bodies. Look at Yalta. We went to war to save Poland, so we said. Now we've handed it to the Russkis on a platter—and half Europe as well. Why worry over all this?' He waved an impatient hand at the stacks of typescript. 'Why not flush it down the toilet and let the politicos have their heads? It comes to the same thing in the end.'

'Because there aren't any politicians in Quellenberg,' said Hanlon quietly.

'The place is crawling with 'em,' said Johnson emphatically. 'We've had 'em in this room—Holzinger, Kunzli, the little bobby—and all the others we haven't met yet.'

'At the moment, they've got no authority. We've got it. I want to see if it can't be used properly, to build something permanent.'

'Like what?'

'Read all about it!' said Hanlon with a grin. He tossed a stack of memoranda into Johnson's lap so that he overbalanced and toppled backward to the floor.

'You haven't answered my question,' said Johnson as he picked himself up and kicked the scattered papers into a heap. 'I don't think you can.'

'There is an answer, you know, Johnny.' Hanlon was suddenly serious again. 'And it's a damn sight simpler than all that rubbish in the memos. We've got to get things organised so that the men can get working and the kids can start eating properly and so that everybody gets a fair share. We've got to weed out any murderers and rapists and professional torturers who've tried to slip back to Quellenberg to live as honest citizens. We've got to restore stolen property to its rightful owners—if they're alive and can be found. We've got to kick out the official exploiters and find honest men to replace 'em so that people get a fair deal in business life and justice in the courts.'

'Better buy yourself a lantern and live in a tub,' said Johnson perkily. 'You can't even get your own mess sergeant to stay honest.'

Hanlon shrugged it off.

'That's the nature of the beast.'

'Does it change, just because he speaks German?'

Hanlon was silent for a while, chewing the cud of the question; then he leaned forward across the table, gesturing in careful exposition.

'Let's get something straight, Johnny, right from the start. I'm a good deal older than you and I've got a lot more reason to be dubious about the good that's in people. But I've learnt something that I think is important. Whatever good there is in this cock-eyed world started small and stayed small for a long time. When it grew, it grew slowly, like a tree, so that folk hardly noticed it, until one day it was big and its branches sheltered a lot of poor devils like you and me. That's what I hope for from this job—to start a small good growing. If I didn't believe it possible I'd be quite happy to whore my way through it and line my pockets at the same time—or blow my brains out! I'm not sure which.'

'Better make up your mind, Major,' said Johnson with a lopsided grin. 'You might come to it sooner than you think.'

'To hell with you, Johnny!' said Hanlon irritably. 'Let's get back to work.'

Together they bent over a verbose instruction on 'The Status of Dependents of Persons Under Remand as Suspected War Criminals'.

Late in the afternoon, when the early dark was already down on the mountains, the leaders of the ski-parties came in to make their reports. All of them tallied with that presented by a hatchet-faced corporal. He had been a school-teacher and his German was good, if pedantic. His intelligence was much higher than his opinion of the Army and those who ran it. For Hanlon he had a grudging respect, which he expressed by an emphatic bluntness of utterance.

'He's around, sir. We all got the same feeling. The farmers are covering up. The police know it and they're covering up too.'

'What makes you say that?'

'First, they say they don't understand our German—which is a lie. The police understand it, so do they. They refuse to speak anything but dialect. That's a pose, too. They lay it on like stage Irish.'

Hanlon nodded thoughtfully. It was an old trick to embarrass the visitor. They played the dumb ox when it suited them, but when their pockets were hit they squawked loudly enough. And in Hochdeutsch too!

'What else, Corporal?'

'The atmosphere, sir: like kids in a classroom. You know there's mischief, by the way they look at you, the elaborate innocence they put on. And you can't get the truth—even if you beat their silly heads against the wall.'

'If we lean on 'em hard enough, they'll crack,' said Hanlon.

'No, sir.'

'Why not?'

'Because they're ready for us. They can see us coming miles away, from those mountain farms. Even if we knew the man was hiding in one of 'em he'd have a two-mile start before we reached the place. We're climbing *up*, remember, on skis. You know how slow that is. To get to the back valleys we've got to go up first, then down—unless we're going to trudge through the drifts in the passes. Even then any look-out would spot us. They've only got to send their visitor out into the pine-belts and we've lost him.'

'Are the police co-operative?'

'Very,' said the corporal dryly. 'They stand around and wait for us to tell 'em what to do. They forget where the tracks are and they find it hard to read a map reference, and they travel slowly even on the best slopes—but you couldn't pin a charge on 'em. We'll never get our man this way. I'll lay odds on it.'

'We're going to keep it up all the same,' said Hanlon with a grin.

'Do you mind saying why, sir?'

'How do you feel, Corporal?'

He got the answer in one expressive word.

'Fine. Now put yourself in the position of the killer. If we have parties out every day, each in a different sector, what happens? He's got to keep moving. If, as I suspect, he's a sick man, sooner or later he's got to stop moving. Then what?'

'They'll hide him.'

'Where? You know what these mountain farms are like. One big building to house the family and the animals and the winter hay. You could turn one upside down in half an hour.'

'They'll shift him down to the town.'

'Then we get him,' said Mark Hanlon with flat finality. And even the doubting corporal was half convinced he would do it.

When the conference broke up, Johnson raised the question of exit papers for Sepp Kunzli.

'I don't see where you're heading on this one, Mark. We had a good report on him. Yet you're starting to put him on the jumps. Why?'

'Stolen property, Johnny. He's a high-class fence. I'd hate him to get away with it, though he probably will.'

'How does that tie up with the report?'

'London said he was a good agent, in war-time. All that means is that he was a good gambler–laying off the risks.'

'Then why let him out of the country?'

'I've got to,' said Hanlon wryly. 'The way the Swiss banks work, I haven't a hope of getting access to his papers unless he brings them to me himself.'

'Do you think he will?'

'Some of them.'

'How do you know he won't skip?'

'He's got too much property inside Austria–and a niece as well. It's my guess he'll decide to sit out his hand and rely on lawyer's tricks to hold most of his property intact. As I say, he'll probably do it. But we'll prise some of it out of him–and a lot of other information as well.'

Captain Johnson cocked a jaundiced eye at his Commanding Officer. 'You're a devious blighter, aren't you?'

Hanlon made a gesture of weary distaste.

'How else do you deal with a devious operator? He sets out to avenge his wife by plucking the Party men, and somewhere along the line the taste for revenge changes to a taste for money. But he still goes on justifying himself as a sort of Monte Cristo. He's nothing of the kind. He's an exploiter, profiting from plundered estates.'

'And his niece sings in the choir,' said Johnson with apparent irrelevance. 'Pretty wench too–in a virginal sort of way.'

'I hadn't noticed,' said Hanlon coolly.

'You're getting old, Mark,' chuckled Johnson with genial cruelty. 'I notice all the girls, all the time.'

Hanlon rounded on him angrily.

'You keep your hands on your change and your mind on the job–and do your leching away from the office! Is that clear?'

Johnson stared at him, surprised at the outburst.

'I'm sorry. It was only a joke. Dammit all . . .'

There was a knock at the door and, in answer to Hanlon's summons, Sergeant Jennings came in with a large red-sealed envelope.

'Just arrived, sir. Safe-hand from Klagenfurt.'

'Thanks, Jennings.'

The sergeant saluted and went out. Hanlon broke the seals and found inside two more envelopes similarly marked. The innermost one contained a long memorandum. He conned it swiftly and then threw back his head and laughed and laughed till the tears ran down his face. Johnson watched him with growing puzzlement until finally curiosity got the better of him.

'Well, what's it about? What's so funny?'

Hanlon recovered himself at last and told him with sardonic deliberation:

'Life's little ironies, Johnny. Just as we're getting ourselves organised they dump this in our lap. By arrangement with the U.S. Command at Salzburg, three hundred displaced persons from three concentration camps will be billeted on us for Christmas and indefinitely thereafter. The International Red Cross will supply medical services and supplies. Accommodation and all other services will be arranged by us. They arrive a week from today.'

'God Almighty!' Johnson swore softly. 'There's a packet of trouble.'

'Bigger than you know.' Hanlon laughed again, humourlessly. 'I wonder what Holzinger will say when I tell him.'

By the time they had got through dinner, Hanlon was sick of his own company and that of his junior. It wasn't the boy's fault. He was agreeable and intelligent; he had a sense of humour and a mordant wit. If he took the world and himself less than seriously, he was to be envied, not blamed. If his commander had a belly-ache or a heart-ache, that was no reason why his own wine should go sour.

But tonight Hanlon was restless. The ornate room stifled him. The mountain of work on his desk appalled him. The exchanges of the dinner-table were stale to him—old tales, familiar and wearisome, new speculations, profitless and impertinent. He wanted to get out for a while.

Where to go? There were no clubs. The bars were closed for want of custom. He had no friends in this alien town. It was unwise for him to drink with the N.C.O.s or the men. He had no taste for solitary tipple.

Huber would be glad to see him at the hospital, but tonight he shrank from the atmosphere of ether and antiseptics, the uncomfortable evidence of suffering and mortality. Father Albertus would welcome him too; but what would they talk of but memories and metaphysics? Uncomfortable subjects, both.

Then he thought of Holzinger. There was business to talk with him, and no valid reason why it shouldn't be talked in comfort. Holzinger had put on a good show at the funeral, he had earned a courtesy. Why not call on him, tender an official thanks, and let him digest the new pill in privacy? If excuse were needed, there it was to hand. He would go.

He checked the position of Holzinger's house on the area map, and went out.

The clouds had cleared away now. The sky was clear and bright with diamond-points. The freeze was beginning and the cold cut into him like a razor. The snow shone, ghostly in the starlight, and the crystals crackled under his feet as he strode briskly through the town and on to the wooded promenade that led to the Bürgermeister's house.

He found himself thinking out his entrance like an actor, planning the words, rehearsing the gestures. 'I will say this, and he will answer me so and so. I will smile to show him that there is no enmity. I will apologise for the intrusion, so that he will understand that I respect his privacy. I will come quickly to the compliment to give him confidence. I must uphold his dignity in the presence of his family. And before the evening is done I must reaffirm my own authority, gently, lest he think that hospitality gives him a hold over me.'

It was a weakness and he knew it. He needed company, diversion, comfort against the bleak loneliness of power. But the lapse was small and easily repaired. The chastest of men leans to the comfort of woman, even if he has no intention to bed with her. He smiled sourly to himself at the thought of all this careful moralising over a simple act. It was a monastic habit and he had never lost it, though he had often succeeded in forgetting it.

A maid in a black dress and a white starched apron opened the door to him. She gaped at his uniform, then stammered an apology and left him standing in the hall while she went to fetch Holzinger. The Bürgermeister was obviously rattled, but he recovered himself quickly and held out his hand in greeting.

'Good evening, Major. This is a pleasant surprise.'

Hanlon smiled and took the offered hand.

'I hope I'm not intruding.'

'Not at all. There is only my family at home. They will be happy to see you.'

Now the compliment, carefully phrased, sedulously rehearsed.

'I was touched by the arrangements you made for the funeral. I wanted to tell you personally . . . informally.'

Holzinger bowed stiffly, and his face softened into a smile of gratitude.

'That was kind, Major.'

'A small courtesy,' murmured Hanlon. 'We have enough unpleasant business to transact in the daytime, without sleeping on it as well.'

Now it was done, decently and in order: the apology, the compliment, the subtle caution. Dignity was assured on both sides. Holzinger took his arm and led him into the bright drawing-room.

The first thing he saw was the two women, tense in their chairs, staring at him. The expression in the mother's eyes was a strange mixture of surprise, puzzlement, fear. The daughter's was cool, appraising, and then suddenly interested.

Holzinger made the introductions and they both looked a little startled when he bent over their hands, continental fashion, and greeted them in his pure colloquial German.

Holzinger led him to a chair.

'Sit down, Major. Make yourself comfortable. A drink? Schnapps? Sliwowitz?'

'Anything you have.'

In the small hiatus that followed, while Holzinger poured the drinks and the two women searched for an opening gambit, he took stock of the room: solid Biedermeier comfort, good pictures, deep carpet, brocaded curtains, Viennese porcelain, Lipizzaner horses, a grand piano, twinkling lustres, an old carved marriage chest from Land Salzburg. On the mantel a photograph of a young man in Alpenjäger uniform, the son probably. . . .

'Where did you learn German, Major?' Liesl Holzinger's voice surprised him, as it did all strangers, with its depth and smoothness.

'I was a student in Graz years ago.'

'Then you know our country well, and understand the people.'

'I like to think so.' Hanlon smiled in careful deprecation. 'Much has changed of course, since I was here.'

'Most Englishmen never speak as well as you.'

'I'm half Irish, perhaps that explains it.'

'Perhaps.'

He had the feeling that she was weighing him, measuring his reactions, listening for the undertones in his voice, watching for any significance of gesture. The women were the strength in this house, he decided, the shrewdness too. He wondered vaguely whether Holzinger was happy with his dark-eyed daughter and this blonde Valkyrie of a wife.

The drinks were brought and they toasted each other.

'*Prost!*' said Mark Hanlon.

'*Prost!*' said Max Holzinger.

'To peace,' said his wife.

The dark girl said nothing at all.

Holzinger laid down his glass and began to talk.

'The Major was telling me, Liesl, that he was very touched by our burial service this morning.' He said it eagerly, almost defensively, as if anxious to affirm his good standing with the Occupying Power.

'It was the least we could do,' said his wife emphatically. 'A thing like that involves us all, even those who were not involved before. Have you found the murderer yet, Major?'

'No. It will take time.'

'The sooner the better,' said Traudl casually. 'Then we can all start living normally.'

Holzinger and Liesl looked at her sharply, but her eyes and her smile were innocent of malice. Hanlon grinned and said gently:

'There's no reason why you shouldn't begin now, Fräulein. The war's over. After a while the rhythm of life will start to pick up again. It always does, you know.'

'Easy to say—for the winner,' said the girl bluntly.

'Traudl!' Her mother turned on her with a sharp exclamation of anger.

'It's all right,' said Hanlon with a smile. 'It's fair comment. It's the young ones who inherit the mess.' He turned back to the girl. 'Don't get the wrong idea about us, Fräulein. The only reason I'm here is to keep order and try to start life moving again. After that I go home—I'd like to be there now.'

'Then why is everybody afraid of you?'

'Are they?'

'You know they are!' She tossed it to him in smiling challenge. 'Everybody, including Father here.'

Holzinger flushed and began to protest, but Hanlon cut him short with a gesture and answered the girl with sober gentleness:

'We're all a little afraid of strangers. Nobody likes a policeman camped on his doorstep. You get used to them in time, then you forget them, and after a while they go home.'

He got up, walked over to the piano and sat down. As the others watched him, curious and vaguely worried, he began to play, stiffly at first, then with fluid grace, the "Kärnter Heimatlied", which is the tenderest of all songs of the motherland province of Austria.

The music seemed to take possession of him, smoothing the lines from his face, relaxing the stiffness in him, so that the drab uniform seemed to sit oddly on his shoulders. The melody flowed from his hands, supple and golden, singing of snowpeak and waterfall, of blossom trees and green meadows, of bird-song and the sparkle of mayflies, and the hunger of an exile for the good land that nurtured him. Its pathos tugged their heartstrings so that they left their chairs and came to him, moving quietly, lest the tenuous magic break. Hanlon neither saw nor heard them. He had surrendered to the memories that flowed out from his finger-tips, old folk tunes, snatches of Schubertlieder, wisps of Mozart and Haydn, a monastery chant, a Tyrolese yodel—scraps and shreds of forgotten happiness stitched into a bright patchwork of melody. Somewhere between the monk and the soldier there had been a musician too, a fellow with a song in his heart and talent in his hands, but he had been thrust into the background, to emerge at this unlikely moment.

Holzinger stood in the background, fighting down a small rush of emotion, but the women stood close to Hanlon, so that the warmth of their bodies went out to him and their perfume was all about him, heady as the music. When his playing faltered, they prompted him, taking up the melody with soft voices, their faces bent to him, their white hands fluttering to the beat. He closed his eyes and played on, surrendering himself to the sound and the perfume and the rhythm of his stirring blood.

Then slowly the pleasure spent itself and the music died in a low minor cadence that lingered a long while in the quiet room. The women moved away, reluctantly, and Hanlon swung round on the stool to face them. His mouth was puckered into a self-conscious grin and he made a little diffident gesture of apology.

'That's all, I'm afraid.'

'*Wunderschön!*' said Liesl Holzinger softly.

'A great kindness,' said Holzinger awkwardly. 'We all appreciate it.' The girl said nothing. She had already turned away to light a cigarette, but her body was alive with the music and with desire for the man who had played it.

'You see,' said Hanlon, mocking her lightly. 'We're not all monsters, Fräulein. Some of us are quite *sympathisch* when you get to know us.'

Even as he said it he remembered that Frank had played Chopin in the butchery of Warsaw, and fiddlers had played Brahms outside the doors of the gas-chambers. But Irmtraud Holzinger was unconscious of such ironies. She raised her head, so that he saw the passion in her eyes and the frank invitation.

'I'll remember it now, Major. I hope you'll play for us again.'

'I hope you'll ask me,' murmured Hanlon, and cursed himself for the easy gallantry.

'You are welcome at any time, Major,' Holzinger assured him with formal courtesy.

'The Major is a busy man. We must not make demands on him,' said Liesl Holzinger, who was still the wisest of them all.

A little while later he took his leave. The women stood in the porch to watch him go, but Holzinger walked down the steps with him to the garden gate. He held out his hand and said in his sincere, uneasy voice:

'I'm glad you came, Major. I hope this may be the beginning of an understanding between us.'

'I hope so too,' said Hanlon politely. 'I'd like you to call on me in the morning. There's a lot to discuss.'

'No more trouble, I hope?' asked Holzinger unhappily.

'No more than usual. Don't let it spoil your rest, Herr Bürgermeister. Good night. And thank you for the hospitality.'

'Good night, Major. Come safely home.'

He stood a long time at the gate, watching the shadowy fligure striding out along the promenade, then he too turned away and walked back to the house, where his women were discussing an important question: whether Mark Hanlon was married or single.

9

When Holzinger presented himself at the Sonnblick at nine-thirty the following morning, he found to his surprise that Fischer and Father Albertus were already there. The three of them sat uneasily in the big room, under the unfriendly eye of Captain Johnson, each wondering why the others had been summoned. Hanlon, it seemed, was busy with the briefing of the search parties and Johnson was content to let them wait and wonder.

Twenty minutes later Hanlon arrived, made a brief apology and plunged straight into business. Cool, detached, he sat behind the big desk with its mountains of paper and read them the official directive on the arrival and reception of displaced persons from the concentration camps. When he had finished he laid down the manuscript and looked at the three faces in front of him. He said calmly:

'There it is, gentlemen. I'd like your comments. You may speak as freely as you want.'

There was a long pause. The three men looked at each other, then back at the official mask of the man behind the desk.

'It's—it's a surprise,' said Holzinger carefully. 'I can't pretend it's a pleasant one.'

'There'll be trouble,' said Fischer bluntly. 'As there has been in other places. Disorder, attempts at rape and murder. I have not the staff to handle them. The Occupying Power must assume the responsibilty.'

Hanlon said nothing. He looked down at the backs of his hands and waited. Then Father Albertus spoke. His deep voice was full of conviction.

'We have a debt to these people. Whatever we do will be too little to repay it. Whatever trouble we have is not too much.'

Hanlon looked up. A small sardonic smile twitched the corners of his mouth.

'Well, gentlemen?'

Holzinger shrugged helplessly.

'We—we can't quarrel with the principle. We shall do what we can.'

'I do quarrel with it,' said Fischer stubbornly.

Hanlon answered him, mildly enough:

'I'd like your view, Fischer.'

The small head jerked forward on the long neck. The bird-like eyes were bright with anger. The hands made jerky, emphatic gestures.

'There is a debt—we admit it. There is a problem of rehabilitation—we admit that too. But we do not solve the problems by dumping these people in the middle of a small community like this one which has no protection against . . .'

'Against what?' Hanlon shot the question at him.

'Hate,' said Fischer bluntly. 'And revenge! Don't tell me they don't want it. You know what happened when the camps were thrown open—bloody murder! Not only of guards and executioners, but of local villagers. These

people know they're protected. Put a D.P. in the dock against a German or
an Austrian. Who wins? Who must win? How do you keep order in a
situation like that? Don't mistake me. I know what was done in the camps. I
know what happenes when you brutalise a man so much that you turn him
into a beast. But they weren't all martyrs. There were rapist and perverts as
well as Jews and politicals. Do you let those loose on us—our women and
children? I can't look at the big issues. I've lived and worked here all my life.
Why dump all this—this corruption on us?'

'Because all of us had our part in it, Karl,' said Father Albertus sombrely.
'All of us co-operated by silence, by cowardice, by eating the fruits that
were manured by millions of dead. You say you know what went on. You
could never know, unless you had been there and endured the horror in
your own body. You talk of vengeance, murder, rape. Wait till you see these
people. They have no heart left for hate—or love either. In many of them
even the will to live is dead. You are afraid of them, you say? What is to be
feared from a skeleton? You fear for our women. Is there lust in a starving
body, whose strength is consumed by the feeblest motion? I will tell you
what you are afraid of—what we're all afraid of—our own guilt staring at us
from dead eyes, our own shame stalking in the sunlight of this town!'

There was a long silence in the ornate room, so that each man was conscious of his own pulse-beat, the small, crepitant rustle of his clothing against
his body. Even Hanlon, who had brought the old priest for this very reason,
was awed by his eloquent condemnation. After a while he said very quietly:

'It seems we're all agreed on the main issue, gentlemen. There are some
practical matters I'd like to discuss with you. First is the requisition of a
suitable building. I'd like your recommendations, Holzinger. Then we'll
inspect it together before I make the order.'

'I'll let you have them tomorrow morning, Major.'

'Good. Next is the question of staffing. The medical nucleus will be
supplied by International Red Cross—doctors, nurses, trained orderlies.
We'll need ward-maids, cleaners, staff for the laundry, the kitchen, the
boiler-room, clerical assistants . . . How do we raise them?'

'You'll have to conscript them,' said Fischer sourly. 'Nobody in his right
senses would volunteer for work in such a place.'

'You underrate our people, Karl,' said the old priest calmly. 'They have
at bottom a Christian conscience. If this proposal is presented to them in the
right fashion, they will respond—many of them anyway. I shall preach about
it on Sunday. If those in authority give the example . . .' He shot a quick,
quizzical glance at Holzinger, '. . . if their families offer voluntary service,
the others will follow. We have time to prepare them. We should make use
of it properly.'

'If you can do that,' said Hanlon, without emphasis, 'you'll make it easier
for me and for yourselves.'

Holzinger nodded, but said nothing. He was wondering what Liesl would
say, and his daughter, when he asked them to take the lead, for an example
to the citizens.

The first ground gained, Hanlon led them carefully through a discussion
of details: rates of payment, the provision of transport from the station to
the hospital, entertainment, recruiting methods. The tension slackened
gradually, and at the end of an hour he ordered coffee to be sent up and
passed round cigarettes. The morning was going well and he wanted to take
advantage of it.

The next question was a ticklish one: the status of Party members and the sequestration of their estates. He saw Fischer and Holzinger tense suddenly when he raised it.

'Understand me, gentlemen. I have a certain latitude in time and action on this matter. I am as anxious as you are to avoid injustice, which profits nobody. The only true balance will be achieved when the first free elections are held and the wish of the people is made known. However, you must understand that I am under the general pressure of policy. I must be able to justify to higher authority my action–or my delay in taking action. Do I make myself clear?'

Holzinger and Fischer nodded. The priest watched him with gentle, perceptive eyes. He went on:

'The first thing I propose is the impounding of documents–city records, Party lists, police files, electoral rolls, registers of births, deaths, marriages; all papers relating to property in the Quellenberg area. Captain Johnson and his men will take possession of these immediately and issue appropriate receipts. The documents will be returned to you after scrutiny and collation.'

Holzinger shifted uneasily and the chair creaked loudly. He flushed and mopped his face. Fischer sat bolt upright, his eyes filmed over like a bird's, unwinking, inscrutable.

'It will be necessary for me to issue a proclamation, which I have already drafted,' he tapped the manila folder at his side, 'making it clear to all citizens that they are free to apply to me with any information of previous misconduct or misappropriation by Party officials. Information may be submitted in the form of charges or as simple requests for inquiry. Its source will be kept secret and a full investigation will be made before legal action is taken. I'm sure you will understand the need for this free access. Many people have lived in fear for a long time. The course of justice has been perverted for many years. I'm sure you are all anxious to redress the balance.'

'You won't do it this way,' said Fischer in his bald emphatic fashion. 'Most of us are condemned out of hand.'

'By opinion perhaps,' snapped Hanlon, 'but not by the law. For the present I am the law. The fact that you are still in office is proof of my impartiality.'

Father Albertus permitted himself a smile behind his broken hand. His old pupil was showing up well. Holzinger said awkwardly:

'Many of the records were destroyed before the surrender.'

'We expected that,' said Hanlon easily. 'We'll make do with what is left. Military records, especially those relating to arms and ammunition dumps, are specially important. It will make your job easier, Fischer, if these can be found.'

Fischer nodded and said irritably:

'You'd better issue a new order on the surrender of firearms. It's like prising out teeth to get 'em now.'

'I'll do that,' said Hanlon. He relaxed and leaned back in his chair, smiling at them amiably. 'That's enough for today, gentlemen. We've covered a lot of ground. We'll get round to the rest of it in time. Any questions before we break up?'

'One,' said Fischer. 'It's small enough, but the people would like to know. The feasts are coming on–St Nicholas the day after tomorrow, Christmas,

New Year, the Three Kings. There are the old customs—St Nicholas and Krampus visit the children, you know how it goes. Do you want them stopped, or do I let them go on?'

'Let them go on. We want to interfere as little as possible with the local life. We thought that . . . if the people cared . . . we'd invite the children here to the Sonnblock for a Christmas party. We'll supply food and the presents.'

'It would be a good thought,' said Father Albertus. 'They haven't eaten well for a long time.'

'Leave it to me, then.' Hanlon stood up. 'Thank you, gentlemen. Captain Johnson will go with you to arrange about the documents. I'll telephone you before our next meeting.'

They rose, bowed stiffly and walked from the room, Johnson first, then Holzinger and Fischer, with Father Albertus bringing up the rear. At the door the old man stopped and looked back. His transparent face was lit with a gentle smile:

'Authority sits wells on you, Brother Mark. I believe you will do good for us here.'

The door closed on him and Mark Hanlon was left alone chewing the butt of a new, disturbing thought . . .

Fischer had started it—the small furtive doubt that lurked behind an apparently simple statement.

'The feasts are coming on . . . The people will want to know.' Fischer was not a man to be interested in feasts or in the people. The question was irrelevant, yet strangely obtrusive among all the big issues they had discussed. Who cared, now, about Father Christmas and his attendant devil? The answer was simple. Fischer cared. But why?'

He puzzled about it for an hour before he found the answer.

On the sixth of December the goat-men came down from the mountains. They wore huge, grotesque wooden masks carved by forgotten craftsmen. They had six horns and jagged teeth and twisted mouths and leering eyes, lit sometimes by torch batteries so that they winked horribly in the darkness. From neck to ankle they were clothed in goat-skins. Their cinctures were rattling chains and on their backs they wore great balls of hollow iron that rattled and drummed as they walked. They came shouting and howling in a curious reverberant chant that filled the valleys and echoed dully against the mountainsides.

When they came to the town they split up into threes and fours to attend the various impersonations of St Nicholas, who went from house to house with gifts for the children. The people called them 'Krampus', which is the name of the attendant devil of St Nicholas who frightens off the robbers and carries the switch to beat naughty boys. But they were much older than Krampus—they were in fact one of the faces of Freya, the wife of Woden, King of the old, bloody Valhalla.

While the Saint went into the houses to distribute his gifts they stayed outside, drumming and howling, peering in at the windows, because the children were afraid of them and often cried. The adults were afraid too, however much they laughed, because this was a memory old in the blood, a memory of twisted horrors dancing in the firelight between the rock tors and in the clearings of the pine wood.

After the giving of gifts, the Krampuses left the Saint and went down to the town, drunk from the wine they had been given at the doors. They paraded the streets, then stood in doors and alleys to catch the girls and bind them with the chains and make them pay a forfeit for their release.

The girls were afraid, but excited too, because this was another memory: the smell of sweat and rough hide, the harsh kisses from under a lifted mask, the hide lifted too sometimes, and the thrust of urgent loins.

Hanlon remembered it all as he paced the room, searching for the significant term what was the key to Fischer's interest. Finally he found it.

All the goat-costumes belonged to old, mountain families, by whom the custom was kept alive. Dress a man in the mask and the hide and his own mother would not know him.

The answer lay before him, pat and final.

On St Nicholas's Day the killer would be brought down to hide in the town, and the man behind the plan was Karl Adalbert Fischer.

'We'll get him, Johnny!' said Hanlon eagerly. 'Given an ounce of luck, we'll get him.'

It was late in the afternoon, the curtains were drawn and the room was bathed in bright yellow light from the chandeliers. They were bent over the map, tracing on its mica cover the ways by which the goat-men might be expected to converge on the town. Johnson nodded approvingly. This was the sort of thing he understood best, a tactical operation, aimed at a limited objective. His questions were brisk and pertinent.

'You want us to wait, Mark. Why not take them as they come in?'

'Because they straggle in,' said Hanlon. 'They come from a dozen different points all over the hills. They use the back paths and mountain tracks. We'd dissipate our forces and reduce our chances of a full check.'

'Fair enough. You want them all to come into town, is that right?'

'Yes. Then we seal off the approaches and let the troops operate in a central area. There's another advantage—most of the Krampuses will be drunk by then. They get a glass of wine at every house.'

'Makes it easier,' said Johnson with a grin. 'But we might have a fight or two on our hands.'

'I doubt it.'

'What's the timing on this, Mark?'

'After dark. They don't start their rounds of the houses until about five-thirty. There's a small ceremony at each home, so they won't start to concentrate down here till about eight. Say nine, to be on the safe side. The housemaids and the nurses won't be free till after that, so we don't stand any risk of losing them.'

Johnson shot him a quick admiring glance.

'You've got this well taped, Mark.'

'I've been here before, remember,' said Hanlon with a grin. 'But it's not quite as watertight as it looks. The first gamble is that our man may not be brought right into town at all. He may be taken to one of the outer homes and left there, before the main business of the evening begins.'

'How do you cover that one?'

'It's a lucky dip. You pays your money and you takes your chance. I'm going to leave the big operation of the evening to you, Johnny. I'm going to dress in ski-clothes and coast around the outer areas from nightfall onwards. I may be wasting my time. I may be lucky.'

'What's the next problem?'

'Surprise,' Hanlon told him crisply. 'How do we filter the best part of a company of troops into the town–all armed–without signalling the punches?'

'We can't,' said Johnson thoughtfully. 'We might lessen the shock a bit, though.'

'How?'

'Day after tomorrow is the big event, right?'

'Right.'

'That gives us tonight and tomorrow night. Why not call Sergeant Jennings up here and talk to him? Tell him the story and have him send the troops out for an airing, both nights. Keep the drunks home and let the others have a drink or two in the *Stüberls*. Let 'em wear side-arms, to get the natives used to the look of those too. A couple of nights of that and they'll be halfway conditioned to having us around.'

'Good.' Hanlon nodded thoughtfully. 'It might work. Let's get Jennings up and give him the drill.'

'Before you do, Mark . . .'

'Yes?'

'What about Fischer?'

'Leave Fischer to me.' Hanlon's tone was bleak. 'Just now I need him where he is; that's why I'm giving him rope. Later I'll hang him with it.'

In his shabby office, under the wine-splashed map of defeats, Karl Adalbert Fischer was planning his own campaign.

He was doing it in characteristic fashion, with his feet on the table, a bottle of schnapps at his elbow, the telephone in one hand and one of Gretl Mertzger's cigars in the other. He was talking to Rudi Winkler.

'I have a present for you, my friend.'

'Charming! Charming!' Winkler's high skittish laugh crackled over the wire. 'I love presents. When do I get it?'

'Day after tomorrow. St Nicholas is calling on you, and Krampus too, of course.'

'To beat me? I'd enjoy that, you know.' He laughed immoderately at the insinuation and Fischer, waiting, frowned till he was calm again.

'You know the ceremony, of course. You give the Saint and his attendants a drink and a small present, then push 'em off. One of the Krampuses will stay behind.'

'Clever!' said Winkler softly. 'I like that. Did you get the–er, sweetmeats I ordered?'

'They're coming. I've placed the order.'

'Good! . . .' He leaned significantly on the next words. 'And you were going to replace some documents for me.'

'That's done too,' said Fischer, grinning to himself. 'I'll bring them round the day after St Nicholas.'

'Careful fellow,' said Winkler petulantly.

Now it was Fischer's turn to chuckle.

'We live in troubled times, my friend. One can never be too careful. *Auf Wiedersehn.*'

'*Auf Wiedersehn.*'

Fischer put down the receiver then lifted it again and began dialling another number. This time it was the widow Metzger who answered, but her voice was strained and off-key. He questioned her quickly.

'Gretl, this is Karl. Are you alone?'

'No.'

'Is it the boy-friend?'

'Yes.'

'Has he brought the stuff?'

'Some.'

'What about the rest?'

'Later.'

'Are you sure of that?'

'Yes.'

'Does he know who it's for?'

'Of course not!' She dropped her voice to a whisper. 'He wants to know how much.'

'I'll name the price when I see the goods,' said Fischer curtly. 'Keep him happy, *Liebchen*–and you'll keep your licence. *Servus*, little one.'

'*Servus*,' said Gretl limply.

Once again he put down the receiver and poured himself a glass of schnapps. He tossed it off at a gulp and he felt it slide down slowly to glow like a warm coal at the pit of his belly.

It was one of the most enduring satisfactions of his life to sit here in this drab room and jerk the strings that made the puppets dance. He enjoyed good liquor but abstinence never irked him. Abstinence from women troubled him more, but he never had been forced to abstain for very long. Now that he was getting older the need was less and the moment required a certain preparation. But the exercise of power was a continuing pleasure. Age only sharpened it, and practice never diminished it. Only one thing could curtail it–the whim of the Occupying Power.

The risk was there, would be there for a long time. He could do nothing but prepare himself for the worst, and hope it never came. Meanwhile, he found a keen delight in this battle to circumvent Hanlon and save this poor maimed devil who was his sister's son. If he succeeded it would be spittle in the Major's eye and a sweet salve to his own pride.

He smoked slowly through the rest of his cigar, then heaved himself out of the chair and picked up the large suitcase that stood in the corner of the room. He laid it on the table, unlocked it and took out its contents–a complete Krampus costume, which until two hours ago had lain, dusty and neglected, in a glass case in the tiny municipal museum.

It was, according to the record, the oldest known costume in the province, dating back four hundred years. The skin was lank and rubbed bare in many places. The chains and iron rattles were hand-forged in some old mountain smithy. The horns were cracked and brittle but the wooden mask was a carver's masterpiece–an evil grotesque, its patina soft as silk under the hand.

Fischer held it up by the horns and stared into the big agate eyes and the gap-toothed mouth. Childhood memories stirred and a sudden shiver of fear shook him. This was the old devil that lurked still in the mountains and in the black forests. This was the grafting of beast and man which has haunted the nightmares of his ancestors and which has sprung up to walk and breed again in the last decade of Europe.

He wondered if this were the face that Father Albertus had seen in the torture rooms at Mauthausen–which he himself might soon see, tormented and terrible, in the frosty sunlight of Bad Quellenberg.

Hastily he thrust the mask back into the suitcase, covered it with the goatskin and piled the chains on top of it. Then he locked the case and carried it out to his car.

Five minutes later he was driving slowly out of town towards the mountain village where his sister and her husband lived. The snow was shining in the starlight, but there was black night between the colonnades of pines. Every shadow was a leaping demon and every tree-hole sheltered a grinning monster with stony malevolent eyes.

10

By five-thirty on St Nicholas's Day all the children of Bad Quellenberg were scrubbed and dressed in their Sunday clothes. They sat, excited but uneasy, in kitchens and parlours, whispering to one another, listening for the howls and the drumming that heralded the coming of the Saint, with his sackful of gifts. Their parents bustled about, laying out the wine and the sugar-cakes and the small money with which the visitors must be welcomed, and if the children stirred too much they warned them: 'Practise your prayers. The Saint will want to hear you recite them. If you fail, the Krampus will take you and beat you with the chains and leave you tied in the snow.'

All of them, parents and children, were touched by the faint panic of fear of the goat-men. This one day was a symbol of their whole lives. There were gifts–but the gifts had to be earned. Behind the smiling giver, with his crown of flowers, stood the twisted demons ready to seize the forgetful and the defaulters.

The houses were lit, but they were small islands of security in the darkness of the mountains. The Advent candles burnt comfortably on the pine wreaths, a symbol of the coming of the Christ-child. But, outside, the baleful eyes of the Krampuses winked horribly and their distorted faces pressed against the window-panes. Childish voices were raised in the *Pater* and *Ave* which the Saint demanded, but they could not wholly exorcise the terror of the gods.

Mark Hanlon felt it too, as he strode out, muffled and hooded, to work his way round the outer approaches, while Johnson and his non-coms made their final plans for the picketing of the town itself.

The house lights were sparse among the trees, the promenades were deserted and the echoing howl of the goat-men was borne to him faintly, mixed with the sound of running water and the creak of the pines bending under weight of snow.

He plunged his hands into the pockets of his parka and felt the butt of his pistol, hard and comforting.

The air was very still. He could hear his own heart beat and the scuff of his boots on the white path. A branch sagged above him, and snow broke over his hood and shoulders. A bat flew out and startled him, and he followed its dipping, uncertain flight back into the forest shadows.

When he reached the high ground, he looked back and saw the town nestling in the neck of the valley, dwarfed to doll-size by the peaks, its lights pale and uncertain against the star-blaze and the high shining snow-field.

The first excitement of his adventure died in him quickly. This too was a small thing—sordid, meaningless. There was no dignity in a man-hunt, no triumph in a hanging.

The chant of the goat-men was nearer now and, as he looked up the path, he saw through the trees the approach of the first small procession: two boys, dressed as pages, each carrying a sack on his back, the Saint, with a high head-dress of paper flowers, and behind them three Krampuses, prancing and howling.

He stepped back into the shadows and waited for them to come.

He took the pistol out of his pocket and released the safety-catch. He threw back his hood and felt the cold strike at his face and neck. They had left the trees now and were advancing down the straight stretch of path towards him. When they came abreast he stepped out and called sharply: 'Wait there!'

They froze in their tracks, their faces turned towards him—the soft faces of the boys, a girl's face, incongruous under the cotton-wool whiskers of the Saint, the distorted faces of the attendants devils. All of them were watching the gun in his hand. He identified himself curtly:

'My name is Hanlon, Occupation Commander. Identity check. Take off your masks.'

They hesitated, looking at one another in doubt and puzzlement.

'Take them off.'

Slowly the Krampus figures raised their hands and lifted the heavy wooden masks from their heads. The change was so comical that he almost laughed aloud. Three doltish faces looked at him, scared and gaping. Their eyes were vacant and hostile. Their cheeks were stubbled and unscarred. None of them was the man he wanted.

'That's all. You can put them on now.'

They settled the masks again and stood there, not understanding what was expected of them. Hanlon grinned and waved them away with his pistol.

'You can go. It's just a formality. *Güte Reise.*'

None of them answered his greeting. The girl-saint prodded the pages furtively and they moved off. But the howling had stopped and the drumming and the dancing. They looked just what they were, a bunch of scrubby mummers playing an old farce, crude and senseless.

Hanlon put his gun back in his pocket and leaned back against the rough bark of a pine tree. He took out cigarettes and lit one, but the sharp mountain air made him cough and he tossed away the cigarette and trod it into a snowdrift. He felt faintly ridiculous. He wondered how many more times this would happen to him before the evening was out.

Four times was the count; each time he felt more uncomfortable and more irritated at having committed himself to the chancy venture. The cold was beginning to eat into him and there was no warmth in these repeated failures. He looked at his watch. Seven-thirty. An hour and a half before Johnson and his men started operations in the town. He decided to work his way round to the other side of the valley along the big path that traversed the neck and linked the two opposing walls of mountains.

He stepped out briskly, head thrust forward, shoulders humped, hands thrust deep into his pockets. He had walked for about ten minutes when he saw something that stopped him in his tracks. Twenty yards ahead was a high stone wall, broken by a big iron gate. Behind it, high among the trees, were the lights of a large house.

Outside the gate were three Krampus figures. Their backs were towards him, and they were talking earnestly among themselves, so that they neither saw nor heard him. The oddity was that they were alone. There was no sign of the Saint or his attendant pages. Unless, of course, they had finished their rounds and were waiting to go down to the town. In any case, they had to be identified.

Hanlon took out his pistol and walked briskly towards them. They turned sharply at his footfall, but he was already upon them and at the sight of the gun they backed carefully against the wall. Hanlon looked at them a moment, noticing with a flicker of interest that one of the costumes was older than the rest, the hide worn and bedraggled, the mask more fantastic and ornate. He told them, as he had told all the previous parties:

'Identity check. Take off your masks.'

A thick voice answered him in dialect.

'Why should we? Can't we even have our feast day in private?'

'It's an order,' said Hanlon mildly. 'Let's get it over and you can go about your business. Take 'em off.'

None of the figures moved. Their agate eyes stared at him, expressionless. The saw-tooth mouths leered at him. 'They're drunk,' thought Hanlon. 'Drunk and stubborn.' He reasoned with them carefully.

'You don't want trouble. Neither do I. But I can make it for you if you play the fool. Take off your masks. Let me have a look at you. Then you can all go down and finish your drinking in town.'

'And if we don't?' The thick voice was truculent now.

'A wise man doesn't argue with a gun,' said Hanlon sharply.

Then another voice spoke, from behind the oldest mask. An educated voice, he noticed, free from the raw peasant accent.

'Do as he says. We don't want trouble.'

'But listen . . .!'

'Do as he says.'

Slowly, the first man raised his hands and began to lift his mask. Hanlon's attention wavered for a moment so that he missed the swift movement as the second man flicked up his chain belt and swung it against the side of his head.

There was a crack like splitting timber and Hanlon went down, spread-eagled in the roadway, his face buried in a drift. A slow spreading of blood stained into the snow and quickly froze. The feet of the goat-men trampled him savagely as they hurried off into the darkness of the trees.

His wakening was a slow nightmare of pain and blindness and nausea and stifling perplexity. He was smothered by darkness and the darkness was a stone-roof against which he battered himself till his head seemed ready to burst. It was a black liquid forced down his throat by faceless torturers. It was fire scalding his face and his hands. It was a horror that enveloped him like the stink of a charnel-house. It was a sea on which he floated, a whirlpool in which he spun dizzily, a swamp in which he gasped helplessly against drowning.

There were leaden pennies on his eyes and when he tried to move them he realised that his hands were bound in cerecloths and his face was swathed like a mummy's He was choked with sickness, and his tongue fell backward into his gullet when he tried to shout. He heard voices that babbled without meaning and names that he had once known but were now alien symbols. He was alive in a world too small for movement. He was adrift in a space without limits.

Then the nightmare passed and a small comforting death took hold of him. The resurrection came slowly. He understood that he was in a bed. He was alive and warm. And if he moved there was pain.

The first thing he saw was the broad, ruddy face of Doktor Huber. It was blurred at first and wavering. Then slowly it came into focus. There was a band around his forehead with a mirror in the centre of it. He held a pencil torch close to Hanlon's eyes and his big fingers were holding up one eyelid and forcing down the lower conjunctiva.

Hanlon blinked and the fingers released their grip. Huber gave a small exclamation of satisfaction and stepped back. Behind him Hanlon saw the tense white face of Captain Johnson and the blonde head of Anna Kunzli. He tried to turn his head to take in the details of the room, but a stab of pain checked him. He closed his eyes and struggled to hold on to consciousness.

When he opened them again, Doktor Huber was smiling at him. He tried to speak, but his voice seemed to come from another man, small and far away.

'What are you doing here, Huber? Where am I. What happened?'

Huber smiled gravely and shook his head.

'It's a long question, Major. Let's leave it awhile. I want to have another look at your eyes. Can you see me quite clearly?'

'Yes.'

'Good.'

Huber bent over him again, peering into the pupils with his tiny light, angling it carefully into the dark lens of the eyeball, searching for any sign of haemorrhage or clotting in the intricate network of blood vessels. Then he straightened up and put the torch back in his pocket.

'You're a very lucky man, Major. You could have been killed. You might have been blinded or deafened.'

'What happened to me?' asked Hanlon weakly.

'Give me a mirror,' said Huber to the girl. She turned away and a moment later she was back with a small hand mirror. Huber held it up in front of Hanlon's face and he stared at the image that confronted him.

His head was bound with swathes of bandage, bloody on the left side. His face was covered with lint held in place by adhesive plaster. When he tried to lift his hands to touch it, he saw that they too were bandaged. He looked at Huber's grave face.

'I–I don't understand.'

'Herr Kunzli's housekeeper found you lying in the snow outside the gate. Your head was laid open by a massive blow. How it didn't crack your skull or give you a brain haemorrhage, I don't know. Your face and hands are badly frost-bitten. If you'd lain there much longer you'd be dead. She called Herr Kunzli and Anna here and they brought you up to the house, then sent for me. I called Captain Johnson.'

'How long have I been here?'

'Thirty-six hours,' said Huber soberly. 'You've had me very worried.'

'Thirty-six hours?' He could feel the nausea coming back, his hold on the world weakening again. He struggled to tell them. 'I–I met the Krampus . . . our man . . . hit me with . . . with . . . chain . . .' Darkness closed over him again. His eyes dropped and his head lolled slackly on the pillow.

Huber stood looking down at him a moment, then turned back to Johnson.

'Did that mean anything to you, Captain?'

'Attempted murder,' said Johnson curtly.

Huber nodded.

'I understand. He spoke to me about this business. It might easily have been murder. It–It could still be . . .'

Johnson stared at him, shocked.

'But I thought you said . . .'

'I can't find any sign of haemorrhage. There may be one, none the less. We can only wait and see how he progresses over the next few days.'

'Shouldn't we get him back to the Sonnblick?'

'No!' Huber was emphatic about it. 'I cannot have him moved in any circumstances. Fräulein Anna here can look after him. You can come to see him whenever you want. I'll visit him twice a day until we are sure there are no complications.'

'I'm–very grateful,' said Johnson awkwardly in German.

Then for the first time the girl spoke:

'We're happy to do what we can, Captain. I promise you I'll give him every care. What should I expect, Doktor? What should I do?'

'He'll be like this for a day or two, drifting between consciousness and unconsciousness. The conscious periods should become longer as he progresses. Feed him a little broth when he can take it. You know how to take a pulse count and a temperature; call me if there is any perceptible slackening, or if there is fever. He may vomit today–let me know if it is severe, or if the unconsciousness lasts too long. I'll change the dressings when I come. No visitors, except the Captain. Even from you, Captain, no long talk until he begins to mend properly.'

Johnson nodded.

'I understand, Doktor.'

'Fräulein?'

'I understand too.'

'If you want medicine, drugs . . .' said Johnson uncertainly.

'I'll call on you,' Huber answered him with a ghost of a smile. Then a new thought struck him and his broad face clouded again. 'There's a murderer in the town, Captain. What do you propose to do about it?'

Johnson told him savagely: 'I'm going to take the town apart, house by house. Why?'

'Advice from a friend,' said Huber slowly. 'Leave it a day or two, until the Major can talk to us. You will lose nothing, I promise you. On the other hand you may gain much.'

'I'll think about it.'

'Do that, Captain. Come, Anna, there are more instructions for you.' He turned and led the girl out of the room.

Johnson stood a long time looking down at the slack figure on the bed, at the frost-bitten hands and the ravaged face and the bandaged head lolling against the white pillow.

Whenever he woke, the girl was there. Sometimes there was sunlight behind her, so that her hair shone like a golden coronet. When he woke, babbling in the dark or moaning with the pain of his burnt face and hands, she would be bending over him, her hair in plaits, her body ethereal in a white gown with lace at the throat and at the wrists. Her hands soothed him and her voice calmed him, and the fragrance of her perfume lingered with him. When he lapsed again it was as if she followed him past the borders of sleep and into the blackness beyond.

He fought his way out of nightmares, shouting her name: 'Anna! Anna!' and she was with him even before he knew it. He submitted without humiliation to be washed and cleansed by her, and, when the dressings were stripped off his wounds and he gasped with the pain, her arms were there to support him. She fed him like a child, spooning the food over his swollen, blistered lips.

He understood now that he was sleeping in her room, and in her bed, and that she had moved to a small cubby-hole across the hall to be within sound of his voice, day and night.

She sat with him through the day, reading, knitting, mending, dozing sometimes because her night had been broken. If he tried to talk she answered once or twice, then hushed him, so that he lay relaxed in a healing doze until the next pains shook him and she came running to his side.

Because he was a man who had been disappointed in one woman he was all the more surprised by the solicitude of this one. Because he was sick he accepted it without question, but gratitude deepened in him as consciousness established itself.

For the first forty-eight hours he tossed uneasily between the brief crests of waking and the long deep troughs of darkness. Then slowly the rhythm changed. There was more day than night; less sleep, more pain; more comfort in the hands and the voice and the young, attentive face under the coronet of corn-gold hair.

One morning when she had finished washing him and smoothing the sheets, she sat down on the end of the bed. He reached out his bandaged hands and laid them in hers. He said languidly:

'You're very good to me, Anna.'

'I like doing it, Mark,' she told him with gentle gravity. His name was a habit with her now, after the watchful hours and their struggle together.

'Why? Sickness is never pleasant, least of all for the nurse.'

'All my life people have cared for me,' she told him simply. 'Now, for the first time, there is someone I can care for; I like that.'

He nodded agreement. It was a thing he understood; something he had once believed in before he had put on cynicism like an armour against the disappointments of passion. Now he was sick and he wore no armour—and who could mistrust such patient innocence? He asked her again:

'Have I been hard to manage?'

She smiled at him.

'Not really. Sometimes you were afraid—and I was afraid too. Sometimes in your sleep you cursed and swore. But men always do that when they're hurt, don't they?'

He tried to smile at her, but his lips were cracked and painful, so that the smile was only in his eyes.

'I'm afraid we do. Was it very bad?'

'Most of it was in English, so I didn't understand it. The German was bad enough.' She was silent a moment, watching his face—the stubble growing up around the dressings, the blue sunken skin under the eyes, the prominent bones of the jaw and the lines etched around his mouth by pain and experience. She reached forward with an oddly intimate gesture and brushed away a wisp of cotton trailing towards his lips. Then she asked him quietly:

'Mark, who is Lynn?'

The smile went out of his eyes. His voice was no longer languid, but tight and strained. 'Where did you hear that name?'

'You were calling it in your nightmares, over and over again.'

'What did I say?'

'I didn't understand. You were talking in English.'

'Oh.'

He relaxed again, closing his eyes and feeling his body limp under the sheets. Anna's voice seemed to come from a long way off:

'I'm sorry. Perhaps I shouldn't have asked. I–I didn't mean to pry. It seemed to trouble you, that's all.'

'It does sometimes.'

He opened his eyes and tried to smile at her again, but when he saw how troubled she was, he drew her a little closer with his maimed hands and said gently:

'It's an old story. Old and unhappy. Lynn is my wife.'

She was not looking at him now, but down at his hands, muffled and shapeless in the bandages, and at her own, clasped over them gently.

'You don't have to talk about it. Unless you want to.'

For the first time in years he did want to talk about it. Here, in the privacy of the sick room, in the sexless intimacy of the first healing day, he could do it without shame. The patient has no pride when the nurse strips him down and bathes him like a babe. Why should he have it when she asks him about his nightmares and he has so much need to purge them out of his soul? So, he told her:

'I was very young, very hungry for love. I had been in a monastery, you see, where passion is suppressed by discipline and love is supposed to be transfigured into a love of God, which the divines call Charity. It is sometimes, when a man is old and the urges of youth have been boned out of him. Sometimes, too, when a man is young–but then only by a special intervention of the Almighty, who wants a saint or two in each century. Me? I should never have been there in the first place; so I was out of both classes.'

'How did you come there?'

'By accident.' He grinned at her disarmingly. 'My father died when I was young. He was a Liverpool Irishman who stayed in Germany after the First War to garrison Hamburg.'

'Just like you, Mark.'

'Just like me. The week before he was due home, he was killed by a runaway car. We were left to fend for ourselves. I was the youngest and a drain on the family. I was lonely too, and I didn't know where I was going or why, so when the good Father came round with his sermon on vocations and his little handful of leaflets, I was in–body, soul and reach-me-down breeches.'

'And you were unhappy?' The wide innocent eyes were fixed on his face.

'Not at first. Not for a long while. But I wasn't happy either. And it's a big truth, Anna—' he leaned on it sombrely–'we're meant to be happy–in monasteries, in marriage, even the Christus on the cross. If we're not, there's something amiss with ourselves, or the folk we live with: generally it's both. So, after a few years, I left. Father Albertus tapped me on the head and gave me his blessing and sent me back to the big wide world I knew nothing about, except that there were girls in it, and I hoped one day one of 'em might love me . . .'

'Father Albertus!' She stared at him, unbelieving. 'You were with him, here? In Austria?'

He nodded, amused at her shock.

'In Graz. He was Novice-Master then.'

She shook her head vaguely as if trying to clear it of some confusion. Her eyes stared past him to some secret speculation of her own.

'So strange, Mark . . . so very strange.'

'What?'

'That you should both be here now and that you should be—what you are.'

'Not so strange, Anna.'

'Why?'

'I wanted to come back. I pulled all the strings I knew to arrange it.'

'What made you want it so much?'

'That's the end of the story,' he told her lightly. 'The riddle you guess at when you have the clues. Three months out of the monastery, I met Lynn. I fell in love with her. Three months after that we were married.'

'Did you really love her?'

'Desperately.'

'What happened then?'

'Nothing.'

'I don't understand you, Mark.'

'Nothing happened, *Liebchen*, nothing at all. We were married. We had two children, who write to me sometimes. Then we didn't have any more because Lynn refused to have them—or me either. It took me a long time to understand that she didn't love me. I was necessary to her, but not as a lover, not as a husband. I thought time might bring love, or patience and tenderness, but I was wrong. I thought passion might bring it, but there was no passion in her—not for me. Then one say I understood something else. Love can die too. It sickens like a plant and wilts slowly, and one day it is dead. Nothing can resurrect it—nothing.'

'You are still married?'

'Yes.'

'Why?'

'For the children's sake—for religion's sake. But there's nothing left in it. I'm here, she's in England, neither of us missing the other.'

'Yet you cry for her in your sleep.'

'Not for her, Anna; for love, yes. The love I spent for no return. The love I pleaded for but never had.'

'One should never plead for love,' said the girl gravely. 'I found that with Uncle Sepp. It is there or it is not there. If it is not, one can never waken it.'

'That,' said Mark Hanlon wryly, 'is one lesson Father Albertus never taught me. I must remind him of it sometime.'

It was out now, and the last of his small strength seemed to have gone with it. He closed his eyes and lay back on the pillow, feeling the drowsiness lap over him in soft, grateful waves. It seemed to him then that Anna Kunzli came and bent over him and touched her lips to his forehead. Illusion? A sweet inconsequent reality? He did not know, and by then he was too tired to care.

II

As soon as Hanlon was able to sustain a coherent conversation, Johnson was there with his list of problems. The young captain was willing enough to accept responsibility, but wise enough to know his limitations. Huber's counsel had left him dubious about precipitate action and he knew Hanlon would disapprove of a hasty application to Klagenfurt. Somewhat to his surprise, Hanlon disagreed with Huber.

'Let's have action, Johnny, by all means. It won't catch our man but it'll worry the hell out of Fischer.'

'What do you want, Mark?'

'House searches first, Johnny, simultaneously, all over the town. Keep the areas as widely separated as possible and stagger the times and places so that there's no apparent pattern. Four men to each search: one to the back door, one to the front, two to work the place over from ceiling to cellar.'

'Do you want him dead or alive?' asked Johnson with a grin. His good-humour was returning now that Hanlon was in the saddle again.

'Alive,' said Hanlon definitely. 'But let's not take crazy risks.'

'Like you, for instance?'

'Like me.'

'Any other ideas?'

'I'd like to tap Fischer's telephone and keep a tail on him twenty-four hours a day. But the town's too small and we haven't the men for it. He'd know in ten minutes.'

'What are you going to do about him, then?'

'Let him sweat. You can lay odds he's doing it now. Very soon I think he'll decide to call on me. Then we'll see what he has to say for himself.'

'What's his connection with the killer, Mark?'

Hanlon frowned and shook his head. He was beginning to tire again and his temples were throbbing.

'I haven't had time to think about it, properly, Johnny. But there's a link that will slip into place soon. Leave it to me.'

'Only too happy,' said Johnson with a grin. 'How long do you expect to stay here?'

'I'll be out as soon as Huber agrees, if not before.'

'Why rush it?' asked Johnson with plaintive envy. 'Home was never like this.' He cast an eye approvingly round the room and sniffed the air for the lingering traces of perfume. 'Maybe we could both function from here?'

'To hell with you, Johnny.' Hanlon laughed in spite of himself.

'Before I go, there's one more question.'

'What's that?'

'What do I tell Klagenfurt about this?'

'Nothing,' said Hanlon flatly. 'I'll write my own report in due course. If they think I'm out of commission they'll have a new commander and half a dozen clodhopping investigators up here in twenty-four hours.'

Johnson looked relieved.

'Just thought I'd mention it for the record. And talking of records . . .'

'Yes?'

'The way the paper's pouring in we're going to need a battery of typists to handle it. It's not only what they're sending in but the stuff they want back–reams of it morning and afternoon.'

'Leave it,' said Hanlon wearily. 'Put the urgent stuff through and stack the rest in a corner. I'll look at the staff position when I'm out of this bed.'

'At least pick 'em beautiful,' pleaded Johnson mockingly. 'I'm too young for this celibate life.'

'Take long walks in the snow, boy. Take one now. My head's buzzing like a hive, and this frost-bite hurts like hell.'

'There's a price tag on everything,' chuckled Johnson. 'Even on pretty nurses. See you later, Mark.'

When he had gone, Hanlon closed his eyes and lay back on the pillows, waiting till the pain should pass and he could think clearly again. He could count on Johnson to keep the situation controlled for a while at least; the important thing was to restore his own strength before Klagenfurt got wind of the trouble and sent in a new man and a new team. The search for the man behind the gun had assumed a new, personal significance. He wanted to finish it himself.

In the evening Huber came again for the painful ritual of dressing his wounds. The first moments were the worst, but Anna was there too with soft hands and steadying voice. When he had removed the bandages, Huber handed him a mirror to see for the first time the extent of the damage.

He was shocked by the first sight of the blotched and crusted frost-burn which covered more than half his face, but Huber reassured him:

'That will clear up quickly enough. We have arrested the infection and now the new skin begins to grow This'–he traced the long open scar that ran from the tip of Hanlon's ear, across his temple and down to the cheekbone–'this is another matter. The chain opened you up like a melon skin. The scar will be ugly.'

'That makes two of us,' said Hanlon thoughtfully. 'He was scarred too. The scores are even.'

Huber was not impressed. He was examining the raw edges of the wound, cleansing them carefully with a swab.

'Later, we will do a little more work on it. A small plastic will repair the worst of the damage. But you will always be . . .'

'Say that again!'

'Say what?'

'A small plastic . . . was that it?'

Huber and the girl looked at him in surprise.

'That's right,' said Huber. 'Why do you ask?'

Hanlon looked from one to the other, debating whether to trust them. His eyes were bright with interest and his head was clear of pain and puzzlement. After a moment he said slowly:

'I'd like a promise from you both. What I have to say must be private to the three of us.'

'As you wish,' said Huber gravely.

Anna Kunzli nodded and said: 'Of course, Mark.'

Then he gave it to them.

'The man who killed Willis and did this to me is scarred too. We know that he has been brought down to the town. I know—or at least I believe—that Fischer is involved in it somewhere.'

'Fischer!' they said it together, on the same rising inflection of surprise.

Hanlon nodded. 'It's a long story. It doesn't matter for the moment. What does matter is this: Fischer has enough experience to know that he can't keep his man here indefinitely. Therefore he must have something else in mind. You gave me a feasible idea. A plastic . . . a new face. That means my identification breaks down. That means the killer, whoever he is, could either stay here or be moved into the U.S. zone without fear of discovery.'

Huber thought about it for a moment. Then he said quietly:

'It could be. But even that would take time.'

'How long?'

'I could not possibly say without seeing the man. Given a fairly easy case, a necessary minimum of skill in the surgeon, and some luck as well, three months. It might be much longer.'

'Take the surgeon first,' Hanlon quizzed him bluntly. 'Who in Quellenberg could do it?'

'I could,' Huber told him. 'And one other member of my staff.'

'Is he likely to be involved with Fischer?'

Huber shook his head.

'I doubt it. Like myself he is a foreigner—a Viennese. He has a wife and children in the British sector. I think he would not risk participation in a thing like this. In any case his movements and contacts would be easy to check.'

'Do you know anybody else—a resident?'

'Nobody. The man who could tell you would be Holzinger—and, of course, Fischer himself.'

Hanlon's puffed mouth twisted into a painful grin.

'Their information mightn't be quite reliable.'

'The town records might help.'

'We'll check 'em, line by line.'

Huber nodded gravely and bent again to the task of cleansing the raw flesh and laying on the new dressing. Anna Kunzli helped him with deft hands. Quite unexpectedly she said:

'Why don't you ask Father Albertus? He knows everybody in Bad Quellenberg.'

Huber looked up from his work and answered in his deep, quiet voice: 'It wouldn't do, little one. A priest is like a doctor; he must preserve the secrets of his flock. To ask him would be an indiscretion.'

Hanlon tried to nod his agreement, but the new antiseptic burned his face and he winced sharply. Instinctively the girl reached out her hand to quiet him. Huber's quick eye caught the movement but he said nothing.

When the dressings were finished and he was settled again, Hanlon turned to Anna and said gently:

'Would you give the doctor a cigarette, Anna, then leave us for a few moments?'

'Of course.'

She rummaged in the drawer of the bedside table, brought out Hanlon's cigarettes, handed one to Huber and put another in Hanlon's mouth. Then she went out, closing the door behind her. Huber lit up for Hanlon and himself, and the two men smoked a few moments in silence. Huber said dryly:

'With training she'd be a very good nurse. She has gentle hands and a warm heart.'

Hanlon ignored the hint and said simply:

'I'm in an awkward position, Huber.'

'How?'

'Sepp Kunzli. I may have to put him through the wringer. Yet I'm a guest in his house.'

Huber eyed him shrewdly through the smoke-drifts.

'Has he said anything to you?'

'I haven't seen him. He sends his compliments through Anna, and asks if there's anything I need, but that's all.'

'He's discreet,' said Huber placidly. 'He understands the situation as well as you do. He prefers to keep it impersonal. It's your own fault if you involve yourself.'

'Meaning?'

Huber jerked his cigarette significantly towards the door.

'The girl. She's more than half in love with you.'

'Nonsense,' said Hanlon curtly.

Huber shrugged and spread his hands eloquently.

'It starts as a nonsense. Afterwards . . . it gets serious.'

'When can I move out?'

Huber smoked for a few moments, considering the question.

'I'd like to keep you here another week, just for safety. But, as things are . . .' He paused. 'I'll send an ambulance and a couple of orderlies tomorrow to move you back to the hotel. You'll have to stay in bed though and stick to the treatment. Otherwise you're in for trouble.'

'I can cope with that sort,' said Hanlon with a grin.

'Better if you can avoid it altogether,' said Huber. 'What else did you want to talk to me about?'

'The killer.'

'What about him?'

'I've met him now,' said Hanlon. 'I think we should revise our opinion.'

'Why?'

'Your first thought was that he was deranged. A shock case . . . something like that.'

'Yes?'

'When I met him, he was with two other men. He was under no restraint. When he spoke his voice was educated and full of authority. He was obeyed. He acted swiftly and with decision.'

'Some of the craziest killers in history have been the most normal in appearance,' said Huber coolly. 'Besides, there's a flaw in your logic.'

'What's that?'

'The man who struck you may not have been the killer at all. It could have been any one of twenty men with a grudge or a bellyful of liquor. It could even have been Fischer himself. There's more than half a chance you're right, but so far it's guesswork.'

'As we're placed now I can't do anything but guess. And eliminate the improbables one by one.'

'I'm puzzled by your attitude in this matter, Major.'

Hanlon looked up, surprised at the blunt challenge.

'What puzzles you, Doktor?'

'The importance you attach to him, the extent of your personal involvement.'

Hanlon gave him a crooked smile and put one muffled hand up to his head.

'Doesn't this explain it?'

Huber shook his head. 'No, you are too intelligent for that. You are too subtle for crude revenge. You would find no pleasure in it. You know better than I how much is to be done here and how secondary is this question of a capture. You will get him in the end. If Fischer is involved, Fischer will do everything he can to keep him under cover so that he is not a danger to anyone else. But you have this–this psychotic drive to get him.'

'Call it a symbol if you want,' said Hanlon casually.

'Of what?'

'Of the things we fought against, the things we came here to stamp out–violence, lawlessness, protected murder.'

'The trouble with symbols,' said Huber calmly, 'is that they mean different things to different people. What one man worships, another draws on a lavatory wall.'

'We have a common interest,' said Hanlon irritably. 'Unless the people see that, there is no profit for either of us.'

'Then find a common symbol,' said Huber with a slow, grave smile.

'What, for instance?'

'Christmas is coming,' said the big Tyrolese, with studied irrelevance. 'There is a child lying in straw and a homeless pair stabled with the cows. There will be millions of them this year, all over Europe. Think about it, Major–for your own sake, and for ours!'

Two hours after Hanlon's return to the Sonnblick, Karl Adalbert Fischer came to see him. He brought with him a large suitcase and a tubby soft-faced fellow whom he introduced as Herr Rudolf Winkler, a retired bookseller from Munich.

Both of them were politely shocked when they saw Hanlon bandaged to the eyes and propped in the ornate bed. He heard them out in sardonic silence, and Captain Johnson watched them with pale unfriendly eyes.

Fischer had a story to tell and he had brought Winkler to corroborate it. He told it carefully and well.

'It seems we both had the same idea, Major: that an attempt might be made to bring the murderer down to the town on St Nicholas's night. You will remember that I raised the question at our last meeting.'

'I remember you made a vague reference.'

'I–I did not pursue it, since to one who did not know our customs it might have seemed laughable. I apologise for underrating your experience.'

'That's always a mistake,' Hanlon told him dryly.

'I realise that when I heard of your accident and when I saw the preparations you had made in the town. It was a clever move, Major. It nearly succeeded.'

'Go on.'

'When the news got around the town Herr Winkler here telephoned me with some information which he thought might be valuable. I think he should tell you about it himself. Then I have my own comments to add.'

The tubby fellow puffed out his smooth cheeks and launched into his story. His voice was high-pitched and faintly effeminate and his soft hands made small fluttering gestures of emphasis.

The time he judged to be about nine o'clock on St Nicholas's night, a little before, or a little after, he could not be certain. At the time it had had no significance. He was at home in his small house at the end of the Mozartstrasse, quiet, withdrawn from the main life of the town. He was not rich. He had to buy modestly and live quietly. However, about this time he heard voices quarrelling outside his gate, men's voices talking in the dialect of the mountains. He was a Bavarian himself and he found them difficult to understand, more so as they seemed to be drunk. He went to the door and looked out. He saw that there were three men dressed in Krampus costumes. Two seemed to be quarelling with the third. He shouted to them to be quiet and move off. One of them shouted a drunken insult. Then they split up: two of them wandered off towards the town, staggering, the third hurried off up one of the tracks that led through the pinewoods. That was all. It was only after the news of the attack on the Major that he attached any significance to the incident. The Major would understand how it was. He was something of a stranger. There was always drinking at provincial feasts. . . .

Then Fischer took up the tale:

'After Herr Winkler's telephone call, I went out immediately to interview him. I followed the track which the third man had taken. About half a mile up the slope there is a woodcutter's hut—a storehouse for wedges and tools. Inside, stuffed behind some boxes, I found this . . .'

He snapped open the suitcase and brought out the Krampus costume which Hanlon had seen on his assailant. Johnson and he stared at it in amazement.

'Do you recognise it, Major?'

'I do.'

Fischer nodded with professional gravity.

'There is a special interest in this costume. It is the oldest known example in the area. It was stolen from a show-case in our museum.'

Johnson and Hanlon looked at each other. The story was so circumstantial it might be true. Even if it weren't, Fischer must be sure it couldn't be broken. The little policeman went on:

'The mask and the show-case and the metal have been wiped clean of fingerprints. So we understand that we are dealing with intelligent people, who are also very familiar with the town.'

'I'd thought of that myself,' said Hanlon.

'I thought it would be wise, therefore, if we co-operated on an immediate search of the area, beginning at Herr Winkler's house and extending in a circular sector back towards the hills.'

'We'll arrange it immediately,' Hanlon told him. 'Captain Johnson will have a detachment ready to move off in ten minutes.'

Fischer nodded approval.

'I wish you to understand, Major, how much we all regret this business, and your own personal misfortune. I promise you our fullest co-operation.'

'Thank you, Fischer. And you too, Herr Winkler. Captain Johnson will go with you and will keep in constant touch until I am on my feet again. *Auf Wiedersehn.*'

'*Güten Tag*, Major.'

They went out; Johnson led them into the corridor and handed them over to Sergeant Jennings. Then he came back to Hanlon.

'Well, Mark? What do you think of it?'

Hanlon shrugged impatiently.

'Fischer's a policeman. He knows a good alibi when he's got it. We'll have to investigate, of course. But I'd take long odds our man is miles away from where Fischer wants us to look.'

'That's my feeling, too. What about Winkler?'

'Either an innocent bystander or an accessory. We'll check his papers, but, knowing Fischer, they'll be in order too. Follow it up, Johnny, but don't expect too much.'

'You want me to go straight away?'

'Yes. Send Jennings up to look after the office.'

'Will do. How are you feeling?'

'Like hell,' said Hanlon unhappily. 'Fischer's made me look a fool and I can't wait to take it out of his hide.'

How big a fool, he could hardly guess.

Forty minutes later Johnson and his non-coms were standing in Winkler's lounge, while the man they were hunting lay, drugged and gagged, under a box-bed, in the room of the trap-mouthed housekeeper.

As soon as Sergeant Jennings arrived, Hanlon dictated a note of thanks to Sepp Kunzli. He enclosed with it a set of travel papers and a detailed list of instructions for the visit to Zürich.

There was a letter for Anna, too, longer, more personal, which the despatch rider was to deliver into her hands.

For the rest of the afternoon he worked steadily through the mass of directives and memoranda that had piled up during his absence.

The amount and complexity of the paper work staggered him at first. Then slowly he began to understand: this was more than half the business of government. The modern world was founded on paper. Without it, chaos would come again.

Policy came first–the broad, deceptively simple statement of ends and means, a document, a manifesto–paper.

Then followed legislation, whose prelude was debate, recorded in sheaves and sheaves of pages, shelves of volumes, millions of words, whose end was more paper–the law: an invocation of authority, a definition of terms, a succession of clauses, a schedule of instructions and of sanctions for offenders, a signature and a seal.

The law was the shortest document of all. But this too began to spawn more words, more pages, more volumes: annotation, glossary, concordance and interpretation.

After the law and the interpretation came the directives handed down from echelon to echelon of administrators through the hands of clerks and typists and messengers, until they came finally to the man who must apply them–the local official.

He need ask no questions. Everything was written for him–on paper. No matter that it might take him a lifetime to find the relevant sheet, it was there, written. Ignorance was no excuse. Every case was covered. Every variant was noted, somewhere.

Then Hanlon began to understand other things, too: how the machinery of government became clogged with paper; how roguery was hidden under a web of words; how administrators hid themselves behind ramparts of books and leaders were insulated from the truth by piles of foolscap; how the voices of reformers were stifled under a vast rubbish of print.

It could happen to him now. He could sit twelve hours a day, reading every word that landed on his desk, replying to them with more words, so that his superiors would name him a careful fellow who kept the record straight–even though men were workless and children were hungry and the hope of a better life was deferred from year-end to year-end.

There was only one answer. Go back to the policy; see the facts first; apply the remedies on the spot. Here in Bad Quellenberg he could. There was a risk, of course.

The man who dispensed with paper got things done. He also dispensed with protection, and if he made a mistake, he lost his head . . .

By five-thirty his own head was spinning and the nausea was back with him again. He dismissed Jennings, made his way painfully to the bathroom, then crawled back between the sheets and dozed off.

When he woke, Captain Johnson was back with a negative report, and the news that Max Holzinger was waiting to see him.

The Bürgermeister was shocked by Hanlon's appearance, and there was a ring of sincerity in his apology and in his expression of concern. Hanlon was touched and tried to spare him embarrassment. He could not know–and Holzinger could not tell him–that there had been a long and heated argument with Fischer, which had ended in a deadlock, since Fischer was not prepared to hand over his nephew and Holzinger was afraid of the revelation of his own duplicity.

Both men were glad when the awkward preliminaries were over and they began to discuss the preparations for the coming of the displaced persons.

The building Holzinger recommended was the Bella Vista, a large, reasonably modern hotel, halfway between the railway station and the church. It was owned by a wealthy Viennese who had not been heard of since the occupation of Vienna. The lease was held by a Swiss syndicate, and the mortgage was in the hands of Sepp Kunzli. The routine of requisition kept them talking for half an hour.

They discussed staffing arrangements, food, fuel, linen, blankets, cutlery, the call-up of private cars to transport the arrivals from the station. At the end of it Holzinger told him with some eagerness:

'You can leave it all to me, Major. Believe me, I am only too happy to take some of the weight off your shoulders, to make some amends for this–this outrage.'

'Forget it,' said Hanlon with a smile. 'It's an occupational hazard. I'm lucky it wasn't worse.'

'We all are,' said Holzinger fervently.

He shifted uneasily in his chair, coughed and stammered over the next gambit.

'My–my wife and daughter are downstairs . . .'

'Good God!' Hanlon stared at him in surprise. 'Why didn't you tell me? They've been waiting an age.'

'It is nothing,' Holzinger assured him awkwardly. 'They insisted on coming. We–that is, I myself–had a talk with Doktor Huber. He told me you were still in need of attention. Now I have seen it myself. My family would like to take over your care. Huber himself is a busy man and this is, after all, a woman's business.'

Hanlon flushed with embarrassment. The offer was patently sincere and singularly attractive as against the cruder ministrations of an Army orderly. But there was the old problem. It set up an obligation, a personal relationship, which might later become embarrassing. He decided to be frank about it.

'I'm very grateful, Herr Bürgermeister. Believe that. I'd like nothing better than to accept.' He grinned disarmingly. 'I like my comfort, and I'm a long way from home. But, don't you see, it could be awkward for both of us. Placed as I am, I may have to enter into dispute with you. Don't misunderstand this, but I may even have to remove you from office. If I am under an obligation to you or to your family . . .'

He broke off and let the sentence hang in mid-air. Holzinger nodded and smiled and then bent forward eagerly.

'I'm glad that you told me, Major. Even if you hadn't I should have known it was in your mind. Understand this first—there are no obligations. Business is business. We both know it. But we are not always in business. We are human too. We like to feel that we can do a kindness and repair a wrong. If only for our dignity, we need that. You would do us a favour, if you would accept.'

Hanlon was beaten and he knew it. A man couldn't play the cynic all the time. If one believed in human kindness one could not for ever choke back its impulses in others. There was no profit in that for either party. Why deny oneself a comfort that pleased the giver as well? He had made his point. He was practising no deception on Holzinger—though he might be deceiving himself. The old monastic itch again! He brushed it away impatiently. A man could scratch himself raw and have no joy at the end of it.

Holzinger was watching him anxiously, trying to interpret his hesitation. Hanlon's cracked lips parted in a rueful smile. He held up his muffled hands.

'You take me at a disadvantage, Herr Bürgermeister. So long as you and I understand each other, I'll be glad to accept.'

A few minutes later Liesl Holzinger and her daughter came up to bathe him and change his dressings. The first breach had been made. The women were moving in to the citadel of the conqueror.

12

Three days later the first train-load of concentration-camp victims arrived in Bad Quellenberg.

The townsfolk heard them coming a long way off, because the sound of the locomotive was like thunder between the hills, and the high scream of the whistle leapt from peak to peak along the winding defile.

They looked at each other, dubious and half-afraid. They remembered the sermon that Father Albertus had preached at the Sunday Masses. They saw his broken hand outflung, and they heard the deep tolling of his voice, challenging them to repentance for a common sin, to restitution for a common injustice, to pity for misery too long ignored.

They remembered, and they were ashamed. They looked away from each other, then reached for coats and hats and began to move, slowly and unwillingly, towards the station.

Soon the approaches and the marshalling yards were jammed and the troops had to clear a passage for the ambulances and the cars and the miscellaneous transport which would carry the sick down to the hospital. On the platform the senior citizens were assembled – the Bürgermeister, the councillors, Karl Adalbert Fischer, Father Albertus. Sepp Kunzli was not there. He was already halfway through the Arlberg, heading for Zürich.

Down by the tracks the troops were drawn up, unarmed and standing easy, with the stretcher-bearers and the drivers waiting behind them. Hanlon and Captain Johnson stood a little apart, watching the final preparations, stamping their feet in the powdery snow, their faces half-turned towards the defile, where the scream and the thunder rang louder as the minutes ticked by.

Hanlon was still in bandages. His face was muffled in a thick scarf and his hands were thrust into a fur muff that gave him a faintly comical appearance. But there was no one to laugh at the comedy. This was the last act of a long-drawn tragedy, the final purging moment of pity and of terror.

Then the train came in, hauled by a squat green engine with grotesque antennae, the snow tossing up in little clouds from under the wheels. It stopped with a rattle and a jerk and the crowd strained forward to catch a glimpse of the occupants; but the windows were misted over and they could see nothing.

The door of the first carriage opened and a tall fellow stepped out. He had a thin hawk-face, a scrawny neck, a prominent chin and grey hair. He wore snowboots and baggy trousers and a windbreaker of American pattern with a Red Cross brassard stitched to the sleeve. When Hanlon stepped forward to greet him he introduced himself in a flat Mid-Western drawl:

'I'm Miller, Chief Medical Officer.'

'Hanlon, Occupation Commander. We're happy to have you.'

'Thanks, Major.' Miller shot a quick glance at the silent crowd and at the little group on the platform. 'Quite a reception.'

'You'd better meet 'em,' said Hanlon. 'They've tried to be helpful.'

He led Miller over to the platform and made the introductions; to Holzinger first, then to Fischer and the councillors. Miller did not offer his hand but nodded curtly and Hanlon was embarrassed by his obvious coldness. He turned away and presented the priest.

'This is Father Albertus, the parish priest. He is himself a camp victim.'

Miller's lined face brightened immediately, and he held out his hand. 'Glad to know you, Father. You'll be able to help us a great deal.'

'Don't misjudge our people, Doctor Miller,' said the priest in his mild, direct fashion. 'They are anxious to help you as much as possible.'

'I wonder if they'll still be as anxious when they see what I've brought them?' He jerked his thumb significantly towards the train. 'Three hundred men, women and children. You'll be burying half of 'em over the next month or two.'

Father Albertus nodded gravely but said nothing. Miller turned away. 'Come, Major, let's get going!'

They walked back towards the train and, at a signal from Johnson, the troops and the stretcher-bearers followed them, and after a moment they all disappeared inside the train. The people waited, tense and expectant, wondering what monsters might be hidden behind the grey misted windows.

When the first stretcher cases were brought out, a low moan of horror shook the crowd. They were wrapped in blankets and their heads were covered with woollen caps, so that only their faces were visible: but these were yellow as parchment and shrunken back to the bone. Their eyes were sunk in dark sockets, their lips were thin and bloodless, drawn back in a rictus of pain, so that they looked more like corpses than living men. The stretcher-bearers carried them lightly, because there was no weight in their bodies. Then the stretchers were stacked, one above the other on the ambulance racks, the doors were closed and the vehicles moved off, lurching through the snow, the wheel-chairs rattling strangely in the silence.

After a while there were no more stretchers, and the bearers stepped out, carrying limp bodies in their arms, so that the crowd saw their skeleton limbs and their necks so weak that they could not support the bony, lolling heads.

When they were seated in the cars, they fell against one another like rag dolls, and the orderlies in front seats had to lean backward and support them.

The walking cases came next, men and women draped in clothes that hung like scarecrow garments. When they walked it was with the shambling, disjointed movements of the very old. Some of them slipped and fell on the icy ground, and when the watchers started forward to help them, they saw the scarred faces and the knotted hands and the shaven scalps and the dead, lustreless eyes.

Last of all came the children, pitiful little bundles with old monkey faces and gapped teeth and twisted, rickety limbs.

When they saw them, the people wept. The women covered their faces with their hands and the men stood, dumb and horror-struck, with the tears rolling down their cheeks. When Hanlon and Miller drove off in the jeep and the troops followed, silent and stony-faced, they fell apart, heads bowed, to hide the shame that was in them. After a while they turned their faces homewards, walking slowly and silently, like folk who have seen a vision of damnation.

In the manager's office at the Bella Vista, Hanlon and Miller were talking over the coffee-cups. The tall American was more relaxed now. He sat sprawled in his chair, chewing on an old pipe, drawling his approval of the preparations that had been made for his patients.

'You've done a good job, Major. I'm grateful. I'll say so in my first report.'

Hanlon shrugged.

'It's unnecessary.'

'I'll do it just the same.' His lined face puckered into a smile. 'Quite a shock, wasn't it?'

'That's an understatement.'

'It's all an understatement,' said Miller laconically. 'This is nothing to what we saw in the camps. These are the lucky ones.'

'You said half of them would die. Did you mean that?'

Miller nodded and took the pipe out of his mouth.

'It's a conservative estimate. They've got T.B. and damaged hearts and ruptured kidneys and a list of ailments as long as your arm. They've been starved and beaten for so long they've got nothing left to fight with. Even the ones who survive will be damaged for life. Still . . . we've got to do the best we can.'

He put the pipe back in his mouth and sucked on it thoughtfully. Hanlon drank the last of his coffee and lit a cigarette. Then he said, simply:

'If there's anything you want, anything I can do, let me know.'

'First thing we've got to do, Major, is talk to the staff.'

Hanlon looked at him surprised.

'I don't understand.'

'They won't either,' said Miller in his drawling fashion. 'We've got to teach 'em some of the facts of life.'

'What, for instance?'

Miller laid his pipe down on the lip of the ash-tray and leaned forward gesturing with his long, knotted hands.

'In twenty-four hours, Major, this place will look more like a madhouse than a hospital. Remember that most of these people have spent years in concentration camps. They lived like animals, fighting for food, sleeping with the dead, envying the dying. Normal life is a strangeness to them. They don't understand it any more. Some of them still eat with their hands, cramming food into their mouths in case it's snatched away from them. They urinate in the corridors, they sleep in their own filth, they scream and struggle when their clothes are taken away to be washed, they fight the orderlies who come to give them injections because that's the way they saw people killed. We're dealing with broken minds as well as broken bodies. We need patience and lots of understanding. Even for my staff it's difficult. But for the locals . . .' He broke off and leaned back in his chair, watching Hanlon with quizzical, ironic eyes.

'Who'll talk to them, Doctor–you or me?'

'I'd prefer you to,' said Miller flatly. 'You hired 'em. You know 'em better than I do.'

'There's a man who could do it better than either of us.'

'Who's that?'

'Father Albertus.'

'Let's get him,' said Miller laconically.

Hanlon reached for the telephone.

Twenty minutes later they were sitting at the back of the big lounge of the Bella Vista, behind the rows of peasant women and elderly men who listened silently to the old priest as he explained their duties as servants of the sick and the problems they would have to face in their daily execution.

He talked simply, persuasively, and Hanlon was struck once again by his compassion and his understanding of the people who were his flock. He told them of his own life as a prisoner: how he had been beaten and starved and his hands broken, so that by repeated torment he had been reduced to the same sub-human state as the others; how after a session of torture he had fouled himself and lain for hours, helpless and filthy, until a scarecrow hand had reached out to help him; how a man's dignity could be so damaged that only patient charity might restore it; how the sick became like children, petulant, ungrateful, obstinate; how the Christus himself had been debased so that he had to depend on his creatures to wipe the blood and spittle from his face and make him clean even for burial. He told them how they must act when they were cursed and struck, how the maimed and the debased were the proper images of Christ, so that a service to them was a service to the Creator. . . .

The old man's eloquence held them all, even Miller, who sat moodily sucking his dead pipe, his eyes fixed on the luminous face under its crown of white hair.

Suddenly Hanlon's attention was wrenched away.

Halfway down the room, wedged between two stout peasant women, sat Anna Kunzli.

From where he sat he could see her golden hair and the profile of her face tilted upward in an attitude of attention. The sight of her shocked him. A child like that in a sad gallery like this one! What part had she in all this wretchedness? What had brought her, and who had permittted her to come?

He was filled with sharp resentment towards Father Albertus and the deep, compassionate voice began to irritate him. No one had the right to lay these burdens on the young. Let the old carry them. They had had their youth and their laughter. This girl had never known either. She was no nun to be bound to such service, she had no sins to demand such penance. Let the others pay their debts first, those who had eaten the fruits of the old triumph–Holzinger's wife, Traudl . . .

Then he remembered, and was ashamed to see how easily he had been tricked. Holzinger's women were waiting for him back at the Sonnblick. They were beyond criticism. They were in service already–the clean, comfortable, dignified service of Caesar's friend. He could dispense with them of course. He could tell them with bland regret that they must go, that there were others who needed them more than himself.

Even as he thought it, he knew he would not do it. No man puts off willingly the panoply of power. He who sits under the eagles has need of comfort in his private rooms.

When Father Albertus had finished speaking, Miller went up to thank him and take him on a tour of the hospital. The small crowd dispersed about their duties, and Hanlon followed Anna out into the corridor and down to a small room stacked with buckets and brooms. She turned suddenly at the sound of his voice and saw him standing in the doorway, blocking her exit. Her face lit up with pleasure.

'Mark! I didn't expect to see you here!'

'I didn't expect to see you either, Anna,' he told her, unsmiling. 'What are you doing? Why did you come?'

The harsh note in his voice puzzled her. She stared at him.

'Why not, Mark? You saw these people. You know how much they need help.'

'There are others to give it to them, Anna.' Her innocence angered him now. 'You're–you're too young for it. You don't understand . . .'

'Didn't you see the children?'

'I did but . . .'

'They need somebody young. Don't you see that? They've got to learn to smile again. I may not be very good at scrubbing floors, but I do like children. They like me too. Why are you angry, Mark?'

The fact that he could not answer her made him angrier still. He said roughly:

'I don't agree with it, that's all. When your uncle comes back I'm going to tell him to keep you at home.'

'Mark!' There was so much hurt in her voice and in her eyes that he softened immediately and reached out his bandaged hands to touch her.

'I'm sorry, Anna. I didn't mean to be rough. But you don't understand what you're taking on. Why do you think we brought Father Albertus here, except to prepare people for something rather terrible? I'd rather you didn't have a part in it.'

For a long moment she did not answer him, but stood holding his hands in her own, looking at the raw discoloured flesh just visible at the edge of the bandages. Then she said softly:

'If it were you that needed me, Mark, I would come gladly. But you don't, do you? It was true what I told you the other night. I must have someone to care for. Without that I am empty. If not you—then the children. Don't deny it me. Please tell me you understand.'

As suddenly as it had flared, the anger was quenched in him. He stood looking down at her with love and pity, smiling wryly at the simplicity of his own defeat. He told her gently:

'Very well, *Liebchen*. Do what you want. The children will be lucky to have you.'

Then he turned away swiftly and walked down the echoing corridor and out into the raw cold of the afternoon.

13

The sun came swinging northward, off the Horns of the Goat and into the Claws of the Crab. The north winds died in a last flurry of snow, a final patter of sleet. The air was warmer and the skies were duller and the days were longer. The first avalanches thundered down from the peaks, dashing themselves into snow-spume on the barriers of pines.

Then the south wind came, shouting up the defiles, and the snow peeled off the lower slopes like a skin, revealing the green flush of the new grass. The bare brambles along the river sprouted into life, the pine-sap flowed, and every valley was full of the noise of water flooding down into the flat country.

The cattle came out of their winter stalls and wandered into the upland, their clappers making a music between the rocks where the late snow was piled in shining drifts. The townsfolk put off their winter grey and the women went shopping in bright dirndls and starched aprons, while the men put on *Lederhosen* and white stockings and hats with jaunty cockades of pheasant tails or chamois hair.

The meadows were dappled with cloud-shadows. The girls walked proudly, swinging their skirts, and the cripples sunning themselves on the promenades whistled as they passed.

Spring was striding over the mountains and the people were opening their hearts and their windows to welcome it.

From his high balcony at the Sonnblick, Mark Hanlon looked down on his small empire and found it good.

He could see the progress now, as he could see the first green shoots that mocked the long death of winter. There was work for the men and food for the children. The first rough patterns of commerce were beginning to shape themselves.

Timber was being cut in the mountains. He could hear the ring of the distant axe-strokes. The logs were trundling down the slides and there were three mills working on the fringes of the town. Raw and unseasoned as it was, the milled pine was being snapped up before it was cut, to rebuild the

bombed areas of a dozen towns. By a system of inter-zone barter, which
Hanlon had designed, half the proceeds of the sale must be delivered in
goods–foodstuffs, clothing material, shoes, medicine. The other half was
paid in Occupation credits which were blocked for future reconstruction.
The schilling was at a discount in the markets and Hanlon refused to sell
good timber for devalued paper.

Out of these credits he had bought two antique stone-crushers which
were now clattering away in the quarries, so that the town had gravel to sell
for spring-time road repairs. The first lapidaries were coming in from
Vienna and Rome and Geneva to buy up the bloodstone and the rock-
crystal which were being chipped out of the old workings.

New bloodstock had been bought on a co-operative scheme to revitalise
the local herds. One of Hanlon's troops was a West Country farmer and
Hanlon had given him a sergeant's stripes and set him in charge of
agricultural enterprises.

The first speculators had appeared with rock-bottom offers for the empty
hotels and guest-houses. He had blocked all sales until titles had been
cleared and had exacted a deposit with any offical quote. The deposits were
paid into a trust fund whose interest gave him a little more credit for local
industries.

Miller's D.P. hospital was functioning smoothly at last. As the first bad
cases died off, others were sent up to replace them, and those who recovered
were now beginning to move about the town, remote, a little ghost-like, but
at least alive–which was no small triumph in the years of the hecatombs.

Huber was getting a small ration of the new drugs, and this victory had
made a bond of friendship between the two men. A Red Cross official was
working in the town, trying to trace the hundreds of missing men from the
Quellenberg Regiment.

His own staff had been increased. An intelligence team had moved in to
investigate Party affiliations and property titles, and with the increase had
come promotion for Hanlon and Johnson.

Batteries of typewriters had been indented for and local girls recruited to
deal with the mountains of paper-work.

A newcomer to Bad Quellenberg would not have noticed a tenth of it. He
would have seen a shabby resort, peopled by mountain folk and sick men
and a small colony of troops, with empty hotels and rationed goods, and at
best a marginal living.

But, standing on the balcony, looking out over the circling town and the
green patchwork valley, Lieutenant-Colonel Mark Hanlon saw the truth of
it. There was progress. There was life. There was hope to match the new
coming of spring.

One thing still irked him. He had not yet found the man behind the gun.
In spite of Johnson's raised eyebrows he had insisted on continuing the
house searches. When the intelligence teams moved in, he had made it part
of their assignment. But the man had not been found. There were rumours,
vague hints and tags of gossip, all of which pointed to the fact that the
murderer was still in the area. But his name and hiding place were still a
mystery.

It was the one sour taste after the sweet wine of success. It was a damage
to his pride. If he could not bring the Quellenbergers to submit this case to a
just trial, then he had failed. The principle of justice was still in breach.

That was what he told himself.

The truth lay deeper than he dared to probe. Huber had touched it sharply in one of their frequent talks. The big Tyrolese had grinned at him and said in his slow, provincial burr: 'You do so much, my friend. You have so much intelligence. And yet you are blind in this matter.'

'How?'

'You are not content to be the consul, the friendly governor. You want to marry yourself to this people.'

'What's wrong with that?'

Huber made a wide emphatic gesture.

'Mixed marriages never work. There is always the reserve, the area of–of incomprehension. Nations are like families. They have their own privacy. They have their own jokes–about the follies of Aunt Matilda and the lecheries of Uncle George. The stranger cannot share them, not ever. They have their scales of judgment which have nothing to do with absolute justice–or perhaps come closer to it than any you can dispense. You will never bring them to this final surrender. They will break your heart first.'

It was sound sense, but Hanlon could not accept it. The memory of his youth in Graz was still strong, still rosy with the afterglow of the lost paradise. The years between had been too barren of comfort. He had no yardstick to measure either hope or illusion.

The door opened behind him and Traudl Holzinger stepped out on to the balcony.

She was dressed, spring-fashion, in a swinging skirt caught at the waist with a belt of tooled leather and a light blouse moulded over her firm breasts. The skin of her face and neck and arms glowed dully with youth and health. Her perfume reminded him of that first night when he had played the piano in the Bürgermeister's house.

She was his secretary now, and though they had come neither to hand's touch nor to kiss, there was a bond between them, a sense of sharing and companionship. Her frank sensuality provoked him, but he was too wary to commit himself to an affair with her. He knew that she was wooing him, carefully and slowly, and the knowledge was a vague comfort, a daily balm to his hurt pride. While she worked with him he was comfortable and good-humoured. When she was away he found himself uneasy and irritable. They were still formal with each other. He called her Fräulein and she addressed him by his title; but he always welcomed her with a smile and she ran his office with efficiency and consideration for his comforts.

Now she had a message for him. Doktor Huber was on the phone. He thanked her and went back into the room and picked up the receiver. Huber's big voice was sharp with interest:

'I think I have something for you, my friend.'

'That sounds promising. What is it?'

'Theft,' said Huber bluntly. 'It's been going on for some time.'

Hanlon frowned in puzzlement.

'That's a matter for Fischer. I can't override his authority in local matters.'

'I think you should know about it before Fischer.'

'Why?'

'Better we don't discuss it on the telephone,' Huber told him carefully. 'How soon can you get down here?'

'How important is it?'

'It could be very important–to you.'

'Twenty minutes,' said Hanlon. '*Auf Wiedersehn.*'

'*Auf Wiedersehn.*'

The line went dead in his ear, but Hanlon still stood there with the receiver in his hand, while Traudl Holzinger watched him thoughtfully. She asked no questions. When he was ready he would tell her, as he told her most things nowadays.

In his small garden at the end of the Mozartstrasse, Rudi Winkler lay sunning himself. He was naked but for a pair of trunks, and his bright, restless eyes were hidden behind a pair of glare-glasses. His fat, pink body was stretched on a rug, his head pillowed on a rubber cushion, and he stared drowsily at the clouds drifting slowly over the pine-tops. The warmth soothed him, and the tang of sap and fresh grass were pleasant in his nostrils. The birds made him a private concert and like a true hedonist he was content with the slow delight of the moment.

He had other reasons for satisfaction as well. Inside the house his patient was sleeping off the anaesthetic. The final operation had been done, the last scar tissue had been pared away, the last new skin had been planted, and, given continuing luck, he would be a new man inside a month. Not quite a man perhaps, but a reasonable facsimile. Now that the scar had been erased, now that he had been fed and rested and calmed into security, his face had lost the wolf-look, and the blue tinge of the grafts was the only sign of the old ravages.

His eyes had changed too. The terror had gone out of them, the hostile animal glare. They were sombre now, but calm. They showed neither eagerness nor hope—but a man who had dodged the hangman should not expect too much. Even a surgeon like Rudi Winkler could not turn a eunuch into a lover or a father of sons.

He smiled at the thought and rolled over to take the sun on his shoulders and the flabby muscles of his back.

In a month he would be rid of this embarrassment. Johann Wikivill would be gone and Rudi Winkler himself would be a new man. Fischer had kept his promise: fresh papers, a fresh identity. His past was safely buried, his future comfortably assured.

Yet even this prospect had its small sour regret. When his patient had gone, he would be lonely. He had come to have a fondness for him, as an artist has for his own creation because it is the best part of himself. And, in his odd fashion, Rudi Winkler was an artist.

There was sensuality in it too. He was a sensual man addicted to refined perversities of pleasure, because the normal passion was beyond him. He had found satisfaction in his service of this damaged body. He had treated it with tenderness and care, denying himself the sharp impulses to cruelty that came on him as passion comes to more normal men. And this denial was itself a pleasure because it affirmed his dignity and seemed to absolve him from the excesses of the past.

It did not trouble him that there was no response to his tenderness and no gratitude in the sombre eyes of his patient. His pleasures had always been solitary ones. They demanded company but not sharing.

Suddenly he began to feel restless. The itch of spring was stirring under his pink hide. Discretion and the demands of his patient had kept him at home these last months. His walks had been confined to the back valleys and the less frequented paths. Now he needed something more—the movement of a town, the sight of new faces, the search for a new friend who might be complaisant to him.

He thought about it for a little while, lazily, chewing on a grass stalk. Then he got up, folded the rug and walked back to the house.

He found Johann Wikivill awake, lying on his back, staring up at the brown beams of the ceiling. The upper part of one cheek was covered with a lint dressing strapped with adhesive tape. He turned his head painfully and looked at Winkler, then asked him in a flat toneless voice:

'How did it go this time?'

Winkler bent over him smiling and touched the fresh tight skin at the side of the bandage.

'Fine. No trouble at all. Unless we get secondary infection, that's the end of it.'

'You're a good surgeon.' It was a statement of fact, not an expression of thanks. Winkler gave a high, shrill chuckle.

'You're a lucky man. I used to charge a lot of money for a job like this.'

'I understand you've been well paid for this one too.'

'Enough.' Winkler was still smiling. It was hard to put him out of countenance. 'You'll be able to start making plans for your future.'

'What sort of plans?'

'Where you'll go, what sort of work you'll do. Unless of course . . .' He let the sentence hang a moment unfinished. 'Unless you'd like to stay with me. We get on well together. We understand each other. . . .'

Somewhat to his surprise, the man on the bed did not reject the suggestion. He nodded slowly and said in the same dead voice:

'I've thought of that too. I've thought about all the things that might be left to make me feel a man again. Even that. But there's nothing.'

Winkler bent to him eagerly.

'There could be. There are so many things. . . .'

'There's nothing,' said Johann Wikivill. 'Unless a man believes . . .'

'In what?'

'In God perhaps. The soul.'

Winkler's red lips curled in contempt. His voice was a silken mockery.

'I have had many men under the knife, my friend. I have explored to the limit their capacity for sensation—and suffering. I have never yet found evidence of a soul. I have heard them scream for God but I have never known Him answer. There is only one reality—this!' He sat down on the edge of the bed and drew the tips of his fingers along the smooth new skin of Wikivill's cheek. 'This body with its million nerve ends, each susceptible to its own delight. When it dies, there is nothing. While it lives, there is still a joy to be coaxed out of it. Why reject what is left, even now?'

The man on the bed made no movement. For all the response he gave he might have been made of stone. He said simply: 'Because there is nothing left for me. Nothing.'

Winkler wrenched away his hand as if he had been burned. He stood up.

'Then I've wasted my time,' he said in a high, harsh voice. 'I should have let you hang.'

He turned abruptly and walked out of the room. The man on the bed lay back and closed his eyes. Five minutes later Rudi Winkler walked out, dressed in his light spring clothes, to take the air in Bad Quellenberg.

On the broad, paved terrace of the Spider-house, Sepp Kunzli too was taking the air. He was pacing slowly up and down, hands clasped behind his back, head thrust forward, busy with a long and complicated thought. Below him the garden fell away in banks of lawn and shrubbery to the screen of pines that gave him privacy from the road. Beside him were the big french windows that gave on to his study, where an elderly Britisher with two Austrian assistants was working through a pile of documents.

They had been there for weeks now, from nine in the morning till six at night, sorting, classifying, indexing, patiently building a schedule of Sepp Kunzli's assets and those of the men, living and dead, for whom he had acted. They were lawyers, like himself, dry, meticulous men appointed by the Occupation Authority to trace expropriated estates and restore them to the rightful owners, provided they were alive.

Now and again they spoke to him, gently, respectfully, as to an honoured colleague. When they needed advice he gave it to them. When there were gaps in the records he supplied them out of his own card-index memory. And all the time he knew that the schedule they were building would be the text of his own indictment.

Yet he was calm about it, almost content.

It was as if he had come to a crisis, survived it, and lived thereafter in a state of syncope, a suspension of all effort and all emotion.

The crisis had come on his journey to Zürich. He had left cheerfully enough, convinced that in the week at his disposal he could sort out his affairs, to leave himself comfortably rich and preserve his standing with the Allied authorities. It was a move he had prepared a long time, and, even at the worst, the salvage would be handsome.

In Zürich he had met a woman. She was charming, witty, willing, and recently divorced from a wealthy exporter. Kunzli was a cool philanderer and the affair had been simple to begin. Its ending had shocked him profoundly.

After their first night she had left him, dry-eyed and bitter, and her last words had rung in his ears ever since:

'It was like mating with a corpse. I hate you for it and I hate myself!'

In the past he had found pleasure in the fear he inspired in the wives of Party men and the daughters of generals. It was all part of his revenge. But this one was different. He had no need to revenge himself on her. He had even looked to her as the beginning of new free life, the first-fruits of the waiting years.

Then, suddenly, he understood. There would be no fruit, ever again. The tree was barren. The tap-root was cut. The sap of passion would never run again. There was only the figment of life, the dead symbol, stark and leafless, better cut down before it became a mockery.

Despair is a strange sin, committed in a strange fashion. Sepp Kunzli surrendered to it in the sad passionless hours of his second morning in Zürich. He saw quite clearly what his end must be, and, like the tidy fellow he was, he set himself to prepare for it.

He met his bankers, arranged for the liquidation of his safest assets and their payment into an account in the name of Anna Kunzli. Then he gathered all his remaining papers together and took them back to Bad Quellenberg. When the inquisitors came, he launched them on their investigations and sat back calmly to await the outcome.

To his niece he presented the same mask of courteous indifference. He neither forbade nor encouraged her work with the displaced persons. He was content to drift through the empty days towards the blank, inevitable future.

The thing that puzzled him now was how he had come to this vacuous state. Other men he knew had lied and cheated and lusted and killed and intrigued and had still retained their taste for living. They still had goals to reach, desires to satisfy. Some of them arrived at love–or a fair copy of it. They still had fears. They still had moments of exaltation.

Yet he, the sanest and soberest of them all, had lost, somewhere along the way, the key to life. Perhaps he had never had it. Perhaps it had dropped out of his hand the day his wife had died. Perhaps this was a reason for her dying–that she knew he was dead already. Now it was all so long ago, so hard and fruitless to remember.

Far back in the house he heard the shrilling of the bell that announced a caller at the iron gate. He stopped his pacing and looked down towards the road. A few moments later Bürgermeister Max Holzinger came hurrying up the steep path.

Kunzli beckoned him on to the terrace and greeted him with a distant smile:

'*Grüss Gott*, Herr Bürgermeister! This is a pleasant surprise. What can I do for you?'

Holzinger cast a quick nervous glance inside the study.

'A word in private, Herr Doktor. A personal matter.'

Kunzli took his arm and led him off the balcony to a sunlit lawn where rustic chairs were set about an iron table.

'Sit down, Herr Bürgermeister. Let's be comfortable. Now . . .?'

Holzinger coughed and fidgeted unhappily. He was never an eloquent man, but now he was tongue-tied with embarrassment. Kunzli encouraged him with gentle irony:

'Come, my friend! Out with it! Times are bad for all of us. Why should we be uneasy with one another?'

'Well then . . .' The Bürgermeister took a deep breath and plunged ahead. 'You–you know the investigations that are going on–into property, into Party affiliations?'

'None better,' said Kunzli dryly.

'You know that I–well, that my record has been at least fairly clean.'

'Cleaner than most.' Kunzli nodded agreement. Then he smiled with a hint of the old malice. 'With luck you might hold your job.'

'I–I am less concerned with that than with my reputation. You will understand that I am in a delicate position. The Occupation authorities trust me. Colonel Hanlon has been a guest in my house.'

'And your daughter works for him.'

'That's right.'

'Fortunate for you–and for her.'

'Quite. But . . .' Holzinger tugged at his collar.

'But a trifle indiscreet of Hanlon. Is that what you mean?'

'Not at all, not at all,' Holzinger assured him hastily. 'There is no question of a liaison. Everything is very correct and official.'

Kunzli cocked a sardonic eye at his visitor.

'Any hopes of marriage?'

'The . . . the subject has not been raised. Later, one might hope, perhaps . . .'

'Then why so sad, Herr Bürgermeister?' Kunzli put it to him bluntly.

'You have more reason than most of us to be glad.'

Holzinger told him, stammering:

'There—there is this question of my house. The title, as you remember, was transferred to my wife on a pre-dated deed. If that were to become known . . .'

Kunzli eyed him coldly.

'How should it become known, my friend, since you and I are the only ones who know it—and the witnesses were unaware of its contents?'

'I—I thought you might give me your assurance . . .'

'Would it make you any more secure? Would it?'

Holzinger was sweating now. The matter was in the open, but he had bungled the diplomacy. Kunzli was baiting him. Later he would set a price. The next question startled him even more.

'Why should I want to betray you, Herr Bürgermeister?'

'Please!' Holzinger held up a shaking hand in deprecation. 'I did not mean that.'

'You did,' Kunzli told him mildly. 'And you should not be ashamed to admit it. There was a time when it might have flattered me.'

Holzinger said nothing. He was trying to read the thoughts that went on behind the metallic, spider's eyes. Kunzli let him sweat a few moments longer, then an idea seemed to strike him. He said briskly:

'I'll make a deal with you, Holzinger.'

Holzinger winced. This was the moment he had dreaded. He asked uncertainly: 'What sort of deal?'

'I shall give you my solemn word of secrecy, in return for a small favour—a personal favour.'

'I don't understand.'

'It's quite simple. I'd like you to ask my niece to dinner, very soon—and have her stay the night with you.'

'Is that all? I mean . . . it would be a pleasure in any circumstance, but . . .'

'In the present circumstance, it would be the biggest favour you could do me.'

'May I ask why?'

'Better you didn't, Herr Bürgermeister.'

And, for the first time in all the years of their acquaintance, Holzinger knew he was getting the truth from Sepp Kunzli. In a secret, shamefaced fashion, he was very glad of it.

To Father Albertus spring brought a new labour—the visitation of his flock. During the winter he was cut off from many of them. He was too old and too frail to make the rounds of the outer farms and the isolated communities in the back valleys.

But when the sun shone and the tracks were dry, and his tired heart beat a little more strongly, he was able to move more freely, sometimes on foot, sometimes riding on a peasant cart.

He had much to do. There were children to be baptised, confessions to be heard, sick folk to be comforted with the Sacraments, bundling couples to be churched. In the outlying villages he would lodge in one of the farmhouses and say Mass in the big living-room where the onions and the smoked hams and black sausages hung from the blackened rafters.

This was his own interpretation of the allegory of spring: the sap of grace beginning to flow again, from the root which was Christ through the trunk which was the Church, out into the spreading branches which were the scattered community of the faithful. Some of the branches seemed dead; and this was a sadness to him. But he never lost hope for them, or ceased to pray. Spring had its miracles every year. Buds broke out on the driest twigs. The oldest trunks pushed out young branches. And on the roughest scree slopes the gentian found room to grow.

On this bright afternoon, while Rudi Winkler was stepping out to see the town and Mark Hanlon was hurrying down for his conference with Reinhardt Huber, the old priest was coming home from a two-day tour of the southern area of his parish.

The woodcutters had given him a lift to the top of the rise. Now he was strolling quietly down a narrow track that gave on to the Mozartstrasse. Sometimes he stopped to feed the birds with a handful of crumbs from his pocket, or coax the little grey squirrels that clung to the tree-boles and stared at him with bright, wary eyes. The sound of water was all about him, and the low hushing of the wind through the new foliages. The peace of it seeped into him, the warmth stirred his ageing blood. Life was renewing itself, hope too. Flowers would grow out of the mouths of dead men. Children would play on the charnel-heaps and never know that they were there.

When he came out into the Mozartstrasse he stopped and looked up at a small chalet of yellow pine with a trim terrace of lawn in front of it. He fished in his pocket and brought out a small notebook, the register of his parishioners. The entry for this house said simply: 'R. Winkler. Visitor. Religion unknown.' He looked up again and saw that the front door was open and the curtains looped back from the windows. He slipped the notebook into his pocket, opened the gate and walked up the stone steps.

When he came to the door, he knocked lightly. There was no answer. He knocked again and waited a moment, then he walked inside.

The first thing he saw was the housekeeper, scared and gaping, framed in the doorway that led to the kitchen. Then he saw the man lying on the bed. He was sleeping, with his face turned to the wall, so that Father Albertus saw the dressings on his cheek and the new skin growing round them.

He turned to the housekeeper and demanded in a low voice:

'How long has he been here?'

She was too frightened to lie and she told him.

'Since St Nicholas's Day. The Herr Doktor has been caring for him. I had nothing to do with it, Father. I am only a servant here and . . .'

He silenced her sternly.

'Hush, woman! You have nothing to fear from me. Leave us.'

'But the Herr Doktor . . .'

'Leave us!'

She went out, closing the door behind her, and Father Albertus sat down to wait until the sleeper should wake again. Silently he began to pray: 'Open Thou my lips, O Lord, and set wisdom on my tongue. . . .'

Rudi Winkler leaned on the parapet of the bridge and looked down at the waterfall that plunged down from the crags and cut clean through the centre of the town. It was swollen now with the melting snows and the thunder of it filled the street and the spray was flung up in a fine mist between the blank walls of the buildings.

There was something hypnotic in this tumult of water and he stood there a long time, watching the patterns of foam and the tossing of the spume about the rock faces. Then he had the uneasy feeling that someone was watching him.

He looked up and saw another man, half a dozen yards away, standing with his back to the water, studying him intently.

He was thin as a bean-pole and his clothes hung on him loosely. He had a long bony face and sunken eyes and a shock of hair that stood straight up on his head like a birch-broom.

Winkler tried to outface him, but he went on staring. The little Bavarian shrugged with annoyance, turned away and walked up the street in the opposite direction, conscious of the bleak eyes fixed on his retreating back.

After a while the shock-haired fellow moved off too. And when he came to the Bella Vista he gathered his friends about him and told them:

'The Butcher's in town! I saw him with my own eyes.'

14

In the shabby office at the 121st Feldlazarett, Mark Hanlon conferred with Reinhardt Huber.

The Doktor was angry. His broad good-humoured face was clouded, his mouth was grim. As he talked he toyed restlessly with a steel paper-knife, now scoring the blotter, now thrusting it, like a scalpel, at Hanlon's intent, sober face.

'I told you once, my friend, I have no local loyalties. I don't belong to this town. My world is inside the walls of this hospital. So I am not concerned to make myself an informer for you or anyone else. If this were any other sort of theft, I should deal with it as a military matter or hand it over to Fischer. But this . . . this is a vile thing. You know how little we have here—how men wake under the knife because I must ration anaesthetic. How I must reserve the sulphas and the penicillin only for the extreme cases and let the others fight out their pain for weeks and months. When the little we have is pilfered, then I begin to think of the thief as a murderer. I call on you. Do you understand?'

'Partly.' Hanlon was non-committal. 'I still point out that in the absence of other circumstances Fischer is the man who has jurisdiction.'

'To hell with Fischer!' Huber exploded. 'Fischer's in this too, up to the neck.'

'If you can prove that,' Hanlon said with a grin, 'I'll be happy to move in.'

'Right!' Huber slammed down the paper-knife and heaved himself out of his chair so that he stood towering over Hanlon, a big angry man, hurt and ashamed. 'Here are the proofs. First, the thefts have been taking place over a long time.'

'Since when?'

'The first losses were noticed just after St Nicholas.'

'Why didn't you do something about it then?'

Huber shrugged unhappily.

'It was the first time. We could not be sure it was theft. The quantities were small—a quarter of a litre of ether, antiseptic solution, a small quantity of sulpha powder. They could have been explained by a careless stocktaking. After that, as you know, things began to be much harder to get. You helped us over the worst. But the small unexplainable losses were there–all in the same categories. Anaesthetic, antiseptics, dressings. Now'–his stubby finger thrust emphatically at Hanlon–'second, the inroad begins on the last and most precious commodity of all. Two capsules of penicillin were taken from the refrigerator. There is no doubt about this one, believe me.'

'Do you know the man who took them?'

Huber nodded.

'This time, yes. A ward-maid saw him leaving the dispensary at a time when he had no right to be there.'

'Have you questioned him?'

'Not yet. I should like you here for that.'

Hanlon frowned and shook his head.

'Not without a reason. Why do you want me to handle it?'

Huber gave it to him, succinctly.

'Our thief has a mistress in the town. Her husband is a patient of ours–incurable, poor devil. She comes to visit him and goes home with a bedfellow . . .'

'What's her name?'

'Gretl Metzger. She holds one of the tobacco licences here.'

'We've got nothing on her in our books.'

'I don't think anybody has,' said Huber with a weary grin. 'But the liaison is significant. It becomes more significant when you know that Gretl Metzger is an old flame of Karl Adalbert Fischer.'

'Can you prove that?' Hanlon shot it at him sharply.

'It shouldn't be hard. It's a small town. Everybody knows the smutty bits about everybody else. So now we have it. Our thief, his girl-friend, Karl Fischer and a handful of drugs in three categories–where do they all point?'

'To my first guess,' said Hanlon tersely. 'Fischer's shielding a murderer and someone's trying to do a plastic on his face. There are no medical supplies on the open market–this is the only way he can get them. Fischer's been using the Metzger women to seduce your staff.'

'Right again, my friend!' Huber eased himself back into the chair. 'Now do you handle the case?'

'I handle it.'

'Good,' said Huber. 'And you also pay me for information received?'

Hanlon looked at him in surprise. The request was so blunt and yet so alien to the man's character. Huber's mouth relaxed into a wry, unhappy smile.

'You are going to replace my drugs, Hanlon, and you are going to increase my supplies. I'm not very proud of myself, you see. I'm selling out my countrymen to the Occupying Power. I want to see a profit in it–for my boys at least.'

'You'll get your supplies,' Hanlon told him quietly. 'And I don't think you should blame yourself. Why should a killer be saved when twenty men die of shock or septicaemia because their supplies have been stolen?'

'No reason at all,' said Huber bleakly. 'But I'm a doctor, not a judge.'

'Like it or not,' said Hanlon grimly, 'we're all judges. You're better off than I am. I'm the hangman too . . .'

'The price of victory,' said Huber with thin humour.

'It buys nothing but a headache,' Hanlon told him sourly.

'And the Mayor's daughter.'

He said it with a smile, but it took Hanlon like a smack in the mouth. His face flushed and he thrust himself out of his chair and stood staring down at Huber. Anger boiled over in a stream of passionate abuse:

'You bastard, Huber! You cruel, dirty bastard! I trusted you. I tried to help you—and that's the muck you fling in my face. Be damned to you! Get your man up here and let me question him. After that you can run your hospital without help from me.'

The big Tyrolese did not move. He sat slumped in his chair, staring at his hands. It was a long time before he raised his head. When he did so, Hanlon saw that his eyes were misty and his face was suddenly aged. The words came out, stumbling and strangely penitent:

'I–I have said an unforgivable thing . . . a malicious joke. I am humiliated by what has happened here, with my own people. I am ashamed of my part in it, so I try to shame you too. I destroy at one stroke a friendship that is precious to me. I am sorry—God only knows how sorry!'

With a sudden weary gesture he put his head down on his arms and slumped forward over the desk. Hanlon stood looking down at him with cold, bitter eyes. His words cracked like a lash over the lolling head:

'I came in friendship, Huber. I came to build, not destroy, to co-operate, and not to rule. What did I get? Murder, cheating, lying, insult. I'm tired of it. I've had enough!'

Slowly Huber raised his head and looked at him, haggardly. His voice was flat and weary.

'That's the trouble, Hanlon. We're all tired. We don't think straight any more. I'm tired of living with all this misery, sick to death of my own helplessness against it. I'm tired of patching bodies that are wrecked beyond repair, tired of preaching a hope I know is a lie, tired of begging for drugs and instruments, sick of the butchery I have to do without them. I can't unsay what I've said, but please believe I'm sorry for it.'

He stood up and faced Hanlon across the desk. Then he held out his hand. After a moment's hesitation Hanlon took it and they looked at each other, shamefaced as schoolboys, until a slow smile broke over Huber's drawn face.

'Nobody believes she's your mistress. And they resent the fact that she isn't. They're afraid of saints, and celibates are dangerous men. We're a primitive folk. We like our rulers comfortably drunk and happily bedded. They're easier to manage.'

'I'm a romantic,' said Hanlon with a crooked urchin grin. 'I'm still crying for the moon. I want a lover more than a mistress.'

Huber's big hands waved away this Celtic folly.

'The moon is cold, my friend. But if a woman is warm in bed you are already halfway to love.'

On that tart little tag-line they were friends again, and they bent themselves to the business in hand: the tracing of stolen drugs and the search for the man behind the gun.

Karl Adalbert Fischer sat under the wine-stained map, with its drooping, melancholy flags, and contemplated his own dubious future. Spring was breaking out all over the mountains, but he was still sunk in a sullen winter of anxiety and disillusion.

His eyes were bloodshot, his mouth was stale with liquor and his body spent from the passion of the night before. He was getting too old for lechery, but the drive of habit was still strong, and hope died more slowly than the loveless ecstasy.

He had spent last night with Gretl Metzger. She had telephoned him late in the afternoon, with the news that there would be no further supplies from the hospital, and that her boy-friend was in daily fear of discovery.

Fischer had gone to see her. She had wept and railed and threatened so that, in sheer weariness, he had had to take her. She had sobbed on his breast and sworn that she would never betray him; but when she had fallen asleep he had lain awake for hours, staring into the darkness, knowing that when the inquisitors came she would tell everything.

That they would come, he had no doubt at all. What he must do was equally clear to him. He must smile and submit and answer no questions until they brought him to trial, when, with luck and a good lawyer, he might assume the character of a martyr, a man driven to petty crime by loyalty to his family and his country. It would make a good case. The press might even build it into a famous one.

The Occupying Powers were in a neat dilemma. They preached democracy and the right of fair trial. In practice they were committed to local autocracy and a doubtful legality in the processes of justice.

He was more troubled about his nephew than about himself. The boy was very near the end of his treatment. Freedom was just around the corner. It would be sweet sarcasm to send him away now. Time was against it, and circumstances too. But somehow a way must be found.

He tilted himself back in the chair, out his feet on the table and lit another cigarette.

Before it was halfway smoked there was a knock on the door and Father Albertus came in.

Fischer swung his legs off the table and stood up to greet him. The old man waved aside the formalities of greeting and came straight to the point.

'I saw your nephew this afternoon, Karl.'

'The devil you did!' Fischer stared at him, irritated and bewildered. 'But I told the young fool to stay inside the house.'

'He did, Karl. I met him by chance. I was making the visitation of the parish, and it brought me to Winkler's house.'

'Oh . . .' It was a long-drawn sigh of relief. 'For a moment you had me frightened, Father.'

Fischer was smiling now, but the face of the old priest was grim. He said crisply:

'There is nothing more Winkler can do for him. I am taking him away from there.'

'What?'

Father Albertus faced him with stubborn dignity.

'The boy is almost healed in body; but in mind he is sick, near to despair. Winkler cannot help him, being so near to damnation himself. I propose to take Johann into my own house and care for him.'

Fischer looked at him stupidly, fumbling for words.

'You mean you would dare . . .'

'For a wandering soul,' said Father Albertus simply, 'a priest should dare anything. Besides, the sanctuary of the Church is a better protection than you or Winkler can give him.'

Fischer shook his head and smiled regretfully.

'There is no sanctuary now, Father. This is the twentieth century, the Secular State. The Church has no immunity any more.'

'Perhaps God may supply what the State refuses,' said the old man mildly. 'In any case, I am taking him. Tonight, after dark, I shall bring him down to my place. He can stay there until he is cured, in body and in spirit.'

'And then . . .?'

'Then he will make up his mind what to do.'

Fischer eased himself slowly back into his chair; then suddenly he began to laugh. The old priest watched him, frowning.

'Perhaps you should tell me the joke too, Karl.'

Karl Adalbert Fischer stopped laughing and waved him irritably to a chair. Then, quite dispassionately, he told him.

The old priest listened intently till the story was finished, then he leaned back in his chair, joined his hands finger-tip to finger-tip and stared musingly at the policeman. His first words were characteristic.

'There is hope for you yet, my friend.'

Fischer shrugged and shook his head.

'There's no hope, believe me. I shall be arrested this evening.'

'I was not thinking of that,' said Father Albertus mildly. 'I was remembering that, for the first time for many years, you have done an unselfish act, at considerable cost to yourself. That is the real hope.'

Fischer cocked a sardonic eyebrow at the old cleric.

'You think you'll get me to confession, Father?'

'I'd like to get you to heaven,' said Father Albertus with a sudden smile. 'That might be less difficult.'

'Get the boy out safely,' Fischer told him sourly. 'That's the big thing.'

'No, Karl. The big thing is to give him hope and a goal. The rest is unimportant.'

A wintry admiration showed in Fischer's canny eyes.

'You priests will never learn, will you?'

'It depends on the lesson, Karl.'

'And what would you have me learn, Father? I'm an old dog. I don't take kindly to new tricks.'

'It's the oldest lesson in the book.' The priest stood up, ready to go. He paused a moment, then quoted softly:

'"*Vanitas vanitatum . . .*" Vanity of vanities, Karl. Everything is vanity but the love of God and the love of His creatures.'

It was a timely thought, but a bitter one. Karl Adalbert Fischer was still chewing on it when Captain Johnson came with two soldiers to place him under arrest.

Rudi Winkler was returning from his walk. He had made the circuit of the town and the lower promenades and now he was retracing his steps, thinking cheerfully of the prospect of a beer in the Goldener Hirsch and a warm bath when he reached his house.

He was tired but relaxed, and he walked slowly, whistling a drinking song and inhaling the last pine-scented warmth of the day. The shadows were lengthening and the shopkeepers were putting up their shutters, but the long winding street was strangely active.

Little groups of promenaders strolled along the narrow footpaths and spilled over on to the roadway. Others stood in the doorways of the shops, talking in low voices.

At first he was hardly aware of them, lapped as he was in a pleasant weariness and in his habitual self-contemplation. Then the strangeness struck him. The time was late for strollers. These were not townsfolk. They looked different; their faces were odd and angular, their eyes hostile, their skin sallow and unhealthy. Their voices were odd too, soft and secretive, tinged with unfamiliar accents. They did not walk freely as the mountain folk did, but shambled, almost furtively, with bent shoulders and heads thrust forward.

Winkler began to be uneasy. He quickened his step, striding out more strongly, looking neither to right nor to left.

The strollers reacted immediately to his change of pace. Those in the doorways stepped out on to the footpath and began to walk steadily in the same direction, keeping pace with Winkler so that they formed a human screen between him and the safety of the doorways.

Those behind strung out in line abreast across the roadway, cutting off his retreat. He dared not look back, but he heard the measured tramp of their feet. Then they began to chant and the beat was in time with the thudding rhythm of their boots—'Butcher! Butcher! Butcher!'

Panic seized him and he began to run, panting and stumbling, up the cobbled road. The others began to run too, not bothering to catch him, but dogging his tracks, outflanking him. They were still chanting, breathlessly but insistently, so that the sound drummed into his ears in a crescendo of terror.

Faster he ran and faster, up the slope that led to the open square where there was usually a policeman on duty. Then he realised that before he reached the square he must cross the bridge over the tumbling waterfall. When he turned the corner he saw it.

Each parapet was lined with lean scarecrow figures, and the exit was blocked by another double rank. Hope died in him and he stopped running. His pursuers stopped too. He stood, motionless in a wide square of people—skeleton faces, scarecrow limbs, dead, hating eyes.

They watched him, silently, as he turned this way and that, looking for a way of escape. They saw his mouth open and heard his scream. Then, without haste, they began to move in on him.

Five minutes later a torn and bloody bundle was hoisted above the heads of the crowd and flung over the parapet. They watched it tossing and leaping in the torrent, then they turned away and shambled back towards the Bella Vista.

The police had refused duty after the arrest of Karl Fischer and Mark Hanlon's troop had not yet arrived to picket the town.

It was seven in the evening before the news of Winkler's murder reached Occupation Headquarters. More than a dozen people had seen it happen, from shop fronts and upper windows. Some had telephoned the police, but authority had collapsed, and none was prepared to apply to the Occupying Power.

Miller, the American, was the first to come at the truth. When his inmates returned, half-scared, half-gloating, the news spread quickly through the wards, and a white-faced nurse came hurrying to the Director's office to tell him the news.

He had acted quickly. All patients were confined to the hospital and a detachment of troops had been called to picket the entrances. Then Miller had driven up to the Sonnblick to make his report.

Hanlon heard him out in silence, approved his prompt action and then settled down to question him closely.

'The name first—you're sure it was Winkler?'

'No doubt of it,' Miller assured him in his flat drawl. 'I got it from half a dozen witnesses. "Butcher" Winkler they called him. He'd served in two camps, Dachau and Mauthausen. Anyway, you'll be able to identify him when you recover the body.'

'I doubt it,' said Hanlon with dry distaste. 'From what you've told me, they must have torn him to ribbons. How many of your people were involved?'

'Upwards of fifty.'

'Can you identity a leader?'

Miller shook his head doubtfully.

'No. I'm not sure we'd be wise to try.'

'Why do you say that?'

'It was a collective act. A scapegoat gives it a different character. It's easier to handle this way, easier to hush up.'

Hanlon gave him a swift, shrewd look.

'What makes you think I want to hush it up?'

'You've got no choice,' Miller told him. 'It's justice of a sort—rough justice if you want—but neither your Headquarters nor mine will want to make a song and dance about it.'

'They can't have it both ways,' said Hanlon abruptly. 'You can't have the courts for some and lynch law for the others. It's a negation of everything we're trying to do here.'

'I agree,' said Miller with a sour grin, 'but I'm talking from experience: this isn't the first case I've seen. There were others, much worse. All of them were hushed up quietly. They'll do it with this one too.'

'This is an area of British jurisdiction,' said Hanlon tartly. 'I think my people will take a different view.'

'I wouldn't bank on it. There's a Four-Power policy involved. Besides, there's a practical point. What are you going to do with fifty D.P.s? Give them a collective trial and a collective sentence? Hand a ready-made propaganda piece to the Russians and the Old Guard? Better bury Winkler and the case too.'

'I'll have to make a report on it,' said Hanlon stiffly, 'and ask Klagenfurt for a directive. I'll send someone down to take depositions and a list of participants. I'd like you to make facilities available.'

'Happy to help,' Miller told him casually. Then his scrawny neck jutted forward and his lined face became unusually grave. 'Don't misunderstand me, Hanlon. I know your views and the situation here. I'm just trying to save you some embarrassment.'

Hanlon grinned lopsidedly and made a small shrugging gesture of helplessness.

'I'm embarrassed already. I've just arrested Fischer and the police are on strike.'

'The hell you have!' Miller threw back his head and laughed. 'What's the charge?'

'Receiving stolen goods. Concealment of a criminal. Accessory after the fact in a murder case.'

'Think you'll make them stick?'

'Not all of them. My intelligence team is sweating him out now. This

Winkler business will help them and me.'

'What's the connection?'

'That's what I'm waiting to find out. I've sent Johnson to search Winkler's house and pull in his housekeeper. If she talks, as I hope she will, I'll confront Fischer with her and see what we get.'

Miller stood up and held out his hand.

'I wish you luck, Hanlon. And a smooth passage with Klagenfurt!'

'To hell with Klagenfurt!'

'To hell with the whole lousy mess. I'd like to go home.'

'Wouldn't we all?'

It was one of the clichés of the Service and Hanlon tossed it off lightly enough. But the truth was quite different. He had no home to go to, and he was too near to triumph to want it, anyway.

Karl Adalbert Fischer was sweating under the lamps.

They had him propped in a chair in a cellar room of the Sonnblick, with lights glaring in his face and the steam heater turned up to full pressure a foot from his back, while three stony-faced interrogaters hammered him with questions, hour after hour.

It was a technique familiar to him and he counted on his years of experience to turn it into a harmless if wearisome ritual. For the first two hours he had done very well. He had stepped round the pitfalls and shrugged off the traps with the bland derision of a man who knows them all by heart.

Then, slowly, the strain began to tell. His clothes became sodden with sweat, his mouth dried out, his fingers twitched, his eyes burned and his head buzzed painfully under the dull repetitive impact of the voices. He had to clamp his mouth shut to stop screaming aloud. He tried vainly to close his ears and withdraw into a state of self-hypnosis, but the lights blazed and the voices drummed on and on so that he wished, in spite of himself, to tell them everything and be done with it.

Then, surprisingly, the inquisition stopped. The lights were switched off. They gave him coffee and a plate of sandwiches and talked genially and casually while he ate them. Then they gave him a cigarette and let him smoke it through to the end, while they reasoned with him like an equal.

The telephone rang and one of the men answered it. Fischer pricked up his ears, but all he heard was the indistinct crackle of the receiver and a noncommittal series of answers. The interrogator put down the receiver and turned to him with a smile.

'You're a lucky man, Fischer. That was Colonel Hanlon. We're going to release you.'

Fischer looked at him, stunned.

'What did you say?'

'We're going to release you. There's no case.'

A warm wave of comfort swept over Fischer's body. He had won. He had told them nothing. He would emerge from this brief ordeal with added prestige and added power. He asked for another cigarette and they gave it to him without question. When he came to light it his hands were trembling violently, but one of the inquisitors leaned forward courteously and snapped a lighter. They poured him another cup of coffee and began gathering up their papers in the shamefaced fashion of men who have finished a distasteful task.

Then the door opened and Mark Hanlon came in—with Rudi Winkler's housekeeper.

In a long bare room at the top of the Pfarrhaus, Father Albertus was dining with Johann Wikivill.

It was a meal the like of which had not graced the presbytery table for many long years: *Rindsuppe*, a trout fresh-caught and stuffed with mushrooms, a roast of chicken, *Apfelstrudel* and fresh whipped cream. There was a Nussberger for the meats and a Muscatel with the sweet, and a long Dutch cigar to match the coffee. The old man had coaxed the ingredients out of the local shopkeepers and handed them all to his grumbling housekeeper, hoping that her skill might not be atrophied after years of ascetic cooking. He had made no secret of the identity of his guest, but had cautioned her to silence and sent her back to the kitchen.

When Wikivill had arrived, furtive and panicky, he had made him bathe and change his clothes and settle himself in a small bedroom with a view over the town and the valley. By the time dinner was served the visitor was calm again and they dined in leisurely fashion, by candlelight, like men remote from disaster.

Father Albertus steered the talk into harmless channels, and his guest responded gratefully, as to a forgotten pleasure. He talked well but with detachment, as if he, like the priest, were no longer part of the world which they discussed. His hands were steady and his eyes were clear but sombre like those of a man accustomed to the contemplation of immense distances, treeless and barren.

It was not until the last of the wine was gone, and the last drops of coffee had been poured, that he asked the critical question:

'You have brought me here, Father. I'm grateful. But what do you hope to do with me?'

The mild, deep-set eyes looked out on him from the luminous face. The grave voice answered him:

'You have come—as every man comes sooner or later—to the end of a road. Behind you is a wreckage. In front, blankness. It is the beginning of despair.'

'It is despair.'

'No.' The priest's voice was gentle but very firm. 'Despair is the loss of hope.'

'I have no hope.'

'I want to try to give you one.'

'Can you?'

It was a clear challenge, but, strangely enough, the old man did not rise to it. He said simply:

'If I promised it to you, my son, I should be lying. Hope springs from faith. At present you have no faith. You do not believe in God—you cannot believe in yourself. I cannot give you faith—it is a gift of the Almighty. The most I can do is bring you to desire it, help you to prepare yourself for it.'

'I desire it,' said Johann Wikivill heavily. 'I need it, as I need love and passion and a whole body—all the things I can never have.'

'You need it more than these, my son. Because the soul endures even after the body is destroyed.'

'If there is a soul.'

'If there were, and if you could believe it, would you bear more easily the maiming and the loss?'

'I–I think so.'

'We begin from there.' The fire seemed to leap up behind the transparent face. 'We reason together. We meditate together. We pray together.'

'I cannot pray. How can I, not believing?'

'You pray as a great Englishman once prayed–he who came from faith to unfaith, and back again, and came to wear finally the dignity of a prince of the Church: "O God–if there be a God–give me light!"'

The sombre eyes of Johann Wikivill were downcast to the table. The candle flames threw strange shadows on his lean, bandaged face. After a while he said softly:

'It is a long journey, Father. I doubt I have courage to make it.'

'There is light at the end of it. And you will not be walking alone. I shall go with you, all the way.'

'You may not be able to. The Englishman wants my head.'

'He shall not have it, unless you choose to give it to him.'

There was so much strength and conviction in the old man's voice that his guest looked up in sharp surprise.

'You can't promise that, Father!'

'I can. I do.'

'You can't. Behind the Englishman is a whole nation–four nations! You cannot fight them all.'

'Not I, my son.' Father Albertus held up his gnarled and broken hands. 'But God Almighty who lifts up the humble and topples the mighty from their seats . . .'

Suddenly the telephone rang, its sound shrill and shocking in the bare room. Father Albertus got up to answer it and his guest sat, tense and up-right, listening. He heard nothing but the disjointed answers of the priest.

'. . . No, I had not heard of it . . . a shocking affair. . . . Yes. . . . I understand that. . . . No. . . . I should prefer to leave it till the morning. . . . I shall be there without fail. . . . Yes, I guarantee that. . . . *Auf Wiedersehn.*'

He replaced the receiver carefully on the cradle and turned to face his guest. He said quietly:

'That was Colonel Hanlon, Occupation Commander. Winkler was murdered this afternoon. Your uncle has been arrested. Hanlon knows you are with me.'

'No . . .!' The sound came out on a long-drawn breath of horror. He pushed back his chair and struggled out of it, shattering a wine-glass as he did so. 'I've got to leave. Get out of here!'

'No!' The deep voice snapped like a thunder-clap. Fire leaped up in the old man like lightning. His frail body seemed to grow in stature, dominating the room and the tense crouching figure of his guest. 'I made you a promise. I shall keep it. They shall not have you, my son. Trust me–in the name of God!'

'I don't believe in God.'

'Then believe in me.'

Slowly, inexorably, the seconds ticked by; the candle flames flickered and the silence crackled with the tension between them. Then, quite suddenly, Wikivill's taut body relaxed and he sat down, resting his trembling hands on the edge of the table. His mouth twisted into a strange smile, half-resigned, half-despairing. His voice was almost a whisper.

'I believe in you, Father. I don't know why, but I do. I'll stay.'

15

'For God's sake, Mark! Have you gone crazy?'

Hanlon had hardly finished his conversation with Father Albertus when Johnson exploded into shocked anger.

'You've been griping for months about this fellow. You've turned the town upside-down to get him. Now, when he's in your hands, you leave him free–to spend the night with a bloody priest! What do you expect him to do–make his confession or something? Walk in here tomorrow morning and hold out his hands for the bracelets? God Almighty! By tomorrow morning he'll be over the hills and far away. And how are you going to explain *that* to Klagenfurt?'

'Finished, Johnny?' Hanlon turned a bleak, unfriendly eye on his subordinate.

'I'm finished, yes. And so will you be if you carry on with this crazy comedy. I know you're a Catholic. I know there's some connection between you and the priest. Fine! It's none of my business. But this is. I don't like it. Burn your own fingers if you like, but not mine.'

'Finished now?'

'Yes, and be damned to you!'

'Then sit down and listen.'

Johnson hesitated a moment, then lowered himself into a chair and sat glaring across the desk at Hanlon. Hanlon reached for a cigarette, lit it and tossed the case over to Johnson. Johnson caught it and put it back on the desk unopened. Hanlon smoked for a few moody moments, then he began to talk, crisply and irritably:

'Item one, Johnny. I'm in command here. If there are orders, you obey 'em. If there are kicks, I take 'em. Right?'

'Right,' said Johnson sullenly.

'Item two. There was a second murder this afternoon. It was committed by people under our protection–the D.P.s. I don't know how to deal with them until I get a clear directive from Klagenfurt. It's high policy, political dynamite. Which brings us to item three. If I arrest Johann Wikivill tonight, I've got to put him through the hoops, immediately! I have to charge one man and let fifty others go free. How's that going to look? What are the people going to say to our protestations of democracy and justice?'

'I–I hadn't thought of that.'

'Item four. The fact that Father Albertus has taken our man under his protection means there's more to the case than you or I know about. I don't want to make any move until I get the score.'

'By then it may be too late.'

'I'm taking Father Albertus's word that it won't be.'

'Why do you put so much stock in him?'

'I've known him a long time, Johnny. He's a bigger man than you and I will ever be, and a wiser one. I trust him.'

Johnson sat quietly for a few moments considering the proposition. Then he said apologetically:

'The only item that carries any weight with me is number two. I see we're in a jam. It could be your way is right, though I'm still not convinced. Anyway, I'm sorry.'

'That's O.K., Johnny. Forget it.'

'What are you going to do about Fischer?'

'Hold him till I can see where we're heading on the whole business.'

'What if he screams for a lawyer?'

'He hasn't yet. I don't think he will.'

Johnson reached for the cigarette case and lit up. Through the spiralling smoke rifts he studied the lean, intelligent face of his commander, noting the deepening care-lines and the new grey hairs and the ugly scar along his temple. He said seriously: 'You puzzle me, Mark.'

'Why so?'

'You're too subtle for me. You think off-centre. I don't say it's a bad thing. In a situation like this it's probably the approach we need. I find you hard to follow, that's all.'

Hanlon nodded thoughtfully and began to worry the thought aloud.

'It's fair comment, Johnny. I think it's a difference of approach, of attitude. You see this job one way, I see it another. We think about it in different terms. To you it's a military operation to be handled according to a certain set of rules. Fair enough. To me it's . . . it's a human enterprise, a problem of people–more than people, persons. You're detached from it, I'm involved. I'm not sure that's a good thing either, but it's a fact and I've got to start from that fact. Can you see that?'

'I can see it, yes. But you're not involved right down the line.'

'How come?'

Johnson smiled a little shamefacedly.

'Take the rest of the officers. Take Wilson, James, Hanneker. We're involved in a different way. They've got their girls and a place to take 'em and a nice cosy domestic set-up. I'm playing the field in a half-hearted sort of way. You're still playing the celibate. You're involved with Fischer and the priest and Holzinger, and even Traudl doesn't get a tumble in the hay, much as she wants it. I'd be happy to give it to her myself, if I thought I had half a chance.'

Hanlon shrugged indifferently.

'Don't let me stand in your light, Johnny.'

Johnson's face creased into a puzzled frown.

'That's what puzzles me, Mark. You're more detached than I am, yet you're risking more than I'd ever risk.'

'Maybe that's it, Johnny,' said Hanlon with a crooked grin. 'Maybe that's why I don't want to be involved with a woman. I'd risk more than you and profit far less. Now get to hell out of here. I want to go to bed!'

Johnson made no move to go, but sat back, grinning at him with the old jaunty impudence.

'You need a change, sonny boy. You need to get out on the town once in a while. I've got a date with a girl at the Zigeuner Café. Why not ring Traudl and have her along? It'd do you good. You'll be dead a long time.'

'Too damn long!' said Mark Hanlon; and, after a moment's hesitation, he reached for the telephone.

The Zigeuner Café was neither a café nor a resort of gipsies. It was a two-storeyed log house, about a mile from the town, perched on the lower pine slopes and looking out across the valley. It took the afternoon sun and was sheltered from the winds at night. There was a terrace in front, planted with blossom trees, and the lower floor was occupied by a kitchen and a long dining-room with a log fire at one end and a big porcelain stove at the other, and half a dozen small guest-rooms.

Its proprietor was a long-headed Carinthian with a stout peasant wife and a quartette of bouncing daughters. They lived on the upper floor, and gave the lower one over to the entertainment of the Occupation troops and their local escorts.

When the proposition had been presented to him, Hanlon had been dubious, but Johnson had sponsored it with enthusiasm. It was quiet, remote from the town. If the boys got drunk there'd be no local disturbance and they would have time to sober up before they came back into the built-up area. It was a useful place for local leave. There were the guest-rooms, the fishing, the mountain walks. . . .

Finally Hanlon had approved. The permit was signed and the Carinthian went away, waving his ration cards, while the more conservative townsfolk muttered unhappily about influence and interlopers.

When the officer staff had been expanded, Johnson had proposed a shrewd amendment. Three nights weekly the place should be private to officers. The rest of the time it should be open to other ranks. This too Hanlon had approved, and the Carinthian was quick to adapt his service and his prices to the different needs of the military castes.

From the official point of view it was a good arrangement. There was privacy for presumptive gentlemen and freedom for those of lower degree. The ladies who accompanied the former could enjoy their seduction in comfort. The soldiers' girls could relax in a more rowdy prelude. The tipple for the troops was tapped from a big cask in the kitchen. The officers' wine came in bottle at double the price. And the bouncing daughters were instructed to keep their mouths shut and their virginity intact, while their father raked in the currency tokens and cashed them at a premium rate.

When Hanlon and Johnson arrived with the girls it was already late. There were half a dozen couples on the floor, dancing to the music of the zither player, a tall blond fellow in *Lederhosen* and a bright peasant shirt. They nodded a perfunctory greeting and settled themselves in a corner near the fire, while the daughters of the house bustled up to light the candles and pour out the wine and lay the table for a meal.

They drank and talked and ate and smoked and laughed and fell silent, watching the dancing couples, while the music played on and on and lost itself in the shadowy, carved beams of the ceiling.

They were restless at first, self-conscious and uneasy with one another. Their talk concealed their thoughts and their laughter had a metallic ring to it. They were lonely, yet not prepared for intimacy. They courted one another yet dared not think of the consummation. But, as the drink relaxed them and the music beguiled them and they watched the hypnotic leaping of the fire, they drew closer to each other and talked more quietly and smiled in the candlelight, but did not laugh any more.

These were the gentle moments: the prelude to passion that had no passion in it; the beginning of love in which there was no thought of love at all.

Then Hanlon took Traudl's hand and led her on to the dance floor. The zither player changed his rhythm to a slow plaintive waltz that swept them into each other's arms in a symbolic surrender.

They danced cheek to cheek, breast to breast, lapped in a mutual harmony of sound and movement. Their lips brushed sometimes, then parted again to whisper small words of satisfaction and endearment.

The other couples fell away from them, then sat down to watch, while they danced on, unconscious of their solitude, of everything but the music and the slow, mounting beat of desire.

Then, abruptly, it was finished. The music stopped. A small clapping broke out. They looked around them in surprise, then walked self-consciously back to the table, where Johnson and his girl were waiting for them.

The room was uncomfortably warm now, heavy with the smell of pine smoke and cigarette and food and spilt wine. Johnson suggested a walk in the garden before they went home. They paid the bill and strolled out into the sharp, scented air under the blossom trees. Then they parted and walked, two and two, into the shadows under the lacing branches.

The moon was riding high over the sleeping valley. The peaks were silver with it, ghostly battlements looking down on the black march of the pines. The river wound brightly through the grey, sleeping meadows, its sound a muted counterpoint to the nostalgic tinkling of the zither.

Hanlon and Traudl Holzinger stood together by the low stone wall looking down over the bright emptiness and upward to the soft scattering of stars, round the fringes of the moonfield. The air was cold, but full of the scent of blossoms that brushed their faces as they turned to kiss and cling to each other.

When the first long kiss was over they drew apart and looked at one another. Their voices were a soft whisper.

'*Du bist so schön, meine Liebe . . .*'

'*Und du, Schatz . . . so schön . . .*'

They were both passionate, both ripe for this moment of starlight and perfume; but neither was ready to make the first demand nor the first surrender. Their passion was strong enough and frank enough, but each, for a different reason, held it in curb. For Hanlon the curb was his marriage and his pro-consular status. For the girl it was the age-old admonition of the Sisterhood: 'Give them everything, yet give them nothing until you have the ring and the promise. We are still unconquered, remember. We must make them pay for our surrender.'

So regretfully they retreated from one another, and after a moment Hanlon said gently:

'Where do we go from here, dark one?'

He looked away from her across the valley and she saw the line of his jaw, tight and stubborn, and his eyes, distant and brooding in the grey moonlight. Her answer came back lightly enough:

'Where do you want to go, Mark?'

'I'd like to go back ten years and start again.'

'With your wife?'

'No. With just myself—with all the world a garden and the girls in it bright as flowers.'

'Why not start now?'

'I might—one day.'

'I'll wait for it, Mark.'

'Kiss me again.'

'*Ach, mein Liebster.*'

After a while the music stopped and they heard the clatter of engines and the laughter of homing couples. Then they too walked slowly out of the perfumed orchard and drove back to Bad Quellenberg under the cold stars.

The following morning, on the stroke of ten, Father Albertus presented himself at Occupation Headquarters. Hanlon received him alone and plunged straight into business.

'You've committed an indiscretion, Father. You've created a delicate political situation. You owe me an explanation.'

'I came to give it to you, Colonel.' The answer was given with careful formality.

'Let me show you where you stand, first. Yesterday three people were arrested–Gretl Metzger, an orderly from the Feldlazarett and Karl Fischer. The charges against the first two are theft and receiving stolen goods. The charges against Fischer are receiving, concealment of a criminal, and being an accessory after the fact of murder. At least one of these charges could be laid against you also.'

Father Albertus nodded thoughtfully, then a faint smile twitched the corners of his mouth. He answered mildly:

'I see your point, Colonel. On the other hand there are circumstances of which you are ignorant. I felt you should know them before–before any decisive action is taken.'

'I am not as ignorant as you suppose, Father,' said Mark Hanlon coldly. 'Karl Fischer made a statement to me, remember. I was prepared to investigate the extenuating circumstances in his nephew's case. Your action in taking him into your house has made that much more difficult.'

'Fischer told you everything? What had happened to the boy? What had been done to him?'

'Yes.'

'And you saw these things only as extenuating circumstances?'

'I saw that they would make a strong defence at his trial.'

'He must not go to trial, Mark!'

Fire snapped in the mild eyes. The old voice rang with passion and authority. Hanlon stared at him, astonished.

'Do you understand what you're saying, Father? This is a legal matter now. The wheels have begun to turn. I couldn't stop them even if I wanted to.'

'Will you hear me out, Mark? Will you answer me some questions and listen to me before you make a final decision? Will you forget for a while that you are Caesar's friend and remember that–that you were once my son? Please.'

Hanlon got up from his desk, walked to the window and stood staring out at the green shoulder of the mountains and the last snow banks near the summit. Without turning round, he said flatly: 'I promise nothing. But I'll listen.'

'Thank you, my son.' The priest paused a moment, as if searching for an opening gambit. Then, almost apologetically, he put the first question: 'Are you still a Catholic, Mark?'

Hanlon swung round to face him.

'What's that got to do with it?'

'Everything, Mark. Before we can talk we must establish a common ground of argument. Otherwise we are both wasting our time.'

'I'm still a Catholic.'

'You don't go to the Sacraments.'

'Let's get it straight, Father.' Hanlon's voice was harsh and irritable. 'I made an unhappy marriage. It gave me none of the things implied in the contract. I've been looking for them ever since—outside the contract. If you want it in moral terms, I'm living in a state of sin. But I'm still a believer. I can recite the Nicene Creed and subscribe to every term of it. Is that enough?'

'For the present, yes. I am sorry for you, Mark. I wish you were happy and at peace with your conscience. But that is for another time. You still have the faith. You believe in God. You believe in the soul, in salvation and damnation.'

'Yes.'

'You will admit that the salvation of a human soul is a greater matter than the fate of empires?'

'As a principle, yes. In practice, the one often depends on the other. It's a paradox and a mystery, Father. You should know that.'

'I do, believe me. But now I am concerned with the principle.'

'I'll admit the principle. Where does it lead us?'

For a while the old man was silent. He seemed to be gathering his strength, praying perhaps for the wisdom to present his argument. Then he bent forward in his chair and with deep, passionate conviction began to speak:

'Johann Wikivill committed this murder in a state of temporary insanity induced by shock and a long accumulation of terror. Whatever a court might decide, I believe that he is morally guiltless. I believe too that he is now completely sane. What concerns me at this moment is that he is a man on the edge of despair. Hope was destroyed in him with the destruction of his manhood. He sees himself as an object of pity and derision, incapable of giving or receiving love because he is incapable of its physical expression. You know, none better, what the denial of love means to a man. You at least have faith in a spiritual destiny, even if you fail to attain it. He has no faith. Life is a blankness to him. The hereafter is a myth and mockery. If he could come to belief, hope might be restored to him. He might even attain, with the grace of God, a great holiness, accepting his loss with patience, bending himself to the service of his fellows. I—I should like to try to lead him on this road. I know that I cannot do it if he still remains in a state of flight and fear. I want to keep him with me, pray with him, talk to him, spend love and courage on him. If you take him away I cannot do it. He will be lost in a black night of disillusion. You see what is at stake, Mark? Not the small symbolic justice of a military court, but a man's soul—his saving or his damnation? Give him to me, my son! Give him to me in the name of God!'

Mark Hanlon was moved. The eloquence and sincerity of his former mentor touched him deeply. His own moral dilemma disposed him to pity. Every impulse urged him to clemency. But he knew that these were traps for the unwary. He was a man under stringent commission, bound by oath to administer a policy. If he made a mistake, he would compromise himself and the man he was trying to save. He began to cast about for a compromise.

'Tell me, Father. If—and it's nothing more than if—I leave Wikivill with you, will you guarantee to surrender him on demand? We might get round the situation by releasing him into your custody, for health reasons.'

The old priest shook his head.

'No, Mark. It is not enough. Don't you see, I cannot begin to help him with a lie? Sooner or later he would discover it, and the whole work would be destroyed. I would hope that one day he might come to you himself and offer to purge himself by trial, being happy in the outcome because of faith and new hope. But I cannot guarantee it. I must leave him free to choose between flight and surrender, between faith and despair. Can't you see that?'

'I see it,' said Hanlon thoughtfully, 'but I don't see what I can do about it. I'm a man under authority. Any decision I make can be reversed overnight. If there were some formula acceptable to Klagenfurt, I'd be happy to give it a try; but I can promise nothing, nothing at all. I'll have to think about it.'

'And in the meantime . . .?'

'Keep Wikivill with you.'

'On what conditions?'

A slow, weary grin broke over Hanlon's lined face. He shrugged and spread his hands in resignation.

'I leave those to your conscience, Father. I'm sure it's more delicate than mine.'

There was no answering smile from Father Albertus. He stood up, twitched his cloak round his thin shoulders and said with grave gratitude: 'Thank you, my son. We understand each other. You are doing more than I expected, if less than I hoped. You are a good man. I pray that one day soon you may come to peace.'

In a cellar room at the Sonnblick, Karl Adalbert Fischer lay on a camp stretcher and stared up at the ceiling. The room was no more than a concrete box in the foundations of the building, with bare grey walls and a blank door and a weak unshaded bulb in the centre of the roof. There was a wash-basin and a toilet-can and a bare table and a kitchen chair. There was no window and the only sound that penetrated was the measured pacing of the guard in the corridor outside. His isolation was as complete as if he had been whisked off to another planet.

He was not too disturbed by his situation. He was warm, he was well fed. The charges against him were formal ones, hard to sustain effectively in the sympathetic atmosphere of a civil court. He had lost his job—but there was comfort even in that for a middle-aged intriguer tiring of the backstairs reek of soiled linen.

What troubled him most was his nephew. The lad was in a mess, mentally and physically. Any new pressures might tip him over the edge into insanity. He would be under arrest by now, possibly in the hands of the interrogators, as he himself had been. He was beyond help, because Karl Adalbert Fischer had no bargaining power left.

Or had he?

A new thought struck him, a new hope, small and weak like the first buds of spring. He nursed it a long while, carefully, then he got up, hammered on the door and demanded to be taken immediately to Hanlon.

He was greeted with ironic courtesy, given a chair and a cup of coffee, and left, at his own request, alone with the Occupation Commander.

Hanlon quizzed him comfortably:

'Well, Fischer, what did you want to see me about?'

'I'd like to make a bargain with you, my friend.'

'You can't.' Hanlon's refusal was blunt. 'Your credit's run out.'

'Nearly, but not quite.' Fischer leaned back in his chair, his small bird-like head tilted jauntily on its long neck. 'You're in a difficult situation, Colonel. More difficult than ever now that Winkler has been killed. I, on the contrary, have nothing more to lose. The scores are even, you see.'

'What have you got in mind?'

Fischer laid the tips of his fingers together in a fastidious churchman's gesture and made his point:

'You told me a long time ago, Colonel, what you wanted to make of this town–"an example of co-operation", wasn't it? "A show-piece for the rest of Austria." You've never been able to do it, because you were never able to touch the wires that made it work. You are further from them than ever now. All you have are scapegoats for your own failure–me and my nephew. When you get us into court, the failure will be shown up very clearly.'

He paused, waiting for the warning to sink in; but Hanlon said nothing. After a moment he took up the thread of his argument.

'For myself, I am not concerned. I shall go through the performance like a well-trained monkey. I might even make some profit out of it in the end. But my nephew is a different matter. He's had enough, poor devil. I don't want to see him crucified again. I know you've got to bring him to trial. I know too that a recommendation to clemency would make things much easier for him. That's what I'm asking. I think I can offer you a good price for it.'

'What's your offer?'

'The keys to this town. The private history of every one of its inhabitants. The knowledge that has kept an incompetent like me safely in office for fifteen years. I know you, Colonel, I know what you need–power. I'm prepared to hand it to you, all in one book. It's worth the price, believe me. I took fifteen years to write it.'

'Where is this book?'

'Hidden. But give your promise on behalf of my nephew and I'll tell you where to find it.' His ridiculous head wagged and his bright eyes shone with malicious humour. 'Tempting, isn't it?'

Hanlon's face was blank, his eyes were hooded, but inside he was bubbling with excitement. Once again Fischer was overreaching himself; and this might be the beginning of the biggest victory of all. He said coolly:

'You might give me the book and I might sell you both down the river.'

Fischer smiled and shook his head.

'I know you better than that. It is an English failing to justify the big betrayal by the small loyalty. If you give me your word, I shall believe you.'

'You've got yourself a deal,' said Hanlon calmly.

When he raised his head, Fischer saw that he was smiling, and the smile chilled him with sudden fear. He had made his last stroke. He had thrown away his shield. Now he was naked to the sword of the invader.

It took Hanlon five hours to draft his report to Klagenfurt, but by seven in the evening it was ready. It was a small masterpiece of concise reporting and meticulous balancing of political possibilities. It ended with a recommendation which he hoped would appeal to the British preference for a workable compromise against a dramatic decision between alternatives.

'. . . We are thus in a neat dilemma. If we proceed against Johann Wikivill, we must perforce proceed against the murderers of Winkler. If we cite one and not the others our credit as impartial administrators is destroyed. If we arraign both parties we find ourselves prosecutors of actions against the sympathies of large numbers of powerful people. The court would undoubtedly return a merciful verdict and award minimum sentences. Shrewd propagandists would make profit out of both cases in the Eastern and the Western press. We ourselves would lose much and gain nothing.

'My recommendation is that both affairs be dealt with quietly at the discretion of the local command. D.P. inmates are now under disciplinary restraint and Johann Wikivill is under the care of the parish priest, a discreet man with a good Resistance record. He is being advised by local medical authorities on the therapeutic treatment of a difficult mental case. I am convinced that no further incidents need be feared.

'We are still considerably in profit. No press disclosures have been made and with the removal of Karl Fischer—a trouble-maker—I have been enabled to remodel the police force and appoint a more co-operative official, without running foul of the interim Austrian Government. I hope you will agree with these recommendations and confirm my discretionary powers in both cases.'

He signed his name with a flourish over the typed subscription, folded the letter, sealed it in a triple envelope and tossed it into the tray for posting.

He had had a big day. He was looking forward to a bath and a cigarette and dinner with Traudl at the Zigeuner Café.

Then the telephone rang. He lifted the receiver.

'Hanlon here.'

A precise, wintry voice answered him.

'Colonel Hanlon? This is Sepp Kunzli.'

'Yes. What can I do for you?'

'If you would be good enough to listen for a few moments, without interruption, I should be very grateful.'

'Go ahead.'

'My niece will be dining with the Holzingers this evening. She will sleep the night in their house. My housekeeper has been given leave to visit her mother. I am therefore alone . . .'

Mark Hanlon frowned at the black mouthpiece but said nothing. The cool, prim voice talked on steadily.

'. . . You have, I believe, an affection for my niece. At least you owe her a small gratitude . . .'

'Yes, but I don't understand what . . .'

'Please, Colonel, no interruptions.'

'I hope therefore that you will be kind to her during the next few days. Your investigators have done a good job, Colonel. In a week at most they will have traced nearly all the expropriated property that has passed through my hands. You will then be forced to take action against me. I propose to save you the trouble. In a few moments I shall kill myself.'

'For God's sake, man!'

'Don't try to do anything, Hanlon. By the time your people got here I should be dead anyway. I am trying to leave you a clean desk. I have made provision for Anna and I know you will believe that the property I have left her is all of clean title. I'd like you to see that she gets it without trouble.'

'I'll do that. But listen, Kunzli, this is crazy. You can't just . . .'

'On the contrary, Colonel, it is the sanest thing I've ever done. I'm saving everybody a lot of trouble, myself included. You'll thank me for it later. You can repay me by being kind to Anna.' There was a moment's pause and the voice came back again, cold and measured as ever.

'I have just taken a cyanide capsule. I expect to be dead in three minutes.'

'Kunzli, listen to me!'

'Good-bye, Hanlon.'

The receiver went dead in his ear. For a long moment he sat there staring stupidly into the black mouthpiece, then, slowly, he put it back on the cradle and walked out into the corridor to find Johnson.

16

Sepp Kunzli was buried the following day in the Lutheran cemetery. The coffin was carried to the graveside by four peasants and the only other mourners were Holzinger, Hanlon, Kunzli's housekeeper and Anna herself. It was a drab, hopeless little ceremony and they were all glad when it was over.

Anna wept a little when the coffin was lowered, and Hanlon put his arm around her shoulders to comfort her. Then he walked her out of the churchyard and along the sunlit promenade, where the birds sang in the overhanging branches and the children played on the dappled carpet of pine-needles.

She was strangely calm. It was as if she had anticipated the tragedy and had prepared for it a long time.

'He was a cold, unhappy man, Mark. His life was very empty. I think he is better quit of it.'

He was wrenched with pity for her, touched with admiration for her small, bright courage, but he had no words to use. He questioned her gently:

'What will you do now? Where will you go?'

'Where should I go, Mark? This is my home. I have work here.'

'Won't you be lonely?'

'I'm used to that. I'd be lonelier somewhere else. I have friends here.'

'I'd like to help you, if I could, Anna.'

'You've helped me already, Mark. Things would have been much worse if you hadn't taken over. There was nothing for me to do, nothing to fear.'

'There was nothing in that. Official routine.'

'You're a good official, aren't you?'

'It's a matter of debate.' He grinned in spite of himself. 'Myself, I'm inclined to doubt it.'

'Herr Holzinger says you are. And Traudl too. She works with you all the time. She should know.'

Her face was turned away from him, so that he could not see whether it was innocence or jealousy that prompted the words. He shrugged them off and said simply:

'If you're in need of help—any kind, any time—I'd like you to come to me first.'

'Please, Mark. . . . Let's not talk about it any more. Here, I want to show you something.'

She laid a hand on his sleeve and drew him off the path into a small bay where there was a stone seat and a bird cote where the birds came to feed in the hungry winter. She made him sit down on the seat, then she scooped up the grain and the nuts which were scattered on the floor of the cote and moved to stand a few yards away, hand outstretched, beckoning the birds.

'Be very still,' she told him. 'Otherwise they won't come.'

She pursed her lips and threw back her golden head and began to whistle a low trilling call. A moment later the birds came fluttering about her, just out of reach. They retreated immediately, then came again, closer this time, while she stood motionless and beautiful in the broad shaft of sunlight, offering the grain in the cup of her hand. Finally they lost their fear and came to settle on her shoulders and on her wrists and to feed from her palm, while Mark Hanlon watched with wonder and delight.

She woke a deeper passion in him than Traudl did; but her innocence was a barrier to courtship. He would not practise on her the soft deceits of love that other women welcomed. Yet he was in love, as he had never been in love before–and this might well be his only memory of her: a dreaming girl, face tilted into the sun, with the birds fluttering down to her hands and their wings an aureole about her golden head.

Traudl's thoughts on the same subject were rather more prosaic. She gave them to him at length when he returned to the office after driving Anna back to the Bella Vista for her day's duty with the D.P.s.

'Little Fräulein Kunzli's nicely set up now. She's her own mistress. She's got a house and a sizeable dowry. She'll be a good catch for someone.'

'She won't marry for a long while yet,' said Hanlon irritably. He was tired and cross-grained, and vaguely uncomfortable under Traudl's clear-eyed scrutiny.

'Why not? She's old enough to carry the milk pails. And she's a big girl too. Or hadn't you noticed?'

'I hadn't.'

'You're slipping, Mark,' Traudl said softly, as she picked a non-existent thread from his lapel. 'She's in love with you . . . or hadn't you seen that either?'

'I've been too damned busy to notice anything,' he snapped at her. 'A riot, a murder, a suicide and three arrests–all in two days! I should interest myself in a girl's green-sickness.'

'You were interested in mine, Mark.'

'Your're different.'

'How different, *Schatz*?'

Her hands were soft on his cheeks. Her perfume was all about him. He took her in his arms and kissed her, just as Johnson opened the door and stepped into the room.

He goggled a moment, then burst into a whoop of joy.

'Lovely stuff! Happiest day in months. The lad's human after all. When are you putting up the banns, Mark?'

Hanlon flushed angrily, then recovered himself. The thing was out now. Best to be good-humoured about it. Traudl stood beside him, head high and proud, her hand lying on his arm in a gesture of possession. Hanlon disengaged himself lightly and said with a grin:

'Shut the door, Johnny. Get the drinks. We could all use one.'

The glasses were filled and they drank, smiling a little shamefacedly at one another.

'To romance,' said Johnson.

'*Prost!*' said Mark Hanlon.

Traudl had a toast of her own, but like a wise woman she kept it to herself. It was Johnson who saved the day with his breezy summing up:

'I'm glad the penny's dropped–for both of you. You've been getting damned hard to live with, Mark. All work and no play makes the Colonel very dull company.'

'Better keep it to yourself, Johnny,' cautioned Hanlon.

Johnson shrugged it off cheerfully.

'Who am I to gossip when there are a hundred others to do it for me? Why should you care, either of you?'

'There's Traudl to be considered . . .'

'Not me,' said Traudl firmly. 'I want to shout it from the mountains. I will too.'

'No,' Hanlon told her bluntly. 'I'm still married, remember, and we're in the middle of a ticklish political situation. The less said the better until it blows over. Same for you, Johnny. You know the score.'

'Yes, Colonel.'

He said it so demurely that they all laughed and the awkward moment was over.

Hanlon had no intention of being jockeyed into a full-scale love-affair and it was fortunate for him that Traudl was not prepared to go beyond the comfortable routines of courtship without a firm promise of marriage. She was as passionate as Hanlon and she had had her own brief encounters with the young bloods of the Reichswehr; but now she was playing for bigger stakes–a marriage that would take her out of this defeated land and into the wider pastures of the West. There were barriers to the leap–Hanlon's marriage, his unwillingness to commit himself to a new gamble, his position as the Occupying Power. None of them was insuperable, but she must lead him gently to the jumps lest he balk and refuse them altogether.

So they settled down to comfortable companionship in work and in playtime, broken by daily passionate interludes that brought them each a little closer to the final surrender. They submitted, willingly enough, to Johnson's amiable conspiracies to bring them into company and force them out again into the spectacular privacy of acknowledged lovers.

They worked late on the accumulated documentation of the Kunzli affair. They dined and danced at the Zigeuner Café. They drove out in the moonlight as far as the roads would take them and bundled for an hour or two in the jeep. They parted at the Holzingers' gate and Hanlon went back to his big bed in the Sonnblick to continue his nightly study of Fischer's black volume of the sins of Bad Quellenberg.

The book fascinated him. The secret life of the town was spread before him like the underside of a carpet–a shabby pattern of lies and cheating and adultery and incest and political bargaining. All the men were there, all the women, even the misdemeanours of their children. Their public successes were set down, side by side with their personal failures. At first he was ashamed of his interest. Then he began to succumb to the fascination of it.

Here, as Fischer had promised him, was the essence of power; to know the sins of all, and the price at which they could be bought. The book was a talisman, like the lamp of Aladdin. Turn one page and a councillor would pour money in your lap. Turn another and his daughter would come to your bed. Point to this line and that and a dozen fearful human beings would run to your most degrading service.

Holzinger was there, the weak, good man making his shoddy compromises between comfort and conscience, never quite sure whether he was wearing the cuckold's horns or the blinkers of a fool.

But Fischer was sure. Fischer had picked up the rumour and traced it back to Hamburg, and proved it for a fact that Liesl Holzinger had lived with a British soldier and possibly become pregnant by him on the eve of her husband's return.

Traudl was there too. Her young war-time loves were listed one by one: the Panzer lieutenant, the official from Vienna, the Luftwaffe pilot who had promised to marry her but had never come back. The geography of her passion was meticulous: the ski-huts were named, the hotel rooms, the glades and glens where she had given herself, and the times were set beside the names of the men who had possessed her.

As he leafed through the sorry little chronicle, Hanlon was touched with horror at his own prurience. He was not in love with this girl, but he had a comradely fondness for her, and a hearty sensual urge for her willing body. Yet here he was peeping like a *voyeur* at the intimate commerce of her bedroom.

It took him a little time to understand why he could read and read and not be jealous. There was nothing to be jealous about. Her past belonged to him, even more than her present. Like all the other citizens of Bad Quellenberg, she was in his power.

Fischer had paid dearly for what he might have had free. He had handed over the keys of the city. He had made Mark Hanlon master of Bad Quellenberg and all the folk who lived there. And yet, not all. There were the few innocent, the many ignorant but unimpeachable. There were the simple ones who were born and loved and married and begot and died unmindful of the greatness they had achieved. They were beyond the reach of malice—like Father Albertus, whom he respected, like Anna, whom he loved but could not have.

They made him ashamed of himself and of this new creeping itch for power. Because of them he closed the book and locked it away in the lowest compartment of the safe, to which he alone had the key.

One night, shortly after the death of Sepp Kunzli, he walked down into the town to call on Reinhardt Huber. A small parcel of replacement drugs had arrived from Klagenfurt and he wanted to give himself the pleasure of delivering them personally.

Huber's broad face lit up with pleasure at the gift and he insisted that Hanlon share a cup of coffee and the last of a bottle of schnapps. They talked and smoked and drank for the best part of an hour, and when Hanlon stepped out into the street again the clock in the church steeple was sounding nine.

The street was deserted. The burghers were all at home supping behind closed blinds. The D.P.s had been under curfew since the murder of Winkler. The troops were drinking in the *Stüberls* or necking with the girls on the promenades or dancing in the Zigeuner Café. Hanlon's footsteps rang hollowly on the cobbles and the moonlight was ghostly on the blank walls and on the pinewoods above the town.

Suddenly, far ahead of him, he heard a woman's scream, high, panic-stricken, quickly stifled. He began to run, swiftly and silently on the balls of his toes. The road narrowed and twisted sharply into the old town, where the shop-fronts were set back under low shadowy arches.

Then he saw them: the woman backed helpless against a stone pillar, the man holding her with one arm locked against her throat while the other tore at her clothing. The man heard him coming, wrenched away and bolted up the narrow street. The woman crumpled at the foot of the pillar.

When Hanlon bent over her he saw that it was Anna Kunzli.

He lifted her gently and carried her the rest of the way to the Spider-house. She woke in his arms, trembling and incoherent with shock, but she gave him the name of her attacker and a rough description of him. When they arrived at the Spider-house he handed her over to the housekeeper to be bathed and put to bed, while he himself sat at Sepp Kunzli's desk and telephoned to Johnson.

'I want you to find me a man, Johnny. His name's Anton Kovacs, a D.P. from the Bella Vista. Phone through to Miller for a full description of him. Comb the town, call in every man jack of the troops and the police if you have to, but get him tonight.'

'What then?'

'Arrest him—and don't be gentle about it. Close confinement.'

'What do I charge him with?'

'Attempted rape.'

'My God! Who's the girl?'

'Anna Kunzli.'

Johnson's whistle of surprise shrilled in his ear.

'Who's the witness?'

'I am.'

'We'll get him, Mark. When will you be back?'

'I don't know. Expect me when you see me. If you want me I'm at the Kunzli house.'

'Roger. Oh, by the way, Traudl rang and wanted you to . . .'

'To hell with Traudl. Jump to it, Johnny.'

'I'm on my way.'

'*Wiedersehn.*'

He put down the receiver and sat with his head on his hands staring down at the burled polished wood of the desk top. He was angry and weary and dispirited. One by one the illusions were being stripped from him. The cynics were proving right. His own blind idealism was a deceit and a sham. Fischer had warned him that the D.P.s would bring murder and rape and violence. All three had happened. Huber had warned him that a man could not be a lover of the people and a good administrator at the same time. The proof of it was on every page of Fischer's black folio. How could one love the rutting, snarling, treacherous animals pictured there? They could be controlled only by strength and cunning. Survival—that was the driving motive. Trample the weak, seduce the strong, take what you want and if you can avoid paying for it, so much the better.

Johnson was right when he derided the compromise of his position. He was involved, but not far enough. He wanted power but was not prepared for the final ruthlessness. He wanted love, but solaced himself with a juvenile courtship. He was neither a contented celibate nor a cheerful lecher. He wanted the best of both worlds and was stuck with the worst of each.

He was still mumbling over this tasteless cud when the housekeeper came and told him that Anna was ready to see him.

He found her propped against the pillows in the same bed where he himself had lain during the days of his illness. She was pale and heavy-eyed and the bruises were beginning to show on the white skin of her throat. He sat down on the edge of the bed and bent to kiss her lightly. Her arms went round his neck and she clung to him in a sudden paroxysm of sobbing.

'Oh, Mark! Mark! It had to be you. There was no one else . . . no one!'

He held her close, soothing her with lover's words until the weeping was over and she was calm again. Then he dried the tears from her face and settled her pillows and sat looking down at her with love and pity.

He told her softly: 'It was a bad dream, *Liebchen*. It's over now. It will never come back.'

She shook her head.

'It was horrible, Mark. He was like an animal. I feel as though I shall never be clean again.'

'You are as you always were, Anna. Clean and beautiful.'

'Am I beautiful, Mark?'

'Very beautiful, *Liebchen*.'

'Will you kiss me please?'

He bent and kissed her lightly on the lips

'Not like that, Mark. I'm not a child. I'm a woman. I want to feel like a woman. I–I love you so much.'

'I love you too, Anna.'

'Kiss me, then.'

Her arms were round him again and their lips met and she made him lead her through all the soft, wild rituals of love, as if only his hands could cleanse her, and only his body could waken her from the nightmare.

When they woke in the morning, the room was full of sunlight. The housekeeper smiled when she brought them their breakfast on the terrace and, when they looked about them, the world was bright and new as if spring were breaking out a second time on the green flanks of the mountains.

When Traudl Holzinger heard the news, she laughed in his face.

'For God's sake, Mark! I thought you'd know better. These mewing virgins are all the same. They're white as milk and soft as butter and so damned innocent you have to teach them the words. They wilt in your arms and beg you to be tender with them–and six weeks later they're yelling that they're pregnant. Men are such fools!'

'It isn't like that, Traudl.'

'It never is, *Schatz,* until they start waving marriage lines under your nose! You wait and see! I'll give you two months, then you'll be back with a bad hangover and indigestion from too much sugar-cake.'

'I'm sorry, Traudl. I'm going to marry her.'

'You won't, you know,' she mocked him cheerfully.

Hanlon was touched by her bright, cool courage. He said gravely:

'Johnny's more than half in love with you.'

She made a small shrugging gesture of resignation.

'He's still a boy, Mark. But I'll probably make a man of him. Don't worry about me.'

She bent forward suddenly and kissed him full on the lips, biting them till the blood flowed and he forced her away from him.

'That's for remembrance. I think you're making a big mistake, Mark, but I wish you luck. Meantime . . .' She was suddenly serious. 'You won't want me round here any more, I suppose.'

'If you're prepared to stay, I'm glad to have you,' said Hanlon stiffly. 'No point in making a song and dance about it. I still need a secretary.'

'You need more than a secretary, Mark,' she told him with sudden malice. 'You need someone to teach you the facts of life. I'm probably the only one who can do it. I'll stay.'

And stay she did—an efficient assistant, a sardonic observer of all the follies of this new mating of May and September.

The first reply from Klagenfurt on the murder cases, reached him the next day:

> Your report received and noted. If possible maintain present position until after High Command Conference Vienna, when further directive will be sent. . . .

Hanlon smiled sourly at the bland official equivocation. He was still in command of the situation, but if he made a mistake they would have his head on a chafing-dish.

He sent a copy of the telegram to Miller and to Father Albertus, then, weary of so many crises, he settled back to the comfortable routine of administration.

He kept his evenings and his week-ends free and he spent all of them with Anna Kunzli. They tramped the back valleys, they fished the trout streams, they sunned themselves in the grass of the uplands, where the gentians bloomed and the small rock orchids and the early columbines. Often he slept in her house and walked back to headquarters in the first warmth of the morning, wrapped in the soft sad contentment that follows after love.

He had been married to one woman. He had slept with many others, in vain pursuit of what the first had refused him. He understood that enjoyment is easily attained, while contentment is as elusive as a marsh-light.

With Anna he had both, and a renewal of his youth as well.

They were in tune with one another—as leaf with wind, as water with the pebbles over which it runs.

Passion rose in them at the same moment, they were calm together and they laughed and kissed and were silent to a common impulse.

Hanlon's young days had been spent in a monastery garden. He looked back on them with a sense of loss. A man has a lifetime to collect wisdom. He has only a few years to store up memories of spring.

Anna Kunzli made good his loss; and because he was wiser now, he was able to be grateful, so that she too was content—at least for a while.

But as the weeks passed, an element of uneasiness began to show itself in the smooth score of their pastorale. In the beginning they had talked, lightly enough, of divorce and re-marriage, yet the more they returned to the subject, the more the difficulties showed themselves. Anna had a Catholic conscience on divorce and a fear of the moral sanctions involved. Hanlon had it too, but he was older, more cynical, more ready to grasp what the years must soon snatch away from him. Anna thought in a woman's terms—the fate of the children, the security of the bond, the breach with the Church.

At first her doubts were easily stifled. Passion ran strongly between them and the warm propinquity of the lovers' bed was all the security they needed. But custom stales even a spring-time affair and often she would wake in the night and cling to him, begging for reassurance which he could not give without a lie, so that he could only make love to her and lull her into a temporary forgetfulness. They had small quarrels, quickly healed with a kiss; but the scars remained, a small accumulation of doubts and indecisions and unspoken regrets. They loved each other but the security of possession was denied them. The bloom was dusting off the flower. The gilt was wearing off the gingerbread house. Traudl Holzinger saw it all and said nothing.

Finally, one night, Anna faced him with it, squarely.

They had dined and drunk a little and made love; but for the first time they were out of harmony and the loving was brief and unsatisfactory. They were lying apart from each other in the big bed in Sepp Kunzli's room, which had become their marriage chamber. The light was burning and they saw each other's faces, strained and dubious. Anna said quietly: 'Mark?'

'Yes?'

'I want to be alone for a few days.'

'Just as you like.'

'Don't be angry with me, Mark. I love you. You know that. I want nothing better than for us to be happy always and always. But I've got to be sure.'

'You can't, you know,' said Hanlon gravely. 'Life isn't like that. Nothing's sure. People drop dead in the streets. Gasworks blow up. Children are crippled with disease. There's war and flood and famine and cankers in the guts. Tomorrow is the most doubtful word of all. The best one can do is live for the day. Take the cash in hand and be glad you've got it.'

'Can you do that, Mark?'

'Nobody can completely.'

'No. . . . That's why I want time to think, to decide. . . .'

'Decide what?' The fear pricked like a sharp knife around his heart.

'Whether to go on with this. Whether to take the cash . . . or play for the future.'

'It's your right, my dear. I don't quarrel with it. How long do you want?'

'I don't know. How can I? Will you leave it to me to get in touch with you?'

'If you want it like that.'

'I do, Mark.'

Without another word he threw back the covers and got out of bed and began dressing himself. The girl lay back on the pillows watching him.

When he was dressed he bent over her and kissed her gently, then walked out of the room without another word. When the door closed behind him, she buried her face in the pillow and sobbed.

Shoulders bent, head thrust forward, Mark Hanlon walked slowly back to the Sonnblick under the cold moon. *Post coitum omne animal triste.* Man is the saddest animal in the world. The act which gives him the keenest delight is the one which brings him closest to death.

17

Father Albertus sat in his high-backed chair, under a wooden statue of St Julian, and looked down at the swollen, tear-stained face of Anna Kunzli. She sat opposite him, pale and straight-backed, her fingers picking nervously at the edges of a small lace handkerchief. The old man's voice was warm with understanding, and even in his chiding there was a gentleness.

'What do you want me to tell you, Anna? That black is white, that adultery is a good thing, that happiness can be built on a lie and an injustice?'

'I want you to help me, Father.' All the youth had gone from her voice. It was weary under the weight of experience. 'You talk about adultery and lies and injustice. These are words to me. All I know is love. I love Mark. He loves me. It's not a dirty word like the others. It's beautiful. How can I make you understand that?'

'I do understand, child, believe me.'

'How can you, never having felt it?'

'You think not?' A ghost of a smile woke in the mild eyes. 'I'm an old man now, but I was young once like you and Mark. The vows of the priesthood don't destroy one's manhood. Only age does that. Do you think I have never felt desire? Do you think I have never held a child in my arms at the baptismal font, and wished that it were my own? What do you think I hear in the confessional? Fairy-tales?'

'Then why are you so pitiless?' She flung it at him desperately.

'I am not pitiless, but I cannot change the truth. Look, Anna . . .' He bent to her, gesturing with his broken hands. 'For the first time in your life you are face to face with the real meaning of religion—the thing that binds, the thing that restricts. People talk of it as if it were a gentle thing, a source of consolation. So it is, but only in part. For the rest, it is a burden, a cross on our backs.'

'Who lays it there?'

'Not I, child, but God Almighty.'

'Then he too must be without pity.'

The wise, luminous face clouded. The white head bent in deprecation.

'He has pity, Anna. He has love too. He framed your lips for kissing and your body for love and child-bearing.'

'And then denies them to me in the end.'

'Because they belong to another woman, Mark's wife.'

'She doesn't want them. She never has.'

'Did Mark tell you that?'

'Yes.'

'How do you know he wasn't lying to you?'

'You've got no right to say that, Father. I know Mark. He hasn't lied to me.'

Father Albertus nodded gravely.

'No, I don't believe he has. I'm sorry. Mark is a good man but an unhappy one. It is hard enough for anyone to be continent when he lives for years away from his wife. It is harder still when there is no love left to preserve loyalty.'

'That's it, don't you see, Father.' She seized eagerly on the tag of the argument. 'There is no love left, there is no injustice. Life will be awfully long for him and for me too. Why shouldn't we enjoy it while we can?'

'You're young, Anna, you can enjoy it with another man–and with a safe conscience.'

She raised her head and faced him squarely. Her young eyes were suddenly cold, her mouth was firm. She said very deliberately: 'Understand something, Father. Whatever I decide in this matter, there is only one man I can ever or will ever love. That man is Mark Hanlon.'

Looking at her then, Father Albertus knew with moral certainty that he was hearing the truth. Anna Kunzli was, in the absolute sense, a simple person, one of those who see quite clearly and choose quite coldly and who hold for ever to their choice, even if it leads to ruin and damnation. This was no country bundling with tears and repentance and marriage lines at the end of it. The girl had come to him in good faith for help in an irrevocable decision. If he failed her now, the damage would be irreparable. He closed his eyes and prayed as he had prayed with Johann Wikivill, for light in his eyes and wisdom on his tongue. Then, very gently he told her:

'I have no consolation to offer you, child. I can only tell you the truth and pray that you may find strength to follow it. If you and Mark stay together you may come to happiness. I say you may, because I know Mark better than you, and I tell you that no woman will ever satisfy him completely. He is one of those touched with a hunger for the lost paradise. He will search for it until he dies, and then, if God is kind to him, he may attain it. I say again, you *may* be happy. If you are, it will be at the expense of your faith, which is the only thing when passion dies and the body begins to wear out.

'And if I give him up?'

'You will be lonely for the rest of your life.'

'What about his child?'

'His child?'

'I'm pregnant, Father,' said Anna Kunzli calmly.

The old man said nothing. He got up, walked to the window and stood a long time staring out over the roof-tops of the town. When at last he turned to her again, she saw that his eyes were misty. His voice was tired and hesitant.

'With all my heart, Anna, I wish I could say to you now, "Go and be happy with your man. Bear his children. Keep his house. Build yourselves a new life in the valley." I love you both, you see. I–I think of you as the son and the daughter I have never had. In your children I might see the continuity which my vows deny me. But I cannot do it. In the camp they beat me and starved me and broke my hands to bring me to betrayal.' He voice faltered. 'I tell you truly it was easy, compared with this.'

Anna Kunzli was touched with sympathy for the old man, but she looked at him with her bright, clear eyes and challenged him:

'You say you love us both, Father. Yet you condemn us to death, a long, slow death, lonely and without love.'

'Not to death, child, to life.'

'Show me anyone who could survive it.'

'I'll do that,' said Father Albertus quietly. 'Perhaps he can help you better than I.'

Without another word he walked from the room, and, a few moments later, he was back with Johann Wikivill.

Two days later Mark Hanlon had a visit from Father Albertus, who handed him a letter from Anna Kunzli. It was short, simple and final.

> My dearest Mark,
> I have decided. I can't go through with it. I know you will understand why. I love you still. I will love you till I die. But please, please don't come to me.
>
> Anna

Hanlon read it through in silence; then, quite deliberately, tore it into small pieces and dropped it in the waste-paper basket. Then he looked up at Father Albertus and said with grim courtesy: 'Thank you, Father. Was there anything else?'

'Except to say that I feel very deeply for both of you.'

'If Anna can survive it,' said Hanlon ironically, 'I've no doubt I can. I've had a good deal more experience.'

The old man brushed aside the irony and answered him warmly: 'You try to hurt me, Mark, but in reality you are tormenting yourself. I did not take Anna from you. I showed her both roads. She made the choice herself. You know that's true, don't you?'

The sardonic mask dropped from Hanlon's face, to reveal the hurt and heartbreak beneath it. He flung out his hands in a passionate appeal.

'Why did she go to you, then? Why didn't she tell me herself? I wouldn't have tried to hold her. Do you think I'd want her unhappy? I know too well what it means. I can't forgive you for that, Father.'

'She was afraid to come, Mark. If she had to hurt you she didn't want to do it with a kiss. Besides, she loved you too much to trust herself in your arms again.'

'Which makes me a pretty sort of lecher, doesn't it?'

'You're not a lecher, Mark,' Father Albertus reproved him mildly.

'What then?'

'A man looking for love,' said the old priest calmly, 'wanting it so much that he may well lose it eternally.'

'Or have it snatched from me.' Hanlon's voice was bitter. 'You took her from me, Father.'

'I did not take her.' The old voice was touched with anger. 'She surrendered you freely. And I tell you now, you will never be happy until you make the same free surrender of her.'

Hanlon's fist slammed down on the desk. His eyes blazed and he shouted at the old priest:

'You want too much for too little. You take everything and give nothing. I gave you Johann Wikivill. You've got Anna. You want me too.'

'I'm a hunter of souls, Mark.' The mild eyes lit with sudden fire. 'I cast the nets as wide as I can.'

'And what do you give to those who surrender, Father?'

'Peace, my son.'

'Peace!' The word was flung back in harsh mockery.

Hanlon heaved himself out of his chair and began to pace angrily up and down the long room, pouring out the resentment and disappointment of years.

'Peace, you tell me! You promised it to me in the monastery close. I never found it. I found pride, ambition, jealousy, and lack of love. You sent me out to look for it in the world. I didn't find it there either. I came, as I came to this place, with love and kindness, and had them tossed back in my face. I loved a woman and was left unloved. I loved my children but their love for me was poisoned. I fought a war to found a peace. I came to this town to establish it. There was no peace. There was murder, rape, suicide, and the death of love. You promise me peace, Father. Where is it? Where?'

The priest was silent a long time. His pitying eyes were fixed in the ravaged face of his old pupil. Then he quoted softly: 'Thou has made us for Thyself, O God, and our hearts will never rest until they rest in Thee.'

'It's too late, Father,' said Hanlon in a dead, flat voice. 'It's too late and I'm too tired.'

'It is never too late, my son.'

'Let's forget it.' Hanlon's voice was crisp again. His face smoothed itself into the old, official mask. 'There's a business matter . . .'

'Yes?'

'I told you, you asked too much and gave too little. It's a bad bargain. You've got Anna. I want you to give me back Johann Wikivill.'

For one disbelieving moment Father Albertus stared at him, and then he stood up and said formally: 'I'll send him to you, Colonel. *Auf Wiedersehn.*'

'*Aug Wiedersehn*, Father.'

A little while later Traudl Holzinger came in with the afternoon's mail from Klagenfurt. She greeted him impersonally and began slitting the envelopes and laying the correspondence in front of him. He worked through them abstractedly, signing them, initialling them and tossing them into their various trays. All the time he never said a word. At last there were only two letters left.

When he opened the first of them, his face changed. He read it through a second time, then abruptly he threw back his head and burst into a great bellow of laughter. He laughed and laughed till the tears ran down his cheeks while Traudl watched him in puzzlement. Then he tossed the paper on the desk in front of her.

'That's it! That's the last bloody straw. Read it! Go on, read it!'

There was little enough to read. There was a file number and a reference and a curt memorandum from the G.O.C. Occupation Headquarters, Klagenfurt: 'Your recommendations on recent incidents in the Quellenberg area are acceptable to this Headquarters, and in line with recent agreements on Four-Power policies in occupied Austria an amnesty for certain classes of military and political prisoners will be proclaimed immediately after the forthcoming elections. We suggest that you take advantage of this to deal with both the displaced persons and with Johann Wikivill.'

'What's so funny about that?' Traudl handed him back the letter. 'You got what you wanted, didn't you?'

'That's the cream of the joke, sweetheart. I got it–and now I don't want it.'

'Like Anna Kunzli?'

He looked up swiftly and caught the bright mockery of her smile.

'I want her, but I've lost her.'

'And now what?'

He picked up the last letter on the tray and tapped it absently on the desk, while he looked at her with bleak irony.

'It's my own damnation, dark one. I'll work it out for myself. Why don't you get Johnny to take you home?'

For a long moment she stared at him, half-pitying, half-resentful, then she turned on her heel and walked from the room. Hanlon picked up a paper-knife, opened the last envelope and began to read:

> My dear Mark,
>   It has taken me a long time—too long, perhaps—to come to the writing of this letter. I can only pray that you will understand my reasons and be kind.
>   The children want to see you. They have heard that arrangements are being made for families of Occupation troops to visit Europe and later to live there with their menfolk. They love you, they miss you. And they are beginning to resent their separation from you.
>   I, too, want to see you. Please, please, believe this! I want it more than anything else in the world. Our marriage foundered a long time ago, but, until recently, I didn't understand that it was I who destroyed it.
>   You knew and you hated me for it. Your hate was a weapon in my hands, just as the children were. Now I don't want weapons. I have no defence. I've been selfish and cold and cruel. I want to say I'm sorry. Then, if you'll have me, I want to try to begin again. I want to give you some of the love I denied you, and, if possible, to build something out of the wreckage of our lives.
>   If you can't forgive me, I shan't blame you. You were always a gentle man and I know will still be gentle for the sake of the children. If you want to know what's brought me to this, it's quite simple.
>   I'm older and wiser—and afraid of the loveless winter. That, too, is a sort of selfishness, but this time at least I'm honest about it. I'm honest too when I say that if we could come together, on any basis, it wouldn't be one-sided, ever again.
>   Will you please write and let me know whether we may come and what arrangements we should make at this end?
>   Some day—soon, please God—I'd like to be able to sign myself
>   Your loving wife,
>   Lynn

He laid the letter down on the desk and covered it with his hands. Then he leaned back in the chair and closed his eyes.

This was the final irony. This was the love he had pleaded for, wept for, tried to fire with anger and nurse with patience through all the bleak years. This was the love whose denial had driven him out, a wanderer, into the arms of other women, to the barren pursuit of power. Now it was being offered, freely and with humility—and he did not want it.

It was meaningless to him: a script in a forgotten tongue, a score jumbled into a hopeless dissonance. Once upon a time the mystery had piqued him—to passion, to tenderness, to the thousand labours of a lover, to a sense of guilt for his own inadequacy. Now he understood that there was no mystery. There was just a woman's body, priced too high; a heart too shallow; a mind bent back too long upon itself and suddenly terrified by the first lonely glimpse of reality.

The children? Yes. They were his other selves, his promise of continuity. They gave love and took it, thoughtlessly. They were the supplement, the annotation, without which the record of life was incomplete. But they were not the full text. They were the third aspect of the human trinity—man, woman, child. They proceeded from both, were independent of either. They could neither supplant nor supply the intimate relationship of body and spirit which is the beginning, the middle and the end of love.

There was still a bond between himself and Lynn; but the bond was a legality. It had nothing to do now with the body or the spirit. Long ago they had ceased to be one flesh. His body now belonged by affinity, if not by law, to Anna Kunzli. His spirit would always be restless without hers to voyage with him.

What could one rebuild out of a situation like that? A home for the children? But where there is no harmony, there is no home. Affection, respect, mutual trust? Impossible, unless both hearts surrender and each accepts the repentance of the other.

He picked up the letter and read it through again, slowly. He was moved by the pity of it. But he resented bitterly the new burden of decision it imposed upon him.

In this small divided kingdom, as in Bad Quellenberg itself, he was being called upon to give judgment, on a cause involving his own happiness, his own peace. The scales were weighted against him but conscience still demanded a meticulous equity.

Other men, he knew, shrugged off such responsibilities. Equity, they said, was a small thing compared with the fundamental need to survive and to find some safe harbour to do it in. If you could not live inside the law, then the law must be wrenched, little or much, to make room. Marriage was a contract, but if the contract proved inequitable, then to hell with it.

The rub was that such practical fellows were more often right in the outcome than men like himself, who clung to the creaky machinery of justice, long after it had seized and lurched to a standstill.

Once again he was face to face with the fundamental problem of his character and education. He needed love, he needed peace. He was not ruthless enough to destroy them in others to guarantee his own attainment.

A word, a visit, a letter, might bring Anna back to him in defiance of Father Albertus, but he would not have her on those terms. A reunion with Lynn would give her security and make a home for the children. It would leave him for ever empty and solitary. Still he could not bring himself to deny her.

For a long time he sat, head on his hands, pondering his situation. Then he drew pen and paper towards him and began to write. It was a long letter, sober, gentle, kind, and it said quite simply: 'Come first and we will talk. The children can follow, later.'

When he scrawled his name at the foot of the page, it was as if he were signing his own death warrant. He folded the letter, sealed it and tossed it into the posting tray. Then he put on his cap and greatcoat and went out to walk in the grey, cool dusk that gathered under the pine trees.

18

In the bare, shadowy room that looked out to the twilight sky and the black humps of the mountains, Father Albertus was taking supper with Johann Wikivill. Their food was almost untouched. They sipped sparingly at their wine and for a long time they did not speak at all. The peace of the moment was precious to them. The wine was like a viaticum–a sacramental preparation for the journey of the pupil and the lonely vigil of the master.

Wikivill's face was in shadow, but the face of the priest still retained its rare luminous quality and his eyes were full of compassion. For him there was a strangeness in the moment. This was his son whom he was sending out to meet that other son who had left him many years since to walk the crooked paths of passion and ambition.

What would happen at their meeting he could not guess. Each in his own fashion had fallen under the harsh disciplines of the Almighty. Each had reacted differently, the one by rebellion, the other by slow submission of the will. One had come to peace, the other was still in torment. He loved them both. He was bound to each by the same paternity of the spirit, yet they might destroy each other under his eyes. He could do nothing but commit them to a common Mercy and wait with resignation on the outcome.

At last he spoke, his voice deep-toned in the vesper silence.

'You should go very soon, my son.'

Wikivill raised his head, so that the old man saw the calm, distant eyes and the firm set of his mouth.

'I'm ready to go.'

'You don't regret it?'

'No. I've always known it must end like this.'

'You must not hate this man.'

'The only man I have ever hated was myself.'

'You must not do that either.'

'I know. That is a thing you've taught me–to live at peace with myself.'

'Are you afraid?'

'Yes.'

The old man got up, walked to the window and stood a long time looking over the misty valleys towards the shoulder of the mountain and the first faint stars pricking out in the soft sky. Then slowly he turned, a black silhouette against the window, and began to speak:

'Let me explain Mark Hanlon to you. If you understand him, you will not be afraid. If you come to him without fear, you may be able to help him.'

'Help him?' Wikivill's voice was sharp with surprise. 'He wants my head. I'll give it to him. After that I've got nothing left.'

The deep voice admonished him firmly: 'You are a man who has walked, like Lazarus, in the valley of the shadow of death. You have endured the wreck of manhood and the destruction of hope. You have survived to a new hope. In that you are rich. You have strength to spend on this man who walks, as you walked, in the place of the dead, in the abyss of desolation. At core, he is a good man, because there is much love in him and no one is lost until he shuts love out of his life and hardens his will against it. Those he has loved have been taken away from him, so he turns to revenge himself on you. He thinks he hates you, but he has no satisfaction in it. He despises the impulse even as he yields to it. He is empty, lost, solitary, yet his pride will not let him confess his need. Even such a pride is not wholly bad, because it will not allow him to take advantage of a man helpless in his hands. Don't fight him. Don't despise him. Don't set your own pride against his. He is poorer than he knows, and you, for all your loss, are singularly blessed. Remember that, my son.'

'But what do I say to him?'

'What your heart tells you.'

'I am still afraid.'

'If you were not, there would be no merit in what you do. There would be no sacrifice if there were no risk.'

'But I risk the only thing left—my liberty.' Wikivill's voice rose in urgent pleading. 'Don't you see that? It's the walls that frighten me, the stones that hem me in. I killed to escape them. Now I must go back to them, freely, on my own two feet. I'm afraid I may lose courage halfway there.'

'There are no walls any more, my son.' Father Albertus moved towards him across the dim room. 'When you accepted the prison of a maimed body, you came at one stride to freedom. No walls can contain you now. No bars can keep you back from the pastures of contentment. Believe that, in the name of God.'

'I believe,' said Johann Wikivill softly. 'God help my unbelief.'

With an odd, pathetic gesture, he leaned forward and buried his face in his hands while the old piest stood towering over him, praying desperately for the infusion of strength in this critical moment. Finally Wikivill raised his head. His eyes were calm again, his face was peaceful. He pushed back his chair and slipped down on his knees at the feet of the old priest.

'Bless me, Father.'

Father Albertus raised his broken hands in the ritual gesture of benediction: '*Vade, mi fili. . . .* Go, my son! In the name of the Father and of the Son and of the Holy Ghost, go in peace.'

Mark Hanlon sat, chilled to the bone, on the small stone bench where once he had watched Anna feeding the birds, and thought about his situation.

It was plain to him now. He had reached the limit of living. All he had loved was lost to him. All he had built was founded on sand. His hopes were folly-fires, his achievements a blown dust on the desert of the past. The future was a wailing emptiness. He could not go back and there was nothing to beckon him forward. The progression of life had been halted and he was caught in the syncope—a timeless, motionless state of naked disillusion.

He was incapable of consecutive thought. All that was left was a series of pictures, a wild kaleidoscope of people and places, unreal, fantastic, strangely terrifying: Willis lying on the roadway; the wolf-mask of the man behind the gun; Anna's face, ecstatic in the moment of love; the claw hands of Father Albertus; the cold, obsidian eyes of Sepp Kunzli; the obscene secrets in Fischer's black book; Traudl in his arms and the movement of her body against his own; Holzinger's weak, handsome face, and behind it the faded, featureless face of his own wife.

The pictures spun dizzily faster and faster until he cried out with the terror of it and buried his face in his hands to shut them out. His body ached as if he had been beaten with rods; his face twitched and his teeth began to chatter uncontrollably. He was deathly cold.

He stood up and began to walk slowly along the promenade in the direction of the town. The trees hung black and motionless in the still air. The sound of running water troubled him like nightmare voices, and when he looked up at the sky he saw only the black mockery of the starlight.

When he reached the town it seemed to him that its aspect had changed. The walls were high cliffs; its yellow windows were caves peopled by monsters who mocked him silently. The shop-fronts mirrored his stooped, shambling figure so that he looked like a shadowy dwarf.

There were ghosts under the black archways. Goat-masks stared at him from behind the chimney-pots and Anna's despairing scream rang in his ears over the pounding feet of her attacker. He walked faster and faster until his body was streaming with sweat and an iron band clamped itself round his rib case.

At the entrance to the Sonnblick the guard stared at his wild, yellow face and put out a hand to support him, but he brushed past and hurried into the lift, slamming the steel gates and jabbing the button in a last frantic effort to reach the safety of his room.

Gasping and retching, he hung over the basin until the nausea had left him; then he stripped off his tunic, douched his face and hands and walked unsteadily back into the office to pour himself a drink. The raw spirit took hold of him quickly; and he drank another glass and another, then sat down at his desk and lit a cigarette. He choked on the first mouthful of smoke and stubbed the cigarette out in the ash-tray.

Then, shrill and shattering, the telephone rang.

Instinctively he reached out and lifted the receiver. Habit and not will dictated the familiar words:

'Hanlon here.'

Sergeant Jennings's voice answered him.

'There's a man to see you, sir. Name Johann Wikivill. He says you sent for him.'

'Send him up–alone.'

'Yessir.'

He replaced the receiver and sat down at the desk. The comedy wasn't quite finished. There was still the antistrophe, the sour epilogue.

A few moments later the door opened and Johann Wikivill stepped into the room.

To Hanlon's heated imagination he looked like a man ten feet tall. He was dressed in the same uniform which he had worn on the day of their first meeting–square, peaked cap, tight jacket, baggy trousers, and the long, theatrical cloak that reached almost to his ankles. The peak of the cap threw a shadow over his forehead, and out of the shadow his distant eyes shone strangely.

It was the cloak that gave him height, but it was the face that lent him the look of an unearthly visitor. One side of it was rough and stubbled, and darkened by shadow. The other was smooth, new and shining. 'Like Lazarus,' thought Hanlon inconsequently, 'caught halfway between death and the renewal of the resurrection.'

The thought amused him. He embellished it, smiling to himself, while

Johann Wikivill stood tall and immobile, watching him. 'At the resurrection there shall be neither marriage nor giving in marriage, but we shall all be like angels of God. . . . The eunuchs will come into their own, the celibates, the barren ones. They'll all have mild, mystical eyes and baby skin like this fellow. They'd be dull company for us poor devils who are content with three meals a day and a little honest loving at night–if we can get it.'

Johann Wikivill announced himself formally.

'I am Johann Wikivill, Colonel. You wanted me.'

'I've been wanting you for a long time,' said Hanlon. 'Tell me . . . Why did you kill Willis?'

'Because I hated myself.'

'That's it!' Hanlon's voice rose. 'Good! It's always that way, isn't it? I know how you felt, man! I'm feeling it myself now! Tell me, what do you see from your end? What do I look like?'

'Like myself.' There was warmth in the voice now, a haunting pity. 'You look weary, hunted, sick . . .'

Hanlon looked up sharply. 'Of course! You're a doctor. I remember now. What's your prescription?'

'There's only one.'

'Name it.'

'Hope,' said Johann Wikivill softly.

Hanlon's mouth drew back into a tight, cheerless grin.

'Father Albertus taught you that, didn't he? I know . . . he taught me, too. But there's a catch in it–a big catch. You know what it is? To hope, you must have something to hope for, a goal, an end! What do you hope for, Wikivill?'

'To be free one day. To practise medicine again. To spend some skill and kindness on poor devils like myself.'

'They won't thank you for it,' said Hanlon with cold irony. 'They never do.'

'I'll be paying a debt. There's no question of thanks.'

'You owe me a debt.' Hanlon's smile was bitter. 'A life for a life.'

'I'm here to pay it,' Wikivill told him calmly.

'You can't!' Hanlon picked up the letter from Klagenfurt and held it out to him. 'Here, read it.'

Wikivill stepped forward and took the letter. The approach diminished him to human size. The shadows fell away from his face so that it became symmetrical again. He read the letter carefully, then handed it back to Hanlon. His eyes were mild; his lips were parted in a smile of great gentleness.

'It seems I owe you a double debt, Colonel.'

Hanlon waved a contemptuous dismissal. 'You owe me nothing. Get out!'

Wikivill did not move. For a long moment he stared at Hanlon, groping for words to convey his gratitude. Then, very quietly:

'I'll look after Anna for you, Colonel. When her time comes, I'll deliver her myself, and care for the child, too. They'll be safe in my hands, I promise!'

Hanlon's head jerked back as if he had been struck in the mouth. His voice was a hoarse whisper. 'What are you saying?'

'I'm sorry,' said Johann Wikivill gravely. 'I thought you knew. Anna Kunzli is going to have your child.'

For one disbelieving moment Hanlon stared at him; then all the pain of the years was wrenched out of him in one despairing cry:

'Dear God in Heaven! No!'

Then he buried his face in his hands and wept like a child.

Johann Wikivill took off his cap and his cloak and stood beside him, patting his shoulder and murmuring small words of comfort, as if they were two brothers, united by a common grief.

'You should go to her,' Wikivill told him firmly. 'No matter what she has said, go to her. Tell her how it is with you and your wife. Tell her you love her and what you want to do for her and the child. That way there will be no bitterness, no regret. . . .'

They were sitting together in the big room where once Hanlon had planned the capture of the man behind the gun. There were drinks between them and the slow, friendly curl of cigarette smoke. Hanlon was still numb with shock, but slowly life seemed to be flowing back to him from the tall, lean man with the calm eyes and the gentle voice.

This was not the surrender he had planned, but if there was no triumph in it, there was also no regret. Now they were men together, conscious of mutual deeds, of common debts. There was no shame between them. The shame of victory was wiped out by the dignity of defeat. The shadow of the lictor's axe was replaced by the shadow of a common cross.

Hanlon leaned forward, questioning awkwardly. 'I'm worried about the child. What happens to him? He has no name, no father. How can Anna still live here and . . .'

Wikivill cut him short with a gesture. 'You forget how it is with our people. They have respect for life—however it comes. The child will be welcomed, and loved, too. Besides, there will be many like it in this land of ours, where the men are dead and the women are lonely. We shall be grateful, all of us, for this new promise of the future. You will see. The women will make clothes, and the woodcutters will bring toys, and there will be flowers and candles for the baptism, so that it will be like the coming of the *Christkind*. I will see that she has a good delivery. If they are sick I will care for them.'

Hanlon was almost stifled by the simple wonder of it.

'I wanted you dead. And now . . .'

'Now you should eat something, then you should sleep, and in the morning go and see Anna.'

'I'd like to see her tonight.'

'It's late,' Wikivill told him soberly. 'You've had a bad day. And night is a treacherous time for lovers.'

Hanlon nodded wearily. 'I know. You're right, of course. I'll wait. But don't go yet,' he added hastily. 'Stay and eat with me. I'm scared.'

'Reaction,' said Wikivill professionally. 'The mind and the body can take just so much, any more and they reject it, violently.'

'That's what scares me. This is only the beginning. There's my work here. There are a dozen personal problems to be worked out. I—I'm so damn tired I'm not sure I can face them.'

Wikivill leaned forward and poured some liquor into the glasses on the table. Without looking up he said gravely: 'You're stronger than you know We all are. But we need a shoulder to lean on sometimes. If you would let me help, it would make me very happy.'

Hanlon gave him a tired grin. 'To pay a debt?'

Wikivill shot him a quick, sidelong glance. 'Not to you.'
'To whom, then?'
'To Father Albertus.' He raised his glass. '*Prost!*'
The old nerve jumped in protest against this shrewd probing.
'Drink that one yourself,' said Hanlon baldly.
Wikivill drank, deeply.

19

He found her waiting in the garden of the Spider-house, colourful as a
flower in dirndl and peasant blouse. The bloom of new pregnancy was on
her cheeks, and when she came hurrying to greet him her eyes were bright
with happy tears.

They kissed and clung together, and then sat down on a rustic seat under
the spread leaves of a copper beech. They held hands and looked at each
other, wordless but content with this first moment of communion after the
long days of separation.

Once again, Hanlon was struck by the extraordinary air of innocence
which surrounded her. Some women were coarsened by passion. Pregnancy
made others uncertain and shrewish. But Anna Kunzli was calm, contained,
fearless. The new life that fed on her seemed to add to her strength instead
of diminishing it.

When he began to speak, she listened gravely, prompting him where he
stumbled, soothing him when he broke out into anger and bitter
resentment. Her gentleness was a balm to him. Her courage shamed him;
and, when his story was done, she put her arms about him and drew his head
down to her breast, so that he felt the beat of her heart and smelt the warm
perfume of her body.

Her voice seemed to reach him from a long way off.

'Rest now, my dear. You've talked enough. There are no lies between us
any more—no blame, no regrets. When your son comes—I know it will be a
son—I will teach him to be proud of his father. When he is old enough, I will
send him to you and you will be proud of him, too.'

Hot tears pricked at Hanlon's eyelids and he dared not look up at the
unbearable tenderness of her face. Anna talked on:

'Sometimes, when you are back in England, you will write to me and I
will write and tell you about your son. Perhaps, even, you may come to visit
us—but not too often, nor for very long. I don't think I could bear to have
you near me and not love you.'

Hanlon straightened up and looked at her. His face was drawn and haggard.
He challenged her: 'How can you take it so calmly? Doesn't it frighten you?'

Her eyes clouded a moment, but she answered him sanely: 'Yes, Mark, it
frightens me. I know that I'll wake in the night and cry for you. I'll look at
other women with their menfolk and mourn for you. But I can bear it,
Mark, because I love you, and I know that this way will be best for both of
us in the end.'

'I wish I thought so, Anna.'

She reached out, imprisoning his hands in her own. 'You do, Mark.

Otherwise you couldn't have made this decision to go back to your wife.'

'I broke my heart when I made it.'

'It will mend, my dear,' she chided him quietly, 'and one day we will both wake up, and find suddenly that we are at peace again.' Her voice faltered a little, but she controlled herself quickly. 'Let's walk round the garden, Mark, just as we used to do.'

They stood up, Hanlon took her arm and they began to stroll up and down the long terrace of lawn between the Spider-house and the lower swathe of pines. The sun was warm on their faces; the air was full of pine scent and the songs of birds. The slow harmony of summer took possession of them, and their talk fell into the sober rhythm of their footsteps.

'I'm afraid, too,' said Mark Hanlon.

'Of what?'

'Meeting my wife. It's been so long, you see. I can't remember when we talked without contention. We're strangers now. I don't even know how to begin.'

'With tenderness, Mark,' said Anna softly. 'She will be feeling the same way, remember. She won't know how you'll receive her. She wants love, but she too has forgotten how to ask for it. Be gentle with her, my dear.'

'What do I tell her–about us?'

'The truth, Mark. But not brutally nor all at once. She'll need time to prepare herself for it. Time to make herself generous. Give her this time, and she will accept it–if only to show you that she loves you.'

'Do you think she does?'

'I don't know, Mark.' For the first time a hint of dissatisfaction came into her voice. 'And–and you mustn't ask me any more, nor tell me when you know.'

'I'm sorry, Anna.'

'Don't be sorry, Mark.' She gave him a small, uncertain smile. 'Just remember that I'm still a woman–and jealous of the man I love.'

'I love you, Anna!'

'Of course you do. And our boy will be a love child, and all the happier for it. But . . .' she hesitated a moment. 'If you and your wife live in peace, you will in the end find a certain love for each other. Not like ours perhaps, but still–love! I–I'd rather not think of that.'

'What if Lynn asks to see you?'

'Send her to me. But don't come with her.'

'Just as you like.'

'Mark?'

'Yes, Anna.'

'Now I'm going to ask you to do something for me.'

'Anything–you know that.'

Gently she disengaged herself and stood facing him, her hair shining golden in the sun, her face up-tilted to his. She waited a moment as if uncertain how to frame her request; then she put it to him simply.

'Mark, I'd like you to make friends with Father Albertus.'

He stared at her, half angry, half puzzled; then he asked her: 'Why?'

'He's an old man, Mark. He's suffered a great deal, and he loves us both.'

'He's got no monopoly of either suffering or love.' Hanlon's answer was harsh. 'And I've given him concessions all along the line.'

'Have you regretted any of them, Mark? Have you regretted Johann Wikivill?'

'I've regretted you,' said Hanlon stonily. 'You were his greatest victory.'

Anna shook her head slowly. 'He didn't take me from you, Mark. He simply pointed out to me what we both believe in–and it broke his heart to do it. Can't you see, Mark? We're suffering–yes. But so is he. He looks on us as his children, you most of all, I think. Can't you bend to him a little, for my sake, for the child's? We must live here, remember. We shall depend on him for so much and you could make him very happy.'

There was so much eagerness in her, so much warm wisdom, that Mark Hanlon was touched in spite of himself. His eyes softened, the taut line of his jaw relaxed. He reached out and drew her to him, holding her against his breast so that his lips brushed the gold of her hair while they stood under the shining bronze leaves of the beeches.

'All right, *Liebchen*,' he told her. 'So be it. I'll make friends with him.'

Then, for the first time, her control broke and she held to him, sobbing as if her heart would break, while Mark Hanlon soothed and coaxed her with words he did not believe and hopes that were already a dusty illusion.

A long time afterwards, when she was calm, and they were both weary, they walked down to the gate and kissed good-bye. Mark Hanlon saluted gravely and turned his face towards the town.

Mark Hanlon lived through the next ten days like a sleepwalker. There were weights on his shoulders and chains round his heart. He had no desires–only needs: the need to eat and work like a galley-rower and sleep a little after the white nights, when he tossed and turned and stretched out groping hands for comfort just beyond his reach.

His body functioned like a protesting machine. One part of his mind worked with precision and clarity, accurate in assessment, prompt in decision, but the rest of him, the feeling part, the part that desired and willed, was caught in a cataleptic state between the horror of living and the mercy of dying.

He dealt with the officers politely but curtly, so that they were glad to be out of his room. With Traudl he was brusque and cold, and for all her affection she could not come within reach of him. When Holzinger or Miller or the local officials came to see him, he dispatched their business so quickly that they went away wondering how they had offended him.

None of his friends could break down his icy reserve. Captain Johnson's awkward advances were snubbed. Huber's invitations were ignored and Father Albertus did not come at all. He lived in a sterile vacuum, solitary, self-sufficient, and desperately afraid.

In spite of his promise to Anna Kunzli he made no move towards a reconciliation with Father Albertus. Resentment had died in him as hope had died; but he lacked the strength even for a simple act of submission. The little energy he had must be husbanded for the moment of his meeting with his wife.

She had not yet replied to his letter, and as the days spun themselves out in painful succession, he felt his resolve weakening and his fears growing daily greater. Questions began to torment him like squawking birds: How should he greet her? Should he kiss her on the lips, could he command a smile to welcome her, or would she sense the revulsion in his touch? How should he tell her about Anna? If she were jealous, how could he master his anger? Was there love enough left in him to share with his legal children and with his coming son? How could he silence the whispers of the townsfolk when they saw him walking arm in arm with Lynn and remembered the pregnant girl in the Spider-house?

There was no answer to any of them, but they fretted him night and day, pecking away at the props of his resolution.

Ten days of this ruthless self-inquisition left him frayed and utterly exhausted. He was smoking too much and drinking more than usual, and his appearance shocked all those who had contact with him.

Then, on the eleventh day, a letter was laid on his desk, franked with a London postmark. His fingers trembled as he slit the envelope and unfolded the thick, scented paper which Lynn used.

> My dear Mark,
>
>   I cannot put into words how deeply your letter touched me, nor how grateful I am. I may not be able to do it, even when I see you. I know I shall be awkward at first, but I beg you to be patient with me. The children are, of course, overjoyed, if rather impatient that they cannot come with me.
>
>   The authorities have arranged for me to fly to Munich on Monday. The arrival time is 3.30 in the afternoon. Can you arrange to meet me? I can't write any more now. I am too excited and afraid to hope too much. The rest must wait till I see you.
>
> Your loving wife,
Lynn

He laid the letter down on the table and sat a long time staring at it, while Traudl watched him curiously from her desk at the other side of the room.

She was tempted to go to him, put her arms about him in the old, frank fashion, and charm the trouble out of him. But the naked grief in his face frightened her. She saw him reach for a cigarette, light it with shaky hands, and draw on it greedily. She saw him walk to the french windows and out on to the small balcony, where he stood, leaning on the balustrade and looking down over the fall of the hills into the green valley, where the houses huddled in mocking peace round the spire of the church.

When he came back into the room, his eyes were dead and his voice was weary and remote.

'Send a note to Johann Wikivill. Ask him to come to see me as soon as possible.'

Traudl scribbled the note on her pad; then, in spite of herself, she stood up and moved towards him.

'Mark! You're ill. What's the matter? Couldn't you tell me?'

He turned towards her, and the dead eyes and the grim mouth stopped her in her tracks.

'I'm quite well, thank you. There's nothing the matter. My wife's coming to visit me. I should be glad about that, shouldn't I?'

'You poor devil,' said Traudl softly. 'You poor unhappy devil.'

Afterwards he remembered that it was the only time he had ever seen her cry.

Early on the Monday morning, Mark Hanlon and Johann Wikivill left Bad Quellenberg for Munich airport. Their way lay northward: over the mountain passes from Carinthia down into the valleys of Land Salzburg, then up again through the Bavarian hills to Munich.

Hanlon drove fast and dangerously, rolling the car round the sharp curves, sliding it through the patches of gravel on the shoulders while the tyres whined and the small echoes whipped back from fence posts and embankments.

Johann Wikivill sat calm and unruffled beside him, lighting his cigarettes, talking inconsequently of legends and landmarks, apparently unperturbed by the danger or by Hanlon's unresponsive silence. There was an odd, reposeful quality in him: the passionless contentment of a man who has seen too much of death to be afraid of it, and too much of life to be disappointed in it.

Hanlon was reminded of the old biblical phrase, 'Strength went out from him.' In spite of his silence, he was grateful to Wikivill, and as the road spun out behind them, he surrendered himself more and more to the cathartic pleasure of speed and to the enveloping virtue of the man he had once hunted.

When they stopped at Salzburg to lunch and refuel, the sky was grey and lowering. By the time they reached the Bavarian foothills a slow drizzle was falling; and when they came to Munich the weather had settled down, cheerless and faintly sinister, after the full blaze of Alpine summer.

The air terminal was like a military installation. A scowling G.I. checked their passes and waved them into the parking area, where trucks and staff-cars were stacked three deep, and gum-chewing drivers lounged under a tin shelter. The aircraft huddled round the aprons. All carried American markings and the waiting-room was a babel of accents from Maine to New Orleans.

To Hanlon, fresh from the isolation of Bad Quellenberg, the scene was a sharp reminder of the nearness of the war and the uncertainty of peace in the scarred cities of Europe. He checked the arrival time on the schedule board, found that the plane would be twenty minutes late, then pushed his way up to the bar with Wikivill to buy coffee and brandies.

Now that the waiting was nearly over he was beginning to be calm again. The sight of the uniforms and the clamour of voices soothed him with a sense of community and comradeship. These men, too, were far from home. They had seen death and disaster as he had. Many of them were involved in war-time loves and post-war heartbreaks. They were his brothers, as Wikivill was. He was neither singular nor separate. He was a unit in the human family, needful, like all the others, of pity and love and wisdom and strength.

He looked up suddenly, to find Wikivill's calm eyes fixed on him. He gave a small, bleak grin. 'It's all right, my friend. I'm ready for it now.'

Wikivill nodded and smiled gravely. 'I told you, didn't I?' You were stronger than you knew.'

Hanlon shrugged ruefully and turned back to his drink. He, too, was conscious of the small, solid core of strength that remained to him, but he knew that he must nurse it carefully against the moment of Lynn's arrival.

The babel of voices began to sort itself out into snatches of dialogue. A corporal from Brooklyn was talking about a girl in Vienna; a dry-voiced major discussed Four-Power politics at command level; an UNRRA official checked off a list of medical supplies with a hatchet-faced woman in Red Cross uniform. A French captain made passes at the fräulein behind the counter.

Hanlon listened, now to this one, now to that, grateful for the distraction, while the minutes ticked away on the electric clock above the schedule board. Suddenly he looked up and saw, with a small shock of surprise, that it was already long past the new arrival time. He pointed it out to Wikivill, who smiled and shook his head.

'In this weather it can be dirty flying from Frankfurt to Munich. Perhaps they will make an announcement soon.'

'The sooner the better,' said Hanlon irritably. 'I wasn't prepared for this.'

'Another drink?'

'Why not?' Hanlon swirled the dregs of liquor in his glass and tossed them off at a gulp. 'Dutch courage! I never believed in it before.'

'So it be courage, who cares?' Wikivill grinned and pushed the glasses across the counter to be refilled. Before Hanlon had time to answer, the speakers crackled into life and a flat, impersonal voice made the announcement:

'Attention please! Would all personnel waiting on passengers from Flight 123, London, Frankfurt, Munich, please come to the Controller's office immediately.'

The crowd in the waiting-room fell silent, and they looked at each other uncertainly as the metallic voice repeated the announcement. Then small knots of people began to disengage themselves and move hesitantly towards the glass-panelled door at the end of the waiting-room.

A few minutes later they heard the news that Flight 123 had crashed fifty miles east of Frankfurt and that there were no survivors.

Johann Wikivill had driven him halfway across Bavaria before Hanlon fully understood what had happened to him.

20

It was a Saturday afternoon, late and drowsy with the heat of high summer.

Father Albertus sat, cramped and tired, in a room a little larger than a coffin, but not quite as big as a grave. In front of him was a velvet curtain, purple in colour, musty with age and human exhalation. On either side of him were walls of pine slab, darkened by age, each pierced by a small grille, which was covered by a Judas door. Behind him was the grey stone wall of the church.

Every week he came here, stifled by the heat or frozen by the winter cold, waiting for his people to come to the shriving of sins. Every week a succession of shadowy faces pressed themselves to the grilles, and their halting whispers counted out the tally of commissions and omissions for judgment and forgiveness.

Children's voices told him of the first small lapses from innocence. Young men, hoarse and ashamed, stumbled through their tales of passion under the pine trees. The married told of their angers and their hates and their occasional adulteries. Spendthrifts came and misers, proud men and humble girls, the wise, the foolish, the selfish and the sorrowing; and over each he pronounced the words of absolution and the counsel suited to their needs.

There were moments—all too few—when his narrow room seemed to grow and lighten like the courtyards of heaven and he was humbled by the manifest workings of God among his creatures. There were other times when the walls closed in on him, like those of the punishment cell at Mauthausen, and he was broken and beaten down by the weight of misery laid on his old shoulders.

He was a priest, like his Master. Like his Master he must make himself the scapegoat of the people. When they did not repent he must count it a failure in himself. When they refused to do penance, he must chastise their follies in his own flesh. This was the meaning of priesthood–a lifelong crucifixion, to merit for others the gratuitous mercies of which he was the channel and the minister.

Sometimes, as it did today, the sheer repetition and continuity of human folly drove him to the brink of despair. In spite of two thousand years of redemption, of renewed martyrdom and crucifixion, the sum of sin never seemed to diminish. A thousand absolutions issued in ten thousand new transgressions. The very patience of God was made a mockery.

When he waited in the stuffy darkness for a new penitent to present himself at the grille, it seemed to him that the years of celibacy and discipline were a monstrous waste. When he struggled to pray against the temptation his lips framed only the desolate words of the dying Christus: 'Eloi, Eloi, lama sabachthani. . . . My God, My God, why hast thou forsaken me?'

Long years ago the Bishop had anointed his fingers and given him all men for his children. But his children left him to follow strange gods, and even after he had forgiven them they went back, like dogs to the vomit, and he could do nothing but wait and hope, and pray for their return.

Age lay on him like a cross and he asked often for the mercy of release from it. But the mercy was withheld, so that he sat here still in the room that was like a coffin and waited for his next patient.

He heard the creaking of the confessional door and the rustle of clothing inside the booth. He slid aside the Judas door, bent his face to the grille, averted his eyes and waited. Then he heard Mark Hanlon's voice, low but firm in the ritual preamble:

'Bless me, Father, for I have sinned.'

The old man's heart leapt, but he kept his face averted and raised his broken hands in blessing.

'*Benedico te, mi fili*. . . . How long since your last confession?'

'A long time, Father. Five years, six maybe.'

'You know that this is itself a great sin, that a man should turn away from the grace that is offered to him daily?'

'I know that.'

'Tell me your sins, my son.'

Then it began–the long count of the locust years, the slow reconstruction of the complex relationship between the old man and the pupil who had left him so many ages ago: the brotherhood of the faith, the fatherhood of the Spirit, the sinner and the judge, priest and penitent, Caesar's friend and the follower of the Crucified.

To each, the moment brought its own pain and its own consolation. The failures of the pupil were the failures of his master. The penitence of the one was humbling to the other. The hands that would confer forgiveness were shaky with gratitude for the restoration of simple, human affection.

When the long recitation was over, Father Albertus asked him: 'Is that all, my son?'

'All I can remember.'

'It is enough.'

The broken fingers were raised and Mark Hanlon bowed his head to receive the absolution. '*Deinde ego te absolvo.* . . . I absolve you from your sins in the name of the Father and of the Son, and of the Holy Ghost. Amen.'

'Thank you, Father.'

'For your penance, you will recite the Sorrowful Mysteries of the Rosary.'

From the other side of the grille came a small, ironic chuckle and Father Albertus looked up sharply, but Hanlon's face was an indistinguishable blur against the wire mesh.

'As easy as that, Father?'

'Forgiveness is always easy, my son,' said Father Albertus soberly. 'The hardest thing of all is to bend the will to ask for it. It has taken these years and a singular mercy to bring you to this moment.'

'There's a harder thing yet,' said Mark Hanlon dryly. 'To live with the memory of the past.'

The old, deep voice admonished him firmly. 'That is part of the penance. To perform it you will need new courage and a new mercy. You dare not despise yourself, because that would be to despise the greatness of God and the good that He has made to flower under your hand. You may regret the past, but you must not resent it. You must not brood upon it, else you may poison the happiness of those with whom you live. You will accept it, humbly, as you will accept what the future offers. You will be grateful that the design of God, through a physical accident, has resolved a dilemma that you could never have resolved yourself. Let the dead bury their dead–but pray for them, because the dead still belong to you, and you to them, through the Communion of Saints. Do you understand?'

'I understand.'

'Go in peace, my son.'

Mark Hanlon stood up and the door creaked again. After he had gone the old priest sat a long time, praying quietly and waiting for the next visitor; then, as no one came, he too got up, stretched his cramped limbs and walked out into the shadowy nave.

The church was empty except for Mark Hanlon, who knelt in the front pew, looking up towards the sanctuary where the dim taper flickered in its bowl of crimson glass. Father Albertus went up and knelt beside him. In a low, clear voice he began to recite the canticle of the Mother of God.

'*Magnificat anima mea Dominum.* . . . My soul doth magnify the Lord.'

'*Quia deposuit potentes* . . .' answered Colonel Mark Hanlon. 'Because he hath put down the mighty from their seats, and hath exalted the humble.'

Together, master and pupil, victor and vanquished, they finished the recitation of the hymn. Then they walked out together through the forest of headboards, past the wooden Christus, out through the lych-gate and up the dappled hillside to the Spider-house, where Anna Kunzli was waiting for them.

Daughter of Silence

DAUGHTER OF SILENCE

For
Hilda

Alta vendetta d'alto silenzio è figlia.
Noble vengeance is the daughter of deep silence.
(Alfieri: *La Congiura de' Pazzi*, Act I. Sc. I.)

I

It was bright noon, high summer, in the upland valleys of Tuscany: a torpid time, a season of dust and languor, of stripped flax and larks in the wheat-stubble, and new wines coming to vintage in the country of the elder gods. It was an hour of bells, undulant in a dry air, tranquil over the tombs of dead saints and the feuds of forgotten mercenaries. It was a persuasion to darkness and drawn shutters; since who but dogs and Americans would expose their foolish foreheads to an August sun at midday?

In the village of San Stefano the first strokes of the Angelus were sounding over the square. The bell-ringer was old and the music of his chimes was muted. The village was drowsy and replete with a good harvest, so the last passages of its morning life were muted too.

An old man stopped, crossed himself and stood with bowed head as the triple tones rang out from the white campanile. A tubby fellow in a white apron with a checker-board napkin over his arm stood at the door of the restaurant and picked his teeth with a match. A mule-faced policeman made a tentative step outside his door, squinted languidly round the square, spat, scratched himself and then wandered back to his wine and cheese.

Water welled sluggishly from the mouths of tired dolphins and spilled into the shallow basin of the fountain, while a skinny boy sailed a paper boat in the eddies. A charcoal-burner trundled his handcart over the cobbles. The cart was piled high with little bundles of twigs and brown bags filled with charcoal. A small girl was perched on top of them, tousle-haired, serious of mien, like a woodland elf. A barefoot woman, with a baby on her hip, came out of the wine-shop and headed for the alley at the far end of the piazza. Five miles away, the towers and tumbled roofs of Siena reared themselves, hazy and magical, against a copper sky.

It was a placid tableau, curiously antique, sparsely peopled, its animation geared to the low pulse-beat of country living. Here, time flowed sluggishly as the fountain, and the only change was the cyclic mutation of age and the seasons. This, one understood, was a tribal enclave, where tradition was more important than progress, where custom was nine points of the law, and old loves were cherished as sedulously as old hates and the tangled loyalties of blood and bondage.

There was a road in and a road out, the one leading to Arezzo, the other to Siena, but their traffic was small and seasonal. The trunk routes of tourism and commerce had always bypassed San Stefano. The valley farms were small and jealously reserved to their peasant owners, so there was no welcome for migrants. Those who went away were the restless or the footloose or the ambitious, and the village was happily quit of them.

Before the last echo of the bell had died away, the square was empty. Shutters were closed, curtains were drawn. The dust settled back into the cracks of the cobbles, the paper boat swam rudderless round the fountain and the cry of the cicadas rose, strepitant and monotonous, from the circling fields. The first watch of the day was over. Peace–or what passed for peace–came down on the village.

It was, perhaps, ten minutes later when the bell-ringer came out of the church: an elderly friar in the dusty habit of St Francis, with a white tonsured head and a ruddy face lined and seamed like a winter apple. He stood a moment in the shadow of the portico, mopping his brow with a red handkerchief; then he twitched his cowl over his head and padded across the square, his sandals flapping tic-tac on the parched stones.

Before he had gone a dozen yards, an unfamiliar sight stopped him in his tracks. A taxi with a Siena number-plate pulled into the piazza and rolled to a halt outside the restaurant. A woman got out, paid off the driver, and watched him drive out of sight.

She was young, no more than twenty-five. Her dress marked her as a city-dweller: tailored costume, white blouse, fashionable shoes, a handbag slung by a leather strap over one shoulder. She wore no hat and her dark hair hung in waves to her shoulders. Her face was pale, calm and singularly beautiful, like that of a wax Madonna. In the empty, sunlit square she looked uncertain and vaguely lonely.

For a while she stood, looking round the square, as if orienting herself in a once-familiar territory; then with a firm, confident step, she walked across to a house between the wine-shop and bakery and rang the bell. The door was opened by a stout matron dressed in black bombazine with a white apron tied round her middle. They talked for a few moments, and the stout one made a gesture inviting her to enter. She declined and the matron went away, leaving the door open. The girl waited, fumbling for something in her handbag, while the friar watched, curious as any countryman about any stranger.

It was perhaps thirty seconds later when the man appeared in the doorway–a tall, thick-set fellow in shirt-sleeves, with a grizzled head, a sallow, lined face, and a table-napkin stuck in his shirt-front. He was still chewing on a mouthful of food, and in the clear light the friar could see a small dribble of sauce at the corner of his mouth. He looked at the girl without any sign of recognition, and asked her a question.

Then she shot him in the chest.

The impact spun him around and flung him against the door-jamb, and in a horrible suspended moment the friar saw her pump four more shots into him and then turn away, walking unhurriedly towards the police-station. The echoes were still shouting around the piazza when the friar began to run, tottering and stumbling, to offer a final absolution to a man who was already beyond it.

Five miles away, in Siena, Doctor Alberto Ascolini was sitting for his portrait–an exercise in futility, an illusion of immortality to which he submitted himself with irony.

He was a tall man, sixty-five years of age, with a pink lively face and a mane of snow-white hair that flowed down in careful disarray over his collar. He wore a silk suit and a silk cravat fastened with a diamond pin. Both the suit and the cravat were immaculately tailored but deliberately old-fashioned as if age and incongruous animation were his stock-in-trade. He looked like an actor–a very successful actor–but he was in fact a lawyer, one of the most successful advocates in Rome.

The artist was a slim, dark girl in her late twenties with hazel eyes, a frank smile and expressive, elegant hands. Her name was Ninette Lachaise. Her apartment was a high attic chamber that looked over the roof-tops of the old city towards the campanile of the Vergine Assunta. One end of it was a studio, meticulous in its order and cleanliness. The other was her living quarters, furnished with the gleanings of provincial craft, waxed and gleaming with Gallic housewifery. Her pictures were an index to her character–full of light, spare in detail, stylized, yet ample in movement, a lineal development of the primitive Tuscan tradition to a twentieth-century idiom.

She was working in charcoal now, making a series of swift bravura sketches of her subject as he sat, half in sunlight, half in shadow, telling scandalous stories of the Roman courts. It was a virtuoso performance on both sides. The old man's stories were full of extravagant wit, clever malice and sly bawdry. The girl's sketches were avid and percipient, so that it seemed as if a dozen men lived inside the sleek pink skin of this very intelligent mountebank.

Ascolini watched her with shrewd, affectionate eyes, and when he had come to the end of his stories he grinned and said with mock pathos: 'When I am with you, Ninette, I mourn my youth.'

'If you have nothing else to mourn, *dottore*,' she told him with gentle irony, 'then you're a fortunate man.'

'What else is there to regret, my dear, but the follies one is incapable of committing?'

'Perhaps the consequences of those one has already committed.'

'Eh! Eh! Ninette!' Ascolini fluttered his eloquent hands and laughed drily. 'No lectures this morning, please! This is the beginning of my holiday; I come to you to be diverted.'

'No, *dottore*.' She smiled at him in her grave fashion and went on sketching with swift, firm strokes. 'I've known you too long and too well. When you come to drink coffee or buy me lunch at the Sordello, then you are content with the world. When you offer me a commission like this or pay me too much for my landscapes, then you have problems on your mind. You offer me a fee to solve them. It's a bad habit, you know–it does you small credit.'

His smooth, youthful face clouded a moment, then he grinned crookedly. 'But you still accept the fee, Ninette. Why?'

'I sell you my pictures, *dottore*, not my sympathy. That you get for nothing.'

'You humble me, Ninette,' said the old man tartly.

'Nothing humbles you, *dottore*,' she told him bluntly. 'And this is where all your troubles begin–with Valeria, with Carlo and with yourself. There now!' She made a last brisk stroke on the canvas and turned to him, holding out her hand. 'The words are said, the sitting is over. Come and look at yourself.'

She led him to the easel and stood, holding his hand while he surveyed the sketches. He was silent for a long time, then with no hint of raillery he asked her: 'Are these all my faces, Ninette?'

'Only the ones you show me.'

'You think there are others?'

'I know there must be. You are too various a man, *dottore*, too dazzling in each variety.'

'And which of them is the real Ascolini?'

'All of them—and none of them.'

'Read them to me, child.'

'This one? The great advocate, the noble pleader who dominates every court in Rome. He changes a little, as you see. Here he is the darling of the *salons*, the wit who makes the men blush and the women squirm when he whispers in their willing ears. That one? A moment from the Sordello: Ascolini drinking wine with the law students and wishing he had a son of his own. There he becomes the chess-player, moving people like pawns, despising himself more than he despises them. In the next one there is a memory—of youth perhaps, and an old love. And last of all, the great advocate as he might have been, had not a country priest pulled him out of a ditch and opened the world to him: a peasant with a load of sticks on his back and the monotony of a lifetime in his eyes. . . .'

'It is too much,' said the old man flatly. 'From one so young it is too much and too frightening. How do you know all this, Ninette? How do you see so many secrets?'

For a moment she looked at him with sombre, pitying eyes. Then she shook her head. 'They are not secrets, *dottore*. We are what we do. It is written in our faces for the world to read. For myself? I am a foreigner here. I came from France like the old soldiers of fortune, to plunder the riches of the South. I live alone. I sell my pictures—and wait for someone to whom I can give myself with confidence. I know what it is to be solitary and afraid. I know what it is to reach out for love and grasp an illusion. You have been kind to me and you have shown me more of yourself than you know. I've often wondered why.'

'Simple enough!' There was a harsh note in his rich actor's voice. 'If I were twenty years younger, Ninette, I should ask you to marry me.'

'If I were twenty years older, *dottore*,' she told him softly, 'I should probably accept—and you would hate me for it ever afterwards.'

'I could never hate you, my dear.'

'You hate everything you possess, *dottore*. You love only what you cannot attain.'

'You're brutal today, Ninette.'

'There are brutal things to be faced. are there not?'

'I suppose there are.'

He released her hand and walked over to the window, where he stood watching the sun pour down over the towers and roof-tops of the old city. His tall frame seemed bowed and diminished, his noble face became pinched and shrunken, as if age had come upon him unaware. The girl watched him, caught in a rush of pity for his dilemmas. After a while she prompted him quietly: 'It's Valeria, isn't it?'

'And Carlo.'

'Tell me about Valeria.'

'We're not two days arrived from Rome and she's started an affair with Basilio Lazzaro.'

'There have been other affairs, *dottore*. You encouraged them. Why should this one bother you?'

'Because it's late in the day for me, Ninette! Because I want grandchildren in my house and a promise of continuity, and because this Lazzaro is scum who will end by destroying her!'

'I know,' said Ninette Lachaise softly. 'I know it only too well.'

'It is news already in Siena?'

'I doubt it. But I was once in love with Lazzaro myself; he was my grand illusion.'

'I'm sorry, child.'

'You must not be sorry for me—only for yourself and Valeria. Carlo too, for that matter. Does he know yet?'

'I doubt it.'

'But he knew about the others?'

'I think so.'

'You laughed about that, I remember, *dottore*. You made a joke about your daughter putting horns on a foolish husband. You said she was following in her father's footsteps, you were proud of her conquests, and her cleverness.'

'He is a fool,' said Ascolini bitterly. 'A sentimental young fool who didn't know what time of day it was. He deserved a lesson.'

'And now?'

'Now he's talking of leaving me and setting up his own legal practice.'

'And you don't approve of that?'

'Of course not! He's too young, too inexperienced; he'll wreck his career before it's half begun.'

'You wrecked his marriage, *dottore*; why should you care about his career?'

'I don't except that it involves my daughter's future, and the future of their children if they have any.'

'You're lying, *dottore*,' said Ninette Lachaise, sadly. 'You're lying to me. You're lying to yourself.'

Surprisingly, the old advocate laughed and flung out his hands in an almost comic despair. 'Of course I'm lying! I know the truth better than you do, child. I made a world in my own image and I don't like the look of it any more, so I need someone to break it over my head and make me eat the pieces.'

'Perhaps this is what Carlo is trying to do now?'

'Carlo?' Ascolini exploded into contempt. 'He's too much of a boy to control his own wife. How can he compete with a perverse old bull like me? I would like nothing better than he should ram my nonsense down my neck, but he's too much a gentleman to do it! ... Eh!' He shrugged off the discussion and walked back to take her hands in his own. 'Forget all this and go paint your pictures, my dear. We're not worth helping—any of us! But there's one thing—'

'What is it, *dottore*?'

'You're dining with us tonight at the villa.'

'No—please!' Her refusal was sharp and emphatic. 'You're welcome here any time, you know that, but keep me out of your family. They're not my people; I'm not theirs.'

'It's not for us, it's for yourself. There's someone I'd like you to meet.'

'Who?'

'He's my house-guest. His name's Peter Landon. He's a doctor and he comes from Australia by way of London.'

'A barbarous country they tell me, *dottore*, full of strange animals and giants in shirt-sleeves.'

Ascolini laughed. 'When you meet this Landon for the first time you may be inclined to believe it. He fills a room when he walks into it. When he talks it seems brusque and too certain for politeness. Then you realize that he is talking pure Tuscan, and that what he says makes a deal of sense, and that he has lived more variously than you or I. There is a strength in him too and, I think, a touch of discontent.' He laid an affectionate hand on her cheek. 'He could be good for you, my dear.'

She flushed and turned away. 'Are you turning match-maker, *dottore?*'

'I am more fond of you than you know, Ninette,' he told her soberly. 'I should like to see you happy. Please come.'

'Very well, *dottore*, I'll come, but you must promise me something first.'

'Anything, child.'

'You will play no comedies with me, no plots like you make with your own family. I could never forgive you that.'

'I could never forgive myself either. Believe me, Ninette.' He took her face in his old hands and kissed her lightly on the forehead. Then he was gone, and she stood a long time looking out over the roof-tops of the town to the tumbled hillsides of Tuscany, where the wine is sweetened by the blood of ancient sacrifices and the cypresses grow out of the eyes of dead princes.

At the Villa Ascolini, perched high on a terraced hill above the village of San Stefano, Valeria Rienzi was drowsing behind closed shutters. She had heard no bells, no shots, no echo of the tumult that followed them. The only sounds that penetrated her room were the bourdon of the cicadas, the clip-clip of a gardener's shears and the pale, plangent music that Carlo was playing in the *salone*.

She had no thought of death this summer noon. The beat of her blood was too strong for such dreary irrelevance. She had only to flex her long body on the bed, twitch the silk robe against her skin, to feel the sweetness and the itch of living. She was in fact thinking of love, which she understood as a pleasant if transient diversion, and of marriage, which she recognized as a permanent, if occasionally irksome, condition.

Marriage meant Carlo Rienzi, the handsome, boyish husband playing his sad piano below stairs. It meant discretion, public propriety, a matronly care for her husband's career. It meant a surrender of liberty, an expense of tenderness which she rarely felt, demands on a body which Carlo had never understood how to waken, exacerbation of a spirit too wilful and too lively to match his melancholy and uncertain temperament. Marriage meant Rome and Roman rectitude—legal dinners and cocktail parties for those who handed fat briefs to her father and his fledgling son-in-law.

Love, in the context of a summer holiday in Tuscany, meant Basilio Lazzaro, the swarthy, passionate bachelor who made no secret of his fondness for young wives. Love was an antidote to boredom, an affirmation of independence. It was a rich joke to share with an understanding father, a goad to prick a too youthful husband into man's estate.

At thirty, Valeria Rienzi was prepared to count her blessings: good health, good looks, no children, a manageable husband, an urgent lover, a father who saw all, understood all and forgave everything with a cynic's indulgence.

It was a pleasant contemplation in the warm, private twilight of her bedroom where painted fauns and dryads disported themselves on the ceiling. There was music whose sadness touched her not at all. There was a promise of a whole summer's diversion, and if Basilio proved too demanding there was the visitor, Peter Landon. She had not measured him yet, but there would be time enough to test this fellow from the New World in the devious, sardonic games of the Old.

And yet . . . and yet . . . there were uneasy ripples on the Narcissus pool, dark currents stirring under the lily-pads. There were changes in herself which she did not fully understand—a sense of emptiness, a demand for direction, a compulsion to new and more passionate encounters, vague fear and occasional poignant regret. Time was when conspiracy with her father assured her of absolution for even her wildest follies. Now it was no longer as absolution but a kind of wry-mouthed tolerance as though he were less disappointed in her than in himself.

He made no secret now that he wanted her settled and breeding a family. The problem was that he still had no respect for Carlo, and could show her no way to restore her own. What he demanded was a new conspiracy: seduction of a husband made indifferent by the indifference of his wife, a loveless mating to bring love to an old epicure who had affected to despise it all his life. It was too much for too little. Too little for her, too much for him—and for Carlo one deception too many.

Time was when he had pleaded with her for love and for the fulfilment of children. Time was when he would barter the last shreds of pride for a kiss and a moment of union. But not now. He had grown older these last months, colder, less dependent, more absorbed in a private planning of his own.

Part of it he had told her. He was determined to leave Ascolini's office and set up his own practice in advocacy. This done, he would offer her a home of her own, a household separate from her father. Afterwards? It was the afterwards that troubled her, when she must stand alone, without buttress, without absolution, subject to the verdict of a wronged husband and the determination of her own turbulent desires.

This was the nub of the problem. What did one want so much that the wanting was a torment in the flesh? What did one need so much that one was prepared to reject all else to attain it? Twenty-four hours ago she had heard the same question from the unlikely lips of Basilio Lazzaro.

She had been standing at the door of his bedroom, fully dressed, with gloves and bag in hand, watching him button a shirt over his brown barrel-chest. She had noted the slack satisfied ease of his movements, his swift indifference to her presence, and she had asked, plaintively: 'Why, Basilio—why must it always be like this?'

'Like what?' asked Lazzaro irritably as he reached for his tie.

'When we meet it is like the overture to an opera. When we make love it is all drama and music. When we part it's . . . it's like paying off a taxi.'

Lazzaro's dark handsome face puckered in a frown of puzzlement. 'What do you expect, *cara*? This is the way it is. When you drink the wine, the bottle's empty. When the opera's over, you don't wait around for the cleaners. You've had your fun. You go home and wait for another performance.'

'And that's all?'

'What else can there be, *cara*? I ask you—what else?'

Which was a neat riddle, but she had found, then or now, no adequate answer. She was still puzzling over it when the ormolu clock sounded a quarter after midday, and it was time to bathe and dress for lunch.

The square of San Stefano was seething and populous as an ant-heap. The whole village was out, babe and beldame, crowding about the house of the dead man, chaffering round the fountain, arguing with the doltish

policeman who stood guard at the door of the station. There was nothing
riotous in their behaviour, nothing hostile in their attitude. They were
spectators only, involved by curiosity in a melodrama of puppets.

From the window of his office Sergeant Fiorello watched them with a
canny professional eye. So far, so good. They were excited but orderly,
milling about the square like sheep in a pen. There was no danger of
immediate violence. The detectives from Siena would arrive to take over the
case in an hour. The family of the murdered man was absorbed in a privacy
of grief. He could afford to relax and attend to his prisoner.

She was sitting, slumped in a chair, head bowed, her body shaken with
rigors. Fiorello's lean, leathery face softened when he looked at her, then he
poured brandy into an earthenware cup and held it to her lips. She gagged
on the first mouthful, then sipped it slowly. In a few moments the rigors
subsided and Fiorello offered her a cigarette. She refused it and said in a
dead, flat voice: 'No, thank you. I'm better now.'

'I have to ask you questions. You know that?' His voice, for so burly a
man, was oddly gentle. The girl nodded indifferently.

'I know that.'

'What's your name?'

'You know it already. Anna Albertini. I used to be Anna Moschetti.'

'Whose gun is that?'

He picked up the weapon and held it out to her flat in the palm of his
hand. She did not flinch or turn away, but answered simply: 'My
husband's.'

'We'll have to get in touch with him. Where is he?'

'In Florence. Vicolo degli Angelotti, number sixteen.'

'Is there a telephone?'

'No.'

'Does he know where you are?'

'No.'

Her eyes were glazed; she sat bolt upright in the chair, pale and rigid as a
cataleptic. Her voice had a formal, metallic quality like that of a subject in
narcosis. Fiorello hesitated a moment, and then asked another question:
'Why did you do it, Anna?'

For the first time a hint of life crept into her voice and eyes. 'You know
why. It doesn't matter how I say it, or how you will write it down. You know
why.'

'Then tell me something else, Anna. Why did you choose this time? Why
not a month ago or five years? Why didn't you wait longer?'

'Does it matter?'

Fiorello toyed absently with the pistol that had killed Gianbattista
Belloni. His own voice took on a brooding, reflective quality, as if he too
were reliving events remote from this place and this moment.

'No, it doesn't matter. Very soon you will be taken away from here. You
will be tried, convicted and sent to prison for twenty years because you
killed a man in cold blood. It's just a question to fill in time.'

'Time . . .' She took hold of the word as if it were a talisman, key to a
lifetime's mysteries. 'It wasn't like looking at a clock or tearing pages off a
calendar. It was like—like walking along a road . . . always the same road . . .
always in the same direction. Then the road ended . . . here in San Stefano,
outside Belloni's house. You understand that, don't you?'

'I understand it.'

But the understanding had come too late—and he knew it. Sixteen years too late. The road had swung full circle and now, like his prisoner, he was stumbling over milestones that he had thought past and forgotten. He laid the gun down on the desk and reached for a cigarette. When he came to light it he found that his hands were trembling. Ashamed, he stood up and busied himself laying out bread and cheese and olives on a plate, pouring a glass of wine and setting the rough meal in front of Anna Albertini. He said gruffly: 'When they take you to Siena you'll be questioned again, for many hours probably. You should try to eat now.'

'I'm not hungry, thank you.'

He knew that she was in shock, but her passivity angered him unreasonably. He blazed at her: 'Mother of God! Don't you understand? There's a man dead a couple of doors down the street. You killed him! He's the Mayor of this town and there's a crowd outside that would tear you in pieces if someone spoke the right word. When the black-suit boys come from Siena they're going to fry you like a fish in a pan. I'm trying to help you, but I can't force you to eat.'

'Why are you trying to help me?'

There was no malice in the question, only the vague and placid curiosity of the ailing. Fiorello knew the answer only too well, but for the life of him he could not give it. He turned away and walked again to the window while the girl sat picking at the food, aimless and pathetic as a bird which has been caged for the first time.

There was a flurry in the street now. The little friar had left the house of the dead man and was hurrying towards the police-station. The people pressed about him, tugging at his habit, besieging him with questions, but he waved them away and stumbled breathlessly into Fiorello's office.

When he saw the girl he stopped dead in his tracks and his eyes filled up with an old man's impotent tears. Fiorello said baldly: 'You know who she is, don't you?'

Fra Bonifacio nodded wearily. 'I think I guessed it the first moment I saw her in the square. I should have expected all this. But it's been such a long time.'

'Sixteen years. And now the bomb explodes!'

'She needs help.'

Fiorello shrugged and spread his hands in a motion of despair. 'What help is there? It's an open-and-shut case. Vendetta. Premeditated murder. The penalty's twenty years.'

'She needs legal counsel.'

'The State supplies that to needy prisoners.'

'It's not enough. She needs the best we can find.'

'Who pays, even if you can find someone to handle a hopeless brief?'

'The Ascolini family is staying at the villa for the summer. The old man's one of the great criminal advocates. At least I can ask him to interest himself in the case. If not he, perhaps his son-in-law.'

'Why should they care?'

'Ascolini was born in these parts. He must have some legal loyalties.'

'Loyalties!' Fiorello vented the word in a harsh chuckle. 'We have so few of our own, why should we expect them from the *signori*?'

For a moment it seemed as if the priest would accept the familiar proposition. His face sagged, his shoulders drooped. Then a new thought engaged him and when he turned back to Fiorello his eyes were hard. He said quietly: 'There is a question for you, my friend. When Anna is brought to trial, how will you testify?'

'On the evidence,' said Fiorello flatly. 'How else?'

'And on the past? On the beginning of this monstrous business?'

'I stand on the record.' Fiorello's face was blank, his eyes cold as agate-stones.

'And if the record lies?'

'Then I am not aware of it, *padre*. I'm paid to keep the peace, not to rewrite old history.'

'Is that your last word?'

'It has to be,' said Fiorello with odd humour. 'I can't hide myself in a cloister like you, *padre*. I can't afford to go beating my breast and making novenas to Santa Caterina when things don't turn out the way I'd like. This is my world. Those folks out there are my people. I have to live with them the best way I can. This one . . .' he made a curt gesture towards the girl–'whatever we do, she's a lost cause. I suppose, anyway, that makes her the Church's business.'

Seconds ticked away as the two men faced each other, priest and policeman, each committed to his separate road, each caught in the consequence of a common history, while Anna Albertini sat a pace away, pecking at her food, remote and contained as a moon-dweller. Then, without another word, the old friar turned away, lifted the telephone and asked to be connected to the Villa Ascolini.

In the noonday quiet of the *salone*, Carlo Rienzi was playing Chopin for the visitor, Peter Landon. They made a curious pair: the burly Australian with his freckled, quirky face and his ham-fist clamped round the bowl of his pipe; the Italian, slim, pale, incongruously beautiful, with sensitive lips and a dreamer's eyes touched with mystery and discontent.

The piece was one of the early nocturnes, tender, limpid, plangent, and Rienzi was interpreting it with simplicity and fidelity. The notes fell pure as water-drops; the phrases were shaped with love and understanding–and with no slur of bravura or false sentiment. This was the true discipline of art: the submission of the executant to the composer's talent, the subordination of personal emotion to that recorded by the long-dead master.

Landon watched him with shrewd, diagnostic eyes and thought how young he was, how vulnerable, how oddly matched with his cool, civilized wife and the flamboyant old advocate who was his master in the law.

Yet he was not all youth, nor wholly unscarred. His hands were strong yet restrained on the keys. There were lines on his forehead and incipient crow's feet at the corner of his eyes. He was on the wrong side of thirty. He was married. He must have suffered his share of the exactions of life. He played Chopin like one who understood the frustrations of love.

For Landon himself, the music woke echoes of a private discontent. A man from the New World, he had assumed without effort the urbanities of the Old. Ambitious, he had abandoned a promising practice in his own country to climb the risky slopes of reputation in London. A rebel by nature, he had disciplined his tongue and his temper and accommodated himself to the stratagems of the most jealous profession in the most jealous city in the world. He had hitched himself to the coat-tails of eminence and now, by industry, talent and diplomacy, had established himself as a senior consultant in psychiatry and a specialist in criminal psycho-pathology.

It was much for a man a year short of forty, but it was still two paces away from the closed perimeter of greatness. Two paces–and yet this was the longest leap of all. One needed a springboard to make it: the opportune case, the fortunate meeting with counsel in need of advice, the moment of illumination in research.

So far opportunity had eluded him and he had lapsed by slow degrees into frustration and the tart dissatisfaction of those who are challenged always within the stretch of their talent.

It was a kind of crisis, and he was wise enough to recognize it. There was a climacteric in every career: a season of resentment, indecision and danger. Many a hapless politician had lost a seat in Cabinet because he lacked patience or discretion. Many a brilliant scholar had missed preferment because he was a mite too brusque with his seniors. In the closed brotherhood of the British Medical Association a man had to swallow his pride and cultivate his friends. And when one ventured into the new science of the spirit, one made sedulous deferment to one's colleagues of the scalpel and the stethoscope. If one were an outlander one was doubly careful, doubly dependent upon the quality of one's performance and the validity of one's research.

So he had chosen a strategy for himself–withdrawal: this sabbatical year among the experts of Europe; three months with Dahlin in Stockholm on institutional practice with the criminally insane, a term with Gutmann in Vienna exploring the nature of responsibility, and now a brief vacation with Ascolini, famous for his use of medico-legal testimony.

And afterwards? He too had his questions about afterwards because now he was faced with a new aspect of the crisis: the ennui of the middle years. How much should a man pay for the fulfilment of ambition? And when he had paid, how much could he enjoy–and with whom? The old, sad music mocked him with its tale of lost hopes and dead loves and the clamour of forgotten triumphs.

There was a long, synoptic moment while the last overtones died away, then Rienzi swung round on the stool to face him. His lips puckered into a boyish, uncertain smile. 'There now, Peter! You've had your music! Money on the table! It's time to pay the piper.'

Landon took the pipe out of his mouth and grinned at him. 'What's the price?'

'Some advice. Some professional advice.'

'About what?'

'About myself. You've been here a week now. I like to think we've become friends. You know some of my problems. You're shrewd enough to guess the rest.' He flung out his hands in an abrupt gesture of appeal. 'I'm caught, Peter! I'm married, in a country where there is no divorce. I'm in love with a wife who has no passion for me. I work for a man whom I admire greatly–and who has as little respect for me as if I were the junior clerk. What do I do about it? What's the matter with me? You're the psychiatrist! You're the fellow who probes the hearts of his patients. Read my wife's and Ascolini's.'

Landon frowned and stuck his pipe back in his mouth. Professional instinct warned him against such untimely intimacies. He had a dozen evasions to discourage them. But the man's distress was patent and his solitude in his own household was strangely poignant. Besides, he had spent more than courtesy on his father-in-law's house-guest, and Landon had been touched to an unfamiliar gratitude. He hesitated a moment and then said carefully: 'You can't have it two ways at once, Carlo. If you want a psychiatrist–and I don't think you do–then you should consult one of your own countrymen. At least you'll have a common language and a set of common symbols. If you want to bellyache to a friend, that's something different.' He chuckled drily. 'Generally it's a better prescription, too. But if you tell my patients, I'll be out of business in a week!'

'Call it a bellyache, if you want,' said Rienzi in his brooding, melancholy fashion, 'but don't you see, I'm trapped like a squirrel in a cage?'

'By marriage?'

'No. By Ascolini.'

'You don't like him?'

Rienzi hesitated a moment and when he answered there was a world of weariness in his voice. 'I admire him greatly. He has a singular variety of talents and he is a very great advocate.'

'But?'

'But I see too much of him, I suppose. I work in his office. My wife and I live in his house. And I am oppressed by his eternal youth.'

It was an odd phrase, but Landon understood it. He had a momentary vision of the first cocktail party in Ascolini's Roman apartment when father and daughter played to their small but distinguished audience while Carlo Rienzi walked solitary on the moonlit terrace. He found himself more gently disposed to this young-old man with the too-sensitive mouth and the restrained artist's hands. He asked quietly: 'Do you have to live with him?'

'I am told,' said Rienzi with soft bitterness, 'I am told that I am in his debt. I am indebted to him for my career. In Italy today the law is an overcrowded profession and the patronage of a great man is rare to find. I am indebted to him also for my wife. And she is in debt to him, being an only daughter whose father has given her love, security and the promise of a rich estate.'

'And Ascolini exacts payment?'

'From both of us.' He made a small, shrugging gesture of defeat. 'From me a loyalty and a conformity with his plans for my career. From my wife a–a kind of conspiracy in which her youth is spent on him instead of on me.'

'How does your wife feel about this?'

'Valeria is a singular woman,' said Rienzi flatly. 'She understands duty, filial piety and the payment of debts. Also she is very fond of her father and finds much pleasure in his company.'

'More than in yours?'

He smiled at that: the boyish, uncertain smile that lent him so much charm. He said gently: 'He has much more to offer than I, Peter. I cannot read the world with my fingertips. I am neither assured nor successful though I should like to be both. I love my wife, but I am afraid I have more need of her than she of me.'

'Time may change that.'

'I doubt it, said Rienzi sharply. 'In this conspiracy there are others involved.'

'Other men?'

'Several. But I am less worried by them than by my own deficiency as a husband.' He stood up and walked to the french doors that gave on to the balcony and the garden terraces. 'Let's walk a little, shall we? It's more private outside.'

For a while they were silent, pacing an alley of cypresses, through whose green pillars they saw the sky within hand's reach and the countryside spread in a multichrome of dark olives, green vineyards, brown fallow and ripe corn shaken by the wind. Cynically, Landon thought that time wrought its changes all too slowly, and that for Carlo Rienzi there was need of swifter remedies. He prescribed them, curtly: 'If your wife makes horns for you, you don't have to wear them. Hand her back to her father and get yourself a judicial separation. If you don't like your job or your patron, change them. Dig ditches, if you must, but cut yourself free–now!'

'I wonder,' asked Rienzi with bleak humour, 'why it is always the sentimentalists who have the pat answers. I expected better of you, Peter. You're a professional. You should understand more than others the obliquities of love and possession: why sometimes a half loaf is better than a basketful of pastry; why hope deferred is often a stronger bond than conquest shared.'

Landon flushed and gave him the tart reminder: 'If a man likes to scratch, he won't thank you for curing his itch.'

'But do you have to tear out his heart to cure him? Cut off his head to teach him reason?'

'Not at all. You try to help him to enough maturity to choose his own remedy. Or, if there is no remedy, to wear his affliction with dignity.'

The words were hardly out before he regretted them, being vain of a tolerance which he did not possess, ashamed of a brusqueness with which clinical practice had endowed him. This was the penalty of ambition: that a man could not sympathize without demeaning himself. This was the irony of self-love: that he could not pity what he had not endured in his own flesh–the kiss given but not returned, the passion spent but unrequited. Rienzi's mild answer was the bitterest reproach of all: 'If I lack dignity, Peter, you must not blame me too much. The meanest actor can play a king. It takes a great one to wear the horns and have his audience weep. If I have not rebelled before this, it is because opportunity was lacking, not courage. It is not as easy as you think to receive the dilemmas of loyalty and love. But I'm plotting revolution, believe me! I know, better than you, that my only hope with Valeria is to beat Ascolini on his own ground–to destroy the legend which he has built up for her and which is the source of his power over her. Strange, isn't it? To prove myself a lover, I must prove myself a lawyer first. I need a brief, Peter, just one good brief. But where the hell do I get it?'

Before Landon had time to frame a reply or an apology, a servant came to call Rienzi to the telephone and the physician of souls was left pondering the problems of love in an old land where passions run in crooked channels and youth carries on its back five thousand years of violent history.

Landon was glad to be alone. A man devoted to the mechanics of success, he found too much company exacting, too many new impressions a burden on the imagination. He felt the need of some restoration before committing himself to an afternoon with his very intelligent but very demanding hosts.

Carlo Rienzi was an attractive fellow, and one could not grudge a gentleness for his dilemmas and indecisions; but it was the problem of all friendships in Italy that one was expected to be involved, to take sides in the most trivial or grandiose issue, to have a care for every sorrow and a blush for every indiscretion. If one were not careful, one was spent like a plenty-purse, sucked dry and left gasping while one's friends waxed riotous on love or pity.

It was a relief therefore to be quit of people and enjoy the simple tourist pleasure of looking at the view from the garden.

The first impact was breath-taking: a bright and palpitating air that challenged the leap of heart and spirit; hills at eye-level, stark against the sky, tufted with pine and chestnut, craggy with ancient rooks and the crumbling castles of Guelph and Ghibelline; a hawk, high-wheeling against the blue; dark pines like spearmen marching the upland slopes.

For all his crust of egotism and ambition Landon was not a gross man. One could not walk the secret ways of the human spirit without a talent for wonder, a minimal grace of compassion, and a small well of tears for man caught in the terror of discontinuity. There were tears rising in him now at the sudden wonder of this old land, peopled with noonday ghosts.

This was the true climate of mysticism, savage yet tender, soft with tillage yet stark with relics of ancient and bloody conflicts.

Here the little Brother Francis was wedded in a wonderful union with the Lady Poverty. Here came the mercenaries of Barbarossa: pikemen from England, bowmen from Florence, bandits from Albania, motley yet terrible in the massacre of Montalcino. The poet-king of Luxembourg, Henry of the love-songs, died here under the cypresses. On the hill of Malmarenda, crowned with four trees, was held that monstrous feast of feasts which ended in the butchery of the Tolomei and the Salimbeni. And under the ancient roofs of Siena the Lady Catherine revealed the sweet substance of her spirit—'Charity does not seek itself for itself . . . but for God. Souls should be united and transformed by charity. We must find among thorns the perfume of roses about to open.'

It was a place of paradox, a field of fusion for historic contrarieties: beauty and terror, spiritual ecstasy and gross cruelty, medieval ignorance and the cold illumination of the age of unreason. Its people, too, were a complex of many strains: ancient Etruscan, Lombard German and soldier of fortune from God knows where. Medieval saints, Florentine humanists, Arab astrologers had all contributed to their inheritance. Their merchants traded from Provence to the Baltic and students came from the four corners of Europe to hear Aldo Brandini lecture on the regimen of the human body.

For Landon it was a strange processional vision—part landscape and part the dredging of old memory—but when it passed he felt a mite more understanding, a shade more tolerant of the passionate, involute people with whom he had broken bread. He did not have to share the damnation they imposed upon themselves. He could forgive them—provided he did not have to live with them.

He caught a drift of perfume and the sound of a footfall and a moment later Valeria Rienzi was standing beside him on the path. She was dressed in a modish summer frock. Her feet were bare in sandals of gold leather and her hair was tied back from her face with a silk ribbon. She looked pale, he thought. There were shadows about her eyes and a hint of weariness in her lips; but her skin was clear as amber and she greeted him with a smile.

'You know, Peter, that's the first time I've seen you looking like that.'

'Like what?'

'Unguarded, unwary. Almost like a boy watching Pulcinella in the square.'

Landon felt himself blushing, but he grinned and tried to shrug off the comment. 'I'm sorry. I didn't know I looked—wary. I don't mean to be, I assure you. You must find me a very stuffy fellow.'

'Anything but stuffy, Peter.' As if it were the most natural gesture in the world she linked hands with him and began strolling down the garden walk at his side. 'On the contrary, you're a very exciting man. Exciting and perhaps a little frightening, too.'

He played games with too many women not to recognize this simple gambit; but his vanity was tickled and he decided to play it a little longer. He asked innocently. 'Frightening? I don't understand.'

'You're so complete . . . so contained. You live from yourself to yourself. You're like my father in many ways. You understand so much that there seems to be nothing other people can give you. You both take life like a dinner party. You eat it, get up satisfied and then pass on. I wish I could do that.'

'I should have said you did it very successfully.'

He delivered the stroke lightly like a fencer opening a friendly match. To his surprise she frowned and said seriously: 'I know. I do it very well. But it isn't real, you see. It's like a pupil going through a lesson that he knows by heart. My father's a good teacher. So is Basilio.'

'Basilio?'

'He's a man I've been seeing lately. He makes an art of irresponsibility.'

The gambit was not so familiar after all. Landon decided that it might be wise to quit the game before it began in earnest. He said, lamely: 'There's a lot of talk about the art of living. In my experience it's mostly artifice: powder and patches and carnival masks.'

'And what's underneath?'

'Men and women.'

'What kind?'

'All kinds—most of them lonely.'

As soon as he had said it, he knew that he made a mistake. This was the beginning of every affair—the first intimacy, the chink in the mailcoat that left the heart bare to the blade. And the blade came probing more swiftly than he had dreamed.

'That's what I read in your face, wasn't it, Peter? You were lonely. You're like that bird up there—high, free, with all the world spread under your wings—and yet you were lonely.' Her fingers tightened on his palm; he felt the warmth of her body and caught the heady drift of her perfume. 'I'm lonely too.'

He was a physician and he understood the uses of pain. He asked coolly: 'With so much, Valeria? With your father and Carlo—and Basilio thrown in for good measure?'

He was prepared for anger and even for a slap in the mouth; but she simply disengaged herself and said with icy scorn: 'I expected better of you, Peter. Because I hold your hand and tell you a little of the truth about myself, does that make me a whore? I make no secret of what I do or of whom I like. But you—you must despise yourself very much. I'm sorry for any woman who tries to love you.'

Then, as if the one shame were not enough, Carlo was standing in the middle of the path and saying with wintry politeness: 'You'll have to excuse me from lunch, I'm afraid. There's been some trouble in the village. I've been asked to help. I'm not sure when I'll be back.'

He did not wait for their comments but left them quickly, hostile actors on an empty stage, without script, prompter or any predictable resolution to their conflict. Awkward as a schoolboy, Landon stammered through an apology. 'I don't know what I can say to beg your pardon. I–I can only try to explain. In my work a man gets bad habits. He sits like a father confessor listening to people's miseries. Sometimes he comes to feel a little bit like God sitting in the judgment seat. That's one problem. The other one is that patients always try to turn their psychiatrist into something else: a father, a mother, a lover. It's a symptom of sickness. We call it transference. We develop defences against it–a kind of clinical brutality. The trouble is we sometimes use the same weapon against people who are not our patients at all. It's a kind of cowardice. And you're right when you say I despise myself for it. I'm very sorry, Valeria.'

For a while she did not answer him but stood leaning against a stone urn, stripping the petals from a wistaria blossom and scattering them at her feet. Her face was averted so that he could not read her eyes and when finally she did speak her voice was studiously grey.

'We're all cowards, aren't we, Peter? We're all brutal when someone probes at the little fester of fear inside us. I'm brutal to Carlo, I know that. He in his own fashion is cruel to me. Even my father, who is as brave as an old lion, makes a purgatory for those he loves. And yet we are necessary to each other. With no one to hurt, we can only hurt ourselves and that is the last terror of all. But how long can we live like this without destroying one another?'

'I don't know,' said Peter Landon sombrely, and asked himself at the same moment how long a man could endure the goads of ambition, how high he could climb alone before he toppled into disillusionment and despair.

2

The police-station in San Stefano was fusty with cigarette smoke and the smell of stale wine and country cheese. Sergeant Fiorello sat ostentatiously detached, copying out a deposition. Fra Bonifacio stood fumbling at his cincture while Carlo Rienzi explained himself to Anna Albertini: 'Fra Bonifacio has told me a little of your history, Anna. I'm anxious to help. But there are things you must understand first.' His voice took on the patient expository tone of a dominie instructing a dullard pupil. 'You must realize, for instance, that a lawyer is not a magician. He can't prove black is white. He can't wave a wand and wipe out things that have happened. He can't bring dead people back to life. All he can do is lend you his knowledge of the law and his voice to plead your case in court. Then a lawyer must be acceptable to his client. You must agree to engage his services. Do I make myself clear?'

It might have been an illusion but it seemed for a moment as if a ghost of a smile twitched at the pale lips of the girl. She said gravely: 'I haven't had much education, but I do understand about lawyers. You mustn't treat me like a child.'

Rienzi blushed and bit his lip. He felt very young and very gauche. But he recovered himself and went on, more firmly: 'Then you must understand what you've done–and what the consequences are.'

Anna Albertini nodded in her placid, detached fashion. 'Oh yes. I've always known what would happen. It doesn't worry me.'

'Not now, perhaps, but later, when you stand in court and hear the sentence. When they take you away and dress you in prison clothes and lock you behind bars.'

'No matter where they put me, it doesn't matter. I'm free now, you see–and happy.'

For the first time the old friar entered the discussion. He said gently: 'Anna, child, today is a strange and terrible day. You cannot say at all how you may feel tomorrow. In any case, whether you want it or not, the court will see that you have a lawyer. I think it's better that you have someone who may care a little, like Mr Rienzi here.'

'I haven't any money to pay him.'

'The money will be provided.'

'Then I suppose it's all right.'

Rienzi was shocked by her indifference and he said testily: 'We'll need something more formal than that. Will you tell Sergeant Fiorello that you accept me as your legal representative?'

'If that's what you want.'

'I heard.' Fiorello looked up with a grin. 'I'll put it in the record, for what it's worth. But I think you're wasting your time.'

'That's what I don't understand,' said Anna Albertini with odd simplicity. 'I know there's nothing you can do for me. So why do you and Fra Bonifacio take the trouble?'

'I'm trying to pay a debt, Anna,' said the friar softly.

Carlo Rienzi gathered up his notes, stuffed them into his pocket and stood up. He said briskly: 'You'll be taken into Siena and charged there, Anna. After that they'll either put you in the remand cells in the city prison, or more probably send you out to the women's house of correction at San Gimignano. Wherever you are, I'll come to see you tomorrow. Try not to be too frightened.'

'I'm not frightened,' said Anna Albertini. 'Tonight I think I shall sleep without nightmares.'

'God keep you, child.' Fra Bonifacio made the sign of blessing over the girl's dark head and turned away.

Rienzi was already at the door talking with Fiorello.

'When we start preparing the defence, I'd like to come and talk to you, Sergeant.'

'Out of order, I'm afraid.' Fiorello's face was a blank, official mask. 'I'll be called for the prosecution.'

'Then we'll talk in court,' said Rienzi curtly and walked out into the buzzing, sunlit square, with the little Franciscan at his heels.

The crowd parted before them. Everyone stared, pointing and whispering as if they were side-show monsters, until they disappeared into the cool confessional shadows of the church of San Stefano.

Lunch at the Villa Ascolini was a three-cornered match, dominated by the flamboyant wit of the old advocate. Carlo's absence was accepted with a shrug and, Landon guessed, a measure of relief. The trouble in the village was dismissed with a gesture of deprecation. Neither Ascolini nor Valeria asked what it was, but when Landon pressed them Ascolini read him an ironic homily on the vestigial practice of the feudal system.

'... We live most of the year in Rome, but our ownership of the villa makes us by definition the padronal family. When we return here, we pay a kind of tribute to our dependency. Sometimes it is a demand for new endowments to the church or the convent. Sometimes we become patrons to a more or less brilliant student. Occasionally we are asked to arbitrate in a local dispute—which is probably what has happened today. But whatever the circumstance, the principle is the same: the lords pay a tax to the lowly for the privilege of survival; the lowly use the lords to protect them from a democracy they distrust and a bureaucracy they despise. It's a reasonable bargain.' He sipped delicately at his wine and added the afterthought, 'I am happy that Carlo begins to assume his share of the tribute.'

Valeria smiled tolerantly and patted the man's sleeve. 'Take no notice of him, Peter. He's a malicious old man.'

Landon grinned and began dissecting a peach. Ascolini's pink face wore an expression of patent innocence. He said, blandly: 'It's the privilege of age to test the metal of youth. Besides, I have great hopes for my son-in-law. He's a young man of singular talent and cultivation.' His shrewd, youthful eyes quizzed Landon over the rim of his glass. 'I hope he has been entertaining you properly.'

'Better than I deserve.' Landon was grateful for the change of subject. 'He drove me out to Arezzo yesterday.'

Ascolini nodded approval. 'A noble city, my friend. Too much neglected by the tourists. Petrarch's town and Aretino's.' He gave a small, amused chuckle. 'You're a student of the soul, Landon. There's a parable for you: the great lover and the great lecher spring from the same soil; the scholarly poet and the satirist scribbling dirty words on public buildings; the Sonnets to Laura and the *Sonetti Lussuriosi*. You've read them, of course?'

'I've read Petrarch,' Landon told him with a grin. 'But they don't reprint Aretino these days.'

'I will lend you a copy.' Ascolini waved an eloquent hand. 'It's a scatological classic which cannot fail to interest a psychiatrist. While you are here, please make yourself free of the library. It's not a large collection, but you may find it interesting and curious.'

'That's kind of you. I didn't know you were a collector.'

'Father is a dozen men rolled up in one,' said Valeria drily.

Again Ascolini gave his spry, old man's chuckle. 'I collect experience, Mr Landon, as I once collected women, who are the key to experience. But I'm too old for that now. So I have books, an occasional picture and the vicarious drama of the law.'

'You're a fortunate man, *dottore*.'

Ascolini fixed him with a bright, ironic eye. 'Youth is the fortunate time, my dear Landon. The best fortune of age is a wisdom to value what is left: the last of the wine, the richness of memory, the ripeness of the season. It is a thing I have tried to explain to Carlo—and to my daughter here—that it is better to be a tree growing quietly in the sun than the monkey scrambling wildly after the fruit.'

'I wonder,' asked Landon with affected innocence, 'whether you were always content to be the tree, *dottore*.'

'I knew I was right about you, my friend. You've dealt with the law too long to be taken in by an old advocate's tricks. Of course I wasn't content;

the higher the fruit, the faster I wanted to climb. But the fact is still the same. It is better to be the tree than the monkey. But how do you put an old truth into a young head?'

'You don't try,' said Landon with some tartness. 'Young heads are made to be beaten on walls. Most of them survive it.'

Surprisingly, Ascolini nodded agreement and said, with an air of regret: 'You're right, of course. I'm afraid I've intruded too much into the lives of these young people. They don't always understand the affection I have for them.'

'What we don't understand, Father . . .' Valeria's voice was high and tight as a fiddle-string, 'what you don't understand either, is the price you exact for it.'

As she stood up, her trailing sleeve caught the rim of her glass so that the crystal shattered on the pavement and the wine splashed red on the grey stones. Landon addressed himself with studious care to the last remnants of his peach until the old man challenged him with sardonic humour: 'Don't let yourself be embarrassed, my friend. Don't try to play the urbane Anglo-Saxon with people like us. This is what we are. This is how we have lived for a thousand years. We make great pictures from our lecheries and grand opera of our most murderous tragedies. You're a student of the human drama. You have a box seat. If we're happy to parade our follies, you have a perfect right to applaud the comedy. Come, my dear fellow, let me pour you a brandy. And if you find it hard to forgive me, remember I'm a peasant who used the law to make himself a gentleman.'

There was no resisting so much urbanity and in spite of himself Landon was charmed back into laughter. But later, as he stretched out on the big Florentine bed to take the ritual siesta, he found himself trying to write his own version of the Rienzi chronicle.

The old advocate was too complex a character to be defined by the somewhat naïve snobberies of a still feudal society. A peasant he might be, with a peasant' shrewdness and harsh ambition, but he was no beggar on horseback. He might have been hewn from rough material, but he was granite-hard and polished by the disciplines of a crowded world. His career was founded on the follies of other men, and passions too ignoble would have destroyed him long since. Landon felt that he owned more stature than either Carlo or Valeria would admit in him. He could see the old man strong in love, hate or a perversion of either, but he could not judge him petty.

Valeria? Here too there was a different reading from the one Carlo had given. He saw her as a kind of intransigent princess, half-awakened to love, yet still enchained by the tyrant magic of childhood. For Carlo there was still an innocence, even in her affairs. But Landon was reminded of the girls Lippo Lippi used for his virgins and angels, with smooth cheeks and limpid eyes and the memory of a thousand nights on their lips. It was a distasteful thought, but he could not rid himself of it. When one sat by the confessional couch one looked at women with calculation and one learnt, sometimes painfully, that innocence was rare and had many counterfeits. Valeria might not be loose, but she was certainly inclined to other satisfactions than those offered by a young and uncertain husband. Landon saw her maternal yet childless, cool but not passionless; not dominated by her father but sustained, like him, by some inner reserves, so that she needed less than other women but could give much more if the mood and the moment were right.

He lapsed into languid contemplation of what such a mood and such a moment might be–and found himself looking into the well of his own emptiness.

All that he saw in these people he had avoided in his own life: cuckoldry, cruelty, the itch in the flesh, the fear of losing what one could only pretend to possess, the vampire tyranny of age, the perverted surrender of youth. He had set himself a limited goal and stood now within measurable reach of it. He had enjoyed women but had never submitted to them. He had preserved the ethics of a healing art while using the art for his own advancement. He had money, position, leisure. He was amenable neither to wife nor mistress. He was free, disciplined–and empty of the wine of life which these others spent with such passionate indiscretion.

Suddenly, it was they who were rich and he the mendicant at their gates; and he wondered, as beggars must, whether he had not lost the stomach for feasting, even were the feasting offered to him.

When the afternoon heat poured like lava over the land, when peasant and burgher burrowed like moles in flight from the sun, Ninette Lachaise packed paints and canvases into her battered car and headed for the open country.

It was an artist's pilgrimage, hardly less painful than that made long ago by the brotherhood of shell and staff. The land was as hot as a chafing-dish; the roads were a dusty misery; the hills, burnt umber, gathered the heat and diffused it in parching waves over the lowland, where the vines drooped and the runnels dried and the olive branches hung listless in the slack air. The cattle gave up their grazing and huddled under the sparse shade, eyes glazed, thirsty tongues lolling. The rare human, caught unaware on cart-track or tillage, seemed shrunken and desiccated as a gnome trudging some lunar landscape.

Yet over it all lay the pervasive miracle of light: the high dazzle of the southward sky, the white flare of stucco and tufa outcrop, bronze shadows in the clefts of the mountains, sheen of pond-water, ochre of roof-top, jewel-fire from bird-wing or locust flight. And this was the justification for the pilgrimage–the harsh newness of aspect, the sudden extension of space, the separation of mass and contour, so that one saw through to the bones of creation and glimpsed the massive articulation of its parts.

For Ninette Lachaise there were other justifications, too. Every pilgrimage was, by definition, a discipline for the spirit, a tempting of the unknown and a stretch towards the unattainable.

Four years before, she had come, in flight, to this city whose devotees called it 'The Home of Souls'. She had fled a Parisian household dominated by an ailing mother and an elderly father whose recreation was a regret for the vanished glories of the military life. She had fled the sterilities of the post-war ateliers and a youth which was a foretaste of old age. Two things had happened swiftly: her painting had exploded into a startling maturity, and a week after her first exhibition she had tumbled headlong into a love-affair with Basilio Lazzaro.

He was a professional amorist, indifferent as a bull, and the affair had lasted six stormy months. They had parted without regret; and she was left, bruised but awakened, aware of her capacity for passion but dubious of another total surrender. She had learnt another wisdom too. This was a man's country and there was no salvation for a woman in promiscuous or ill-considered loving. So she had made the disciplines of art a discipline for the flesh as well, while she waited, too cautiously for the most part, on the moment of fortunate meeting.

But it was not enough to wait, unknowing, on the fairy-tale promise of love, Prince Charming and happiness-ever-after. There were elements in her nature and her situation which, as yet, she did not fully understand. How far might her talent drive her? How soon might she challenge the legend of woman's incapacity for greatness in creation? How much equality did she need to survive after the first flush of courtship and bedding? Why was she drawn to men like Ascolini–the cynical and the wise–and why did she so mistrust the young ones, all ardour and so little endowed with understanding? What was the profit in recording visions for others to enjoy while the green years waned into the loneliness of autumn?

Since Ascolini's visit, all these questions and a dozen others had moved into sharp focus like the crags and crenellations of the Tuscan hills. It was a measure of her uneasiness that she had accepted his invitation to dine at the villa–with Valeria, who was now playing lover to Basilio Lazzaro, and with an unknown outlander who was being presented like bloodstock for her inspection.

Then, abruptly, the humour of the situation took hold of her and she began to laugh–a clear, free sound that rang across the valley, startled the cropping goats and flushed a ground lark into the shimmering summer air.

In the library of the villa, Alberto Ascolini, advocate and actor, staged a reconciliation with his daughter. It was a scene had had played many times and his role had the patina of long practice. He stood, leaning against the mantel, trim, dapper and impressive, with a glass of brandy in his hand, a small conspiratorial smile twitching the corners of his mouth. Valeria sat, curled in his armchair, chin on hand, her feet tucked under her like a small girl. He shrugged eloquently and said: 'Child, you mustn't resent me too much. I'm a perverse old goat who laughs at his own jokes. But I love you tenderly. It's not easy for a man to be father and mother to a girl-child. I know my failures better than you. But that I should seem to sell my love–this is new to me. Painful, too. I think you should explain yourself a little.'

Valeria Rienzi shook her head. 'You're not in court now, Father. I'm not going into the witness box.'

'Perhaps not, child.' His tone was unruffled, touched only with a hint of sadness. 'But you put me in the dock. Surely I have the right to hear the indictment? How do I make you pay for love?'

'You take a share of everything I do.'

'Take? Take?' The noble brow wrinkled in puzzlement and he ran a hand through his white mane. 'You make me sound like a tax-gatherer. I have a care for you–true! I have an interest in your happiness–is this an exaction? Have I denied you anything, even the right to be young and foolish?'

For the first time she tilted up her head to face him, half hostile, half appealing. 'But don't you see, half of it has always been for yourself. Carlo? He was your creation first. You groomed him and handed him to me like a pet pony, but you always had one hand on the bridle. The others? They were yours, too–diversions for the unhappy bride, *cavalieri serventi* provided by the indulgent father. They were romances to recall your own youth.'

'And you accepted them, my dear. You were grateful, as I remember.'

'You taught me that, too.' The words came out in a rush of bitterness. 'Say thank you for the sweetmeats like a good girl. . . . But when I wanted and took something for myself—like Basilio—ah, that was different!'

For the first time a flush of anger showed in his pink, shining cheek. 'Lazzaro is scum! Not fit company for a woman of breeding!'

'Breeding, Father? What is our breeding? You were a peasant's son. You married poor and regretted it when you came to reputation. You despised my mother and you were glad when she died. Me? You know what I was to be? The model of the woman you wanted but never had. You know why you never married again? So that no one could ever match you. So that you could always despise what you needed and own what you loved!'

'Love?' Ascolini laid down the word with bleak contempt. 'Tell me about love, Valeria. You have loved Carlo perhaps? Or Sebastian? Or the South American, or the son of the Greek who had money running out of his ears? Or have you found it rutting in a third-floor apartment with this Lazzaro fellow?'

She was weeping now, head buried in her hands, and he thought that he had won. He said gently: 'You and I should not hurt each other, child. We should be honest and say that what we have between us is the best we have known of love. For me it is all I have known worth having. For you there will be more, much more, because the world is still young for you. Even with Carlo there can be something, but you must make at least half the step towards it. He's a boy, you're a woman, rich with experience. But you must begin to prepare like a woman for a home and children. In a year or two I shall want to retire; Carlo will naturally step into my practice. You will have a secure estate. And there must be children with whom you can enjoy it. The locust years will come to you too, my dear, as they have already come to me. It is then you will need the little ones.'

Slowly she heaved herself out of the chair and then stood, facing him with the brutal question: 'And whose children will they be, Father? Carlo's? Mine? Or yours?'

Abruptly she turned away and left him alone in the vaulted library with two thousand years of wisdom on the shelves and no remedy at all against winter and disillusion.

There was a legend in San Stefano that Little Brother Francis had built the first chapel there with his own hands. The frescoes in the church commemorated the event, and in the cloisters of the brown friars there was a garden with a shrine where the *Poverello* stood with outstretched arms welcoming the birds who came to bathe in the fish-pond at his feet. The air was cool, the light subdued, and the only sounds were the splash of water in the pond and the flapping of sandalled feet along arches of the colonnade. Here, seated on a stone bench, Carlo Rienzi found himself listening to the confession of Fra Bonifacio.

It was a chastening experience, like watching a man read his own indictment in open court or hearing a physician diagnose his own malignancy. The old man's face was scored and shrunken, his back bent as if by a heavy load. As he stumbled through his exposition, his knotted fingers laced and unlaced the cord of his cincture.

'I told you earlier, my son, that what happened today was the last chapter of a very long story. There are many people involved in it. I am one of them.

Each of us bears a measure of guilt for what happened today.'

Rienzi held up a warning hand. 'Let's wait here a moment, Father. Let me show you first a little of the law. Murder was done here today. On the first evidence the crime was a premeditated act of revenge for a wrong done some years ago to Anna Albertini. There is no dispute about the act, its circumstances or its motive. The prosecution has an iron-clad case. The defence has only two pleas: insanity or mitigation. If we plead insanity we have to prove it by psychiatric testimony, and the girl's case is hardly better than if she suffers the normal penalty for murder. If we plead mitigation we have a choice of two grounds: provocation or partial mental infirmity. A court is not a confessional. The law takes only a limited cognizance of the moral guilt of an act. It concerns itself with responsibility, but in the social order and not in the moral one.' He smiled and spread his hands in deprecation. 'I read your lectures, Father. Forgive me. But this time our roles are reversed. For my client's sake, you must not lead me into irrelevance.'

The old man digested the thought slowly and then nodded approval. 'Every act of violence is a kind of madness, my son, but I would doubt whether you will find Anna Albertini legally insane. As to mitigation, here I think I can help you, though I cannot say how you may use what I tell.' He paused a moment and then went on slowly. 'There are two versions of this history. The first is the one which will be presented in court, because it is a matter of official record. The second . . .' He broke off and waited a long moment, staring down at the backs of his knotted, freckled hands. 'I know the second version, but I cannot tell it to you, because it came to me first under the seal of confession. I can only say that it exists and that you will have to ferret it out for yourself. Whether you can prove it is another problem again. And even then I am doubtful whether it will have validity in court.' His voice trembled and his eyes filled up with the rheumy tears of age. 'Justice, my son! How often is it abrogated by the very processes and the very people who are meant to preserve it! You saw Anna today. She is twenty-four years old. The last time I saw her was sixteen years ago—a child of eight putting flowers on her mother's grave and scratching an inscription on the cemetery wall with a piece of tin. It's still there. I'll show it to you afterwards.'

For all his professional detachment and his private preoccupations, Rienzi was moved by the pathos of the old man's situation. He himself was a man familiar with guilt, familiar too with the impotence to purge it. This was the tragedy of the human condition: that every single act was contingent upon another in the past and spawned a litter of consequences for the future. Sin might be expiated, forgiveness might be granted, but the consequences spread out, ripples in a limitless pool, currents eternally moving in a dark sea.

Rienzi prompted the friar gently: 'The official story, Father—where does it begin? Where is it written? Who tells it?'

'Everyone in San Stefano. The record is in Sergeant Fiorello's files, attested by half a dozen men. It begins in the last year of the war, when the Germans were in control of this area, and Gianbattista Belloni was the leader of a Partisan band operating in the hills. It was, as you know, a time of confusion, suspicion and blood-feud. Anna was living in the village with her mother, Agnese Moschetti, who was the widow of a man killed in the Libyan campaign. For a while there was a small detachment of Germans quartered in the village and some of them were billeted in Agnese Moschetti's house. When they moved out, she was accused of consorting with them and of betraying Partisan movements and personnel. She was arraigned before a drumhead court martial of Partisans, found guilty and executed by a firing-squad. Gianbattista Belloni presided at the court and signed the order for the execution. After the armistice, the proceedings of the court martial were attested and recorded in the police records of the village. A few years later, Belloni was made Mayor of the village and decorated with a gold medal by the President for gallantry in the service of his country . . .'

He broke off and wiped his lips as if to erase an unpleasant taste. Rienzi asked him: 'And what does the record say about Anna Albertini?'

'Her existence was noted,' said the old man drily. 'And the fact that she was handed in to the care of Fra Bonifacio of the Order of Friars Minor, who had her sent away to Florence in the care of relatives.'

'Where was she while her mother was tried and executed?'

'The record makes no mention of that.'

'But you know?'

'Under the seal.'

'Anna herself never told you?'

'From the time of her mother's death until this day I never heard a single word from her lips. Neither did anyone else in the village. At her mother's grave she did not even cry.'

'She's married now. Do you know anything about her husband?'

'Nothing. The police have sent for him, of course.'

'Other relatives?'

'The aunt who took her to Florence. I'm not even sure she's alive.' His old shoulders drooped despairingly. 'It's been sixteen years, my son. Sixteen years. . . .'

'You told me she wrote something on the cemetery wall. Could I see it, please?'

'Of course.'

He led Rienzi round the circuit of the cloisters, through a creaking postern and into the walled confine of the Campo Santo, where marble cherubs and wreathed columns and shabby immortelles gave their mute testimony to mortality. The grave of Agnese Moschetti was marked by a rough headstone which recorded only the date of her birth, the date of her death, and the last pathos: *'Requiescat in pace.'* There was hardly a pace between the headstone and the cumbling wall of the cemetery, and they squatted and wedged themselves close to the ground to read the painful childish etching: 'Belloni, one day I will kill you.'

Rienzi stared at the words for a long time, then asked sharply: 'Has anyone else seen this?'

'Who knows?' The old man shrugged helplessly. 'They've been there so many years.'

'Produce them in court,' said Rienzi softly, 'and we are dead before we begin. Find me a mallet and a chisel, man—and hurry!'

At three-thirty in the afternoon Landon woke from an uneasy doze to find Carlo Rienzi sitting in his armchair smoking a cigarette and flipping through a magazine with moody disinterest. His shoes were dusty, his shirt crumpled. His face looked drawn and tired. He gave Landon a telegraphic account of the events in San Stefano and ended with the wry summation: 'So that's it, Peter. The dice are cast. I've accepted the brief. I've found a pair of associates to act with me and give me entry to the Sienese courts. I have my first case.'

'Have you told your wife or Ascolini?'

'Not yet.' He gave a little lopsided grin. 'I've had enough excitement for a while. I'll leave the announcement until after dinner. Besides, I wanted to talk with you first. Would you do me a favour?'

'What kind of favour?'

'Professional. I'd like to retain you informally as psychiatric adviser. I'd like you to see the girl, make your own diagnosis and then indicate a possible use of medical evidence.'

'That's a tall order.' Landon frowned dubiously. 'It raises questions of ethics and medical politeness and my own status under the law.'

'If you were assured that informal consultation would give no offence?'

'Then I'd consider it. But I would still owe your father-in-law the courtesy of an explanation. After all, I'm his guest.'

'Would you wait until after I've spoken with him?'

'Naturally. But there's something I'd like to ask you, Carlo . . .' He hesitated a moment and then put the bald question: 'Why this case? On the face of it, the odds are all against you. It's your first brief and I don't see that you have a hope in hell of winning it.'

Rienzi's drawn face relaxed into a rare, boyish smile, and then grew serious again. He said quietly: 'It's a fair question, Peter, and I'll try to answer it, as I've already answered it for myself. It's a naïveté to believe that legal eminence is founded only on victories. The lost cause is often more profitable than the safe brief. New light on classic antinomies, contentious applications of accepted principles, a strategy that takes advantage of the perennial paradox of legality and justice–these are the foundations of reputations in advocacy. It's like medicine, you see. Who makes the greatest name–the fellow who cures an apple-colic or the man who massages ten seconds of life into a failing heart? There's no cure for death, my dear Peter, but there is a high art in its deferment. In law there is a correlative art of illumination, and on this great careers are built. Ascolini's for instance. And, I hope, mine.'

Landon was shocked by the cool cynicism of the exposition. He could not believe that this was the nostalgic poet who had played Chopin, the pained lover whose world had blown up in his face. His lips seemed too young to have framed the argument, his heart too young to have surrendered to so bleak an ambition. Yet, in all justice, Landon had to agree with him. He had undertaken to beat Ascolini on his own ground, that narrow field of contention where the law defines itself by contradiction as an instrument of rule or an instrument of justice. Carlo Rienzi could only contend on the traditional terms, divesting himself of feeling as he divested himself of the common dress, clothing himself in the black inhuman habit of the inquisitor.

Still, Landon had committed himself to friendship and he had to know how far Rienzi understood his own commitment. So he faced him harshly with a new question: 'Do you understand what you're saying, Carlo? You've engaged yourself to a client–and on the basis of hope. Not a great hope, maybe, but at least a small one. It's a personal relationship that reaches far beyond legality.'

'No, Peter!' His denial was swift and emphatic. 'It is based simply and solely on legality. I cannot make moral judgments on the state of my client's soul. I cannot commit myself to sympathy or sentiment in her regard. It is my function to induce such sympathies in others, to advocate favourable judgment by others, to bend every provision of the law to her advantage. These are her claims on me. I can admit no others. I am neither priest nor physician, nor custodian of sick minds.'

If he were as precise and as eloquent as this on the floor of the court there could be great hopes for him. But Landon wondered how many were the pupil's words and how many were the master's. He wondered, too, how far Rienzi understood that the detachment of the great lawyer or the great surgeon was the fruit of bitter experience, the mature conviction of ultimate futility. He asked himself whether it were not as great a mistake for Rienzi to commit himself too early to the detachment of age as to surrender too readily to the compassions of youth. But he was the spectator and Rienzi was the actor, so he shrugged and said lightly: 'I should stick to my own cobbling. Anyway, if your client is as beautiful as you tell me you'll make an impressive pair in court.'

Rienzi's face clouded and he said thoughtfully: 'She's like a child, Peter. She's twenty-four but she talks and thinks like a child–simple and unaccountable. I doubt she's going to be much help to me or to herself.'

'An insanity plea?'

Rienzi frowned. 'I'm no expert, but I doubt it. This is why I need your expert advice. I confess I'm relying more heavily on mitigatory evidence which I hope to dig up in San Stefano.'

'Investigations like that can be expensive.'

'Fra Bonifacio has undertaken to raise the expenses for the defendant. But I shouldn't be surprised if I have to meet some of them from my own pocket.'

'You're gambling a great deal, aren't you?'

'The biggest gamble of all is Valeria,' said Rienzi gravely. 'But I am resigned to that, so the rest is bagatelle.' He held out his hand. 'Wish me luck, Peter.'

'All the luck in the world, Carlo. Go with God.'

Rienzi gave him a swift, searching look. 'I think you mean that.'

'I do. I'm no great example of devotion, but I know that no matter how far you fall you'll never quite fall out of the hand of God. You may need to remember it some time.'

'I know,' said Rienzi moodily. 'Tonight I think I shall need it most of all.'

Then he was gone and Landon felt an oddly poignant grief for him. There were swords at his back and a battle looming ahead, but Landon could not shake off the uneasy conviction that he was fighting with the wrong weapons and for the wrong cause–and that victory for Carlo Rienzi might well prove the subtlest defeat of all.

Ascolini's dinner party began, genially enough, with cocktails in the library. The old man was urbane and eloquent, Valeria was affectionate to him and attentive to her guests, if a shade more reserved than the occasion seemed to demand. For Landon, his fellow guest was a pleasant surprise. He found her decorative, diverting and agreeably feminine. She had none of the studied languor of her Italian cousins, none of their giddy coquetry which promised much but was apt to be niggardly in fulfilment. She talked well and listened with flattering interest – and she was more than a match for the ironic malice of the advocate.

Ascolini was making a patent comedy out of his role of matchmaker. He said heartily: 'We must provide some diversion for you, Landon. A pity you're not in the marriage market. You'd be the rage of the town.'

'Don't you provide for bachelors in Siena?'

Ascolini laughed and tossed the question to Ninette Lachaise. 'How would you answer that, Ninette?'

'I would say that bachelors generally manage to provide for themselves.'

'It's a legend,' said Landon with a grin. 'Most bachelors get what they ask for and end by finding it isn't what they want.'

'We have our legends, too,' said Ascolini with tart humour. 'Our virgins are virtuous, our wives content, our widows discreet. But love is always a lottery. You buy the ticket and wait on your luck.'

'Don't be vulgar, Father,' said Valeria calmly.

'Love is a very vulgar business,' said Doctor Ascolini.

Ninette Lachaise raised her glass in a toast. 'To your conquest of Siena, Mr Landon.'

He drank to it cautiously. There was no coquetry in her frank brown eyes, but a faint smile clung to the corners of her mouth. Good-humoured women were rare enough in his life, and the intelligent ones were either boresome or unbeautiful. He toyed with the thought that with this one he could risk more than he had ever dared before of confidence, intimacy and perhaps even love. He saw Ascolini watching with a smile of thin amusement, and wondered if the thought were patent to the old man. Then Carlo came in, immaculate and apparently in the best of humour, to pour himself a drink and join in the conversation.

The change in the climate was immediate and startling and yet curiously hard to define. It was as if half the lights in the room had been switched off, so that they stood in a rosy glow of amiability. Ascolini became suddenly benign and Valeria took on an aura of prosy tenderness. The talk lost its edge and lapsed into comfortable digression. It was the kind of conspiracy which is practised on the ailing; the vague euphoria which is imposed on those for whom the impact of the world has proven too harsh.

Carlo himself seemed unaware of it, and Landon was quite prepared to admit that his own perception might have been heightened by fatigue and that cautious suspicion which one brings to a new situation. The fact remained that from the last cocktail till the first cup of coffee he could not remember one single significant phrase or gesture. But when the brandy was poured and the servant had retired, Carlo Rienzi took the stage and light came up again to full glare.

'With the permission of our guests I should like to make a family announcement.' Valeria and her father exchanged a swift, questioning glance and Valeria shrugged her ignorance. Carlo went on, calmly: 'I haven't discussed this with either of you, because I felt it was my private decision. Now it is made and I hope you will accept it. I was called to the village today, as you know. The Mayor was murdered by a former village girl, Anna Albertini. It's a long story that I won't bother you with now. The end of it is that Fra Bonifacio asked me to undertake the girl's defence. I agreed to do it.'

Ascolini and Valeria watched him blank-faced. He waited a moment and then turned to Ascolini with the not ungraceful compliment: 'I have served a long apprenticeship under a great master. Now it is time I made my own road. I'm resigning, *maestro,* to wait for my own briefs and plead my own causes.' He fished in his pocket and brought up a small package which he handed to the old man. 'From the student to the master, a gift which says my thanks. Wish me luck, *dottore.'*

Landon felt a singular respect for him at that moment and prayed that they would be kind to his shortcomings. Whatever the basis of their tacit union against him, he had acquitted himself like a man.

Rienzi waited, standing in a pool of silence while his wife and her father sat with heads bowed and eyes downcast to the table. Then he too sat down and Ascolini began to open the package with sedulous deliberation.

Finally the gift was revealed: a small, gold fob watch of exquisite Florentine workmanship, hung on a close-linked chain. Ascolini showed no sign of pleasure or regret, but held the watch in his hands and spelt into Italian the classic Latin of the inscription: 'To my illustrious master, from his grateful pupil, this gift and my first case are dedicated.'

Ascolini let the watch drop from his hands so that it swung like a pendulum from its intricate chain. His eyes were hooded, his voice a dusty contempt: 'Keep it, boy—or send it to the pawnbroker. You may need it sooner than you think.'

He laid the watch carefully on the table, pushed back his chair and walked from the room. Carlo watched him go, then he turned to Valeria and said, quite calmly: 'And you, *cara?* What do you have to say?'

Slowly she raised her head and looked at him with eyes full of condemnation. She said softly: 'I am your wife, Carlo. Wherever you go, I must walk too. But you've done a terrible thing tonight. I'm not sure that I can ever forgive you.'

Then she too walked out, and Landon, Ninette and Rienzi sat facing each other over the wreckage of the dinner party. Carlo cupped his hands round the warm bubble of the brandy goblet and raised it to the level of his lips. He gave them a small, crooked smile and said: 'I'm sorry you both had to see that, but it was the only way I could guarantee my own courage.' Then he added the saddest words they had ever heard: 'Strange, you know . . . all my life I was afraid of being alone, and all my life I was alone and never knew it. Strange!'

'All my life,' said Peter Landon moodily, 'I have dealt with sick minds. I don't think I've ever been so shocked.'

Ninette Lachaise laid a cool hand on his wrist and said calmly: 'That's your mistake, I think, Peter. These people are not sick, only selfish. Their whole life is a battle, one against the other. Each wants too much for too little. They're entrenched like enemies in their own egotism.'

'You're a wise woman, Ninette.'

'Too wise for my own good, perhaps.'

They were sitting in her car, half a mile from the gates of the villa where three separate lights burned yellow in the blank walls and the moonlight shone cold on the spear-points of the cypresses. When Carlo had left the dining-room, Landon had felt suddenly stifled by the atmosphere of hostility, and with unaccustomed humility he had begged Ninette to lend him her company for a while before bedtime. She had agreed calmly and driven him out along the winding road to a spot where the land fell away into a pool of darkness and the hills climbed steeply towards the late, faint stars.

He felt no need of caution with this woman, and she made no drama of this first intimate nocturne. He was thankful to her and he sensed in her quiet talk a return of this gratitude of the lonely. It gave him pleasure to open to her a thought that had puzzled him for a long time. 'You know the rarest thing in the world, Ninette? A man or woman wise enough to look the world in the eye and accept it, good or bad, for what it is at that moment. When people come to me or when I am summoned to them in prison or hospital, it's because I am the last milestone in their long flight from reality. Their flight is a symptom of sickness—and the sickness is the subtlest one of all: fear! They're afraid of loss, of pain, of loneliness, of their own natures, of the obligations which any normal life lays on them.'

'And what's your cure, Peter?'

'Sometimes there is no cure. Sometimes the mechanisms of the mind seize up or refuse to work except in a psychotic groove. For the rest, I try to take them by the hand and lead them back, step by step, to the moment of primal terror. While I am doing it I try to rebuild their courage to face it. If I succeed, they begin to be well again. If I fail . . .' He hesitated a moment and sat staring out over the dark valley where a sparse huddle of lights marked the village of San Stefano '. . . If I fail, then the flight begins once more.'

'And where does it end?'

'In nothingness. In the ultimate negation of being, when the world contracts to the dimensions of a man's own navel, when there is no splendour, no profusion, and even a capacity for love is destroyed. There are times,' he added softly, 'when I wonder if I am not destroying in myself what I'm trying to build in others.'

'No, Peter!' The warmth in her voice surprised him. 'I watched you tonight with Carlo. You were careful of him. You had the grace to be gentle. So long as you keep that, you needn't be afraid.'

'But how do you renew in yourself what you spend on others?'

'If I could be sure of the answer to that,' said Ninette softly, 'I would feel safer than I do now. But I think—no, I believe—that the spending is the growing too, that the flowers fall to make the fruit grow, and that this is the way it was intended to be from the beginning.' She laughed lightly and withdrew her hand. 'It's late and I'm getting sentimental. Go to bed, Peter. You're a disturbing man.'

'May I see you again?'

'Any time. You'll find me in the phone book.'

'I think I may leave the villa tomorrow.'

'Where will you go?'

'If it weren't for Carlo I'd go back to Rome. But I've promised to help him with his case and I can't retract now. I'll probably get myself a room in Siena.'

'I'm glad of that,' said Ninette Lachaise simply. 'It gives me a little hope, too.'

She turned and kissed him lightly on the lips and when he held her to him she pushed him away gently. 'Go home, Peter. Golden dreams.'

He stood watching a long time as her rickety car clattered down the hillside; then he turned away and trudged back to the iron gates of the villa, where a sleepy gate-keeper bade him a truculent goodnight.

He slept badly that night and woke, stale and sour, to raw summer in Tuscany. A shave and a bath refreshed him, but he could not shake off the burden of being a guest in a hostile house. He wished fervently that he had not obliged himself either to Ascolini or Rienzi; but the damage was done and he had at least the comfort of a partial retreat. He packed his bags for a swift departure after breakfast and then walked out to take the early morning air on the terrace.

To his surprise he found Valeria Rienzi there before him. There was more than a hint of embarrassment in her greeting. 'You're up early, Peter.'

'I had a restless night. And it is a beautiful morning.'

She made a rueful mouth and said quietly: 'I'm glad to find you here. I want to apologize for last night. We behaved very badly.'

He was in no mood for a fencing match, so he shrugged and said boldly: 'I don't need an apology. This is your house. You're free to behave in it any way you want. But I think Carlo deserved better.'

'I know that.' She accepted the reproof without protest. 'I hurt him very badly. I've told him I'm sorry.'

'Then there's nothing more to be said. The rest is private to you both.'

'You're very angry, aren't you?' Her hand imprisoned his against the stone balustrade and she turned on him the charm of a very penitent smile. 'I don't blame you. But Carlo took me by surprise. I'm sorry that you had to be involved.'

'I'm not involved and I'm not angry. Not now. But I think it's better that I leave after breakfast.'

She made no attempt to dissuade him but nodded assent. 'Carlo told me. I can understand how you feel. He told me, too, that you had promised to stay a few days in Siena. I'm grateful for that. He needs a friend just now.'

'I think he needs his wife more.'

She flushed at the reproach and turned away, covering her face with her hands. Landon waited, half guilty, half glad, staring over the cypresses to the distant crags of Amiata. In a little while she was composed again, but there was a winter in her voice and her look was sombre when she turned to him. 'Perhaps I deserved that. Perhaps, for Carlo's sake, you have the right to say it. But now will you do me a favour?'

'What sort of favour?'

'Walk with me in the garden. Talk with me a while.'

'Of course.'

'Thank you.'

She took his hand and led him down the broad stone steps that gave on to the garden walks. By the classic contrivance of the old gardeners they followed the contour of the land, winding imperceptibly downwards through ranks of pines, rose arbours, banks of flowering shrubs and pergolas trailing the purple blossom of wistaria. Sometimes the house was hidden, sometimes the walk was screened, as if for the privacy of old lovers, but always the valley was in view. There was no sound but the buzzing of insects, the occasional chitter of a bird and the brisk rustle of a lizard from the leaves to a warm rock.

'Sometimes at night,' said Valeria, 'we hear nightingales in the garden. Father and I come out very softly and listen. First one starts, then another, until the whole valley seems full of singing. It is so very beautiful.'

'Lonely too, sometimes.'

'Lonely?' She looked up at him in mild surprise.

'For the one who sits inside playing Chopin in the dark.'

'Carlo?'

'Who else?'

'You don't understand, do you?'

'I'd like to, but I don't have to. After all, it's not my affair.'

'Carlo has made it so. And I'd like to explain myself.'

'Listen to me, Valeria!' He stopped pacing and faced her under the branch of a grey fig tree where a robin surveyed them with a beady, critical eye. 'Understand who I am and what I am. I'm a healer of sick minds. I spend the best part of my life listening to other people's troubles and getting paid for it. If I extend myself outside the consulting-room I give myself no chance at all of a normal life. I'm often touched by people's misfortunes, but I can't be obliged because I have so little to give. By the same token, you owe me no explanation, even if you choose to do hand-springs on the roof of the Duomo. Now, if that's understood, I'll listen. If I can help, I will. After that–*basta!* Enough for me, enough for you, too.'

'I wish I had half your detachment.' Landon was startled by the bitterness of her tone. 'But you're right. There are no claims on you. I talk; you listen; you go away. *Basta!* But you're not half so cold as you want others to believe.' She took his hand again and made him fall into step beside her while the robin flirted cheekily along the fringe of their progress. He found himself admiring the assurance with which she entered on subjects and issues that earned her no credit at all. She did not minimize or attempt to make a drama. There was an essential simplicity in her which was damnably disconcerting. She said first of all: 'I know, Peter, that you find something unnatural in my relation with my father. It colours what you think about my marriage with Carlo.'

'Let's settle on another word–"unusual"–and start from there.'

'Very well–"unusual". You're more courteous than some of my friends.'

'It's the way of the world. People gossip. They love the smell of scandal.' It was a banality, but she thought on it gravely for a few moments, then asked him: 'Do you find it scandalous, Peter?'

He smiled and shook his head. 'I'm a doctor, not a censor of morals. I take the clinical view. Find out all the facts before you make a diagnosis.'

'Then here is the first fact, Peter. For a long time I lived only in one world and I found it very satisfying. I had no mother, but a father who loved me tenderly and who opened the world to me door by door. Each new revelation was a kind of wonder. He denied me nothing, yet somehow managed to teach me the disciplines of enjoyment. He did what most fathers cannot do–taught me to understand what it means to be a woman. He answered every question I ever asked and I never found him out in a lie. Was it unnatural that I should love him and be glad always to have him near me?'

'No, not unnatural, but perhaps unfortunate.'

'Why do you say that?' For the first time he caught an edge of anxiety in her voice.

'Because, generally, it is the shortcoming of parents which forces a child to find wholeness elsewhere–in a wider world, with other people, with other kinds of love. It is not your relationship which is unnatural, only that you should find it complete and sufficient. Your father's a very remarkable man, but he's not all men nor all the world.'

'That's what I found out,' said Valeria Rienzi quietly. 'Does that surprise you?'

'A little.'

'I told you I had never found him out in a lie. Until recently that was true. It dawned on me quite slowly. Always he had told me that all his care and counsel was directed to my well-being. Instead I found that my well-being was a fund set for himself. I was a capital he had created to replenish the youth he had lost.' Her face clouded and she stumbled, shamefaced, to the conclusion. 'He wants me to be all the things I can't be—wife, mistress, son . . . and a mirror image of Alberto Ascolini!'

'And what do you want to be, Valeria?'

'A woman! My own woman.'

'Not Carlo's?'

'Anybody's who can give me the identity my father has taken from me!'

'Can't Carlo do that?'

For the first time he heard her laugh; but there was no humour in it, only an unhappy irony. 'You feel so much for Carlo, don't you, Peter? He's a boy! A passionate boy! And when you've lived with a man all your life, it isn't half enough!'

'He looked very much like a man last night,' said Peter Landon flatly.

'You didn't go to bed with him,' said Valeria Rienzi. He was still digesting that sour little morsel when she offered him another one. 'What's your prescription, Doctor, when a girl wants to be kissed and tumbled in the hay, and all she's offered are chocolates for breakfast!'

Then, because he was challenged in his own manhood, because he was sick of playing the wise owl while others played *'baciami'* in the bushes, he took her in his arms and kissed her and tasted the sweetness of her mouth mixed with the salt tang of blood.

'Charming!' said Doctor Ascolini with dry good humour. 'Quite, quite charming—if a trifle indiscreet.' Landon broke away roughly and saw the old man standing in the middle of the path, his pink face bright with merriment. 'I must disapprove on principle, but in the circumstances I find it a commendable diversion for both of you.'

'Oh—go to hell!'

Sick with anger and humiliation, Landon pushed past Ascolini and hurried away. The rich actor's laugh followed him like the laughter of a child delighted with the antics of a painted clown.

3

When Landon reached the terrace, breakfast was already laid and Carlo Rienzi was working through coffee and a stack of morning newspapers. He greeted Landon with grave courtesy, passed him a cup of coffee and a dish of warm country bread, then told him calmly: 'I saw what happened, Peter. It was almost as if it were contrived that I should.' He pointed down into the garden where Ascolini and his daughter were clearly visible through a gap in the shrubbery. 'You understand now, perhaps, what it is that I have to fight.'

Landon felt himself blushing under a new humiliation. He said awkwardly: 'It was my fault. I'm sorry it happened.'

Rienzi waved aside the apology. 'Why blame yourself? It's happened before. It will happen again.'

Unreasonably, Landon was angry with him. 'Then why are you so damned complacent about it? Why don't you punch me on the nose? And if my wife were unfaithful I'd break her neck, or walk out!'

'But she is not your wife, Peter,' said Rienzi in a flat voice. 'She is mine—and I am half responsible for what she is. You've known her for a few days. I've lived with her for years. You judge her as you would judge any other wife who wants to play hot cockles in the summertime. But in her this is a kind of childish wilfulness in which her father has indulged her for his own purposes. She is never wilful with him, you see, although she often resents it. The pattern of order and authority has been set, as it would have been set with us in a normal marriage. Outside the pattern Valeria recognizes no claim, no obligation. The world and all the creatures thereof were made for the sole use and benefit of the Ascolini family.'

'And do you think you can break the pattern and reset it?'

'I know I must try.'

'I wish you luck!'

Rienzi smiled and shook his head. 'Peter, my friend, don't play the cynic with me. I know what you are and how you feel. This is a marriage—not a very satisfactory one, but it's a contract binding until death and I must make it work as best I can. In the beginning I made a bad mistake. I had too much love, too little wisdom. Now I am wiser and there is, I think, still enough love. You must not despise me because I try to do a good thing. You must not despise Valeria because she has never been taught what is good.'

The dignity of the man, the pathos of his situation, shamed Landon more than he cared to admit, but there was still a warning to be given: 'It takes two to keep a contract, Carlo. You may do all that you hope, and more—and you can still fail with Valeria. You should at least be prepared.'

He shrugged and said with a kind of sad self-contempt: 'What have I to lose, Peter?'

'Hope.'

For a long moment Rienzi stared at him, then nodded a bleak assent. 'This is the last terror, Peter. You must not ask me to face it yet. Start your breakfast and let's see what the press has to say about our client.'

The affair at San Stefano had made headlines in every morning paper. Their accounts were lurid, full of gory rhetoric and sadistic detail. The photographs ran the gamut of vulgarity, from a grisly shot of the dead man lying in state in the parlour to a close-up of Anna Albertini being bundled into a police car with her skirt rucked up to her thigh. But, out of the welter of ill-chosen words, the lines of the story emerged clearly enough.

The dead man was Gianbattista Belloni, formerly a peasant farmer, then a Partisan leader and later Mayor of San Stefano and a landowner of ample means. After the war he had been decorated with a gold medal and a citation from the President for distinguished military service. He was married, with two grown sons. His wife's name was Maria. All local testimony confirmed him as a man of good character, generous habits and modest eminence. His murder had raised the village to passionate resentment.

Anna Albertini—named variously in the press as 'the young assassin', 'the beautiful but ensanguined murderer', 'the killer of Satanic charm'—was born Anna Moschetti, daughter of a conscripted soldier killed in the Libyan campaign and a mother executed by the Partisans for collaboration with the Germans. She was twenty-four years of age and had lived away from San

Stefano for sixteen years. At twenty she had married a young Florentine named Luigi Albertini who worked as night-watchman in a textile factory.

On the day of the murder, she had made breakfast for her husband, then, when he was asleep, had taken his gun and left the house. She had caught an early train which arrived in Siena just before midday. She had hailed a taxi at the station and driven to San Stefano to murder Belloni. The motive for her crime was manifest: vendetta–reprisal for her mother's death on the man who had presided at the drumhead court.

The newspapers made much of this motive. Most of them discussed it with singular sobriety and one leading journal spread itself in an editorial condemning in the strongest terms 'any revival of this ancient and malevolent practice' and demanding 'the utmost vigilance on the part of the police and the judiciary lest any false benignity should seem to justify the barbarity of the blood-feud which has disfigured so many pages of our history'.

Which, it seemed to Landon, was fair enough. The *lex talionis* marked rock-bottom in human relations. It was a bloody, mutinous, wasteful cult which had no counterpart even in the jungle. Wherever it was practised, communities lived in daily terror, one step from breakdown and chaos. In this affair he had to admit that his sympathies were all on the side of the angels. And no matter how Carlo Rienzi framed his plea, the angels would give him a rough passage through the court.

In the last journal of all he came on a startling photograph of Anna Albertini: a two-column plate, marred somewhat by hasty etching, but still a portrait of tragic beauty and terrible innocence. There was no malice in the softly curving lips, no hate in the eyes, but almost a touch of wonder at some magnificence invisible to others. If the old moralists spoke truth when they said that the eyes were windows of the soul, then Anna Albertini's soul was a mirror of primitive purity. Carlo Rienzi leaned across the table and tapped the photograph with a coffee spoon.

'That's exactly how she looks, Peter, and you have to tell me what goes on behind that face.'

'I'll need time,' said Landon, in dry, professional fashion, 'time and a certain freedom in consultation. That part's up to you.'

'I'll have to consult with Galuzzi. He's the consultant to the Department of Justice on Mental Health. If he agrees, we won't have too much trouble with the prison authorities. It may take a little time to arrange a meeting with him, but I'll do it as soon as I can. I've arranged a lodging for you in Siena. I'll get in touch with you there.'

'It's an awkward situation for everybody,' said Landon with sour discomfort. 'It's best I leave the villa.'

'You told me you wanted to talk with Ascolini before you did any work with me.'

'I'll dispense myself from the courtesy. I don't think it matters now.'

'Good,' said Carlo briskly. 'Let's get your bags and hit the road.'

The drive into Siena was a short and barren one for both. Carlo was preoccupied and Landon was moody and exacerbated. The splendid countryside slipped by unnoticed and Rienzi soon gave over his half-hearted attempts at diversion. When they arrived, he installed Landon in an astonishing *pensione* with the arms of the Salimbeni over the portal, immense rooms with coffered ceilings and a thirteenth-century fountain playing in the courtyard. As a final gesture he announced that the rent was paid for a week. When Landon blushed at so much generosity, Rienzi laughed. 'Call it a bribe, Peter. I need you here. You've seen the worst of us. Now I'd like to show you the better side. Today you need time to yourself and so do I. I'll pick you up here at nine-thirty tomorrow morning. Stay out of mischief!'

Landon had no heart for mischief just then, but he was glad when Rienzi was gone. He needed time and privacy to shake off the depression which had been laid upon him. The day was still young and he decided to wander round the city. Its lovers had named it long ago 'The Home of Souls'. He hoped it might do something for his own, which presently was in a very sorry state.

In fact, it did nothing at all but make him feel more miserable. There is a disease which afflicts many travellers, an endemic malaise whose symptoms are an acute melancholy, a sense of oppression by what is old and distaste for what is new. The faces one sees take on a sinister character, like the cartoons of da Vinci. The gaudy cavalcade of history becomes a procession of spavined caricatures shambling forward to the tolling of the *miserere* bell. One is conscious of solitude and strangeness. The effort of communication in an alien tongue becomes an intolerable burden. The food presents itself as a garbled mess. One longs for the thinnest wine of one's own country.

There is no remedy for the disease. One tolerates it like a recurrent bout of malaria, and then it goes away, with no perceptible harm to mind or body. The best treatment is to ignore it and keep moving; to go through the motions of interest and activity. A pretty girl is a great help. A half-bottle of brandy is an unreliable substitute.

But Landon had drunk too much brandy the night before and was too jaded to go looking for the fillies in a new town! So, after two hours of footloose wandering, he settled for an indifferent lunch, a siesta and a phone call to Ninette Lachaise. Her reaction was immediate and warm. She would be delighted to see him. They should meet for dinner at the Sordello, a cavernous, lively resort near the Campo, frequented by artists and students from the faculties of the University.

When they met she greeted him affectionately. When they made their entrance into the smoky cellar heads were turned and there was a whistling chorus of approval which made Landon feel a foot taller and singularly grateful to Ninette Lachaise.

For the practised traveller or the practising bachelor there was no time for long overtures in friendship. One either achieved a quick rapport or abandoned the effort. One became jealous of time because so much was dispersed on the mechanics of getting from one place to another. Even a railway ticket was a warrant for the minor death of parting. When one boarded an aircraft one was launched into a suspension which was a troubling image of eternity. So one resented those who demanded proof of identity, elaborate tokens of aptitude for their company. One was impatient of women who doled out their smiles and made a grand opera out of an invitation to dinner. And one sometimes despised oneself for so much need of company on the pilgrim road.

When Landon explained it to Ninette Lachaise she accepted it as a compliment and gave him her own good-humoured version of the theme. 'It's the penalty of freedom, Peter, the tax we pay for being bachelors or artists. When the strolling players come to town, husbands keep a close eye on their wives. When the pedlars come with their trays of novelties, honest merchants tighten their purse-strings and keep their daughters at home. You are still Scaramouche, *chéri*; I am still Pierrette, light in love and ready to seduce their sons to the altar. It is only when we are old and famous that they want to have us to dinner.'

'And yet they need us, Ninette. It's only people like you and I who can show them how to hold up the world by the heels and spit in its eye.'

She laughed happily and bit into an olive. 'Of course they need us, Peter, but not quite as we want to be needed. The walls are bare without a picture or two. It's as fashionable to have an analyst today as it used to be to have a personal confessor. For the rest—' her fine hands embraced the chattering concourse in the cellar–'they would rather we stayed in Bohemia and came out only at carnival time. I'm sure we're happier here, anyway.'

'What happens when we get old?'

She shrugged and pouted like a true Parisienne. 'If we are old and foolish we hit the pavement and the bottle. If we are old and wise we still come back sometimes, ancient masters to receive the homage of youth . . . like that one, for instance.'

She pointed across the room to a shadowy corner where a white-haired man sat with half a dozen students who listened to him with rapt attention. On the hat-stand beside the table were hung three or four of those curious medieval caps whose colour denoted the Faculty of Law. At the same moment the old man turned his head and Landon saw with a shock of surprise that it was Doctor Ascolini. He was too far away, too absorbed in his séance, to notice Landon, but Landon felt a faint flush of embarrassment mount to his cheeks. Ninette quizzed him, smiling: 'You haven't told me what happened this morning, Peter. Do you want to talk about it?'

He did. He talked through the soup and the *pasta*. He talked through one bottle of wine and ordered another, while Ascolini sat, eloquent and honoured, among his student entourage, while Ninette probed with an occasional question towards the core of the provincial drama. When he had finished, she laid one slim hand over his and asked gently: 'Do you want to know what I think, Peter?'

'I do.'

'Then I think Valeria is more than half in love with you. Carlo leans on you too much for his own good, and Ascolini respects you more than you know.' Before he had time to challenge her, she went on: 'I think, too, that you are more deeply touched by all this than you admit. You like to play the misanthrope, but the mask slips off because it doesn't fit you very well. Underneath, you are a soft man, too easily hurt by malice and mistrust. You judge these people too curtly. You make all your pictures black and white, with no room for half-tones.'

'You mean Ascolini?'

'All of them, but Ascolini first, if you want.'

A burst of laughter went up from the old man's table and Landon saw him tapping the shoulder of the youth who had caused it. He saw him signal the waiter for another bottle of wine and then bend attentively to the question of another student. Ninette Lachaise asked another question: 'How do you read that, Peter? What brings him here?'

'You said it yourself. The old master receives the homage of youth!'

'Is that all, *chéri*? No kindness? No fear? No loneliness?'

Landon surrendered ruefully. 'All right, Ninette. You win. So the devil has a gentle heart–but not for his own.'

'Has he shown you his heart, Peter? Or have you read it only through someone else's eyes?'

The reproof was so gentle that he had perforce to accept it. He grinned at her and said: 'You're the artist. Your eyes are sharper than mine. Maybe you should read him for me.'

'I know him, Peter,' she said calmly. 'I have known him for a long time. He buys my pictures and he comes often to look at what I'm doing, to drink coffee and talk.'

For no good reason, Landon felt a pang of jealousy that this malign old mountebank should enjoy the privacy of Ninette's house. But Siena was a small town and he had fewer rights in the girl than Ascolini. He shrugged and said: 'I know he has a lot of charm.'

Ninette Lachaise refilled his glass and handed it to him with a laugh. 'Drink your wine, *chéri*. It is you who will be seeing me home, not the venerable doctor. But seriously, there is a tragedy in his life. He has a daughter who disappoints him and a son-in-law who resents him.'

Now it was Landon's turn to laugh. 'Valeria disappoints him? What's he got to grumble about? He made her in his own image.'

'Self-portraits are not always the best art, Peter.' Her lovely hands reached out and turned his face towards her. Her eyes challenged him, half in jest, half in earnest. 'We all love ourselves, Peter, but we are not always happy with what we see in the mirror. Are you?'

He capitulated as gracefully as he could. He took her hands and kissed them, and said lightly: 'You win, Ninette. You're a better advocate than Ascolini. I'll reserve judgment.'

'Would you do me a favour?'

'Name it.'

'Let me ask Ascolini to our table for a drink.'

To refuse would have been a grossness. Besides, he wanted to see more of this woman and a few minutes of embarrassment were a modest price for the privilege. She gave him a swift, grateful smile and walked across the room to another chorus of whistles and applause. Ascolini greeted her with lavish courtesy and, after a few moments of talk, walked back with her to Landon's table. He held out his hand and said, with the old wilful irony: 'You're keeping better company, my friend. I'm glad to see it.'

'We have much in common,' said Ninette Lachaise.

'You're a fortunate fellow, Landon. If I were twenty years younger, I should take her away from you.' He sighed theatrically and settled into his chair. 'Ah youth! Youth! A fugal time! We prize it only when we have lost it. Every one of these boys wants to be as wise as I am. How can I tell them that all I want is to be as lusty as they?'

Landon poured wine for him and drank the toast he made to Ninette. They talked desultorily for a few moments and then abruptly Ascolini said: 'I seldom make apologies, Landon, but I owe you this one. I'm sorry for what happened in my house.'

'It's forgotten. I'd like you to forget it, too.'

Ascolini frowned and shook his white mane. 'You must not promise too much, my friend, even in courtesy. It is not possible to forget, only to forgive—and that is difficult enough, God knows.' As curtly as he had raised the subject, he dropped it and turned to another. 'You've been with Carlo today, Landon?'

'I have.'

'You're embroiled in the affair then?'

'Hardly embroiled.' Landon's tone was testy. 'I've offered Carlo my professional advice on the side of the defence.'

'Carlo is fortunate in his friends,' said Ascolini drily.

'More fortunate than in his family, perhaps!'

Before the old man had time to answer, Ninette Lachaise moved into the argument. 'You are both my friends. I will not have you quarrel in my company. You, Peter, have too quick a tongue. And you, *dottore*'–she laid a restraining hand on his sleeve–'why do you make yourself a monster with horns and tail and fire coming out of your ears? You have the same loyalties as Peter, though you will not admit them.'

For Landon it was a reminder to better manners from someone whose respect he wanted. He tried awkwardly to repair the breach. 'Please, Doctor! I'm a stranger caught up in a family affair against his will. I'm irritable and confused. Carlo gave me his confidence in the first instance, so, naturally, I'm prejudiced in his favour. But really none of it is my concern. Only a fool wants to arbitrate a domestic dispute.'

The old man surveyed him with a bright, ironic eye. 'Unfortunately, Landon, it is not arbitration we need, but forgiveness of our sins and a grace of amendment. I am too old and too proud to ask for it, Carlo is too young to admit the need. And Valeria . . .' He broke off to sip his wine and consider how he should express the thought. 'I have opened the world to her–and robbed her of the innocence to understand it. You're the wise woman, Ninette; how do you prescribe for a sickness like ours?'

'You may not buy any more pictures if I tell you.'

'On the contrary, I may surprise you and buy them all.'

'Then, *dottore mio*, here is my prescription. Unless you want to end by killing each other, someone has to say the first gentle word. And you are the one who has the least time left.'

For a long moment Ascolini was silent. The fire went out of his eyes, his pink cheeks sagged, and Landon understood for the first time how old he was. Finally, he stood up, took the girl's hand and pressed it to his lips. 'Goodnight, child. Sleep in peace.' To Landon he said formally: 'If you will lunch with me at Luca's tomorrow I should like to talk with you.'

'I'll be there.'

'One o'clock, then. Enjoy yourselves with my blessing.'

They watched him across the room, picking his old man's way between the crowded tables, until the students stood to welcome him back like sons careful of an honoured parent.

Landon felt Ninette's eyes on him, but he had nothing to say and he sat staring down at the checked tablecloth, abashed and faintly ashamed. Finally, she said, with a touch of tenderness: 'There are other places, other people, Peter. Let's go and find them.'

There were no whistles as they walked out. Even the Sordello had its private chivalries, but Landon could not say whether it was the aegis of Ascolini that protected them or whether even then he had the look of a man fallen in love–a noble occasion in Tuscany, only a trifle less solemn than a funeral or the coronation of a Pope.

It was three in the morning when he walked Ninette home from the last place and the last people. In the shadow of her doorway, they kissed and clung together, drowsy and passionate, until she pushed him away and whispered: 'Don't rush me, Peter. Promise me you won't rush me. We're not children and we know where this road goes.'

'I want it to go a long way.'

'I, too. But I need time to think.'

'May I come tomorrow?'

'Tomorrow–any day!'

'You may get sick of me and turn me out.'

'And then I'll curse myself and call you back. Now go home, *chéri*, please!'

The old city lay magical under a summer moon, her columns silver, her towers serene, her fountains full of faint stars. Her bells were silent, but her squares were murmurous with ancient friendly ghosts. One of them asked him a question which he thought to have heard before: 'What happens, my friend, when the world blows up in your face?'

In a third-floor room near the Porta Tufi, Valeria Rienzi lay awake and watched the moon-shadows lengthen over the rooftops. Beside her in the tumbled bed, Basilio Lazzaro slept and snored, his heavy, handsome face slack with satisfaction. Even in repose, there was a gross, animal vitality about him: in the broad barrel-chest, tufted with swart hairs, in the flat belly and the thick, muscly shoulders. He was like a stud beast, bred for coupling, proud of his potency, graceless but dominant in the act of union.

Yet even while she despised him she could not regret him. His violence bruised her, his egotism angered her, yet he never failed to bring her to a kind of fulfilment. He did not ask her to be other than she was, an attractive woman, apt for mating, happy to play lovers' games and not ask too many questions about love. There was a panic urgency in his wooing that brought her swiftly to excitement. He was content with submission but delighted with co-operation.

He did not demand, like Carlo, that she play the seducer or, like her father, that she should relive an episode in prurient fiction. He was simple as the animal he resembled; and his simplicity was a guarantee of her freedom. She could go or stay. If she stayed, there was a price. If she went, there were twenty other women to be called with a snap of his stubby fingers. He treated her like a whore and made her feel like one, but at least she was not involved beyond the night's contract.

He was purge for her confusions, a partner and a symbol of her rebellion. Yet he would never be permanent or sufficient to her. Which brought her by a round turn face to face with the answered question: what else was left when the opera was over?

Her father had one answer: convenient marriage and a clutch of children with whom she could decline gracefully into the middle years. But his answer was coloured by an old man's demand for possession and continuity. When the children came, he would bind them to him with affection and hold them over her like a reproach.

Carlo? His answer was different again. Marriage was a contract, love a mutual bargain. He held up his love like a posy of flowers and demanded to be kissed for the offering. If he brought off a victory in this case or another he would become more arrogant, but no less demanding to lay it at her feet as the price of love. In a sense his exaction was more brutal than Lazzaro's, who gave and took and went away. Carlo loved himself in her, as a child loves itself in a mother, and, self-centred as a child, demanded a gratuitous gift of affection.

He was full of uncertainty, but he could not tolerate uncertainty in her. He had submitted, in his own fashion, to Ascolini's tyranny, but he refused to understand how much more subject she herself had become. He demanded allegiance to his own rebellion, but could never understand that hers must be made elsewhere and in subtler fashion. He, too, wanted children—but as a proof and not as a fruit of loving.

But these were not the only answers, and she knew it. She was wilful and demanded to be tamed, passionate and in need of satisfaction. There were fears buried deep inside her that she wanted shared, by someone cool and wise but unpaternal. There were shames to be talked out and memories to be accepted without reproach; so that when the time came to give, she could give gratefully and freely—whether as wife or mistress made no matter.

As the moon waned and the pale shadows climbed from floor to ceiling, she thought of Peter Landon and the brief, passionate interlude with him in the garden. Given time and the occasion, she could draw him to her again, unless—and the thought gave her a sharp pang of jealousy—unless Ninette Lachaise were to take him first.

Peter Landon was not the only subject of contention between herself and this interloper from over the border. She had watched for a long time the growth of Ascolini's affection for her, sensed his unspoken regrets that his daughter could not match the footloose bohemian, painting in her garret. Even Lazzaro talked of her with a kind of regret. And tonight, with a perverse enjoyment, she had made him talk again.

She had flattered him and tickled his sensuality, until in the end he had revealed with a base man's vanity the intimate details of his affair with Ninette Lachaise. It was a shameful victory at best, but a wise Valeria might well turn it into a nobler one. Love was a war in which the spoils were to the subtle and the knowing—and a man once kissed was already half disarmed.

Spilt milk could not be poured back into the pitcher, lost innocence could never be restored. But Landon was no innocent either and perhaps . . . perhaps . . . The cold grey of the false dawn was creeping into the eastern sky as she dressed hurriedly and crept down the stairs to where her car was parked in the alley. Basilio Lazzaro would wake and find her gone—and would smile with relief at having found a woman who knew the rules of the game.

Punctually at nine-thirty the next morning, Carlo Rienzi arrived at the *pensione* to read Landon the report of the first day's activity. The opening summary of it was unpromising. Anna Albertini had been charged with premeditated murder and lodged in the women's house of correction at San Gimignano. Carlo had interviewed her and found her quite unco-operative. The thing was done. She was content. She did not want to talk about it any more. Her husband was to be produced as a witness for the prosecution and no one in San Stefano was prepared to open his mouth except in support of police evidence. Fra Bonifacio's expectations had exceeded his purse and Rienzi would have to pay his colleagues' expenses from his own pocket.

There was one entry on the credit side. Professor Galuzzi would be happy to welcome his distinguished colleague from London and to open informal discussions on the psychiatric aspects of the case. Carlo and Landon were bidden to coffee with him at his rooms in the University.

Landon warmed to him from the first moment of meeting. He was a lean, tall fellow in his late forties with grey hair, a grey goatee, gold pince-nez and a faintly pedantic address. But the pince-nez concealed a shrewd, twinkling eye, and the pedantry masked a quick wit and a ready sympathy. Landon had the feeling that he might be a formidable and expert fellow in court. His private summation was brisk but genial: 'A formula exists under which Mr Landon might be called in an Italian court as an expert witness for the defence. For my part–and please don't mistake my intentions–I would advise against it. Local sympathies, even among the judiciary, might run against a foreign expert. On the other hand, I should be happy to have my distinguished colleague work with me as a clinical observer on the case.' He bent sedulously over his coffee. 'Of course if any distinguished colleague chose to advise defence privately, that would be his own affair.'

'You go further than I had hoped, Professor,' said Rienzi cautiously.

'But you don't understand why?' Galuzzi surveyed him with a bright, birdlike eye. 'Is that it? I think perhaps Mr Landon will understand me better than you do. We are both medical men. Our prime concern is to care for the health of the human mind and, when we meet with the law, to mitigate the consequences of any mental infirmity that may exist. Don't misunderstand me!' He held up a warning hand. 'When I am called to the witness stand, I must answer fully and truthfully any questions which are asked on the subject of my clinical knowledge. I'm not a judge. I cannot determine what use the court may make of my testimony. If you felt it necessary to call other experts to challenge my diagnosis, they would of course be given full facilities to examine the accused.'

'It's a fair offer, Carlo,' said Landon warmly. 'I'm flattered by it. I think you should be grateful. Tell me, Professor, have you seen Anna Albertini yet?'

'Not yet. I make my first visit to her this afternoon. For that I should like to be alone. Afterwards it will be easier to introduce you as a visiting observer. However, I do have one item of interest. As you know, every new prisoner is submitted to a medical examination by the prison doctor. The purpose of the examination is to detect the presence of communicable disease which may infect other inmates. Anna Albertini has been given a clean bill of health. It is also noted in the record that she is *virgo intacta*.'

Rienzi gaped at him. 'But she's been married four years.'

'Interesting, isn't it?' Galuzzi's goatee bobbed up and down as he laughed. 'Something for you, also, to sleep on, Mr Landon! And there is another thing. No sign of depression or mania. No violence, no hysteria. My colleague at the prison describes the accused as calm, good-humoured and apparently content. But we shall see. . . .' He hesitated a moment and then asked: 'Would you do me a favour, Mr Landon?'

'Of course.,

'Your work is not unknown here, and you speak excellent Italian. I should like to improve our acquaintance–and perhaps, if it is not too much of an imposition, have you lecture to some of my senior students.'

'I'd be delighted. You can contact me at any time at the Pensione della Fontana.'

'I'll be in touch with you.' He scribbled the address on a desk pad, then stood up. 'And now, if you'll excuse me, gentlemen, I have a lecture in five minutes.'

As they made their tortuous way back to the centre of the city, Carlo was voluble in his satisfaction with the meeting, but Landon added a rider or two of caution. 'Don't lean too much on this kind of thing. Carlo. I like

Galuzzi. He's a pleasant fellow, freer than most with the courtesy of the trade. But the courtesy doesn't cost him anything—and in the witness box he'll stand up like a rock, because his professional reputation is at stake.'

'I keep forgetting,' said Rienzi wryly, 'that you must have been through this kind of thing many times. Tell me one thing: is it likely that your diagnosis of a case would vary much from Galuzzi's?'

'I doubt it. There might be some divergence of opinion on a complex disorder. There might be a greater divergence on the question of treatment. But it seems to me you're begging the question. You're assuming that all abnormal conduct is a symptom of mental illness. There are some extreme practitioners who hold that view. I don't. I'm sure Galuzzi doesn't, either. If your client is insane, we'll both agree on the point—and your case will be over in twenty minutes. If she's not, then you're back to mitigatory circumstances.'

'That's what I'm working on now. But so far I've met only closed doors.'

'There's one that might open.'

'What's that?'

'Anna Albertini's husband.'

'He's refused to talk to anyone but the police, and he's already gone back to Florence.'

'Take a drive up there and ask him why his wife's still virgin after four years of marriage.'

'My God!' said Rienzi softly. 'My God, it might just work!'

'It's always a reasonable bet. Challenge a man in his virility and he's only too ready to talk. Whether he gives you the truth is, of course, another matter.'

'If we knew what inhibited the marriage we would have some leading questions to ask Anna herself. And from there . . .'

'From there,' said Landon with a grin, 'you cook your own dinner, Carlo. I can help you stir the soup, but in the end you're the fellow who has to eat it. And talking of eating, Ascolini's asked me to lunch with him today. I met him last night with Ninette Lachaise.'

'The old, old charm!' said Rienzi resentfully. 'Honey for the flies. If you were a woman, he'd have you in bed before sunset. Don't sell me out, Peter!'

He said it with a smile, but Landon was instantly and bitterly angry. 'To hell with you, Carlo! If that's the way you read a simple politeness, to hell with you!'

Ignoring Rienzi's protest, he turned and hurried away, plunging into a tangle of alleys, stumbling over refuse and runnels of filthy water until he emerged, breathless and furious, into the blinding sunlight of the Campo. When he looked at his watch it was only midday, so he turned into a bar, drank two brandies and smoked half a dozen tasteless cigarettes until it was time for lunch with Alberto Ascolini.

He found the old man in the favoured corner of Luca's, enthroned in a red-plush chair at the feet of a Renaissance nude. A brace of waiters hovered at his elbow, attentive and obsequious, while Ascolini sipped yellow vermouth and made notes in a pocket-book covered with purple morocco. Landon could not repress a smile at the care with which he stage-managed every occasion. Peasant he might be, but he had the knack of imposing distinction even on the baroque spendour of Luca's, which is part restaurant, part club and part monument to the vanished pomps of the nineteeth century.

He greeted Landon absently, had an aperitif in his hand in ninety seconds, and then asked him bluntly: 'Have you been reading the papers, Landon?'

'I have.'

'What do you make of the affair?'

'Barring insanity, I can't imagine a simpler case for the prosecution.'

'And the defence?'

'Has a hopeless task. I've said as much to Carlo.'

'Does he agree?'

'Not altogether.'

'He must have other information, then.'

'It would seem so.'

He let it rest there and smiled—a canny old swordsman disengaging after the first perfunctory passes. 'Let's call a truce, Landon. I have, believe me, no wish to embarrass you. And I would like you to trust me a little. It may be hard for you to understand, but I do have a very real interest in Carlo's welfare.'

Landon digested that for a moment and then said, carefully: 'It might help us both if you would explain that interest.'

Ascolini leaned back in his chair, spreading his soft hands and joining them, fingertip to fingertip, in an episcopal gesture. His eyes filmed over like those of a dozing bird and his voice took on a dusty, didactic quality.

'As one of your English writers has said, Landon, youth is wasted on the young. When one is old, one resents the waste. One also has the means to indulge the resentment, as I have done in Carlo's case. This is the problem of age, my friend—and you will face it sooner than you imagine: the catalogue of available pleasures contracts so that one clings even to one's baseness for want of more robust diversion. I am not proud of this. Neither can I say that I am sorry for it. I explain it to you as an experience. I am a jealous man, my friend: jealous of what I have, jealous of what I have lost, jealous of the extravagance with which the young indulge their conscience or their illusions. Take Carlo, for instance. In his marriage he plays the patient gentleman. That is a folly with all women—most foolish with a woman like Valeria. With me he plays the respectful pupil, the dutiful son-in-law. He refuses to see that I am an old hard-head, who needs his nose rubbed in the dust. The old bulls, Landon! They stand, diminished but defiant, waiting for the one last fight which will ennoble them even while it destroys them and despising the uncertain youngsters who refuse the combat. Does this make any sense to you? You of all people should understand.'

'I do understand,' Landon told him quietly. 'I'm grateful that you've explained it. But there's something you should understand, too. Carlo has begun his fight. What he has done so far is his challenge to you. You must not despise him because he fights in another fashion than yours.'

'Despise him?' The old man was suddenly vehement. 'For the first time I begin to respect him!'

'Then why humiliate him as you did when he offered you a gift and his thanks?'

Ascolini gave him a wintry smile and shook his head. 'You too are still young, my dear Landon. When the old bulls fight they use all the dirty tricks.' He shrugged off the argument as if he had no further interest in it. 'Now let me order you dinner and a wine to put blood in your veins. You'll need it with a woman like Ninette Lachaise.'

The waiters came scurrying at his signal and they were served like princes of a nobler age. As they ate, the old man talked, quietly and persuasively, of his peasant boyhood in the Val d'Orcia, of his education at the hands of the parish priest, his student days at the University of Siena, his struggle to find a foot-hold in Rome, his first successes, his eclipse under the Fascist régime, his rise to new eminence after the war.

The narrative was bold and vivid, touched sometimes with sardonic humour, sometimes with poignant regret for the simplicities of a lost time. He talked, without rancour, of the failure of his marriage, of his desire for a son, and of his hopes for the daughter who had arrived instead.

By the time they reached the fruit and the cheese, Landon had the picture of a man who had attained greatly but who had lost, somewhere along the road, the key to happiness. Of himself, Ascolini said whimsically: 'I have eaten the apples of Sodom, my friend, but I cannot regret them too much because I can still remember the taste of good fruit and of some noble wines.' Of Valeria he said bleakly: 'I tried to arm her with knowledge against the day when love might fail her. I have understood too late that it was my love which failed her first. I wanted to possess in her what her mother had failed to give me. What I found, finally, was a replica of myself. But . . .' He shrugged and swept away regret with the crumbs on the tablecloth. 'This is life. One must wear it with good grace or walk out of it with dignity. I have elected to wear it.'

To which Landon had nothing to say. He could neither comfort the man nor judge him. So he asked a question: 'Do you think Carlo can ever re-establish himself with Valeria? Will she ever content herself with him?'

'I don't know. As it lies now, Carlo would seem to be the lover, she the one who accepts love but sets no value on it. It may be that, if the love were withdrawn, she might be afraid and reach out to hold it. If not–*chi sa?* There are women who play games with their hearts and seem to live satisfied.'

'Do you care which way it goes?'

He fixed Landon with a cold, lawyer's eye and said, emphatically: 'I care greatly, though not, perhaps, for the reason you think. I want this marriage to last–and last as happily as possible, not for Carlo's sake, not for Valeria's, but because I want a grandchild–some promise, at least, of continuity.' Before Landon had time to comment, he hurried on. 'That is why I have asked you here today. I want Carlo to know that he has my support in this case and in his relations with Valeria.'

Landon stared at him in blank disbelief. Everything that had happened in the last forty-eight hours gave the lie to what the old man was saying. As if aware of Landon's thought, Ascolini brought out from his pocket a buff-coloured envelope and pushed it across the table. 'I'd like you to see that Carlo gets this. It contains a cheque for a million lire and some notes which I have made on the case. I'd like you to explain to Carlo my attitude and urge him to accept the money and the advice to further his client's cause. Will you do it?'

'No!'

'You don't believe me? Is that it?'

'I think you're making a mistake.'

'Why?'

'First, I don't believe Carlo will accept. Second, even if he did accept, you would put him in your debt again. His triumph–if any–would still belong partially to you.'

'You think that's what I want?'

'No. But on your own confession you would use it. The old bulls—remember?'

For a long while Ascolini sat silent, staring down at the table, drawing meaningless patterns with a fork on the white cloth. Then he picked up the envelope, put it back in his pocket and said quietly: 'Perhaps you're right, Landon. You have no good reason to trust me, and I have no right to salve my vanity by making you a messenger. Will you do me at least one favour?'

'If I can, certainly.'

'Tell Carlo what I have said, what I have offered.'

'You see him every day. Why not tell him yourself?'

'I hope that you may explain me better than I can explain myself.'

'I'll try, but I can't guarantee how he will judge.'

'Of course not. Who can guarantee that even the judgment he makes on himself is not a lie to make life bearable?' He gave Landon a cool, ironic smile. 'You, for example, Landon, you can take a man's mind to pieces and put it together again like a watch. Have you explained to yourself why you are so deeply committed to our affairs?'

It was so neatly done that Landon had to laugh at the sheer virtuosity of the man. Besides, it was a fair question and it was time he gave it a fair answer. He thought about it for a moment and then said, soberly: 'Sympathy is part of it. I like Carlo and I think he deserves better. Ambition is part of it, too. You know that I've been looking for a theme of original research to herald my return to London. This case might provide me one. More than that,'—he spread his hands palms downward on the tablecloth and studied them intently for a few moments—'in a sense, I too am in crisis—a crisis which I think you will understand. I have been too long solitary and self-sufficient. My involvement is, I believe, part of a subconscious drive to community and competition.'

Ascolini nodded approval. 'I appreciate your frankness, Landon. Let me ask you a little more. How do you regard me?'

'With singular respect,' said Landon.

'Thank you. I believe you mean it.' He waited for a fraction of a second and then probed more shrewdly. 'How do you regard Valeria?'

Again Landon felt the swift rise of anger but he fought it down and said in a flat voice: 'She's an attractive woman and she has her own problems.'

'Do you think you can solve them?'

'No.'

'Do you think she may create problems for you?'

'Any woman can create problems for any man.'

Landon grinned crookedly into his wine-glass. Ascolini frowned and resumed his tracing on the tablecloth. After a few moments he looked up. 'Strangely enough, Landon, at another time I should not have disapproved of an association between you and Valeria. I think you are the kind of man she needs. But now, for all the reasons that I have explained to you, I would set my face against it.'

'I, too,' said Landon lightly. 'I have hopes elsewhere.'

The old man brightened immediately. 'Ninette Lachaise?'

'Yes.'

'I'm glad to hear it,' said Ascolini with grave satisfaction. 'I have a great affection for Ninette. I should give much to see her happy. For this reason only I say to you, be very sure of yourself–and don't try to have it all on your own terms. Thank you for your patience, Mr Landon, and your company.'

For all Ascolini's urbanity, Landon left the restaurant still angry and bitterly resentful. If it had not been for Ninette Lachaise he would have damned them all to hell and taken the first train back to Rome. He was sick of their intrigues. He hated them heartily for seducing him into friendship and then laying at his door the guilts they blamed in one another.

It was the kind of situation he had avoided sedulously all his life, believing that a man had enough bother compassing his own salvation without acting as judge, jury and wet-nurse to the rest of mankind. But to be trapped like a green boy with his first widow–this was too much! He decided then and there to close his accounts with them and began to walk off his ill-temper by a tramp through the narrow alleys to Ninette's studio.

The moment she was in his arms again, he knew for certain that he loved her. Everything that he had ever dreamed of in a woman seemed to have flowered in this one: simplicity, passion, courage. She had none of the tricks that other women used to evoke tenderness while refusing to return it. What she had she would spend freely and make no usurer's demand for payment. She looked out on the world with an artist's eyes, serene, grateful, compassionate. For the first time in his life, the bachelor's caution deserted him and he told her the truth.

'I had to come. I had to tell you. I love you, Ninette.'

'I love you, too, Peter.' She clung to him for a moment and then withdrew herself gently and walked over to the window to stand, face averted, looking out over the red-tiled roofs of the ancient town. 'Now that it's said, Peter, let's live with it a while. Let's make no contracts, just wait and enjoy what we have. If it grows, it will be good for us both. If it dies, it will not hurt us too much.'

'I want it to grow, Ninette.'

'I, too. But we have both said before what we say now–and it didn't last.'

'I know it will last, for me.'

'Then just keep saying it, *chéri*, all the time, until you believe down to the bottom of your heart that it's true.'

'And you?'

'I'll do the same.'

They stood together at the window, arms laced, bodies close, savouring the first sweets of confession, watching the light pour down, golden and tender, from the Tuscan sky. Then she made him sit down, stripped off her smock and bustled about like a housewife to prepare him coffee. He told her of his lunch with Ascolini and of his anger with Rienzi; told her too of his decision to withdraw, as soon as possible, from the whole shabby business. She listened in silence while the coffee-pot bubbled a comic counterpart to the story. Then she sat down, took his hands between her own, and said, in her frank fashion: 'I know how you feel, Peter. I don't blame you. These are not your people or mine. The pattern of their lives is twisted and distorted in a fashion that neither you nor I could endure. They bear, as we could never do, the burden of old and bitter histories. And yet, in a curious way, they need us–you much more than me.'

'How can you say that, Ninette?'

'Because I need you almost as they do, Peter. You're dissatisfied with yourself, I know; but to us you are the new man from the New World, proof that it is possible to live without history, to start with a clean canvas in a land with new light. It's a symbol, you see, which represents the only solution for these folk and for many others. Someone has to say, "I'm sorry", and begin again. Otherwise the old history corrupts the new and there is, in the end, no hope at all. . . .' She faltered then and broke off as if searching for words to define a troublesome thought. 'It's like ourselves, you see, we've both known other people, loved some and hated the rest. But if we go on living in the past there is no hope for either of us. We have to accept that the present is important and tomorrow is always a question mark. I love you because you are able to do that. Rienzi and Ascolini need you for the same thing. You can afford to be generous with them.'

Landon shook his head. He was troubled by a vague guilt that even then he could not expose to her. 'Don't overrate me, my dear. There are times when I feel very empty.'

'You give more than you know, *chéri*. That's why you're dear to me.'

Then, to his own surprise, a thought which he had concealed from himself found utterance. 'I'm afraid of these people, Ninette. I can't tell you why, but they terrify me with their capacity for malice. They know what they're doing, they confess it, and some of the shame rubs off. It's like listening to a man tell dirty stories about his wife.' He gave a small, harsh laugh. 'I should be used to it—I get it every day from my patients—but here I'm not so well armed.'

'I know,' said Ninette softly. 'I've been here longer than you. They torment themselves because they don't know how to love. But we do. So they can't hurt us—and we may be able to help them.'

'Is that what you really want, Ninette?'

'I'm so rich, Peter, so very rich at this moment, I'd like to spend a little on the rest of the world.'

He took her in his arms and kissed her. The coffee-pot boiled over and they laughed and laughed with the simple, foolish joy of being alive.

In the fall of the afternoon they drove out in Ninette's battered Citröen to San Gimignano—'San Gimignano of the Wondrous Towers', that miniature town where the Middle Ages are preserved, unenlarged, almost unchanged, in the context of the twentieth century.

The land lay placid under the long shadows of cypress and olive, brown where the ploughshare had turned it, grey under the overhang of the vines, green where hidden springs still watered the young grass. The light was soft, the air calm but warm with the breath of a land still living, still fertile after a lapse of hungry centuries. The peasants, fresh from siesta, were working the terraces and the vegetable plots—men, women and children humped over the mattock or the weeding-fork. The peace of it slid into Landon's soul and he lapsed into that pleasant dichotomy where the body concentrates on the mechanical exercise of progress and the mind ranges free over the timeless panorama of men.

Ninette, too, was silent, absorbed in an artist's contemplation of colour, contour and mass. They were separate but united, private but harmonious, like notes in the same chord, colours in happy complement. They had no needs that were not fulfilled by the simple presence of one to the other, no fears that could not be allayed by a hand's touch or a smile of reassurance. If this were not love, then Landon was ignorant indeed. And if love were a folly, then he was well content to be a fool.

When they came in sight of the grim old monastery which was now the women's house of correction, Ninette shivered as if a goose had walked over her grave. She drew close to Landon and said in a low voice: 'Sometimes, Peter . . . sometimes I, too, am afraid.'

'Of what, dearest?'

'Of all this.' Her gesture took in the sunlit *campagna* and the distant dreaming towers of San Gimignano. 'It is so peaceful, as you see. The peasants are simple folk—narrow like their kind everywhere, but kind and very gentle with their children. Yet every little while something explodes—pam!—and there are violence, hate, and a very animal cruelty.'

'Like the affair at San Stefano?'

'Just like that. That girl, Peter. Before you came, I sketched her face from the photographs in the newspapers. I tried to dissect it as an artist does, and I could find nothing but childhood, yet look what happened.'

'I've had the same thought ever since I read the papers this morning. It's hard to believe in the malice of children, but it exists.'

'They inherit it sometimes, like spirochetes in the blood. Sometimes they accept it as a substitute for love. Nobody can live with an empty heart.'

'Yet this one was married. She must have known something of love.'

'It doesn't follow, Peter. Sometimes the capacity for love is destroyed. A swamp weed will die in sweet soil. An animal bred in the dark is blind in the sunlight. Look at Ascolini's daughter. Has she ever lacked love?'

'What made you think of her?'

Her answer took him by surprise: 'I dreamed of her last night, Peter—and of you, too. You were holding hands like lovers in a garden. I called out to you, but you would not listen. I tried to go to you but I was held back. I awoke calling your name and crying.'

'Darling, you're jealous.'

'I know. Silly, isn't it?'

'Very silly. Valeria means nothing to me.'

'I keep asking myself whether you may mean something to her.'

'What should I mean?' He felt a pang of shame and embarrassment.

'Kiss and come hither! What do they always mean?' She broke off and gave a little rueful chuckle. 'Bear with me, *chéri*. Every woman has her whims and it's mine to be jealous of the man I love. Let's forget them all and talk about ourselves.'

And talk they did, in the happy, extravagant manner of lovers, while the roof-tops and belfries of San Gimignano hardened themselves against the sky. Finally Landon told her that he would stay in Siena until after the trial and that then he would ask her to marry him.

Oddly, the talk of marriage seemed to trouble her, as if it were asking too much too soon and tempting the old gods of Etruria to a prankish humour. Landon tried to tease her out of it, but the mood persisted. Like many courageous people who accept life on the best terms available, she had a deep, unreasoned fear of demanding too much promise from the future, of counting the crop before the fruit had come to ripeness.

When they came to the city they stopped to drink wine in the old square which was called 'The Place of the Cistern'. Landon made a silly ceremony of pouring a libation to placate the deities. Ninette frowned, and said with a touch of irritation: 'Don't do things like that, Peter!'

'It's a joke, sweetheart. It means nothing.'

'I know, Peter, but I don't like making pacts with tomorrow. I want today just as it is, good and bad. I feel safe that way. I don't want to face the great perhaps.'

'Perhaps what?'

'Perhaps I shall die. Perhaps you will grow tired of me and go away. Perhaps I shall go blind and not be able to go on painting.'

'That's nonsense.'

'I know, *chéri*. Everything that hasn't happened is nonsense. But when it does happen, it is better to be prepared. I like to discount the future until I see the sun rise on a new day.'

'But someone has to plan for tomorrow. Life's not just an accident—or a chess game played by an overruling destiny.'

'Then you must plan for both of us, Peter. I'll just try to keep us both happy from one hour to the next.' She stood up and pulled him to his feet. 'Come on, now! There's so much to show you before sunset!'

For the next two hours they explored the tiny city—each step a regression into the violent history of the province. In the twelfth century the citizens had cast out the tyrant, Volterra. In the fourteenth it had surrendered to Florence, bled dry by the Medici bankers and by the bloody factions within its own gates. Benozzo Gozzoli painted here and Folgore, its poet son, was damned from here to Dante's hell with the eleven great spendthrifts of Siena. When one tower tumbled down, another was built 'furnished with arrows and mangonels and every warlike need'. Niccolo Machiavelli put the trainbands through their paces just outside the walls, and Dante himself led an embassy to the Grand Council from the Guelph League. To the outward aspect, the place was little changed by the centuries, and as the shadows lengthened one almost expected to hear the tramp of men-at-arms and the clatter of horsemen as merchant and knight and wandering friar squeezed themselves in at the gate before sunset.

By the time they had finished their tour they were hot, dusty and panting for a drink. Ninette suggested that they stop at a small roadside restaurant on the way to Siena, which was half eating-house, half rustic wine-shop and, by reputation, a rendezvous for country lovers. They parked the car by the roadside and as they entered the shaded courtyard they saw, five seconds too late, that Valeria Rienzi was seated with a male companion at one of the little marble tables. Landon saw Ninette flush and stiffen, and at the same moment Valeria waved them to her table. There was no option but to be polite. Valeria presented her companion: 'Peter, I should like you to meet a friend of mine, Basilio Lazzaro. Basilio, this is Peter Landon. You know Ninette, of course, Basilio?'

'Of course. We're old friends,' said Lazzaro smoothly. 'And it's a pleasure to meet you, Mr Landon.'

Ninette said nothing. Valeria watched her with feline amusement while Lazzaro and Landon measured each other and decided on instant dislike. There was a stiff little pause and then Valeria said: 'I was trying to telephone you this morning, Peter. I wanted to see you for a little while tomorrow.'

'I've been out most of today,' said Landon awkwardly. 'And I'm not quite sure what goes on tomorrow.'

'May I telephone you then? It is rather important.'

There was nothing to do but to agree. Landon and Ninette disengaged themselves as quickly as possible, took their drinks in silence and hurried back to the car. After a while, Ninette said, irritably: 'I told you, Peter, didn't I? She has interest in you and she will not give it up without a fight.'

'It seemed to me,' said Landon tartly, 'that Basilio what's-his-name had interests in you.'

And there, brusquely, the conversation ended. A small chill wind scurried across the countryside and then dropped. For all their love they could not find words to reassure each other and they drove back to Siena, moody and withdrawn, while the grey dusk settled on the olive groves and the sad funereal cypresses.

In every love-affair, however precipitate, there are moments when the swift, intuitive communion is broken, when the man and the woman are thrust back into that loneliness which first disposed them to each other. The vision that each has of the other is too perfect, the balance of interest is too precarious to sustain the smallest defect or the mildest shock of disappointment. Their first surrender appears so complete that neither can admit the reserves that still exist. They are so tender that they cannot believe themselves intolerant. The resentments flare swiftly into lovers' quarrels. There are anger, separation and withdrawal into privacy which presently becomes intolerable and drives them back, more needy than before, into each other's company.

This is the true anatomy of love: simple and patent to those who have survived it, but complex and painful to those who, like Ninette and Landon, had still to undergo the dissection.

They did not quarrel that night but were reserved with each other. Ninette's jealousy of Valeria Rienzi seemed to Landon petty, childish and contradictory, small compliment to a man who was prepared to sign a marriage contract at the drop of a lace handkerchief. It was Ninette who urged him back into alliance with Rienzi. It was she who had persuaded him that these people had need of his friendship. If now she regretted the decision, there was no good reason to make him pay for it.

For her part, she demanded reassurance, indulgence for her whim. She needed, as women do, a partnership in the apparent folly of the love-game. She resented his raillery as much as his sour disinclination.

There was only one remedy: throw away the book, forget the words and turn to kisses. But they both sheered away from this simplicity. They were afraid of each other that night. They talked contrariwise; they knew that the truth was only a step away—the big Florentine bed with its shadowy drapes and long memories of other loves. Neither of them was innocent of passion, neither lacked experience or inclination, but both of them felt, without being able to put it into words, that the disciplines of continence promised better for them both than the intemperate surrender of other days. It was a folly perhaps. Life is too short to waste so much of it in sterile anger. But everything in love is a folly and they parted, only half-reconciled, with the hope that things would be better in the morning.

4

At ten-thirty the following day Professor Emilio Galuzzi sat in private consultation with his English colleague. There was a subtle change in his manner as if, without witnesses, he were prepared to expose himself more freely to one of the esoteric brotherhood of medicine. He began with a personal apologia.

'You will agree with me, I think, Landon, that we are still the pioneers of an inexact science. Our methods are often fumbling and awkward. Our definitions are sometimes inaccurate. We have had great masters—Freud, Jung, Adler and all the rest—but we know that even their most illuminating researches have often been inhibited by a too dogmatic adherence to unproven hypothesis. For myself, I would like to say that I am an eclectic. I like to reserve to myself the right of choice when one or other of the masters seems to point a clearer way to the truth. From what I have read of your work, I believe that you have a similar attitude.'

'That's true enough.' Landon nodded agreement. 'I think it's true of all sciences that the great leaps of discovery have been made by bold speculators whose very errors have served in the end to elicit another fraction of the truth. The science of the mind is still inexact, but we've come a long way from Bedlam and the primitive notions of diabolical possession or divine madness.'

'Good.' Galuzzi seemed relieved. 'From this point we can begin to co-operate.' He shrugged and made a small, fastidious gesture. 'I have been too often bedevilled by colleagues who seem to think that they hold in their hands the answer to the ultimate riddle of the human mind. We cannot afford to be so arrogant. We are neither gods nor soothsayers. So . . . we come to our patient, this Anna Albertini. I was with her for several hours yesterday. I made a tape-recording of our interview which I should like you to hear. Before we do, however, I should like to make clear to you a point of criminal law as it is presently framed in this country. We have, like you, the normal plea of insanity, whose definition approximates very closely to that currently in use in British courts. We have also another plea, less clearly defined, which is called "*semi-infermità mentale*", or partial mental infirmity. At one end of the scale this definition wears a little of the colour of the American plea of "uncontrollable impulse". At the other, it rests on an acceptance of the principle that certain mental states do diminish the legal responsibility of the individual without entirely destroying it. Do I make myself clear?'

'Admirably,' said Landon with a smile. 'I shouldn't like to face you in court without a well-prepared brief.'

'Rienzi will be facing me,' said Galuzzi drily, 'and I am guessing that this is the ground on which he will have to stand.'

'You rule out insanity altogether?'

'I do.' His answer was quite emphatic. 'When you have seen the girl I think you will agree with me. I believe that by all the legal norms the girl is quite sane. I see no evidence of mania, schizophrenia or paranoid tendencies. There is no amnesia, no evidence of hysteria. There is some residual shock, but she sleeps calmly, eats normally, takes singularly good care of herself, and seems to accept her situation with reasoned resignation. There is trauma, of course, associated with her mother's death. There is also obsession, reduced but not wholly eliminated by the cathartic effect of the act of revenge. Their degrees and ramifications will need much longer exploration.'

'Do they constitute mental infirmity under the Italian definition?'

Galuzzi laughed and threw out his arms in Latin exuberance. 'Ah! Now we come to the core of it! We are all in difficulty here. The definition is unclear. And too often the judicial mind in this country reacts very strongly against any suggestion that a person legally sane is not fully responsible for his actions. On this point, Landon, you know as well as I that the development of mental science and the evolution of the law do not march at the same pace. Often it is a matter of advocacy to swing the bench to a favourable decision. Often justice is inhibited by the lack of definition in the codex. This is a service that men like you and I can render to the law: to make our findings so clear that they cannot fail to be accepted as a basis for future legislation. But in this case we have to accept the situation as it exists. The best we can do is explore the mind of the accused and determine as clearly as we can the limit of her legal responsibility. Now, before we hear the tape . . . you tell me you have not seen this girl?'

'Not yet. Rienzi saw her and gave me a somewhat colourful description.'

Galuzzi chuckled. 'I shouldn't blame him too much for that. I am older than he is but I confess I, too, was curiously impressed. She has a quite extraordinary beauty, an almost nun-like charm. They dress them like nuns, too, in San Gimignano–drunks, thieves, abortionists and the little whores who sell themselves on street corners. But this one! You could paint an aureole around her head and put her on a pedestal in the church. Anyway, let's listen to her.'

He crossed to the desk and switched on the recorder and a few seconds later Landon was immersed in the dialogue.

Galuzzi's voice took on the cool, informal tone of the trained analyst. The girl's voice was pleasantly pitched, but remote and indifferent; neither dull nor bored, but strangely dissociated, like that of an actor speaking through a Greek mask.

'You understand, Anna, that I'm a doctor and that I'm here to help you?'

'Yes, I understand.'

'Tell me, did you sleep well last night?'

'Very well, thank you.'

'You weren't afraid?'

'No. I was very tired because of all the questions. But nobody was unkind to me. I wasn't afraid.'

'How old are you, Anna?'

'Twenty-four.'

'How long have you been married?'

'Four years.'

'What sort of a house do you live in?'

'It's not a house. It's an apartment. It's not very big, but it was enough for Luigi and me.'

'How old is Luigi?'

'Twenty-six.'

'What did you do after you were married?'

'What everyone else does. I cleaned the house and did the shopping and looked after Luigi.'

'This was in Florence?'

'Yes.'

'Did you have any friends in Florence?'

'Luigi had friends from work, and he had his family. I didn't know anyone there.'

'Didn't you feel lonely?'

'No.'

'Was Luigi good to you?'

'Yes. He used to get angry with me sometimes but he was good to me.'

'Why did he get angry?'

'He used to say I didn't love him like I should.'

'And did you?'

'Underneath I did.'

'Underneath what?'

'Inside me. You know, in my head. In my heart.'

'Did you tell Luigi that?'

'Yes. But it didn't stop him getting angry.'

'Why?'

'Because he used to say it wasn't enough. Married people did things to show they loved each other.'

'Did you know what he meant?'

'Oh yes.'

'But you didn't want to do them?'

'No.'

'Why not?'

'I thought he would hurt me.'

'What else did you think?'

'I thought about his gun.'

'Tell me about the gun.'

'He used to take it to work with him every night. That was his job. He had to guard the factory at night. In the morning, when he came home, he would put it away in the drawer of the bureau.'

'Were you afraid of it?'

'Only when I dreamed about it. In the daytime I used to take it out and hold it in my hand and look at it. It was cold and hard.'

'What did you dream about the gun?'

'That Luigi was holding it in his hand and pointing it at my mother. Then it wasn't Luigi. It was someone else. I couldn't see his face, but I knew it was Belloni. Then I would try to get to him, but I couldn't, and I would wake up.'

'Belloni was the man you killed?'

'That's right.'

'Why did you kill him?'

'He shot my mother.'

'Tell me about that, Anna.'

'I'd rather not talk about it. It's over now. Belloni's dead.'

'Does it frighten you to think about it?'

'No, I just don't want to talk about it.'

'All right. Then tell me about your father.'

'I don't remember much about him. He went away in the Army when I was five. Then we heard he was killed. Mother cried a lot. Then she got over it. She moved me into her room and I slept with her.'

'Until the Germans came to the village?'

'No, all the time.'

'When the Germans were there, did you still sleep with her?'

'Yes. She used to lock the bedroom door at night.'

'Where did you go to school?'

'In San Stefano with the Brown Sisters.'

'What did they teach you?'

'Reading and writing and figures. And the Catechism.'

'In the Catechism, Anna, doesn't it say that it's wrong to kill anybody?'

'Yes.'

'But you killed Belloni. Wasn't that a sin?'

'I suppose so.'

'Don't you care?'

'I never thought about it that way. All I knew was I had to kill him because he killed my mother.'

'Did you know it all the time?'

'Yes.'

'How did you know it?'

'I just knew. When I woke up in the morning, when I cooked the dinner or washed the floor or went out shopping, I knew all the time.'

'How did you make up your mind to kill him?'

'It was the gun.'

'But you told me the gun was there all the time. Luigi would take it to work at night and put it in the bureau drawer in the morning. You told me you used to take it out and look at it. Why did you wait all that time?'

'Because it was different. On that morning, Luigi didn't put the gun in the drawer. He emptied his pockets and left the gun on the table beside the bed. When he was asleep I took it and went to San Stefano and killed Belloni. . . . Please, can we stop for a while?'

'Of course.'

Galuzzi got up and switched off the machine. Then he turned to Landon, who was sitting at the desk scribbling notes on the back of an envelope.

'Well, Landon, that's the first part of it. What do you think so far?'

'So far, it's almost classically simple. Shock and trauma caused by the circumstances of her mother's death; the child's incapacity to master the situation, and a consequent blocking of the ego-function; hence the obsession, the nightmares, the sexual incompetence, the transference of symbols.' He shrugged and grinned. 'That's talking off the cuff, of course. I shouldn't commit myself so quickly. One interesting point is the emergence of the vestigial primitive conscience from beneath the overlay of convent education—violence must be purged by violence. It's the archaic attempt to master a situation beyond control by the usual means. You see it again in the acceptance of a magical moment like the discovery of the gun exposed on the table, as a motive for the final act of vengeance. But I'm reading you lectures, Professor. You know all this as well as I do.'

Galuzzi nodded, and said soberly: 'As you say, my friend, it is almost a textbook case. We shall dig further, of course, and we shall come sooner or later to a description of what we are at present refused—the moment of the mother's death. I have no doubt that we shall discover many more complexities than are revealed to us in this first discussion. But even if our first guesses are confirmed, even if we present ourselves with a classic set of symptoms and a perfect pathology of traumatic psychosis, where do we stand then?'

'We're back on the coda,' said Landon grimly: 'the nature and the determining factors of human responsibility. The old moralists had a point, you know, when they refused to surrender too easily the doctrine of free-will.'

Galuzzi nodded and embellished the theme in his pedantic fashion: 'My point exactly, Landon. I cannot believe the determinists who say that there is no real responsibility and that every human act is an inevitable consequence of a thousand others, like a ball bouncing off an unseen wall. The question we have to answer, the question the court will demand to be answered, is whether there remains in this girl enough of free-will, enough of intelligence, to judge the nature of her action and to have been able to choose against it.'

Landon shrugged helplessly. 'Who answers that one, except God Almighty?'

'And yet,' said Galuzzi sombrely, 'every time we set up a court we arrogate to ourselves a divine function, the exercise of the power of life, death and ultimate judgment. Times are when I stand in the witness box and tremble for my own sanity. Do you want to hear any more or would you rather see the girl first?'

'I'd like to see her with you,' said Landon. 'You can ask the questions, I'll just listen. It's hard enough to conduct an investigation in one's own language without trying to read the colours into another.'

'Let me buy you lunch and a bottle of wine,' said Emilio Galuzzi. 'I think we may have a difficult afternoon.'

Dusk was declining over the old city when Landon returned to the Pensione della Fontana. He felt tired and dispirited, oppressed by the memory of the grim prison and the faces of the unfortunates confined there.

The interview with Anna Albertini had been long and tedious and, for all Galuzzi's skill and Landon's prompting, they had not been able to induce her to reveal anything about the circumstances of her mother's death or her own participation in it. Landon himself had felt frustrated by having to watch another professional in control of a familiar operation.

His depression was increased by the fact that there was no message from Ninette. There were, however, two other messages: a telegram from Carlo in Florence and a request to call Valeria Rienzi at a Siena number before eight that evening.

Carlo's telegram was brief and cryptic: 'It was a joke, but I apologize. Have made progress. Further interviews San Stefano tonight. With client tomorrow morning. Please contact me Hôtel Continentale midday tomorrow.' Landon stuffed the telegram in his pocket and rang for the maid to draw him a bath.

As he soaked himself in the ornate marble tub, he took stock of his situation. For a man on his sabbatical year he had surrendered too much of his freedom, too much of his personal interest, to a group of people in whom he had no stake at all. If the case of Anna Albertini were what it seemed to

Daughter of Silence

be–a textbook history–it would add nothing to his experience or his reputation. He could discharge his promise to Carlo Rienzi by writing him a summary of his own and Galuzzi's conclusions and then indicating lines of questioning for the defence. To Ascolini he owed nothing but the courtesies of a guest. A polite note and a graceful gift would discharge them adequately. To Valeria he owed as much or as little as a summer kiss was worth.

To Ninette? This was a different question. He was in love with her. He had told her he wanted to marry her. She had shied away from an answer. She had told him he was free to wait or to go. So now the question took a different shape. What did Peter Landon want? How much was he prepared to pay? What road would he walk in double harness?

He was still piqued by Ninette's failure to call him. He knew himself unreasonable in demanding so much of her, but when a man had had women at his beck for so many years the habit of demand was hard to break. There were other fears, too. If the lute was rifted so early and so easily, what sort of music would it play after a couple of years of marriage? Perhaps, after all, it was better to pack and go, resigning oneself to the cash guarantee of contentment. Happiness was a doubtful credit in any ledger, and who should know it better than a doctor of sick souls?

Then, by swift reaction, his mood changed from irritation to recklessness. To the devil with them all! He was still free, white and long past the age of consent. He had spent enough of himself; he deserved a night on the town. And if a maid or matron wanted to be kissed, then why not oblige her and himself at the same time? The comic thought came to him that Ascolini would probably approve him heartily at that moment. He stepped out of the tub, dried himself with brisk satisfaction, dressed himself with extra care, and then sat down to telephone Valeria Rienzi.

After a discreet interval she answered, grateful but reserved: 'Peter? It's kind of you to call. Could you spare me a little time this evening?'

'Yes, I can.'

'Could you take me to dinner?'

'Certainly. Where shall we meet?'

She told him she was having cocktails with friends in an apartment on the Via del Capitano. She suggested that he call for her at eight-thirty and then take her to dinner at a near-by restaurant. He liked the idea of company at their first meeting, so he agreed. She thanked him with disarming courtesy and hung up.

Moved by a vague impulse of guilt, he tried to telephone Ninette, but there was no answer from her studio. He felt resentful and then decided, with masculine naïveté, that a little separation would be good for both of them. It was still only seven-thirty, so, having an hour to kill, he decided to deal with some of his neglected correspondence.

As he worked through the pile of letters, he found himself bathed in a rosy glow of righteousness. He was a sensible fellow who knew where he was going, a sane citizen in credit with his banker, a professional who did noble service to his fellows. The rest–Ninette Lachaise excepted–was a provincial excursion, a pastoral interlude which would be forgotten as soon as it was ended.

Then, without any warning, he found himself projected into one of those moods in which the terror and the mystery of life became suddenly manifest, when the most trivial actions revealed themselves as matters of cosmic consequence.

He had presented a letter of introduction in Rome and now he was acting as unwilling catalyst in a drama of family intrigue. He had been charmed by a fledgling lawyer and was now to counsel him on the fate of his client. He had dined with a new woman, as he had done a thousand times before, and now was committed to the resolution of marriage, to the promise of children and the unending chain of human continuity. Now he was to dine with another, reckless but not wholly unaware that this meeting, too, might start another chain of consequences.

It was a curious experience, like standing on a high mountain looking into a valley flooded with darkness. The valley was empty and soundless. One was solitary in eminence, a creature thrust up from nowhere, going to no place. Then a light pricked out, another and another. The moon rose and the valley was abruptly alive with man and all his works and one must, perforce, go down to join the concourse or die, in the cold election of pride, empty and naked.

It was not good for man to be alone. But there was a price to pay for joining the pilgrim train and a tax for every day of the journey. One must break bread with tears and drink thin wine with gratitude. One must submit to be envied and hated as much as to be loved. And if the caravan did not arrive where the master first promised, then one must wear out the sojourn in the desert with resignation, if not with joy. This was the real terror of the human condition, that men were yoked one to another in an ineluctable bondage so that a sickness in one might be a plague upon the whole fraternity and the guilt of a few make scapegoats of all. The small compassion might be a great affirmation and a petty injustice spread to a whole corruption.

A comfortless thought for a summer evening in Tuscany. So he thrust it away and took himself off to dine with Valeria Rienzi.

Give the lady her due, she had a singular charm and could be generous with it when she chose. She flattered him to her friends, but gave him no time to be bored with them. Then she handed him the keys of her car and had him drive her out beyond the walls of the old city to a country restaurant where they ate under a lattice of vines and drank wine pressed in the local vineyard. The wine was potent, there was a trio of sentimental musicians and within twenty minutes Landon was more relaxed and less cautious than he had been for days.

Valeria, too, seemed grateful for the occasion and began to tease him good-humouredly: 'It seems, Peter, that you're beginning at last to enjoy yourself—a little drama, a little comedy, a little romance.'

'It's about time, don't you think?'

'Of course. But until tonight I would never have dared to say it.' She pouted and frowned in comic mime. 'Every time I talked with you I felt like a girl going to her confessor.'

'Not tonight, I hope.' Landon laughed and stretched out a hand to her across the table. 'Let's dance, and I'll make my confession to you.'

It was said lightly, but she held him to it with the same light touch. As they danced close and harmonious, as they sat sipping wine in the pale lamplight, she drew him out so that he talked freely about himself, his family, his career, and of the situation which had brought about his withdrawal from the London scene. Valeria was a good listener, and when she was not playing coquette she dispensed a warmth and a simplicity which he would not have believed in her. Later they talked about Carlo, and she asked him: 'Do you still think he's doing the right thing, Peter?'

'I think it's right for him: though he may win less than he hopes, I think it's good that you and your father have decided to support him.'

She gave him a swift, sidelong glance. 'Do you think he cares at this moment whether we support him or not?'

'I think he cares greatly, though he would not admit it for fear of seeming weak.'

'Have you seen his client–this Anna Albertini?'

'Yes, I had a long session with her this afternoon.'

'What is she like?'

'Young, beautiful–and quite lost, I think.'

She gave a dry little laugh. 'It would be funny if Carlo fell in love with her. Lawyers and doctors do fall in love with their clients, don't they?'

'I think Carlo's in love with you, Valeria.'

She shook her head. 'Not that way, Peter. If I were a lame puppy, perhaps he might be. I know he believes that what he feels for me is love, but I'm afraid it's not my kind. And you, Peter, are you in love with Ninette Lachaise?'

It was as neat as a conjurer's trick. A flick of the silk handkerchief and a white rabbit pops out of the empty hat while the conjurer smiles at his innocent audience. And Landon, caught unawares, was as innocent as the moths fluttering around the shaded lamps. He sidled away from the question. 'Don't rush me, Valeria. As you say, I'm just beginning to enjoy myself.'

She reached out and patted his hand with sisterly approval. 'That's good, Peter. And I'm glad for you. It's always best with an experienced woman. If it doesn't work there are no complications, no regrets. Dance with me again. Then we must go.'

After that it was all too easy. The languor of the night took hold of them and when they drove back to Siena she dozed with her head on his shoulder, comfortable as a cat. When they reached the Pensione della Fontana he asked her in for a last drink. She accepted drowsily. But when they were closed in the old room with its high coffered ceiling and its shadows of former loves, passion lifted them like a wave and set them down in darkness and tumult on the tumbled sheets.

In the small morning hours, Landon woke to find her sitting on the edge of the bed fully dressed. She cupped his face in her hands and kissed him on the lips. Then she smiled, and her smile was full of the old wisdom of women. 'I'm happy now, Peter. I wanted you first, you know, and you'll never be able to despise me again. . . . No, don't say anything. It was good for me, and I think it may be good for you. I wanted to hurt you very much. Now I can't. You needn't be afraid of me any more. Carlo will never know, nor Ninette. But you and I won't forget. Goodnight, darling Sleep well!'

She kissed him again and left him, and he lay wakeful until dawn, fumbling through the dictionary of his trade for words to describe what had happened to him.

He was too old to panic like a youth after his first lapse with a married woman, but he was too experienced not to be honest about its consequences. There was a guilt in what he had done: a personal guilt, an injustice to Ninette, a greater one to Carlo Rienzi. He could blame no one but himself–and he could not afford the luxury of confession. So, with a consummate irony, he was forced back to the prescription which he imposed on all his patients: accept the guilt, know yourself for what you are, wear the knowledge like a Nessus shirt on your own back and bear the pricks and the poison with as much dignity as you can muster.

He wore it all the morning. He tramped the city aimlessly, through sun-parched squares and stinking lanes. He drank too much coffee and smoked too many cigarettes. He cursed himself for a fool but found that he could not curse Valeria. He ended an hour before midday sitting alone in a pavement café, exhausted and humbled by the knowledge that this was a crisis in his life and that he was ill-prepared to meet it.

He had travelled too far and too long not to know that there were twenty agreeable substitutes for the grand passion. One could survive contentedly with any one of them, as most folks survived without truffles for breakfast or champagne for every supper. The parched traveller was happy with a mug of water from the village pump and asked no sweeter or more magical spring. His life could extend itself into a succession of episodes like the one with Valeria, each episode becoming a shade more inconsequent as vitality diminished with the years. And if there were no ecstasy, at least there would be none of the painful commitments of love.

Love was an exotic state, close kin to agony, but when a man had once endured it he was plagued ever after by the memory and the bitter nostalgia for the lost paradise. How many times could the world blow up? And after the one wild splendour, who could clap hands for fireworks and sex in suburbia?

A romantic might make of this moment a tale of spiritual insight and noble resolution. But Landon was deficient in these things as he felt himself to be in so many others. He simply waited, stiff and tired, until calm came over him and he felt ready to face Ninette Lachaise.

His heart was pounding and his hands were clammy as he climbed the stairs and knocked on the door of her studio. Ten seconds later she was in his arms, anxious and reproachful.

'*Chéri*! Where were you all day yesterday? Why didn't you call? I telephoned a dozen times this morning, but nobody knew where you were. We mustn't do these things to each other! Not ever again—promise me!' Then, sensing a strangeness in him, she held him at arm's length and looked into his face. 'Something's happened, Peter. What is it?'

The lie came out more easily than he had hoped. 'Nothing's happened, except that I've been a fool. I'm sorry. I was busy all yesterday. I telephoned you in the evening, but you weren't at home. I went out on the town. I was angry and I shouldn't have been. Forgive me?'

He took her in his arms to kiss her, but she drew away, pale and cold as a statue, and walked over to the window. When at last she spoke, her voice sounded strained and hollow across the big room. 'This is what I have been afraid of, Peter: the moment when what we have been comes to threaten what we want to be. This is why I wanted to wait and give our loving time to grow.'

'Do you still want that?' Studiously, he held himself back from her, held his voice neutral and reserved.

'Yes, Peter, I do, but only if you want it as much as I. And you mustn't lie to me, not ever. If there's something you don't want to tell me, keep it to yourself, but don't lie. I'll make you the same promise.'

'Is there anything else?'

'Yes. I still want time, Peter, before we make up our minds to marry.'

'How much time?'

'Until after the trial.'

'I'd hoped we might leave before then.'

For the first time she turned to face him and he saw that she was fighting to hold control of herself. Her answer was very firm.

'No, Peter. Don't ask me to read you the whole book. But I think you know by now that you owe Carlo a debt and you won't be happy till you pay it. I know I won't either.'

To which he had nothing to say, and he stood, shamed and irresolute, until she came to him and put her arms about him and he felt for the first time the promise of an unspoken absolution.

It was a quarter after noon when Landon reached the Continentale. He found Rienzi in his shirt-sleeves, working through a sheaf of notes at a desk piled high with textbooks. His face was grey, his eyes heavy with fatigue, and he was driving himself through the work with brandy and black coffee—a poisonous combination for a man already half drugged with body-toxin. Landon himself was tired, embarrassed and in no carnival humour, so he decided to share the poison. He poured himself a cup of coffee and two fingers of brandy, then stretched out on the bed while Rienzi talked.

'We make progress, Peter. It's slow, but at least we're going in the right direction. I went to Florence, as you know. I talked to Luigi Albertini. He's an insignificant little character and he'd been well coached by the police. However, as you guessed, he opened up a little when I asked him why his wife was still a virgin after four years of marriage.' Rienzi grinned and mimicked the back-alley dialect of Florence: '"She didn't want to. She thought it would hurt her. I took her to a doctor but he couldn't do anything. What's a fellow to do with a wife like that?" After that he closed up like a shellfish. I had the feeling he was hiding something else, but I couldn't spare the time to find what it was. However, I wanted to keep him worried, so I paid a private investigator to dig up some more information about him. He'll write me if he gets anything.'

'You told me in your telegram you were going to San Stefano. Did you get anything new there?'

'Again, some progress. Fra Bonifacio wanted to see me. One of his penitents had come to him with a trouble of conscience. He wouldn't tell me his name, but apparently it was someone who had been associated with Belloni in the Partisans. Fra Bonifacio told him that he had an obligation in conscience to reveal anything that would help the girl. He wanted time to think about it. If he decides to open up, Fra Bonifacio will get in touch with me immediately. I tried again to talk to Sergeant Fiorello but got nowhere. I've appointed another private investigator to scout the villages and see what he can dig up about Belloni's war-time history. A man like that must have had some enemies. . . . And this morning I saw Anna.'

'I saw her myself yesterday,' said Landon.

'I know. She told me. She was grateful that you and Galuzzi were so gentle with her.'

'Apparently she was more communicative with you than she was with us.' Landon grinned and sipped his brandy. Rienzi came over and sat on the edge of the bed. He asked anxiously: 'What do you think, Peter? What does Galuzzi think?'

'You rule out insanity,' said Landon definitely. 'There is evidence of trauma, obsession and other psychotic symptoms. Galuzzi wants more time to determine how far her condition reduces legal responsibility. I agree with him.'

'Is that all?'

'What more do you want?'

Rienzi began to pace the floor, running his fingers through his hair, talking in sharp, hurried sentences. 'I'm looking for a place to stand, Peter, a position from which to fight. I'm horrified by what has been done to this girl—much more than by what she herself has done. You know what she's like? Like someone who has lived all her life in one room, looking out of the same window on the same small garden. You know what she said to me today? "Now I can make love. Now I can begin to make Luigi happy." How could she have known what she was doing? She's like someone dropped on to a new planet!'

'The court will have another view, Carlo,' said Landon soberly. 'Best you keep it clearly in your mind. She knew what a gun was. She knew enough to plan a tour by train and taxi. She knew that murder was a police matter. She understood its consequences. She lived in a big city. She kept house for her husband. She had a basic education and dressed like a big girl. She was neither crazy nor cretinous and she waited sixteen years to kill a man. I don't say that's the full story—I know it isn't—but that's where the court starts. And you know as well as I do that at the back of their minds are the question of public order and the fear that any clemency will bring back the practice of vendetta to the mountains.'

It was the last thought that sobered Rienzi the quickest. He chewed on it for a moment and then said quietly: 'I know everything you say and more, Peter, but there's something that troubles me deeply and that may possibly give us a starting point for the defence. This murder was premeditated for sixteen years. If that is true, then Anna Albertini decided on it at the age of eight, which is not an age of legal responsibility. The decision was taken, Peter, although the act was performed in another time. What happened during those sixteen years? What was the state of this girl during all that time? What was the shock that first projected her into it?'

'You're asking Galuzzi's question and mine, in another form.'

'Then unless you give me the answer, Peter, there will be no justice done.'

Landon put down his coffee cup and swung himself off the bed. Then he in his turn began pacing the floor while he pieced out his argument.

'The law does justice by accident, Carlo. Any law. First and foremost it's a code of public order, a deterrent, a punitive weapon. Justice is still in the hands of God—and He takes a long time to deliver a verdict!'

'Perhaps this time,' said Carlo Rienzi, 'we may be able to persuade Him to work a little faster.' He hesitated a moment and then, moved by a sudden resolution, he swung round to face Landon. 'I have no right to ask this of you, Peter. I can offer you nothing for your services except my gratitude, but I want you to stay in Siena and help me. In spite of Galuzzi, and provided I can get the court to approve, I want to put you in the witness box for the defence!'

'Just as you like.'

Landon said it so casually that he felt he had betrayed himself; but he had no heart for more acting, and when Carlo gaped at him in surprise and delight he snapped irritably: 'For God's sake, man, you knew all along I'd say yes! Let's not make a drama out of it. And by the same token don't expect miracles. The best I can offer you is an authority to match Galuzzi's.'

Rienzi laughed, a full, boyish laugh of relief and pleasure. 'Miracles, Peter? This is already a miracle.'

'There's another one,' said Landon moodily, anxious to be quit of the subject. 'I lunched with Ascolini, as you know. He wants to help you. He offers you a million lire and a set of notes he has made on the conduct of the case.'

'I can't accept,' said Rienzi with cool emphasis.

'I told him you probably wouldn't, but it might be an idea to send him a note of thanks.'

'I'll do that.' He added quietly: 'You know, Peter, at this moment I am able to feel more kindly to Valeria and her father than I have ever done before. You know why? Because I have you for my friend and because there's someone who needs me more than they do–Anna Albertini. All of a sudden there's a focus for my life, a cause to be anxious about–and it makes me very happy.'

Happy? To Landon he sounded more like a man on the scaffold making a hollow joke while the noose was fitted round his neck. But what was there to say? When you've slept with a man's wife can you rob him of his illusions as well? It was the bitterest draught Landon had ever swallowed in his life. He drank it with a smile, but the taste was sour on his tongue every hour of every day until Anna Albertini was brought to trial.

5

The opening of a criminal trial is an oddly theatrical occasion. Tradition and the public instinct demand not only that justice should seem to be done, but that its dispensation should provide a dramatic diversion: a purging by pity and terror of the passions which have been aroused by the criminal act.

There are those who hold that British court procedure makes better theatre than its continental equivalents; but let no unwary delinquent underrate either of them. The British tradition derives directly from the old Germanic system of trial by combat. The court is a place of contest and disputation, arbitrated by a judge and a jury. Prosecution and defence elicit their evidence by examination and cross-examination. They dispute fact and interpretation. They engage in wordy battles like knights in the ancient lists.

The Latin mode, by contrast, is one of inquisition, based on Roman law and modified by the method of the Canonists. It consists of a preliminary inquiry by a magistrate into all available evidence, which is then summarized and submitted to the court in the form of a prepared brief, on whose merits the case is heard. The prisoner does not plead guilty or not guilty. There is no contest, simply a public revelation of facts, a plea on the basis of facts by the defence and the prosecution, and then a decision–not a verdict–delivered by the president on the votes of five judges: two from the judiciary and three representing the people.

For one bred in the British tradition, there is always something a trifle sinister in the inquisitorial method since it seems to deny the accepted principle that the onus of proof rests on the Crown and that a man is innocent until he is proven guilty. The Latin method assumes in practice, if not in fact, that truth is at the bottom of a deep well and that the accused is guilty until the inquisition has enough facts to prove him innocent. In the end it seems that justice is as well or ill served by the one method as by the other.

Every court has something of the aspect of a theatre. There is a stage where the personages act out the rituals of revelation, conflict and resolution. There is a symbolic montage: the arms of the republic over the judges' dais, the carved chair which sets the president above his assisting judges, the rostrum which sets them apart from the officials of the court. There are stalls for the audience, who must conduct themselves decorously while transferring their partisan sentiments to the actors on the stage. There is a gallery for the critics and the censors of the press. The principals are in costume. The movement is stylized. The dialogue is formal and traditional, so that, as in all theatres, reality is revealed through unreality and truth is exposed by a mummer's fiction.

Landon and Ninette arrived early, to find the antechamber choked with a press of people: reporters, photographers, witnesses, spectators, harassed officials, all talking at once, all making their own buskers' drama before the official programme began.

Old Ascolini pushed his way through the crowd to greet them. He looked tired, Landon thought. His pink cheeks were paler, his skin transparent, as though the lively spirit were burning through the tissues of his body; but he greeted them with the old quirky humour: 'So the love-birds show themselves at last! Let me look at you, young woman. Good! So far, love is an agreeable pastime, eh? Maybe soon you will be able to finish my portrait. And you, Landon, you are to be the expert witness, eh? You're a stubborn fellow, aren't you? You surprised us, Valeria most of all, I think!'

'Is she here today?' It was Ninette who asked the question.

'Over there, sulking in a corner. I've seen very little of her these last weeks. She has troubles of her own, I think. And I am afraid I cannot reach her.'

It was a touchy subject. Landon tried to talk him away from it. 'How's Carlo this morning?'

'Feeling the strain.' Ascolini gave him a crooked, sardonic smile. 'You should know better than I, Landon. You've been working with him.'

Landon chose to ignore the barb and asked quietly: 'What's your feeling about the trial, Doctor?'

Ascolini spread his hands in a rueful gesture. 'What I expected. A hostile climate and a vague rumour of surprises. Carlo has told me little. But if you are free at any time, Landon, I should like to drink a glass of wine with you both.'

'Any time, *dottore*,' said Ninette with a smile. 'Just knock on the door.'

'With young lovers it is usually safer to telephone. But I shall see you.'

There was a flurry in the crowd as the door opened and they were thrust forward, willy-nilly, into the court-room. It took ten minutes to subdue the rabble into a whispering audience; then the actors began to drift on to the set.

First came the Public Minister, who would conduct the prosecution: a tall, hawk-faced official with iron-grey hair. He took his place at a table on the right of the judges' rostrum and began a whispered discussion with his assistants. Next came the Chancellor and the Clerk of the Court, detached, faintly pompous fellows who sat at a table near the prisoner's dock facing the Prosecutor across the floor.

Carlo Rienzi came in next with two seedy, middle-aged colleagues and they settled themselves at a table facing the rostrum. Carlo had aged much in the last few weeks. He had lost a great deal of weight. His clothes hung baggily on his thin shoulders. His face was drawn and yellow. There were deep lines scored around his mouth and at the corners of his eyes. In his black gown, with the white, starched jabot, he looked like a monk harried by conscience and ascetic practice.

Ninette touched Landon's arm and whispered: 'We must look after him, Peter. He looks so dreadfully alone.'

Landon nodded absently. She had not meant it so, but it was a sharp reminder that even after weeks of common labour his debt to Rienzi was still unpaid.

Suddenly there was a gasp and a flutter of talk as Anna Albertini was brought in and led to the prisoner's dock. The noise was quickly hushed by the Clerk, but the girl gave no sign that she had heard it. She stood stock-still, hands gripping the brass rail of the dock, eyes downcast, her face bloodless but still beautiful under the harsh, yellow light.

Finally the court was called to order for the entrance of the judges and the President and the crowd stood in silence until they had settled themselves on the rostrum and spread out their papers.

The President was an imposing figure: a tall, stooping man with white hair and an old, wise face in which understanding and the impersonal majesty of the law seemed constantly at war with one another. He frowned at the rustle as the crowd sat down, but he offered no comment. Then the Chancellor stepped forward and announced: 'May it please the President and members of the court–the Republic against Anna Albertini; the charge, premeditated murder.'

Landon felt Ninette's hand tighten on his arm. There was a small flutter of fear at the pit of his belly. The flails of the law were beginning to beat on the threshing-floor and they would not cease until the chaff had been winnowed and the last grains of truth had been piled for the mills.

The President's first words were addressed to the girl in the dock: 'You are Anna Albertini, born Anna Moschetti in the village of San Stefano, lately resident in Florence?'

Her answer was firm, flat and colourless. 'I am.'

'Anna Albertini, you are charged in this court with the wilful and premeditated murder of Gianbattista Belloni, Mayor of San Stefano, on the fourteenth day of August this year. Are you represented by counsel or do you require the assistance of a public advocate?'

Carlo Rienzi rose and made the formal announcement: 'The accused is represented, Mr President. . . . Carlo Rienzi, advocate.'

He sat down and the President bent for a moment over the papers on his desk. Again he addressed the prisoner: 'According to the indictment before me, you, Anna Albertini, arrived by taxi-cab in San Stefano at midday on the date named. You walked to the Mayor's house and asked to see him. You were invited to enter, but you refused and waited at the door. When the Mayor came out, you shot him five times and walked to the police-station, where you surrendered the weapon, were taken into custody and later charged. You made a statement: "He shot my mother in the war. I promised I would kill him. I have done it." Do you now wish to withdraw or challenge this statement?'

Carlo Rienzi answered for her. 'We do not wish to withdraw or challenge the statement made by the prisoner. We are satisfied that it was made freely and without coercion.'

The President gave him a puzzled, frowning look. 'Counsel has read the statement?'

'Yes, Mr President.'

'You understand fully its incriminating character?'

'Fully, Mr President. But it is our submission that for justice's sake this statement must be read in the light of evidence still to be presented in this court.'

'The submission is valid, Mr Rienzi. My colleagues and I will take note of it at the proper time.' He turned to the prosecution. 'The Public Minister may present his case.'

'Permission granted.'

The tall, hawk-faced fellow stood up and announced, quite mildly: 'Mr President, gentlemen of the court, the events in this crime are so simple, so clear and brutal, that they require no oratory from me to bring you to condemn them. With the permission of the President, I propose simply to present my witnesses.'

'Permission granted.'

The first witness was the burly Sergeant Fiorello. In spite of his rugged face and his country accent, he cut a notable figure in the box. His answers were concise, his narrative fluent. He identified himself as Enzo Fiorello, rank of sergeant in the service of Public Security. He had spent twenty-five years in San Stefano and was now in charge of its station. He identified the prisoner and the weapon she had used. He sketched the circumstances and the aftermath of the murder and earned a word of commendation from the President for his expert handling of the situation. He earned another for his moderate interrogation of the accused and his swift suppression of disorder in the village. By the time the prosecution had finished with him, he stood up like some local Hampden–a champion of order but a sympathetic guardian of his people.

Then Carlo Rienzi produced his first minor surprise. He declined to examine the witness but requested that he be recalled later for questioning by the defence. The President raised a dubious eyebrow. 'This is an unusual request, Mr Rienzi. I feel it must be justified to the court.'

'It is a question of clarity in our presentation, Mr President. We propose to elicit certain information from later witnesses and on some of it we shall need to re-examine Sergeant Fiorello. If we examine him now, the questions will have no relevance.' He bowed formally to the Prosecutor. 'At this moment we are in the hands of the Public Minister and we must follow his sequence of witnesses.'

There was a moment of whispered conference on the rostrum, then the President agreed. Rienzi thanked him and sat down.

Landon looked across the court to see what Ascolini had made of the tactic, but his face was hidden and Landon saw only the serene, classic profile of Valeria.

It was as hard to read malice in her as it was to read murder in the white virginal face of the girl in the dock. Landon was reminded of the Japanese legend of those beautiful mask-faced women who changed by malignant magic into foxes when the moon was full. And yet she had kept her bargain. Whatever Ninette had guessed, Valeria had told her nothing. When, during the past weeks, he had met her in Carlo's presence, she had maintained discretion. Once only, coming on him in an empty room, she had rumpled his hair and whispered: 'I miss you, Peter. Why do girls like me always pick the wrong ones?'

For the rest, Landon trusted her and was forced to a reluctant respect.

Now a new witness was being led to the stand: Maria Belloni, wife of the dead man, the stout motherly woman who had stood in the doorway of the Mayor's house and greeted Anna Albertini. Now, dressed in widow's weeds, she seemed shrunken and old, burdened beyond endurance by loneliness and grief. When the oath was administered, the Prosecutor approached her, gentle as an undertaker. His fine voice intoned the words like the syllables of a psalm: 'Signora Belloni, we share your grief with you. We regret that you should be exposed to the pain of a new questioning, but I want you to try to compose yourself and answer the questions of the President.'

'I'll–I'll try.'

'You are a very courageous woman. Thank you.'

He remained near her while the President worked through the formal gambits.

'Your name is Maria Alessandra Belloni and you are the wife of the deceased?'

'Yes.'

'The court would like to hear in your own words what happened just before your husband was killed.'

For a moment, it seemed that she might break down completely. Then she recovered herself and began her testimony, hesitantly at first, then on a rising note of passion and hysteria.

'We were sitting down to eat like we always do . . . my husband, the boys, me. There was wine and *pasta* and a special *risotto*. It was a feast, you see: my husband's birthday. We were happy like a family should be. Then there is the ring at the door. I go out. This one is standing there.' She flung an accusing hand towards Anna Albertini. 'She says she wants to see my husband. She looks so small and lonely I think to do her a charity. I ask her to come and eat with us. She says no; it is a private matter, it will take only a moment I . . . I go back and call my husband. He gets up from the table. He still has his napkin round his neck and a little sauce at the corner of his mouth. . . . I . . . I remember that still . . . the sauce at the corner of his mouth. He goes out. Then . . . then we hear the shots. We rush out, we find him lying in the doorway with blood all over his chest. She killed him!' The words came out in a wild scream. 'She killed him like an animal . . . she killed him . . .' The scream broke off and she buried her face in her hands, sobbing.

Landon looked across at Anna Albertini. Her eyes were closed and she was rocking on her feet as though she was going to crumple in a faint. Rienzi was on his feet in an instant. His voice was sharp with protest. 'Mr President, my client is under a great strain. I must ask that she be given a chair and a glass of water.'

The President nodded. 'The accused may sit during the evidence. Bring her a drink.'

One of the guards went out and brought in a chair. The Clerk of the Court offered a glass of water from his own table. The girl drank it, gratefully, and then sat down. All the while, the Prosecutor stood by Maria Belloni, comforting her with practised gentleness. It was, perhaps, three minutes before the President was able to resume his questioning.

'Signora Belloni, had you ever seen the prisoner before she came to your house?'

'Not since she was a little girl during the war.'

'Did you recognize her?'

'Not then. Only later.'

'Do you know why she killed your husband?'

'Because he did his duty.'

'Will you explain that, please?'

'During the war, my husband was the leader of the Partisans in this area. There were lives in his hands, many lives. There were also traitors who sold information to the Germans and to the *Fascisti*. This girl's mother was one of them. Because of her, some of our boys were taken, tortured and then killed. So she was arrested. There was a trial and she was condemned to death. My husband presided at the court and later at the execution. But this was war. He had to protect his men–and their women, too.' Quite suddenly, she seemed to become vague and dissociated, as if she were lapsing out of the reality of the court into a privacy of grief and terror. 'But that was long ago, it was finished, done, like all the other things that happened in the war. Then . . . this happens. . . . It is all crazy like a nightmare. I keep thinking that I must wake up and find my man beside me. But he doesn't come . . . he doesn't come!'

Her voice trailed off and she lapsed into low, broken sobbing. A whisper of pity went round the court like a breeze in a wheatfield, but the President silenced it instantly. He said: 'Does the defence have any questions for this witness?'

'We have three questions, Mr President. The first is this: how did Signora Belloni know of the charges against Anna Albertini's mother, of the trial and execution?'

'Will you answer that, please?'

Maria Belloni raised her head and stared vaguely at the rostrum. 'My husband told me, of course, and the others who were there. How else would I know? I had children to care for, a house to keep.'

'Thank you. The next question, Mr Rienzi?'

'With the permission of the court, I should like to put them directly to the witness.'

'Permission granted.'

Rienzi got up and walked slowly across to the witness box. His manner matched that of the Prosecutor for mildness and compassion. 'Signora Belloni, was your husband a good husband?'

Her answer came back, swift and bitter. 'A good husband! A good father! He loved us–took care of us. Even in the worst days, we were always fed and warm. He never did anyone any harm. The President of the Republic sent him a gold medal and called him a hero. That's the sort of man he was. Then she came along and killed him like a dog!'

Rienzi waited a moment until she relaxed, and then asked her with deceptive mildness: 'Was your husband always faithful to you?'

The Prosecutor jumped to his feet. 'Mr President, I object!'

The President shook his head. 'We find the question relevant to the summary before us. The witness is required to answer it.'

'I repeat the question, *signora*,' said Rienzi, patiently. 'Was your husband always faithful to you?'

'Of course he was! A woman always knows, doesn't she? He was a good husband and a good father. There was nobody else.'

'Thank you, *signora*. That is all.'

For the life of him, Landon could see small relevance in the question. The spectators in the court saw no drama in it either. Landon felt, with vague disappointment, that Carlo Rienzi was fumbling badly against unchallengeable witnesses.

As Maria Belloni was led from the witness box, there was a whispered consultation between the President and the other judges. Then the President addressed himself to the Prosecutor: 'My colleagues point out, quite rightly, that, given the evidence of the witnesses so far called, given also the signed statement of the accused which the defence accepts as true and voluntary, there is no doubt in their minds as to the fact and material circumstances of the murder of Gianbattista Belloni. They point out, however, that the second part of the charge must be sustained by the Public Minister: namely, that the murder was wilful and premeditated.'

The hawk-faced Prosecutor smiled. He could afford to be indulgent with a watertight brief that was already half proven. He said genially: 'We have established fact and motive, Mr President. We submit that premeditation will be proven by the testimony of our next witness. The first of these is Giorgio Belloni, son of the dead man.'

Giorgio Belloni proved to be a thin, narrow-faced youth with restless hands and a strident country accent. His testimony was simple and damning. He had been confronted twice with Anna Albertini–first on the day of the murder, later at the preliminary examination. They has been schoolchildren together and he had recognized her instantly. Both times he had challenged her to tell him why she had killed his father and on each occasion she had given, before witnesses, the same answer: 'I have no quarrel with you, Giorgio, only with him. I had to wait a long time, but it's finished now.'

When Rienzi declined either to challenge the testimony or to examine the witness, the President frowned and the judges on the rostrum leant towards each other whispering. Ninette turned to Peter and asked anxiously: 'What's he doing, Peter? How can he possibly fight now?'

'Give him time, sweetheart. This is only the first round.'

'Look at Doctor Ascolini.'

He glanced across the room and saw the old man leaning forward with his head in his hands, while Valeria sat erect beside him, a small, ironic smile on her lips. The Prosecutor announced his next witness with unctuous satisfaction: 'Luigi Albertini, husband of the accused.'

All heads were turned at a stifled cry from Anna.

'No, Luigi . . . no!'

It was the first sign of emotion she had shown since the trial began. Her eyes stared, one hand holding a crumpled handkerchief went to her mouth and it seemed for a moment as if she wanted to rush from the dock to the pale, handsome youth who was taking the stand. Then one of the guards placed a restraining hand on her shoulder and she sat rigid again, closing her eyes as if to blot out an impending horror. The young man was sworn and the President questioned him in a level voice: 'Your name is Luigi Albertini and you are the husband of the accused?'

'Yes.'

The reply was barely audible and the President admonished him sharply: 'This is a painful occasion, young man, but you are here to be heard by the court. Please speak up! How long have you been married?'

'Four years.'

'You have lived with your wife all that time?'

'Yes.'

'What work do you do?'

'I'm a night-watchman in the Elena textile factory in Florence.'

'What are your hours of work?'

'From nine in the evening until six in the morning.'

'In the course of your work, do you carry a gun?'

'I do.'

At a sign from the President, the Clerk of the Court walked across to the witness box and held out the weapon.

The President asked again: 'Do you recognize the weapon?'

'Yes, it's mine.'

'When did you last see it?'

'After I came off duty on the morning of the fourteenth of August. I put it on the bedside table. I usually put it in the bureau drawer, but this time I was tired and I forgot.'

'The gun was loaded?'

'Yes.'

'What do you usually do when you come off duty?'

'I have a meal and go to bed.'

'You did that on the morning of the fourteenth of August?'

'Yes.'

'What time did you wake up?'

'Three in the afternoon.'

'Was your wife at home?'

'No.

'Where was she?'

'I didn't know. She left a note saying not to worry about her and that she would be back in a couple of days.'

'When did you discover your gun was missing?'

'As soon as I found the note.'

'When did you see it again?.

'When the police brought me to Siena to see my wife.'

'Thank you.'

The President looked up questioningly at Rienzi.

He stood up slowly and said: 'Once again, Mr President, we must ask the indulgence of the court. I should like this witness recalled for defence examination at a later time.'

The President frowned and said, tartly: 'I would advise Counsel for the Defence that the judgment of the court will be given on the facts contained in our brief and interpreted in evidence. He would be strongly advised not to rely upon tactical manoeuvres.'

'With respect, Mr President,' said Rienzi, firmly, 'this court exists to dispense justice and it would be a sorry day if too a rigid a procedure were to inhibit such dispensation.'

Even to untutored observation, it was a risky move. The assisting judges looked up, displeased, and then turned to the President for a direction. The old man sat silent for a moment, toying with a pen. Finally, he frowned and said: 'In view of the dubious situation of the defence, we are inclined to grant his request. The witness is excused but he will be recalled later.'

'Thank you, Mr President.'

Rienzi sat down and the Public Minister took the floor with placid triumph.

'May it please the President and members of the court, it is the submission of the Republic that without further testimony murder is proved and premeditation as well. However, in order to anticipate any submission that may be made by the defence on the grounds of insanity or mental incapacity, I should like to call as my last witness Professor Emilio Galuzzi.'

Professor Galuzzi made an impressive progress to the stand. He spoke slowly and pedantically, but there was no doubting either his authority or his competence. With the consent of the President, the Prosecutor led him personally through the examination.

'Professor Galuzzi, what are your official appointments?'

'I hold the Chair of Psychiatric Medicine at the University of Siena. I'm the Director of Psychiatric Treatment at the Santa Caterina Hospital in this city. I act as adviser to the Department of Justice on Mental Health and Criminal Psychology.'

'Have you examined the prisoner Anna Albertini?'

'Yes. Acting under instructions from the Chancellor of this court, I made a series of psychiatric and medical examinations of the accused.'

'Will you tell the court your findings, please?'

'I found no evidence of any physical disorder or of any hysteric symptoms. There was evidence of residual shock, but this was consonant with a normal reaction after a crime of this nature and with the processes of arrest, imprisonment and interrogation to which the accused had been subjected. I did note, however, strong evidence of psychic trauma directly related to the circumstances of her mother's death. This was revealed by the classic symptoms of obsession, emotional incapacity and an apparent perversion of moral sense in respect of the crime.'

'Would you say, Professor, that the accused was, in the legal sense, a sane person?'

'Yes.'

'For this reason you agreed that she was fit to stand trial in this court.'

'Yes.'

'Again in the legal sense, Professor, she is to your view a responsible person?'

'You're asking me to repeat myself,' said Galuzzi, mildly. 'Legal sanity implies legal responsibility.'

The Prosecutor acknowledged the reproof with a thin smile. 'I have one more question. In your view, and in the same legal sense, was Anna Albertini a responsible person at the moment of the crime?'

'I would say so, yes.'

'That is all. Thank you.'

Carlo Rienzi stood up. 'With the permission of the President, I should like to ask the witness some questions.'

The President looked up at the clock, which showed five minutes to midday. He said, with tart humour: 'The court welcomes any display of activity on the part of the defence, but we are coming close to midday recess. Will Counsel's questioning take long?'

'It may take some time, Mr President.'

'In that case it would be better to take the recess now. Counsel may begin his examination when we resume sitting. The court is adjourned until three o'clock this afternoon.'

He gathered up his papers and walked out, followed by his colleagues. The guard led Anna Albertini from the dock and the court broke into a hubbub of talk. Landon and Ninette pushed forward to speak to Carlo, but before they reached him Valeria was already there and they were close enough to catch the first terse exchanges. Valeria asked irritably: 'Are you coming to lunch, Carlo? I don't want to hang around here too long.

Carlo stared at her vaguely. 'No, don't wait for me. I want to talk to Anna. I've ordered lunch in her cell.'

'Charming!' said Valeria with contempt. 'Charming, if a trifle bizarre! Then you won't mind if Basilio takes me to lunch?'

Rienzi shrugged wearily and turned away. 'You must do whatever you want, Valeria. I can't fight two battles at once.'

'You're not doing very well in this one, are you, darling?'

'I'm doing my best,' said Carlo moodily, 'and there's a long way to go yet.'

'A lifetime for your little white virgin!'

She turned away to follow the crowd from the court, but Landon, bitterly angry, blocked her retreat. 'Drop it, Valeria! Stop acting like a bitch! No man deserves what you're trying to do to Carlo.'

'You should be more polite, darling. I can do worse things if I want to.'

She gave him a little indulgent pat on the cheek and left him, flushed and impotent, counting once more the cost of a night's indiscretion. He turned back to the defence table, where Ninette, mercifully, was talking with Carlo: 'You're looking tired, Carlo. You must take care of yourself.'

Rienzi smiled ruefully. 'It's been a rough time. Except for Peter here I've been much alone. And Valeria is playing games to make it harder.' He turned to Landon. 'How does it sound from the front, Peter?'

'As we planned it–a preliminary skirmish.'

A brief, boyish grin lit up Rienzi's drawn face. 'I think we may do a little better this afternoon. Now, if you'll excuse me, I want to see my client. She needs a great deal of support just now.'

'Why not dine with us this evening?'

He hesitated, but Ninette gave him her most winning smile. 'Please, Carlo! You owe us a little of your company. We'll wait for you after the next session and then we'll dine at my apartment. You can relax there and perhaps play us a little music.'

'I'd like that. Thank you.'

He gathered his papers and walked, a stooping, tired figure, towards the door that led to the remand cells. Landon and Ninette watched him go and were touched by a common pity for so much lonely talent and so much genuine good will. Ninette exploded angrily: 'Valeria's a monster! If she can't break him one way she'll try another. What did you say to her, Peter?'

'I told her she was a bitch–and to leave Carlo alone.'

'You're not afraid of her, are you, Peter?' The question took him unawares and for a moment he had no answer. To his surprise, Ninette laughed quietly. 'Never let a woman blackmail you, Peter. Not even me. I love you, *chéri,* and I too can fight for what I want. Come on! You can buy me a drink and something to eat.'

The ante-room of the court was almost empty, but Dr Ascolini was waiting for them near the outer door. Without so much as a by-your-leave, he linked arms with Ninette and said, positively: 'I refuse to eat alone. You will both have lunch with me at Luca's. I want to talk with you.'

There was little time to talk as they threaded their way along the narrow, crowded pavements. But when they were settled in the baroque comfort of Luca's Ascolini challenged Landon: 'Well, my friend, what do you think of Carlo's chances?'

'It's too early to say.'

'And you, Ninette?'

'Frankly, *dottore,* I don't know what to think. I cannot believe that he is so inept as he has seemed to this point. But he has made no impression on me, and I think very little on the members of the court.'

The old man chuckled with satisfaction. 'So now perhaps you are prepared to agree that I might have been wise to dissuade him from this case?'

Ninette Lachaise shook her head. 'Not wholly. Even if he fails, and Peter thinks the odds are that he will, he will have tried his strength. He cannot fail to make some profit.'

'Even if he wrecks his career?'

'A career is less important than self-respect, *dottore.* You know that.'

'*Touché!*' said Ascolini with a grin. 'You have a formidable prize in this woman of yours, Landon. Now I should tell you both something which may surprise you: I think Carlo is doing remarkably well.' He waited a moment, savouring their surprise. 'You, my dear Landon, are bred to the forensic fireworks of a British court. You think in terms of a duel between opposing Counsel. You want one fact balanced against another, one argument qualified by an opposite one. You demand the sway of sympathy and the clash of personality. So you miss the strategy which our system demands.' He sipped his drink and wiped his lips fastidiously with a silk handkerchief. 'Consider what Carlo has done so far. He has reduced himself in the eyes of the judges so that they are concerned whether adequate justice is being done to the accused. Therefore they are inclined to allow him more latitude than they would otherwise do. He has permitted the prosecution to expend its whole argument in one morning's session. His timing allows him to examine a key prosecution witness at the beginning of a fresh session and to re-examine others in the light of defence evidence. This is sound campaigning—most sound with an unpromising brief.'

'Carlo would be encouraged to hear you say that.'

The old man frowned and answered unhappily: 'I doubt it. The climate between us is less favourable than ever. Valeria is now flaunting this Lazzaro fellow under Carlo's nose. He cannot fail to believe that I approve it.'

'She's destroying herself,' said Ninette with sudden anger. 'Can't she see that?'

'More clearly than you, I think,' said the old man sombrely. 'But there are matters that have no aptitude for contentment. I am one, she is another. Our sole satisfaction is to wrest from each moment whatever it holds of sweet or bitter. It is, if you want, an impulse of conquest and not of enjoyment. We seek to dominate and, if we cannot, we are happier to destroy. Carlo has withdrawn himself from us. All his interest is centred in this case–and, I'm afraid, in his client.'

'I'm afraid of that too,' said Landon with sharp interest. 'I've watched it happening these last weeks. I've tried to show him where it leads. I've pointed out the dangers to him and his client, but I'm afraid he's in no condition to measure them. I'm worried about him. In this profession, as in any other, a man needs a line of retreat from the demands which are made on him. If he doesn't find it at home, then he may attempt either an impossible dedication or a dangerous identification with his client.'

Ascolini nodded agreement, and asked with grave interest: 'Which way is Carlo leaning?'

'He thinks it is to dedication. I'm afraid it's the other way. He makes no secret of his compassion for Anna Albertini. He spends himself to ensure her comfort and to offer her reassurance. For her part, she is coming to lean on him for everything. Which makes a double danger.'

'I know,' said Ascolini. 'Valeria makes sordid jokes about it, and this is bad for any man working on the edge of his nerves. But he fights back now. He will not let us play games with him as we once did. The boy has become a man, and there is a fund of anger in him.'

He broke off, as if weary of so much unhappiness, and signalled a waiter to attend them. While they ate, they talked of more amiable matters, but by the time the coffee was brought they were back to the trial again, and the old man was expounding in sober, legal fashion his views on the problems of the defence.

'. . . In a case of this kind, where the facts and circumstances of a crime are beyond doubt, there is no hope of acquittal. No society can condone a murder. Between you and Carlo you have framed a plea of mitigation on the grounds of provocation and partial mental infirmity. Your problem is, of course, that you are brought immediately into areas of dubious definition where success depends as much on the skill of the advocate as on the legality of his plea. This is where experience comes in–and Carlo is deficient in experience.'

'I think you still underrate him, *dottore*,' said Ninette gently.

'Perhaps.' Ascolini smiled wryly. 'Even so, child, I'm afraid this court will be more stringent than you think, since too liberal a decision may lead to public disorders.'

'The vendetta?'

'The vendetta, the crime of passion–any circumstance where the law has failed to prevent or punish injustice, and the individual takes redress into his own hands. No society can permit this, however great the original wrong, because society dares not take liberties with its own survival.' His fine hands dismissed the subject as a riddle beyond solution. 'This is why justice is represented by a woman. She is fickle, paradoxical, relentless, but she has always an eye to the main chance.'

They laughed at his cynicism and he was pleased. Yet Landon felt in the same moment a pang of pity for him: a man with a touch of greatness, a cool analyst, a doughty fighter, a stoic humorist, yet robbed of the repose of age by the passions he had indulged in himself and others. It was not their place to judge him, but Landon understood all too clearly the dilemma in which he found himself. He had derided too long the man he now needed as a son. He had loved too selfishly the daughter who now used love as a weapon against him. Ambition was satisfied and passion spent. All that was left to him was the fierce peasant pride–weak buttress against the siege of years and solitude.

Landon was glad when Ninette said to him in her quiet, percipient fashion: Carlo's having dinner with us tonight. Why don't you come, too, *dottore*? It would give you both a chance to relax together.'

He smiled and shook his head. 'You have a gentle heart, young woman, but don't let it run away with you. It is Carlo who needs your company. And I'm a crooked old devil who will say the wrong thing from sheer perversity.' He pushed back his chair and stood up. 'Let's get a little fresh air before the next session.'

Twenty paces from the court-room, in the narrow, whitewashed remand cell, Advocate Carlo Rienzi was serving luncheon to his client. He had ordered the meal from a neighbouring restaurant, complete with wine, silver cutlery and fresh linen napery. Now he was busy as a housewife, spreading the cloth, laying the places and serving the food while the girl stood looking out of the single barred window towards a patch of blue sky.

The cell was austere as a monk's hole–with a truckle-bed, a crucifix on one wall, a pair of stools and a rough wooden table–but to Carlo Rienzi it wore for the moment an air of comfort and intimacy.

For the past weeks he had visited Anna Albertini almost daily, but had never once been private with her. There was always a guard within earshot whose menacing presence imposed a formality on their exchanges. Here, for the first time, they were truly alone. The heavy door was bolted, the Judas shutter was closed, and the languid guard was eating his lunch and washing it down with the wine Rienzi had brought for him.

Anna Albertini, however, showed no sign of pleasure or surprise at the new situation. She had thanked him gravely when the meal was brought in, and then had left him to serve it. When it was finished, he called her: 'Come and eat something, Anna.'

'I don't want anything, thank you.' She did not turn to answer him but spoke to the sky in a flat, toneless voice.

'It's a good meal,' said Rienzi with forced brightness. 'I ordered it myself.'

She turned then, and there was a hint of warmth in her reply: 'You shouldn't have taken all this trouble.'

Rienzi smiled, poured two glasses of wine and handed one to her. 'If you're not hungry, I am. Won't you join me?'

'If you want me to.'

Remote and placid, she moved to the table and sat down facing him. Rienzi began eating immediately, questioning her between mouthfuls.

'How do you feel, Anna?'

'Quite well, thank you.'

'It was rough this morning. I'm afraid it's going to be worse this afternoon.'

'I'm not afraid.'

'You should be,' said Rienzi roughly. 'Now stop being silly and eat your lunch.'

Obedient as a child, the girl began picking at her food while Rienzi sipped his wine and watched her, wondering as he always did at her uncanny air of innocence and detachment. After a while, she asked him: 'Why should I be afraid?'

For all his experience with her, Rienzi was staggered. 'Don't you understand, Anna? Even now? You saw the court, you heard the evidence. If the Prosecutor has his way you'll be in prison for twenty years. Doesn't that scare you?'

Her small, waxen hand pointed round the room. 'Isn't this prison?'

'Yes.'

'This doesn't scare me.' She was wide-eyed at his obtuseness. 'People are kind and considerate. I'm happy here. I'm happy at San Gimignano, happier than I've ever been in my life.'

'Because you killed a man?' Rienzi's tone was sharp with irritation.'

'No, not really. Because I sleep quietly, don't you see? I don't have nightmares. I wake in the morning and I feel new, a new person in a new world. There's nothing to hate, nothing to fear. For the first time I feel that I am myself.'

Rienzi stared at her, caught between pity and wonder and a little wordless fear. 'What were you before, Anna?'

Her face clouded, and her eyes became suddenly vague. 'I never knew. That was the trouble: I never knew.'

Then, as always, he was shaken with pity for her. He bent over his plate and ate a while in silence. Then, more genially, he told her: 'We do have a chance, you know, Anna. It's a slim one. But we may be able to get you off with a very light sentence.'

'I hope so,' said Anna Albertini placidly, 'for your sake.'

Rienzi gaped at her, startled. 'For my sake?'

'Yes. I know this case means a great deal to you. If you win it, it will make your reputation. You'll be the great advocate you've always wanted to be.'

'How do you know that?'

'I'm not a child, you know,' said Anna Albertini.

Rienzi digested the wry morsel for a few moments and then tried another line of questioning: 'Tell me, Anna, if we do succeed and you get a light sentence, what will you do when you come out of prison?'

'What I've always wanted to do—go back to my husband, be a good wife, bear him children.'

'Are you sure you could?'

'Why not? I told you, I'm a new person. The nightmares are over.'

'You may find worse ones waiting for you,' said Rienzi harshly. He pushed back his chair and walked away from the table, to stand as Anna had stood, looking through iron bars at a pocket-handkerchief sky. The girl watched him with childish puzzlement. She said, unhappily: 'I don't understand you at all.'

Rienzi swung round, stared at her for a moment, and then launched into a simple, passionate appeal: 'Anna, I'm trying to make you understand something. At this moment, and until the end of your trial, you are in my hands. I act for you, think for you, plead for you. But afterwards, whichever way it goes, you will have to do all these things for yourself. You will have to build a new life—inside the four walls of the prison or outside in the world of men and women. You have to begin preparing yourself now for whatever may happen. You will be alone, do you understand?'

'How can I be alone? I'm married to Luigi. Besides, you'll help me, won't you?'

Rienzi hedged his answer: 'A wise advocate interests himself only in the case, Anna, not in the private life of his client.'

'But you're interested in me aren't you–privately, I mean?'

'What makes you say that?'

'I feel it, that's all. When I'm standing there in the court, I tell myself that as long as I think of you everything will be all right.'

'That's not true, Anna. I'm just an ordinary lawyer with a bad brief. I can't work miracles. You mustn't expect them.'

It was almost as if she had not heard him, could not even see him. She went on with the pathetic earnestness of a child trying to explain herself: 'So far as I'm concerned, you are the only one in the court. I hardly see the others. I hardly hear them or know what they say. It's as if . . . as if . . .'

Rienzi prompted her sharply, 'As if what?'

'As if you were holding my hand, as my mother used to do.'

'God Almighty, no!'

The girl stared at him in distress. 'Did I say something wrong?'

'Eat your dinner, Anna,' said Rienzi dully. 'It's getting cold.'

He turned away from her and began pacing thoughtfully up and down the narrow room while the girl picked listlessly at the meal. After a few moments, a new thought seemed to strike her, and she asked: 'Where's Luigi? Why hasn't he come to see me?'

'I don't know, Anna.'

In her odd, absent fashion she seemed to accept the answer. Rienzi hesitated a moment and then asked her: 'Tell me, Anna, why did you marry Luigi?'

'My aunt said it was time for me to settle down. I wanted it, too. Luigi was a nice boy, gentle and kind. It seemed we could be happy together.'

'But you weren't?'

'When we were courting, yes. I was proud of him and he seemed to be proud of me. We would walk and talk and hold hands and kiss. We would make plans about what we were going to do–about names for our children, the sort of apartment we'd like. . . .'

'But afterwards?'

Anna Albertini looked at him strangely, and for the first time he saw the hint of a break in her composure. 'Afterwards was my fault. I just couldn't help myself. Every time he took me in his arms I . . .' She broke off and threw out her hands in a gesture of appeal. 'Please! I don't want to talk about it. It's all over now. I'm changed. I know I'll make him a good wife.'

'Does he still mean so much to you?'

'He's the only one I have.'

'What did he say to you when they brought him to see you in the prison?'

'Nothing. He just looked at me. I tried to explain to him, but they wouldn't let me talk. And then he went away. I don't blame him. I'm sure he'll understand in the end. Don't you agree?'

'I hope so,' said Rienzi deliberately, 'but I wouldn't count on it.'

For the first time, the real point of his interrogation made itself clear to her. Her hand went to her mouth and her face crumpled into a mask of horror. 'He doesn't love me any more?'

'No, Anna. I'm going to put him in the witness box again this afternoon. You may not like what you hear.'

She did not weep or cry out, but got up slowly from the table and walked to the window, where she stood, tight and trembling, the palms of her hands pressed against the white stone wall. Rienzi asked her: 'Were you really in love with him, Anna?'

'I don't know.' Her voice was dull and toneless. 'That's the point. Until now I've really never known about anything—even myself. So long as Belloni was alive things seemed to make sense, there was just a long, straight road, with me at one end of it and Belloni at the other. So long as I kept walking, I knew I must meet him sooner or later. Now he's dead, and there's nothing . . . no road, nothing!'

'Then you must find a new road, Anna.'

There was an infinite pathos in her reply: 'But a road always goes somewhere. I don't know where I want to go. I don't even know if there's a me. There's just my name, Anna Albertini, but no me. Can you see one?'

'I can, Anna.' He went to her and took her cold hands in his own. 'I can see one, touch one. She is made to have children of her own and hold them in her arms. She is very beautiful. She can love and be loved.'

'The only one who ever loved me was my mother.'

'She is dead, Anna.'

'I know.'

He pleaded with her passionately: 'But you're alive, Anna. You will go on living. You have to have something to live for.'

'I used to have Belloni. Now he's dead, too.'

'That was hate, Anna. You can't go on hating a dead man!'

'I wanted to love Luigi, but he doesn't love me. Where do I start? Where do I go?'

Sombrely, he told her again: 'If we lose our case, you'll go to prison for twenty years.'

'You know I'm not afraid of that. In a way it's been quite good. They tell me what to do, how to do it, where to go.'

'But this is not living.' He was angry now, and vehement. 'This is death! This is like the princess in the enchanted wood. You will have no nightmares, but you will have no life either! You will be led this way and that, like a clockwork figure, until beauty dies and love dies and there is no hope for you any more!'

'Please don't be angry with me.'

He caught her shoulders in a savage grip and shook her. 'Why not? You're a woman, not a rag-doll. You can't go on any longer shifting the responsibility for your life to someone else. It was you who broke Luigi. He wanted love and you couldn't give it to him. I want something from you now—help, co-operation! You're giving me nothing!' He released her and she stood rubbing her bruised shoulders, her eyes filled with the first tears he had ever seen in her. Instantly his anger was gone and he was overwhelmed by tenderness. He put his arm about her and drew her dark head against his breast. 'I'm not blaming you, Anna. I'm not God. I'm trying to get you to blame yourself.'

Then, for the first time, she began to weep, clinging to him desperately while her body shook with sobbing. 'Don't leave me. Don't leave me, please. I feel safe with you!'

Brutally, he thrust her away and blazed at her again: 'You can't feel safe! You've got to feel naked and alone and scared! You've got to want something so badly that it breaks your heart. You're a woman, Anna, not a child!'

Pitifully, she pleaded with him: 'I want to be a woman. Can't you see I want to be, but I don't know how? Help me! For God's sake help me!'

She clung to him again, her dark head on his shoulder, her hair brushing his lips. Rienzi tried awkwardly to comfort her while he stared, unseeingly, beyond her towards all the bleak implications of her dependence on him. Then he disengaged himself gently.

'I'll have to go now, Anna. We're due in court in a few minutes.'

'Don't go. Don't leave me!'

'I must, Anna,' said Rienzi with sober pity, 'I must.'

He turned away, walked to the door and called the guard to let him out. When it slammed behind him Anna Albertini stared blank-faced at the Judas window, then, seized with sudden terror, she flung herself on the bed, weeping like a lost child.

6

The afternoon session opened tamely, on a note of academic calm. Professor Galuzzi took the stand and Carlo Rienzi led him through a short résumé of the testimony he had given in the morning. Then Rienzi began to ask for definitions.

'Professor, I wonder if you will be good enough to explain to the court the meaning of the words "trauma" and "traumatic psychosis".'

Galuzzi smiled, coughed, adjusted his pince-nez, and explained: 'Literally, the word "trauma" means a wound. In the medical sense, it signifies a morbid condition of the body caused by some external disorder. In the psychiatric sense, it means much the same thing—a scar caused by emotional or mental shock. The words "traumatic psychosis" describe a disordered state of mind induced by the trauma. If I may explain more clearly, a scar in the finger is a trauma—not a very serious one. The scars left by major surgery are also traumas. There are similar degrees of scarring to the human psyche.'

'And the more serious traumas are always persistent?'

'Always. Though time and treatment may diminish their effects.'

'Correct me if I am wrong, Professor, but does not the word "psychosis" describe a deep-seated, grave and more or less permanent mental disorder?'

'In general terms, that's true.'

'So that a psychotic patient is always, in greater or less degree, handicapped?'

'Yes.'

'Let us take some simple examples, Professor.' Rienzi's tone was mild, almost deferential. 'A child loses a beloved parent. Would you call this an emotional shock?'

'Most certainly.'

'It would leave a scar?'

'Yes.'

'Which might reveal itself through some psychic infirmity in later life?'

'It might—yes.'

There was a small silence in the court. All eyes were on Rienzi as he walked back to his table, picked up some papers and then returned to Galuzzi. There was a change in him now. His shoulders straightened, his tone became crisper, the tempo of his questions grew faster.

'Let us take the case of Anna Albertini. She had lost both her parents by the age of eight. According to the evidence of the prosecution, her mother was executed by a firing-squad. How would you judge the scar inflicted on her young mind?'

'A very grave one.'

'Another question, Professor. You say you carried out tests on the prisoner. What was the nature of these tests?'

'In general terms, they consisted of a medical examination, a neurological survey and a modified form of analysis.'

'You know, then, that although she has been married for four years she is still a virgin?'

'Yes.'

'You would agree that this indicated an abnormality in her relations with her husband?'

'Yes.'

'How did you diagnose that abnormality?'

'As a condition of sexual incapacity in the accused related to and probably induced by her childhood experiences.'

'In other words, by the trauma, or scar, we have been talking about? Would you describe Anna Albertini as a psychotic subject?'

'Yes.'

'In other words, Professor, what you are saying is that she is mentally infirm?'

The Prosecutor stood up, protesting: 'I object, Mr President. The question leads the witness to a conclusion which is properly the function of the Bench.'

'The objection is upheld. Counsel for the Defence must confine himself to eliciting information in terms of the brief before us.'

'With respect, Mr President,' said Carlo Rienzi firmly, 'I am concerned to define clearly to the court the nature of the information elicited. However, in deference to the President's wishes, I will reframe the question. Tell us, Professor, is it or is it not true that a psychotic patient is mentally infirm?'

'It is true.'

'No more questions.'

'You are excused, Professor,' said the President.

There was a moment of whispered consultation on the rostrum and Ascolini turned to Landon and Ninette with a grin of triumph. 'You see? I told you he had cards in his sleeve! This is good–very good!'

To judge from the murmur that ran through the court, most of the spectators had taken the point too. The pressmen were scribbling notes and the Prosecutor was conferring with his associates. Alone of all the people in the court Anna Albertini sat calm and unmoved, like a priestess presiding over some ancient rite which had long since lost relevance or meaning.

The President rapped with his gavel and there was silence again while the Prosecutor stood up and addressed himself to the panel of judges: 'Mr President, gentlemen of the court, the indictment which is in your hands is so clear and simple, the testimony of the witnesses so concise and unanimous, that I hesitate to waste any more of the court's time by calling other testimony which is available to us. We have submitted proof of the crime, we have submitted proof of the premeditation. Both are confirmed by the voluntary statement of the accused. It is not for me to comment on the new line opened by the defence, but we would point out that it has accepted or left unchallenged all our testimony. We should appreciate a direction, Mr President.'

For a reason which Landon did not understand, the President seemed piqued by the suggestion. He said, acidly: 'I fail to see any reason for new direction in this case. If the prosecution has no more witnesses to call, then the defence may present its own testimony. Mr Rienzi?'

'With the permission of the court, I should like first to recall Luigi Albertini.'

At the mention of the name, the girl in the dock seemed to waken. Her hands fumbled restlessly on the brass railing and her eyes, wide and troubled, followed every step of the weak, puzzled youth towards the witness stand. Rienzi let him stand there a few moments, then began to question him with cool deliberation.

'Mr Albertini, how long have you been married?'

The boy looked up, startled and irritated. 'I said it before: four years.'

'Has your marriage always been a happy one?'

There was a pause, a shamed look towards his wife and then a mumbling, sullen answer: 'It's never been happy.'

'Why not?'

'I–I'd rather not say.'

'You must say,' Rienzi told him, flatly. 'Your wife is on trial for murder.'

Albertini flushed and stammered unhappily: 'I–I don't know how to say it.'

'Say it as you know it–simply, bluntly. Why was your marriage not happy?'

'We–we never made love together as married people should.'

'Why not?'

'Because whenever I took Anna in my arms she would start screaming: "They're killing her! They're killing my mother!"'

'Do you understand why she did this?'

'Of course I do!' A sudden feeble anger flared out of him, and then died. 'Anna understood it, too. But it didn't help either of us. Four years that went on.'

'During those four years–difficult years, I admit–did you ever seek medical advice?'

'Many times and with many doctors. They all said the same thing.'

'What did they say?'

'"Give her time and patience and she might get better."' He burst out, bitterly: 'But she never did! What kind of life is that?'

'And now, Mr Albertini?'

The boy looked puzzled. 'I don't know what you mean.'

Cold as a swordsman, Rienzi moved in for the kill. 'I think you do. Is it not a fact that ten days after your wife's arrest you made application, first to the Archbishop of Florence and then to the civil authorities, for the annulment of your marriage on the grounds of non-consummation?'

There was a moment of dead silence and then a scream of pure horror from the girl in the dock. 'No, Luigi, no!' The next instant, she was grappling with the guards and crying in a long, moaning ululation: 'Don't do it, Luigi! Don't leave me! Don't! Don't!'

The President's voice cut across the tumult: 'Remove the prisoner.'

In the body of the court, Professor Galuzzi jumped to his feet. 'With respect, Mr President, I suggest the prisoner be given immediate medical attention.'

'Thank you, Professor. The court would appreciate your attendance on the accused and your later advice on her fitness to continue the hearing.'

As Anna was wrestled out, moaning and struggling, her husband stood, downcast, in the dock and Carlo Rienzi turned a pale, composed face to the judges. 'I am finished with my witness, Mr President. I regret the disturbance, but I had no choice.'

For the first time, a wintry smile of approval showed on the old man's face. 'You are new to this court, Mr Rienzi. I hope we may see more of you.' He picked up his gavel. 'The court is adjourned for thirty minutes or until such time as the prisoner is fit to attend.'

In the disorder that followed his exit, Ninette and Landon sat with Doctor Ascolini and waited for the chattering crowd to disperse. Carlo picked up his papers and walked out of the court towards the remand cells.

Ascolini was as excited as a schoolboy, bouncing in his chair and making a whirlwind pantomime for Ninette's benefit. 'You see where the instinct shows, child? The method, the dramatic sense? This is the talent of great advocacy. You saw what he did. First he takes a hostile witness and borrows straw from him for his own bricks. He takes the specialist word "trauma" and all of a sudden it is a new one–"mental infirmity". We have the first brick laid. But Carlo knows and we all know that each of us is infirm in one fashion or another. So he stages a big drama, tears, shrieks and disorder, to show what infirmity may mean–a pretty girl who can't enjoy a tumble in bed. This is another brick: sympathy. And we all ask the same question: "How can this happen to a pretty girl that we'd all like to sleep with?" For the moment we forget that she has killed a man and that another woman sleeps lonely because of her. Two bricks! They are not yet a foundation for any defence. But the promise, girl! The promise in the man! I'm proud of him!'

'Then go and tell him so, *dottore*,' said Ninette firmly. 'A dozen steps and a dozen words and it is done. Go on now.'

'It's not time yet.'

'There will never be a better time, *dottore*. Swallow your pride.'

For a moment he hesitated, then he stood up, smoothed down his coat and walked with firm steps towards the far door of the court-room. Landon was dubious and said as much, but Ninette was jubilant over the success of her manoeuvre. 'It's important, don't you see, Peter? To Carlo, if he can call on Ascolini's support and advice for the rest of the case. To Ascolini, who has come to his own crisis. The best things we do are done quickly, from the heart.'

'We know what's in our own hearts, darling: I'm not sure we understand what's in theirs.'

'You make mysteries, Peter, where none exist. These two are ready for friendship. There is a respect on both sides. Let a good moment pass and there may not be another for a long time.'

To which he had no adequate reply, and besides it was easier to kiss her than argue with her. He surrendered with a shrug and a smile and they walked out hand in hand to the babble of the ante-room. The talk was deafening. It rose on high waves of emphasis and tumbled into frothing troughs of confusion. Words, phrases, scraps of interpretation were tossed up like spume-flakes and blown away. Women laughed, men looked subtle and knowing. Secrets were touted as freely as backstage gossip at an opera.

It was a bitter little commentary on the need of human nature to make a circus out of death and spectacle out of the scapegoat driven into the desert. Pity is a comforting indulgence, easily turned to contempt or ribaldry, but compassion is a rare virtue, founded on the admission that each hides in his own heart the weakness that he damns in his fellows, and that pain or thwarted desire may drive him to great excesses than they have committed. The cruelty of a crowd is less terrifying than the fear which it hides, the despair of personal forgiveness which inhibits the forgiveness of others.

'Peter, look!'

Ninette's fingers dug into his palm and he glanced up to see Valeria Rienzi pushing her way through the crowd towards them. Her face was white and strained and she accosted them abruptly: 'I want to talk to you two. Come and have a cup of coffee with me.'

Without waiting for an answer, she linked arms with them and hurried them to a little bar a hundred yards down the street. They had hardly settled themselves at the table before she burst out: 'I thought you'd both like to know. Basilio's left me. He told me so at lunch. Just like that ... the comedy's over!' She gave a sharp, hysterical laugh. 'Oh, I know what you're thinking! He would have done it sooner or later, just like he did it to you, Ninette. But it wasn't like that ... it wasn't like that at all. You know who organized it? My wise, loving father. He likes people of breeding, you know. Only the best stallions come to the Ascolini stud! So he telephoned Basilio and threatened to make trouble in his business if he didn't stop seeing me. Clever, isn't it? Everybody's mated now except me and Father. Carlo has his little virgin, you have each other. That leaves Father and me. What do I do now, Peter? Where do I look?' Her voice rose higher and heads were turned in their direction. 'You know how I am in bed. What's your prescription?'

Under the astonished eyes of the drinkers at the bar, Landon leaned across the table and slapped her hard on both cheeks so that the rising wave of hysteria broke into weeping. Ninette said nothing, but sat, shamed and blushing, while Landon fished a handkerchief from his pocket and pushed it across the table to Valeria. He said calmly: 'Dry your eyes, girl. You're making a fool of yourself!'

His tone sobered her and she began dabbing at her cheeks while Ninette and Landon looked at each other and at the stark revelation between them. Landon was the first to speak. He said quietly: 'I think you'd already guessed it, Ninette. I'm sorry you had to hear it this way.'

She shook her head, not trusting herself to speak. But she stretched out an impulsive hand and laid it over Landon's. In the same calm voice Landon spoke again to Valeria: 'Why don't you say the rest of it? You want revenge. You know the way to get it. Tell the story to your father. Then tell Carlo. This is the best time, isn't it, right in the middle of this case?'

'I want to.' Valeria's voice was almost a whisper. 'You don't know how much I want to.'

'But you won't,' said Ninette sharply.

'Why not?'

They faced each other like duellists across the table and Landon felt himself as far excluded as if he stood on the moon. Ninette Lachaise said quietly: 'You won't do it, Valeria, because, whether you know it or not, Carlo's your last hope. I know it because I've been part of the way you've gone. You can't survive too many men like Lazzaro. And after a while that's all we get, any of us. It doesn't really matter whether Carlo wins or loses, but if you break him before he has had his chance you break yourself too.' In the same breath she turned to Landon, and said with a twisted little smile: 'You go back to the court, Peter. It's women's business from here on.'

When he walked out into the flare of the midday sun, he felt like a man reprieved from the noose. Five minutes later he was back in the court with Ascolini at his side, waiting for the prisoner to be brought in and the judges to make their entrance. The old man was curiously subdued. When Landon questioned him about his meeting with Carlo, he answered absently: 'We talked a while. He was quite friendly. I made some suggestions. He seemed grateful.'

'But it was a progress?'

'Oh, yes. I should call it progress.' After a moment he added: 'Carlo took me into the cell to see the girl. I talked with her and with Galuzzi.'

'How did she impress you?'

'A pathetic child—a tragic woman. What else can one say?'

Landon would have said that the old man had matters on his mind that he was not prepared to discuss, but he made no comment and a few moments later Anna Albertini was brought into the dock and the judges filed in to continue the hearing.

The girl was a pitiful sight. She was sitting bolt upright in the chair, her hands gripping the brass rail of the dock. Her face was pinched and elongated, her eyes ringed with deep shadows, her hair no longer sleek but damp and clinging about her cheeks and temples. But when the President asked her whether she felt well enough to continue, she answered in a firm, flat voice: 'Yes, thank you.'

Rienzi confirmed her assent and then called his first witness for the defence: a countrywoman in her late thirties with a faded, sensual charm that contrasted vaguely with the dress of a peasant matron. She took the stand serenely and smiled self-consciously as the Clerk administered the oath. The President's method with her was brisk and businesslike.

'Tell the court your name, please.'

'Maddalena Barone.'

'Where do you live?'

'Pietradura. Ten kilometres north of San Stefano.'

'Are you married?'

'No.'

'Have you any children?'

'Yes. One son.'

'How old is he?'

'Sixteen.'

'Who was his father?'

'Gianbattista Belloni.'

There was an anguished cry from Maria Belloni: 'It's a lie—a dirty lie!'

The President slammed the gavel on the bench. 'If there is any more disturbance, I shall have you removed from the court!'

The Prosecutor jumped to his feet. 'Mr President, I protest! A man is dead—murdered! His past sins can have no relevance in this court.'

The President shook his head. 'We must overrule the objection. The Public Minister has been at pains to elicit facts about the character and reputation of the dead man. The defence must have the same latitude.' He went on questioning the witness. 'Did the father of your child ever make any contribution to his maintenance?'

'Yes. He paid every month. It wasn't much, but it helped.'

'How was this money paid to you?'

'By Sergeant Fiorello.'

'Did he deliver it personally?'

'No. It came through the post.'

'How do you know it came from Sergeant Fiorello?'

'After my boy was born, I wrote to his father asking him to help me. He didn't answer, but then Sergeant Fiorello came to see me.'

'What did he say?'

'He said I would get regular money. He would post it to me every month. But it would stop if I opened my mouth about who the father was.'

'Why are you now prepared to reveal this fact to the court?'

'Fra Bonifacio came to see me and told me it was my duty to tell the truth.'

'Thank you. You may step down.'

In the brief, tense pause that followed, the only sound was the muffled weeping of Maria Belloni. The Prosecutor made another, more restrained appeal: 'Mr President, I should like to call to the court's attention the fact that payment of maintenance through an official and confidential channel reflects credit and not dishonour on the memory of Gianbattista Belloni.'

The President assented, urbanely. 'No doubt my colleagues will take this fact into consideration at the proper time. Mr Rienzi?'

'With the permission of the court, I should like to re-examine Sergeant Fiorello.'

'Permission granted.'

The burly sergeant took the stand and again Landon was struck by his air of competence and composure. He blinked a little when Carlo requested permission to conduct the interrogation himself, but otherwise he showed no sign of emotion. Carlo's examination began in a flat, prosy style: 'Sergeant Fiorello, I want to recall to you some of the details of your service as a police officer. You entered the service twenty years ago under the Fascist administration and after training you were posted to San Stefano. You remained there all through the war. And after the war you were promoted to the rank of sergeant and given charge of the post. Is that correct?'

'Yes.'

'After the war many of your colleagues in the service were dismissed on the grounds of Fascist sympathies or on charges of oppression and cruelty?'

'That's right.'

'And during the war some of them had been shot by the Partisans for the same reason?'

'Yes.'

'How did you escape? How did you achieve promotion?'

'The official inquiry showed that I had been active in the underground movement and had worked in secret with local Partisan leaders.'

'Especially with Gianbattista Belloni?'

'Yes.'

'And the records of the inquiry contain an official letter of commendation from Belloni?'

'That's true.'

'What was your opinion of him?'

'A patriot and a brave man.'

'You have since had no reason to change that opinion?'

'No.'

'I call your attention, Sergeant–and I call the attention of the court–to item number 75 in the summary of evidence handed down to this court from the judicial inquiry.' He waited a moment while the judges leafed through their papers and then went on: 'This item is a photostatic copy of an entry annexed to the Records and Charges Book of the Public Security Division in San Stefano. The entry is in fact an account of the trial, sentence and execution of Agnese Moschetti, mother of Anna Moschetti, in November 1944. The account is attested by Gianbattista Belloni and five other participants in the military court. You will note that the date of the statement is 16 November 1944–three days after the death of Agnese Moschetti. But it was not annexed to the police record until 25 October 1946, long after the armistice, a month after the appointment of Sergeant Fiorello to command the post. Can you explain these dates to the court, Sergeant?'

'I can. The account of the trial was made and attested while the Fascist administration was still in power and the Germans were in occupation of the country. It was, therefore, an incriminating document. Belloni kept it until after the war and then handed it to me for inclusion in the official record.'

'Would you regard it as an unusual document?'

'In what way?'

'In the context of the times and the local conditions, the trial and execution of Agnese Moschetti were acts of war. Why did Belloni feel it necessary to record them? Can you tell me of any other Partisan proceedings that were similarly recorded?'

'No, I can't.'

'Then why did Belloni take this unusual step?'

'As he explained it to me, the execution of a woman was a bitter business–those were his words, "a bitter business"–and he wanted the facts recorded and known.'

'And that was the only reason?'

'I don't know of any others.'

'There had not been, for instance, any demand for a public inquiry?'

'Not that I know of.'

'No rumours or doubts or questions about the real nature of the Moschetti affair?'

'None.'

'As a matter of interest, Sergeant, where did the trial take place?'

'That's in the statement. Anna Moschetti's house in San Stefano.'

'Where were the police on that night–and, specifically, where were you?'

'We were out on patrol, miles away. Belloni had faked a telephone call and a report of a Partisan attempt to blow up the railway line.'

'Did you know what was being planned?'

'No.'

'But I thought you had his confidence and that you co-operated with him?'

'It was the method–nobody knew more than he had to. It was safer that way. I did what I was told and asked no questions.'

'Sergeant, you understand that you are testifying under oath.'

'I do.'

'Then let me repeat an earlier question. After you were appointed to command the post, did anybody at any time ask you to open an inquiry into the circumstances of Agnese Moschetti's death?'

'No!'

Rienzi's finger stabbed at him like a scalpel. 'You lie, Sergeant! You lie under solemn oath–and I shall prove it to this court!' He turned and made a small, apologetic bow to the judges. 'I am finished with this witness, Mr President.'

'But the court is not finished with him!' The President turned a cold eye on the burly, impassive fellow on the stand. 'You still have time to amend your testimony, Sergeant. If later testimony proves you guilty of perjury, you may face grave punishment.'

For a moment, Landon thought he would brazen it out, but at the last moment he wavered and stammered: 'I–I answered the questions as put to me. There was no demand for an inquiry, but–but there was talk about having one. It didn't come to anything.'

Carlo leapt to his feet. 'Please, Mr President, I should like to have the Clerk read a transcript of my earlier question which specified "rumours, doubts or questions".'

'We may dispense with the transcript,' said the President firmly. 'The question is still fresh in our minds. The Chancellor and the Public Minister will take note of the conduct of this witness and that charges may eventually lie against him for perjury, obstruction of justice and conspiracy. Step down, please.'

As Fiorello walked back to his place, he seemed to have shrunk about six inches in height and girth. Rienzi, on the other hand, seemed to take on new stature with every moment. For all his grey, insomniac complexion and his drawn, peaked face, strength went out from him and authority increased in him. In the intervals of interrogation or while the judges conferred, as they were conferring now, he seemed able to efface himself from one's attention, so that each new appearance had a new impact and each interrogation a new aspect of drama. After the short discussion on the rostrum, the President recalled the court to order and put a new question to Rienzi: 'My colleagues point out, with some justice, that the testimony of the defence seems to be placing considerable emphasis on the character of the deceased and on an event which took place sixteen years ago–the execution of Agnese Moschetti. They feel, and I feel too, that the defence should help us by establishing the relevance of such testimony.'

'It is our submission, Mr President, that the testimony is relevant to every issue in this case: to the nature of the crime, to motive, provocation, premeditation, to the moral and legal responsibility of the accused and to the question which is paramount in the mind of every member of the judiciary and every member of the body politic: how justice may be done within the limitation of the law.'

A faint smile of approval twitched the thin lips of the old jurist. 'If the evidence of the Counsel for Defence matches his eloquence, the court will be well served. Your next witness, please.'

'I call Fra Bonifacio of the Order of Friars Minor, parish priest of San Stefano.'

There was a curious pathos in the spectacle of the stooped, weather-beaten cleric padding across the court in his sandalled feet. In spite of his tonsure and habit of an ancient Order, he looked exactly what he was—an ageing shepherd of an unruly flock who had found the world to big for him.

The Clerk stepped forward to administer the oath: 'Do you swear before God to tell the whole simple truth without concealment or addition?'

The friar hesitated a moment and then turned to the judge. 'May it please the President?'

'Yes, Father, what is it?'

'I cannot swear to tell the whole truth—only that part of it which lies outside the seal of confession and which comes within my knowledge as a public citizen.'

'We will accept your oath on those terms.'

'Subject to the seal, then, I swear.'

'Defence may question this witness.'

Rienzi's method with the old priest was deferent and almost humble. Once more, Landon was struck by his chameleon talent for adaptation to a situation and a person. He asked quietly: 'How long have you lived in San Stefano?'

'Thirty-two years.'

'You know everybody in the town?'

'Everybody.'

'You knew the mother of the accused, Agnese Moschetti?'

'I did.'

'And you knew the accused as a child?'

'Yes.'

'After her mother's death, you were the one who took care of her and later made arrangements to send her to relatives in Florence?'

'That is correct.'

'During the war you were a member of a Partisan band fighting against the *Fascisti* and the Germans.'

'That is not quite correct. My first duty was always that of a priest ministering to the spiritual needs of my flock. I did, however, on many occasions work with local Partisans.'

'Specifically, you worked with Gianbattista Belloni?'

'I did.'

'What did this work entail?'

'Carrying information, hiding fugitives, looking after the wounded, sometimes transporting guns, food and ammunition.'

'You did all these things right up to the armistice?'

'No.'

'Will you explain that to the court, please?'

'In the last stages of the war and immediately afterwards, I felt bound in conscience to withdraw from Belloni and in fact to reprove him openly.'

'Why?'

'I believed that many of his actions were dictated not by the needs of war but by a desire for private vengeance or private gain.'

'Can you give the court any examples?'

'Belloni and his men took away our local doctor and shot him, simply because he had given medical care to a wounded German. He ordered the execution of a peasant and his wife whose land adjoined his own property. Later he bought this land at a trifling price. Immediately after the armistice he directed the summary trial and execution of seven townspeople. Continued complaints were made to me by women and girls who had been molested by him or by members of his band.'

A flutter of comment broke out in the court and the Prosecutor leapt to his feet. 'Mr President! I must protest in the strongest terms against the irregularity of these proceedings. Belloni is dead and beyond the jurisdiction of this court. We are concerned only with a charge of murder against Anna Albertini, which I submit we have proved beyond question. Belloni is not here to answer for himself. We are not trying him but Anna Albertini.'

For the first time, Rienzi made his own emphatic rebuttal: 'Mr President, gentlemen of the court! Our concern is justice, an assessment of guilt. Our judicial system defines and graduates the crime of murder, not only in terms of the act, not only in terms of premeditation or provocation, but in terms of motive and mitigation. I submit with all respect that you cannot arrive at a just decision without knowing all the circumstances and all the characters concerned in it, including the character of the dead man.'

The President nodded assent. 'The Counsel for the Defence may continue his examination.'

'Thank you, Mr President.' He turned back to the witness. 'Now, Father, the court would like to hear what you know of the death of Agnese Moschetti, mother of the accused.'

'I'm sorry.' The old man drew himself up and answered firmly: 'I cannot answer that question. I was not an eyewitness. Much of the knowledge I have came to me first under the seal of confession. I do not feel free, therefore, to give any evidence on the point.'

'Would it be true to say, Father, that people gave you this information in the confessional because they were afraid to give it publicly?'

'I cannot answer that, either.'

Reinzi accepted the answer respectfully. He waited a moment and then moved off on to another tack. 'Let me ask you a personal question, Fra Bonifacio. Did you yourself make any public protests about the trial and execution of Agnese Moschetti?'

'I did. I condemned it in the strongest terms from my pulpit. I made mention of other acts of violence committed not only by the Partisans but by those in power. I tried to initiate punitive action through the former police representative, Sergeant Lopinto.'

'But after the armistice, when Sergeant Lopinto was dead and Sergeant Fiorello was in charge, and Belloni was back as Mayor and master of the village—did you take any action then?'

'Yes. I asked Sergeant Fiorello to reopen the case and institute a public inquiry. He refused.'

'Did he give any reason?'

'Yes. He said many things had been done during the war which were better forgotten. People had to start living normally again. There was no point in continuing old hates.'

'And you agreed with that?' asked Rienzi, softly.

For the first time the old man hesitated. His face clouded, his lips trembled and he seemed to stoop a little more as though weighed down by the burdens of guilt and memory. 'I—I was not sure. There was much to recommend the thought. This is the tragedy of war, that men of good will are committed to evil courses and wicked things are done in the name of good. Besides, we had to rebuild our lives and we could not rebuild them on bitterness.'

'So you did nothing more about the inquiry?'

'Until the death of Gianbattista Belloni-no.'

'So, in fact, Father,' said Rienzi, with cold precision, 'you too lent yourself to a conspiracy of silence on this matter?'

'A man can only take the path he sees at his feet. It appears I chose the wrong path. I am sorry for it now. A priest has so much more to answer for.'

There was no one in court who did not feel for the old man in this moment of bitter avowal. But Rienzi was not finished with him yet. He walked back to his table and unwrapped, with theatrical deliberation, a small, brown-paper parcel. Then he walked back to the witness stand, holding in his hands what appeared to be a piece of broken masonry. He held it out to the friar. 'Do you recognize this?'

'I do. It's a piece of stone from the wall of the churchyard at San Stefano.'

'There are words written on it. I do not ask you to read them, only to tell me by whom they were written.'

'By Anna Albertini, the accused.'

'Do you know when they were written?'

'The day after her mother's death.'

'Did you see them written?'

'I did. I came on her scratching them into the wall with a piece of tin.'

'Thank you, Father, that is all.'

As the friar stepped down from the box, a bowed, shambling man, Rienzi turned to the judges' rostrum. 'With the permission of the court, I propose to return to this object in later evidence and to identify it more fully for the court. For the present, I would direct the attention of the court to the condition of my client. She has been, as you know, under grave strain. She is, as you see, very much reduced and in need of rest and medical attention. I beg the clemency of the court and request that this hearing be adjourned until tomorrow, when we shall present the final evidence for the defence.'

The President looked up, sharply. 'The court has already allowed a great deal of latitude to Counsel in the presentation of his case. I must warn him against leaning too much on tactic and stratagem.'

'This is not a stratagem, Mr President,' said Rienzi hotly. 'It is a request made out of consideration for my client, who is on trial on the gravest possible charge. We are content to abide by the decision of the Bench, but we submit that medical advice may be indicated.'

The President bent down to talk with his judicial associates and then with the people's judges. After a moment, he said: 'Will Professor Galuzzi step forward, please?'

The whispering in the court went on unchecked as Galuzzi conferred with the President and the other members of the Bench. Finally, the President announced, formally:

'In compliance with the request of the defence, this court is adjourned until ten o'clock tomorrow morning.'

'Thank you, Mr President,' said Carlo Rienzi, and walked back to his table like a man who had just staked his life's savings on the last roll of the dice.

'I hope—' muttered Ascolini, 'I hope he has good cards for tomorrow. If not, they will crucify him.' Then, abruptly, he said: 'Carlo's dining with you tonight. I want to talk with you before you see him.'

Landon frowned dubiously. 'I doubt I'll have time. Ninette's not here, and I promised to wait for him after the session.'

'Then send him a note.' The old man's tone was testy. 'Tell him to go directly to the apartment an hour from now.'

'But why, Doctor?' There was a note of irritation in his voice. His patience was frayed thin by the exactions of these people.

Ascolini was subtle enough to take the point. He spread his hands in apology: 'I know! I know! We ask too much and give too little. We draw you into our intrigues and wound you because you are our friends. I'm sorry. I promise you this will be the last time.' He fished out a small note-book and a silver pencil. 'Please indulge me this time. Write a note to Carlo and have one of the clerks take it to him.'

Reluctantly, Landon scribbled the note and the old man handed it to an official to deliver to Rienzi. Then he steered Landon out of the court-room, through the clamour of the dispersing spectators and into the pale, late sunlight of the city.

Three minutes' devious walking brought them to a small square with a time-scarred fountain in the centre of a surprising little café that offered iced tea and sweet pastries. The square was still hot and humid, but inside there were deep shadows and a grateful cool. They were served quickly, and Ascolini began, brusque and unsmiling, to set down his thoughts.

'Carlo has done much, much better than I expected. He cannot win, of course. Tomorrow will be a dangerous day for him, but if he survives it he will have scored a professional triumph. There will be twenty briefs on his desk before the week is out. And this will be only a small presage of what is to come. His first battle will have been won, as indeed it is won already–to prove himself a good advocate and an independent spirit. But one battle is not a campaign and there are others, more bitter, still to be fought. For this one he has been armed with education and training. For the others I'm afraid he is quite unprepared.'

'I advised him weeks ago,' said Landon bluntly. 'He can win them only by walking away. Valeria is no good to him. She'll take everything and give nothing. He'll spend the rest of his life trying to tame her–and end an old man living with a shrew.' Then he added, regretfully: 'I'm sorry, Doctor. I have a great respect for you and she's your daughter. But I can't be polite any more.'

'You don't have to be polite,' said Ascolini mildly. 'I know she's jealous of you and Ninette and that she wants to make trouble between you. But you did make some of it yourself when you slept with her.'

Shamed and shocked, Landon gaped at him. 'How did you know that?'

Ascolini waved an inconsequential hand. 'She told me the day after your little escapade.' He chuckled with sour amusement. 'Oh, I imagine she promised discretion and secrecy, but you should have known better than to be taken in by such protestations.'

'I should,' said Landon, 'but I didn't. What was the point in telling you?'

'A threat,' said Ascolini quietly. 'An assertion of power by a jealous woman. If I interfered any more in her relations with Lazzaro she would tell Carlo and she would tell Ninette.'

'She told Ninette at lunch.'

Ascolini nodded sagely. 'I expected she might. How did Ninette take it?'

'Better than I deserved,' said Landon. 'I left them together. What happens now I wouldn't know. When you knew, Doctor, why didn't you come to me?'

Ascolini gave one of his eloquent shrugs. 'I saw a profit in not telling you. I thought, and thought rightly, that you would feel obliged to Carlo and would stay to help him. For the rest,' he chuckled again in self-mockery, 'I could understand it. I've done it myself with other men's daughters and other men's wives. And there was a satisfaction in watching a man like you squirm a little. I shock you, I know, Landon. But I told you a long time ago this is the kind of people we are. My only credit is that I am honest enough to admit it. I'm not a noble father putting a virgin daughter on the auction block. I've connived at too many follies not to wear this small one with equanimity.'

Landon burst out, bitterly: 'Then why the hell did you make such a fuss about Basilio Lazzaro?'

Ascolini answered in the same equable tone: 'Even in a society like ours, Landon, old, sophisticated and often corrupt, there are limits beyond which a woman cannot go and still preserve her place. We are amused by the diversions of convenient marriage. We object to vulgarities like Lazzaro. This affair had to stop or Valeria would have no retreat at all.'

'Do you think she has now?'

'Just one–Carlo.'

'Ninette said the same thing. I'm not sure that I agree. The road may be closed already.'

'Do you think I don't know that?' For the first time, there was a flash of anger from the old advocate. 'Why else do you think I give you so much confidence? I want to use you, Landon. . . . Look! I saw Carlo this morning. I spoke with him and with Galuzzi. I am too old not to understand how matters stand between him and his client. You're a professional. You know what this means. Carlo has affection for this girl. I read the signs. I've had clients of my own to whom I have been drawn in circumstances much less favourable. I was cynical enought to enjoy the opportunity. But Carlo is no cynic, and he has been starved of love too long.'

Landon shook his head and leaned back wearily from his untasted coffee. 'I'm sorry, Doctor. I can prescribe for Carlo–and I've already done it–but I can't make him drink the medicine. Besides I don't think it can go too far. The girl is mentally infirm!'

'And have you, my dear Landon, never met those who need an infirmity in the beloved?'

'Sometimes.' Landon's impatience was rising. 'But what the devil do you expect me to do? Read him a little lecture and send him back to the loving Valeria?'

'I'm sorry, Landon,' said Ascolini with grave dignity. 'We have spun webs for you and now you are as enmeshed as we are. One day, perhaps, we may have grace enough to make amends, but you've asked me a question and this is my answer.' He paused a moment and then laid it down with an almost touching simplicity. 'Tell Carlo, from one who knows, that it is sometimes better to be content with a small, sour apple than to eat strange fruit in an alien country.'

When Landon reached the apartment, he found Ninette alone, bustling about the preparation of Carlo Rienzi's dinner. They embraced, but without passion, and then Ninette told him: 'I had a long talk with Valeria. I understand her, Peter, and I'm sorry for her. All her supports have been knocked away with one stroke–and Ascolini is responsible. I'm fond of him, as you know, but he has been brutally selfish in this matter, as in so many others. All his life he has tried to centre Valeria's affection on himself. Now, because he wants children, because Carlo suddenly begins to look like the son he wanted, he turns away from Valeria. She's lost, Peter, lost and bitter and jealous. So she tried to strike at anyone in reach.'

'She still has Carlo to strike at,' said Landon unhappily. 'I think I should tell him before she does.'

'No, Peter!' Ninette was firm. 'So long as there's a chance that he won't know I think we have to take it. After my talk with Valeria I think there is that chance. She knows at least that I feel no malice towards her—and that you don't either.'

'I think I'd feel better if I talked it out with Carlo.'

'Would he, Peter?'

'I don't know.'

Then she faced him with the question he had been dreading all the afternoon: 'And how do you feel now, Peter—about us?'

'I'm ashamed of myself, if that's any help.'

'Why are you ashamed, Peter? Because you're not the man you thought you were?'

'Partly. We all have our pride, you know. And partly because you deserve better from me.'

'Do you mean that, Peter? Even though you know about Lazzaro and me?'

'Lazzaro was an old episode for you. Mine was something different. There was no excuse for it.'

'There's always an excuse, Peter. That's what worries me. I'm not perfect, God knows. If we were married I'd probably give you twenty more excuses in a month, but if you took them I would hate you. I don't want that kind of marriage, Peter. I don't want a union that flowers inevitably into the kind of cruelty we've seen practised in the last few weeks. I'm not built to endure it. I'd wither under it very quickly. I love you, *chéri*, but I want to see you content. I love you enough to want you gone if you can't be content with me.'

'I love you too, Ninette, more desperately than I ever thought possible.' He moved towards her, but she drew away. He went on, slowly, piecing out the thought with difficulty: 'All my life, for a thousand reasons and one, I've tried to be self-sufficient, self-dependent, beyond the touch of the pain that other people can inflict. That's the way they know me in my profession—the driving man, the ambitious fellow they'd like to trip but can't because he knows too much and feels too little. I can go back to that, but I can't be content with it any more. I know what I need. I know that I need you. I want to tell you something, sweetheart. I've never said this to another person in my life. At this moment I'm almost like Carlo Rienzi. You can put any price on yourself. I think I'd pay it.'

For a long moment she stood slack and irresolute, measuring him, measuring the risk to herself. Then she shook her head and said in a whisper: 'There's no price, Peter. Just love me. For God's sake, just love me.'

Then she came to him running and clung to him and they kissed and were glad and it seemed almost possible that youth and all its illusions might be reborn again.

When Carlo came he found them happy as birds in an apple tree. They hustled him into the studio and settled down to lay the foundations of a convivial evening. Chianti and Barolo and Tuscan brandy are rough remedies for the megrims, but they worked for them that night. They drank deeply and laughed immoderately and made a lavish production of Ninette's dinner and then lapsed by degrees into drowsy contentment, while Carlo sat at the piano and played Scarlatti and Brahms and old plaintive melodies from the folk music of the mountains.

It was a good time, a gentle time: a recall of youth and the high untarnished hopes of innocence. Their doors were locked against intrusion. Their windows opened on silver roof-tops and a sky rich with stars. Harsh memories were muted to mezzotint. The music laid a balm to new wounds and was lenitive to old regrets. When it was done, they sat quiet in the half-dark, the talk floating between like straws in slack water. Carlo said softly: 'I am grateful for tonight–more grateful than I can tell you. Tomorrow is a critical day for me, and you have made me ready to face it.'

'How will it go, Carlo?' asked Ninette.

'Who knows? We are on the knees of the Blind Goddess. I dare not hope too much.'

'Are you satisfied so far?'

'For myself, yes. I think we have done better than anyone believed possible. I can look at myself in a mirror and know that I have proved what I set out to do. At the beginning, I thought this would be enough. Now, it is all too little.' He broke off to light a cigarette and the flare of the match lit up his face, peaked and pale, but endowed with the new maturity of experience. 'It is Anna who troubles me now. She trusts me so far. She has so little fear, so little understanding of what my failure may mean to her. This is a nightmare to me.'

'Perhaps to her it is a mercy,' suggested Ninette.

'Oh no!' His reaction was swift and passionate. 'You don't understand. In the beginning it was a mercy–but not now. How can I explain it? When I first met her, she was like a child–no–like a woman who had wakened out of one world into another, strange but much more beautiful, in which there was nothing to hate, nothing to fear, nothing to desire. Even the prison seemed to her a comfortable place. I thought at first that she did not understand her situation, but she understood it very well and could look forward to twenty years of confinement without a single terror. Her only interest in her defence seemed to be that she should not disgrace me. I spoke to you about it, Peter, and you explained it to me as the euphoria of shock, the well-being of those who have survived a massive onslaught on the tissue of mind and body and have lapsed into the anaesthesia which nature provides beyond the powers of the physician. Then, slowly, awareness began to grow in her. She began to talk to me of her husband, of the failure of their life together, of her hope to come now to the consummation of love and bear him children. I did a brutal thing when I put him in the witness box, but it was necessary. And it has had a strange effect. For the first time, she has begun to be aware not only of tragedy but of hope. If she is robbed of it now, God knows what may happen to her!'

His voice trailed off and they sat smoking in silence while the shadows closed in on them and the cigarette smoke drifted up, grey and ghostly, into the darkness of the ceiling. After a while, Ninette asked: 'How do you see her, Peter? What kind of a person is she?'

Landon thought about it for a moment and then said, judicially: 'The answer is, I think, that she's not yet a person at all. She's twenty-four years of age, familiar as any of us with the motions of a workaday world, but still a child, with a child's innocence and a child's wonder and a child's dependence.'

'That's it, Peter!' Carlo's voice was eager. 'Valeria and her father think I'm in love with Anna. Perhaps I am, but not as they imagine. Valeria has never given me a child, but I think I have the same feeling for Anna as I should have for a daughter: a care, a tenderness, and a pity for so much simplicity.'

'Will she ever grow up?' It was Ninette who asked the question and Landon who answered it.

'It's possible, but it will be a slow process. Carlo has already seen some of the signs. The act of murder was, in effect, an attempt by violent means to shake off the burden of her past. The next step is the one we see now: she is groping, as children grope, for an affirmation of identity.'

'Like this afternoon.' Carlo took up the thread of the argument. 'For the first time, she was angry with me because I told her she must be afraid for herself, instead of leaving me to carry the burden of her fears.'

There was a moment's pause, and then Landon spoke, quiet and shrewd, out of the shadows. 'What did she say to that, Carlo?'

'That I was impatient with her, that I asked too much too soon, that she wanted to be a woman, but could not grow alone.'

'Poor child!' said Ninette softly. 'Poor lost child!'

'But don't you see!' Rienzi's voice took on a new, vibrant urgency. 'She is looking for herself now, she is looking for a new road. If we lose our case and she is sent to prison for twenty years, she will sink back into the absolute calm of despair. She will end like those poor creatures who sit all their lives in one corner, seeing nothing, hearing nothing, saying nothing, without even the thought of death to comfort them. But if we can win, if we can give her hope of release within a reasonable time, then she may continue the search, and, given a little love, she may well succeed. Even the care which she senses in me has done much for her. A little more—and who knows?'

In spite of himself, Landon gave voice to the final question: 'Can you spare so much, Carlo, and have you the right?'

His answer came back, sharp and strong: 'I think I have. I have spent so much for no return—why should I not spend a little on this lost one?'

'The time may come,' said Landon deliberately, 'when your child is a woman and will ask more than you have to give.'

'I cannot think of that,' said Carlo Rienzi. 'I cannot think past tomorrow.'

7

The following morning Landon and Ninette arrived at the court forty minutes before the session was due to open; but the ante-room and the pavement were already choked with people clamouring for entrance. It took twenty minutes of argument with a harassed official before they were admitted into the court-room, where other privileged visitors were already seated.

Ascolini was there with Valeria. She was dressed more soberly than usual.

Her face was pale, her eyes heavy and her manner was oddly absent and distracted. Landon and Ascolini sat side by side between the two women. The old advocate, too, was tense and preoccupied. He answered Landon's questions vaguely and summed up the morning's prospects in short, irritable phrases: 'So far, it has been a matter of tactics. Carlo has gained ground. The main lines of his plea have clarified themselves. The dispositions of the court seem slightly in his favour. From this point, everything depends on the testimony he has to offer and on the use he makes of it in his final summation. I'd have liked to discuss it with him, but he, too, has a hard head. I feel old this morning. It is time I thought of retirement. . . .'

The doors each side of the court opened and the personages began filtering on to the stage for the final act of the legal drama. The Chancellor and his clerks settled themselves at their table. The Prosecutor talked in low tones to his assistants. Carlo Rienzi came in with his two seedy colleagues trailing behind him. He sat down at his table and began leafing through his briefs and making notes on a scratch-pad beside him. There was a burst of excited talk as Anna Albertini was brought in by her gaolers. Then, as if to forestall any more discussion, the President and his assisting judges filed in briskly and took their places on the rostrum. There was whispering and scuffling as the spectators settled themselves and then the dry clatter of the gavel reduced the crowded room to deathly silence.

Carlo Rienzi stood up. His voice was cool, clear and impersonal. 'Mr President, gentlemen of the court, we have two more witnesses to offer and then our testimony is complete. With the permission of the court, I should like to examine Ignazio Carrese.'

'Permission granted.'

The man who approached the witness stand was a short, stocky peasant nearing fifty, with gnarled hands and a shuffling gait and a dark, sun-tanned face, seamed and scored like the weathered rocks of his own countryside. When the oath was read, he mumbled an assent and stood, arms limp, shoulders humped, eyes downcast to the floor in front of him.

Rienzi let him sweat a moment and then stood a pace away from him until the peasant lifted his head and faced him with frightened eyes.

'Tell the court your name, please.'

'Ignazio Carrese.'

'What do you do for a living?'

'I'm a farmer in San Stefano.'

'Do you own your own land?'

'Yes.'

'Have you always owned it?'

'No. I bought it after the war.'

'Where did you get the money?'

'Belloni lent it to me.'

'What interest did he charge you?'

'None at all.'

'Was he always as generous at that?'

Carrese dropped his eyes, hesitated, and then mumbled his answer: 'I–I don't know. He was to me, anyway. I–I was his number two in the Partisans.'

'Do you understand that by answering some of the questions I am going to put to you, you may do yourself harm?'

The witness looked up and then straightened himself as if to meet a destiny long deferred. His voice took on a new, firmer tone. 'I–I understand that.'

'Why have you agreed to give evidence?'

'I talked to Father Bonifacio. He told me . . .' His mouth trembled and it seemed for a moment as if he were about to break down.

Rienzi checked him sharply: 'Told you what?'

'That it wasn't enough to be sorry. I had to make amends.'

'A tardy wisdom,' commented Rienzi drily, 'which I hope may commend itself to this court.' His silence challenged them for a moment, then he went on, more quietly: 'Ignazio Carrese, I want you to take your mind back to a day in 1944. It was a Saturday, I believe.'

As if anxious to purge himself as swiftly as possible, the witness stumbled on, lapsing occasionally into the raw country dialect. 'That's right, it was a Saturday night. We were all at the hide-out in the hills . . . me . . .the other boys. We were waiting for Belloni. When he got in, we saw he was hopping mad. He had that crazy look he used to get when someone crossed him. He said: "That's it! Nobody slaps Belloni and gets away with it! There's a job tomorrow, a big job!"'

'Did he tell you what this big job was?'

'Yes, he did.'

'What did he say?'

'He said . . . he said . . .' Beads of sweat broke out on his lined forehead and he wiped them away with a grubby handkerchief.

Rienzi pressed him, firmly. 'What did he say?'

He said: 'It's the Moschetti bitch. Her husband's a bloody Fascist and she's no better. She's got to go!'

There was a low moan from the dock and all heads were turned to see Anna Albertini swaying in her chair, eyes closed, her face chalk-white.

Rienzi's words rang across the court like a pistol crack: 'Control yourself, Anna.'

There was a gasp of surprise in the court.

The President looked up, startled and displeased, but the effect on Anna Albertini was instantaneous. She opened her eyes, sat bolt upright and steadied herself on the edge of the dock. She said in a low voice: 'I'm sorry. I'll be all right now.'

Rienzi turned back to his witness. 'Belloni said: "Her husband's a bloody Fascist and she's no better." Did you understand what he meant?'

The old peasant seemed to shrink again and his voice lapsed into a low undertone. 'Sure. Everybody knew. He'd been trying to get her to sleep with him for weeks, but she wouldn't have him.'

'He was prepared to kill her for that?'

'Yes.'

'Didn't any of you protest?'

'Sure! Sure!' He tried with feeble animation to justify himself. 'I tried . . . and a couple of others . . . but Belloni did the same thing as always–he pulled out a gun and said: "You know the rules. You do as you're told or you get shot. Take your pick."'

'And the next day,' said Rienzi softly, 'you killed the mother of Anna Albertini?'

'We didn't kill her! Belloni did. We . . . we just went along like we had to.'

There was a long rigid silence in the court. All eyes were turned to the shabby, stooping countryman on the stand. Then, as if by common impulse, they turned to the girl, who sat like a stone woman, staring sightlessly into the distance. Very calmly, Rienzi took up his examination again. 'Will you tell us, please, how the killing took place?'

The old peasant took a deep breath and began struggling through the last revelation. 'It was Sunday night . . . we . . . we all went along to the Moschetti house. We found Agnese Moschetti with the girl . . .'

'This girl?' Rienzi's outflung hand pointed to Anna Albertini.

'Yes . . . she was only a kid then, of course–eight or nine, I think. We–we held her, while Belloni took the mother into the bedroom. The kid screamed and kicked like a wild thing until we heard the shots. . . . Then . . . then she stopped . . . didn't say another word, just stood there, staring . . . staring like she was dead. . . .' His voice broke and the last words came tumbling out of him in tearful agony: 'Oh God, I'm sorry! But I couldn't stop it . . . I couldn't!' He buried his face in his gnarled hands and sobbed uncontrollably while Anna Albertini sat motionless, caught in the old, cataleptic horror.

Slowly Rienzi walked back to his desk and picked up the piece of masonry which he had shown to Fra Bonifacio. He held it out to the old peasant, who stared at it dumbly.

'Have you ever seen this before?'

Carrese nodded, unable to speak.

Rienzi pressed him quietly: 'Can you read?'

'Yes.'

'Will you please read the words written on this stone?'

Carrese turned away, his face contorted. 'Please . . . please, don't ask me.'

Rienzi shrugged and turned to face the President. 'With the permission of the court, I shall read them. They are simple words, gentlemen, scratched deep with a piece of tin. They are weathered by sixteen years of wind and rain, but they are still legible. They say: "Belloni, one day I will kill you!" '

He handed the stone to the President, who glanced at it briefly, then passed it down for the scrutiny of his colleagues.

Slack and exhausted, Rienzi stood in the clear space before the judges' rostrum. He waited while the stone was passed from hand to hand, then he took it back and crossed the court to the prosecution table. He laid the stone down in front of the Public Minister and announced: 'I should like the prosecution to read the words, too: words written by a child of eight the day after her mother's death, three days before a kindly relative came and took her away to live in Florence.' His voice rose on a note of sharp anger. 'They prove his case! Premeditation! Premeditation by a child of eight, who saw her mother raped and murdered by a hero of the Partisans! I am finished with this witness, Mr President.'

The countryman shuffled back to his place in the hushed court. The President scribbled a note on his pad and passed it down to his senior assistant. Then he said, in a flat, tired voice: 'Call your next witness, please, Mr Rienzi.'

'I call Mr Peter Landon!' After the dramatic testimony of Carrese, Landon felt that his own entrance was an anti-climax; but his appearance and the English sound of his name caused a buzz of comment in the court. He took the stand, assented to the oath and identified himself. Rienzi elaborated a moment on his qualifications and appointments, and then asked the court to accept him as an expert witness of equal status with Galuzzi.

As if to detract even further from the dramatic impact of the previous testimony, Rienzi then called on the Clerk of the Court to re-read the transcript of Professor Galuzzi's testimony. The Clerk shuffled his papers, coughed, adjusted his spectacles, and then read, parrot-fashion, the long, definitive passages. While they were being read, the crowd shifted and stirred uneasily. Landon threw a cautious glance at Rienzi, but there was no response from the pale, drawn face and the bleak inquisitor's eyes. When the Clerk had finished the transcript, Rienzi thanked him formally and then began to interrogate Landon: 'You would agree, Mr Landon, with Professor Galuzzi's definitions?'

'I would—yes.'

'You would agree, in general terms, that psychic traumas reveal themselves in various forms of mental infirmity, often long after the event which has caused them?'

'In general terms—yes.'

'You heard the testimony of the last witness. You heard how this accused, as a child of eight, was witness to the brutal circumstances of her mother's rape and murder. You would agree that this would be sufficient to cause a psychic wound of the gravest possible kind?'

'I would.'

'Mr Landon, how would you define the word "obsession"?'

'In psychiatric terms, it means a persistent or recurrent idea, usually strongly tinged with emotion and frequently involving an urge towards some form of action, the whole mental situation being pathological in character.'

' "Pathological" meaning, in this case, diseased or infirm?'

'That's correct.'

'Could you make your definition a little clearer to the court?'

'Well, some patients have obsessions of guilt, so that they are prepared to accuse themselves of crimes they had never committed. Others are obsessed by unreasonable anxieties, so that they will not cross a street for fear of being killed. There are some people who will go around the house twenty times at night to assure themselves that the doors and windows are locked. This, too, is an obsessive condition.'

'Is this condition curable?'

'Sometimes it can be alleviated by analysis, which reveals to the patient the roots of his disorder. Sometimes, however, the idea and the emotional pattern become so fixed as to be incurable—except perhaps by that type of surgery known as pre-frontal lobotomy.'

'From your examination of the accused and from the evidence elicited in this court, would you say she was the victim of an obsessive condition?'

'Undoubtedly.'

'Which began with the psychic shock inflicted on her by her mother's death?'

'Yes. Her failure to consummate marriage, for instance, is an obsessional symptom directly associated with the violence done to her mother.'

'Now, Mr Landon, I want you to be very clear on the import of my next question. I want the court to be clear on it, too, lest I should seem to be leading this witness away from fact and into a domain of speculation. This is, I hasten to assure the President, no part of my intention. The testimony of Dr Galuzzi raised the crucial question of moral sense and moral responsibility. I should like to be more specific on this point.' He turned to Landon and asked with great deliberation: 'Does the obsession which we have been discussing—the fixed idea, the fixed emotional pattern—deprive the patient of moral responsibility? Does it diminish this responsibility so that the patient cannot help what he does, but is compelled to it by forces outside his control?'

It was a loaded issue and Landon new it. He took time to digest the question and his answer was studiously exact. 'Modern psychology points to many states in which the subject is or seems to be deprived of responsibility for his actions, or in which his moral sense and therefore his moral responsibility are diminished. However, it must be said that such states are not yet matters of legal definition, and the patient who commits a criminal act may still be amenable to the law as it is now framed.'

'Would you say that the infirmity of the accused would diminish her moral responsibility?'

'Most certainly.'

'Would it retard in any fashion her growth as a person?'

'It's elementary, I think. The human psyche develops, as the body does, by organic growth, environmental influence and education. Its development may be inhibited by bodily infirmity, by trauma or maleducation.'

'And, as in the case of the body, one psychic function may be inhibited while all the others are normal?'

'That's true. A brilliant mathematician, for instance, may have the emotional responses of a child.'

'Would it be true to say, Mr Landon, that in certain psychic shocks, not only is normal growth inhibited, but the sufferer is left, shall we say, fixed and anchored at the moment when the shock took place?'

'This is one mode of obsession—not an uncommon one.'

'An act committed under such an obsession would, therefore, have the same moral character, the same emotional pattern, as if it were committed at the time of the first shock?'

Landon frowned and pursed his lips. 'It might. You must not ask me to go further than that. One could only establish the fact by long, controlled clinical analysis.'

'But you would admit at least the possibility?'

'Any psychiatrist must admit that much.'

'Remembering what happened to Anna Albertini, remembering the evidence of her later incapacity, remembering your own clinical examinations, would you admit the possibility in her case?'

'One could not discount it.'

'Let us be clear on this, Mr Landon. You admit, without any doubt, grave shock, grave psychic damage?'

'That's right.'

'You admit an obsessional state with diminished moral responsibility?'

'Yes.'

'You admit at least the possibility that the murder of Gianbattista Belloni might have, in the mind of the accused, the same character as if it had taken place immediately after her mother's death?'

'On this point I am not prepared to go further than I have gone already.'

'Thank you, Mr Landon.' Rienzi turned away. 'The defence rests at this point, Mr President.'

'The witness may step down.'

Although they had planned the questionnaire together, Landon had the uneasy feeling that Rienzi had mistimed it and treated it in a fashion altogether too casual. To the spectators also, it was a tame, almost pathetic conclusion. The storm which Rienzi had seemed to promise them had blown out in a single squall. Landon said as much to Ascolini, but the old man shook his white mane and muttered testily: 'It is not you who are trying the case but the fellows on the rostrum. The boy did well. He gave them their moment of drama–then a draught of cool reason. Besides, there is more to come. Listen!'

The tall, hawk-faced Prosecutor had taken the floor and, in grave, measured tones, was addressing the judges: 'Mr President, gentlemen of the court, no one has been more deeply moved than I by the evidence of the defence. No one has greater sympathy than I for the burden which has lain, all these years, on the shoulders of this unfortunate young woman. But . . .' An orator's pause, well timed and pregnant with admonition. 'But I must take my stand, as you, the members of the judiciary, must take yours, on the law. The law is a wall between order and chaos. There is a sense in which the law is more important than justice. Suspend the law–as it was suspended in this country for too many years–and you let in violence and disorder of every kind. Try to bend the law even in favour of the deserving, try to modify it because of your own sympathies, and you create a precedent for new and greater crimes; you say that violent revenge is lawful, that political assassination is allowable; you bring back to this country the vendetta, in which a tradition of murder is handed down from generation to generation. You dare not do this! On the evidence submitted to you, you must convict this woman. The crime itself is proven beyond a shadow of a doubt; premeditation is proven–sixteen years of premeditation, the record of which was written first on a cemetery stone and then in the blood of Gianbattista Belloni. Much has been said in this court of the dubious character of this man. We challenge none of it. But we take our stand on the most primitive principle of the law: that murder, for whatever motive, is an immoral and illegal act. You may, at your discretion, consider a merciful punishment for the unfortunate girl who stands in the dock. But you must recognize her crime for what it is–wilful and premeditated murder! I am the servant of the law, gentlemen, as you are. I need say no more than this–I submit that you cannot do less.'

It was so simply done that one almost missed the talent behind it: the nice judgment, the meticulous timing, the actor's verve and the gambler's shrewdness that made him refuse even to skirmish round the outer edge of his phalanx. Sympathy might run against him, but the currents of interest, precedent and judicial responsibility ran strongly in his favour. He had a pat case, and a gratuitous plea for leniency would dent it not at all. He sat down, sober and a trifle smug, as the President called Carlo Rienzi to present his plea and summation.

Carlo got up slowly, twitching his gown up on his shoulders and gathering himself for the final moments of his first forensic adventure. He glanced briefly at Anna Albertini and then, in quiet, persuasive fashion, addressed himself to the judges: 'Mr President, gentlemen of the court, my learned friend has spoken to you of the law. To hear him, you would believe that the law is something fixed, immutable, beyond dispute or interpretation. This is not so. The law is a body of traditions, precedents and ordinances, some good, some bad, but all dedicated in principle, if not in fact, to the security of the subject, the maintenance of public order and the dispensation of moral justice. Sometimes these ends accord with one another. Sometimes they are in contradiction, so that justice may be ill served while order is most securely maintained. Sometimes the ordinance is too simple, sometimes it is too detailed, so that there is always need for gloss and annotation and the conflict of opinions to arrive at its true intent. The decalogue says bluntly: "Thou shalt not kill". Is this the end of it? You know it is not. You put a uniform on a man's back and a gun in his hands and you say: "It is a holy and blessed thing to kill for one's country", and you pin a medal on his chest when he does it. Let us be clear on this issue, gentlemen. The law is an instrument and not an end. It is not, and never can be, a perfect instrument of justice.

'It is not merely the law which is imperfect. There is imperfection also in its ministers–the police and the judiciary. If these fail in their duty, if their power is perverted, as it was perverted during the war in San Stefano, so that evil men flourish and the innocent are left defenceless, what then? If, at the moment when Belloni dragged this girl's mother away to be raped, Anna Albertini had shot him dead, would you then have charged her with murder? No! You would have commended her as a brave child defending her mother's honour. You might even have pinned on her breast the medal which a grateful country gave to Gianbattista Belloni!

'I do not say this, Mr President, to claim for the defence a ground of argument outside the law. I say it in affirmation of a principle to which great jurists in this country and elsewhere have subscribed: that it is the duty of a court not merely to uphold the law, but to ensure that the greatest justice possible is done within its imperfect framework.

'I know and you know that you will never be able to give justice to my client. You cannot bring back her dead mother. You cannot draw back the veil and hide from her young eyes the horror of rape and murder. You cannot restore to her the years which she has spent in the syncope of obsession. You cannot bring back the husband who has withdrawn himself from her, nor the capacity to enter even the elementary relationship of marriage. All you can do is lay new burdens upon her, of guilt, punishment and reparation.

'You are in dilemma in this matter, gentlemen. We are all in dilemma. We are obliged to that which we cannot perform. We believe that which we cannot affirm in this court, because the vocabulary of the codex lacks words to define it. We are committed to that which we condemn in the accused–the *lex talionis*, an eye for an eye, a tooth for a tooth!

'You will, because you must, find Anna Albertini guilty, *de facto*, of an act of homicide. Yet you know and I know that had the act been committed in another time–though in the same context of shock and provocation–you would have praised it as an act of virtue. You know that this act might never have been committed, had not a guardian of the law conspired many years ago to deny Anna Albertini a legal redress. But when you retire to reach your decision, you will not be able to take effective cognizance of that fact. You will consider, and I believe you will decide favourably on, the defence plea of mitigation on the grounds of partial mental infirmity. You will reject out of hand the prosecution's case for premeditation, understanding that the evidence of trauma and obsession puts it completely out of court.

'But the tragedy, gentlemen, the bitter tragedy of your situation is that you will fail to dispense justice; not for want of knowledge or good will, but because our law has never adequately defined the nature of moral responsibility, because its evolution has not kept pace with the findings of modern psychiatry on the intricate ills of the human mind.

'What can you do, being dedicated to truth and to justice but knowing them beyond your noblest reach? I submit that you must define this act in the most lenient terms sanctioned by the law. You must mete out a minimum penalty, not only in terms of duration, but also in terms of place and condition. If you must confine this girl, who is still only a child, let it not be in a house of correction, but in a place where she may find love and care and a hope of cure for the infirmities which have been laid upon her. . . .'

For the first time, he faltered. His shoulders shook and he stood with head bowed, fighting to recover himself. Then he straightened up and flung out his arms in a final impassioned plea: 'What more can I say, gentlemen? How else can I show you how to conform the cold unreason of legality with the truth and the justice to which the human instinct points with unerring finger? Like you, I am a servant of the law, and, like you, I am this moment ashamed of my servitude. God help us all!'

Without another word, he turned away, walked to his table and sat down, burying his face in his hands.

It was a magnificent moment, an instant of vision such as great preachers sometimes impose on their audience. The paradox of the human estate was suddenly laid bare, the pathos of it and the pity and the massive terror that attend the most banal imperfection. In the court a woman sobbed brokenly. Ninette dabbed at her eyes and old Ascolini blew his nose in a great trumpet blast. The white-haired President wiped his spectacles and his assistants tried vainly to mask the emotions that this youthful advocate had stirred in them. Only Anna Albertini sat, wraith-like and withdrawn, oblivious of the high climax of the scene.

The President bent forward in his chair. 'Mr Rienzi. . . .'

Rienzi looked up, vaguely, and all saw that his face was wet with tears. 'I–I beg your pardon, Mr President.'

The President nodded sympathetically. 'The court understands that Counsel is under a great strain, but it is customary after the pleas of both prosecution and defence to give the accused the opportunity of making a personal statement.'

Rienzi glanced across at Anna Albertini and then shook his head. 'We waive the privilege, Mr President. There is nothing to add to our defence.'

'Then the court is adjourned while my colleagues and I consider our decision.'

He was hardly on his feet before a woman's hysterical voice shouted from the back of the court: 'Let her go! Hasn't she had enough? Free her!'

A couple of officials rushed towards the woman, but before they reached her the whole audience had taken up the cry, stamping and shouting: 'Free her! Free her!' in a fury of shame and pity and frustration.

In the disorder that followed, the judges made a hurried exit, Anna was whisked back to the cells and Ascolini hurried Valeria, Ninette and Landon into the enclosure of the court, where the four of them stood with Rienzi and his colleagues watching with slack amazement as the policeman herded the people like sheep through the ante-room and into the street, and the cries went up more loudly and fiercely, 'Free her! Let her go!'

The doors slammed shut and they were left with their own private drama of confusion and wonder. For a moment, no one said a word, then old Ascolini threw his arms around Carlo and embraced him in the ardent fashion of the South. 'Wonderful, my boy, wonderful! I'm proud of you! You will do great things, but you may never have another moment like this for twenty years! Look at him, Valeria! Look at the man you married! Aren't you proud of him?'

'Very proud, Father.' With the practised charm of an actress, she put her arm round Carlo and pressed her lips to his cheek. Landon was standing near enough to catch her words: 'You win, Carlo! I won't fight you any more. I promise that.'

There was an infinite weariness in his whispered reply: 'Did it need so much, Valeria? Did it need all this?'

Then he kissed her lightly on the cheek and came forward with a tired smile to receive their congratulations. The Prosecutor gathered up his papers and strolled across with casual professional friendliness. 'My compliments, Rienzi! The best handling of a bad brief I've seen in many a long day!' He turned to smile at Ascolini. 'A star pupil, eh, *dottore*? We old dogs will have to learn new tricks to match this one!'

Rienzi flushed and murmured vaguely: 'Kind of you to say so!'

'Not at all, my dear fellow, you deserve it. And you'll do very well out of the case. The press will give you a very good run. The President's not a man to throw compliments round either. Give it a week or two and you'll have more briefs than you can handle!'

Rienzi grinned ruefully. 'We still haven't got the decision.'

'Nonsense, my dear fellow!' The Prosecutor smiled and patted him genially on the shoulder. 'The decision is unimportant. It's your performance that counts, and you made a startling début.'

As he drifted away, Ascolini snorted irritably: 'The fellow's a fool! Take no notice of him.'

Rienzi shrugged abstractedly. 'He meant to be kind. Tell me, *dottore*, how do you think it will go?'

Ascolini pursed his thin lips and then said, carefully: 'I think you have a good chance. Medical evidence works strongly in your favour. You did well to underline in your plea the judicial dilemma. This always disposes to sympathy for the accused. On the other hand, the judiciary is always concerned with legal precedent. It cannot lend itself, or appear to lend itself, to condonation of the vendetta. I should not like to be in their shoes at this moment. But you, my boy, you have done as well as any man.' He smiled a little self-consciously and said: 'If you haven't pawned the watch, I'd like to have it back.'

'You make me very happy, *dottore*,' said Carlo gravely. 'But in fact I did sell the watch.' He grinned boyishly. 'This has been an expensive venture for me.'

'It will pay you back a hundred times over,' said Ascolini warmly, 'and then you will buy me another watch.'

Rienzi turned to Ninette and Landon. 'I owe you a great deal, Peter—and Ninette also. You've been more patient than I—than any of us—deserve.'

Landon flushed and said in a low voice: 'Let's keep that part of it for later, Carlo. I have things to say, too.'

There was a small, embarrassed pause, but before anyone found words to bridge it, Professor Galuzzi came in from the remand cell and walked across to join them. Rienzi asked him anxiously: 'How is Anna, Professor?'

'Better than I expected. I've given her a light sedative and a tranquillizer. We'll get her through the rest of the day without any trouble. I'd like you to join me in her cell in a few moments. You made a remarkable plea, young man. I found myself deeply moved by it.'

'Did you agree with it, Professor?'

'In the main, yes. The definition of criminal responsibility is one of our great problems in forensic medicine. Your examination of Mr Landon here brought it in very clear focus. With your permission, I should like to quote from it in a paper which I am preparing for the *Medical Record*.'

'That's a great compliment, Professor.'

'Not at all. You have done us all a service.'

Rienzi hesitated a moment and then put the blunt question: 'You will naturally be asked to make a report on this case and recommendations for treatment of my client. Would it be an indiscretion to ask how you will frame it?'

'Not at all,' said Galuzzi, amiably. 'I shall suggest minimum confinement, preferably in one of our more modern psychiatric institutions where patients have a large degree of freedom, comfort and constructive activity. In addition to this, I shall recommend regular observation, analysis and therapy.'

'You will recommend this, even if we lose our plea?'

'Certainly. I must point out, of course, that the final decision rests with the court.'

'I understand that. I'm sure you will understand that I have a personal interest in the girl's future.'

'I'll be happy to keep you in touch with her progress. Now, if you'll excuse me, I'm likely to be called at any moment to consult with the magistrates.'

He made a little formal bow and left them. Rienzi looked after him with anxious eyes. Valeria watched her husband shrewdly but said nothing. Ascolini said gently: 'Each to his own profession, my boy. Your client will be in good hands.'

'I know,' said Carlo moodily. 'I know.'

Valeria's voice, tinged faintly with irritation, cut across the talk: 'How long will the judges be out? We can't just stand around here all the morning.'

'They'll be some time, I think,' said Carlo. 'Why don't you all go out and get some coffee? If I know where you are, I'll send a clerk round to call you when they're ready.'

'Why not come with us, Carlo?'

'No, my dear. I'll wait around here. I want to talk with Anna. There may be very little time—afterwards.'

'Send word to the Caffè Angelo,' said Ascolini briskly. 'It's the nearest place. We'll be there. Relax, my boy, it will soon be over.'

When they were leaving the court, Valeria said, with a curious touch of pity: 'He'll be lonely without his little virgin.'

'He's been lonely so long,' said Ascolini harshly, 'he's probably accustomed to it. You're a fool, Valeria. He's survived his crisis. Yours is still to come.'

Ninette said tactfully: 'It's a nervous time, *dottore*. We all need to be patient with each other. Why don't you two men take a stroll and meet

Valeria and myself later at Angelo's?'

It was Landon's cue and he took it gratefully. 'Let's do that, *dottore*. I could use something stronger than coffee.'

The two girls left them and they began to stroll in leisurely fashion round the sunlit perimeter of the Campo. Ascolini seemed tired. He leant heavily on Landon's arm and talked in halting, meditative fashion as if all his trenchant confidence had deserted him.

'Valeria is beginning to be jealous, which is a good thing. But it is not enough. She will need to be generous as well. When this is over, Carlo will be spent and lonely; he will need gentleness and consideration.'

'Will Valeria be able to give them?'

'I hope so. But they need practice and—and a certain humility. She, like me, is deficient in both. I am troubled, Landon. I am old enough to see the magnitude of my mistakes, too old to avert their consequences. I have lived a long time without belief. Now ... I begin to be afraid of death and judgment. Strange!'

'Valeria's afraid too, isn't she?'

'Of other things. Of losing me. Of being forced to submit herself to other standards than mine. Of losing the easy absolution which she has had from me.'

'Of losing Carlo?'

'Of having him reject her—which is not quite the same thing.'

'Reject her for what? A mistress?'

'No. This would not trouble her too much, I think. It would justify her own follies. His guilt would preserve her power over him. And Carlo is not a man to find happiness in a backstairs liaison. The danger for both of them is more subtle—that Carlo will borrow dignity and satisfaction from apparently noble aims, while Valeria is left with no dignity and diversions already stale.'

'You're thinking of Anna Albertini?'

'This is the beginning of it, though not necessarily the end. It is a worthy enterprise, you see: a lost one to be rescued and guided to safe harbour; innocence to be protected; the unloved to be cherished back to normal growth. There will be others, more and more as he gets older: cheats, murderers, violent husbands, unhappy wives, with all of whom he will become involved in greater or less degree. I can understand it.' He chuckled grimly. 'I have played the merry lecher with too many women; yet there have been one or two for whom I have been the white and gallant knight, who took them home to mama instead of taking them to bed. This is how we justify ourselves, Landon. You know it as well as I.'

Landon knew it only too well, but he did not know what he could do about it. Marriage was an uneasy bargain at the best of times, and stiff-necked virtue could often destroy it more quickly than amiable sin. Mutual dependence was a habit, mutual care was a grace of rare cultivation, but both must begin from a moment of common need, and Rienzi and his wife seemed to have missed it by a long, long way. He said as much to Ascolini, and he nodded, gravely: 'The need is there, Landon, but Carlo has grown tired of telling and Valeria has never learnt the words. I tried last night to teach them to her, but I'm not sure that she understood. Perhaps Ninette will do better.'

'I hope so.'

'The trouble is, there's not much time, Carlo's career was begun today.

Soon it will begin to roll like a railway train. After that, there will be no leisure for lovers' games.'

After which melancholy summary, 'there was little to be said, so they turned into a bar and drank a glass of brandy together. Then they walked back slowly to the Caffè Angelo to meet the womenfolk.

To Landon's relief, they found them talking companionably over the coffee-cups. Valeria was pale and subdued and it seemed that she had been crying, but she smiled wanly and said: 'Ninette has been kind to me, Peter. I've treated you both very badly but I hope we may be friends from now on.'

'We won't talk about it any more,' said Ninette firmly. 'It's finished–done! And tonight there will be a celebration.'

'A celebration?' Ascolini cocked a shrewd eye at his daughter. 'Where?'

'At the villa,' Valeria told him quietly. 'A homecoming for Carlo. There will be Peter and Ninette, and you, Father, will bring Professor Galuzzi and anyone else you think Carlo might like. I've telephoned and Sabina has everything in hand. We need something like this, Father.'

Ascolini chuckled happily. 'Child, we shall make a *festa* to end all *festas*. Leave the guest-list to me. Are you sure they'll be ready for us at home?'

'I'm sure of it, Father.'

'Good. Now, let's write down the names. Then I'll borrow Angelo's telephone and we'll be organized.'

Ten minutes later, he was perched like a cheerful gnome on a high stool summoning the worthies of Siena to attend him at the family triumph.

In the white conventual cell, Anna Albertini lay tranquil in a drugged sleep while Carlo Rienzi kept vigil beside her. Her face was waxen but relaxed in a strange, empty beauty. Her hands, outflung on the grey blanket, were slack and undemanding as those of a sleeping baby. Her hair, tumbled on the pillow, was like a dark halo around her ivory brow. Her small, virginal breast rose and lapsed in the languid rhythm of repose. Passion and guilt and terror were strangers at such a sleeping, and Carlo Rienzi, at this penultimate moment of the battle, felt himself floating like a straw in the backwater calm of the narrow room.

All that he could do had been done. All that he had promised had been fulfilled. The outcome lay now in the lap of the Blind Goddess. For himself, he felt spent, empty and parched as a summer brook; but as he looked down at the pale, innocent face, he felt the first grateful runnel of tenderness break out inside him like a spring bursting out of dry sand. It was a kind of refreshment after the arid discipline he had imposed upon himself and, moved by a sudden impulse, he stretched out a tentative hand to brush away a trailing hair from the girl's forehead.

He drew it back with a guilty start when he heard the rattle of bolts, the creak of the opening door, as Professor Galuzzi was admitted into the cell.

Galuzzi surveyed him for a moment with a shrewd, scholarly eye, and asked: 'How is she, Mr Rienzi?'

'Sleeping quietly.' Rienzi stood up and moved away from the bed. Galuzzi picked up one slack hand, took a short pulse-count and then laid the hand back on the blanket. 'Good. We can let her sleep a while. I think the judges will be out some time. You've given them a great deal to think about, Rienzi.'

'Have you consulted with them yet?'

'I have. I've given them my opinion in the same terms as I gave it to you.'

'I'm grateful,' said Carlo Rienzi.

Galuzzi looked at him for a moment, hesitating over the lines of fatigue and strain in his young, handsome face. Then he said, in meditative fashion: 'One day, Mr Rienzi, I think you will be a very great advocate. You have the mind for it: the dramatic quality, the single-mindedness amounting almost to obsession. All the great ones have it—surgeons, philosophers, inventors, jurists. But, like all greatness, it requires discipline.'

'What are you trying to tell me, Professor?' asked Rienzi quietly. 'Has it something to do with my client?'

'A great deal, I think,' said Galuzzi in the same thoughtful vein. 'You're not content with what you've done in court—and I doubt whether any other advocate could have done half as much. You want to go further. You want to reshape her life after the trial.'

Rienzi was nettled. He said sharply: 'Someone would have to do it.'

'Why you?'

Rienzi made a small, shrugging gesture of puzzlement. 'Put it that way and I hardly know how to answer. But, don't you understand, until this point I've held the life of this girl in my hands. She has depended on me utterly. I can't just drop her like a stone in a pool and forget her. Surely you see that?'

Galuzzi ignored the question and asked another of his own: 'This is your first big case, isn't it?'

'Yes.'

For a moment Galuzzi said nothing more, but walked back to the bed and stood looking down at the sleeping girl. Then, very softly, he began again: 'There will be so many others, Mr Rienzi. Can you carry them all as you propose to carry Anna Albertini?'

'No, I suppose not.'

'Take the surgeon—and I myself practised surgery for a long time. How often does he stand with a human life held literally in his own two hands? Sometimes it slips away. Sometimes, mercifully, he holds it safe. Can he regret what he has lost, or carry for the rest of his life the burden of what he has saved?' He swung round and faced Rienzi with the sharp challenge: 'Are you in love with this girl, Mr Rienzi?'

'I—I don't think so.'

'But you're not sure?'

For a long moment Rienzi did not answer. Finally, he made the reluctant admission: 'No, I'm not sure.'

Galuzzi turned away and walked to the window. After a while he came back to face Rienzi. His eyes were touched with pity and his voice was gentle: 'I should have guessed it. No one could have made the case you did without a touch of passion.'

'I told you I'm not sure.' Rienzi's voice was edged with anger.

'I know. But she is sure.'

Rienzi stared at him, startled. 'You mean she's in love with me?'

'I didn't say that. I don't think she knows what love is. But the only objects of passion in her life—her mother, her husband, even Belloni—have dropped out of it. Her obsession has fixed itself on you.'

Rienzi took a deep breath. 'I was afraid of that.'

Galuzzi looked at him with a half-smile on his thin, fastidious lips. 'But flattered too, eh?' He gave a little, humourless chuckle. 'If I have learnt one thing in twenty years of psychiatric medicine it is this, Mr Rienzi: the human mind never works simply. When it appears to do so, then it is at its most complex. It is like those ivory balls which the Chinese carve so skilfully, one inside the other. No matter how deep you probe there is always something else to surprise you.'

To Galuzzi's surprise, Rienzi smiled and quoted lightly: '"I went to my uncle the Mandarin to question him about love. He told me to ask my wayward heart." Don't worry too much, Professor, it may never happen.'

'If it does happen,' said Galuzzi in his grave, academic fashion, 'if you do commit yourself to any involvement, the consequences for both of you may be more terrible than you can imagine.'

He turned on his heel and left, and when the door closed behind him Carlo Rienzi sat down by the bed and took the hand of the sleeping girl in his own.

The police were taking no chances of a disturbance at the close of the trial of Anna Albertini. The approaches to the court were picketed with motor-cycle police. There were guards on every door, stocky, tough fellows with short batons and pistols in holsters of black leather. Justice was about to be done and folk could either like it or lump it; but either way they would keep their mouths shut or have their heads broken.

The court was full of whispers. Even the character of the light seemed to have changed so that every feature of every personage was etched sharply, like mountains under a stormy sky. Rienzi was standing by the dock, talking in low tones with Anna Albertini. When the judges came in, he gave her an encouraging smile, patted her head and walked back to his table. Silence, tense and explosive, settled on the room as the President sat down and began, with maddening deliberation to arrange his papers. Then he began to speak:

'I have presided over many cases in this court, but I say now that none of them has laid so heavy a burden on me and on my colleagues. We are not monsters. We are men of average understanding, pity and sympathy. But, as the prosecution has so justly stated, we are also the representatives of the law–its keepers, its interpreters, its arbitrators. Upon our decisions later decisions will be based. The precedents we create will influence the course of justice long after we are dead. If we judge falsely or foolishly, we may pervert justice for many, many others.'

He paused and looked around the court, a white-haired image of temperance and orderly reason.

'If you want an example of how this may happen, you have it in the present proceedings. There was a time when the law no longer functioned in this country. There was a time when men were confused by what were called "the necessities of war"–when the only court was the drumhead, when those who claimed to mete out summary justice were, in fact, using their accidental power for revenge or private gain. The law was perverted by politics, by power, by deliberate conspiracy. The crime for which Anna Albertini has been tried began in this time of disorder, but . . .' he waited a moment, and then went on firmly: '. . . it ended in another when the rule of law had been re-established. Now, Anna Albertini must be judged according to the codex.'

No word was spoken, but one felt the ripple of interest moving through the room like a shock-wave through water. The President turned over a page of his notes and continued soberly: 'However, as Counsel for the

Defence pointed out in his most eloquent plea, the law takes consideration not only of the act itself, but of the intention, the provocation, the responsibility of the person committing it. To all these things my colleagues and I have given the greatest reflection. The intention, in this case, was clear: murder for revenge. The provocation was great—greater than any of us might care to sustain. But to say that provocation excuses the act is to open the door to every sort of violence, to bring back to this country the ancient and horrible practice of traditional vengeance.

'The question of responsibility is much more complex and on this we have debated long and studiously. At no time has the defence suggested that Anna Albertini was insane at the time of the act. At no time was it intimated that she was incompetent to stand trial in this court. Counsel has argued with considerable weight that the traumatic shock of her mother's death left her in a state of mind in which time and the change of circumstances did not exist for her. His view is supported, at least in part, by expert medical testimony.

'From this point, he developed—with considerable forensic skill—a double plea. His first submission was that the act of murder committed by Anna Albertini had the same character in law and morals as if it were committed at the time of her mother's death. A psychiatrist might build a feasible hypothesis on this point, but,' he laid it down with singular deliberation, 'it is my view and the view of my colleagues that this hypothesis has no value in law.

'His second argument, that the state of the accused represented a mental infirmity and that her criminal responsibility was diminished thereby, was much more cogent and, in arriving at our decision, we have given full weight to it. We have taken note also of the terrible provocation which preceded the act, albeit by many years. We have taken into account also the many years of mental torment which this young woman has suffered, the wreck of her marriage and the dubious future which she now faces.'

He turned over the last page of his notes, gathered himself for a moment and then, more dispassionately, began to deliver his decision.

'The prosection has requested a verdict of premeditated murder. It is our view that this charge is too grave to be sustained. We have, therefore, found on a lesser one.'

He turned towards the dock and made the cold official pronouncement: 'Anna Albertini, the decision of this court is that you are guilty of the lesser charge of homicide while in a state of partial mental infirmity, for which the law prescribes a sentence of imprisonment from three to seven years. In view of all the mitigating circumstances, we have decided to award the minimum penalty of three years, which you will spend in such place or places as may be determined from time to time by our medical advisers.'

The words were hardly out of his mouth before Carlo Rienzi slumped forward in his chair and buried his face in his arms. Anna Albertini sat in the dock, pale, cold and virginal, while the court broke out into a tumult of cheering that even the scurrying police were powerless to stop.

8

'Tomorrow,' said Ninette firmly, 'tomorrow we pack and go. We'll get ourselves married in Rome and find ourselves a villa out near Frascati, a place with a garden and a view where you can study and I can paint. We need it, *chéri!* We've spent too much of ourselves in this place. It's time to go!'

They were walking in the garden of Ascolini's villa, watching the light spread westward over the valley, while the cicadas made their crepitant chorus and a languid bird chirped in the shrubbery. Carlo was asleep. Ascolini was drowsing in his library, and Valeria was playing the diligent *châtelaine*, arranging flowers, bustling the servants about the kitchen in preparation for the evening's entertainment.

In spite of protests from Landon and Ninette, Ascolini had insisted that they come directly from the court to the villa. Valeria, too, had pleaded urgently for their presence. It was as if they were afraid of being alone with one another, as if they needed a catalyst to start the slow process of restoration and reunion. Landon and Ninette were tired and resentful, but they comforted themselves with the thought that on the morrow they should be quit of courtesies and free to address themselves to their private affairs.

After the drama of the court and the confusion of the aftermath, the countryside imposed a welcome calm on them all. Valeria drove, Carlo sat beside her, rehearsing the morning's triumph. Then, he, too, lapsed into silence while the vineyards and the cornfields swept past and the olive leaves drooped, dusty and listless, on the hillside.

They lunched on the terrace, chatted vaguely for a little while and then dispersed. Carlo was in the grip of a fierce reaction. Valeria was conducting herself with self-conscious discretion and Ascolini was simply watching the gambits like a wary old campaigner. Landon's own position was summed up in Ninette's verdict: '*Finita la commedia!* Time to be quit of all others but ourselves. Let them play out their own epilogue. We mustn't wait for the curtain call.'

So, in the long decline of the afternoon, they strolled in the pleasances of the villa and talked in the happy, inconsequent fashion of new lovers. They talk of Frascati and how they should live there: not penned in the town, not among the princely villas of the Conti and the Borghese and the Lancellotti, but in some small estate in the folds of the Alban hills, with a vineyard, perhaps, and a tenant farm with a green garden to walk in and watch the sun go down on the distant sprawl of imperial Rome. They talked of an exhibition for Ninette, of friends who would come to share their pastoral, of how their children might be born citizens of the Old World and of the New.

Then, as the shadows lengthened, Ascolini came out to join them, chirpy as a cricket after the siesta. 'A great day, my friends! A great day! And we owe you a debt for your part in it. You know what we need now.' He jerked an emphatic thumb in the direction of the house. 'A love-philtre for those two. Don't laugh. The grandmothers in these parts still make them for peasant lovers. We, of course, are too civilized for such nonsense, but . . . it has its uses.'

Ninette laughed and patted the old man's arm. 'Patience, *dottore*! No matter how much you prod him, that little donkey will trot at his own pace!'

Ascolini grinned and tossed a pebble at a scuttling lizard. 'It is not I who am impatient, but Valeria. She is eager now for reunion. She demands proofs of forgiveness. But I tell the same thing: "*Piano, piano!* Soft words, soft hands, when a man is tired like this one." ' He chuckled happily. 'With me, it was different. After every big case, I was wild and roaring for woman! Maybe Carlo will come to it, too—when he gets Anna out of his blood.'

'Where will they put her, do you know?'

'It's not fixed yet. They've taken her back to San Gimignano, but I understand Galuzzi has hopes of transferring her to the Samaritan Sisters at Castel Gandolfo. They have a big hospice there for mental cases. It's very beautiful, I believe. Very efficient, too.' He shrugged off the subject and asked: 'What will you two do now?'

'We're going to Rome,' Landon told him, 'just as soon as we can pack and close Ninette's studio.'

'I hope we may see you there. We, too, will be leaving in a few days. I want Carlo to begin taking over my practice.'

'How does he like the idea?'

'It appeals to him, I think, now that we can meet on equal terms. For my part, I need leisure to set my life in order. If these two can content themselves, then I, too, can begin to be happy.' He plucked a twig from an overhanging bush, sat down on a stone bench and began drawing slow cursive patterns in the gravel. 'Life is a twisted comedy, my friends. Had you told me six weeks ago that I should come to this—that I should be playing Cupid and dreaming of grandchildren and even thinking of going to confession—I should have spat in your eye! But this is what has happened. I wonder, sometimes, whether it is not too easy, and whether there is not a fellow waiting round the corner with a bill of reckoning in his hand.'

'Why should there be, *dottore*?' asked Ninette warmly. 'Life is not all debit and credit. Sometimes there are gifts for which the only price is gratitude.'

'Sometimes,' said Ascolini, drily, 'Perhaps I'm a suspicious fellow who doesn't deserve his good fortune.'

'Then let me tell you ours,' said Ninette with a smile. 'We're going to be married.'

Ascolini stared at her for an instant. Then his shrewd old face lit up with genuine delight. He threw his arm around her and waltzed her up and down the path. '*Maraviglioso!* Wonderful! And you will have a sack of children, all beautiful. And you will be the most beautiful mother in the world! All this and talent, too! Landon, you are a fortunate fellow! *Fortunatissimo!* And you owe it all to us. If we hadn't sent you back to Siena with a flea in your ear, you'd still be playing kiss-me-quick with the models and the telephone girls. But what an omen! There is double reason for a *festa* tonight.' Breathless and excited, he grasped their arms and trotted them both up the gravelled path towards the house. 'You must tell Valeria, child. And you, Landon, will read Carlo a sermon in marriage and the joys of fatherhood and all the fun you have arriving there. When the first baby comes, we'll have a great christening and I'll guarantee a cardinal in a red hat to do the job for you. Then you must make me godfather so that I can look after his faith and morals!'

'We'll have to reform you first, *dottore!*'

'By that time, child, I shall probably be wearing a hair shirt and beating my chest with a brick, like San Geronimo!'

It was a comic picture and it made them laugh. They were still laughing when they reached the terrace and Ascolini shouted for a servant to bring wine and glasses. Valeria came out to join them, and when Ascolini told her the news her eyes filled up with tears and she embraced Ninette ardently.

Her friendliness surprised Landon. Ascolini's conversion was easier to accept. He was getting old and, faced with the great 'perhaps', he was clinging to the simple certainties of life: pride and irony were too thin a diet for the winter years. Passion was being disciplined by the sheer diminution of age; native shrewdness and perverse experience were maturing into wisdom. But Valeria was a different case. She was still young, still wayward, initiated too early to the taste of truffles for breakfast, and Landon could see no good reason for so swift a reform.

Then, slowly, understanding began to dawn. This was the whole nature of these people. This was the essential paradox of their character and history. Old Cardinal du Bellay had called them *'peuple de grands enfants.... Ç'est une terrible beste, que cette villa-là, et sont estranges cerveaulx'* a terrible beast of a city ... great children ... strange brains ...Their own San Bernardino, a very modern psychologist in the fifteenth century, had characterized them even better: 'I understand the weakness of your character. You leave a thing and then return to the same thing; and seeing you now in so many divisions with so many hatreds, I believe that, had it not been that you are very, very human, you would have ended in doing yourselves some great harm. However, I say that your condition and you yourselves are very changeable. And how very changeable you are, also with evil, for you soon return to good.'

They were very human people: too human for colder spirits to live with in comfort. They were violent by nature, incapable of compromise. The same mould produced the mystic and the murderer, the political assassin and the ascetic who took the Kingdom of Heaven by storm.

The valley below was still filling with shadow, but the place where they stood was still bathed in sunlight, a symbol, Landon thought, of the gentler feelings which seemed to pervade the Ascolini household. He asked himself whether he had discovered, at last, the root of Carlo's problem: that he understood Valeria and her father too little and demanded too much—a Roman constancy, an urban rectitude—when all they had to offer was courage, a fluent passion, and the high, visionary folly of an older day.

The wine was brought and they drank a toast to mutual happiness. They talked a while of simple things. Then Valeria took Ninette inside to find her a dress while Landon went in search of Carlo to borrow a clean shirt for dinner.

He found him rubbing the sleep out of his eyes in a small room that must have been his retreat when the marital chamber was too cold for comfort. Rienzi greeted him cheerfully, lit a cigarette and then said, laughing: 'There's a commentary for you, Peter! I stage a great triumph. My name will be in every newspaper and I end like this—sleeping in my underpants in the spare room!'

'Just as well, laddy. You have a big night ahead of you.'

'I know.' He frowned in distaste. 'I'm not sure I want to face it.'

'Nonsense, man! It'll do you good. And besides it's a graceful gesture and you've got to accept it gracefully.'

'It was the old man's idea, of course.'

'No, it wasn't. It was Valeria's.'

He gave Landon a sharp look. 'Are you sure of that?'

'Of course I'm sure. She and Ninette cooked it up between them. Ascolini simply telephoned the invitations. I was there. I should know.'

'She means it then,' he muttered, moodily.

'Means what?'

'A new start. An attempt to patch up our marriage.'

'Yes, she does mean it. I hold no brief for her, as you know, but I'm convinced that she's sincere in this. How do you feel about it?'

Rienzi chewed on the question a moment, then lay back on the bed and blew smoke-rings towards the ceiling. He said, slowly: 'That's a big question, Peter—and I don't know how to answer it. Something's happened to me and I don't know how to explain it, even to myself.'

'It's simple enough, for God's sake! You're tired, played out. You've fought a big case at a critical time of your life. Now you need rest and a little readjustment.'

'No, Peter. It's more than that. Look!' He heaved himself up on his elbow and talked eagerly. 'You know the way I used to imagine this day—the day of my first success? I'll tell you: just as it happened in the court. The decision, the acclamation, the congratulations of my colleagues, Ascolini's surrender. Then? Then I would come to Valeria and take her in my arms and say: "There it is! I've tumbled the stars in your lap. Now stop being a child and come to bed and let's make love and start a baby!" And she would come happily and there would be no more fighting—except lovers' quarrels that would still end in bed.'

'That's exactly as she wants it at this moment. If you don't believe me, try it!'

'I know,' said Rienzi, flatly. 'I don't need you to tell me. But don't you see? I don't want it any more! I don't have the feeling. You know what it's like.'

Landon knew, but he could not find words to tell Rienzi, who hurried on, explaining himself in an urgent tumble of words: 'When I was a student in the first year of law, we had a great party. It was the night when the results were posted and I had passed. We got drunk and sang songs and felt twice as large as life. Then we all decided to finish the evening at a house of appointment, the biggest and most luxurious in Rome. Wonderful! We were young, full of sap, puffed with success. Then, when we got there, eh! It was nothing. I wasn't afraid, I wasn't innocent, but the thing was a cold transaction. Too many feet had walked over the doorstep. Too many fools had walked up the same stairs.'

'Did you go to bed?'

He laughed wryly. 'No. I walked home and held hands with the landlady's daughter, who was so innocent she thought a kiss would make her pregnant.' His face clouded again. 'But seriously, Peter, that's how I feel now with Valeria. I just don't care. I have no interest. What do I do?'

'Lie a little. Give it time. Blow on the coals long enough and you have fire again.'

'But if there are no coals, Peter—only charcoal and ashes?'

'Then you're in a bad way, brother! There's no divorce in the Church or in this country, and you've got no talent for a double life. So give it a try, man, for pity's sake! You're not a baby. You know the words. And women are happy to believe what they want to hear.'

'You're right, of course.' He jerked himself off the bed and stubbed out his cigarette. 'Except that I'm a bad liar and Valeria knows the words backwards. Still . . . *vesti la giubba*! On with the motley and see what sort of a play we make! Now, let's see if we can find you a shirt.' He burrowed in a drawer and came up with a beautiful creation in cream silk which he tossed to Landon with a grin. 'Wear it to the wedding, *amico*, and drink a toast to the reluctant groom!'

It was a bad joke, but Landon let it pass. This was no time to read Rienzi a lecture on marriage and the joys of fatherhood, so he let it pass, too. He thanked Rienzi for the shirt and walked back towards the guest-room to get ready for dinner. He wondered why Rienzi has said no word of Anna Albertini, and he asked himself, cynically, whether the boyhood history were not repeating itself in fantasy: the shamed man and the little white virgin holding hands at the top of the stairs while the big lusty world rolled on about its business.

The first act of Ascolini's dinner party was a formal success. More than twenty people sat down in the big dining-room: local pundits and their wives, a member of the Chamber of Deputies, a brace of legal eminences, the doyen of the Siena press, Professor Galuzzi, and an astonishing marchesa, fragile as a Dresden doll, who scolded Ascolini with the frankness of an old lover.

Ascolini gave one of his bravura performances. Valeria smiled and directed the whole affair with a deft hand. Carlo walked through his part with a vague charm that disarmed the men and left the women crooning with satisfaction. Ninette was radiant and besieged by elderly gentlemen who had discovered all too late an interest in art. Landon had small talent for this kind of social charade and he was rescued from complete boredom only by Professor Galuzzi, who proved himself an urbane and witty talker and a satirist of formidable dimension.

When the meal was over, they took their brandies out on to the terrace and watched the moon climb slowly over the distant ridges of Amiata. Valeria's nightingales were not singing yet, but Galuzzi was a diverting story-teller and Landon did not miss them at all. Inevitably, Galuzzi worked his way round to the Albertini affair and, after a cautious glance to assure himself that they were still alone, he delivered himself of some disturbing reflections.

'One day, Landon, this young Rienzi will be a very great jurist. But there's a flaw in him somewhere and I cannot put my finger on it.'

'What kind of flaw?'

'How shall I define it? A confusion, a conflict still unresolved.'

'The conflict's clear enough, I think. It's not a very happy marriage.'

'I've heard this before. It's common talk. One observes the incompatibility, but this is not what I mean. I've watched him closely with this client of his, a curious relationship, to say the least.'

'How—curious?'

'On the girl's part,' said Galuzzi carefully, 'it is, shall we say, normally abnormal. The mind in disorder seeks a focus for its dissociated faculties, a relief from the burden of its fears and frustrations and infirmities. It demands a scapegoat for its guilts, a protector for its weakness, an object for its ailing love. This is what Rienzi has become for the girl. You know as well as I how this kind of transference works.'

Landon said uneasily: 'Carlo's quite aware of that part, I think.'

'I know he's aware of it,' said Galuzzi tartly. 'I warned him.'

'How did he take the warning?'

'Very well. And I must say that his conduct has been professionally impeccable. But it is precisely at this point that the flaw begins to show: an arrogance, an attitude of possession, a subtle conviction that he exercises a benign influence over this girl, a too great readiness to assume responsibilities beyond his function.'

Everything that Galuzzi said Landon was prepared to echo and affirm. But the nagging sense of guilt made him attempt at least a token defence of Rienzi. 'Isn't this a fairly normal reaction–the first client, the first big case?'

'On the face of it, yes. But there is another element which I find it hard to define.' Galuzzi sipped his brandy in meditative fashion, and then lit a cigarette. He went on, slowly: 'You know what I think it is, Landon? A tale of innocence and the lost paradise . . . I see you smile–and well you may! We are cynics, you and I. In our profession we have to be. We lose innocence early and seldom regret it until we are old. It's a wasteful way to live, because we spend a whole lifetime getting back to the first point of departure. But it's a very human way–and for most of us it's the only way we learn to tolerate ourselves and tolerate others. We come in the end to forgive because we cannot endure without forgiveness for ourselves. We learn to be glad of half a loaf and not too proud when we achieve half a virtue.' He laughed and threw out his arms in a spacious gesture. 'Why should I read you a lecture on innocence, Landon? You have as much experience as I have. Fellows like you and me can pick a virgin at twenty paces and an honest man blindfolded. There aren't too many of either! The world is full of half-virgins and near-liars.' His face clouded again and he went on: 'Rienzi is no more innocent than most, but he has never been able to forgive the lack in himself or in the world. He wants the moon and the sixpence too. He wants to be loved by a virgin and solaced by a whore, because each in her own way gives him the illusion of virtue. His ambition is nourished, his whole career is built on other men's sins. But this is not enough. He must play the little priest and read sweet lectures to his client in prison. A fellow like this is impregnable! Nothing can touch him because everything is food for his delusions!'

'By the same token,' said Landon sombrely, 'nothing can make him happy.'

'I agree. Nothing can make him happy because he judges everything in the light of the lost paradise.'

Abruptly, Landon faced him with a new question: 'Do you propose to let Rienzi keep in touch with the girl?'

Galuzzi smoked for a moment in silence and then answered slowly: 'I've thought about that a great deal. I doubt whether I could prevent what is a reasonable contact between lawyer and client. I doubt also whether I would want to. To this point, Rienzi has been good for the girl. He may continue to help her for a long time. So I have decided to compromise.'

'How will you do that?'

'I'm trying to have Anna Albertini transferred to an institution at Castel Gandolfo, just near Rome. That may take a little time. For the present, she will be placed in the care of the Sisters of the Good Shepherd who run a similar, but smaller, mental home near Siena. I've told Rienzi he can visit her there immediately after she has been admitted. Then I want her left alone for a while so that I can keep her under my control and devise a regimen of analysis and treatment.'

'How did Rienzi take the idea?'

'He had to take it, but he didn't like it.' Galuzzi shrugged, flipped away his cigarette, and stood, a dark, imposing figure against the rising moon. 'How does one draw pictures for the blind? How does one fight the potent magic of self-deception?'

Bluntly, Landon faced him with the last question: 'Do you think Rienzi's in love with the girl?'

'Love is a chameleon word,' said Galuzzi, absently. 'Its colour matches a gamut of diverse experiences. Who can say that, even when we protest it most nobly, we are not loving ourselves?'

On that comfortless thought they left it and walked inside to join the other guests.

The party was tapering off now, fragmenting itself into little groups which, having exhausted their stock of civilities, were busy with local gossip and provincial reminiscence. Landon rescued Ninette from a too talkative politician and suggested that they arrange a ride back to Siena with the first party to leave. Carlo wandered up at the same moment with a glass in his hand and waved away the suggestion: 'Nonsense! You can't leave yet! Let's get rid of this stuffy bunch and we'll finish the evening together. Then I'll drive you back myself.'

His eyes were glazed, his voice slurred, and Landon had no intention of letting him get within fifty feet of a car, so he grinned and said: 'Not tonight, Carlo! You're tired and you're tipsy and it's time you went to bed!'

'To bed!' He gave a drunken chuckle and gagged on another mouthful of liquor. 'Everybody wants me to go to bed! Valeria, the old man, and now you! Nobody asks me what I want. I'm just a stallion, that's all! A noble sire led out to service. You know what they want me to do?' His voice rose higher and the liquor slopped from the glass on to the polished floor. 'People the place with advocates–great advocates, like Ascolini and me!'

It was time to do something. Landon took his arm firmly and steered him towards the door, humouring him as best he could. 'That's fine, Carlo! Nobody wants you to do anything that doesn't suit you. Ninette and I will stay around, but you've got to sober up a little.'

'Who wants to be sober? This is a great day. I'm a success! And I'm going to be married again!' Landon had him out of the *salone* now and was working him up the stairs, out of earshot, when Valeria appeared on the landing above them. Rienzi raised his hand in a maudlin salute: 'There she is! The little bride who wants to be the mother of the Gracchi. How many children do you want, darling? Shall we have them all at once or in easy stages?'

'Get him to bed, for God's sake!' said Valeria bitterly, and tried to hurry past them down the stairs.

Rienzi reached for her, but Landon fended him away and wrestled him back against the banisters. He surrendered with a drunken laugh.

'You see, my friend, she despises me! You don't despise me, do you,

Peter? You know I'm a great man! Little Anna doesn't despise me either. I saved her, you know that! Nobody believed I could do it, but I saved her. Poor little Anna! Nobody's giving her a party tonight.'

He leaned against the banisters and began to cry. Half-pushing, half-carrying, Landon got him up the stairs and into the small bedroom, laid him on the bed and took off his jacket, shoes and tie. He was still moaning and mumbling when Landon closed the door and went downstairs. Ninette signalled to him from the door of the library and he went on to join her while Ascolini and his daughter farewelled the last of their guests. She kissed him and said: 'Thanks, *chéri*. You did that very neatly. I don't think anybody saw too much. Valeria's going to drive us back to town. Poor girl, I feel very sorry for her.'

'It's a bloody mess, sweetheart. But this one they'll have to clean up for themselves.'

'What's the matter with Carlo?'

'He's tired. He drank too much. And he's all mixed up, like a country omelette.'

He told her of his talk with Carlo and of Galuzzi's uneasy diagnosis. She sighed and made a shrugging Gallic gesture of despair. 'What more can one do, Peter? What is there to say? Is there any hope for these people?'

'None at all!' said Ascolini from the doorway. He was leaning against the door-jamb—a white-haired, grey-faced old man in a dinner jacket that seemed suddenly too large for him. 'We never forget anything and we never forgive anything. There's a blight on us. Worms in the fruit and weevils in the wheat! Go home, my friends, and forget us.'

He crossed the room with a slow, tottering step and slumped into a chair. Landon poured him a glass of brandy and he drank it at a gulp, then sat, slack and listless, staring at the floor. Valeria came hurrying in with a coat thrown over her dinner-frock and a small suitcase in her hand. She was white with anger.

'We're going now, Father. Don't wait up for me. If Carlo wants to know where I am, tell him I've gone to ask Lazzaro to have me back. He's no great prize—God knows—but at least he's a man!'

'Please, child, don't do it!' A last flush of anger and animation galvanized the old man. 'Let our friends take the car. You stay here and wait out one more day with me.'

'With you, Father?' Her voice was high, harsh and bitter. 'You told me last night I must stand alone now; you had your own life, you said, and I must live mine and take the consequences! Well, I'm doing just that! Carlo doesn't want me. You're tired of reliving the dead years through me! So I'm free. Goodnight, Father! I'll see you two in the car.'

Without a backward look, she hurried out. Landon shook the old man's limp hand and muttered a phrase or two, but he did not seem to hear. Only, when Ninette bent to kiss him, he stirred himself and patted her cheek and said softly: 'Bless you, child! Look after your man—and be gentle to each other!'

'You'll come to see us in Rome, *dottore*?'

'In Rome . . .? Oh yes—yes, of course.'

They left him then, shrunken and defeated, in the big chair, and walked out into the cold moonlight where Valeria was waiting for them at the wheel of the car. Her face was wet with tears, but she said nothing and slammed the car fast and dangerously down the drive and out on to the moonlit ribbon of the Siena road. For the first mile or so, she was silent, wrestling the car savagely round the curves of the hill, while the tyres screamed and the offside wheels spun dangerously in the gravel of the verge. Then she began to talk–a low, passionate monologue that brooked neither comment nor interruption.

'Dear Carlo! Dear sweet Carlo! The noble boy with the great talent and the great future and the wife who didn't love him! You didn't believe me, did you? You thought I was just a cold bitch who was warm to everyone but her husband! The music was the trick, you know! Soft music for bleeding hearts. Nocturnes for unrequited lovers. God, if you only knew how much I hoped from that man! I was my father's girl. He gave me everything and I was grateful, but the one thing he couldn't give was myself. He couldn't surrender that, you see, and I didn't know how to take it from him. He made himself a partner, even in my foolishness. That's what I wanted from Carlo: what you two have and what I hated you for–partnership. I wanted him to stand with me, match me with love and anger, tame me and make me free at the same time! But he didn't want that. Not Carlo! He wanted possession, surrender–to grind me small and boil me down and swallow me up so that there was nothing left. He wasn't strong enough to do it one way so he tried another! The wilting smile, the melancholy mood, tantrums and tenderness. Take me back to the womb and let me eat your soul out like a grub in a walnut! . . .' The car lurched and skidded as she wrenched it round a hairpin bend, but she talked on, heedless of Ninette's cry and Landon's protest. . . . 'I thought today his pride–or whatever it is that drives him–would be satisfied and I could go to him as a woman. But he doesn't want a woman! He wants a doll to play with, to croon over and spill the sawdust out of when he feels strong and cruel. That's why he's fallen for this Anna, a poor, empty, pretty child, with nothing inside her but what he's put there. Well, he's welcome to her. I'm free of him now–free of my father, too! I'm my own woman and I don't care what . . .'

She screamed and hit the brakes as a shadowy mass scrambled out of the ditch and ambled across the road in front. Ninette screamed, too, and threw herself against Landon. The wheels locked and they skidded in a sickening circle while the bumpers ripped open against the trunk of a roadside poplar. They ended, bruised and shaken, facing in the direction from which they had come. Ninette was breathless and trembling and Valeria sat slumped and sobbing over the steering-wheel. Landon was the first to recover. He said harshly: 'That's enough for tonight! We're going back to the villa!'

Valeria made no protest when he thrust her roughly out of the driver's seat and took over the wheel. They were all silent through the rattling, grinding drive up the hill, and when they reached the house Landon gave Ninette a curt order: 'Get her up to bed. Stay with her until I come. I'm going to talk to the old man!'

Ninette opened her mouth to protest, but, seeing his white, angry face and his tight trap mouth, she thought better of it and, taking Valeria's arm, she led her, submissive as a hospital patient, up the stairs to the bedroom.

Ascolini was still sitting in the library, slumped in his chair, staring into emptiness with a glass of brandy half-drunk at his elbow. Landon gave him no greeting but launched at once into a bitter tirade: 'This has got to stop, Doctor–all of it–now! If it doesn't there will be death in your house before the week is out. All three of us were damn near killed on the road ten minutes ago. Valeria's desperate. Carlo's a drunken mess. And you're sitting here feeling sorry for yourself because the bill collectors are in at last and you don't want to pay the score. If you want to destroy yourselves this is the way to do it!'

The old man lifted his white, lion mane and fixed Landon with a vague but hostile eye. 'And why should you care, Landon, what happens to us? Death, dishonour, damnation, what the hell does it matter to you?'

Landon's anger drove him on. He thrust an accusing finger in the old man's face and blazed at him: 'Because I've got debts to pay, that's why! To you, to Carlo, to Valeria. This is the only way I can pay them, and it's the last chance I've got. It's your last chance, too–and you know it! This is where it began–with you. If there's any hope at all it's in your hands. The bailiffs are in, my dear Doctor, and if you don't pay they'll tumble the house down about your ears!'

He broke off, splashed brandy into a glass and drank it at one swallow while the old man stared at him with cold, resentful eyes. Finally, with a hint of the old sardonic humour, Ascolini asked: 'And what's the payment, eh, my friend? What's the penance from our confessor? I'm too old to scourge myself in the market place and crawl to Mass on my knees!'

'You're old, Doctor,' said Landon with soft malice, 'and you'll soon be dead. You'll die hated and leave nothing behind but an unhappy memory. Your daughter will make herself a whore to spite you. And the man who could breed children for your house will die barren because there's no love to teach him better.' Swiftly as it had come, the anger died in him and he turned away with a gesture of despair. 'Damn it all! What more's to be said? Nothing is good enough for your gratitude, nothing can humble you enough to beg what the rest of us would give our eyes for!'

There was a long silence while the mantel clock ticked off the seconds like a death-watch beetle in the woodwork. Then, slowly, Ascolini heaved himself out of his chair and took a pace towards Landon. In a shaky, old man's voice that still had in it a note of dignity, he said: 'All right, Landon! You win. The old bull surrenders. Where does he go from here?'

Slowly, Landon turned to face him and saw in his aged face so much of ravaged pride, so much of pain long hidden, that he felt himself stifled by the sudden rush of pity. He gave the old man a pale, crooked smile. 'The first step is the hardest. After that it gets simpler all the time. A little loving, Doctor: a little tenderness, a little pity, and the grace to say one is sorry.'

'You think it's as easy as that?' A ghost of a grin twitched the lips of the cynic. 'You overrate me, Landon. Now go to bed like a good fellow. A man has a right to be private before the last surrender!'

When he left the old man, Landon walked out on to the terrace and lit a cigarette. The moon was riding high and magical over the mountains and from the recesses of the garden he heard, for the first time, the sweet lament of the nightingales. He stood stock-still, one hand resting on the cold stone of the balustrade, while the plangent song rose and fell in the still air. It was a ghostly music, echoing the plaint of dead lovers and the ardour of passions long cold. It was a lament for lost hopes and vanished illusions and words unsaid but now never to be spoken. And yet there was a peace in it and the cool absolution of time. The moon would wane and the song would lapse into the sad silence of the cypresses, but in the morning the sun would rise and the scent of the garden would waken again, and so long as one was alive there was the hope of morning and maturity.

Not so long ago, he had come to this place, obsessed by the conviction of futility, convinced that the jargon of his trade was like a shaman's incantation—a passport to eminence in the tribe, but a fruitless remedy for the manifold ills of the soul. Now, for the first time, he began to see a virtue in their use, a virtue in the experience he had gathered, and perhaps a small promise of virtue in himself.

With Ascolini he had won a battle and paid one debt. But there were others still to be fought and he was grateful for the restoration of this hour of moonlight and nightingales. He finished the cigarette and then walked slowly upstairs to Valeria's room.

She was in bed, propped against the pillows, her face pale, her eyes absorbed in the painful self-contemplation of the sick. Ninette was sitting on the edge of the bed, brushing Valeria's hair. Landon stood at the foot of the bed, looking from one to the other, and groping for the words he needed. To Ninette he said affectionately: 'I want you to go to bed, sweetheart. Valeria and I have things to talk about. I'll come in to see you before I go to sleep.'

Ninette Lachaise nodded agreement, but he caught a swift flash of resentment in her eyes. She bent and kissed Valeria and then kissed Landon too. 'Don't be too late, *chéri!*' There was a note of caution which belied the lightness of her tone. 'I'll be waiting up for you.'

She left him then and Landon sat down on the side of the bed. Valeria Rienzi watched him, half curious, half afraid. Landon said, with professional casualness: 'It's been a rough day, hasn't it?'

Her eyes filled up with weak distressful tears, but she did not answer. Landon talked on, skirmishing round his theme, lest any injudicious word might destroy the relationship between them.

'I know how you're feeling, girl, because I feel with you. I know the danger you're in, because I've been dealing a long time with hurt minds. You had a look at death tonight, but at the last minute you drew back. If you get reckless and take another look, you may wait a second too long. After that—*kaput!* There's a cure for most things, but not for the kiss of the Dark Angel. You're asking yourself why I care what you do. I'll tell you. There was a night we had—and there was good in it, because there was some love. Not enough for a lifetime, perhaps, but enough for that little while. So I care! And there's more. I'm a physician. People come to me with soul-sickness and heart-sickness, but most of them come too late when the sickness has a hold and won't let go. You're not sick, yet. You're hurt and tired and lonely in a dark country. I'm offering you a hand to hold while you walk out of it.'

He could see the war in her: need and defiance struggling for the first utterance. She closed her eyes and lay back, dumb on the piled pillows. Landon laid a firm hand on her wrist.

'There are two ways you can have it. You can fill yourself with sleeping pills and wake in the morning with the ghosts still sitting on the bed. Or you can talk the troubles out and let someone else cut them down to size for you. Me, for instance. I know all the words—even the dirty ones.' He laughed softly. 'There's no fee. And if you want to cry, I can lend you a clean handkerchief.'

She opened her eyes and looked at him in doleful wonderment. 'You really mean that?'

'I mean it.'

'But what happens then? Do you gather me up and put me together again? Do you fill up all the empty places where there's no me at all?'

'No.'

'Do you pat me on the head and tell me I'm forgiven, provided I'm a good girl in future?'

'Not that either.'

'Do you teach my father to love me and Carlo to want me for a wife?'

'No.'

'Then what do you give, Peter? For God's sake, what do you give me?'

'Courage and a strong back! For the rest you need God Almighty. But without courage you won't find Him either. Well . . . it's the best offer I can make. Do you want to talk or do you want a sedative capsule?'

She broke then, and began to pour herself out, in tears first and then in a flood of talk, sometimes wild and incoherent, sometimes tragically lucid. Landon listened, prompted, probed and wondered, as he always did, at the miscellany of faces one human being could wear. Bitch, lover, liar, mother, mistress and lady in a mirror, small girl sitting on a father's knee and selling him the world for a kiss. In one night, or in a month of nights, there was no time to read even a single one of them. What he was attempting now was not a clincial analysis but the dispensation of a simple mercy: to conjure away grief for a few hours, to plant a hope that he knew might not survive the first dawn.

Finally the torrent of talk spent itself, and Valeria lay back, exhausted but calm and ready for sleep. Landon bent and kissed her lightly on the lips and she responded with a sleepy murmur. Then, bone-weary, he went to his own room.

Ninette Lachaise was sleeping fully dressed on his bed. He slipped off coat and shoes and tie and lay down beside her. She stirred and muttered and threw her arm across his breast, then he too lapsed into sleep with her lips brushing his cheek. When he woke, she was no longer there and it was, once again, high noon in Tuscany.

When Landon came downstairs he found the villa bathed in a glow of triumph and familial unity. The maid-servant sang as she polished the furniture, the old gate-keeper whistled as he raked the gravelled drive, Ninette and Valeria were picking flowers in the garden, while Ascolini and Carlo Rienzi sat at coffee on the terrace working through a stack of newspapers and a pile of congratulatory telegrams.

They greeted him smiling. Ascolini rang for fresh coffee and then launched himself into an enthusiastic tally of Rienzi's successes. 'It is magnificent, Landon—like a great night at the opera. Read for yourself what they say. "A forensic victory . . ." . . ."a vindication of the noblest principles of justice" . . . "a new star in the legal firmament". I haven't seen anything like it for twenty years. And these.' He waved expansively at the pile of telegrams. 'Our colleagues in Rome are delighted. From this moment Carlo can have his choice of a dozen major cases. I'm proud of him. He has made me eat my words but I'm proud of him.'

Rienzi himself was flushed with pleasure. His face had lost its pinched and anxious look and he too launched into voluble compliments. 'It's your success, too, Peter. Without your counsel I should not have done half so well. I'm fortunate in my teachers, and, believe me, I know it.' Then, with boyish awkwardness, he made his apology. 'I'm sorry about last night. I hadn't eaten all day and I was very drunk.'

Ascolini laughed indulgently. 'A bagatelle, my boy! Forget it. I've seen better men than you carried to bed after smaller occasions. Besides, it's the future we have to think of. Before you came, Landon, we were discussing a partnership for Carlo. I'm not quite ready to pack up yet, but I will be soon. And then he can have the whole practice. But I still have a few lessons to give him, eh, my boy?'

There was so much patent good will between them that Landon wondered for a moment whether he had not read too much drama into the events of the night. Then Carlo said, casually enough: 'I had a call from Galuzzi this morning. They're transferring Anna today to the Sisters of the Good Shepherd. He says I can visit her this afternoon. I was wondering, Peter, if you'd like to come with me.' He gave a deprecating smile and added: 'I know how much I've asked of you, Peter, believe me. Valeria told me you and Ninette were getting married, and I know you want to be gone as soon as possible. But I would appreciate it if you'd take a last professional look at Anna.'

'If you like, of course, though I think there's nothing I can add to Galuzzi's knowledge. He's a good man. I would have great confidence in him.'

'I know. But he is, after all, a government official. I'd appreciate a little private guidance.'

'How would Galuzzi feel about my visit?'

'He's already approved it. Please come, Peter. We can leave about three o'clock and we'll be back here by five.'

'Valeria and I will look after Ninette,' said Ascolini. 'We shall all dine together tonight and then we shall send you away with our love.'

It was all so simple and bland that Landon almost missed the point. Carlo needed a privacy with the girl. Ascolini needed Ninette as his ally with Valeria. Galuzzi was shrewd enough to want a monitor for this first crucial meeting between the advocate and the client whom he had started on the dubious road to freedom. They were still using him and there would be no freedom until Ninette and himself had left this home of troubled souls and made their own retreat in the green hills of Frascati.

The first touch of autumn was in the air as Landon and Rienzi drove out along the Arezzo road to the Hospice of the Good Shepherd. Carlo's good humour seemed to have deserted him and he was fretful and preoccupied. When they reached the first high ridges he swung the car off the road into a craggy indentation from which the land fell steeply away into a wild and sombre valley. When they stopped, he produced cigarettes, lit one for Landon and one for himself, and then began to talk in the nervous, staccato fashion of a man too long deprived of intimacy.

'We have to talk, Peter. There are things I want to discuss with you.'

'Go ahead.'

'Valeria first. I'm sorry and ashamed for what happened last night, but in fact what I said was all true. I have no feeling for her any more. More than ever, at this time, I need a good marriage. I know what's going to happen. My career's going up like a balloon. You know what that means as well as I do. Pressure, demands, labour—from which there is no retreat. Without some kind of love in my life I shall be spending without renewal—a bankrupt's course. An understanding mistress would help, but I have not that either. I'm lonely, Peter. I feel old and empty beyond my years.'

His self-pity irritated Landon, but, remembering his debt, he tried still to be gentle. 'Look, Carlo. This kind of reaction is the most natural thing in the world. You've just fought a tremendous case. The pendulum is bound to swing back from triumph to depression. Don't be too hasty. Why don't you and Valeria give it another try?'

Rienzi's face hardened and he shook his head. 'We've forgotten the words, Peter. For me, too many nights in a cold bed. For her, too many other beds. Where do you start after that?'

Landon gave him Ninette's answer first. 'Someone has to make the first step and say "Sorry". I suggest it should be you.'

'And after that? How do you wipe out the waste and the hurt and all the memories?'

Landon gave him another answer to that, blunt and bawdy as anger could make it. 'You live with them, brother! You live with them and learn to be grateful for what you've salvaged. Damn it, Carlo! You're a big boy now! What do you want? A new book every night with the pages uncut and nothing written on them anyway? A new maidenhead every bedtime and people cheering when you hang out the sheets in the morning? Where's the comfort in that, for God's sake? It's a twelve-hour wonder—and a tedious business at best!'

To his surprise, Rienzi laughed. 'At least you haven't forgotten the words, Peter!'

'Neither have you. Neither has Valeria.'

'I'm afraid you'll never understand.' Rienzi smoked in silence for a few moments and then said, more calmly: 'You give me small credit, Peter. I'm not going to toss my cap over the windmill. I'm not going to go chasing the little models on the Via Veneto. I'm not built that way. I wish I were. Believe it or not, I've almost resigned myself to the situation. Convenient marriage is a very old institution in this country. Valeria can do what she wants so long as she's discreet about it. For myself, I can begin to see a kind of purpose in my life. Not wholly satisfactory, perhaps, but in part, yes.'

'You mean Anna Albertini?'

'Yes. In three years she'll be free. During that time she has to be prepared for an entry into the common world. When she does enter it she will need some kind of framework of interests and affection to step into.

'And you think you can provide it?'

'I do.'

'At what price?'

'Less than I've paid for the little I have now.'

'Do you want to know what I think?' Landon's voice was chilly.

'That's why I'm talking to you, Peter. More than ever now I need your friendship.'

'Then for God's sake listen in friendship to what I'm going to tell you!' He broke off and gathered himself for a moment, then began to talk, warmly and persuasively, knowing that now or never the last debt must be paid. 'First, let me explain to you, Carlo, that I don't agree with many of my colleagues who claim that every human aberrration is a symptom of mental illness. I believe, as I think you do, that man is a responsible being, endowed with free-will. But this is no reason to confuse the issue. There is a moral infirmity as well as a mental one. There is evil in the world. There are calculated depravity and indulgence. And there is also a special sickness that follows from these things: a state of fugue, a flight from the knowledge of guilt, man pulling the blankets over his head to escape the beaks of the Furies.

'This is why modern psychiatry splits itself into two schools. The determinists say that man is not responsible for his actions. Therefore, when we've revealed to him the source of his disorder, he will cure himself by forgiving himself. You're a lawyer. You see where this ends—in the destructive absurdity that evil is its own absolution. The other school says, more reasonably, that when the source of the disorder is revealed, man must be given a hope of forgiveness, but he must also be led to the motions of self-reform. . . .' He broke off and laughed a little self-consciously. 'You wonder why I'm reading you this little lecture, Carlo? I'm no plaster saint, God knows. I know when I'm doing wrong and so do you. You're doing it now because you refuse any sort of forgiveness to Valeria and demand all of it for yourself. You know that you're preparing the way for a greater wrong. So you're creating a fiction that you can absolve yourself by the very act which will damn you—a cultivation of Anna Albertini.'

'You're lying to me, Peter,' said Rienzi coldly.

'Not this time, believe me.' He was pleading now and the knowledge of his own guilt lent him an urgent humility. 'Listen to me, Carlo, and think for a moment about Anna. You won your case on the plea you and I set up for her—that at the time of the murder she was mentally infirm, robbed of moral sense and legal responsibility by the shock of her mother's death. Now this could be true. On the other hand, it could be equally true that she was a responsible person, that she was conscious of guilt, and that, after the act—after it, remember—she projected herself into the state of fugue in which she has remained virtually ever since. Think about that for a moment. And if there's half a chance of its being true, see where it leads. She clings to you because you are the only one who continues to absolve her as you did in the legal sense in court. This could be why she has no regret for her husband, because he rejected and did not forgive her!'

'That's a monstrous thought!'

'Monstrous indeed,' said Landon quietly, 'and the consequences are more monstrous still. You could be the one who robs her totally and completely of any hope of cure.'

'I don't understand that.'

'Then let me explain it to you, Carlo.' He laid a tentative, friendly hand on Rienzi's shoulder, but Rienzi withdrew resentfully from the contact. 'Believe me, man, I'm being as honest as I know how. I'm not raising bogies to frighten you. This is my profession, as the law is yours. All successful psychiatry depends upon the patient's willingness to seek a cure because of his knowledge that he is sick. He will resist treatment, of course, but if the distress is acute enough he will come to co-operate—except for instance in cases of paranoia where the mind closes itself utterly against reason. In Anna Albertini's case there is no distress, no sense of need. So long as she has you she is not sick but cured, so her mind closes itself to further inquisition. You have forgiven her. Therefore she is totally forgiven. So the long flight continues and you, Carlo—you, my friend!—are her partner in the flight.'

'But only,' said Rienzi in the ironic fashion of the law, 'only if your guess is true, and in court you proved to the satisfaction of the judges that it was not. Where do you stand now, Peter?'

'On the same ground,' said Landon flatly, 'but for a different reason. You have made yourself a necessary prop to her infirmity. She will continue to cling to you. She will accept any condition, any relationship you impose on her, but you'll never be able to get rid of her. And if you fail her . . .'

He broke off and let the thought hang, a discordant note between them. Rienzi prompted him caustically: 'And if I fail her, Peter?'

'Death is familiar to her now,' said Landon sombrely. 'It holds no terrors and solves all problems. She will either kill herself or try to kill you.' It was out now, the untimely thought: death in the Tarot cards, death written on the palm of a man's hand, and he too blind to see it. Landon let him sweat over it for a few moments and then asked: 'Do you believe me, Carlo?'

'No,' said Carlo Rienzi, 'I'm afraid I don't.'

He started the engine, turned the car back on to the highway, and headed once more into the uplands towards the Hospice of the Good Shepherd.

In the late afternoon, Alberto Ascolini made his final capitulation to his daughter and to Ninette Lachaise. He sat with them on a low stone bench facing a small fountain where a dancing faun played his pipes and disported himself among the water jets. For once in his life, he gave no thought to stage management nor to the rhetoric of his trade. He did not attempt to persuade or to dominate the occasion, but sat, leaning on a stick, with a peasant hat perched on his white head, making the first and last apologia for his mountebank's career.

'This is the way it ends, my children. This is the way I think it is meant to end—an old fool sitting in the garden with the women. I used to be afraid of it, you know. Today, for the first time, I can see there might be a pleasure in it. When I was young, and that was a long time ago, the *signori* who owned this villa used to drive through San Stefano in their carriages on the way to Siena. They had coachmen and outriders, and the women—they looked like princesses to me—used to sit holding their handkerchiefs to their noses as they drove through the village. I remember myself, a snot-nosed urchin with the backside out of his breeches, shouting for coppers while the coachman flicked at me with his whip. A long time ago, but I remembered it every month, every year, as I was climbing up out of the dung-heap. One day I would have a coach and the woman with the lace handkerchief would be my woman, and I would sit in grand array at the opera and ride on the Corso in Rome and kiss hands in the *salons*. I did it all, as you know. I've dined with kings and presidents and walked into a reception with a princess of the blood on my arm . . . eh! What is it now? Not dust and ashes. I can't say that. A rich time? Yes. But every so often I would dream of the snot-nosed boy and reach out my hand to lift him into the coach—yet I could never touch him. Neither could I escape him. He would always come back and I could never be sure whether he mocked me or blamed me. So, for him, I think, I took my revenges on the world into which I had climbed, even on you, Valeria, my child. It has taken me a long time to understand that they were revenges on myself as well. When I married your mother I was poor and ambitious and I loved her. When I was famous and courted I regretted her. In you I tried to make her over again in the image of what I had desired. A strange thing, you know. She was wiser than I. She told me many times the price was too high and that when I had paid it I would regret it. You, child, I regret most of all. You were right, you know, when you said I made you pay for everything I gave. Nothing for nothing! It was the bitterest lesson my snot-nosed urchin had to learn. He could never believe in gratuity–the kiss that cost nothing or the hand to help a neighbour out of a ditch. He's learnt it now, from you, Ninette, even from that pig-headed Landon of yours. But you, my Valeria, have had to pay for the lesson. . . .' His voice faltered and he blew his nose violently. 'Forgive me, child, if you can. If you can't, believe at least that I love you.'

'It's enough, *dottore*,' said Ninette Lachaise softly. 'The loving is enough–and that Valeria should know that the loving is there.'

She lifted the old straw hat and kissed him on the forehead and laid one cool hand for a moment on his cheek. Then she left them, Valeria with her tears and the old advocate with his regrets, to the healing of the last summer sun.

'Now!' said the old man in his brisk, pragmatic style, 'now we dry our eyes and see if we have grown any wiser. You will know now, child, that I am telling you the truth?'

'Yes.'

'Then let's see what we can do about this marriage of yours. Tell me honestly now: what's the trouble between you?'

Valeria Rienzi lifted a ravaged face and stared at him blankly. 'It's plain enough, isn't it, Father? I've been a fool and Carlo needs something that I can't give him.'

'We'll admit the foolishness,' said Ascolini with his old sardonic grin. 'We'll lock it away and bring it out occasionally to remind us not to be fools again. But what about Carlo? What does he want?'

She shrugged unhappily. 'I wish I knew. A mother, perhaps, or a child bride fresh from convent school!'

'He has the child bride,' said Ascolini cynically. 'But she's no good to him because she'll be locked away for three years. As for the mother, he can't do much about that unless he finds a clucking widow with a forty-five-inch bust.'

'Don't make jokes about it, Father. It's serious.'

'I know it's serious, child!' The old man was testy again. 'But we don't throw up our hands and go wailing through the town. We do something about it.'

'What, for instance?'

'This girl, Anna Albertini. Ignore her. If Carlo wants to go hanging round the convent garden with the girl on one arm and a nun for a watchdog on the other, let him. He'll get sick of it in time. Pity's a thin diet for a man of thirty-five. If he wants to try the widow or a chicken from a pavement café, ignore that, too. Swallow your pride and take him for what he is, and while you've got him see if you can't make him into something better. It's been done, you know. And you do have something to work on. You saw him in court. He was another man. You're a woman. You may be able to bring the same man out in bed. Look, child.' He turned to her and imprisoned her wrists in his old strong hands. 'There's always one who kisses and one who turns the cheek. Sometimes the one who turns the cheek learns to like the taste of kissing. It's worth a trial, isn't it? You've had your playtime. There's autumn after summer. If it doesn't work, what have you lost?'

'Nothing, I suppose. But don't you see, Father, I'm lonely now. I'm scared.'

'Wait till you get to my age,' said Alberto Ascolini with a grin '–the last winter, when you know for certain there'll never be another spring.

Courage, girl! Go and put on a new face and let's see what carrots we can find for this noble ass you've married!'

The Hospice of the Good Shepherd Sisters reared its grey bulk over a spread of garden and farmland and dark cypresses. Its nearer aspect was forbidding: a big wall of tufa stone topped with spikes and broken glass, wrought-iron gates backed with a close mesh of chain wire, and, beyond them, the hospice itself, an old monastery building, four storeys high, solid as a fortress, with barren windows and a television antenna rising incongruously above its ancient tiles. An elderly porter opened the gates and raised his hand in a half-hearted salute as they passed. A pair of inmates shuffling across the lawn turned and stared at them with glazed, indifferent eyes. A young nun, with the sleeves of her habit rolled up, was clipping flowers, trailed by a group of women, aimless as hens in a barn-yard. A vague oppression crept over Landon as he thought of all the misery penned in this place, last refuge of those who, by act of God and self-delusion, had failed to come to terms with life.

Yet not all the deluded were behind bars. There were all too many who, like Carlo Rienzi, created for themselves situations charged with explosive and destructive possibilities. Carlo had become, overnight, a public figure, thrust into limelit eminence, and yet the shrewd eye could see already how the pillars and buttresses of his personality were slowly withering away. The cracks were plainly visible, the dangerous cant towards indulgence and self-deception. How, or which way, he would fall was anyone's guess, but Landon was prepared to give long odds that he would decline inevitably in the direction of Anna Albertini.

Even for a middling sensual man, the association with an attractive young woman of twenty-four was fraught with danger. Add to that the character of the girl herself—her enforced dependence, her immaturity, her capacity for tragic decision—and there were all the elements of a classic melodrama.

How many times could the world blow up? The answer was plain to Landon now, plainer than it had ever been: as often as a man chose to reject the simple pragmatic rules of human experience and arbitrate his private destiny without respect to duty, obligation and his nature as a dependent animal.

The Greeks had a word for that, too: Nemesis—the ultimate and inevitable catastrophe, when a man pulled down the roof-trees of the world on his own hapless head. The trouble was that other heads were broken as well and he generally did not survive to mend them.

Landon was still chewing on that tasteless cud when the Sister Portress, a horse-faced woman with gentle eyes and an uncertain smile, opened the door to them. She showed them into the visitors' room, a large, bare chamber, furnished with high-backed chairs, twin statues of the Sacred Heart and Our Lady of Lourdes, and smelling vaguely of lamp-oil and floor-wax; then she trotted off to find the Mother Superior.

Landon wilted at the thought of spending a couple of hours in this ascetic atmosphere, but Carlo reassured him with an unexpected smile: 'Don't worry, Peter. This is just to condition us to piety. They keep it for chaplains and doctors and visiting bishops. When Anna comes I imagine they'll give us the freedom of the garden.'

'Thank God for that!' said Landon drily.

Rienzi gave him a rueful, boyish smile. 'Don't be too angry with me,

Peter. After all, this is my decision and I have to carry the conse-quences–good or bad.'

'Do you, Carlo?' Landon was still smouldering. 'If that's what you believe, then you'll do what you damned well please. I'm leaving tomorrow anyway, so why should I care?'

'I want us to be friends,' said Carlo Rienzi. 'I have a great affection for you, Peter. But that doesn't mean I have to agree with you all the time, does it?'

'A man who pleads his own cause has a fool for a lawyer, Carlo. A man who wants to be his own doctor is a bigger fool still. You've had my advice. I can't force you to act on it. Now please drop the discussion, like a good fellow.'

At that moment the Mother Superior came in: a small, grey woman with a fine-boned face, who reminded Landon of Ascolini's marchesa. She had the air of a great lady born to wield authority, and Landon thought she could be a very formidable superior indeed.

When Carlo presented himself she gave him a warm greeting: 'I followed your case with great interest, Mr Rienzi. The men of my family have been associated with the law for many years, so I had a special interest. You made a magnificent plea.' To Landon she extended a graver courtesy: 'We're very happy to see you here, Mr Landon. Professor Galuzzi speaks of you with great respect. If you would care to visit us at any time to see our methods or talk to our staff you will be most welcome.'

Landon bowed his acknowledgement and the Mother Superior went on with what was obviously a well-prepared exordium: 'We are all very interested in Anna's case, gentlemen. She was admitted early this afternoon, as you know, and we had none of the difficulty usual with new patients. Professor Galuzzi has given instructions that she is to be allowed as much freedom and responsibility as she can take. She will have all the privileges accorded to our advanced patients: a room of her own, time to read and sew, an hour of television each day, and a few cosmetics. These are special privileges, but so long as our people are orderly in their habits, obedient in their demeanour, there is no reason for them to be reduced. With regard to visits, there is a normal visiting day once a month. However, Professor Galuzzi suggests that for the present it would be best for Anna if we arranged a visiting day every six weeks. If she makes good progress, then we shall go back to the usual schedule.'

'Neatly done,' Landon thought. Galuzzi had a clear head and shrewd eye, and in this little grey woman he would have a strong lieutenant.

She went on in her crisp, businesslike fashion: 'We have another rule, too, which we have found most useful. When visitors come they are generally accompanied–unobtrusively of course–by one of our Sisters. However, as Mr Landon is here with you today, I think we can dispense ourselves from the practice.'

For the first time, Rienzi was able to get a foothold in the conversation. Anxious as a Dutch uncle, he said: 'I have a great personal interest in Anna, as you know. If there is anything I can do to make her happy you have only to call me.'

The Mother Superior smiled indulgently. 'I assure you, Mr Rienzi, she will have the best of care. Our medical staff is well trained and devoted. Professor Galuzzi is a constant visitor. Our Sisters are especially trained to maintain a reasonable discipline while spending as much kindness as possible on our patients. Today you may find Anna a little restless. This is natural. It is her first day and she is new and strange; but she will settle down quickly. Also, she is a healthy young woman and it is natural that from time to time she will be irked by confinement and by the lack of the company of the opposite sex. But we are trained to watch for these things and to offset them.' She stood up and smoothed down the skirt of her habit. 'If you've brought any gifts for her I'd like to see them now.'

Awkward as a schoolboy, Rienzi displayed the packages: a box of chocolates, a hair ribbon, a religious medallion on a small gold chain, a sewing kit. The old nun passed them all with a smile, but insisted on taking the scissors out of the sewing box. 'Not because of Anna, Mr Rienzi, but because of the danger of their falling into other hands.'

Rienzi blushed and apologized. 'It was thoughtless of me. I'm sorry.'

'On the contrary, Mr Rienzi, you're a very thoughtful man. Anna is lucky to have your support.'

At the same moment, Anna Albertini walked hesitantly into the room and Rienzi held out an eager hand in greeting. 'Anna, my dear! How good to see you!'

'And you, Mr Rienzi.'

The formal address and the tentative handshake belied the pleasure in her eyes. Rienzi presented her to Landon. 'You remember Mr Landon, Anna? He was a great help to you before the trial and during it.'

'Of course.' She gave him a cautious smile. 'Mr Landon was very kind to me. I won't forget that.'

'You look well, Anna. I know you're going to be very happy here.'

The girl said nothing and the Mother Superior cut in briskly: 'I must be off. I have work to do. Take the gentlemen into the garden, Anna. Walk them down to the place where you saw the Sisters saying their prayers.' She explained herself with a smile to Landon: 'It's the Sisters' garden. You'll be more comfortable there. You won't be bothered by the inmates wandering around the grounds. Before you go, Anna will bring you back here for coffee.'

When she was gone, Carlo displayed his gifts, and while they were admiring them together Landon took a long look at Anna Albertini. She was dressed, like all the inmates, in a frock of grey cotton with long buttoned sleeves and a cloth belt sewn to the frock itself. She wore black stockings and black shoes. Her hair was shorter now, drawn back from her face and tied with a wisp of blue ribbon. Her hands were uneasy, but her face still wore the look of calm and classic repose which he had noticed on the day of their first meeting. There was more colour in it now, more animation in the eyes and in the voice. Her gestures were restrained, her movements studiously modest, so that she looked more like a fledgling nun than a prisoner serving sentence for murder.

For all his past judgments of Rienzi, Landon had to admit that he could see nothing but innocence in this first moment of meeting. There was no trace of sensuality, not so much as a hand's touch or a glance to hint at intimacy or collusion. Anna was now calling Rienzi by his first name, but the most suspicious eavesdropper would have found nothing to blame in the tone or the affection.

When her first excitement was over, Anna piled her gifts on one of the chairs and then took the two men out into the garden. She walked between them reserved as a novice, rehearsing with simple pleasure the details of her first day after the trial.

'Everyone was so kind to me. At San Gimignano they made me a special supper and the nurses were allowed to come in and talk to me. One of them did my hair, another brought me a prayer-book. In the morning I was allowed to walk by myself in the garden and the warden's wife gave me coffee. Everyone said how lucky I was and what a wonderful thing you had done for me. I felt very proud. They've given me a nice room here. There are bars on the windows, but there are curtains, too, with flowers on them, and everything is white and clean. Sister Eulalia took me for a walk and showed me some new kittens in the gardener's shed. She told me funny stories about the people we saw, and tonight there is to be a concert with some very famous singers from Rome.'

Landon's first impression was of her extreme simplicity, her preoccupation with trivial things, her contentment with the narrow ambit of enclosed existence. But when Carlo began to question her about what she had read, about how she like to spend her time, about the programmes she had watched on television, Landon caught a glimpse of a lively, if limited, intelligence and a very adequate judgment.

For the first time, she expressed an interest in what she might do after her release. She had once seen a fashion show and she wondered whether she might later qualify as a mannequin. If this failed, she thought she might like to train as a stenographer. She wanted to know whether there was any training available in the hospital. She asked questions about Carlo's work and Landon's, and her queries, if elementary, were still eminently sensible.

Carlo's method with her was sound. He probed for her interest, stimulated it with questions and then set about filling in the blank spaces in her information. His talk ranged widely, but he avoided any subject which might arouse her to discontent or revive old memories of childhood or married life. He made jokes for her and laughed at her mild comedies. And all the time he walked separate from her, hands clasped behind his back like a genial parent at finishing-school.

But for Landon there was something missing from the picture. It was too placid, too sober. Its pathos was too muted, its motif too mild. There was nothing in it to justify Carlo's desperate hope, or his own fears, or its importance to Anna herself. Landon could not believe that the performance was being staged for his benefit. Rienzi was too poor an actor to bring it off and Anna had had no warning to prepare for a deception.

Then understanding began to dawn on Landon. This was not the whole performance, but a prelude, a ritual entry into another stage of communion. He saw, or thought he saw, how they would both need something like this. They were poles apart in nature, education and experience. They would meet too rarely and for too short a time to leap at once into a high ground of understanding. The girl would be subdued by the daily disciplines of the institution. Carlo would have to discipline himself lest the exacerbations of his life drive him into indiscretion. So each of their meetings would begin like this: slow talk to skim the surface of the sleeping thoughts, a slow pavane along the garden paths—to what?

Their walk brought them finally to a low stone wall, broken by a wicket gate which led into private domain of the Sisters: a croquet lawn screened on all sides by close-grown shrubs and, beyond it, more private still, a sunken garden with a fish-pond and a shrine of Our Lady of Fatima.

This was where the nuns came for their recreation and to say the Rosary in the cool of the evening. This was their retreat from the thankless labours of the hospice and from the intrusion of the sick ones shambling about the grounds.

'Here—' said Anna suddenly, 'here I felt for the first time that I'm free. Not free as I used to be, but as I will be one day.'

She was not looking at her companions, but around the garden and over the tips of the cypresses to the pale sky where a solitary hawk wheeled and hovered in the slack air. Her eyes shone, her face was transfigured by a swift glow of vitality.

'You see that fellow up there? When I was a little girl in San Stefano, they used to call him the chicken-stealer. You know what I call him now? I call him Carlo. He hangs about up there for hours and hours and you think he's never going to come down. Then, all of a sudden, he drops–plop!–like a stone.' She turned to Landon, flushed and laughing. 'Just like Carlo! All the time I was in prison, all the time during the trial, he seemed to be so far away–miles and miles away among the great ones. Now–look!–he's here with me, in this garden.'

Landon stole a quick glance at Rienzi, but he was bending over a rose bloom, studious as any botanist. The girl laughed again in childish mockery.

'Carlo doesn't think he's a hawk. He likes to make out he's a wise old stork with long legs and a long advocate's nose with a pair of spectacles on it. You should have heard the lectures he read me when he came to see me! He sounded just like Mother Superior today. "Anna must be a good girl. Anna must do as she is told. She must learn her lessons and be tidy and patient and co-operative."'

'Anna's a lucky girl,' said Carlo coldly, 'but she laughs at the wrong things.'

'You told me once I needed to laugh!'

'I know, child, but . . .'

'I'm not a child! I'm a woman. That's what you want me to be, isn't it? That's what you were saying all the time, during the trial. Now you call me a child.'

She said it petulantly, as if it were an old complaint, and then stood, downcast, biting her thumbnail, waiting for Carlo to reprove her again. This time he was more gentle with her. He smiled benignly and said: 'Anna, the things I tell you are the things that will make you free. You're much better off than we ever expected you to be. Three years isn't such a long time and they'll go much quicker if you live each day for itself. This is a good place to be. The Sisters are kind people. If you're obedient and easy for them to handle we may have a chance to get you out of this place sooner. That's not a joking matter.'

'But I've been cooped up so long. Now I want to fly free like the chicken-stealer. I want to wear nice clothes again and look in shop windows and . . .'

'I know, I know.' His voice took on a softer, crooning tone. 'But I'll come to see you as often as I can. I'll bring you presents. You'll find the days will go faster and faster. Besides, it takes a whole winter to make the spring flowers–but in the end they come.'

She was penitent now, like a calculating child who asks for cake only to win a caress. She said humbly: 'I'm sorry, Carlo. I'll try better. I want so much to please you.'

'I know you do, Anna. Now forget it like a good girl and let's talk about something else.'

For Landon it was an embarrassing experience, like stumbling on a drunken courtship half-way down the stairs. Anna was seducing Carlo with pity while he struggled with the clumsy fiction of paternal solicitude. How long they could keep it up Landon did not know. By all the signs, they had been practising for some time, and perhaps they had developed a stronger tolerance than most for this courtship by mutual deception. But sooner or later one would crack. The fairy-tale would come apart at the seams, and then–caps over the windmill and hell to pay!

Landon had had more than enough for one afternoon, but he endured it for another half hour, pacing with them up and down the croquet lawn, listening to their talk, adding an occasional banality of his own, and watching how easily and unconsciously they lapsed into the conventions of their unconventional attachment. Finally, he gave up and suggested to Carlo that it was time to leave.

Carlo looked at his watch and said, resentfully: 'Well, if you feel you must . . . but it will be some time before I can see Anna again.'

Anna was even more reluctant. She laid an urgent hand on Rienzi's arm and demanded: 'Please, Carlo! Before you go, could we have a few words in private?'

'Would you mind, Peter?'

No, he would not mind. He would be glad to be rid of them for a while. He would smoke a cigarette and stroll for ten minutes more while they exchanged whatever secrets they had with the Madonna in the sunken garden. Carlo led Anna to the stone steps that separated the two enclosures and when she disappeared down the other side he came back for a hurried word with Landon.

'I'm sorry, Peter. All this must be very boring to you. But you see how it is. This is her first day here. She's restless. And I'd feel guilty if I left her unsettled. I shan't be very long.'

Guilty or innocent, Landon had to tell him. Once outside the gates of the hospice, chameleon love would change colour again and crawl back into the pigeon-hole marked 'grand illusions', a high, secret place beyond all reach of reason. He clamped a firm hand on Carlo's wrist and gave him the warning: 'Carlo, you're my friend and I've got to say it. You're walking on eggs in this affair. Whatever she says, however she says it, this girl is hot for you. And you're at least warm to her. Pull out now like a sensible man! Say goodbye to her and call it a day. Please, Carlo!'

Carlo tried to wrench away, but Landon held him as the other blazed in low, bitter invective: 'If today hasn't shown you the truth, Peter, nothing will. You've got a dirty mind! You've said all this before. Now it's once too much. Let me go, please!'

'One more thing, Carlo!' It was on the tip of Landon's tongue to tell him of his talk with Galuzzi and of the suspicion under which he lay aready. Then he thought better of it. Why the hell play hangman to a man plaiting his own rope? Landon shrugged and let him go. Carlo stalked angrily out of sight into the sunken garden while Landon settled himself under an autumn tree and smoked a tasteless cigarette.

He smoked another, and a third. He paced the lawn for ten minutes, fifteen, twenty. Then, utterly exasperated, he went in search of Rienzi and Anna. He had hardly set foot on the first stone step when he heard their voices, and for the first time in his life he played the keyhole spy.

Rienzi and Anna were sitting on a stone bench in an alcove opposite the shrine. They were facing each other with half the length of the bench between them, but Anna was holding Carlo's hand and pleading with him: 'You've told me many times, Carlo, that no one can live without love–some kind of love. I know you're married, so I mustn't ask that kind. But I'm not a child, so you mustn't offer me that kind either. What have we got, Carlo? What can you give me to keep me alive in this place?'

Landon could not see Rienzi's face, but he could sense the uneasiness in him and his effort to hedge his answer in that bland dominie's voice: 'You're very precious to me, Anna, my dear–for many reasons. All those weeks I held your fate in my hands. You were and still are my prize. Of course I care for you deeply.'

'Is that all?'

It was the voice Landon had heard first on Professor Galuzzi's tape–dead, flat and colourless. Rienzi protested feebly: 'No, Anna. You know it isn't all. But, for the rest, I'm not even sure myself. I doubt I could put it into words.'

'But I have words, Carlo . . . I love you!'

Rienzi was badly shaken, but he still tried to humour her like a child. 'Love is a big word, Anna. It means different things at different times. The way you love me today may be a lot different from the way you love me tomorrow.'

'Do you love me, Carlo?'

Landon saw him hesitate a moment and then heard him surrender: 'I–I love you, Anna.'

But she was not satisfied yet. She pressed him urgently, raising his reluctant hands and holding them to her breast. 'How do you love me, Carlo? How?'

It was Rienzi's last ditch and he knew it. Landon could feel him gathering himself, fumbling for the words that were his final defences against her. 'I–I don't know that yet, Anna. That's why you must be patient with me. I need time, we both need time to get to know each other, not in the crisis of a court-room, not here in this place, but outside, in a world of normal people. This thing between us, Anna, needs to grow naturally, like a plant. If the flower looks different from what we expected, it will still be beautiful, still good for us both. Can you understand that?'

To Landon's surprise and Carlo's evident relief, she accepted it. She hesitated for a moment and then said, in her childish voice: 'Yes. I do understand. I can be happy now, I think. . . . Will you please kiss me goodbye?'

Rienzi looked at her for a long moment, then, with touching tenderness, but with no vestige of passion, he cupped his hands under her chin and kissed her lightly on the lips. Then he released her and stood up. Puzzled and disappointed, she faced him, picking a scrap of lint from his lapel with nervous fingers.

'You did that as if I were a little girl.'

Rienzi smiled gravely and shook his head. 'No, Anna! You're a woman. A very beautiful woman.'

'Then kiss me like one! Make me feel like a woman. Just once . . . just once!'

Landon wanted to shout to him: 'No, don't do it!' but shame held him back. The next moment the girl was in Rienzi's arms and they were kissing passionately like lovers, while the marble Madonna looked on dumbly and any wandering nun might shout their ruin over the roof-tops.

Then, without any warning, it happened. With a single, convulsive gesture, Anna thrust Carlo away from her. Her face was a contorted mask of terror and hate. As Carlo stared at her, unbelieving, she opened her mouth in a high, hysterical scream: 'They're killing her! They're killing her!' The next moment she was tearing at his eyes and face, tiger-wild and shouting in insane accusation: 'You're the one! You're the one who killed her! You . . . you!'

It took all their efforts to wrestle her back to the hospice, where four muscular nurses buckled her into a strait-jacket and carried her away. The Mother Superior looked at them with shrewd, dubious eyes and then called a Sister to dress Carlo's torn face.

9

Ten minutes later, in the bleak reception-room where Carlo's gifts to Anna still lay piled on the chair, the little grey nun faced them with the cold question: 'Well, gentlemen, how did it happen?'

Carlo Rienzi was a very great advocate, but now he was in the dock and in need of another's counsel. Before he could open his mouth, Peter Landon hurried into an explanation: 'I think, Reverend Mother, I probably saw more of what happened than Mr Rienzi. All three of us were in the garden together. Mr Rienzi was just saying goodbye to Anna and I was standing about three paces away, watching them. Anna seemed perfectly normal, but when Mr Rienzi held out his hand she put her arms around his neck and tried to kiss him. He pushed her away gently and told her not to be silly. Then she started to scream that he was the one who had killed her mother. Immediately after that she attacked him.'

Landon hoped desperately that the narrative sounded as shocked and ingenuous as he tried to make it. This grey, competent lady held, at this moment, power of life and death over Advocate Rienzi, and Landon had no doubt she would damn him without mercy if she suspected the truth, so, for good measure, he added a professional opinion. 'This is a tragic business, Reverend Mother, but, speaking professionally, I am not too surprised. Both Professor Galuzzi and I were gravely concerned about certain unstable elements in this girl's case. I know Professor Galuzzi hoped to explore them more fully by deep analysis. If I could use your phone I think I should call Galuzzi from here.'

The Mother Superior gave him a cool, appraising look and then, apparently satisfied, turned to Rienzi. 'Mr Rienzi, do you agree with Mr Landon's account of what happened?'

Shaken as he was, Rienzi was still a good lawyer. He knew that half a lie is worse than no lie at all. His answer came back pat and convincing: 'That's exactly how it happened.'

The Mother Superior nodded and then said in a crisp, decisive fashion: 'I'm afraid it doesn't end here. You both know that people committed to our care from the courts are wards of the State. Everything that happens to them becomes the matter of an official report. I shall need affidavits from both of you—four copies, each copy notarized.'

She must have been convinced, Landon thought sourly, otherwise she would know that she was committing them to perjury, and the consciences of the worthy Sisters were too tender for such wilful irony.

Carlo Rienzi murmured some words of regret, but the Mother Superior waved them aside with an old, imperious hand. She had no time for lamentations. Her vocation was the care of sick minds and Anna Albertini was sick beyond recovery. She led Landon down a bare, echoing corridor into her office and then telephoned Professor Galuzzi.

Her own report was made first, in the clear decisive tones of a staff officer. Then she handed the receiver to Landon. It was a relief to him to hear Galuzzi's dry, academic voice from the other end of the line: 'So, my friend, it happened sooner than we expected, eh? Well, perhaps it's better this way—for everybody. Mother Superior tells me you were there and saw it all?'

'That's right.'

'I presume it's your version I've just heard?' There was an edge of irony in Galuzzi's question.

'Mother Superior reported exactly what I told her. I'll be attesting it in an official report.

Surprisingly, Galuzzi chuckled. 'One young advocate is fortunate in his friends. Your eyewitness report will, of course, close the matter, since it carries such a weight of professional reputation. If you have time, however, in the next few days, I'd like to drink a glass of wine with you—and perhaps consult you about our patient.'

'I'm very grateful,' said Landon, 'more grateful than I can tell you. But I'll be leaving Siena in a couple of days. I'm getting married.'

'My felicitations!' said Galuzzi warmly. Then he added drily: 'I think you're wise. Miss Lachaise is a charming woman—and it's time you had some diversion. Good luck, my friend. Go with God.'

'Good luck to you,' said Landon softly. 'And thank you.'

The old nun looked at him with a canny, cultivated eye. 'So your case is closed, Mr Landon. Mine is just beginning. Thank you and good day.'

Landon drove Rienzi's car out of the iron gates and heard them close with a clang. As they climbed out of the valley towards the high road, Carlo sat huddled and silent beside him, fingering his scarred face and staring with blank eyes at the road ahead. After a while, he roused himself slightly and said, in a toneless voice: 'Thank you for what you did, Peter.'

'Forget it.'

'I can't say how sorry I am.'

'Forget that, too.'

Landon could hardly have said less, but he had no heart to say more. He knew that if Rienzi uttered one word of self-pity he would stop the car and punch him on the nose and make him walk every step of the way back to Siena. He understood what the man must be suffering, he was prepared to perjure himself to save Rienzi's neck, but the memory of Anna Albertini, lost to all hope, buckled in a canvas bag and carted off to oblivion, would haunt him for a long time.

Dusk was coming down when they reached the Villa Ascolini. Mercifully, everyone was dressing for dinner, so Landon settled Carlo in the library with a whisky decanter and a siphon of soda and then hurried upstairs to talk to Ninette. She heard him out in silence and then chided

him firmly: 'I know you're angry, *chéri*, but you can't give way to it now. I
know how badly you feel about having to perjure yourself. I agree that all
your debts are paid. But we can't just work on debit and credit. This is a
crisis for Carlo and we must help him to survive it.'

'Don't you think it's time he helped himself?'

'Do you think he can at this moment?' Her hands reached out to caress his
angry face. 'Peter, Peter, can't you see? What he's done today must seem
like murder to him.'

'Wasn't it just that?'

'Who knows, *chéri*? Who knows how much or how little was needed to tip
the balance for Anna? Who knows whether without Carlo it might not have
happened much sooner? Don't judge him, Peter. Not today. Not yet
awhile.'

He could not resist her then. He took her in his arms and kissed her and
surrendered with a weary grin. 'All right, sweetheart, what do you want me
to do?'

'Leave Carlo to me for a while. You go up and talk to Ascolini and
Valeria.'

'Do you think it's wise to tell them?'

'I'm sure of it.'

Landon was far from sure, but at bottom he was too indifferent to care. A
few moments later, Ninette went down to the library to see Carlo while
Landon walked along the corridor to talk with Doctor Ascolini.

The old man took the news calmly enough. He made a quick canvass of
the legal possibilities and then, satisfied that both Rienzi and Landon were
beyond impeachment, he shrugged and said calmly: 'For the girl, of course,
it's a terrible thing. For us—all of us—it may be the mercy we have been
waiting for. Carlo is alone now. Perhaps he will turn back to Valeria.'

'Perhaps. It seems he has no other place to go.'

The old man cocked a quizzical eye at Landon. 'You've had enough,
haven't you, my friend?'

'More than enough. We'll say goodbye tonight, Doctor.'

Ascolini nodded a grave agreement. 'You're right, of course. If I say I am
grateful it will mean too little. Let me tell you simply that all your debts are
paid to Carlo and that we are now in debt to you. I have never perjured
myself for any man, though I've often sworn false oaths to women. But
that's a different matter. I thank you, Landon, and wish you well. I think
you will be good for Ninette and I know she'll be good for you. Leave me,
like a good fellow. I'll come down and see Carlo in a few minutes. What will
you tell Valeria?'

'The truth,' said Landon flatly. 'What else? This is the end of the road.'

When he had told her the news, Valeria Rienzi echoed the tag of his own
thought, 'It is the end of the road, as you say, Peter. If we can't come
together after this there's no hope at all. We part and go separate ways.
There are limits to all endurance.'

There was a question that had to be asked and he gave it to her baldly:
'How do you see this coming together?'

'Only with love, Peter.' She was very emphatic about it. 'No more of this
cold salad of convention. I don't expect too much, I don't even count on an
equal bargain, but there must be some love on both sides, a touch of passion
sometimes. What else can we build on?'

'Nothing else. Do you love Carlo?'

'I can begin to, I think.'

'Does he love you?'

'I don't know, Peter. But he must tell me tonight.'

'Do you think he will know tonight?'

'If not tonight, then never!' She turned back to her mirror and began brushing her hair. 'I'll see you downstairs, Peter . . . and when you go don't kiss me goodbye.'

He walked back to his own room, flung himself on the bed and closed his eyes. He was bone-weary, but there was no rest for him yet. By his own reckoning, all debts were paid and he was free to go. But there was still the last exaction and he had no heart to face it just yet. He lay, spent and empty, trying to set his own tangled thoughts in order.

It was not only Carlo Rienzi who had come to the end of the road. Peter Landon, too, had reached a moment of conclusion and a point of new departure. For a long time now he had been involved, knowing and unknowing, in the diverse and delicate anatomies of love and justice: in the loyalties of the one and the legalities of the other. He had found that, while both were attainable, neither was perfect.

One arrived at each by conflict and contradiction. Love was affirmed by the contract of marriage, but the contract was not enough to preserve it. Justice was deemed to be preserved by the manifold provisions of the codex. But plead for both with a thousand voices, give a thousand advocates a thousand briefs, and you would not attain to love or justice without the slow search, the meticulous balance of right and duty, the probe for truth, the ruthless weeding out of error and egotism.

A lifetime's efforts and you were not yet at the end of it. Love was a flower of low nurture, justice was a fruit of vigilant cultivation. The flower would wither and the fruit would drop under the hands of a shiftless gardener. And–God save their miserable souls!–men were all too careless of the charge committed to them: the love by which they might live happy and the justice by which they might live safe, two steps and a spit from chaos.

On which disturbing thought he heaved himself off the bed, splashed water in his face, ran a comb through his hair and went downstairs.

He found Ascolini and Valeria talking with Ninette outside the closed door of the library. Ninette looked strained and anxious and her eyes were swollen with weeping. When Landon asked her about Carlo she shook her head. 'I can't tell you, *chéri*, because I don't know myself. For a while it was quite terrifying. I've never seen a man so distraught. He told me everything–the most secret things of his life. Then he just sat on the floor with his head on my knees and didn't say a word. He's calm now, but what's he feeling or thinking I don't know. He wants to see us all now.'

'Did he say why?'

'No, just that he wanted to see us all together.'

For a few moments they stood, irresolute, searching one another's faces. Finally, Valeria shrugged and pushed open the door of the library.

The first sight of Carlo Rienzi stopped them all in their tracks. He seemed to have aged ten years in a couple of hours. His face was sallow and shrunken, his eyes burning like those of a man in high fever. His hair hung damp and lank over his forehead. He stood propped against the marble mantel as if the slightest move would topple him.

'Hello, Carlo,' said Valeria softly.

'Hello, Valeria.'

After that, there was a pause. Carlo looked at them vaguely and then blinked and shook his head as if to chase away the trailing mists of a nightmare. Then he said, in a dead level voice: 'I'm glad you're here, Valeria. I'm glad our friends are here. I want to tell you something.'

Landon could see Valeria struggling against a swift impulse of pity, but she stood her ground and waited for Carlo to go on. Then he began to speak: 'I'm an empty man tonight. I am nothing and I have nothing. I've done a terrible thing today and I can't even feel guilty about it any more. I can't even feel what I'm saying to you now. All I know is that I want to feel it and I want you to believe it because I will never be able to say it again. I'm not sorry for myself, but I'm sorry for what I've done and for what I've been—to you, Valeria, to your father, to Peter and Ninette here. This will sound strange from a man who cannot feel anything, but this too must be said. I love you all. I hope you'll forgive me and let me go in peace.'

'My God!' thought Landon, 'it can't be true!'

But it was true, and so patent that Landon wondered why they did not all burst out laughing. Advocate Rienzi was fighting his own cause with the greatest piece of mountebankery he would ever pull in any court. He was pleading for the thing he denied—the right to go on pitying himself, the right to have life always on his own terms and yet always have a breast to cry on. As a final stroke of genius, he was making himself the whipping-boy, knowing that, in the end, the stripes would fall on other backs than his own. He would never make a shrewder plea, never a less worthy one.

Landon thought he was winning it, too, when he saw Valeria move a pace towards him with hands outstretched. Then, abruptly, she checked herself and asked him, in a clear, cool voice: 'Where will you go, Carlo?'

He turned vaguely towards her and said, almost apologetically: 'You mustn't ask me to talk about that. I've caused you enough grief already. But there'll be no more trouble, I promise.' He laughed, unsteadily. 'I told Peter today I didn't know the words. Funny! It turns out I knew them all the time. It's just that I'm saying them too late. That's always been my trouble. Too little a man growing up too late. I'm sorry.'

Landon almost expected to hear him say, 'The defence rests.' But he was too shrewd a craftsman for that—and besides he was exhausted, like every actor after a great performance. He heaved himself away from the mantel and began to walk with slow, dragging steps, towards the door. Then, clear as a trumpet, old Ascolini's rich voice challenged him: 'Nonsense, boy! Every damned word of it! So you've made a fool of yourself. That's every man's right. But you have no right in the world to inflict a maudlin confession on the rest of us! Pull yourself together, man! Cry in a tavern if you must, or in a bawdy-house, but in this place you stand up like a man and keep your mouth shut!'

For a moment, Rienzi stood blank-faced and rocking under the impact. Then, in a curious moment of transformation, his face seemed to harden and what might have been a smile twitched at his bloodless lips. He raised one hand in a mocking salute: 'You're a better advocate than I am, Doctor. You always will be!'

Then his knees buckled under him. Landon caught him as he lurched forward, and carried him over his shoulder to the guest-room. He tossed him on the bed and left him to Valeria. She said nothing, but gave him a small, bitter smile and began unlacing Rienzi's shoes.

Landon was grateful for her discretion. He had never liked curtain speeches and he had no patience with drunken actors. But Carlo Rienzi was a great actor–which in an advocate was a talent, and, for some women, a passable substitute for manhood. At least Valeria was accepting it without illusions. Or perhaps she was creating a new one, since love was a blind goddess, sister to her who sat with naked sword and scales in balance, peeping from under her handkerchief at the comedies enacted in her name.

'Time to go, Peter,' said Ninette Lachaise. 'Time to spend ourselves on ourselves. We've been too long in this town.'

They were standing together on the terrace of the villa, watching the rise of the moon and hearing the first solitary song of the nightingales. The valley stretched itself placid in the moon-glow and, above the crenellations of the mountains, they saw the pricking of the first faint stars. The land had surrendered itself to the night, and for Landon, too, it was the time of surrender. He drew Ninette to him and said, more gently than he had ever spoken before: 'I love you, girl. I never thought I could love anyone so much. But are you sure you want to risk me?'

'It's always a risk,' said Ascolini from behind them, 'but only the wise ones know it. Go home, both of you. Get yourselves churched if you must, but do it quickly. Time's the most precious thing you have, and who should know it better than I?'

He handed them the keys of the car and then fished out of his pocket two old and beautiful volumes, one of which he handed to Ninette with the sardonic dedication: 'For you, my dear. All the things your man feels for you but won't be able to say because he's a dull fellow who knows only the jargon of the clinic. They're Petrarch's Sonnets to his Laura, and the book was made by Elzevir. It's a wedding present. My heart goes with it–and all my love.'

Ninette threw her arms round the old man and kissed him. He held her for a long moment and then pushed her gently away.

'Take her, Landon, before I change my mind and rush her to the altar. Here's something for you, my friend!' He handed Landon the companion volume, and said, whimsically: 'It's an Aretino–"The Luxurious Sonnets"! You're old enough to enjoy them and young enough not to need them!' He took their arms and urged them swiftly off the terrace towards the car. 'No more words! No long farewells. They remind me of death and I have enough reminders already!'

As they drove down the winding path to the gates, they could see him solitary and gallant on the terrace, the moonlight silver on his lion's mane, listening to the lament of the nightingales.

The Salamander

THE SALAMANDER

For
Silvio Stefano

wise counsellor, honest advocate
friend of my heart

If we could learn to look instead of gawking
We'd see the horror in the heart of farce.
If only we would act instead of talking,
We would not always end up on our arse.
This was the thing that had us nearly mastered!
Don't yet rejoice in his defeat, you men.
For though the world stood up and stopped the bastard,
The bitch that bore him is on heat again.

From *Arturo Ui* by Bertolt Brecht,
translated by George Tabori

PART I

Scrupulous people are not suited to great affairs.

Turgot

Between midnight and dawn, while his fellow Romans were celebrating the end of Carnival, Massimo, Count Pantaleone, General of the Military Staff, died in his bed. A bachelor in his early sixties, a soldier of spartan habit, he died alone.

His servant, a retired sergeant of cavalry, brought the General's coffee at the accustomed hour of seven in the morning and found him lying on his back, fully clothed, gape-mouthed and staring at the coffered ceiling. The servant set down the coffee carefully, crossed himself, closed the dead eyes with two fifty-lire pieces, then telephoned the General's aide, Captain Girolamo Carpi.

Carpi telephoned the Director. The Director telephoned me. You will find my name on the Salamander dossier: Dante Alighieri Matucci, Colonel of Carabinieri, seconded for special duty to the Service of Defence Information.

The Service is usually called by its Italian initials, SID (Servizio Informazione Difesa). Like every other intelligence service, it spends a huge amount of taxpayers' money perpetuating itself, and somewhat less in scavenging information which hopefully will protect the Republic against invaders, traitors, spies, saboteurs and political terrorists. You will gather I am sceptical about its value. I have a right to be. I work in it; but every man who works in it becomes disillusioned in some fashion. The Service encourages the loss of innocence; it makes for pliable instruments of policy. However, that's a digression. . .

Massimo, Count Pantaleone, General of the Military Staff, was dead. I was appointed to stage a clean exit for the corpse. I needed help. The Army supplied it in the shape of a senior medical officer, rank of Colonel, and a military advocate, rank of Major. We drove together to the General's apartment. Captain Carpi received us. The General's servant was weeping over a glass of *grappa* in the kitchen. So far, so good. No confusion. No neighbours on the landing. No relatives yet informed. I had no great respect for Carpi, but I had to commend his discretion.

The medical officer made a cursory examination and decided that the General had died from an overdose of barbiturates, self-administered. He wrote a certificate, countersigned by the military advocate, which stated that the cause of death was cardiac arrest. It was not a false document; simply a convenient one. The General's heart had stopped. A pity it hadn't stopped years ago. A scandal would benefit no one. It might harm a great many innocent people.

At eight-thirty, a military ambulance arrived and removed the body. I remained in the apartment with Carpi and the servant. The servant made us coffee and while we drank it, I questioned him. His answers established a series of simple facts.

The General had dined out. He had returned twenty minutes before midnight and retired immediately to his bedroom. The servant had secured doors and windows, set the burglar alarm and gone to bed. He had risen at six-thirty and prepared the morning coffee. ... Visitors? None. ... Intruders? None. The alarms had not been triggered. Telephone calls, in or out? No way to know. The General would use the private line in his bedroom. Certainly the domestic telephone had not sounded. ... The General's demeanour? Normal. He was a taciturn man. Hard to know what he was thinking at any time. That was all. ... I gave him a pat on the shoulder and dismissed him to the kitchen.

Carpi closed the door behind him, poured two glasses of the General's whisky, presented one to me and asked a question:

'What do we tell his friends—and the Press?'

It was the sort of question he would ask: trivial and irrelevant.

'You saw the death certificate, signed and notarized: natural causes, cardiac arrest.'

'And the autopsy report?'

'My dear Captain, for an ambitious man you are very naïve. There will be no autopsy. The General's body has been taken to a mortuary where it will be prepared for a brief lying-in-state. We want him seen. We want him honoured. We want him mourned as a noble servant of the Republic—which in a certain sense he was.'

'And then?'

'Then we want him forgotten. You can help us there.'

'How?'

'Your patron is dead. You did well for us. You deserve a better appointment. I'd suggest something far away from Rome—the Alto Adige, perhaps Taranto, or even Sardinia. You will find promotion a lot quicker in places like that.'

'I'd like to think about it.'

'No time, Captain! You pick up your transfer papers this morning. You deliver them, completed and signed, by five o'clock this afternoon. I guarantee you will have a new posting immediately after the funeral. ... And, Captain?'

'Yes?'

'You will remember that you are in a very delicate position. You accepted to spy on a superior officer. We of SID are grateful; but your officer colleagues would despise you. The slightest indiscretion would therefore damage your career, and might well expose you to great personal danger. I trust you understand me?'

'I understand.'

'Good. You may go now. ... Oh, a small matter.'

'Yes?'

'You have a key to the apartment. Leave it here please.'

'What happens next?'

'Oh, the usual routine. I examine papers and documents. I file a report. Please try to be sad at the funeral. ... *Ciao!*'

Carpi went out, wrapping the rags of his dignity around him. He was one of those weak, handsome fellows, who always need, and generally attract, a patron: and who will always betray him to a more potent one. I had used him to report on Pantaleone's movements, contacts and political activities. Now he was a redundant nuisance. I poured myself another glass of whisky and tried to set my thoughts in order.

The Pantaleone affair had all the makings of a political time-bomb. The irony was that you could shout the name up and down the Corso and not one in a thousand of the citizens of the Republic would recognize it. Of those who did recognize it, not one in ten would understand its potency or the magnitude of the conspiracy which had been built around it. The Director understood; so did I. I had dossiers on all the principal participants. For a long time I had chafed at my impotence to do anything about them. They were not criminals—at least not yet. They were all high men—ministers, deputies, industrialists, service officers, bureaucrats—who looked to a day when the confusions of Italy—unstable government, industrial unrest, a faltering economy, an inept bureaucracy and a very frustrated people—would bring the country to the brink of revolution.

On that day, which was closer than many people imagined, the conspirators hoped to seize power and present themselves to a bewildered populace as the saviours of the Republic and the conservators of good order and human rights. Their hope was tolerably well-founded. If a Junta of Greek Colonels had done it, there was no good reason why a much larger and more powerful group of Italians could not do it better . . . especially if they had the support of the Army and the active co-operation of the Forces of Public Security.

Their figure-head had been named for a long time: that noble soldier, one-time junior aide to Marshal Badoglio, passionate patriot, friend of the common man, General Massimo Pantaleone. Now the General had removed himself from the scene. Why had he done it? Who, or what, had nudged him towards the final act; and why again? Was there a new man waiting in the wings? Who was he? When and how would he reveal himself? And was the day already at hand? I was commissioned to answer all these questions; and the margin for error was very slim indeed.

Even a hint that an investigation was in progress would split the country down the middle. If the Press got half an idea that a dubious document had been notarized and uttered by the Army, there would be headlines in every newspaper in the world.

Conspiracy is endemic to Italy, always has been, since Romulus and Remus began horse-trading from Tiber Island; but if the dimension of this plot were made known and the very real possibility that it might succeed . . . Dio! There would be barricades in the streets and blood on the tram-tracks within a day: one could not rule out even mutiny in the armed services, whose political loyalties were deeply divided between Left and Right. I had made no idle threat to Captain Carpi. If he tried to sell himself or his information to new masters, an accident would be speedily arranged for him. Meantime, I had my own work to do.

I drank the last of the whisky and began to comb the apartment for papers. I opened drawers and cupboards and tested each one for secret hiding-places. I went through the pockets of each garment in the wardrobe. I shook out every book in the library and removed the blotting paper from the desk-pad. I made no attempt to examine what I found; but simply piled it into a heap. There would be hours of work to sift and analyse it all—and very little value at the end. The General was too old a fox to have left dangerous documents lying about his house.

Still, I could not afford to take risks; so I moved pictures and mats in search of a concealed safe. Then I made a final circuit, lifting ornaments, upending cups and vases, prising up the felt beds of the jewel-cases which held the General's orders and decorations. Even so, I nearly missed the card.

It was lying on its edge against the skirting board, behind the bedside table; a small rectangle of stiff paste-board with a design on one side and an inscription on the other. Both the design and the inscription had been done by hand in black Indian ink. The design had been executed at a single stroke, in a series of intricate whorls and flourishes. It showed a salamander with a coronet on its head, couched in a bed of flames. The inscription was four words of perfect copperplate: *'Un bel domani, fratello'*.

'One fine tomorrow, brother' . . . It was a very Italian phrase, which could preface a variety of sentiments: a vain hope, a promise of reward, a threat of vengeance, a rallying cry. The word 'brother' was ambiguous, too, and the salamander made no sense at all, unless it were the symbol of a club or a fraternity. Yet there was no association with any sign or code-name in my dossiers. I decided to refer it to the specialists. I went back to the study, picked up a clean envelope, sealed the card inside it and put it in the pocket of my jacket.

Then I decided it was time for a private chat with the sergeant of cavalry. I found him in the kitchen, a dejected old man ruminating over an uncertain future. I consoled him with the thought that the General had probably remembered him in his will, and that, at least, he was entitled to severance pay from the deceased's estate. He brightened then and offered me wine and cheese. As we drank together, he became garrulous; and I was happy to let him ramble.

'. . . He didn't have to be a soldier, you know. The Pantaleone always had money running out of their ears. Not that they were free with it. Lord, no! They looked at both sides of a coin and wept before they spent it. Probably that's why they stayed rich. Lands in the Romagna, apartment buildings in Lazio, the old estate in Frascati, the villa on Ponza—of course, she's got that now.'

'Who has?'

'You know—the Polish woman. The one he had dinner with last night. What's her name? . . . Anders—that's it—Anders. She's been his girl-friend for years. Although, I must say, he was pretty close about it. He never brought her here. Funny that. . . . He didn't want people to think he was enjoying himself. Like we used to say in the Army, he was born with a ram-rod up his backside. I knew about her, of course. I used to take her calls. . . . Sometimes I went to her place to deliver things for the General. Good-looking woman, not over the hill yet, either. Which reminds me. . . . Someone ought to tell her what's happened.'

'I'll do that. Where does she live?'

The question was a blind. I knew the answer and a great deal more about Lili Anders.

'Parioli. The address is in the General's pocket book.'

'I'll find it.'

'Hey! Now that's a thing! You're not taking any of the General's stuff away are you? I'm responsible. I don't want any trouble.'

'I'm taking all his papers, and I'll borrow a valise to carry them.'

'But why?'

'A matter of security. We can't leave confidential documents lying around. So, we'll go through the lot, take out the ones that belong to the Army and return the private ones to his lawyer. You won't have any trouble, because I'll give you an official receipt before I leave. Clear?'

'If you say so.... Wait a moment! Who are you? I don't even know your name.'

'Matucci. Carabinieri.'

'Carabinieri! ... There's nothing wrong is there?'

'Nothing at all. ... Normal procedure with an important man like the General.'

'Who's going to make all the arrangements, tell his friends, that sort of thing?'

'The Army.'

'So, what do I do? Just sit around here?'

'There's one thing you could do. People will telephone. Take their names and numbers and we'll arrange for someone to call them back.'

'I'll still be paid?'

'Don't worry. You have to be paid. It's the law. ... I meant to ask you something else. Where did the General dine last night?'

'At the Chess Club.'

'You're sure?'

'Of course, I'm sure. I had to know always where he was. Sometimes there were calls from Headquarters or from the Ministry.... Another drop?'

'No, thanks, I'll be on my way.'

'And you're sure about the money?'

'I'm sure. And you'll remember to record the telephone calls?'

'Trust me, friend. The General did. I never let him down. You know, he was as cold as a fish; but I'll miss the old bastard. I really will.'

The fellow was becoming maudlin now and I was ready to be quit of him. I scribbled a receipt, picked up the bag of documents and walked out into the thin spring sunshine. It was ten minutes after one. The shop-keepers were closing their shutters and the alleys were busy with Romans homing for lunch and siesta.

I have to tell you frankly I don't like the Romans. I'm a Tuscan born and these people are first cousins to the Hottentot. Their city is a midden; their countryside a vast rubbish tip. They are the worst cooks and the most dyspeptic feeders in Italy. They are rude, crass, cynical and devoid of the most elementary graces. Their faces are closed against compassion and their spirits are pinched and rancorous. They have seen everything and learned nothing, except the basest arts of survival. They have known imperial grandeur, papal pomp, war, famine, plague and spoliation; yet they will bow the knee to any tyrant who offers them an extra loaf of bread and a free ticket to the circus.

Yesterday, it was Benito Mussolini, drunk with rhetoric, haranguing them from the balcony in the Piazza Venezia. Tomorrow it might be another. And where was he now, at this very moment on Ash Wednesday, in this year of doubtful grace? ... One thing was sure, he wouldn't be standing like Dante Alighieri Matucci, flat-footed in the middle of the Campo Marzio.

I shook myself out of the reverie, walked half a block to my car, tossed the documents on to the seat and drove back to the office. I might have saved myself the trouble. My two senior clerks were out at lunch; number three was flirting with the typist and the data bank was out of action because the power supply had been interrupted by a two-hour strike. There was a message from the Ministry of the Interior requesting 'immediate contact on a most urgent matter'. When I called, I was told that my contact was entertaining some foreign visitors and might possibly be back at four o'clock. Body of Bacchus! What an oafish lot! Judgment Day might come and go, the Maoists might even now be storming the Angelic Gate at Vatican City, but the Romans must finish siesta before they did anything about it.

I dumped the bag of documents on the desk and shouted for number three clerk to sort and collate them. Then, because the strike had put the elevator out of action, I climbed three flights of stairs to the forensic laboratory, where there had to be someone alive, even at lunch time. As usual, it was old Stefanelli who, according to local legend, slept every night in a bottle of formaldehyde and emerged fresh as a marmoset at sunrise every morning. He was a tiny wizened fellow, with wispy locks and yellow teeth and skin like old leather. He must have been ten years past retirement age, but still managed by a combination of patronage and sheer talent to hang on to his job.

What other technicians burst their brains to learn, Stefanelli knew. Sprinkle a peck of dust in his palm and he would name you the province and the region and even make a reasonable guess at the village from which it came. Hand him a swatch of fabric and he would fondle it for a moment, then tell you how much cotton was in it and how much polyester, and give you a list of the factories that might have made it. Give him a drop of blood, two nail clippings and a tress of hair and he would build you the girl who owned them. He was a genius in his own right, albeit a tetchy and troublesome one, who would spit in your eye if you crossed him, or slave twenty-four hours at a stretch for a man who trusted him. He read voluminously and would bet money on his technical knowledge. Only a very new or a very vain junior would bet against him. When I came in, puffing and sour-faced, he greeted me, exuberantly.

'Eh, Colonel! What have you got for Steffi today? I've got something for you. ... Death by suffocation ... green alkaloids in the blood ... no punctures, no abrasions, no apparent means of entry into the blood system. Five thousand lire if you can tell me what it is.'

'Put it that way, Steffi, and I know I'll lose my money. What is it?'

'It's a shell-fish. Comes from the South Pacific. They call it the Cloth of Gold. On contact, the fish injects microscopic needles full of alkalide which paralyse the central nervous system. Case in point—a marine biologist working with the Americans in the South Pacific. ... If you're interested, I'll send you a note on it.'

'Thanks, Steffi, but not today. I have troubles on my own doorstep.' I fished out the salamander card and handed it to him. 'I want a full reading on that: paper, penmanship, the meaning of the symbol and any prints you can lift. I want it fast.'

Stefanelli studied the card intently for a few moments, and then delivered himself of a peroration.

'The card itself is made from Japanese stock—fine quality bonded rice. I can tell you who imports it within a day. The penmanship–fantastic! So beautiful it makes you want to cry! I haven't seen anything like it since Aldo the Calligrapher died in 1935. You remember him, don't you? Of course, you wouldn't. You're too young. Used to have a studio over near the Cancelleria. Made a fortune forging stock certificates and engrossing patents of nobility for fellows who wanted to marry wealthy Americans. . . . Well, Aldo's dead, so he can't help you. We have to go to the files to find who's in practice now. . . . The design? Well . . . it's obviously a salamander, the beast that lives in the fire. What it means here, I don't know. It could be a trade-mark. It could be a *tessera*–a member's card for a club. It could be adapted from a coat-of-arms. I'll put it up to Solimbene. . . . You don't know him. Old friend of mine. Works in the Consulta Araldica. Knows every coat-of-arms in Europe. He can read them like another man would read a newspaper.

'Good idea. In fact, why don't you do some copies now, before the others get back from lunch. I'll need one for my own inquiries anyway.'

'Where did you get this, Colonel?'

'General Pantaleone died last night. I found it in his bedroom.'

'Pantaleone? The old *fascista*! What happened to him?'

'Natural causes, Steffi . . . and we've got a notarized certificate to prove it.'

'Very convenient!'

'Very necessary.'

'Suicide or murder?'

'Suicide.'

'Eh! That smells bad.'

'So, Steffi, for the present, this business is between you and me, and the Director. Keep the card in your own hands. No files, no discussion in the laboratory. Dead silence until I tell you.'

Stefanelli grinned and laid a bony forefinger on his nose–the gesture of knowing and agreeing a conspiracy.

'I don't like Fascists any more than you do, Colonel–and we've got our share of them in this Department. Sometimes I wonder if we've got any democrats left–or whether we ever had any in Italy–except you and me. If we don't get a stable government soon, we'll get a *colpo di stato,* with a Fascist in the saddle. The week after that there'll be civil war–or something very like it–Left against Right, North against South. I'm an old man. I can smell it in the wind. . . . And I'm scared, Colonel. I have sons and daughters and grandchildren. I don't want them to suffer as we did . . .'

'Nor I, Steffi. So we have to know who steps into the General's shoes. Get busy on the card. Call me day or night as soon as you have anything.'

'Good luck, Colonel.'

'I'll need it. . . . *Ciao*, Steffi.'

Now I was at a loose end. I could make no sense of the Pantaleone documents until they were listed and collated with the General's dossier. The Director was the only man to whom I could talk freely and he was out of the office. I could, of course, call on Francesca, the little model who was always available after midday. But that would leave me drugged and dozy for the rest of the afternoon. I settled for a cup of coffee in a bar and then drove out to Parioli to see Lili Anders.

Her apartment was on the third floor of a new condominium, all aluminium and glass, with a porter in livery and an elevator panelled in walnut. The place had cost, according to the lady's dossier, sixty million lire; the upkeep according to the contract was a hundred and twenty thousand a month. The fiscal records of the Comune di Roma showed that Lili Anders was taxed on a visible standard of living of a million lire a month. Since she paid the tax without demur, it was obvious she must be living at twice the scale assessed. I was keeping an apartment, a servant, a three-year-old Fiat and an occasional playmate on six hundred thousand a month less taxes and I thought Lili Anders was a very fortunate woman. By the time I came to ring the bell, therefore, I was feeling bad-tempered and resentful. An elderly house-keeper, dressed in black bombazine and starched white linen, confronted me like a true Roman, laconic and hostile:

'Yes?'

'Matucci. Carabinieri. I wish to see the Signora Anders.'

'You have an appointment?'

'No.'

'Then you'll have to come back later. The Signora is asleep.'

'I'm afraid I must ask you to wake her. My business is urgent.'

'Do you have any identification?'

'I offered my card; she took and read it slowly, line by line, then swept me into the hallway like a pile of dust, and left me.

I waited, grim and dyspeptic, but touched with a sour admiration for this ancient matron, whose ancestors had tossed rooftiles on popes and cardinals and puppet princelings. Then Lili Anders made her entrance. For a woman in her middle thirties, she was singularly well-preserved; a little plump for my taste, but still most definitely on the right side of the hill. For a woman who had just been sleeping, she was beautifully turned out; every blonde hair in place, no slur in the make-up, no wrinkle in skirt, blouse or stockings. Her greeting was polite but cool.

'You wished to see me?'

'Privately, if that is possible.'

She passed me into the salone and closed the door. She prayed me to be seated and then stood herself by the mantel under an equestrian portrait of Pantaleone.

'You are, I believe, from the Carabinieri.'

'I am Colonel Matucci.'

'And the reason for this visit?'

'A painful matter, I'm afraid.'

'Oh?'

'I regret to inform you that General Pantaleone died early this morning.'

She did not weep. She did not cry out. She stared at me, wide-eyed and trembling, holding on to the mantel for support. I moved towards her to steady her; but she waved me away. I crossed to the buffet, poured brandy into a goblet and handed it to her. She drank it at a gulp, then gagged on the raw spirit. I gave her the clean handkerchief from my breast pocket and she dabbed at her lips and the front of her blouse. I talked to her, quietly:

'It's always a shock, even in our business. If you want to cry, go ahead.'

'I will not cry. He was kind to me and gentle, but I have no tears for him.'

'There is something else you should know.'

'Yes?'

'He died by his own hand.'

She gave no sign of surprise. She simply shrugged and spread her hands in a gesture of defeat.

'With him it was always possible.'

'Why do you say that?'

'There were too many dark places in his life, Colonel; too many secrets; too many people lying in wait for him.'

'Did he tell you that?'

'No, I knew.'

'Then, perhaps, you know this. Why did he choose last night to kill himself? Why not a week ago, or next month?'

'I don't know. He had been moody for a long time, a month or more. I asked him more than once what was troubling him. He always put me off.'

'And last night?'

'One thing only. During dinner a waiter brought him a message. Don't ask me what it was. You know the Chess Club–it's like being in church, all whispers and incense. He left me at the table and went outside. He was away about five minutes. When he came back, he told me he had had a telephone call from a colleague. Nothing more was said. Later, when he brought me home, I invited him in. Sometimes he stayed the night, sometimes he didn't. This time he said he had work to finish at home. It was normal. I didn't argue. I was tired myself, anyway.'

I took out the photo-copy of the salamander card and handed it to her.

'Have you seen this before? Or anything like it?'

She studied it intently for a few moments and then shook her head.

'Never.'

'Do you recognize the animal?'

'Some kind of lizard . . . a dragon, perhaps.'

'The crown?'

'Nothing.'

'The words?'

'What they say . . . "One fine tomorrow, brother" . . . that's all.'

'Have you ever heard them before anywhere?'

'Not that I can remember. I'm sorry.'

'Please, dear lady! You must, in no sense, reproach yourself. You have had a grievous shock. You have lost a dear friend. And now. . . . How to say it! . . . I have to distress you still further. It is my duty to warn you that from this moment you stand in grave personal danger.'

'I don't understand.'

'Then permit me to explain. You have been for a long time the mistress of an important man, whom certain elements have considered an explosive man. A mistress is presumed to be a confidante, a repository of secrets. Even if the General told you nothing, others will believe he told you everything. Inevitably, therefore, you will come under surveillance, under pressure, possibly even under threat.'

'From whom?'

'From extremists of the Right and of the Left, persons who are trained to use violence as a political weapon; from foreign agents, operating within the confines of the Republic; even–though I blush to confess it–from officials of our own Public Security. As a foreigner, residing here on a sojourn permit, you are especially vulnerable.'

'But I have nothing to tell! I lived a woman's life with a man who needed comfort and affection. His other life, whatever it was, I did not share. When his door closed on us, the world was shut out. He wanted it so. You must believe that.'

She was shaken now. Her face seemed to crumple into the contours of middle-age. Her hands fumbled restlessly at the balled handkerchief. I leaned back in the chair and admonished her.

'I wish I could believe you. But, I know you Lili Anders. I know you chapter and verse, from your first birthday in Warsaw, to your latest despatch to one Colomba, who is a printer and book-binder in Milan. You identified yourself, as usual, by the code-word 'Falcone'. All the members of your network are called by bird-names, are they not? You are paid by Canarino from account number 68-Pilau at the Cantonal bank in Zurich. . . . You see, Lili, we Italians are not really as stupid or inefficient as we look. We are very good conspirators, because we love the game and we make the rules to suit ourselves. . . . Another brandy? I'll have one myself, if you don't mind. Relax now, I'm not going to eat you. I admire a good professional. But you are a problem, a real problem. . . . *Salute!* To your continued good health!'

She drank, clasping the glass in both hands as if it were a pillar that would support her.

'What happens to me now?'

'Eh! That's a very open question, Lili. As I see it at this moment there are two alternatives. I take you into custody on charges of conspiracy and espionage. That means a long interrogation, a stiff sentence and no hope even of provisory liberty. Or, I could leave you free, on certain conditions, to continue your comfortable life in Rome. Which would you prefer?'

'I'm tired of the game, Colonel. I'd like to be out of it. I'm getting too old.'

'That's the problem, Lili. You can't get out. You can only change sides.'

'Which means?'

'Full information on the network and all your activities, and a contract with us as a double-agent.'

'Can you protect me?'

'As long as you're useful, yes.'

'I was a good mistress, Colonel. I kept my man happy and gave value for money.'

'Let's try some more questions then. Who arranged your first meeting with the General?'

'The Marchesa Friuli.'

'What is her code-name?'

'Pappagallo.'

'It suits the old girl. She even looks like a parrot. What was your directive?'

'To give early warnings of any attempt at a *coup d'état* by neo-fascist groups, and of actions designed to provoke it.'

'Such as?'

'Acts of violence planned against police or Carabinieri during labour demonstrations, bomb attacks that could be attributed to Maoist or Marxist groups, the spread of disaffection among conscripts and new levies in the armed services, any contracts, secret or open, between the Greek regime and officials of the Republic of Italy, shifts of influence or changes of political groups in the Italian High Command.'

'Had there been any such changes recently?'

'No . . . at least not to my knowledge.'

'Then why was the General depressed?'

'I don't know. I was trying to find out.'

'Money problems?'

'I wouldn't think so. . . . He was never a lavish man–even to me.'

'Political pressures–blackmail?'

'I had the feeling that it was a personal and not a political matter.'

'What gave you that impression?'

'Things he said when he was relaxed here with me.'

'For example?'

'Oh, odd remarks. He had a habit of saying something–how would you call it?–something cryptic; then passing immediately to another subject. If I pressed him to explain, he would close up like a shell-fish. I learned, quickly to hold my tongue. . . . One night, for example, he said: "There is no simple future for me, Lili, because my past is too complicated." Another time he quoted from the Bible: "A man's enemies are those of his own household." . . . Things like that.'

'Anything else?'

'I'm trying to remember. . . . Oh, yes, about three weeks ago we met in Venice. He took me to the opera at the Phoenix Theatre. He talked about the history of the theatre and he explained the name to me. He said that the Phoenix was a fabulous bird that rose again, alive, from its own ashes; then he said that there was another animal more fabulous and more dangerous–the salamander that lived in fire and could survive the hottest flames. . . . Wait! That's your card . . . the Salamander!'

'So it is, Lili. You see how far we come when we talk like friends? What else did he say about the salamander?'

'Nothing. Nothing at all. Some friends joined us. The subject was dropped and forgotten.'

'Let's leave it then. There will be other times and other questions. From now on you will be under constant surveillance. There is my card with day and night numbers. You'll be notified of the date of the funeral. I'd like you to be there.'

'Please, no!'

'Please, yes! I want tears, Lili. I want deep grief and black mourning. You will not move back into society until I tell you. Naturally, you will have telephone calls from your masters and from friends of the General. Your house-keeper will want to know the reason for my visit. You will tell them all the same story. The General died of a heart attack. It would not hurt to confess that he had an ailment which sometimes interfered with his love-making. . . . One other thing. No new boy-friends until you are out of mourning. That would make an ugly figure. If you find a live one after that, I'd like to check him out before you adopt him.'

She managed a weak and watery smile.

'Him or me, Colonel?'

'I admire you, Lili, but I can't afford you. If you could make an old fossil like Pantaleone sit up and beg, God only knows what you'd do to a hungry fellow like me. Still, it's a thought to keep. One fine tomorrow, we just might play a little chamber music. Be good now. And there's a prize for every tear of the requiem. . . . Where's your telephone?'

Half an hour later I was seated in a glass booth on the Veneto, with a sandwich and a *cappuccino*, scanning the afternoon editions of the Roman and Milanese papers. The General's death was reported only in the stop press. The terms of each report were identical, a direct quotation of the

Army announcement. There were no obituaries, no editorial comments. There might be some in the final editions but the bloodhounds would not be in full cry until morning. By that time, the General would be safely embalmed and lying in state in the family chapel at Frascati, with the cadets of his old regiment standing the death watch.

The obsequies of Massimo Count Pantaleone, General of the Military Staff, made a splendid piece of theatre. The requiem was sung by the sub-urbicarian Bishop of Frascati, Cardinal Amleto Paolo Dadone, assisted by the choir of the monastery of Sant' Antonio della Valle. The panegyric was delivered in classic periods and ringing tones by the Secretary-General of the Society of Jesus, a former class-mate of the deceased. The Mass was attended by the President of the Republic, Ministers of the Council, Members of both Chambers, Prelates of the Roman Curia, Senior Officers of all Services, representatives of NATO and the Diplomatic Corps, relatives and friends of the deceased, family retainers, press-men, photographers and a motley of Romans, countrymen and casual tourists. Six field-officers carried the bier to the vault, where the regimental chaplain consigned it to rest until resurrection day, while a detachment of junior officers fired the last volley, and the Penitentiaries of Sant' Ambrogio recited the Sorrowful Mysteries of the Rosary. The door of the vault was closed and locked by the President himself, a gesture of respect, gratitude and national solidarity not lost upon the gentlemen of the Press. Lili Anders was there, heavily veiled and leaning on the arm of Captain Girolamo Carpi, who was visibly moved by the passing of his beloved patron.

I was among the mourners, too; but I was less concerned with the ceremonies than with the efforts of my camera crew to produce a clear photograph of every person at the funeral, from the Cardinal celebrant to the florist who laid the tributes. I hate funerals. They make me feel old, unwanted and disposed to sexual exercise which is a kind of defiance of my own imminent mortality. I was glad when the rites were over, so that I could drive down to see Francesca, while my colleagues were still guzzling spumante and sweet pastry at the Villa Pantaleone.

At three-thirty in the afternoon, I went back to the forensic laboratory to talk to Stefanelli. The old fellow was jumping like a grass-hopper.

'. . . I told you, Colonel! Bet with old Steffi and you have to win! I showed the card to Solimbene and he recognized it at first glance. The crowned salamander is the emblem of Francis the First. It recurs, with certain modifications, in arms derived from the House of Orleans, the Duchy of Angoulême and the Farmer family in England. I've retained Solimbene to get us a list of existing Italian families who use the symbol. You'll have to authorize the payment. The pen-work? We say it's based on Aldo the Calligrapher but probably executed by Carlo Metaponte who used to be a forger, made papers for the partisans during the war and has been going straight ever since. The card itself . . . I was wrong about that. It's not Japanese at all. It's a very passable Italian imitation made in Modena by the Casaroli Brothers. They're supplying us with a list of their principal customers in Europe. The inscription makes no sense yet; but we're coming to it. How's that, eh! Not bad for forty-eight hours. Tell me you're happy, Colonel, otherwise I'll drown myself in the toilet.'

'I'm happy, Steffi. But we need a lot more. Fingerprints for instance.'

'I'm sorry, Colonel. The only ones we've been able to lift belong to the

late lamented General. You didn't expect anything else, surely?'
'I want miracles, Steffi. I want them yesterday.'
'Spare us a little pity, Colonel. Everything takes time. . . . How was the funeral?'
'Beautiful, Steffi. I cried all through it! And the eloquence! . . . "That noble spirit snatched untimely from among us, that dedicated servant of the Republic, that Christian patriot, that hero of many battles . . ." *Merda!*'
'*Requiescat in aeternum.*' Stefanelli crossed hands on his bony chest and rolled his eyes heavenwards. 'If he's in heaven, I hope never to go there. Amen! . . . Have you read today's papers?'
'Now, when have I had time to read, Steffi?'
'I've got them in my office. Come on! They're worth a look.'
The obituaries were, like the obsequies, an exercise in grandiloquence. The Right wing was fulsome; the centre was respectful and only mildly censorious of the General's Fascist period; the Left achieved a kind of poetry of abuse, culminating in a pasquinade, which for form's sake was attributed to some anonymous Roman:

'*Estirpato oggi,*	'*Uprooted today,*
L'ultimo della stirpe,	*The last of his line,*
Pantaleone,	*Pantaleone,*
Mascalzone.'	*The rogue.*'

I was not unhappy with the things I read. They were good reviews for a bad score and a book full of contradictions. Not one of them called in question the official version of the General's demise; which was not to say they believed it but only that it suited all parties to accept it. The pasquinade worried me a little. Take it at face value and it was a harmless squib. The General was the last of the Pantaleone line, and an old rogue to boot. Read it another way and it might mean that the Left had taken a hand in rooting him out and that happily no successor was in sight. If one were very subtle—and I was paid to read meaning even into blank pages—one might see it as the opening gambit of a campaign to vilify the General and bring all the skeletons out of his family vault. A pity if it happened, but there was nothing I could do about it. I was still drowsy and disinclined to exert myself, so I began leafing through the journals, while Stefanelli added a spicy commentary.
'. . . Now, here's a pretty thing: "The Principessa Faubiani presents her summer collection!" You know about her, don't you? Came from Argentina originally, married young Prince Faubiani, set him up with a boy-friend, and then petitioned for separation on the grounds of his impotence. That way she kept her freedom, the title and a right to maintenance. Since then, she's had a new protector every couple of years—old ones now, and all rich. They finance the collections and improve her standard of living as well. That last one was the banker, Castellani. . . . Wonder who it is this year? Funny thing, she still stays friends with them all. See, there's Castellani, next to the model in the bikini. Ah, there's the new one, in the front row, behind Faubiani and the Editor of Vogue. That's the place of honour. Ritual, you know. When the High Priestess gets tired of you, she hands you down to the models. Still, if you're sixty or over, who cares? The girls come cheaper than a whole summer collection, eh? . . . I must find out who the new one is.'

'And what's your interest in fashion, Steffi?'

'My wife has a boutique on the Via Sistina ... high mode for rich tourists.'

'You crafty old devil!'

'I'm a lucky man, Colonel. I married for love and got money for my old age as well. Also the staff is decorative and the gossip's always interesting. .... Which reminds me. Pantaleone is supposed to have a brother floating around somewhere.'

'Not in my dossier, Steffi. The old count, Massimo, had two daughters in the first three years of his marriage and a son about ten years later. One daughter married a Contini and died in childbirth. The other married a Spanish diplomat and lives in Bolivia. She has three adult children who all have Spanish nationality. The son, our General, was the only male issue. He inherited the title and the bulk of the real estate. That's the record, verified at Central Registry, and from the baptismal files at Frascati.'

'Well, I agree she's not as official as the Central Registry, but the old Baroness Schwarzburg has been a client of my wife's for years. She's tottering on the edge of the grave, but she still spends a fortune on clothes. She claims she knew the General's father–which is very possible, because the old boy was chasing girls until the day he fell off his horse on the Pincio and broke his neck. According to her story, the Count bred himself a bastard from the girls' governess. He paid her off and she married someone else who gave the boy a name, though what the name was the Baroness couldn't remember. She's getting doddery, of course, so it could be nothing but scandalous rumour. You know what these old girls are. They've never got over their first waltz, and the time King Umberto showed them his coin collection. .... Anyway, it's a note in the margin, if you're interested.'

'Not really, Steffi. Now, if you could find me a suicide note or a blackmail letter that would tell me why Pantaleone killed himself, I'd be much happier. .... *Dio!* It's nearly five. The funeral photographs should be ready. If they're not, I'll send you three heads for pickling. See you later, Steffi. Keep in touch.'

Naturally enough, the photographs were not ready, and the Chief of Photographic Records was liverish and unhappy. Everyone understood the urgency, but I must be reasonable. Could I not see that the tanks were clogged with film, the enlargers were working overtime, and even with three photographers and two photo-file experts, it would take hours yet to identify all the personages. Even then there would be gaps. This was like an epic at Cinecitta, the whole set crowded with hundreds of extras–and how did one put names to farm-labourers and three bus-loads of tourists?

After ten minutes of snappish dialogue, I gave up in disgust and went back to my own office. Here, at least, there was a semblance of order and efficiency. The documents I had brought from the General's flat were all indexed and filed, and number one clerk had made some interesting discoveries.

'Brokers' advice notes, Colonel. All sales. The General has unloaded about eighty million lire worth of prime stock in the last four weeks. Covering letters from the Brokers, each one in the same terms ... "We have remitted proceeds in accordance with your instructions". Question: Where did the proceeds go? Not into his bank, because there's his last statement, issued a week ago. Then there's a letter from the Agenzia Immobiliare della Romagna. They advise that though the Pantaleone property has been on open offer for more than two months, there has been no serious interest at the figure named. They recommend withdrawing the property until the credit situation in Europe eases a little, and the new agricultural agreements have been announced for the Common Market. . . . Now come to this little piece. It's a handwritten note from Emilio del Giudice in Florence. You know him; a big name, a heavy dealer in important art works. Here's what he says: "Strongly advise against any transactions which involve you personally in a commitment to export works from the Pantaleone collection. As vendor you offer the works for sale subject to the conditions of the laws in force. After that, full responsibility for export formalities rests on the purchaser" . . .'

'So, he was trying to sell up. Any indication why?'

'Not in these papers.'

'What else have we got?'

'Cheque stubs, household accounts, bank statements, correspondence with estate managers and renting agencies, desk directory, pocket address-book. I'm still checking those against the names in our dossiers and so far, no surprises. This is the General's key-ring with a key to a safe-deposit box at the Banco di Roma. I'd like to see the inside of that.'

'We will–as soon as the banks open in the morning.'

'His lawyer is howling for us to release the documents.'

'I'll worry about him later. I'll also have a chat with the General's brokers. I'd like to know where they remitted the sale money. . . . If you want me in the next hour, I'll be at the Chess Club. After that, at home.'

The Chess Club of Rome is an institution almost as sacred as the Hunt Club. You enter it, as you hope one day to enter Heaven, through a noble portico, and find yourself in a courtyard of classic dimension. You climb a flight of stairs to a series of ante rooms, where servants in livery receive you with cautious deference. You tread softly and speak in muted tones, so as not to disturb the ghosts who still inhabit the place, Kings and Princes, Dukes, Barons, Counts and all their consorts. In the salone, you are dwarfed by soaring pilasters and frescoed ceilings, and gilt furniture designed for the backsides of grandees. In the dining-room you are awed by an afflatus of whispers, the talk of men who deal with great affairs like money and statecraft and spheres of commercial influence. You are daunted by the cold eyes of dowagers, sour with the virtue of age. You are hounded by waiters so disciplined, that even a crumb upon the shirt-front seems a sacrilege. . . . And you will look in vain for chess players, although it is rumoured that they do exist, cloistered as Carmelites in some secret cell.

I was not coming to play chess. I was coming to wait upon the Secretary, who might condescend to present me to the head-waiter, who, might if the stars were in favourable conjunction, put me in touch with the steward who had served General Pantaleone on the eve of his death.

I did not relish the prospect. The Chess Club is one of those places that makes me despair of my countrymen. In the uplands of Sardinia, where I once served as a junior officer, there are shepherds who live a whole winter on corn-bread and black olives and goat-cheese, and turn to banditry to feed their families, while their landlords lobby senators and ministers over brandy in the Club. In the mortuary at Palermo, I have identified the body of a colleague murdered by the Mafia, while the man who ordered him killed was lunching with a Milanese banker–at the Chess Club, of course. The economists weep tears of blood over the flight of capital from Italy to Switzerland, but the men who put wings to the money, sit sober and respectable over lunch at the corner table. Here, the survivors of the old order and the exploiters of the new, make truce and treaty and marriages of convenience, while the people, poor, ill-educated, impotent, fume at the chicanery of politicians and the tyranny of petty bureaucrats.

Time was when I toyed with the idea of joining the Communists who promised at least a levelling and a purging and one law for all. My enthusiasm died on the day when I saw a high Party official sharing smoked salmon and fillet steak with the president of a large chemical corporation. The more things change in Italy, the more they are the same. The scion of an old house joins the Christian Democrats; the cadet is free to flirt with Left or Right; and no matter who wins the last race, the bets will still be settled in the Chess Club. . . . Eh! Philosophers are as big a curse on the country as politicos: and a muddled conscience is bad medicine for an investigator. Let's be done with the job and go home!

It was still only eight-thirty and the guests were sparse. The Secretary was unusually urbane and the head-waiter was disposed to be helpful. He installed me in the visitors' room, brought me an aperitif, and, five minutes later, reappeared with the head-porter and the steward who had served the General's last meal. I explained my mission with suitable vagueness. Sometime during dinner the General had been called to the telephone. For reasons connected with military security, I wished to trace the call and contact the person who had made it. Then I had my first surprise.

'No, Colonel.' The head-porter was very definite. 'You have been misinformed. The General was called from the dining-room, but not to the telephone. A senior member of the Club had asked to speak with him in private. He waited in the card-room. The steward conducted the General to him. They spoke for a few moments, the General returned to his table, the member collected his coat and left the Club. I saw him leave.'

'And who was this member?'

'A gentleman from Bologna. The Cavaliere Bruno Manzini. He's in the Club now. Came in about twenty minutes ago with the Principessa Faubiani.'

'La Faubiani, eh?' I permitted myself a small grin of satisfaction. At least I was one up on old Steffi. The head-porter coughed eloquently.

'Colonel . . .?'

'Could you tell me something about the Cavaliere?'

'I could, sir, but—with respect—that sort of request should be addressed to the Secretary.'

'Of course. My compliments on your discretion. Would you give the Cavaliere my card and ask him to spare me a few moments?'

In any company, the Cavaliere Manzini would have been an impressive figure. He must have been nearly seventy years old; his hair was snow-white, brushed back in a lion's mane over his coat-collar; but his back was straight as a pine, his skin was clear, his eyes bright and humorous. His clothes were modish, his linen immaculate and he carried himself with the air of a man accustomed to deference. He did not offer his hand but announced himself with calm formality.

'I am Manzini. I understand you wished to see me. May I see your official identification?'

I handed him the document. He read it carefully, passed it back and then sat down.

'Thank you, Colonel. Now, your question.'

'You were, I believe, a friend of General Pantaleone?'

'Not a friend, Colonel, an acquaintance. I had small respect for him, none at all for his politics.'

'How would you define his politics?'

'Fascist and opportunist.'

'And your own?'

'Are private to myself, Colonel.'

'On the night before he died, the General dined here with a lady. I understand you had a conversation with him.'

'I did.'

'May I know the substance of it?'

'Certainly. I am the client of an art-dealer in Florence. His name is del Giudice. He had told me that Pantaleone was about to sell the family collection. I was interested in certain items, an Andrea del Sarto and a Bosch. I told Pantaleone I would like to negotiate with him directly. It would save us both money.'

'And . . .?'

'He said he would think about it and write to me soon.'

'You didn't press him for a date?'

'No. I could always buy through del Giudice. May I know the reason for these inquiries?'

'At this moment, sir, I am not at liberty to disclose it. Another question. The Pantaleone collection is an old and important one. Why would the General want to disperse it?'

'I have no idea.'

'May I ask you to keep this conversation private?'

'No, you may not! I did not invite it. I gave no prior promise of secrecy. I stand upon my right to discuss it or not, as I please—and with whom I please.'

'Cavaliere, you know the organization which I represent?'

'The Service of Defence Information? I know of its existence. I am not familiar with its activities.'

'You know, at least, that we deal with highly sensitive matters, both political and military.'

'My dear Colonel, please! I'm an old man. I lost my milk teeth years ago. I have no taste for spies, provocateurs or those who treat with them. I know that intelligence services can become instruments of tyranny. I know that they tend to corrupt the people who work in them. If you have no more questions, I trust that you will excuse me. . . . Good evening!'

He stalked out of the room, stiff as a grenadier, and I let out a long exhalation of relief. This was a sturdy one for a change, hard to coax, impossible to frighten. He looked you straight in the eye and gave you clean answers crack-crack-crack, knowing that you dared not gainsay him. But there were important questions still open. Why would Pantaleone, with suicide on his mind, engage in the long and tedious business of selling an estate? If he did embark on it, why not complete it? And why promise a letter he knew he would never write?

Boh! It was enough for one day and more than enough. My head was full of cotton wool and my heart full of envy for a seventy-year-old Cavaliere who could afford expensive pets like the Principessa Faubiani. I walked out of the Club into a soft spring rain, prised my car out of the court-yard and drove reluctantly homeward, to a hot dinner, a tepid hour of television and a cold bed afterwards.

In fact, I had a very troubled night. Shortly after ten, a colleague from Milan telephoned with the news that a young Maoist, under questioning in a bomb case, had fallen to his death from the window of the interrogation room. There would be headlines in every morning paper. The Left would swear he had been pushed. The Right would affirm that he had jumped. Either way, they had a martyr on their hands. My colleague was evasive, but when he mentioned the name of the interrogator, I knew the truth. The man was a sadist, a rabid idiot who didn't care how he got his evidence, or where he made it stick. He also had friends in high places who would spray him with rosewater at any inquiry. This was the kind of madness that bedevilled the whole country and brought the police and the judicial system into disrepute. There would be troops on every street corner for a week and this, too, would heighten the tension and polarize the factions, the one crying tyranny and repression, the other shouting law and order and an end to anarchy. *Dio!* What a nightmare mess! If I had any sense I should pack my bags and take the next boat to Australia.

At eleven-thirty, Lili Anders telephoned in panic. Her network contact had called and summoned her to a rendezvous at the Osteria del Orso. She was due there at midnight. What should she do? I told her to keep the rendezvous, rehearsed her three times in her story and then spent an anxious fifteen minutes trying to regroup my surveillance team.

I was just about to crawl into bed, when the telephone rang again. This time it was Captain Carpi's shadow. The Captain was drunk and mumbling darkly to a bar-girl at the Tour Hassan. What did I want done about it? For God's sake! Let him drink himself silly on bad champagne. The girls at the Tour Hassan wouldn't leave anyway until four in the morning. After that, if Carpi was still on his feet—or even if he wasn't—bundle him into a taxi and take him home. . . . Expenses? Have them put the drinks on Carpi's bill. They'd be padding it anyway. Goodnight and the devil take the pair of you!

At nine-thirty next morning, I sat in conference with a senior official of the Banco di Roma. He was courteous but very firm. There could be no access to the late General's safe deposit until every juridical requirement was met. He understood perfectly my position. He was sensible that matters of national security were involved. However, they were equally involved in his own case. The bank was a national institution. Public confidence depended on the rigid performance of contracts between banker and client. The law demanded it. The Carabinieri were servants of the law. Besides—he paused before delivering the *coup de grâce*—the strong box was empty. The General's lawyer had taken possession of its contents under an existing authority. I acknowledged defeat and went to see the General's brokers.

The brokers, an affiliate of a large American house, were much more co-operative. They had indeed sold large parcels of stock for the late General. They had remitted the proceeds, under instruction, to the General's legal representative, Doctor Sergio Bandinelli. So far as they were concerned, the transaction was closed at that point. They had no information as to the ultimate disposition of the funds. They were brokers only. They offered market advice under the normal disclaimers. They bought and sold under instruction. They functioned rigidly within the prevailing laws. End of conference.

Back in my office, I signed an *invito* requesting Doctor Sergio Bandinelli to wait on me within forty-eight hours. Then I spread the funeral photographs on the desk and settled down to examine them minutely against the accompanying check-list. It was not the names or the personages which interested me so much as the juxtapositions: who was talking to whom, which group seemed the most cohesive and intimate. Sometimes, in a crush like that, public enemies were revealed as secret allies. Sometimes, by a thousand to one chance, one saw a sign given or a message passed from hand to hand. At the end of an hour, I was left with one small surprise.

The surprise was the Cavaliere Manzini, the old autocrat from the Chess Club. He appeared in three shots, once talking to Cardinal Dadone, once with the Minister of Finance and the third time, a little removed from the cemetery vault, standing beside an elderly peasant who was listed as employed at the Villa Pantaleone. For a man who had small respect for Pantaleone, who regarded him as a Fascist and an opportunist, it was a singular gesture. I wondered why he had troubled to make it. I made a telephone call to a colleague in Bologna and asked that a copy of the Cavaliere's dossier be sent post-haste to Rome. Then I called the laboratory and summoned Stefanelli for a private talk.

Old Steffi was bursting with news, little of it good. First, his wife had told him that the new protector of the Principessa Faubiani was one Bruno Manzini, a Bolognese, richer than any one had a right to be–big enterprises, textiles, electrics, steel, food processing. Eat any pie you liked, Manzini owned a slice of it.

'I know all that, Steffi.'

'The hell you do? How?'

I told him at length and in detail. Then I spread the photographs on the desk.

'Now, tell me, Steffi. What's he doing at the funeral of a man he disliked and despised?'

'Easy, my friend. The Club. Members may not like each other; but they don't insult each other either. You may not like me, but you'll come to bury me, won't you? How else can you be sure I'm dead?'

'Maybe . . . maybe. . . . What else have you got for me?'

'The Casaroli Brothers sell rice-paper to wholesalers only; one in each province of Italy. The wholesalers sell to retail printers and stationers. That's the list of the wholesalers. The retailers will run into hundreds, possibly thousands.'

'Body of Bacchus! Don't you have any good news, Steffi?'

'Solimbene called me from the Consulta Araldica. He'll have his list ready tomorrow morning. So far, he's found fifteen surviving families in Italy who use the salamander in their coat-of-arms. Another paper-chase, I'm afraid. . . . Did you read the headlines this morning?'

'I did.'

'I'm scared, Colonel. When the police look like gangsters . . .'

'Or are made to look like gangsters, Steffi.'

'Either way, there's trouble ahead. They had two thousand Carabinieri on the streets of Milan this morning. And there's another thousand on extra duty in Rome; to say nothing of Turin and down south in Reggio. Right now, we've got the country clamped down tight–but we're not curing anything, we're not reorganizing anything.'

'It's not our job, Steffi. We're an arm of government–but we're not the Government itself.'

'We don't have a Government, friend. We have parties, factions, warring interests; and the man in the street doesn't know where to turn. Who represents the Government to him? A cop who walks away from a traffic jam; some little clerk in the pensions office who slams a window in his face. If things don't change soon, our man in the street is going to start shouting for a leader . . . a new *Duce!*'

'And who would that be, Steffi? Go on, toss me names! Pantaleone's dead. He's off stage. Who enters next–and from where–left, right or centre? That's what I'm trying to find out.'

'And when you do?'

'Say it, Steffi . . .'

'You buried an embarrassing corpse yesterday–under orders. Suppose you stumble on another embarrassment, a live one this time–a man in our own service for example. Suppose you're ordered then to close the file and keep your mouth shut. What will you do? Tell me honestly, friend to friend.'

'Steffi, I'm damned if I know. Old Manzini was right. This trade corrupts people. I know it's corrupted me; I don't like to ask how much.'

'You may have to ask very soon, Colonel. Look! Last night in Milan a suspect under questioning jumped or was pushed from a window. He's dead now. He can't be brought to trial. Nobody else can, either. You and I are guardians of public security. What do we do? What does the whole service do? We absolve ourselves. Why? Because we can put ten, twenty thousand armed men in the streets to keep the people cowed and stifle the questions. Who are the real rulers of Milan at this very moment? The Government? Hell! We are–the Carabinieri and our colleagues of the police. That's a tempting blue-print, you know. Terribly tempting. We don't have to offer bread and circuses any more; just public order, peace in the streets and the buses running on time. I told you I'm scared. Now I'll tell you why. I'm a Jew, Colonel. You didn't know that? Well, here and now, it doesn't pay to advertise the fact. I live over behind the synagogue in the old Ghetto. In the synagogue we've got a list of names, three hundred men, eight hundred women and children. They were shipped out of Rome to Auschwitz on the Black Sabbath of 1943. After the war, fifteen came back. Fourteen men and a woman. Do you know why I joined the service? So that I'd know in advance if it were ever going to happen again. . . . How old are you, Colonel?'

'Forty-two. Why?'

'You were a boy when it happened. But every time I see an election poster now, I get nightmares. I'm sorry if I've offended you.'

'You haven't, Steffi. I'm glad you told me. Now, why don't you go play with your microscope, eh?'

When the old man had gone, I sat a long time staring at the littered desk, the photographs, the memoranda, the tapes recorded last night in the Osteria del Orso. Suddenly, it all seemed irrelevant, trivial to the point of absurdity. What was at issue was not politics, not power-games and the sordid ploys of espionage, but myself, Dante Alighieri Matucci, who I was, what I believed and what price I would accept for my soul–if indeed I had one.

To be a servant of the State was easy. The State was like God. You couldn't define it. Therefore, you didn't have to ask questions about it. You didn't even have to believe that it existed. You had only to act as if you did. This was the difference between the Anglo-Saxons and the Mediterraneans. For the Anglo-Saxon, the State was the people. Parliament was its voice. The bureaucracy was its executive. For the Latin, the State was the *res publica*–the public thing had little, if anything, to do with people. The Latin, therefore, was always in an attitude of defence against the State, of opposition to its directives, of compromise with its exactions. The policeman was not his servant, but the factor of his master. In England they called their bureaucrats 'public servants'. In Italy they were *'funzionari'*, functionaries of the impersonal State.

But I, Dante Alighieri Matucci, was a person–or hoped I was. How much of me did the State own? How far could it legitimately direct me? To toss a living man out of a window? To shoot a rioter? To stifle a citizen with papers so that he couldn't even piss without a permit? And then there was the other side of the coin: fifty million people locked in a narrow peninsula, poor in resources, rich only in sap and energy, turbulent in spirit, easy prey to demagogues and agitators. How did you stop them tearing each other to pieces if you didn't break a few heads from time to time? It was all too easy to live underground like a mole nibbling at the roots of other people's lives, never caring to stick your dirty snout into the sunlight. . . .

I was still chewing on that sour thought when the boys from the surveillance team presented themselves to report on Lili Anders. Their tapes of the night-club meeting were almost unintelligible. I wanted to know why.

'No time to plant anything effective, Colonel. A crowded night-club, haphazard table placement, half-an-hour's notice . . . no chance. Anyway, they only stayed half an hour. We followed them back to Anders' apartment. The contact dropped her there and drove off. Giorgio followed him. I stayed to get a report from the lady.'

'Who was the contact?'

'Picchio . . . the woodpecker.'

'What did sweet Lili have to say for herself?'

'I've got it here: Woodpecker asked what the General died of? She replied a heart attack. Had she known he was sick? No, but he did have occasional chest pains that he called indigestion.

'Good for Lili. Go on.'

'Who brought her the news? A Colonel of Carabinieri. What was his name? Matucci. Why a full Colonel? She didn't know. She'd been wondering. How long had he stayed? Twenty minutes, half-an-hour. She'd been upset. The Colonel had been kind. Had he asked any significant questions? Only about Pantaleone's movements and contacts on the night of his death. She had told him the truth, there was nothing to hide. Woodpecker asked who were the General's heirs. She didn't know. She had never seen his will. Did she know the General's lawyer? Yes. Was she friendly with him? Reasonably. Then she was ordered to cultivate his acquaintance and if possible his friendship; and find out all the things she could about the General's estate. Had she ever met a Major-General Leporello?'

'He's one of ours, for God's sake.'

'It shook me a little, too, Colonel.'

'What did Lili say?'

'She'd never met him. Had the General ever spoken of him? No. At least not that she remembered. What would her next assignment be? Sit tight, concentrate on the lawyer, await further contact and instructions. . . . Fade out, *fine*. That's it, Colonel. . . . And, by the way, I didn't get to bed until three in the morning.'

'Poor fellow! I hope you slept well and chastely. Anything from Lili's phone tap?'

'Nothing since her call to you, Colonel.'

'Good. . . . Now, let's hear about our little Captain Carpi.'

'Nothing to tell, Colonel. He passed out cold about three in the morning. I paid the girl and the drink bill from his wallet and then took him home. He's a bad drunk, Colonel.

'That's something new. Anyway, he's off to Sardinia tomorrow. That should sober him up. Thank you, gentlemen. You may now resume your sleep. Make sure you're fresh and sharp by eight this evening. You're still on night roster. . . .'

They slouched out, bleary-eyed and grumbling and I grinned at their discomfiture. This was what the Americans called the name of the game. You walked your feet off. You knocked on doors. You stood watch on street-corners and cruised round smoky clubs. You waded through reams and reams of useless information, until you came up with one fragment of fact, that began or completed a whole mosaic. I had one now: why was Woodpecker, a Polish agent, interested in Marcantonio Leporello, Major-General of the Carabinieri?'

As an investigator I have many shortcomings and two special talents. The first is a photographic memory. The second is that I know how to wait. Comes a moment in every investigation when there is nothing to do except wait, and let the chemistry of the case work itself out. If you try to hurry the process, to satisfy yourself or a superior, you make mistakes. You accept false premises, create a fictional logic. You harry your operatives so that they make myopic observations and give you half-answers to keep you happy. You snatch at facile solutions and come up with a handful of smoke.

The Italians love bustle and brouhaha. Sketch them a scene and they will build you an opera inside an hour. They are glib; they are dilatory; they are evasive. They hate to commit themselves either to an opinion or an alliance, lest tomorrow they be held to the consequences. They would rather lose a tooth than sign a binding document. I am a colonel at forty-two because I have learned to make a virtue out of the vices of my countrymen.

The Minister of the Interior wanted action? He got it, scored for brass and tympani. NATO needed a spy care to tighten up security? *Bene!* There were twenty scripts to choose from and authentic villains to fit them. There was a stink over a procurement contract? For that, too, there was a magic formula: sabotage by enemy agents, at source, in transit, or on delivery site. But when a big thing came up, the trick was to create a zone of quiet and sit there, visible but enigmatic, digesting the facts in hand, calm as a Buddha waiting for the next turn of the wheel of life. It was a tactic that disconcerted many of my colleagues and irritated some of my superiors: but, most times, it worked—with a little sleight of hand to help the illusion.

At that moment in time, the Pantaleone affair was in suspense. The meaning of the salamander card was not yet deciphered. The General's papers and his money were in the hands of his lawyer who would probably wait until the last moment before he answered the *invito* and then stand pat on legal privilege. The man at the funeral might mean nothing. The Cavaliere Manzini was simply a buyer of expensive art. There was nothing yet from the heraldic expert. Nothing . . . nothing . . . nothing. Except that a Polish agent, named Woodpecker, was interested in Major-General Leporello. It seemed an appropriate time to have a chat with the Director.

The Director of the Defence Information Service was a character in his own right. He was related on his mother's side to the Caraccioli of Naples and on his father's to the Morosini of Venice. In the Service they called him Volpone–the old fox. I had another name for him: Cameleonte, the chameleon. One moment you saw him plain, the next you had lost him against the political undergrowth. He had the manners of a prince and the mind of a chess-player. He had a sense of history and a conviction that it always repeated itself. He was an ironist in eight languages, and had made conquests in all of them. He played tennis, sailed a keel-boat, collected primitive art and was a devotee of chamber music in which he sometimes played viola. He was inordinately rich, generous to those he liked and ruthless as a public executioner to those he did not. He insisted that I, Dante Alighieri Matucci, was one of those he liked; one of the few he respected. We had clashed often. He had tempted me, more than once, but I had sniffed at the bait and turned away from it with a grin and a shrug. I made no secret of my weakness, but I was damned if I would be blackmailed with them, by the Director or anyone else. And if the Director wanted to play games, I had a few of my own, with rather complicated rules.

I was playing one now. Major-General Leporello was a big man in the Carabinieri. I wanted to know whether the Director was big enough to handle him if ever there were a need. So, without ceremony, I put the question:

'Woodpecker is interested in Leporello. Why?'

The Director was instantly alert, the old fox sniffing a hostile air. He said, evenly:

'Isn't it your job to tell me?'

'No, sir, not yet. Leporello's dossier is marked "Reserved to Director".'

'Forgive me, I'd forgotten. Let me see now. General Leporello has spent the last five months abroad.'

'Where?'

'Japan, Vietnam, South Africa, Brazil, the United States, Great Britain, Greece, France.'

'Who paid the fare?'

'The tour was official. The General was on a study mission.'

'Studying what?'

'Riot control and counter-insurgency.'

'Do you know the General personally, sir?'

'Yes. He's a sound man.'

'Vulnerable?'

'He's a patriot, a devout Catholic, a Christian Democrat and financially independent. I doubt he could be bought or frightened.'

'Attacked? Assassinated?'

'Possibly.'

'Seduced?'

'By what, Colonel?'

'The ultimate infirmity—ambition.'

'For example . . .?'

'The man who devises the strategy of counter-revolution might decide to put it into practice on his own account . . . or on account of a potent minority.'

'Any evidence?'

'Indications only. Woodpecker and his network have a commission which I quote: ". . . to give early warning of any attempt at a *colpo di stato* by neo-fascist groups, or of actions designed to provoke it." If Woodpecker is interested in Leporello, we have to be interested, too.'

'You're in unicorn country, Matucci.'

'Half our lives, we deal with fables. Sometimes the fables come true.'

'In Leporello's case, I think not. However, let me play with the idea. I'll come back to you. For the moment, no action.'

'Yes, sir.'

'Anything else?'

'No, sir.'

'Then, permit me to offer you a compliment. I like your attitude to your work, careful and open-minded. That's rare, necessary, too, in these times.'

'You are kind, sir. Thank you.'

'Until later then.'

I walked out a very pensive man. If the Director was scared, everybody else should be running for cover. If the Director was committed to a cause or a compromise, nothing would divert him but a bullet in the head. He was the perfect *cinquecento* man, with a confessor at his right hand and a poet on his left, while his enemies rotted, howling, in the dungeons beneath his feet. I was named after a poet and needed a confessor; but I had no slightest wish to end my days in the dungeons of official disfavour. And yet . . . and yet. . . . A man who could control rioters and urban guerrillas might, one fine tomorrow, control the country, especially if he were a patriot, a good Christian and didn't have to worry about his rent or his dinner.

I was hardly back in my office when my secretary announced that Doctor Sergio Bandinelli had answered my *invito* and was waiting to see me.

The advocate was short, fussy and very irascible. I debated for a moment whether to play the bureaucrat or the gentleman, and then decided to smother him with courtesy. I regretted the need to disturb a busy man. I was grateful for so prompt a response. I trusted to dispose quickly of the few matters in question. I understood the relationship between advocate and client. It was my duty to protect that relationship and to discourage any breach of it. However. . . .

'. . . In cases where national security is involved, Avvocato, we both need to be slightly more flexible. I am sure you understand that.'

'No, Colonel, I do not. I am here to protest the illegal seizure of my client's papers and to require their immediate delivery into my hands.'

'No problem at all. You may take the papers with you when you leave. As for the protest, what's the profit? The Defence Information Service works under presidential directive, and to rather special rules. Of course, if you wish to press a complaint . . .'

'Well . . . under the circumstances. . . .

'Good! I am encouraged now to take you into our confidence, to solicit your assistance in a matter of importance.'

'I am happy to assist, Colonel, provided I may reserve my position in the event of conflict of interest.'

'Of course. Let us proceed then. General Pantaleone was an important man. His death has political consequences. I am directed to study those consequences. I am interested, therefore, in every aspect of the General's activities. He was, for example, engaged in liquidating his estate, selling shares, preparing to disperse his art collection. Why?'

'I am not at liberty to say.'

'His brokers inform us that the proceeds of his shares were transmitted to you. What were you directed to do with the money?'

'I cannot tell you that, either.'

'I am afraid you must.'

'No, Colonel. Legal privilege.'

'Before you invoke it, let me tell you something else. Your late client maintained relations with a member of a foreign espionage network.'

'I don't believe it.'

'It's true, nevertheless. You, yourself, are under surveillance by the same network.'

'Is this some kind of threat, Colonel?'

'No threat, Avvocato, a statement of fact. So ... when you refuse to disclose what has happened to large sums of money, you put yourself in some jeopardy. Crime is involved, a threat to the security of the State. Your client is dead. You are answerable for your part in his affairs. So, I ask you again. What happened to the money?'

'I was instructed to reinvest it.'

'Where?'

'Abroad. In Switzerland and in Brazil for the most part.'

'And if the art collection had been sold, and the land?'

'The same instruction applied.'

'Such exports of funds requires approval from the Ministry of Finance. Did you have it?'

'Well, no ... but the nature of the transaction. ...'

'Don't tell me, Avvocato. The transaction would involve intermediaries who have safe channels for currency export. They charge five per cent for their services. For this, they guarantee immunity to the client. It's an old story. It doesn't hold water and you know it. You can be charged with conspiracy to circumvent the law. You're lucky I'm an intelligence investigator and not a policeman ... but I can change my hat any moment I choose. So talk, Avvocato! Don't play children's games! ... Why was Pantaleone exporting funds?'

'In sum, he was afraid. He had joined himself with the new Fascists as their military adviser and as commander-in-chief in case of a *colpo di stato*. Their provocative tactics worried him. He felt they were not strong enough to risk a *colpo di stato* and that, if they tried, it would lead to civil war. All the strength of the Movement is in the South. In the North, the Left is in control and far better organized. So the Movement began to lose faith in Pantaleone. They wanted to move him out in favour of a bolder man.'

'Who?'

'I don't know.'

'Did Pantaleone know?'

'No. All he knew was that it was someone who was not in the Movement but who might be attracted into it when the time was right.'

'A military man?'

'Obviously. If they were provoking a disturbance, they had to be able to offer military action to suppress it. That's the whole point of provocation, no?'

'So, the General was frightened. Of a rival or of something else?'

'Of action against himself.'

'What sort of action?'

'I don't know.'

'Then guess.'

'Damage to his reputation. Some kind of revelation of his past.'

'Blackmail, in fact?'

'Yes. He had a chequered career and many enemies.'

'Had he received any direct threats?'

'Well . . . in a legal sense, no.'

'In common sense, Avvocato?'

'About a week ago he received a communication by messenger.'

'What sort of communication?'

'It consisted of a very complete and accurate biography which, if it had ever been published, would have damaged his reputation beyond repair and banished him forever from public life.'

'He showed it to you?'

'Yes. He asked whether there might be any defence against publication or any means of tracing the author. I advised him there was not . . . at least not without risk of spreading the information dangerously.'

'But a threat of publication was made?'

'I read it so.'

'Read what?'

'A card, attached to the typescript.'

I laid the salamander card on the table before him.

'This card?'

The advocate picked it up, gingerly, examined it and agreed.

'Yes, that's the one. Where did you get it?'

'I found it in the General's bedroom. What happened to the biography?'

'He lodged it in his strong box at the bank.'

'Which you emptied yesterday.'

'Yes.'

'I want it. I want all his documents.'

'I'll give them to you, happily—on a judge's order. Without it, no.'

'This card, Avvocato, what does it signify?'

'To me, nothing.'

'What did it signify to the General?'

'I can only tell you what he said.'

'Yes?'

'He was a taciturn man, given to aphorisms. He said . . . "Well, Saint Martin's day at last."'

'And what the devil was that supposed to mean?'

'He wouldn't explain it. He never did. I puzzled over it for a long time; then I found the reference. It's in Don Quixote: "To every pig comes Saint Martin's day." In Spain, pigs are usually killed on the feast of St Martin.'

'Doctor Bandinelli, I am sure you are a very good advocate. You never tell a lie. You simply bury the part of the truth that really matters and the law protects you while you do it. However, you've stepped outside the law and put yourself and your privilege in jeopardy. You can fight me, of course.'

You can delay me, by tactics and quibbles, but your St Martin's day will come in the end. If you want to avoid it, I'm prepared to make a bargain with you. I'll forget the currency question. I'll send a man with you now to assemble every paper you hold on the Pantaleone family. He will list the papers, then lock and seal them in your safe. Tomorrow I will come to your office and go through them with you. That way you keep your privilege and I get the information I want. Agreed?'

'I seem to have no choice.'

'Very little.'

'Then I agree.'

'Good. You can sign for the papers we hold and take them back with you. When you go home this evening, leave the key of your office with my man. He will spend the night there.'

'Why?'

'Protection, Avvocato. Politics is a risky business these days.'

I meant it as an irony. I was the old-line professional patronizing a civilian. I should have known better. In this trade, in this country, you are always standing on a trap-door with a hangman's noose around your neck.

The which being said, I agree an explanation is needed. This so-called Republic of Italy, we so-called Italians, are not a nation at all. We are provinces, cities, countrysides, tribes, factions, families, individuals–anything and everything but a unity. Ask that fellow over there, the street-cleaner, what he is. He will answer, "I am a Sard, a Calabrese, a Neapolitan, a Romagnolo." Never, never, will he tell you he is an Italian. That girl in the Ferrari, she's a Venetian, a Veronese, a Padovan. Wife, mistress, mother or rare virgin, she names herself for a place, a plot of separate earth. I, myself, as I have told you, am a Tuscan. I serve, because I am paid to serve, the nebulous public thing called the State; but my belonging is else-where–Florence and the Medici and the Arno and the pines planted over the graveyards of my ancestors. The consequence? A kind of anarchy, which the Anglo-Saxons will never understand; a kind of order which they understand even less. We know who we are, man by man, woman by woman. We despise the outlander because he is different. We respect him because he knows and we know who he is. So, my dilemma: I can never say, "This is the enemy, destroy him!" I must say, "This is the enemy of the moment, but he comes from my country, his sister is married to my cousin and tomorrow we may need to be friends. How must I comport myself so that the links are not broken even though the chain be stretched to breaking-point?'

There are many who say that, in this system, there is no place for patriots, only for pragmatists and opportunists. These are dirty words–or are they? We have to survive: a practical problem. We have one life, one opportunity to come to terms with it. So long as the terms are negotiable, we try to negotiate. If we are forced to a base bargain, we accept it and wait for a tomorrow when the contract may be annulled or varied by mutual consent. As you see, I know it all. So there is no excuse for the follies I began to commit that afternoon.

The first was my contemptuous bargain with Doctor Sergio Bandinelli. I judged him for a frightened and pliable man. I gave him for guardian a junior agent, one Giampiero Calvi. I issued a set of simple instructions. Calvi would accompany Bandinelli to his office. He would take possession of the Pantaleone papers, list them, lock them in the advocate's safe, seal the safe and remain in the office until I relieved him at nine the next morning. During the night, he would call the duty-officer at headquarters every hour on the hour. Calvi was a promising young man. I read him no lectures. I presumed on the training I, myself, had given him.

Then, because I was tired, I decided to mix business with pleasure. Because I was—and am—too arrogant for my own good, I elected to play out my little game against the Director. I telephoned my maid and told her that I would not be home for dinner and that I might have to spend the night outside Rome. Then I called Lili Anders and told her that, in line of duty, I would call on her at eight-thirty for a cocktail and take her out to dinner afterwards. Where? A discreet place, but elegant, where she could forget her grief and relax. My intentions? Dear Madam, those of a colleague and collaborator; no more, no less.

I walked down the corridor to chat with my associate Rigoli, who concerns himself with the movements and the security of public and not-so-public officials. Rigoli is a grey, mousey fellow with a card-index mind. What he does not know, he can guess with seventy per cent accuracy: where the Minister of Finance can be found at three on Friday morning, what First Secretary took what flight to Venice and who had the seat next to him. He told me that Major-General Leporello was presently in Rome, lodged at the Hassler, and engaged in a series of conferences with senior service officers. I called the hotel and, after a brief passage-at-arms with a junior aide, was put through to the General. The conversation was brief and terse.

'General, this is Colonel Matucci, SID.'

'Yes?'

'An urgent matter. I should like to see you.'

'How urgent?'

'Very.'

'I am busy until six. I can spare you half an hour after that. Call me from the lobby. Suite 10.'

'Thank you, sir.'

'The name again?'

'Matucci. Section E.'

I put down the telephone and waited. If I judged my man aright, he would check back either to me or to the Director. If he called the Director, I was in for an uncomfortable hour. I was gambling on the fact, well-known in the Service, that the Director was a very secretive fellow who refused casual contacts, even to senior officials. Sure enough, within three minutes my phone rang and Leporello came on the line.

'Who is this, please?'

'Matucci, Section E.'

'This is Leporello. We have an appointment I believe.'

'Yes, sir. Suite 10 at 1800 hours.'

'Please be punctual. Goodbye.'

Boh! I might well need a little relaxation after half an hour with this hard-head. I made one more call, this time to a curious little office on the Via Bissolati which feeds to the Press and to private subscribers news of the comings and goings of celebrities. I don't subscribe to it. I use it and pay my way by encouraging my colleagues at the Questura to overlook a few irregularities in procedure—German telephonists whose sojourn permits are out of date, English typists who don't pay social service contributions and the like. It's a kind of corruption, but there is a more historic name for it–*toleranza,* live and let live, but remember always that the law has a long memory and a heavy boot. My contact is a busty Dane, who lives, unhappily, with a Spanish journalist accredited to the Holy See. Her civil status is highly dubious, but her information is always accurate.

'Faubiani . . . ? Well, old Manzini's in town, so she's doing the rounds with him. Let's see. . . . Yesterday Valerio was showing knitwear. Tonight Fosco is displaying jewellery and they've tied in the Lavezzi who is launching a coffee-table book on Renaissance goldsmiths. Faubiani will probably be there. It's a buffet supper at Fosco's, eight-thirty until the champagne runs out. If you want a ticket, I can let you have mine. Claudio's working tonight and I only get envious when I look at all that expensive junk.'

'You're an angel, Inge.'

'Don't tell Claudio that. He's getting demonic again. . . . When am I going to see you, Dante?'

'When I pick up the card at seven-thirty. *Ciao, bambina!*'

And so, with my evening laid out, hour by shining hour, one small decision remained: what number should I leave with the night duty-officer? I gave him two–Lili Anders' and my house. Now I was ready for grooming; a change of clothes, a trim, a shave, a massage to tone up my sagging face muscles and half an hour of instructive gossip from my favourite manicurist.

At eighteen hundred hours precisely, I telephoned Major-General Leporello from the front desk of the Hassler. He commanded me to wait until his aide came to fetch me. The aide, I noted, was a muscular young blood with red hair and freckles and a Trentine accent. He was respectful but laconic, and he wanted to see my card before we moved from the lobby. I suspected that when he left me with the General, he posted himself just outside the door of the suite. Leporello, himself, was a surprise. He was a tall man, blond and ruddy, more German than Latin. His chest was broad, his belly flat. His gestures were restrained and his manner brisk and businesslike. He had no sense of humour at all.

'Your identification, please.'

I gave it to him. He studied it, line by line, and then handed it back to me.

'What do you wish to discuss, Colonel?'

'Matters arising out of the death of General Pantaleone.'

'Such as?'

'This card, sir. It was found in the General's room after his death.'

'What does it signify?'

'That's what I am trying to establish. It was attached to a set of records which were delivered to Pantaleone before his death.'

'What sort of records?'

'Incriminating documents of the General's past life.'

'Blackmail?'

'We believe so.'

'Where are they now?'

'In his lawyer's office, in custody of an officer of SID.'

'The card?'

'Is our only clue to the identity of the blackmailer.'

'The symbol?'

'A salamander.'

'That's odd.'

'Why, sir?'

'During the war, one of the most important partisan groups in the Valpadana was led by a man who called himself the Salamander.'

'What was his real name?'

'I don't know. He dropped out of sight about 1943. There was a rumour the Germans had got him.'

'Did he use a card like this?'

'My memory is vague, because all my information at the time was second or third hand; but I seem to remember some talk of a calling card pinned to the chest of victims of the band.'

'Was this a Marxist group?'

'Most groups in the North had real or imputed connections with the Marxists.'

'Did you ever work with such groups, General?'

'I? Never. My loyalties were to the Crown. I never changed them—even when it might have been convenient to do so. I disliked the Fascists, I loathed the Germans; but even for that I could not make myself a turncoat soldier. Today I am able to be both honest and proud.'

'I am sure you are, sir. You are also a natural target for the terrorists of the Left.'

'I must presume so.'

'Which brings me to the real purpose of my visit; which is to inform you that you are under surveillance by at least one network of foreign agents.'

He gave me a thin, humourless smile.

'That's hardly fresh news, Colonel. I have always assumed surveillance by all groups—foreign or local.'

'The news is, General, that this group regards you as a possible successor to General Pantaleone.'

'In what capacity?'

'As a military and political leader in the event of a right-wing coup.'

'Which is nonsense, of course . . .'

'Of course, sir. But it does make you vulnerable.'

'To what?'

'To blackmail or assassination.'

I had thought to shake him or at least to interest him. Impossible. He was hard and smooth as cemetery granite.

'Blackmail, Colonel? Quite impossible I assure you. My life is an open book. I am not ashamed of any single page. As for attempts on my life, these have been foreseen, and security measures arranged to protect me and my family. I am more concerned by the suggestion—even from hostile elements—that I might have political ambitions. I have none. I believe in hierarchy and order. I see myself only as a servant of duly constituted authority.'

'I understand perfectly, sir.'

'A question, Colonel.'

'Sir?'

'Have you discussed this matter with your Director?'

'I have.'

'His opinion?'

'That no action is required by SID. I have, in fact, exceeded my brief by seeking this interview with you.'

'Why did you seek it then?'

'We are colleagues, General, you and I. We are members of the same corps. I felt that a point of honour was involved. I decided to act on my own initiative and at my own risk.'

'What risk, Colonel?'

'Well . . . to put it gently, the Director is a very formidable character.'

'Are you afraid of him?'

'No, sir–but I have a healthy respect.'

'So, you would prefer I did not report our meeting to him?'

'I have not said that, sir. Nor would I say it. I have done my duty as I read it. I was, and am, prepared to accept all consequences.'

For the first time, Leporello relaxed. He offered me a cigarette from a gold case, and condescended to light it for me. He leaned back in his chair and surveyed me with grim approval.

'You impress me, Colonel. If you need a friend in the Service, you have one in me. I shall instruct my staff that you may have instant access to me at any time.'

'That is very generous, sir.'

'Not at all. We have a common aim: the security and stability of the Republic. We must co-operate whenever we can. Pantaleone was a dangerous fool and more than half a rogue. Today we need strong men who are prepared to risk themselves in public service. I judge that you are such a one. Your present experience is, of course, most valuable. If ever you felt an inclination to join my personal staff, I should be happy to have you.'

'That's a great compliment.'

'You deserve it. And, Colonel . . .?'

'Sir?'

'I have no intention of discussing this meeting with your Director.'

'Thank you, sir.'

He shook my hand and ushered me out, commending me to the care of his athletic aide, who escorted me downstairs with a trifle more grace and favoured me with a salute as I drove away.

In the gardens of the Pincio I stopped the car and sat for twenty minutes trying to make sense of Major-General Leporello. I have an instinctive fear of characters who act as if they were first cousins to God Almighty. Their virtue dazzles me. Their ruthlessness never ceases to amaze me. Their passion for order sets them beyond reason or pity. They have all the rectitude of a grand inquisitor, and a Jesuit skill in casuistry. They are dogmatists all, and they have no hesitation about rewriting the codex to suit themselves. They attract minions and satellites and suborners who feed their ambition and bloat their conscious virtue into a legend of impeccability. In short, I loathe their guts and I am more afraid of them than of all the venal villains I meet in my trade. They make me afraid of myself, too; because they provoke me to anger and misjudgment and savage reaction.

Still there was a tenuous profit. Leporello was tempting me into an alliance, first with a scrap of information, true or false, on the Salamander, then with a promise of friendship and advocacy. An alliance pointed to a strategy; a strategy pointed to a goal. What goal? What was the next ambition of a man who was appointed to control ant-heap cities and their millions of volatile humans? Even if he had not yet defined it for himself, there were others ready to prescribe it for him. Eh! It was too late and too early for Dante Alighieri Matucci to read the future. I started the car and drove through the dappled alleys of the gardens to drink cocktails with Lili Anders.

The apartment had changed since my last visit. The equestrian portrait of Pantaleone was gone from the mantel, and in its place was a bright surrealist piece of Spiro, a landscape of flowers with smiling human faces, and a procession of musical instruments playing them into a dance. The furniture had been rearranged, the ornaments culled to produce an air of undiluted feminity. Lili herself was changed in some subtle fashion that I could define only by details; the hair more softly swept, the clothes more modish and extravagant, her manner more relaxed and confident. Even the house-keeper was a shade less brusque, if still suspicious and unwelcoming. When I commented on the changes, Lili smiled and shrugged.

'I am my own woman now. Not as much as I would wish, but a little more anyway. What will you drink?'

'Whisky, please.'

'You are changed, too.'

'How?'

'More human, perhaps. Less professional. How am I to call you, Colonel?'

'My name is Dante Alighieri.'

'Dante was a very sombre man. You?'

'Sometimes. Not tonight.'

'What is different about tonight?'

'There is business to be done; but I would still like us to enjoy ourselves.'

'That's hardly possible is it?'

'Why not?'

'Because, Dante Alighieri, you own me. You direct me like a puppet. I have no choice of what or how I may enjoy. . . . Your drink, master.'

'Your health, Lili.'

'Where are we dining?'

'We are guests at an exhibition and a champagne supper afterwards. Fosco is displaying his new season's jewellery.'

'That should be interesting. Do you like jewellery, Dante?'

'I do—even though I can't afford it.'

'Would you like to see mine?'

'If you like.'

'I'll show it you when we come back. I presume you will bring me back after the supper.'

'You're being rough with me, Lili.'

'No. I want you to know that I understand our relationship. I promised value for money and protection.'

'I'm not a whore-master, Lili.'

'Then what are you?'

'Would you believe me if I told you?'

'I might.'

'It's very simple. I'm a self-indulgent bastard who likes pretty women.'

'Now tell me the rest of it.'

'I'm tired and I want to laugh. I'm puzzled and I want to stop thinking. I'm scared and I don't really want to ask why.'

'You, scared?'

'Yes. This is the age of the assassins, Lili—the age of the fanatics and the destructors. They want a new world. They'll tear down twenty centuries of civilization to achieve it. What they don't see is that when they're sitting in the ruins, the old gang will have to come back, the technocrats to build the factories, the financiers to create a new illusion of money, the police to bully people into order, even the city rat-catchers like me. It's a madness, Lili, and I'm at the centre of it. So are you. There's no escape for either of us, but I thought, just for an hour perhaps there might be a zone of quiet in the eye of the hurricane. I was a fool. Forget it. I'm not a sadist. So, for Christ's sake, don't be insulted! . . . Now, please, may I have another drink?'

She took the glass from me without a word, refilled it and brought it back. Then she laid a cool hand on my cheek and said, very calmly:

'Even if you mean only half of it, I'll believe you. And I'm not insulted.'

I wasn't sure I believed myself; but I wanted to feel less like a pimp and more, much more, like a man who could face the sunlight without shame. I drew her hand down to my lips and kissed it lightly.

'Now, let's start the scene again. Enter Dante Alighieri Matucci, who is welcomed by Lili Anders. Her greeting is formal but not unfriendly. . . .'

'Correction. Her greeting is friendly though not yet intimate.'

She bent and kissed me on the forehead and then moved away to pour herself another drink. Twenty minutes later we were driving down to Fosco's and we joined the gathering, hand in hand, like lovers.

I had not told Lili; but I knew a small something about Fosco, the jeweller. He was–still is for that matter–a phenomenon: a young and talented homosexual who leapt from a back-alley apprenticeship in Florence to establish himself in five years as one of the best private goldsmiths in Rome. He showed up once in our files as the friend of an Arab Embassy official; but the association lapsed quickly and we lost interest in him. We are very tolerant in moral matters but highly sensitive to Middle Eastern politics. Sometimes, because his shows attracted a motley group of titled somebodies and monied nobodies, I planted an observer among his guests or his security guards. But, though the exercise was profitable in minor ways, Fosco himself always showed clean: a good craftsman, with exquisite manners, and an iron-clad egotism that enabled him to impose his taste and his exorbitant price-list on a wide spectrum of Roman matrons, diplomatic wives, rising film-stars and vagrant notables.

The presentation of his spring collection was a gala occasion. The best titles in Rome staged a slow pavane round the show-cases. The most expensive models disposed themselves at strategic points in the gallery. A master chef presided over the buffet. An army of handsome young waiters distributed champagne and canapés; and even the security guards contrived to look like Milanese captains of industry. It was a sophisticated social ballet and Fosco directed it with considerable charm and only a hint of contempt for the performers.

We arrived in the middle of the first movement; the early diners who would come, be seen, drink a cocktail or two and leave. The serious ones, the friends of the Master, would come later, linger over the buffet and leave at midnight. Fosco received us with vague courtesy, and waved us into the concourse. We snared two glasses of champagne and a pair of catalogues and began our circuit of the exhibits. One fact was immediately clear: Fosco had made a killing. Half the items were already pre-empted, some marked 'sold' others 'reserved', optioned in advance to great houses–Bulgari, Cartier, Buccellati, Tiffany. Not that he did not deserve it. He was a master of every style, the baroque, the antique, the avant-garde. His designs were original, his craftsmanship superb. The poorest stones looked like gems of the first water. The best were set like sacred relics alive under the artful lights.

He was not modest about them either. He labelled every exhibit as if it were a museum piece, described the genesis of the design, the particulars of the stones and their setting, and whenever he could, the name and title of the person who had commissioned it. The older houses sniffed at such vulgarity, but Fosco demolished their snobbery at a stroke.

'I want my jewels to be talk-pieces. How can a woman talk about what she doesn't know. I explain my work and thus emphasize its value. Right or wrong? Look at the result! I carry no dead stock. I am liquid after every exhibition. . . .'

After this one, it seemed, he would have money running out of his ears. We were about half-way round the gathering when Lili tugged at my sleeve and pointed to the catalogue. The section she indicated was entitled, 'A Fantasy of Rare Beasts' and referred to a collection of jewelled butterflies, birds and animals to be worn as brooches, pendants, clasps, buckles, earrings and symbolic guardians of women's chastity. Lili was pointing to number 63 of which the description read:

> Salamander. Brooch in the form of an heraldic beast. Emeralds in pavé. Crowned with brilliants and ornamented with Burma rubies. Adapted from a calligraphic design. Commissioned by Cav. Bruno Manzini, Bologna.

The piece itself was twenty feet away, laid on a bed of black velvet, in a small show-case, mounted on a pillar of alabaster. It was not a gaudy jewel, but the craftsman had preserved the character and sweep of the original calligraphy, so that when I compared it with the card there was no shadow of doubt that the designs were identical.

I drew Lili away from the show-case into the crush of people round the buffet. At the same moment, the Cavaliere Bruno Manzini entered the gallery with the Principessa Faubiani at his side and a small retinue of friends in attendance. Fosco greeted them effusively, snapped fingers at his minions to bring them champagne and catalogues and then led them on his own personal tour of the masterworks.

Immediate problem: how to confront Manzini before he left the gallery. I had him under my hand here. Once he left, I could be chasing him all over the peninsula. On the other hand, with the Press and the gossips of the city turned out in force, I could not risk a scandal. Leaving Lili at the buffet, I made my way to the entrance where an agreeable young man was deputizing as host for Fosco. I flashed my card at him.

'Carabinieri. Who is in charge of your security guards?'

'Over there, by the stairwell, tall fellow with grey hair. There's no trouble, I hope?'

'None. Just routine.'

I drew the tall fellow into the shadows and showed him my card too, but this time I made sure he read it carefully before I instructed him.

'This is important. We can't afford a mistake. You will take me to Fosco's private office. I'll give you a note to the Cavaliere Bruno Manzini. You will escort him to the office, then leave us alone. Stay outside the door and let no one in while we're talking–clear?'

'Clear. There's no trouble, I hope.'

'No trouble. I've noted your security arrangements. First class.'

He was happy then. He led me to Fosco's office–a fairy bower done in Pompeian red. I scribbled a note to Manzini on the house note-paper. The text was respectful but cryptic:

Regret intrusion but have urgent and official communication. Please accompany messenger to office.

Matucci SID

He was with me in three minutes, cool and condescending as ever. He would not sit down. He had guests waiting. He demanded that I state my business and be done with it.

'My business is still the late General Pantaleone.'

'So?'

'Shortly before he died, he received a communication which was, in effect, a dossier of his past life.'

'And what has that to do with me?'

'Attached to the dossier was this card. You will note the design–a crowned salamander. We have established that the design corresponds exactly with exhibit No. 63 in the Fosco catalogue. We are confident you will wish to explain the connection.'

'Why should I wish to explain it, Colonel?'

'A matter of national security is involved.'

'Is that fact or opinion?'

'Fact.'

'And you could establish it as such to my satisfaction?'

'I believe so.'

'Is there any suggestion of criminal activity in this case?'

'As yet, none.'

'Then what do you want from me, Colonel?'

'At this stage an informal discussion.'

'When?'

'Now, Cavaliere.'

'Quite impossible. I am occupied with friends.'

'Afterwards then. At your hotel, perhaps?'

'My dear Colonel, I am seventy years old. By midnight I am near to dying. You would get no sense out of me at all. Say, nine in the morning at the Grand Hotel, and I'll do my best to enlighten you. Now, may I be excused?'

'Some questions before you go, Cavaliere.'

'Yes?'

'The salamander, what does it signify?'

'Survival. It was my code-name during the war. The rest is too long to tell you now.'

'The inscription?'

'That's a long story too.'

'The beginning of it then, if you please.'

'The beginning and the end, Colonel. Pantaleone was my half-brother. Only he happened to be conceived on the right side of the blanket.'

I stared at him, open-mouthed like an idiot. He smiled at my discomfiture and made a small gesture of deprecation.

'Please! I am not trying to make theatre, only to show you that we do need time to be clear with each other. Agreed?'

'Agreed.'

'Now, Colonel, will you answer one question for me?'

'If I can, yes.'

'Who killed Pantaleone?'

'The death certificate states that he died of a cardiac arrest.'
'But that's what kills us all, Colonel.'
'Exactly.'
'No other comment?'
'None. Until tomorrow, Cavaliere.'
'My compliments, Colonel. Goodnight.'

Why didn't I hold him? Why didn't I hammer him with questions while I had him off-balance? I told you before, this was a very special one, the best of the breed. Off-balance? Never for an instant. I was the unsure novice, groping for hand-hold and foot-hold on a bare mountain. Besides—let me make it plain to you—this is Italy, where the law goes back to Justinian, and half of it hasn't been dusted off for centuries, and the rules of the game are written in sand. Three people in Manzini's retinue could immobilize me for a month by lifting a telephone. Twenty names at Fosco's party could consign me forever to the limbo of the retired list. And if you've ever tried to collect a debt or enforce a claim against the Republic, then you'll know what I'm talking about. In China, they drowned their enemies in a bath of feathers. Here in Italy, they stifle them with silence and bury them under a tumulus of *carta bollata*.

It was still only ten-thirty. I rescued Lili from the crush at the buffet and carted her off to dinner at a place I knew in Trastevere, where the food was honest Tuscan, the wine was honourable and the waiters were proud to serve you, and there was a great open fire for the winter and an arbour of vines for the summer nights. There was music, too; a skinny, plaintive fellow with a guitar, who would come to your table, when you were ready for him, and sing the soul out of your body with the old songs of the South. I was known here, but not for my trade, only because I prized the cook, and sometimes drank enough to sing and strum a song or two while the sad fellow ate his supper.

I had friends there: Castiglione, who used to be a great locksmith until the arthritis got him; Monsignore Arnolfo Ardizzone of the Vatican Secretariat of State, a cleric, knowledgeable and discreet, who had renounced marriage to serve God and adopted the bottle as the only mistress acceptable to Mother Church; Giuffredi, the poet, who wrote satires in Romanesco which nobody read any more; and Maddalena, who sold yesterday's roses at five hundred lire a bloom and was said to own a whole apartment block on the Tuscolana. True or false? I had never cared to inquire. This was one place where I was myself—whoever that might be. I accepted everyone at face value. I used no one. I paid the score and was welcome in the house. Enough! Everyone needs a bolt-hole. This was mine.

I tried to explain all this to Lili as we walked the last hundred metres through lanes hung with laundry and came out into a tiny square guarded by a dusty virgin in a glass case. I wanted to explain, which in my trade is a weakness. She seemed happy to listen, holding close to me as we stepped over foul runnels and spilt refuse, while the cats of the quarter slunk back into the shadows. Sometimes, when the rare light fell on her face, she looked like a young girl. When she crossed herself at the shrine of the little virgin, she looked like a peasant woman, weary from a long day in the fields. You may not believe me, but I did not care. I was not hunting now, I was simply glad not to be alone.

When we were settled at the table, with bread and wine and a fresh candle, Lili leaned across to me and laid her hands on mine.

'You look different now, Dante Alighieri.'

'How?'

'At Fosco's you were tight, wary, like a fox. Now you are loose, free. You greet people like human beings. They, too, are glad to see you.'

'This is Trastevere, my love. Across the river. You know what these people call themselves? *Noantri*—we others. They refuse to belong to anyone but themselves.'

'I like that. For now, we, too, are *noantri*. Please, may I have some wine?'

'I may get drunk and sing.'

'I'll sing with you.'

'And who will drive us back across the river?'

'Perhaps we won't go back—ever again.'

It was a happy thought and we nursed it with all sorts of fantasies through the *zuppa* and the *pasta* and the *griglia* and the *dolci*. We embroidered it with the music of the plaintive one as he perched on the stool next to Lili, and played her the curiosities of his repertoire—The Song of the Washer-woman of Vomero; Friend Don't Trust the Spinster; The Undressing Song and the Tale of the Lecherous Clogseller.

Midnight came and we were still singing. At one-thirty in the morning we were vaguely drunk, and the waiters had begun to wilt; so we wandered into the square, said goodnight to the lonely virgin and strolled towards the riverside car-park. Lili said, drowsily:

'Do you know something?'

'What?'

'I want to go to bed with you; but I don't want to go home.'

'Why not?'

'Because home is yesterday. I want to forget it.'

'And tomorrow?'

'Tomorrow starts when the sun comes up, and this place will be ugly and smelly and full of sad people afraid of each other and you'll be all wise and wary again.'

'So let's drive out along the ring-road. There's a place I know. . . .'

'Anywhere you say, *caro mio*. Anywhere you say.'

'I have to make a phone call first.'

'Why?'

'I left your number with my duty officer. I'll have to check in and give him a new one.'

'There's no escape is there?'

'We escaped tonight.'

'So we did. But you still have to telephone. . . .'

'Please, Lili.'

'Please, just kiss me. . . .'

In case you're hoping—as I was—for a happy tale of love and lechery, forget it! The evening of liberty ended with that kiss. I called Headquarters from the corner phone booth. The time was 0210 hours. The duty-officer told me agent Calvi had not made his hourly call. What did I want done about it? I ordered two cars of our mobile squadron, one to pick up Stefanelli, one to meet me at the lawyer's office. I flagged a passing taxi, bundled Lili into it and sent her home. Then I climbed into my own car and drove like a madman across the sleeping city.

The office of Doctor Sergio Bandinelli was on the fifth floor of a large modern block on the Via Sicilia, only two hundred metres from the bustle of the Via Veneto. When I arrived, one car of the mobile squadron was already parked outside the entrance. The second, carrying Steffi and his little black bag, came hurtling round the corner a few seconds later. Before we entered the building, I gave a few sharp directions to the squadron leaders: this was a high security matter; no police, no Press, no curious sightseers; two men standing by the cars, one on guard with the concierge, three to accompany Steffi and myself to the fifth floor. Then we rang the bell.

The porter, bleary-eyed and grumbling opened the door, and immediately launched into a babble of questions. We flashed our cards, left him still babbling and took the elevator to the fifth floor. Bandinelli's office was in darkness, the door was closed but unlocked. I entered first and switched on the lights.

The scene was curiously tranquil. Doctor Bandinelli lay stretched on a leather settee. Agent Giampiero Calvi was seated in a chair behind the desk, head pillowed in his arms. On the desk beside him was a Moravia novel, a loaded pistol, two ham rolls, a hard-boiled egg and a flask of coffee. The coffee was warm. The two men were stone-cold. Old Steffi sniffed the air, made a brief examination of the bodies and pronounced his verdict.

'Dead. Cyanic acid gas. Pistol or pressure-pack.'

I examined the safe. The seals were broken, the door was open, the Pantaleone papers gone. The immediate temptation was to plunge into action; forensic procedure, interrogation of witnesses, all the rest of it. It was a temptation hard to resist for any man with police training, but in my work it could be fatal to a sensitive project. I picked up the phone and called the Director's private number. He answered with surprising promptness. I told him:

'. . . We're in trouble. Documents missing and two bundles of dirty linen for immediate disposal–one of them ours.'

'So . . .?'

'As soon as the situation is tidy, I'll report in person!'

'When might that be?'

'Before breakfast, I hope.'

'I'll expect you for breakfast then–the earlier the better.'

Steffi cocked his head and cackled at me, for all the world like an ancient scruffy parrot.

'When everything's tidy! Eh! So now we're in the miracle business!'

The boys from the mobile squadron were fidgeting on their feet, waiting for me to make some decisions. The problem was that every decision carried highly explosive consequences. If I made a big scene with police procedures and interrogations, the Press would come swarming like wasps to a honey-pot. Once they found the Pantaleone papers were involved, they would immediately start asking questions about Pantaleone's death and hasty burial. On the other hand, if we could not interrogate freely, we would be grievously handicapped in reconstructing the events of the evening, and, therefore, in our search for the Pantaleone documents. Besides, there were two bodies to be disposed of in a convincing, if not legal fashion. Steffi was right as usual. Willy-nilly, we were in the miracle business. So it was time to get the ritual started.

The first problem was to get the two bodies out of the building without fuss or comment. I sent Steffi down to question the porter in his own cubby-hole, out of view of the entrance. Steffi's talk would hypnotize a fighting-cock. I counted on having the porter so bemused that he would miss a herd of elephants six feet from his nose.

Next we emptied Bandinelli's pockets and Calvi's as well. The boys of the mobile squadron carried the bodies into the elevator, rode them to the ground floor and bundled them into the waiting cars like a pair of late drunks. One car drove Bandinelli's remains to the casualty department of the Policlinico; the other deposited Calvi at the hospital of the Blue Sisters. In each case the story was the same; the mobile squadron had found a man lying, apparently unconscious, in an alley. They were consigning him to hospital while they pursued inquiries as to his identity. Dead on arrival? Dear me! Then give us a receipt and hold him in the mortuary while we complete our inquiries!

It sounds naïve! Then let me explain that even if your grandmother, with all her documents in her purse, falls sick on the Corso and is carted off to a public hospital by some street samaritan, it may well take you the best part of a week to trace her. We have small talent for administration at the best of times; but our public health service is a mess beyond description. Unless you go to an expensive private clinic, you may find your blood report really belongs to a ballet-mistress and your urine was supplied by a fellow who caught clap in Fregene. So, by all the rules of the game, two unidentified bodies should stay unclaimed until we were ready to deal with them.

While Stefanelli was questioning the porter, I drank Calvi's coffee and ate one of his ham rolls, while I examined the entries in his notebook.

20.00 hrs.	Bandinelli's staff left.
20.30 ,,	Completed indexing of Pantaleone documents. Locked and sealed safe in presence Bandinelli. Signed receipt for papers and keys. Bandinelli left.
21.00 ,,	Telephoned duty-officer H.Q.
21.25 ,,	Office cleaners arrived.
21.55 ,,	Office cleaners left.
22.00 ,,	Telephoned duty-officer H.Q.
23.00 ,,	Telephoned duty-officer H.Q.
23.36 ,,	Made final check of fifth floor.
24.00 ,,	Telephoned duty-officer H.Q.
00.37 ,,	Bandinelli telephoned. He wished pass by office for late night conference with two clients. He explained it as a police matter. He would not disturb me, but would use outer office for conference. Since my instructions referred only to custody of safe and contents, I had no authority to refuse him access to his own office. I agreed.
01.00 ,,	Telephoned duty-officer. Asked him note Bandinelli's request and my decision.

The entries ended at that point. I called the duty-officer myself. He confirmed the entries from his own log. Which left me with a vital question: had Bandinelli come to the office under duress, or had he come as an accomplice who was liquidated when his usefulness was ended? I was still puzzling over it when Steffi came back, cross-grained and unhappy.

The porter knew nothing, had seen no one. He worked strictly by the book and the terms of his contract, which stated that he would remain awake and on duty until midnight or until the cleaners left, whichever was the later. After that he might go to bed. All tenants had pass-keys to the front door. They had free access to their offices at any hour. Non-tenants were refused admission outside office hours unless they were identified as cleaners or contractors.

'. . . So, in fact, Steffi, anyone with a pass-key could bring a whole army into the building after midnight, with no one any the wiser?'

'That's the size of it, Colonel.'

'Where was Bandinelli when he telephoned at thirty-seven minutes after twelve?'

'One way to find out, Colonel. Ring his house.'

I lifted the telephone again and called Bandinelli's villa on the Cassia. The phone rang for a long while and then a very surly male answered:

'Villa Bandinelli! Who is this?'

'Carabinieri. We wish to speak to the Advocate.'

'He's not here.'

'His wife then.'

'The Signora is in Naples.'

'Who are you?'

'De Muro, Major-domo.'

'Where can I find the Advocate?'

'At this hour, God knows!'

'What time did he go out?'

'He hasn't been home since yesterday morning. He telephoned in the evening to say he wouldn't be home for dinner.'

'No idea where he might be?'

'None at all.'

'Thank you. Good morning.'

He did not return the greeting. He hung up in my ear. Steffi grinned.

'No luck?'

'No. His wife's away. He didn't go home for dinner.'

'Which helps your little fiction about an unidentified body.'

'But it doesn't tell me who did the killing and took the documents.'

'Does it matter, Colonel?'

'For God's sake, Steffi! What sort of question is that?'

'A very good one I thought, Colonel. Look! This is a professional job, neat, tranquil, simple as walking. Which do you want? The liquidators or the people who paid them? This is not police work, friend; it's intelligence analysis, an exercise in pure reason. Start from the bottom and you'll be wandering round the sewers six months from now. Start from the top and you halve the work and double your chances–believe me!'

'I do believe you, Steffi. But sometime in the next three hours I have to face the Director. What do I offer him?'

'Human sacrifice! . . .' Steffi favoured me with a gallows grin. 'So why don't you pour me some coffee, Colonel, and let's discuss the candidates.'

The Director's apartment was the top floor of a sixteenth-century palace just off the Via della Scrofa. The revenues from the rest of the palace–dwellings and fashionable shops–would keep him in kingly state for a lifetime. His paintings, sculptures and objects of virtue were a fortune in themselves. His library was a minor treasure-house of rare editions, specialist studies and exotic poetry in a variety of languages. The Director was an exotic himself, resplendent in a brocaded dressing-gown, attended by a wiry Sicilian who was both butler and bodyguard. At six in the morning, grubby, unshaven and very unsure of myself, I was in no mood to appreciate the dramatic effect.

The Director offered me a cool welcome, and an English breakfast—tea, toast, scrambled eggs and marmalade. I asked for coffee and pastry. The Director conceded the point with a smile and then proceeded to make a few of his own.

'You knew the Pantaleone papers were important, Colonel. Why did you not take immediate possession of them?'

'I needed a judicial order. To get it, I would have had to appear against Bandinelli in the presence of a judge. I thought it unwise.'

'So, you made an arrangement which resulted in the death of agent Calvi and of Bandinelli himself?'

'Yes.'

'Any excuses?'

'No excuse. An explanation. I was trying to scare Bandinelli into further revelations. I thought the security risk was minimal. In the event, I was wrong.'

'Who else knows the facts at this moment?'

'Only SID. We had the bodies out and the place cleaned up by four this morning. We're in a holding situation for a few days at least.'

'But we don't know who has the Pantaleone papers?'

'No.'

'So, let's guess, Colonel. Local group or foreign?'

'Local, I think.'

'Right wing or Left?'

'Right.'

'Why?'

'The Left have a lot of dirt they haven't published yet. The Right have a lot of dirt they want to bury—I think last night was a funeral party.'

'You don't convince me, Colonel.'

'I'm not trying to convince you, sir. I'm telling you what I believe. If you're thinking of Woodpecker and his network, forget him. I had him pulled in at four this morning. I worked on him myself, for nearly two hours, before I came to see you. I know what his brief is. Assassination is not part of it. Besides, he's been under constant surveillance and he doesn't have the resources or contacts to set up a job like this in half a day. Now, let's look at the other side of the coin. Bandinelli was on the Right wing. He served Pantaleone. He could have sold out to a successor. . . .'

'And been killed for his pains?'

'That, too.'

'Name me a possible successor.'

'Major-General Marcantonio Leporello.'

For the first time, the Director was shaken and he showed it. He set down his tea-cup with a clatter and sat a long moment staring at me with bleak and hostile eyes. Then he said, quietly:

'I presume you have evidence in support, Colonel?'

'Some. I interviewed the General yesterday at the Hassler Hotel.'

'You what?'

'I interviewed Leporello.'

'In spite of my orders that no action was to be taken with that subject?'

'Yes, sir.'

'And what did you tell him?'

'That he was under surveillance by a foreign network who had tipped him as political candidate for the Right.'

'What else?'

'The whereabouts of the Pantaleone papers.'

'Oh . . . !'

'And the fact that I was acting against direct orders.'

'And what was his reaction to that?'

'He promised to keep the interview secret—and he offered me a job on his own staff.'

'I'm tempted to make you immediately available, Matucci.'

'That's your privilege, sir—and, even from the point of view of the Service, it mightn't be a bad idea.'

'You're bargaining with me, Matucci. I don't like that.'

'And you're threatening me, sir. I don't like that either.'

'You disobey orders and that's dangerous.'

'It was a risk. I took it. I think it paid dividends.'

'It gave you a convenient suspect, nothing more.'

'Something more.'

'What?'

'I've identified the Salamander.'

That brought him up short. He held a piece of buttered toast half-way between the plate and his thin lips. Then he popped it into his mouth and chewed on it pensively. Finally, he said:

'And do you propose to tell me who he is?'

'Yes, sir. If I'm still in the Service at nine o'clock this morning, I'll be keeping an appointment with him. He's the Cavaliere Bruno Manzini. He tells me, and I hope to confirm it from the records, that he is the bastard brother of General Pantaleone.'

'First Leporello, now Manzini. Leporello is your military superior. Manzini is one of the most powerful financiers in Italy. You're flying very high, my friend.'

'And you can shoot me down now, if you choose.'

'I mightn't need to do it. Whoever killed Calvi, could as easily kill you.'

'I know.'

'So, if I let you go on?'

'I want a free hand, and access to the Leporello file.'

'Can I trust you, Matucci?'

'You can, but you'd rather not.'

'Do you trust me?'

'With reservations, yes.'

'What reservations?'

'You're the Director. I know what you are commissioned to do. What I don't know is how you interpret your commission and to what secret ends you direct the activities of SID.'

'Do you have any right to know?'

'Legally, I suppose not. I'm a serving officer, I do as I'm told . . . *basta!* Personally? That's another matter. If you'd asked me the same question a week ago, I'd have given you a nice, complaisant answer: bless me father, lead me in the way of salvation and look after my pension rights! This morning, it's different. I'm middle-aged and tired and I haven't had a shave and I lost a good lad because I didn't think straight. So, I don't want to be manipulated any more. I want to know where I'm being directed and why—and if I don't like it, I'll resign my job with you and go back to desk duty or police work.'

The Director drank the last of his tea and dabbed at his lips with a linen napkin. He pushed back his chair, walked to the window and stood a long time looking out at the tumbled roof-tops of Rome, gold and umber and crimson in the early light. When he turned, the light was at his back and the contours of his face were in shadow. He began to talk, quietly at first, then with mounting passion and eloquence.

'You are a presumptuous fellow, Colonel. Yet, I can forgive you, because I, also, presume too much and too often. I presume on wealth and family and myself as a product of all the alliances and misalliances of our history. In a way, I am yesterday's man; but then Italy is yesterday's country as well as today's. We build our houses on tombs. We built our prosperity on ruins and papal monuments and the genius of our ancient dead. Our law is an idiot confusion of Justinian, the Codex Canonicus, Napoleon, Mussolini and the founding fathers of the United States. Our nobility is a hodge-podge of ancient families and the last upstarts ennobled by the House of Savoy. In politics, we are Marxists, Monarchists, Socialists, Liberals, Fascists, Christian Democrats—opportunists all! We have the best business men and the worst bureaucrats in the world. We're a nation of anti-clericals and we've manipulated the Catholic Church for centuries. We shout federal republican democracy—yet every province is a separate continent. A man's country is whatever miserable village he was born in. . . . Now you, my dear Colonel, demand that I should tell you to what I am committed and to what end I direct the Defence Information Service. . . . Let me turn the question then and ask you where you would walk if you were in my shoes—as you may be one day if you are cool enough and clever enough and understand the price to be paid? . . . No answer? Then, here is mine. Our problems will not be solved by an election, by a coalition of parties, by the victory of one system over another. We are Mediterranean men, Colonel. We are, whether we like it or not, a mongrel breed of Greek and Latin and Phoenician and Arab and Iberian Celt and Viking and Visigoth and the Huns of Attila. We live, as we have lived for centuries, in a precarious balance of tribal and family interests. When the balance tips, ever so slightly, we are plunged into disorder and civil strife. When the strife becomes too bloody for us all, we cry halt and beg to be delivered—by the Church, by a personal saviour—or, most pathetically of all, by politicians and bureaucrats who are as bloodied and confused as we are ourselves. The Spaniards and the Greeks and the Portuguese turned to dictators. The Arabs threw out the Colonial powers and replaced them with local autocrats. We Italians have tried one dictator and made a shambles of democracy. Now, we don't know what we want. Me? I don't know what the people want. I can't even judge what they will tolerate. So, I manipulate information and situations to hold things in balance as long as I can. I don't want dictatorship. I don't want Marxism. I'm sure the kind of democracy we have is too unstable to last. But, come one or the other, I'll try to make it as tolerable as I can. Politics is the art of the possible. Mediterranean politics is the art of the impossible and I understand it better than most. You're worried about Leporello, but you have no evidence against him and I'm not going to antagonize him just at a moment when we may need him. You're worried about your Salamander, who, I confess, makes no sense to me at all just now. You want a free investigation? I'll give it to you, but, understand me, Matucci, when I move, in whatever gambit, I am king of the board and you are a pawn. Take it or leave it.'

I gave him the answer without a second's hesitation.

'I'll take it. And I'll give you an honest report. If I don't like what you do, I'll argue it face to face. If we don't agree, I'll fight you; but I'll do it in the open.'

'It's a rash promise, Matucci. I won't hold you to it. If ever you fight me, you'll have to lie like a whore and cheat like a card-sharp, just to save your skin. . . . By the way, you can't meet Manzini looking like that. My valet will show you to the guest-room and find you a razor and a clean shirt.'

At eight o'clock on the same spring morning, with an hour to kill before my meeting with Manzini, I rejoined old Stefanelli as he strolled whistling down the Spanish Steps. The sun was bright; the air was crisp; every tread of the staircase blossomed with girls. I had been up all night, but I felt miraculously refreshed and I could see the sap rising even in Steffi's withered trunk.

This was the best of Rome: the smell of dust and women and new bread and fresh violets; the clatter of the gossips on their way to market, the honk of taxis, the solemn parade of tourists, pale from the mists of Denmark and High Germany; the tumble of cupolas and campaniles and russet roofs crowned with clothes-lines and television antennae. This was the fountain of youth that gave a man fantasies, put birds in his head and wings on his bunioned feet.

At the foot of the steps, we paused so that Steffi could buy himself a carnation for his button-hole, then we turned into Babington's Tea Rooms, where Steffi had promised to buy Solimbene tea and English muffins. Solimbene was a pedant but an amiable one, who affected small eccentricities—velvet smoking jackets, fin-de-siècle cravats, gold fob-seals and eyeglasses on a ribbon of watered silk. He also nourished a passion for red-headed women and English manners, though he had never in his life travelled further than Paris.

We found him enthroned in a corner of the tea-room, clasping the hand of a blonde waitress and pouring out his passion in execrable German. He let her go, reluctantly, and turned the flood of his eloquence on Steffi:

'My dear colleague! My brother in arms and in art! I have revelations for you, Steffi mine! Revelations, mysteries and scandals. Don't laugh! Your trade is horrible—blood and dust and excrement and clothing from the dead. Me? I live with fairy-tales—gryphons rampant and unicorns couchant, allocamels and lioncels and dancing dolphins and magical swords in disembodied hands. . . . But, when you need a simple little fact, who finds it? Me! Solimbene, the herald! . . . Yes, my love, my dove, tea, muffins and English marmalade. Coffee is a madman's drink. It produces dyspepsia and dries out the kidneys. . . . Now, my friends, we begin with this.' He laid the salamander card on the table and stabbed at it with a cake-fork. '. . . Which is not heraldry at all, but calligraphy, a monkish art. Even the crown is corrupted. However, notwithstanding, *mutatis mutandis*, I was prepared to accept an heraldic origin. Result? I found myself chasing salamanders across every escutcheon in Europe. Insanity! Total insanity! Finally, I reduced the number of possibles to five. Insanity again!' He spread a set of glossy photographs on the table and annotated them. 'These two families are extinct. The only survivor of this one is a monk in the Certosa of Florence. Which leaves us, my dear friends, with this last photograph. I found it listed in our files under *"curiosa* and *exotica"*. There is your salamander in the first and fourth quarterings; the supporters are lions rampant. It's beautifully executed, as you can see. Only one problem: it is not a coat of arms at all. It is an artist's conceit. It belongs to no known family.'

Stefanelli shrugged and spread his hands in a Levantine gesture.

'So, it's beautiful and it means nothing. Why show it to us?'

'Oh, it does mean something, dear colleague. It means a great deal—fraud, fakery and scandals juicy as a beefsteak. How old are you, Steffi?'

'None of your business.'

'Come now, don't be touchy. I'm doing you a favour.'

'No favour, you're being very well paid—provided the Cononel here authorizes the invoice. Now, let's see the meat in the sandwich.'

The waitress came back with tea and muffins and Solimbene detained her again with compliments and cajolery. Then, when she whisked herself away, he began another comedy with notebook and eyeglasses and a new flourish of rhetoric.

'In the year of Our Lord, nineteen hundred and ten, when Pius X was gloriously reigning, and you, dear Steffi, were still wet behind the ears, there lived not a stone's throw from here a very notable lady of fashion, who called herself the Countess Salamandra. She entertained only the noble and the wealthy—among them a certain opera singer, who, as he left her house early one morning, was shot and killed, presumably, by a jealous rival. There was, of course, a scandal. The lady, assisted by some of her clients, fled the country and went to live in Nice. Police inquiries revealed that the Countess Salamandra was not a countess at all, but a young Scots lady named Anne Mackenzie, who, having fallen from grace in a noble bed, decided to enrich herself by the same means. . . . How's that for a prelude, Colonel? Will you authorize the invoice now? Or are you bored already?'

'Go on! Go on, man!'

'This coat of arms was used by the Countess Salamandra. She had caused it to be forged for professional purposes.'

'Is that all?'

'All?' Solimbene was outraged. 'My dear Colonel, when I do a job, I do it properly. I have tramped this city in your service. I have burrowed like a badger into the files of Central Registry. I have spent hours of my life with withered old dowagers, who have almost, but not quite, cured me of concupiscence. Miss Anne Mackenzie was once in service with the Count Massimo Pantaleone, as nurse and governess to his daughters. She became pregnant to the old Count and left his service. In August 1900, she married one Luca Salamandra, described in the marrage certificate as a circus performer, who, two days after the wedding, fell from a high-wire and broke his neck. The child, a boy, was born a week after his demise and was baptized Massimo Salamandra in the Capuchin church in the Via delle Zoccolette. In proof of which I offer certificates of marriage and birth and baptism, all dated 1900. In October of the same year, a lady calling herself the Countess Salamandra set herself up in the Palazzo Cherubini, just down the road here, and began to prepare her entry into Roman society. It is a reasonable guess, supported by the gossip of my dowagers, that she was financed in her venture by a generous allowance paid by old Count Pantaleone.'

'And what happened to the boy?'

'His mother took him with her when she fled to Nice. After that, no record until 1923, when a young man named Massimo Salamandra presented himself before a tribunal in Rome and applied to change his name to Bruno Manzini. The tribunal approved the application and the transaction was entered at the Central Registry in Rome–which is where I found it yesterday. . . . Now, gentlemen, do I get my money?'

I didn't tell him; but at that moment he could have tripled the price without a murmur from me. When you are playing against the house it always pays to have a spare ace in your sleeve. Even that doesn't help, of course, when the rest of the deck is stacked against you.

The Cavaliere Bruno Manzini received me in a suite large enough to house a division of infantry and still leave room for the camp followers. His morning face was benign. His manners impeccable. He was even solicitous for my health.

'You look a little peaked this morning, Colonel. A late night?'

'A long one, Cavaliere. I haven't been to bed yet.'

'My dear fellow! Had I known, we could have made a later appointment.'

'Kind of you, but I need, desperately, whatever information you can give me.'

'Let's save time then. How much do you know already?'

'That your mother was one Anne Mackenzie, some-time nurse to the Pantaleone family. That you are the son of her union with the old Count. That you were baptized Massimo Salamandra in Rome in 1900. That your mother, for reasons of business, adopted a spurious title and a coat-of-arms to match it. The device of the salamander appears in that coat-of-arms. In 1923 you changed your name to Bruno Manzini . . .'

'And how did you come by all that information?'

'Some luck, some heraldry, and the Central Registry.'

'What else can you tell me?'

'That depends, Cavaliere, on how much you are prepared to tell me.'

'Anything you wish to know.'

'Do you mean that?'

'I would not say it otherwise.'

'Then, why were you blackmailing your brother?'

'Blackmail? My dear Matucci, since the war I have become inordinately rich. I could have bought and sold him twenty times over. I was threatening him with public disgrace! If he had persisted in these crazy politics of his, I should have exposed him without mercy.'

'Instead you killed him.'

'I beg your pardon?'

'He died of an overdose of drugs–self-administered.'

'A fact which was not made public. Why?'

'Bluntly, Cavaliere, for fear of a political scandal which might lead to civil disorder.'

'Now I could make the scandal.'

'Will you?'

'No. It would defeat my purpose; which is the same as yours. To avoid political disruption and civil violence.'

'Next question then. If the document you sent your brother fell into other hands, what use could be made of it?'

'Now that he is dead, very little. Oh a newspaper could publish it and make a ten-day wonder, but politically—in my view at least—it would be a damp fire-cracker. Why do you ask?'

'Because all the Pantaleone papers were stolen last night from the offices of Doctor Sergio Bandinelli. Bandinelli and one of our agents were murdered.'

'There was no news of this in the Press.'

'Nor will there be, unless you choose to release it.'

He stared at me in blank disbelief. Then he shook his head like a man waking from a dream and wondering where he was. He pieced out the next words, slowly, as if they were quite inadequate to express his thought.

'I do not believe . . . I cannot believe . . . that any intelligent man would . . . would be so rash as to commit himself to a stranger in this way. You have put an atomic bomb into my hands, Colonel. I could blow up the country with it. . . . My God, don't you see! You, a serving officer, have just admitted to falsifying the records of a suicide and . . . concealing two murders! How do you know that I will not lift this telephone and call the Press—some of which I own—and splash the news all over the world?'

'I don't know, Cavaliere. I'm gambling.'

'Then you're a madman.'

'Only if you lift the telephone. If you don't, if you place your knowledge at my disposal, then I'm the sanest man in Rome.'

'But you have no guarantees have you?'

'In this dog's world, Cavaliere, there are no guarantees and you know it. The law is no more than a thin crust over a nest of soldier ants. Even death is big business now—international business. You want someone dead in Israel, you fly the killers in from Japan. You want a murder in Venice, you phone London or Munich and your assassin arrives the next day. Hijack an airliner? Simple. You let the contract in New York, embark your people in Stockholm, fly the damn thing to Libya if it suits you. . . . I have to trust someone. Let's say I trust you because you despise the trade I'm in and make no secret of it. . . . Now, can we go on?'

'You'll check my answers, of course?'

'As if I were the Grand Inquisitor himself.'

'That's better. Please begin.'

'Cavaliere, what would you expect to find in the Pantaleone papers that would be worth two lives and the risk of the crime itself?'

He pondered that for a long while before he answered:

'In the family papers themselves, very little. There would be title-deeds, business transactions, wills, settlements, old correspondence, some of it scandalous perhaps, but of interest only to the social historian. In my brother's personal papers . . .? Well, let's think of him as a political soldier, playing a power-game. He would assemble dossiers on friends and enemies alike. Some of those might be very valuable either to the subjects themselves or to political rivals. But murder . . . ? Somehow I don't see it. You're an expert on dossiers. I use them, too, in business. But, truly, how important are they? Everybody in Italy knows a little dirt—or a lot—about the man next door. We're all gossips and scandalmongers, and what we don't know, we invent. It's a social disease, tolerable only because it's endemic—like syphilis among the Cossacks. Our sexual morals are special, our social ethics non-existent. After the Fascists and the war, and the occupation and the scrabble for world trade and the late history of the Vatican and all the chicanery of

our recent politics, who has clean hands anyway? No matter what my
brother wrote in his notebooks, you can safely wager twenty other people
knew it before he did. I'm not saying the stuff couldn't be valuable. . . . But
the murder of a lawyer and a Government agent . . . ? No, I can't see it.
There must be something else.'

'For example . . . ?'

'Plans, more likely. The tactics and strategy of a *colpo di stato*. The
political and military organization that must be ready to take over at a
moment's notice. The list of participants, active and passive. The location
of arms, the disposition of available forces in sympathy with the plotters.
Even your own service might do murder for such things.'

'In this case they didn't.'

'So now, Matucci, we are at the heart of the artichoke. We have to decide
whether or no we can trust each other. Who makes the next move?'

'It's your turn, Cavaliere!'

'Before you arrived your Director telephoned me.'

You know that strange sensation of disembodiment that comes in
moments of shock. You are suddenly outside yourself, looking at the antics
of a body that doesn't belong to you. I had it then. I watched myself
tumbling into the trap which opened under my unwary feet. Then the
hallucination passed and I was back in my own skin, writhing under the
irony of my situation. Manzini watched me, grave and unsmiling. He went
on:

'You are angry. You have a right to be. I know your Director very well.
He is sometimes too clever for his own good and always as vain as Lucifer.
He wanted to display his cleverness to me and also, I think, to teach you a
lesson for some delinquency.'

'That's true, at least. Now what, Cavaliere?'

'Now I am going to give you a piece of information which your Director
does not yet possess. At eight o'clock yesterday evening, I signed, on behalf
of one of my companies, a procurement contract with the Government. The
contract calls for the urgent supply of large quantities of riot-control
equipment. The specifications were drawn up by Major-General Marcantonio Leporello; and the equipment will be used by troops under his
command. . . . I have drawn certain conclusions from this situation. You
may care to hear them.'

'Please . . . !'

'If I were a new Fascist or an old one, if I were looking for a new leader, I
should be very ready to bargain with Marcantonio Leporello.'

'Perhaps the bargain has already been struck.'

'No, Colonel. Leporello was waiting on the contract which would put
fire-power and bargaining power into his hands. He was waiting for
something else, too.'

'What?'

'He would not commit himself until the Pantaleone papers were safe in
his own hands.'

'And he has them now?'

'I believe so.'

'It seems to me, Cavaliere, you're something more than a business man.'

'I'm a salamander, Colonel—a perennial survivor. You?'

'A servant of the State. Except that I'm not sure what the State is
today—and I'm scared of what it may be tomorrow.'

'That makes us allies.'

'In a lopsided league.'

'That frightens you?'

'Yes, Cavaliere, it frightens me.'

'Then, let me offer you a small reassurance. I shall write you a name and an address. If you go there you will hear part of the truth about me. If it satisfies you, you will come to see me in Bologna. If it doesn't, you will still be in profit.'

He took a business card from his wallet, wrote a name and address on the back of it and handed it to me. The name was Raquela Rabin; the address, a street near the Theatre of Marcellus. He made no explanation. I did not ask for one. We shook hands, he led me to the door and held it open for me.

'One other thing, Colonel. . . .'

'Yes?'

'Advice from an old campaigner. Always walk close to the wall, and sleep with one eye open. . . . I hope we meet again soon.'

'I hope so, too, Cavaliere. Good day!'

When I hit the street, it was exactly ten o'clock. The bells of Santa Susanna were tolling the hour; the traffic made a dramatic discord, the vast indifference of the city was a blow in the face. All of a sudden I was maudlin tired, rocking on my feet. I climbed into my car and drove, in a perilous daze, all the way to Parioli. I hammered on Lili's door and almost fell into her arms when she opened it herself. She asked no questions but led me by the hand into the bedroom and helped me to undress. I don't know what I said or tried to say; but she hushed me like a child and drew the covers over me and let me collapse into sleep.

That sleep was a journey into the underworld, so deep I could not hope to escape from the nightmares that beset me: I was harried by faceless huntsmen, bayed through dark tunnels, stood naked in a desert under the eyes of a hundred accusers, I was arraigned in a graveyard by dead men, I was hung by the thumbs in my own interrogation room, while a masked executioner held a vial of poison under my nose. I screamed as he crushed it in his giant fingers; and woke, sweating and trembling, with the sheets knotted about me like a shroud.

The smell of my own body offended me. It was the odour of fear, dammed up too long, souring the body juices, spilt like the voidings of an animal for the predators to follow. I was marked now—by the Director as an intransigent, by Leporello as a man who must be bought or seduced, by Manzini as a collaborator, useful one moment, dispensable at the twitch of an eyebrow. I was in danger because I knew too much. I was exposed because I could do too little. I was a silly goat tethered to attract the tiger—and if the tiger did not come, the marksman in the tree could pick me off at a whim.

Lili could be picked off, too: by her own people, if not mine. I had pulled in Woodpecker. His network was in disorder. Lili was compromised. In the code of the trade she was marked for liquidation. If the assassins did not get her, the Director would order her arrested, if only to teach me a lesson. I looked at my watch. Three o'clock. Siesta time still. I lifted the bedside phone and called Stefanelli's house.

'Steffi? Matucci!'

'Don't you ever sleep, for God's sake?'

'Steffi, the roof's falling in. Have you got a spare room?'

'For you?'

'No. To store a very sensitive package.'

'Now sensitive?'

'It has to be kept away from heat and light until other storage is arranged.'

'*Porca miseria!* I was up all night with you. I had breakfast with you. I've had two hours of bad sleep and I'm still in my pyjamas!'

'Steffi–the package may explode and blow my head off!'

'Eh-Eh-Eh . . . ! Where do I collect it?'

'I'll bring it to you. Go back to sleep.'

'Thank you for nothing, dear friend.'

I had just put the phone down when Lili came in, frowning and solicitous.

'I thought you were talking in your sleep. Earlier you were shouting and groaning.'

'I had bad dreams, Lili.'

'You look like a bad dream yourself. What happened after you left me last night?'

'Don't ask. Just listen to me.'

'But . . .'

'Lili, it's condition red for you. I want to try to get you out of the country into Switzerland. That needs time and planning. So, I'm taking you to a safe house. You stay there until I'm ready to move you. Yes or no?'

I felt the sudden tension in her hands; saw the suspicion in her eyes.

'If I say no . . . ?'

'You get killed by your own people or gaoled by mine.'

'I don't believe it. Last night . . .'

'Last night was a million years ago. While you and I were singing the Undressing Song, two men were murdered–one of them mine, the other Pantaleone's lawyer. It's not in the papers because we did some stage-management. I arrested Woodpecker at four this morning. The network is broken. You're compromised. I can't protect you more than a few days; and I'm putting myself at risk to do it.'

'Why?'

'Just to prove to myself I'm not a whore-master. Will that do? You've got fifteen minutes; which is about how long it will take me to shower and dress. After that, you're on your own.'

'Please . . . ! Hold me. I'm frightened.'

'I want you frightened, Lili. I want you to do exactly as I tell you and don't for Christ's sake try to make second guesses. Understand?'

'Yes.'

'Start now. Pack a small overnight bag. Take your jewellery, your cheque books, whatever cash you have in the house.'

At that moment, the doorbell chimed: four musical notes, ominous in the silence. I laid a finger on Lili's lips and whispered:

'The house-keeper?'

'Out. Her day off.'

I rolled out of bed, ridiculous in my nakedness, and crept from the bedroom, through the salon and into the hallway. A letter had been thrust through the letter-box and was lying about a foot from the door. I bent to pick it up and then drew back. This was siesta time. No self-respecting postman would be on the streets at the sacred hour. I went back into the bedroom.

'Lili, do you have a kitchen spatula or anything like that?'

'I think so, why?'

'Get it for me, please.'

While she was rummaging in the kitchen, I dressed. Then, incongruously armed with a fish-slice, I walked back into the hall, lifted the letter by sliding the fish-slice under it and carried it gingerly to the coffee-table in the centre of the salon. The address was typed. The stamp was Italian. But it had not been franked by a post office. I left it there, walked back into the bedroom, snapped at Lili to get the packing done, and telephoned a friend of mine in the security section of Posts and Telegraphs. He gave me the cheerful news that a normal letter-bomb contained enough explosive to kill the man who opened it and maim anyone else in a normal sized room. He promised to have an expert on the doorstep in thirty minutes. I told him I couldn't wait that long. He told me to call the police and put a man on guard until the expert arrived.

I hurried Lili through the packing. We locked the apartment and then, avoiding the elevators, walked down four flights of stairs to the lobby. The porter was sitting at his desk, his nose buried in the *Corriere dello Sport*. The street was lined on both sides with parked vehicles. My own car was jammed beautifully between a Mercedes and a Fiat 600.

I left Lili in the foyer and walked outside. The road was deserted except for a woman walking a dog, an old street cleaner, laboriously pushing a tin can on wheels, and the flower-seller dozing at her booth on the corner. I looked up at the buildings on the opposite side. All the windows were closed, some where shuttered. There was no place for a marksman. I walked back into the building and dialled *Pronto Soccorso,* the police emergency service of the Carabinieri.

Five minutes later a squad car pulled up at the entrance to the apartments and the two-man crew came in at a run. The *brigadiere* was cool and efficient. He would call the explosives squad to handle the letter and to check my car for booby traps. Meantime, if I would give him a deposition ... ? My card convinced him he could wait for it. I needed his car and his driver to deliver the lady and myself to the Excelsior Hotel.

Senz'altro! . . . We took off at speed and he dropped us diagonally opposite the hotel. We waited five minutes window-shopping at Rizzoli's, then took a taxi to the Theatre of Marcellus and walked through the maze of alleys to Steffi's house.

Steffi received us with characteristic flourish. He clucked over Lili, showered her with compliments, insisted on settling her into her room himself and then stormed downstairs to give me the rough edge of his tongue.

'Matucci, you're a madman! That little baggage upstairs is dangerous! When the Director hears of this—and he will, sooner or later—you'll be cooked, screaming, like a lobster. God Almighty! It's a ready-made case to put you away for twenty years: SID Colonel sells out to Polish Agent! I could write the indictment myself, blindfolded. And all this other melodrama—letter-bombs and calling the Carabinieri to defuse your car. Wait till that paper-work starts going the rounds!'

'Steffi, have you got a whisky?'

'For you, hemlock and soda.'

'Then pour me a big one and shut up.'

'Shut up, he says! The next thing you'll be wanting to sleep with the woman under my roof.'

'I might at that, Steffi.'

'Oh, no you don't! This is a good Jewish house. If anybody's going to defile it, it won't be a dumb goy like you. There's your drink.'

'Chin-chin, Steffi.'

'I hope it rots your gullet! . . . Now, can we be serious a minute?'

'I'm serious, Steffi. I'm sweating blood.'

'Good! Sweat a little more for me.'

'Tell me. Who is Raquela Rabin?'

'Will you repeat the question, Colonel?'

'Who is Raquela Rabin?'

'Why do you want to know?'

'I have an introduction. I'd like to know something about her before we meet.'

For a moment he stared at me, blank-faced and hostile; then he sat down heavily on a chair, cupped his hands round the glass and sat staring into the liquor. An old man ravaged by time and history.

'. . . Fifteen came back from Auschwitz, Colonel. Raquela Rabin was the only woman. In the ghetto, when you say her name, you say it with respect–great respect. She did not have to go away; she had powerful protectors. But when the trucks came she was here, standing in the *piazza*, waiting like a daughter of David. She was an artist, Matucci, an angel voice, one of the greatest of her time. When you see her, you will say she is older than I, but she is still only sixty-six. Everything that should not happen to a woman happened to her; but she is still sane and splendid as the evening star. . . . You will be very gentle with her. What she tells you, you will believe without question. You will not mix her in this stinking business of ours. You will not mix her–understand that!'

'Easy, Steffi. . . . Easy!'

'I'll take you to her, because I want you clean when you go in–clean and humble, because this is a great woman. I've done you a favour, Colonel. Your woman–and she is your woman, no?–is under my roof, at my risk. Now you will tell me, who gave you this introduction?'

'Bruno Manzini.'

'Why?'

'He said that if Raquela Rabin spoke well of him I might be prepared to trust him. I need that, Steffi. You warned me once I would be put on the auction block. I'm there now, Steffi. Tomorrow or the next day someone's going to open the bids. They'll be high and tempting. I'm not sure I'll be able to resist them. . . . A wise friend would help. A strong one might lend me courage. I'm running out of it, Steffi, because I don't know what to believe any more. I don't even know who I am.'

He brightened at that, as if I had read him the best news in the world. He cocked his head with that old parrot pose and surveyed me with grudging approval.

'So! History is being made. The *Risorgimento* of Dante Aligheiri Matucci. So you don't know what you are? Who does? But sure as breathing, you'd better see what's being done to you.'

'I see it. I don't understand it.'

'Because you refuse to come to terms with yourself. You don't want to decide what you are–a patriot or a mercenary.'

'Hard words from a friend!'

'True words, because I am your friend.'

'I've seen too many rogues wearing too many bright labels, Steffi.'

'A simple question then. Today you might have been killed. Tomorrow the risk is bigger. Why do you take it? When you stake your life, what are you staking it for—or against?'

'Maybe for a dream, Steffi. . . . I don't know. Maybe against a madness I smell every day in the streets. The land is the centre of it somehow. The vines greening on the terraces, the white hills and the brown stubble and the river sedge with the mist on it. My land! I will not live in it by sufferance and privilege. The people? That's another thing. I hate the crowds that jostle me, the silly functionaries who bedevil me from dawn till dark; but then, I see a woman bursting like a grape with love; I am served by a peasant who says "*Salve!*" and offers me wine and bread and salt as if I were his brother. . . . These are the good things, Steffi, painted on the walls of Etruscan tombs, celebrated in the songs of fishermen. . . . Boh! This is home. And I don't want it trampled by jackboots, or desecrated by mindless mobs. . . . Now, let's leave it, eh?'

'I can leave it, friend. You can't. You're the man who knows the underside of politics, the cogs in the power machine. You have to decide how you will use that knowledge.'

'I'm not paid to use it—only to collect it.'

'You collect it, but you filter it, too. You suppress, you emphasize, you interpret. To what end?'

'For Christ's sake, what do we all want? A quiet life. Some dignity in our living and dying.'

'Not enough! Not half enough! Look . . . !'

'Be quiet, old man!' Lili challenged him from the doorway, cold and angry. 'Let him find his own answers in his own time.'

'He has no time.' Steffi was brusque and brutal. 'He robbed himself, when he gave it to you.'

'I am here to give it back. May I sit down, please?'

Steffi pointed to the chair and she sat down between us. She laid her palms flat on the table as if to hold herself erect and in command. She was silent for a few moments, gathering herself, then she told us:

'You are friends. I am the outsider. I accept to be here because I am afraid. I don't want to be killed. I don't want to spend the rest of my life in a Roman prison. But I am not a beggar. I can pay for what you give me.'

'You were not asked to pay.'

'No; but I will.' She turned to me and laid her hands on mine. 'You are going to be very angry with me, Dante Alighieri.'

'Am I?'

'There's something I haven't told you. I might have told you last night if . . . if things had been different. Then again . . . I might not. We were still bargaining then. This morning, you held my life in your hands. You did not bargain. Neither did your friend.'

'So . . . ?'

'Massimo Pantaleone did not leave all his documents in the bank.'

'Where are the rest?'

'In the villa on Ponza.'

'What are they, Lili?'

'Microfilms and maps.'

'How long have they been there?'

'He took them on our last visit to the villa—a week before he died.'

'But you didn't tell Woodpecker or any of your own people?'

'No.'

'Why not?'

'I had no control over what Woodpecker might do. If he stole the stuff, I was finished. Only Massimo and I could possibly know the hiding-place.'

'Could you describe it to me?'

'No. I would have to take you there.'

'That means new arrangements. You have to wait here while we make them. Steffi, you and I have a visit to make. Don't leave the house, Lili. If there are any callers, don't answer. We'll be back in an hour or so.'

'I may never come back,' said Steffi, mournfully. 'I may drown myself in the Tiber. I do not want to be alive when you try explaining this madness to the Director.'

He did not drown himself. He withdrew, quite deliberately, into his own yesterdays and forced me to withdraw with him, as if it were some rite of passage that I must undergo before I met Raquela Rabin. As we strolled–he would not let me hurry–through the alleys of the old ghetto, he conjured ghosts out of every doorway: old Marco the furniture-maker who whittled a piece of pine into the shape of a fearsome brigand and carved his name on the underside; Ruggiero, the pharmacist, who once made him privy to mysteries: a mummified hand and waters that changed colour when you mixed them; Blasio, the gunsmith, who showed him pistols which had killed five men in duels of honour.

As he talked, his narrative became more vivid, his gestures more ample and exotic. He swept away all traces of the present and planted me firmly in the city of his own childhood. Over there, for instance, was Salamone, called by the folk of the Quarter, Salamone Vecchione. He was so old that he looked like a twin brother to Methuselah, so shrunken that one more year must see him disappear altogether. He wore a long black caftan that was green when the sun shone on it, a little black cap perched on his wispy scalp and a silver chain with a star pendant on his wheezy, hollow bosom. He trundled a barrow from which he sold old prints and books with mildewed bindings and metal tubes with scrolls inside and clay tablets that looked as though birds had walked on them before they were fired in the oven.

The market people were afraid of Salamone and treated him with the exaggerated respect due to a magus or a caster of spells. When he passed they made the sign against the evil eye, and muttered, balefully, about the fire that would consume all Jews and pagans. But to the young Stefanelli, he was like the imp out of a bottle, with a wonder in every pocket.

Not all of Steffi's ghosts were friends. Some were sad traitors; some were nightmare enemies. Luca, the hunch-back, for instance, who sat on his stool outside the hairdresser's and allowed his hump to be touched for a coin. Luca was a police pimp who spied on the ghetto people for the Fascists. Balbo was a ruffian policeman who took tribute from every shopkeeper on his beat and Fra Patrizio was a shave-pate Franciscan who in every sermon railed against the perfidious Jews who crucified the Saviour every day. . . .

'Sometimes,' said Steffi, moodily, 'I would like to forget them all. But God is an ironist who keeps the key to memory in his own hands. . . . Here we are, Colonel. I will present you to Raquela Rabin and then leave. You will come directly to the point with her and not stay too long. She is very frail.'

She was frail indeed, white-haired, pale as milk, almost transparent, so that you felt the next *scirocco* might blow her away. Only her eyes were alive, dark and lustrous, and strangely pitying. She sat erect and calm, listening in silence while I explained who I was and why I had come. When I had finished, she seemed to lapse into meditation like an ancient pythoness waiting for the spirit of divination to animate her. I felt oddly diminished–an ignorant neophyte in the presence of a woman who had seen and suffered everything. Even when she spoke–and she was very gentle with me–there was a hieratic quality in her tone that diminished me still further.

'Do you know why Bruno sent you to me?'

'No, Madam.'

'We were lovers for a long time. Not happy lovers always, because I was famous and courted and Bruno was haunted by his own past: a mother who was a once famous courtesan, a father who lavished money on him, but was never prepared to acknowledge him. But the love was there. It is still there.'

'Even though you were taken; and he stayed.'

'We had parted long before. I went of my own free will. He stayed to fight against those who had taken me. He is still fighting.'

'How?'

'He is a strange man. He believes in forgiving. He does not believe in forgetting.'

'Is there a difference?'

'He thinks so.'

'You?'

'I accept what is: that I am alive and others are dead; that I cannot change it; that people must forget because they cannot bear to remember.'

'Can I trust Bruno Manzini?'

'To be what he is, yes.'

'What is he, Madam?'

'A man who has built himself, cell by cell, from nothing. . . . He is very strong, very faithful. What he promises he will do, however much it costs him. Each year, on the anniversary of the Black Sabbath, he sends me a card. In the right-hand drawer of the desk you will find a folder. Please pass it to me.'

The folder was of tooled leather made by a Florentine craftsman. On the cover, embossed in gold, was a Star of David. I handed it to her. She spread it open on her knees, took out the cards and handed them to me. The cards were identical with that which I had found in Pantaleone's bedroom. Only the inscriptions were different.

Hans Helmut Ziegler
Sao Paolo–3 January 1968

Emmanuele Salatri
London–18 August 1971

Franziskus Loeffler
Oberalp, Austria

'What do these mean, Madam?'

'They are the names of men connected, each in his own way, with what happened to me and to others in 1943. I have fifteen so far. There are nine to come. Bruno Manzini traced them all. A labour of years, because they were spread all over the world. When he traced them, he sent each man a card and a dossier on his past.'

'What do the dates mean?'

'The days on which they died.'

'Who killed them?'

'They killed themselves.'

'There is no date on this one.'

'He is still alive. . . .'

'The difference?'

'Bruno told me that this was the best gift of all–a man who had found a way to live honourably with himself. I was very content to know that.'

'Are you happy with Bruno Manzini–a man who plays God?'

'He does not see it that way.'

'How then?'

'He says that every man must be allowed to judge himself; but he must not be allowed to bury the evidence.'

'And you, Madam?'

'I agree with him, Colonel. I gave evidence at Nuremberg–for and against those in the dock. I hate no one now. I am afraid of nothing. But the terror has come again–in Vietnam, in Brazil, in Africa, here in Europe. Is not that why you have come to me; because you, too, are afraid?'

'Yes, Madam, I am very much afraid.'

'Then trust my Bruno, but not blindly, because then he would have no respect for you. Argue with him, fight him, friend to friend. You may not convince him; you may even end as adversaries; but he will never, never betray you. . . .'

'Thank you, Madam.'

'Thank you for coming. I wish peace on your house and in your heart.'

I was grateful for the blessing; but I walked out into the sunlight a very pensive man. A new conviction was crystallizing out of the murky fluid of my own thoughts. There was no cure for the human condition because every man read the present and plotted the future in the light of his own past. There was no such thing as a clean start, because no one truly forgave and no one wholly forgot. In the end, the folk memory betrayed us all. The wrongs of the fathers were revenged on the children. I understood Manzini and his cold conviction that, even in exile, the tyrants should not be allowed to flourish. I understood the Director and his willingness to settle for a balance, however precarious. I understood Leporello and his fanatic belief that order at any price was cheaper than chaos. The only person I did not understand was myself. . . .

On the way back to Stefanelli's, I stopped in a bar and made a telephone call to Manzini at the Grand Hotel. Our conversation was brief.

'Cavaliere, I have just spoken with Raquela Rabin.'

'And . . . ?'

'I am very glad we met. I should like to see you as soon as possible.'

'I leave for Bologna in half an hour. I am happy to receive you there at any time. When may I expect to see you?'

'In two or three days at the latest. Sooner if I can make it.'

'Good! What is your own situation?'

'Difficult. It may improve soon. I hope so, anyway.'

'Good luck then!'

His wish must have had some potency because when I called the Director, his aide told me he had been called to an urgent conference at the Ministry. Was there a message? None that I could deliver safely on an open line. He should tell the Director that there were new developments in my current investigation and that I would be out of contact for forty-eight hours. I was only putting off the bad day; but if I could get to Ponza and lay my hands on the rest of the Pantaleone files, I might still cheat the headsman.

I was faced now with a problem in space and time. The island of Ponza–which is not my favourite place in all the world–lies about sixty-five kilometres south-west of Gaeta. Legend says Pontius Pilate was born there. The Fascists used it as a place of exile for political prisoners. After the war, islands being scarce and getting scarcer in the twentieth century, people started to buy land and build villas on the slopes and around the shore line. The island is served by ferries from Anzio, Formia and Naples, but whichever way you choose, it still means a road journey from Rome and a three or four hour sea-trip, which in rough weather is a purgatory. At all costs I wanted to avoid using public transport, and to cut the time of the operation to a minimum. If the Director decided to send out a panic call for me, I would be as conspicuous as a wart on the Mona Lisa.

Besides, there was another and more sinister possibility. The papers, stolen from Bandinelli's office were now in the hands of persons unknown. By now it would be clear that the codex was incomplete. Conclusion: the hunters would be on the prowl again and by simple logic they must come back, sooner or later, to Lili Anders and to the villa which she had shared with Pantaleone. Postscript to the conclusion: I needed help in a hurry.

By the time I got back to Steffi's house, it was five-thirty. I put through a priority call to a certain Colonel Carl Malinowski at NATO headquarters in Naples. Malinowski is an agreeable American–sometimes too agreeable for his own good. Two years ago I managed to prise him out of an embarrassing situation which involved his Neapolitan girl-friend and a Russian agent operating in the naval dock areas. Malinowski owed me a favour. I needed it now, in the shape of the big Baglietto, which he used for drinking parties and seduction and which could do twenty-five knots in any reasonable sea.

Malinowski was happy to oblige. He could write himself a leave-pass. He also had a new girl-friend who would appreciate the outing. If we could be at Mergellina docks by first light, he would drive us to the island himself. Better still, if we care to come down to Naples tonight, he would feed us dinner and offer us a bed in his own apartment. The bed was matrimonial size. He presumed it would suit. If it wasn't that sort of party I could sleep on the divan and to hell with me. The rest was easy. I hired a Fiat 130 from a rental agency and by seven in the evening–to Steffi's infinite relief–we were out of Rome and heading south along the *autostrada* to Naples.

I enjoyed that drive; the sudden sense of relief as the city fell away behind us, the dusk gentling the hills of Lazio, the lights pricking out from the mountain farms, the processional sweep of the traffic along the highway, the rise of the yellow moon behind the crags of the Appennines, the brief but grateful privacy of man and woman in a small floating world.

Lili was tense at first, openly resenting my high-handed dealings with her person. I had leaned heavily on the dangers of her situation; but now,

homeless and rootless she could see no hopeful future, and I was in no
position to promise her one. She sat, stiff and withdrawn, as if she could not
bear to be near me. I turned on the radio to a session of Neapolitan music,
and affected to ignore her. After a while, she began to nod; and when I drew
her towards me, she did not resist but laid her head on my shoulder and
dozed, fitfully, until we passed Monte Cassino.

She was calmer then. She sat close and we talked, quietly and
disjointedly, until the mood of the first evening came on us again.

'Know something, Dante Alighieri?'

'What?'

'At this moment we really are *noantri*. I can't go home. You don't know
where you're going.'

'True, my love, true.'

'I like your Steffi.'

'Yes. . . . He's quite a character.'

'He's very fond of you.'

'We understand each other.'

'But he's afraid you'll make wrong decisions, isn't he?'

'I'm afraid too, *bambina*.'

'I hope you don't sell out—to anyone. Once you do, there's no way back. I
know. . . .'

'Why did you come into the game, Lili?'

'Haven't you got that in your dossiers?'

'The how of it—not the real reason.'

'There's a whore in every woman, *caro*, and you know it. Come the low
moment when she's lonely and unloved and the first crow's-feet are
beginning to show, she'll sell, provided the price looks like a gift and the
words are said gently, and tomorrow doesn't look too near. No excuses. No
pity, thank you.'

'Suppose we get you out of the country, what then?'

'I'm a bachelor girl of modest means, in the market for a man.'

'What sort of man?'

'That's a private dream; and I won't have you laugh at it.'

'I wouldn't laugh.'

'What kind of a woman do you want, Dante Alighieri?'

'I've had all kinds, Lili—except the one I'd settle down with and make
children.'

'Aren't you ever lonely?'

'Often. But it's a tolerable condition. At least it has been. . . .'

'Now?'

'I don't like the fellow who lives in my skin.'

'I like him—sometimes.'

'You don't know him very well, Lili.'

'Well enought to put a name to him.'

'What name?'

'*Bufalo Solitario*—the rogue male.'

'Paid to protect the herd.'

'From what? The Marxists, the Fascists, the Monarchists? I don't believe
this "protection", neither do you. You're a political instrument. Any hand
can lift you and use you for any work.'

'Let's talk about something else, eh?'

'If you like. What do you do when you can't bear to be alone. . . . ?

'I go out and play.'

'Like last night in Trastevere?'

'Like that. . . .'

'I wish we didn't have to go to Ponza.'

'So do I.'

'What happens when we come back?'

'It depends on what we find and how well I can hide it. . . . That's Capua over there where Spartacus raised the revolt of the slaves.'

'I know about Spartacus, *caro*. I just hope we have better luck than he did.'

Major Carl Malinowski of the United States Marines was a tonic for our jaded spirits. He was six feet tall, all brawn and muscle, with ham fists and a big laugh and a magnolia drawl which, although I speak tolerable English, was often hard for me to understand. He had an unshakeable conviction that the world was still a Garden of Eden, full of willing Eves and congenial serpents. His apartment, furnished in American style, was a bachelor's paradise, with a view across the Bay, from Vesuvius to Capo di Sorrento, a bewildering liquor cupboard and piped music in every room. His new girl was a Swede, culled from the summer crop of tourists and blooming after the transplant. He took one look at Lili and shouted his approval to the neighbourhood.

'*Bella! Bellissima!* Dante, my boy, your taste's improving. This is a real Southern-style woman! Honey, you be good to this man now. He's the best Eyetalian I known–all heart and sex-urge. Bright, too–though you wouldn't think it to look at him. Helga, why don't you take Lili and get her settled while Dante and I build some drinks.' He clamped an iron fist on my shoulder and steered me to the bar. 'Tell me now, Colonel, sir, is this business or pleasure?'

'Business, Carl.'

'So what do you want me to do?'

'Get us to Ponza, get us back fast.'

'In this weather it's three hours each way–more if the wind freshens. How long do you want to stay?'

'Two hours should do it.'

'We leave at six in the morning, we're back mid-afternoon. Suit you?'

'Fine.'

'Expecting trouble?'

'An outside chance.'

'What's with you and Lili-belle?'

'Some business, some pleasure. Too much of one, not enough of the other.'

'I read you, Colonel, sir. I read you loud and clear. So, tonight we drink Christ's tears, and have ourselves a love-in. Tomorrow we hit the beach at Ponza!'

It was a long night and a merry one. We dined like kings on caviar and beefsteak and Neapolitan ice-cream. We drank two litres of Lacrima Christi and half a bottle of Courvoisier, talked the world to rights and told bawdy stories and sprawled on the rug, drowsing to taped music. Sometime after midnight we paired off and went to bed, and I must tell you there is no bed in all the world more comfortable, more apt for love-making, than a big, brass Neapolitan *letto matrimoniale*.

It was a good night for both of us. We did what pleased us and we pleased each other. We were glad, we were grateful, and, for a while, not solitary. We slept deeply and we did not dream at all. We were awake and enjoying each other again when Malinowski hammered on the door and summoned us to breakfast.

I have told it badly; I might have used the same words for a dozen encounters; because I am—and I say it gratefully—a man who has been fortunate in most of his women. But this time there was a difference, a sense of consequence if not yet of commitment. There was another difference, too: I was disposed to be sentimental afterwards, while Lili would have none of it.

She told me so, bluntly, as we stood together on the after-deck of the Baglietto and watched the green cone of Ischia fade against the dawn.

'*Caro*, sometimes you treat me as if I had no brains at all. I know what's at stake. If the material at the villa is important, it puts power into your hands. You think it will also buy me a free passage out of Italy.'

'I hope it will.'

'And salve your conscience about me.'

'If you like to put it that way.'

'But you won't promise anything?'

'I can't.'

'Nonsense! I don't need you to get me out of Italy, Dante Alighieri.'

'You think you can run the frontier guards yourself? Don't try it, Lili.'

'I wouldn't have to do that. I could hire any fisherman on Ponza to run me into Corsica tomorrow.'

'What are you trying to say, Lili?'

'That you need me, like you need the Pantaleone records, as a bargaining card. Let me go and you rob yourself of power, you castrate yourself. I understand that. I accept it. But, you insult me when you try to dress the thing up like a confidence trick. Your friend Steffi was right. You always refuse to come to terms with yourself. . . . Now can we go inside please? I'm cold.'

It was cold. The wind was freshening from the north-west, whipping up an uncomfortable sea; and Malinowski was driving the boat hard, pitting his helmsman's skill against the yaw of the high-powered craft and the short, tricky chop. We settled ourselves in the saloon and I tried, with a kind of desperation, to salvage the argument and my own pride.

'Let's have it clear, Lili. I made a treaty with you. So far I've honoured it. So far, you're free and protected. Agreed?'

'Agreed.'

'Now you want to change it. You want me to turn a blind eye while you make a run for Corsica.'

'No! I want you to be sure what kind of treaty you are making with other people, and what it will do to you in the end.'

'And why the hell should you care?'

'Poor Dante Alighieri! So many women and you've learnt so little. What a waste!'

'At least I don't have any illusions.'

'Boh! Let's not argue then. You write the script; you say the words; you pull the strings; and when the play's over Lili, the puppet, is packed up in her box. Just so we know, my love.'

'And you said there'd be no blackmail! God!'

'Blackmail involves a threat, doesn't it? How can I threaten you? With the Pantaleone records? You will have those as soon as we reach the villa. With a night in bed? That's the custom of the trade isn't it? With your promise of protection? That's the trade, too–every little policeman plays the same trick at every interrogation. So . . . what frightens you, my brave Colonel, if not yourself?'

'If that's the way you read it–fine! Right or wrong, it doesn't change anything. . . . Let's go up on the bridge.'

'I'd like to be alone for a while.'

'This is business, Lili.'

'At your service, Colonel.'

Malinowski welcomed us with a blue-eyed smile, all health and innocence, and spread on the chart-table a small-scale map of Ponza. On this, Lili identified the site of the villa, a small promontory on the eastern shore of the island. The villa was noted in the Pilot as a landmark for mariners: '. . . a large square building of grey stone, due east of which the pillars and arches of a Roman ruin are clearly visible. In winds W to NW the southern inlet offers fair shelter to small vessels. The bottom is sand and rock with some weed.' I asked Lili:

'If we put in there, can we get to the villa from the beach?'

'Yes. There's a rough cart track that goes up to the ruins.'

Malinowski cut in with a sailor's question.

'If we anchor, we'll have to put down the dinghy and winch it up again. You'll have a wet and uncomfortable ride to the beach. Why don't we moor in the harbour itself and you take a taxi to the villa?'

'Strategy, Carl. In the port we'd be conspicuous. It's out of season. The locals would talk. I'd rather not have that.'

'Clear, Colonel, sir. We anchor.'

'The villa itself, Lili. Any servants?'

'No. Out of season it's closed up. A village family comes in once a week to clean it and turn on the heating for a few hours. But we don't have to go near the villa. What we want is there, in the ruins.'

'Why the ruins?'

'You will see when you get there.'

'Can you overlook the ruins from the house?'

'Only the top of them. Our domain is walled all the way round. The ruins are on Government land, part of the shoreline. The *demanio* line runs here.'

'Better still. Take a look at the chart, Carl. How close in can you anchor?'

'Let's see. . . . For safety, a cable's length.'

'Visible from the house?'

'On the approach, yes. When we're anchored, probably not. I don't understand your problem though. That's public terrain. Anyone can land from the sea. That's one piece of Italian law I do know.'

'I'm not worried about trespass, Carl. Lili owns the villa anyway. Let's say I'm concerned with hostile intruders.'

'Those, Colonel sir, we can take care of very nicely.' He opened the cupboard under the chart-table and brought out an automatic rifle. 'I carry this little baby in case the sharks chase one of my girls while she's swimming bare-ass. So, while you and Lili-belle go ashore, I stand deck watch for hostile intruders. . . . Satisfied?'

'No. I can't have an American officer involved in an Italian domestic drama. So, if you don't mind, I'll take the gun ashore with me.'

'Just as you like. Switch on the radio, will you? We should get the news in a minute and I'd like to catch the weather report afterwards.'

'If you don't want me any more,' said Lili, 'I think I'll lie down in the saloon. I'm feeling a little seasick.'

'You should have told me, Lili-belle. I've got just the thing to . . .'

'No, thank you, Carl. I'll be all right. Excuse me!'

When she left us, Carl grinned and fixed me with a knowing eye.

'Problems, brother? Need a little post-nuptial counselling?'

'As a matter of fact, I do.'

'Okay, tell Uncle Carl.'

'What would you say if I told you Lili was a double-agent working for me and for the Marxists?'

'I'd say half your luck—and forget you told me.'

'And if I told you I might have to toss her in gaol to satisfy my people?'

'I'd say you were in a nasty jam.'

'And if I then asked you to keep her on board and run her up to Corsica out of Italian jurisdiction, what would you say?'

'I would tell you, Colonel sir, that you are my very good friend, and I owe you a big favour which I am now repaying. But I would tell you also that I am a natural-born, dyed-in-the-wool Republican, that I have seen my buddies die in Korea and in Vietnam and I don't much like niggers, though I've learnt to live with 'em, but Commies of any sex or breed I can't abide. And so, if you asked me—and I'm sure you wouldn't—I would have to say no sir, no thanks, no way at all. You do read me, Colonel?'

I read him so clearly I couldn't believe it. For a moment I thought he was joking. He joked about most things. The shock was that he was in deadly earnest. I suppose I had never really believed that a great and vigorous people could survive on such simplistic formulas of faith. But then we Europeans had a much longer and bloodier experience and we were still not half as sceptical as we needed to be. . . . Carl Malinowski held out his hand.

'No hard feelings, eh, Dante?'

'No, Carl.'

'And I'm not saying you're a Red. You know that.'

'Of course.'

'And I'm not judging Lili-belle either. Just ducking the issue you might say.'

'I understand.'

'And I'm still with you against the hostile intruders.'

'Thanks.'

'Now, let's listen to the news, eh?'

The news, read in the bland, euphoric style of R.A.I., was the usual mixture: the tribal feuds of Africa, strikes in England, strikes in Italy, another piece from the Pope on the Italian divorce law, another Italian parliamentary squabble, this time over the allocation of provincial subsidies, and finally, a terse postscript: an Arab employee of the Libyan Embassy in Rome had been shot dead outside his house on the Aventine Hill. The victim was the Roman representative of the Palestine guerrilla organization, Al Fatah. The police were treating the murder as a political crime, probably organized by Israeli agents.

The item made the hair stand up on the nape of my neck. In the SID I was regarded as an expert on Arab-Israel terrorist activities. I had built up our first files on Palestinian guerrillas, resident or active in the Republic. I had

good informants among the Jordanians and the Egyptians. I knew the
director of the Jewish counter-terrorist organization, a cool-eyed Lett, who,
in my view was one of the best intelligence men in the world. Once, in a very
private gathering of experts, I had heard him discourse on the true nature of
terror, both as a political weapon and a social infection.

'As a weapon, it is almost irresistible. In infuses fear and doubt. It
destroys confidence in democratic procedures. It immobilizes police
agencies. It polarizes factions: the young against the old; the have-nots
against the haves; the ignorant against the knowing; the idealists against the
pragmatists. As a social infection it is more deadly than the plague: it
justifies the vilest of remedies, the suspension of human rights, preventive
arrest, cruel and unusual punishment, subornation, torture and legal
murder. The most moral of men, the sanest of governments, is not immune
from the infection. Violence begets violence; blackmailers are paid from the
public treasury; reprisals fall as heavily on the innocent as on the guilty. . . .
You Italians made a hero of a man who hijacked an airliner. When we strike
at an Arab who plants a bomb in Rome, we have to accept that we will waken
all the latent anti-semites in Italy and give a scape-goat to the new Fascists.
Every Marxist beaten in a police cell raises twenty recruits for the
revolution. Every bomb thrown in the streets brings out a new brigade of
riot-police with gas-guns and water-cannon. Every big city has its own
university of terror. And the lessons are circulated from Ulster to the
Udine, from Vietnam to Venezuela, from Rio to Athens to Rome. . . .'

For me, therefore, the murder on the Aventine was more than bad news,
it was a personal disaster. Here I was cruising like a tourist between Naples
and Ponza, in very mixed company, while the Director would be pressing
panic buttons and combing the country for one delinquent expert on
Semitic affairs. If I brought back the Pantaleone papers and Lili Anders, I
might just escape the rack and thumb-screw. If I came back empty-handed,
he would rend me limb from limb and feed me to the lions in the zoo.

For one panic moment I thought of trying to contact him by ship's radio,
at least to report myself on duty. Then I realized that this would only
compound the mistakes of the last two days and broadcast my business to
the whole of the Western Mediterranean. To the devil with it then. He had
given me a free hand. I would nail the brief to his door like Luther's articles;
if he didn't like what he read he could eat it for supper. I rather hoped it
might choke him.

We raised Ponza in a squall of wind and driving rain, and we had to coast
slowly right under the lee of the island before we could make any positive
identification of the promontory and Lili's villa. Even the Pilot book fell
short of its promise. The shelter offered by the inlet was less than fair and
the anchor-hold was dubious at best. There was one small profit. If there
were any watchers in the villa, they would have no better visibility than we
had. Lili and I draped ourselves in oilskins and scrambled into the bobbing
dinghy. Carl handed me the rifle and after the customary struggle to start
the outboard, we motored through a choppy surf to the beach.

The beach was deserted. On the promontory itself there was no sign of
life. The track which led to the ruins was steep and greasy, and at one point
we were scrambling on hands and knees, hauling ourselves upward by
tussocks and the stalks of wild rosemary. By the time we reached the top, I
was breathless and irritable. I was convinced that either Pantaleone was
mad, or Lili had deliberately led me on a fool's errand. I could not, for the

life of me, understand why, with a great fortress of a villa at his disposal, any man would hide valuable documents in a mouldering ruin, on land that didn't even belong to him. I said as much—and heatedly—to Lili, who burst out laughing.

'You look so silly—like a clown in a circus! And that little popgun. What are you going to shoot with it—seagulls?'

She took me by the hand and led me through an archway into the shelter of a vault which had, somehow, withstood the ravages of the centuries. The outer walls were of hewn stone, but the inner ones were of reticulated brickwork thrust upwards and inwards into a shallow dome. The floor was paved with slabs of marble, cracked, discoloured and sagging in places, but still mostly intact. The place smelt of stale droppings and seaspray. Lili threw back the hood of her oilskins and stood, hands on hips, surveying the shadowy interior.

'You think Massimo was crazy? So did I when he brought me here. But think again. The villa is left all winter. Servants poke into everything when the *padrone* is away. Look around. Go on, examine! What do you see?'

The brickwork of the walls revealed nothing. I walked the floor testing for hollow spaces beneath it. Again nothing. Lili stood there grinning at me in triumph.

'See, Dante Alighieri, you are not half so clever as you think you are. And Massimo was not always so stupid as he looked. Watch!'

She moved to a small sunken patch of floor, where the rain, driving in through the archway, had created a puddle, perhaps three or four centimetres deep. She knelt down and with her bare hands prised up a small triangular piece of marble. She held it up for my inspection. It was the size of my palm, coated on the underside with a thick wad of cement.

'Like a bath-plug, eh, Dante? You didn't walk in the puddle, but even if you had, the floor would have sounded solid.'

She plunged her fingers into the aperture and drew out a long aluminium tube such as architects use for plans and specifications. It was sealed at both ends with black adhesive tape. Immediately she removed the tube, the puddle emptied itself into the hole. Lili replaced the marble plug and handed the tube to me.

'It is exactly as we left it. The maps are rolled inside. The microfilms are in small capsules.'

'There's nothing else?'

'Nothing.'

'Let's go. You carry this.'

'Not even a thank you for puppet Lili?'

'Thank you, puppet Lili. Now you follow me until we come to the beach track. Then you go first.'

I released the safety catch on the rifle and made for the entrance to the vault. Half-way to the entrance I stopped to scan the narrow vista framed by the archway. All I could see was the rise of the land, covered with tussocks and boulders and stunted bushes and the lower courses of the wall surrounding the villa domain. So far, so good. I moved closer so that the vista widened and the upper courses of the wall became visible and then the top of it, a layer of cement stuck with fragments of broken glass. Then I heard a shout, amplified and distorted by a loud-hailer.

'You, in there! Come out with your hands up. This is the Carabinieri. I repeat—this is the Carabinieri.'

I turned back to Lili and snatched the tube from her.

'Now listen and understand. Stay close to me. Do nothing, say nothing, unless I tell you. Clear?'

'Clear.'

'We're going out now.'

I threw back the hood of my oilskins and then, holding the rifle and the tube high above my head, I walked through the archway with Lili at my heels. Twenty yards from the entrance, just outside my last field of vision, there were five men, two on one side, three on the other. Four were in uniform and armed with sub-machine guns. The fifth was in civilian clothes and carried the loud-hailer. I recognized him immediately: the freckle-faced red-head, aide to General Leporello. He recognized me, too, and the expression on his face gave me a singular pleasure.

The troops began to close in, guns cocked and ready. The young man followed, a little less confidently. I let them come to within five metres before I halted them in my best parade-ground style. They stopped, looking uncertainly from me to the red-head. Then I told them:

'I will identify myself in proper form. Whoever is in command will check my documents. I am Matucci, Dante Alighieri, Colonel in the Service of Defence Information. The person accompanying me is Anders, Lili, in my custody and assisting me in my investigations. Now, we shall lower our hands, and the officer in command will approach to complete the identification and explain this situation to me.'

The red-head found voice and courage at last. He approached, gave me a tentative salute and presented himself.

'Roditi, Matteo, Captain, aide to Major-General Leporello. May I see your papers please, sir?'

I fished them out from under the oilskins and handed them to him. He made a great play of reading them then handed them back.

'Thank you, sir. The situation, sir, is as follows. I am under orders from General Leporello to maintain surveillance of the Villa Pantaleone and its environs and to inhibit any attempt to remove papers or property of whatsoever kind from the premises. In pursuance of these orders I am empowered to call upon the assistance of local units. That explains the presence of this detachment.'

'May I see those orders please, Captain?'

'Certainly, sir.'

He handed them to me and I took a little longer than I needed to study them. Then I quizzed him, loud enough for the local boys to hear and take note.

'It would appear, Captain, that you have misread these orders.'

'Sir?'

'The orders refer specifically and exclusively to, and I quote, "the villa and the domain dependent thereon which is called the Villa Pantaleone". That's right, isn't it?'

'Yes, sir.'

'You will note that the land on which we are now standing, and the ruins at my back, are outside the domain of the Villa Pantaleone and are, in fact, public property delimited by the *demanio* markers on the land and the low water-mark on the shore. Correct?'

'Correct, sir.'

'Therefore you have exceeded your orders. You have impeded a senior officer of the Service of Defence Information in the discharge of highly secret duties. You have placed him and the person in his custody at considerable risk. One incautious move by any of your troops might have caused a fatal accident. You do see that?'

'Respectfully, I submit the danger was minimal.'

'No doubt that submission will be considered at the proper time and place. Anything else, Captain?'

'I should like a private word with you, sir.'

'Not possible at this moment, Captain. I suggest you return to your duties and leave me to carry out mine.'

'That vessel, sir, in the bay. . . .'

'Has been made available to me by courtesy of our friends and allies in NATO. Further questions?'

'No, sir.'

'My compliments to General Leporello. I shall telephone him on my return to Rome. Dismiss! Come, Miss Anders. Walk in front of me, please.'

It is hard to make a dignified exit with four guns at your back. It is harder still to make it down a slippery goat track in driving rain, carrying a rifle and a long tube of explosive documents. In point of fact, we slid the last thirty feet on our backsides and floundered into the dinghy like seals.

By the time we reached the Baglietto, we were both in shock. I was sweating from every pore and Lili was retching over the side of the dinghy. Helga hauled us inboard and made the dinghy fast. Carl—God bless the Marines!—had the anchor up and was charing seaward at twenty-five knots before I had poured our first brandy. Lili, grey and trembling, lay on the settee while I forced the liquor between her chattering teeth. She stared at me as if I were a stranger.

'Back there . . . they were going to kill us!'

'They didn't, Lili. And they can't touch us now.'

'Not now. But tomorrow, the day after. . . .'

'Finish your drink. Close your eyes. Try to sleep. . . .'

'Who was that man, Roditi . . . ?'

'You heard.'

'I heard. I didn't understand.'

'I'll explain later. Relax now. . . . Relax. . . .'

'I don't know you at all, Dante Alighieri. Your face changes all the time. I can't tell which one is yours.'

'I'm a bad actor. That's all. Trust me, *bambina*.'

'I have to . . . there's no one else.'

'Another drink?'

'I couldn't.'

'Close your eyes. . . . That's better. . . . *Lasci'andare, bambina* . . . let go. Let everything go.'

After a while, she lay quiet and the surge of the sea made her dozy. I poured myself another brandy, stripped the seals from the metal tube and examined the contents: a set of overlay maps on transparent paper, each labelled with the name of a city and references to standard ordnance maps, and half a dozen metal capsules, each containing a spool of microfilm. The maps were easy to interpret. They showed the positions of police posts, military installations, communication centres, traffic control points, military and civilian airfields. The microfilms were impossible to decipher without projection equipment. However, I borrowed the chart enlarger from the bridge and was able to establish that they consisted of documents and letters and nominal rolls, and lists of figures. I had no doubt at all that they supplied the best possible motive for the murders in the Via Sicilia, and were, in fact, the blue-prints of a *colpo di stato*. It would need a team of experts to interpret them accurately, and a very wise statesman to decide how to use them. I sealed them back in their container and went up on the bridge to talk to Carl. I found him poring over his charts while Helga stood wheel-watch. I asked him.

'How much fuel have you got, Carl?'

'Plenty. Why?'

'Enough to get us into Ostia?'

'Ostia! For Chrissake, that wasn't in the schedule at all!'

'I know, Carl. But could you get us there?'

'I could. Would you like to tell me why?'

'Because I've just identified a murderer and we could have been murdered ourselves.'

'The Commies?'

'No, Carl. The other ones.'

'So, we go to Ostia. Take five while I lay me a course.'

'Can you give me an estimated time of arrival?'

'I'll give it to you firm, little brother.'

'Then I'd like to make a ship-to-shore radio call.'

'Can do. Sit tight now, while I play with my slide rule.'

While Carl was doing his arithmetic, I jotted down the coded message which would convey to the Director my immediate needs: a car and an armed escort to meet us at Ostia, an emergency conference immediately on our arrival in Rome, safe lodgings and an agent to guard Lili Anders, until her future was decided. Forty minutes later I had the Director's answer.

'Communication acknowledged. Arrangements agreed.'

We do have code-words for thanks and commendations. He didn't use them. Under the circumstances I could hardly blame him.

In the event, the Director was extremely civil. He was a little frosty at first; but he thawed like an ice-cube in whisky when I handed over the maps and the microfilms and made my first verbal report. He approved, without reserve, my concern for Lili Anders; in proof whereof he countermanded a previous order and lodged her, in state, under a fictional name, at the Grand Hotel. He even changed the guard for a more presentable type who would not detract from the ambience.

He invited me to dinner at his apartment. He commended me for my imagination, my finesse, my courage in risking my career and perhaps my life to conclude an important investigation. He saw good sense in my suspicions of Leporello, although he was not yet ready to pass judgment. He sat with me through a private screening of the microfilms and was sedulous to weigh my opinions of the documents and the personages named therein. He read the maps with me and agreed the major points of my interpretation. At the end of the session, which lasted until after midnight, he ordered fresh coffee, brought out his best brandy and offered me the rewards of virtue.

'This Lili Anders . . . I agree with your submission. She had done us a service. She is no longer a security risk. She could be an embarrassment. Let's get her out of the country–tomorrow.'

'Thank you, sir.'

'Now, let's talk about your own future. How much leave have you accumulated?'

'About four months.'

'I'd like you to take it, now. After you return from leave, I propose to detach you for extended studies with friendly agencies abroad. You will have the best possible introductions, a very flexible brief, and your pay and allowances will be supplemented by a generous grant from the funds of this Service. How does that sound?'

'Like an obituary notice.'

The Director smiled and spread his elegant hands in a gesture of depreciation.

'My dear Matucci! You and I live in an upside-down world. You will be buried for a while but you will not be dead, just enjoying yourself while you wait for resurrection day.'

'No alternatives?'

'There are always alternatives, my friend, but I do not think they would recommend themselves to an intelligent man. I could, for example, retain you on the Leporello investigation; in which case you would be at constant risk, an abrasive element, a prime target for assassination. I could, on the other hand, bow to the pressure which inevitably will be applied, to remove you from the Service altogether and return you to your own Corps of Carabinieri, where you would fall under the direct authority of Major-General Leporello. He knows you for a nuisance. He may consider you a threat.'

'I see what you mean.'

'You see everything except the core of the apple.'

'Which is?'

'You know too much. You lack the authority and—forgive me—the experience to make use of the knowledge.'

'And . . . ?'

'You would not be content as a passive instrument of a complicated and highly variable policy.'

'Also I would not submit to pressure by a murder suspect, however high he stood.'

'And you would be very unwilling to treat with political conspirators, however high they stood.'

'Exactly.'

'So, because I respect you and because I should like to be in a position to recall you at an appropriate moment, I immobilize you. I offer you as a propitiatory victim to the powerful people whose names we know. I buy myself time to deal with them by the classic formula: divide and rule. I told you once before, this is the only course I see as possible for Italy at this moment in history. You would polarize the factions, Matucci. You have already done it.'

'That, too, is a classic formula.'

'And like every formula it has limited application. I am not blaming you, Matucci. On the contrary, since I do not often choose to explain myself, I am paying you a compliment with I believe you merit. . . . Well?'

'I'd like to pay you a compliment, too, sir. I think you're a very civilized man. I couldn't ask for a more stylish funeral.'

'Excellent! More brandy?'

'Thank you.'

'Now, as to details. As from this moment you are officially on vacation for four months, and relieved of all duties and responsibilities in the Service–except one. You will escort Lili Anders to Zurich tomorrow morning. Your flight has been booked. A hotel reservation has been made for you at the Baur au Lac. I shall hand you the tickets and the necessary currency before you leave tonight. You will remain outside Italy for at least a month. After that, you may make whatever arrangements you choose for the rest of your vacation. If you choose to divert yourself with the lady–to whom obviously you have some attachment–that is your business. The Service has no further interest in her, provided she does not attempt to re-enter the Republic. It's all a little rushed I'm afraid, but I am sure you will find the financial arrangements more than generous. . . . Questions?'

'No. A minor worry. I'd hate to spend a long vacation waiting for a bullet in the back. I'd much rather stay on duty where there's a certain amount of protection.'

'I thought we had covered that. The whole purpose of the tactic is to demonstrate that you are no longer a threat to Leporello or anyone else and that action against you would violate what I might call your very useful neutrality. . . . There is a danger period, however: from the moment you leave this house until you take off for Zurich tomorrow.'

'I was wondering about that, too.'

'So I've assigned a two-man team to cover for all your movements. They've already packed your clothes and delivered the suitcases to the Grand Hotel. Your room adjoins that of Miss Lili Anders. You will leave the hotel together at eight-thirty. Much simpler from a security point of view.'

'Of course.'

'Now, . . . two air tickets, ten thousand Swiss francs in varying denominations and an order of the Union Bank in Zurich for another twenty thousand. That's a bonus with my personal thanks. Your salary will be credited in the normal way to your bank account in Rome. . . . That's all, I think. The car is waiting to take you to your hotel. I wish you a pleasant trip and a very restful vacation. *Sogni d'oro*, Matucci–golden dreams.'

We parted with a handshake, firm and fraternal. The Sicilian bodyguard escorted me to the ground floor and handed me into the care of two junior colleagues, who drove me like a visiting potentate to the Grand Hotel.

It was one-thirty in the morning. The foyer was deserted. They steered me past the reception desk and the concierge, rode up with me in the elevator and installed me in my bedroom. One of them checked cupboards and bathroom and even under the beds, while the other pointed out the beautiful job of packing, and how my suits had been pressed, and that if I wished to speak with the Signorina Anders the key was on my side of the communicating door. . . . As the Director had prescribed maximum precautions, I could sleep soundly. They bade me goodnight and retired like lackeys from the presence of a prince.

Perhaps they were right. I was the Prince's man, bought and endowed. His money was in my pocket. His gift was sleeping next door. His brand was on my forehead like slave-mark. Still, give the devil his due, he was a very rare specimen. He recognized merit. He enjoyed malice but never practised it wastefully. He had been scrupulously polite. He had exacted my consent with just the right amount of pressure and finesse. He was the king. I was the pawn. He had swept me off the board to wait for another game. Never once had he suggested that I was making a slave's bargain. He knew it, of course. So did I. Which is why, much as I wanted her, I could not turn the key and go to Lili, but, instead, lay dressed and wakeful until dawn, scheming revolt like Spartacus in Capua.

At dawn I abandoned the futile exercise and went to Lili Anders. With a very refined irony, the Director had kept her in ignorance of the arrangements, so that at six in the morning, sleepless and in need of loving, I was forced to explain the whole complicated play, step by step. When I explained that she was to be set at liberty in Switzerland, she was hysterically delighted. When I told her I would go with her, it was Christmas, Epiphany and all her birthdays rolled into one. After that I had no wish or heart to tell her the price. From the moment I left Italy I would be, in effect, an exile. From the moment I became an exile I would be subject to a clinical change which the Director had calculated to a nicety. For most Europeans, for all Anglo-Saxons and Americans, the word exile has an old-fashioned ring. Whatever crimes a man may commit he is never deprived of his citizenship or his primal relationship with his homeland. He may be imprisoned, he may be brutalized, but he is never robbed of that essential element of his identity, his contact with the mother earth.

For us Italians, however, for us whose identity depends upon a small terrain, a tribal group, a dialectal area, exile is a constant and sinister reality. We can still be legally transported and confined to a distant province, a depressed island, to a community whose tongue and customs and history are totally foreign to us, where we will be strangers until the day we die. We cannot move from it without permission from the police. We cannot flourish in it because we are an alien corn. We exist only by sufferance and under surveillance.

The personal consequences are as deep and as demoralizing as if we had been transported to Siberia or dumped like castaways in the dry Tortugas.

The terror begins subtly with a sense of disorientation and discontinuity. It can end with a trauma of impotence, when every act seems pointless, every step ends at a barred gate, every hope is proved an illusion.

The Director knew this because he had used it many times as a means of immobilizing men who were hostile to him. I knew it because my father had been in exile under the Fascists and I had seen him come home a broken man. But how could I explain it to Lili who had survived her own exile and was now breaking out into freedom. . . . Perhaps it was just as well, the loving would not have been half as sweet nor our exit from Italy half as impressive.

At eight twenty-five, our baggage was removed under the supervision of an agent. At eight-thirty, with no bills to pay, and as many bows as if we had paid them twice over, we were led from the foyer into an official limousine. At nine-fifteen, we were conducted into the V.I.P. lounge at Fiumicino and held in comfort and respect until fifteen minutes before take-off. Then, spurning the crush of common travellers, we were escorted to the aircraft and deposited in a pair of first-class seats. Our agent hovered over us until the moment before the doors were closed. Then, with a final salute on behalf of a grateful Republic, he left us. Five minutes later—this being a fair and strike-free day at Fiumicino—we were airborne in the care of the Swiss. We held hands. We made foolish jokes. We toasted each other in champagne. Then I fell asleep and did not wake until we were in the final approach to Kloten Airport in Zurich.

When we arrived at the Baur au Lac, we found that the Director had provided against all contingencies. We were accommodated in separate rooms, each communicating with a large salon, furnished already with flowers, fruit, liquor and a welcome note from the management. There was also a telegram from the Director: 'Second Samuel Seven One.' Zurich is a sound Calvinist town so I deciphered the joke from the Bible on my bedside table: 'The Lord gave him rest from all his enemies.'

Later in the day, a second telegram arrived, two words only: 'Tekel Stefanelli.' I didn't need a Bible for that one. I remembered the riddle from my religious youth: 'Tekel: Thou art weighed in the balance and found wanting!' I had to answer him and I did it with Deuteronomy one sixteen; 'Judge righteously between every man and his brother and the stranger that is with him.' By then the joke was stale and bitter. I had to make an end of it. I told Lili the truth.

The moment of telling had a curious quality about it. It was seven in the evening. We had decided to dine early in the suite, to relax after the alarms and excitements of the last few days. Lili, glowing from a visit to the hairdresser, the masseuse and the manicurist, was dressed in a house-coat she had bought to celebrate her new liberty. She had presented me with a silk shirt and a rather exotic cravat. I was mixing drinks like an amateur barman, feeling very domestic, very comfortable and yet somehow remote and passionless, as if I were recovering from a long illness. The story told itself in the same remote fashion and I heard myself speak it as if I were listening to a report from another man:

'. . . Everything the Director says is true and yet it all adds up to a lie, which you still cannot disprove. He is a very great actor. He conjures you into a world that doesn't exist and yet makes you believe that every leaf on every tree is real. He shows you another self–and makes you believe it is you. . . . "You lack authority, Matucci. You lack experience. You are an abrasive element. You polarize the fractions." All true, but true in an opposite way. . . . "You are not dead, just buried for a while." . . . But I knew, the moment I stepped on that plane, I was dead; because he has all my files and records now and he can reprocess history in any way he choose. He says he wants to divide and rule. But suppose he doesn't? Suppose he wants to unite and conquer, and then play Fouché to Leporello's Napoleon? I've given him the means to do it. . . . And he paid me for them: with you, with a long holiday, with a sinecure that half the men in the Service would give their eyes for. And he'll honour the payment, have no doubt of it, so long as I play the game according to his rules and wait on the word of the Lord. . . .'

'Why did you accept the payment, Dante Alighieri?' There was no reproach in the question. There was no compassion, either. She was calm and composed as an examining magistrate. 'Because I was part if it?'

'No. I believe that, even if I had fought him, he would still have let you go, if only to demonstrate that I was obstinate and unreasonable. He might even have worked to set you against me. . . . He spins webs so fine you cannot see the threads.'

'So, why did you consent? For me, this is freedom; for you, exile.'

'Strange, but at this moment I'm enjoying it.'

'If you could go on enjoying it, with me or without me, then it would be another story. Could you?'

'I don't know. . . . Yes, by God, I do know! Last night I dined with him and enjoyed him. After dinner we worked together on the documents and I respected him–because he respected me. So, when he asked me to step out of the picture, and gave me his reasons, I had to respect those, too. Then, after I had agreed, he had to show me how clever he was, how he knew in advance that I must consent. He was so certain that he had arranged everything in advance–even to this liquor and the roses in your bedroom. Suddenly, I was not a man any more, I was. . . .'

'A puppet, my love! A marionette, life-size and helpless, with no manhood left at all. It's a bitter experience, isn't it?'

'I think it's funny, very funny!'

'Is it?'

'The joke of the century! Dante Alighieri Matucci, tenor castrato in the puppet choir!'

'Why don't you laugh then?'

'I'm a clown puppet, Lili. I make other people laugh. That is his final triumph, don't you see? He's spread the news all round the Service. How else would Steffi know? Why else would he send me that telegram: 'weighed in the balance and found wanting'. Mother of God! What a beautiful, beautiful comedy!'

'I'd like to see the end of it.'

'This is the end, Lili. Don't you understand that?'

'It's the end he wrote. I think there's a better one.'

'I'd love to hear it.'

'The puppet becomes a man, scrapes off the clown's paint, and rides out to confront his enemy.'

'It's a fairy-tale, Lili.'

'No! It's a truth–my truth. And now that we're quits, I can tell it. I know you for a man, much more–and not just in bed, Dante Alighieri.'

'Thanks. That helps a little.'

'But not enough. Where's your wallet?'

'In the bedroom, why?'

'There's a card in it, remember? A salamander and an inscription: "One fine tomorrow, brother!" A good motto, don't you think? And a very appropriate device: the lizard that lives in the fire. Get the card, my love. And find the telephone number of the Cavaliere Bruno Manzini. I think you should call him in Bologna.'

The idea was seductive. But I was still gun-shy and suspicious of any new entanglement. Bruno Manzini belonged to another world, with another set of rules: the world of the *condottieri*, the free-booters, who had taken over the ruins of a cardboard empire and built a new one of steel and concrete and international gold. They dispensed enormous power; but the dispensation was in another currency than that to which I was accustomed. True, Bruno Manzini had invited me to trust him. Through Raquela Rabin, he had offered me proof of good faith. But, if he betrayed me, then I was lost beyond redemption; since the jurisdiction of money is universal and its minions are devoid of pity.

I argued this with Lili–the new Lili who had flowered overnight into another woman, serene, mature and wholly confident in herself. She abolished my doubts with a simple challenge:

'What have you to lose? Nothing. What have you to gain? At best a powerful friend. At least an alliance of interest that you can dissolve at will. Most important of all, you will have begun to fight. Please! Telephone him now!'

To make the call was easy. To speak to the Cavaliere was only less difficult than having a Sunday chat with the Pope. I was passed from a telephonist to a woman secretary, from the secretary to a male assistant, very efficient, very *alt'Italia*, who informed me that the Cavaliere was conducting an important conference and could in no wise be interrupted. I took a risk then and used the magical name of the Service, threatening all sorts of vague crises if the Cavaliere were not called immediately to the telephone. I waited another three minutes before he came on the line. I told him:

'Cavaliere, yesterday I recovered certain records from Ponza. I delivered them to my superior, our mutual friend. I am now on four months' leave and will later be transferred to other activities in the Service. I am under orders not to return to Italy for a month and I am lodged at the Baur au Lac in Zurich.'

There was a moment's silence, then a series of brusque questions:

'Have you yourself examined the records?'

'Yes.'

'Important?'

'As you suggested in Rome.'

'Do you know what will happen to them now?'

'Only what may happen. There are several possibilities.'

'Which you can no longer control.'

'Precisely.'

'Do you need assistance, financial or otherwise?'

'I need the man whom Raquela Rabin recommended to me, provided, of course, he is still available.'

'He is. He will be with you tomorrow evening. . . . By the way, how is our mutual friend?'

'Very pleased with himself.'

'No doubt. And you?'

'Happier. Now that I have spoken with you.'

'Are you in good health?'

'Our mutual friend assures me I have nothing to fear.'

'He would know, of course.'

'Yes. But he never tells all he knows.'

'Remember it, my friend. Walk close to the wall.'

'Thank you, Cavaliere. . . . Goodnight.'

When I put down the phone, I was trembling and the palms of my hands were wet. I was truly afraid, now. The old man's parting words had demolished the last frail illusion of security and revealed the full, refined malice of the Director's design. I was a stranger in a land stuffed with money and indifferent to the point of callousness. I was a member of a legal underworld, suspect everywhere and nowhere loved. I could be shot down on any street corner and the Swiss would have the blood hosed off and the traffic flowing before you could say John Calvin. I told you I am a Tuscan born. In that moment I tasted the full, Florentine flavour of the Director's revenge. Then, Lili came and put her arms around me and we held each other close while she whispered the words over and over like an incantation:

'One fine tomorrow, brother . . . one fine tomorrow. . . .'

Tomorrow was a gift of God: no wind, no cloud, the lake a-dazzle under the spring sun, snow on the uplands, the lower meadows ankle-deep in spring grass, the herdsmen moving the cattle up the slopes to a music of bells. I hired a car and we drove eastwards along the lake into the Grisons, aimless and happy as a honeymoon pair. Lili was in a rapture of contentment. She sang, she clowned, she played word-games and love-games and built dream-houses, furnished and demolished them, plucked children out of nowhere and blew them away like thistledown.

Me? I was happy, too. I had been a stranger too long to this kind of simplicity. My relationships with women had been too haunted by time, too frail and feverish to issue in any kind of peace. I hunted; they challenged; we joined, we parted, tomorrow was another day and another hunt, with a tip of the hat and *ciao, ciao bambina* at the end of it. I knew nothing of home-comings and kisses at the door and the daily loving absolution from all the sins of my trade. I was the *bufalo solitario*, always on the fringe of the herd, cutting out the errant females, leaving them for other males to breed and cherish. I used to boast of it, because this is our national pastime to prove that we are infinite in potency. But, today, humbled by fear, diminished with self-respect, I was, perhaps for the first time, truly grateful to a woman.

For the first time, too—and this may sound strange from a man who is trained to observe and fit every human being on to an anthropometric chart—I saw her to remember: the honey-colour of her hair, escaping from under the scarf, the high Slavic cheekbones flushed with the wind and the excitement, the little flecks of gold in her eyes, the half-smile that haunted the corners of her mouth, the lift of chin and shoulder and breast and the way she fluttered her hands when she spoke, even the first faint touch of time in the texture of her skin. She was no girl this Lili. She had lived too strangely for too long. But I was no boy either; and I was tired of baby-talk and lovers' lies and all the gossip of the model circuit.

We lunched in a mountain inn, perched high over the valley. We ate cheese soufflé and beef fondue and drank a thin petillant wine, much different from the rich vintage of my Tuscan hills. The girl who served was blonde and pink and white and dressed like a doll in dirndl and embroidered blouse. We sat in front of a big log fire and drank coffee and pear brandy; and we loved the solid, smug Swiss comfort of it all. We talked of the future and Lili assessed her own without resentment.

'. . . I am on file now. Any policeman who knows my record can harass me like a street-walker. So, I have to be careful. If I live modestly and soberly, the Swiss will give me a temporary sojourn. They will extend it grudgingly; but with a good lawyer in a small canton, I may be able to live in peace for a long while. If I married, it would be different. I would have a new civil status and a new life. So I have to think of that . . . but not yet. I have money here, enough for two years of simple living. I have the villa on Ponza which can be sold and will bring a good price. Massimo told me he had provided for me in his will; but that is stolen now. And, in any case, there is bound to be litigation and I base nothing on it . . . especially as I cannot return to Italy ever again. . . . Still, I am very lucky. Lucky in you, too, my love. . . . I did not believe you would have so much concern for me.'

'Boh! I didn't believe I would ever need a woman in this way. To be calm, to prove nothing, just to be glad that she is in the room. What would you say if I asked you to spend this month with me?'

'I would say yes. But I would also say, please leave me before you get bored; please let us have no quarrels and no bad words. Let it be as it is now, simple and easy, one hour, one day at a time.'

'One day at a time. Good. . . .'

'And when you go away—you must, I know that—and you find yourself lonely, come back again. We do not have to spell the words, you and I. We do not even have to say them. You must be very free now, free to risk or enjoy, as you choose. You have to begin to know the man who lives in your skin.'

'I'm afraid of him, Lili.'

'So, one day you must confront him in the mirror. After that, please God, you will be able to be happy.'

'I hope so. But there is something that must be said, Lili.'

'What?'

'If a day should come when you have to choose between me and yourself, consider your own interest first. I would want that.'

'I don't understand.'

'Listen, *bambina!* We are not here by accident. We are not lodged side by side in a beautiful hotel because people want us to be happy. This was arranged by the Director so that we would become tied to each other, the more closely the better. Then, a threat to one would be a pressure on the other. He has thought to buy me. Perhaps he is convinced he has bought me. But he is also buying insurance against a day when I may cheat on the contract. You see . . .?'

'I do. And I want you to cheat him. Tell me something.'

'What?'

'I have never heard you name this man. You speak of him only as the Director. Why?'

'A rule of the game that has become second nature. But, now that you ask, there is another reason. This is a very attractive man. He can seduce you, as he has seduced me, many times, with a smile, a handshake, a show of confidence and infinite good sense. He was born with that talent. It was bred into him through twenty generations. I envy it—God, how much! I am awed by it. I have grown more and more afraid of it. So, I force myself to think of him not as man, but as a function, like the Pope or the President. That way I can cope with him. I can obstruct, inhibit, redirect, as I have often done in the past. Strange! I've never admitted that to another living soul.'

'Perhaps one day will come when you will be able to name the two in one breath—the man who lives in your skin, and the other of whom you are still afraid.'

'Am I so great a coward, Lili?'

'There is one fear that makes each of us a coward!'

'And what is yours?'

'The little room, the light shining in my eyes, the faces I cannot see, the questions and the blows that come from nowhere. You saved me from that, and there is nothing I would not do to repay you.'

'We're both rewarded, *cara* . . . the good day is enough.'

'And tonight your Cavaliere Manzini arrives. . . . Are you going to tell him about me?'

'I can hardly avoid it. Does it worry you?'

'No. But it's an odd situation. I was his brother's mistress. Now he finds me with you. I wonder what he will think or say.'

'Do you care?'

'Yes. I want him to be a friend to you.'

'He calls himself the Salamander. He must have paid his own price for survival. We start with the hope that he will understand ours. After that . . .

who knows? There are no signs in the sky and I cannot read a crystal ball. . . . We should go back now. It's an hour and a half to Zurich.'

At eight-thirty in the evening, the Cavaliere Bruno Manzini received me in his suite at the Dolder Grand. Once again, the setting was opulent: the vast salon, the vista of dark woodland and moonlit lake and the lights of the nestling city; yet the man, himself, was aloof, austere, so that you knew, if all the rest were swept away, he would still stand there, straight as a pillar, with his proud eyes and his patrician beak, and his hair like snow on a great alp. His greeting was warm and smiling; but, from the moment I entered he was reading me by stance and attitude and intonation. His first comment was characteristic:

'You are changed, Colonel.'

'How so, Cavaliere?'

'Every way. You wear your clothes as you enjoyed them. You are more loose, more forthcoming. I would guess that you had found yourself a satisfactory woman and a little more courage than you had yesterday.'

'Both true.'

'A drink?'

'Whisky, please.'

He served me himself and I noticed that he drank very lightly. He raised his glass in a toast:

'Health, money and love . . .'

'And time to enjoy them, Cavaliere.'

'That above all, Colonel. . . . I have ordered dinner to be served here in half an hour. I thought you would trust me to choose the menu.'

'Of course.'

'Now, tell me everything that has happened since we met in Rome.'

I told him. I recited all the facts without gloss or interpretation, up to, and including, my arrival in Zurich with Lili Anders, and the relationship which had begun to mature between us. During the whole narrative he did not utter a word, but his eyes never left my face and I knew that he was weighing every phrase and inflection. When I had finished, he sat a long time in silence and then began to question me. His tone was curt and inquisitorial.

'You are convinced that Major-General Leporello has allied himself with the neo-Fascists?'

'I am convinced that he was and is a candidate for such an alliance. I cannot prove he has concluded it.'

'You infer, therefore, that he ordered, or connived at, the murders in the Via Sicilia and the theft of the Pantaleone papers.'

'I state that there is a case to be investigated.'

'And the evidence in support?'

'Leporello knew, from me, where the papers were, and the steps that had been taken to guard them. If and when the papers came into his possession he would have known instantly that they were incomplete. He would–and in fact he did–take steps to trace the remainder, to wit the microfilms and the maps on Ponza. His aide was there, armed with an authority signed by Leporello.'

'And why would he be stupid enough to sign an order that would incriminate him and his aide?'

'The order would not necessarily incriminate him. He could justify it quite simply as an investigative measure under his own counter-insurgency programme. You know how our services and agencies are organized. Sometimes they run parallel, at others, they overlap; sometimes they run contrary to each other. There are rivalries between them and the ministries that control them.'

'There are also internal conflicts, yes?'

'Of course.'

'Conflicts of policy?'

'Always.'

'What is the ground of dispute between you and your Director?'

'There are several. I asked for an investigation of Leporello. He deferred it. I disobeyed a direct order and made contact with Leporello.'

'In effect you may be responsible for two murders and the theft of vital documents.'

'I believe I am responsible.'

'So your Director was perfectly justified in taking you off the investigation.'

'If he did it on disciplinary grounds, yes.'

'You suggest he had other reasons?'

'He stated them clearly: I lacked the authority and experience to deal with a complex political situation; I would polarize existing factions who would be better kept divided; I was a convenient victim who would buy him time.'

'Good reasons or bad?'

'Eminently sound.'

'And he has treated you very generously?'

'Very.'

'So what is your quarrel with him? Why do you object to the way he has acted?'

'I have no quarrel. I have no objection that I can validly sustain. But. . . .'

'But what, Colonel?'

'I said it to his face and I say it still. I do not trust him.'

'His answer?'

'I quote it verbatim: "I don't want dictatorship. I don't want Marxism. I'm sure the kind of democracy we have is too unstable to last. But, come one or the other, I'll try to make it as tolerable as I can."'

'A laudable ambition, surely?'

'That depends on the interpretation. He, himself, put a gloss on it: "I am king on the board and you are the pawn."'

'And you don't like being a pawn, Colonel?'

'No, I don't.'

'You would prefer to be king, no doubt?'

'Cavaliere, my father was an old line socialist, who spent five years of exile on Lipari under the Fascists. They let him come home to die.'

'I'm sorry, I didn't know that.'

'No reason why you should.'

'So, what would you like to be?'

'A servant of an open society.'

'But you joined a closed service, more subject than any to the corruption of secrecy. Why?'

'I was recommended, Cavaliere. I seized the opportunity.'

'Why?'

'I have a talent for investigation.'

'And intrigue?'

'That, too, if you like.'

'And a taste for influence without responsibility.'

'No. I like responsibility.'

'And you resent the fact that you can no longer exercise it?'

'Yes, I do.'

'And what do you resent most of all?'

'That one man can, at a whim, make me less than I am—and that the same man can if he choose, bury, manipulate or trade information that may determine the political future of this country. My country, Cavaliere . . . yours, too.'

'How much do you know about this country of ours, Colonel?'

'Too little. And too much from the wrong side. I know criminals, agitators, propagandists, policemen, politicians; but the people—eh!—there are times when I feel like a little green man from Mars, all brain and antennae but no heart at all.'

'Can you be bought, Colonel?'

'I was, Cavaliere, forty-eight hours ago.'

'Can you be frightened?'

'I am frightened now. I know too much. I'm isolated. I'm an easy target.'

'And who would want to eliminate you?'

'The Director for one. Leporello for another.'

'Or both, working together.'

'That's the real nightmare. And it could be true. Look what happened in Greece. And look how quickly the Colonels have become respectable. Pantaleone, your half-brother, had the first blue-prints for a military coup, and they are still very formidable. With Leporello and the Director acting in concert they could be twice as formidable, very quickly.'

'And when you called me yesterday, what did you think I could do about it?'

'I thought you might advise me how to stay alive and use the knowledge I have to prevent a *colpo di stato*.'

'What knowledge do you have, Matucci?'

'I know every name on the microfilms. I could reproduce every document. I could reconstruct every map. I have a photographic memory, Cavaliere. I'll back it for ninety per cent accuracy.'

'Does the Director know that?'

'Yes.'

'Then he told you the truth. You are a natural victim.'

'And you, Cavaliere?'

'I, too, told you the truth. We are natural allies. But you have to accept that it will be—what did you call it?—a lopsided league.'

'How will it be loaded?'

'Enormously in my favour. I will introduce you into a new world. You will have to learn its history, its language and its symbols. I have everything you lack: influence, money, friends or servants in every country of the world. Also I am old and obstinate. So I have to hold the advantage.'

'I understand that and accept it.'

'There is one more condition.'

'Yes?'

'This Lili Anders. . . . She is a danger to you, an embarrassment for me. Pay her off and forget her.'

'I can't do that, Cavaliere.'

'I insist on it, if we are to work together.'

'Cavaliere, thirty years ago I am sure you had many friends who gave you the same advice about Raquela Rabin. As a Jewish celebrity, she was a danger to you and a nuisance to them. What did you do?'

'I took their advice.'

'Raquela Rabin told me a different story.'

'I know, but mine is the true version.'

'And yet you ask me to do the same thing to another woman?'

'For a different reason.'

'The same reason, Cavaliere.'

'You are making a great mistake.'

'Probably. But you offer me the same stale bargain as the Director. Submit and be safe. I'm sorry. The market's closed. No deal.'

'Another whisky?'

'No thank you. And if you'll excuse me, I'll dispense myself from dinner.'

'You will not dispense yourself, Colonel. You will stay and humour me, if only because I'm thirty years older than you and I have some excuse for bad manners.'

'Cavaliere, I have excuses, too. I may be dead very soon. I should like to enjoy the time I have left.'

'Sit down, man, for God's sake! The game is over now.'

'I beg your pardon.'

'I offered you a shabby contract, my friend. Had you consented, I would have sold you myself to the assassins. . . . Now, ring the bell, please. I think we are ready to eat.'

The man who sat with me at dinner that night in the Dolder Grand was a phenomenon, different from any image I had formed of him. He was seventy years old, an age at which most men are content to lapse into comfort and idiosyncrasy. Not this one. He bubbled like champagne. He talked books, women, painting, money, oil, films, fashion, religion, game-parks, wine and the growing of roses. He was so various that he dazzled me, and yet, so complete in what he was and did that he shamed me with the waste of my own good years. It was not simply that he was eloquent or interested; he knew, and knew profoundly. He enjoyed. He savoured. He had made his own sense of the mad mathematics of creation. Above all, he still had respect for mystery and though he judged trenchantly, there was always a touch of reserve and compassion in the verdict. Between the fruit and the cheese, he opened a new line of talk:

'We are all inheritors, Matucci, and we can no more shed our past than we can slough off our skins. We are free only to make the best of what we have, in the now-time at our disposal. We send men to the moon and believe we have discovered tomorrow; but tomorrow is still growing out of all our yesterdays, and we decipher it in scraps and fragments like the arithmetic of the Incas. You and I, for instance, we have shared bread and salt and wine. We have begun a friendship. But you will never understand me unless you remember that I was born in an attic above a brothel, on the feast of the Assumption of the Virgin, the day the acrobats came to town. You are curious? . . . I'm glad. When you get to my age, Matucci, you will find there are few left with whom you can share your past. The old go away. The young have no interest. You are there, a broken pillar in a wheatfield, the triumphs you celebrate long forgotten, the hands that raised you, crumbled into dust and blow away. Let me tell you of my birthday. Most of it is true; some of it is uncertain; the rest, perhaps, I have dreamed into myself; but, none the less, it is part of me. Please pour yourself some wine. It may help you to be patient with my fairy-tale.'

And that is exactly how he told it, like a fairy-tale, in old-fashioned language, with ample gestures and quite obvious enjoyment. He was playing the *gigione*, the ham actor, and watching sidelong to see how I would react to his improvisation.

'. . . The time, my dear Matucci, was 1900. Victor Emmanuel III was king of Italy and Leo XIII was gloriously reigning as Pontiff of the Holy Roman Church. The place is the Piazza delle Zoccolette, the Square of the Little Wooden Shoes, in Rome. . . .

'I didn't see it, Matucci; but I can reconstruct it for you because I saw the acrobats many times in my childhood. . . . They came twirling and prancing and tumbling in their gaudy patchwork while the fifers tootled and the drummers made boom-boom-boom, rat-tat-tat and the mountebank tossed his ribboned staff and announced to one and all the wonders that would soon be enacted in the Piazza delle Zoccolette. . . . They set up a stage for the mummers and a booth to sell favours and cure-all potions . . . and a little theatre for Pulcinella. They hoisted poles and ladders and stretched a tight-wire so that the *funambolo* could do his death-defying walk high above the crowds from one corner of the Piazza to another. . . . They made a square of cords to hold back the crowds and laid down bright mats for the tumblers and rolled out the great bar-bells which only Carlo the Magnificent could lift . . . though he would pay a gold coin to any man who could match him. And, all the while, the mountebank strode about distributing handbills, crying the talents of his company and the virtue of his nostrums and the surpassing beauty of his female contortionists. . . .

'. . . In the old days, Matucci, there was a brothel in the Piazza called, by courtesy, a house of appointment, and run by a bawd called Zia Rosa. It wasn't the most fashionable place in town, yet again, it wasn't the seediest. I don't remember it but my old nurse Angela, who was Zia Rosa's sister, would sometimes tell stories about it to the goggling maidservants in my mother's house. . . . For Zia Rosa the feast day and the arrival of the acrobats spelt money in the cash box. The feast day meant eating and drinking and strolling by the river and afterwards every young fellow with red blood in his veins was ready for a bout in bed. The show meant crowds and a press of bodies in the Piazza; and the sight of the girl acrobats bouncing about in their tights, was enough to send St Anthony screaming for solace from his mid-summer lust. . . . I know, Matucci, I lusted after more than one myself in my salad days. . . .

'. . . On that day, Matucci, my mother was in labour in the attic of Zia Rosa's house. How she came there was simple enough; a pregnant girl, disgraced, with little money, found her way almost inevitably to Zia Rosa or to someone like her. Zia Rosa provided a double service. Her sister Angela was both midwife and abortionist. And afterwards she recruited the more likely girls for service in the house.

'I once overheard Angela describe my mother as she was then. She called her "an original", a *furbacchiona*, sideling and hard to read. She had pale skin and blue eyes and honey-coloured hair. She spoke Italian and English and Romanesco. Her clothes were good but a trifle too modest for someone who obviously knew more than her prayers. She had money in her pocket too–at least enough for Angela to attend her at the birth; for Angela would do nothing without cash in hand . . .

'. . . Even then apparently, my mother was arrogant and demanding, in spite of her swollen belly and her need of so mean a shelter. She wanted clean sheets and towels, and soap, and two good meals a day from the kitchen and a list of medicines from the pharmacy. She stated flatly that she would stay a week after the birth of the child and she would pay a maid to attend her during her convalescence. She was a tough one too. Most women by this time would have been screaming and tossing and clamouring to be spared the birth pangs. Not this one, said Angela. Every groan had to be wrenched out of her as if she were a martyr on the rack. As each spasm passed, she forced herself to talk in that cool matter-of-fact voice that made even Italian sound strange. What she said made little sense, especially from a woman sweating out her labour in the garret of a bawdy house. But then most women were a little mad at such a time so Angela humoured her until the pains came sharper and faster and she was compelled to cry continuously. . . . Does this sound strange to you, Matucci, that I should be reliving my own birth? There is a meaning at the end of it. At least I think there is.

'Down in the Piazza–and this I know, Matucci, because Angela was watching–Luca Salamandra, the wire-walker, was about to begin his pilgrimage across the sky. He was dressed all in black with plastered hair and curled moustaches. Half-way up the ladder he turned and saluted the cheering crowds. Then he climbed to the little platform on the top of the pole and stepped on to the wire. There was a gasp from the crowd as they saw it sag under his weight and watched him come perilously into balance. Then they fell silent. . . .

'. . . He moved slowly at first, testing the strength of the breeze and the tension of the cable under his footsoles. In the centre of the Piazza, he stopped and began bouncing himself on the wire. Then he flipped into a somersault and landed upright on the swaying cable. He was, perhaps, five metres from the end of the wire when he stopped, staring straight into Angela's eyes. She remembers him smiling at her, beginning to walk towards her. . . . At which precise moment, Matucci, my mother screamed and I poked my reluctant head into the world and Luca Salamandra toppled into eternity.

'Ten days later, a woman in deep mourning, with an elderly companion, presented herself at the General Registry Office to deposit a set of notarized documents. The first was a certificate of marriage, between Anne Mary Mackenzie, a spinster, of Great Britain, and Luca Salamandra, bachelor, acrobat. The second was the surgeon's certificate of the death of Luca Salamandra. The third was a notification of the birth of Massimo Luca Salamandra, male, infant, issue of Anna Maria Salamandra and Luca Salamandra, deceased.

'This extraordinary concatenation of documents was the result of a long discussion between Anne Mary Mackenzie and Zia Rosa, followed by three hours' hard bargaining between Angela, the midwife, Zia Rosa, the mountebank, and Aldo the Calligrapher, an elderly forger who lived in a lane behind the Piazza and specialized in the reproduction of historic manuscripts. The fact that the registry clerk accepted the documents without question was a tribute to his calligraphic skill.

'The result of the whole transaction was that Anne Mary Mackenzie became a respectable Roman widow, and I was endowed with a spurious legitimacy which would enable me to enter the service of the Crown or even to take Holy Orders, in the unlikely event that I should ever aspire to the priesthood. . . .

'Of course, I have never wanted to be a priest, Colonel, but I sometimes think I should have made a splendid Cardinal, under the Borgias, of course, when celibacy was less stringently demanded. . . . Shall I tell you what you are thinking at this moment? You are asking yourself what is the point of that long story; whether I am making fun of you or indulging myself with a captive listener. You are right on both counts. But I have also shown you a parable. I was sired by a nobleman, fathered by a dead acrobat. I am, and always have been, a contradiction. To treat with me you will need patience and as much faith as it takes to believe in the blood of San Gennaro. Now, you are the man on the tight-rope. You want to save yourself and serve a very divided country and a very contentious people. You will need steady nerves, because you, too, will see monsters borning, and if you slip once you are dead. . . . I hope you understand that.'

'I do. But where do we begin?'

'You are under orders not to return to Italy for a month. We use that month to establish an insurance. Tomorrow morning at nine, you and Lili Anders will check out of the Baur au Lac. A limousine will be waiting to drive you by a circuitous route into Liechtenstein, where you will be lodged in a house which belongs to one of my companies. It's actually a converted hunting lodge, quaint but comfortable. There you will record everything you know of the Pantaleone affair, the microfilms, the maps . . . everything. This material will be copied and the copies will be lodged in a series of banks inside and outside Italy. During this same month you will receive other material from me. You will study it, carefully, because it will prepare you for the next stage of the operation: your return to Italy. We shall, of course, remain in close personal contact. You will have two of my staff on constant call as guards and couriers.'

'And when I go back to Italy?'

'You will still be on leave, an underpaid career officer with specialist qualifications. I shall, to use a cant phrase, take you up, professionally and socially. I shall offer you substantial fees as a consultant on economic intelligence. This will be an open transaction, sanctioned by regrettable custom. Every public functionary in the country tries to supplement his income by private business. Of course, your Director will hear of it. In fact, I shall make it my business to secure his approval.'

'Are you sure he will give it?'

'Why not? It will give him another means of compromising you whenever he wishes. It will demonstrate that you are, what he hopes you are, a venal man, easily bought and silenced. Under cover of this situation, you will continue your investigations into the new Fascist movement and Leporello's connection with it. You will report your findings to me and we shall agree a course of action. Does that make sense to you?'

'With one reservation, Cavaliere.'

'Which is . . .?'

'The Director. . . . I have seen him write the script of similar comedies. I do not believe he will buy this one.'

'Nor I. But he will try to make us believe he has bought it–which is all we need. The real problem is rather different: we have to keep you alive.'

The hunting lodge was ten kilometres south of Triesen, where the peaks of the Rhatikon join with the Glarner Alps and the pine-forests climb, haunted and dark, towards the snow line. It was built at the neck of a high valley, accessible only by a single track of bitumen which ended at a massive gate of stout pine, tipped with steel spikes and slung between pillars of hewn stone. Inside the gate a paved driveway wound through tall trees to the lodge itself, a long, freestone building, raftered with logs, roofed with zinc on timber, standing squat and solid against the lift of the pines and the heave of the misty peaks.

Outside, it looked cold and unwelcoming, ready to withstand invasion or avalanche. Inside it was simple but warm, with firelight gleaming on panelled walls, and polished copper and peasant pottery. The house was kept by an elderly Tyrolese and his wife and there were two other staff: Heinz, a big taciturn fellow from the Grisons, and Domenico, a swarthy young Varese, who was garrulous in English, French, Italian and Switzerdeutsch. They were an odd, but formidable, pair; Heinz, a deadly shot with a rifle, Domenico, a circus athlete, who was also accomplished in pistol and karate. There were always one of them on duty patrolling the grounds, surveying the road, scanning the high defiles for herdsmen or climbers. Each morning, Heinz drove into Triesen to do the shopping and pick up mail. Each evening at sunset the gates were locked, a complicated series of alarms was set and the two men shared the night-watch.

There was a telephone in the house; but we were warned not to use it. We could walk freely in the confines of the estate, but always and only with Heinz and Domenico in attendance. For the rest, there was a typewriter, papers, carbons, a copying machine, and, if I needed anything else, I had only to ask for it and Heinz would procure it, even from as far away as Zurich.

For the first few days I felt caged and restless; but Lili was as carefree as a bird; and she scolded me into relaxation and a simple routine of work. We rose early and, after breakfast, I settled down to the task of reconstructing from memory the material in the microfilm. It was a tedious job, which depended on a whole series of mnemonic tricks, each of which triggered off a sequence of visual memories. With trained interlocutors and a stenographer to record the material immediately, I could have done the job in half the time. As it was, I had to interpose the mechanical labour of transcribing each sequence on a typewriter. I had therefore to reckon with a fatigue factor and stop work immediately it inserted itself into the memory equation. In effect, I could work only about four hours a day on the reconstruction. The rest of the time I spent sorting and annotating the despatches which arrived each day by mail from Bruno Manzini.

All the despatches were posted from Chiasso, which is the frontier town of the Swiss canton of Ticino. The information was beautifully codified and it covered a startling variety of subjects: the organization and control of labour unions, the location of Marxist cells, and the pattern of their activities; charts showing the financial and management structure of large companies, with dossiers on their principal directors; lists of contributors to political parties, matrimonial alliances among the great families; investment holdings by foreign organizations, credit reports, notes on the editorial policies of newspapers and publishing houses; the activities of foreign embassies; the names and private histories of prominent functionaries and a schedule of their visits to Greece and Spain; a whole set of illuminating documents on Vatican finances and the political activities of the Vatican Secretariat of State.

I had been in the intelligence trade a long time, but much of this material was new even to me, and it argued the existence of an enormous and expensive organization, not merely to gather the information, but to classify and process it for constant use. The more I read, the more I was in awe at the complexity of Italian life and the problem of maintaining even a semblance of order in a modern industrial nation. The tension was so high, the balance of forces so precarious that even the most sanguine could not ignore the daily threat of disaster.

I understood, vividly, the frustation of the revolutionary who wanted to sweep the whole mess out of existence and begin again. I understood the despair of the young, who wanted to drop out, like the Poverello of Assisi, and live in fraternal simplicity on cannabis and corn-bread. I understood the seductive illusion of dictatorship: that one messianic man, armed with plenary power, could impose order and unity with a wave of his sceptre. More slowly, I began to see the meaning of Bruno Manzini's belief that we were all prisoners of our genes and our history and that our future was written by scribes long perished.

There were days—bad ones—when memory was sluggish and reason balked, and I was oppressed by a sense of total futility. I was a vain fool, shouting down the avalanche. I was a prancing ape, crying to be a king of human-kind. What right had I to determine, however minutely or indirectly, the text of a single line of history? I found myself drawn with poignant yearning, back to the beliefs of my childhood: a personal God to whom not even the fallen bird was unimportant, who would, in one grand glorious judgment, redress and stabilize and make all things new. And then I knew that I had reasoned Him out of my universe and that He was forever beyond my appeal.

In those desert days, Lili was an oasis of comfort. She refused to be put out by my snappishness. She lavished tenderness on me. She coaxed me out of the house and walked with me through the pine-woods, forcing me to attend to every small wonder: the contour of fungus on a tree-bole, the music of mountain water, the texture of stone and bark, the play of sunlight on the high crags. Whatever was left of dreamer in my dried-out self, she woke and nurtured with extraordinary patience. She chided me, too, and shamed me back into sanity.

'. . . I know how you feel, my love. Everything passes. You and I will pass, too, and the horror of the world will still remain. But think of this while we are still fighting, we hold it back if only for a little while. If everyone gave up the fight, the barbarians would take over for another thousand years. Even if we are ignorant and misguided, the cause is still good. You must believe that, you must never let yourself forget it. Look . . . even I am one small triumph for you. No, please, hear me out. I cannot remember how long it is since I belonged to myself. Today I do. Even when I give myself to you, I give as a free woman. If you had not cared, even a little, I should be dead, or locked up with the prostitutes in the Maddalena. This is good, isn't it—this day, this place? We should not be enjoying it if you had not made your fight and your mistakes as well. . . . Now, why don't you take me home and make love to me. It's much too damp out here.'

The love-making was always good; but it was haunted, too, by the thought that all too soon it must end. We talked very little about that; I was a man without resources, too old to make another career in exile. She had to be reborn out of the dark womb of the trade into another existence. I was the cord that tied her to the past. The cord must be snapped before she could be wholly free. There was no hope for either of us in a day-dream future; but the thought of lonely tomorrows weighed heavily on us both and our nights were the more desperate and the more precious because of it.

We had been about two weeks at the lodge when Bruno Manzini came to visit us. It was a Sunday. He arrived just after lunch, tired and brusque. He took possession of my notes and retired to his bedroom and we did not see him again until he joined us for a drink at seven-thirty in the evening. He apologized for his ill-humour and made a special effort to set Lili at ease:

'You are good for this man, Lili Anders. I am sure you were good for Pantaleone. Please don't be embarrassed with me. Life is much too short to entertain ghosts at the dinner-table. . . . and I am old enough to value beautiful women. I've studied your notes, Matucci. Excellent! But very disturbing. Have you made any sense out of the stuff I've sent you?'

'Some, yes. I'd like to discuss it with you after dinner.'

'That's why I'm here. We will shut you out, young lady, but you are going to forgive me in advance; because the more you know, the more you are at risk, and our friend here has a singular concern for you. Have you told her, Matucci?'

'Told me what, Cavaliere?'

'That I ordered him to send you away and threatened to withdraw my help if he refused. He defied me. Meeting you now, I am glad he did.'

'Thank you, Cavaliere. He did not tell me.'

'Matucci, you're a fool.'

'That's old news. Let's not labour it, eh?'

He laughed, put his arm round Lili and toasted her with old-fashioned gallantry, then launched us into a cascade of small talk and reminiscences that swept us from soup to coffee without a noticeable pause. Afterwards, when we were alone, with the brandy warming in our hands, he told me:

'. . . Things are bad, Matucci, very bad. First we have this business of Bessarione. The police say he blew himself up while he was attempting to sabotage a power pylon. The Left say he was framed and assassinated by the Right. I knew the man: an eccentric if you like, a wealthy romantic, who was also a very good publisher. What's the truth? Who knows? But, at least, it should be open to public debate. What happens? A series of arrests of journalists and students. The charge? "Spreading news calculated to disturb public order." For God's sake! That's the old Fascist dragnet. I remember the day it was promulgated. Result? More division. More unrest. Tomorrow there will be another walk-out from Fiat. In Rome the garbage-collectors will be on strike and the city will be a dungheap in three days. After that, with Easter coming and the tourist season beginning, the hotel employees will walk out. In between we shall have a bomb or two and maybe a child hit by a police bullet. . . . You see how beautifully it works. The Fascists blame the Marxists, the Marxists blame the Fascists. Each provokes the other. Each blames the other for the consequences of violence. In the middle are the people: the students who cannot get an education because we do not build enough schools, the housewives who cannot get home because the buses do not run; the sick, who are lined three-deep in our hospital wards. Let me tell you something, Matucci. I am on notice to rush deliveries of every piece of riot equipment I can fabricate. What I cannot make, I am to buy, borrow or steal, and no limit on foreign valuta either. The markets are beginning to panic, too. If I told how much money went out of the country last week, it would make you weep. So, how does it add up? The Marxists can, and maybe will, disrupt the country: but they are not ready to run it. I am not sure they want to run it, at least not from the Quirinal Hill. Their support is at the local level, in the cities and the communes and the provinces. They can practise terror and intimidation with urban guerrilla groups; but they cannot mount a military coup. The Right could do that, as you know, provided they had enough tacit support from the centre and from the confessional. As for outside encouragement, they would have it from America, which has huge investments in the country and the Sixth Fleet bottled in the Mediterranean playing cowboys and Indians with the Russians. They would get it from Spain and Greece and very probably from France. After that, who cares? ... Your notes confirm all this, Matucci. But they tell more: my half-brother was less a fool than I believed. He planned better than I knew. With certain modifications, his strategy is still valid today or tomorrow. .... I have kept the worst news till last. Leporello has made his deal. He has stepped into Pantaleone's shoes.'

'And the Director . . .?'

'Has joined him. .... They met last weekend at a houseparty at the Villa Baldassare.'

'How do you know this?'

'I was there, too. They wanted me to join the club.'

'And . . .?'

'I agreed, of course. A natural union when you come to think of it. Heavy industry, textiles, newspapers, banking and a stable government pledged to law and order.'

'Why had they never asked you before?'

'Because Pantaleone would never hear of it. And at that time, they needed him more than me.'

'Why now?'

'Because, thanks to your investigation and to the information in my brother's papers, the Director and General Leporello knew all about my connection with my brother's death. So, the time was very ripe for a civilized arrangement. Don't you think so?'

'I think, Cavaliere, that I am going quietly mad.'

'Not yet, please, Matucci. I need you very sane. I joined to be inside the conspiracy. I want this precious junta broken and brought down. Between us, I believe we can do it.'

'In God's name, how?'

'Convict Leporello of murder and the Director of conspiracy with a murderer. Could you do it?'

'I'd be willing to try.'

'The dangers are doubled now.'

'I know.'

'Hesitations?'

'Some. I think we need a new script.'

'Let's discuss that in a moment. Do you have any conditions?'

'That I conduct the affair in my own way, without interference from anyone.'

'Agreed.'

'That I call on you for information, money and such other help as I need from time to time.'

'Agreed. What about financial arrangements?'

'No financial arrangements, thank you. I'm not a mercenary and I can hardly ask you to pay life insurance in advance. I have a request, that's all.'

'Name it.'

'From the moment we leave this place, I want Lili Anders protected. If I succeed in the job, I want a Presidential amnesty for her so that she can be free to re-enter Italy, if she chooses. Can you guarantee those things?'

'The first, yes. The second, no. But I would break my back to procure it.'

'That's all, then. Now, let's talk about the script.'

He sipped his brandy, slowly, set down his glass, then made a small cathedral with his fingertips and smiled at me across the roof of it. He said, placidly:

'My friend, I have already sold this script to the Director.'

Suddenly and unreasonably, I was angry. My gullet was sour with bile and my head full of buzzing wasps. I thrust myself out of the chair and stood over him, mouthing a vehement abuse.

'You are an arrogant old man. Arrogant and dangerous. This is my life, mine! . . . You can't play knuckle-bones with it! What you do is your own business. You're rich, protected. You can buy yourself advocates, bodyguards, diplomatic privileges, immunity from everything but cardiac arrest. I can't. I have to carry my own insurance—sole risk! So, you don't make arrangements that I haven't approved. You don't close sales that I haven't ratified. You haven't bought me, Cavaliere. Understand that. You haven't bought me! Oh, I know you're the Salamander and you've survived longer than I'm ever likely to do. But you wrote that history for yourself. I have to write mine, even if it's only two words: *Hic jacet!*'

Without thinking what I was doing, I slammed the brandy-glass into the fire, where it exploded in a rush of flame. The flames died in a few seconds and I turned to see Manzini still smiling at me over the tips of his fingers. Then, he stood up and faced me across the hearthrug, still bland and benign.

'My dear Colonel, truly you underrate me. Or perhaps I am too cryptic for a late evening. When we talked in Zurich two weeks ago, did we not agree on a strategy?'

'We did. But the circumstances are different. You are now inside the Club. That colours any public relationship I have with you.'

'May I suggest that the colours make a better camouflage than before?'

'You may suggest what you like. I need proof.'

'Let me try to give it to you, then. When I talked with your Director and with Leporello at the Villa Baldassare, your name was mentioned several times.'

'Who introduced it?'

'The Director first. Then Leporello. Naturally, I had comments to make, too.'

'What was said?'

'The Director, with his usual delicacy— said you were a nuisance. Leporello used the words, "grave risk"! The Director said you were immobilized. Leporello said he required the risk eliminated altogether.'

'And you, Cavaliere?'

'I pointed out that you were a very senior and very intelligent officer, and that if I were in your shoes I should have taken certain precautions, for example, by lodging documents in a bank, for publication in the event of your death. I offered the opinion that an untimely accident might demoralize your friends and colleagues in the Service. I then ventured a small fiction: that after your arrival in Switzerland you telephoned me and asked whether I could find a place for you in my organization. You told me that you had been badly treated and that you were thinking seriously of resigning your commission and seeking civil employment. I told the Director I had invited you here this weekend to discuss the matter. I thought it might be a good idea if I offered you temporary employment while he still retained you at the disposal and under the authority of the Service. In sum, I managed to persuade the Director that you were safer alive than dead, at least for the moment.'

'And Leporello?'

'Did not agree. The Director overrode him.'

'For how long, I wonder?'

'Good question. And I don't know the answer. However, as you see, the arrangement is not yet concluded because your consent is necessary. You may have changed your mind. You may still elect to conduct this operation in secret and without any overt connection with me. I would agree to that, too, if it left you more free and efficient. For the rest, I am often arrogant, though I do not wish to be so with you. I am also old, and I can be dangerous; but never to my friends, Matucci, believe that!'

'I do believe it, Cavaliere. I was rude. But I'm tired of people playing games with my life.'

'Do you often break out like that?'

'Not often.'

'I'm glad to hear it. That's expensive brandy. Have another.'

'Let's finish this discussion first. If I work underground, I am constantly on the run. I have to use false papers, perhaps two or three identities, and often unsuitable addresses. I've done it before. I can do it again; but I am handicapped. I should prefer to work in the open as your employee, but I may compromise your position and expose you to personal risk. So, it's your decision.'

'I've already taken it. You join me.'

'When?'

'I telephone the Director tomorrow, tell him I want to employ you on trial and ask his permission to bring you back to Italy with me.'

'So soon?'

'The answer's in your own notes. There is very little time.'

'I haven't finished the notes yet.'

'Finish them at my house. I'm lodging you there until you make other arrangements.'

'What do I tell Lili?'

'Whatever she needs to keep her happy. I'll instruct her on the security arrangements before we leave. You concentrate on the love passages.'

'Talking of love passages, Cavaliere. . . .'

'Yes?'

'What is your exact relationship with the Principessa Faubiani?'

It was his turn to be angry now. He flushed red as a cock's comb. His head jerked up and the nostrils of his patrician beak flared out. He snapped at me: 'And how the devil does that concern you?'

'I have to ask, Cavaliere. I've known several good men talked to death in bed.'

He stared at me for a long hostile moment. He gulped the last of his brandy and tossed the glass into the fire as I had done. Then he relaxed and smiled and the smile made him look twenty years younger.

'Let's say that I'm a wealthy patron who has visitor's privileges whenever I'm in Rome. But I do take your point, Matucci. The arrangement isn't exclusive and the lady does gossip. Perhaps I should introduce you and let you judge for yourself. Who knows? You might even find her useful. I also have other relationships, Matucci. Do you propose to intrude on them all?'

'If my life is involved, yes, Cavaliere.'

'*Dio!* We do snarl at each other, don't we? I don't mind. I need an argument occasionally to keep me honest. But let's not do it too often. I'll give you a thought to take to bed. Comes a moment when all you have left is sap for one good loving and courage for one good fight. Don't waste the loving on a whore, or the fight on a paper dragon. Goodnight, friend!'

It was an actor's exit; and I wondered, irritably, why he took the trouble to make it so obvious. He had nothing to prove. He commanded so much power, he had survived so many storms, that the teasing and the mystification only cheapened him. Then, I began to wonder whether he were not trying to cheapen me, to make me more pliant to his designs. I told the thought to Lili, as we lay together in the dark, spelling out the hours of our last night together. She disagreed, passionately.

'. . . You have to trust him, my love. I think he is a rather wonderful old man, so alert, so vigorous; but he resents the passing of time. He is lonely as he told you. So he preens himself to command your interest and respect. You can be a rough man, Dante Alighieri. You have lived an adventurous life. Manzini has been an adventurer, too. He sees you as a friend, but also as a rival. Indulge him a little. You will not lose in the end.'

I told her then the promises I had exacted to keep her safe and to claim an amnesty afterwards. To my surprise, she rejected the idea out of hand.

'No! You want to be kind. But this is not the way. Don't you see? You tie me to the past. You tie me to yourself in a way I do not want. When you come to me again—if you come—you will visit me in my house, you will drink my wine and eat at my table. I will not be empty-handed as I am now. I need that, my love. As for the risks, I do not care. We will arrange addresses where we can write to each other. There's another reason, too. You will be doing a dangerous work. You cannot do it with a divided mind. You will need other women. You must be free in the end to choose between them and me. I must be free, too. . . . Please, let's not be tense and desperate. Love me gently tonight, gently and slowly. I am so fond of you. . . .'

Somewhere, in the small dark hours, while we were sleeping in each other's arms, the alarm went off; a shattering noise of bells and sirens. I leapt out of bed and ran to the window. The grounds were lit with blazing floodlights, and I saw Heinz and Domenico loping across the open space towards the pine-woods. We threw on dressing gowns and hurried into the lounge where we found Manzini standing, erect and calm, at the window. It was impossible to speak. The noise went on and on, a vicious assault on the eardrums, until twenty minutes later, perhaps, Domenico came hurrying back, switched off the system and reset it. A few moments later he reported to Manzini.

'We got him, Cavaliere. Up on the northern boundary.'

'Alive or dead?'

'Dead. Heinz got him with the first shot.'

'Who was he?'

'Italian, I think. No one we know. No papers, no identifying marks. No labels in the clothes.'

'Armed?'

'Grenades, plastic explosive and fuses and a Walther pistol.'

'How did he get in?'

'He had to come over the mountain on foot. We might be able to trace his route when the sun comes up.'

'Not worth the trouble.'

'Do we call the police?'

'In Liechtenstein? No! Bury him.'

'With respect, Cavaliere, the alarm can be heard for miles.'

'So far as we know, a deer fouled one of the trip-wires.'

'As you say, Cavaliere.'

'Bury him deep, Domenico.'

'Leave it to me, Cavaliere. . . . Goodnight.'

When he had gone, Manzini poured three glasses of brandy and passed one to each of us. His hand was steady. He raised his glass in a kind of grim salute.

'Like the old days in the Partisans, Matucci, which you are too young to remember.'

He meant to proclaim it like an ancient battle-cry. To me it sounded like an epitaph.

PART II

The practice of politics in the East may be defined by one word: dissimulation.
Benjamin Disraeli: Contarini Fleming

We did not go directly into Italy, but drove by way of Salzburg, where Manzini wanted to discuss a lumber contract with an Austrian mill, and then down through the Brenner to Mestre where one of his companies was building a graving dock for small tankers. It was a tedious journey, because the weather closed in, with heavy snowfalls, north and south of the Alps, and the roads were a mess of churned snow and dangerous ice.

Manzini, however, was in high spirits, determined, as he put it, that we should divert ourselves before we stepped into the lions' cage. He had a taste for legend and for local history, and he understood the continuity of it all, and how the old feudal families were still mixed up in the omelette of modern Europe. He did not ramble as some old men do; but talked his themes through to a wholeness. He was a natural dramatist and even when he invented dialogues and situations, you were left with a sense of concordance and probability.

Time and again, he returned to his own childhood, as if his deepest need was to purge himself of old rancours and remember forgotten joys:

'I grew up in a spacious time, Matucci, in a tolerant and cynical city. I lived in a palace behind the Condotti; a house full of doting women, from which men were never absent. I had all the illusions I needed and no guilts at all. In this, I think, I was a very fortunate child. Strange as it may seem, I was most fortunate in my mother. There were so many of her, you see—a new one for every day.

'I remember her, naked in the bath, smooth and appetizing as a peeled peach, whistling and singing and sipping champagne from a glass perched on a stool beside the bath. I remember her in corset and camisole, all ribbons and laces, pirouetting before the mirror and chattering about my uncles. . . . No boy in all the world had as many uncles as I.

'There was Colonel Melchior, who had one hand made of wood, covered with a black leather glove, because he had lost his hand in Abyssinia at the slaughter of Adowa. There was Uncle Burckhardt, who wore a gold chain across his belly and huffed when he bowed and puffed when he talked and who bored my mother to distraction. There was Uncle Freddie, who bought me my first clockwork train and taught me to play chess. He was English and his name was ffolliot-Phillimore, and the servants called him the "pope's angel", because he had a high piping voice like the eunuch tenor in the papal choir. A lot of people hated him. Even Mamma hated him sometimes, because he could be very malicious. But I loved him. . . .

'He opened a new world to me. He took me down the Tiber in a row-boat. He read my first Latin and Greek with me. He showed me how to dig for shards and seals on Testaccio. He would sit with me on a tumbled pillar in the Forum and make me close my eyes and see the Vestals garlanded with flowers and the augurs telling the future from the flight of birds, and Petronius walking proud and elegant among the orators. . . . One day, he said to me; "When you grow up, young fellow, you must be an elegant man, else I shall be miserably disappointed in you. Look out there. That's your city. You must impose yourself on it as Petronius did, with brains and good taste and a talent for mockery. You must learn from it, too. Learn the art of survival and being reborn every day. When you have your first woman, let her be a Roman, all fire and fury, tears and tenderness. This is a rogue's city. Learn to be a rogue, too, if you must, but for God's sake be a rogue with style."

'Strange! I remember that as if it were yesterday. I didn't know anything about style, of course. So, I asked him what it was. He pointed up to the sky and said: "Look up there. See the swifts, how they fly, riding the wind as if they owned the whole heavens. Now, look over there. See that poor dumb donkey hauling the wine-cart. He's a useful creature. We couldn't live without him. But which would you rather be, the swift or the donkey? . . . The swift, of course! That's style, young fellow. That's style . . ."

'My father? Well, that's a hard one, Matucci. You see, I believed for a long time that my father was dead. I accepted it as children do, without question and truly without too much regret. Even after I had met him in the flesh, I was allowed for years to believe that he was just another kind uncle. That is one of the things I have found hardest to forgive. You told me I have too many enemies. I wonder sometimes if all the enemies are not one man: Massimo Count Pantaleone. I wonder if that is not why I hated my own brother, because he bore the name that should have been mine. And yet, given the custom of the time, given the laws of legitimacy and inheritance, I should not blame him too much.

'The first time I saw him, I was riding with Mamma on the Pincio. Uncle Melchior had bought me a pony and Mamma had given me a jacket and breeches in the English style and this was my first day out with her. You should have known the Pincio in those days. Matucci. It was the place where you would see the most stylish landaus and some of the best horses in Rome. The Cardinals would drive up in their carriages, and they would walk solemnly under the pines, while their retainers, all in livery, would gossip together. The nobles of Rome would ride and salute each other and flirt in the fashion of the time. Not everybody saluted Mamma. Most of the ladies held their heads high and looked through her as if she were a windowpane. I remember she used to toss her head and swear at them in Romanaccio: "Old farts! The only thing they can ever get under their skirts is a horse."

'Well, this morning, a gentleman reined up and fell into talk with Mamma. He was tall and bulky with a big eagle's beak–like mine, probably–and a shock of grey hair. He rode a black stallion with flaring nostrils and he looked like a giant statue come to life. Mamma was like a doll beside him, but she sat straight and smiling and held out her hand as if he were the humblest of men. They talked for a long time. Then suddenly he swept me off my pony and on to his saddle, and took me on a wild gallop through the woods. He rode the stallion into a lather and then dismounted in a small grove–long gone!–where there was a statue of Pan and a runnel of clear water. He put both his hands on my shoulders and looked at me, silent and frowning. Then he smiled and said: "Good boy. You have good manners and a stout heart–a trophy for any man in his autumn days. I wish I had the courage to claim you." . . . I didn't know what he meant, only that he was pleased with me. Then he took me back to Mamma. . . .

'Eh, Matucci! If you are bored, blame yourself. You wanted to know me. Here I am! Now, let's talk a little business. You will stay for a few days at my country place outside Bologna. Then I suggest you establish yourself in Milan. I have a furnished apartment, which I can place at your disposal, together with servants you can trust. You will need a bank account and credit facilities, and a cover-story for your activities in my employ; after that, good luck and a very active guardian angel.'

'More, Cavaliere. I need a list of safe houses and two or three sets of papers. The best forgeries.'

'Surely you know how to get those?'

'How and where and how much, but I cannot appear in the negotiations.'

'I know the best forger in the business.'

'I know him, too . . . Carlo Metaponte, pupil of Aldo the Calligrapher. He engraved your Salamander card. He's on our files.'

'Still usable?'

'If you can control him, yes.'

'I can control him. . . . Matucci, will you take a little advice from me?'

'Yes.'

'Please try to be generous with me. I'm old enough to be your father. Strange as it may seem, I still have a conscience; because I try to live by logic and conscience is the last term of a syllogism. I have tried to examine this conscience on our relationship. I conclude, rightly or wrongly, that what divides us is not principle but history . . . the class struggle, the class image. Your father was an old-line socialist, exiled to Lipari. Mine was an old-line aristocrat, who exploited the poor and broke his neck chasing women on the Pincio. But when you were thirteen years old, Matucci, I was making petrol bombs in a barn near Pedognana. When you were fourteen, I was hung by my thumbs in a Gestapo cell in Milan. What I fought for then, you are trying to preserve now, a liberty, however precarious and imperfect. I cannot risk what you risk; because I have only the tag-end of a life at my disposal. But it's still sweet and I savour every second of it. This is not a reproach, believe me. It is–how can I call it?–a plea that we should enjoy this fight. Go down, if we must; survive, if we can, singing and shouting. Can you understand that?'

'I can. I do. I'm grateful, Cavaliere.'

'Please! Not "cavaliere" anymore. I am Bruno. You are Dante Alighieri . . . *Bene?*'

'*Bene, grazie!*'

'And I want you to develop some style, my Dante. New uniforms for special occasions. A Colonel should look like a Colonel, not a conscript corporal. New suits, too, the best fashion, a modish cut. And don't be mean with money; spread it like sauce on spaghetti. . . . Good! That's the first time I've heard you laugh like a happy man!'

Then, because he must still play the conjuror, he hit me with a new surprise. We would stay, not in Mestre, which was a barbarous town, but across the water in Venice at the Gritti Palace–and the Director would join us for dinner. After all the charm he had spent on me, I had to take it with good grace. That pleased him almost as much as his own cleverness and he explained the reason at length and in detail:

'... You would have to confront him sometime. Better with me than alone. Better in his own city where he feels most a Prince. Across the water he will see some of the enterprise that makes me what I am. He will see you, too, in another light: a bought man enjoying the fruits of judicious compromise. We are at home, now, where these subtleties matter. Not that you will demean yourself. Never! You will be courteous, a little reserved, but not insensible of his magnanimity. He will goad you, of course; but you will still fight back, though not so strongly as before, because you have less to lose. He will ask you about Lili Anders. You will shrug her off, a ripe peach tasted and thrown away. When you think you have had enough, you leave. You have to meet a woman in Harry's Bar. She will be there, too. Her name is Gisela Pestalozzi. She will be on your list of safe houses. . . . The barman will know her. You will say that the Salamander sent you. . . . Clear?'

'Clear. Except how you manage it all.'

'It's a game, my Dante. One of the few I can still play well.'

We came to Venice in the early dark. There was mist on the canals, a thick pestiferous haze, heavy with the fumes of sulphur and the exhalations of the canals. Domenico parked the car and we took a gondola to the hotel because, said Manzini, the gondoliers were all vultures, but even vultures had a right to survive. At the Gritti we were welcomed like mediaeval Cardinals and lodged in adjoining suites overlooking the Grand Canal. Not that there was much to see, because the fog sat low on the water and the lights of the sparse traffic made dull yellow blotches in the murk. I shaved and bathed at leisure, while my clothes were pressed. I dressed with more care than usual and managed to make my entrance just as Manzini and the Director were settling themselves at the table. The Director received me like the prodigal son.

'My dear Matucci! I'm delighted to see you. Filthy weather, isn't it?'

I agreed it was; but Venice was still Venice after all.

'You look well and rested. That's good. Did you have a good journey?'

'Brutal!' said Manzini, testily. 'Chains all the way! Still, it should bring the skiers out. Did you invest in that little project I recommended at Bolzano?'

'Regrettably, no. I bought a Picasso instead.'

'Rubbish! There's too much of him and more to come when he's dead. You should have waited until the Pantaleone collection came on the market. It has to, you know.'

'My dear Bruno! What's the use, if you can't export the stuff when you're tired of it. Are you interested in painting, Matucci?'

'I am, sir; but I can't afford it. Not yet, anyway.'

'Take my advice. Start with the young ones. If you have a good eye, you can't fail to pick at least one in ten. At that you'll still make a profit. Wouldn't you say, Bruno?'

'I want him interested in my profits first. That's the quickest way he'll make them for himself. Do you have any idea how many milliards of lire we lose a year through pilfering, large-scale theft, industrial sabotage and bad book-keeping? Matucci here, has made some intelligent suggestions. If he can put them into action, I'll be prepared to bid very high for him.'

'Provided, my dear Bruno, that the Service is prepared to waive claims on his valuable talents. . . . Still, I must say I'm glad to see him have this opportunity. He deserves it. I owe you some thanks, Matucci. You behaved very well in a difficult diplomatic situation. I don't blame you for feeling angry. I'm glad to see you had the enterprise to contact Bruno here. It's a situation that could work out very well for all of us, even for the Service; because, as you have often said, we are weak in the high industrial sector. Still, that's for another time. . . . We've made a few changes at headquarters since you left.'

'Oh?'

'Gonzaga moves into the Middle-East section and Rampolla takes over the Balkan desk. The rest are minor, except that we've retired Stefanelli from Forensics. He was getting much too old and crotchety. . . . Ah, the menu! What do you recommend, Bruno?'

'My dear fellow, you should know by now, I never recommend food, horses or women. It's the surest way to lose friends. Wine is another matter altogether. I believe you had a very good vintage last year.'

'One of our best in a decade. It's too early yet, but when it's ready, I'll reserve you a few cases.'

'Thank you. I'd appreciate it. By the way, have you recovered the Pantaleone will yet?'

'Not yet. Which reminds me, Matucci. We were lucky about Bandinelli. It appears the wife was having an affair with a young singer at San Carlo. She was only too pleased to consent to a quiet funeral with no embarrassing questions.'

'I'm delighted to know it, sir. I'm afraid I didn't handle that situation very well.'

'We all make mistakes. And you were under a big strain. Let's order shall we? I hate having waiters breathing down my neck.'

I was glad of the respite and the small talk that followed it: the talk of high men who played with power and people as if they were coloured counters on a gaming table. They were well matched these two: the Director so firmly entrenched in history that you had only to change his costume to set him back in the Council of the Ten; Manzini, the old technocrat, straddling the past and the present and the future like a colossus in a business suit. But the language was the same and the power was the same as in the days when one galley a day slid down the slips, and half the treasure of Byzantium poured into the Venice of the Doges. For a while they ignored me, and I was very content to listen and begin to learn the stylized language of this other world.

After a while, inevitably, the talk became spicy and scandalous: who was taking advantage of the new divorce law and who was not and why. Then, without warning, the Director tossed a question to me.

'By the way, Matucci, what happened to the Anders woman?'

'I took your advice, sir.'

'Oh, forgive me, Bruno, I forgot there was a family connection.'

'Please! I am not in the least concerned. I only hope Matucci enjoyed himself.'

'Did you, Matucci?'

'Briefly, sir.'

'Where is she now?'

'She was talking of going to Klosters for a while. I didn't inquire too closely. You know the way it is.'

'Do you think she'll go back to the trade?'

'Not our trade, sir. I think she has marriage in mind.'

'Any prospects?'

'Not with me, I assure you. Which reminds me, if you gentlemen will excuse me from coffee, I have an appointment with another lady.'

'By all means, unless Bruno here. . . .'

'No, no! Go ahead. Enjoy yourself while you can. You'll have little enough time later.'

'Oh, before you go, Matucci. . . .'

'Sir?'

'This dual employment of yours. I'm quite happy about it, of course. I'm glad to oblige my friend Bruno here. But you will be discreet about it, won't you? It's faintly illegal and I'd hate to raise discontent among your Service colleagues. You do understand?'

'Perfectly, sir. And I'm very grateful. Goodnight, gentlemen.'

'Good luck with the lady.'

'It's a dirty night,' said Bruno Manzini, with a grin. 'Don't fall into the canal.'

It was a fair warning and I took it seriously. I went up to my room, put on a top-coat and slipped a pistol into my pocket. I spent a moment at the desk in the lobby buying postage stamps from the concierge and then stepped out into the alley between the Palazzo Pisani and the Gritti. You know the place. The alley opens into a piazza in front of the Zobenigo. You turn right, cross over a small bridge and come into the Largo Ventidue Marzo, which brings you slap against the façade of the Basilica of San Moise. Even by day, it is a quiet route. There are few shops and nothing to see except the Basilica; and the stale backwater under the bridge is jammed with gondolas and barges. But at night, with choking fog, and every window shuttered, it was like a city of the dead.

I paused a moment under the light and heard a murmur of voices from the left; boatmen, probably, waiting to ferry some of the diners back home. I could not see them, but I could hear the boats bumping against the piles. I began to walk, not fast, but steadily, holding to the wall for direction, listening for the sound of other footfalls. Nothing, except the wash of the canal, and the sound of distant music and the wail of foghorns from the basin at Mestre. When I turned out of the Piazza Zobenigo, I stopped and listened again. This time I heard, or thought I heard, the faint slap-slap of rubber-soles, running tip-toe on the cobbles; but the sound was so vague, so muted by the mist that it could have been an illusion. I began to walk, faster now, towards the vague yellow glow that marked the hump of the bridge. Then, from behind me, I heard a long high whistle. I stopped, flattened myself against the wall, took the pistol from my pocket and slipped off the safety catch. The situation was clear now. Behind me was one man. Ahead, where the canal cut across the alley, there would be two, one at either corner of the *traghetto*. Before I reached the bridge they would close the trap and kill me inside it.

Backed against the wall, I began to ease myself slowly along it, feeling for a doorway or any projection of the wall that would give me the slightest shelter. I heard rubbershoes make a few swift, running steps. I saw a faint movement near the bridge, which might have been a man, but could just as easily have been a swirl of mist. Then my fingers slid off the rough surface of the wall and groped in emptiness. It was not a doorway. It was an open archway, low and narrow, leading back into the courtyard of a palace or a tenement. Thanks be to God! Now they would have to come for me. I slid down on one knee and peered out cautiously. It was, perhaps, ten seconds before they began to move, two hugging the wall on my side, the third moving down the opposite side of the alley. This was the one I must take first, if I could see clearly enough to hit him.

They moved irregularly, in a series of short runs, first one, then the others, never in the same sequence. I had to have them nearer. I dared not let them come too close, in case they were armed with grenades or a nail-bomb. Then, mercifully, the man on the opposite side made a run that brought him into range. I could not see him clearly. I had to guess him between a barred window and the deeper shadow of a doorway. I took careful aim and fired. In the narrow space the explosion was deafening. He did not fire back. He turned and ran. The others ran, too. I fired two more shots, wild into the mist. Then, because shutters were opening, and heads were showing at lighted windows, I, too, bolted down the alley and over the bridge. I did not stop running until I reached the shelter of Harry's Bar.

Mercifully, the bar was busy; so my breathless entrance attracted no attention at all. I ordered a large drink, carried it to the telephone booth and called Manzini at the hotel. They called him away from his coffee and I told him:

'Thanks for the warning. I nearly did fall into the canal.'

'What happened?'

'A well-laid trap. Three men. I fired shots. They got away.'

'Where are you now?'

'Where you sent me. I haven't met the lady yet.'

'Come to my room when you get back.'

'How's our mutual friend?'

'Smug as a cat. I think I'll stir him up a little. Until later, eh?'

I carried my drink back to the bar, nudged myself on to a stool and waited for a slack moment to chat to the barman. When I asked him about Gisela Pestalozzi, he grinned.

'Interested in a little fun, eh? Well, she's expensive, but she's got the best girls in town.'

'How expensive?'

'Sixty to a hundred thousand a night in season. At this time, maybe less; but you'll have to haggle. Still, they've all got their own apartments; and that's something in this weather. Where are you staying?'

'Friends of the family. Very stuffy people.'

'Eh! Then Gisela's your best bet.'

'How will I know her?'

'She sits over in the far corner. Big red-head in her middle forties. Wears lots of junk: bangles, neck-chains, big earrings, that sort of thing. You can't miss her. She's an old cow, but always good for a laugh. Give you a tip, though. Don't cross her. She's got lots of friends.'

'Police?'

'A few. More of the other kind.'

'Thanks. . . . And here's something for the service.'

'Thank you. Staying long in Venice?'

'I doubt it. Why?'

'Well, as I say, I wouldn't want to cross Gisela; but if you're interested, I have a few numbers of my own. . . .'

'Thanks. I'll remember. Pour me another drink and send it over to the corner.'

I spread myself over the banquette. The waiter brought the drink and I sipped it, slowly, while I thought about the Cavaliere Bruno Manzini, called the Salamander. Everything he said was magical but how much was true and how much was fairy-tale, I could not guess. Bruno Manzini, partisan hero, joined with the Fascists and then called on me, Colonel Nobody, to destroy them. I felt like a whirling dervish, dancing himself into oblivion to prove that God was God and all His works were a splendid inconsequence.

Then Gisela Pestalozzi came in, scattering greetings and perfume, and sat down beside me. She had rings on her fingers and dangling bells in her ears and enough chains to moor the *Galileo*. She had arms like a wrestler and bosoms bountiful enough to feed a continent. Her hair was titian red, her lips geranium and her voice was like pebbles in a gravel-grinder. She was sweating profusely and she fanned herself with a table napkin. She ignored me for a full half-minute, then she announced:

'This is my place, young man. You must be new here.'

'And you must be Gisela?'

'That's right. How did you know?'

'A friend told me.'

'What friend?'

'Can you lower your voice a little, please?'

'Why should I? It's my voice. It's my place. If you want to talk business, that's another thing.'

'I want to talk business.'

'Sixty thousand a night, dinner and drinks extra. Yes or no?'

'No. The Salamander sent me.'

'Eh!' She collapsed like a vast balloon and her voice dropped ten decibels. 'Why didn't you say so straight off? What do you need?'

'A safe house.'

'How long?'

'I don't know yet. Weeks, months.'

'With or without?'

'With or without what?'

'A woman, of course. What else?'

'Without.'

'Two rooms, kitchen and bath. Fully furnished, light, heat and telephone. Two hundred thousand a month. Suit you?'

'It's a murderous price.'

'It's a safe house. Private entrance. No porter and two other exits.'

'Where?'

'A hundred metres from San Marco.'

'Quality?'

'Well, it's not the Ca' d'Oro; but it's comfortable.'

'Where do I get the key?'

'From me. With a month in advance and a month's deposit.'

'I'll think about it. Where do I find you when you're not here?'

'The Salamander has my number.'

'Good. A drink?'

'What's your name?'

'I change it every day. Just call me lover.'

'Do you want a girl?'

'Not tonight.'

'Then move over, lover! This is working hours.'

'*Ciao*, Gisela! We'll be seeing each other.'

And that was it, pointless and purposeless as everything else that was happening to me. I left my drink unfinished on the table and paid a sleepy boatman one thousand lire to deliver me two hundred metres down the canal at the front door of the Gritti, which, being a civilized hotel, has a good telephone service and booths where you need not discuss your business with the world and his girl-friend. I ordered a call to Stefanelli in Rome and, two minutes later, I had him on the line. In ten seconds I knew that I was not a welcome caller.

'Steffi, this is Matucci.'

'I remember the name. Yes?'

'I'm in Venice, Steffi.'

'Happy you. Happy Venice.'

'Steffi, stop clowning for Christ's sake! This is serious.'

'I know. I am out of a job. Every *fascista* in the Service has jumped two grades and you are eating lobster in Venice. It can get more serious?'

'I want to see you.'

'I'm at home all the time—midnight to midnight.'

'Listen, please!'

'No! You listen. You sold out, little brother! You took a long leave and a lush sinecure and now you're on the payroll of private industry. You're a *stronzo*, Matucci. The worst I've ever known.'

'Where did you hear all this?'

'Does it matter?'

'Yes, it does. And if you hang up, Steffi, I'll spit on your grave. Now tell me!'

'I heard it from the great talking horse himself, our dear Director, on the day he retired me. I quote: "You are still active, Stefanelli. Why don't you emulate your colleague, Matucci, and direct your talents, your very considerable talents, to civilian occupation." I still quote: "The rewards are very great, as Matucci will tell you. We had our disagreements, but we were able to resolve them, and I venture to suggest that Matucci will end a very rich man." End of quote. Do you want to hear any more?'

'No, thanks. Did you get my telegram?'

'I got it.'

'But you didn't believe it?'

'No.'

'Will you do me one favour?'

'Flowers for your funeral maybe.'

'Save your money. It could be sooner than you think. Go talk to Raquela Rabin instead. Ask her what we discussed the day I went to see her.'

'And then?'

'I'll call once more. Then, if you want, you can call me all the names in the book. Goodnight, Steffi.'

After that I went upstairs to talk to Bruno Manzini. I was surprised to find that the Director was still with him; but the atmosphere had changed. They were tense with me and tense with each other. Manzini plunged straight into interrogation.

'Tell us what happened, Matucci.'

I told them. I drew a map on the hotel notepaper to make it clear. I made it even clearer that someone had set me up like a clay pigeon and I wasn't very happy about it. Manzini cut me off in the middle of this theme and said, flatly:

'I have already told your Director what happened at the lodge.'

'I see.'

'And I have conveyed to him your suspicion that both these attempts were officially inspired.'

'And I am shocked at the suggestion, Matucci.' He looked it, too. For the first time I caught a hint of unease under his sardonic mask. 'Did you really believe that, after we had settled an amicable arrangement, after I had agreed to your return to Italy and your private employment with my old friend, I would put out a contract for your life?'

'It had to be you or Leporello. You were kept constantly informed by the Cavaliere. You knew I had an appointment at his lodge. You knew I was coming to dinner here tonight. Knowing the trade as we both do, it's not too illogical is it?'

'From my point of view, Matucci, it's madness. I would stamp you out with no compunction at all if I had to; but, as things are, I have a vested interest in keeping you alive.'

'I will not work with fools,' said Bruno Manzini flatly. 'I will not tolerate threats against my staff. You will talk sense into that upstart Leporello.'

'Please!' said the Director softly. 'Please, Bruno. We're too old for tantrums. I will deal with it. . . . Sleep well, Matucci.'

When he had gone, Bruno Manzini lay back in his chair and surveyed me with ironic amusement.

'Well, my Dante, what did you make of that?'

'I think he's telling the truth.'

'I know he is. And I know he's worried. If he can't control Leporello now, he'll never be able to do it afterwards. . . . All profit, my Dante! When thieves fall out it's gold in the pockets of the godly.'

I laughed. What else could I do? I laughed until tears ran down my cheeks; while the old man sat chuckling in his chair like a spider who had just made a meal of a gad-fly.

There were lions at the gates, twin beasts of lichened stone, supporting beneath their upraised paws an illegible escutcheon. The gates were of black iron, scrolled and curlicued, twice the height of a man. The gate-keeper was a dwarfish manikin who came running to the door of the car to greet his master with a simian chatter of dialect. Beyond the gate a gravelled drive wound through an avenue of cypresses and opened into a geometer's fantasy of flowerbeds and miniature hedgerows, beyond which a stairway of white marble led to the villa, a small Palladian jewel, light and beautiful even under the grey sky and the steady drenching rain.

This was Pedognana, country seat of the Cavaliere Bruno Manzini, and he displayed it to me with child-like pride:

'Home, my Dante! The one place in all the world where I am truly myself. My mother bought it, in the good years, and sold it in the bad ones. When I made my first real money, I bought it again, and I have held it ever since. The arms over the gate are the ones my mother invented for herself. You can still make out the Salamander if you look closely enough. I defaced it in the partisan days, because this was my headquarters until the Germans arrested me and shoved me into gaol. There's everything here: orchards, farmland, mulberries for the silkworms, rice on the river flats, grapes and olives on the foothills. Something of the old life, too, as you will see for yourself. Come inside. . . .'

In the pillared entrance, under a dome resplendent with Tiepolo fantasies, the household was assembled: Gualtiero, the factor, six feet tall and solid as an oak-tree; Lanfranco, major-domo of the villa; Don Egidio, chaplain to the estate; Donna Edda, the housekeeper, a stout country-apple woman, full of flounce and fluster; and with them, a small hierarchy of maids, gardeners and grooms. Manzini saluted them all by name, and I had perforce to repeat the salutation, so that, by the time the ceremony was over, I was convinced that I had been translated into the nineteenth century.

The greetings over, I was consigned to the care of Donna Edda, who bustled me upstairs with such a fervour of welcome that I felt giddy. The splendour of the room overwhelmed me—the canopied bed, the vast buhl desk, the fire blazing behind the brass screen, the bookcase that climbed to the ceiling, full of leather-bound tomes. Suddenly, it was all too much; and I wondered irrationally whether this were not a tactic: to stifle me with grandeur and bind me like another serf to his service. However, he put himself at pains to explain himself and the scope of his design.

'. . . Try to understand, Dante Alighieri. I am a free man. I understand liberty in the Anglo-Saxon way, because my mother was a Scot and a free woman in her own right. She fought Pantaleone to establish an estate for me and he did it. She made a long nose at society; but she never complained when society looked down its nose at her. But freedom like this is a rare state of mind. People have to grow to it, be educated to it. And this country is still only half-educated, in parts not educated at all. Many prefer tyranny to freedom, because tyrants can be corrupted while liberty demands a drastic innocence, a daily battle like that of Sant' Antonio with the demons. . . . I am not innocent; neither are you; but we don't want to be whores all our lives. Remember Raquela Rabin? . . . Well, that's a story that says it all. We were lovers, as you know. We parted . . . each for the same reason. I bowed to social pressures. She found herself a more powerful protector—a vice-President of the Jewish Council, a man high in Fascist affairs. You are too young to remember, Dante Alighieri, but even the Jews believed in the *Duce* and trusted till the last that he would save them from the German holocausts. . . . In the end, we knew that we had both betrayed ourselves. Raquela went to Auschwitz—a willing victim. I went underground to fight. . . . Remember the Bible? "A man's enemies shall be those of his own household." It is like that still. So, I had to test you. I will go on testing you; because you have not yet been hung by the thumbs or been shocked with electrodes clipped to your testicles. . . . Forgive me. I am too vehement. I am still not as wise as I should like to be. . . .'

Later that evening, with maps and documents spread all over the table, we sketched the first plan of campaign. Once again I marvelled that so old a man could be so precise and ruthless in his designs.

'State the purpose of the exercise, Colonel.'

'To convict Major-General Leporello of conspiracy to murder Avvocato Bandinelli and Agent Calvi. To discredit the Director by showing him joined in the conspiracy.'

'And where do you begin?'

'With three facts: Leporello knew the location of the Pantaleone papers and my arrangements to guard them; his aide, Captain Roditi, appeared on Ponza with orders to claim the other documents; later, the Director joined Leporello in a plot to establish military rule.'

'Given those facts, where do you probe first?'

'At the weakest point. Captain Roditi.'

'Next?'

'Leporello.'

'Why not the Director? You know him better.'

'As he stands, he's almost impregnable. He can justify any action by the secret needs of the Service.'

'Come back to Leporello, then.'

'I've never seen his dossier. We can build one easily enough, but it will take time. Apart from that, we have two versions of him: his own and the Director's.'

'Quotes?'

'The Director: "A patriot, a devout Catholic, a Christian Democrat and financially independent. Doubt he could be bought or frightened."'

'His own?'

'Verbatim quote . . . "My loyalties were to the Crown. I never changed them—even when it might have been convenient to do so. I disliked the Fascists. I loathed the Germans; but even for that I could not make myself a turncoat soldier. Today I am able to be honest and proud." Quote ends.'

'*Dio mio*! A resolute virgin! I don't believe it.'

'Neither do I. What is your impression of him?'

'Cold, ambitious, more than a little paranoid. But put him on that balcony in the Piazza Venezia and many people would go mad for him. I'd like to examine him in social circumstances. I'll invite him to a suitable gathering in Milan. He's based there, so that's easy. He'll bring his aide, so that should give you a starting point, too. We'd better install you in the apartment as soon as possible. Which raises another question, Dante *mio*, . . . women!'

'Oh?'

'How do you propose to arrange yourself, for business and pleasure?'

'I'm organized for both.'

'I believe you. However, I suggest you take an interest in the marriage market as well.'

'You must be joking!'

'On the contrary. You're a bachelor, a full Colonel, with interesting prospects. So, you're a good candidate for any woman's guest list. Use that, my friend, especially here in the North where money talks and those who have it gossip like nuns. Now . . . since gossip is important, let's discuss your cover-story. You are appointed as my personal adviser on all aspects of industrial security. You enter at managerial level. You have free access to all plants and offices. You will be supplied with a company credit card and a car for your personal use. You will make as many friends as you can inside my companies and you will allay as far as possible any jealousies that may arise out of your privileged position. When I am absent from the country, as I am frequently, you will work at your own discretion and report to me in a code which I shall supply to you. My secretary will be instructed to inform you of my movements. If she does not know them—and they are sometimes secret—I shall inform you in advance. My banker arrives at ten tomorrow morning to open your account and establish a credit rating backed by me. Now, what else is on the list?'

'Personnel.'

'Employ whomever you wish. But check with me before you use any of my staff. Next?'

'You've written here: "The Church".'

'Oh yes. This is a delicate one, Matucci. Mother Church is up to her neck in Italian politics. We know that. She's a very old and very shrewd lady, and she has friends to the Left and Right as well as in the centre. Sometimes it's hard to distinguish them, because the cassock makes all priests look alike and everybody in the Vatican uses the same language—with very subtle overtones that make all the difference to the meaning. If you find you're treading on a cassock, tread lightly until you know who's wearing it. . . . Are you religious, by the way?'

'I was baptized, communicated and confirmed and the good brothers beat me into unbelief. Why the question?'

'It helps to know what a man thinks about dying—his own or another's.'

'I think about it as little as possible. I find that helps. You?'

'I'm old. It makes a difference.'

'I see that it might.'

'I've lived the discord, but I think I hear a harmony. I hear it plainest in the old words and the old signs of grace. Maybe it's an illusion, but I'd rather die with it than without it. . . . Still, each to his own. My God! I really must get you to a good tailor. That suit was cut by a pork-butcher.'

In the morning, the banker came, and in the afternoon, whirled from Milan, a tailor, who measured me for more clothes than my father had worn in a lifetime. In between, and late into the dusk, I played my memory game on the microfilms and sweated over the mountain of material from the data-bank. In the evening, with an odd feeling of trepidation, I called Stefanelli. This time, he was his old truculent self:

'So, I apologize Matucci; then what?'

'Then I say, don't mention it.'

'Then what?'

'Then I say, how would you like to work for me. Good salary, expenses, a little travel.'

'What sort of work?'

'Now, Steffi, if I were fool enough to tell you on an open line, you would be a fool to work for me.'

'Oh? That sort of work.'

'Yes, Steffi. What do you say?'

'I'll have to ask my wife.'

'You're a millstone round her neck and you know it. She can't wait to get you out of the house.'

'Now, that's a great truth, little brother. How soon?'

'A week. Ten days at most.'

'How long?'

'No idea.'

'How much?'

'Your Service salary.'

'You've bought me.'

'Good. I'll be in touch soon. And, Steffi, please. . . .'

'I know. Don't tell me. Once there were three wise monkeys. . . .'

'Steffi, you're a jewel.'

'I am also stark raving mad. But I'll be madder still if I stay in this house too long.'

'One more thing. Do I have any friends left?'

'Still a few. . . . Need something?'

'Yes. Roditi, Matteo, Captain of Carabinieri, aide to Major-General Leporello. Any background you can get.'

'Should be easy enough.'

'Thanks, Steffi. Soon, eh?'

'Shalom. . . .'

I felt happier after that. I sat down and typed a short note to Lili, who was staying at a small hotel in the Bernese Oberland. The note would be carried across the border by a courier and posted inside Switzerland. There is no official censorship of mails in Italy, but letters do get opened and a lot of private information finds its way into the files. I could not say very much because Lili might still be under surveillance and someone just might go through her things. And it's hard to be very passionate when you sign a letter 'Uncle Pavel'. Still she would know I was well and she would be able to answer through the accommodation address in Chiasso, provided by Manzini.

For the next week, I worked like a galley slave on notes and mnemonics, daily conferences with Manzini, broken only by sessions with the tailor who arrived every two days with a new batch of fittings, and who by some miracle of Italian industry would have everything ready for delivery the day I took possession of the apartment. I was inclined to be flippant about the tailor; but Manzini became quite testy and read me a five-minute lecture on the subject.

'This isn't a joke, Matucci. And don't let that Tuscan snobbery of yours cloud your judgment. We're talking about some of the most potent people in the world today – the image-makers, the dream merchants, the illusionists. Put eight hundred million people in black button-up tunics and what have you got – Mao's China, and the whole world goggle-eyed at the wonder of it. I make textiles, Matucci, and I know what the fashion business means. . . . Tourism is our second most important industry – and if you took the bikini off the travel posters, it would slump by half overnight. Have you read that batch of cuttings I put on your desk this morning?'

'Not yet. Why?'

'Because the image-makers are working on Leporello right at this moment. There are two picture stories, four excerpts from recent speeches on law and order, and twenty-three other references on various themes. It's the beginning of a campaign, Matucci. They're testing the market before they strike a line. There's a big agency behind it – Publitalia – and if you check your notes you'll find the name of the man who owns it. . . . Now, for God's sake, stop being coy and let's attend to business!'

He was a rough old pirate; but I was beginning to love him. He had so much talent, so much zest and drive that he made me feel sometimes like a country clod. No detail was too small for his attention; the names I should use on my false papers, the decoration of the apartment in Milan, the clubs at which he might present me, whether I should play tennis or take a few lessons in golf, and even the make of car I should drive. He instructed me in the workings of the bourse, so that I could talk stocks and bonds intelligently. He sketched the histories of the great families, the Torlonia, the Pallavicini, the Doria, the Orsini. He read me the careers of the modern merchant adventurers and the follies of their wives and offspring. He showed me where the American money was, and the German and the Swiss, and how the oil war was fought, and how the tentacles of the Honourable Society reached even into the North. Over and over again, he repeated the same lesson:

'. . . Think always in the frame of history, Dante. It takes more than a hundred and fifty years to build a nation and a national consciousness. Once Mussolini was toppled, we were back to the days of the warring dukedoms. Even the Marxists are split. Now we are looking for another point of focus; and that's the appeal of the new Fascism. What people don't see is that we have to grow out of disunity, not be bludgeoned out of it, by new blackshirts. If they try it . . . God! I hate to think of the consequences . . .!'

Then, abruptly, as always, he dropped the subject and took me out on a tour of the estate, reminiscing all the while about his youth and his relations with his father.

'. . . He was the perfect mirror of his time, Dante; an unblushing pragmatist who was convinced that money and a title could command anything, even immortality. He believed in God but found Him agreeably absent from most human transactions. He believed in the Church, as one of the more stable and useful human institutions. He believed in marriage as a social contract, but not as a solace for a normal man's desires. Diplomacy was an art for gentlemen, but politics was a trade for arrivistes and rogues. He was happy to profit from it but he refused to engage himself in it, being content with a public affirmation of loyalty to the Crown and a private manipulation of conflicting parties to the sole and singular interest of Pantaleone. . . .

'I see you smile, my friend. You're right. I'm very like him. He was a good business man, too. He invested in steel and electricity and shipbuilding and insurance and banks, and bought no stock at all in colonial adventures. As I told you, my mother fought him to make a settlement on me, and that was the foundation of what I have today. After that first meeting on the Pincio, he began to take an interest in me, and I accepted him as the best and most exciting of all my uncles. . . .

'Looking back now, I see his intentions very clearly. He wanted to get me out of the harem atmosphere of my mother's house and thrust me into a world of men. It was a wonderful world then, Matucci, especially if you didn't see the underside of it–and I was spared that for many years. Once each week, I would go to the *salle d'armes*, where Pantaleone practised sabre and épée with the master, Carducci. Sometimes, at first light, we would drive out along the Appia Antica to the stud at Tor Carbone where he bred racehorses from British and Irish stock. We would watch the morning gallops, make the rounds of the stables and then sit down to breakfast in the kitchen of the old farmhouse with the stud-master and the trainer. . . .

'On other days he would take me to visit the craftsmen who flourished under his patronage and that of his wealthy friends. They were wonderful men, Dante, all gone now. There was Ascoli, the antiquarian, a wizened old gnome who could take a handful of shards and rebuild them into an Etruscan urn, and read you a whole history from it. There was Haro, the Spaniard, a gunsmith who lived over on the Prati and whom even the British ranked with their own masters. He had a pistol range in his cellar and pigeon-traps and a line of butts in the fields where his gentlemen clients could test their skill. That was where I first learned to handle a gun and to care for it, too. . . . Eh, memory is a treacherous gift!'

'You look troubled. Something bothering you?'

'I've just recalled something. A lesson Pantaleone taught me. I hated him for it. Now–God knows why–it makes me want to weep.'

'Do you want to talk about it?'

'Why not? It's very short. One day at the gallops, I slipped and fell in the mud. A stable-boy laughed and I flew at him, clawing and punching and screaming in Romanaccio. Pantaleone hauled me away and cuffed me till my ears sang, and I was sobbing with pain. He was quite cold about it, brutal and deliberate. Then he told me: "You will never do that again. The boy did you no harm. You looked a fool and he laughed. He could not hit back because he is a poor peasant who depends on me for work. You are supposed to be a gentleman. You acted like an animal out of control. You will go now and apologize." I refused. He gave me a look of such contempt that I felt crushed. Then he walked away and left me. Later, I did apologize, but by then he was gone and the farm people had to drive me back to Rome in a wine-cart. I didn't see him for months afterwards. I thought he had rejected me because of my disobedience. I did not know until long afterwards that his wife had given him a legitimate son, and that I had been relegated to the shadows. . . . That's all.'

'Not quite all, I think.'

'What do you mean?'

'The lesson wasn't lost. I was talking to Gualtiero, your factor. He told me you've turned this place into a co-operative, so that your people can have tenure after your death.'

'Oh, that! Well, it's something, I suppose. I'm bowing to social necessity. Eh! Let's change the subject. Look at those blossoms, Dante. The whole hillside is in flower. You'll be gone soon. But I want you to know that you are welcome here whenever you choose to come. You're good for me.'

'And you for me, Bruno. I'll be sorry to leave this place.'

'Have you no land of your own?'

'None.'

'Then buy yourself a plot, however small. Plough and plant and love it a little. Every man needs one earth he can call his own.'

'Perhaps, after this is over. . . .'

The rest of the thought remained unspoken; but we both understood the big perhaps. If things went wrong, I should have all the earth I needed: two metres long, a metre and a half deep–a grave in the Campo Santo.

The apartment in Milan was the penthouse of a new block, built by Manzini, not far from the centre of the city. I had two bedrooms, two bathrooms, an American-style kitchen, a large salon, a dining-room and a study, as well as separate quarters for two servants. There was a terrace on three sides, planted with shrubs and spring flowers in urns. The only access was by private elevator whose entrance and interior could be scanned by closed-circuit televison from inside the apartment. The servants had one key to the elevator. I had another. The doors of the apartment were equipped with double locks and chain-bolts and the windows with steel shutters. There were two independent alarm systems, each connected by telephone circuit to the headquarters of the Mobile Squadron.

Everything in the place was new and designed for a rich and sociable bachelor: deep leather furniture, a well-stocked bar, a high-fidelity system, racks of records, a television set, bright modern canvases, books, new and old, for lonely nights. There was a typewriter, a Xerox copier, a tape machine, boxed notepaper with my name on it, two sets of visiting cards, one for civilian, the other for military occasions. Behind the bookshelves, concealed by a false panel, was a modern safe with an electronic locking device and an alarm connected to the central system. Even the telephone index on my desk was typed up to date with all the numbers I might need within Manzini's organization and with the addresses of tradesmen, doctor and dentist. Manzini made me free of it all with a smile of satisfaction.

'There, my dear Dante. All yours. Now you have nothing to do but to work and divert yourself profitably. Let me introduce you to the servants.'

There were two of them, twin brothers from Sardinia, small dark men, taciturn and dignified as grandees. They were named Pietro and Paolo, so that they could share the same feast-day. Pietro was cook and butler. Paolo was houseman and valet. There was always one of them on duty night and day. They had served Manzini for ten years, and, if first impressions meant anything, they would keep me like a filmstar. Within ten minutes of my arrival, my suits were ranged in the closet, my toilet things laid out, my soiled clothes whisked out of sight. They came from Nuoro, Manzini told me, and they had served a prison term for banditry. He had hired them for a season on his yacht and then offered them a permanence. They were fiercely loyal and so discreet that they would not give the time of day to a stranger.

We toasted the enterprise and blessed the house with a glass of champagne and then, before he left, Manzini did a touching thing. He put his hands on my shoulders and embraced me, cheek to cheek, as if we were brothers. Then he loosened his tie and took from round his neck a thin gold chain with a medallion. He slipped it over my head and said, quietly:

'It's a Saint Christopher. I had him all through the war. You don't have to believe. Just wear him for me, eh?'

An instant later he was his old ironic self, with a wave and a gibe as he walked out the door.

'Let's have some style now, Danto Alighieri. *Fregiamo i non-credenti!* Let's bugger the ungodly. Good luck!'

It was the first obscenity I had ever heard him use; but somehow it gave me courage and the will to be up and doing. I telephoned Steffi and told him to heave his backside out of the chair and get himself to Milan as soon as possible. He told me he had managed to pull a file on Captain Matteo Roditi, but there was nothing in it worth a second thought. Allora! I would have to start digging for myself.

There is a club in Milan called the Duca di Gallodoro. It was founded by an Englishman who sold it, under pressure, to some Milanese bandits and then, I am told, married an American widow and went to live in Boston. I never bothered to check the story; but I did use the club whenever I came to Milan, because it was one of the few surviving places where you could eat reasonably well, dance in comfort and not be beaten into insensibility by shouting oafs with a million-watt amplifier. The drinks were honest, the girls better than average, and the prices high enough to discourage the sweat-shirt brigade. It was also close enough to headquarters for the officers of the Carabinieri to drop in for a drink and see the kind of citizens they were paid to protect. I decided to go there, alone for once, so that I could drift and gossip and make my escape before I got bored or the girls got too eager.

It was about ten-thirty, when I arrived. The restaurant was full but the bar was slack, so I perched myself in my favourite corner and made small-talk with Gianni, the barman, who knew everybody and told everything in a thick Genovese accent. He was kind enough to notice my new clothes and pay me what he thought was a compliment.

'Eh! Beautiful! English cloth, virgin lambswool. And the cut—perfect! What is this, Colonel—a legacy or a rich widow?'

'My life's savings, Gianni, I'm on leave. I thought I owed myself a present. What's going on in town?'

'The same, only more so. Strikes every third day. Students marching. Police on every street corner. Takings are down, too. Twenty per cent last week. People are scared. They're buttoning their pockets and staying home to watch television. All this violence! There was another smash and grab raid this afternoon. Fabbri, the jeweller. Broad daylight and they got clean away. . . . Maybe we need a new *Duce* to pull things into line.'

'Maybe.'

'This new fellow's shaking things up though. What's his name? Lep-something. That's it—Leporello. I hear your boys talking about him. They say he doesn't care how many heads get broken, so long as we have a quiet city. And he's right! He doesn't sit on his backside either. He's out and about every night with the patrols. They tell me he's training new riot squads, like the French have. You know, slam-bam, clear the streets and no questions asked. You must know him, though. Big fellow. Looks like a German. The boys call him old Iron-jaw.'

'Good name. Do you know any of his staff?'

'Sure. Some of them come in here. Never on duty, though. He's stopped all that. One offence and out. That's the rule now they tell me. He even wants to know the kind of women they hang around with. Ask some of the girls. They'll tell you. . . . Hullo, isn't this a friend of yours?'

He sidled up to the bar, all two metres and a hundred and twenty kilograms of him: Giorgione, Big George, Major Marinello, on the official lists of the Corps. He looked like a great spaniel with sad eyes and dewlaps; but when he saw me, he brightened a little and raised a big fist in greeting.

'Hello, Matucci. Good to see you.'

'You too, Giorgione.'

'What are you doing in this town?'

'I'm on leave.'

'Chasing a woman, I'll bet.'

'Winding up to it. Let me buy you a drink.'

'Thanks, I need it. Old Iron-jaw's been snapping at my heels all day.'

'Big changes, eh?'

'Changes? God! He's ramming the whole United Nations down our necks. How the Greeks do it and the French and the Brazilians and the British and the Japanese. . . . *Salute!*'

'Chin-chin!'

'I tell you, Matucci, you should be glad you're seconded. This Leporello is a one-hundred-per-cent armour-plated bastard. And you should see the types he's getting around him. *Mamma mia!* He's bringing in brains, he says, computer boys and statisticians and, God help me, psychiatrists even! But that's not the end of it. He's building up a little private group of musclemen, for special duties! Something funny's going on. I wish I knew what it was. . . . He's got that Roditi fellow running round like a fart in a bottle. Do you know him?'

'I've met him. I don't know him.'

'You haven't lost anything. He's a real weird one. . . . God, I'm tired.'

'Have another drink.'

'Thanks.'

'How do you mean, weird?'

'Oh, you know: big front, big secrets, the General presents his compliments, sir . . . that sort of stuff. No friends, except among the new bunch. I wouldn't trust him very far.'

'Does he ever come here?'

'No, no! This is girl-territory, Matucci. You know that. I think our friend Roditi sits down to pee.'

'Any proof?'

'Proof? Hell, no! I'm running so fast these days, I can't tell whether I'm married or single.'

'Is Leporello that way, too?'

'I wouldn't say so. He's married, got two kids. Goes to lunch with the Cardinal Archbishop. Very proper!'

'Why Roditi then, and the other odd bunch?'

'I don't know. I think he just likes the idea of the elite guard and all that stuff. . . . Say, what's your interest anyway? You've got a nice sweet job with SID; why should you care what happens to us poor sweats? Hey, wait a minute. . . .' He set down his glass and swivelled himself round to face me. 'Come on, Matucci, give, eh?'

'How would you like to take a walk, Giorgione?'

'Where?'

'My place. It's quiet and the drinks are free. Come on, it's only half a dozen blocks; then you can put your feet up.'

'Well, all right. But don't think I'm letting you off the hook, Matucci. I want to know. . . .'

'Shup up, or I'll make you pay for the drinks.'

The walk gave me time to think. For all his vast bulk and his shambling ways, Giorgione was as cunning as a badger. He would never make promotion, but he was one of the mainstays of the division that dealt with fraud and corrupt practices. If I wanted his help, I had to give him enough of the truth to keep him happy and discreet. Strangely enough, the apartment helped. He smelt money and he smelt power and he had a healthy respect for both. Pietro helped, too. His cool wooden-faced service would have cowed a Cardinal. So, when I judged Giorgione ready and relaxed, I gave him the story.

'Facts for the record, Giorgione. You can tell these to the street-cleaner, if you like. I'm on leave. Four months. I'm working, all above board, for a big company, as security adviser. This apartment goes with the job. Everything else is off the record—and I mean so far off you can't see it with a telescope.'

'Listen, Matucci, I didn't mean to. . . .'

'I know you didn't, Giorgione; and you may be able to help me. First, I'm still with SID, active, you understand. All this is a cover; and I don't want the boys wandering up for a drink or a visit of inspection.'

'Understood.'

'Second. I'm on a job I can't tell you about. Maximum security and dangerous. That you don't even guess at. Check?'

'Check.'

'Third. We're interested in Roditi, too. I've been asked to check him out while I'm here and to do it without upsetting General Leporello. If he is a *finocchio*, we don't want him in a sensitive post. If he's a disruptive influence, that's another good reason for moving him out. So, I have to move carefully; but because of this other business, I can't waste time. If you can help me, fine! If not, there's no harm done, provided you sit quiet, as I know you will. That's the story, Giorgione. . . .'

'Well, thanks for telling me. I appreciate it. What do you want to know about this fellow?'

'The full sheet, Giorgione. Or as much of it as you can get.'

'You know I can't help you with eyewitness material. I'm too big and conspicuous.'

'You tell me where and when. I'll arrange the rest of it. Two main points: what's his relationship with Leporello, and what, if anything, does he have to do with the musclemen? Any immediate thoughts?'

'Some, yes. Roditi's a bit of a muscle-man himself. Cheer leader to the health and physical fitness squad. Works out every day in the gymnasium—weight-lifting, judo, karate. Anything that's going, he's in it. Pistol shoots, automatic weapons training. . . . How he gets time for it all, I don't know. Then he's doing some kind of recruiting job round the country, inside the Corps that is. From what I hear they're setting up some kind of commando group. It sounds like that French lot—what were they called?'

'The Barbouzes?'

'That's it. Real thugs from what I hear.'

'Where do they train?'

'Oh, that's one of the big secrets. Nobody seems to know and the boys themselves won't talk. Still, I'll smell around a bit and let you know.'

'Where does Roditi live?'

'I don't know that either, but it must be on file. I'll get Rita to dig it out. You remember Rita, don't you? Dark, gypsy type. Last time you were here, you and she. . . .'

'Let's not go into that, Giorgione. And for God's sake, don't tell her I'm in town. . . . Now, you think Roditi's a *finocchio*. Any evidence?'

'Well, no. But no girl-friends and all this body-building stuff. It points that way doesn't it?'

'It might. Any boy-friends at headquarters?'

'No. The women watch him like vixens at mating time. There are half a dozen who'd love to give him a tumble; but they haven't noticed anything.'

'How does Leporello treat him?'

'Oh, very formally, but—how shall I say it?—very much like a man of confidence. You know the sort of thing . . . "If you need any further direction, Captain Roditi will make himself available . . . Captain Roditi will call you to arrange a conference . . ." I know he visits Leporello's home.'

'Where's that?'

'On the road to Linate airport. Big villa with a high stone wall.'

'Does Leporello have any women working in his office?'

'Three. A senior secretary and two typists. Nothing for you there, Matucci. The secretary's a dragon and the two juniors are straight from the nunnery.'

'What about Leporello's wife?'

'Never seen her. I don't think she's ever come to headquarters. If she had, I'm sure we'd have heard of it.'

'When he made this study trip, did his wife travel with him?'

'No. . . . But Roditi did, by God! Yes he did.'

'It doesn't prove anything, Giorgione.'

'You're right. It doesn't.'

'What's the general feeling in the Corps about Leporello?'

'Well . . . I know I was sounding off about him at the bar. He is a bastard. He drives us like a slave-master. And it's easier to get milk from a chicken than it is to wring a word of praise out of him. . . . But he is good. He's very good. And a lot of the things he's done are real improvements. How do we feel about him? You know the Service, Matucci. You can cut it like a deck of cards. There's the big middle group who do their job and don't ask questions, and gripe about everything just to affirm their rights. There's the bottom group that I call the earth-brothers. They serve and serve willingly in country posts and small communes and outlying provinces. They're pretty good guardians of the peace. They're close to the people and, all in all, sympathetic with them. Then you've got the top group, the hard-nose boys, everything by the book, we serve the State, and it's three years' hard labour if you poke us in the nose when you're drunk. They like Leporello. The middle group are uneasy about him. The earth-brothers loathe him. Not always for the right reason, mark you, because some of them can be pretty sloppy as you know. But instinctively–did I say that right? I'm a little fuzzy–instinctively they mistrust him.'

'What about you, Giorgione?'

'Me? I just hate his tripes. But that's natural, too. I'm good enough at my job; but look at me! I'm no great ornament to the Service. And Leporello makes me feel it all the time. God! It's late! My wife will kill me! How soon do you want this stuff?'

'Yesterday, if possible.'

'How do I get it to you?'

'Phone me here. If I'm out, leave a message with the servants. Name a place and time and I'll meet you, or call you back if I can't make it. Thanks, Giorgione.'

'Don't mention it. Good to see you again. Oh, Matucci, if you change your mind about Rita . . .?'

'Do you think she fits this place, Giorgione?'

'Come to think of it, not quite. . . . Still, she's a nice girl. Take care now. There aren't too many of us good ones left.'

He shambled out, a great, kindly freak of a man who was beginning to find his Gulliver's world too complicated to live in. He left me both pleased and worried. Roditi, my first quarry, was an unpopular type with a dubious reputation. Leporello was a hard-nose with an unhappy staff. Therefore, the preliminary investigation could move quickly, and there would be plenty of enthusiastic helpers to dig up the dirt. On the other hand, the news about the new riot squads was very disquieting. It was a regressive step, a new threat to privacy and personal rights. It argued an official sanction for intimidation and police brutality.

Italian law was, in any case, heavily loaded in favour of the State and against the individual. Many of the old Fascist enactments were still on the books and could be invoked at will. We had never, God knows why, adopted the British system of *habeas corpus*. A man could be held almost indefinitely on a trumped-up charge; and a complaisant magistrate could delay inquiries and shuffle his documents till doomsday. Our judiciary was overworked, our documentation systems were hopelessly outdated. Our interrogation methods were brutal at the best of times, and our prison system a public shame. To compound all this, with an open or tacit brief of terror, and a deliberate exploitation of the Mediterranean vice of cruelty, was a leap back into the dark ages. I understood Manzini's anxious conviction that the twenty-third hour was past and the minute hand was climbing already to midnight.

I was restless now, itchy for company and action, so I flipped through my pocket-book in search of another contact among the night-owls. I settled on Patrizia Pompa, a Lesbian lady of singular beauty and metallic charm, who made a handsome living decorating the apartments of rich Milanese. To my certain knowledge, Patrizia never went to bed before three in the morning. In my salad days, I had tried to get her there, and I was raw from the experience for a long time afterwards. However, we understood each other in the end, and we had managed to maintain over the years a prickly kind of friendship. I called her. She answered in that deep, husky voice that promised all sorts of wild experience. She sounded faintly hostile.

'Who the hell is this?'

'Dante Alighieri Matucci, sweetheart. Did I interrupt something?'

'Nothing important. What do you want at this hour?'

'Information—and a little company.'

'You can have mine if you bring a bottle of whisky. . . . What sort of information?'

'Clubs for the gay boys. Know any?'

'A couple. Why?'

'I'm looking for a man.'

'I didn't think you'd be looking for a girl, lover. What sort of answer is that?'

'He's a nasty man. I think he killed a friend of mine.'

'Oh! Then try the Pavone and the Alcibiade. They're both open till four in the morning.'

'Do they admit girls?'

'Only nice girls, lover—like me.'

'Care to come along and hold my hand?'

'Why not? I am just bored enough to enjoy the sight of Matucci among the fennel-flowers.'

'You've got a dirty mind, sweetheart.'

'Don't say no till you've tried it, lover. I'll be ready in twenty minutes. Bring transport, eh? Where are you staying, by the way?'

'In a convent. Where else? See you!'

I picked her up in my own car, a red Mercedes sports model. She was dressed for the fray in a man-tailored suit with a white shirt and a flowing black cravat. When she saw my new rig, she chuckled.

'My God, Matucci, I believe you have passed over. You didn't do all this on a Colonel's salary. Who's keeping you?'

'Sweetheart, you embarrass me.'

'You'll be more embarrassed where you're going. Were you serious about . . .?'

'Yes, I was. So listen, darling, and get the story straight. I'm an old friend and you're showing me the town.'

'Suppose we meet someone you know.'

'Same story. And if you get any telephone calls afterwards, you stick to it. Don't play funny games. It could be dangerous.'

'With a friend like you, Matucci, I need extra life-insurance.'

'I'm the best insurance you've got, sweetheart. Who's going to touch you with a handsome youth like me around?'

It was a bad joke, and it got worse when we entered the Pavone—a smoky cellar-dive near the Duomo. The bouncers at the door set the tone of the place: two muscle-bound Adonises from the local athletic club, with tight jeans and studded belts and high-necked sweaters. They made a couple of cute remarks, collected four thousand lire by way of entertainment tax, and bowed us through. Inside there was more of the same, big boys and little boys, all in jeans and jumpers, and not a woman in sight. There was a fug you could cut with a knife, and just to help the atmosphere, a stuffed peacock with moulting tail-feathers, preening himself on a pedestal in the centre of the room. There was a piano-player and a pockmarked youth with an electric guitar pounding out a steady rock-beat and the talk was a low secretive chatter that stopped dead as we entered and made our way to the bar. Then there was a chorus of whistles and cat-calls, and Patrizia murmured in my ear:

'Somehow, lover, I think we've come to the wrong place.'

It was going to cost us two drinks anyway, so we ordered and sipped them slowly until the boys had finished their fun and settled back to their whispering. Then we turned to face the room and I peered through the murk to distinguish a familiar face. The barman tapped me on the shoulder with a soft, fat finger:

'Looking for someone, darling?'

'Yes, a friend.'

'What's he look like?'

'Big red-head with freckles. Looks like a German, but actually comes from Trento. Lovely boy. But I don't see him here.'

'Does he have a name?'

'He told me it was Matteo.'

'But not the rest of it.'

'No. . . .'

'You must miss him, darling.'

'I do.'

'How much do you miss him?'

I slid a ten-thousand-lire note across the counter and held it under my hand.

'That much . . . for a start.'

'Well, I think I've seen him in here a few times. Can't be sure, you know. There's a bunch that drops in every couple of weeks, three or four together. I never had much to do with them because they're too quiet . . . and they're interested in very rough trade. If I see him again, what would you like me to do?'

'Give me a call at this number.' I scribbled it on the back of a paper coaster and handed it to him. 'It's worth another ten if I make contact.'

'And when I ring, who do I ask for?'

'Just Dante. Like the poet, you know. My friend here is a poet. Aren't you, sweetheart?'

'I feel like a horse's arse,' said Patrizia, unhappily.

'You look like it too, darling,' said the barman, sweetly. 'Why don't you go where you belong and leave us girls to our knitting.'

The Alcibiade was a different proposition altogether, strictly plush, strictly for the carriage trade—and there was a great deal of it to be had, in both sexes. The place was designed in a complete circle, like the Pantheon, with a bar at one end of the diameter, and a curved stage at the other, and the tables ranged round a small dance floor at the centre. It was air-conditioned; which was a mercy, because there was a lot of smoking going on and not all of it tobacco. The decor was ingenious and furiously expensive. The walls were covered in black velvet, broken at regular intervals by illuminated niches in each of which was a white plaster figure, half-life and fully sexed, representing a classic male hero of antiquity. Woman was honoured only on the black dome, where a snow-white Leda was mounted by a very sinuous swan.

The clients were the most elegant bunch I had seen in a long time; mostly young, but with a sprinkling of grey-haired males and mannish dowagers, with short hair and long cigarette holders. This time our entrance attracted no attention at all. The stage was occupied by three youths in baggy gold pants and turned-up slippers. One of them was playing a sitar, the other was tootling soulfully on a pipe, while the third was executing some kind of slow dance which left me cold as Narcissus by his lily-pool.

The barman was a splendid boy, beautifully barbered and ineffably polite. The drinks cost an arm and a leg, but they were served in crystal goblets, with a fresh canapé to help the digestion. Patrizia purred with satisfaction.

'Lover, I'm glad you brought me. I think I've been out of circulation too long. If I strike it lucky, just pay the bill and leave me.'

'Anything you say, sweetheart.'

'Can you see your man?'

'Not yet. Wait till the act's over and the lights go up.'

We waited a small eternity before the last notes faded and the dancer sank like a tired petal to the floor, to a rather pallid applause. The lights were rather pallid, too, but they were bright enough to show me Captain Matteo Roditi, in a midnight blue jacket, seated with two other young men, at a table on the edge of the dance floor.

I turned back to the bar and whispered to Patrizia:

'I've seen him.'

'What do you want to do?'

'Talk to him . . . alone.'

'I'll wait for you.'

'Better you're not seen with me.'

'This is exciting.'

'It doesn't look it, but it's dangerous. Order another drink and make your own arrangements.'

I pressed some notes into her hand and then wandered down through the tables, like any other client surveying the local talent. Roditi and his friends were so busy with each other that they did not notice me until I stood over the table and offered my little greeting.

'Captain Roditi, isn't it?'

He didn't recognize me for a moment, then he leapt to his feet and stammered:

'Colonel Matucci! Forgive me, I didn't recognize you.'

'Relax, Captain, we're not on parade now.'

'What are you doing in Milan, sir?'

'Enjoying some leave.'

'Forgive me, but I heard you were retired from the Service.'

'It's under discussion. Nothing definite yet. I'm still on the active list. Won't you introduce me to your friends?'

'Oh, I'm sorry, sir. Franco Gozzoli, Giuseppe Balbo, Colonel Matucci.'

'Are you gentlemen in the Service, too?'

He was quick, but not quick enough, to intercept their swift looks of inquiry.

'No, sir, no. They're both in business here.'

'What sort of business?'

'Oh-er-architectural draughtsmen.'

'How very interesting. Please sit down, gentlemen. Do you come here often, Captain?'

'Occasionally. It's a change from the usual kind of club. You, sir?'

'Oh, I just dropped in for a drink–coasting you might say.'

'Indeed . . . ?' He reacted instantly to the familiar word, and a faint hint of conspiracy crept into his smile. 'Will you be staying long in Milan?'

'A few weeks, possibly. Why don't you come and have a drink with me one evening, Captain?'

'I'd like that, sir.'

'Good. I'll call you at headquarters. Please give my compliments to General Leporello. Tell him I hope to see him soon.'

'I'll do that, sir, with pleasure.'

'Goodnight, Roditi. Enjoy yourself.'

As I walked past the bar, I saw Patrizia Pompa deep in talk with a small doll-like blonde in a green pant-suit. She gave me a wink and a farewell twitch of the fingers. She didn't need me any more, she was back in circulation again.

It was three in the morning when I got back to the apartment. I was desperately tired; but I could not sleep until I had set down a summary of the evening's encounters. We were in profit on several heads. In Giorgione, I had a friend and a source of information. Roditi was vulnerable, by reason of his sexual interests. Leporello was unpopular with his staff, some of whom might be persuaded to inform against him. The debit column, however, was alarming. Leporello had in training an apparatus of terror which could operate at will inside or outside the law. Such a group attracted social delinquents and put enormous power into the hands of a political manipulator. If the manipulator achieved political success, the apparatus became an arm of government, self-perpetuating and self-justified. There was a debit against my personal account as well. If the murders in the Via Sicilia were the work of the apparatus, it would be difficult, if not impossible, to prove charges against Roditi and Leporello. If Leporello wanted me removed, he had a whole pack of well-trained bully-boys to stalk me into ambush.

It was a chill thought. It haunted me through a restless sleep, and was still with me when I woke, blear-eyed and irritable, at ten in the morning.

At midday, Steffi arrived, chirpy as a cricket. He brought me blessings from his wife, who, he claimed, was happy to be rid of him. He recited greetings from some of our colleagues in Rome and a litany of curses against the time-servers. He surveyed every inch of the apartment and concluded mournfully that only a whore could enjoy such luxury without a twinge of conscience. Purged at last of wisdom and bile, he listened in silence while I told him what had happened to me since our last meeting. Then, sober and subdued he gave me his own version of events in Rome:

'... We liberals are out of date, little brother. Every current flows against us. Every wind blows contrary. Just when we think we have a moment of quiet to water the flowers, the Arabs Hijack another airliner, or the Zionists knock off an agent, or some twenty-year-old idiots hold up a bank or the police fire on demonstrators in some depressed province. If it's not happening inside the country, it's just next door. Look, a simple thing! When I arrived at the airport this morning, the computer system had broken down. A little mechanical fault, but suddenly there was chaos. The booking clerks wouldn't handle the inquiries. The airline officials went into hiding. And five thousand passengers on domestic and international flights didn't know whether they were coming or going. We're not like the English. We don't form a queue and read *The Times*. We shout and scream just for the merry hell of it. But someone only had to scream too loud or jostle too hard this morning, and there could have been a riot. . . . For what? A blown fuse that cost maybe a hundred lire. . . . That's the terror of it, Matucci. Nobody blames the fuse. Everybody wants a scapegoat who can be kicked into a bloody mess because the plane's late. They're daubing slogans on the bridges of Rome now: "Death to the Fascists", "Down with the Marxists". And where I live, it's "Zionist pig!" . . . I wonder if you know what you're really fighting, my friend?'

'Do you?'

'Sometimes I wish I didn't. *Simia quam similis*. . . .'

'I don't know that one, Steffi.'

'The ape, the vilest of the beasts, how like to us! Cicero. . . . We haven't changed much since his time, have we?'

'No, except we've got computers to multiply the vileness. Steffi, understand something. This is a damn dangerous project. I don't want you too close to me. You work from the Europa Hotel. We meet in a variety of places.'

'What do you want me to do?'

'We're investigating murder. So, it's old-fashioned detective work, Steffi. On Leporello and Roditi first. I want to know what they eat for breakfast and what brand of toothpaste they use. If you've got any friendly colleagues at Milan Headquarters, use them; but for God's sake be careful.'

'I should give you the same advice, little brother. The Director doesn't love you any more.'

'But he has a vested interest in keeping me alive. His own words, Steffi!'

'He didn't tell you what the interest was, did he?'

'No.'

'So, let me give you more bad news. He has a man working full-time on your record.'

'Who told you this?'

'Rampolla. He was making a big joke of it. Some joke! You've sailed very close to the wind in your time, Matucci. You need a very sympathetic biographer to make you halfway respectable. At this moment, they're writing a Black Book on you.'

'I'm writing a Black Book of my own, Steffi.'

'The big question for the big money—who gets into print first? One more item. . . . Woodpecker has been under interrogation every day since you left Rome. He's sold out his whole network. And your girl-friend, Lili Anders, figures prominently in the transcript.'

'They can't touch her now. The Swiss don't extradite for political offences.'

'They do for criminal acts.'

'Oh, come on, Steffi. I know her dossier backwards. There's nothing like that against her.'

'There wasn't when you last looked at it. There may be now. If you're fond of the woman, it's a thing to think about. . . .'

'Steffi, you make me feel like Job on his dunghill.'

'So, bless the Lord for your afflictions, little brother, and pray loud and strong for His mercies. Also, don't underrate the Director. He wants you alive—but buried up to your neck in the same dunghill. . . . Do you have a drink in this bawdy-house?'

'For news like that, I should feed you cyanide.'

'Make it Scotch whisky and I'll give you a few good words for a change.'

'The words first, you old vulture.'

'Remember the letter-bomb that was posted in Lili Anders' flat?'

'Yes?'

'The police sent us a forensic report on it. The report came across my desk, together with a nice clear set of prints, matched from their files. I brought a copy with me, in case they might be useful.'

'And?'

'The prints belonged to Marco Vitucci, age twenty-eight, one-time steward with the Flotta Bernardo, wanted in Rome and Naples on several counts of larceny and robbery with violence.'

'Never heard of him.'

'Nor I. But it's a start—a link in the chain. The police are working actively to trace him. He is known to use two other names, for which he has false documents. The names are Turi Goldoni and Giuseppe Balbo. . . .'

'Say that last one again.'

'Giuseppe Balbo.'

'Steffi, you're a genius! You're a towering transcendental magician!'

'I know it; but since when have you discovered it?'

'Now . . . this minute! I told you I met Roditi last night at the Club Alcibiade. One of the boys with him was called Giuseppe Balbo.'

'If it's the same one, that's almost enough to nail Roditi as well.'

'Almost, but not quite. Not with the protection he's got. But it's a beautiful beginning and, since it's a police report, SID can't bury it. Steffi, the soup's beginning to cook . . . !'

'So, please may I have my whisky?'

We talked it upside down and roundabout, through lunch and into the afternoon. We arranged codes, meeting places, a schedule of telephone contacts; then Steffi left to rest his aged bones at the hotel and plot his own campaign of investigation. I had just finished transcribing the new information on to tape, when the telephone rang and Major-General Leporello came on the line. He was brisk, but surprisingly cordial:

'Welcome to Milan, Colonel.'

'Thank you, sir.'

'Captain Roditi delivered your message. I should be delighted to see you.'

'I simply wanted to pay my respects, sir. I know how busy you are.'

'Dinner on Thursday. How would that suit?'

'Yes, sir. I'm free on that night.'

'Good. My house at eight-thirty for nine. I'll send you a confirmation with directions how to get there. Strictly informal–a family foursome. Er–is there someone you would care to bring?'

'No, sir.'

'Leave it to my wife, then–she's the party girl. You and I can have a private chat over the coffee. By the way, have you ever thought about my offer?'

'Yes, sir, I have.'

'Let's talk about it again. Until Thursday then.'

'I look forward to it, General.'

I had expected some approach–drinks in the Mess perhaps, coffee at the Club–but this was out of all character and proportion. Two weeks ago he wanted me dead; now he wanted me to dinner. The two wishes were not necessarily in contradiction–there have been many notable treacheries at Italian dinner-tables–but they were certainly anomalous. I could hardly wear side-arms to a family foursome, but I had only forty-eight hours to find a very long spoon.

Steffi's news had disturbed me, profoundly, not because it was unexpected, but because, once again, I had lapsed into dangerous inattention, selecting only one issue and ignoring the whole complex of threats and problems behind it. The Black Book was an ingenious perversion, first designed by the Director as a training exercise and then refined into a technique of blackmail. The trick was to take a man's dossier and by editing, emphasis and interpretation, distort it into a criminal caricature. For 'bachelor' read 'not interested in women', for 'likes card games' read 'known gambler' and you have the art in a nutshell. It's a filthy game, but it works, because every man has some guilts, and the simple exhibition of the dossier to the victim is a crushing display of cynical power.

I knew the game, because I had played it often. I knew, too, that I was the easiest victim in the world, a secret agent working always on the outer margin of the law and sometimes a long way beyond it. Lili Anders was in a similar position, a known subversive, guest in a neutral country. It needed only a telephone call from the Director to his counterpart in Switzerland, and she, too, would be helpless as a leaf in a winter storm. I was still chewing on that sour thought when a courier arrived with two messages from Bruno Manzini.

The first was a note in which, apologizing for short notice, he requested me to dine with him this night at the Bankers' Club, in order, as he put it, 'to meet money and see whether it smells or not'. He suggested we meet in the card-room half an hour before dinner for a private briefing. The second was a letter from Lili:

> My dear,
>   It is so long since I have written to a man, that I hardly know how to begin. I would guess that you, my careful amorist, have never written letters to a woman at all. Uncle Pavel doesn't count, because he doesn't exist; but it was nice to hear from him just the same.
>   I am sitting on my balcony, bathed in sunshine, with a marvellous vista of green valley and snow-covered peaks, and farms that look like dolls' houses–all

mine to enjoy. And I am enjoying it, my dear, in a way I would never have thought possible. I do very little. I walk. I read. I have taken up petit point. I chat to the other guests. In the evenings, I play bridge. I am in bed by ten and I sleep until the maid brings my breakfast. It is all so simple, I wonder how I let it escape me for so long.

I worry sometimes, because I am still so transient and insecure; but my lawyer, Herr Neumann, reassures me. He is a little old man with white hair and gold pincenez. He calls me 'young woman'–which is always a help. He knows all about me now–except some very intimate things–and he says that perhaps I may be able to apply for political asylum. He has taken a lot of depositions and is seeking advice from colleagues in Zurich. I rather like the idea of asylum. It sounds almost like finding refuge in a church, where everything is confessed and everything is forgiven and you can begin again without fear.

The people here are simple folk, sober and kind. The guests are pleasant, too. There are a couple of elderly ladies, one of whom is my bridge partner. There is a honeymoon couple who make me envious sometimes; an American professor, rather elderly, who is writing a book on the Germanic migrations; and there is a very dashing fellow from Lugano, who talks to me in Italian and buys me a cocktail before dinner and keeps offering me whirlwind tours in his Maserati. I haven't accepted yet; but I may soon. He's attentive. He's not bad-looking and quite intelligent–an engineer or something on a construction project ten miles from here.

And you, my Dante Alighieri, how are you? I don't ask what you are doing because I know too much and can do nothing to help. I love you and I miss you; but I dare not let myself depend on the loving, and I must get used to the missing. I tell you only that I dream of you often and when I wake I half-expect to find you there beside me. As I write, I am jealous of every woman you meet or will meet. I wonder if you are jealous of my engineer. I'd like to think so.

Take care, my dear. Think gently of me as I do of you.

One fine tomorrow, perhaps I'll be

Yours Lili.

I read it three times, then tore it up and burned the shreds in the ashtray. I was jealous and I had no right to be. If I wasn't in love, then I was as near to it as I had ever been in my life. I couldn't risk the distraction. I couldn't afford the luxury. Forget it then! There were too many dangerous tomorrows to survive, and Lili's bright and shining day might never come.

The Bankers' Club in Milan is only a whit less venerable than the Chess Club in Rome. It is, however, much more impressive, because the focus of its power is clearer and all its members are fluent in a single, international language–money. It is a religious language reserved to priests and acolytes, like Church Latin or the time-symbols of the Incas. It is precise, flexible, subtle and quite unintelligible to the profane populace. It is proof of the cyclic nature of history: because the first banks in the world were the temples of Babylon, Greece and Rome, where you could raise loans, make deposits, arrange credit and have your coinage tested by assay under the vigilant eyes of the local deity.

If you ask why a fellow like me should know or care about such things, then I must remind you again that I am a Tuscan, and that I was bred to the history of the Bardi and the Frescobaldi and the Petruzzi, who were bankers to the English Crown in the fourteenth century and that my father was an old line socialist, who talked me blind about the need to nationalize the banks and put the speculators out of business. I like money. Who doesn't? I am also fascinated by its history, its forms, its potency why some men make it and most men lose it and even Charon, the ferry-man, demands a coin to row you across the Styx into eternity.

So, I found a certain propriety in the fact that my first entry into the world of Bruno Manzini should be made throught the portals of the Bankers' Club. I was also curious to know why he had chosen so sensitive and sacrosanct a place to present me. I put the question to him in so many words, as we sat over cocktails in the card-room, a privilege reserved to the most senior priesthood. He answered me, with a grin:

'It's an exercise in logic, my dear Dante. Here everyone has money. Money imposes discretion. Discretion conduces to free speech. Here, therefore, there is free speech–quite a lot of it, in fact. There are six of us who meet for dinner once a month. We talk about everything under the sun. Any member may bring a guest, provided he guarantees him as a safe man with a secret.'

'Thanks for the compliment.'

'I can pay you compliments anytime, my dear Dante. There are two men I want you to meet tonight. One is Ludovisi from the Banco Centrale, the other is Frantisek, from the Opera Pontificia at the Vatican. He's one of the shrewdest bankers in the business. The fact that he's an American and a Bishop is incidental. Both these men can be very useful to you.'

'How?'

'They can tell you, quicker than anybody, where the big money is going, and why. There's another reason, too. Ludovisi is the brother-in-law of your Director.' He chuckled and held up his hand. 'No, don't be alarmed. They love each other like cat and dog. Ludovisi is suing for divorce. He blames his wife's family for the failure of the marriage. He's very eloquent and very well briefed on the subject. Frantisek, on the other hand, is a very complex character. He looks like a football player, talks Italian with a Brooklyn accent, has a golf handicap of five, and stands in high favour with the reigning Pontiff. He helped to reorganize the Vatican's financial arrangements and negotiate the tax settlement with the Italian Government. He's not a very good theologian. His philosophy is pure pragmatism. His noblest virtue is a fanatical loyalty to the Holy See. Still, he does smell the wind, and if he likes you, he can be a very powerful friend. The rest? Well, they're agreeable and well-informed. One's a Liberal, the others are Christian Democrats of varying shades. Paolini's an out and out Fascist, but on a personal basis he's so agreeable you can almost forgive him.'

'And what do you expect me to do?'

'Whatever you like. Talk, listen, argue. If you make a gaffe, don't worry; it's the privilege of the Club. Now, tell me, what have you been doing?'

He heard me out in silence and then gave a long, low whistle of satisfaction.

'Good! Good! As you say the soup is beginning to cook. What do you propose to do now?'

'Wait until I have more evidence, much more. It's a risk. You must understand that. I may lose Giuseppe Balbo, who is our only link with what happened in Rome. But if I take him now, and hand him to the police, I may lose the big ones, Roditi and Leporello. You know the way things are. We need a brass-bound case before we open proceedings, and a notarized copy of every document in our own hands.'

He frowned over that for a long while and then, finally, nodded agreement.

'I hate the thought of losing a key witness; but the risk of premature action is even less palatable. These new riot squads worry me. It's only one step from those to the Brazilian *Esquadras de la Muerte* . . . police assassins. Let's take some soundings round the table tonight and see if there's any news floating around. I know Leporello is in high favour with the business men just now. He gave a talk here last week on the theme of Order and Progress. Very seductive, I hear. Very well received. I wonder why he's asked you to dinner, and who the fourth guest will be. Woman bait?'

'Possibly. Though it hardly seems his style.'

'If he's recruiting homosexual gymnasts and criminals, I shouldn't think he'd balk at simple seduction. Let's go in, shall we? The others should be here by now.'

We were eight people at a round table so that there was no question of precedence. Protocol was honoured by an opening grace from Bishop Frantisek, who, indeed, did look like a football player. His accent was appalling, but his grammar was faultless, his talk fluent and his manners affable. Ludovisi was the wit of the group, a lean, grey-eyed dandy, with a faun's grin and a fund of scandalous stories. The others, with the exception of Paolini, were typical of their breed, well-barbered, well-fed, eloquent about everything to do with money, agreeably cynical about any other human concern. Paolini I found an enigma. His manners were impeccable and he radiated charm, but his mind was closed to every logic but his own—which I must confess was hard to refute. His hobby-horse was multinational companies, the great concerns which spanned the frontiers of the world and operated in all jurisdictions, with no allegiance to any.

'. . . Four thousand companies making fifteen per cent of gross world product, that's what we're talking about. They control more assets than many of the countries in which they operate. Look at General Motors! Twenty-eight billion dollars in annual sales. Royal Dutch Shell, twelve and a half billion. . . . What single government can regulate enterprises like that? No democracy certainly. The lobby's too powerful, the leverage in employment and capital is too great, to say nothing of external pressures exercised through commerce and diplomacy. . . . And they're getting bigger all the time, like a fat man who can't stop eating. You fellows laugh at me and label me a Fascist, but show me any authority as strong and belligerent as a board of a giant company. De Gaulle saw it. The Labour unions see it, and it's the best argument they have for Marxism. . . . Even the Americans are seeing it now, as the Japanese apply the lesson and build multinationals of their own. . . .'

'So, what do you want?' Ludovisi cut in with a laugh. 'A junta that can be bought quicker than a parliament, because there's no one left to ask questions? Come now! Be realistic.'

'I am being realistic, my dear fellow. Look what happened in Greece. A few years ago you could hardly raise a dollar for investment. Now, they've got some law and order, the money's pouring in. Even expatriate capital is coming back. And the Government controls the terms. That's a much better situation than we've got at this moment.'

'Correction, old friend.' The Monsignore cut in with a tart reminder. 'The Colonels suspended law and imposed order.'

'It's a proper distinction,' said Bruno Manzini, mildly, 'but I wonder if it really makes any difference to the man in the street. We've got so many laws that we can't enforce them, and we end up with Government by regulation.

We've got so many parties that the people are not represented at all, only factional interests.'

Ludovisi gave him a quick questioning glance. Paolini applauded.

'Bravo! If Bruno here can see the light, why not the rest of you?'

'It's not the light,' said Manzini, with an impish grin. 'I think it may be a pillar of cloud with a very familiar demon inside it. Did anybody hear the speech General Leporello made here last week?'

'I did,' said Paolini. 'I thought he made excellent sense.'

There seemed to be a tepid agreement on that from everyone, except Ludovisi, who threw up his hands in despair and groaned aloud.

'My God! The fellow used every cliché in the handbook . . . "liberty is not licence; the desire of the people for a peaceful society; provocative elements; strong security measures" . . . Oh, dear, dear, dear! It sounded like my brother-in-law talking with his tongue in his cheek. Paolini, have you met this fellow personally?'

'I have. I think he's the kind of man we need, resolute, clear-headed, absolutely incorruptible.'

'I've yet to meet an incorruptible man. Has anyone else met this paragon?'

I saw, or thought I saw, a faint signal from Manzini, so I moved into the discussion.

'I know him.'

The Monsignore's eyebrows went up and he leaned his bulky body across the table to question me.

'And what's your opinion of him, Matucci?'

'I'd rather not make a judgment of him as a man. I will say he's embarked on a highly dangerous policy.'

'What policy is that?'

'Surely you gentlemen know. It's all over town. I'm new here, but I get it in every bar. He's recruiting special riot squads on the lines of the French Barbouzes. It's a secret operation and that worries me. I know where some of the recruits are coming from and that worries me even more.'

'Where do they come from, Matucci?'

'Resorts of known criminals and social delinquents.'

'That's a serious statement.' Paolini was visibly shocked.

'I know. I make it in the privacy of this gathering. I shall be presenting some evidence in support to Major-General Leporello himself next Thursday.'

'Perhaps he knows it already,' said Ludovisi, grimly. 'Have you thought of that? You mentioned the Barbouzes. You could also have mentioned the *Esquadras de la Muerte* in Brazil. It's a familiar pàttern: pull the rowdies off the streets and set them breaking heads under legal sanction. If your information is correct, Matucci, I'd say we were in for a very bloody mess.'

'I agree.'

'I think we're making a morbid pre-judgment.' Paolini was too bland and urbane to be true. 'Why don't we change the subject. No offence, Matucci, but you don't know my colleagues as well as I do. If you spread panic and alarm like that, you'll rattle the market for a month. Eh, Bruno?'

'I hope not.' Manzini chuckled like a happy child. 'I'm coming into the market myself tomorrow. The English have just come out with an electron welder that will join two plates of twenty centimetre steel in a single welding pass. I want to buy rights in it and finance a local manufacture. Any of you fellows interested, or do I have to go to the Vatican? You'll come in, won't you, Monsignore? Just what his Holiness needs to repair the rifts in the Church.'

They all laughed at that and the tension relaxed. As we moved from the dining-room to take coffee in the salon, Ludovisi laid a hand on my arm and steered me towards the men's room. He was sombre and preoccupied.

'That was bad news, Matucci. How sure are you?'

'Very sure.'

'Do you know where it's pointing?'

'Yes.'

'How do you know?'

'I work for SID, as well as for Manzini.'

'Then you know my brother-in-law.'

'Yes.'

'Where does he stand in this matter? Before you answer, it must be obvious that I don't like him. I think he's both devious and dangerous.'

'As a serving officer, I couldn't comment. As a guest in your Club, I would say that I agree with you. For the public record I would deny ever having made such a statement.'

'Thank you. Here's my card. If ever I can help, please call me.'

'Thank you, but I doubt you can help me with this mess.'

'You keep an open mind. I'll keep an open door. *D'accordo?*'

At eleven-thirty, the guests dispersed; but Manzini held me back for a final coffee in the card-room. He was obviously tired. There were dark circles under his eyes and his skin had a curious yellow tinge. Even his waspish wit had deserted him. When I asked if he were unwell, he shrugged wearily.

'That dinner tonight. . . . Truly, I could go out and cut my wrists in a bath-tub! You shoved a live grenade under their noses and only two had sense enough to see it. . . . The others didn't want to see it. . . . Have you never thought, friend, that if you die one night in a back street, you will be dying for men like these?'

'You must have thought about it, too.'

'I did, many times. Remember my telling you about my Uncle Freddie? I thought of him this evening when you were telling me about these types that Roditi is recruiting. Freddie could be vicious, too: mostly when he was short of money or frustrated in some affair, which happened more and more as he got older. He used to sponge on my mother, and if weeping didn't open her purse, he would try a little blackmail. . . . That's how I found out that Uncle Pantaleone was my father. I must have been—let me see—oh, about ten, I suppose. I had a new toy, a jack-in-the-box. I wanted to surprise Mamma with it. I crept into the salon where she was talking with Uncle Freddie and I hid behind the settee. I found myself in the middle of a bitter quarrel. Freddie wanted money. Mamma was refusing vehemently. Then Freddie threatened to spread the story of my parentage all over town. He must have been very desperate, because never before had he shown me anything but kindness. Finally, I couldn't stand it any longer. I burst out of my hiding-place and begged them to stop quarrelling. I don't remember what was said; but I do remember a long strange silence and how ill Freddie looked and how I had never seen Mamma so fierce and angry. . . . After that, I never saw Freddie again. . . . I know what happened to him. I could read by then. I saw it in a newspaper. One night, not long afterwards, he was wandering drunk and maudlin along Lungotuvere. He was accosted by a young sailor, who invited him on to a river barge. There he was bound, gagged and beaten until he died. A fowler discovered his body, ten days later, tangled in the reeds half-way to Ostia. . . . He wasn't very popular. Indeed, in his latter years, he was very disreputable. But he was well-connected in England, so the police were diligent in their inquiries and they made a voluminous report to the British Consul. It seems the people who killed him were paid for the job. . . .'

'By whom?'

'Oh, I didn't know that for a long time. Not until my mother died and I had to go through her papers and possessions. I found Freddie's signet ring with a tiny label on it: "In memoriam . . . Pantaleone". My father was a very thorough man, you see; and like me, he had a taste for irony. . . . There's a sequel, my Dante. It may answer the question you've been too polite to ask. When the Gestapo had me in gaol—I'd been under interrogation for about a week, I think, and I wasn't in very good shape—my half-brother came to see me. He was Captain, then: very chic, very General Staff. He offered me a bargain. In return for the list of the Salamander network, the Gestapo would release me and I could live out the war in comfortable retirement at the Pantaleone Villa in Frascati. . . . I didn't spit in his eye, like a hero. I was too sick and tired. I told him the story I have just told you. I thought I was signing my death warrant, which would have suited me very well at that moment. . . . But my brother was only half the man my father was. I was handed back to the interrogators. They worked on me for another month. Then, one day, without warning, I was released into house arrest. I was put into a closed car and driven to Frascati. The servants at the Villa nursed me. My brother was away on army business. I couldn't leave the house. And, anyway, I was unwell and I had no place to go and no papers to take me. One day, my brother came to see me. He told me he had procured my release. He told me why: he wanted to discharge his father's obligations to me! I'm afraid I did spit in his eye then; though, looking back, I think he meant at least half of it. That was the half that took me to his funeral. The other half. . . . Well, you see what I mean about motives for martyrdom, don't you? Sometimes they're simple: and sometimes they're very confused. . . .'

Early next morning, while I was still rubbing the sleep out of my eyes, Giorgione telephoned me from his home. He had good news. From a word dropped in the canteen and a few careful inquiries from Rita in the file room, he had discovered the location of a new camp. He thought it could be one of those used for the training of the riot squads. He gave me a name and a map reference: Camerata, a small Lombard town in the mountains north of Bergamo, about an hour's run from Milan. He told me I would have no difficulty finding the place, but I might have difficulty getting inside it. The location was classified as a maximum security area. He had other information, too. Captain Roditi lived, in some style, in a new apartment block not far from the Europa Hotel. The rents were higher than he could afford on a Captain's stipend. So, either he had private income, or someone was subsidizing him.

I called down blessings on Giorgione's tousled head and then sat down to a very meditative breakfast. After breakfast, I rang Roditi's office to set our appointment for drinks. His sergeant told me Roditi had left for Turin with General Leporello and would not be back until Thursday afternoon. At nine, Stefanelli called in. I told him we were going for a run into the country. I would pick him up at his hotel in thirty minutes. By ten, we were out on the autostrada, cruising westward to the Bergamo exit.

My plan was simple but risky. As a serving officer of SID, I was still in possession of my official identity document, which would procure me entrance to any military or civilian installation, and access to all documents, however classified. The risk was that the commanding officer could insist on his right to check the document back to its origin before admitting me to his area. I proposed, therefore, to drop Steffi off in Bergamo with instructions to telephone Manzini if I were detained beyond a reasonable time. Steffi was not enthusiastic.

'I think you're crazy, Matucci. If they do check your document, you're up to your neck in trouble.'

'I know, Steffi; but the omens are good today. Leporello and Roditi are out of town. I think I can bluff my way past any questions.'

'What's the reason for the visit–the official reason?'

'The best. I'm looking for a man named Marco Vitucci, wanted on charges of subversion and murder. We feel he may have slipped through the screening into a sensitive organization. I won't find Vitucci, of course. But if I do find Giuseppe Balbo, then we're in big profit.'

'Enough to buy you a beautiful tombstone, little brother.'

'Relax, Steffi. It's a beautiful day. . . . I'll be back in a couple of hours and I'll buy you the best lunch in Bergamo.'

'And what am I supposed to do for two hours in Bergamo?'

'Let's see . . . you could make a pilgrimage to the house of Papa Giovanni. After all he did make the Jews respectable again, and a lot of people didn't like him for it. . . . You could read some Tasso, you could listen to some Donizetti or even dance the *bergamasca*, if you can find a girl old enough to remember it.'

'Regular little tourist guide, aren't you, Matucci?'

'You wouldn't believe it, Steffi, but I was just that in my student days–until I made an improper suggestion to one of the clients. She was willing enough but her husband caught us holding hands in the Cappella Colleoni and I lost my job. You might pay a little visit there, just for my sake.'

'I've got a much better idea, little brother. Let's keep driving until we get to Switzerland. You can settle down with your girl and I'll peddle cuckoo clocks to the tourists. That way we both stay alive a little longer.'

From Bergamo the road wound upwards through the Brembo Valley, curving along the flanks of the Lombard hills. I drove carefully, rehearsing myself for the touchy moments of my first entry into the camp. At Camerata I stopped to ask directions, and ran against the first security perimeter. The three people I asked knew there was a camp somewhere, but had no idea where is was. Finally, I had to call on the local police and produce my card to the *brigadiere*, who drew me a map on a sheet of yellow paper. Even then, I nearly missed the turn-off, a narrow corrugated defile enclosed at the end of a stockade of logs surmounted by a watch-tower with a searchlight and a machine gun.

There were guards at the gate as well, two husky fellows who halted me ten yards from the entrance and demanded to know my business. I showed them my card and told them I wanted to see the Commandant. One of them took my card and went back to his box to telephone. I waited five minutes and then they waved me through the gates and closed them behind me.

Inside, the place was grim and unwelcoming: twin rows of log huts with a broad parade-ground in between, and beyond, a vast basin, half-cleared, half still under timber, which was obviously the training area. I parked my car outside the Commandant's office and went inside. A desk sergeant took my card and disappeared into the next room. I waited another five minutes, before I was ushered into the presence of a slim bullet-headed Major, who looked as though he could straighten horse-shoes and tear telephone books with his bare hands. His desk was a mess of papers and he was quite self-conconscious about it. He fumbled with this sheet and that, as if he were still not sure what was written on it. His greeting was respectful, uneasy.

'Major Zenobio at your service, Colonel. I'm afraid I had no notice of your visit.'

'There were good reasons, Major.'

'Oh?'

'General Leporello left for Turin early this morning. I was still waiting on information from Rome, which came through just before ten o'clock. I left immediately. I am required to report to the General on his return. In fact, we're dining together tomorrow evening. If you feel the need to check that, please telephone his secretary immediately. I'd like to get down to business.'

He hesitated for a moment, took another look at my card, then closed it and handed it back to me. His tone was one degree less frigid.

'No, I don't think we'll need that, Colonel. Now, your business is . . . ?'

'Reserved to you and me at this stage, Major. I have to insist on that from the outset.'

'I understand.'

He fumbled with the papers again, tossing them about like confetti. For me, a man whose life depended on paper, it was a kind of sacrilege.

'Major, I'm looking for a man. The police want him for attempted murder. We want him because he is a known subversive, and we need to talk to him before anyone else.'

'And you hope to find him here, Colonel?'

'There's a certain logic in the idea that appeals to my people. These new groups of yours constitute a sensitive project, highly political. Your recruiting methods are, shall we say, unorthodox. To put it more bluntly, it has been decided, as a matter of high policy, that even social delinquents are acceptable, provided that they can be retrained to certain essential skills. Correct?'

'Correct.'

'Next. The project is secret, the requirements special. A man who wanted to go underground might well present himself for enlistment. If his dossier didn't look too disastrous, you would accept him.'

'A question, Colonel. The project is secret. How does your man know about it?'

'Ah, that's one of the matters I have to discuss with the General tomorrow night. It doesn't affect you, Major, but it does affect another officer who has been less than discreet. . . . However, that's confidential until the General gives clearance. Take it for granted that the man would know and could present himself. . . . Now, we're not interested in the police side of it at all. But a known subversive, an active Marxist agent, inside this kind of group—well! You do see my point?'

'Too clearly, Colonel. What's the name of your man?'

'Marco Vitucci.'

'Let's take a look at the nominal roll.'

'We'll come to that in a moment. What other records do you keep on your troops?'

'Each man has a record card, which contains his personal details and the reports of the training staff.'

'Photographs?'

'Each card carries a photograph, a thumbprint and a list of distinguishing marks. These are recorded also on the subject's identity document, which he carries at all times in addition to his civilian identification.'

'Good. Now, let's have a look at the nominal rolls.'

It took him three minutes to find them under the mess on his desk and in his trays. It took only a minute to establish that in a list of four hundred men in two training groups, there was no Marco Vitucci.

'Well, we do have one other alias.' I thumbed ostentatiously through my notebook. 'Here it is—Barone, Turi.' That landed me among the B's. There was no Barone either; but I did light on the name, Balbo, Giuseppe, and I pointed it out to the Major.

'Balbo, eh? Nothing to do with the case, of course. I was just wondering if he's any relation to General Balbo, who marched with the *Duce*?'

The Major smiled for the first time.

'I doubt it. But let's take a look, just for curiosity. Funny if it were though. Balbo was one of the first quadrumvirate of Fascism. We could be the new beginnings. . . . Here you are.'

He opened a filing cabinet, took out a card and handed it to me. I scanned it carefully. The identification was clear. This was the same man I had met with Roditi in the Club Alcibiade. If the thumbprint tallied with the one on the police files, then I had everything I needed. I handed the card back to the Major, who tossed it on to the littered desk, and then half-buried it under the nominal rolls.

'No connection, I'm afraid. The old General was a Ferrarese. This one comes from Gaeta. Well, it was a pleasant fantasy. That's all, I think, Major. Painless for you, disappointing for me. Still, we'll keep trying. I wonder if I could ask you one favour?'

'Anything, Colonel.'

'Could I have a cup of coffee?'

'Certainly.'

He yelled for the sergeant, and when there was no answer, he went through the door at a run and I could hear him shouting across the parade-ground. I slipped the Balbo card in my pocket and followed him out.

'Please, Major, don't disturb yourself. I'll be on my way. Just a reminder. This visit is strictly reserved.'

'Of course, Colonel. Have a good journey.'

He was glad to see me go; but not half so glad as I was to hear the gates of the stockade slam behind me. The moment I was out of sight of the watch-tower, I stepped hard on the accelerator and drove fast and dangerously all the way to Bergamo. I snatched a plaintive Steffi from the square of the High Town and drove straight back to Milan. The prints on the Balbo card matched those which Steffi had brought from Rome. We made four Xerox copies and locked the original in the safe. Then we rang for Pietro and ordered champagne and a gourmet meal to celebrate this first real rape of the ungodly.

It was one of those jubilant hours that only a professional can understand and share. It was like winning a lottery or having the prettiest girl in the room wilt into your arms. I was the shrewdest fellow in the world, as racy a gambler as ever bet his wife's virtue on the turn of a card. But–*post coitum triste, post vinum capitis dolor!* at four in the afternoon, sober but sleepy, we still did not know what to do with the Balbo document. Steffi, who had missed his siesta, summed it up irritably.

'*Ebbene!* We now have evidence to put one Giuseppe Balbo in prison for life. You don't want that. You want him here, in this room, singing like a love-bird, telling you all he knows about Roditi, and the letter-bomb, and the murders in the Via Sicilia. Then you want Roditi here, singing another song about General Leporello. Then, when you've copied down the whole melody, what are you going to do with it? Like the Rabbi who played golf on the Sabbath and got a hole-in-one, whom do you tell? And when you tell, who's going to want to believe you? And, much more important, who's going to do anything about it? Matucci, little brother, big wooden-head, you have to answer all those questions!'

'Give me time, Steffi, for God's sake!'

'You don't have time, little brother. Suppose your Major Zenobio has missed the card?'

'I'm hoping he hasn't. He's careless with papers.'

'Suppose he rings Leporello to check on you.'

'I'm gambling he won't.'

'Gambling, hoping! On a thread like that you could hang yourself.'

'I know, I know! Let's take it one step at a time. I want doubt, confusion and panic. . . . What's the time?'

'Three thirty. Why?'

'How far is it to Chiasso?'

'Less than fifty kilometres. Again, why?'

I grabbed the telephone and dialled Bruno Manzini's private number. When he came on the line, I told him what I wanted.

'. . . A courier, Bruno. I want him now. He's to drive to Chiasso and post some letters. They have to be delivered in Milan with tomorrow's mail. And I'd like to see you as soon as possible, here, at the apartment. I'm sorry to bother you, but it's very urgent.'

Crotchety he might be, but he always ran true to form. The courier would be with me in fifteen minutes. He, himself, would join me at six. Steffi was looking at me as if I were an amiable lunatic. I unlocked the safe, took out the Balbo document, rubbed it clean with a new handkerchief and laid it on the desk. Then, I rang for Paolo and asked him to bring me a pair of his clean white gloves. Finally, Steffi could bear it no longer:

'So, tell me, Matucci! Or do I just stand here and watch you make like Inspector Maigret?'

'Step one. We make two fresh copies of the Balbo document. This time without our fingerprints all over the copy-paper. Step two. We clip Balbo's thumbprint off each copy. Step three. I type two identical notes to accompany the thumbprints. Step four. The said notes and thumbprints are posted to catch tonight's mail from Southern Switzerland.'

'And what will be in the notes?'

'Two names: Bandinelli, Calvi. A place: Via Sicilia, Rome. And the date on which they died.'

'And who gets the notes?'

'Major-General Leporello and Captain Roditi–at their private addresses.'

'And how long does it take them to run the print through records?'

'Forty-eight hours at least.'

'And how long to tie everything back to you through a stolen card?'

'Another twenty-four. Those are inside limits. We might do better.'

'Then what, little brother?'

'Then there is the beautiful scene, Steffi. I think we'll get Fellini to film it. I, Dante Alighieri Matucci, am standing solitary and noble in the middle of the Olympic Stadium. All the stands are full. All the spectators look exactly like the Director. They all have guns and they're all pointing at me. . . . What happens after that, I'm not sure.'

'I'm sure, Matucci. I'm going home to mother.'

'Oh, no you're not. Not tonight anyway. At ten o'clock we are going to make a private visit to the apartment of Captain Matteo Roditi. How does that sound?'

'Like madness, little brother. Like old-fashioned dancing madness!'

Bruno Manzini arrived punctually at six. When he heard of my day's exploits, he was not amused. He gave me no tolerant elegies either. He was coldly and eloquently angry.

'. . . Matucci, you shock me! You do not lack talent. You have vast experience. You have at least a rudimentary sense of politics. So this children's game you have played today is an incredible and inexcusable folly.'

'Now, listen, Cavaliere. . . !'

'No! You hear me first! You have compromised yourself. You have compromised me. You have set in motion a whole train of events for which we are quite unprepared, and for which we have no time to prepare! Good God, man! Have you learnt nothing? This is high politics. We are talking of revolution, Matucci, barricades in the streets, gunfire and bombs! Yet, you behave like some fly-brained agent from a comic book! Truly I despair!'

'I think you despair too quickly, Cavaliere.'

'Do you, indeed. Then show me half a grain of sense in this crack-brained escapade and I'll die happy.'

'Then, here it is. Locked in that safe, there is a document, perhaps the only existing document which can tie Roditi and Leporello to a conspiracy of murder. I procured it by a risky act with awkward consequences, but. . . .'

'Awkward! Mother of God! Is that what you call it?'

'. . . But, Cavaliere, if you don't take risks in my business, you're left standing like a clown while people pour buckets of water over your head. Next point, we agreed on a policy of doubt and confusion. I have begun to create it. . . .'

'Prematurely. Without foresight!'

'With hindsight then. We are dealing with conjurors, Cavaliere: people who can make files disappear, people who can suborn witnesses and silence politicians and buy perjurers with straw in their shoes–if we give them enough time. I am trying, rightly or wrongly, to deny them time. I'm a fly-brained agent, because I don't have the luxury to be Lorenzo di Medici compassing the downfall of his enemies by slow and princely degrees. I'm the opportunist, because I have to fight the skirmishes and the street-battles, and if I lose those, your campaign is so much scrap-paper! . . . Eh! This is madness! Let's drop it!'

He stared at me for a long moment, bleak-faced and hostile; then, he nodded, slowly, as if assenting to some private proposition of his own. Then, he set it down for me.

'*Ebbene!* You are right and I am right, and we are both equally wrong. Let's start from there and see what we can salvage.'

'No, Cavaliere. Let's see what we can build.'

A small reluctant smile twitched at the corners of his mouth.

'You're a real wooden-head, Matucci. What am I to do with you?'

'Wear me, Cavaliere. Like a hairshirt, if you must, but wear me. And give me some advice. We project from the evidence we have in hand. We establish a case that involves Balbo as an assassin, and Roditi and Leporello as conspirators. Where and how do we present our case? And how do we tie the Director into it? You say we're not prepared. I know we're not. So I need help against the high men, before they close ranks. Can you give it to me?'

'It's the Director who bothers you, isn't it?'

'Yes. He's got a perfect position. He can excuse everything he has done on the grounds that he was infiltrating a conspiracy that threatened the security of the State. He knows so many secrets that everyone's afraid of him, even his own Minister.'

'I'm not afraid of him, Dante.'

'That's hardly enough. You have to have the lever that will topple him.'

'We have the lever, my Dante. It's the fulcrum we need; and you, without knowing, may have provided it.'

'I don't understand.'

'I know you don't. And that is what makes me angry with you. In the fervour of a crusade, in the heat of a new situation, you slip out of gear. You change from logician to opportunist. You chase the marsh-light and forget the bale-fires burning on the hills behind you. Remember what happened at the lodge? In Venice? The same thing is happening now. This is why you are vulnerable to such a man as the Director. You have every talent he has, and some he lacks, but you cannot or you will not focus them. So, always until now, you have been a tool of other men's designs. . . . I'm sorry if I've offended you; but I have so much regard for you that I cannot bear what you do to yourself. . . . Let me show you what I mean. When you left my brother's house on the morning after his death, you left an old servant weeping into his liquor. You had asked him to record telephone calls for you. He did that. You never went back to collect the messages. I did. I went there to see to the wants of an old man who had known my father, Because he was afraid, he told me that he had lied to you. He was not awake when my brother came home from the Chess Club. He was drunk and snoring. He lied because he thought he would be blamed, for not putting on the alarms. They were off when he woke in the morning. . . . No, please don't interrupt. Let me embarrass you a moment longer. The night after my brother's funeral, I had his body removed from the vault. An autopsy was performed in the mortuary of a private clinic. My brother did take barbiturates. He probably took quite a large dose, but not enough to kill him. He was killed by an injection of air into the femoral artery. The mark of the syringe was clearly visible under the pubic hair. You see what happened, Dante? You connived with the Director to hush up a suicide. You were made an accomplice in murder.'

'Why didn't you tell me this before?'

For a full minute he said absolutely nothing. His eyes were filmed over like those of a bird, so that he seemed not to be looking at me, but away and beyond into some immeasurable distance. He sat quite rigid, with his fingertips joined and laid against his thin pursed lips. When he spoke, his voice was frosty, remote, like the first chill wind of autumn.

'To teach you a lesson, Matucci. Trust no one. Not even me. Don't believe that the old Adam is dead until you've screwed down the coffin and seen the grave-digger stamp the last sod on top of him.'

He was right, of course. The old bastard was always right. We Latins are the most logical people in the world. We mistrust our mothers when they give us the teat. The only things we believe happily are unprovable propositions like weeping Madonnas, and flying houses and infallible Popes.

Our visit to Roditi's apartment began auspiciously. There was a party on the sixth floor; the foyer was busy with guests in evening-dress and the porter had lost count of the arrivals. Steffi and I rode with the party-goers as far as the fifth floor and stepped out on to a deserted landing. We rang the bell on Roditi's apartment; and, when there was no answer, I used a pick-lock and opened the door in thirty seconds. It was as simple as shelling green peas.

The interior of the apartment was a surprise. I had expected an epicene elegance or perhaps a feminine clutter. I found, instead, a place as aseptic and impersonal as a hotel room. The furniture was Danish modern. The pictures, arranged in a severe symmetry, were all of soldiers in historic costumes. There was a cabinet for drinks and a stereo-player with a collection of popular songs, film-scores and American musicals. The desk was bare, except for a blotting pad of tooled leather and a leather cup full of ball-point pens and freshly-sharpened pencils. The place was spotless and the teak furniture glowed with wax and recent polishing.

We began our search in the kitchen. We found coffee and bread and butter and cheese and a carton of milk. The dining-room was furnished with linen, cutlery and glassware for six persons. Everything was of good quality. None of it distinguished. In the liquor cabinet there was one spare bottle of each drink and perhaps a dozen assorted mineral waters. The books in the salon were innocuous: paperback novels, a few biographies. There was no pornography, no sign of sexy prints or photographs. The drawers of the desk were unlocked. They contained notepaper and envelopes and a few blocks of ruled drafting paper. The bathroom revealed nothing except that the Captain's toiletries were expensive, though not exotic.

The bedroom was more rewarding. Roditi had ten suits and four uniforms, all made by an expensive tailor. His shirts were handmade and monogrammed. He was prolific in shoes, ties, scarves and costly accessories. He was either a very tidy man, or he had a jewel of a maid, because his drawers were set with mathematical precision and his dressing-table was laid like a show-piece in a store.

In the right-hand drawer of the dressing-table, face-down, was a photograph in a silver frame. It was a portrait, obviously taken by a professional, of a woman in her early thirties, who bore a striking resemblance to Rafael's Donna Velata in the Pitti Gallery in Florence. There were the same dark eyes, large and lustrous, the same nose, a little large for perfect beauty, the same mouth, soft and enigmatic in repose. Even the hair-style was similar: dark, straight tresses drawn back over her ears and braided behind the head. The photograph was inscribed in a bold, round hand, 'To my dearest Matteo, for memory and for promise, Elena'.

Beside the photograph I found a bundle of letters, more than thirty, held together by a rubber band. They were written in the same hand, signed with the same name. I read them and passed them one by one to Steffi. They were love-letters, lyrical, tender, totally uninhibited in their celebration of the nights and days of a passionate affair. I have thumbed through many letters in my time, but these moved me deeply and I felt a sudden shame at my invasion of the privacy of this unknown woman. The letters were undated. There was no address. From the text and the references, it was clear that they had been written over a period of several years and that the last was written no more than a week ago. Elena was married, unhappily, to a husband older than herself. Roditi, whatever his other vices or virtues, was obviously a passionate and thoughtful lover. There was no reproach in any of the letters, only yearning and gratitude and a vivid, sensual poetry. Even old Steffi was awed. He handed the last note back to me and said, sombrely:

'Eh, Matucci! If you and I could move a woman like that. . . .'

'It doesn't make sense, Steffi. A fellow like Roditi. . . .'

'He makes sense to her, little brother, the most beautiful sense in the world.'

'A *finocchio* like that! Never.'

'Now hold it, Matucci. Maybe you're wrong from the beginning. You've seen him at the Alcibiade. You've heard–only heard, mark you–that someone like him chases rough trade at the Pavone. Giorgione told you he's a physical culture addict. That's all you've got. The rest is imagination and inference. This apartment now, does it smell of fennel-flowers? Not to me. Does the lady sound cheated? Not to me. Maybe you have to rethink this fellow. . . . Hand me that photograph a minute.'

He unfastened the clip at the back of the frame and slid out the photograph. On the back of it was the address of the photographer, together with a file number: A. Donati, Bologna, 673125. Steffi scribbled the notation in his notebook and put the photograph back in the frame.

'Tomorrow, Matucci, I should take a little trip to Bologna and trace that print, no?'

'Do that, Steffi. . . . Wait a minute though. There's something strange.'

'What?'

'We are looking at half a house, half a man. The place is incomplete, as though not enough important things have happened here yet. It's as neutral as a showroom.'

'But whichever way you read him, Roditi's not neuter.'

'Exactly.'

'So, why don't you take one of those letters from the middle of the bundle and let's haul our tails out of here. I feel like a criminal.'

'Which is exactly what you are, Steffi. But you bring me back the lady's name tomorrow and I'll pin a medal on you.'

We left the apartment pristine as we found it and rode down, innocent as babes, to the foyer. The porter was locked in his little booth watching television. We could have been trailing a bloodied corpse across the Garrara marble and he would not have blinked an eyelid.

It was still only a little after eleven. The night was balmy and the streets were still lively with strollers and traffic. Steffi was tired, so I dropped him at his hotel. I was too restless to sleep. Bruno Manzini had taught me a rough lesson. My thinking was confused. My judgments were hasty. My actions were precipitate and dangerous. The Director had judged me long before and made me a facile actor in his sardonic dramas. Even Lili knew my weakness, and would not commit to me until I had mastered it, if indeed I ever could.

The prospect of a solitary evening in the apartment daunted me, so I drove across town to the Duca di Gallodoro, where at least I could share my loneliness and have it set to music.

They gave me a table in a shadowy corner. I ordered a drink and sat watching the shuffle of the dancers and the drift of the drinkers around the bar. A couple of girls wandered past with hopeful smiles; but I waved them away. I was too morose to endure their inevitable small-talk and their constant thirst for bad champagne. I had been there for perhaps twenty minutes, when two men came in and sat three tables away on my right. One was a big sturdy fellow, with the lumpy battered face of a pugilist; the other was small, dark and dapper, with ferret eyes and a wide flashing smile.

The small one I knew. Everyone in the Corps knew him, at least by name and reputation. They called him the Surgeon, because, they said, he would cut the brain out of a living man and dissect it for the last morsel of information. They even had a proverb about him: Fall into the hands of God, not into the Surgeon's paws! The suspect, who had jumped or been pushed from the high window, had been under his studious care. The big fellow was obviously his bodyguard—and probably his assistant butcher. I sat back further into the shadows lest he see me and salute me and I be forced to acknowledge him.

A few moments later, the band stopped playing and the dancers drifted back to their tables. A microphone was set up in the middle of the floor and a master of ceremonies announced the presence of the eminent and well-beloved Patti Pavese, who would sing for us. Then all the lights went out and there were five seconds of darkness until a spot splashed in the centre of the dance floor and revealed the singer in a splendour of fishnet and sequins. She looked better than she sang, but the audience loved her and clapped handsomely. When she delivered her big number, *Una Manata d'Amore*, they went wild and called her back for two repeats of the chorus and sang the last one with her.

When the lights went up again, I glanced across at the Surgeon. He was lying slumped across the table in a welter of spilt liquor. His bodyguard was sprawled sideways on the banquette. They had both been shot in the head by a small-calibre pistol. I tossed a pair of notes on the table and made for the entrance. I was half-way to the door before I heard a woman's scream and the commotion that followed it.

The killing of the Surgeon made headlines in the morning press, and the foreign agencies made a big meal of it as well. The police announced a nation-wide hunt for the assassins and appealed for information from the public, especially from anyone who had left the Duca di Gallodoro before the arrival of the police.

Manzini, who had telephoned me at breakfast and bidden me on a tour of his factories in Milan, was gloomy and dispirited.

'. . . A fellow like that is better dead, but there are fifty others waiting to step into his shoes. So nothing is soled. The factions are polarized still more. The tyrants look so much more attractive to a scared and dispirited people. Watch, Dante! Watch and listen! Note the tension, the undercurrent of unrest and suspicion. You will see the groups of workers coalesce, each wary of the other, each on the look-out for spies and provocative agents. These are good people, Dante. We have fewer labour troubles than most, because we sign reasonable agreements and keep them. I am not hated as the *Androne*; I am even respected, I think. But as a man I am remote as the moon. I personify power. I am identified with all the excesses of power in this country. I had a telephone call from Rome this morning. The Government is considering a new regulation that will give the police even wider powers of search and arrest. They are talking of ninety-two hours preventive detention on mere suspicion. . . . Preventive detention! That's madness! It puts us back forty years. Your Surgeon is the symbol of the terror necessary to control the restless mass. In the old days he would have worn a mask and carried a headsman's axe. In part I am guilty of him, too. I have guards on my gates and plant detectives to stop pilfering. Forgive me, I am morbid today. We will have lunch with the managers and then I will show you something a little more cheerful.'

We drove ten miles outside the city towards Como and turned off the main road into a private parkland where twenty bungalows, all new, were grouped around a central building, which looked rather like a clubhouse, set about with lawns and flower-gardens. Manzini explained it to me with ironic deprecation.

'. . . A sop to my pirate's conscience, Dante. One of the things I hope may earn me a late reprieve from damnation. It's a home for mongoloid children who cannot be cared for within their own families. They tend to have a short life span, as you may know. If they are submitted to undue stress, for example, in an old-fashioned institution, some of them may become violent and anti-social. So, we've tried here to reproduce a family situation. Each house has six to ten children under the care of a married couple. The central building contains class-rooms, a clinic, a recreation hall and staff quarters. We're experimenting all the time and this place has become a prototype for others in different parts of Italy. In this country the Church used to be the fountain of charity; but too many of the old orders of monks and nuns have become sclerotic and outdated. As for the State institutions, the less said the better. I have seen orphanages, my friend, where children did not learn to speak until they were seven and eight years old, because no one ever talked to them. . . . Here, we are both teaching and learning, and every week there is some small revelation that makes it all worth while.'

To me, the greatest revelation of all was the old man himself. The staff adored him, men and women alike. Each one had something special to show him: a therapy project, a piece of recent equipment, a diet chart, a game that seemed to have a special fascination for their charges. With the children, he was like a happy grandfather. He fondled them, kissed them, squatted on the floor and played games with their blocks and models. He drew comic pictures on a black-board, and even pounded out a tune on the piano. He swung one tiny mite on his shoulders and carried him round the place, while half a dozen others tugged at his coat-tails for attention. There was nothing organized about the chanted chorus of welcome or farewell. He came and went as the patriarch of a frail family which without him would have remained ungathered and forgotten. The odd thing was that he needed to justify himself–and to me of all people.

'. . . There is a man in Rome, Dante, a priest I know, who deals only with monsters. I mean it, literally. Man still begets and women still throw monstrosities with one eye and three arms and half a brain and two hearts. Some of them survive. God only knows why and He never explains though I think He should if He wants us to believe in mercy and loving-kindness and all the rest! However, this man told me once, that he was, perhaps, the only one in all the world who could truly affirm miracles. Now, you have to understand, Dante, that the creatures we talk about are truly subhuman, beyond reason, beyond imagining, beyond even compassion. But this man told me that, sometimes at the strangest moments, he would feel, see, hear a response that shook the foundations of his sanity. These vegetables, these montrous nothings knew! They knew . . .! For how long, and how much? Eh! Impossible to say; but for one flash of time there was lightning on Tabor. This work I do is far easier than his. It costs me nothing but money. The rest is pure joy. I go back to the ant-hill changed, if only a little. I know that life is not all vendetta and woe to the vanquished. The mystery is that we still must fight, to hold room even for so small a loving. If we didn't, they would burn the monsters and sterilize those babies of mine and hand them over to the brutes of the world for anatomical experiment. . . . You are seeing Leporello tonight?'

'Yes.'

'Worried?'

'A little. If he opens a door, I have to walk through it, even if I'm not sure what's on the other side. You may not approve what I do.'

'Do you care whether I approve or not?'

'Yes, I care.'

'A warning, Dante Alighieri. Shut the door on today. Forget it until a calmer time. We are going back into the jungle. You cannot afford illusions.'

'What illusions, Bruno?'

'That the Salamander will always survive. That's a myth, a beautiful legend, like the Holy Grail and the Golden Apples of the Hesperides. I've had my warning, Dante. I have a mitral stenosis which will kill me–probably sooner than later. If I go before this is finished, you will be alone. What then?'

'Another test, Bruno?'

'No. A simple question.'

'Answer one: I finish my leave and go back to SID, an obedient servant. Answer two: I take the job which Leporello will offer me at dinner tonight.'

'Answer three?'

'I emigrate and live happily ever after, mining bauxite in Australia.'

'Is that all?'

'No. There's one more possibility. Write me into your will. Leave me the engraver's plate from which you print your cards. I'll set up in business as the Salamander. Who knows? I may write a new legend, before they hose me out from the ashes.'

It was a bad joke, but he laughed at it. I laughed, too–at the wondrous spectacle of Dante Alighieri Matucci, perched on his dunghill, flapping his wings and crowing defiance at principalities and thrones and dominations and all the dark powers of this sunlit Latin world.

I gave great thought to the manner in which I should dress for Leporello's dinner. The suit should be sober, but not too sober lest I look like some pettifogging clerk come to dine with the bank manager. Modish? Yes. The ladies like a man who has a little colour about him, and the General would not want another grey mouse on his staff. The shirt, white cambric, with gold cufflinks, just for a hint of money. The General should know where the bidding started. It was all *figura* . . . the thing we live by here in Italy. The inwardness is something else. The women share it with their confessors. We males disclose it to our friends, or, given grace and time in our advancing years, to God, who, by then may have lost interest in such trifling matters.

My car was polished; Pietro had seen to that. There was no cloud on the bright-work, no speck of dust in the interior. There was a basket of flowers for my hostess and a bottle of brandy for my host, to honour my first footing in their house. If my dinner companion proved willing, there was champagne in the refrigerator and coffee on the stove and sweet music would flood the place at the touch of a switch. All in all—saving the ravages of time and middle age—the *figura* was not bad. Pietro flicked the last speck of fluff from my lapels and swept me out into the night.

I drove carefully, because there were police at every intersection and trucks full of carabinieri parked at strategic points. The murder of the Surgeon was no small matter in this city of a million and a half people, restive under the twin threats of violence and repression. I was stopped twice on the way and a third time at the gates of Leporello's villa, where two carabinieri checked my papers, waved me inside and closed the gates behind me. Leporello was taking himself and his job very seriously. There were two plain-clothes men inside the grounds. One of them opened the door of the car and delivered me, unscathed, at the front door, where a maid took charge of me and led me into the salon.

Leporello was alone. Even in civilian clothes he was still an impressive figure, tall, straight and formal to the point of stiffness. Still, his greeting was warm, his handshake firm and welcoming. He apologized for the ladies, who were chatting upstairs. They would join us presently. A manservant offered drinks, whisky or champagne. We toasted each other. Leporello made a joking reference to the guards and the security men. I told him I thought it wise and necessary to take precautions. I asked about his investigation into the murder of the Surgeon. He frowned and shrugged:

'You know how it is, Colonel. The murder took place in a crowded nightclub, while the attention of the clients was focused on a popular performer. Most of the place was in darkness. The assassins used silenced pistols, small calibre, low velocity. Where do we begin?'

I was lavish with sympathy for his problem. I wished, fervently, that I could offer some constructive suggestion. I was happy to be on leave and dispensed from responsibility. He smiled, faintly, and said that we must discuss that over the brandy. Then the ladies came—and it was as if the roof had fallen on my unwary head. The woman in Roditi's photograph was the wife of General Leporello.

I stammered God knows what by way of greeting and bent over her hand in a panic of embarrassment. It is one thing to look into a woman's cleavage when you know beyond all doubt that she has put it on show for you. It is quite another to look into her eyes when you have read all her secrets in a bundle of love-letters. You feel the small shameful triumph of the voyeur and you wonder that she cannot read it in your face. You feel a guilt that makes you withdraw from her touch, a fear that some unguarded word may expose the secret knowledge that you possess.

Fortunately, for me, my table-partner provided an adequate diversion. Laura Balestra was a lively *biondina*, with big, bedroom eyes and a little-girl smile and a talent for amusing chit-chat. She loved dressy men. She hated stuffy soldiers. She had an uncle in Bolivia who mined emeralds and lavished them on mistresses in six different countries. She had just come back from Austria where she had almost, but not quite, fallen in love with a ski-instructor. Didn't I love Elena's dress and wasn't this a beautiful villa? And why anyone would want to live in Milan, she couldn't imagine. She much preferred Florence, but then Mamma was ailing and she had to play duenna for Papa who was enjoying his second youth in a rather embarrassing fashion. . . . And dear, oh dear, she did carry on, didn't she?

She did, but I was so grateful I wanted to kiss her, and thought I would afterwards. Then, she turned to Leporello and left me to make my halting way with the lady of the love-letters.

I will say it once and be done with it: she was a beautiful woman; she wakened the old Adam in me the moment I set eyes on her. The photographer had flattered her a little because he had caught her in a moment of repose and contentment. I wondered how a ramrod like Leporello had managed to marry her. She was wondering about me, too. Her first question was a challenge.

'You're older than I expected, Colonel.'

'I try hard to conceal it, Madam.'

'I didn't mean that. My husband likes to surround himself with very young officers.'

'Oh? I've only met one member of the staff, Captain Roditi.'

'Do you know him well?'

'Hardly at all. We've met only three times and we've had very little to say to each other.'

'He's rather exceptional. He's been with my husband nearly seven years now. Are you married, Colonel?'

'No.'

'Not interested?'

'Very dubious–about marriage that is.'

'My husband tells me he's invited you to join his staff.'

'Yes.'

'You don't like the idea?'

'I have some reservations. I'll be discussing them with the General.'

'You're very tactful.'

'And you're very beautiful, Madam. Do you know the Veiled Lady?'

'I'm afraid not. Should I?'

'Rafael painted her. She's in the Pitti. You're her living image, even to the hairstyle.'

'Thank you for the compliment.'

'I'm sure you get many, from all those dashing young officers.'

'Very few, Colonel. I'm a respectable married woman with two children.'

'Girls or boys?'

'Twin girls. They'll be five this August.'

'Summer children! That's nice.'

'Summer or winter, does it make any difference?'

'Isn't there a proverb that says, "Spring loving's the brightest, but summer's the sweetest?"'

'I've never heard it. Is that your experience, Colonel?'

'Well, yes. I suppose it is.'

'You must tell me about it one day.'

'I'd be delighted; but I never tell names or write letters.'

'Very gallant–and very discreet.'

'In my business I have to be discreet.'

'Oh, yes, you're something in intelligence, aren't you?'

'That's right.'

'Do you like your work?'

'Not always. It destroys one's illusions too quickly.'

'Do you have any left, Colonel?'

'Some. . . . And you?'

'Ask me some other time.'

'I'll do that. It's a promise.'

Dinner was announced at that moment, so there was no chance to finish the gambit. But if I guessed my lady right, she was playing the old game of spite-my-husband, and playing it very recklessly indeed. Leporello, on the other hand, was punctiliously polite, though never casual or intimate. For a man, who was normally brusque and imperative, his attitude to his wife was surprisingly deferential. It was as if he had acquired the habit of stepping round arguments and avoiding the simplest discussions. I had the curious impression that he was afraid of her and that she, knowing it, was prepared to push him to the limit of endurance. At table, he concentrated his first attention on me. He was persuasive and complimentary. He wished most earnestly to have me on his staff. Men with my training and experience were precious. He hoped the women might persuade me if his own eloquence were not enough. Laura Balestra was on his side, teasing and inconsequent. Elena Leporello played her own game, flattering me and denigrating her husband in a dozen subtle ways. By the time we had finished the pasta, I was tired of their comedy. I began to devise one of my own.

'By the way, General, did you know someone tried to kill me in Venice?'

He was a very good actor. He choked on his wine and, as he set down the glass, he spilt the dregs on the tablecloth. The women were shocked and excited. Leporello silenced them with a gesture and demanded a full account of the affair. I shrugged it off.

'Well, I'd just had dinner with my Director and the Cavaliere Manzini. I was on my way to Harry's Bar to meet a girl. I was waylaid by three men who tried to bottle me up in an alley. I fired some shots. They ran away.'

'You reported the matter to the Director, of course?'

'Yes. . . . He told me he would make some inquiries and come back to me.'

'But you haven't heard from him yet?'

'Not yet.'

'This worries me, Colonel. It seems this kind of violence is becoming epidemic. You heard what happened here in Milan last night?'

'I was there, General.'

He was not acting now. He gaped at me, fish-eyed; I explained with elaborate discretion.

'You won't find my name in your reports because I slipped out before the panic started–to avoid embarrassing questions. I was sitting three tables away.'

'And you saw nothing?'

'Only the bodies, when the lights went up. It was obviously a professional job. I shouldn't think you'll get far with normal inquiries. Myself, I wouldn't be inclined to push them too hard.'

'That's an odd thing to say, Colonel?'

'Not really, General. Let's face it, both sides are in profit. The Left have their victim. You're rid of a discreditable nuisance.'

Elena Leporello was quick to see the point and turn it against us both.

'That sounds like a loaded proposition, Colonel.'

'Not at all. It's a statement of fact–unless you want me to say that your husband approved of sadism in police interrogations. However, I agree it's not the sort of thing one shouts about in public.'

Leporello brightened at that and nodded a vigorous approval.

'Very proper, Matucci. . . . Very proper. Our public image is very important at this time.'

'And what do you think of the image, Colonel?' Elena Leporello was a very persistent adversary. 'I get the impression it's rather tarnished just now.'

'In some respects, yes. On the other hand, your husband's reputation is growing.'

'His reputation for what, Colonel?'

'Firm policy, decisive action. . . . I was at the Bankers' Club the night before last. Your speech on Order and Progress made a big impression, General. I've heard other talk as I've been moving around. There's a great deal of popular support for your programme. These riot squads you are training. . . .'

'Where did you hear about those, Colonel?'

'They're being talked about in every bar and club in town, General.'

'It's supposed to be a secret project.'

'I assure you it isn't any more.'

'Could you name me any places where you've heard this talk?'

'Certainly. The Duca di Gallodoro, the Hilton Bar, the Club Alcibiade. . . .'

The mention of the Alcibiade produced a variety of reactions. Elena looked blank. The General developed a sudden interest in the strawberry flan. Laura Balestra quizzed me, pertly:

'The Club Alcibiade? And what were you doing there, Colonel?'

'Just looking.'

'Did you find what you were looking for?'

'Yes, I did, as a matter of fact. I found a man I've been chasing for weeks.'

'I didn't think you'd find a man within a kilometre of the place.'

'Indeed, yes. I was there. Captain Roditi was there. . . .'

'Matteo?'

It was Elena who asked the question, and she addressed it, not to me, but to Leporello, who smiled over it as if it were the first real victory of the evening.

'Don't ask me, my dear. I wasn't there. . . . Now, if you don't mind, the Colonel and I will take coffee in the library. We'll join you when we've had our talk.'

No sooner were we settled and private than his manner changed, dramatically. He was every inch the soldier again: curt, decisive, dogmatic, as if he were addressing a staff conference.

'Matucci, the time has come for us to be frank with each other.'

'I'd welcome that, sir.'

'Your Director thinks you're a trouble-maker. I think you and I would get on well together. Why do you hesitate to join me?'

'Two reasons to begin with: I want to finish my leave. I want to test myself in civilian employment.'

'With Bruno Manzini.'

'Yes.'

'He's an old rogue–dangerous.'

'Dangerous?'

'He's a bad enemy. He has blackmailed a number of people into suicide. Before you leave this evening, I shall give you copies of two dossiers. I should like you to study them, carefully, and return them to me. I make no further comment. You will come to your own conclusions.'

'You seem sure they'll agree with yours.'

'We'll see. . . . If you decide to join me, you may finish your leave without curtailment.'

'That's very fair.'

'Now, as to the appointment itself. There is no establishment as yet, no title, no table of organization. You would be required to set up a completely new section, subject only to me and to my personal directives. You would model this section on the Service of Defence Information, with such variations as your experience dictated and we agreed together. Interested?'

'So far, very. What would be the purpose of this section?'

'Political intelligence, in the widest sense. If certain events take place, if certain projects mature, the scope of the work would be greatly enlarged, and your position would be one of considerable power.'

'Can you specify the events and the projects, General?'

'I can, but not yet.'

'May I ask why?'

'Because I must first be sure, Colonel, where your loyalties lie.'

'I should have thought that was obvious, General.'

'Indeed?'

'Yes, sir. We are both commissioned officers in the same Corps. We took the same oath of service. That specifies everything very clearly, I think.'

'Unfortunately, it doesn't. It does not specify, for instance, your political affiliation.'

'Am I required to have one?'

'For this post, yes.'

'Then you should nominate it, General.'

'I need a very conservative man.'

'That could be a contradiction in terms. Intelligence deals both with the actual and the possible. I could quote my Director at length on that subject.'

'Would it help if I told you that your Director has become a very conservative man.'

'I already know that, sir.'

'What do you know?'

'The meeting was held at the Villa Baldassare, was it not?'

'How the devil . . .?'

'I dined with the Director and with Bruno Manzini in Venice.'

'What did they tell you?'

'I could not depose that they told me anything. Let's say I became aware of certain situations and arrangements. For instance, there was a discussion as to whether I should be eliminated. There were two votes against, one for killing me—your vote, General. So you see, I'm rather puzzled by this offer of yours.'

I had thought to shake him. I was disappointed. Whatever he was as a husband, in his character of soldier and strategist, he was impregnable. He reproved me, quietly.

'Why? You know the trade. We're all at risk. I voted yes. Then, I changed my mind.'

'Why?'

'I have never trusted your Director. I have always regarded him as a useful but fickle ally. So, when I left the meeting at the Villa Baldassare, I thought very carefully. I concluded I had need of a rival and an ultimate substitute for the Director. . . . You, my dear Colonel. Simple, isn't it?'

'Too simple.'

'Why so?'

'Everyone carries life insurance, except me. Manzini has wealth and influence. The Director has a presidential appointment. You have general rank in the Carabinieri. Me? I'm out on the limb of the cherry-tree.'

'Join me and you will have my personal protection. Don't underrate that, Colonel.'

'I don't. But I was thinking of the Surgeon.'

'What about him?'

'He's dead.'

'I wasn't protecting him.'

'Oh, I see.'

'You said it yourself: the man was a discreditable nuisance. . . . More brandy?'

'Thank you. . . . Do you mind if I ask a few questions?'

'Please!'

'This aide of yours, Captain Roditi . . . explain him to me.'

I had touched him on the raw. His head jerked up. He was suddenly tense and threatening.

'I think you should explain yourself, Colonel.'

'*Ebbene!* You want me to join you. I am interested; but I am not prepared to walk blind into a new situation. I have studied you, General, as you have studied me. I hear that this Roditi is a court favourite. He is resented. Because of him, you are resented, too. I want to know why.'

He considered the question for a long time. He turned it over and over, as if it were a piece of putty from which he might mould an answer that would suit me. Finally, he said:

'Roditi is dispensable. You come, he goes, if that's what you want.'

'What was he doing at the Club Alcibiade?'

'He recruits there.'

'And at the Pavone?'

'Yes.'

'I'm curious to know why you're using these types.'

'We need men without ties, with no ambition beyond money and the companionship of their own kind. They, too, will be dispensable in time, like the Congo mercenaries.'

'General, if you were sitting in my chair, would you accept that answer?'

'If I were sitting in your chair, Matucci, I should not expect to have all the words spelt out for me.'

'Fair comment, General. . . . I accept it. However, you must be patient with me. You offer me patronage, protection. I have to know where the power lies, and the weakness, too.'

'I'm listening.'

'Your marriage is obviously unhappy.'

'Is it so obvious?'

'To me, yes. A man like you, with ambitions like yours, cannot afford an enemy in the house. You must be very lonely, General.'

'I am. I confess that these are desert days for me, Matucci. But I am prepared to endure them a while longer.'

'So, you lean on Roditi?'

'More than I should, perhaps. He's become like a son to me. But I need someone much stronger, much wiser. You, my friend.'

'But you're still not prepared to trust me. . . . Please, General, let's not play games. There's a dossier on you at SID. The Director knows what's in it. I don't, because he has always reserved it to himself. That's why you wouldn't move until you had him as an ally. You still don't trust him, and you want to set me up against him. I'm impotent, unless I know as much as he does. I can't protect you, unless I know what weapons he can use against you. . . . Now, why don't you think about that? If you still want me, we can meet again and discuss final questions. After that, we can sign transfer papers.'

'You might decide not to join me after all.'

'And you might decide to withdraw your protection. In which case, I could end like the Surgeon, with a bullet in the head. If that happened. . . .?'

'Yes, Colonel?'

'There is a data-bank in Switzerland, which would immediately circulate a lot of information to the Press and other interested parties.'

'Blackmail, Colonel?'

'No, General. That begins when I try to extort money or preferment. I have done neither. I have simply taken out insurance. But, talking of blackmail, are you sure you yourself are not a victim?'

'I told you once, Colonel, I tell you again. My life is an open book.'

'That's the public record, General. The secret one is what they hit you with on the day when you're proclaimed saviour of the country. . . . Look, I didn't ask for the job. You offered it. If you're unhappy with my terms, let's forget it.'

'Let's define them more clearly.'

'Full disclosure on both sides.'

'Very well. I'll be in touch with you again in a few days. Meantime, you can study the Manzini dossiers. . . . More brandy?'

'No, thank you. I should be getting home. It's been a long day.'

'Not too unprofitable, I hope?'

'Far from it, General. I think we've come a long way towards an understanding.'

'Good. . . . By the way, would you mind dropping Laura in town, otherwise I'll have to call a staff car. I don't like taxis calling at the house here.'

'No trouble at all. I'll be delighted.'

'I like her. She's a cheerful soul. A little stupid, perhaps, but rich in her own right–and still unattached. A word to the wise, eh?'

Cheerful she was, and more than a little drunk, and she chatted like a feather-brain; but stupid she wasn't. As we drove back to town, she gave me a zany but revealing commentary on the dinner-party.

'Meow-meow-meow! Talk about the cat in the pigeon-loft! You were very naughty tonight, Dante. You know you were. You've still got feathers all over your whiskers. You're the first man I've seen who was able to handle Elena in one of her moods. Eek! She really had her claws out for Marcantonio tonight. . . . Not that I blame her, really. He's no joy in bed and no fun anywhere else, as far as I can see. . . . You don't really want to work for him, do you? I can't see you fitting into the bunch of *finocchi* he's got around him. But then, I don't know you very well, do I? And you never did say what you were doing at the Alcibiade. And what was Matteo Roditi doing there? You didn't see Elena's face when you dropped that hot brick. I thought she was going to burst a gusset and pop that big bosom of hers in the gravy. You know they're lovers, of course? My dear man, everybody knows–even the General. If my arithmetic's right, Roditi has to be the father of the twins. . . . Why? Oh, come on, Matucci! Why do you think the old boy uses Matteo to do all his dirty work. . . . Me? I'm the little friend of all the world. But I am Elena's friend first. And I'll make a bet with you. If she doesn't call you in the next twenty-four hours, I'll give you a night in bed, myself. . . .'

'No bet. You're already invited.'

'I hate to be rushed.'

'No rush. There's champagne and caviar and soft music and. . . .'

'And Elena will hate me ever after.'

'Who's to tell, *bambina*?'

'That's right, who's to tell. She'll still ring you though. She's wild for you, Matucci. I know her.'

'You told me she was wild for Roditi.'

'Oh, that's special. The others–and there have been a lot of others–are her revenge on her husband. If you're going to join him, she'll get you to bed, if she has to scream rape and murder to do it.'

'She sounds like a candidate for the *manicomio!*'

'Wouldn't you be, if you were married to a middle-aged *finocchio* with delusions of grandeur.'

'God forbid!'

'Amen! Now, tell me about your love-life, Colonel. I'd like to know what I'm getting into before I have too much champagne.'

As it turned out, three glasses were more than enough. She passed out cold to the music of Henry Mancini. I undressed her, tucked her into the big double bed, hung up her clothes, stuck a get-well note to the bathroom mirror and closed the door on her.

It was now one in the morning in Milan; where, if her citizens are to be believed, money will buy you anything, day or night. My needs were essentially simple; an atomizer and a one-eyed notary, deaf and dumb, insomniac and avaricious. I record, as a matter of historic interest, that, even with my contacts, it took me an hour to find him, twenty minutes to haggle with him and a hundred thousand lire in cash to coax him out of the house.

I can be flippant about it now; but at that moment in time I was desperate. To explain: I wanted to take a legal deposition from a witness. I was prepared to exercise duress, threats, intimidation and physical violence, if necessary. So, I needed a notary, with a stack of *carta bollata* and a rubber stamp, and a flexible conscience.

At three-fifteen, armed and accompanied by the said notary, I presented myself at the apartment of Captain Matteo Roditi. The Captain was out, absent, abroad about the business of his master—or his mistress, as the case might be. I entered the apartment, closed the notary in the bedroom to doze awhile, made myself a cup of coffee in the kitchen and settled down to wait. At three-forty-five, red-eyed and almost sober, Roditi came home. I pushed him against the wall while I patted him for concealed weapons. Then I sat him in the Danish armchair and perched myself on the desk, with the pistol and the atomizer beside me. After that, I was able to talk to him like a country uncle.

'Captain, you don't know me very well. You may, therefore, be tempted to believe I am playing games. I am not. If you don't give me truthful answers, I'm going to kill you. I shall spray cyanic acid gas in your face and you will be dead in four seconds. If you co-operate, I may offer you a way out of the mess you're in now. Clear?'

'Yes.'

'In your bedroom there is the signed photograph of a woman, and a bundle of love-letters from a woman called Elena. Who is Elena?'

'She's the wife of General Leporello.'

'How long have you been lovers?'

'About six years.'

'Are you the father of her children?'

'I believe so.'

'Does the General know of your association?'

'Yes.'

'And condones it?'

'Yes.'

'Tell me why?'

'It gives him a hold over both of us.'

'Explain that.'

'He is the legal father of the children. His name is on the registration of birth. He could remove them from Elena's care and custody.'

'And what is his hold over you?'

'I have performed services for him which put me in legal jeopardy.'

'What services?'

'I have procured for him.'

'Inside or outside the Service?'

'Both. I have another apartment, near the Duomo. The lease is in my name. He uses that as a meeting place. I pay the people and make sure there's no trouble afterwards.'

'How do you do that?'

'Threats mostly. Action, if necessary.'

'You have people beaten up, that sort of thing?'

'Yes.'

'I'll need names and dates and places, but we'll come to that later. Do you know Major Zenobio, the Commandant of Camerata?'

'Yes.'

'Have you heard from him today?'

'There was a message to call him. I haven't done it yet.'

'Did you get a letter from Chiasso today?'

'Yes.'

'Did the General get one?'

'Yes.'

'What did you do about them?'

'I passed them to forensics to check the fingerprint and the typewritten sheet.'

'Have you had any answers yet?'

'No.'

'When would you expect the answers?'

'Tomorrow, or the next day.'

'Did you know whose print it was?'

'I had an idea. I wasn't sure.'

'Whose?'

'It could have belonged to Balbo.'

'Did he kill Bandinelli and Calvi?'

'Yes.'

'Did he plant a letter-bomb in the apartment of one Lili Anders?'

'Yes.'

'Who gave the orders?'

'I did.'

'Who gave you your orders?'

'The General.'

'Where are the Pantaleone papers?'

'I gave them to Leporello.'

'Where are they now?'

'I don't know. Possibly at his house.'

'Where is Giuseppe Balbo?'

'I think he's dead.'

'You think . . .!'

'I was told to take him to the Club Alcibiade tonight and make sure we left at two forty-five.'

'Who told you?'

'The General.'

'Because of the letter from Chiasso?'

'Yes.'

'Who was going to do the job?'

'I don't know. I wasn't told.'

'Any ideas?'

'Leporello talked of killing two birds with one shot–the Surgeon and Balbo.'

'Very neat. Did you ever think he might want to get rid of you one day?'

'Yes.'

'Did you never take out any insurance?'

'Yes, I did. I had the other apartment bugged. There are tapes and photographs.'

'Where are they?'

'Elena has one set. I have another in safe deposit at the Banco Centrale.'

'I'll need the key and an authorization of access.'

'Very well.'

'How do you feel about Elena now?'

'I love her, for God's sake! Why else do you think I've stayed in this rotten business?'

'Because you didn't want to get out. . . . When Leporello brought off his coup, you'd be a very big man.'

'What are you going to do now?'

'Not I, Roditi, you! You're going to write a deposition. There's a little man in your bedroom who will notarize the document. When that's done, we'll talk about the rest of it. . . . Now, there's the *carta bollata*, there's the pen. I'll dictate. You write.'

It took half an hour to compose the document and half a minute to stamp and notarize it. I sent the notary on his drowsy way, had Roditi write a letter to his bank, stuffed the documents into my breast pocket, and settled down to a more cosy chat. Roditi was utterly defeated, sallow and trembling, so I let him have a whisky to revive himself while I laid out the deal.

'. . . Your deposition buys you a life sentence, Roditi. A phone call from me to Leporello gets you killed before morning. So, you're going absent without leave. You'll pack a bag. I'll drive you to a safe place in the country and you'll stay there until I've built the last brick into my case against Leporello. You'll be interrogated. You'll make more depositions than you've ever dreamed of. But at least you won't be in gaol, and waiting for some cell-mate to put a skewer in your back. Then, before the case breaks, you'll have twenty-four hours to get out of the country with Elena and the children. . . . It's the best I can do. Take it or leave it.'

'It's no good. It won't work.'

'Why not?'

'It just won't, that's all.'

'Have you got a better idea?'

'Yes. Leave me free until you've finished your case. I can bluff it out. That's one thing I'm good at. I can feed you information–better information than you would get any other way. Things are starting to happen, Matucci, and they're going to happen very fast. . . .'

'What sort of things?'

'I can't tell you yet. But I will as soon as I know.'

'I'm sorry. I don't like it. Pack your bag, now.'

'I'm not going.'

'Then you're going to tell me why.'

'All right. You've been followed all the evening. While your car was at the General's house, they fixed a bleeper on it.'

'Which means they know where I am now?'

'Yes, yes.'

'And they're waiting for me, downstairs?'

'I don't know.'

'Then let's take a walk and find out. If they're not there, we'll take a little drive–to Balbo's place first, then over to the General's house. . . . If we have to finish it now, let's finish it. On your feet!'

'I'm not going. You can kill me here if you like, but I'm not going.'

'So, that's why it was all so easy, eh? They cut me down as I walk out the front door! Or they've taped the car with plastic and when I switch on the ignition, it blows me sky-high. Now, little man, which is it?'

'I don't know. I swear I don't know.'

'Then, let's find out.'

I fished out my pocket-book and found the number of the SID agency in Milan. I dialled it and spoke to the duty officer, quoting my identification number.

'. . . I am questioning a suspect. My car is parked outside the building. It's a red Mercedes with a Milan number plate. I know it has been bugged. It may have been planted with an explosive device. It is also possible there may be an attempt to assassinate me as I leave the building. The suspect is an officer of Carabinieri, so I'd rather not have them brought in. Can you manage it by yourselves? And without making a fuss? I don't care about the car, you can deliver that for me when it's clean. But I'll need another vehicle at my disposal when I leave. When you're ready, send a man up to the apartment to let me know. Code-word "Dragon". . . . That's right– "Dragon". Don't let him forget it. He might get shot as he comes in. . . . Thanks. Hurry it up please. Oh, and just for safety, check me back on this number as soon as I hang up.'

He checked back and told me the boys would be with me in thirty minutes. It was a long time to wait and a lot could happen in that time. I switched off the lights and crossed to the window and parted the drapes. It was already happening. Three police cars were already parked outside the building, a third was turning into the street. Already the men were piling out of them and grouping themselves round the officer in command. The plot was very clear now. Arrest and search and ninety-two hours' detention on any charge in the book. I could think of two that would stick–breaking and entering and withholding information from the police on the killing of the Surgeon. By the time I got out, if I ever got out, the depositions would have disappeared into thin air. I hauled Roditi to his feet, thrust a wadded handkerchief into his mouth, poked my gun into his kidneys and hustled him out of the apartment.

There was no way down, except by the elevators, or the concrete stairs. Either way would land me in the arms of the Carabinieri. We went up. We climbed four flights until we came to a door that gave access to the roof and the watertanks on top of it. The door was locked. It took me a minute to pick the lock. I pushed Roditi out on to the roof and relocked the door from the outside. Then I leaned him, face against the door, and chopped him hard on the back of the skull. He went down like a sack. I dragged him into the shelter of the water-tanks and took the gag out of his mouth. I didn't want him to choke just yet. He had a lot more talking to do, if ever I could get out of this very neat trap.

I made a cautious circuit of the roof and found that the two adjoining buildings were similar in height and construction. It would be an easy matter to climb across the parapets and make my escape through the third building. It would be quite impossible if I had to take Roditi with me. I left him and a few minutes later I found myself in a deserted office block. I waited, frozen and disconsolate in a toilet, wondering what had happened to Roditi and why no one had bothered to check the rooftop. When the workers began to arrive in the morning, I walked out into the crowded, sunlit streets and took a taxi to Steffi's hotel.

For all his cavils and quirks, Steffi in crisis was a treasure. While I bathed and shaved, he strolled around to the Xerox offices and made copies of the deposition on a coin-in-the-slot machine. Then he went to the Milan office of his bank, cashed a cheque and deposited the original document for safekeeping against my signature or his own. After that, he surged, larger than life, into Manzini's office and demanded to see the old man. He presented my compliments, a photostat copy and a second-hand account of the night's events. The pair of them came back to the hotel for breakfast, chatting as if they had known each other all their lives.

Breakfast, however, was a sober meal. Manzini telephoned the editor of his newspaper and came back with three stories which would feature in the afternoon editions. The lead story dealt with a gun battle in which one, Guiseppe Balbo, a suspect in the murders at the Duca di Gallodoro, had been killed by police officers while resisting arrest. Also on the front page was the account of a mysterious occurrence in a fashionable apartment block. Answering an anonymous telephone call, the details of which could not yet be released, the police had visited an apartment on the fifth floor, occupied by Captain Matteo Roditi, personal aide to Major-General Leporello. The apartment was empty and in disorder. There was no sign of the Captain, who, at the time of going to press, was still missing. The police had already detained one man who was known to have visited the apartment in the early hours of the morning. They were also seeking to question a certain Dante Alighieri Matucci, member of a Government agency, whose car was parked outside the building and whose fingerprints were found in the apartment of the missing man. There was full and accurate description of me and a photograph obviously supplied by wire from the files of SID.

'... And that, gentlemen,' said Manzini, flatly, 'disposes of our case. Balbo is dead. Roditi is dead or in protective custody. Your notary is now under the lamps; and, by the time they have finished with him, he will sign whatever they want. Roditi's deposition is worthless, because they will produce a counter-deposition proving duress. You, my Dante, are now a man on the run. If they take you ... *Buona notte!* It's the Matteotti affair all over again.'

'You're forgetting something, Bruno. I have a key and an authority that will open Roditi's safe-deposit at the Banca Centrale. If he was telling me the truth, there's enough material there to finish Leporello at one stroke.'

'There are three ifs in that proposition, Dante. If Roditi was telling the truth.... If Leporello hasn't already got a judical order to open the box.... If you could open it yourself.... Remember, you have to present identification. An hour from now, your description will be all over the streets of Milan. Which means also we have to get you out of here fast.'

'Let me answer first. I believe Roditi was telling the truth. I don't believe he would hand his last insurance to Leporello.'

'Not even if he were threatened with death? You broke him easily.'

'Only because he thought he was protected. If he sold out to Leporello, he would know he was leaving his woman and her children defenceless. I think he would cling to one last hope–that I, or someone else, might bring Leporello down.'

'I agree,' said Steffi, vehemently. 'One crumb of hope keeps a man going for a long time.'

'Access to the box, then.' Manzini was still gloomy. 'How do you manage that?'

'What does a banker need–not at the moment itself–but on his record after the customer is gone?'

'A signature and a note of the document of identification.'

'You have my document of identification. You have a very good calligrapher in Carlo Metaponte, who did your Salamander card. And you have your friend Ludovisi at the Banca Centrale who promised his help if ever we needed it. Well, Bruno . . .?'

'It depends on Ludovisi, doesn't it?'

'That's right.'

'I'll try him. Let me have your documents and the key. . . . Now, Matucci, what are we going to do with you?'

'I'll have to go underground. For that I'll need the false papers which are in the safe at the apartment.'

'I'll go there and get them. Meantime, where do we put you?'

'Where's your car?'

'Parked in front of the hotel. The doorman's been paid.'

'Could you get me out to Pedognana and keep me there for a couple of days?'

'Not in the house. I think we might have a visit from the Carabinieri. On the estate, certainly, if you don't mind a little peasant living. What about Stefanelli here?'

'I'll stay in town, Cavaliere. This big oaf needs me more than he admits.'

'I don't like it, Steffi. It's a very rough game now.'

'So, what do you need if not someone who understands the trade? Besides who cares about an old sorehead on a holiday he can't enjoy?'

'Thanks, Steffi. When I call, I'm Rabin. It should be a lucky name for us all.'

Manzini ignored the reference. He was still wrestling with a private problem. He asked, abruptly:

'Suppose Ludovisi won't play. What then?'

'There's one last hope. . . . Leporello's wife.'

'When she reads that report, she'll think you killed or kidnapped Roditi.'

'The report came from her husband. I don't think she'd believe him if he told her the day of the week.'

'It's an awful gamble.'

'I know a worse one.' said Steffi, sombrely. 'Leporello for *Duce* and the bully-boys keeping order with truncheons and castor oil.'

I spent four days at Pedognana, three of them lodged in the attic of the factor's house. The Carabinieri came once and spent an afternoon prowling the estate. I spent that same afternoon in a barn loft and emerged with a beautiful dose of hay fever. On the fourth day, Manzini arrived with my documents, and a suit-case of ready-to-wear clothes to fit my new identity as one Aldo Carnera. Thorough as ever, he had procured me a back-dated employment as a travelling salesman with one of his small off-shoot companies. I would never have to put in an appearance, but, if anyone checked back, my false name and personal details were on file.

He brought discouraging news, too. Ludovisi was in New York at a conference. He was flying from New York to Mexico City and thence to Buenos Aires. He was not expected back for ten days. Manzini was fretful. All his careful plans to introduce me into society, to elevate me to the status of a diplomatic agent, were now in ruins. I was back in the underworld from which he had taken me. I was, by presumption, disreputable and because of me, he, too, had fallen into some discredit with the Movement. He was excluded from its inner councils. The Director had sent him a caustic little note suggesting that, until his credit was restored, he might confine his activities to financial contribution, of which the Movement stood in constant need.

We dined together that night and I tried to coax him back into his anecdotal mood; but he refused to be drawn until I mentioned the two dossiers which Leporello had given to me, but which I had not had an opportunity to read. All I remembered were the names: Hans Helmut Ziegler and Emmanuele Salatri. He mused over them for a few moments and then threw up his hands, casting off ill-humour like a cloak.

'Eh! Why not? What is the past for, if not to renew our hope in the future. Hans Helmut Ziegler. . . . That one goes a long way back. It began, let me see, in nineteen-thirty. I was in Sao Paolo then, spending my first big money, making my first investment in the New World. In those days, my Dante, there were more Italians than Brazilians in Sao Paolo. Most of them were migrants, but some like myself were investors—in sugar and coffee land, in textiles and pharmaceuticals, small companies at first but immensely profitable. Those were wild days. I was coining money and spending it and coining more. . . . And the women, *Dio*! They dropped into your hands like ripe papayas.

'One night in a gambling club, I was standing next to a young fellow about my own age. He was Brazilian and he was playing higher than I was on roulette. I was having a run of luck. He was losing and chasing his losses. In the end, about midnight, he was cleaned out. He looked so disconsolate, so utterly despairing, I couldn't bear it. I put my hand on his sleeve and invited him to stay and share a stake with me—just for luck, my luck if not his. For a moment, I thought he was going to strike me. Then he laughed and said: "Why not? It's fools' money." Well, to cut it short, I put a big green chip on thirty-five. It won. We split the money and walked away from the table, arm in arm, friends for life. His name was Paolo Pereira Pinto and he is now one of the best bankers in Brazil. When he got his first directorship he sent me an emerald, five carats, square-cut, as a souvenir of that night. I had the emerald set in a brooch for Raquela Rabin.

'. . . That's the first part of the story. The second part is much later. Hans Helmut Ziegler was the Gestapo man who worked me over in prison. He loved his job and he was expert at it. A dialogue with him, in the interrogation cell, was like a confrontation with the evil one himself. Even now, old as I am, I remember him with terror and loathing. After the war, he disappeared, swallowed up in the chaos. In 1965 the daughter of my old friend, Pinto, was left a widow with two young children. A year later, she remarried and Pinto sent me the wedding photograph. The man she had married was Hans Helmut Ziegler. . . . It took two years' work and twenty-thousand dollars to build a dossier on him. I sent it to him with a Salamander card. He couldn't even manage a clean exit. He drove himself over a cliff at one hundred and fifty kilometres an hour. Old Pinto read the dossier and thought the Israelis had killed him. He was glad to be rid of Ziegler. He didn't want the Zionists operating in his bailiwick. He called in the police who sent the dossier to Interpol. Eventually, they found their way to me, by way of the Italian authorities—which is, I suppose, how the dossier came into Leporello's hands. You may not believe it, but Pinto and I are still friends. . . .

'That ought to be the end of the story, my Dante, but it isn't. In the days before the Black Sabbath, the Jews of Rome believed they had a deal with the Germans to ransom themselves. A fund was set up to which everyone contributed in gold and jewellery. Women even gave their wedding rings. All to no avail. The Germans took the gold and took the people as well. . . . However, one of the collectors was a man called Emmanuele Salatri. It was to him that Raquela gave the emerald brooch. Salatri never delivered what he had collected. He simply vanished with the loot. In 1969, there was an important auction of jewellery in Zurich. Among the pieces advertised in the catalogue, was that brooch. I was, therefore, in a position to trace its provenance. I traced it through two other owners to Emmanuele Salatri, who was then a prosperous gem-dealer in Hatton Garden in London. I sent him a dossier and a card. He blew his brains out. Once again, the dossier was traced back to me. Once again, nothing could be done about it because I had committed no crime. I gave the brooch back to Raquela. She would not accept it. There was blood on it, she said, and it would bring no joy to anyone. I sold it to Bulgari who broke it up and reset the stone.

'. . . Old history! Am I wrong to dig it up? I have thought so, many times, but always I have come back to the same question: why should the villains flourish while the victims still suffer the effects of their villainies? This is your question now, Matucci. It is one of the ironies of history that Leporello could wade through a whole ocean of crimes and still prove a potent and even a good ruler. But even if he did, should we still suffer him? Even if he came now in sackcloth with a halter round his neck, should we, in the same breath, forgive him and consecrate him to power? I cannot see it. I cannot. . . .

'There's one more story, my Dante; and then we must go to bed. Come over to the window. You see those far hills and the cluster of light at the top? . . . That's Vincolata. It's nothing much of anything, a little hill town with maybe five hundred people inside its old walls. In the Partisan days, I used it as an observation point, and sometimes I slept there in the house of a widow woman called Bassi.

'One day we ambushed a small German detachment a kilometre from the town, and killed two men. There were immediate reprisals. The Germans arrested twenty men, young and old, as hostages, and ordered them to be shot in the square of Vincolata. The officer in charge of the firing squad was a young Austrian Oberleutnant named Loeffler. . . . You can imagine the horror of such an event in a small place like Vincolata. Twenty men. . . . It is a loss and a trauma that can never be repaired. They were my people. They had suffered because of orders I had given. So, I promised, one day justice would be done.

'. . . Loeffler survived the war, went back to Austria and entered the pastoral priesthood. It takes us different ways you see. Me, it made an instrument of vengeance, him, it turned into an apostle. I had lost Loeffler by then and the more I came back here and saw the peace of this place, the less I wanted to disturb it.

'. . . Late in the sixties, I was in Austria, negotiating a contract for iron-ore. In the local press I read the news that the Right Reverend Franziskus Loeffler, parish priest of Oberalp, had been nominated to a Bishopric and would be consecrated in Rome by the Holy Father. I wasn't sure if it was the same man; so I went to see him. It was the same Franziskus Loeffler, and I didn't like him. I found him shallow, stubborn, vain, the kind of churchman I have always resented, half tyrant, half father-figure. I told him why I had come. I asked him whether he did not consider his elevation to a Bishopric an affront to his co-religionists in Vincolata.

'I could not come within a hand's touch of him. He was so secure in his conversion, it was as if he carried a private brief from the Almighty. I went away angry and bitter. I wrote to the Vatican. I incited a press campaign against the nomination, and suggested that Loeffler could and should be extradited to Italy to stand trial as a war criminal. Loeffler declined his nomination, resigned his parish and retired into obscurity.

'There is, however, an epilogue. About eighteen months ago, the parish priest of Vincolata came to see me, and asked as a special favour that I attend his Sunday Mass. Loeffler was there. He was dressed in clerical grey, with a white collar and a black tie and was kneeling in the front pew, by the nave. After the recitation of the Confiteor, he stood up, faced the congregation and announced very simply: "I am Franziskus Loeffler. I attended the execution of your relatives and friends during the war. I gave the firing order. I am here to beg your pardon if you feel you can give it. If not, I am prepared to offer myself for whatever retribution you may exact. I cannot bring back the dead. I wish I could. Please forgive me." He knelt down again and the Mass went on. Afterwards, I waited to see what the folk of Vincolata would do. . . . Nothing, my Dante! Absolutely nothing! They ignored him. They walked away and left him in what must have been the cruellest solitude of his life.

'. . . What could I do? I invited him home for lunch. I still didn't like him; but he was a bigger man than I, for whom the simplest apology is like drawing a tooth. Afterwards I thought he would probably have made a very good Bishop. . . . I'm sorry you won't meet him now. I'd have liked to know your opinion. . . . See you in the morning, my Dante. Sleep well!'

I didn't sleep. I sat up late, and, desperately lonely, wrote a letter to Lili; not from Uncle Pavel this time, but from Dante Alighieri Matucci, fugitive, who tomorrow must go back to the half-world of those who cannot conform or will not submit to the discipline of the ant-heap.

My dearest Lili,
This letter is from your puppet-man who has discovered, late and painfully, how little he can control his own destiny.
It is very late. The moon is full and high and all the land is silver. It is very still, so still that I can almost hear the mice breathing behind the panelling of my bedroom. The fire is almost dead and I am beginning to be cold; but I do not want to go to bed, because you will not be there and I cannot dream you back. I tore up your last letter because I wanted to put you out of my mind until all this business was finished. It was no use. I cannot forget you. I cannot bear the empty room in my heart. I am jealous that you may have found someone else to take my place in yours.
I love you, Lili. There! Now! It is said. I love you. I have clowned the words before. I have lied them and have traded them. This is the first time there has ever been a truth in them. Will you marry me, Lili? If I call you one day, to some tiny place that is hardly a name on a map, will you come and join hands and lips and body with me for always and a day more than always? Don't answer until you are sure; because when you are sure and I am free, I shall follow you to the last frontiers and home again.
Home? I have no home now, Lili. I am a man on the run. Things have gone badly for us, but there is still hope of a good outcome. Tomorrow I must leave this pleasant refuge and go back into the underworld, where the beggars plot against the tyrants and the tyrants use beggars for spies. I am looking for a legacy, left by a man I think is dead. If I find it, everything will be simple. If not, you may see me in Switzerland sooner than you expect.
I am afraid, but not too afraid; because I am learning slowly, to live with the man who lives in my skin. I haven't seen him full-face yet. That, too, will come. The Salamander still flourishes; and I am learning from him, too, the arts of

survival. . . . You will smile; but I never thought I could survive so long without a woman's company. Perhaps the truth is that my woman is never so far absent that I am without her utterly.

Strange how the words come back: '*Quella che 'mparadisa la mia mente!*' . . . she who makes my mind a paradise. My namesake wrote some very good things in his day. A pity he didn't write more about the body. That's very lonely just now.

Always yours,
Dante Alighieri . . .

I have the letter still, because it was returned to me in circumstances which belong later in this record.

I came back to Milan in the early afternoon, and settled myself in a modest *pensione* near the Ambrosian Library. It was clean, comfortable and economical, the right sort of lodging for a travelling salesman whose only visible possessions were a cardboard valise and a leather attaché case, with a combination lock just to impress the customers.

After I had unpacked, I strolled out to look at the Sforza Castle, the vast fortress of red brick built by Francesco, Fourth Duke of Milan and founder of the Sforza dynasty. He began as a simple *condottiere* with a horse and a sword and three pieces of advice from his father: never beat a servant, never ride a horse with a hard mouth and never make love to another man's wife. He made himself the sword-arm of Filippo Visconti, last of the line, fathered twenty-two bastards, married Filippo's daughter, and, when the Visconti died, rode into a starving city with all his men-at-arms festooned with bread. He died of the dropsy in 1466; but the bastion he built is still the pride of Milan.

They were wild men in those days; but their genius and their vices perpetuate themselves in the Italians of today, and all who deal with us do well to understand it. To the foreigner, we look like characters out of an opera, exaggerated and larger than life. The reverse is true. The opera is only a pale shadow of our history; and our history repeats itself in shorter cycles than theirs. Filippo Visconti, for instance, was just like the Surgeon. He, too, threw people out of windows. He conjured up plots and spies and filled the city with soldiers of fortune to protect him. Galeazzo Maria was murdered in the Church of St Stephen by three young men who went to Mass first to tell St Stephen they were sorry for messing up his Church. Where Leonardo wrote his Atlantic Codex, the Pirelli building stands, as a monument to Leonardo's successors.

Aimless thoughts, perhaps, from a man too disengaged for safety, in a city where every policeman had his name. And yet not aimless, not so irrelevant. Major-General Leporello was vaulting higher than the Visconti and the Sforza had even dreamed. They were content with duchies and provinces. He wanted all Italy under his first. He had arms and communications beyond their imagining and he had no Emperor or Pope breathing down his neck.

As I wandered through the galleries and corridors of the fortress, I wondered how I should best approach Elena Leporello. She was my last chance: the last filly in the last race. If I lost her I might just as well head for the Alps. I could write her a note. Her husband or a household spy might intercept it. I could accost her in the street. She might scream for the nearest policeman. I could telephone. She might, and probably would, slam down the receiver in my ear. I decided to telephone. I bribed a custodian to let me use the telephone in his office. A maidservant answered. I asked:

'May I speak with the General please?'

'I regret. The General is not at home. I suggest you try headquarters.'

'This is headquarters. Is the Signora at home?'

I waited a very long moment, and when Elena Leporello came on the line, I talked fast and eloquently:

'Please, madam, whatever I say, do not hang up until I have finished. This is Dante Alighieri Matucci. There is an order out for my arrest. I have been in hiding for several days. I read the papers. I do not know whether Captain Roditi is alive, dead or going about his normal duties. Can you tell me, please?'

'I can't tell you, not at this moment.'

'The reports give the impression that I either kidnapped him or murdered him. Neither is true. If he is alive, I must find him. Are you willing to talk to me?'

'Yes.'

'When?'

'Any day between ten and six.'

'Thank you. Now listen, carefully. At ten-thirty tomorrow morning go to the Ambrosian Library. Ask to see Petrarch's Virgil. The librarian will bring it to you. He will stay with you while you inspect it. A friend of mine will contact you then and bring you to me. Is that clear?'

'Yes, thank you.'

'Are you being watched?'

'I don't know.'

'If you think you are, don't keep the appointment. The same arrangement will stand for three days. If we have not made contact in that time, I will telephone again and make other arrangements.'

'I understand.'

'My friend will give you a recognition signal. He will ask: "Are you Raquela Rabin?" You will answer, "Yes!" Then do whatever he asks. Expect to be out of town for four or five hours.'

'I understand that.'

'I want to ask you some other questions. Just give me yes or no. . . . Can I trust Laura Balestra?'

'No.'

'Can you trust your servants?'

'No.'

'Will you trust me?'

'Until we meet–yes.'

'Thank you. I will now repeat. The Ambrosian Library, ten-thirty for three days. Petrarch's Virgil. Are you Raquela Rabin?'

'Yes. Thank you. Goodbye.'

So far, so good; but how far is far when you are dealing with a woman practised in intrigue? I put another slug in the telephone and dialled the number of Steffi's hotel.

'Steffi? This is Rabin. Shalom.'

'And to you, too, old friend. How are you?'

'Surviving. Are you free for dinner?'

'When you get to my age, you're always free for dinner. Where?'

'Rent yourself a car. Pick me up at six at the entrance to the Sforza Castle.'

'Who dines at six o'clock?'

'Nobody. We're going for a drive first. Do you like red-headed women?'

'With green hair even.'

'Any news?'

'Only that I'm bored.'

'That's good news. *Sbrigati eh!* Move it! There's a long way to go and the traffic's heavy.'

It was six-thirty when he found me and another forty minutes before we were on the autostrada, bowling along at a hundred and twenty kilometres an hour in the direction of Venice. As we drove, through warm, soft air and a misty countryside of poplars and orchard trees, I told him of my conversation with Elena Leporello and what I proposed to do about it.

'... If Roditi was telling the truth—and we always come back to that—then Elena Leporello has films and tapes that will hang Leporello higher than Haman's gibbet.'

Steffi slewed himself round in the seat and regarded me with limpid, compassionate eyes. He smiled and nodded his head, vigorously, up and down, up and down, like one of those silly Chinese mandarins. He admonished me with doleful patience.

'Matucci, little brother, it is as plain and large as the nose on my face that you have never been married. What do you know about this woman? She writes beautiful love-letters to a frightened pimp who procures for her husband! She bitches her husband at a dinner-party. What wife doesn't? You should hear mine sometimes, when I spill sauce on my tie or make a remark about one of the pretty little tarts who work for her. And her girl-friend says she has fallen for you! Oy-oy-oy! How much is that to gamble your life on? The trouble with you bachelors is that you don't hear a word that's said between hullo and goodbye. Now, listen little brother. Keep your eyes on the road and hear what an old married man has to tell you. This woman is sick. Worse, she knows it and loves it. She needs a husband she can kick around and humiliate. If he's a big shot in his profession, so much the better. That's spice for the turkey. She needs a lover of the same kind. Sure, she writes him love-notes ... better than Petrarch even! But she saddles him with two kids after a summer loving, and the poor bastard takes it; because he is a poor bastard and a rotten little pimp as well....'

'I know all that, Steffi, but....'

'But nothing, Matucci. Keep your eyes on the road and let me finish. Now, you come waltzing to her party all done up like a wedding-cake. You're new, you're male. Sure, she is interested. You're a challenge. She has to prove she can pat you down and make you eat out of her hand like the others. She's got something you want—no matter that it isn't what she'd like you to want—and she's going to make you sit up and beg for it. And beg, and beg.... And if you won't beg, she'll turn you in, just to show you who holds the whip.... So, you don't like it, you don't have to buy it; but that's how I read the story of Elena Leporello.'

'Even if you're right, Steffi, it still doesn't solve my problem. She has got something I want. How do I get it?'

'First question: where has she got it?'

'I don't know.'

'Second question: who shares it with her?'

'I don't understand.'

'A woman like that, with a wonderful dirty story and pictures to match. . . . You think she keeps it all to her lonely self? Never in a million years! She has to tell it. Else, where's the fun?'

'Laura Balestra?'

'Possibly. Probably. What do you know about her?'

'Not much. I'm told she's rich. I know she's unmarried.'

'How old is she?'

'Oh, thirty . . . thirty-five.'

'What else?'

'She's amusing and she likes to flirt and I'd guess she likes to get drunk so she doesn't have to say yes, and she can always blame the man when she wakes up in the wrong bed. I'd say she's an almost girl: almost in love and almost engaged and almost never likely to get married.'

'She sounds a likely candidate for the scandal session. . . . Matucci, do you always drive like this? Please, I'm dyspeptic. Let me live to enjoy my dinner.'

'So, Laura knows where the stuff is hidden. She tells me. What then?'

'Then, little brother, you have the whip. You threaten the lady. If she doesn't hand over the material, you will tell her husband she has it.'

'It would never work, Steffi.'

'I told you. You'll never understand women . . . until you marry one and then it's too late!'

'Let me think about it.'

'While you're thinking about it, here's a little bet. Ten thousand to a thousand the lady doesn't show at the Ambrosiana tomorrow.'

'Done! Now what do you fancy for dinner?'

'First, I would like a Bacardi cocktail, in company with a red-headed woman. . . .'

He got his Bacardi in Harry's Bar. He got his red-headed woman: but Gisela Pestalozzi was too much even for Steffi's jaded palate. Her appearance struck him dumb, her loud, bawdy talk reduced him to idiot confusion, so that I expected him at any moment to go into fugue and retreat under the table. However, the apartment she showed us was a little gem: with a front entrance that gave on to a quiet alley, a rear one from which you could step straight into a boat and an attic window from which you could climb over the rooftops, as long as the tiles would hold. The heating was more than adequate, the telephone worked, the furniture was worm-free and the linen was fresh. At our first meeting she had called the price at two hundred thousand a month. We settled on a hundred and fifty. There was no lease; the Salamander's name was good enough on both sides. I paid two months rent in cash. She handed me the key and some advice by way of a bonus:

'If you want a boatman, call me. If you want to bribe a policeman, check with me before you hand over any money. If you're in trouble, stay out of Harry's Bar and use the phone. For false documents, there's a forty-eight-hour service. It costs less if you can give me more time. No wild parties. No brawls. You get resident's discount on my girls. . . . And you, old man, don't be shy. I've had eighty-year-old cripples throw away their crutches. . . .'

She left us with a clatter of baubles and a toss of that extraordinary hair. Steffi collapsed into a chair and spluttered:

'My God! She's straight out of the Wax Museum! . . . Safe house indeed! With a man-eating monster like that, you'd be safer in a slaughter-yard. But what do you want the place for?'

'Don't laugh, Steffi! After tomorrow you may be on the run yourself.'

Looking at him then, pop-eyed and speechless, I remembered one of the less useful facts of history. Pietro Aretino died in Venice. He was no mean pornographer himself; and he died of apoplexy, laughing at a dirty joke.

At ten o'clock the next morning, dressed in a mechanic's cap and overalls and smeared with engine oil, I was tinkering with a scrubby Fiat, sixty metres from the entrance of the Ambrosian Library. There was nothing wrong with the engine; but I was nervous and twitchy, half-hoping that Steffi would win his bet and I could call the whole thing off with a good conscience. At ten-fifteen, Steffi himself marched down the street, looking for all the world like an elderly professor, who could decipher fifteenth-century cursive or decide a disputed interpretation at the drop of his black fedora. He was whistling, 'The Hills are in Flower', which, if you could recognize the tune, was a sign that, so far at least, there were no *poliziotti* on the horizon.

At ten twenty-five Elena Leporello drove up in a white Lancia. She was alone, which was another good sign. She locked the car, put the keys in her handbag and, without a backward glance, walked into the library, calm and unflustered as any Milanese matron out for a morning's shopping. I straightened up, wiped my hands on the greaserag, lit a cigarette and surveyed the street, up and down, from the entrance. There was the usual passage of people. There were no suspicious loiterers; no convergence of cars or men that would indicate the imminent arrest of a dangerous character. *Ebbene*! There was nothing to do but wait and the waiting could be fairly long, because the inspection of Petrarch's Virgil is one of the most serious ceremonies at the Ambrosiana.

The volume is huge. The Chief Librarian, himself, must authorize the inspection. An attendant, reverent and watchful, must stand beside you as you turn the pages, illuminated by Simone Martini of Siena. If you cannot read the inscription, written in the poet's own hand, the attendant will translate it for you:

> Laura, with all her illustrious virtues and long celebrated in my poems, first appeared before my eyes, in my young manhood, on the sixth day of April, in the year of our Lord 1327 in the early morning, in the Church of St Claire in Avignon . . .

I have always had a sentiment for the ceremony. In my days as a tourist guide, I found a reading of Petrarch in the original worked wonders with impressionable young women. Now, impatient and sweating with nervousness, I cursed myself for an idiot. I tossed away my cigarette, closed the bonnet of the car and sat inside, watching the entrance through the rear-vision mirror.

At ten fifty-five, Steffi came out with Elena Leporello. They got into the Lancia and drove off. I followed far enough behind to see whether any shadow car had joined our cavalcade. In the howling chaos of Milan's traffic, it was difficult to be sure of anything, even my own sanity. I saw, or thought I saw, one or two likely followers, but they dropped away. When we came on to the autostrada, I hung well back, letting the cars build up between me and the Lancia; but by the time we passed the Verona exit, I was fairly confident that we were free of shadows. By Padua, I was sure of it; so, I let them drive far ahead of me all the way to Mestre. Steffi's instructions were to cross to Venice, buy the lady a sandwich in St Mark's Square and leave when I made my appearance. He would then go to the safe house and wait for me. Elena Leporello could drive back to Milan alone. I hoped the strategy might establish in her mind the fact that I had left Milan and was holed up somewhere in the city of the Doges.

I went straight to the house, washed and tidied myself, and then, dressed in slacks and a green pullover, walked round to St Mark's Square. Steffi saw me coming and left before I reached the table. Elena Leporello gave me a frosty welcome:

'I hope, Colonel, there is some sense in this sordid little drama.'

'I hope, madam, you will help me make sense of it. Have you heard from Captain Roditi?'

'Not a word.'

'Does your husband know where he is?'

'No. He has a team of investigators working night and day on the case. He says he knows what happened at Matteo's apartment. You forced him to write a false and incriminating document, then had him killed or kidnapped.'

'And how does he know that?'

'From the notary who witnessed the document in Matteo's apartment. He's been arrested and he has signed a confession.'

'Has your husband seen the document?'

'He hasn't said so.'

'Then how does he know it's false and incriminating?'

'Obviously the notary told him.'

'The notary didn't read the document. He simply stamped and signed it.'

'But a document does exist?'

'Yes.'

'Is it incriminating?'

'Yes . . . but not false. Would you like to see it?'

'Please.'

I handed her a photostat copy of Roditi's confession and watched her, closely, as she read it. The colour drained from her face. She trembled violently and I thought for a moment she was going to faint. I put out a hand to steady her, but she rejected me with a gesture and continued her reading. By the time she had finished, she was in control of herself again; and the sudden mastery of her emotions was frightening to see. She folded the document carefully and handed it back to me. Then she faced me, cold-eyed and contemptuous.

'That's a tissue of lies, Colonel—monstrous, horrible lies.'

'That is Roditi's handwriting.'

'But you dictated it; the notary heard you from the bedroom.'

'I dictated it after interrogation. Did he hear that, too?'

'He heard your threats, he must have heard the rest of it.'

'Are you sure, madam, that everything is false?'

'Everything!'

'Then you and Roditi were not lovers?'

'Of course not.'

'I read your letters, madam. I saw your signed photograph. Roditi kept them in the drawer of his dressing-table.'

'No, Colonel. There are no letters.'

'You mean they were removed on your husband's orders. Not all. I have one in my pocket now. I can tell you that the photograph was taken by Donati in Bologna. He made an extra copy for me. . . . Let me tell you something else. Roditi, your lover, was a friend of Giuseppe Balbo who was killed by the police a few nights ago. I met them together in the Alcibiade. No, Madam. The statement doesn't lie. I'm not lying. You are. Why? Are you afraid of your husband? Of what he may do to you or the children?'

'No, Colonel.'

'Then, listen to me, please. Roditi told me you have material, photographs and tapes which prove against your husband all the charges in that document.'

'I have no such material, Colonel.'

'But, if your letters mean anything, you loved Roditi. He loved you. He told me so.'

'Old love is cold comfort, Colonel.'

'He also told me that the tapes and photographs were your only insurance against your husband.'

'I have no such material. And I need no insurance.'

'Why? Because Roditi's dead?'

'You said that, not I.'

'Or because his evidence is discredited and your husband's giving up his little games for the time being? . . . What about you? What sort of a woman are you?'

'I'll tell you the sort of woman I am, Colonel. If my husband is clever enough to handle this mess, then he's clever enough to climb right to the top of the tree. I want to be there, too. If my husband can't make it . . . Boh! There's always another day for me.'

'You can settle that question now, madam. There's a policeman over there, and two carabinieri at the entrance to St Mark's. Call them. Tell them who I am and have me arrested.'

'No, my dear Colonel, I'm not quite sure yet how clever you are and whether you're a match for my husband. It's a game, don't you see? I'm the privileged spectator, I just sit back and enjoy it. I could even enjoy an hour in bed with you, now, if you're interested, and your place isn't too far. . . . No? Another time, perhaps. I'm much better than Laura. . . . By the way, did you hear what happened to her?'

'What?'

'She drove her car into a tree last night. She drinks too much as you well know. I've warned her many times; my husband has, too.'

'Is she badly hurt?'

'The doctors think she'll live, but she could end up as a vegetable. . . . Pity! She was such a pretty girl. Goodbye, Colonel.'

She offered me her hand. I could not take it. I would not even stand to salute her going. I sat and watched her walk across the square, head high, hips swinging, jaunty as any girl on the beat. The pigeons rose in clouds as she passed and the waiter, counting my change, sighed, dolefully, at the waste of so much woman. He was a Venetian, but he had forgotten the cynical wisdom of his forebears. When they sent an ambassador abroad, they let him take his cook. They made him leave his wife at home.

It was all defeat and disaster, and there seemed no way to mend it. Steffi summed it up in a terse valediction.

'... Checkmate! You have no place to go, little brother. Your last hope—and that's a slim one—is the safe-deposit box. I wish I could help you. I can't. I'm going back to Rome. If there's something you need, call me. But take a little advice ... cut out now and join your girl in Switzerland. Let Manzini handle the rest of it. Here, you're in a trap. Worse, you're in a vacuum, which is demoralizing. You know the system. They've immobilized you. All they have to do is wait. Sooner or later, you'll make a small mistake and they'll spring the trap. I'm fond of you, Matucci—God knows why, because you've given me grief and ulcers! I don't want to see you lopped before you've had a chance to grow up. ...'

When he had gone, I called Manzini, who was equally gloomy. He told me he had been contemplating a press campaign to stir up the muddy waters; but that the risks were too great: risk of libel action, risk that old laws might be invoked to stop publication, risk that timid friends on the Quirinal might be lost by untimely action, risk of fomenting public disorder. He, too, suggested I move out to Switzerland. He sounded tired and spiritless and I wondered about the state of his health.

When I put down the phone, I found myself, suddenly, in the grip of a violent reaction. I cursed and swore and slammed about the apartment in a frenzy of frustration. It was incredible that with so much evidence, we could do nothing. It was monstrous that one man could manipulate an arm of the law to make it an instrument of crime. It shamed me that a bastard like Leporello could turn me into a fugitive while his bitch of a wife sat laughing and offering to go to bed with me. And, for a last straw, here I was, in an empty house, with no food or liquor, and suddenly afraid to poke my nose outside the door. To hell with it! I wasn't a criminal. Why should I behave like one? To hell with the whole rotten crew! I would stay!

... How I was going to stay was another matter. I needed to think that one out over a meal and a bottle of wine. I didn't bother to change. I strolled down the Calle dei Fabbri and found myself a simple place where the food smelt good and the waiter was friendly. The night was balmy, so I sat outside, where I could look at the girls of Venice, who are better in the flesh than Titian ever painted them. I ordered a risotto and a dish of sea-food and a bottle of Barolo and settled down like any honest citizen to enjoy my supper. It was a good meal and I relished every mouthful. I was relaxed and happy over my coffee, when two carabinieri picked me up like an orange from a basket and carted me off to the Questura.

They were very polite. They spared me all the usual routine and took me straight to the Commandant. The Commandant looked at my papers and asked me if I was the person therein described: Aldo Carnera, travelling salesman. I assured him I was. I asked whether I was charged with any offence. He assured me I was not. It was simply a question of the green pullover. Had I been in St Mark's Square that afternoon? I had. Ah! That explained everything.

It told me exactly nothing and I begged to know whether there was anything special about a green pullover. He admitted that he could see nothing special in it, except that he, himself, was not overly fond of green. However ... at three in the afternoon, a woman, who declined to give her name, had telephoned the Questura with the information that she had identified a man wearing such a garment as one Dante Alighieri Matucci, wanted for questioning in Milan. She had seen his photograph in the papers.

Now, the Commandant had been informed of the Matucci affair, which was a highly political matter in which he did not wish to embroil himself. He understood that an agent of a secret service often carried a false identification. So, if in fact I was Colonel Matucci, the matter of the forged papers could be easily dealt with. Then, he brought out a photograph of me and a set of fingerprints from the SID files. I smiled and he smiled and we agreed that it was the luck of the game.

He offered me a cup of coffee. I asked whether I might make a telephone call. He smiled again and produced an order stating that, when and if Dante Alighieri Matucci were apprehended, he should be held *incommunicado*, pending instructions from Milan Headquarters. He was going to telephone Milan now. He hated to do this to a senior colleague in the Service. He hoped I understood that there was nothing personal. He begged me to make myself comfortable until he returned.

A wink being as good as a nod to a blind elephant, I used the telephone on his desk, asked for an outside line and dialled an interurban call to Manzini's Milan apartment. The old man was out. His manservant took the message. It was a disappointment, but at least Manzini would know what had happened to me. There was one other crumb of comfort. The Surgeon was dead and I should be spared his tender attentions.

The Commandant was gone a long time. He came back looking grave and preoccupied. He told me that I was now formally under arrest and that I should surrender all my personal belongings, for which he would issue a receipt. His orders were to detain me overnight at the Questura, and send me, in the morning, to Milan.

A *brigadiere* escorted me to the detention cell. A turn-key locked me in. About fifteen minutes later the *brigadiere* returned accompanied by a guard and a man in a white coat carrying a kidney-dish covered with a towel. He introduced himself as the police surgeon and asked me to roll up my sleeve. He told me he wanted to give me a sedative. I protested, vigorously, against this invasion of my rights and my person. The surgeon suggested it would be simpler if I complied, otherwise he would be forced to put me under restraint. I did as I was told. I rolled up my sleeve and twisted it into a tourniquet. I made a fist and presented my arm for the injection. I winced at the prick of the needle and began counting one-two-three. . . .

Then all the lights went out.

PART III

We have changed all that.

Molière: Le Médecin malgré lui

I woke–or dreamed I woke–in absolute darkness and absolute silence. I was–or dreamed I was–floating in undetermined space in a timeless continuum. I was not sad; I was not happy; I was not in pain; I simply was. At first, that was enough: the floating and the dreaming and the simply being. Then I began to be uneasy, faintly at first, then more and more acutely. Something was absent. I could not define what it was. I could not define anything. My mind was a swirl of mist. I was groping, without hands, into nowhere.

The mist dispersed slowly in drifts and eddies. Slowly and intermittently, I began to collect the scattered parts of myself. My thumb encountered my fingertips. My tongue met my palate. My eyelids blinked. Somewhere out in the fog my feet brushed, one against the other. Then the parts became a whole and I was aware that my body and I were still together. I was able to lift my hand–both my hands–and run them over my face and shoulders and breast and belly and genitals. I was there, naked and lying on a hard flat surface, warm to the touch.

Then, panic engulfed me. I was buried alive. I was blind. I was deaf. I was dumb. When I cried out, no sound would issue from my parched constricted throat. I broke out into a sweat of terror and curled myself into a foetal ball, huddling away from the horror of nothingness. The panic rose and fell, endlessly, like waves on a beach, but slowly, slowly, it subsided to a ripple, constant, threatening, but, mercifully, no longer a madness. The mist about my mind was tendrils now and cobwebs, but at least I knew I had a mind, and must, somehow, begin to use it.

First I directed my body to uncurl itself; and, reluctantly, my body obeyed. Then I asked my fingers to explore my immediate ambience. The slab on which I lay felt like marble or smooth stone. It terminated a few centimetres either side of my body; and above it and all around there was empty space. Below it, my fingers encountered a floor, not paved, but rough to the touch. The floor was colder than my slab. How far it stretched, I did not know. Enough that I had found a foot-hold in reality.

Now I must make a search of my inward self, testing for time-holds and memory-pegs. This was more difficult. Inside my skull was a kaleidoscope that made patterns, fragmented them, rearranged them, dissolved them into monochrome fluid. I was lifted on a wave of panic, dropped into despair, tumbled over and over in an undertow, floated free again.

At last one picture held, one peg was firm; a woman walking through a cloud of pigeons, a man in a green pullover sitting at a table watching her. I could go forward from that. I could go back from it. I found myself weeping quietly in the dark. The tears were good. They fell like oil on the panic waters. When they were spent, I knew that I was still a man. I knew, and I knew that I knew, what had happened to me and what would happen very soon.

If you walk through the museums of the world you will find a variety of instruments of torture: racks, thumbscrews, barbed whips, iron maidens, pincers, branding irons, machines for electric shocks. The most potent instruments of all you will never see. They are darkness and silence. Each is an absence, a negation. Darkness is a negation of light. Silence is a negation of sound. Evil, said Thomas Aquinas, is an absence of good. My namesake, Dante Alighieri, wrote a poem about hell which has become one of the world's classics. I stand now to witness that he did not know what he was talking about. Hell is nothing but a dark and silent room. Damnation means to be locked inside it—alone.

Please let me explain. It is necessary to me. Come the day of the tyrants, it may be necessary for you, too, to understand it. Do you know the word 'parameter'? Many people use it, too few understand its meaning or its importance. The dictionary defines it as 'a quantity constant in the case considered, but varying in different cases'. Admit is now: the definition means little, if anything, to you. But suppose one night, you went to sleep and when you woke in the morning the campanile or the oak-tree that was always framed in your window was not there. Suppose you opened the door to your kitchen and found instead a rose garden. The constant quantities in your life would be gone. You would be lost. You would say: I do not know where I am. If the changes continued, day after day, you would become a victim of their inconstancy. You would say in the end: I do not know who I am.

But suppose. . . . Suppose, suddenly, all the constants are gone: the steeple and the kitchen and the sunrise and the sunset and the sun and the moon and the stars and even the light . . .? Suppose the inconstants, too, are taken away; the cars in the street, the doves in the cabbage garden, the dripping tap, the passing clouds, the wind, the sound of rain, the vagrant human voices . . .? Then you are damned beyond redemption.

This is what happens when you close a man inside a dark and silent room and leave him. He has nothing against which he can measure himself, except the confines of the floor, and the monotony of that measurement helps to drive him mad. He has no sense of height, no sense of time. He is cut off from his past. He has no expectation of the future. His present is darkness and silence. He cannot divert himself with the minutest things—a fly buzzing against a windowpane, an ant crawling across the floor, dustmotes in a sunbeam. His only points of reference are the contours of his body, the fixed contours of the walls and the floor and his sleeping-place, and the little world of memory inside his own skull-case. And there are less, much less, than enough to keep him sane.

I can tell you what happens, because it happened to me. It was planned to happen. It was contrived, inflicted, as the subtlest vengeance any man could contrive against another. . . . You are alone in this dark and silent nowhere. You say to yourself: I know who I am. I know what they are trying to do to me. I will not let them do it. I will retreat into my skull-case and live there, feeding on memory and hope and faith and love, the whole capital of a lifetime. I will hold fast to the facts I know: that this nowhere is, in truth, a somewhere; that outside there are humans and animals and solid, tangible things. I know that they will have to feed me, or at least give me something to drink. This perpetual non-motion is as impossible as perpetual motion. Something has to break, sometime; else why would they take all this trouble to torment me. Someone will come, if only to gloat. Otherwise, it would have been simpler to put a bullet in my head and toss me in a ditch.

 ... Eh-eh-eh! It is an illusion. Nobody comes. The silence and the darkness remain unbroken. You discover, in your first circuit of the walls that they have left three plastic demi-johns of water, enough to keep you alive for a long, long time. You discover other things, too. The world inside your skull-case becomes quickly confused. You grasp for one memory and find another. Pictures flash by and you cannot hold them in focus. You lean on hope and collapse into weeping despair. You try to pray and find yourself cursing. You recite poems and hear yourself babbling nonsense. After three days, though you have long since forgotten time, you are hallucinating constantly; and, even if anybody came, you would not know whether they were real or not.

 This is the trick of it, you see. They do come, but you do not know. They scoop you up from the floor and pump barbiturates into you to continue the hallucination. They drip enough glucose into your veins to keep you alive; and they feed you with new fears to drive you closer and closer to the cliff-edge of permanent derangement. I learned later that I was there fifteen days. When they brought me out, I was blind for a while, and dumb and ataxic, shambling like an animal, bearded and filthy from my own droppings. They put me under deep sedation for forty-eight hours, and when I came out of it, I was sure I had died and arrived, by some cosmic mistake, in Paradise.

 There was so much light, I could only bear it for the shortest while and then must close my eyes and shut it out. There were flowers on a table. I remember that they were iris, blue and yellow and plum purple. Always, when I opened my eyes, there was a pretty nurse in the room, sometimes close to the bed, sometimes sitting in the armchair, reading. For a time I thought she was Lili; but later, when I could concentrate a little, she told me her name was Claudia and that I had been very ill, but now I was getting better.

 Whenever the light began to fade, I would become restless and fretful, scared that it would go out altogether. But it never did. Always another nurse came in and turned on the lamps; and even when I slept there was always a small light burning. The night nurse was not so pretty as Claudia, but she was very gentle and solicitous. She was very patient, too. Sometimes I talked and talked until I couldn't stop myself. At others, I was morose and silent, staring at the small circle of light on the ceiling, hating myself, hating everything, unable to change the fixed and horrible trend of my thoughts. When I talked, she listened. When I was silent, she talked, a steady stream of soothing meaningless gossip that lulled me at last into a doze.

 Every day the doctor came and examined me and chatted for a little while about my illness, which he said was a psychic dysfunction induced by my experience in confinement. It would cure itself, he told me. All it needed was time and patience, a little sedation and the simple therapy of human communication. A couple more days of complete rest and he would let me walk in the garden. When I asked him where I was, he told me I was clinic and left it at that.

I told him I was troubled with nightmares. He nodded sagely, and said that this, too, was a curative process: the subconscious mind working on the intolerable to make it tolerable. I told him that I had difficulty in remembering; that I could not concentrate even on a page of print; and that to reason through the simplest proposition was an enormous effort. He explained that this was the natural response of an organism taxed beyond endurance. It simply refused to function until it was rested and ready. When I asked whether I was still under arrest, he smiled and told me that I was free; but that I needed to be prepared if I were to enjoy the freedom I had.

It was all pleasantly vague; but gradually, one by one, new parameters were established and I began to take a more confident hold on the realities around me. The distant realities were still vague. I thought often about Lili and Manzani and Steffi; but I could not grasp them as present or regret them too much as absent. They would come, or I would go to them, in some near future, which I did not need, as yet, to determine by days or weeks. My whole concept of time was still rather uncertain. I never once asked the date or the time of day. The inimical realities, Leporello, his wife, the Director, were so vague as to be almost irrelevant. In some fashion, which I could not yet describe, I had survived them. I had walked through them as if they were a paper wall and come out on the other side. When I looked back I saw only tattered images blown by the wind.

When they allowed me out of bed for the first time, I was astonished to find how weak and insecure I was. My sense of balance had been impaired and I felt as though I were listing, now to one side then to the other. If I turned my head too suddenly, I became dizzy. And the first short walk to the window, left me weak and trembling. Even the view outside proved a shock. I saw it first in a single dimension. Then, quite suddenly, it solidified and fell into perspective.

There was a belvedere, set with cane-chairs and bright umbrellas. Beyond the belvedere was a lawn, broken by flower-gardens, and then an unbroken wall of cypresses, dark against a limpid sky. It was pleasant to look at, but it told me nothing. There were no people, no landmarks. After a few moments, I was bored with it and glad to go back to bed. Claudia sponged my damp forehead and smoothed my pillows and closed my eyes with the tips of her fingers and told me to go to sleep.

When I woke, the night-light was burning and Bruno Manzini was standing at the foot of my bed. He came to me and took my hands between his own and held them a long time in a wordless greeting. Suddenly, and without reason, I was weeping. Manzini took the handkerchief from his breast-pocket and wiped the tears from my cheeks. Then, he perched himself on the edge of the bed and talked me back to composure.

'. . . Eh! It's been a rough road, hasn't it, my Dante. But you've survived it. Another ten days will see you out of here. Then I'm taking you home with me to Pedognana. You'd like that, wouldn't you?'

'Yes, I would. I feel so weak and lost. I don't know what's the matter with me.'

'You've had your season in hell, my friend. It takes time to recover from that.'

'I suppose so. Where is this place?'

'Near Como. It's a small psychiatric clinic. I finance it. . . . Oh, don't worry, you're quite sane; but you wouldn't have been if they'd held you much longer.'

'How did I get here?'

'I brought you. It took me ten days and a lot of bribery to find where they were holding you. Then I had to get a judicial order for your release. That was harder; but we managed it. You're on provisional liberty, of course. Charges still lie against you.'

'I can't imagine why Leporello let me go.'

'He was convinced you were broken beyond repair. And the Movement would have lost a large cheque from me. He may still get you into court. Fortunately, we now have medicial evidence of the treatment to which you were submitted; and I don't think he wants that revealed just yet.'

'You've no idea what it's like . . . no idea. . . .'

'It's over now–finished. I am proud of you, my Dante.'

'Everything's in pieces. I–I can't put them together.'

'You put it all together before this happened. We have everything in our hands. Your notes on the microfilms, the tapes and the photographs from the bank. We can break Leporello now–and the Director after him.'

'Do you know what happened to Roditi?'

'Oh, yes. He's on indefinite sick leave. They put him through the treatment, too. He's no danger to Leporello now and no use to anyone else.'

'I'm afraid I'm not going to be much use to you, either.'

'Listen to me, my Dante, and listen well. . . . You are a lucky man, too lucky to have pity for yourself. You cannot surrender now. You will not; because if you do, you hand the victory to Leporello and all you have suffered will be useless. Also you have cost me an enormous sum of money. . . . Come, man! I have been where you are now. I have climbed the dark mountain and come down into sunlight on the other side. You will, too. . . .'

'I'm so tired. . . .'

'Try a little hating, my friend. It's the best stimulant in the world.'

'It's all too big and complicated. I just want to drop it and get out.'

'Easy now, relax. We'll talk about it another time. I'll see you again in a few days.'

I was glad to see him go. I wanted to feel sorry for myself. I deserved a little pity and this terrible old man had none. I would put him out of my mind. Later, when I was well, I would shut him out of my life.

Next day, I was stronger and I sat for an hour on the terrace looking at the pictures in the scandal magazines. The day after, I made my first circuit of the garden with Claudia and found that I could walk without staggering and talk without confusion and fatigue. In the evening I watched a cabaret show on television and found myself laughing at the comedian and beating time to the music and wondering why my nurse wasn't there to share the pleasure with me.

My sedatives were withdrawn that night for the first time, and I was swirled through a series of disconnected dreams; so that I woke, red-eyed and irritable, but aware that I had gained much ground on the climb up the dark mountain. After that I walked in the garden every morning, ambling like a monk in meditation, from one end of the lawn to the other, soaking up the sun and the colour of the flowers, knowing that the parameters were holding firm, and I was beginning to be a man again. I was reading print now, colour magazines and light novels, which I never finished, because my concentration still waned after an hour. The newspapers were brought to me, but I did not open them. Newspapers were today. Newspapers were a responsibility which I was not yet ready to shoulder.

Then Manzini came to see me again. He brought a bottle of champagne and a pot of fresh caviar and we made a picnic on the terrace, and afterwards strolled around the garden. He approved the change in me; but I was wary of him. I did not want him to disturb my still precarious comfort. He did not disturb it. He shattered it with a single stroke.

'I have bad news for you, my Dante. Lili Anders is back in Italy. She is in prison in the Maddalena in Rome.'

'No . . . it can't be true.'

'It is. Your Director called me yesterday to announce the good news. He asked me to pass it on to you.'

'But why? How? Did the Swiss deport her?'

'She came back of her own accord. She entered the country by way of the Brenner and was arrested by the border police.'

'But that's madness! I don't understand it!'

'It seems you called her back, by telegram.'

'How could I? I've been out of action for nearly four weeks.'

'That's the way the Director tells it. Your telegram said she was free to return. You would meet her in Bolzano and you would make immediate arrangements to get married. She was carrying the telegram in her handbag. She produced it when the frontier police looked her up in the black-book and questioned her.'

'It was a trap!'

'Of course. But she walked into it.'

'We've got to get her out.'

'How, my Dante? You collected the evidence against her. You prepared her dossier. You broke her network, and gaoled her master, the Woodpecker. You can hardly refute your own testimony, can you?'

'But the Director promised to let her go.'

'He did. She came back. Illegal entry for a start.'

'Mother of God! What a stinking filthy mess! I've got to get out of here, Bruno!'

'I'm not sure that's wise.'

'I don't give a curse whether it's wise or not. I can discharge myself. Let's go back. I'll do it now.'

'If that's what you want, so be it.'

We were half-way back across the lawn, when a sudden thought stopped me dead in my tracks. I caught his arm, and heedless of his age and his infirmity, swung him round to face me. I challenged him, brutally:

'Did you arrange this, Bruno?'

There was not a tremor in him. He stood straight and firm as a pine-tree, staring me down. His eyes were cold. His mouth, under that great eagle's beak, was tight as a trap.

'Do you think me capable of it?'

'Yes, I do.'

'Good. Then you have learned something.'

'Did you do it?'

'I might have–if I had thought it useful. In fact, I did not. I think you did, sometime in that fifteen days of dysfunction and hallucination. I know that you told things about me; because I had to lie about them later. I know we nearly missed the safe-deposit box, because Leporello did get a judicial order to open it the day after we had extracted the contents.'

'Oh Christ, I'm sorry.'

'Don't be sorry. Think about those who made a traitor out of you against your will.'

'I'll kill the bastards.'

'They'll expect you to try. They'll be waiting for you. And if they take you a second time, there'll be no escape. . . . No, Dante, this time we'll do it my way. . . . Now, let's talk to the doctor. You're not setting foot outside the gate until he tells me you're ready.'

'The doctor was hesitant and very dubious. He was prepared to let me go only on condition that I understood the risks. I was still convalescent. There were still dysfunctions which would become acute again under stress. My memory would play tricks. My concentration would be limited for a long time. I would be subject to fits of depression and anxiety. I should not throw away too quickly the crutch of sedatives and tranquillizers. For the rest, I should trust to nature and not to try to force myself too fast along the road.

It was easy to say, impossible to do, with the guilt of Lili's betrayal nagging at me like an aching tooth. The moment we drove out the gates of the clinic and into the sunny countryside of Lombardy, I lapsed into deep despondency. It was Lili who should be at liberty and not I. It was Lili who should be travelling in luxury with the sun on her face and all the world smiling back at her. Instead, she was penned with thieves and prostitutes and child-slayers in a mediaeval hell-hole on the banks of the Tiber. Manzini let me brood awhile, and then faced me with a blunt question:

'How serious are you about this woman of yours?'

'I love her.'

'Enough to marry her?'

'I've already asked her.'

'When?'

'I wrote her just before I left Pedognana last time. I gave you the letter to mail through Chiasso.'

'I thought you were supposed to be her Uncle Pavel.'

'I wasn't when I wrote the letter.'

'Wasn't that rather foolish?'

'On the face of it, yes.'

'So, you don't know whether she wants to marry you or not?'

'No. . . . Why?'

'A vague thought. Let me play with it awhile. . . . There's something else more important. I think we know the date of the *colpo di stato*.'

'When?'

'October thirty-first, mid-autumn. The tourists have gone home. Diplomats have returned from the summer holidays. Training programmes have been completed. Transport still functions freely, which it doesn't in mid-winter. More importantly, the word is being whispered among the initiates . . . and it checks with dates mentioned in your notes on the microfilms.'

'That's five months ahead.'

'Never count on time, Dante. It runs away too quickly. Opinion is hardening on both sides. Leporello is a splendid organizer; and you are not the only one he has eliminated or immobilized. The Milan bomb cases have not been brought to trial. Several important witnesses have disappeared; others have been systematically intimidated. No, we have to move before summer.'

'What do you want me to do?'

'For the moment, exactly what the doctor has ordered—rest and recuperate. However, there is one thing which you can do without prejudice to your health.'

'What's that?'

'Entertain your friends. I presume you do have friends of your own rank and standing in the Corps?'

'Some, yes. But they're scattered up and down the country. I'm a bad correspondent. It's hard to keep in touch.'

'Now you will have time. Write a few letters. Make some direct calls. You've been ill. You've been in personal strife. You would like to see them sometime at Pedognana. We have plenty of guest-rooms. There is riding and shooting. . . . They'll come.'

'What are you looking for now, Bruno?'

'A pretorian guard. Ten men would be enough, so long as they were resolute and understood what was at stake. On your own showing, there's quite a large amount of disaffection from Leporello and his policies.'

'If you're asking me to stage a revolt of the armed forces, Bruno, forget it. I'm not very bright at this moment; but that's mystical madness.'

'Who said anything about revolt? On the contrary, we need men proud of the traditions of the Corps, jealous of its honour and its oath; old-fashioned patriots, who don't like seeing their fellow-citizens kicked in the teeth and justice denied by perjured witness.'

'Buy me a tub and a lamp, Bruno. I might have a better chance.'

'We're bitter today, aren't we, my Dante? But I agree. Go play Diogenes. But find me ten good men willing to put their heads on the block for one night. . . . Oh, by the way, I brought your clothes back from the apartment. You've lost some weight, but they'll still fit. I can't bear that rubbish you're wearing now.'

He would not tell me any more and I was too tired to press him. I lay back in the seat and dozed fitfully until we drove through the gates of Pedognana.

At cocktails that evening, I discovered there was another guest at the Villa: the Principessa Pia Faubiani, prima donna of Roman fashion, mistress of Bruno Manzini. She was slim, dark, leggy, flat-busted and, if you favour the pinched and glacial *modella*, very attractive. At first meeting, I did not favour her at all. I was edgy, jealous of my privacy and in no mood to lavish on her the attention which she very obviously demanded. I was also mistrustful, because of Manzini's equivocal description of his relations with her. However, this was his house and he could open it to whom he liked. The least I could do was to exert myself to be agreeable.

I was amply rewarded for my pains. Pia Faubiani was a witty and intelligent woman with enough malice to survive in the rough world she exploited, and more than enough affection and good humour to spend on her friends. I was glad I wasn't married to her; her claws were too sharp for comfort; but for playmate and boon companion . . . yes, without a second thought. She was wearing the salamander pin from Fosco's exhibition, and when I commented on it, she announced, cheerfully:

'It's a parting gift. This is my first and last season with Bruno.'

Manzini chuckled and held up his glass in a toast.

'You're too young and I'm too old, my love; and I hate to be second-best at anything. Besides, the way you're going, you'll need a bank of your own, just to pay the interest bills. This woman, Dante, is the best designer and the worst accountant in the business. I keep telling her she'll either marry a gold-mine or end in debtor's prison.'

'I was thinking of a convent, darling; now that you've deserted me.'

'I've never deserted a woman in my life and you know it. I've just retired from the field–with honour.'

'With honour! Listen to the man! You're an old fox, Bruno! *Buon giorno–buona notte, ciao bambina*–and you're over the hills and far away licking your chops as you go. This man, Dante, has had many mistresses as I've had birthdays, and I don't think he's ever been in love in his life. . . . Have you ever been in love, Dante?'

'Handle him gently, Pia. He's in love and his woman's in gaol.'

'Oh, I'm sorry. . . .'

'So, you're going to cheer him up for me.'

It was obviously as much of a shock to her as it was to me. She sat, with a morsel of cream-cake poised precariously on the end of her fork, and gaped at Manzini.

'I am? I'm glad you told me, darling.'

'If you drop that cake, you'll spoil a very expensive dress. Put it in your mouth, like a good girl. . . . No wonder God gets bored, Dante. Nobody ever gives him any surprises. Now, where was I? Oh, yes: what you, my Pia, are going to do for me. When do you open your show in Bologna?'

'Next Wednesday.'

'And in Milan and Turin?'

'Each one ten days after the other?'

After that, you're free.'

'Well, not exactly free, darling. I have to go back to Rome and. . . .'

'I know, but you'd come for at least a couple of says, wouldn't you? For last season's sake?'

'Of course, but why?'

'I want you to hostess a party for me, here, at Pedognana. I've been promising to introduce Dante to people ever since he came to Milan. He's had a rough time, as I told you, and I think he needs some diversion.'

'Please, Bruno! A party's the last thing I need.'

'It may be the last one you'll get, if you go to trial. Besides, there's a month yet to get used to the idea. Enjoy, man! Enjoy! They'll be toasting our funerals soon enough. . . . You'll do it for me, won't you, Pia?'

'You know I will.'

'And if you see this fellow moping around like a barnyard owl, take him out, introduce him to your girls, seduce him yourself if you like. . . . But bounce him out of his miseries, understand?'

'Your servant, Cavaliere.'

'I wish you were, my love. I think we'd have lasted longer. Still, it's been fun hasn't it . . .?'

She laid a hand on his and said, gently:

'It's been fun, *caro*. And I'm sorry about . . .'

'Enough, please! I've had a good life and I'm very grateful for it. Also I'm tougher than they think. . . . And I'll tell you something, my Pia. I have been in love, twice, in my life. That's more than enough for any man.'

'I know about Raquela, darling. That's something even I wouldn't joke about. But who was the other one?'

'My wife.'

We both stared at him then. He gave us an odd, embarrassed, little smile and a shrug of apology.

'I'm sorry. I wasn't trying to surprise you this time. I've been thinking a lot about her lately, wondering if we'll meet again, and if we do will we recognize each other. . . . I married her in Paris in 1934. She was nineteen years old. I was thirty-five. I had travelled all over the world and I thought she was the most beautiful creature in it. I brought her back here to Pedognana and she fell in love with the place at first sight. Ask some of the old ones and you'll find they still remember her riding the rounds with the factor, kneeling in the chapel on Sunday, with all the children about her.

'She was born to the land. Her people farmed a big estate near Poitiers. This place flowered under her hand in those two strange years. . . . You're too young to remember it, my Pia, but they were very strange. We had an empire then. We took Addis Ababa and annexed Ethiopia. Ciano became Foreign Minister, Farouk became King of Egypt and Germany occupied the Rhineland, and Charlie Chaplin made *Modern Times*. . . . But, here at Pedognana, we were almost able to forget the madness that was going on around us. We were ludicrously happy. My affairs were prospering. If things went wrong in Europe, I had capital planted and growing abroad, and, best of all, Marie Claire became pregnant. For a man like me, who had never known a family life, this was like the announcement of the Second Coming. I was out of my mind with delight. I was bubbling with wild plans for my son's future—because, of course, it had to be a son.

'In the fourth month of her pregnancy, Marie Claire fell sick and died within a week, of cerebro-spinal meningitis. . . . She's buried in the chapel here on the estate. I know you're not a praying man, Dante, but you'd have seen the inscription if you'd bent that stubborn neck of yours. Marie Claire, beloved wife of Bruno Manzini. Born Paris, April 20, 1915. Died Pedognana, June 17, 1936. Requiescat . . . Boh! Long ago and far away. Let's have coffee in the study. It's cosier there.'

When the coffee was brought, he refused it and announced, abruptly, that he was going to bed. Pia Faubiani made a move to go with him, but he pushed her gently back into the chair and bent to kiss her on the forehead. His tone was very tender.

'Stay here, my love. I'm very tired tonight.'

'But, darling. . . .'

'Don't worry. I'll sleep. Tomorrow we'll talk about the party. . . . Goodnight, my Dante. Think about the pretorian guard, won't you? It's very important. Golden dreams to you both.'

When he had gone, Pia Faubiani kicked off her shoes, curled herself in the armchair and gave a deep sigh of relaxation and contentment.

'*Dio!* I'm so glad it's ended like this! He's one man in the world I wouldn't want to hurt. I never thought I'd let any man dismiss me; but that one—God bless him—is very particular.'

'I know what you mean.'

'You're rather particular, too, Dante Alighieri. I can't quite read you yet.'

'Don't try, Pia. I'm a mess just now. You'd get the wrong reading anyway.'

'Bruno loves you.'

'I know. He's told me.'

'How do you feel about him?'

'I don't know. I admire him very much. I wish sometimes I could be like him. I fight him often. I never quite understand him. . . . How sick is he?'

'He's not sick at all, really. He's an old man. His heart's tired and wearing itself out. He could go quickly and he knows it. I think he's more afraid of lingering too long. His big regret is that he doesn't have a son. . . . Wasn't that a sad little story about his wife?'

'Very. It's the shortest story I've ever heard him tell. . . . What are you going to do now?'

'Me? The same, with someone else's money. I'm a pretty hardy plant, you know. Give me a little sun and I can grow anywhere. Tell me about yourself.'

'What's to tell? I am an intelligence man who thought he could break the system. Instead the system broke me.'

'You don't believe that.'

'I do. Look at my hands. I can't hold a glass steady. Do you know why? I'm scared to go to bed and switch off the light. I know it will pass: but I'm still scared.'

'Did they hurt you in prison?'

'No. Nobody touched me. Would you like another brandy?'

'Yes, please. I don't want to go to bed either.'

'What are you afraid of?'

'If I told you, you wouldn't believe me.'

'Try me.'

'Getting old and raddled like Coco Chanel and having some bright boy write a musical about me.'

'I promise you, Pia *mia*, it will never happen.'

'Can you swear that?'

'On the bones of my ancestors.'

'Then I'll make you a promise, too, Dante. You'll sleep well tonight.'

And I did sleep well. I had no nightmares either. In the morning across the breakfast table, Bruno Manzini blessed us with a grin and a Venetian proverb: '*El leto xe' una medicina* . . . Bed is a medicine'. As usual the old monster was right.

I found I could not write letters; so I made telephone calls from one end of the country to the other. I talked to men who had once been friends and were no longer. I talked to friends who were no longer. I talked to friends who were delighted to gossip but were always too busy to make a train journey to a place so outlandish as Pedognana. There were others who said they would be delighted to come, but found it hard to set a date. There were a few, six only, who expressed a care for an old friend, and a concern about what they heard had been done to him. These would give up their leave and come on various days to have a meal and a chat with me. I wondered, with growing disillusion, why there were so few of them. As we sat in the study, examining papers and photographs and tapes, Manzini gave me his own answer:

'Cattle smell the wind, my Dante. They turn their tails to it and wait for it to pass. Reeds bend with the wind, and sing whatever music it plays on them. Chaff blows away in the gusts and only the good grain settles. Be grateful, however small the harvest. I talked to Frantisek at the Vatican today. If you want, he will visit your Lili in the Maddalena. If she wants to marry you, we can, perhaps, arrange for you to visit her so that you can become betrothed in the prison. The regulations provide for that, but you must be very sure what you want. You cannot live a lifetime on guilt and pity. Besides, you have to face the fact that we may not get her out. The law in this country is a madness out of the Dark Ages. People can rot in prison for years without a trial. And there is nothing so destructive as a disappointed hope. So, think carefully before you lay new burdens on the girl. . . .'

I knew I must. I knew equally that I could not determine myself to a lifetime of lonely fidelity. I was not proud to admit it—God help me!—but the fact was there, brutal and inescapable. I tried to put it out of my mind and concentrate on the work in hand, which was the collation of all the material at our disposal to see if it added up to a case which would unseat Leporello and the Director.

There were two problems. My notes on the microfilms from Ponza were third-hand material collated from memory. Even the originals had belonged to Pantaleone and represented his plans for a military coup, not those of Leporello. From an intelligence point of view, my material was valuable. From a judicial one, it was quite invalid. All we had left, therefore, were the photographs and tapes of Leporello's sexual activities in Roditi's apartment in Milan. With these, we could make a scandal; but, in Italy at least, the scandal could be suppressed, because the law forbids the publication of obscene material. We could publish the material outside the country, but then we would be open to suspicion of forgery and the accusation of political chicanery. However, we might yet be forced to take that risk.

Whether we could make a case out of the obscene material was even more problematic. Photographs can be forged very easily. Roditi could testify to their authenticity, but Roditi had succumbed to the brain-washing and was no longer a competent witness. The tapes were even more dubious evidence. Leporello could be identified by a voice print, but the defence could claim that the tapes themselves had been edited and thus constituted a forgery.

There was another problem, too. Sexual misdemeanour is the commonest human aberration; and while everyone loves scandal, public sympathy is generally on the side of the offender—unless children are involved, which in this case they were not. If we could identify Leporello's partners as junior members of his own service, then we would have a case, and a strong one, to have him cashiered. . . . But, as Manzini pointed out, this was a long way from murder and political conspiracy and the high men, including the Director, would still go untouched. Roditi could have proved murder. Balbo had committed it. But Balbo was dead and Roditi lost to us.

At the end of an hour's discussion, we decided to concentrate our case on the photographs. I borrowed a magnifying glass from Manzini and settled down to study them minutely. There were more than thirty in all, some of them clear, some of them out of focus, some so contorted in their poses that it was impossible to identify the participants. We had Leporello. There was no doubt of that. I was concerned to see if I could identify any of his partners. The problem was that we had only contact prints of thirty-five-millimetre size and each one had to be examined minutely. It would have been easier in a studio, with full equipment available, but the material was so explosive we dared not yet commit it to other hands.

Finally, I was lucky. In one frame there was a man whom I could almost certainly identify–Giuseppe Balbo. In another there was a face which, though less clear, was very familiar to me. I groped vainly for the name, but my memory, jolted and jarred by my experience, failed me every time. I called Manzani and showed him what I had found. He was jubilant.

'If that's Balbo, then we have all we need. A known criminal, probably a murderer, whom we can identify from a thumbprint and your testimony, and who was killed by Leporello's men in Leporello's zone of command. Yes, that would do it! The other one. . . . Well, he'll come back to you. . . . Now, listen! We can't afford to let this stuff out of our hands. We'll have to bring all the equipment we need into the villa. Can you do the job?'

'No, only the basics. This needs an expert. One we can trust.'

'Then let's bring one in from outside. I'll call my people in Zurich and they can find a man and fly him down. We're coming closer, my Dante . . . two steps closer. Maybe your party will be a victory celebration after all. I'll call Zurich now. You lock that stuff away. We mustn't scandalize the servants.'

It was still an hour to lunch-time, so I walked out on to the terrace and paced up and down, trying to reason, calmly, about Lili's situation. Wherever I looked, there was no way out for her. Escape was impossible. Acquittal was unthinkable. There was enough material in my dossiers alone to convict her twenty times over. The Director could recommend deportation or exchange if he saw a political advantage in either. All his advantage lay in keeping her in Italy.

The afterthought was even less comforting. Lili knew her own plight better than I. The thing she feared most was now a present reality: the small room, the lights, the questions that came from nowhere. She could not bargain even for a respite. I had robbed her of the last face cards in the pack. Having once tasted liberty and hope, how would she tolerate despair?

Manzini came out to join me, rubbing his hands with satisfaction. The equipment we needed was already being packed in Milan. His expert would fly in from Zurich tomorrow. When the news failed to cheer me, he frowned and snapped at me:

'Matucci, stop it! I refuse to spoon-feed you any more. Your Lili is no child. She will survive if she wishes. So long as she survives, there is hope. You do her no service with self-torment or self-denial either! Now, have you put a name to that face in the photograph?'

'Not yet.'

'Keep trying. I have set the date of the party for four weeks from now. My secretary is working on the guest list and the invitations. It will be a gala affair. This old place needs some life put into it. So do I, for that matter–and you.'

'Truly, Bruno, I don't see. . . .'

'You don't see the nose on your own face, Dante Alighieri! That's your problem. Look! You think you can go back to the Service again? Never– even if they wash you in the blood of the lamb and give you a new baptismal robe. So, you have to start again. Where do you start? As a *spazzolino*, sweeping up rubbish on the streets? Of course not. You want to begin as far up the ladder as you can. For that you need friends and recommendations. Hence the party. . . . And, because it's my party too, it must be something everyone will want to attend and everyone will remember. "*Che vale petere . . . e poi culo stringere. . . .* If you're going to fart don't tighten up. It strains the arse." I've left a book in your bedroom, you might find it instructive. . . .'

The book was the *Ricordi of Francesco Guicciardini*, and I read it after dinner in the study, because Bruno retired early and Pia Faubiani was not returned from Bologna. My father was a great reader, and I had learned the habit from him; though latterly, between chasing information and chasing women, I had fallen out of it. Now, like sick Satan, I was disposed to be contemplative, and I found the experience rather pleasant. I also found that Messer Francesco Guicciardini was very entertaining company.

Like me, he was a Tuscan born, a Florentine, who at twenty-nine was named by the Republic as ambassador to the King of Spain. Pope Leo X, Medici of the Medici, made him Governor of Reggio and Modena and Parma, and Pope Clement VII made him Lieutenant General of the Papal armies. He was utterly without mercy, but he knew how to govern and he loved women of all kinds and ages and conditions. The only man who could handle him was Cosimo de Medici, who climbed to power on his shoulders and then kicked him into retirement. But Guicciardini was a natural survivor. He retired gracefully, grew vines, wrote books and died peacefully of a stroke at fifty-eight.

The *Ricordi* were his secret memorials, a kind of diary of opinion and experience, which he was wise enough never to expose in his lifetime, and which were published centuries after his demise. Manzini had marked several passages and annotated them in his precise script:

'To be open and frank is a noble and generous thing, but often harmful. On the other hand, it is useful and often indispensable to dissemble and deceive, because men are evil by nature.' (So smile, my Dante. Show them you are a man who has no care in the world, because you have aces in your sleeve!)

'I do not blame those who, on fire with love of country, confront dangers to establish liberty . . . though I think that what they do is very risky. Few revolutions succeed and, even if they do, you find very often they didn't win what you hoped. . .' (Which is why I draw back from public disorder and seek rather to seduce the ungodly in secret.)

'Nearly all men are more concerned for their own interest than for glory and honour.' (Remember this when you come to confront the Director, who is a quite unbearable patriot.)

'I believe that a good citizen . . . should maintain friendly relations with the tyrant, not only for his own security, but also for everyone else's good.' (Which is why I pay money to the Movement and dine the Director, and plot with you to bring them down. You have wondered, and I know it!)

'Do not take people too seriously when they prate the advantages of freedom. . . . If they could find a good job in a tyrannical state, they would rush to take it.' (I would go further. If they could be tyrants themselves, they would climb over a mountain of skulls to arrive.)

'My position under several Pontiffs has forced me to seek their glorification for my own profit.' (I wonder if the Director had this in mind when he cast his vote in favour of Leporello. Think about this as a motive for murder. Old Guicciardini had a lot of people executed in his time.)

'The past illuminates the future; the world has always been the same. . . . The same things come back with different names under different colours. . .' (You and I, my Dante, are trying to change the course of history. But let's not expect too much. The river is still the same.)

'Nobody knows his subjects as little as their ruler.' (This is what we are betting on, you and I. They think they have bought me. They know they have frightened you. They do not understand we have not yet begun to fight back.

It was, at that point, that I laid down the book and went upstairs to bed. I still could not turn out the light; but lay a long time, wakeful, staring at the ceiling, until Pia Faubiani came home from Bologna.

Next day, a variety of things began to happen at Pedognana. The artisans of the estate marched in force to the villa, and in the space of a few hours converted an attic suite into a very passable photographic studio. The expert arrived from Zurich, was briefed, sworn to secrecy, and set to work installing the new equipment which had arrived from Milan. Early in the evening Corrado Buoncompagni, the editor of Manzini's newspaper, arrived in company with a tubby little Torinese, whom he presented as Milo de Salis, the noted film director.

We were five at dinner that night—Manzini, Pia, Milo de Salis, Buoncompagni and myself. The photographer dined alone in his suite and continued working into the night. The meal turned into a council of war, at which Manzini exposed, for the first time, the scope of his design. I had seen him in many moods and acting out many roles, but I had never quite grasped him as the director of giant enterprises, a strategist of great and risky campaigns. Now, at last, I saw him plain, and was amazed at the subtlety and the audacity of his genius. He was calm, dispassionate, unhurried and yet he held us as no orator could have done.

'. . . I ask no oaths of you, my friends. From this moment, we are all conspirators. We are all at risk. All of you understand the nature of the risk. We shall have to use other people. That is unavoidable. We give them only the information they need to carry out their tasks. For the rest, we lie, conceal, confuse and obfuscate, so that the true issue is clear only to us, inside this room.

'I will define that issue. We are attempting to discredit and remove from power men who wish to impose by force, or threat of force, a government by dictation. We believe that this form of government is unacceptable to the vast majority of the people. We know, however, that it can be imposed, as it has been in the past, and that with all the modern mechanisms of control, it could be held in power for a very long time. Therefore, we must abort the *colpo di stato*, which we know is already planned.

'The means at our disposal are limited. They are limited by considerations of humanity and common prudence, and by the nature of the democratic process itself. We have in our hands, explosive information, which, if improperly handled, would confuse the public mind and lead to civil disorders, which themselves would provide the best excuse in the world for an imposed order. We cannot appeal directly to the people who are already torn between the factions. We must appeal to those in power on the basis of their own self-interest, whether that interest be blind or enlightened. In other words, we work within the context of the history of this country, and not of any other. Here the people speak, but are not heard. Therefore, we do not attempt to manipulate the many-headed monster. Instead we threaten those who are afraid of the monster: ministers of state, big public functionaries, members of the elected assembly, industrialists like myself, all who have a vested interest in order and public security.

'The threat will not be overt, but implicit. It will not be protracted, but sudden and surprising. It will call for immediate action. The action must be such as to command the approval of all those who see themselves endangered. We must be prepared to take it.

'The preparations begin now. Corrado, commencing with Thursday's edition, you will reverse the editorial and news policy of the paper. We are no longer Centrists, we are swinging very rapidly to the Right. I know you don't like it. I know the staff won't. It's your job to keep them happy, with the best lies you can tell. I don't think they'll go as far as a strike; but, even if they do, it may help us. I want editorials that my Fascist friends will read and applaud. I want a big feature on the work of Major-General Leporello. Let's call it an accolade, modified by stringent and critical recommendations. In other words, let us not be cretinous or fulsome. I don't want to lose staff or circulation, but I want it known that I am prepared to support the Right under conditions. I want them to call me and invite me to lunch. Then I can invite them here instead.

'Milo, your job is more difficult, because of the time and the technical problems involved. Upstairs, we have a mass of documents and notes collated by Matucci, of which the most important are the military maps and the campaign plans. In addition, we have a collection of obscene photographs and sound tapes. You have access to certain other material from film files and newreels. You have three weeks in which to write, film and edit a ten minute film based on all that material. The film will say that Major-General Leporello is a pederast with his own troops, a murderer and a conspirator against the security of the State. Matucci, here, will edit the film with you. He will also appear as commentator and final accuser. As an actor, he needs much direction. I trust you will succeed where I have failed.

'Matucci, you will work with Milo on the film. You will recruit and have at my disposal within the same three weeks, a pretorian guard of senior officers, who will agree to attend with you at an official function and act with you if a certain expected crisis should arise. Now, this is the riskiest point of the plan, because it involves a nice consideration of how and when the nature of the crisis is to be revealed to them. I do not know your friends. I cannot pretend to decide how you will treat with them. I can tell you only this: if they fail us at the last moment, we may all be brought low, and the ungodly may survive, stronger than ever.

'Now, let me describe the moment at which our plan comes to fruition or disaster. I have just completed plans for one of the biggest ventures of my career, a chain of tourist hotels and marina developments around the southern coastline of the peninsula. This enterprise will bring a flow of tourists and dependent tourist industries into the depressed South. It is, therefore, of major interest to the Government. I am now able to announce that a consortium of Italian and foreign banks has agreed to finance the whole project. I propose to make that announcement at a gathering in this house a little over three weeks from now. The party will be private. No Press will be invited, but Corrado will attend as my personal guest, and as pipeline to the communications media. If we fail here, we shall, for our own protection, publish all the material we have.

'The guest list is already prepared. It includes senior ministers and functionaries—all the people of whom I have already spoken. Major-General Leporello and his wife are on that list, as also is the Director of SID. I believe that the tone of our new editorials and features will encourage them both to attend. . . .

'I am still not decided what will happen on that night. We shall have to wait until acceptances have been received, before we can arrange a protocol and an order of ceremonies. I will consult with all from time to time before decisions are made. However, let me make one thing clear to all of you. If we win, no one will thank us. If we lose. . . . Eh! We'd better take the next plane to Rio!'

The next day, I identified the second man in the Leporello photographs. It was Captain Girolamo Carpi, one-time aide to Pantaleone. This was a stunning surprise. It established a direct link between Leporello and Pantaleone. It also revealed a yawning hiatus in my own information on Carpi, since there was no hint of any deviate practices in his army dossier. I had hired him. I had dismissed him and arranged for his safe exile to a training base in Sardinia. Now I had to rethink, and, if possible, arrange for his return to the mainland. Neither was going to be easy. I was no longer on active duty. Therefore, I had no access to files and could not make any formal requests to Army authorities.

I took the news and the problem to Bruno Manzini. He frowned over it for a long while and then announced:

'Dante, this man could be the most important witness we have. We must get him here, question him, break him and, if possible, get him on the film in time for our function. How do we do that, without showing our cards to the Army?'

'I go to Sardinia with the photograph in my pocket and frighten him into talking.'

'No, Dante. I can't risk you outside the gates of Pedognana.'

'If we could get Carpi posted to Bologna, we could arrange access easily enough. You must have friends in the Army high enough to swing a transfer.'

'I have. The problem is how far I can trust any of them at a time like this. . . . Leave this with me, Dante. I need to think about it quietly. What about your pretorians?'

'One is coming tomorrow, two more over the weekend, the others during the following week.'

'Have you decided what you're going to tell them?'

'I can't decide that until I've talked to them. How important is the number?'

'Less important than the security. Ten field officers in full uniform would be very impressive, but I would rather have three, primed and resolute, than risk a single waverer.'

'I'll report back to you after I've talked with each one.'

'Let me ask you something else about Carpi. How did you come to use him in the first place?'

'Let me see now. . . . He was appointed as aide to your brother about eighteen months ago. About six months after that, the Director called me and suggested we enlist Carpi as a domestic spy. He gave me Carpi's dossier, which showed that he was living beyond his means and was heavily in debt to a money-lender in Rome. I approached him with the proposition that if he worked for SID, we would pay his debts and give him a monthly stipend as well. He leaped at the offer. . . .'

'But his dossier was given to you by the Director. You didn't call for it yourself from the Army?'

'No.'

'And knowing the Director's way with dossiers, what does that suggest to you?'

'It could have been doctored before I saw it.'

'Exactly. Now I will tell you something else, my Dante. The Director knew my half-brother quite well. You remember he was selling his art collection?'

'Yes. He was in correspondence with Del Giudice.'

'And your Director was bidding against me for certain items.'

'I thought he wasn't interested in old masters.'

'He isn't—except as negotiable currency. He buys them as non-exportable commodities. He sells at a big profit to another dealer, not as honest as Del Giudice. This dealer has them copied by an expert, gets an export licence for the copy and sends the original out of the country. Three of my father's paintings have gone on this route. This was the substance of my talk with Pantaleone on the night of his death.'

'Can you prove that?'

'Yes. But don't delude yourself, Dante. It's a good point for a dossier. It is not enough to bring down the Director, who is in a strictly legal position. We have to prove murder.'

'For what motive?'

'Profit—on every level. Pantaleone dies. Leporello replaces him as military leader. Since Leporello has organized the murder, the Director moves in as head of State, just to keep the record pure. Don't you see? It's the classic method. They are like bull-leapers, vaulting over the horns. The one who vaults the last beast and gives it the last pat on the rump is champion. Yes, we need your Captain Carpi. Somehow I will get him here. . . . Tell me, how are you feeling?'

'Better. You were right. Bed is a good medicine; and hate's a better one. What are our chances?'

'*Cosi-cosi* . . . fifty-fifty. It all depends on the mood of the gathering. If they walk out, we are sunk. If they stay, we shall win. It's an opera, my Dante, staged for an operatic people. Everyone knows the score backwards. It's a question of how well it is staged and sung. . . . I know this is positively my last performance. I hope I can hit the high note and hold it till the last chord and take the final bow. I hope . . . that's all. But if you see me wilting, prop me up until the curtain comes down. . . . Dante, even if I can get Carpi here, there will be no time for a full inquiry. You may have to bluff with him.'

'I don't relish that. Let's wait and see whether you can get him and what I can do with him. . . . There's something that's bothering me, Bruno.'

'Oh, what's that?'

'You're going to have a hundred, a hundred and fifty, highly sophisti-cated men and women who come to your house for a celebration party. How are you going to get them to sit for ten minutes through a very sordid film, which impugns some of their fellow-guests, casts suspicion on others and makes them all feel very uncomfortable?'

'Would you believe, my Dante, I have been so bothered by that same question I have a certain Professor Mueller flying in tomorrow from Munich. He is an acknowledged expert on mass psychology and group manipulation. I want to pose the problem to him in the most precise terms, and in the ambience where it will arise. I should have preferred someone more familiar with our own Latin character, but I dare not use any of our own people. The old story, my friend: "A man's enemies shall be those of his own household." Sad, isn't it?'

'That's strange . . .'

'What?'

'Pantaleone used the same words to Lili Anders.'

'In what connection?'

'Let me think now. . . . I want to get it right, and my memory still plays tricks. Oh, yes. Apparently Pantaleone had a habit of making cryptic remarks and then refusing to explain them. Lili linked two such remarks: "There is no simple future for me, because my past is too complicated" and the words you have just used.'

'In what connection were these remarks made?'

'As I understood it, in connection with the Salamander.'

'Could he have been referring to Carpi, who was a domestic spy?'

'Very possibly.'

'Think about it, Dante. Think of Carpi as an intimate of Leporello, as an emissary of the Director, as a man with free access to the Pantaleone apartment . . . as the man who killed my half-brother.'

'And myself, as the man who employed him. That's very pretty!'

'I'm glad you've seen the point. You told me the Director was preparing a Black Book on you. If we indict Carpi, you could be in bother, too.'

'Bruno, let's face it now. You can stay me with apples and pomegranates, you can surround me with angelic choirs. I'm still up to my neck in the *merda*. I'm the man who started all this. I'm the man who must finish it. That's the way I'm constructing the film with Milo. If things go wrong, you must walk away from me.'

He lifted his white head and gave me a small enigmatic smile.

'Dante, son of my heart, never underscore the obvious. If we lose I can't afford you. If we win–touch wood!–we shall both be very busy men. Too busy for dramatic gestures. . . .'

The next three weeks were a period of mounting panic, suppressed only by the calm generalship of Manzini. The ballroom of the villa was invaded by an army of painters, decorators and electricians. A barn was transformed into a studio, offices and cutting room for Milo and his crew. Manzini worked, sometimes at home with a battery of secretaries, sometimes in Milan, from whence he would return, grey-faced and tired, but always with some new word of encouragement. His guest list was filling up. His press campaign had been well received by the Right. Leporello and the Director had consented to come. This minister or that had sent him words of personal greeting.

Milo and I quarrelled our way through the film, he concerned with the visual impact of his work, I troubled always by the legal logic of the case we must present. My friends came, one by one, to visit me and I probed them like a confessor before I dared a single hint of the project on which we were embarked. All of them were troubled by the situation of the Republic and the divisions within the armed forces. They, themselves, were divided on the remedies. In the end, there were only four of whom I felt I could commit with any real confidence. To these, I proposed as follows:

'You will be invited as guests to an official ceremony, here at the villa. It's a big occasion and you will wear formal mess uniform. I guarantee you each a pretty girl as escort. Now, here's the reason. The place is going to be full of important people, ministers, functionaries, that sort of thing. There'll be the usual contingent of security men in attendance, but we don't want them inside the dining-room. That's why I want you there, looking like happy guests.... We've been told something may happen on that night. I can't tell you what it is. I don't want you to ask. I want you to trust me and come for friendship's sake ... and maybe for the sake of all the things we've talked about. You are committed to nothing beyond attendance. You will receive the same invitation card as every other guest. Now, can you accept that or not? If you can, will you accept one other condition? This is a State secret and you'll have to keep it like that.'

They accepted and I believed them. They were friends of the heart, close as family, which is the one thing on which you can depend in this troubled disparate land of mine. When I told Manzini, he nodded a curt agreement and dimissed the matter. This was my province. I was on my own responsibility. When I asked him about Carpi, he frowned and shook his head:

'Nothing yet. Tomorrow I am flying to Rome to see a friend of mine in the Ministry of Defence. There is a risk involved and some very devious staff work. But I hope we shall get him here in time.'

In the event, he was disappointed. The last week passed in a flurry of frantic activity. On the day of the dinner party, Captain Carpi had still not arrived.

At the final council of war, which was held at three o'clock in the afternoon, it was decided that I should not attend the function at all, but should present myself only in its closing moments. The reason was simple and perfectly valid. My presence could prove an embarrassment to Leporello and the Director and introduce a dangerous note of uneasiness into a gathering whose success depended upon a careful contrivance of atmosphere.

After the meeting, Manzini walked us round on a final tour of inspection. In the foyer, the guests would be received by four of Pia's girls, and led to the first reception room, to be presented to Manzini and Pia and circulate for cocktails round a huge illuminated projection of the development—a large scale-relief map of the boot of Italy, showing the tourists arteries and the location of the development sites, and a series of models showing the completed installations.

After cocktails, they would proceed to the ball-room, which had been converted into a dining-room for the occasion. The place was ablaze with flowers and the lighting was contrived to flatter the least beautiful of women. The seating was unusual for such a function: a series of small rectangular tables, each seating three persons a side, so that the guests faced each other in a small closed community. At one end of each table was a silver bucket in which were six flat rectangular packages wrapped in gold paper and tied with ribbon—party favours for each guest. At the other end of each table was a small television set of the most advanced design, connected by closed circuit to a central control in an adjoining room. The host's table at the far end of the room was arranged as a horseshoe, with the television receiver placed between the points of the shoe.

Each guest was supplied with a programme card, illuminated by Carlo Metaponte, and, for a final impudent irony, the place-cards were set in small silver mounts in the shape of a salamander. The programme was simple: a toast to the President and the Republic, an opening address by the Minister for Tourism, a reply by Bruno Manzini and the showing of a short television film on the new development, produced and directed by Milo de Salis.

There were other refinements, too: three television scanners were placed at various points of the room. Two were focused on the tables where Leporello and the Director were to be seated. The third covered the room, so that all the proceedings could be monitored and recorded on tape for later evidence. Leporello and the Director were seated at opposite sides of the room, out of each other's line of vision. One of my pretorians was seated at each of their tables, with another at the table next in line. What Manzini had spent in terms of money was staggering. What he had spent of imagination and ingenuity were unbelievable from a man of his years. When the tour was over, he took me back to his study, poured brandy for both of us and made a last toast to the venture.

'. . . I will not say, good luck, my Dante. What has brought us to this point is believing and working and daring. What happens tonight will depend on how nicely we have calculated the interaction of small groups of people submitted to a sudden and shocking experience. According to Mueller, we are gambling that their curiosity will overcome their repugnance and hold them seated until the end. However, he does say there will be a crisis point at which either Leporello or the Director may attempt to leave, calculating that a sudden move may upset the audience. You must prevent that at all costs. You will be armed, of course, but for a threat only. There must be no violence. What happens at the end, of course, is in the hands of God . . . and though you may not believe it, Dante, He has to have an interest in tonight's affair. . . . Perhaps that should be my toast, I pray that He may hold you safe, my Dante, and bring you to a quiet harbour.'

I said amen to that and it was the closest I had come to praying for a long time. We drank and set down our glasses. Then Manzini sprang his last surprise.

'Dante, my friend, have you thought about tomorrow?'

'Tomorrow?'

'Yes. It will come, you know—unless we both die in our sleep.'

'So?'

'So if our strategy succeeds you will have the Director and Leporello under arrest on a variety of charges. How will you proceed from that point?'

'According to the book. Deposition by the arresting officer, desposition by the accused. Documents forwarded to the magistrate. Examination by the magistrate, indictment, submission of pleas by the defence and public trial.'

'Which will of course make an international scandal?'

'Yes.'

'And have profound political consequences?'

'Inevitably.'

'Consequences for which neither the Government nor the country are as yet prepared.'

'True.'

'Read me the consequences as you see them.'

'We shall have aborted a Fascist coup. We shall have damaged public faith in the senior bureaucracy. We shall have given vast new strength to the Left. . . . On the other hand we shall have affirmed that the State is capable of purging and regulating itself to the benefit of the people.'

'And the final outcome?'

'Potentially healthy.'

'Potentially?'

'That's my best estimate.'

'Which leaves us still at risk–grave risk.'

'Yes.'

'The first risk is yours. You have passed the film. You will make the arrest, you will prefer the charges. You must file the indictment. Is the case complete?'

'Against Leporello, yes. Against the Director, no. A good laywer could win it for him.'

'And then you would go to the wall.'

'Obviously.'

'Are you ready for that?'

'I hope so.'

'You could avoid it.'

'How?'

'Accidents happen–fortunate accidents.'

'I know. .... "The prisoner was shot while attempting to escape. The prisoner suffered a cardiac seizure while under normal interrogation and the police surgeon deposed to a long-standing mitral defect. The suspect was granted provisional liberty on the instance of his attorneys and failed to appear at the court hearing. ...." No, Bruno! Not this time! Not for me. Not for you. Not for the Minister or the President himself.'

'Not for the people either? Your people, my Dante.'

'The people belong to themselves. I am the only man who belongs to me. You taught me that lesson, Bruno. I can't unlearn it now.'

He gave me a long, quizzical look, grinned and dismissed the matter with a shrug. Then he went to his desk, unlocked a drawer and brought out a small velvet box. He handed it to me and said simply:

'It's a gift. I hope you like it.'

I opened the box and found, slotted in the velvet bed, a gold signet ring. The symbol engraved on the seal was a crowned salamander.

My emotions were still unsteady; and I was deeply moved. Manzini, however, would not indulge me in any expressions of gratitude. He stood towering over me, like a sardonic sage, and read me his last cautionary tale.

'. . . We are the victims of those who love us, my Dante. They dream our destinies and plunge us into nightmares. They plot fabulous voyages and blame us when the voyages end in shipwreck. Yet, we have no recourse, because we, too, are born dreamers and conspirators. . . . My father robbed me of his name and the inheritance of his history and thought to recompense me with the foundations of the fortune which I have today. Your father dreamed his noble dreams of a new world, and his family suffered for them. In the end, you, my Dante, came to wear the uniform of the men who arrested him.

'Yet, each of us learned the same lesson: there are no guarantees; there is no permanence; life is a riddle propounded by a Divine comedian, whose answer is so simple, we never see it until it is too late. I have never told you this, but after the war when we were, for a long while, a nation of beggars, subsisting on reconstruction funds from America, making all sorts of shabby bargains which today we are trying to undo, I toyed with the idea of quitting Europe altogether and investing what remained of my life and my fortune in the New World. Here I was entangled by history, caught like a lamb in a bramble-bush, torn and scarred and totally confused. There, I felt I could be another man, a builder looking only to the future. . . .

'I came back here to Pedognana. One evening, I walked down to the chapel and sat a long time looking at the slab which covered Marie Claire's grave. I tried to talk to her. There was no answer; because that is the nature of the Divine riddle: the eloquence of those who do not understand it, the silence of those who have solved it at last. I wept then, the last tears I have ever shed. Old Don Egidio came in. You've met him. He's the typical peasant priest, not very learned, slipshod and cross-grained, something of a tippler too, but, with it all, very shrewd.

'He did not try to comfort me. He knew me too well for that. He knew that I should have rejected him as a man too ignorant to understand the complexity of my condition. He sat down beside me, and told me the tale of the puppy with the straw tail. . . . You have never heard it? It's very simple. There was once a puppy who was born with a short tail. He was very ashamed of this defect, so he made himself a long and beautiful tail of golden straw. He was proud of himself then. He wagged his tail twice as vigorously as any dog in the village. He strutted and preened himself and was courted by all the bitches. Then, one day, as he lay by the fire in his master's cottage, his tail caught fire. . . . He couldn't get rid of it, of course. He ran around yelping until his master tossed him in the pond to put out the flames.

After that, he had another problem. His real tail was still shorter and now his rump was scarred and all the other dogs laughed at him. What did he do? He had been very happy with his straw tail, so he made himself another one; but ever afterwards he was careful to stay away from the fire. . . . He could, of course, have made another choice. He could have shed his false tail, and worn his scars and slept comfortably through the winter, close as he wanted, to the fire.

'. . . The moral, you would think, was obvious. Not to Don Egidio. His conclusion was quite different: man is not a puppy dog; he embraces all elements and is embraced by all and can survive them all: he can write his own bargain with life; the only thing he cannot haggle over is the final price: death and solitude. . . . You will be lonely tonight, my Dante. You will be lonely afterwards; because there is no credit for anyone in the company of the public executioner. The ring I have given you is a symbol, not a talisman. The only magical thing about it, is the love that goes with the giving. Remember that, when I leave you, as I shall, as I must. . . .'

I had a long wait ahead of me. The guests would not arrive until eight-thirty. They would not sit down to dinner until nine-thirty, when I would go down to the control room and follow the proceedings on closed circuit with Milo and his crew. The moment Manzini finished his speech, the lights would be extinguished and the television screens illuminated. I would move immediately to the ball-room, take up my post inside and lock the door. If anyone tried to leave, unless it were a woman, I would detain them until the end of the screening. It still lacked twenty minutes to six. I went to my room, set the alarm for eight, read a few pages of Guicciardini and lapsed into a deep and dreamless sleep.

I woke refreshed and strangely calm. I shaved, carefully, bathed and put on my new uniform. When I looked at myself in the mirror, I saw a man I hardly recognized: a serving officer of a Corps whose oath still had a ring of royalty about it, whose tradition of service, however besmirched by individuals, still carried a blazon of honour. The badges of rank I had earned myself. I, the son of a political exile, could claim some service to the country for which he, in his own way, had sacrificed himself. For all the sordid shifts of my trade, I could still feel some pride, and a small, hesitant affection for the man inside my skin. Enough! It was time to go.

As I walked down the stairs into the empty foyer, the major-domo opened the front door and let in Captain Carpi. For a moment, he did not recognize me; and when he did, he was non-plussed. He told me that he had been sent from Sardinia with urgent despatches to be delivered personally into the hands of Major-General Leporello. His plane had been delayed at Cagliari, and he had been forced to hire a car to bring him out to Pedognana. I told him the General was at dinner, but that I would take him in as soon as the function was over. He asked me what I was doing. I told him I was on special duty. That seemed to satisfy him. He was quite in the dark about the whole affair. All he knew was that his commanding officer had called him, told him he was to act as courier on a special mission and sent him on his puzzled way. I wondered what devious staff work had gone into that manoeuvre. I took him into the control room, fed him a glass of champagne and a canapé and drew Milo aside to warn him not to make any indiscreet comment. Then we settled down to watch the show, while I tried frantically to figure how I should make use of this very untimely arrival. By the time Manzini stood up to announce the Presidential toast, I had made my decision.

The Minister of Tourism made an elegant and witty speech, a little long, perhaps, but then he had important people to impress: his colleague, the Minister for the Interior among them. He noted the variety and the magnitude of Manzini's enterprises. He praised the boldness of his vision, which he said made a lot of people blink, and others close their eyes and wait for the thunderclap. He complimented the bankers on their foresight and their confidence in the economy of the country, and its political stability. He was grateful for the lavish welcome extended by the Cavaliere to his guests. He saw it as the symbol of the welcome extended by Italy to the millions who came visiting each year. He wished the project well, assured all the participants of the benevolence of the Government, added a flourish or two of metaphor and sat down to polite applause.

Then Bruno Manzini stood up and began his own speech.

'I thank the Minister for his kind words. I thank him for his confidence in our enterprise, which is, itself, an act of faith in the future of this beloved country of ours. This act of faith is the more sincere, because my colleagues and I have committed huge sums of money to Italian development at a time when, despite the optimism of my good friend, the country is divided on many issues. I can say this here, in this gathering, because there are no Press to report my remarks, and you are intelligent men and women concerned as I am for the future of this country and its children. The divisions of which I speak, are very deep. Some of them are historic; some of them are political; some are social. We are one people under one flag, but we are also many peoples with many different histories. We have too many parties and too little consensus to achieve easily a government for the people and by the people. Too much wealth is concentrated in too few hands, my own among them. However, to attempt to reconcile these differences, as some seek to do, by violent and sinister means, is a dangerous folly; so dangerous, indeed, that it could negate at one stroke all that we have achieved since the war, all that we hope to build in the coming years. . . .'

They applauded him then. It was a proposition they could all accept; because they didn't have to examine it too closely. Divisions they knew, and violence they knew; and they all had sinister symbolic scapegoats to carry their sins into the wilderness of forgetting. Manzini hushed them, slowly, with a smile and a gesture. His manner changed. He was happy now, and teasing.

'. . . Have you ever thought of this, my friends: right through our history, dinners have been important occasions. That's strange, because we are not gross feeders, like the Germans, nor big drinkers like the French. We enjoy the food and we enjoy the wine and we enjoy the company of beautiful women, of whom there are so many here tonight. But the fact is, we do make history at meal-times. There was Trimalchio's supper. You all remember that: very gross, very disgusting, even when dignified by the art of the great Petronius. Then, there was the fatal supper of the Tolomei and the Salimbeni, which those of you here who are privileged to be Tuscans will remember. That one ended in murder. But I assure you all, dear friends, there will be no murder here, tonight. Then, there were the *canacoli* of the Blessed Catherine of Siena, where souls were elevated by spiritual discourse and bodies were mortified by a very restricted diet. Saving the reverence of Monsignor Frantisek, who is here with us tonight as unofficial representative of the Holy Father, I regret we have not attained to this degree of spiritual perfection. However, I dare to think that this is an historic occasion.

'. . . In the silver buckets at the end of each table, you will find a number of packages. If the gentlemen will pass them round the tables, please . . . No, no, don't open them yet. They will make no sense until you have seen the film–which is not, I must tell you, the one promised on your programme. . . . This one is a privileged document. The Press does not know of its existence. The public will never see it–only you, my friends and compatriots. You will find it a strange experience. Some of you, especially the ladies, may be discomfited and embarrassed. I beg you to be patient and tolerant until the film justifies itself. . . . Now, if you will turn your chairs a little you should all have a comfortable view of the television screens at the end of each table.'

This was the cue. In the movement that followed, two of my pretorians stood up and leaned casually against the wall, so that a single pace would bring them to Leporello and Baldassare. The other men did the same, so that the whole thing had the air of a casual and comfortable reshuffle. Manzini went on:

'If anyone of you hesitates to share this experience with us, I beg him or her to leave now. . . . You are all resolved? Good! In a moment the television screens will light up: and this room will be plunged into darkness. I think you will agree with me that secrets should be told in the dark and enjoyed in the light.'

That was my signal. I hurried Carpi out of the control room and we reached the dining-room just as the lights went down and the television screens lit up. I locked the door, put the key in my breast pocket and focused on the nearest screen.

Milo de Salis had settled on a film method that was as simple as a child's primer and as devastating as a death sentence. It consisted of a series of direct and unqualified statements, in image and commentary. The image was too distant for comfort, but I knew the commentary by heart.

'. . . This is a photograph of Major-General Massimo Pantaleone, who died in Rome this year, on Carnival night.

'This is the death certificate which states that he died of natural causes. . . . In fact, he died of an injection of air into his femoral artery. He was murdered. . . .'

There was a gasp of surprise, a rustle of movement, a flurry of whispers, then silence, as the commentary began again.

'This is a photograph of the later autopsy report, signed by three very reputable physicians.

'This is a photograph of an office block in the Via Sicilia, where the General's papers were stored after his death. The papers were stolen and two men were murdered–Avvocato Bandinelli and Agent Calvi of the Service of Defence Information. . . .

'This is the identity card of the man who murdered them: Giuseppe Balbo, a criminal who used a number of aliases.

'Among the General's papers were these maps: Turin . . . Milan . . . Rome . . . Naples . . . Taranto . . . These are military maps which have since been altered in detail but not in substance. They show how, on the thirty-first of October of this year a military junta plan to overthrow the legitimate Government of Italy and establish a government by dictation.

'The moving arrows illustrate how the plan would operate.

'The maps and plans you have just seen are in the possession of this next man, Major-General Leporello, who is a guest here tonight.'

Once again there was a stir as all heads were turned to identify Leporello. They could not see him in the dim light, so once again the image and the commentary commanded their attention.

'This is a recent photograph of General Leporello's aide, Captain Matteo Roditi. He is at present under psychiatric care because he was tortured into insanity to prevent his giving testimony in court.

'This is another photograph of Giuseppe Balbo, murderer, who was shot down while resisting arrest by General Leporello's men.

'This is the Club Alcibiade, a resort of deviates, where Captain Roditi met often with Giuseppe Balbo, who was, strange to say, an enlisted member of the Carabinieri, under General Leporello's own command.

'This woman, shopping with her children in Milan, is the wife of the Major-General Leporello.

'This is a love-letter, one of thirty, which she wrote to Captain Roditi, her husband's aide and true father of her children. Their love-affair was condoned by the General, for good reason.'

This was the crisis point which Mueller had predicted. Leporello could not defend himself, he would and must defend his wife. Instantly he was on his feet, his tall frame monstrous in the half-dark. He shouted: 'This is an outrage against an innocent woman. I demand. . . .'

He demanded nothing. My pretorian was at his side with a pistol rammed into his ribs. Manzini's voice rang like a trumpet blast from the rostrum:

'Sit down, General. Ladies and Gentlemen, I beg that you control yourselves. We are not here to insult a woman, but to prevent an imminent bloodshed.'

There was a gasp of horror which I could feel physically. They did not settle immediately. They watched and waited until Leporello subsided into his chair then, lost and leaderless, they submitted in silence to the last brutal revelations.

'These next photographs will distress you, but I beg you to look at them carefully. This one shows Major-General Leporello engaged in a sexual act with Giuseppe Balbo, murderer.

'This one shows him in another act with the man identified as the personal aide, and probable murderer, of the late Major-General Pantaleone. His name is Captain Girolamo Carpi.

'This man, Major-General Leporello, ladies and gentlemen, was chosen to lead the *colpo di stato*. He, himself, however, would never have assumed power. There was another man behind him. . . .

'. . . This man–Prince Filippo Baldassare, Director of the Service of the Defence Information. This man plotted the death of Pantaleone, hired Carpi to kill him, and then arranged for Leporello to replace him.'

Again the audience slewed round in the darkness to identify Baldassare. I was one of the few who could see him. He sat calm and unmoved, sipping brandy from a crystal goblet.

'Who am I? I am Colonel Dante Alighieri Matucci of the same service. I collected this information. I too was imprisoned and submitted to psychological torture to prevent my revealing it. I take full responsibility for the substance and presentation of this film. I depose it as true and I shall offer to the appropriate authorities documents in support.'

The screens went dark. The lights went up and a hundred and fifty people sat there, dumb and ashamed to look at each other. I moved forward into the silent room with Carpi, like a sleepwalker, at my side. I had one moment of blind panic. Then I found the words.

'The officers present will place the General and Prince Baldassare under arrest.'

I did pray then. I said, 'Dear Christ, please make them move, please!'. . . . They moved. They placed their hands on the shoulders of the two men. The act was final and complete. Now I had to speak again. I heard myself say:

'Cavaliere, Ladies and Gentlemen, I have with me, under arrest, Captain Girolamo Carpi who will testify in the proper place to his part in this affair.'

Then, from his own table, Bruno Manzini took command:

'My countrymen! You have been insulted tonight. You have been shocked and shamed. You may choose never to pardon me for the pain I have inflicted upon you. I will not apologize. I tell you only that it is a small price to pay to prevent the bloodshed and the misery of a civil uprising and the oppression of a new tyranny. . . . Now, may I ask you to retire to the salon where coffee and liqueurs will be served.'

They got up, slowly, and moved away blank-faced, like automatons, each carrying the supper gift, a dossier of the damned, with a complimentary card from the Salamander. Elena Leporello left too, and she passed me without a glance of recognition. Finally, there was no-one left but the pretorians and the accused and Manzini and the Minister for the Interior and myself.

Manzini and the Minister stepped from the high table and walked slowly down the room towards me. They stopped. They faced me, bleak and expressionless. The Minister said:

'Thank you, Colonel. You will do what has to be done with these gentlemen. I shall wait here. You will report to me before you leave.'

Bruno Manzini said nothing. He did exactly as he had promised. He walked away.

It was an eerie moment. Three prisoners, three gaolers, silent among the debris of a rich man's feast. We were like actors, frozen on an empty stage, waiting for the Director to move us. Then, I understood that I was the Director and that, without me, the play would neither continue nor conclude. I must move. I must speak. I must decide. I heard the words as if they issued from the mouth of another man.

'Prince Baldassare, General Leporello, will you please remain seated. You other gentlemen, will you please conduct Captain Carpi to the monitor room and wait there till I call you.'

Two pretorians linked arms with Captain Carpi and led him mute and unprotesting from the room. Those standing guard over the Director and Leporello left their posts and walked out. If I read their looks aright they were very glad to be gone. When the door closed behind them I was, at last, alone with my enemies. I felt no triumph, only a strange sense of disillusion and of loss, and a vague humiliation as though my best-told joke had fallen flat. Both men sat bolt-upright in their chairs, hands flat upon the tables, their faces averted from me. They were so far apart that unless I stood far away like a ring-master or a theatrical tyrant I could not address them together, nor even compass them with a single glance. I had to confront them, one by one, face to human face. I went to Leporello first. I straddled a chair in front of him and found myself staring into a death mask. I told him:

'General, it is your privilege to be held under arrest, in barracks under custody of service officers, and you may elect to be tried under military law. If you waive this privilege you become immediately subject to civil process. Which do you choose?'

He did not answer. He sat like a stone man, cold and motionless. I tried again.

'General, there are formalities. I want to make them as simple and easy as possible. If you would like to speak to your wife, I can have her brought to you. Afterwards, as you know, it will not be so easy. If you are unwell, I can call a doctor. For your own sake, General, I advise you to answer me.'

He had not even heard me. His lips were locked: his eyes blank as pebbles. I stretched out a hand and laid it on his wrist. There was pulse, but nothing more. The muscles were rigid as iron, there was no twitch of recognition or aversion. Then I heard the Director's voice, cool and ironic as always:

'Classic fugue, Matucci. Total withdrawal. You'll get nothing out of him tonight—if ever. To cover yourself I'd call a doctor and have the wife present when he makes his diagnosis.'

I swung round to see him, calm and smiling, sipping a glass of brandy and puffing a cigar. He raised the glass in a toast:

'My compliments, Matucci. . . . Trial by television! I wonder why I never thought of that. It's hardly a democratic process, but it's very effective.'

He poured a goblet of wine and pushed it across the table towards me.

'Sit down! Relax. I'm a co-operative witness. You can afford to be pleasant to me. I imagine you've had rather a tense evening. Still, you must be very satisfied. You've got everything now; except the fellow singing "Sic transit" and burning flax under your nose. What's the next move?'

'You know the code as well as I do, sir.'

'And I know the trade better, Matucci. You made your case against Leporello—though I doubt he'll ever stand to answer it. The man was always a psychotic, in full flight from reality. Tonight you pushed him over the edge and I doubt he'll ever come back. Even if he does, a good lawyer will plead him unfit and the State will, in its own interest, concur. Against me, what have you got? Carpi, a man with straw in his shoes, who will be frightened, suborned or eliminated before you get a line of decent testimony out of him. Still, it's your case, and you must make it, win or lose. Unless of course. . . .'

'What?'

'Unless you are open to a little lesson in statecraft. You were always weak in that discipline, as I told you. That's what held you back in your career.'

'If you're proposing a deal, the answer's no.'

'My dear Matucci! Why do you always underrate me? Do you think I would be so naïve as to propose a deal to a man both righteous and triumphant? On the contrary, I invite you to a mature consideration of realities. . . . Statecraft has nothing to do with morals, has nothing to do with justice relative or absolute. It is the art and craft of controlling large masses of people, of holding them in precarious equilibrium with one another and with their neighbours. All means are open to the statesman and he must be prepared to use them all in their seasons from the headsman's axe to the circus holiday. He must never overrate his triumph nor lose courage in temporary adversity. From time to time he needs a victim, if he is to avoid a holocaust. Clemency for him is not a virtue but a strategy. . . . Only the aim is constant, to hold the many-headed monster in control, to calm him when he growls, to curb him when he gets too playful, to wonder at his visions but sedate him before they turn into nightmares. . . . You, Matucci, are still a servant of the state. . . . You are not yet a statesman. Tonight you have the opportunity to become one.' He broke off, sipped his brandy, drew on his cigar and smiled at me though the eddies of fragrant smoke. I said nothing and after a while, he began on a new tack.

'At this moment, Matucci, you are in a position of great strength. You have forestalled a military coup. You have discredited the authors of it. You have two important victims to toss to the lions, Leporello and myself. In Manzini you have a powerful friend. In the Minister you have an important patron who is waiting only for you to give him the right advice. . . . Think about the Minister, Matucci. He is a politician—a thinking reed, blown by every gust of popular vociferation, by every whisper in the corridors of the Assembly. What does he want? What would you want if you were in his shoes? A discreet and well-managed triumph or a platter full of bleeding heads . . .? One head is useful. You can stick it on a pike and display it for a warning to the populace. More than one is a carnage. . . . Which head would you select for the pike? In my view—which I admit could be prejudiced—the one with the fewest brains. You've got it, over there. . . . Mine is worth much more to you and the Minister if you leave it on my shoulders. I am discredited; so I can't do any harm unless you bring me to trial—when, my dear Matucci, I can promise you scandals that will be shouted from Moscow to the Golden Gate. On the other hand, if clemency were offered, I should respond to it gratefully. I would remove myself from the scene and leave a rich legacy of information to my successor. . . . Do I make myself clear?'

I was ashamed for him then. For a moment he had been eloquent. Now he was merely plausible. I told him bluntly: 'I must be equally clear. I have no authority to offer clemency.'

'My dear fellow, I know that. I will go further. It would be useless and dangerous for you to treat with me at all. You should and you must treat only with the Minister.'

'What are you asking of me then?'

'I want to speak to the Minister privately, now.'

'He may not want to speak to you.'

'He will. And afterwards he will ask to see you.'

'And?'

'All I ask is that you give him an honest professional answer to any questions he asks you.'

'Can you be sure I'll do that?'

'No. I hope you will. You have no reason to love me. I would not blame you if you pressed to the limit the advantage that you have now. In fact I'd be rather surprised if you didn't. However, I've read you the lesson; make what you like of it. Will you convey my request to the Minister?'

'Give me a hand with Leporello, we'll get him to a bedroom. I'll call a doctor and then I'll see the Minister.'

The interview between Prince Baldassare and the Minister lasted more than three hours. I was not present. I was closeted with Professor Malpensa of the Army Psychiatric Unit in Bologna who had been roused from his bed and brought by helicopter to Pedognana. With him was Doctor Lambrusco, a guest at the party and Manzini's personal physician. I had asked them to examine Leporello separately and in concert, and then render me a joint diagnosis. They expressed in in writing: '. . . a catatonic or pseudo-catatonic state, expressive of a profound fugal impulse induced by guilt and shock. It is our joint recommendation that the patient by institutionalized for clinical observation. It is our opinion that the patient is at present incapable of rational communication, and that to submit him to interrogation or confinement would be pointless and dangerous. Prognosis, doubtful.'

I accepted the document, signed the General into the hands of Professor Malpensa, who flew him back to Bologna. Then I went in search of Manzini. His guests had gone, long since and he was sitting alone in the drawing-room. He was grey about the gills but still alert and cheerful. He greeted me with a smile and a grim, dry chuckle: 'Well, Matucci, we did it!'

'Yes. . . . It's very quiet now.'

'What did you expect? Garlands and a triumph?'

'Blessed is he who expects nothing; because he is sure to get it. . . . I think I'd like a brandy.'

'Help yourself.' He gestured in the direction of the study. 'Our friend Baldassare is trying to strike a bargain with the Minister.'

'I know.'

'Would it surprise you to know that I have recommended it?'

'In what terms, Bruno?'

'I have represented that without the co-operation and connivance of the Director we should never have been able to stage this evening's drama.'

'That's not true.'

'I know it. You know it. The Minister knows it. But it happens to be a fiction that fits the moment. Objections?'

'None.'

'You approve?'

'I don't approve. I think it's expedient.'

'You're learning, my Dante.'

'The hard way. How much of tonight's affair will reach the Press?'

'By direct report, nothing. By leaks and gossip, quite a lot. It's unfortunate, but inevitable.'

'Could you reach your editor now?'

'Of course. Why?'

'I'd like him ready to file a report to the wire services. We've missed the morning editions; but we'll make the evening papers and the international correspondents will have it on the teletype when the bureaux open in the morning.'

'What do you have in mind?'

'I can't tell you, until I've spoken with the Minister.'

He gave me a swift appraising glance and then a nod of satisfaction.

'*Bene*! At last I can approve you, Dante Alighieri. For a long time, I wondered. . . .'

'Wondered what?'

'How much of you was man and how much a confection of circumstance. Forgive me! How does one know whether a nut is sound until one cracks the shell? You are a man full of contradictions, my Dante. You are coward and hero. You are wise and foolish. You are soft as putty and hard as iron. A friend can buy you with a smile. A purse of gold will not corrupt you. How you will end, God knows; but I am happy to know I have not wasted myself on you. . . . Excuse me, I'll call my editor.'

He was gone perhaps three minutes, when the door of the study opened and the Minister came out. When he saw I was alone, he announced brusquely:

'I have some questions to ask you, Colonel.'

'At your service, sir.'

'I need direct answers: yes or no.'

'I understand, sir.'

'The charges which you made public tonight, are they true?'

'Yes.'

'Can you sustain them in court?'

'I can sustain those against General Leporello. Those against Prince Baldassare will be more difficult to prove.'

'Could you guarantee a conviction in his case?'

'Guarantee, no.'

'But you would be willing to proceed?'

'As an officer of Public Security, yes.'

'You have qualified that statement. Why?'

I handed him the medical report on Leporello and waited in silence while he read it. He folded it and handed it back to me.

'I repeat the question, Colonel. Why did you qualify your last statement?'

'Because, sir, I am commissioned to act and advise as an officer of Public Security. I have not been asked to tender an opinion of a political nature.'

'I take your point. I now ask you to offer, without prejudice, a political opinion. We have, thanks to your efforts, averted a national crisis. How should we act to avoid a national scandal?'

'We have two important men under arrest, sir. One is clearly incompetent by reason of a psychotic condition. The case against the other is incomplete; and even if we could complete it we should risk embarrassing revelations prejudicial to public security. We should risk also deep and divisive enmities in the Republic and between the Republic and her allies. I would advise, with deference and respect, that Prince Baldassare be permitted to retire from public life and remove himself within twelve hours from the confines of the Republic.'

'Could that be done without raising a public outcry?'

'There would be hostile comment, a great deal of it. There would be political embarrassment. In my view that would be a lesser evil than a celebrated and scandalous trial.'

'What are your personal feelings about Prince Baldassare?'

'I admire his talent greatly. I have learnt much from him. I disapprove his politics and his personal ambitions. I have very private reasons for wishing to see him brought down.'

'What are those reasons?'

'He has imprisoned a woman, once a foreign agent, with whom I am in love. He has damaged my career. He has conspired to submit me to psychological torture from which I am only recently recovered.'

'But you would still recommend his release?'

'As a political expedient, yes.'

'Would you arrange it and supervise it?'

'What you mean, sir, is will I accept personal responsibility for it?'

'Yes.'

'And will I, by consequence, absolve the Ministry and the Government and place myself in jeopardy?'

'You express it very accurately, Colonel.'

'We could of course do it another way, sir.'

'How?'

'You give me a ministerial directive. I execute it. Very simple.'

'Too simple, Colonel, and you know it. A politician cannot afford to be a patriot. The moment he is elected, he abjures the luxury. I know it's a difficult decision. Would you like a little time to think about it?'

'There is no time, sir.'

'A condition then? A gift to sweeten the risk?'

'No, sir. I'm not for sale—not any more. I'll do it. I'll get him across the border tonight. The Cavaliere Manzini will help me to handle the Press.'

'Thank you, Colonel.'

'Is there anything else?'

'One other matter. I should like you to report to me as soon as possible in Rome. We have to begin cleaning house.'

'May I remind you, sir, that I am still on provisional liberty, under charges laid by General Leporello.'

'The charges will be withdrawn. As of this moment you are restored to active duty.'

'Answerable to whom?'

'To me, Colonel. By the time you return to Rome I trust to be able to confirm your appointment as Director.'

He meant it as an accolade—manna in the hungry desert of a bureaucrat's career. Instead it tasted like Dead Sea fruit, dust and ashes on the tongue. For a moment I had felt like a patriot; then, for reward, he had made me a whore again. Still, that was the rule of the game. I had no choice but to play it or toss the cards back on to the table. I bowed and smiled and said: 'Thank you, sir. You do me a great honour.'

'Thank you, Colonel. Goodnight.'

It was strange sitting in the Director's chair. For a man so elegant, he kept a very dingy office. There were no ornaments, no pictures, no photographs, not even a lictor's axe. The only symbols of power were the grey filing cabinets and the scrambler telephone and the intercom switchboard, which would bring twenty people running to attend me. Old Steffi sat on the other side of the desk, cocked his parrot head at me and cackled:

'Eh-eh-eh! So, you've arrived, Matucci! How does it feel? Does your backside fit the seat of the mighty? And what now, little brother? What's the policy? Left, Right or Centre?'

'Middle of the road, Steffi. *Toleranza.* I think we all need to breathe a little.'

'Same as before, eh? Until somebody tosses a bomb in Turin, or the police fire on rioters in Catanzaro and the boys up top get panicky and scream for action. I wonder how tolerant you'll be then! . . . Well, *speriamo bene!* Here's hoping!'

'Come on, Steffi, give me time!'

'I can give you time. All the time you want. But what about them? . . . What about you?'

'Please, old friend . . .!'

'So, I'm still without a job and my nose is twisted out of joint. I'm sorry. What do you want me to do?'

'I've called the Commandant at the Maddalena. He's expecting you. You present the Minister's letter and mine. Lili is released to you. You deliver her to her apartment. I'll be there when you arrive.'

He stared at me as if I were some curious animal, kicked up from under a stone. There was contempt in his eyes and a kind of wondering sorrow.

'My God! What kind of a man are you, Matucci? She's your woman, why don't you fetch her yourself? What have you got in those veins of yours, icewater?'

I was angry then, bitterly and desperately angry. I poured out on him all the pent-up fury of the last months.

'I'll tell you what kind of a man I am, Steffi. I bleed like everyone else. I bruise like everyone else. I'm sick and tired of being pushed and shoved and used and mis-used and mis-judged and mis-read by every clot who thinks he knows the secrets of the universe. I'm sick of all the smug bastards like yourself who think they can sum me up in a line and pay me off like a whore after an hour in bed. I'm sick of friends who make like Father Confessors and expect me to walk round ever afterwards in sackcloth and ashes. You want to know why I'm not going to the prison? I'll tell you! Because the first time Lili sees me I'll be in company with the Commandant and a notary and a turnkey with a pistol at his belt. I'll look exactly the way they do and I don't want her to see me like that; because that's not the kind of man I am . . . at least not to her. I'll want to take her in my arms and kiss her and comfort her and I won't be able to do that while every whore and pickpocket in the gallery makes a dirty joke of it and every little jack-in-office smiles behind his hand. . . . I won't submit her to that. I asked you to go because I thought you were my friend. Instead you sit there and insult me and make lousy ghetto jokes as if God gave you the right to be the conscience of the world. Now get the hell out of here! I'll find someone else.'

He did not move. He sat there, downcast, his lips working as if he could not frame coherent words. Finally, he faced me and there was compassion in his look and a new kind of respect. He said quietly:

'I'm an old fool with a bird's brain and a frog's mouth. I'm sorry. I'll be glad to do it for you.'

'Thank you.'

'You're scared, aren't you?'

'Yes, Steffi, I'm scared.'

'*Piano, piano*, eh! . . . Take it very easy!'

Even for a Director, formalities are long in Rome. Functionaries come and go, but the great paper machine goes round and round, churning out hundreds and thousands and millions of reams of *carta bollata*, signed and countersigned and stamped and sealed and stuffed into pigeon-holes and dumped into subterranean repositories, until one fine or cloudy day, some poor devil goes to gaol and stays there while they dig, or say they dig, for the one line of evidence that may prove him innocent.

I filled the apartment with baskets of flowers. I had champagne cooling in a bucket, and canapés on a silver tray and a whole refrigerator full of food. I had documents from the *Comune* to put up the marriage banns on Capitol Hill. I had even an emerald betrothal ring, especially designed by Bulgari. I still had to wait an hour and a half before Lili came home.

The ring at the door was like camel-bells in the desert. When I opened it, she was standing alone and very still. I swept her into my arms and was astonished at how light she was. I kissed her and hugged her, and wondered where all the passion had gone. I sat her in the armchair and served her like a princess. And then I looked at her. . . . She was so pale, she was almost transparent. She had shrunk to skin and bone. Her clothes hung on her like scarecrow garments. Her mouth was pinched, her hands fluttered nervously. Her eyes, those eloquent eyes, were glazed and dull as pebbles. She ate and drank, not hungrily, but mechanically, and when I laid my hands on her brow and her cheeks, she submitted but did not respond. I knelt beside her and begged.

'Tell me, Lili, what happened. What did they do to you?'

'Not much. Sometimes they questioned me. Most times they left me alone.'

'Lili, you know I didn't send the telegram. . . .'

She stared at me, blankly:

'What telegram?'

'I was told you came back because of a telegram from me?'

'There was no telegram.'

'Then why did you come back?'

'I got your letter. I used to read it every night before I went to bed. One night it wasn't there. I thought I had mislaid it. The next day, I was out walking. My friend from Lugano stopped and offered me a lift in his car. I got in. Someone put a pad over my face. The next thing I remember we were in Italy, near Bolzano. Then two other men took over and drove me here to Rome. That's all. Except they told me you were in prison, too.'

'Oh, darling, darling. . . . I'm so sorry.'

'It doesn't matter.'

'Listen, sweetheart. This is what's going to happen. I'm going to move in here with you. I'm going to nurse you and get you well and we're going to be married. The notice goes up on Capitol Hill tomorrow. After that, no problems! You're my wife. You're under the personal protection of the Director of SID, for ever and ever, amen. . . . How does that sound?'

'It sounds the most beautiful thing in the world, Dante Alighieri. But I don't want it.'

As I stared at her, not understanding, I saw the first flush of life in her cheeks, the first dawning of emotion in her eyes. She put out her hands, not soft now, but thin and creped like raw silk, and cupped them round my face. Then she told me, very gently:

'Dante, I know you love me. Your letter was the most touching compliment I have ever read in my life; but I'm going to give it back to you. I couldn't bear to keep it. I don't want to destroy it.'

'But you said the letter was gone.'

'They gave it back to me in prison. I don't know why, but they did. They do strange things, cruel and kind; and you never know which will be next. I love you, too, Dante. I suppose I'll always love you . . . but not to marry, not to live with for ever and ever.'

'Lili, please. . . .'

'No, listen to me, Dante! You have to know . . .! I don't understand you Italians any more. You are so warm and kind; then, suddenly, you are devious and cold and so cruel, it makes my blood run cold. You smile at each other in the morning, and plot against each other at night. You have no loyalties, Dante—only to the family and to today. Outside the family, after today, everything is doubt and calculation. Oh, Dante Alighieri, I hate to hurt you, but I have to say it. You're the people who always survive, no matter what happens to you. That's a wonderful, a hopeful thing. But it is also very terrible, because you will trample each other down to get the last drop of water in the world. . . . Even you, my Dante, even your Bruno! I can't face that any more. I want to live secure, with a little book that tells me what to do. I want to be sure that if I keep the rules, the rules will keep me safe—safer than marriage, Dante Alighieri, safer than promises, safer even than loving. In Switzerland, I can do that. Not here . . . I cannot risk you any more.'

What could I say? It was all true. The ring on my finger symbolized it: the fabulous beast that survived the hottest fire. And yet, it wasn't true. Not the way she said it. The book of rules wasn't the answer. Not for us, the sun-people. The light was too clear. It showed the cross-wise writing on the palimpsest. How could we believe in permanence, who walked to the office over the bones of dead emperors? We couldn't trust tomorrow; we could only make do with today. I knelt there a long time, face buried in her hands, whose pores still exuded the stale smell of prison. I pitied her. I loved her. I could find no words to comfort her or myself. Then, I heard her say:

'Will you help me to pack, please, Dante; and see if you can get me a flight to Zurich. I'd like to leave as soon as I can.'

It was then I discovered how important it was to be the Director. I was able to command a first-class seat on an over-booked aircraft. I was able to park the car in a prohibited zone at Fiumicino. I was offered free drinks in the distinguished visitors' lounge. I was able to walk Lili all the way to the aircraft and settle her in the seat and commend her to the good offices of the Chief Steward. All that came out of a small piece of card in a black leather folder, stamped with the Arms of the Republic.

I didn't wait for the take-off. I drove back to Rome and telephoned Pia Faubiani. She wasn't at home; she had gone to Venice to open her show there. I called an agency and commissioned them to find me a larger apartment in a more fashionable district. I needed a better *figura*, no that I should be dealing with high men and large affairs. I dined at my old place in Trastevere; but found it suddenly cramped and provincial. Even the musician seemed to have lost his touch. I went home early and tried to read a little of my namesake before I went to bed. I was too sleepy to concentrate on his ponderous imagery—and besides, I didn't believe a word of him. . . . No, that's not true. There were three lines I had to believe:

> *E quella a me, 'Nessun maggior dolore*
> *Che ricordarsi del tempo felice*
> *Nella miseria; e cio sa 'l tuo dottore.'*
> And she said to me: 'There is no greater grief
> Than to remember happy times, in misery;
> And your teacher knows it, too.'

The Shoes of the Fisherman

THE SHOES OF THE FISHERMAN

For
Christopher, Paul and Melanie

ACKNOWLEDGMENTS
Rome is a city older than the Catholic Church.
Everything that could happen has happened there, and
no doubt will happen again. This is a book set in a
fictional time, peopled with fictional characters, and no
reference is intended to any living person whether in
the Church or out of it.

I cannot ask my friends to accept the responsibility for
my opinions. So those who have helped me with this
book must remain anonymous.

To those who gave me their stories, to those who
placed their learning at my disposal, to those who
spent upon me the charity of the faith I offer my
heartfelt thanks.

Thanks are due also to Penguin Books Ltd for
permission to reprint three extracts from the Philip
Vellacott translations of Euripides (*Alcestis*, *Iphigenia
in Tauris*, *Hippolytus*).

Also to Reverend Father Pedro A. Gonzales O.P. for a
passage from his thesis on Miguel de Unamuno, which
is incorporated without quotes in the body of the text.
                                                    M.L.W.

I

The Pope was dead. The Camerlengo had announced it. The Master of Ceremonies, the notaries, the doctors had consigned him under signature into eternity. His ring was defaced and his seals were broken. The bells had been rung throughout the city. The pontifical body had been handed to the embalmers so that it might be a seemly object for the veneration of the faithful. Now it lay, between white candles, in the Sistine Chapel with the Noble Guard keeping a death watch under Michelangelo's frescoes of the Last Judgment.

The Pope was dead. Tomorrow the clergy of the Basilica would claim him and expose him to the public in the Chapel of the Most Holy Sacrament. On the third day they would bury him, clothed in full pontificals, with a mitre on his head, a purple veil on his face, and a red ermine blanket to warm him in the crypt. The medals he had struck and coinage he had minted would be buried with him to identify him to any who might dig him up a thousand years later. They would seal him in three coffins—one of cypress; one of lead to keep him from the damp and to carry his coat of arms, and the certificate of his death; the last of elm so that he might seem, at least, like other men who go to the grave in a wooden box.

The Pope was dead. So they would pray for him as for any other: 'Enter not into judgment with thy servant, O Lord ... Deliver him from eternal death.' Then they would lower him into the vault under the High Altar, where perhaps—but only perhaps—he would moulder into dust with the dust of Peter; and a mason would brick up the vault and fix on a marble tablet with his name, his title and the date of his birth and his obit.

The Pope was dead. They would mourn him with nine days of Masses and give him nine Absolutions—of which, having been greater in his life than other men, he might have greater need after his death.

Then they would forget him, because the See of Peter was vacant, the life of the Church was in syncope and the Almighty was without a vicar on this troubled planet.

The See of Peter was vacant. So the Cardinals of the Sacred College assumed trusteeship over the authority of the Fisherman, though they lacked the power to exercise it. The power did not reside in them but in Christ and none could assume it but by lawful transmission and election.

The See of Peter was vacant. So they struck two medals, one for the Camerlengo, which bore a large umbrella over crossed keys. There was no one under the umbrella, and this was a sign to the most ignorant that there was no incumbent for the Chair of the Apostles, and that all that was done had only an interim character. The second medal was that of the Governor of the Conclave: he who must assemble the Cardinals of the Church, and lock them inside the chambers of the conclave and keep them there until they had issued with a new Pope.

Every coin new-minted in the Vatican City, every stamp now issued, bore the words *sede vacante,* which even those without Latinity might understand as 'while the Chair is vacant'. The Vatican newspaper carried the same sign on its front page, and would wear a black band of mourning until the new Pontiff was named.

Every news service in the world had a representative camped on the doorstep of the Vatican press office; and from each point of the compass old men came, bent with years or infirmity, to put on the scarlet of princes and sit in conclave for the making of a new Pope.

There were Carlin the American, and Rahamani the Syrian, and Hsien the Chinese, and Hanna the Irishman from Australia. There were Councha from Brazil, and da Costa from Portugal. There were Morand from Paris, and Lavigne from Brussels, and Lambertini from Venice, and Brandon from London. There were a Pole and two Germans, and a Ukrainian whom nobody knew because his name had been reserved in the breast of the last Pope and had been proclaimed only a few days before his death. In all there were eighty-five men, of whom the eldest was ninety-two and the youngest, the Ukrainian, was fifty. As each of them arrived in the city, he presented himself and his credentials to the urbane and gentle Valerio Rinaldi, who was the Cardinal Camerlengo.

Rinaldi welcomed each with a slim, dry hand and a smile of mild irony. To each he administered the oath of the conclavist: that he understood and would rigorously observe all the rules of the election as laid down in the Apostolic Constitution of 1945, that he would under pain of a reserved excommunication preserve the secret of the election, that he would not serve by his votes the interest of any secular power, that, if he were elected Pope, he would not surrender any temporal right of the Holy See which might be deemed necessary to its independence.

No one refused the oath; but Rinaldi, who had a sense of humour, wondered many times why it was necessary to administer it at all—unless the Church had a healthy disrespect for the virtues of its princes. Old men were apt to be too easily wounded. So, when he outlined the terms of the oath, Valerio Rinaldi laid a mild emphasis on the counsel of the Apostolic Constitution, that all the proceedings of the election should be conducted with 'prudence, charity, and a singular calm'.

His caution was not unjustified. The history of papal elections was a stormy one, at times downright turbulent. When Damasus the Spaniard was elected in the fourth century, there were massacres in the churches of the city. Leo V was imprisoned, tortured, and murdered by the Theophylacts, so that for nearly a century the Church was ruled by puppets directed by the Theophylact women, Theodora and Marozia. In the conclave of 1623 eight Cardinals and forty of their assistants died of malaria, and there were harsh scenes and rough words over the election of the Saint, Pius X.

All in all, Rinaldi concluded—though he was wise enough to keep the conclusion to himself—it was best not to trust too much to the crusty tempers and the frustrated vanities of old men. Which brought him by a round turn to the problem of housing and feeding eighty-five of them with their servants and assistants until the election should be finished. Some of them, it seemed, would have to take over quarters from the Swiss Guard. None of them could be lodged too far from bathroom or toilet, and all had to be provided with a minimum service by way of cooks, barbers, surgeons, physicians, valets, porters, secretaries, waiters, carpenters, plumbers, firemen (in case any weary prelate nodded off with a cigar in his hand!). If (God forbid!) any Cardinal were in prison or under indictment, he had to be brought to the conclave and made to perform his functions under military guard.

This time, however, no one was in prison—except Krizanic in Yugoslavia, and he was in prison for the faith, which was a different matter—and the late Pope had run an efficient administration, so that Valerio Cardinal Rinaldi even had time to spare to meet with his colleague, Leone of the Holy Office, who was also the Dean of the Sacred College. Leone lived up to his name. He had a grey lion's mane and a growling temper. He was, moreover, a Roman, bred-in-the-bone, dyed-in-the-wool. Rome was for him the centre of the world, and centralism was a doctrine almost as immutable as that of the Trinity and the Procession of the Holy Ghost. With his great eagle beak and his jowly jaw, he looked like a senator strayed out of Augustan times, and his pale eyes looked out on the world with wintry disapproval.

Innovation was for him the first step toward heresy, and he sat in the Holy Office like a grizzled watchdog, whose hackles would rise at the first unfamiliar sound in doctrine interpretation, or practice. One of his French colleagues had said, with more wit than charity, 'Leone smells of the fire.' But the general belief was that he would plunge his own hand into the flame rather than set his signature to the smallest deviation from orthodoxy.

Rinaldi respected him, though he had never been able to like him, and so their intercourse had been limited to the courtesies of their common trade. Tonight, however, the old lion seemed in gentler mood, and was disposed to be talkative. His pale, watchful eyes were lit with a momentary amusement.

'I'm eighty-two, my friend, and I've buried three Popes. I'm beginning to feel lonely.'

'If we don't get a younger man this time,' said Rinaldi mildly, 'you may well bury a fourth.'

Leone shot him a quick look from under his shaggy brows. 'And what's that supposed to mean?'

Rinaldi shrugged, and spread his fine hands in a Roman gesture. 'Just what it says. We're all too old. There are not more than half a dozen of us who can give the Church what it needs at this moment: personality, a decisive policy, time and continuity to make the policy work.'

'Do you think you're one of the half-dozen?'

Rinaldi smiled with thin irony. 'I know I'm not. When the new man is chosen—whoever he is—I propose to offer him my resignation, and ask his permission to rusticate at home. It's taken me fifteen years to build a garden in that place of mine. I'd like a little while to enjoy it.'

'Do you think I have a chance of election?' asked Leone bluntly.

'I hope not,' said Rinaldi.

Leone threw back his great mane and laughed. 'Don't worry. I know I haven't. They need someone quite different; someone—' he hesitated, fumbling for the phrase—'someone who has compassion on the multitude, who sees them, as Christ saw them—sheep without a shepherd. I'm not that sort of man. I wish I were.'

Leone heaved his bulky body out of the chair, and walked to the big table where an antique globe stood among a litter of books. He spun the globe slowly on its axis so that now one country, now another, swam into the light. 'Look at it, my friend! The world, our vineyard! Once we colonized it in the name of Christ. Not righteously always, not always justly or wisely, but the

Cross was there, and the Sacraments were there, and however a man lived—in purple or in chains—there was a chance for him to die like a son of God. Now . . .? Now we are everywhere in retreat. China is lost to us, and Asia and all the Russias. Africa will soon be gone, and the South Americas will be next. You know it. I know it. It is the measure of our failure that we have sat all these years in Rome, and watched it happen.' He checked the spinning globe with an unsteady hand, and then turned to face his visitor, with a new question. 'If you had your life over, Rinaldi, what would you do with it?'

Rinaldi looked up with that deprecating smile which lent him so much charm. 'I think I should probably do the same things again. Not that I'm very proud of them, but they happened to be the only things I could do well. I get along with people, because I've never been capable of very deep feelings about them. That makes me, I suppose, a natural diplomat. I don't like to quarrel. I like even less to be emotionally involved. I like privacy and I enjoy study. So I'm a good canonist, a reasonable historian, and an adequate linguist. I've never had very strong passions. You might, if you felt malicious, call me a cold fish. So I've achieved a reputation for good conduct without having to work for it . . . All in all, I've had a very satisfactory life—satisfactory to myself, of course. How the recording angel sees it, is another matter.'

'Don't underrate yourself, man,' said Leone sourly. 'You've done a great deal better than you'll admit.'

'I need time and reflection to set my soul in order,' said Rinaldi quietly. 'May I count on you to help me resign?'

'Of course.'

'Thank you. Now, suppose the inquisitor answers his own question. What would you do if you had to begin again?'

'I've thought about it often,' said Leone heavily. 'If I didn't marry—and I'm not sure but that's what I needed to make me halfway human—I'd be a country priest with just enough theology to hear confession, and just enough Latin to get through Mass and the sacramental formulae. But with heart enough to know what griped in the guts of other men, and made them cry into their pillows at night. I'd sit in front of my church on a summer evening and read my office and talk about the weather and the crops, and learn to be gentle with the poor and humble with the unhappy ones . . . You know what I am now? A walking encyclopaedia of dogma and theological controversy. I can smell out an error faster than a Dominican. And what does it mean? Nothing. Who cares about theology except the theologians? We are necessary but less important than we think. The Church is Christ—Christ and the people. And all the people want to know is whether or no there is a God, and what is His relation with them, and how they can get back to Him when they stray.'

'Large questions,' said Rinaldi gently, 'not to be answered by small minds or gross ones.'

Leone shook his lion's mane stubbornly. 'For the people they come down to simplicities! Why shouldn't I covet my neighbour's wife? Who takes the revenge that is forbidden to me? And who cares when I am sick and tired, and dying in an upstairs room? I can give them a theologian's answer. But whom do they believe but the man who feels the answers in his heart, and bears the scars of their consequences in his own flesh? Where are the men like that? Is there one among all of us who wear the red hat? Eh . . .!' His grim mouth twitched into a grin of embarrassment, and he flung out his arms in mock despair. 'We are what we are, and God has to take half the responsibility even for theologians! . . . Now tell me—where do we go for our Pope?'

'This time,' said Rinaldi crisply, 'we should choose him for the people and not for ourselves.'

'There will be eighty-five of us in the conclave. How many will agree on what is best for the people?'

Rinaldi looked down at the backs of his carefully manicured fingers. He said softly, 'If we showed them the man first, perhaps we could get them to agree.'

Leone's answer was swift and emphatic. 'You would have to show him to me first.'

'And if you agreed?'

'Then there would be another question,' said Leone flatly. 'How many of our brethren will think as we do?'

The question was subtler than it looked, and they both knew it. Here, in fact, was the whole loaded issue of a papal election, the whole paradox of the Papacy. The man who wore the Fisherman's ring was Vicar of Christ, Vicegerent of the Almighty. His dominion was spiritual and universal. He was the servant of all the servants of God, even of those who did not acknowledge him.

On the other hand, he was Bishop of Rome, Metropolitan of an Italian see. The Romans claimed by historic tradition a pre-emption on his presence and his services. They relied on him for employment, for the tourist trade and the bolstering of their economy by Vatican investment, for the preservation of their historic monuments and national privileges. His court was Italian in character; the greater number of his household and his administrators were Italian. If he could not deal with them familiarly in their own tongue, he stood naked to palace intrigue and every kind of partisan interest.

Once upon a time the Roman view had had a peculiarly universal aspect. The numen of the ancient empire still hung about it, and the memory of the Pax Romana had not yet vanished from the consciousness of Europe. But the numen was fading. Imperial Rome had never subdued Russia or Asia, and the Latins who conquered South America had brought no peace, but the sword. England had revolted long since, as she had revolted earlier from the legions of Roman occupation. So that there was sound argument for a new, non-Italian succession to the papal throne—just as there was sound reason for believing that a non-Italian might become either a puppet of his ministers or a victim of their talent for intrigue.

The perpetuity of the Church was an article of faith; but its diminutions and corruptions, and its jeopardy by the follies of its members, were part of the canon of history. There was plenty of ground for cynicism. But over and over again the cynics were confounded by the uncanny capacity for self-renewal in the Church and in the Papacy. The cynics had their own explanations. The faithful put it down to the indwelling of the Holy Ghost. Either way there was an uncomfortable mystery: how the chaos of history could issue in so consistent a hold on dogma or why an omniscient God chose such a messy method of preserving His foothold in the minds of His creatures.

So every conclave began with the invocation of the Paraclete. On the day of the walling-in, Rinaldi led his old men and their attendants into St Peter's. Then Leone came, dressed in a scarlet chasuble and accompanied by his deacons and subdeacons, to begin the Mass of the Holy Spirit. As he watched the celebrant, weighed down by the elaborate vestments, moving painfully through the ritual of the sacrifice, Rinaldi felt a pang of pity for him and a sudden rush of understanding.

They were all in the same galley, these leaders of the Church—himself along with them. They were men without issue, who had 'made themselves eunuchs for the love of God'. A long time since they had dedicated themselves with greater or less sincerity to the service of a hidden God, and to the propagation of an unprovable mystery. Through the temporality of the Church they had attained to honour, more honour perhaps than any of them might have attained in the secular state, but they all lay under the common burden of age—failing faculties, the loneliness of eminence, and the fear of a reckoning that might find them bankrupt debtors.

He thought, too, of the stratagem which he had planned with Leone, to introduce a candidate who was still a stranger to most of the voters, and to promote his cause without breaching the Apostolic Constitution which they had sworn to preserve. He wondered if this were not a presumption and an attempt to circumvent Providence, whom they were invoking at this very moment. Yet, if God had chosen, as the faith taught, to use man as a free instrument for a divine plan, how else could one act? One could not let so momentous an occasion as a papal election play itself like a game of chance. Prudence was enjoined on all—prayerful preparation and then considered action, and afterwards resignation and submission. Yet however prudently one planned, one could not escape the uncanny feeling that one walked unwary and unpurged on sacred ground.

The heat, the flicker of the candles, the chant of the choir, and the mesmeric pace of the ritual made him drowsy, and he stole a surreptitious glance at his colleagues to see if any of them had noticed his nodding.

Like twin choirs of ancient archangels they sat on either side of the sanctuary, their breasts hung with golden crosses, the princely seals agleam on their folded hands, their faces scored by age and the experience of power.

There was Rahamani of Antioch, with his spade beard and his craggy brows and his bright, half-mystical eyes. There was Benedetti, round as a dumpling with pink cheeks and candyfloss hair, who ran the Vatican Bank. Next to him was Potocki from Poland, he of the high, bald dome and the suffering mouth and the wise, calculating eyes. Tatsue from Japan wanted only the saffron robe to make him a Buddhist image, and Hsien, the exiled Chinese, sat between Ragambwe, the black man from Kenya, and Pallenberg, the lean ascetic from Munich.

Rinaldi's shrewd eyes ranged along the choir stalls, naming each one for his virtues or his shortcomings, trying on each the classic label *papabile*, he-who-has-the-makings-of-a-Pope. In theory every member of the conclave could wear it; in practice very few were eligible.

Age was a bar to some. Talent or temperament or reputation was an impediment to others. Nationality was a vital question. One could not elect an American without seeming to divide East and West even further. A Negro Pope might seem a spectacular symbol of the new revolutionary nations, just as a Japanese might be a useful link between Asia and Europe. But the princes of the Church were old men and as wary of spectacular gestures as they were of historic hangovers. A German Pope might alienate the sympathies of those who had suffered in World War II. A Frenchman would recall old memories of Avignon and tramontane rebellions. While there were still dictatorships in Spain and Portugal, an Iberian Pope could be a diplomatic indiscretion. Gonfalone, the Milanese, had the reputation of being a saint, but he was becoming more and more of a recluse, and there was question of his fitness for so public an office. Leone was an autocrat who might well mistake the fire of zealotry for the flame of compassion.

The lector was reading from the Acts of the Apostles. 'In those days, Peter began and said, Men, Brethren, the Lord charged us to preach to the people and to testify that He is the one who has been appointed by God to be judge of the living and of the dead. . . .' The choir sang, '*Veni, Sancte Spiritus* . . . Come Holy Spirit and fill the hearts of your faithful ones . . .' Then Leone began to read in his strong stubborn voice the Gospel for the day of the conclave: 'He who enters not by the door into the sheepfold, but climbs up another way is a thief and a robber. But he who enters by the door is the shepherd of the sheep.' Rinaldi bent his head in his hands and prayed that the man he was offering would be in truth a shepherd, and that the conclave might hand him the crook and the ring.

When the Mass was over, the celebrant retired to the sacristy to take off his vestments, and the Cardinals relaxed in the stalls. Some of them whispered to one another, a couple were still nodding drowsily, and one was seen to take a surreptitious pinch of snuff. The next part of the ceremony was a formality, but it promised to be a boring one. A prelate would read them a homily in Latin, pointing out once again the importance of the election and their moral obligation to carry it out in an orderly and honest fashion. By ancient custom, the prelate was chosen for the purity of his Latin, but this time the Camerlengo had made another arrangement.

A whisper of surprise stirred round the assembly as they saw Rinaldi leave his place and walk down to the far end of the stalls on the Gospel side of the Altar. He offered his hand to a tall, thin Cardinal and led him to the pulpit. When he stood elevated in the full glare of the lights, they saw that he was the youngest of them all. His hair was black, his square beard was black too, and down his left cheek was a long, livid scar. On his breast, in addition to the cross, was a pectoral ikon representing a Byzantine Madonna and Child. When he crossed himself, he made the sign from right to left in the Slavonic manner; yet, when he began to speak, it was not in Latin but in a pure and melodious Tuscan. Across the nave Leone smiled a grim approval at Rinaldi, and then they surrendered themselves like their colleagues to the simple eloquence of the stranger:

'My name is Kiril Lakota, and I am come the latest and the least into this Sacred College. I speak to you today by the invitation of our brother the Cardinal Camerlengo. To most of you I am a stranger because my people are scattered, and I have spent the last seventeen years in prison. If I have any rights among you, any credit at all, let this be the foundation of them—that I speak for the lost ones, for those who walk in darkness and in the valley of the shadow of death. It is for them and not for ourselves that we are entering into conclave. It is for them and not for ourselves that we must elect a Pontiff. The first man who held this office was one who walked with Christ, and was crucified like the Master. Those who have best served the Church and the faithful are those who have been closest to Christ and to the people, who are the image of Christ. We have power in our hands, my brothers. We shall put even greater power into the hands of the man we elect; but we must use the power as servants and not as masters. We must consider that we are what we are—priests, bishops, pastors—by virtue of an act of dedication to the people who are the flock of Christ. What we possess, even to the clothes on our backs, comes to us out of their charity. The whole material fabric of the Church was raised stone on stone, gold on golden offering, by the sweat of the faithful, and they have given it into our hands for stewardship. It is they who have educated us so that we may teach them and their children. It is they who humble themselves before our priesthood, as before the divine Priesthood of Christ. It is for them that we exercise the sacramental and the sacrificial powers which are given to us in the anointing and the laying-on of hands. If in our deliberations we serve any other cause but this, then we are traitors. It is not asked of us that we shall agree on what is best for the Church, but only that we shall deliberate in charity and humility, and in the end give our obedience to the man who shall be chosen by the majority. We are asked to act swiftly so that the Church may not be left without a head. In all this we must be what, in the end, our Pontiff shall proclaim himself to be—servants of the servants of God. Let us in these final moments resign ourselves as willing instruments for His hands. Amen.'

It was so simply said that it might have been the customary formality, yet the man himself, with his scarred face and his strong voice and his crooked, eloquent hands, lent to the words an unexpected poignancy. There was a long silence while he left the pulpit and returned to his own place. Leone nodded his lion's head in approval, and Rinaldi breathed a silent prayer of gratitude. Then the Master of Ceremonies took command and led the Cardinals and their attendants with their confessor and their physician and surgeon, and the Architect of the Conclave, and the conclave workmen out of the Basilica and into the confines of the Vatican itself.

In the Sistine Chapel they were sworn again. Then Leone gave the order for the bells to be rung, so that all who did not belong to the conclave should leave the sealed area at once. The servants led each of the Cardinals to his apartment. Then the prefect of the Master of Ceremonies, with the Architect of the Conclave, began the ritual search of the enclosed area. They went from room to room pulling aside draperies, throwing light into dark corners, opening closets, until every space was declared free from intruders.

At the entrance of the great stairway of Pius IX they halted and the Noble Guard marched out of the conclave area, followed by the Marshal of the Conclave and his aides. The great door was locked. The Marshal of the Conclave turned his key on the outside. On the inside the Masters of Ceremonies turned their own key. The Marshal ordered his flag hoisted over the Vatican, and from this moment no one might leave or enter, or pass a message, until the new Pope was elected and named.

Alone in his quarters, Kiril Cardinal Lakota was beginning a private purgatory. It was a recurrent state whose symptoms were now familiar to him: a cold sweat that broke out on face and palms, a trembling in the limbs, a twitching of the severed nerves in his face, a panic fear that the room was closing in to crush him. Twice in his life he had been walled up in the bunkers of an underground prison. Four months in all, he had endured the terrors of darkness and cold and solitude and near starvation, so that the pillars of his reason had rocked under the strain. Nothing in his years of Siberian exile had afflicted him so much, nor left so deep a scar on his memory. Nothing had brought him so close to abjuration and apostasy.

He had been beaten often, but the bruised tissue had healed itself in time. He had been interrogated till every nerve was screaming and his mind had lapsed into a merciful confusion. From this too he had emerged, stronger in faith and in reason, but the horror of solitary confinement would remain with him until he died. Kamenev had kept his promise. 'You will never be able to forget me. Wherever you go, I shall be. Whatever you become, I shall be part of you.' Even here, in the neutral confines of the Vatican City, in the princely room under Raphael's frescoes, Kamenev, the insidious tormentor, was with him. There was only one escape from him, and that was the one he had learned in the bunker—the projection of the tormented spirit into the arms of the Almighty.

He threw himself on his knees, buried his face in his hands, and tried to concentrate every faculty of mind and body into the simple act of abandonment.

His lips commanded no words, but the will seized on the plaint of Christ in Gethsemane. 'Father, if it be possible, let this Chalice pass.'

In the end he knew it would pass, but first the agony must be endured. The walls pressed in upon him relentlessly. The ceiling weighed down on him like a leaden vestment. The darkness pressed upon his eyeballs and packed itself inside his skull-case. Every muscle in his body knotted in pain and his teeth chattered as if from the rigors of fever. Then he became deathly cold, and deathly calm, and waited passively for the light that was the beginning of peace and of communion.

The light was like a dawn seen from a high hill, flooding swiftly into every fold of the landscape, so that the whole pattern of its history was revealed at one glance. The road of his own pilgrimage was there like a scarlet ribbon that stretched four thousand miles from Lvov, in the Ukraine, to Nokolayevsk on the sea of Okhotsk.

When the war with the Germans was over, he had been named, in spite of his youth, Metropolitan of Lvov, successor to the great and saintly Andrew Szepticky, leader of all the Ruthenian Catholics. Shortly afterwards he had been arrested with six other bishops and deported to the eastern limits of Siberia. The six others had died, and he had been left alone, shepherd of a lost flock, to carry the cross on his own shoulders.

For seventeen years he had been in prison, or in the labour camps. Once only in all that time he had been able to say Mass, with a thimbleful of wine and a crust of white bread. All that he could cling to of doctrine and prayer and sacramental formulae was locked in his own brain. All that he had tried to spend of strength and compassion upon his fellow prisoners, he had had to dredge out of himself and out of the well of the Divine Mercy. Yet his body, weakened by torture, had grown miraculously strong again at slave labour in the mines and on the road gangs, so that even Kamenev could no longer mock him, but was struck with wonder at his survival.

For Kamenev, his tormentor in the first interrogations, would always come back; and each time he came, he had risen a little higher in the Marxist order. Each time he had seemed a little more friendly as if he were making a slow surrender to respect for his victim.

Even from the mountain-top of contemplation, he could still see Kamenev cold, sardonic, searching him for the slightest sign of weakness, the slightest hint of surrender. In the beginning he had had to force himself to pray for the jailer. After a while they had come to a bleak kind of brotherhood, even as the one rose higher and the other seemed to sink deeper into a fellowship with the Siberian slaves. In the end, it was Kamenev who had organized his escape–inflicting on him a final irony by giving him the identity of a dead man.

'You will go free,' Kamenev had said, 'because I need you free. But you will always owe me a debt because I have killed a man to give you a name. One day, I shall come to you to ask for payment, and you will pay, whatever it may cost.'

It was as though the jailer had assumed the mantle of prophecy, because Kiril Lakota had escaped and made his way to Rome to find that a dying Pope had made him a Cardinal 'in the breast'–a man of destiny, a hinge-man of Mother Church.

To this point the road in retrospect was clear. He could trace in its tragedies the promise of future mercies. For every one of the bishops who had died for his belief, a man had died in his arms in the camp, blessing the Almighty for a final absolution. The scattered flock would not all lose the faith for which they had suffered. Some of them would remain to hand on the creed, and to keep a small light burning that one day might light a thousand torches. In the degradation of the road gangs, he had seen how the strangest men upheld the human dignities. He had baptized children with a handful of dirty water and seen them die unmarked by the miseries of the world.

He himself had learned humility and gratitude and the courage to believe in an Omnipotence working by a mighty evolution toward an ultimate good. He had learned compassion and tenderness and the meaning of the cry in the night. He had learned to hope that for Kamenev himself he might be an instrument, if not of ultimate enlightenment, then at least of ultimate absolution. But all this was in the past, and the pattern had still to work itself out beyond Rome into a fathomless future. Even the light of contemplation was not thrown beyond Rome. There was a veil drawn, and the veil was the limit imposed on prescience by a merciful God . . .

The light was changing now; the landscape of the steppes had become an undulant sea, across which a figure in antique robes was walking toward him, his face shining, his pierced hands outstretched, as if in greeting. Kiril Cardinal Lakota shrank away, and tried to bury himself in the lighted sea; but there was no escape. When the hands touched him and the luminous face bent to embrace him, he felt himself pierced by an intolerable joy, and an intolerable pain. Then he entered into the moment of peace.

The servant who was assigned to care for him came into the room and saw him kneeling rigid as a cataleptic with his arms outstretched in the attitude of crucifixion. Rinaldi, making the rounds of the conclavists, came upon him and tried vainly to wake him. Then Rinaldi too went away, shaken and humbled, to consult with Leone and with his colleagues.

In his cluttered and unelegant office, George Faber, the greyhaired dean of the Roman press corps, fifteen years Italian correspondent for the New York *Monitor*, was writing his background story on the papal election:

'. . . Outside the small medieval enclave of the Vatican, the world is in a climate of crisis. Winds of change are blowing and storm warnings are being raised, now in one place, now in another. The arms race between America and Russia goes on unabated. Every month there are new and hostile probes into the high orbits of space. There is famine in India, and guerrilla fighting along the southern peninsulas of Asia. There is thunder over Africa, and the tattered flags of revolution are being hoisted over the capitals of South America. There is blood on the sands in North Africa, and in Europe the battle for economic survival is waged behind the closed doors of banks and board rooms. In the high airs above the Pacific, war planes fly to sample the pollution of the air by lethal atomic particles. In China the new dynasts struggle to fill the bellies of hungry millions, while they hold their minds chained to the rigid orthodoxy of Marxist philosophy. In the misty valleys of the Himalayas, where the prayer-flags flutter and the tea-pickers plod along the terraces, there are forays and incursions from Tibet and Sinkiang. On the frontiers of Outer Mongolia, the uneasy amity of Russia and China is strained to the point of rupture. Patrol boats probe the mangrove swamps and inlets of New Guinea, while the upland tribes try to project themselves into the twentieth century by a single leap from the Stone Age.

'Everywhere man has become aware of himself as a transient animal and is battling desperately to assert his right to the best of the world for the short time that he sojourns in it. The Nepalese haunted by his mountain demons, the coolie hauling his heart muscle into exhaustion between the shafts of a rickshaw, the Israeli beleaguered at every frontier, everyone all at once is asserting his claim to an identity; everyone has an ear for any prophet who can promise him one.'

He stopped typing, lit a cigarette and leaned back in his chair, considering the thought which he had just written–'a claim to identity'. Strange how everyone had to make it sooner or later. Strange for how long one accepted with apparent equanimity the kind of person one seemed to be, the state to which one had apparently been nominated in life. Then all of a sudden, the identity was called in question . . . His own for instance. George Faber, long-time bachelor, acknowledged expert on Italian affairs and Vatican politics. Why so late in life was he being forced to question what he was, what he had so far been content to be? Why this restless dissatisfaction with the public image of himself? Why this doubt that he could survive any longer without a permanent supplement to himself? . . . A woman, of course. There always had been women in his life, but Chiara was something new and special. . . . The thought often troubled him. He tried to put it away and went again to his typewriter:

'Everywhere the cry is for survival, but since the supreme irony of creation was that man must inevitably die, those who strived for the mastery of his mind or his muscle have to promise him an extension of his span into some semblance of immortality. The Marxist promises him a oneness with the workers of the world. The Nationalist gives him a flag and a frontier, and a local enlargement of himself. The Democrat offers him liberty through a ballot box, but warns that he might have to die to preserve it.

'But for man, and all the prophets he raises up for himself, the last enemy is time; and time is a relative dimension, limited directly by man's capacity to make use of it. Modern communication, swift as light, has diminished to nothing the time between a human act and its consequences. A shot fired in Berlin can detonate the world within minutes. A plague in the Philippines can infect Australia within a day. A man toppling from a high wire in a Moscow circus can be watched in his death agony from London and New York.

'So, at every moment, every man is besieged by the consequences of his own sins and those of all his fellows. So, too, every prophet and every pundit is haunted by the swift lapse of time and the knowledge that the accounting for false predictions and broken promises is swifter than it has ever been in history. Here precisely is the cause of the crisis. Here the winds and the waves are born and the thunderbolts are forged that may, any week, any month, go roaring round the world under a sky black with mushroom clouds.

'The men in the Vatican are aware of time, though many of them have ceased to be as aware as they need to be. . . .'

Time . . .! He had become so vividly conscious of this diminishing dimension of existence. He was in his mid-forties. For more than a year he had been trying to steer Chiara's petition of nullity through the Holy Roman Rota so that she might be free from Corrado Calitri to marry him. But the case was moving with desperate slowness, and Faber, although a Catholic by birth, had come to resent bitterly the impersonal system of the Roman Congregations and the attitude of the old men who ran them.

He typed on vividly, precisely, professionally:

'Like most old men they are accustomed to seeing time as a flash between two eternities instead of a quantum of extension given to each individual man to mature toward the vision of his God.

'They are concerned also with man's identity, which they are obliged to affirm as the identity of a son of God. Yet here they are in danger of another pitfall: that they sometimes affirm his identity without understanding his individuality, and how he has to grow in whatever garden he is planted, whether the ground is sweet or sour, whether the air is friendly or tempestuous. Men grow, like trees, in different shapes, crooked or straight, according to the climate of their nurture. But so long as the sap flows and the leaves burgeon, there should be no quarrel with the shape of the man or the tree.

'The men of the Vatican are concerned as well with immortality and eternity. They too understand man's need for an extension of himself beyond the limit of the fleeting years. They affirm, as of faith, the persistence of soul into an eternity of union with the Creator, or of exile from His face. They go further. They promise man a preservation of his identity and an ultimate victory even over the terror of physical death. What they fail too often to understand is that immortality must be begun in time, and that a man must be given the physical resources to survive before his spirit can grow to desire more than physical survival. . . .'

Chiara had become as necessary to him as breath. Without her youth and her passion, it seemed that he must slide all too quickly into age and disillusion. She had been his mistress for nearly six months now, but he was plagued by the fear that he could lose her at any moment to a younger man, and that the promise of children and continuity might never be fulfilled in him . . . He had friends in the Vatican. He had easy access to men with great names in the Church, but they were committed to the law and to the system, and they could not help him at all. He wrote feelingly:

'They are caught, these old and deliberate men, in the dilemma of all principality: that the higher one rises, the more one sees of the world, but the less one apprehends of the small determining factors of human existence. How a man without shoes may starve because he cannot walk to a place of employment. How a liverish tax collector may start a local revolution. How high blood-pressure may plunge a noble man into melancholy and despair. How a woman may sell herself for money because she cannot give herself to one man for love. The danger of all rulers is that they begin to believe that history is the result of great generalities, instead of the sum of millions of small particulars, like bad drainage and sexual obsession and the anopheles mosquito . . .'

It was not the story he had intended to write, but it was a true record of his personal feelings about the coming event . . . Let it stand then! Let the editors in New York like it or lump it . . .! The door opened and Chiara came in. He took her in his arms and kissed her. He damned the Church and her husband and his paper to a special kind of hell, and then took her out to lunch on the Via Veneto.

The first day of the conclave was left private to the electing Cardinals, so that they might meet and talk discreetly, and probe for one another's prejudices and blind spots and motives of private interest. It was for this reason that Rinaldi and Leone moved among them to prepare them carefully for the final proposal. Once the voting began, once they had taken sides with this candidate or that, it would be much more difficult to bring them to an agreement.

Not all the talk was on the level of eternal verities. Much of it was simple and blunt, like Rinaldi's conversation with the American over a cup of American coffee (brewed by His Eminence's own servant because Italian coffee gave him indigestion).

His Eminence, Charles Corbet Carlin, Cardinal Archbishop of New York, was a tall, ruddy man with an expansive manner and a shrewd, pragmatic eye. He stated his problem as baldly as a banker challenging an overdraft:

'We don't want a diplomat, and we don't want a Curia official who will look at the world through a Roman eyeglass. A man who has travelled, yes, but someone who has been a pastor and understands what our problems are at this moment.'

'I should be interested to hear Your Eminence define them.' Rinaldi was at his most urbane.

'We're losing our grip on the people,' said Carlin flatly. 'They are losing their loyalty to us. I think we are more than half to blame.'

Rinaldi was startled. Carlin had the reputation of being a brilliant banker for Mother Church and of entertaining a conviction that all the ills of the world could be solved by a well-endowed school system and a rousing sermon every Sunday. To hear him talk so bluntly of the shortcomings of his own province was both refreshing and disquieting. Rinaldi asked:

'Why are we losing our grip?'

'In America? Two reasons: prosperity and respectability. We're not persecuted any more. We pay our way. We can wear the faith like a Rotary badge—and with as little social consequence. We collect our dues like a club, shout down the Communists, and make the biggest contribution in the whole world to Peter's Pence. But it isn't enough. There's no—no heart in it for many Catholics. The young ones are drifting outside our influence. They don't need us as they should. They don't trust us as they used. For that,' he added gravely, 'I think I'm partly to blame.'

'None of us has much right to be proud of himself,' said Rinaldi quietly. 'Look at France—look at the bloody things that have been done in Algeria. Yet this is a country half-Catholic, and with a Catholic leadership. Where is our authority in this monstrous situation? A third of the Catholic population of the world is in the South Americas yet what is our influence there? What impression do we make among the indifferent rich, and the oppressed poor, who see no hope in God and less in those who represent Him? Where do we begin to change?'

'I've made mistakes,' said Carlin moodily. 'Big ones. I can't even begin to repair them all. My father was a gardener, a good one. He used to say that the best you could do for a tree was mulch it and prune it once a year, and leave the rest to God. I always prided myself that I was a practical fellow like he was–you know? Build the Church, then the school. Get the nuns in, then the brothers. Build the seminary and train the priests, and keep the money coming in. After that it was up to the Almighty.' For the first time he smiled, and Rinaldi, who had disliked him for many years, began to warm to him. He went on whimsically, 'The Romans and the Irish! We're great plotters, and great builders, but we lose the inwardness of things quicker than anybody else. Stick to the book! No meat on Fridays, no sleeping with your neighbour's wife, and leave the mysteries to the theologians! It isn't enough. God help us, but it isn't!'

'You're asking for a saint. I doubt we have many on the books just now.'

'Not a saint.' Carlin was emphatic again. 'A man for the people, and of the people, like Sarto was. A man who could bleed for them, and scold them, and have them know all the time that he loved them. A man who could break out of this gilded garden patch and make himself another Peter.'

'He would be crucified too, of course,' said Rinaldi tartly.

'Perhaps that is just what we need,' said His Eminence from New York.

Whereupon Rinaldi, the diplomat, judged it opportune to talk of the bearded Ukrainian, Kiril Lakota, as a–man-with-the-makings-of-a-Pope.

In a somewhat smaller suit of the conclave, Leone was discussing the same candidate with Hugh Cardinal Brandon from Westminster. Brandon, being English, was a man with no illusions and few enthusiasms. He pursed his thin, grey lips and toyed with his pectoral cross, and delivered his policy in precise, if stilted Italian:

'From our point of view, an Italian is still the best choice. It leaves us room to move, if you understand what I mean. There is no question of a new attitude or a fresh political alignment. There is no disturbance of the relations between the Vatican and the Republic of Italy. The Papacy would still be an effective barrier to any growth of Italian communism.' He permitted himself a dry joke. 'We could still count on the sympathy of English Romantics for Romantic Italy.'

Leone, veteran of many a subtle argument, nodded his agreement and added almost casually, 'You would not then consider our newcomer, the one who spoke to us this morning?'

'I doubt it. I found him, as everyone did, most impressive in the pulpit. But then eloquence is hardly a full qualification, is it? Besides, there is the question of rites. I understand this man is a Ukrainian and belongs to the Ruthenian rite.'

'If he were elected, he would automatically practise the Roman one.'

His Eminence of Westminster smiled thinly. 'The beard might worry some people. A too Byzantine look, don't you think? We haven't had a bearded Pope in a very long time.'

'No doubt he would shave it.'

'Would he still wear the ikon?'

'He might be persuaded to dispense with that, too.'

'Then we should be left with a model Roman. So why not choose an Italian in the first place? I can't believe you would want anything different.'

'Believe me, I do. I am prepared to tell you now that my vote will go to the Ukrainian.'

'I am afraid I can't promise you mine. The English and the Russians, you know . . . Historically we've never done very well together . . . Never at all.'

'Always,' said Rahamani the Syrian in his pliant, courteous fashion, 'always you search a man for the one necessary gift–the gift of co-operation with God. Even among good men this gift is rare. Most of us, you see, spend our lives trying to bend ourselves to the will of God, and even then we have often to be bent by a violent grace. The others, the rare ones, commit themselves, as if by an instinctive act, to be tools in the hands of the Maker. If this new man is such a one, then it is he whom we need.'

'And how do we know?' asked Leone dryly.

'We submit him to God,' said the Syrian. 'We ask God to judge him, and we rest secure in the outcome.'

'We can only vote on him. There is no other way.'

'There is another way, prescribed in the Apostolic Constitution. It is the way of inspiration. Any member of the conclave may make a public proclamation of the man he believes should be chosen, trusting that if this be a candidate acceptable to God, God will inspire the other conclavists to approve him publicly. It is a valid method of election.'

'It also takes courage–and a great deal of faith.'

'If we elders of the Church lack faith, what hope is there for the people?'

'I am reproved,' said the Cardinal Secretary of the Holy Office. 'It's time I stopped canvassing and began to pray.'

Early the next morning, all the Cardinals assembled in the Sistine Chapel for the first ballot. For each there was a throne and over the throne a silken canopy. The thrones were arranged along the walls of the Chapel, and before each was set a small table, which bore the Cardinal's coat of arms and his name inscribed in Latin. The Chapel altar was covered with a tapestry upon which was embroidered a figuration of the Holy Ghost descending upon the first Apostles. Before the altar was set a large table on which there stood a gold Chalice and a small golden platter. Near the table was a simple potbellied stove whose flue projected through a small window that looked out on the Square of St Peter.

When the voting took place, each Cardinal would write the name of his candidate upon a ballot paper, lay it first on the golden platter, and then put it into the Chalice, to signify that he had completed a sacred act. After the votes were counted, they would be burned in the stove, and smoke would issue through the flue into the Square of St Peter. To elect a Pope, there must be a majority of two-thirds.

If the majority were not conclusive, the ballot papers would be burned with wet straw, and the smoke would issue dark and cloudy. Only when the ballot was successful would the papers be burned without straw, so that a white smoke might inform the waiting crowds that they had a new Pope. It was an archaic and cumbersome ceremony for the age of radio and television, but it served to underline the drama of the moment and the continuity of two thousand years of papal history.

When all the Cardinals were seated, the Master of Ceremonies made the circuit of the thrones, handing to each voter a single ballot paper. Then he left the Chapel, and the door was locked, leaving only the Princes of the Church to elect the successor to Peter.

It was the moment for which Leone and Rinaldi had waited. Leone rose in his place, tossed his white mane, and addressed the conclave:

'My brothers, I stand to claim a right under the Apostolic Constitution. I proclaim to you my belief that there is among us a man already chosen by God to sit in the Chair of Peter. Like the first of the Apostles, he has suffered prison and stripes for the faith, and the hand of God has led him out of bondage to join us in this conclave. I announce him as my candidate, and dedicate to him my vote and my obedience . . . Kiril Cardinal Lakota.'

There was a moment of dead silence, broken by a stifled gasp from Lakota. Then Rahamani the Syrian rose in his place and pronounced firmly:

'I too proclaim him.'

'I too,' said Carlin the American.

'And I,' said Valerio Rinaldi.

Then in twos and threes, old men heaved themselves to their feet with a like proclamation until all but nine were standing under the canopies, while Kiril Cardinal Lakota sat, blank-faced and rigid, on his throne.

Then Rinaldi stepped forward and challenged the electors. 'Does any here dispute that this is a valid election, and that a majority of more than two-thirds has elected our brother Kiril?'

No one answered the challenge.

'Please be seated,' said Valerio Rinaldi.

As each Cardinal sat down, he pulled the cord attached to his canopy so that it collapsed above his head, and the only canopy left open was that above the chair of Kiril Cardinal Lakota.

The Camerlengo rang a small hand bell and walked across to unlock the Chapel door. Immediately there entered the Secretary of the Conclave, the Master of Ceremonies, and the Sacristan of the Vatican. These three prelates, with Leone and Rinaldi, moved ceremoniously to the throne of the Ukrainian. In a loud voice Leone challenged him:

'*Acceptasne electionem?* Do you accept election?'

All eyes were turned on the tall, lean stranger with his scarred face and his dark beard and his distant, haunted eyes. Seconds ticked away slowly, and then in a dead flat voice, they heard him answer:

'*Accepto . . . Miserere mei Deus!* I accept. God have mercy on me!'

EXTRACT FROM THE SECRET MEMORIALS OF KIRIL I PONT. MAX.

No ruler can escape the verdict of history; but a ruler who keeps a diary makes himself liable to a rough handling by the judged. . . . I should hate to be like old Pius II, who had his memoirs attributed to his secretary, had them expurgated by his kinsmen and then, five hundred years later, had all his indiscretions restored by a pair of American blue-stockings. Yet I sympathize with his dilemma, which must be the dilemma of every man who sits in the Chair of Peter. A Pope can never talk freely unless he talks to God or to himself—and a Pontiff who talks to himself is apt to become eccentric, as the histories of some of my predecessors have shown.

It is my infirmity to be afraid of solitude and isolation. So I shall need some safety valves—the diary for one, which is a compromise between lying to oneself on paper and telling posterity the facts that have to be concealed from one's own generation. There is a rub, of course. What does one do with a papal diary? Leave it to the Vatican library? Order it buried with oneself in the triple coffin? Or auction it beforehand for the Propagation of the Faith? Better, perhaps, not to begin at all; but how else guarantee a vestige of privacy, humour, perhaps even sanity in this noble prison house to which I am condemned?

Twenty-four hours ago my election would have seemed a fantasy. Even now I cannot understand why I accepted it. I could have refused. I did not. Why?...

Consider what I am: Kiril I, Bishop of Rome, Vicar of Jesus Christ, Successor of the Prince of the Apostles, Supreme Pontiff of the Universal Church, Patriarch of the West, Primate of Italy, Archbishop and Metropolitan of the Roman Province, Sovereign of the Vatican City State.... Gloriously reigning, of course...!

But this is only the beginning of it. The Pontifical Annual will print a list two pages long of what I have reserved by way of Abbacies and Prefectures, and what I shall 'protect' by way of Orders, Congregations, Confraternities and Holy Sisterhoods. The rest of its two thousand pages will be a veritable Doomsday Book of my ministers and subjects, my instruments of government, education and correction.

I must be, by the very nature of my office, multilingual, though the Holy Ghost has been less generous in the gift of tongues to me than he was to the first man who stood in my shoes. My mother tongue is Russian; my official language is the Latin of the schoolmen, a kind of Mandarin which is supposed to preserve magically the subtlest definition of truth like a bee in amber. I must speak Italian to my associates and converse with all in that high-flown 'we' which hints at a secret converse between God and myself, even in such mundane matters as the coffee 'we' shall drink for breakfast and the brand of petrol 'we' shall use for Vatican City automobiles.

Still, this is the traditional mode and I must not resent it too much. Old Valerio Rinaldi gave me fair warning when an hour after this morning's election he offered me both his retirement and his loyalty. 'Don't try to change the Romans, Holiness. Don't try to fight them or convert them. They've been managing Popes for the last nineteen hundred years and they'll break your neck before you bend theirs. But walk softly, speak gently, keep your own counsel, and in the end you will twist them like grass round your fingers.'

It is too early, Heaven knows, to see what success Rome and I shall have with one another, but Rome is no longer the world, and I am not too much concerned—just so I can borrow experience from those who have pledged me their oaths as Cardinal Princes of the Church. There are some in whom I have great confidence. There are others ... But I must not judge too swiftly. They cannot all be like Rinaldi, who is a wise and gentle man with a sense of humour and a knowledge of his own limitations. Meantime, I must try to smile and keep a good temper while I find my way round this Vatican maze.... And I must commit my thoughts to a diary before I expose them to Curia or Consistory.

I have an advantage, of course, in that no one quite knows which way I shall jump–I don't even know myself. I am the first Slav ever to sit on the Chair of Peter, the first non-Italian for four-and-a-half centuries. The Curia will be wary of me. They may have been inspired to elect me but already they must be wondering what kind of Tartar they have caught. Already they will be asking themselves how I shall reshuffle their appointments and spheres of influence. How can they know how much I am afraid and doubtful of myself? I hope some of them will remember to pray for me.

The Papacy is the most paradoxical office in the world; the most absolute and yet the most limited; the richest in revenues but the poorest in personal return. It was founded by a Nazarene carpenter who owned no place to rest His head, yet it is surrounded by more pomp and panoply than is seemly in this hungry world. It owns no frontiers, yet is subject always to national intrigue and partisan pressure. The man who accepts it claims Divine guarantee against error, yet is less assured of salvation than the meanest of his subjects. The keys of the kingdom dangle at his belt, yet he can find himself locked out for ever from the Peace of Election and the Communion of Saints. If he says he is not tempted by autocracy and ambition, he is a liar. If he does not walk sometimes in terror, and pray often in darkness, then he is a fool.

I know–or at least I am beginning to know. I was elected this morning, and tonight I am alone on the Mountain of Desolation. He whose Vicar I am, hides His face from me. Those whose shepherd I must be do not know me. The world is spread beneath me like a campaign map–and I see balefires on every frontier. There are blind eyes upturned, and a babel of voices invoking an unknown. . .

O God, give me light to see, and strength to know, and courage to endure the servitude of the Servants of God . . .!

My valet has just been in to prepare my sleeping-quarters. He is a melancholy fellow who looks very like a guard in Siberia who used to curse me at night for a Ukrainian dog and each morning for an adulterous priest. This one, however, asks humbly if my Holiness has need of anything. Then he kneels and begs my blessing on himself and his family. Embarrassed, he ventures to suggest that, if I am not too tired, I may deign to show myself again to the people who still wait in St Peter's Square.

They acclaimed me this morning when I was led out to give my first blessing to the city and to the world. Yet, so long as my light burns, it seems there will always be some waiting for God knows what sign of power of benignity from the papal bedroom. How can I tell them that they must never expect too much from a middle-aged fellow in striped cotton pyjamas? But tonight is different. There is a whole concourse of Romans and of tourists in the Piazza, and it would be a courtesy–excuse me, Holiness, a great condescension!–to appear with one small blessing. . .

I condescend, and I am exalted once again on wave after wave of cheering and horn-blowing. I am their Pope, their Father, and they urge me to live a long time. I bless them and hold out my arms to them, and they clamour again, and I am caught in a strange heart-stopping moment when it seems that my arms encompass the world, and that it is much too heavy for me to hold. Then my valet–or is it my jailer?–draws me back, closes the window and draws the drapes, so that, officially at least, His Holiness Kiril I is in bed and asleep.

The valet's name is Celasio, which is also the name of a Pope. He is a good fellow, and I am glad of a minute of his company. We talk a few moments and then he asks me, blushing and stammering, about my name. He is the first who has dared to raise the question except old Rinaldi, who, when I announced that I desired to keep my baptismal name, nodded and smiled ironically and said, 'A noble style, Holiness–provocative, too. But for God's sake don't let them turn it into Italian.'

I took his advice, and I explained to the Cardinals as I now explain to my valet that I kept the name because it belonged to the Apostle of the Slavs, who was said to have invented the modern Cyrillic alphabet and who was a stubborn defender of the right of people to keep the faith in their own idiom. I explained to them also that I should prefer to have my name used in its Slavic form, for a testimony to the universality of the Church. Not all of them approved since they are quick to see how a man's first act sets the pattern of his later ones.

No one objected, however, except Leone, he who runs the Holy Office and has the reputation of a modern St Jerome, whether for his love of tradition, a spartan life, or a notoriously crusty temper I have yet to find out. Leone asked pointedly whether a Slavic name might not look out of place in the pure Latin of Papal Encyclicals. Although he is the one who first proclaimed me in the conclave, I had to tell him gently that I was more interested in having my encyclicals read by the people than in coddling the Latinists, and that since Russian had become a canonical language for the Marxist world, it would not hurt us to have the tip of one shoe in the other camp.

He took the reproof well, but I do not think he will easily forget it. Men who serve God professionally are apt to regard Him as a private preserve. Some of them would like to make His Vicar a private preserve as well. I do not say that Leone is one of these, but I have to be careful. I shall have to work differently from any of my predecessors, and I cannot submit myself to the dictate of any man, however high he stands, or however good he may be.

None of this, of course, is for my valet, who will take home only a simple tale of missionary saints and make himself a great man on the strength of a Pontiff's confidence. *Osservatore Romano* will tell exactly the same tale tomorrow, but for them it will be 'a symbol of the Paternal care of His Holiness for those who cleave, albeit in good faith, to schismatic communions ...' I must, as soon as I can, do something about the *Osservatore*. ... If my voice is to be heard in the world it must be heard in its authentic tones.

Already I know there are questions about my beard. I have heard murmurs of a 'too Byzantine look'. The Latins are more sensitive about such customs than we are; so perhaps it might have been a courtesy to explain that my jaw was broken under questioning and that without a beard I am somewhat disfigured ... It is so small a matter, and yet schisms have begun over smaller ones.

I wonder what Kamenev said when he heard the news of my election. I wonder whether he had humour enough to send me a greeting.

I am tired–tired to my bones and afraid. My charge is so simple: to keep the faith pure and bring the scattered sheep safely into the fold. Yet into what strange country it may lead me I can only guess ... Lead us not into temptation, O Lord, but deliver us from evil. Amen.

2

In the white marble lounge of the Foreign Press Club, George Faber stretched his elegant legs and delivered his verdict on the election:

'To the East a stumbling block, to the West a foolishness, to the Romans a disaster.'

A respectful laugh fluttered around the room. A man who had spent so many years on the Vatican beat had a right to make phrases—even bad ones. Sure of the attention of his audience, he talked on in his calm, confident voice:

'Look at it any way you like, Kiril I means a political mess. He's been a prisoner of the Russians for seventeen years, so at one stroke we wipe out any hope of rapprochement between the Vatican and the Soviets. America is involved too. I think we can expect progressive abandonment of neutralist policies, and a gradual lining up of the Vatican with the West. We are back again to the Pacelli-Spellman alliance. For Italy—' He flung out eloquent hands that embraced the whole peninsula. 'Beh!—What happens now to the Italian miracle of recovery? It was created in co-operation with the Vatican—Vatican money, Vatican prestige abroad, Vatican help in emigration, the confessional authority of the clergy holding the Left in check. What happens now? If he starts making new appointments the links between the Vatican and the Republic can be broken very quickly. The delicate balance can be tipped—' He relaxed again and turned on his colleagues a smile of charm and deprecation, the smile of king-maker. 'At least that's my story and I'm sticking to it. You may quote me with acknowledgments, and if anyone steals my lead lines, I'll sue!'

Collins of the London *Times* shrugged fastidiously and turned back to the bar with a German from Bonn. 'Faber is a mountebank, of course, but he does have a point on the Italian situation. I'm quite staggered by this election. From all I hear most of the Italians were in favour of it—though none of them gave any hint of it before they went into conclave. It's a wonderful weapon for Right or Left. The moment the Pope talks about any Italian business they can label him a foreigner, interfering in local politics. . . . That's what happened to the Dutchman—who was it, Adrian VI? The historical evidence shows him a wise man and a sound administrator, but when he died, the Church was in a bigger mess than before. I've never liked the kind of baroque Catholicism which the Italians hand out to the world, but in affairs of state they have a great political value—like the Irish, if you understand what I mean.'

'. . . for a picture story the beard is wonderful'—this from a hungry-mouthed brunette at the other end of the bar. 'And it might be fun to have a few Greek and Russian ceremonies at the Vatican. All those odd robes and those lovely dangling ikons on their chests. One could start a craze with those—pendants for the new winter fashion! Quite a line, don't you think?' She gave a high-pitched braying laugh.

'There's a mystery about it,' said Boucher, the fox-faced Frenchman. 'A complete outsider after the shortest conclave in history! I talked with Morand and with some of our own people. The impression was of desperation—as if they saw the end of the world and wanted someone special to lead us toward it. They could be right. The Chinese have gone to Moscow and the word is that they want a war now, or they will split the Marxist world down the middle. They may get it too, and then there is an end of politics, and we had all better begin to say our prayers.'

'I heard an odd one this morning.' Feuchtwanger the Swiss sipped a coffee and talked in a whisper with Erikson the Swede. 'A courier arrived in Rome yesterday from Moscow, by way of Prague and Warsaw. This morning a personage from the Russian Embassy called on Cardinal Potocki. Of course nobody is saying anything, but I wonder if Russia expects something from this man. Kamenev is in trouble with the Chinese, and he has always seen a lot further than the end of his nose. . . .'

'Strange,' said Fedorov the Tass man softly, 'strange! Wherever you turn today you feel the finger of Kamenev, even in this—name him or not you see his touch.'

Beron the Czech nodded wisely but said nothing. The great Kamenev was beyond the reach of his humble pen, and after twenty years of survival he had learned that it was better to say nothing for a year than to permit himself a moment's indiscretion.

The Russian talked on with the quiet zeal of the orthodox. 'Months ago I heard a rumour—it was only a rumour then—that Kamenev had organized this man's escape, and that the Praesidium would have his head for it. Now, although we have been told to say nothing, the secret is out. It was Kamenev. And he must be laughing in his sleeve to see a man on whom he has left his mark, sitting on the Apostolic throne.'

'And what does the Praesidium think of it?' asked the Czech cautiously.

Fedorov shrugged and spread his stubby fingers on the table. 'They approve, of course—why should they not? Kamenev's mark is on every one of them too. Besides, the man is a genius. Who else could have done what all the Five Year Plans could not do—brought the Siberian plains into flower? From the Baltic to Bulgaria, look what he has done! For the first time we have peace in the Western marches. Even the Poles don't hate us too much any more. We are exporting grain. Think of it! I tell you, whatever this man does the Praesidium and the people cannot fail to approve.'

The Czech nodded soberly and then asked another question. 'This, this mark of Kamenev—what is it?'

The Tass man sipped his drink thoughtfully, and then said, 'He spoke about it once, I believe. I was not there but I heard echoes of it. He said, "Once you have taken a man to pieces under questioning, once you have laid out the bits on the table and put them together again, then a strange thing happens. Either you love him or you hate him for the rest of your life. He will either love you or hate you in return. You cannot lead a man or a people through hell without wishing to share a heaven with them too." That's why our own people love him. He put them on the rack for three years and then suddenly showed them a new world.' He downed his drink at one gulp and slapped the glass on the table. 'A great man, the greatest we have had since Peter the Emperor!'

'And this Pope—this Kiril—what sort of a man will he be?'

'I don't know,' said the Russian thoughtfully. 'If Kamenev loves him, strange things may happen. Strange things may happen to both of them.'

He was not yet crowned, but already Kiril the Pope had felt the impact of power. The shock of it was greater than he had ever dreamed. Two thousand years of time and all of eternity were now given into his hands. Five hundred million people were his subjects, and his tribute came in every coinage of the world. He could walk, as he walked each day now in the gardens of the Vatican, and measure the confines of his kingdom in a day's stroll; yet this narrow domain was only a foothold from which his power reached out to encompass the tilted planet.

The men who had made him, he could now unmake with a word. The treasures of the centuries which they delivered to him with the Keys, he could dispense at will or dissipate with a fool's gesture. His bureaucracy was more complex and yet more cheaply run than any other in the world. The toy soldiers who guarded his sacred presence were backed by thousands of levies bound to him by vow to serve with their talent, their hearts, their will and all their celibate lives. Other men held dominion by the fickle voice of voters, by the pressure of party alignment, or by the tyranny of military juntas. He alone in all the world held it by divine delegation, and no one of all his subjects dared gainsay it.

Yet the knowledge of power was one thing, the use of it was quite another. Whatever his plans for the Church, whatever changes he might make in the future, he had for the present to use the instruments at his disposal and the organization which his predecessors had transmitted to him. He had to learn so much so quickly; and yet in the days before his coronation, it seemed almost as if there were a conspiracy to rob him of the time to think or plan. There were moments when he felt like a puppet being dressed and rehearsed for the theatre.

The cobblers came to measure him for new slippers, the tailors to stitch his white cassocks. The jewellers offered their designs for his ring and his pectoral cross. The heralds presented their drawings for his coat of arms: crossed keys for Peter's charge, a bear rampant on a white ground, above it the dove of the Paraclete, and, beneath, the motto, '*Ex oriente lux*. A light out of the East.'

He approved it at first glance. It appealed to his imagination and to his sense of humour. It took time to lick a bear into shape–but once he was full-grown he was a very formidable fellow. With the Holy Ghost to guide him, he might hope to do much for the Church. And perhaps the East had been dark too long because the West had given too local a shape to a universal Gospel.

The chamberlains led him through audience after audience–with the press, with the diplomatic corps, with the noble families who claimed place about the papal throne, with prefects and secretaries of congregations and tribunals and commissions. The Chancellery of Briefs and the Secretariat of Briefs to Princes kept his desk piled with replies in impeccable Latin to all the letters and telegrams of felicitation. The Secretariat of State reminded him daily of crisis and revolution and the intrigues of the embassies.

At every step he stubbed his pontifical toe on history, ritual, and protocol and the cumbersome methodology of Vatican bureaucracy. Wherever he turned there was an official at his elbow directing His Holiness's attention to this or that–an office to be filled, a courtesy to be bestowed, or talent to be elevated.

The setting was grandiose, the stage management was sedulous, but it took him nearly a week to find out the title of the play. It was an old Roman comedy once popular, but now fallen into some disrepute: its title was, 'The Management of Princes'. The theme was simple–how to give a man absolute power and then to limit his use of it. The technique was to make him feel so important and to keep him so busy with pompous trifles that he had no time to think out a policy or put it into execution.

When he saw the joke, Kiril the Ukrainian laughed privately and decided to make a joke of his own.

So, two days before his coronation, he summoned without warning a private meeting of all the Cardinals in the Borgia rooms of the Vatican. The abruptness of the call was calculated, and the risk of it was calculated too.

The day after his coronation, all but the Cardinals of the Curia would leave Rome and return to their own countries. Each could prove a willing adjutant or a discreet hindrance to papal policy. One did not become a prince of the Church without some ambition and some taste for power. One did not grow old in office without some hardening of heart and will. They were more than subjects, these hinge-men, they were counsellors also, jealous of their own Apostolic succession and of the autonomy conferred by it. Even a Pope must deal delicately with them and not strain too far their wisdom, their loyalty, or their national pride.

When he saw them seated before him, old and wise and shrewdly expectant, Kiril's heart sank and he asked himself for the hundredth time what he had to offer to them and to the Church. Then once again it seemed as though power renewed itself in him, and he made the Sign of the Cross, an invocation to the Holy Ghost, and then plunged into the business of the Consistory. He did not use the 'we' of authority, but spoke intimately and personally, as if anxious to establish a relation of friendship:

'My brothers, my helpers in the cause of Christ—' His voice was strong, yet strangely tender, as if he pleaded with them for fraternity and understanding. 'What I am today you have made me. Yet if what we believe is true, it is not you, but God who has set me in these shoes of the Fisherman. Day and night I have asked myself what I have to offer to Him or to His Church–I have so little, you see. I am a man who was wrenched out of life like Lazarus, and then drawn back into it by the hand of God. All of you are men of your time. You have grown with it, you have been changed by it, you have contributed to change it for better or for worse. It is natural that each of you should guard jealously that place and that knowledge, and that authority which you have earned for yourselves in time. Now, however, I must ask you to be generous with me and lend me what you have of knowledge and experience in the name of God.' His voice faltered a little, and to the old men it seemed for a moment as if he were about to weep. Then he recovered himself, and seemed to grow in size, while his voice took on a stronger tone. 'Unlike you I am not a man of my time–because I have spent seventeen years in prison and time has passed me by. So much of the world is a novelty to me. The only thing that is not new is man, and him I know and love because I have lived with him for so long in the simple intimacy of survival. Even the Church is strange to me because I have had to dispense for so long with what is unnecessary in it, and I have had to cling the more desperately to that which is of its nature and its essence–the Deposit of Faith, the Sacrifice and the Sacramental Acts.'

For the first time he smiled at them, sensing their uneasiness and trying to calm them. 'I know the thought that is in your mind—that you may have for Pope an innovator, a man avid for change. This is not so. Though much change is necessary, we must make it together. I try simply to explain myself so that you may understand me and help me. I cannot cling as zealously as some to ritual and to traditional forms of devotion because for years I have held to nothing but the simplest forms of prayer and the bare essentials of the Sacraments. I know, believe me, I know, that there are those for whom the straightest road is the safest one. I wish them to be as free as possible inside the bond of the faith. I do not wish to change the long tradition of a celibate clergy. I myself am celibate as you are. Yet I have seen the faith preserved under persecution by married priests who have handed it to their children like a jewel in silk. I cannot grow hot over the legalities of the canonists or the rivalries of religious congregations because I have seen women raped by their jailers, and I have delivered their children with these consecrated hands.'

Once again he smiled and threw out his crooked hands to them in a gesture of pleading. 'I am perhaps the wrong man for you, my brothers—but God has given me to you and you must make the best of me.'

There was a long pause and then he went on more strongly still, not pleading, not explaining, but demanding with all the power that surged within him:

'You ask me where I want to lead you, where I want to lead the Church. I will show you. I want to lead you back to God, through men. Understand this, understand it in mind and heart and obedient will. We are what we are, for the service of God through the service of man. If we lose contact with man—suffering, sinful, lost, confused men crying in the night, women agonizing, children weeping—then we too are lost because we shall be negligent shepherds who have done everything but the one thing necessary.' He broke off and stood facing them, tall, pale and strange, with his scarred face, and his crooked hands, and his black Byzantine beard. Then he handed them like a challenge the formal Latin question:

'*Quid vobis videtur?* How does it seem to you?'

There was a ritual to cover this moment, just as there was a ritual to cover every act of Vatican life. The Cardinals would remove their red caps and bow their heads in submission, and then wait to be dismissed to do or not to do that which they had been counselled. A papal allocution was rarely a dialogue, but this time there was a sense of urgency and even of conflict in the assembly.

Cardinal Leone heaved his lion's bulk out of his chair, tossed his white mane, and addressed himself to the Pontiff. 'All of us here have pledged to Your Holiness and to the Church the service of our lives. Yet we should not discharge this service if we did not offer counsel when we believed counsel was necessary.'

'This is what I have asked of you,' said Kiril mildly. 'Please speak freely.'

Leone made a grave acknowledgment and then went on firmly. 'It is too early yet to measure the effect of Your Holiness's election upon the world at large, and especially upon the Roman and Italian Church. I mean no disrespect when I say that until we know this reaction there should be a prudence, a reserve in public utterance and public action.'

'I have no quarrel with that,' said Kiril in the same mild fashion. 'But you must not quarrel with me when I tell you that I want the voice of Kiril to be heard by all men—not another voice, in another accent or another mode, but my voice. A father does not speak to his son through an actor's mask. He speaks simply, freely, and from the heart, and this is what I propose to do.'

The old lion held his ground and went on stubbornly. 'There are realities to be faced, Holiness. The voice will change, no matter what you do. It will issue from the mouth of a Mexican peasant and an English academician and a German missionary in the Pacific. It will be interpreted by a hostile press or a theatrical television correspondent. The most Your Holiness can expect is that the first voice shall be yours, and the first record shall be the authentic one.' He permitted himself a grim smile. 'We too are your voices, Holiness, and even we may find it hard to render the score perfectly.' He sat down amid a small rustle of approval.

Then Pallenberg, the lean, cold man from Germany, took the floor and presented his own problem. 'Your Holiness has spoken of changes. It is my view and the view of my brother bishops that certain changes are long overdue. We are a divided country. We have an immense prosperity and a dubious future. There is a drift of the Catholic population away from the Church because our women must marry outside it, since our males were decimated during the war. Our problems in this regard are legion. We can only solve them at the human level. Yet here in Rome they are being dealt with by Monsignori who cannot even speak our language, who work solely by the canons and who have no sense of our history or of our present problems. They delay, they temporize, they centralize. They treat the affairs' of souls as if they were entries in a ledger. Our burden is great enough, we cannot carry Rome on our backs as well–for myself and for my brethren, *Appello ad Petrum*. I appeal to Peter!'

There was an audible gasp at so much bluntness. Leone flushed angrily and Rinaldi hid a smile behind a silk handkerchief.

After a moment Kiril the Pope spoke again. His tone was as mild as ever, but this time they noticed he used the plural of royalty. 'We promise our German brothers that we shall give immediate and full consideration to their special problems and we shall confer with them privately before they return to their homeland. We would urge them, however, to patience and to charity with their colleagues in Rome. They should remember, too, that often things are left undone from habit and from tradition, rather than from lack of good will.' He paused a moment, letting the reproof sink in; then he chuckled. 'I have had my own troubles with another bureaucracy. Even the men who tormented me did not lack good will. They wanted to build a new world in one generation, but the bureaucracy beat them each time. Let us see if we can find ourselves more priests and fewer bureaucrats–fewer clerks and more simple souls who understand the human heart.'

Now it was the turn of the Frenchman, and he was no less blunt than Pallenberg. 'Whatever we do in France–whatever we propose from France comes here to Rome under the shadow of old history. Every one of our projects, from the worker priests to studies in the development of dogma and the creation of an intelligent Catholic press, is greeted as if it were a new tramontane rebellion. We cannot work freely or with continuity in this climate. We cannot feel ourselves helped by the fraternity of the Church if a cloud of censure hangs over everything we plan or propose.' He swung around angrily and flung out a challenge to the Italians. 'There are heresies here in Rome too, and this is one of them: that unity and uniformity are the same thing, that the Roman way is best for everyone from Hong Kong to Peru. Your Holiness has expressed the wish to have his voice heard in its true tone. We too wish to have our voice heard without distortion at the throne of Peter. Appointments need to be made, men who can represent us and the climate in which we live, truthfully and with understanding.'

'You touch on a problem,' said Kiril carefully, 'which preoccupies us as well. We ourselves carry the burden of history so that we cannot always deal with the simplicity of a matter but must consider a complexity of colorations and historic associations.' He raised a hand to his beard and smiled. 'Even this I understand to be a source of scandal to some although our Master and the first Apostles were all bearded men. I should hate to think that the rock of Peter should split for want of a razor. *Quid vobis videtur?*'

In that moment they laughed and loved him. Their anger with one another subsided, and they listened more humbly while the men from the South Americas told of their own problems: impoverished populations, a scarcity of trained clergy, the historic association of the Church with the wealthy and the exploiters, lack of funds, the strength of the Marxist idea held up like a torch to rally the dispossessed.

Came then the men from the East, telling how the frontiers were closing one by one on the Christian idea. And how one by one the old missionary foundations were being destroyed while the idea of an earthly paradise took hold of the minds of men who needed it so desperately because they had so little time to enjoy it. It was a brutal balance sheet for men who had to make their reckoning with the Almighty. And when finally it was done, there was a silence over the whole assembly, and they waited for Kiril the Pontiff to make his final summation.

He rose then in his place and confronted them—a figure oddly young, oddly alone, like a Christ from a Byzantine triptych. 'There are those,' he told them solemnly, 'who believe that we are come to the last age of the world because man has now the power to destroy himself from the face of the earth, and every day the danger grows greater that he will do it. Yet we, my brothers, have no more or no less to offer for the world's salvation than we had in the beginning. We preach Christ and Him crucified—to the Jews, indeed a stumbling block and to the Gentiles, foolishness. This is the folly of the faith, and if we are not committed to it then we are committed to an illusion. What do we do, therefore? From this point where do we go? I believe there is only one way. We take the truth like a lamp and we walk out like the first Apostles to tell the good tidings to whoever will listen. If history stands in our way we ignore it. If systems inhibit us we dispense with them. If dignities weigh us down we cast them aside. I have one commission now for all of you—for those who are going away from Rome and those who stay here in the shadow of our triumphs and our sins—find me men! Find me good men who understand what it is to love God and love His children. Find me men with fire in their hearts and wings on their feet. Send them to me, and I will send them out to bring love to the loveless and hope to those who sit in darkness . . . Go now in the name of God!'

Immediately after the Consistory, Potocki, the Cardinal from Poland, presented a petition for an urgent and private audience with the Pope. To his surprise it was answered within an hour by an invitation to dinner. When he arrived at the papal apartment, he found the new Pontiff alone, sitting in an armchair, reading a small volume bound in faded leather. When he knelt to make his obedience, Kiril stretched out a hand and raised him to his feet with a smile.

'Tonight we should be brothers together. The cooking is bad, and I haven't had time to reform the papal kitchens. I hope your company will give me a better dinner than usual.' He pointed to the yellowed pages of the book, and chuckled. 'Our friend Rinaldi has a sense of humour. He gave me a present to celebrate my election. It is an account of the reign of the Dutchman, Adrian VI. Do you know what they called the Cardinals who elected him? "Betrayers of Christ's blood, who surrendered the fair Vatican to foreign fury, and handed the Church and Italy into slavery with the barbarians." I wonder what they are saying about you and me at this moment?' He shut the book with a snap and relaxed once again in the chair. 'It is only the beginning, and yet I do so badly, and I feel myself so much alone . . . How can I help you, my friend?'

Potocki was touched by the charm of his new master, but the habit of caution was strong in him and he contented himself with a formality. 'A letter was delivered to me this morning, Holiness. I am told that it comes from Moscow. I was asked to deliver it directly into your hands.' He brought out a bulky envelope sealed with grey wax and handed it to Kiril, who held it a moment in his hands and then laid it on the table.

'I shall read it later, and if it should concern you as well, I shall call you. Now tell me . . .' He leaned forward in his chair, begging earnestly for a confidence. 'You did not speak in the Consistory today, and yet you have as many problems as the others. I want to hear them.'

Potocki's lined face tightened and his eyes clouded. 'There is a private fear first, Holiness.'

'Share it with me,' said Kiril gently. 'I have so many of my own, it may make me feel better.'

'History sets snares for all of us,' said the Pole gravely. 'Your Holiness knows this. The history of the Ruthenian Church in Poland is a bitter one. We have not always acted like brothers in the faith, but like enemies one to another. The time of dissension is past, but if Your Holiness were to remember it too harshly, it could be bad for us all. We Poles are Latin by temper and loyalty. Time was when the Polish Church lent itself to persecution of its brothers in the Ruthenian rite. We were both young then, but it is possible—and we both know it—that many might have lived who are now dead had we kept the unity of the Spirit in the bond of faith.' He hesitated and then stumbled awkwardly through the next question. 'I mean no disrespect, Holiness, but I must ask with loyalty what others will ask with a false purpose: how does your Holiness feel about us in Poland? How do you regard what we are trying to do?'

There was a long pause. Kiril the Pontiff looked down at his gnarled hands and then abruptly heaved himself from the chair and laid his hands on the shoulders of his brother bishop. He said softly, 'We have both been in prison, you and I. We both know that when they tried to break us, it was not with the love we had, but with the resentments that we had buried deep inside us. When you sat in the darkness, trembling and waiting for the next session with the lights, and the pain, and the questions, what tempted you most?'

'Rome,' said Potocki bluntly, 'where they knew so much, and seemed to care so little.'

Kiril the Pontiff smiled and nodded gravely. 'For me it was the memory of the great Andrew Szepticky, Metropolitan of Galicia. I loved him like a father. I hated bitterly what had been done to him. I remembered him before he died, a hulk of a man, paralysed, torn with pain, watching all that he had built being destroyed, the houses of education, the seminaries, the old culture he had tried so hard to preserve. I was oppressed by the futility of it all, and I wondered whether it were worth spending so many lives, so many more noble spirits, to try again. . . . Those were bad days, and worse nights.'

Potocki flushed to the roots of his thin hair. 'I am ashamed, Holiness. I should not have doubted.'

Kiril shrugged and smiled wryly. 'Why not? We are all human. You are walking a tightrope in Poland, I am walking another in Rome. Both of us may slip, and we shall need a net to catch us. I beg you to believe that if I sometimes lack understanding, I do not lack love.'

'What we do in Warsaw,' said Potocki, 'is not always understood in Rome.'

'If you need an interpreter,' said Kiril briskly, 'send me one. I promise him always a ready hearing.'

'There will be so many, Holiness, and they will speak in so many tongues. How can you attend to them all?'

'I know.' Kiril's thin frame seemed suddenly to shrink as if under a burden. 'Strange. We profess and we teach that the Pontiff is preserved from fundamental error by the indwelling of the Holy Spirit. I pray but I hear no thunder on the mountain. My eyes see no splendours on the hills. I stand between God and man, but I hear only man and the voice of my heart.'

For the first time the harsh face of the Pole relaxed, and he spread his hands in a gesture of willing defeat. 'Listen to that, Holiness. *Cor ad cor loquitur*. Heart speaks to heart, and this may well be God's dialogue with men.'

'Let's go to dinner,' said Kiril the Pontiff, 'and forgive my nuns their heavy hand with the sauce. They are worthy creatures, but I will have to find them a good cookery book.'

They ate no better than he had promised, and they drank a thin young wine from the Alban hills; but they talked more freely, and a warmth grew between them, and when they came to the fruit and the cheese, Kiril the Pontiff opened his heart on another matter.

'In two days I am to be crowned. It is a small thing, perhaps, but I am troubled by so much ceremony. The Master came into Jerusalem riding on a donkey. I am to be carried on the shoulders of nobles between the plumed fans of a Roman Emperor. All over the world are barefoot men with empty bellies. I am to be crowned with gold, and my triumph will be lit with a million lights. I am ashamed that the successor of the Carpenter should be treated like a king. I should like to change it.'

Potocki gave a thin smile, and shook his head. 'They will not let you do it, Holiness.'

'I know.' Kiril's fingers toyed with the broken crumbs on his plate. 'I belong to the Romans, too, and they must have their holiday. I cannot walk down the nave of St Peter's because I could not be seen, and even if the visitors do not come to pray, they do come to see the Pontiff. I am a prince by treaty, they remind me, and a prince must wear a crown.'

'Wear it, Holiness,' said Potocki with grim humour. 'Wear it for the day and do not trouble yourself. Soon enough they will crown you with thorns!'

An hour away at his villa in the Alban hills, Valerio Cardinal Rinaldi was giving his own dinner party. His guests made a curious yet powerful assemblage, and he managed them with the skill of a man who had just proved himself a king-maker.

Leone was there, and Semmering the Father General of the Jesuits, whom the vulgar called the 'Black Pope'. There were Goldoni from the Secretariat of State, and Benedetti, the prince of Vatican finances, and Orlando Campeggio, the shrewd, swarthy fellow who was the editor of *Osservatore Romano*. At the foot of the table, as if for a concession to the mystics, sat Rahamani the Syrian, soft, complaisant, and always unexpected.

The meal was served on a belvedere which looked down on a classic garden, once the site of an Orphic temple, and beyond it to the farmlands and the distant glow of Rome. The air was mild, the night was full of stars, and Rinaldi's assiduous servants had coaxed them into comfort with one another.

Campeggio, the layman, smoked his cigar and talked freely, a prince among the princes. '. . . First it seems we have to present the Pontiff in the most acceptable light. I have thought a great deal about this, and you will all have read what we have already done in the press. The theme so far has been "in prison for the faith". The reaction to this has been good—a wave of sympathy—an expression of lively affection and loyalty. Of course this is only the beginning, and it does not solve all our problems. Our next thought was to present "a Pope of the people". We may need some assistance with this, particularly from an Italian point of view. Fortunately, he speaks good Italian and therefore can communicate himself in public functions, and in contacts with the populace. . . . Here we shall need both direction and assistance from the members of the Curia . . .' He was a deft man, and he broke off at this point, leaving the proposition for the clerics.

It was Leone who took it up, worrying it in his stubborn fashion, while he peeled an apple and sliced it with a silver knife. 'Nothing is quite as simple as it sounds. We have to present him, yes, but we have to edit him and comment him as well. You heard what went on in the Consistory today.' He thrust the knife blade at Rinaldi and Rahamani. 'Print what he said baldly and without explanation, and it would read as if he were ready to throw two thousand years of tradition out of the window. I saw his point, we all did, but I saw too where we have to protect him.'

'Where is that?' Semmering, the spare, blond Jesuit, leaned forward in his place.

'He showed us his own Achilles' heel,' said Leone firmly. 'He said he was a man who had dropped out of time. He will need, I think, to be reminded constantly what our times are and what instruments we have to work with.'

'Do you think he is unaware of them?' asked the Jesuit again.

Leone frowned. 'I'm not sure. I have not yet begun to read his mind. All I know is that he is asking for something new, before he has had time to examine what is old and permanent in the Church.'

'As I remember,' said the Syrian mildly, 'he asked us to find him men. This is not new. Men are the foundation of every Apostolic work. How did he say it? "Men with fire in their hearts and wings on their feet."'

'We have forty thousand men,' said the Jesuit dryly, 'and they are all bound to him by solemn vows of service. We stand, all of us, at his call.'

'Not all of us,' said Rinaldi without rancour. 'And we should be honest enough to confess it. We move familiarly where he must move for a while awkwardly and strangely, in the headquarters of the Church. We accept the inertia and the ambition, and the bureaucracy, because we have been bred to it, and in part we have helped to build it. You know what he said to me yesterday?' He paused like an actor waiting for their attention to focus on him. 'He said, "I celebrated Mass once in seventeen years. I lived where hundreds of millions will die without having seen a priest or heard the word of God, yet here I see hundreds of priests stamping documents and punching time-clocks like common clerks . . ." I understand his point of view.'

'What does he expect us to do?' asked Benedetti acidly. 'Run the Vatican with IBM machines, and put all the priests in the mission fields? No man can be as naïve as that.'

'I don't think he is naïve,' said Leone. 'Far from it. But I think he may discount too readily what Rome means to the Church—for order and discipline, and a stewardship of the faith.'

For the first time Goldoni, the grey, stocky man from the Secretariat of State, entered the argument. His harsh, Roman voice crackled like twigs in a fire, as he gave his own version of the new Pontiff. 'He has been in to see me several times. He does not summon me, but walks in quietly and asks questions of me and of my staff. I have the impression that he understands politics very well, especially Marxist politics, but he is little interested in details and personalities. He uses one word often, *pressure*. He asks where the pressures begin in each country, and how they act on the people, and on those who rule them. When I asked him to explain, he said that the faith was planted in men by God, but that the Church had to be built on the human and material resource of each country, and that, to survive, it had to withstand the pressures that were suffered by the mass of the people. He said something else too: that we have centralized too much, and we have delayed too long to train those who can maintain the universality of the Church in the autonomy of a national culture. He spoke of vacuums created by Rome—vacuums in classes and countries—and local clergies . . . I do not know how enlightened his own policies may be, but he is not blind to the defects of those which already exist.'

'The new broom,' said Benedetti tartly. 'He wants to sweep all the rooms at once . . . He can read a balance sheet too! He objects that we have so much in credit, while there is so much poverty in Uruguay, or among the Urdus. I ask myself if he really understands that forty years ago the Vatican was almost bankrupt and Gasparri had to borrow ten thousand sterling pounds to finance the papal election. Now at least we can pay our way, and move with some strength for the good of the Church.'

'When he spoke to us,' said Rahamani again, 'I did not hear him mention money. I was reminded how the first Apostles were sent out with neither scrip nor stave nor money for the road. As I heard the story, that is how our Kiril came from Siberia to Rome.'

'Possibly,' said Benedetti irritably. 'But have you ever looked at the travel bills for a pair of missionaries—or worked out how much it costs to train a seminary teacher?'

Abruptly Leone threw back his white mane and laughed, so that the night birds stirred in the cypresses and the echoes rolled down over the starlit valley. 'That's it. We elected him in the name of God and now suddenly we're afraid of him. He has made no threat, he has changed no appointment, he has asked nothing but what we profess to offer. Yet, here we sit weighing him like conspirators, and making ready to fight him. What has he done to us?'

'Perhaps he has read us better than we like,' said Semmering the Jesuit.

'Perhaps,' said Valerio Rinaldi, 'perhaps he trusts us more than we deserve. . .'

EXTRACT FROM THE SECRET MEMORIALS OF KIRIL I PONT. MAX.

. . . It is late and the moon is climbing high. The Square of St Peter is empty, but the rumour of the city still reaches me on the night wind—footsteps sounding hollow on stones, a scream of motor tyres, the bleat of a horn, snatches of far-away song, and the slow clip-clop of a tired horse. I am wakeful tonight, and I resent my solitude. I want to walk out through the Angelic Gate and find my people where they stroll or sit together in the alleys of Trastevere, or huddle in narrow rooms with their fears and their loves. I need them so much more than they need me.

One day soon I must do this. I must shrug off the bonds which are laid upon me by protocol and precaution, and confront this city of mine, so that I may see it and it may see me as we truly are. . .

I remember the stories of my childhood, how the Caliph Haroun disguised himself and walked out with his vizier at night to search the hearts of his people. I remember how Jesus the Master sat at meat with tax-gatherers and public women, and I wonder why His successors were so eager to assume the penalty of princes, which is to rule from a secret room and to display oneself like a demi-God only on occasions of public festivity. . .

It has been a long day but I have learned something of myself and of others too. I made a mistake, I think, in the Consistory. When men are old and powerful, they need to be drawn by reason and calculation, because the sap of the heart dries up with age. . .

When one is in a position of power, one must not show oneself publicly humble, because the ruler must reassure with strength and a show of decision. If one displays one's heart, it must be in private, so that the man who sees it will believe that he has received a confidence. . .

I am writing like a cynic, and I am ashamed of it. Why? Perhaps because I was confronted with strong men who were determined to bend me to their opinions. . .

Leone was the one who irritated me most of all. I had hoped for an ally, and instead I found a critic. I am tempted to appoint him to another office, and remove him from the position of influence which he now holds. Yet this, I think, would be a mistake, and the beginning of greater ones. If I surround myself with weak and compliant men, I shall rob the Church of noble servants . . . and in the end I shall be left without counsellors. Leone is a formidable fellow and I think we shall find ourselves opposed to each other on many issues. But I do not see him as an intriguer. I should like to have him for my friend, because I am a man who needs friendship, yet I do not think he will surrender himself so far. . .

I should like to keep Rinaldi by me, but I think I must consent to his retirement. He is not, I think, a profound man, though he is a subtle and an able one. I sense that he has come to grips with God very late in his life and that he needs a freedom to audit the accounts of his soul. This, fundamentally, is why I am here, to show men the staircase to union with God. If anyone stumbles on my account, then I shall be the one to answer for it. . .

Kamenev's letter is open before me, and beside it is his gift for my coronation—a few grains of Russian soil and a package of sunflower seeds.

'I do not know,' he writes, 'whether the seeds will grow in Rome, but perhaps if you mix a little Russian earth with them they will bloom for next summer. I remember that I asked you during one interrogation what you missed most of all, and you smiled and said the sunflowers in the Ukraine. I hated you at that moment because I was missing them too, and we were both exiles in the frozen lands. Now you are still an exile, while I am the first man in Russia.

'Do you regret us? I wonder. I should like to think so because I regret you. We could have done great things together, you and I; but you were wedded to this wild dream of the hereafter, while I believed, as I still believe, that the best a man can do is make barren earth fruitful and ignorant men wise, and see the children of puny fathers grow tall and straight among the sunflowers.

'It would I suppose be courteous to congratulate you on your election. For what they are worth, you have my compliments. I am curious to know what this office will do to you. I let you go because I could not change you, and yet I could not bring myself to degrade you any more. It would shame me now if you were to be corrupted by eminence.

'We may yet have need of each other, you and I. You have not seen the half of it, yet I tell you truly we have brought this country to a prosperity she has not known in all her centuries. Yet we are ringed with swords. The Americans are afraid of us; the Chinese resent us and want to drag us fifty years back in history. We have fanatics inside our own borders who are not content with bread and peace and work for all, but want to turn us all back into bearded mystics from Dostoevsky.

'To you perhaps I am anti-Christ. What I believe you reject utterly. But, for the present, I am Russia, and I am the guardian of this people. You have weapons in your hands, and I know, though I dare not admit it publicly, how strong they are. I can only hope you will not turn them against your homeland, nor pledge them to a base alliance in East or West.

'When the seeds begin to grow, remember Mother Russia, and remember that you owe me a life. When the time comes to claim payment, I shall send you a man who will talk of sunflowers. Believe what he tells you, but deal with no others, now or later. Unlike you I do not have the Holy Ghost to protect me, and I must still be wary of my friends. I wish I could say that you were one. Greetings. Kamenev.'

. . . I have read the letter a dozen times, and I cannot decide whether it brings me to the fringe of a revelation or to the edge of a precipice. I know Kamenev as intimately as he knows me, yet I have not reached down to the core of his soul. I know the ambition that drives him, his fanatic desire to exact some goodness from life to pay for the debasement he inflicted on himself and others for so many years. . .

I have seen peasants scoop up a handful of soil from a new plot and taste it, to see whether it was sweet or sour. I can imagine Kamenev doing the same with the soil of Russia.

I know how the ghosts of history threaten him and his people because I understand how they threaten me too. I do not see him as anti-Christ, nor even as an arch-heretic. He has understood and accepted the Marxist dogma as the swiftest and sharpest instrument yet devised to trigger a social revolution. I think he would throw it aside the moment he saw it fail of its purpose. I think, though I cannot be sure, that he is asking my help to preserve what he has already won of good for the people, and to give it a chance to grow peacefully into other mutations.

I believe that having thrust himself up so high he has begun to breathe a freer air and to wish the same fortune for a people he has learned to love. If this be true, then I must help him. ...

Yet there are events which give him the lie at every moment. There are invasions and forays on every frontier, under the banner of the sickle and the star. Men are still starved and beaten, and locked away from the free commerce of thought and the channels of Grace.

The great heresy of the earthly paradise still creeps across the world like a cancer, and Kamenev still wears the robe of its High Priest. This I am pledged to fight, and I have already resisted it with my blood...

Yet I cannot ignore the strange working of God in the souls of the most unlikely men, and I believe I can see this working in the soul of Kamenev. . . . I see, though only dimly, how our destinies may be linked in the divine design. . . . What I cannot see is how to comport myself in the situation which exists between us. . . .

He asks for my friendship, and I would gladly give him my heart. He asks, I think, for a kind of truce, yet I cannot make truce with error, though I can ascribe the noblest motives to those who propagate it. I dare not, however, place the Church and the faithful in jeopardy for an illusion, because I know that Kamenev could still betray me, and I could still betray myself and the Church.

What do I do?

Perhaps the answer is in the sunflower–that the seed must die before the green shoots come, that the flower must grow while men pass by, heedless that a miracle is taking place under their noses.

Perhaps this is what is meant by 'waiting upon the mercy of God'. But we cannot only wait because the nature with which He has endowed us drives us to action. We must pray too in darkness and dryness, under a blind sky...

Tomorrow I shall offer Mass for Kamenev, and tonight I must pray for light for Kiril the Pontiff, whose heart is restless and whose vagrant soul still hungers for its homeland . . .

3

For George Faber, the coronation of Kiril I was a long and elaborate boredom. The ovations deafened him, the lights gave him a headache, the sonorities of the choir depressed his spirit, and the gaudy procession of prelates, priests, monks, chamberlains and toy soldiers was an operatic cavalcade, which pricked him to resentment and gave him no entertainment at all. The exhalation of eighty thousand bodies, jammed like sardines into every corner of the Basilica, made him feel faint and nauseated.

His copy was already written and filed for transmission: three thousand glowing words on the pageantry and symbolism and religious splendour of this Roman festal day. He had seen it all before, and there was no reason for him to repeat the tedium except, perhaps, the snobbery of sitting in the place of honour in the press box, resplendent in a new frock-coat, with the ribbon of his latest Italian decoration bright upon his chest.

Now he was paying for the indulgence. His buttocks were jammed tight between the broad hips of a German and the angular thighs of Campeggio, and there would be no escape for at least two hours, until the distinguished congregation broke out into the Square to receive the blessing of the new-crowned Pope with the humbler citizens and tourists of Rome.

Exasperated, he slumped forward in his seat and tried to find a grain of consolation in what this Kiril might mean to himself and Chiara. So far the Curia had kept him tightly in wraps. He had made few public appearances, and no pronouncements of any moment at all. But the word was already about that this was an innovator, a man young enough and strange enough to have a mind of his own and the vigour to express it in action. There were rumours of rough words in the Consistory, and more than one Vatican official was talking of changes, not only in personnel, but in the whole central organization as well.

If changes were made, some of them might affect the Holy Roman Rota, where the petition of nullity for Chiara's marriage had lain in the pigeonholes for nearly two years. The Italians had a wry-mouthed joke for the workings of this august body: '*Non c'e divorzio in Italia.* There is no divorce in Italy–and only Catholics can get it!' Like most Italian jokes, this one had more than one barb to it. Neither Church nor State admitted the possibility of divorce, but both viewed with apparent equanimity a large-scale concubinage among the rich and a growing number of irregular unions among the poor.

The Rota was by constitution a clerical body, but much of its business was in the hands of lay lawyers, specialists in canon law, who formed, for mutual profit, a union as rigid and exclusive as any in the world so that the business of marital causes banked up in a bottleneck, regardless of the human tragedies which underlay most of them.

In theory the Rota must adjudicate equally for those who could pay and for those who could not. In practice the paying petitioner, or the petitioner with Roman influence or Roman friendship, could count on quicker decisions by far than his poorer brethren in the faith. The law was the same for all, but its decisions were dispensed more swiftly to those who could command the best service from the advocates.

The tag of the joke made another point as well. A decree of nullity was much easier to obtain if both partners to the marriage consented to the first petition. If *Error* had to be proved in the contract, or *Conditio*, or *Crimen*, it was much easier to do it with two voices. But if one partner only made a petition and the other presented contradictory evidence, the case was doomed to a slow progress and to very probable failure.

In such cases, the Rota made a neat, if hardly satisfying distinction: that, in the private forum of conscience–and, therefore, in fact–the contract might be null and void; but until it could be proved so in the external forum, by documented evidence, the two parties must be regarded as married, even though they did not live together. If the aggrieved party obtained a divorce and remarried outside the country, he or she would be excommunicated by the Church and prosecuted for bigamy by the State.

In practice, therefore, concubinage was the easier state in Italy, since it was more comfortable to be damned inside the Church than out of it, and one was much happier loving in sin than serving a prison sentence in the Regina Coeli.

The which precisely was the situation for George Faber and Chiara Calitri.

As he watched the new Pontiff being vested by his assistants in front of the High Altar, Faber wondered sourly how much he knew or could ever hope to know of the intimate tragedies of his subjects, of the burdens which their beliefs and loyalties laid upon their shoulders. He wondered too whether the time had not come to throw aside the caution of a lifetime and break a lance, or his head, for the most contentious cause in Rome, the reform of the Holy Roman Rota.

He was not a brilliant man, and certainly not a brave one. He had a capacity for close observation and urbane reportage, and a slightly theatrical knack for ingratiating himself with well-bred people. In Rome these things added up to a valuable talent for a correspondent. Now, however, with the climacteric looming, and the lonely years, the talent was not enough. George Faber was in love, and, being a Nordic Puritan and not a Latin, he needed at all costs to be married.

The Church, too, wanted him married, being concerned for the safety of his soul; but she would rather see him damned by default or rebellion than seem to call in question the sacramental bond which she counted, by divine revelation, indissoluble.

So, like it or not, his own fate and Chiara's were held between the rigid hands of the canonists and the soft, epicene palms of Corrado Calitri, Minister of the Republic. Unless Calitri slackened his grip—which he showed no sign of doing—they could both stay suspended till Doomsday in the limbo of those outside the law.

Across the nave, in the enclosure reserved for dignitaries of the Republic of Italy, Faber could see the slim patrician figure of his enemy, his breast resplendent with decorations, his face pale as a marble mask.

Five years ago he had been a spectacular young deputy with Milanese money behind him and a Cabinet career already in promise. His only handicaps were his bachelor estate and a fondness for gay young men and visiting aesthetes. His marriage to a Roman heiress, fresh from convent school, had put the ministry in his pocket and set the Roman gossips laughing behind their hands. Eighteen months later, Chiara, his wife, was in hospital with a nervous breakdown. By the time she had recovered, their separation was an accomplished fact. The next step was to file a petition for a declaration of nullity with the Holy Roman Rota, and from this point began the tedious dialogue of the tragicomedy:

'The petitioner, Chiara Calitri, alleges first a defect of intention,' so the lawyers deposed on her behalf, 'in that her husband entered into the bond of matrimony without the full intent to fulfil all the terms of the contract, with respect to cohabitation, procreation, and normal sexual commerce.'

'I had the fullest intention to fulfil all the terms of the contract . . .' Thus Corrado Calitri in reply. 'But my wife lacked both the will and the experience to assist me to carry them out. The married state implies mutual support; I did not get support or moral assistance from my wife.'

'The petitioner alleges also that it was a condition of the marriage that her husband should be a man of normal sexual habits.'

'She knew what I was,' said Corrado Calitri in effect. 'I made no attempt to conceal my past. Much of it was common knowledge. She married me in spite of it.'

'Fine!' said the auditors of the Rota. 'Either of the pleas would be sufficient for a decree of nullity, but a simple statement is not proof. How does the petitioner propose to prove her case? Did her husband express his defective intentions to her or to another? Was the condition made explicit before the contract? On what occasion? In what form of speech or writing? And by whom can the condition be verified?'

So inevitably the wheels of canonical justice ground to a halt, and Chiara's lawyers advised her discreetly that it was better to suspend the case while new evidence was being sought than to force it to an unfavourable conclusion. The men of the Rota stood firm on dogmatic principle and the provisions of the law; Corrado Calitri was safely married and happily free, while she herself was caught like a mouse in the trap he had set for her. The whole city guessed at the next step before she made it. She was twenty-six years old, and within six months she and George Faber were lovers. Rome in its cynical fashion smiled on their union and turned to the merrier scandals of the film colony at Cinecittà.

But George Faber was no complaisant lover. He had an itch in his conscience, and he hated the man who forced him to scratch it every day. . . .

He felt suddenly dizzy. A sweat broke out on his face and palms, and he struggled to compose himself as the Pope mounted the steps of the altar supported by his assistants.

Campeggio cocked an astute eye at his queasy colleague and then leaned forward and tapped him on the shoulder. 'I don't like Calitri either; but you'll never win the way you're going.'

Faber sat bolt upright and stared at him with hostile eyes. 'What the devil do you mean?'

Campeggio shrugged and smiled. 'Don't be angry, my friend—it's an open secret. And even if it weren't, you have it written on your face . . . Of course you hate him, and I don't blame you. But there are more ways than one of killing a cat.'

'I'd like to hear them,' said Faber irritably.

'Call me for lunch one day and I'll tell you.'

And with that, Faber had to be content, but the hope buzzed in his head like a gadfly while Kiril the Pontiff chanted the Coronation Mass, and the voices of the choir pealed around the dome of the Basilica.

Rudolf Semmering, Father General of the Society of Jesus, stood rigid as a sentinel at his post in the nave and addressed himself to a meditation on the occasion and its meanings.

A lifetime of discipline in the Ignatian exercises had given him the facility of projecting himself out of the terms of time and space into a solitude of contemplation. He did not hear the music, or the murmur of the concourse, or the sonorous Latin of the ceremony. His subdued senses were closed against all intrusion. A vast stillness encompassed him, while the faculties of his spirit concentrated themselves upon the essence of the moment: the relationship between the Creator and His creatures which was being affirmed and renewed by the installation of His Vicar.

Here, in symbol, ceremony and sacrificial act, the nature of the Mystical Body was being displayed—Christ the God-man as head with the Pontiff as His Vicar, enlivening the whole body by His permanent presence and through the indwelling of the Paraclete. Here was the whole physical order which Christ had established as the visible symbol and the visible instrument of His working with humankind—the *ecclesia*, the hierarchy of Pope, bishops, priests, and common folk, united in a single faith with a single sacrifice and a single sacramental system. Here the whole mission of redemption was summarized—the recall of man to his Maker by the dispensation of grace and by the preaching of the New Testament.

Here, too, was the darkness of a monstrous mystery: why an omnipotent God had made human instruments capable of rebellion, who could reject the divine design or deface it or inhibit its progress: why the All-Knowing should permit those whom He had made in His own image to grope their way to union with Him on a knife-edge path, in daily danger of losing themselves for ever from His face. Here finally was the mystery of the *ministerium*, the service to which certain men—himself among them—were called: to assume a greater responsibility and a greater risk, and to show forth in themselves the image of the Godhead for the salvation of their fellows.

Which brought him by a round turn to the application of his whole meditation: what he himself must do for service to the Pontiff, the Church, and the Christ to whom he was bound by perpetual vow. He was the leader, by election, of forty thousand celibate men, dedicated to the bidding of the Pontiff in whatever mission he might choose to give them. Some of the best brains in the world were at his command, some of the noblest spirits, the best organizers, the most inspired teachers, the most daring speculators. It was his function, not merely to use them as passive instruments, but help each one to grow according to his nature and his talent with the spirit of God working in him.

It was not enough, either, that he should present the massive network of the Society to the Pontiff and wait for a single command to set it working. The Society, like every other organization and every individual in the Church, had to seek and to propose new modes and new efforts to further the divine mission. It could not surrender itself either to the fear of novelty or to the comfort of traditional methods. The Church was not a static body. It was, according to the Gospel parable, a tree whose whole life was implicit in a tiny seed, but which must grow each year into a new shape and a new fruitfulness, while more and more birds made nests in its branches.

But even a tree did not always grow at the same rate or with the same profusion of leaf and flower. There were times when it seemed that the sap was sparse, or the ground less nourishing, so that the gardener must come and open up the soil and inject new food into the roots.

For a long time now, Rudolf Semmering had been troubled by the reports that came to him from all over the world, of a slackening of the influence of his Society and of the Church. More students were drifting away from religious practice in the first years after college. There were fewer candidates for the priesthood and for religious orders. The missionary drive seemed to lack impetus. Pulpit preaching had declined into formality—and this in an age when the whole world lived under the shadow of atomic destruction, and men were asking more poignantly than ever before to what end they were made, and why they should breed children into so dubious a future.

In his younger days in the Society, he had been trained as an historian, and all his later experience had confirmed him in the cyclic and climatic view of history. All his years in the Church had shown him that it grew and changed with the human pattern in spite of—or perhaps because of—its perennial conformity with the Divine One. There were seasons of mediocrity and times of decadence. There were centuries of brilliance when genius seemed to spring from every lane and alley. There were times when the human spirit, burdened too long by material existence, leapt from its prison and went shouting free and fiery across the rooftops of the world, so that men heard thunders out of a forgotten heaven and saw once more the trailing splendours of divinity.

When he looked up at the great altar and saw the celebrant, moving stiffly under sixty pounds of gilded vestments, he asked himself whether this might not be the forerunner of such a time. Remembering the Pope's plea for men with winged feet and burning hearts, he wondered whether this were not the first offering he should make out of the resources of the Society—a man who could speak the old truths in a fresh mode and walk as a new apostle in the strange world that had been born out of the mushroom cloud.

He had the man, he was sure of it. Even in the Society he was little known because most of his life had been spent in strange places, on projects that seemed to have little relation to matters of the spirit. Yet now it appeared from his writing and his correspondence that he was ready to be used otherwise.

His meditation over, Rudolf Semmering, the spare methodical man, took out his notebook and made a memorandum to send a cable to Djakarta. Then from the dome of the Basilica the trumpets broke out in a long melodious fanfare, and he lifted his eyes to see Kiril the Pontiff raise above his head the body of the God whom he represented on earth.

On the night of his coronation, Kiril Lakota dressed himself in the black cassock and the platter hat of a Roman priest and walked alone out of the Angelic Gate to survey his new bishopric. The guards at the gate hardly glanced at him, being accustomed to the daily procession of Monsignori in and out of the Vatican. He smiled to himself and hid his scarred face behind a handkerchief, as he hurried down the Borgo Angelica toward the Castle of Sant' Angelo.

It was a few minutes after ten. The air was still warm and dusty, and the streets were alive with traffic and the passage of pedestrians. He strode out freely, filling his lungs with the new air of freedom, excited as a schoolboy who had just broken bounds.

On the Bridge of Sant' Angelo he stopped and leaned on the parapet, staring down at the grey waters of the Tiber, which had mirrored for five thousand years the follies of emperors, the cavalcade of Popes and princes, and the dozen births and deaths of the Eternal City.

It was his city now. It belonged to him as it could never belong to anyone else but the successor of Peter. Without the Papacy it could die again and crumble into a provincial relic, because all its resource was in its history, and the history of the Church was half the history of Rome. More than this, Kiril the Russian was now Bishop of the Romans—their shepherd, their teacher, their monitor in matters of the spirit.

A long time ago it was the Romans who elected the Pope. Even now they claimed to own him; and, in a sense, they did. He was anchored to their soil, locked within their walls until the day he died. They might love him, as he hoped they would. They might hate him as they had many of his predecessors. They would make jokes about him as they had done for centuries, calling the hoodlums of the town *figli di papa*, sons of the Pope, and blaming him for the shortcomings of his Cardinals and his clergy. Provoke them enough and they might even try to murder him and throw his body in the Tiber. But he was theirs and they were his, though half of them never set foot in a church, and many of them carried cards which showed them to be Kamenev's men and not the Pope's. His mission was to the world, but his home was here, and, like any other householder, he must get along with his neighbours as best he could.

He crossed the bridge and plunged into the network of lanes and alleys between the Street of the Holy Spirit and the Via Zanardelli, and within five minutes the city had engulfed him. The buildings rose on either hand, grey, pitted and weather-stained. A pale lamp glimmered at the shrine of a dusty Madonna. An alley cat, scrabbling in a heap of refuse, turned and spat at him. A pregnant woman leaned in a doorway under the coat of arms of some forgotten prince. A youth on a clattering Vespa shouted as he passed. A pair of prostitutes, gossiping under a street lamp, giggled when they saw him and one of them made the sign against the evil eye. It was a trivial incident, but it made a deep impression on him. They had told him of this old Roman custom, but this was the first time he had seen it. A priest wore skirts. He was neither man nor woman, but an odd creature who probably was *mal' occhio*. It was better to be sure than sorry and show him the horns.

A moment later he broke out into a narrow square at whose angle there was a bar with tables set on the sidewalk. One of the tables was occupied by a family group, munching sweet pastries and chattering in harsh Roman dialect; the other was free, so he sat down and ordered an Espresso. The service was perfunctory, and the other guests ignored him. Rome was full of clerics, and one more or less made no matter.

As he sipped the bitter coffee, a wizened fellow with broken shoes sidled up to sell him a newspaper. He fumbled in his cassock for change, then remembered with a start that he had forgotten to bring any money. He could not even pay for his drink. For a moment he felt humiliated and embarrassed; then he saw the humour of the situation and decided to make the best of it. He signalled the bartender and explained his situation, turning out his pockets as evidence of good faith. The fellow made a surly mouth and turned away, muttering an imprecation on priests who sucked the blood of the poor.

Kiril caught at his sleeve and drew him back. 'No, no! You misunderstand me. I want to pay and I shall pay.'

The newsvendor and the family waited silently for the beginning of a Roman comedy.

'Beh!' The barman made a sweeping gesture of contempt. 'So you want to pay! But when and with what? How do I know who you are or where you come from?'

'If you like,' said Kiril with a smile, 'I'll leave you my name and address.'

'So I'm to go trotting all over Rome to pick up fifty *lire*?'

'I'll send it to you or bring it myself.'

'Meantime, who's out of pocket? Me! You think I have so much that I can buy coffee for every priest in Rome?'

They had their laugh then and they were satisfied. The father of the family fished in his pocket and tossed a few coins expansively on the table. 'Here! Let me pay for it, Padre. And for the paper too.'

'Thank you . . . I'm grateful. But I would like to repay you.'

'Nothing, Padre, nothing!' Paterfamilias waved a tolerant hand. 'And you must forgive Giorgio here. He's having a bad time with his wife.'

Giorgio grunted unhappily and shoved the coins into his pocket. 'My mother wanted me to be a priest. Maybe she was right at that.'

'Priests have their problems too,' said Kiril mildly. 'Even the Pope has a few, I'm told.'

'The Pope! Now there's a funny one.' This from the paper vendor, who, being a seller of news, claimed the right to comment upon it as well. 'They've really cooked us beautifully this time. A Russian in the Vatican! Now there's a story for you!' He spread the paper on the table and pointed dramatically to the portrait of the Pontiff which covered nearly half the front page. 'Now tell me if he isn't an odd one to foist on us Romans. Look at that face and the . . .' He broke off and stared at the bearded visage of the newcomer. His voice dropped to a whisper. '*Dio!* You look just like him.'

The others craned over his shoulder, staring at the portrait.

'It's queer,' said Giorgio, 'very queer. You're almost his double.'

'I am the Pope,' he told them, and they gaped at him as if he were a ghost.

'I don't believe it,' said Giorgio. 'You look like him. Sure! But you're sitting here, without a *lira* in your pocket, drinking coffee, and it's not very good coffee at that.'

'It's better than I get in the Vatican.'

Then seeing their confusion and their trouble, he asked for a pencil and wrote their names and their addresses on the back of a bar bill. 'I'll tell you what I'll do. I'll send each of you a letter and ask you to come to lunch with me in the Vatican. I'll pay you back the money then too.'

'You wouldn't joke with us, Padre?' asked the newsvendor anxiously.

'No. I wouldn't joke with you. You'll hear from me.'

He stood up, folded the newspaper and shoved it into the pocket of his cassock. Then he laid his hands on the old man's head and murmured a benediction. 'There now. Tell the world you've had a blessing from the Pope.' He made the sign of the cross over the little group. 'And all of you, tell your friends that you have seen me and that I didn't have enough money for coffee.'

They watched him, stupefied, and he strode away, a dark, gaunt figure but oddly triumphant from his first encounter with his people.

It was a petty triumph at best, but he prayed desperately that it might be the presage of greater ones. If Creation and Redemption meant anything at all, they meant an affair of love between the Maker and His creatures. If not, then all existence was a horrible irony unworthy of Omnipotence. Love was an affair of the heart. Its language was the language of the heart. The gestures of love were the simplicities of common intercourse, and not the baroque rituals of ecclesiastical theatre. The tragedies of love were the tragedies of a waiter with sore feet and a wife who didn't understand him. The terror of love was that the face of the Beloved was hidden always behind a veil so that when one lifted one's eyes for hope, one saw only the official face of priest or Pope or politician.

Once, for a short space in a narrow land, God had shown His face to men in the person of His Son, and they had known Him for a loving shepherd, a healer of the sick, a nourisher of the hungry. Then He had hidden Himself again, leaving His Church for an extension of Himself across the centuries, leaving, too, His vicars and His priesthood to show themselves other Christs for the multitude. If they disdained the commerce of simple men and forgot the language of the heart, then, all too soon, they were talking to themselves. . .

The alleys closed around him again, and he found himself wishing that he could peer beyond their blank doors and their blind windows into the lives of their inhabitants. He felt a strange momentary nostalgia for the camps and the prisons, where he had breathed the breath of his fellows in misfortune and wakened at night to the muttering of their dreams.

He was halfway along a reeking lane when he found himself caught between a closed door and a parked automobile. At the same moment the door opened and a man stepped out, jostling him against the panels of the car.

The man muttered an apology and then, catching sight of the cassock, stopped in his tracks. He said curtly, 'There's a man dying up there. Maybe you can do more for him than I can. . .'

'Who are you?'

'A doctor. They never call us until it's too late.'

'Where do I find him?'

'On the second floor . . . Be a little careful. He's very infectious. T.B.–secondary pneumonia and haemothorax.'

'Isn't there anyone looking after him?'

'Oh yes. There's a young woman. She's very capable–better than two of us at a time like this. You'd better hurry. I give him an hour at most.'

Without another word, he turned and hurried down the alley, his footsteps clattering on the cobbles.

Kiril the Pontiff pushed open the door and went in. The building was one of those decayed palaces with a littered courtyard and a stairway that smelled of garbage and stale cooking. The treads cracked under his feet, and the banister was greasy to the touch.

On the second landing he came on a small knot of people huddled around a weeping woman. They gave him a sidelong, uneasy stare and when he questioned them, one of the men jerked a thumb in the direction of the open door.

'He's in there.'

'Has he seen a priest?'

The man shrugged and turned away, and the wailing of the woman went on, unchecked.

The apartment was a large, airless room, cluttered as a junk shop and full of the morbid smell of disease. In one corner was a large matrimonial bed where a man lay, fleshless and shrunken, under a stained counterpane. His face was unshaven, his thin hair clung damp about his forehead, and his head rolled from side to side on the piled pillows. His breathing was short, painful, and full of rales, and a small bloody foam spilled out of his mouth.

Beside the bed sat a girl, incongruously well groomed for such a place, who wiped the sweat from his forehead and cleansed his lips with a linen swab.

When Kiril entered she looked up, and he saw a young face, strangely serene, and a pair of dark, questioning eyes.

He said awkwardly, 'I met the doctor downstairs. He thought I might be able to do something.'

The girl shook her head. 'I'm afraid not. He's in deep shock. I don't think he'll last very long.'

Her educated voice and her calm professional manner intrigued him. He asked again, 'Are you a relative?'

'No. The people around here know me. They send for me when they're in trouble.'

'Are you a nurse, then?'

'I used to be.'

'Has he seen a priest?'

For the first time she smiled. 'I doubt it. His wife's Jewish and he carries a card for the Communist Party. Priests aren't very popular in this quarter.'

Once again Kiril the Pontiff was reminded how far he was from being a simple pastor. A priest normally carried in his pocket a small capsule of the Holy Oils for the administration of the last sacraments. He had none, and here a man was dying before his face. He moved to the bed, and the girl made place for him while she repeated the doctor's warning:

'Just watch yourself. He's very infectious.'

Kiril the Pontiff took the slack, moist hand in his own, and then bent so that his lips touched the ear of the dying man. He began to repeat slowly and distinctly the words of the Act of Repentance. When it was done he urged quietly, 'If you can hear me, press my hand. If you cannot do that, tell God in your heart you're sorry. He's waiting for you with love, it needs only a thought to take you to Him.'

Over and over again he repeated the exhortation while the man's head lolled restlessly, and the fading breath gurgled in his gullet.

Finally the girl said, 'No use, Father. He's too far gone to hear you.'

Kiril the Pontiff raised his hand and pronounced the absolution. '*Deinde ego te absolvo a peccatis tuis.* . . . I absolve you from your sins in the name of the Father, and of the Son, and of the Holy Ghost. Amen.'

Then he knelt by the bed and began to pray passionately for the soul of this shabby voyager who had begun his last lonely pilgrimage while he himself was being crowned in the Basilica of St Peter.

In ten minutes the little tragedy was over, and he made the prayers for the departed spirit while the girl closed the staring eyes and composed the body decently in the attitude of death. Then she said firmly:

'We should go, Father. Neither of us will be welcome now.'

'I would like to help the family,' said Kiril the Pontiff.

'We should go.' She was very definite about it. 'They can cope with death. It's only living that defeats them.'

When they walked out of the room, she announced the news bluntly to the little group. 'He's dead. If you need help call me.'

Then she turned away and walked down the stairs with Kiril at her heel. The high mourning cry of the woman followed them like a malediction.

A moment later they were alone in the empty street. The girl fumbled in her handbag for a cigarette and lit it with an unsteady hand. She leaned back against the car and smoked a few moments in silence. Then she said abruptly, 'I try to fight against it, but it always shakes me. They're so helpless, these people.'

'At the end, we're all helpless,' said Kiril soberly. 'Why do you do this sort of thing?'

'It's a long story. I'd rather not talk about it just now. I'm driving home–can I drop you off somewhere?'

It was on the tip of his tongue to refuse; then he checked himself and asked, 'Where do you live?'

'I have an apartment near the Palatine, behind the Foro Romano.'

'Then let me ride with you as far as the Foro. I've never seen it at night–and you look as though you need some company.'

She gave him an odd glance, then without a word opened the door of the car. 'Let's go then. I've had more than enough for one night.'

She drove fast and recklessly until they broke out into the free space where the Forum lay, bleak and ghostly, under the rising moon. She stopped the car. They got out together and walked over to the railing, beyond which the pillars of the Temple of Venus heaved themselves up against the stars. In the terse fashion which seemed habitual to her, she challenged him:

'You're not Italian, are you?'

'No, I'm Russian.'

'And I've seen you before, haven't I?'

'Probably. They've printed a lot of pictures of me lately.'

'Then what were you doing in Old Rome?'

'I'm the Bishop of the City. I thought I should know at least what it looked like.'

'That makes us both foreigners,' said the girl cryptically.

'Where do you come from?'

'I was born in Germany, I'm an American citizen, and I live in Rome.'

'Are you a Catholic?'

'I don't know what I am. I'm trying to find out.'

'This way?' asked Kiril quietly.

'It's the only one I know. I've tried all the others.' Then she laughed, and for the first time since their meeting she seemed to relax. 'Forgive me, I'm behaving very badly. My name is Ruth Lewin.'

'I'm Kiril Lakota.'

'I know. The Pope from the steppes.'

'Is that what they call me?'

'Among other things . . .' She challenged him again. 'These stories they print about you, your time in prison, your escape, are they true?'

'Yes.'

'Now you're in prison again.'

'In a way, but I hope to break out of it.'

'We're all in prison, one way or another.'

'That's true . . . And it's the ones who understand it that suffer most of all.'

For a long moment she was silent, staring down at the tumbled marbles of the Forum. Then she asked him, 'Do you really believe that you stand in God's shoes?'

'I do.'

'How does it feel?'

'Terrifying.'

'Does He speak to you? Do you hear Him?'

He thought about it for a moment and then answered her gravely. 'In one sense, yes. The knowledge of Himself which He revealed in the Old Testament and in the New pervades the Church. It is there in the Scripture and in the Tradition which has been handed down from the time of the Apostles, and which we call the Deposit of Faith. This is the lamp to my feet . . . In another sense, no. I pray for divine light, but I must work by human reason. I cannot demand miracles. At this moment for instance, I ask myself what I must do for the people of this city—what I can do for you. I have no ready answer. I have no private dialogue with God. I grope in the dark and hope that His hand will reach out to guide me.'

'You're a strange man.'

'We are all strange,' he told her with a smile, 'and why not, since each of us is a spark struck off from the fiery mystery of the Godhead?'

Her next words were uttered with a poignant simplicity that touched him almost to tears:

'I need help, but I don't know how, or where, to get it.'

For a moment he hesitated, torn between prudence and the promptings of a vulnerable heart. Then once again he felt within him the subtle stirring of power. He was the Pastor and none other. Tonight one soul had slipped through his fingers; he dare not risk another. 'Take me home with you,' he told her. 'Make me a cup of coffee, then talk it out. Afterwards you can drive me back to the Vatican.'

In a small apartment huddled under the shadow of the Palatine Hill she told him her story. She told it calmly and gravely, and with no trace of that hysteria which every confessor feared in his relations with women.

'I was born in Germany thirty-five years ago. My family was Jewish, and it was the time of the pogroms. We were chased about from one country to another, until finally a chance came to enter Spain. Before we applied for visas we were told it might help if we became Catholics. . . . So my parents went through the motions and became converts—Moriscos might be a better name! We took the new identity and we were admitted.

'I was a child then, but it seemed that the new country and the new religion opened their arms to welcome me. I remember the music, the colour, the Holy Week processions winding through the streets of Barcelona, while little girls like me, with white veils and flower wreaths in their hair, threw rose petals before the priest who carried the Monstrance. I had lived so long in fear and uncertainty that it was as if I had been transported into a land of fairy tale.

'Then, early in 1941, we were granted visas for America. The Catholic Charities Bureau took care of us, and with their help I was placed in a convent school. For the first time I felt thoroughly safe and, strangely enough, thoroughly Catholic.

'My parents did not seem to mind. They too had reached safe harbour, and they had their own lives to rebuild. For a few years I was serenely happy; then—how do I say it?—my world and I myself began to crack down the middle. I was a child still, but the minds of children open more quickly than adults ever believe.

'In Europe millions of Jews were dying. I was a Jew and I was oppressed by the thought that I was a renegade who had bought my safety by forswearing my race and my religion. I was a Catholic too, and my belief was identified with the freest and happiest time of my life. Yet I could not accept the freedom or the happiness because it seemed they had been bought with blood-money.

'I began to rebel against the teaching and the discipline of the convent and yet all the time I knew that I was rebelling against myself. When I began to go out with boys, it was always with the rebels, the ones who rejected any kind of belief. It was safer that way. Perhaps in the end it would be better to believe nothing than to be torn apart by a double allegiance.

'Then, after a while, I fell in love with a Jewish boy. I was still a Catholic, so I went to discuss the case with my parish priest. I asked for the usual dispensation to marry someone outside the faith. To my surprise and my shame, he read me a bitter lecture. I heard him out and then walked out of the rectory, and I have never set foot inside a church since. He was a foolish man, blind and prejudiced. For a while I hated him, and then I understood that I was really hating myself.

'My marriage was happy. My husband had no fixed belief nor, it seemed, did I; but we had a common race, and a common heritage, and we were able to live in peace with one another. We made money, we made friends. It was as if I had achieved the continuity which my life had lacked from the beginning. I belonged to someone, to a settled order, and, at long last, to myself.

'Suddenly, and for no apparent reason, a strange thing happened. I became morbid and depressed. I would wander around the house disconsolate, tears rolling down my cheeks, sunk in utter despair. Sometimes I would break out into violent rages at the slightest provocation. There were times when I contemplated suicide, convinced that I would be better dead than inflicting so much unhappiness on myself and on my husband.

'In the end my husband forced the issue. He demanded that I see a psychiatrist. At first I refused angrily, and then he told me bluntly that I was destroying myself and destroying our marriage. So I agreed to begin treatment, and entered on a course of analysis.

'This is a strange and frightening road; but once you begin to walk it you cannot turn back. To live life is hard enough. To relive it, to retrace every step in symbol and fantasy and simple memory, is a weird experience. The person who makes the journey with you, the analyst, assumes a multitude of identities: father, mother, lover, husband, teacher—even God.

'The longer the journey the harder the road, because each step brings you closer to the moment of revelation where you must face once and for ever the thing from which you have been fleeing. Time and again you try to step off the road or turn back. Always you are forced forward. You try to defer, to temporize. You create new lies to deceive yourself and your guide, but the lies are demolished one by one.

'In the middle of my analysis my husband was killed in an automobile accident. For me it was another guilt added to all the others. Now I could never restore to him the happiness of which I had robbed him. My whole personality seemed to disintegrate under the shock. I was taken to a nursing home, and the therapy began again. Slowly the nature of my hidden fear became clear to me. When I reached the core of myself I knew that I should find it empty. I should not only be alone, but hollow as well, because I had built a god in my own image, and then destroyed him, and there was no one to take his place. I must live in a desert without identity, without purpose since, even if there were a God, I could not accept Him because I had not paid for His presence.

'Does this seem strange to you? It was a terror to me. But once I stood in the desert, empty and solitary, I was calm. I was even whole. I remember the morning after the crisis when I looked out from the window of my room and saw the sun shining on the green lawn. I said to myself: "I have seen the worst that can happen to me, and I am still here. The rest, whatever it is, I can endure."

'A month later I was discharged. I settled my husband's estate and came to Rome. I had money, I was free, I could plan a new life for myself. I might even fall in love again . . . I tried it too; but in love one must commit oneself, and I had nothing to commit.

'Then I began to understand something. If I lived for myself and with myself I should always be hollow, always in solitude. My debts to my people and my past were still unpaid; I could accept nothing from life until I had begun to pay them.

'You asked me tonight why I do this kind of service. It's simple enough. There are many Jews in Rome—the old Sephardic families who came from Spain in the time of the Inquisition, immigrants from Bologna and the Lombard cities. They are still a people apart, many of them are poor like the ones you saw tonight . . . I can give them something. I know I do. But what do I give myself? Where do I go? . . . I have no God although I need one desperately . . . You tell me you stand in His shoes—can you help me?'

EXTRACT FROM THE SECRET MEMORIALS OF KIRIL I PONT. MAX.

. . . I am troubled tonight. I am solitary and perplexed. My installation in the see of Peter is complete. I have been crowned with the Triple Tiara. The Ring of the Fisherman is on my finger. My blessing has gone out to the city and to the world. In spite of it all—because of it all, perhaps—I have never felt so empty and inadequate. I am like the scapegoat driven into the desert with the sins of all the people on my back . . .

I must ask Rinaldi to find me a wise priest to whom I can confess myself each day, not only for absolution and the sacramental grace, but for a purging of this pent, stopped-up spirit of mine. I wonder if the faithful understand that the Vicar of Christ has often more need of the confessional than they themselves . . .

I have seen many men die, but the sad and solitary exit which I witnessed tonight in a Roman tenement afflicts me strangely. The words of the woman who saw it with me still ring in my ears—'They can cope with death. It's the living that defeats them.' It seems to me that this defeat is the measure of our failure in the ministry of the Word.

Those who need us most are those who are bowed the lowest under the burden of existence—whose life is a daily struggle for simple sustenance, who lack talent and opportunity, who live in fear of officials and tax-gatherers and debt-collectors, so that they have no time and hardly any strength to spend on the care of their souls. Their whole life becomes a creeping despair . . . If it were not for the infinite knowledge and the infinite mercy of God, I too could easily despair.

The case of the woman, Ruth Lewin, gives me more hope. While I was in prison and under the long ordeals of interrogation, I learned much about the intricate functioning of the human mind. I am convinced that those who devote themselves to the study of its workings, and of its infirmities, can do a great service to man and the cause of his salvation . . . We should not, as shepherds of souls, treat this infant science with suspicion or hasty censure. Like every other science it can be wrested to ignoble ends. It is inevitable that many who explore the misty country of the soul will make mistakes and false guesses; but every honest research into the nature of man is also an exploration of the divine intent in his regard.

The human psyche is the meeting ground between God and man. It is possible, I think, that some of the meaning of the mystery of Divine Grace may be revealed when we understand better the working of the subconscious mind, where buried memories and buried guilts and buried impulses germinate for years and then break out into a strange flowering . . . I must encourage competent men inside the Church to pursue this study, and to co-operate with those outside it, to make the best use possible of their discoveries . . .

The sick mind is a defective instrument in the great symphony which is God's dialogue with man. Here perhaps we may see a fuller revelation of the meaning of human responsibility and God's compassion for His creatures. Here we may be able to illuminate the difference between formal guilt and the true status of the soul in the sight of God . . .

It might scandalize many if I declared openly that in a woman like this Ruth I see—or think I see—a chosen spirit. The key to such spirits is their recognition that their wrestling with life is in reality a wrestling with God . . .

The strangest story in the Old Testament is the story of Jacob, who wrestled with the angel and conquered him and forced the angel to tell his name . . . But Jacob went away from the struggle limping.

I too am a limping spirit. I have felt reason and the foundations of my faith rock in the dark bunker and under the lights and the relentless inquisition of Kamenev.

I believe still. I am committed more completely than ever before to the Deposit of Faith, but I am no longer content to say, 'God is thus. Man is thus', and then make an end of it. Wherever I turn on this high pinnacle, I am confronted with mystery. I believe in the godly harmony which is the result of the eternal creative act. . . . But I do not always hear the harmony. I must wrestle with the cacophony and apparent discord of the score, knowing that I shall not hear the final grand resolution until the day I die and, hopefully, am united with God. . . .

This is what I tried to explain to Ruth, though I am not sure that I did it very well. I could not bring myself to present her with blunt theological propositions. Her troubled spirit was not ready to receive them.

I tried to show her that the crisis of near despair which afflicts many people of intelligence and noble spirit is often a providential act, designed to bring them to an acceptance of their own nature, with all its limitations and inadequacies, and of the conformity of that nature with a divine design whose pattern and whose end we cannot fully apprehend.

I understand her terrors because I have endured them myself. This I am sure she understood. I advised her to be patient with herself and with God, who, even if she could not believe in Him, still worked in His own fashion and His own secret time.

I told her to continue the good work she was doing, but to regard it always as a payment of debts. No one of us could pay his debts, were it not for the redemptive act, consummated on the cross by Christ.

I tried to show her that to reject the joy of living is to insult Him who provides it, and gave us the gift of laughter along with the gift of tears . . .

These things I think I should write for others because the sickness of the mind is a symptom of our times, and we must all try to heal one another. Man is not meant to live alone. The Creator Himself has affirmed it. We are members of one body. The cure of a sick member is a function of the whole organism . . .

I have asked Ruth to write to me, and sometimes to come and see me. I dare not let this office separate me from direct contact with my people . . . For this reason, I think I should sit in the confessional for an hour each week and administer the Sacrament to those who come into St Peter's.

The nearest I came to losing my faith and my soul was when I lay naked and solitary in an underground bunker . . . When I was brought back to the huts, to the sound of human talk–even to the sound of anger and ribaldry and blasphemy–it was like a new promise of salvation . . .

I wonder whether this is not the way in which the creative act renews itself daily: the spirit of God breathing over the dark waters of the human spirit, infusing them with a life whose intensity and diversity we can only guess . . .

'*In manus tuas, Domine.* Into thy hands, O God, I commend all troubled souls . . .'

4

It was nearly six weeks after the coronation before George Faber arranged his luncheon with Campeggio. He might have put if off even longer had not Chiara argued him into it with tears and tantrums. He was by nature a prompt man, but he had lived long enough in Rome to be suspicious of any gratuitous gesture. Campeggio was a distinguished colleague, to be sure, but he was in no sense a friend, and there was no clear reason why he should concern himself with the bedding and wedding of Chiara Calitri.

So somewhere in the offing was a *combinazione*–a proposition–with the price tag carefully hidden until the very last moment. When one lunched with the Romans, one needed a long spoon and a steady hand, and George Faber was still a little shaken by his quarrel with Chiara.

Spring was maturing slowly into summer. The azaleas made a riot of colour on the Spanish Steps, and the flower-sellers did a brisk business with the new roses from Rapallo. Footsore tourists found refuge in the English Tearoom, and the traffic swirled irritably around Bernini's marble boat in the Piazza.

To stiffen his small courage, George Faber bought a red carnation and pinned it jauntily in his buttonhole before he crossed the Square and entered the Via Condotti. The restaurant which Campeggio had named for their rendezvous was a small, discreet place, far away from the normal haunts of newsmen and politicians . . . In a matter of such delicacy, he claimed, one should not risk an eavesdropper, though Faber saw little point in secrecy since the Calitri story was common property in Rome. However, it was part of the game that every *combinazione*, every *progetto*, must be dressed up with a little theatre. So he submitted with as much good grace as he could muster.

Campeggio entertained him for half an hour with a vivid and amusing chronicle of the Vatican, and how the clerical dovecotes were fluttering as the new Pope asserted himself. Then, with a diplomat's care, he steered the talk toward Faber:

'. . . It may please you to know, my dear fellow, that your own dispatches have been very favourably noticed by His Holiness. I am told he is anxious to make more direct contact with the press. There is talk of a regular luncheon with senior correspondents, and your name is, of course, first on the list.'

'I'm flattered,' said Faber dryly. 'One tries always to write honestly, but this man is an interesting subject in his own right.'

'Leone too has a soft spot for you, and you are well regarded in the Secretariat of State . . . These are important sources and important voices, as you know.'

'I'm well aware of it.'

'Good,' said Campeggio briskly. 'Then you understand the importance of preserving a good relation without, shall we say, embarrassing incidents.'

'I've always understood that. I'm interested to know why you bring it up now.'

Campeggio pursed his thin lips and looked down the backs of his long, manicured hands. He said carefully. 'I make the point to explain my next question. Do you propose setting up house with Chiara Calitri?'

Faber flushed and said testily, 'We've discussed it. So far we haven't made any decision.'

'Then let me advise you very strongly not to do it at this moment . . . Don't misunderstand me. Your private life is your own affair.'

'I'd hardly call it private. Everyone in Rome knows the situation between Chiara and myself. I imagine the rumour has reached the Vatican long before this.'

Campeggio gave him a thin smile. 'So long as it remains a rumour, they are content to suspend judgement and leave you in the hands of God. There is no question of public infamy which could damage your case with the Rota.'

'At this point,' Faber told him bluntly, 'we have no case. The whole business is suspended until Chiara can get new evidence. So far she hasn't been able to find any.'

Campeggio nodded slowly, and then began to trace an intricate pattern on the white tablecloth. 'I am told by those who understand the thinking of the Rota that your best hope of a verdict rests on the plea of defective intention. In other words, if you can prove that Calitri entered into the marriage contract without the full intention of fulfilling all its terms—and that intention includes fidelity—then you have a good chance of a favourable decision.'

Faber shrugged unhappily. 'How do you prove what's in a man's mind?'

'Two ways: by his own sworn statement or by the evidence of those who heard him express the defective intention.'

'We looked for people like that. We couldn't find any, and I'm damn sure Calitri won't give evidence against himself.'

'Put enough pressure on him and I think he might.'

'What kind of pressure?'

For the first time Campeggio seemed uncertain of himself. He was silent a while, tracing long flowing lines with the point of his fork. Finally he said deliberately, 'A man like Calitri who holds a high position and who has, shall we say, an unusual private life, is very vulnerable. He is vulnerable to his party, and to public attack. He is vulnerable to those who have fallen out of his favour ... I don't have to tell you that this is an odd world he lives in—a world of strange loves and curious hates. Nothing in it is very permanent. Today's favourite is rejected tomorrow. There are always bleeding hearts ready to tell their story to a good listener. I've heard some myself. Once you have enough stories you go to Calitri.'

'I go to him?'

'Who else? You report the news, don't you?'

'Not that sort of news.'

'But you know plenty who do?'

'Yes.'

'Then I don't have to draw pictures for you.'

'It's blackmail,' said George Faber flatly.

'Or justice,' said Orlando Campeggio. 'It depends on the point of view.'

'Even if we did frighten a testimony out of him, he could then allege undue pressure and the whole case would be thrown out of court for good.'

'That's the risk you have to take. If the stakes are high enough, I think you might be wise to take it. . . . I should add that I may be able to give you a little help in your inquiry.'

'Why?' asked Faber sharply. 'Why should you care a row of beans what happens to Chiara and me?'

'You've become a Roman,' said Campeggio with cool irony. 'Still, it's a fair question. I like you. I think you and your girl deserve better than you're getting. I don't like Calitri. Nothing would give me greater satisfaction than to see him destroyed. That's almost impossible, but if your Chiara wins her case it will damage him a great deal.'

'Why do you dislike him so much?'

'I'd rather not answer that question.'

'We have common interests. We should at least be honest with each other.'

The Roman hesitated a moment, and then threw out his hands in a gesture of defeat. 'What does it matter anyway? There are no secrets in Rome. I have three sons. One of them works in Calitri's department and has, shall we say, fallen under his influence. I don't blame the boy. Calitri has great charm, and he doesn't scruple to use it.'

'A dirty business!'

'It's a dirty town,' said Orlando Campeggio. 'I'm the last man who should say it, but I often wonder why they call it the City of Saints.'

While George Faber was still chewing unhappily over his luncheon dialogue, Chiara Calitri was sunning herself on the beach, at Fregene.

She was a small dark girl, lithe as a cat; and the youths who passed, idling along the beach, whistled and preened themselves for her attention. Safe behind her sunglasses, she watched them come and go, and stretched herself more decoratively on the coloured towel.

A sense of comfort and well-being pervaded her. She was young, the admiration of the youths told her she was beautiful. She was loved. Faber in his uneasy fashion was committed to fight her battles. She was freer than she had ever been in her life.

It was the freedom which intrigued her most of all, and each day she became more conscious of it, more curious about it, and more eager for its enlargement. This morning she had wept and shouted like a market woman at poor George because he had seemed unwilling to risk a talk with Campeggio. If he wavered again she would fight him again because from now on she could not love without the liberty to be herself.

With Corrado Calitri she had felt herself torn apart, blown this way and that like paper shredded on the wind. For a time–a terrifying time–it was as if she had ceased to exist as a woman. Now at last she had put herself together again–not the same Chiara but a new one, and no one ever again must have the power to destroy her.

Deliberately she had chosen an older man because they were more tolerant and less demanding. They asked a more placid life. They offered affection as well as passion. They moved with authority in a wider world. They made a woman feel less vulnerable . . .

She sat up and began to toy with the warm sand, filtering it between her fingers so that it spilled out and made a small mound at her feet. Inconsequently she thought of an hourglass in which time measured itself inexorably in a spilth of golden grains. Even as a child she had been obsessed with time, reaching out for it as she now reached for freedom, spending it recklessly as if, by so doing, she could bring the future into today. When she was at home she had cried to go to school. At school she had wanted always to grow up. Grown up at last, she had wanted to be married. In marriage–the bitter fiasco of her marriage to Corrado Calitri–time had suddenly and dreadfully stood still, so that it seemed she must be anchored eternally to this union with a man who despised her womanhood and debased it at every opportunity.

It was from this terror of static time that she had fled finally into hysteria and illness. The future toward which she had reached so eagerly was now intolerable to her. She no longer wanted to advance but only to retreat into the dark womb of dependence.

Even here time was still her enemy. Life was time; an unendurable extension of loveless years. The only ways to end it were to die or to stay for ever in retreat. But in the hospital the vigilant nurses held death away from her, while the physicians drew her slowly and patiently back to another meeting with life. She had fought against them, but they too were inexorable. They stripped her illusions away one by one like layers of skin until the naked nerves were exposed, and she screamed in protest against their cruelty.

Then they had begun to show her a strange alchemy: how pain might transmute itself into a mercy. Endure it long enough and it began to diminish. Run from it, and it followed, always more monstrous like a pursuer in a nightmare. Fight it and in the end you could come to terms with it–not always the best terms, not always the wisest, but a treaty that was at least bearable.

She had made her own treaty with life now, and she was living better than she had hoped under the terms of it. Her family disapproved of the bargain, but they were generous enough to give her love and a measure of affection. She could not marry, but she had a man to care for her. The Church condemned her, but so long as she preserved a public discretion, it would withhold a public censure.

Society, in its paradoxical fashion, registered a mild protest and then accepted her with good enough grace ... She was not wholly free, nor wholly loved, nor wholly protected, but she had enough of each to make life bearable, and time endurable, because each now held a promise of betterment.

Yet it was not the whole answer, and she knew it. The treaty was not half as favourable as it looked. There was a catch in it–a dragnet clause which, once invoked, could cancel all the rest.

She looked out at the empty water of the Tyrrhenian Sea and remembered her father's tales of all the strange life that inhabited its deeps: Corals like trees, whales as big as a ship, fish that flapped their wings like birds, jewels that grew in oyster slime, and weeds like the hair of drowned princesses. Under the sunlit surface was a whole mysterious world, and sometimes the waters opened and swallowed down the voyager who risked them too boldly. Sometimes, but not always ... The most unlikely sailormen survived and came to safe harbour.

Here precisely was the risk of her own contract with life. She believed in God. She believed in the Church's teaching about Him. She knew the penalty of eternal ruin that hung over the heads of those who rashly dared the divine displeasure. Every step, every hour, was a tightrope venture of damnation. At any moment the contract might be called in. And then ... ?

Yet even this was not the whole mystery. There were others and deeper ones. Why she and not another had been submitted to the first injustice of a false marriage contract. Why she and not another had been forced into the suicidal confusion of a breakdown. And this precipitate grasping at any straw for survival. Why? Why?

It was not enough to say, like the parish confessor, that this was God's dispensation for her. It was Corrado's dispensation first. Did God compound injustice, and then hold damnation over the heads of those who wilted under its weight? It was as if the sea rose up and swirled her back into the confusion of her illness.

There was no cure for the untimely thought, that came in night-time or daytime, prickling along the flesh like a cold wind. One could not surrender to it for fear of a new madness. One could not blot it out except by the exercise of love and passion, which in a strange way seemed to affirm what the preachers said they denied: the reality of love and mercy, and the hand that helped the most hapless sailormen out of the damnation of the deep ...

She shivered in the warm air and stood up, wrapping the towel about her. A brown youth with the figure of a Greek god whistled and called to her, but she ignored him and hurried up the beach toward the car. What did he know of life who vaunted it like a phallic emblem in the sun? George knew better–dear middle-aged, uneasy George, who shared her risk and was at least working to rid her of it. She longed for the comfort of his arms and the sleep that came after the act of love ...

Rudolf Semmering, Father General of the Society of Jesus, sat in the airport at Fiumicino and waited for his man from Djakarta. To those who knew him well, his vigil was of singular significance. Rudolf Semmering was an efficient man, adapted by nature and ascetic exercise to the military spirit of Ignatius Loyola. Time to him was a precious commodity because only in time could one prepare for eternity. A waste of time was therefore a waste of the currency of salvation. The affairs of his order were complex and pressing, and he might easily have sent a deputy to meet this obscure member who was already thirty minutes late.

Yet the occasion seemed to demand a more than normal courtesy. The newcomer was a Frenchman, a stranger to Rome. He had spent more than twenty years in exile–in China, in Africa, in India, and the scattered islands of Indonesia. He was a simple priest, and a distinguished scholar, whom Rudolf Semmering had held in silence under his vow of obedience.

For a scholar the silence was worse than exile. He was free to work, to correspond with his colleagues all over the world, but he was prevented by a formal obedience from publishing the results of his research or teaching on any public rostrum. Many times in the last decade, Rudolf Semmering had questioned his own conscience about this prohibition laid on so brilliant a mind. Yet always he had come to rest on his first conviction that this was a chosen spirit which discipline could only refine, and whose bold speculations needed a term of silence to found themselves firmly.

A man with a sense of history, Semmering was convinced that the effectiveness of an idea depended on the temper of the time into which it was first introduced. It was too late in history to risk another Galileo affair or the burning of a new Giordono Bruno. The Church was still suffering from the sad debates over the Chinese rites. He was less afraid of heresy than of a climate of thought which could make heresy out of a new aspect of truth. He lacked neither compassion nor understanding of the sacrifices he demanded of a noble mind such as this one, but Jean Télémond, like every other member of the Society, had vowed himself to obedience, and when it had been exacted of him, he had submitted himself.

For Semmering this was the final test of the mettle of a religious man, the final evidence of his capacity for a godly work in a position of trust. Now the test was over, and he wanted to explain himself to Télémond and to offer him the affection that every son had a right to expect from his father in the spirit. Soon he would be asking Télémond to walk a new road, no longer solitary, no longer inhibited, but exposed, as he had never been exposed before, to the temptations of influence and the attacks of jealous interests. This time he would need support more than discipline, and Semmering wanted to offer them with warmth and generosity.

Diplomacy was involved as well. Since the time of Pacelli, the Cardinals of the Curia and the Bishops of the Church had been afraid of any attempt to introduce a Grey Eminence into the counsels of the Pontiff. They wanted, and so far they had had, a return to the natural order of the Church where the Curia were the counsellors of the Pontiff and the bishops were his co-workers, acknowledging his primacy as the successor of Peter, but holding equally to their own apostolic autonomy. If the Society of Jesus gave any appearance of attempting to push a favourite into the Papal Court, it would inevitably meet suspicion and hostility.

Yet the Pontiff had called for men, and the question was now how to offer this one without appearing to canvass for him . . . The voice of the traffic-caller crackled over the amplifiers announcing the arrival of a B.O.A.C. flight from Djakarta, Rangoon, New Delhi, Karachi, Beirut. Rudolf Semmering stood up, smoothed down his cassock and walked toward the customs entrance to meet the exile.

Jean Télémond would have been a striking man in any company. Six feet tall, straight as a ramrod, lean of visage, with grey hair and cool, humorous blue eyes, he wore his clerical black like a military uniform, while the yellow malarial tinge of his skin and the furrows about his upturned mouth told the story of his campaigns in exotic places. He greeted his superior with respectful reserve, and then turned to the porter who was struggling with three heavy suitcases.

'Be careful with those. There's half a lifetime of work in them.'

To Semmering he said with a shrug, 'I presumed I was being transferred. I brought all my papers with me.'

The Father General gave him one of his rare smiles. 'You were right, Father. You've been away too long. Now we need you here.'

A spark of mischief twinkled in Télémond's blue eyes. 'I was afraid I was to be hauled before the inquistion.'

Semmering laughed. 'Not yet . . . You're very, very welcome, Father.'

'I'm glad,' said Télémond with curious simplicity. 'These have been difficult years for me.'

Rudolf Semmering was startled. He had not expected a man so brusque and aware. At the same time he felt a small glow of satisfaction. This was no vague savant, but a man with a clear mind and a stout heart. Silence had not broken him, nor exile subdued him. An obedient spirit was one thing, but a man with a broken will was no use to himself or to the Church.

Semmering answered him gravely. 'I know what you've done. I know what you've suffered. I have, perhaps, made your life more difficult than it needed to be. I ask only that you believe I acted in good faith.'

'I've never doubted that,' said Jean Télémond absently. 'But twenty years is a long time.' He was silent a while, watching the green meadows of Ostia, dotted with old ruins and new excavations, where red poppies grew between the cracks of ancient stones. Suddenly he said, 'Am I still under suspicion, Father?'

'Suspicion of what?'

Télémond shrugged. 'Heresy, rebellion, a secret modernism, I don't know. You were never very clear with me.'

'I tried to be,' said Semmering mildly. 'I tried to explain that prudence was involved, and not orthodoxy. Some of your early papers and lectures came under the notice of the Holy Office. You were neither condemned nor censured. They felt, and I agreed with them, that you needed more time, and more study. You have great authority, you see. We wanted it used to the best advantage of the Faith.'

'I believe that,' said Jean Télémond. 'Otherwise I think I should have abandoned the work altogether.' He hesitated a moment and then asked, 'Where do I stand now?'

'We have brought you home,' said Semmering gently, 'Because we value you, and we need you. There is work for you here, urgent work.'

'I have never made conditions; you know that. I have never tried to bargain with God or with the Society. I worked as best I could within the limits imposed on me. Now . . . now I should like to ask something.'

'Ask it,' said Rudolf Semmering.

'I think,' said Télémond carefully, 'I think I have gone as far as I can on this lonely road. I think what I have done needs to be tested by discussion and debate. I should like to begin to publish, to submit my thesis to open criticism. This is the only way knowledge grows, the only way the horizons of the spirit are enlarged . . . I have never asked for anything before, but in this I beg for your support, and for the support of the Society.'

'You have it,' said Rudolf Semmering.

In the cramped seats of the speeding automobile they faced each other, superior and subject, the man under obedience, the man who exacted the fulfilment of the vow.

Télémond's lean face crumpled a little, and his blue eyes were misty. He said awkwardly, 'I–I did not expect so much. This is quite a homecoming.'

'It is better than you know,' said the Father General gently. 'But there are still risks.'

'I've always known there would be. What do you want me to do?'

'First you have to pass a test. It will be a rough one, and you have less than a month to prepare yourself.'

'What sort of test?'

'July 31st is the feast day of Saint Ignatius Loyola.'

'I was ordained on that day.'

'It makes a good omen than, because on that same day His Holiness will visit the Gregorian University, which you know owed its beginning to our founder and Saint Francis Borgia . . . I want you to deliver the memorial lecture in the presence of His Holiness, the teaching staff, and the students.'

'God help me,' said Jean Télémond. 'God help my stumbling tongue.'

As they turned into the clamour of the city, through the Lateran Gate, he buried his face in his hands and wept.

Ruth Lewin sat under a striped umbrella on the Via Veneto, sipped an *aranciata*, and watched the lunchtime crowds disperse toward siesta. The soft air of summer lifted her spirits and she felt as if all the weight of the world could be shrugged off with one long, comfortable yawn. Even the city seemed to have taken on a new face. The clamour of the traffic was a friendly sound. The folk were better dressed than usual. The waiters were more courteous. The ogling of the men was a compliment.

Nothing had changed in her situation. None of her doubts or dilemmas had resolved themselves, yet their burden was lighter, and she wore it with a better humour. It was as if her long convalescence was over and she could take her place confidently in the normal commerce of the world.

It was not all an illusion. She had suffered too long the perilous alternations of exaltation and depression to deceive herself about her cure. But the swings were shorter now–the heights less dizzy, the deeps less terrifying. The pulse of life was returning to a regular beat. The fever had broken at last and the moment of crisis had been her meeting with Kiril the Pontiff in a Roman back alley.

Even now the memory was lit by a kind of wonder. His aspect was so strange–the scar, the beard, the contrast between his office and his humble dress. Yet when she had confronted him in her own house, over the banality of coffee and biscuits, the impression was not of strangeness but of extraordinary simplicity.

Ever since her break with the Church, she had had a creeping distaste for clerical talk and the forms of clerical convention. This man had none of them. He wore his belief like a skin, and his convictions were expressed with the gentleness of one who had acquired them at a price he would not ask others to pay. His words came out new-minted and ringing with sincerity:

'. . . All life is a mystery, but the answer to the mystery is outside ourselves, and not inside. You can't go on peeling yourself like an onion, hoping that when you come to the last layer you will find what an onion really is. At the end you are left with nothing. The mystery of an onion is still unexplained because, like man, it is the issue of an eternal creative act . . . I stand in God's shoes, but I can't tell you any more. Don't you see? This is what I am here to teach—a mystery! People who demand to have Creation explained from beginning to end are asking the impossible. Have you ever thought that by demanding to know the explanation for everything you are committing an act of pride? We are limited creatures. How can any one of us encompass infinity . . .'

In the mouth of another the words would have sounded dry and stilted; but from this Kiril, they came endowed with a quality of healing, because they were not read from a book, but from the palimpsest of his own heart. He had not reproached her for the dereliction of a baptismal faith, but had talked of it with kindness, as if it were even a sort of mercy in itself.

'No two people come to God by the same road. There are very, very few who reach Him without stumbling and falling. There are seeds that grow a long time in darkness before they push up shoots into the sun . . . There are others that come to the light at one thrust in a single day . . . You are in darkness now, but if you want the light, you will come to it in time . . . The human soul, you see, meets barriers that it must cross, and they are not always crossed at one stride. The direction in which the soul travels is the important thing. If it travels away from itself, then it must ultimately come to God. If it turns back upon itself, this is a course of suicide because without God we are nothing . . . Everything, therefore, that urges you to an outward growth—service, love, the simplest interest in the world—can be a step toward Him . . .'

Disturbed as she was on that night, she had not taken in the full import of all that he had said. But the words had remained imprinted on her memory, and each day she found in them a new meaning, and a new application. If now she could sit calm in a summer sun watching the folly and flirtation of the town, passing no judgement on it or on herself, it was because of this Kiril, who sat in the seat of judgement and yet withheld verdict. If love were possible again, it would be because of him who lived solitary in the celibate City of the Vatican.

Love . . . ! It was a chameleon word and she had seen more of its changes and colorations than she could admit without blushing.

Every big city had its enclave of cripples and oddities and vagrants who sustained life on the best terms they could get, and were grateful for the most temporary easement from lonely misery. Here in Rome the kingdom of the beggars of love was a weird and polyglot domain and in her time she had wandered over most of it.

It was a treacherous journey for a widow of thirty-five with money in the bank and a heart empty of resources. Unhappy boys had wept at her breast for their mothers. Straying husbands and playing tourists had come knocking on her door. Men with noble names had made her the confidant of their exotic attachments. The secret sisterhood had offered her entry to the sapphic mysteries. In the end she had emerged, shaken and unsatisfied, knowing that even in the half-world of the odd ones, there was no place for her.

Love . . . ! Here on the Via Veneto, pretty girls with poodles on a leash sold it by the night's instalment. In the clubs and bars any woman with a foreign accent could buy it for a smile and the flirting of a lace handkerchief . . . But where and how did one find the person on whom to spend this newly discovered self–so fragile and suddenly so precious?

Miraculously, Humpty-Dumpty had been picked up and put together again. He was sitting back on the wall, smiling and clapping hands at the concourse. But if he tumbled again and the glue came unstuck . . . who then could patch the eggshell? O little white wandering spirit, please, please stay in one piece!

Out of the clamour of the traffic she heard her own name spoken. 'Ruth Lewin! Where have you been hiding yourself?'

She looked up to see George Faber, grey-haired and dapper as any Roman dandy, looking down at her.

In his private study, Kiril the Pontiff was closeted with two of his senior ministers: Cardinal Goldoni, his Secretary of State, and Cardinal Clemente Platino, Prefect of the Congregation for the Propagation of the Faith. The purpose of their meeting was a day-long stocktaking of the affairs of the Church, Holy, Universal, and Apostolic. The study was a large room bare of ornament save for a carved wooden crucifix behind the Pontiff's desk and, on the opposite wall, a case full of maps showing the distribution of Catholic communities throughout the world.

In another setting and another dress they might have been a trio of international businessmen: the Pontiff, dark, bearded and exotic; the Secretary of State, grey, stocky and harshly eloquent; Platino, tall, olive-skinned, urbane, with a great eagle beak inherited from some Spanish ancestor.

But in this place and in this time they were dedicated, each to the limit of his own talent, to a folly that promised small profit to any business: the preparation of all men for death and for union with an unseen God. Their talk ranged over a multitude of subjects: money, politics, military treaties, economic agreements, personalities in high places round the globe; yet the core of the discussion was always the same: how to spread throughout the world the knowledge of Christ, His teaching, and the society which He had set up to preserve and disseminate it.

For them every question–how a man married, how he was educated, what he was paid, his national allegiance–was at root a theological proposition. It had to do with the Creator and the creatures and the eternal relationship of one with the other. Everything that was done in the dimension of time had its roots and its continuity in eternity.

When the Secretary of State appointed an ambassador to Austria or a legate to Uruguay, his function was to maintain an official relationship with the government, so that in a climate of accord between Church and State human souls might be led the more easily to the knowledge and the practice of a saving truth.

When Platino appointed this missionary congregation or that to go into the jungles of the Amazon, he did so with the fullest conviction that he was obeying a clear command of Christ, to carry a Gospel of hope to those who sat in darkness and the shadow of death.

It was, however, a point of view that raised special problems of its own. Men who did a godly work were apt to become careless about the human aspect of it. Men who dealt with the currency of eternity were apt to rest too hopefully on the future and let the present slip out of their control. Those who were sustained by the two-thousand-year-old structure of the Church were protected too softly from the consequence of their own mistakes. With so much tradition to rest on, they were often prickly and suspicious about new modes of Christian action.

Yet in spite of all, men like Platino and Goldoni had an acute awareness of the world in which they lived and of the fact that, to do the work of God, they had to come to terms with what man had done for himself or to himself. Platino was making this point now. His long brown finger pointed to a spot in South-east Asia.

'. . . Here, for example, Holiness, is Thailand. Constitutionally it is a monarchy. In fact it is a military dictatorship. The religion of the state is Buddhism. At one time or another in his life every male of the royal family, and every senior official, takes the saffron robe and spends some time in a monastery. We have schools here. They are run by nuns and teaching priests. They are free to give religious instruction but not within normal school hours. Those who wish to be instructed in the faith must come outside these times. This is our first difficulty. There is another. Government appointments–and any position of consequence is a government appointment–are only open to Buddhists. Officially, of course, this is not admitted, but in fact it is true. The country is under-developed. Most commerce is in the hands of Chinese, so that, for all practical purposes, a man who becomes a Christian must give up all hope of economic or social advancement . . . The temper of the people, which has also been conditioned by Buddhist belief, is resistant to change and suspicious of outside influence . . .

'On the other hand, there is evident among the young men a growing interior conflict. They are being brought every day into closer contact with Western civilization through American military and economic aid; but there is little opportunity or work for them. I have been given what I believe is a reliable statistic, that twenty-five per cent of senior male students are addicted to heroin before they leave school. You see the problem. How do we move to make a real penetration of the minds and hearts of the people?'

'How do you summarize the work we are doing now?' asked the Pontiff gravely.

'Basically as a work of education and charity. On the human level we are helping to raise the standard of literacy. We run hospitals which are used as training centres. There is a home for the rehabilitation of girls who have been taken out of the brothels . . . We serve the community. We display the faith to those who pass through our hands. However, the number of conversions is small, and we have not yet entered effectively into the mind and heart of the country.'

'We have a worse position in Japan,' said Goldoni in his brisk fashion. 'We have a concordat which gives us much more effective working conditions than we have in Thailand, but here again we have made no real break-through.'

'Yet we did once make a break-through,' said Kiril with a smile. 'It was begun by one man. Saint Francis Xavier. The descendants of his are still there–the Old Christians of Nagasaki and Nara. Why do we fail now? We have the same message. We dispense the same grace as the Church of the catacombs. Why do we fail?' He heaved himself out of the chair and stood by the map, pointing to one country after another and measuring the failures and retreats of the Church. 'Look at Africa. My predecessors proclaimed constantly the need for the swift training of a native clergy: men identified with their own people, speaking their language, understanding their symbols and their special needs. Too little was done too slowly. Now the continent is moving toward a federation of independent African nations, and the ground has been cut from under our feet . . . Here in Brazil you have an immense industrial expansion, and a huge population of peasants living in the most grinding poverty. To whom are they turning to champion their cause? To the Communists. Do we not preach justice? Should we not be prepared to die for it as for any other Article of Faith? I ask you again. Where do we miss?'

Goldoni breathed a silent sigh of relief and left the answer to his colleague. After all a Secretary of State had to deal with a situation as it was, with diplomats and politicians as they were–good or bad, pagan or Christian. Platino, on the other hand, was charged directly with the spread of Christian belief throughout the world. His authority was enormous, and inside the Church they called him 'The Red Pope' as the Father General of the Jesuits was called the black one.

Platino did not answer directly, but picked up from the desk two photographs which he held out to the Pontiff. One of them showed a fuzzy-haired Papuan in a white shirt and white lap-lap, with a small crucifix hung round his neck. The other was the picture of a native from the uplands of New Guinea with a head-dress of bird-of-paradise feathers and a pig tusk thrust through his nose.

As the Pontiff examined the photographs, Platino explained them carefully:

'Perhaps these two men will answer Your Holiness's question. They both come from the same island, New Guinea. It is a small place, economically unimportant, but politically it may become so as the pivot of a federation of South Pacific Islands. In two years, five at most, New Guinea will be an independent country. This man . . .' He pointed to the photograph of the man who wore the crucifix. 'This is a mission boy. A teacher in one of our Catholic shools on the Coast. He has lived all his life in a mission colony. He speaks English and Pidgin and Motu. He teaches the catechism, and has been proposed as a candidate for the priesthood . . . This one is a tribal chief from the mountains: a leader of twenty thousand men. He speaks no English, he understands Pidgin, but speaks only his own upland dialect. He is wearing now a ceremonial dress. He still holds to the old pagan beliefs . . . Yet, when independence is granted to this country, he is the most likely leader, while our mission boy will have no influence at all.'

'Tell me why,' said Kiril the Pontiff.

'I have thought about it a long time, Holiness,' said Platino deliberately. 'I have prayed much. I am still not sure that I am right, but this is what I believe. With our mission boy, we have in one sense succeded admirably. We have educated a good human being. We have set him in the way of salvation. He lives chastely, deals justly, and displays in himself the example of a godly life. If he becomes a priest, he will teach the Word and dispense the Grace of the Sacraments to those with whom he comes in contact. In him and those like him, the Church fulfils her prime mission–the sanctification of individual human souls . . . In another sense, however, we have failed because in this boy–how shall I say it?–we have limited the relevance of the faith . . . In the mission we have created a small, safe world for him. A Christian world, yes, but one that has cut itself off from the larger world which is still God's vineyard. We have made him an apolitical individual, and man by his nature is a political and social animal who has an immortal soul . . . We have left him, in large part, unprepared for the dialogue which he must sustain throughout his life with the rest of his fellows in the flesh . . . Look at our friend here, the one with the tusk through his nose. He is a man of power because he practises polygamy and each wife brings him a plot of land and then cultivates it for him. He holds to the old beliefs because these are his ground of communication with his tribe. He is their mediator with the spirits as he is their mediator with men of other tongues. He understands tribal law and tribal justice. In the difficulty and confusion which will follow the granting of independence, he will speak with more authority and more relevance than our mission boy, because he has not been divorced from the realities of social existence . . . Your Holiness spoke of Brazil and the South Americas. There is an analogy between the two situations. The Church has to deal with man in the circumstances in which he lives. If he is hungry we have to feed him; if he is oppressed we must defend him so that he may have, at least, a minimum freedom to set his soul in order. We cannot preach from the pulpit, "Thou shalt not steal", and then stand by inactive while political or social injustice is done to those who sit and listen to our preaching . . . We see a strange example in Poland, where the church has had for very survival to enter actively into a conversation with elements hostile to it. It has had to prove itself relevant, and it has done so. It lives the more strongly for that very reason, even though it lives more painfully . . .'

He broke off and mopped his forehead with a handkerchief.

'Forgive me, Holiness, if I speak more strongly still. We have all seen the progress that was made under your predecessor toward a growth of unity between the separated Christian communities. Our work in this field has only begun, but it seems to me that where we have been defensive, where we have retreated, holding the faith to ourselves as though it could be tarnished by contact with the world, there we have failed. Where we have held it up for a witness, where we have affirmed most boldly that the Gospel is relevant to every human act and every situation, there we have done well.'

'You affirm it,' said Kiril the Pontiff bluntly. 'I affirm it, as do our brother bishops scattered across the world, but affirmation does not reach the people with the same clearness and the same fruitfulness—it does not even reach my Romans here. Why?'

'I think,' said the Secretary of State brusquely, 'the world is educating itself more quickly than the Church. Put it another way. The knowledge that is necessary to make an Act of Faith, and an Act of Repentance, is not enough to found a Christian society or create a religious climate. In the last twenty years men have been projected into a new and terrifying dimension of existence . . . The graph of human science from the invention of the wheel to the internal-combustion engine is a long, gradual slope. It covers—what?—five, ten, fifteen thousand years. From the internal-combustion engine to this moment, the line leaps almost vertically, pointing to the moon . . . *Tempora mutantur* . . .' He quoted wryly, 'Times change and man changes with them. If our mission means anything, it means that each new enlargement of the human mind should be an enlargement of man's capacity to know, love, and serve God.'

'I think,' said Kiril the Pontiff with a smile, 'I should send you both out on a missionary journey . . .' He crossed to his desk and sat down, facing them. He seemed to gather himself for a moment and then very quietly, almost humbly, he explained himself. 'I am as you know an eager man. It has been my fear, since I have sat in the Chair of Peter, that I should act too hastily and damage the Church which is given into my hands ... I have tried to be prudent and restrained; I have understood also that one man in his lifetime cannot change the world. The symbol of the Cross is a symbol of the apparent failure and folly of God Himself ... But it is my office to teach and to direct, and I have decided now where I want to begin ... What you have told me confirms me in the decision. I am grateful to you both. I want you both to pray for me.'

The two Cardinals sat silent, waiting for him to go on. To their surprise he shook his head. 'Be patient with me. I need time and prayer before I declare myself. Go in the name of God.'

'I suppose,' said George Faber in his uncomfortable fashion, 'I suppose you're wondering why I'm telling you all this about Chiara and me.'

Ruth Lewin laughed and shrugged. 'That's the way it goes in Rome–everybody's got a story. And a stranger's usually the best listener.'

'We're not really strangers, though. How many times have we met? Half a dozen at least. At the Antonellis' and at Herman Seidler's and ...'

'So I'm convinced we're not strangers. Take it from there.'

'I was feeling low–and I was delighted to see you.'

'Thank you, kind sir.'

'And I don't tell my life story to every girl I meet on a street corner.'

'I don't think it matters in Rome whether you tell it or not. People know it just the same–in different versions, of course!'

Faber grinned and looked for a moment like a self-conscious boy. 'I've never heard your story, Ruth.'

She parried the probe with a smile. 'I've never told it. And I don't belong to the cocktail set.'

'Where do you belong?'

'I've often wondered that myself.'

'Do you have many friends here?'

'A few. They call me for dinner sometimes. I visit them when I feel inclined. I do a little work amongst some lame ducks in Old Rome. For the rest ... *Mi arrangio.* I get along one way and another.'

'Are you happy?'

Once again she hedged the answer. 'Is anyone? Are you?'

'I'm in a mess,' said George Faber bluntly.

'That's not your reputation.'

Faber looked up sharply, wondering if she were mocking him. He had a small humour, and banter always made him suspicious. 'What's my reputation?'

'You have the tidiest life in Rome ... and a beautiful mistress to round it out.'

'That's not the way I see it. I want to get married. It seems the only way I can do it is to mix myself up with blackmail and backstairs politics, and a bunch of gay boys and Lesbians.'

'Don't you think the risk is worth it?'

His heavy handsome face clouded and he ran a nervous hand through his grey hair. 'I suppose it is. I haven't really had time to think it out.'

'That means you're not sure.'

'No, I'm not sure.'

As if to divert her attention he signalled the waiter to bring him another cup of coffee. Then he lit a cigarette and stared moodily at the shop-front on the other side of the pavement. For all her detachment, Ruth Lewin felt herself touched by a pang of pity for him. He was no longer young, though most women would find him attractive. He had built himself a comfortable career and a respectable name in his trade. Now he was being asked to risk them both for a girl who, once free, might grow tired of him and look for younger loving. She dropped her teasing tone, and questioned him more gently.

'What does Chiara want?'

'Freedom at any price.'

'Even at the price of your career?'

'I'm not sure of that either.'

'Don't you think you should ask her?'

'That's what bothers me . . . I'm not even clear myself what the risks are. All I know is that, on the one hand, there's an element of blackmail, and I'm to be the blackmailer . . . Don't misunderstand me. I've been in this game a long time. I know that every newsman is tempted at some time or another to use his position for his own profit. My experience is that those who do it always lose in the end. I've never been a muckraker, and I'm rather proud of it . . . On the other hand, I'm fighting for something and someone very precious to me.'

'If you start a fight with Corrado Calitri,' said Ruth Lewin soberly, 'I can promise you it will be a very rough one.'

He stared at her, surprised. 'Do you know Calitri then?'

'I know some of the people he knows. They play very dirty when their feelings are hurt.'

He hesitated a moment and then faced her with the question, 'Could you help me to meet some of them?'

'No.' She was very definite about it.

'Why not?'

'I lived in that little Arcady for a while. I didn't like it. I don't want to go back. Besides, you're a newsman. You have your own contacts.'

'Not too many I can trust. Would you be willing to give me names . . . information?'

To his surprise she burst out laughing and then, seeing his discomfiture, she laid an apologetic hand on his wrist. 'Poor George! I shouldn't laugh at you. But I wonder . . . I really wonder . . .'

'What?'

'About you and Chiara. Are you both so sure you can go through with this fight–win or lose? If you lose, you know, they'll tear you into little pieces and feed you to the lions like early Christians. The Church won't have either of you. You'll never be welcome again at the Vatican or on the Quirinale. Are you both ready for that? Do you have enough love for Chiara? Does she have enough for you?'

He shrugged and spread his hands in a Roman gesture of puzzlement. 'Beh! Everybody in Rome talks about love. Everybody plays at it in his own fashion. I've played, too, but now it's late in the day for me. I don't want to make a mistake.'

'I'd like to help you,' she told him quietly, 'but it's your life and your girl . . . I should go now, it's getting late.'

'Would you let me take you home?'

'Better not. I'll get a taxi.'

'Could I see you again?'

'Why, George?'

He flushed unhappily. 'I've enjoyed talking to you. I hope you'll decide to help me. And if I go ahead with this Calitri business, I'll need to talk to someone I can trust.'

'What makes you think you can trust me?'

'You said yourself you don't belong to the gossip circuit. I'd like to add that you're a very grown-up girl.'

'Is that the best recommendation you can give me?'

Once again his rare humour asserted itself. 'Give me time and I may think of others.'

'If and when you do, you can call me. I'm in the telephone book.'

On which indecisive note they parted. As she rode home through the clamour of the afternoon traffic, she remembered that it was late in the day for her, too, and she felt again the pang of treacherous pity for George Faber and his puzzled, middle-aged heart.

EXTRACT FROM THE SECRET MEMORIALS OF KIRIL I PONT. MAX.

. . . It is an hour after midnight–the beginning of a new day. An important day for me because for the first time I shall begin to address myself to the whole Church. Late last evening I asked my confessor to come to me so that I might purge myself from the sins of the day, and purify myself for the task I am about to undertake.

Afterwards I begged him to stay with me a little while and serve the Mass which I wanted to celebrate immediately after midnight . . . It is strange how much variety there can be for a priest in the offering of the Sacrifice. Sometimes one is dry and unmoved, one has to make an effort of will to concentrate on the familiar ritual and on the staggering significance of the Act of Consecration. At other times it is as if one is caught out of oneself and 'into the spirit', as Saint John puts it. One is aware of God. One is at the same moment humbled and exalted, afraid and rapturously glad . . .

Tonight is was different again. I began to understand in a new fashion the nature of my office. When, at the moment of elevation, I lifted the Host above my head I saw the real meaning of the 'We' with which the Pontiffs have addressed themselves customarily to the world. It is not 'I' who am to speak or to write, it is the Church through me and Christ through me and the Church.

I am myself, yes. But if I speak only of myself and for myself, I am nothing. I am like the wind bells whose sound changes with every breeze . . . But the Word cannot change. The Word is immutable . . . 'In the beginning was the Word, and the Word was with God, and the Word was God.' . . . Yet in another sense the Word must renew itself in me as the redemptive act of the crucifixion renews itself at the hands of every priest when he says Mass. I am the reed through which the voice of the spirit must be blown so that men may hear it in the mode of their own times . . .

The paper is blank before me, the pens are ready. Is Kiril ready? I pray that he may be. What must he write? And how and to whom?

My subject is education, the preparation of a man to take his place in this world and in the next. My letter will be a discussion of the educative office of the Church–its mission to 'lead out' the soul of man from the darkness of ignorance, from the bondage of the flesh, into the light and the freedom of the Sons of God . . .

How shall I write? As simply as I can because the deepest truth is the most simply stated. I must write from the heart—*cor ad cor loquitur*. And I must write in my own tongue because this is the best fashion for every man to talk of God, and to Him. Later the Latinists will take my words and harden them into the antique form which will preserve them for a permanent record in the Church. After them will come the translators who will turn them into a hundred other tongues in which the Word of God must be preached . . . The world is a Babel Tower of conflicting voices, but inside the Church there is and must always be 'the unity of the spirit in the bond of Faith'.

Outside the Church, too, there is a unity which we neglect too often. It is the unity of men who suffer together a common existence, delight in common joys, and share the same confusions, regrets, and temptations . . .

I am reminded of something forgotten too often by us the shepherds, Tertullian's 'Testimony of the Soul' . . . 'Man is one name belonging to every nation upon earth. In them all is one soul though many tongues. Every country has its own language, yet the subjects of which the untutored soul speaks are the same everywhere.'

There is another reason why I want to write in Russian. I want Kamenev to see my letter as it came from my own hand. I want him to hear through it the tones of my voice so that he may know that I love him and the people among whom I was born. If it were possible I should like him to have my manuscript, but it may be difficult to get it into his hands, and I could not risk compromising him.

To whom shall I write? . . . To the whole Church—to my brother bishops, to all priests and monks and nuns, to all the faithful, without whom our office is meaningless. I must show them how their mission is not merely to teach but to educate one another with love and forbearance, each lending of his own strength to the weak, of his own knowledge to the ignorant, of his charity to all . . .

And when I have written, what then? I must begin to act through the administration of the Church to see that reforms are made where they are needed and that the inertia of a large and scattered organization does not stand in the way of God's intention. I must have patience, too, and tolerance, understanding that I have no right to demand of God a visible success in all I attempt. I am the gardener. I plant the seed and water it, knowing that death may take me before I see the bud or the flower. It is late and I must begin . . .

'Kiril, the servant of the Servants of God, to the Bishops and Brethren of all the Churches, peace and apostolic benediction . . .'

5

The homecoming of Jean Télémond, S. J., was a drab little affair that belied the warmth of his superior's welcome.

The headquarters of the Society, at No. 5 Borgo Santo Spirito, was a large grey building, bleak as a barracks, that nestled under the shadow of St Peter's Dome. Its furnishings were sparse, functional, and without discernible beauty. The only man to greet him was the brother porter, a grey and crusty veteran who had seen so many members come and go that one more made no matter.

The whole aspect of the place was cheerless and temporary, a shelter for men whose training was to divest themselves of comfort and human attachment and make themselves soldiers of Christ. Even the religious emblems were ugly and mass-produced, reminders only of the interior life which no symbol could properly convey.

After they had prayed together, the Father General led him to his room, a small, whitewashed box, furnished with a bed, a prie-dieu, a crucifix, a desk, and a set of bookshelves. Its dusty windows looked out on a courtyard, chill and deserted even under the summer sun. Jean Télémond had lived more harshly than most and in less friendly places, but this first look at the Mother House plunged him into a deep depression of spirit. He felt solitary and naked and strangely afraid. The Father General gave him the timetable of the House, promised to introduce him to his colleagues at suppertime, and then left him to his own devices.

It took him only a few moments to unpack his meagre personal belongings, and then he set about the task of laying out the mass of notes, manuscripts, and bulky folders which represented his lifework. Now, when the time had come to make the tally of it and present it to the world, it seemed small and insignificant.

For twenty years he had worked as a palaeontologist, in China, in Africa, in America, and the Far Indies, plotting the geography of change, the history of life recorded in the crust of the earth. The best scientific minds had been his colleagues and co-workers. He had survived war and revolution and disease and loneliness. He had endured the perilous dichotomy between his function as a scientist and his life as a religious priest. To what end?

For years the conviction had been growing in him that the only intelligible purpose of so much effort and sacrifice was to display the vast concordance of creation, the ultimate convergence of the spiritual and physical which would mark the eternal completion of an eternal creative Impulse. Many times he had pondered the significance of the old proverb, 'God writes straight with crooked lines', and he was convinced to the marrow of his bone that the final vector of all the diverse forces of creation was an arrow pointing straight to a personal divinity.

Many another before him had attempted this justification of God to men. Their achievements and their failures were the milestones of human thought–Plato, Saint Augustine, Albertus Magnus, Thomas of Aquin . . . Each had used the knowledge of his own time to build a theology or a philosophy or a cosmology . . . Each had added another stage to the journey of unaided reason; each had elevated man thus much above the jungle that spawned him.

For Télémond the project presented itself in another form; to trace, from the text of the living earth, the journey from unlife to life, from life to consciousness, from consciousness to the final unity of Creation with its Creator.

The study of the past, he believed, was the key to the pattern of the future. The justification of the past and of the present lay in the tomorrow that would thrust out of them. He could not believe in a wasteful Creator or in a diffuse, accidental, purposeless Creation. At the root of all his thought and, he belived, at the root of every human aspiration was an instinctive desire for a unity and a harmony in the cosmos. Once men abandoned their hope for it, they condemned themselves to suicide or madness.

That the harmony did exist, he was convinced beyond doubt. That it could be demonstrated he believed also—though in another mode of credence. The pattern was laid but it was not yet complete. He believed he had grasped the main lines of it; but his problem was to explain them in terms intelligible and acceptable. So vast an exposure needed new words, new levels of thought, new analogies and a new boldness in speculation.

For too long Western thought had been disinclined toward a unified knowledge of the world. Even in the Church the spiral thinking of the Eastern fathers, the traditional Christian *gnosis*, had been overshadowed by the nominalist and rationalist tradition of Western theologians. Now, if ever, the hope of the world's survival seemed to rest on a leap out of mere logic into a recognition of new and bolder modes of communication.

Yet the terror of this first moment in Rome was that under the first impact of this noisy, brawling city, where past and present rubbed elbows with each other at every step, his conviction seemed to be weakening. Rome was so sure of itself, so sophisticated, so sceptical, so certain that everything that had happened or could happen had been weighed and judged beyond dispute—that his own voice must sound small and meaningless.

A long time ago, from a hut on the fringe of the Gobi desert, he had written, 'I understand now how little mere travel gives to a man. Unless the spirit expands with the explosion of space about him, then he returns the same man as he went out.' Here in the Mother House of the Society, where all the rooms looked the same, where everyone was dressed in the same black cassock and attended the same exercises of devotion, and ate at the same table, he wondered whether in truth he had changed at all, and whether the enlargement which he thought to have attained was not a bitter illusion.

With a gesture of impatience, he stacked the last manuscripts on the desk, closed the door on them, and walked out to view the city which threatened him so vividly.

A few moments' walking brought him out on to the broad reach of the Street of Conciliation and in full view of the Piazza of St Peter's. The slim finger of the obelisk pointed to the sky, and on either hand Bernini's colonnades swept backward to the sunlit dome of the Basilica. The sudden majesty of it all—the towering cupola, the gigantic figures of windy stone, the rearing masses of columns and pilasters—oppressed him and he felt drunk with the suddenness of sun and space.

Instinctively he lowered his eyes to the human aspect: the straggle of afternoon tourists, the coachmen gossiping at their horses' heads, the pedlars with their little boxes of rosaries, the buses and cars, and the slim jets of the fountains. Once again the cogs of memory slipped into gear and he remembered what he had written after his first look at the Grand Canyon of the Colorado . . . 'I am either unmoved or tremendously troubled by the sight of natural grandeur, or even by a spectacular artifact deserted by its makers. As soon as man appears I am comforted again because man is the only significant link between the physical order and the spiritual one. Without man the universe is a howling wasteland contemplated by an unseen Deity. . . .' If man deserted even this ageless splendour of St Peter's, it would decay and rot into a goat-cropping, where tree roots grew out of the stones and animals drank from the muddy basins of the fountains.

Encouraged, he strolled across the Piazza toward the entrance of the Basilica, pausing to look up at the papal apartments and ask himself what manner of man now dwelt in them. Soon they would meet face to face, and Jean Télémond would have to justify his own life's work to a man charged to perpetuate the life of the whole Church. Already rumours were rife about the new Pontiff and his challenge to the reactionaries and the extreme traditionalists in the Vatican. There were those who saw him as the prime mover of a second Renaissance within the Church, a new and unexpected link between the logical West and the illuminated East.

If the rumours were true then there was hope that Jean Télémond might be freed at last from his exile. If not . . .

On the opposite side of the Piazza lay the Palace of the Holy Office, where the Hounds of God kept watch over the Deposit of Faith. To them Jean Télémond was known already. Once a priest came under their scrutiny he was never forgotten, and everything he wrote must pass through their hands before it could be printed. Cardinal Leone was still there, too, he of the white mane and the cold eye and the uncertain temper. It was an open secret that Leone had small liking for the Father General of the Jesuits and that he favoured more the opinions and the manners of the older orders in the Church. Télémond wondered what had prompted Semmering to risk the displeasure of the old lion by bringing back to Rome a man of suspect opinions.

There were politics inside the Church as well as out of it. There were questing minds and reluctant ones. There were blind traditionalists and too eager innovators. There were men who sacrificed order to growth, and others who reached so boldly for change that they held it back for centuries. There were rank pietists and fierce ascetics. There were administrators and apostles–and God help any luckless fellow who was caught between the millstones.

There was only one refuge; one committal which he had made a long time ago. A man could walk only the path he saw at his own feet or that which was pointed out to him by a lawful superior. After that he was in the hands of God . . . And their compass was more generous, their hold more reassuring, than the hands of any man.

In spite of the warmth, he shivered and quickened his steps toward the interior of the Basilica. Looking neither to right nor left, he walked down the echoing nave toward the sanctuary, and then knelt for a long time praying at the tomb of Peter.

In the small cold hours between midnight and dawn, George Faber lay wakeful and grappled with his new situation. Beside him Chiara lay sleeping like a child, satiated and tranquil. Never in the months of their loving had he experienced a passion so tumultuous, a mating so abandoned, as on this night. Every sense had quickened, every emotion had surged up and spent itself in a climax of union so intense that death itself had seemed only a whisper away. Never had he felt so much a man. Never had Chiara shown herself so generously a woman. Never had speech been stifled so swiftly by the outpourings of tenderness and the transports of desire . . . Never in all his life had he been so suddenly overwhelmed by the sadness of the afterward.

When their loving was done Chiara had given a small contented sigh, buried her face in the pillow and lapsed immediately into sleep. It was as if she had left him without warning and without farewell to embark on a private journey—as if having touched the limit of love he were left solitary to face the darkness and the terrors of an endless night.

The terrors were more real than they had ever been before. For so rich a pleasuring, some time, somehow, a price must be paid. And he knew beyond the shadow of a doubt that he would be the one to pay it. What he had felt this night was a springtime flowering which might never repeat itself, because for him it was late summer, late harvest, with the tax man waiting at the gate to claim his due.

For Chiara life was still her debtor. Payment had been deferred too long and her body was greedy for the tribute. For himself, a man on the wrong side of forty, the case was far other. He knew where the price tags were hidden. He knew the needs that followed the brisk satisfaction of the act of union: the need of continuity, the need of children to be born of the seed so richly spent in lust or love, the need of quiet harbour and a morning sunlight after the storms of the night.

Even as he thought about it, Chiara stirred and turned toward him for warmth. It was a gesture made in a dream but it was more eloquent than words. Until her marriage to Calitri she had been protected at every step—by rich and doting parents, by cosseting nuns, by the traditions of her class. When her marriage had failed she had found another refuge, and now she had come to rest in his arms to forgetfulness in his practised embrace. So long as he held her strongly and securely she would stay. But the moment his grip slackened or his courage faltered, she would slip away.

The strange thing was that she saw nothing one-sided in the bargain. She had given her body, she had given him her reputation; what else was there to demand? Had he told her, she would never have understood. Married and the mother of children she would grow in the end to maturity, but in this halfway state she would always be the girl-woman, half delighted by the adventure, half afraid of its consequences, but never wholly understanding that the debt of love was not all paid in the coinage of the flesh.

For her even tonight's encounter, rich, ruinous and wonderful, was a kind of flight—and he was too old, too wise, or too calculating to make it with her. Instinctively he turned, threw his arms about her and drew her to him, wondering even as he did so why the miraculous oneness of the flesh should last so short a time, and why in the end two lovers must lie so often and so long like islands in a dark sea. Her slack hand lay across his body, her hair brushed his lips, her perfume surrounded him. But sleep would not come, and he rehearsed over and over again their dinner-table talk, when he had told her of Compeggio's advice, and where it might lead the pair of them . . .

She had listened attentively, chin cupped in her hands, her dark eyes bright with eagerness, intrigued by the prospect of a plot.

'Of course, darling! It's so simple. Why didn't we think of it before? There must be twenty people in Rome who'd be happy to give evidence against Corrado. All we've got to do is find them.'

'Do you know any of them, Chiara?'

'Not really. Corrado was always fairly discreet with me. Still, I'm sure if we talked around we'd get a whole list of names.'

'The one thing we mustn't do,' he told her firmly, 'is talk around. If word gets out about what we're doing, we're finished. Don't you understand? This is a conspiracy.'

'George, darling, don't be so melodramatic. All we're trying to do is get justice for me. You couldn't call that conspiracy, surely.'

'It wears the colour of it. And in the eyes of the Church, and civil law, it comes to the same thing. There are only two things we can do—employ a professional investigator or I'll have to do the investigation myself. If we use an investigator it will cost me more money than I can afford, and in the end he could sell me out to your husband. If I do the job myself . . . I'm immediately embroiled up to the neck.'

She stared at him, wide-eyed and innocent. 'Are you afraid, George?'

'Yes, I am.'

'Of my husband?'

'Of his influence, yes.'

'Don't you want to marry me, darling?'

'You know I do. But once we're married we have to live. If I lose my reputation in Rome I can't work here any longer. We'd have to go back to America.'

'I wouldn't mind that . . . Besides, what about my reputation? I didn't throw that in your face, did I?'

'Please, Chiara! Please try to understand this isn't a matter of morals, it's a matter of authority, professional status . . . the credit I live by. If I'm held up as a common blackmailer . . . where do I start again? This is the double standard, sweetheart. You can sleep around as much as you like. You can make a million by exploiting the poor. But if you pass a bad cheque for ten dollars or breach the code of professional ethics, you're dead and buried and there's no coming back. That's the way the world is, rough as guts. Do what you want. Take what you want. But if you trip—God help you! That's what we have to face—together.'

'If I'm not afraid, George, why should you be?'

'I've got to be sure that you know what's involved.'

'I wonder if you really know what's involved for me. A woman needs to be married, George. She needs to have a home and children, and a man who belongs to her. What we have is wonderful, but it isn't enough. If you won't fight for it, George, what can I do?'

. . . And there it was, the challenge that had taken him at one stride to her arms—a challenge to his virility, a challenge to the one folly he had never indulged—to count the world well lost for love. But George Faber was a man of his own world. He knew himself too well to believe that he could live without it. He had made the gesture, to be sure. He had flung his cap at the whirling windmills, but when the time came to assault them with a sword and lance, how would he be then? A knight in shining armour with his lady's favour on his helm . . . ? Or an ageing Quixote on a spavined nag, an object of laughter for men and angels?

Valerio Cardinal Rinaldi sat on the terrace of his villa and watched the day decline toward the sea. The folds of the land were full of purple shadows, the hills were touched with gold and bronze, and the rooftops of village and farmhouse shone russet in the glow. A small breeze stirred across the land, carrying the scent of lilac and roses, and mown grass. The sound of childish laughter rose from the garden below, where his niece's daughter played among the Orphic marbles.

This was the good time—the hour between day and dusk, when the eye was rested from the harshness of the sun and the spirit was not yet touched by the melancholy of twilight. The cicadas were still, and the crickets had not begun their mournful chirping. He picked up the book that lay on his lap and began to read the crabbed Greek characters which hid the magical words of Euripides:

> *'And O for that quiet garden by the Western sea*
> *Where the daughters of Evening sing*
> *Under the golden apple-tree;*
> *Where the bold sailor wandering*
> *Finds the Ocean-god has barred*
> *His Westward path over the purple waste!*
> *Where huge Atlas lives to guard*
> *The solemn frontiers of the sky!*
> *Where in Zeus' palace fountains of ambrosial wine*
> *Flow by the festal couch divine,*
> *While holy Earth heaps high*
> *Her fruits of rarest taste*
> *To bless the immortal feast with bountiful supply!'*

He was a lucky man and he knew it. It was given to few to arrive at eminence and then survive it with a strong heart and a good digestion to enjoy the quiet garden where the daughters of Evening sang. It was given to few in his profession to hear the voices of children in his own orchard close, to have them cluster about his knee for a story, to give them a kiss and an old priest's blessing at bedtime.

Others he knew had died before their time. Others again survived painfully, with blear eyes or palsied limbs or slow cankers, on the charity of the Church. Some lapsed into senility or a poverty of possession and spirit. But he sat here in the splendour of a fading day—prosperous, independent, the last of the princely Cardinals of the Church. He had few regrets, because regret had always seemed a vanity and alien to his nature. He was ready for retirement—prepared for it, too, by a curious and scholarly mind and a diversity of friendships and interests. He did not fear death because in the normal course it was still a long way off, and he had lived an orderly life, investing his talents as best he knew for the service of the Church.

Yet sometimes—in the twilight hour, in the wakeful nights of an old man, or when he watched the peasants bending over the tillage of his estate—the poignant question presented itself: why have I so much? Why am I endowed so richly and others in so niggardly a fashion? Or is this all a divine irony whose point will be revealed only in eternity?

Old Euripides had raised the same question and yet answered it no better:

> *'They wander over the waves, visit strange cities,*
> *Seeking a world of wealth,*
> *All alike sure of achievement; yet*
> *One man's aim misses the lucky moment,*
> *Another finds fortune in his lap.'*

And there was another question still. What did one do with all this fruitage of life? Toss it away, like little Brother Francis, and walk the world singing the praise of Lady Poverty? It was too late in the day for that. The grace of abandonment had passed him by–if, indeed, it had ever been offered. For better or for worse he was saddled with the career he had built.

He was neither gluttonous nor spendthrift. He was educating his sister's children, and a pair of needy students for the priesthood. When he died half his wealth would go to his family, the other half to the Church. The Pontiff himself had approved the disposition. For what then should he reproach himself? For nothing, it seemed, except, perhaps, a certain mediocrity of spirit, a need of his nature to have the best of both worlds. And yet God Almighty had made them both, the seen and the unseen, for man's habitation and benefit. He had made man too, and it was the nature of His mercy to exact no more than a just return on the talent He had given to each one.

Valerio Rinaldi was wise enough not to rejoice too freely in his good fortune. Yet he could not weep because there was nothing to weep for. So he sighed a little as the shadows drew closer over the land and went on reading the story of Hippolytus, the son of Theseus:

> *'To go into the dark! Now let me die, and pass*
> *To the world under the earth, into the joyless dark!*
> *Since you, dearer than all, are at my side no longer,*
> *And the death you have dealt is more than the death that*
> *   has swallowed you.'*

When twilight came at last, he closed his book and went in to say evening prayers with his household, and then prepare himself for dinner with Cardinal Leone.

The white-haired inquisitor was growling and crusty as ever, but he softened instantly at the entry of the children. When they bobbed before him, three dark-haired little maids, to receive his blessing, his eyes clouded and his hands trembled as he laid them on their foreheads. When the children backed away respectfully, he drew them to him and talked gravely as any grandfather about their lessons and their dolls and the momentous event of a day at the zoo. Rinaldi smiled secretly to see the old lion tamed so swiftly. He was even more surprised when the man who was the guardian of so many mysteries fumbled his way through a jigsaw puzzle and begged for time for the children to finish it with him.

When at last the children were dismissed and dinner was announced, Leone was strangely subdued. He said soberly, 'You're a lucky man, Rinaldi. For this you should be grateful to God all the days of your life.'

'I am grateful,' said Rinaldi. 'It troubles me that I have done so little to deserve my happiness.'

'Enjoy it, my friend. It's the purest one you will ever know.' Then he added the poignant afterthought, 'When I was in the seminary one of my old masters said that every priest should be given a child to rear for five years. I didn't understand what he meant then. I do now.'

'Do you have any relatives?' asked Rinaldi.

'None. I used to think that, as priests, we didn't need them. That's an illusion, of course . . . One gets lonely in the cloth as well as out of it.' He grunted and gave a wintry smile. 'Eh! We all get sentimental when we're old.'

They dined alone as befitted a pair of princes, men who were charged with the weightiest secrets of the Church. An elderly manservant waited on them and withdrew after each course was served, so that they might talk freely. Leone seemed oddly moved by his meeting with the children, and as he picked absently at his fish he reverted once more to the problems of a celibate life.

'. . . Every year, as you know, we get a small crop of cases at the Holy Office: priests who get into trouble with women, unsavoury affairs between teachers and pupils, and allegations of soliciting by priests in the confessional. It's inevitable, of course. There are bad apples in every barrel, but the older I get, the less sure I am of how to deal with them.'

Rinaldi nodded agreement. He himself had served as a commissioner of the Holy Office and was privy to its most diverse deliberations.

Leone went on: 'We have a very bad case in front of us now, affecting a Roman priest and a young woman of his congregation. The evidence is pretty conclusive. The girl has fallen pregnant, and there is possibility of open scandal. I felt bound to bring the affair to the personal notice of the Holy Father.'

'How did he take it?'

'More calmly than I expected. The priest in question has, of course, been suspended from his duties; but His Holiness ordered that he be required to submit to a medical and psychiatric examination before the case is finally decided . . . It's an unusual step.'

'Do you disagree with it?' asked Rinaldi quizzically.

'The way it was put to me,' said Leone thoughtfully, 'I was in no position to disagree. His Holiness pointed out that no matter what a priest does, he is still an erring soul in need of help; that punishment was not enough; that we had to help the man to mend his error and his life. He went on to say that modern research had shown that many sexual aberrations had their roots in a real sickness of the mind, and that the celibate life raised special problems for those of a psychotic disposition . . . The ruling of the canons is guarded on this point, but not, of course, prohibitive. A priest may seek or be given psychiatric treatment only in grave cases and with the permission of the bishop. The authority of the Holy Father is supreme in the matter.'

'You still haven't said whether you agreed with his decision,' said Rinaldi in his mild, ironic fashion.

Leone chuckled. 'I know, I know. I have a bad reputation. To the Church at large I am still the Grand Inquisitor ready to purge out error by rack and fire . . . But it isn't true. I am always in dilemma in these matters. I have to be so careful of discipline. I am torn always between compassion and my duty to enforce the law . . . I've met this man. He's a sad, troubled creature. We can break him with a word, and set him with the same word in the way of damnation. On the other hand, what about the woman, and the child which is to be born?'

'What did His Holiness have to say about that?'

'He wants the child made a ward of the Church. He wants the girl provided with employment and a dowry. Once again, you see, there is a question of precedent. But I admire his attitude even though I am not sure I can agree with all of it. He has a soft heart . . . The danger is that it may be too soft for the good of the Church.'

'He has suffered more than we. Perhaps he has more right to trust his heart than we have.'

'I know that. I could wish he trusted me a little more.'

'I know he trusts you.' Rinaldi made the point firmly. 'I know he has a great respect for you. Has he moved against you in any way?'

'Not yet. I think the real test is still to come.'

'What do you mean?'

Leone cocked a shrewd eye at his host. 'Don't tell me you haven't heard. The Father General of the Jesuits has brought this Télémond fellow back to Rome. He's arranged for him to speak in the presence of the Pope on the feast of Saint Ignatius Loyola.'

'I heard about it. I'm invited to be present. I don't think it means too much. Télémond is a distinguished scholar. I think it's only natural that Semmering should want to reinstate him and give him a wider field of action in the Church.'

'I think it's a calculated step,' said Leone bluntly. 'Semmering and I rub each other the wrong way. He knows that Télémond's opinions are still suspect.'

'Come, come, old friend! He's had twenty years to revise them, and you certainly can't call him a rebellious spirit. He submitted, didn't he, when silence was imposed on him? Even the Holy Office can't refuse him the opportunity to restate his position.'

'The occasion is too public. Too symbolic, if you want. I think Semmering has committed an indiscretion.'

'What are you really afraid of, my friend? A victory for the Jesuits?'

Leone growled and tossed his white mane. 'You know that isn't true. They do God's work, as we try to do it, in our own fashion.'

'What then?'

'Have you met this Jean Télémond?'

'No.'

'I have. He's a man of great charm and, I think, of singular spirituality. I think he may make a very favourable impression on the Holy Father. I believe that's what Semmering's expecting, too.'

'Is that a bad thing?'

'It could be. If he has the patronage of the Pontiff, then he is much freer to promulgate his opinions.'

'But the Holy Office is still there to monitor them.'

'It would be much more difficult to move against a man under papal patronage.'

'I think you're making two unfounded assumptions–that he will get papal patronage, and that you will have to move against him.'

'We have to be ready for anything that happens.'

'Isn't there a simpler way? Why not raise the matter with the Holy Father now?'

'And what do I tell him? That I mistrust his discretion, or that he doesn't trust me enough?'

'I can see that might be difficult.' Rinaldi laughed and rang the bell for the next course. 'I'll give you my advice. Relax. Enjoy your dinner, and let the affair take its own way. Even the Holy Office can't do as well for the Church as the Holy Ghost . . .'

Leone smiled grimly and addressed himself to the roast. 'I'm getting old, my friend–old and stubborn. I can't get used to the idea that a youngster of fifty is wearing the Triple Crown.'

Rinaldi shrugged like a true Roman. 'I think the tiara fits him very well. And there is nothing in the faith which prescribes that the Church must be a gerontocracy–a government of old men. I have time to think now, and I am sure age doesn't always make us wiser.'

'Don't mistake me. I see the good that this man brings to us. He goes out like a true shepherd among the flock. He visits the hospitals and the prisons. Last Sunday, believe it or not, he sat through three sermons, in three different Roman churches . . . just to hear what kind of preaching we had in our pulpits.'

'I hope he was impressed.'

'He was not,' said Leone with tart humour. 'He made no secret of it. He talked of "turgid rhetoric" and "vague devotion" . . . I think we may hear something of this in the encyclical which he is preparing now.'

'Is it ready yet?'

'Not yet. I hear he is still working on the first Russian version . . . We may be in for some surprises . . .' He laughed ruefully. 'I've already had a few myself. His Holiness disapproves of the tone of certain Holy Office proclamations. He feels they are too stringent, too harsh. He wants us to refrain from outright condemnation, especially of persons, and to adopt a tone rather of admonition and warning.'

'Did he say why?'

'He put it very clearly. He said we must leave room to move for men of good will, even when they are in error. We must point out the error, but we must not do injustice to the intentions of those who commit it.'

Rinaldi permitted himself a thin smile. 'I begin to see why you are worried about Jean Télémond.'

Leone ignored the joke and growled, 'I'm inclined to agree with Benedetti. This man *is* a reformer. He wants to sweep all the rooms at once. He is talking, I believe, of a reform of the Rota, of changes in seminary training, and even of separate commissions to represent the various national Churches in Rome.'

'That could be a good move,' said Rinaldi thoughtfully. 'I think that everyone but us Romans agrees that we have centralized too much. We live in troubled times, and if there is another war, then the churches of the world will be much more isolated than they have ever been. The sooner they can develop a vigorous local life the better for the faith.'

'If there is another war, my friend . . . it may well be the end of the world.'

'Thank God things seem to be a little calmer at present.'

Leone shook his head. 'The calm is deceptive, I think. The pressure is building up, and before another year is out I think we may see a renewal of crisis. Goldoni was talking to me about it only yesterday. He is making a special report to the Pontiff.'

'I wonder,' asked Rinaldi softly. 'I wonder how the crisis looks to a man who has sat for seventeen years in the shadow of death?'

To Kiril the Pontiff the crisis presented itself in a variety of aspects.

He saw it first in microcosm, on the battleground of his own soul. At the lowest level—the level at which he had lived in the prison bunker—there was the simple impulse to survival: the desperate effort to cling to that single spark of life which, once extinguished, could never be lit again. There was only one infusion of life into the frail vessel of the body. Once the vessel was broken it would never be put together again until the day of the last restoration. So, with infusion of life was infused also the instinct to preserve it at all costs against whatever threatened, or seemed to threaten it, from within or without.

Every animal contained within himself a mechanism of survival. Only man, the last and noblest of the animal kingdom, understood, however dimly, that the mechanism must run down and that sooner or later he must make a conscious act of abandonment of the gift into the hand of the Creator, who had first given it. This was the act for which all his living was a preparation; to refuse it was to commit the final rebellion from which there was no recanting.

Yet every day of every man's life was a series of small rebellions against the fear of death or of sporadic victories for hope in the unseen. Even for Kiril, the Vicar of God on earth, there was no retreat from the daily war. The impulse to survival took many forms: the delight in power which gave a man the illusion of immortality; the fear of oppostion which might limit the illusion; the desire for friendship to buttress the weak body and faltering spirit; the urge to action which affirmed a man's potency against threatening circumstance; the desire to possess what must in the end be forgone; the cowardice which thrust him into isolation as if he could close every crack against the ultimate invasion of death. Even for a Pontiff, who stood by presumption nearest to God, there was no guarantee of victory over himself. Each day brought its own tally of defeats which must be repented and purged in the penitential tribunal.

But what of other men, so much less enlightened, so much more vulnerable, so much more oppressed by the terror of bodily extinction? On them the pressures of existence built up to breaking point every day. For them he must find in himself a strength to lend, and a charity to spend, lest they collapse utterly under the burden, or turn and rend each other in a feral war, which would blot them out quicker than the merciful death from which they fled.

This was the other aspect of the crisis which he read in every report which was laid on his desk, in every newspaper and bulletin which came under his notice.

When a man in a capsule was shot into a new dimension of space and time, the world exulted as if he came back with a promise of eternity in his pocket.

When a new programme of armament was announced, it seemed that those who promoted it wrote with the one hand a new profit into the stock market while with the other they inscribed their own epitaph.

Each economic treaty brought advantage to those who signed it, and a degree of injustice to those whom it excluded.

The populations of the East and the Africas were exploding into a new magnitude, and yet men put their trust in islands of colour or race, as though they were endowed with a divine right of election to an earthly paradise.

Every new victory over disease made a corresponding drain on the diminishing resources of the planet. Every advance in science was another patch on the shabby cloak which man wrapped about himself against the cold wind of dissolution.

And yet . . . and yet this was the nature of man. This was the historic method of his progress—a tightrope walk toward a destiny dimly perceived, but profoundly felt. The Church was in the world, though not of it—and it was her function to hold up the truth like a lamp to light the further shore of man's ultimate arrival.

So Kiril the Pontiff, caught like all his fellows in the human dilemma, sat at his desk and traced in the formal words of his Secretary of State the shadows of the gathering storm.

'The pivot of the present situation is China. The most reliable reports indicate that the agricultural programme has again broken down and that there will be a very light harvest this summer. This will mean, almost inevitable, a military push toward the rice-bowl areas of South-east Asia immediately after the next monsoons. Military training is already being stepped up, and there are reports reaching us every day of repressive measures against disaffected elements. Our own people are being subjected to new campaigns of surveillance and open persecution.

'In America the economic recession has eased, but this is largely due to an increase in the programme of military armament. Our sources in the United States inform us that any new Chinese expansion toward Burma or Indo-China or Siam would create an immediate danger of war . . .

'In Bonn and Paris there is new talk of France and Germany participating in a joint programme for the development of atomic weapons. This is a logical outcome of their status as senior partners in the European bloc, but it is clear that it must present itself as an open threat to East Germany and Moscow . . .

'It has been our hope for some time that Russia's fear of the Chinese might bring about a betterment of her relations with the West, but this situation introduces a dangerous and contrary element.

'It would seem timely for Your Holiness to make some clear and public comment on the dangers of this new armament race, which is being justified as a strengthening of the Western alliance against communism.

'It is difficult to see how it could be done, but if it were possible for us to make any contact with the Praesidium in the Kremlin and to introduce ourselves as a mediating element in East-West relations, there would be no time better than the present. Unfortunately our opposition to the doctrines of communism is all too easily interpreted as a political alliance with the West. We have instructed our legates and nuncios everywhere to emphasize, both in public and in their conversations with political personalities, the dangers of the present situation.

'As Your Holiness knows, we are now maintaining friendly relations with representatives of the Orthodox Church, and with senior members of other Christian bodies. We may look with confidence to their co-operation in this matter. However, the creation of a moral climate always lags far behind the creation of a political one, and we do have to face the fact that the next six or twelve months may well bring the world to the threshold of another war . . .

'In Africa . . .'

Kiril the Pontiff put down the typescript and covered his tired eyes with the palms of his hands. Here again in macrocosm was the struggle for human survival. The Chinese wanted a bowl of rice. The Russian wanted to hold the civilized comfort which had just become familiar to him. A hundred and eighty million Americans had to be kept working, lest the precarious consumer economy should collapse. France and Germany, stripped of their colonies, had to maintain their bargaining power in the European community of nations.

'What we have we hold, because it is ours, because we have earned it. All that increases us is a good. All that diminishes us is a threat . . . Jungle law . . . Survival of the fittest . . . There are no morals in politics . . .'

Yet, boil it down, survival even for the individual was never a simple equation. The definition of rights and duties had occupied theologians and legalists for two thousand years of the Christian dispensation, and for thousands of years before that. It was one thing to state the law, but to apply it, to bring all the diverse millions of mankind to see it with the same eye, to recognize it as a divine decree . . . This was, on the face of it, a rank impossibility. Yet there was the promise. 'I, if I be lifted up, will draw all things to myself.' And without the promise there was no foothold of reason left in the universe. If one did not believe that the spinning orb of the earth was held safe by the continuance of a creative act, then one might well despair and wish it dissolved in fire, to make place for a better one.

Once again memory struck off at a tangent, to a conversation he had had with Kamenev nearly ten years before:

'The difference between you and me, Kiril, is that I am dedicated to the possible while you are dedicated to a nonsense . . . "God wishes that all men should be saved and come to the knowledge of truth." . . . That's what you preach, isn't it? Yet you know it's folly. A sublime folly, I agree. But still–a folly . . . It doesn't happen. It won't happen. It can't happen. What is your heaven but a carrot to make the donkey trot? What is your hell but a rubbish heap for all your failures–God's failures, my friend! And you say He's omnipotent. Where do you go from here? Do you come with me to achieve the small possible or go chasing after the great impossible? . . . I know what you want to say: God makes all possible. Don't you see? I am God to you at this moment because you can't even move from that chair until I give the order . . . Here! God gives you a little gift. A cigarette '

He had taken the cigarette, he remembered, and smoked it gratefully while his tired mind grappled with the paradox which Kamenev had presented to him. . . . The little gain or the great loss? Which? The limited wisdom or the monstrous folly? He had chosen the folly, and been consigned again to stripes and starvation and solitude to purge it out of him.

And now the paradox had reversed itself. Kamenev was faced with a situation impossible to resolve, while Kiril, the abject prisoner, stood in the shoes of God to whom all things were possible.

For a long time he sat pondering the gigantic humour of the situation. Then he lifted the receiver and called Goldoni in the Secretariat of State.

'I'm reading your report. I'm impressed. I'm grateful. I'm also very worried. Now tell me something . . . If I wanted to get a message to the Premier of Russia–a private message–how would I do it?'

EXTRACT FROM THE SECRET MEMORIALS OF KIRIL I PONT. MAX.

. . . It is well that I have kept a sense of humour; otherwise I should be harassed to madness by the consequences of my most trivial actions. When a man in my position asks a simple question the whole Vatican begins to flutter like a nest of birds. If I make the smallest motion it is as if I were trying to shake the foundations of the world. I can only do what I believe to be right but there are always twenty people with as many reasons why I should not move at all . . . And I am a fool if I do not at least listen to their opinions.

When I proposed to Goldoni that I should make a pastoral visitation of the whole of Italy, and see on the spot the problems of my local clergy, he was aghast. Such a thing had not been done for centuries. It would create problems with the Italian government. It would raise God knows what questions of protocol and logistics and local ceremony. He pointed out that I was a prince and that the paying of princely honours would impose hardship on poor and depressed areas. I had to be very firm with him on this point and tell him that I am first and foremost a pastor, successor to a fisherman who was executed like a common criminal in the City of the Emperors. Even so we have not yet agreed how and when I shall make this journey; but I am determined to do it before very long.

I want to make other journeys too. I want to cross the frontiers of Europe and the oceans of the world, to see my people–where and how they live, and the burdens they carry on their journey to eternity . . . This, I know, is a project not easily accomplished. It will involve opposition from governments, a risk to myself and to the administration of the Holy See . . . But it would, I believe, restate as nothing else could the Apostolic mission of the Pontiff . . . For the present, however, I have a more pressing concern: to establish and maintain a personal contact with Kamenev.

Immediately after my telephone call, Goldoni came rushing across from the Secretariat of State to talk with me. He is a shrewd man, much practised in diplomacy, and I have great respect for his opinion. His first counsel was a negative one. He could see no possible ground of communication with those who preach an atheistic heresy and who are engaged in an active persecution of the faithful . . . He made the point, too, that all those who are members of the Communist Party are automatically excommunicated from the Church. I could not help remarking that in the twentieth century excommunication was a blunt weapon and very possibly an outmoded one . . . He offered then the very valid caution that even a private dialogue with the Kremlin might constitute a diplomatic affront to Western governments.

I could not disagree with him, but I am obsessed by the belief that the prime mission of the Church is a pastoral and not a diplomatic one. I showed Goldoni the letter which Kamenev had written to me, and he understood my anxiety to begin some kind of conversation. Goldoni gave me, however, another warning: any step that I take may be misinterpreted as a sign of weakness and may be used as a propaganda weapon by the Communists . . .

Goldoni is right, of course; but I do not believe he is wholly right. The truth has a virtue of its own; the good act has a virtue of its own, and we must never discount the fructifying power of the Almighty . . .

I have never believed that everyone who comes to Rome must come there by way of Canossa. This, I think, has been one of our historic errors. The good shepherd seeks out the lost sheep and carries them home on his shoulder. He does not demand that they come crawling back, draggle-tailed and remorseful, with a penance cord around their necks . . . It was St Augustine who said, 'It takes a big mind to make a heresy.' And there are noble minds and noble spirits from whom the gift of faith is withheld and for whom salvation comes by way of the uncovenanted mercy of God. With all such we must deal in patience, tolerance and brotherly charity, humbled always by the gratuitous mercy of God in our own regard. For them we must exercise in a special fashion the *ministerium* of the faith and not insist too harshly upon its magistracy.

So, finally, Goldoni and I agreed on a compromise. We would try to get a message to Kamenev to tell him that I have received his letter and that I have nothing but the most friendly disposition toward him and toward my own people. The problem was, of course, how to deliver the message, but Goldoni in his subtle fashion proposed an amusing solution. A South American diplomat who has social contacts in the Kremlin will seek an opportunity to speak with the Premier at a cocktail party and tell him that a friend of his would like to talk more about the growing of sunflowers . . . In this way neither one of us will be compromised and the next effective move will be for Kamenev to make. God knows where the move may point, but I must pray and rest in hope . . .

It is curious but I am more deeply perturbed by the case which Leone has transmitted to me from the Holy Office: a priest accused of soliciting in the confessional, who is now in danger of being cited in a civil paternity suit . . . This sort of scandal is, of course, sporadic in the Church, but I am troubled by the spectacle of a soul in a mortal sickness.

There are men who should never be priests at all. The system of seminary training is designed to filter out unsuitable candidates, but there are always the odd ones that slip through the net. There are those whose sole hope of a normal and fruitful life is in the married state; yet the discipline of the Western Church imposes on all priests a perpetual celibacy.

It is within my power as the Pontiff to dispense this unfortunate man from his vows and permit him to marry. My heart urges me to do it, and yet I dare not. To do so would be to create a precedent which might do irreparable damage to clerical discipline and to a tradition which has its roots in Christ's teaching on the state of dedicated virginity.

I have the power, yes, but I must use it to build and not to demolish what has been given into my keeping. I am aware that I may be increasing the danger of damnation of this unhappy soul. I want to deal with him as mercifully as I can, but I dare not, for one soul, put ten thousand others in jeopardy . . .

The Keys of the Kingdom are given into my hands; but I do not hold them absolutely. They are mine in trust under law . . . There are times—and this is one of them—when I wish I could take upon myself the sins of all the world and offer my life in expiation for them. I know, however, that I am only a man, and that the expiation was made once for all on Calvary. Through the Church I administer the fruits of redemption. I cannot change the covenant of God with man which governs their distribution . . .

It is late and my letter to the Church is still unfinished. Tonight I am working on the text, 'A chosen generation, a kingly priesthood'. A priest is only a man, and we have only a few short years to train him for the burden of kingship . . . To those who stumble under its weight, we must extend the maternal love of the Church. For them we must invoke the patronage of the Virgin Mother of all men . . .

It is warm tonight. Summer is coming in, but there are those who walk in a lifetime winter, lost and alone. Let me not fail them who have felt the winter in my own bones, who have cried at night for love in a loveless prison . . .

6

The Princess Maria Caterina Daria Poliziano was a small, grey woman who admitted to seventy-five years and was prepared to sue anyone bold enough to dispute her accounting.

Her hair was thin, her skin was shrunken. Her sharp beak and her black agate eyes gave her the look of a mummified eagle dug from some ancient tomb. But the Princess Maria-Rina was very far from dead and was, on the contrary, a very formidable old lady.

She kept an apartment in Rome—which she rarely used 'because all Romans are beginning to look like commercial travellers'—a villa in Fiesole, where she held habitual court, estates in Sicily, farms in the Abruzzi, and holdings in beet and rice in the Romagna and along the valley of the Po. Her portfolio, begun by her father and augmented by the fortunate deaths of two husbands, was full of the fattest stocks in Italy, and she traded them as shrewdly as a gypsy tinker.

Her bony finger stirred every political pudding north of Lazio, and those whispers of power which did not begin in her drawing-room circulated there, inevitably, before they blew into a wind. A summons to her table was either a warrant for execution or a promise of promotion. And more than one too bold politico had braved her anger only to find himself running out of funds, favour, and votes at the next election.

Her dress was antique, her manner more tyrannical than regal. She drank Scotch whisky and smoked Egyptian cigarettes in a long gold holder. She had a scandalous tongue, a dangerous memory—and an unexpected discretion. She despised the old and courted the young like a crotchety but humorous vampire who could pay richly for youthful blood. In her villa garden, among the fountains and the cypresses, and the avenues of weathered marbles, it seemed, in very truth, as if time stood still at her aged, but imperious bidding.

Her favourite resort was an arbour hung with maturing grapes and fronting a small fountain where an antique Leda was courted by languid swans to the sound of water music. In a younger time the Princess Maria-Rina had been courted there as well—now, instead, she bargained with the legacies of her youth: power, money, and prestige. Once a month the Archbishop of Florence came to drink coffee with her. Once a week someone from the Quirinale came to lunch and made a private report from the Premier. Where the dandies of another age had bent over her small hand, now the bankers and the stockbrokers came to pay her a reluctant homage, and a tribute of secret confidence.

She was sitting there now, this summer morning, reading a blunt lecture to a Minister of the Republic, her nephew, Corrado Calitri:

'You're a fool, boy! You come a certain way and you think it is the end of the journey. You want to sit down and play with the flowers. It's delightful, I'm sure, but it isn't politics.'

Calitri's pale classic face flushed, and he put down his coffee cup with a clatter. 'Now listen, Aunt, you know that isn't true. I do my work. I do it very well. Only yesterday the Premier was good enough to say . . .'

'Was good enough to say!' Her old voice crackled with contempt. 'Why should you care what he says? What is praise, anyway, but breakfast for the prisoner before they cut his throat? You disappoint me, Corrado. You're a baby. You can't see past your nose.'

'What do you expect me to see, Aunt?'

'The future!' said the Princess crisply. 'Twelve months from now when the election comes. Are you prepared for it?'

'Of course I am. The funds are there. My committees are working day and night, even now. I don't think there is any doubt I shall be re-elected . . . I think the party will have a reduced majority. We'll have to open out a little further in coalition with the Left, but even so I'm assured of a seat in the Cabinet.'

'And that's the end of the story?' Her dark agate eyes bored into him; her withered lips twitched into a smile of pity.

Calitri shifted uneasily in his chair. 'Do you see another ending, Aunt?'

'Yes!' Her old hands reached across the table and fastened like talons on his wrist. 'You have twelve months left to plan it, but if you plan aright, you can lead the country.' He stared at her gape-mouthed and she gave a high, cackling laugh. 'Never underrate your old aunt, my boy. When you're as old as I am you've learned to see round corners and I tell you without a doubt you can lead the Republic . . .'

'You really believe that?' Calitri's voice was almost a whisper.

'I never tell fairy tales, my boy–and I gave up listening to them a long while ago. At lunch today you will meet some people who will show you how you can do it. There will be a certain amount of—' she rubbed her fingertips together in the gesture that signified money '—but that part we can handle. I want to talk to you about something else. There's another price to be paid, and you're the only one who can pay it.'

Corrado Calitri cocked a shrewd eye at his relative. 'And what is the price, Aunt?'

She fixed him with a beady and predatory eye and told him. 'You'll have to clean up your life and do it quickly. Get rid of this bunch of pimps and playboys that you hang around with. Push this marriage business through the courts. Get rid of Chiara. She's no good to you. And get yourself married again, quickly and quietly. I'll find you a woman who can manage you. You need a strong one–not a dewy-eyed shoolgirl.'

'I won't do it!' Corrado Calitri exploded into sudden anger. 'I won't be bought and sold like a piece of merchandise!'

He heaved himself out of his chair and began to pace restlessly up and down the flagged pathway between the arbour and the fountain, while the old princess watched him with a calm and calculating eye.

When his anger had spent itself a little, she went to him and linked her arm in his and led him slowly round the circuit of the villa plantations. She was a different woman now. She made no effort to tease or provoke him, but talked soberly and quietly as if he were her son:

'. . . I told you I don't listen to fairy stories any more–even about myself. I know what I am, Corrado–a dried-up old woman with paint on her face, and her past a million years away . . . But I've lived, my boy. I've lived every minute of every hour. I've sucked the orange dry and spat out the pips. So listen to me, please . . . I know you're not like other men. You were always different, even as a little boy . . . Watching you, I used to think of someone trying to rub out the world, and paint it new and clean again. I could have made it different for you, I think; but your father would never have me near the house . . .' She gave a short, bitter chuckle. 'He thought I was a corrupting influence. He was a strait-laced fellow with no sense of humour. I never could see what your mother found in him.'

'Misery,' said Corrado Calitri harshly. 'Misery and loneliness, and no love at all. I hated that man from the bottom of my heart.'

'But you can't run away from him any longer,' said the old woman softly. 'He's dead and the daises are growing out of his ears. I know what you look for–the love you didn't get from him. I know you find it sometimes; but it doesn't last. I know the dangers when you go on looking desperately and without caution.' Her thin hands clutched at his arm. 'You do have enemies, don't you?'

'Who hasn't in a job like mine?'

'Have you ever been blackmailed?'

'It's been tried a couple of times.'

'Then you know what I'm talking about. The enemies get more and they grow bigger–bigger than you realize. Take Campeggio, for instance . . .'

'Campeggio!' He swung round to face her, genuinely startled. 'Campeggio! I've never done him any harm.'

'You have his boy,' said Maria-Rina gravely.

'So that's the story.' Calitri threw back his patrician head and laughed, startling the birds in the olive trees. 'The boy works for me. I like him. He has talent, and charm and—'

'Beauty?'

'That, too, if you want. But not for me. You think I want to fall foul of Campeggio and the Vatican?'

'You've already done it,' said the Princess Maria-Rina. 'And without the Vatican you can't lead the country at the next election. Now–now do you see what I'm talking about?'

For a long moment he did not answer her, but seemed to shrink back into himself. His youthful face furrowed. His eyes misted with sudden emotion. Finally he said softly, 'Life is very long, Aunt. Sad, too, sometimes, and solitary.'

'You think I don't know that, boy? You think when Louie died I wasn't sad and solitary? You think I didn't know what it was like to be middle-aged and rich, and able to buy what I couldn't get for love? I tried it, too, for a little while. Does that shock you?'

'No. I understand it.'

'Then I woke up as you have to wake up. You can't get out of bed every morning fearing to lose what you don't own anyway. You can't wait and weigh the risks of the blackmailer. You can't govern your life by the snap of a pretty boy's fingers. No! One day you have to say to yourself: What have I got that is really mine? How best can I enjoy it? . . . When you come to add it up, you find there's a great deal. And there may even be a little loving as well.'

'In marriage?' he asked with heavy irony.

'In it or outside. It makes small matter. For you . . .' Her skeleton finger stabbed at him like a dagger. 'For you marriage is necessary. Very necessary.'

'I tried it, remember.'

'With a baby who was still playing with dolls.'

'And this time?'

'First,' said the old woman briskly, 'we must get you out of the mess you're in now, and this is where you make your first payment.'

'How much?' asked Corrado Calitri.

'In money, nothing. In pride . . . a great deal, perhaps. You will have to approach the Rota and reverse all your previous testimony.'

'How do I make them believe me?'

The Princess Maria-Rina laughed again. 'You repent. There will be joy in Heaven and in the Vatican when you come to repair the grave injustice that you have done to an innocent girl. You will be mending your ways, too, and they will be happy to have you back in the fold.'

'I can't do it,' said Corrado Calitri heavily. 'It's a monstrous hypocrisy.'

'It needn't be,' said the princess. 'And even if it is, the Quirinale is worth a Mass, isn't it?'

In spite of himself Calitri smiled and laid an affectionate hand on the old woman's cheek. 'Sometimes, Aunt, I think you're descended directly from the Borgias.'

'I am,' said the old princess. '—but on the wrong side of the blanket! . . . Now . . . Will you do what I ask?'

'I'll have to think about it.'

'You have thirty minutes, boy. At lunch they will want your answer and mine.'

In a third-floor tenement, a stone's throw from the Pantheon, Ruth Lewin was caught up in another of the daily dramas of Old Rome. From the evening angelus until nearly midnight, she had been working with a twenty-year-old wife to help her give birth to her first child. For the last two hours the doctor had been with her, a haggard young man who seemed far too embroiled in the drama for his own good, or for that of his patient.

When finally they had dragged the child into the light with forceps, it was a monster—a tiny, whimpering deformity with a human head and a penguin body, whose feet and hands were attached directly to the trunk.

Ruth Lewin stared at it in horror, and the young doctor swore savagely. 'Sweet Jesus! Sweet suffering Jesus, look at it!'

Ruth Lewin found herself stammering helplessly, 'But why? What caused it? What . . . ?'

'Shut up!' said the doctor harshly. 'Shut up and give me water and a towel.'

Mechanically she did as he asked and watched in fascinated horror while he swaddled the deformed body, and then poured a few drops of water on the head and muttered the ritual words: 'I baptize thee in the name of the Father, and of the Son, and of the Holy Ghost. Amen.'

Ruth Lewin found voice again. 'What's going to happen now?'

'That's my business. You get the mother cleaned up.'

Angry and near to tears she set about the menial task, bathing the torn young body, comforting the girl as she struggled back, moaning, into consciousness. When finally it was done and the young mother lay composed and decent on the pillows, Ruth Lewin looked up. 'What now, Doctor?'

He was standing by the table, his back toward her, fumbling with the wrapping that covered the child. He turned a stony face to her and said:

'It's dead. Get the father in.'

She opened her mouth to ask a question, but no sound issued. She searched his face for an answer but his young eyes were blank as pebbles. He repeated the order. 'Please call the father.'

Ruth Lewin went to the door and beckoned to a tall, muscular boy who was drinking a glass of wine and talking with a group of neighbours on the landing. 'Will you come in, please?'

Puzzled, the youth approached her with the neighbours at his heels. She drew him inside and closed the door against the other curious faces.

The doctor confronted him, holding the swaddled body in his arms. 'I have bad news for you, my friend. The baby was born dead.'

The boy stared at him stupidly. 'Dead?'

'It happens sometimes. We don't really know why. Your wife is well. She will be able to have other children.'

Dumbly the boy moved toward the bed and bent crooning over the pale, half-conscious girl.

'Let's go,' said the doctor abruptly. 'I want to deliver this to the general hospital.'

To the boy he said, 'I have to take the body away. It's the law. I'll be back in the morning to see your wife, and give you a death certificate.'

Neither the boy nor the wife seemed to hear him, and he went out carrying the small pathetic bundle, with Ruth Lewin following like a professional mourner. The crowd on the landing stared silently at their passing and then crowded into the door of the room, whispering excitedly among themselves.

When they reached the street, the doctor laid the body of the child on the back seat of his car and slammed the door. Then he faced Ruth Lewin and said abruptly, 'Don't ask any questions. I'll deliver the cadaver to the general hospital and make a report.'

'Won't there be an autopsy?'

'No. Even if there were it would show nothing. The child died of asphyxiation . . .'

In a single moment all his control seemed to drain away. His body was shaken with rigors, and his young face twisted as if with an intolerable pain. Suddenly in a fury of desperation he was pleading with her. 'Don't leave me now. For God's sake don't leave me. Come to the hospital and then . . . then let's go somewhere. Somewhere sane. If I'm alone tonight I think I'll go mad.'

'Of course I'll come with you. But you can't blame yourself for this. You're a doctor; you know these things happen every day.'

'I know! Oh yes, I know.' He tried to smile but it was more like a rictus of agony. 'I'll tell you something you don't know. I've got twenty more babies to be born in the next eight weeks, and at least half of them are going to be like that.'

'Oh God,' said Ruth Lewin softly. 'Oh God Almighty, why? . . .'

In her quiet house under the haunted shadow of the Palatine he told her the why. He told her savagely and brusquely as if the whole paradox of the healing art–its half promise of perpetuity, its ultimate surrender to mortality–had proved too much for him.

'. . . It's a crazy thought . . . But medical pharmacy always seems to come with the elixir of life in one hand, and a phial of poison in the other . . .

There are antibiotics that cure some people and kill others. There was the French drug that boiled men's brains. There was Thalidomide that gave sleep, and then grew monsters in the womb. Now there's another one. It came on the market about twelve months ago–a combination formula to prevent nausea in pregnancy, and reduce the danger of toxaemia . . . Three months ago we started to get the first warnings from Germany about deformities induced by the drug . . . It looks like Thalidomide all over again, only this time everyone's trying to hush it up . . .'

He lay back in his chair, an image of dejection, fatigue and pure misery. 'I used to think I was a kind of medical apostle. I paid for drugs for poorer patients out of my own pocket. I bought the bloody stuff for that girl tonight, and for all the others in the quarter.'

'There's no hope that the other births will be different?'

'Some of them will be normal. But the rest . . .' He flung out his hands in passionate appeal. 'What do I do? I can't murder them all.'

'First, you must never use that word again. I saw nothing tonight. I heard nothing.'

'But you know, don't you?'

'I don't know anything–except this. You mustn't blame yourself, and you mustn't ever again play God. There's a kind of madness in that.'

'Madness is right.' He ran a shaking hand through his hair. 'It was a madness tonight, and yet . . . What equipment do those people have to cope with such a situation? You know what they would have said if they'd seen that birth tonight? *"Mal' occhio!"* The evil eye. Someone looked on the mother and laid a curse on her while the child was still in her womb. You have no idea of the power of superstition over the minds of these poor folk. What would they do with the child? Some few might care for it. Others might stifle it or try to throw it in the river. Some few might sell to professional beggars who would make profit from its deformity . . . What about all the others still to come? What do I do about them? Sweet Jesus, what do I do?'

Without warning he was racked by deep weary sobs, so that Ruth Lewin ran to him and threw her arms about him for comfort and soothed him with soft and helpless words. When he was calm at last, she made him lie down on her bed, and covered him with a blanket, and then sat beside him holding his hand until he lapsed into the mercy of sleep. Then she was alone–alone in the mournful hours, confronted by the ultimate mystery of life and death and pain, and the bloody stinking mess of the world.

She had seen a monster come to birth as the result of an act of healing and kindness. She had seen murder done in the name of mercy and found her heart more than half approving the act. Here in little was the whole mighty tragedy of man, the whole bleak mystery of his existence and his destiny.

Confronted by that pitiful embryo, how could one say that the cogs of creation did not slip out of kilter and grind into a monstrous confusion? How could one talk of Omnipotence and Omniscience and an ever-present Goodness? How could one find a soul or spirit in the weak, puling, fishlike creature, swimming blindly out of the fluid of the womb to affront the light of day?

Where now were the foundations of faith, and hope, and love? Where was one vestige of sanity in this madhouse of sick, maimed, helpless victims of civilization? If there were none, then it was time to quit and be gone. The exit was easy enough and once she had almost passed through it. One could not go on blundering wildly through a hall of mirrors confused, disordered, purposeless, and afraid. If there were no resolution to the discord, then pack up the band and send it home. But if there were, then it must be soon, before the tattered nerves frayed themselves into a screaming horror.

The weariness of the vigil crept into her bones, and she stretched out on the bed beside the sleeping man. But the contact of his body troubled her, and when he muttered and turned to her in sleep, she withdrew and went into the kitchen to make herself a cup of coffee.

She remembered another night with another man in this same house, and how for a while she had glimpsed a beginning of light. She asked herself what he would have made of tonight's affair, and what would have been his answer for the horrors that were still to come. Then the thought struck her, cold and reviving. This was his city. He had claimed it for his own. He had named himself as the shepherd and servant of its people . . .

Ruth Lewin was still awake when the grey of the false dawn crept across the Palatine Hill. And before the city had rubbed the sleep out of its eyes, she had written her letter begging a private audience with Kiril the Pontiff.

His own letter to the Church was already finished, and the Russian draft was in the hands of the translators. Now that it was done, he felt strangely empty, oppressed by a sense of futility and frustration.

While he was writing he had felt seized as never before by the power of the Word, by the conviction of its inevitable fruitfulness in the hearts of good men. Yet now he was faced with cold fact that without the grace of God—and men co-operating with the grace of God—the seed might lie fertile but fruitless for a hundred years. Among the millions of believers who professed an obedience to the Word, and to his authority as its Supreme Preacher, how many were there from whom he could exact a full performance?

He saw all too clearly what would happen to his letter. It would be read within a few months in every Catholic pulpit in the world. He would receive acknowledgments from bishops pledging their loyalty to his counsels and promising to carry them out as best they could. But between the promise and the fulfilment stood a hundred obstacles: shortage of men, shortage of money, shortness of sight and courage sometimes, and the natural resentment of the man at the point of action, who wondered why he was being asked to make so many bricks with so little straw.

The best one could hope was that, here and there, the Word would take fire in the soul of a man, would brighten his eyes with vision, and set him striding out to achieve a divine impossible. For himself he knew there was no other choice but to go on preaching, teaching, urging to action, and to wait, empty of all but hope, on the promise of the Paraclete.

There was a knock on his door, and the Maestro di Camera entered to inquire whether His Holiness was ready to begin the morning's audiences. Kiril glanced briefly at the list and saw that the first name was that of Ruth Lewin.

Her letter had troubled him deeply because it had reached him in a moment of temptation—the temptation to immerse himself in the political aspects of the Church and to challenge, by a display of power, those men like Leone who made no secret of their disagreements with him. There were those, he knew, who found his encyclical something of a novelty. It was too personal they felt, too specific. It was too openly critical of past policy. It called for new modes of action in the training of the clergy and in the direction of missionary education. For himself, the man at the top, it was all too easy to thrust his authority down the throats of his subordinates and stifle their criticism by a summons to religious obedience.

Ruth Lewin's letter reminded him that the real battleground was elsewhere—in lonely rooms and solitary hearts, among folk who had no theology but only an intimate and frightening familiarity with the problems of living and dying. Ruth Lewin represented a contact with such people. If he could make the faith efficacious for her, than whatever the outcome of his pontificate, he would not have failed uttterly.

When she was ushered into his presence, he greeted her warmly and then, without preamble, addressed himself to the subject:

'I had you called as quickly as I could because I know that you must be suffering a good deal.'

'I'm grateful to Your Holiness,' she told him in her blunt fashion. 'I have no right to bother you, but this is a terrible affair.'

'For you?' asked Kiril quizzically.

'For me it calls everything into question. But I want to talk about the others first.'

'What others?'

'The women who are going to give birth to these children. Most of them, I believe, are quite unprepared for what is going to happen.'

Kiril's lean face clouded, and a nerve began throbbing under the scar in his cheek. 'What do you want me to do?'

'We . . . that is, the mothers need help. They need a place where they can leave these children if they're not capable of looking after them themselves. The children have to be cared for. I'm told the expectation of life is short, but they will need a special kind of care—a special kind of loving.'

'You think the Church can provide it?'

'It has to,' said Ruth Lewin flatly. 'If it means what it teaches.' She flushed, understanding that she had committed an indiscretion; then she hurried into an explanation. 'I'm a woman, Your Holiness. I asked myself the other night what I would do, how I would feel, if I were the mother of such a child. I don't know. I don't think I should behave very well.'

Kiril the Pope gave a small wintry smile of approval. 'I think you underrate yourself. You have more courage than you realize . . . Tell me. How many of these births are there likely to be in Rome?'

'We expect about twenty in the next two months. There may be many more.'

He sat for a moment, silent and thoughtful. Then he gave a crooked, boyish grin and said:

'Well! Let's see what sort of authority I have in the Church.' He picked up the telephone and dialled the number of the Secretary of the Sacred Congregation of Religious.

Crisply he explained the situation and then asked, 'Which of our nursing nuns in Rome are best equipped to look after these children?'

There was an indistinguishable clatter of talk from the other end of the line, and Ruth Lewin saw the Pontiff's mouth tighten in anger. He said sharply, 'I know it is difficult. Everything is difficult. But this is an urgent work of charity, and it must be done. If money is needed we will provide it. It will be your business to find the accommodation and the nursing aid. I want it arranged within the next twenty-four hours.'

He put down the phone with a bang and said testily, 'These people live in a little world of their own. One has to bounce them out of it into reality . . . Anyway you can take it for granted that we shall provide care and hospital accommodation for those who need it. You will be informed by letter and telephone of the details. Then I shall have an announcement published in the *Osservatore* and circulated to the Roman press.'

'I'm very grateful to Your Holiness.'

'I'm grateful to you, young woman. Now, what can I do for you?'

'I don't know,' said Ruth Lewin unhappily. 'I've been asking myself the same question all the way to the Vatican. Why do these things happen? Why does a good God let them happen?'

'If I could tell you that,' said Kiril the Pontiff soberly, 'I'd be God myself. I don't know, though I sometimes wish I did. You mustn't imagine that the mystery of Faith is any simpler for me than it is for you. The Act of Faith is an act of acceptance—not an explanation. I'll tell you a story about myself . . . When I was first taken to prison it was in the bad time in Russia. There was much torture, much cruelty. One night a man was brought back to my hut who had been handled more brutally than any other I had ever seen. He was in agony, and he kept crying over and over again for someone to kill him and put him out of his misery. I tell you truly I was tempted. It's a terrible thing to see so much suffering. It degrades and terrifies those who see it but cannot alleviate it. That's why I can understand, though I cannot condone, what your doctor friend did. It seems almost as though one would be bestowing a divine mercy with the gift of death. But one is not divine, one cannot dispense either life or death.'

He broke and seemed for a moment to sink back into a private contemplation.

Ruth Lewin prompted him gently. 'What was the end of the story, Holiness?'

'The man died in my arms. I should like to tell you that he died in a godly fashion, but I have no way of knowing. I could not penetrate through his pain to touch the springs of his will. He just died, and I had to commit him to God . . . That's the only answer I can give you.'

'It's a leap into the dark,' said Ruth Lewin gravely. 'I'm not sure I can make it.'

'Is it any less hard to stay where you are?'

'It's harder, I think.'

'But you have already made one step into the dark.'

'I don't understand.'

'You could not condone this murder, even of a monstrous birth.'

'Not wholly, no.'

'And you have turned to me for help not for yourself, but for the children.'

'I just felt so inadequate. I needed someone who could act . . .'

'Perhaps,' said Kiril the Pontiff softly. 'Perhaps that is part of the meaning of pain—that it challenges our arrogant possession of life; that it confronts us with our own frailty and makes us aware, however dimly, of the sustaining power of the Creator.'

'I wish I could believe that. But how do you see God in a human child that looks like a fish?'

'It's not a new mystery, Ruth. It's a very old one. How do you see God in a dying criminal nailed on a gallows tree?'

'It isn't enough to say that,' said Ruth Lewin harshly. 'There has to be some loving somewhere. There has to be.'

'True . . . There has to be some loving. If the mystery of pain is not a mystery of love, then all this . . .' His crooked hands embraced the ornate room and all the Sacred City beyond it. 'Then all this is an historic nonsense. And my office is a role for a mountebank.'

His bluntness took her by surprise. For a moment she stared at him, caught by the contrast between his crooked, quizzical face and the religious formality of his dress. Then she said:

'Your Holiness really believes that?'

'I do.'

'Then why can't I?'

'I think you do believe it,' said Kiril the Pontiff gently. 'That's why you are here to see me. That's why you act within a context of belief, although you are still wrestling with God.'

'If I could only know that I was loved–that I was worth loving.'

'You don't ask that of someone you love–why should you ask it of yourself?'

'Your Holiness is too clever for me.'

'No! I am not a clever man. I understand you, Ruth Lewin, better than you know, because I have walked on the same road that you are walking now. I'm going to tell you another story, and then I'm going to send you away because there are lots of people waiting to see me . . . My escape from Russia was arranged, as you know. I was released from prison and sent to hospital because I had been very ill for some time. The doctors treated me well, and I was nursed solicitously. After seventeen years of endurance it was a strange experience. I did not have to fight any more. It was as if I became another human being overnight. I was clean, and well fed. I had books to read and leisure, and a kind of freedom. I enjoyed it. I was proud to be decent . . . It took a little time to understand that I was being submitted to a new temptation. I felt loved again. I wanted to be loved. I used to look forward to the coming of the nurse, to her smile and her service of me. Then came a moment when I understood that what Kamenev my tormentor had not been able to do to me I was doing to myself. I was demanding an experience of love. In spite of my priesthood and my bishopric, I was being tempted by this attraction of a simple human communion . . . Do you understand what I'm trying to say?'

'Yes, I understand it. It's what I feel every day.'

'Then you will understand something else. That the taking and the demanding is only one side of the medal of love. The giving is the side that proves the true minting. If I took I should have nothing to give. If I gave, the giving renewed the resource and it was this that had kept me whole for seventeen years of imprisonment.'

'And the return of love?'

'You are part of it,' said Kiril the Pontiff gently. 'You and these children whom we shall love together, and those whom I shall reach here and there in the Church, because my voice echoes in their hearts . . . I am still lonely often, as you are. But to be lonely is not to be unloved, but only to learn the value of love–and that it takes many forms, and is sometimes hard to recognize.' He rose and held out his hand. 'Now I must send you away, but we shall see each other again.'

She had long since rejected the authority which he represented; yet she bowed her knee and laid her lips to the Fisherman's ring on his finger, and listened with gratitude to the words of the blessing:

   'Benedictio dei omnipotentis descendat super te et maneat semper . . .'

For Kiril the Pontiff, it was a startling irony that his encyclical on Christian education made far less stir than his statement in the *Osservatore Romano* on the victims of the new drug. Every correspondent in Rome cabled the full text of the *Osservatore* release, which was interpreted in Europe and America as a clear papal command to place the medical and social resources of the Church at the disposal of mothers and offspring who were affected by the deadly medicine.

For a week afterwards, his desk was piled with letters and telegrams from bishops and lay leaders, commending his action as a timely demonstration of the charity of the Church. Cardinal Platino wrote expansively:

'. . . It seems to me that Your Holiness has shown in a very special fashion the relevance of the Church's mission to every act and circumstance of human life. It may well be that Your Holiness's pronouncement points the way to a missionary method of great importance–the reintroduction of the Church into private and public life through works of practical charity. Historically speaking, this method has been the beginning of the most permanent evangelical activity, and it is, in fact, a true copy of the work of the Master, who in the words of the Gospel, "Went about healing the sick and doing good . . ."'

Another man might have been flattered by so spontaneous a response to an executive action; but Kiril Lakota was preoccupied by those aspects of the problem which the press either ignored or built into a factitious drama.

Day and night he was haunted by the picture of a woman, waiting through nine months of fear and uncertainty to give birth to a deformity, of a doctor urged to intervene before the tragic moment, of the child itself, and what might happen to it when it grew to maturity. For all these, the charity of the Church was at best a postscript, at worst an unwelcome prolongation of grief and despair.

The mission of the Church to all these people was far other than a dispensation of kindness. It was to confront them with the naked fact of their existence, with all its risks and all its terror, and the other fact that their existence set them in a precise relationship with the Creator, who had called them into being. The Church could not change the relationship. It could not eliminate one single consequence of it. Its sole functions were to interpret it in the light of reason and revelation and to dispense the grace by which alone the relationship was made workable.

In theory, every one of the thousands of priests who trotted about the streets of Rome, in platter hats and black skirts, was an official interpreter of doctrine, an official dispenser of grace, and a shepherd with a sackful of compassion for his flock. In fact, there were all too few with the talent or the understanding to participate truly in these intimate tragedies of human-kind.

It was as if the symbiosis of the Church failed at a certain point and the lives of its people diverged thenceforward from the lives of its clergy. It was as if the interpretation of God to man became a didactic exercise, and the realities of God's grace were blotted out by the realities of pain and loss.

In the methodology of the Church, the priest was always available to the people of his parish. If they did not turn to him, it was because of their own negligence and want of faith. This at least was the text of many a Sunday sermon, but, in truth, the breakdown came because the cleric no longer shared the tragedy of his people, was even protected from it by his cloth and by his education.

... Education! He came back to it again by a round turn, seeing more clearly than he had ever done before that the fruit of his mission to the world must never be judged by spectacle or acclamation, but only by its flowering in the secret heart of the individual.

Buried under the pile of congratulations there were other and more disquieting letters. Like the one from Cardinal Pallenberg in Germany:

'... With the greatest respect, therefore, I would beg Your Holiness to undertake an examination of the present constitution and method of working of the Holy Roman Rota. Your Holiness is well aware that, because of our special circumstances in Germany, a large number of marital cases are being referred each year to Rome. Many of these have been delayed for three and four years, with consequent hardship and grave spiritual danger to the parties concerned. It seems to me and my brother bishops that there is need of swift reform in this matter, either by way of fuller reference of powers to provincial courts or by an increase in the number of Rota officials and the institution of a speedier method of examination. It is suggested that instead of all documents being translated into Latin–a slow and expensive progress–they might be presented and examined in their original vernacular . . .'

On the face of it the Holy Roman Rota was a far shout away from an act of infanticide in a third-floor slum. Yet the causes which found their way into the slow files of this august body were no less dramas of love and passion. The Holy Roman Rota was the last court of appeal for marital cases within the Church, and every marital case was a history of love or the lack of it, and of a human relationship–defective or not–which had to be measured beside the divine one.

To the theologian and the canonist, the function of the Rota was very simple. It had to render a decision as to whether or no a marriage was valid according to the moral law and the prescriptions of the canons. To many inside the Church, it seemed that this view was altogether too simple. The Rota was meticulously careful that justice should be done. It cared not one whit that it should seem to be done. Its methods were antique and often dilatory. Every document and every deposition had to be translated into Latin. The number of personnel, both clerical and lay, was hopelessly inadequate to handle the volume of business with any degree of speed. The least sympathetic of men could not fail to guess at the hardship which such slowness inflicted on those who had appealed to the tribunal.

Kiril the Pontiff understood the problem more clearly than others, but he had already learned that to accomplish a reform in Rome, one had to prepare slowly and act strongly at the right moment; otherwise one ended fighting the bureaucracy, which was tantamount to fighting oneself.

He pencilled a note on his calendar to discuss the question with Valerio Rinaldi, who, having retired from the politics of the Church, might give him good advice about how to beat them.

From Ragambwe, the black Cardinal in Kenya, came a note of even greater urgency:

'... Events in Africa are moving much more swiftly than would have seemed possible two years ago. Within the next twelve months I believe we may see a bloody uprising of black against white in South Africa. This is an almost inevitable consequence of the brutal repressive measures exercised by the South African government under the banner of Apartheid, and by the archaic, feudal and often brutal methods of the Portuguese. If this revolution is successful–and with the support of other African nations there is reason to believe it will be–then it may well be the end of Christianity for a hundred years in the southern continent of Africa. We are training catechists as fast as we can, but we cannot hope to train even a minimal number of native priests in the time at our disposal. I know that this may well seem a revolutionary suggestion, but I ask myself whether we should not consider very seriously a new programme of training in which the local language, and not Latin, will be the basis of instruction, and in which the whole liturgy will be celebrated in the vernacular. If this course were approved it might be possible to train a native clergy in about half the time it takes now to train them under the system laid down by the Council of Trent.

'I understand very well that this would mean a clergy less well educated than that in other lands, but the question is whether we shall have such a clergy, preaching the Word and dispensing the Sacraments validly and religiously, or whether we shall have no clergy at all. Your Holiness will understand that I speak of desperate measures for a desperate time, and that . . .'

Once again he was brought back to the subject of his letter, the education of the ministers of the Word. Once again he was faced with the intangible x that dominated the whole thinking of the Church–the infusion of the Holy Spirit supplying what was defective in man, so that the Mystical Body was kept always alive. How far, therefore, could one go in entrusting the Church to this dominating influence of the Spirit? How far was it lawful to risk the Word and the Sacraments to men partly instructed, trusting to the Paraclete to supply the rest? And yet who but himself was to say what was a partial and what was a sufficient instruction? Did the Holy Ghost work less strongly now in the twentieth century than in the primitive Church, when twelve fishermen were entrusted with the deposit of faith and the mission to preach it to all nations . . . ?

Outside, the summer day was dying. The bells of the city were tolling their vain cry for recollection and withdrawal. But the city was full of other sounds, and it was left to Kiril the Pontiff to gather his household about him for vespers and a remembrance of the hidden God.

'You've done a very thorough job, my friend.' Campeggio laid down the typescript and looked at George Faber with a new respect. 'That's the most complete dossier I've ever seen on Corrado Calitri and his friends.'

Faber shrugged unhappily. 'I was trained as a crime reporter. I have a talent for this sort of thing . . . But I can't say that I'm very proud of it.'

'Love's an expensive business, isn't it?' Campeggio smiled as he said it, but there was no humour in his shrewd dark eyes.

'I was going to talk to you about that. The information in that document cost me a thousand dollars. I may have to spend a lot more.'

'On what?'

'To get a signed statement out of one or more of the people mentioned in the dossier.'

'Have you any idea how much it will cost?'

'No. But from what I've gathered so far, several of them are short of money. The most I can afford is another thousand dollars. I want to know if you're prepared to put up any more.'

Campeggio sat silent a while, staring down at Faber's littered desk. Finally he said deliberately, 'I'm not sure that I should discuss the proposition in those terms.'

'What do you mean?'

'From the point of view of the Rota, and of civil law, it could amount to a subornation of witnesses.'

'I've thought of that myself.'

'I know you have. You're an honest man—too honest for your own comfort, or mine. Let's look at it from another angle. How do you propose to approach your prospective witnesses?'

'I've marked three names in the document. Each one of them has open animosity to Calitri. One is an actor who hasn't had a good part for twelve months. One is a painter. Calitri financed one exhibition for him, and then dropped him. The third is a woman. I'm told she's a writer though I've never seen anything she's published. The two men always spend the summer at Positano. The woman has a house on Ischia. I propose to go south during the summer holidays and try to make contact with each one.'

'Are you taking Chiara with you?'

'No. She wants to come, but I don't think it's good diplomacy. Besides I . . . I need to test myself away from her.'

'You may be wise at that.' Campeggio's shrewd eyes searched his face. 'I wonder if any of us knows himself before his middle years? . . . Now tell me something else. Why do you think your witnesses will ask for money?'

'It's the way of the world,' said George Faber wryly. 'Nobody really wants to be persecuted for justice's sake. Everybody wants to make a profit on the process.'

'You're a Catholic, Faber. How do you feel in conscience about this transaction?'

Faber flushed. 'My conscience is compromised already. I'm committed to Chiara, I can't afford the luxury of scruples.'

Campeggio agreed sourly. 'It's a very Nordic point of view. It's probably more honest than mine.'

'And what is your point of view?'

'About the money? I'm prepared to give you another thousand dollars. But I don't want to know what you do with it.'

Faber's rare wintry humour asserted itself for a moment. 'And that leaves your conscience clear?'

'I'm a casuist,' said Campeggio with a thin smile. 'I can split hairs as well as the Jesuits. It suits me to be in doubt. But if you want the truth . . .' He stood up and began to pace up and down Faber's office. 'If you want the truth, I'm in deep confusion. I think Chiara has justice on her side. I think you have a right to try to get it for her. I think there is justice on my side too, when I want to remove my son from Calitri's influence. I'm doubtful about the means; so I don't want to question them too closely. That's why I'm co-operating with you, while leaving you to carry the burden of moral and legal decision . . . It's a very Latin trick . . .'

'At least you're open with us,' said Faber with odd simplicity. 'I'm grateful for that.'

Campeggio stopped his pacing and looking down at Faber, who sat slumped and vaguely shrunken behind his desk. 'You're a soft man, my friend. You deserve a simpler loving.'

'It's my fault more than Chiara's . . . I have to work double time to be free for the vacation. I'm worried about money. I'm scared that I may not be able to control the consequences of what we are doing.'

'And Chiara?'

'She's young. She's been hurt. She's in an uncomfortable position for a woman . . . So she wants to be diverted . . . I don't blame her. But I don't have the stamina for five nights a week at the Cabala or the Papagallo.'

'How does she occupy herself while you're working?'

Faber gave a small, rueful grin. 'What does any young matron of fashion do in Rome? . . . Luncheon parties, mannequin shows, cocktails . . .'

Campeggio laughed. 'I know, I know. Our women make good lovers and good mothers. As wives, even as unofficial ones, they lack something. They resent their husbands, and spoil their sons.'

For a moment Faber seemed to lose himself in a private contemplation. He said absently, 'The loving is still good . . . But I have the feeling that we're both starting to calculate. When Chiara came to me first she was almost broken. I seemed to be able to supply everything she needed. Now she's back to normal and I am the one with the needs.'

'Doesn't she understand that?'

'That's the sixty-four-dollar question . . . By nature she's impulsive and generous, but living with Calitri has changed her. It's as if . . .' He fumbled uneasily for the words. 'As if she thinks men owe her a special kind of debt.'

'And you're not sure you can pay it all?'

'No, I'm not sure.'

'Then if I were you,' said Campeggio emphatically, 'I should cut loose now. Say goodbye, cry into your pillow, and forget the whole business.'

'I'm in love with her,' said Faber simply. 'I'm ready to pay any price to hold her.'

'Then we're both in the same galley, aren't we?'

'What do you mean?'

Campeggio balked a moment and then explained himself deliberately. 'In the beginning—possession always seems the ultimate triumph of love. You have your Chiara now, but you cannot be wholly happy until you possess her by legal contract. Then, you feel, you will be safe. You pluck the rose and put it in a vase in the drawing-room, but after a while the bloom fades, and it is no longer so important that you own a wilting flower. When children come they are another kind of possession. They depend on you utterly. You hold them to you by their need of sustenance and security. As they grow, you find that the bond weakens, and that you no longer possess them as you once did . . . I want my son. I want him to be the image and the continuum of myself. I tell myself that what I do is for his good, but I know, deep in my heart, that it is also for my own satisfaction. I cannot bear that he should withdraw himself from me and give himself to another—man or woman—whom I consider less worthy . . . But in the end he will go, for better or for worse . . . Look at me now. I am a man of confidence at the Vatican. As editor of *Osservatore* I am the mouthpiece of the Church. I have a reputation for integrity and I believe I have earned it. Yet today I am beginning to compromise myself. Not for you! Don't think I'm blaming you! It is for my son, whom I shall lose anyway, and for myself, because I have not yet begun to come to terms with age and loneliness . . .'

George Faber heaved himself out of his chair and stood facing his colleague. For the first time he seemed to take on an unfamiliar strength and dignity. He said evenly, 'I have no right to hold you to any bargains. You're in a more delicate position than I am. You're free to withdraw your offer.'

'Thank you,' said Orlando Campeggio simply. 'But I can't withdraw. I'm committed . . . because of what I want, and what I am.'

'And what are you? What am I?'

'We should have been friends,' said Orlando Campeggio with dry irony. 'We've known each other a long time. But we missed the chance. So I'm afraid we're just conspirators—and not very good ones at that!'

Ten days before the feast of Saint Ignatius Loyola, Jean Télémond received a letter from His Eminence Cardinal Rinaldi:

> Dear Reverend Father,
>
> This is not an official communication, but a personal one. Just before your arrival in Rome, the Holy Father granted me permission to retire from office, and I am now living privately in the country. I am, however, invited to be present next week when you address the students and faculty at the Gregorian University. Before that day I should very much like to have the opportunity of meeting and talking with you.
>
> Already I know a great deal—more perhaps than you realize—about you and your work. I judge you to be a man favoured by God with what I can only call the grace of commitment.
>
> This grace is a rare gift. I myself have missed it, but for this reason, perhaps, I am the more aware of it in others. I am aware too that it comes to the recipient more often as a cross than as a consolation.
>
> I believe that your recall to Rome may be an event of great importance to the Church. I know that it is a decisive one for you. I should like therefore to offer you my friendship, my support, and perhaps my advice in your future activities.
>
> If it is convenient, perhaps you would be good enough to visit me next Monday and spend the afternoon with me. You will be doing me a favour, and I hope sincerely I may be of some service to you.
>
> Yours fraternally in Christ Jesus,
> Valerio Rinaldi
> Cardinal Priest

For a man in crisis, it was a princely encouragement and it touched Télémond deeply. It reminded him—when he needed the reminder most—that, for all its monolithic faith, the Church was a habitation of diverse spirits amongst whom still dwelt a virtue of fraternity and compassion.

In the clattering, gregarious, clerical society of Rome, he felt like an alien. Its conventions irked him. Its brusque orthodoxy troubled him as if he were being reproached for his twenty-year solitude among the mysteries of Creation. The melancholy of the climacteric weighed upon his soul. On the one hand he found himself dreading the moment when he must present the speculation of a lifetime to the public view. On the other he found himself approaching the moment with a kind of calculation which made the risks he had sustained, in flesh and spirit, seem futile and even guilty.

Now suddenly there was a hand stretched out to welcome him, and a voice that spoke with an accent of rare understanding and gentleness. He had not lacked friendship in his life. His work had not wanted patronage and encouragement. Yet no one had ever seen it so clearly for what it was. A gamble, a commitment to living and knowing and believing, with a complete conviction that every moment of existence, every extension of knowledge, every act of faith was a step in the same direction, toward God-made-man, and man made in the image of God.

What had troubled him most in Rome was the feeling that certain people in the Church regarded his work as an arrogance. Yet an arrogant man could not have embarked upon such a journey, nor risked so much in a single-minded search for truth.

He had never been afraid of error since all his experience had shown him that knowledge was self-corrective and that a search honestly pursued must bring a man closer to the shores of revelation, even though their outline remained for ever hidden from his view.

There was an attitude of orthodoxy which was itself a heresy: that to state the truth, as it had been stated and restated in every century of the Church, was to display it for ever in all its fullness. Yet the history of the Church was the history of an immutable revelation unfolding itself into greater and greater complexity as men's minds opened to receive it more fully. The history of spiritual progress for an individual was the history of his preparation of himself to co-operate more willingly, more consciously, and more gratefully with the grace of God.

For Jean Télémond the letter of Valerio Rinaldi wore the aspect of such a grace. He accepted it thankfully, and made an appointment to visit the Cardinal in his country retreat.

They were instantly at ease with each other. Rinaldi walked his guest round the pleasances of the villa and rehearsed its history from the first Etruscan tomb in the orchard to the Orphic temple whose pavement lay uncovered in the sunken garden. Télémond was charmed by the urbanity and kindness of his host, and he opened himself more freely than he had done for a long time, so that the old man looked out through his visitor's eyes on exotic landscapes and a cavalcade of histories, new and strange to him.

When they had finished the circuit, they sat beside a marble pond and drank English tea, and watched the fat carp browse languidly among the lily pads. Then, amiably but shrewdly, Rinaldi began to probe the mind of Jean Télémond.

'Rome is a chameleon city. It wears a different colour for every visitor. How does it look to you, Father?'

Jean Télémond toyed with the question for a moment and then answered it frankly. 'I am uneasy. The idiom is strange to me. I am a Gaul among the Romans, a provincial among the metropolitans. I came back sure that I had learned so much in twenty years. Now I feel that I have forgotten something—some essential mode of speech, perhaps. I don't know what it is, but the lack of it troubles me.'

Rinaldi put down his teacup and wiped his fastidious hands with a linen napkin. His lined, patrician face softened. 'I think you rate yourself too humbly, Father. It's a long time since Gaul was a province of Rome, and I think it is we who have lost the art of communication . . . I don't deny that you have a problem, but I am inclined to read it differently.'

Télémond's lean, disciplined features relaxed into a smile. 'I should be grateful to hear Your Eminence's interpretation.'

The old Cardinal waved an eloquent hand, so that the sunlight gleamed on the emerald ring of his office.

'There are some, my friend, who wear the Church like a glove. Myself, for instance. I am a man who was made to grow comfortably within an established order. I understand the organization. I know where it is rigid and where it can be made flexible . . . There is no merit in this, no special virtue. It is at bottom a matter of temperament and aptitude. It has nothing to do with faith, hope or charity. There are those who are born to be good servants of the State. There are those who have an aptitude for the government of the Church . . . It is a talent if you want, but a talent which has its own temptations, and I have succumbed to some of them during my life . . .'

He broke off and stared down at the lily pond, where the fish swam gold and crimson, and the flowers spread their creamy petals under the afternoon sun. Télémond waited while the old prince gathered the rest of his thoughts.

'. . . There are others, my friend, who wear the Church like a hair-shirt. They believe no less. They love perhaps more richly and more daringly; but they move, as you do, uneasily inside the discipline. For them obedience is a daily sacrifice, whereas for me and those like me, it is an accommodation—often a rewarding accommodation—to circumstance. Do you understand what I mean?'

'I understand it; but I think that Your Eminence underrates himself to be kind to me.'

'No! No!' Rinaldi's answer was swift and emphatic. 'I am too old to pay idle compliments. I have entered into judgement with myself and I know how much I am found wanting . . . At this moment you are a troubled man . . .'

'So very troubled, Eminence,' said Télémond, softly. 'I came to Rome under obedience; but there is no peace for me here. I know that.'

'You are not born to peace, my friend. This is the first thing you must accept. You will not come to it, perhaps, till the day you die. Each of us has his own cross, you know, made and fitted to his reluctant shoulders. Do you know what mine is?'

'No.'

'To be rich and content and fulfilled, and to know in this twilight of living that I have deserved none of it and that, when I am called to judgement, I must depend utterly upon the mercy of God and upon the merits of others more worthy.'

Télémond was silent a long time, touched and humbled by this glimpse of an intimate and private agony. Finally he asked quietly, 'And my cross, Eminence?'

'Your cross, my son . . .' The old man's voice took on a new warmth and passion. 'Your cross is to be always divided between the faith which you possess, the obedience which you have vowed, and your personal search for a deeper knowledge of God through the universe which He has made. You believe that there is no conflict between the two, and yet you are involved in conflict every day. You cannot recant the Act of Faith without a personal catastrophe. You cannot abandon the search without a ruinous disloyalty to yourself and to your own integrity. Am I right, Father?'

'Yes, Eminence, you're right; but it isn't enough. You show me the cross, but you do not show me how to carry it.'

'You have carried it for twenty years without me.'

'And now I am staggering under its weight. Believe me, I am staggering . . . And now there is a new burden—Rome!'

'Do you want to go away?'

'Yes. And yet I should be ashamed to go.'

'Why?'

'Because I hope that this may be the time of resolution for me. I feel I have been silent long enough for my thought to take shape. I feel that I have a duty to expose it to debate and dialectic. This exposure seems as much a duty as all my years of study and exploration.'

'Then you must do your duty,' said Rinaldi mildly.

'That makes another problem, Eminence,' said Télémond with a flash of humour. 'I am not a publicist. I do not present myself very well. I do not know how to accommodate myself to the climate of this place.'

'Then ignore it,' said Rinaldi bluntly. 'You come armed with a right heart and a private vision of the truth. That is armour enough for any man.'

Télémond frowned and shook his head. 'I mistrust my courage, Eminence.'

'I could tell you to trust in God.'

'I do, and yet . . .' He broke off and stared unseeing across the reaches of the classic garden.

Rinaldi prompted him gently. 'Go on, my son.'

'I'm afraid–desperately afraid!'

'Of what?'

'That there may come a moment when this conflict in myself splits me in two, and destroys me utterly. I can't put it any other way. I lack the words. I can only hope that Your Eminence understands.'

Valerio Cardinal Rinaldi stood up and laid his hands on the bowed shoulders of the Jesuit. 'I do, my son, believe me! I feel for you as I have felt for few men in my lifetime. Whatever happens after your address next week, I want you to count me your friend. I told you you would be doing me a favour if you allowed me to help you. I put it more strongly. You may give me the opportunity of winning some small merit for myself . . .' His habitual humour asserted itself again, and he laughed. 'It's a tradition in Rome, Father. Painters, poets, and philosophers all need a patron to protect them from the Inquisition. And I may be the last real one left!'

EXTRACT FROM THE SECRET MEMORIALS OF KIRIL I PONT. MAX.

. . . All this week I have been besieged by what I can only call a temptation of darkness. Never since my time in the bunker have I been so oppressed by the wild absurdity of the world, by the wastefulness of man's struggle for survival, by the apparent idiocy of any attempt to change human nature or bring about a corporate betterment in the human condition.

To reason with the temptation was simply to create another absurdity. To reason with myself was to invite a new confusion. A spirit of mockery seemed to inhabit me. Whenever I looked at myself I saw a jester in cap and bells, perched on a mountain-top, waving his silly wand at the hurricanes. When I prayed, my spirit was arid. The words were like an incantation from some ancient witchcraft–without virtue and without reward. It was a kind of agony which I thought would never come my way again; yet this time I was more deeply wounded by it than ever before.

In my confusion, I addressed myself to a meditation on the passion and death of the Master. I began to understand dimly the meaning of the agony in Gethsemane garden, when the trouble of His human spirit communicated itself so poignantly to His body that its mechanism began to break down and He suffered, as a leukaemia patient does, the bloody sweat which is a foretaste of dying.

For a moment also I glimpsed the meaning of His final desolate cry from the Cross: 'My God, my God. Why hast Thou forsaken me?' In that moment, I think He must have seen—as I see now—the wild folly of a world gone mad, bursting itself asunder in a tangential flight from its centre.

At that moment His own life and death must have seemed a vast futility, just as my life and all my effort as His Vicar seem to me. Yet He endured it, and so must I. If He, God-man, could suffer, uncomforted by the Godhead, shall I refuse the cup which He hands on to me?

I held to the thought with a kind of terror, lest it should slip away from me, and leave me for ever a prey to blackness and despair. Then, slowly, the darkness dissipated itself and I found myself shaken, almost physically ill, but comfirmed once again in the essential sanity of belief. I did, however, see something very clearly: the plight of those who have no God to infuse a meaning into the monstrous nonsense of the whole human effort.

For a believer, life is at best a painful mystery made acceptable by a partial revelation of a divine design. To an unbeliever—and there are hundreds of millions from whom the grace of belief has been withheld—it must present itself at times as a kind of madness, always threatening, at times almost unendurable. Perhaps this is the meaning of what I am, and what has happened to me: that being poor in all else, I can offer to the world the love of an understanding heart . . .

Today a second letter arrived from Kamenev. It was delivered in Paris to the Cardinal Archbishop and forwarded to me by special messenger. It is more cryptic than the first, but I sense a greater urgency in it:

> I have your message and I am grateful for it. The sunflowers are blooming now in Mother Russia, but before they come to flower again, we may have need of each other.
>
> Your message tells me that you trust me, but I have to be honest and say that you must not trust what I do or what I am reported to say. We live in different climates, as you know. You command an obedience and a loyalty impossible in my sphere of action. I can only survive by understanding what is possible, by yielding to one pressure in order to avoid a greater one.
>
> Within twelve months, even sooner, we may come to the brink of war. I want peace. I know that we cannot have it with a one-sided bargain. On the other hand, I cannot dictate its terms even to my own people. I am caught in the current of history. I can tack across it but I cannot change the direction of the flow.
>
> I believe you understand what I am trying to say. I ask you, if you can, to interpret it as clearly as possible to the President of the United States. I have met him. I respect him. In a private dealing I could trust him, but in the domain of politics he is as subject to pressure as I am—more so, perhaps, because his tenure is shorter, and the influence of public opinion is stronger. If you can communicate with him, I beg you to do so, but secretly and with the greatest discretion. You know that I should have to repudiate violently any suggestion that there is a private channel of talk between us.
>
> I cannot yet suggest a secure method by which you can write to me. From time to time, however, you will receive applications for a private audience from a man named Georg Wilhelm Forster. To him you may speak freely, but commit nothing to writing. If you succeed in a conversation with the President

of the United States, you should refer to him as Robert. Foolish, is it not, that to discuss the survival of the race, we must resort to such childish tricks?

You are fortunate that you can pray. I am limited to action, and if I am half right for half the time I am lucky.

Again I repeat my caution. You believe you stand in God's shoes. I must wear my own and the ground is very slippery. Trust me no further than I can trust myself. Martyrdom is out of fashion in my world.

Greetings. Kamenev

No man remains unchanged by the experience of power. Some are perverted to tyranny. Some are corrupted by flattery and self-indulgence. Some very few are tempered to wisdom by their understanding of the consequences of executive action. I believe this is what has happened to Kamenev.

He was never a gross man. When I knew him he had surrendered himself to cynicism, but this surrender was never quite complete. This was proved by his action in my regard. I would say that there is in his thinking no truly spiritual or religious domain. He has accepted too fully a materialist conception of man and of the universe. However, I do believe that, within the limits of his own logic, he has arrived at an understanding of the dignity of man, and a sense of obligation to preserve it as far as he can. I do not think he is governed by moral sanctions as we understand them in the spiritual sense. But he does realize that a certain practical morality is essential to social order, and even to the survival of civilization as we know it.

I think this is what he is trying to tell me: that I can trust him to proceed logically in his own system of thought, but that I must never expect him to work inside mine. For my part I must not forget that, while man is limited to the covenanted channels of grace, made available to him by the redemptive act of Christ, God is not so limited, and that in the outcome Kamenev's logic may be turned into a divine one. Even in the human order, Kamenev's letter has an historic importance. The man who embodies in his office the Marxist heresy, who has tried violently to extirpate the faith from the land of Russia, now turns to the Papacy to provide a free and secret mode of communication with the rest of the world.

I see very clearly that Kamenev offers me nothing—no entry for the faith into Russia, no slackening of oppression or persecution. Cardinal Goldoni points out that at this very moment our schools and seminaries in Poland, and Hungary, and East Germany, are in danger of being closed altogether by the imposition of new and savage taxation. He asks me what Kamenev proposes to offer either to the Church or to the United States by way of a down payment towards peace . . .

On the face of it he offers nothing. One might even make a good case for the opinion that he is trying to use me to his own advantage. I have to weigh this opinion very carefully. Yet I cling to the deep conviction that there is a divine design in this relationship between us and that it must not be allowed to degenerate into a political gambit . . .

It is an historic fact that, when the temporal power of the Church was greatest, her spiritual life was at its lowest ebb. It is dangerous to read divine revelation into every paragraph of history, but I cannot help feeling that, when we are like the Master, poorest in temporality, then we may be richest in the divine life.

From me the occasion demands prayer and prudence . . . Normally we should communicate with the government of the United States through our own Secretariat of State. In this instance we dare not do so. I have, therefore, sent a cable to the Cardinal Archbishop of New York, asking him to come to Rome as quickly as possible so that I may brief him on the situation and have him communicate directly with the President of the United States. Once I have spoken with Cardinal Carlin, we shall all be walking on eggs. If any hint of the matter is revealed to the American press, this small hope of peace may be lost to us for ever . . . In the morning I must offer Mass as a petition for a favourable outcome . . .

Today I held the first of a series of conferences with the Congregation of Religious and with the heads of the major religious orders. The purpose of the conferences is to determine how they may best adapt themselves to the changing conditions of the world and participate more actively and more flexibly in the mission of the Church to the souls of men.

There are many problems involved, and we shall not solve them all at one stroke. Each order holds jealously to its tradition and its sphere of influence in the Church. All too often the tradition is a handicap to apostolic effort. Systems of training differ. The 'spirit of the order'–that mode of thought and action which gives it a special character–tends too often to harden itself into 'the method of the order', so that it reacts too slowly and too stubbornly to the demands of the times.

There is another problem, too. The rate of recruitment of new members has become dangerously slow because many willing spirits find themselves too limited and constrained by an archaic constitution and even by a mode of dress and life which separates them too sharply from the times in which they live . . .

Once again I am faced with the fundamental problem of my office–how to translate the Word into Christian action; how to scrape off the overburden of history so that the lode of the primitive faith may be revealed in all its richness. When men are truly united with God, it matters little what dress they wear, what exercises of piety they perform, what constitution they live under. Religious obedience should set a man free in the liberty of the sons of God. Tradition should be a lamp to his feet, lighting his pathway into the future. To renounce the world is not to abandon it, but to restore it in Christ to the beauty of its primal design . . . We inherit the past but we are committed to the present and to the future.

It is time, I think, for a deeper exploration and a clearer definition of the function of the laity in the life of the Church. Anticlericalism is a symptom of dissatisfaction among the faithful. For the fact is that rebellion against the doctrine of the Church is less common than the gradual desertion of a religious climate which seems to be at irreconcilable odds with the world men have to live in. Those whose aspirations exceed the dimensions of the local pastor's mentality gradually fade from the pews in search of substitutes and partial truths, which as a rule bring them neither peace nor joy, but certainly a sense of dedicated integrity. The number of these cases has become large enough to achieve some sort of recognizable status in the Church, which, though ambiguous, is radically different from the category of those whose militant darkness attempts to eradicate from human consciousness the very notion of man's existence dependent on God . . .

In this world of ours, when men are reaching swiftly for the moon, the dimension of time seems to narrow daily, and I am perturbed that we cannot adjust ourselves more quickly to the change . . .

In a couple of weeks the holiday season will begin in Europe. It is customary for the Pontiff to leave the Vatican and spend a vacation at Castel Gandolfo. In spite of my impatience, I find myself looking forward to the change. It will give me time to think, to sum up for myself the thousand diverse impressions of these first months in office.

I have not dared to mention it to the Secretary of State, but I think I shall take the opportunity to travel a little in private, round the countryside . . . I shall need a good driver. It would be embarrassing to me, and to the Italian government, if we had any accidents on the road–it would make a wonderful picture if the Pontiff were discovered in the middle of a highway arguing with an Italian truck-driver . . . I find myself wishing for an agreeable companion to spend the vacation with me, but I have not yet found time to cultivate any real friendship. My Isolation is all the greater because I am so much younger than the members of the Curia, and–God help me–I do not want to become an old man before my time.

I understand now how some of my predecessors have lapsed into nepotism and surrounded themselves with relatives, and how others have cultivated favourites in the Vatican. It is not good for any man to be wholly alone . . .

Kamenev is married and has a son and a daughter. I should like to think he has made a happy match . . . If not, he must be much more isolated than I. I have never regretted my own celibacy, but I envy those whose work in the Church is with children . . .

A sudden dark thought. If there is another war, what of the little ones? They are the inheritors of our misdeeds, and how will they fare in the broadcast horror of an atomic Armageddon?'

It must not be . . . it must not!

7

In his bachelor apartment on Parioli, Corrado Calitri, Minister of the Republic, was conferring with his lawyers. The senior advocate, Perosi, was a tall, spare man with a dry, academic manner. His junior had a round dumpling face and a deprecating smile. In the far corner of the room, the Princess Maria-Rina sat withdrawn and wary, watching them with hooded, predatory eyes.

Perosi laid the tips of his fingers together, like a bishop about to intone a psalm, and summed up the situation:

'. . . As I understand it, you have been troubled in conscience for some time. You have taken counsel with a confessor, and he has advised you that it is your duty to change your testimony with respect to your marriage.'

Calitri's pale face was blank, his voice devoid of expression. 'That's the position, yes.'

'Let us be very clear, then, where we stand. Your wife's petition for a decreee of nullity is made under the terms of Canon 1086, which states two things: first, the internal consent of the mind is always presumed to be in agreement with the words or signs which are used in the celebration of the marriage; second, if either party or both parties, by a positive act of the will, exclude marriage itself, or all right to the conjugal act or any essential property of the marriage, the marriage contract is invalid.' He rustled his papers and went on in his professional fashion. 'The first part of the canon does not really concern us. It simply expresses a presumption of the law, which may be overcome by contrary proof. Your wife's plea leans on the second part. She claims that you deliberately excluded from your consent her right to the conjugal act, and that you did not accept the contract as unbreakable, but as a form of therapy to be laid aside if the therapy failed. If her plea could be sustained, the marriage would, of course, be declared invalid. You understand that?'

'I've always understood it.'

'But you denied in a written and sworn statement that your intention was defective.'

'I did.'

'Now, however, you are prepared to admit that the statement was false and that, in fact, you perjured yourself.'

'Yes. I understand that I have done a grave injustice, and I want to repair it. I want Chiara to be free.'

'You are prepared to make another sworn statement, admitting the perjury and the defective intention?'

'I am.'

'So far so good. This will give us a ground to reopen the case with the Rota.' Perosi pursed his pale lips and frowned. 'Unfortunately it will not be sufficient for a decree of nullity.'

'Why not?'

'It's a question of procedure covered by Canon 1971, and by commentaries on the code dated March 1929, July 1933, and July 1942. A party to a marriage who is the guilty cause of the nullity is deprived of the right to impugn the contract. He has no standing in court.'

'Where does that leave us?'

'We need one or more witnesses to testify that you expressed to them, clearly and explicitly, your defective intentions before the marriage took place.'

The brisk old voice of the princess intruded itself into the conversation. 'I think you can take it for granted that such testimony would be available.'

'In that case,' said Advocate Perosi, 'I think we have a sound case, and we may look with some confidence to a favourable outcome.'

He sat back in his chair and began rearranging his papers. As if on a prearranged signal, the dumpling man added a footnote to the discussion:

'With respect to my senior colleague, I should like to make two suggestions. It would be an advantage if we had a letter from your confessor indicating that you are acting under his advice in trying to repair the injustice done. It might help, too, if you wrote a friendly letter to your wife, admitting your fault and asking her to forgive you . . . Neither of these two documents would have any value in evidence, but they might, shall we say, help the atmosphere.'

'I'll do as you suggest,' said Calitri in the same colourless fashion. 'Now I'd like to ask a couple of questions. I admit default, I admit perjury. On the other hand I do have a public position and a reputation to protect.'

'All the deliberations of the Rota, and all the depositions made before it, are protected by rigid secrecy. You need have no fear on that score.'

'Good. How long do you think the business will take?'

Perosi considered the question a moment. 'Not too long. Nothing can be done, of course, during the holiday period, but if all the depositions were in our hands by the end of August, we could have the translation done in two weeks. Then, in view of your position and the long suspension of the case, I think we would get a speedy hearing . . . I should say two months at the outside. It might even be sooner.'

'I am grateful,' said Corrado Calitri. 'I'll have the papers ready by the end of August.'

Perosi and his colleague bowed themselves out. 'We are always at the disposal of the Minister.'

'Good day, gentlemen, and thank you.'

When the door closed behind them, the princess threw back her bird's head and laughed. 'There now. I told you, didn't I? It's as simple as shelling peas. Of course we have to find you a confessor. There's a nice understanding Monsignore who attends me from Florence. Yes, I think he'd be the one. He's intelligent, cultivated, and quite zealous in his own way. I'll have a talk with him and arrange an appointment . . . Come on now, smile. In two months you'll be free. In a year you'll be leading the country.'

'I know, Aunt, I know.'

'Oh, there's one more thing. Your letter to Chiara. There's no need to be too humble about it. Dignity, restraint, a desire to make amends, yes. But nothing compromising. I don't trust that girl. I never have.'

Calitri shrugged indifferently. 'She's a child, Aunt. There's no malice in her.'

'Children grow up—and there's malice in every woman when she can't get what she wants.'

'From what I hear, she's getting it.'

'With the dean of the foreign press. What's his name?'

'George Faber. He represents one of the New York dailies.'

'The biggest one,' said the old princess firmly. 'And you can't shrug him off like a cold in the head. You're too vulnerable now, my boy. You have the *Osservatore* against you, and Chiara in bed with the American press. You can't afford a situation like that.'

'I can't change it.'

'Why not?'

'Campeggio's son works for me. He likes me and dislikes his father. Chiara will probably marry this Faber as soon as she gets the decree of nullity. There's nothing I can do about either situation.'

'I think there is.' She fixed him with a shrewd and rheumy eye. 'Take young Campeggio first. You know what I should do?'

'I'd like to hear it.'

'Promote him. Push him forward as fast as you can. Promise him something even bigger after the election. Bind him to you with trust and friendship. His father will hate you, but the boy will love you, and I don't think Campeggio will fight his own son . . . As for Chiara and her American boy friend, leave them to me.'

'What do you propose to do?'

The old princess gave her high birdlike chuckle and shook her head. 'You have no talent with women, Corrado. Just sit quietly and leave Chiara to me.'

Calitri spread his eloquent hands in a gesture of resignation. 'Just as you say, Aunt. I'll leave her to you.'

'You won't regret it.'

'I'll take your advice, Aunt.'

'I know you will. Give me a kiss now, and cheer up. You'll have dinner with me tomorrow night. There are some people from the Vatican I want you to meet. Now that you're back in the bosom of the Church, they can begin to be useful to you.'

He kissed her withered cheek and watched her leave, wondering the while that so much vitality should reside in so frail a body, and whether he had enough to sustain the bargain he had made with his backers.

All his life he had been making deals like this one. Always the price had to be paid in the same coin—another fragment of himself. Each depletion made him less assured of his identity, and he knew that in the end he would be altogether empty, and the spiders would spin webs in the hollow of his heart.

Depression came down on him like a cloud. He poured himself a drink and carried it over to the window-seat from which he could look down on the city and the flight of pigeons over its ancient roofs. The Quirinale might be worth a Mass, but nothing—nothing—was worth the lifetime damnation to emptiness which was demanded of him.

To be sure, he had made a contract. He would be the White Knight without fear and without reproach, and the Christian Democrats would let him lead them into power. But there was room still for a footnote, and the Princess Maria-Rina had spelled it out for him . . . Trust and friendship . . . Perhaps even more! In the sour bargain he had made, there was suddenly a hint of sweetness.

He picked up the telephone, dialled the number of his office, and asked young Campeggio to bring the afternoon's correspondence to his apartment.

At ten-thirty of a cloudless morning, Charles Corbet Carlin, Cardinal Archbishop of New York, landed at Fiumicino airport. An official of the Secretariat of State met him at the steps of the aircraft and hurried him past the Customs and Immigration officials into a Vatican limousine. An hour and a half later, he was closeted with Kiril the Pontiff and Goldoni the Secretary of State.

Carlin was by nature a peremptory man, and he understood the usages of power. He was quick to see the change that a few months of office had wrought in the Pope. He had lost some of his charm, none of his swift, intuitive warmth. Yet he seemed to have reached a new dimension of authority. His scarred face was leaner, his speech more brisk, his whole manner more urgent and concerned. Yet, characteristically, he opened the discussion with a smile and an apology:

'I'm grateful that Your Eminence came so promptly. I know how busy you are. I wanted to explain myself more fully, but I could not trust the information even to a coded cable.'

Then in crisp, emphatic sentences, he explained the reason for the summons and showed Carlin the text of Kamenev's two letters.

The American scanned them with a shrewd and calculating eye, and then handed them back to the Pontiff. 'I understand Your Holiness's concern. I confess I am less clear on what Kamenev hopes to gain by this manoeuvre.'

Goldoni permitted himself a faint smile. 'Your Eminence's reaction is the same as mine . . . A manoeuvre! His Holiness, however, takes a different view.'

Kiril spread his crooked hands on the desk top and explained himself sharply. 'I want you to understand first that I know this man. I know him more intimately than I know either of you. For a long time he was my interrogator in prison. Each of us has had a great influence on the other. It was he who arranged my escape from Russia. I am profoundly convinced that this is not a political manoeuvre, but a genuine appeal for help in the crisis which will soon be upon us.'

Carlin nodded thoughtfully. 'Your Holiness may be right. It would be folly to discount your experience with this man and your intimate knowledge of the Russian situation. On the other hand—and I say it with all respect—we have another kind of experience with Kamenev and with the Soviets.'

'When you say "we", do you refer to the Church or to the United States of America?'

'To both,' said Carlin flatly. 'So far as the Church is concerned, the Secretariat of State will bear me out. There is still active persecution in the satellite countries. In Russia the faith has been totally extinguished. Our brother bishops who went to prison with Your Holiness are all dead. The Soviet frontiers are sealed against the faith. I see no prospect of their being opened in our time.'

Goldoni added agreement. 'I have already put this view very clearly to his Holiness.'

'And I,' said Kiril the Pontiff, 'do not disagree with it . . . Now tell me about the American view.'

'At first blush,' said Carlin, 'this looks to me like another version of the old summit meetings. We all remember the arguments . . . "Let's bypass the lower echelons and let the leaders talk freely and familiarly about our problems. Let's skip the details and get down to the fundamental issues that divide us . . ." Well, we had the meetings. They were always abortive. In the end every discussion was wrecked by the details, if not wholly destroyed. In the end, you see, the lower echelons of government are more decisive than the upper ones, because under our system, and under the Russian one, the leader is always subject to the pressures of political and administrative advice from below. No single man can sustain the burden of decision on major issues.' He smiled expansively at the Pontiff. 'Even in the Church we have the same situation. Your Holiness is the Vicar of Christ. Yet the effectiveness of your decisions is limited by the co-operation and obedience of the local ordinaries.'

Kiril the Pontiff picked up the letters from his desk and held them out to his two counsellors. 'So what would you have me do about these? Ignore them?'

Carlin side-stepped the question. 'What does Kamenev ask Your Holiness to do?'

'He is very clear, I think. He asks me to communicate the letters to the President of the United States, and communicate also my own interpretation of his mind and his intentions.'

'What is his mind, Holiness? What are his intentions?'

'Let me quote again what he says. "Within twelve months, even sooner, we may come to the brink of war. I want peace. I know that we cannot have it with a one-sided bargain. On the other hand, I cannot dictate its terms even to my own people. I am caught in the current of history. I can tack across it but I cannot change the direction of the flow . . . I believe you understand what I am trying to say. I ask you, if you can, to interpret it as clearly as possible to the President of the United States . . ." To me, in my knowledge of the man, the message is quite evident. Before the crisis becomes irreversible, he wants to establish a ground of negotiation, so that peace may be preserved.'

'But what ground?' asked Goldoni. 'Your Holiness must admit that he is somewhat less than precise.'

'Put it another way,' said Carlin in his pragmatic fashion. 'I go back home. I call Washington and ask for a private interview with the President of the United States. I show him these letters. I say: "It is the view of the Holy See that Kamenev wants to begin secret talks to fend off the crisis we all know is coming. The Pope will be the intermediary of the talks . . ." What do you think the President will say or do then? What would Your Holiness do in his place?'

Kiril's scarred face twitched into a smile of genuine amusement. 'I should say, Talk costs nothing. So long as men can communicate, however haltingly, then there is a hope of peace. But close all the doors, cut all the wires, build the walls even higher–then each nation is an island, preparing in secret a common destruction.'

Abruptly Carlin challenged the argument. 'There is a flaw in the logic, Holiness. Forgive me, but I have to show it to you. Talk always costs something–this kind of talk especially. Secret parleys are dangerous because once they are brought into the open–and inevitably they must be–then they can be denied by those who took part in them. They can be used as weapons in political dealings.'

'Remember!' Goldoni added the potent afterthought. 'There are no longer two grand powers in the world. There is Russia, and the United States. There is the European bloc. There is China, and there are the uncommitted nations of Asia and Africa and the South Americans. There is not only the arms race. There is the race to feed the hungry and the race to align vast numbers of mankind with one ideology or another. We dare not take too simple a view of this very complex world.'

'I hesitate to say it, Holiness,' said Carlin gravely. 'But I should not like to see the Holy See compromised by offering itself as an intermediary in bilaterial and probably abortive discussion . . . Personally I mistrust a truce with the Russian bear, no matter how prettily he dances.'

'You have him in the papal coat of arms,' said Kiril tartly. 'Do you mistrust him there too?'

'Let me answer the question with another. Can Your Holiness trust himself completely in this matter? This is not doctrine or dogma, but an affair of State. Your Holiness is as open to error as the rest of us.'

He had been dangerously frank and he knew it. To be Cardinal Archbishop of New York was to sit high in the Church, to dispose great influence, to command money and resources vital to the economy of the Vatican. Yet, in the constitution of the faith, the Successor of Peter was paramount, and in its history many a Cardinal Prince had been stripped of his preferment by a single word from an outraged Pontiff. Charles Corbet Carlin sat back in his chair and waited, not without uneasiness, for the papal answer.

To his surprise, it was delivered in a tone of restraint and real humility. 'Everything you tell me is true. It is, in fact, a reflection of my own thought on the matter. I am grateful that you have chosen to be open with me, that you have not tried to bend me by diplomatic words. I do not want to bend you either. I do not want to force you to act against your own prudence. This is not a matter of faith or morals, it is a matter of private conviction, and I should like to share mine with you . . . Let us have lunch first, and then I want to show you both something. You have seen it before, but I hope today it may take on another meaning for you.'

Then, seeing the doubt and surprise on their faces, he laughed almost boyishly. 'No, there are no plots, no Borgia subtleties. I've learned something in Italy. One should never discuss weighty matters on an empty stomach. I think Goldoni will agree that I've reformed the Vatican kitchens if nothing else. Come now, let's relax for a while.'

They ate simply but well in Kiril's private apartment. They talked discursively of men and affairs and the hundred intimacies of the hierarchic society to which they belonged. They were like members of an exclusive international club, whose fellows were scattered to every point of the compass, but whose affairs were common knowledge in all tongues.

When the meal was over and the Vatican had lapsed into the somnolence of siesta time, Kiril put on a black cassock and led his two guests into the Basilica of Saint Peter.

The tourists were sparse now, and no one paid any attention to three middle-aged clerics halted by the confessional boxes near the sacristy. Kiril pointed to one of them which carried on its door the laconic legend, 'Polish and Russian.'

'Once a week I come and sit here for two hours, to hear the confession of anyone who chances to come. I should like to hear them in Italian as well, but the dialects escape me . . . You both know what this ministry of the tribunal is like. The good ones come. The bad ones stay away; but every so often there arrives the soul in distress, the one who needs a special co-operation from the confessor to lead him back to God . . . It's a lottery always–a gamble on the moment and the man, and the fruitfulness of the Word one plucks from one's own heart. And yet there, in that stuffy little box, is the whole meaning of the faith–the private speech of man with his Creator, myself between as man's servant and God's. There, encompassed by the smell of blood sausage and cabbage water, and the sweat of a frightened man, I am what I was ordained to be: a sublime opportunist, a fisher of men, not knowing what I shall catch in my net or whether I shall catch anything at all . . . Now come over here.'

He beckoned to an attendant to accompany them. Then he took the arms of the two Cardinals and walked them across to the steps that led down to the confession of Saint Peter, in front of the great altar of Bernini. They descended the steps. The attendant unlocked the bronze grille in front of the kneeling statue of Pope Pius VI. When they entered the recess, he closed the door on them and retired to a respectful distance. Kiril led his two counsellors to the space where a dark hole plunged down toward the grottoes of the Vatican. Then he turned to face them. His voice dropped to a murmur that echoed softly round the enclosure.

'Down there, they say, is the tomb of Peter the Fisherman. Whenever I am afraid or in darkness, I come here to pray, and ask him what I, his inheritor, should do. He was an opportunist too, you know. The Master gave him the Keys of the Kingdom. The Holy Ghost gave him the gift of wisdom and the gift of tongues. Then he was left, still a fisherman, an alien in the empire of Rome, to plant the seed of the Gospel wherever there was earth to receive it . . . He had no method. He had no temple. He had no book but the living Gospel. He was conditioned by the time in which he lived, but he could not be bound by the condition ... Neither can I. Do you remember the story of Paul coming into the city of Athens, among the philosophers and the rhetors, and seeing the altar of the Unkown God? Do you remember what he did? He cried out with a loud voice: "Men, brethren! What you worship without knowing, I preach!" Is not this an opportunist also? He does not reason with the moment. He does not appeal to a system or a history. He gambles himself and his mission on a word tossed into a milling crowd. Don't you see? This is the meaning of faith. This is the risk of belief.'

He turned a luminous face on Carlin, not commanding but pleading with him. 'Before Your Eminence came to see me I was in darkness. I saw myself as a fool shouting a folly to a heedless world. So be it! That is what we preach: transcendent nonsense which we trust in the end will make a divine logic ...'

Abruptly he relaxed and grinned at them mischievously. 'In prison I learned to gamble, and I found that in the end the man who always won was he who never hedged his bets. I know what you're thinking. I want to navigate the barque of Peter by the seat of my papal breeches ... But if the wind is blown by the breath of God, and the water is rocked by His hands ... how better can I do it? Answer me! How better can I do it?'

In the narrow enclosure, Goldoni shifted uneasily on his feet.

Carlin stood as obstinate and unshakable as Plymouth Rock. He said evenly, 'This is perhaps the faith that moves mountains, Holiness. I regret that it has not been given to me in the same measure. I am compelled to work by normal prudence. I cannot agree that the affairs of the Church can be administered by private inspiration.'

Kiril the Pontiff was still smiling when he answered. 'You elected me by inspiration, Eminence. Do you think the Holy Ghost has deserted me?'

Carlin was not to be put off. He pressed his argument stubbornly. 'I did not say that, Holiness. But I will say this: no one is large enough to make himself the universal man. You want to be all things to all men, but you can never truly succeed. You're a Russian, I am an American. You ask me to risk more on this Kamenev than I would risk on my own brother, if he were President of the United States. I cannot do it.'

'Then,' said Kiril, with unexpected mildness, 'I will not ask you to do it. I will not ask you to risk anything. I will give you a simple command. You will present yourself to the President of the United States. You will offer him these letters, and one which I shall write myself. If your opinion is asked, you will be free to say whatever you wish, as a private cleric and as an American, but you will not attempt to interpret my mind or Kamenev's. This way I hope you will feel free to discharge your duty to the Church and to your country.'

Carlin flushed. He said awkwardly, 'Your Holiness is generous with me.'

'Not generous, only logical. If I believe the Holy Ghost can work through me and through Kamenev, why should he not work though the President of the United States? It is never wise to discount Omnipotence. Besides,' he added gently, 'you may do better for me in opposition. At least you will guarantee the good faith of the Holy See toward the United States of America ... I think now, perhaps, we should pray together. It is not expected that we should agree on what is prudent, only that our wills should be set toward the service of the same God.'

As the month of July drew to a close, and the summer exodus from Rome began, Ruth Lewin found herself caught up once more in the cyclic drama of mental distress.

The onset of the action was always the same: a deep melancholy, a sensation of solitude, a feeling of rootlessness, as though she had been set down suddenly on an unfamiliar planet where her past was meaningless, her future was a question mark, and communication lapsed into gibberish.

The melancholy was the worst sensation of all. As a symptom it was familiar to her; yet she could neither reason with it nor dispel it. It drove her into fits of weeping. When the tears stopped, she felt empty and incapable of the simplest pleasure. When she looked in a mirror she saw herself old and ravaged. When she walked out into the city, she was a stranger, an object of derision to the passers-by.

The flaw in her personality must be evident to everybody. She was a German by birth, a Jew by race, an American by adoption, an exile in the country of the sun. She demanded belief and refused it with the same gesture. She needed love and knew herself impotent to express it. She wanted desperately to live, yet was haunted by the insidious attraction of death. She was everything and nothing. There were times when she huddled helpless in her apartment like a sick animal, afraid of the clamorous health of her kind.

All her relationships seemed to fail her at once. She moved like a stranger among her protégés in old Rome. She made expensive telephone calls to friends in America. When they failed to answer she was desolate. When they responded with casual thanks, she was convinced she had made a fool of herself. She was oppressed by the prospect of summer, when Rome was deserted and the heat lay like a leaden pall over the alleys and the sluggish life of the piazzas.

At night she lay wakeful with aching breasts, tormented by a fire in the flesh. When she drugged herself into sleep, she dreamed of her dead husband and woke sobbing in an empty bed. The young doctor with whom she worked came to visit her, but he was too immersed in his own problems, and she was too proud to reveal her own to him. He was in love with her, he said, but his demands were too blunt, and when she drew away he was quickly bored, so that in the end he stopped coming, and she blamed herself for his neglect.

A couple of times she tried the old prescription for unhappy widows in Rome. She sat herself in a bar and tried to drink herself into recklessness. But three drinks made her ill, and when she was accosted, she was brusquely and unreasonably angry.

The experience was salutary. It made her cling with a kind of desperation to the last vestige of reason. It gave her a little more patience to support the illness which she knew must pass, even though she dare not wait too long upon the cure. Each petty crisis depleted her reserves and brought her one step nearer the medicine cabinet, where the bottle of barbiturates mocked her with the illusion of forgetfulness.

Then, one heavy and threatening day, hope stepped into her life again. She had awakened late and was dressing listlessly when the telephone rang. It was George Faber. He told her Chiara was out of town. He was feeling lonely and depressed. He would like to take her to dinner. She hesitated a moment, and then accepted.

The incident was over in two minutes, but it wrenched her out of depression and into an almost normal world. She made a hasty appointment with her hairdresser. She bought herself a new cocktail frock for twice the money she could afford. She bought flowers for her apartment, and a bottle of Scotch whisky for Faber; and when he came to call for her at eight o'clock, she was as nervous as a débutante on her first date.

He was looking older, she thought, a trifle stooped, a little greyer than at their last meeting. But he was still the dandy, with a carnation in his buttonhole, an engaging smile, and a bunch of Nemi violets for her dressing-table. He kissed her hand in the Roman fashion, and while she mixed his drink he explained himself ruefully:

'I have to go south on this Calitri business. Chiara hates Rome in the summer, and the Antonellis have asked her to go to Venice with them for a month. They've taken a house on the Lido . . . I hope to join them later. Meantime . . .' He gave a little uneasy laugh. 'I've lost the habit of living alone . . . And you did say I could call you.'

'I'm glad you called, George. I don't like living alone either.'

'You're not offended?'

'Why should I be? A night on the town with the dean of the foreign press, that's an event for most women. Here's your drink.'

They toasted each other and then fenced their way through the opening gambits of talk.

'Where would you like to dine, Ruth? Do you have any preferences?'

'I'm in your hands, good sir.'

'Would you like to be quiet or gay?'

'Gay, please. Life's been all too quiet lately.'

'That suits me. Now, would you like to be a Roman or a tourist?'

'A Roman, I think.'

'Good. There's a little place over in Trastevere. It's crowded and noisy, but the food's good. There's a guitar player, an odd poet or two, and a fellow draws pictures on the tablecloth.'

'It sounds wonderful.'

'I used to like it, but I haven't been there in a long time. Chiara doesn't like that sort of thing.' He blushed and fiddled nervously with his liquor. 'I'm sorry. That's the wrong beginning.'

'Let's make a bargain, George.'

He gave her a quick, shamefaced glance. 'What sort of bargain?'

'Tonight nothing is wrong. We say what we feel, do what we like, and then forget it. No strings, no promises, no apologies . . . I need it like that.'

'I need it too, Ruth. Does that sound like disloyalty?'

She leaned across and placed a warning finger on his lips. 'No second thoughts, remember!'

'I'll try . . . Tell me about yourself. What have you been doing?'

'Working. Working with my *juden* and wondering why I do it.'

'Don't you know why?'

'Sometimes. At others it's pretty meaningless.'

She got up and switched on the radio-player, and the room was filled with the saccharine tones of a Neapolitan singer. Ruth Lewin laughed. 'Pretty schmalzy, isn't it?'

Faber grinned and lay back in his chair, relaxed for the first time. 'Now who's having second thoughts? I like schmalz–and I haven't heard the word three times since I left New York.'

'It's the Yiddish in me. It slips out when I'm off my guard.'

'Does that worry you?'

'Occasionally.'

'Why should it?'

'That's a long story, and it's not for now. Finish your drink, George. Then take me out and make a Roman of me, just for tonight.'

At the doorway of the apartment he kissed her lightly on the lips, and then they walked, arm in arm, past the ghostly marbles of the Forum. Then for a final surrender to whimsy, they hailed a carrozza and sat holding hands while the tired horse carried them clippity-clop over the Palatine bridge and into the populous lanes of Trastevere.

The restaurant was called 'o Cavalluccio. Its entrance was an old oaken door, studded with rusty nails. Its sign was a prancing stallion, roughly carved into the weathered stone of the lintel and picked out with whitewash. The interior was a large, vaulted cellar, hung with dusty lanterns and set with heavy wooden refectory tables. The clientele was mostly families from the quarter, and the spirit of the place was one of amiable tyranny.

The proprietor, a dumpy fellow in a white apron, set them down in a dark corner, planked a flask of red and a flask of white wine in front of them, and announced his policy with a flashing smile:

'As much wine as you can drink! Good wine, but no fancy labels. Two kinds of pasta only. Two main dishes—a roast of chicken and a stew of veal in Marsala. After that you're in the hands of God!'

As Faber had promised, there was a guitar player, a swarthy youth with a red bandana round his neck and a tin cup tied to his belt for an alms-box. There was a bearded poet dressed in blue denims, home-made sandals and a sackcloth shirt, who turned an honest penny by mocking the guests with verses improvised in the Roman dialect. For the rest, the entertainment was provided by the clowning of the guests themselves and an occasional raucous chorus called by the guitar player. The pasta was served in great wooden bowls, and an impudent waiter tied a huge napkin round their necks to protect their noble bosoms from the sauce.

Ruth Lewis was delighted with the novelty, and Faber, plucked out of his normal ambience, seemed ten years younger and endowed with an unsuspected wit.

He charmed her with his talk of Roman intrigues and Vatican gossips, and she found herself talking freely of the long and tortuous journey which had brought her at last to the Imperial City. Encouraged by Faber's sympathy, she exposed her problems more freely than she had ever done, except to an analyst, and found to her surprise that she was no longer ashamed of them. On the contrary they seemed to define themselves more clearly, and the terror they had once held for her was magically diminished.

'. . . For me everything boiled itself down to a question of security, and the need to put down some kind of roots in a world that had shifted too quickly for my childish understanding. I never seemed to be able to do it. Everything in my life, people, the Church, the happiness I enjoyed—and I did have moments of great happiness—everything seemed to have the look of "here one day and gone the next" . . . I found that I could not believe in the permanence of the simplest relationship. The worst moments were when I found myself doubting that anything that had happened to me was real at all. It was as if I had been living a dream—as if I, the dreamer, were a dream too. Does that sound strange to you, George?'

'No, not strange. Sad, yes, but rather refreshing too.'

'Why do you say that?'

He sipped his wine thoughtfully, and then gave her a long, searching look over the rim of his glass. 'I suppose Chiara is just the opposite. In spite of everything that has happened to her, she seems completely certain of what she wants in life, and how she's going to get it. There's only one way to be happy–her way. There's only one way to be amused or content–the way to which she has been bred. Her marriage to Calitri shocked her dreadfully, but basically it didn't change her view of life . . . I think in the end you may be more fortunate than she is.'

'I wish I could believe that.'

'I think you must. You may not be happy yet. You may never be truly secure. But you're more flexible, more ready to understand the thousand ways people live, and think, and suffer.'

'I often wonder if that is a good thing–or whether it's just another illusion on my part. You know, I have the same dream over and over again. I talk to someone. He does not hear me. I reach out for someone. He does not even see me. I am waiting to meet someone. He walks right past me. I'm convinced that I don't exist at all.'

'Take my word for it,' said George Faber with a rueful smile. 'You do exist and I find you very disturbing.'

'Why disturbing?'

Before he had time to answer, the bearded poet came and took his stand by their table, and declaimed a long rigmarole that sent the diners into roars of laughter. George Faber laughed, too, and handed him a bank note for reward. The poet added another couplet that raised another roar of laughter, then backed away, bowing like a courtier.

'What did he say, George? I missed most of the dialect.'

'He said we weren't young enough to be single, but we weren't too old to look like lovers. He wondered if your husband knew what you were doing, and whether the baby would look like him or me. When I gave him the money he said I was rich enough not to care, but if I wanted to keep you I'd better marry you in Mexico.'

Ruth Lewin blushed. 'A very uncomfortable poet, but I like him, George.'

'I like him too. I wish I could afford to be his patron.'

They were silent a while, listening to the clatter and the muted, melancholy music of the guitar. Then, casually enough, Faber asked:

'What will you do with yourself during the summer?'

'I don't know. Just now I'm dreading it. In the end I'll probably take one of those CIT tours. They can be pretty dull, I know, but at least one isn't alone.'

'You wouldn't think of joining me for a few days? Positano first, then Ischia.'

She did not shrink away from the question, but faced it in her forthright fashion. 'On what terms, George?'

'The same as tonight. No strings, no promises, no apologies.'

'What about Chiara?'

He gave her a shrugging, uneasy answer. 'I won't question what she does in Venice. I don't think she'll question me. Besides, what harm is there? I'll be working for Chiara. You and I are both grown up. I'd like you to think about it.'

She smiled and refused him gently. 'I mustn't think about it, George.

You're finding it hard enough to cope with the woman you have. I doubt you could handle me as well.' She reached out and took his hand between her palms. 'You have a rough fight ahead of you, but you can't win it if you split down the middle. I can't divide myself, either . . . Please don't be angry with me. I know myself too well.'

He was instantly penitent. 'I'm sorry. I guess it sounded pretty crude, but I didn't mean it like that.'

'I know you didn't, and if I try to tell you how grateful I am, I'll cry. Now will you please take me home?'

Their driver was still waiting for them, patient and knowing, in the darkened alley. He roused his dozing horse and set him on the long way home: the Margherita bridge, the Villa Borghese, the Quirinale Piazza, and down past the Colosseum to the Street of St Gregory. Ruth Lewin laid her head on Faber's shoulder and dozed fitfully while he listened to the clip-clop of the ancient nag and searched his troubled heart.

When they reached Ruth Lewin's apartment, he helped her alight and held her for a moment in the shadow of the doorway.

'May I come up for a little while?'

'If you want to.'

She was too sleepy to protest, and too jealous of the little that was left of the evening. She made him coffee, and they sat together listening to music, each waiting for the other to break the dangerous spell. Impulsively, George Faber took her in his arms and kissed her, and she clung to him in a long and passionate embrace. Then he held her away from him and pleaded without reserve:

'I want to stay with you, Ruth. Please, please let me stay.'

'I want you to stay too, George. I want it more than anything in the world . . . But I'm going to send you home.'

'Don't tease me, Ruth. You're not a girl like that. For God's sake don't tease me!'

All the needs of the years welled up in her and forced her towards surrender, but she drew away from him and pleaded in her turn. 'Go home, George. I can't have you like this. I'm not strong enough for it. You'll wake in the morning and feel guilty about Chiara. You'll thank me and slip away. And because you feel disloyal I won't see you again. I do want to see you. I could be in love with you if I let myself, but I don't want half a heart and half a man . . . Please, please go!'

He shook himself like a man waking out of a dream. 'I will come back, you know that.'

'I know it.'

'You don't hate me?'

'How can I hate you? But I don't want you to hate yourself because of me.'

'If it doesn't work out with Chiara . . .'

She closed his lips with a last light kiss. 'Don't say it, George! You'll know soon enough . . . Perhaps too soon for both of us.'

She walked with him to the portico, watched him climb into the carozza, and waited until the fading hoof-beats had died into the murmur of the city. Then she went to bed, and for the first time in months she slept dreamlessly.

In the Great Hall of the Gregorian University, Jean Télémond stood facing his audience.

His address lay before him on the rostrum, translated into impeccable Latin by a colleague of the Society. His back was straight. His hands were steady. His mind was clear. Now that the moment of crisis had come, he felt strangely calm, even elated by this final and resolute commitment of a lifetime's work to the risk of open judgement.

The whole authority of the Church was here, summed up in the person of the Pontiff, who sat, lean, dark, and oddly youthful, with the Father General on one side of him, and Cardinal Leone on the other. The best minds of the Church were here: six Cardinals of the Curia; the theologians and philosophers, dressed in their diverse habits—Jesuits, Dominicans, Franciscans, and men of the ancient order of St Benedict. The future of the Church was here: in the students with scrubbed and eager faces, who had been chosen from every country in the world to study at the seat of Christendom. The diversity of the Church was here, too, expressed in himself, the exile, the solitary seeker, the exotic who yet wore the black tunic of brotherhood and shared the ministry of the servants of the Word.

He waited a moment, gathering himself. Then he made the sign of the Cross, delivered the opening allocution to the Pontiff and the Curia, and began his address:

'It has taken a journey of twenty years to bring me to this place. I must therefore beg your patience while I explain myself, and the motives which prompted this long and often painful pilgrimage. I am a man and a priest. I became a priest because I believed that the primary and the only perfectly sustaining relationship was that between the Creator and the creature, and because I wished to affirm this relationship in a special fashion by a life of service. But I have never ceased to be a man, and as a man I have found myself committed, without recourse, to the world in which I live.

'As a man, my deepest conviction—confirmed by all my experience—is that I am one person. I who think, I who feel, I who fear, I who know and believe, am a unity. But this unity of my self is part of a greater unity. I am separate from the world, but I belong to it because I have grown out of its growth just as the world has grown out of the unity of God as the issue of a single creative art.

'I, therefore, the one, am destined to participate in the oneness of the world, as I am destined to participate in the oneness of God. I cannot set myself in isolation from creation any more than from the Creator.

'From the moment that this conviction became clear to me, another followed it by inevitable consequence. If God is one, and the world is one issue of His eternal act, and I am a single person spawned out of this complex unity, then all knowledge—of my self, of creation, of the Creator—is one knowledge. That I do not have all knowledge, that it presents itself to me by fragments and in diversity, means nothing except that I am finite, limited by time and space and the capacity of my brain.

'Every discovery I make points in the same direction. No matter how contradictory the fragments of knowledge may appear, they can never truly contradict one another. I have spent a lifetime in one small branch of science, palaeontology. But I am committed to all sciences, to biology, to physics, to the chemistry of inorganic matter, to philosophy, and to theology, because all are branches of the same tree, and the tree grows upwards toward the same sun. Never, therefore, can we risk too much or dare too boldly in the search for knowledge, since every step forward is a step toward unity—of man with man, of men with the universe, of the universe with God . . .'

He glanced up, trying to read in the faces of his audience a reaction to his words. But there was nothing to read. They wanted to hear his whole case before they committed themselves to a verdict. He turned back to the typescript and read on.

'Today I want to share with you a part of the journey which I have made for the past twenty years. Before we begin it, however, there are two things I want to say. The first is this. An exploration is a very special kind of journey. You do not make it like a trip from Rome to Paris. You must never demand to arrive on time and with all your baggage intact. You walk slowly with open eyes and open minds. When the mountains are too high to climb you march around them and try to measure them from the lowlands. When the jungle is thick you have to cut your way through it, and not resent too much the labour or the frustration.

'The second thing is this: When you come to record the journey, the new contours, the new plants, the strangeness and the mystery, you find often that your vocabulary is inadequate. Inevitably your narrative will fall far short of the reality. If you find this defect in my record, then I beg you to tolerate it and let it not discourage you from contemplation of strange landscapes which, nevertheless, bear the imprint of the creative finger of God.

'Now to being . . .'

He paused, twitched his cassock over his thin shoulders, and lifted his lined face to them in a kind of challenge.

'I want you to come with me, not as theologians or philosophers but as scientists—men whose knowing begins with seeing. What I want you to see is man: a special kind of being who exists in a visible ambience at a determinable point in time and space.

'Let us look at him in space first. The universe which he inhabits is immense, galactic. It stretches beyond the moon and sun into an enormity of dimension which our mathematics can only express by an indefinite extension of zeros.

'Look at man in time. He exists now at this moment, but his past goes back to a point where we lose him in a mist. His future prolongs itself beyond our conception of any possible circumstance.

'Look at man by numbers, and you find yourself trying to count the grains of sand on a shoreline without limit.

'Look at him by scale and proportion and you find him on the one hand a minuscule dwarf, in a universe without apparent limits. Measure him by another scale and you find him in partial control of the enormity in which he lives . . .'

The most sceptical of his bearers—and there were many in the audience who were disposed to be dubious of him—found themselves being caught up and carried by the strong current of his eloquence. The passion of his conviction expressed itself in every line of his weathered face, in every gesture of his thin, expressive hands.

Rudolf Semmering, the grim, soldierly man, found himself nodding approval of the noble temper of his subjects. Cardinal Rinaldi smiled his thin, ironic smile and wondered what the pedants would make of this valiant intruder into their private domain. Even Leone, the harsh old watchdog of the faith, leaned his craggy chin on his hand and registered a reluctant tribute to the unflinching courage of this suspect spirit.

In Kiril the Pontiff the conviction grew, swift as a conjurer's mango plant, that this was the man he wanted: a man totally committed to the risk of living and knowing, yet anchored firm as a sea-battered rock to belief in a divinely planned unity. The waves might tear at him, the winds might score his spirit, but he would stand unshaken and unshakable under the assault. He found himself murmuring a message to sustain him. 'Go on! Don't be afraid. Your heart is right, and it beats in time with mine. No matter that the words stumble and the record falters. The vision is clear, the will points straight and true toward the Centre. Go on! . . .'

Télémond was in full course now, expounding to them his view of matter–the material of the universe which expressed itself in so many different appearances, and finally in the appearance of man.

'. . . "God made man of the dust of the earth!" The Biblical image expresses aptly the most primitive conviction of man–a conviction confirmed by the most advanced scientific experiment–that the stuff of which he is formed is capable of indefinite scaling down to particles infinitely small . . . At a certain point of this scaling down, man's vision of himself becomes blurred. He needs spectacles, then a microscope, then a whole array of instrumentation to supplement his failing sight. For a moment he is lost in diversity–molecules, atoms, electrons, neutrons, protons . . . so many and so different! Then suddenly they all come together again. The universe, from the farthest nebulae to the simplest atomic structure, is a whole, a system, a quantum of energy–in other words, a unity. But–and I must ask you to lean and linger and think upon this most important "but"–this universe is not a static whole, it is in a constant state of change and transformation. It is in a state of genesis . . . a state of becoming, a state of evolving. And this is the question which I ask you to face with me now. The universe is evolving and man is evolving with it–into what? . . .'

They were with him now. Critics or captives of the idea, they were with him. He could see them leaning forward in their benches, intent on every phrase and every inflection. He could feel their interest projected toward him like a wave. He gathered himself once again and began to sketch, with swift, decisive strokes, the picture of a cosmos in motion, rearranging itself, diversifying itself, preparing itself for the coming of life, for the coming of consciousness, for the arrival of the first subhuman species, and the ultimate arrival of man.

He was on his own ground now, and he marched them forward with him, out of the misty backward of a crystallizing world to the moment when the change to life from non-life took place, when the megamolecule became the micro-organism, and the first biotic forms appeared on the planet.

He showed them how the primitive life-forms spread themselves in a vast network around the surface of the spinning globe; how they joined and disjoined into a multitude of combinations; how some conjunctions were swiftly suppressed because they were too specially adapted to a time and a condition of the evolutionary march; how others survived by changing themselves, by becoming more complex in order to guarantee their own endurance.

He showed them the first outlines of a fundamental law of nature–the too specialized life-form was the first to perish. Change was the price of survival.

He did not shrink from the consequences of his thought. He took his audience by the scruff of their necks and forced them to face the consequences with him.

'. . . Even so early in the evolutionary chain, we are faced with the brutal fact of biological competition. The struggle for life is endless. It is always accompanied by death and destruction, and violence of one kind or another . . . You will ask yourselves, as I have asked myself a thousand times, whether this struggle necessarily transfers itself, at a later stage of history, into the domain of man. At first blush the answer is yes. But I object to so crude and total an application of the biological pattern. Man does not live now on the same level at which he lived when he first made his appearance on the planet. He has passed through successive levels of existence; and it is my belief, supported by considerable evidence, that man's evolution is marked by an effort to find other less brutal, and less destructive modes of competition for life . . .'

He leaned forward over the rostrum and challenged them with the thought that he knew was already in their minds.

'You ask me why I do not invoke at this moment a divine intervention in the pattern of human evolvement. It is because we must continue to walk along the exploratory path which we have set ourselves. We are limiting ourselves only to what we see. And all we are seeing at this moment is man emerging as a phenomenon in a changing universe. If we are troubled by what we see, we must bear the trouble and not seek too easy an answer for it. I make this point although man has not yet appeared to our exploring eyes. We have leapt forward to meet him. Now we must go back.'

He could almost feel their tension relax. He stole a swift glance at the front row of the audience. Leone was shaking his white head and making a whispered comment to a Cardinal on his left. Rinaldi was smiling and he lifted one hand in an almost imperceptible gesture of encouragement. Kiril the Pontiff sat erect in his chair, his scarred face immobile, his dark eyes bright with interest.

Gently now Télémond led them back to the main stream of his story. He showed them the primitive life-forms reproducing themselves, multiplying, joining and rejoining, groping ingeniously but indifferently toward stability and permanence. He drew for them the tree of life and showed how it branched and yet grew upwards; how certain twigs died and fell off; how certain branches ceased to grow; but how, always, the main thrust of growth was upwards in the direction of the large brain and the complex organism, and the most flexible mechanism of survival. He showed them the first subhuman species—the hominoid, which was the prelude to the human—and finally he showed them man.

Then, brusquely, he presented them with a puzzle.

'. . . From where we stand now we see a continuity and a unity in the evolutionary process. But if we look closely, we see that the line of advance is not always a firm and definite stroke. It is dotted in places, or broken. We cannot say where, in point of time, life began. Yet we know that it did begin. We know that the pterodactyl existed. We have dug his bones out of the earth. But where and by what mutations he came to be is not wholly clear to us. We see him first as plural . . . many pterodactyls. But was there a first couple or were they always many? We do not know . . . So, with man, when we first find him on the earth, he is many. If we speak as scientists, there is no record of the emergence of man as a single couple. In the historic record written in primal day, men are suddenly present. I do not say that they came suddenly, any more than that the pterodactyl came suddenly. All the evidence points to a slow emergence of the species, but at a certain point in history man is there, and with man something else is there as well . . . Consciousness . . . Man is a very special phenomenon. He is a being who knows, he is also a being who knows that he knows. We have come, you see, to a very particular point of history. A creature exists who knows that he knows . . .

'Now, my friends, I want you to address yourself to my next question only as scientists, only as witnesses of the visible evidence. How did this special phenomenon emerge?

'Let us step back from him a moment. Let us consider all those phenomena which preceded him, many of which still coexist with him, from the micro-organism to the hominoid ape. All of them have something in common—a drive, a groping, an urge to fit themselves for survival. To use an overworked and imprecise term, it is an instinct to do those things, to enter into those combinations and those associations which will enable them to proceed along their proper line of continuity. I prefer to choose another word than *instinct*. I prefer to say that this drive, or this capacity, is a primitive but evolving form of what culminates in man ... Consciousness . . .'

Once again he had brought them to a crisis and he knew it. For the first time he felt really inadequate to display to them the whole range and subtlety of the thought. Time was against him and the simple semantic limitation and the rhetorical power to persuade them into a new, but still harmonious view of the nature and origin of humankind. Still, he went on resolutely, developing for them his own view of the cosmic pattern—primal energy, primitive life, primitive consciousness, all evolving and converging to the first focal point of history, thinking man. He took them further yet, by a bold leap into their own territory, showing all the lines of human development converging to a final unity, a unity of man with his Creator.

More vividly than ever before he could feel the mood of his audience shifting. Some were in awe, some were dubious, some had settled themselves into complete hostility to his thought.

Yet, when he came to his peroration, he knew that he had done the best he could and that for all its sometime vagueness, and sometime risky speculation, his address had been the true reflection of his own intellectual position. There was nothing more he could do but commit himself to judgement and rest courageous in the outcome. Humbly, but with deep emotion, he summed it up for them.

'I do not ask you to agree with me. I do not put any of my present conclusions beyond reconsideration or new development, but of this I am totally convinced: the first creative act of God was directed toward fulfilment and not destruction. If the universe is not centred on man, if man as the centre of the universe is not centred on the Creator, then the cosmos is a meaningless blasphemy. The day is not far distant when men will understand that even in biological terms, they have only one choice: suicide or an act of worship.'

His hands trembled and his voice shook as he read the words of Paul to the Colossians:

'"In Him all created things took their being, heavenly and earthly, visible and invisible . . . They were all created through Him and in Him; He takes precedence of all, and in Him all subsist . . . It was God's good pleasure to let all completeness dwell in Him, and through Him to win back all things, whether on earth or in heaven, unto union with Himself making peace with them through His blood, shed on the Cross."'

He did not hear the thunder of applause as he stepped down from the pulpit. As he knelt to pay his respects to the Pontiff, and lay the text of his address in his hands, he heard only the words of the blessing and the invitation—or it was a command?—that followed:

'You're a bold man, Jean Télémond. Time will tell whether you are right or wrong; but at this moment I need you. We all need you.'

EXTRACT FROM THE SECRET MEMORIALS OF KIRIL I PONT. MAX.

. . . Yesterday I met a whole man. It is a rare experience but always an illuminating and ennobling one. It costs so much to be a full human being that there are very few who have the enlightenment, or the courage, to pay the price . . . One has to abandon altogether the search for security, and reach out to the risk of living with both arms. One has to embrace the world like a lover, and yet demand no easy return of love. One has to accept pain as a condition of existence. One has to court doubt and darkness as the cost of knowing. One needs a will stubborn in conflict, but apt always to the total acceptance of every consequence of living and dying.

This is how I read Jean Télémond. This is why I have decided to draw him to me, to ask for his friendship, to use him as best I know in the world of the Church . . . Leone is uneasy about him. He has said so very bluntly. He points, quite rightly, to ambiguities and obscurities in his system of thought, to what he calls a dangerous rashness in certain of his speculations. He demands another full examination of all his writings to the Holy Office, before he is permitted to teach publicly or to publish his research.

I do not disagree with Leone. I am not so bold that I am prepared to gamble with the Deposit of Faith, which is, after all, the testament of Christ's new covenant with man. To preserve it intact is the whole meaning of my office. This is the task which has been delegated to Leone in the Church . . .

On the other hand I am not afraid of Jean Télémond. A man so centred upon God, who has accepted twenty years of silence, has already accepted every risk, even the risk that he can be mistaken. Today he said so in as many words and I believe him . . . I am not afraid of his work either; I do not have the equipment or the time to judge truly of its ultimate value. This is why I have counsellors and experts learned in science, theology and philosophy to assist me . . .

I am convinced, moreover, that honest error is a step toward a greater illumination of the truth, since it exposes to debate and to clearer definition those matters which might otherwise remain obscure and undefined in the teaching of the Church. In a very special sense the Church too is evolving toward a greater fullness of understanding, a deeper consciousness of the divine life within itself.

The Church is a family. Like every family it has its home-bodies and its adventurers. It has its critics and its conformists; those who are jealous of its least important traditions; those who wish to thrust it forward, a bright lamp into a glorious future. Of all them I am the common father . . . When the adventurers come back scarred and travel-worn from a new frontier, from another foray, successful or unsuccessful, against the walls of ignorance, I must receive them with the charity of Christ and protect them with gentleness against those who have fared better only because they have dared much less. I have asked the Father General of the Jesuits to send Jean Télémond to keep me company at Castel Gandolfo during the summer. I hope and pray that we may learn to be friends. He could enrich me, I think. I, for my part, may be able to offer him courage and a respite from his long and lonely pilgrimage . . .

In an odd fashion he has given me courage as well. For some time now I have been engaged in a running debate with the Cardinal Secretary of the Congregation of Rites on the question of introducing the vernacular liturgy and a vernacular system of teaching into the seminaries and churches of missionary countries. This would mean inevitably a decline of the Latin liturgical language in many areas of the world. It would mean also an immense task of translation and annotation, so that the works of the Fathers of the Church would be made available to clerical students in their own language.

The Congregation of Rites takes the view that the merits of the change are far outweighed by its disadvantages. They point out that it would run counter to the decisions of the Council of Trent, and to the pronouncements of later Councils and later Pontiffs. They claim that the stability and uniformity of our organization depend much on the use of a common official tongue in the definition of doctrine, the training of teachers, and the celebration of the liturgy.

I myself take the view that our firsty duty is to preach the Word of God and to dispense the grace of the Sacraments, and that anything which stands in the way of this mission should be swept aside.

I know, however, that the situation is not quite so simple. There is, for example, a curious division of opinion in the small Christian community in Japan. The Japanese bishops want the Latin system preserved. Because of their unique and isolated position, they are inclined to be timorous about any change at all. On the other hand, missionary priests working in the country report that work is handicapped when the vernacular is not used.

In Africa the native Cardinal Ragambwe is very clear that he wants to try the vernacular system. He is very aware of the risks and the problems, but he still feels that a trial should be made. He is a holy and enlightened man, and I have great respect for his opinion.

Ultimately the decision rests with me, but I have deferred it because I have been so vividly aware of the complexity of the problem and of the historic danger that small and isolated groups of Christians may, for lack of a common communication, be separated from the daily developing life of the Church. We are not building only for today, but for tomorrow and for eternity.

However, listening to Jean Télémond, I felt myself encouraged to make a decisive step. I have decided to write to those bishops who want to introduce the vernacular system and ask them to propose to me a definite plan for its use. If their plans seem workable, and if at the same time a certain select number of the clergy can be trained in the traditional mode, I am disposed to let the new system be tried . . . I expect strong opposition from the Congregation of Rites, and from many bishops in the Church, but a move must be made to break the deadlock which inhibits our apostolic work, so that the Faith may begin to grow with more freedom in emerging nations.

They are all jealous of their new identity, and they must be led to see that they can grow in, and with, the Faith toward a legitimate social and economic betterment. We are not yet one world, and we shall not be for a long time, but God is one, and the Gospel is one, and it should be spoken in every tongue under heaven . . . This was the mode of the primitive Church. This was the vision which Télémond renewed for me: the unity of the spirit in the bond of Faith in the diversity of all knowledge and all tongues . . .

Today I held the last series of audiences before the summer holidays. Among those whom I received privately was a certain Corrado Calitri, Minister of the Republic. I had already received most of the Italian Cabinet, but I had never met this man. The circumstance was sufficiently unusual for me to comment on it to the Maestro di Camera.

He told me that Calitri was a man of unusual talent, who had had a meteoric rise in the Christian Democratic Party. There was even talk that he might lead the country after the next elections.

He told me also that Calitri's private life had been somewhat notorious for a long time, and that he was involved in a marital case presently under consideration by the Holy Roman Rota. Now, however, it seemed that Calitri was making serious efforts to reform himself and that he had put himself and his spiritual affairs into the hands of a confessor.

There was, of course, no discussion of these matters between myself and Calitri. An audience is an affair of state and has nothing to do with the spiritual relationship of Pastor and people.

None the less, I was curious about the man, and I was tempted for a moment to call for the file on his case. In the end I decided against it. If he comes to power, we shall have diplomatic connections, and it is better that it should not be complicated by a private knowledge on my part. It is better too that I do not interfere too minutely in the varied functions of the tribunals and the congregations. My time is very limited. My energies are limited, too, and presently they are so depleted that I shall be glad to pack and go from this place, into the comparative serenity of the countryside.

I see very clearly the shape of a great personal problem for every man who holds this office: how the press of business and the demands of so many people can so impoverish him that he has neither time nor will left to regulate the affairs of his own soul. I long for solitude and the leisure for contemplation. 'Consider the lilies of the field . . . They labour not, neither do they spin!' Lucky the ones who have time to smell the flowers, and doze at noonday under the orange trees . . .!

8

George Faber left Rome early on a Saturday morning. He headed out through the Lateran Gate and down the new Appian Way toward the Southern autostrada. He had a five-hour drive ahead of him, Terracina, Formio, Naples, and then out along the winding peninsular road to Castellamare, Sorrento, Amalfi, and Positano. He was in no hurry. The morning air was still fresh, and the traffic was heavy, and he had no intention of risking his neck as well as his reputation.

At Terracina he was hailed by a pair of English girls who were hitch-hiking down the coast. For an hour he was glad of their company, but by the time they reached Naples he was happy to be rid of them. Their cheerful certainty about the world and all its ways made him feel like a grandfather.

The heat of the day was upon him now–a dry, dusty oppression which made the air dance and filled the nostrils with the ammoniac stink of a crowded and ancient city. He turned into the Via Carocciolo and sat for a while in a waterfront café, sipping iced coffee and pondering the moves he should make when he reached Positano. He had two people to see: Sylvio Pellico, artist, and Theo Respighi, sometime actor–both of them, according to the record, unhappy associates of Corrado Calitri.

For weeks now he had been puzzling over the best method to approach them. He had lived long enough in Italy to know the Italian love of drama and intrigue. But his Nordic temper revolted from the spectacle of an American correspondent playing a Latin detective in raincoat and black fedora. Finally he had decided on a simple, blunt approach:

'I understand you knew Corrado Calitri . . . I'm in love with his wife. I want to marry her. I think you can give me some evidence against him. I'm prepared to pay well for it . . .'

For a long time he had refused to reason beyond this point. Yet now, three hours from Rome, and a long way further from Chiara, he was prepared to come to grips with the *if*. If all failed he would have proved himself to himself. He would have proved to Chiara that he was prepared to risk his career for her sake. He would be able to demand a two-way traffic in love. If that failed, too . . .? At long last he was beginning to believe that he would survive it. The best cure for love was to cool it down a little, and leave a man free to measure woman against woman, the torment of a one-sided loving against the bleak peace of no loving at all.

One could not bounce a middle-aged heart, like a rubber ball, from one affair to another; but there was a crumb of comfort in the thought of Ruth Lewin and her refusal to commit his heart or her own to a new affliction without any promise of security.

She was wiser than Chiara. He knew that. She had been tested further and survived better. But *love* was a rainbow word that might or might not point to a crock of gold. He paid for his drink, stepped out into the raw sunshine, and began the last leg of his journey into uncertainty.

The Gulf of Naples was a flat and oily mirror, broken only by the wake of the pleasure steamers and the spume of the *aliscafe*, which bounced their loads of tourists at fifty miles an hour toward the siren islands of Capri and Ischia. The summit of Vesuvius was vague in a mist of heat and dust. The painted stucco of the village houses was peeling in the sun. The grey tufa soil of the farm plots was parched, and the peasants plodded up and down the rows of tomato plants like figures in a medieval landscape. There was a smell of dust and dung, and rotting tomatoes and fresh oranges. Horns bleated at every curve, wooden carts rolled noisily over cobblestones. Snatches of music swept by, mixed with the shouts of children and the occasional curse of a farmer caught in the press of summer traffic.

George Faber found himself driving fast and free, and chanting a tuneless song. On the steep spiral of the Amalfi drive he was nearly forced off the road by a careering sports car, and he cursed loud and cheerfully in Roman dialect. By the time he reached Positano, the shabby, spectacular little town that ran in a steep escalade from the water to the hilltop, he was his own man, and the experience was as heady as the raw wine of the Sorrentine mountains.

He lodged his car in a garage, hefted his bag, and strolled down a steep, narrow alley to the city square. Half an hour later, bathed and changed into cotton slacks and a striped sailor shirt, he was sitting under an awning, drinking a Carpano, and preparing for his encounter with Sylvio Pellico.

The artist's gallery was a long, cool tunnel that ran from the street into a courtyard littered with junk and fragments of old marbles. His pictures were hung along the walls of the tunnel–gaudy abstracts, a few portraits in the manner of Modigliani, and a scattering of catchpenny landscapes to inveigle the sentimental tourist. It was easy to see why Corrado Calitri had dropped him so quickly. It was less easy to see why he had taken him up in the first place.

He was a tall, narrow-faced youth with a straggly beard, dressed in cotton sweatshirt, faded blue denims, and shoes of scuffed canvas. He was propped between two chairs at the entrance to the tunnel, dozing in the sun, with a straw hat tipped over his eyes.

When George Faber stopped to examine the pictures he came to life immediately and presented himself and his work with a flourish. 'Sylvio Pellico, sir, at your service. My pictures please you? Some of them have already been exhibited in Rome.'

'I know,' said George Faber. 'I was at the show.'

'Ah! Then you're a connoisseur. I will not try to tempt you with this rubbish!' He dismissed the landscapes with a wave of his skinny hand. 'Those are just eating money.'

'I know, I know. We all have to eat. Are you having a good season?'

'Eh!.... You know how it goes. Everyone looks, nobody wants to buy. Yesterday I sold two little pieces to an American woman. The day before, nothing. The day before that . . .' He broke off and cocked a huckster's eye at George Faber. 'You are not an Italian, Signore?'

'No. I'm an American.'

'But you speak beautiful Italian.'

'Thank you . . . Tell me, who sponsored your exhibition in Rome?'

'A very eminent man. A Minister of the Republic. A very good critic, too. Perhaps you've heard of him. His name is Calitri.'

'I've heard of him,' said George Faber. 'I'd like to talk to you about him.'

'Why?' He leaned his shaggy head on one side like an amiable parrot. 'Did he send you to see me?'

'No. It's a private matter. I thought you might be able to help me. I'd be happy to pay for your help. Does that interest you?'

'Who isn't interested in money? Sit down, let me get you a cup of coffee.'

'No coffee. This won't take long.'

Pellico dusted off one of the chairs, and they sat facing each other under the narrow archway.

Crisply Faber explained himself and his mission, and then laid down his offer. '. . . Five hundred dollars, American money, for a sworn statement about Calitri's marriage, written in the terms I shall dictate to you.'

He sat back in his chair, lit a cigarette, and waited while the artist cupped his brown face in his hands and thought for a long time. Then he lifted his head and said, 'I'd appreciate an American cigarette.'

Faber handed him the pack and then leaned forward with a light.

Pellico smoked for a few moments, and then began to talk. 'I am a poor man, sir. Also I am not a very good painter, so I am likely to remain poor for a long time. For one like me, five hundred dollars is a fortune, but I am afraid I cannot do what you ask.'

'Why not?'

'Several reasons.'

'Are you afraid of Calitri?'

'A little. You've lived in this country, you know the way things run. When one is poor, one is always a little outside the law and it never pays to tangle with important people. But that's not the only reason.'

'Name me another.'

His thin face wrinkled, and his head seemed to shrink lower between his shoulders. He explained himself with an odd simplicity. 'I know what this means to you, sir. When a man is in love, eh! . . . It is ice in the heart and fire in the gut . . . One loses for a while all pride. When one is out of love the pride comes back. Often it is the only thing left . . . I am not like you . . . I am, if you want, more like Calitri. He was kind to me once . . . I was very fond of him. I do not think I could betray him for money.'

'He betrayed you, didn't he? He gave you one exhibition and then dropped you.'

'No!' The thin hands became suddenly eloquent. 'No. You must not read it like that. On the contrary, he was very honest with me. He said every man has the right to one trial of his talent. If the talent was not there, he had best forget it . . . Well, he gave me the trial. I failed. I do not blame him for that.'

'How much would you charge to blame him? A thousand dollars?'

Pellico stood up and dusted off his hands. For all his shabbiness, he seemed clothed in a curious kind of dignity. He pointed at the grey walls of the tunnel. 'For twenty dollars, sir, you can buy my visions. They are not great visions, I know. They are the best I have. Myself I do not sell. Not for a thousand dollars, not for ten thousand. I am sorry.'

As he walked away down the cobbled street, George Faber, the Nordic Puritan, had the grace to be ashamed of himself. His face was burning, his palms were sweating. He felt a swift, unreasonable resentment toward Chiara, sunning herself in Venice five hundred miles away. He turned into a bar, ordered a double whisky, and began to read through the dossier of his next contact, Theo Respighi.

He was an Italo-American, born in Naples and transported to New York in his childhood. He was a middling bad actor who had played small parts in television, small parts in Hollywood, and then returned to Italy to play small parts in Biblical epics and pseudo-classic nonsense. In Hollywood there had been minor scandals—drunken driving, a couple of divorces, a brief and turbulent romance with a rising star. In Rome he had joined the roistering bunch who kept themselves alive on hope and runaway productions and the patronage of Roman playboys. All in all, Faber summed him up as a seedy character who should be very amenable to the rustle of a dollar bill.

He ran Respighi to earth that same evening in a cliff-side bar, where he was drinking with three very gay boys and a faded Frenchwoman who spoke Italian with a Genoese accent. It took an hour to prise him away from the company, and another to sober him up with dinner and black coffee. Even when he had done it, he was left with a hollow, muscular hulk who, when he was not combing his long, blond hair, was reaching nervously for the brandy bottle. Faber stifled the wavering voice of his own conscience and once again displayed his proposition:

'. . . A thousand dollars for a signed statement. No strings, no problems. Everything that goes before the Roman Rota is kept secret. No one, least of all Calitri, will ever know who gave the testimony.'

'Balls!' said the blond one flatly. 'Don't try to con me, Faber. There's no such thing as a secret in Rome. I don't care whether it's in the Church or Cinecittà. Sooner or later Calitri has to know. What happens to me then?'

'You're a thousand dollars richer, and he can't touch you.'

'You think so? Look, lover boy, you know how films are made in this country. The money comes from everywhere. The list of angels stretches from Napoli to Milano, and back again. There's a black list here, too, just like in Hollywood. You get on it, you're dead. For a thousand crummy bucks, I don't want to be dead.'

'You haven't earned that much in six months,' Faber told him. 'I know, I checked up.'

'So what? That's the way the cookie crumbles in this business. You starve for a while, and then you eat, and eat good. I want to go on eating. Now if you were to make it ten thousand, I might begin to think about it. With that much I could get myself back Stateside, and wait long enough to get a decent start again . . . Come on, lover! What are you playing for? The big romance or a bag of popcorn?'

'Two thousand,' said George Faber.'

'No deal.'

'It's the best I can do.'

'Peanuts! I can get that much by lifting a phone and telling Calitri that you're gunning for him . . . Tell you what. Give me a thousand and I won't make the call.'

'Go to hell!' He pushed back his chair, and walked out. The laughter of the blond one followed him like a mockery into the darkened street.

'The longer I live,' said Jean Télémond musingly, 'the more clearly I understand the deep vein of pessimism that runs through so much of modern thought, even the thought of many in the Church . . . Birth, growth, and decay. The cyclic pattern of life is so vividly apparent that it obscures the pattern that underlies it, the pattern of constant growth, and—let me say it bluntly—the pattern of human progress. For many people, the wheel of life simply turns on its own axis, it does not seem to be going anywhere.'

'And you, Jean, believe it is going somewhere?'

'More than that, Holiness. I believe it must go somewhere.'

They had taken off their cassocks, and they were sitting relaxed in the shade of a small copse, with a bank of wild strawberries at their backs and, the flat bright water of Lake Nemi. Jean Télémond was sucking contentedly on his pipe, and Kiril was tossing pebbles into the water. The air vibrated with the strident cry of cicadas, and the little brown lizards sunned themselves on rock and tree-trunk.

They had long since surrendered themselves to bucolic ease and the comfort of one another's company. In the mornings they worked privately–Kiril at his desk, keeping track of the daily dispatches from Rome; Télémond in the garden, setting his papers in order for the scrutiny of the Holy Office. In the afternoons they drove out into the country, Télémond at the wheel, exploring the valleys and the uplands and the tiny towns that had clung to the ridges for five hundred years and more. In the evenings they dined together, then read or talked or played cards until it was time for Compline and the last prayer of the day.

It was a good time for both: for Kiril, a respite from the burden of office; for Télémond, a true return from exile into the companionship of an understanding and truly loving spirit. He did not have to measure his words. He felt no risk in exposing his deepest thoughts. Kiril, for his part, confided himself fully to the Jesuit, and found a peculiar solace in this sharing of his private burden.

He tossed another pebble into the water and watched the ripples fan out toward the farther shore, until they were lost in the shimmer of sunlight. Then he asked another question:

'Have you never been a pessimist yourself, Jean? Have you never felt caught up in this endless turning of the wheel of life?'

'Sometimes, Holiness. When I was in China, for instance, far to the north-west, in the barren valley of the great rivers. There were monasteries up there. Enormous places that could only have been built by great men–men with a great vision–to challenge the emptiness in which they lived ... In one fashion or another, I thought God must have been with them. Yet, when I went in and saw the men who live there now–dull, uninspired, almost doltish at times–I was afflicted by melancholy ... When I came back to the West and read the newspapers and talked with my brother scientists, I was staggered by the blindness with which we seem to be courting our own destruction. Sometimes it seemed impossible to believe that man was really growing out of the slime toward a divine destiny ...'

Kiril nodded thoughtfully. He picked up a stick and teased a sleeping lizard, so that it skittered away into the leaves. 'I know the feeling, Jean. I have it sometimes even in the Church. I wait and pray for the great movement, the great man, who will startle us into life again ...'

Jean Télémond said nothing. He drew placidly on his pipe, waiting for the Pontiff to finish the thought.

'... A man like Saint Francis of Assisi, for instance. What does he really mean? ... A complete break with the pattern of history ... A man born out of due time. A sudden unexplained revival of the primitive spirit of Christianity. The work he began still continues ... But it is not the same. The revolution is over. The revolutionaries have become conformists. The little brothers of the Little Poor Man are rattling alms-boxes in the railway square or dealing in real estate to the profit of the order.' He laughed quietly. 'Of course, that isn't the whole story. They teach, they preach, they do the work of God as best they know, but it is no longer a revolution, and I think we need one now.'

'Perhaps,' said Jean Télémond with a twinkle in his shrewd eyes. 'Perhaps Your Holiness will be the revolutionary.'

'I have thought about it, Jean. Believe me, I have thought about it. But I do not think even you can understand how limited I am by the very machinery which I inherit, by the historic attitudes by which I am enclosed. It is hard for me to work directly. I have to find instruments apt to my hand. I am young enough, yes, to see big changes made in my lifetime. But there will have to be others to make them for me . . . You, for instance.'

'I, Holiness?' Télémond turned a startled face to the Pontiff. 'My field of action is more limited than yours.'

'I wonder if it is?' asked Kiril quizzically. 'Have you ever thought that the Russian revolution, the present might of Soviet Russia, was built on the work of Karl Marx, who spent a large part of his life in the British Museum and is now buried in England? The most explosive thing in the world is an idea.'

Jean Télémond laughed and tapped out his pipe on a tree-bole. 'Doesn't that rather depend on the Holy Office? I have still to pass their scrutiny.'

Kiril gave him a long, sober look, then quizzed him again. 'If you fail to pass, Jean, what will you do then?'

Télémond shrugged. 'Re-examine, I suppose. I hope I shall have the energy to do it.'

'Why do you say that?'

'Partly because I am afraid, partly because . . . because I am not a well man. I have lived roughly for a long time. I am told my heart is not as good as it should be.'

'I'm sorry to hear that, Jean. You must take care of yourself. I shall make it my business to see that you do.'

'May I ask you a question, Holiness?'

'Of course.'

'You have honoured me with your friendship. In the eyes of many —though not in mine—it will seem that you have given your patronage to my work. What will you do if it is found wanting by the Holy Office?'

To his surprise Kiril threw back his head and laughed heartily. 'Jean, Jean. There speaks the true Jesuit. What will I do? I shall always be your friend, and I shall pray that you have health and courage to continue your studies.'

'But if I should die before they are done?'

'Does that worry you?'

'Sometimes . . . Believe me, Holiness, whatever the outcome, I have tried to prepare myself for it. But I am convinced that there is a truth in my researches . . . I do not want to see it lost or suppressed.'

'It will not be suppressed, Jean. I promise you that.'

'Forgive me, Holiness, I have said more than I should.'

'Why should you apologize, Jean? You have shown me your heart. For a lonely man like me, that's a privilege . . . Courage now. Who knows? We may see you a Doctor of the Church yet. Now, if it will not offend your Jesuit's eyes, the Pope of Rome is going for a swim.'

When Kiril stripped off his shirt and made ready for the plunge, Jean Télémond saw the marks of the whip on his back, and he was ashamed of his own cowardice.

Two days later, a courier from Washington delivered to the Pontiff a private letter from the President of the United States:

> ... I read with lively interest Your Holiness's letter and the copies of the two letters from the Premier of the U.S.S.R. which were handed to me by His Eminence Cardinal Carlin. I agree that we shall need to preserve the most rigid secrecy about this whole situation.
>
> Let me say first that I am deeply grateful for the information which you give me about your private association with Kamenev, and your views on his character and his intention. I was also deeply impressed by the frank disagreement of Cardinal Carlin. I know that he would not have spoken so freely without the permission of Your Holiness, and I am encouraged to be equally frank with you.
>
> I have to say that I am very dubious about the value of private conversations at this level. On the other hand, I am happy to pursue them so long as there seems the slightest hope of avoiding the explosive crisis which is inevitable in the next six or twelve months.
>
> The problem as I see it is both simple and complex. Kamenev has expressed it very well. We are caught in the current of history. We can tack across it, but we cannot change the direction of the flow. The only thing that can do that is an action of such magnitude and such risk that none of us would be allowed to attempt it.
>
> I could not, for example, commit my country to one-sided disarmament. I could not abandon our claims for a reunification of Germany. I should very much like to be quit of Quemoy and Matsu, but we cannot relinquish them without a serious loss of face and influence in Southeast Asia. I can understand that Kamenev is afraid of the Chinese, yet he cannot abandon an alliance–even a troublesome and dangerous one–which guarantees a solid Communist block from East Germany to the Kuriles.
>
> The most we can hope is to keep the situation elastic, to give ourselves a breathing space for negotiation and historic evolution. We must avoid at all costs a head-on clash, which will inevitably cause a cataclysmic atomic war.
>
> If a secret correspondence with Kamenev will help at all, I am prepared to risk it, and I am very happy to accept Your Holiness as the intermediary. You may communicate my thoughts to Kamenev and make known to him the contents of this letter. He knows that I cannot move alone, just as he cannot. We both live under the shadow of the same risk.
>
> I do not belong to Your Holiness's faith, but I commend myself to your prayers and the prayers of all Christendom. We carry the fate of the world on our shoulders, and if God does not support us, then we must inevitably break under the burden ...

When he had read the letter, Kiril breathed a sigh of relief. It was no more than he had hoped, but no less either. The storm clouds were still piled, massive and threatening, over the world, but there was a tiny break in them and one could begin to guess at the sunlight. The problem was now to enlarge the break, and he asked himself how best he might co-operate in doing it.

Of one thing he was certain: it would be a mistake for the Vatican to assume the attitude of a negotiator, to propose grounds for a bargain. The Church, too, carried the burden of history on her back. Politically she was suspect; but the very suspicion was a pointer to her task–to affirm, not the method, but the principles of a human society capable of survival, capable of ordering itself to the terms of a God-given plan. She was appointed to be a teacher, not a treaty maker. Her task was not to govern men in the material order, but to train them to govern themselves in accordance with the principles of the natural law. She had to accept that the end product–if, indeed, one could talk without cynicism about an end–must always be an approximation, a stage in an evolutionary growth.

It was this thought that led him once more into the garden of Castel Gondolfo, where Jean Télémond, studious and absorbed, was annotating his papers under the shade of an old oak tree.

'Here you sit, my Jean, writing your visions of a world perfecting itself, while I sit like a telephone operator between two men, each of whom can blast us into smithereens by pressing a button . . . There's a dilemma for you. Does your science tell you how to resolve it? What would you do if you were in my shoes?'

'Pray,' said Jean Télémond with a puckish grin.

'I do, Jean. Every day–all day, for that matter. But prayer isn't enough, I have to act too. You had to be an explorer before you came to rest in this place. Tell me now, where do I move?'

'In this situation, I don't think you move at all. You sit and wait for the appropriate moment.'

'You think that's enough?'

'In the larger sense, no. I think the Church has lost the initiative it should have in the world today.'

'I do, too. I should like to think that in my Pontificate we may be able to get some of it back. I'm not sure how. Do you have any ideas?'

'Some,' said Jean Télémond crisply. 'All my life I've been a traveller. One of the first things a traveller has to do is learn to accommodate himself to the place and time in which he lives. He has to eat strange food, use an unfamiliar coinage, learn not to blush among people who have no privies, search for the good that subsists in the grossest and most primitive societies. Every individual, every organization, has to sustain a conversation with the rest of the world. He cannot talk always in negatives and contradictions.'

'You think we have done that?'

'Not always, Holiness. But of late, all too often. We have lived to ourselves and for ourselves. When I say *we*, I mean the whole Church–pastors and faithful alike. We have hidden the lamp of belief under a cover instead of holding it up to illuminate the world.'

'Go on, Jean. Show me how you would display it.'

'This is a plural world, Holiness. We may wish it to be one in faith, hope and charity. But it is not so. There are many hopes and strange varieties of love. But this is the world we live in. If we want to participate in the drama of God's action with it, then we must begin with the words we all understand. Justice, for instance. We understand that . . . But when the Negroes in America seek justice and full citizenship, is it we who lead them? Or we who support most strongly their legitimate demands? You know it is not. In Australia, there is an embargo on coloured migrants. Many Australians feel that this is an affront to human dignity. Do we support their protests? The record shows that we do not. In principle, yes, but in action, no. We proclaim that the Chinese coolie has a right to work and subsistence, but it was not we who led him toward it. It was the men who made "The Long March". If we object to the price they put on the rice bowl, we must blame ourselves as much as we blame them . . . If we want to enter once more into the human dialogue then we must seek out whatever common ground is available to us–as I take it Your Holiness is trying to do with Kamenev–the ground of human brotherhood and the legitimate hopes of all mankind . . . I have thought often about the Gospel scene when Christ held up the coin of the tribute and proclaimed: "Render to Caesar the things that are Caesar's, and to God the things that are God's . . ." To what Caesar? Has Your Holiness ever thought about it? . . . To a murderer, an adulterer, a pederast . . . But Christ did not abrogate the conversation of the Church with such a one. On the contrary He affirmed it as a duty . . .'

'But what you show me, Jean, is not one man's commitment. It is the commitment of the whole Church–Pope, pastors, and five hundred million faithful.'

'True, Holiness–but what has happened? The faithful are uncommitted, only because they lack enlightenment and courageous leadership. They understand risk better than we do. We are protected by the organization. They have only God's cloak to shelter them. They grapple each day with every human dilemma–birth, passion, death, and the act of love . . . But if they hear no trumpets, see no crusader's cross lifted up . . .' He shrugged and broke off. 'Excuse me, Holiness. I am too garrulous, I think.'

'On the contrary, Jean. I find you a very serviceable man. I am glad to have you here.'

At that moment a servant approached, bringing coffee and iced water, and a letter which had been received that moment at the gate. Kiril opened it and read the brief, unceremonious message:

'I am a man who grows sunflowers. I should like to call upon you at ten-thirty tomorrow morning.'

It was signed: 'Georg Wilhelm Forster.'

He proved a surprise in more ways than one. He looked like a Bavarian incongruously dressed by an Italian tailor. He wore thick German shoes and thick myopic spectacles, but his suit and shirt and his tie came from Brioni, and on his small pudgy hand he wore a bezel ring, half as large as a walnut. His manner was deferent, but vaguely ironic as though he were laughing at himself and all he stood for. In spite of his German name, he spoke Russian with a strong Georgian accent.

When Kiril received him in his study, he went down on one knee and kissed the papal ring; then he sat bolt upright in the chair, balancing his panama hat on his knees, for all the world like a junior clerk being interviewed for a job. His opening words were a surprise too. 'I understand Your Holiness has received a letter from Robert.'

Kiril looked up sharply to catch a hint of a smile on the pudgy lips.

'There is no mystery about it, Holiness. It is all a matter of timing. Timing is very important in my work. I knew when Kamenev's letter would reach the Vatican. I knew when Cardinal Carlin returned to New York. I was told the date and time of his interview with Robert. From that point it was a simple deduction that Robert's letter would reach you at Castel Gandolfo.'

Now it was Kiril's turn to smile. He nodded aprroval and asked, 'Do you live in Rome?'

'I have lodgings here. But as you can guess, I travel a good deal . . . There is an extensive business in sunflower seeds.'

'I imagine there is.'

'May I see Robert's letter?'

'Of course.'

Kiril handed the paper across his desk. Forster read it carefully for a few moments, and then passed it back.

'You may have a copy if you like. As you see, the President is perfectly willing that Kamenev should see the letter.'

'No copy will be necessary. I have a photographic memory. It's worth a lot of money to me. I shall see Kamenev within a week. He will have an accurate transcript of the letter and of my conversation with you.'

'Are you empowered to talk for Kamenev?'

'Up to a certain point, yes.'

To Kiril's amazement he quoted verbatim the passage from Kamenev's second letter:

'"From time to time ... you will receive applications for a private audience from a man named Georg Wilhelm Forster. To him you may speak freely, but commit nothing to writing. If you succeed in a conversation with the President of the United States, you should refer to him as Robert. Foolish, is it not, that to discuss the survival of the human race, we must resort to such childish tricks."'

Kiril laughed. 'That's an impressive performance. But, tell me, if you know of whom we are speaking why do I have to refer to the President as Robert?'

Georg Wilhelm Forster was delighted to explain himself. 'You might call it a mnemonic trick. No man can guard altogether against talking in his sleep, or against verbal slips when he is under questioning ... So one practises this kind of dodge. It works too. I've never been caught out yet.'

'I hope you won't be caught out this time.'

'I hope so too, Holiness. This exchange of letters may have long consequences.'

'I should like to be able to guess what they may be.'

'Robert has already pointed to them in his letter.' He opened again. '"An action of such magnitude and such risk that none of us would be allowed to attempt it."'

'The proposition contradicts itself,' said Kiril mildly. 'Both Kamenev and the President—excuse me, Robert—point to the need for such action, but each in the same breath says that he is not the man to begin it.'

'Perhaps they are looking to a third man, Holiness?'

'Who?'

'Yourself.'

'If I could promise that, my friend, believe me I should be the happiest man in the world. But as our countryman, Stalin, once remarked, "How many divisions has the Pope?"'

'It is not a question of divisions, Holiness, and you know it. It is at bottom a question of influence and moral authority. Kamenev believes that you have, or may come to have, such an authority ...' He smiled and added an afterthought of his own. 'From the little I have learned I should say that Your Holiness has a greater stature in the world than you may realize.'

Kiril considered the thought for a few moments and then delivered himself of the firm pronouncement. 'Understand something, my friend. Report it clearly to Kamenev as I have already reported it directly on the other side of the Atlantic. I know how small are our hopes of peace. I am prepared to do anything that is morally right and humanly possible to preserve it, but I will not allow myself or the Church to be used as a tool to advantage one side or the other. Do you understand that?'

'Perfectly. I have only been waiting for Your Holiness to say it. Now may I ask a question?'

'Please do.'

'If it were possible, and if it seemed desirable, would Your Holiness be prepared to go to another place than Rome? Would you be prepared to use another channel of communication than the Vatican radio and the Vatican press, and the pulpits of Catholic churches?'

'What place?'

'It is not mine to suggest it. I put the proposition as a generality.'

'Then I will answer it as a generality. If I can speak freely, and be reported honestly, I will go anywhere and do anything to help the world breathe freely for however short a time.'

'I shall report that, Holiness. I shall report it very happily. Now there is a practical matter. I understand the Maestro di Camera has a list of those who may be admitted readily to private audience with Your Holiness. I should like my name added to the list.'

'It is already there. You will be welcome at whatever time . . . Now I too have a message for Kamenev. You will tell him first that I am not bargaining, I am not pleading, I am not making any conditions at all for the free passage of talk through me. I am a realist. I know how much he is limited by what he believes and by the system to which he is subject, as I am subject to mine. This being said, tell him from me that my people suffer in Hungary and Poland and East Germany and in the Baltic. Whatever he can do to ease their burden—be it ever so small—I shall count as done to myself, and I shall remember it with gratitude and in my prayers.'

'I shall tell him,' said Georg Wilhelm Forster. 'Now may I have Your Holiness's leave to go?'

'Go with God,' said Kiril the Pontiff.

He walked with the strange little man to the gate of the garden and watched him drive away into the bright and hostile world beyond.

The Princess Maria-Rina was a doughty old general, and she had planned her nephew's campaign with more than usual care. First she had set him to rights with the Church, without which he could neither arrive at power nor begin to rule comfortably. Then she had isolated Chiara for a whole month from her American lover. She had set her down in a gay playground surrounded by young men, one at least of whom might be ardent enough to seduce her into a new attachment. Now she was ready for her next move.

Accompanied by Perosi, and with Calitri's letter tucked into her handbag, she drove to Venice, plucked Chiara off the beach, and hurried her off to lunch in a quiet restaurant on Murano. Then she added her own brusque commentary to Calitri's letter:

'. . . You see, child, all of a sudden it is very simple. Corrado has come to his senses. He has set his conscience in order and in a couple of months you will be free.'

Chiara was still shocked and delighted by the news. She was prepared to trust the whole world. 'I don't understand it. Why? What made him do it?'

The old princess dismissed the question with a wave of her hand. 'He's growing up. For a long time he was hurt and bitter. Now he has better thoughts . . . For the rest, you need not concern yourself.'

'But what if he changes his mind?'

'He won't, I promise you. Already his new depositions are in the hands of Perosi here. The final papers will be ready for presentation to the Rota immediately after the holidays. After that it's just a formality . . . As you will see from his letter, Corrado is disposed to be generous. He wants to pay you quite a large sum by way of settlement. On the understanding, of course, that you will make no further claims on him.'

'I don't want to make any claims. All I want is to be free.'

'I know, I know. And you're a sensible girl. There are, however, a couple of other matters. Perosi here will explain.'

It was all so neatly done that she was totally disarmed. She simply sat there, looking from one to the other, while Perosi explained himself with smooth formailty:

'You understand, Signora, that your husband is a public figure. I think you will agree that it would be most unfair, after this generous gesture, to expose him to comment and notoriety.'

'Of course. I wouldn't want that either.'

'Good. Then we understand each cther. Once the affair is over, then we should let it die quietly. No publicity. No word to the newspapers, no hasty action on your part.'

'What sort of action? I don't understand.'

'He means marriage, child,' said the Princess Maria-Rina gently. 'It would be most undesirable for you and for Corrado if you were to rush into a hasty union, as soon as the decree of nullity is granted.'

'Yes, I see that.'

'Which brings us to the next question,' said Perosi with elaborate care. 'Your present association with an American correspondent. His name, I believe, is George Faber.'

Chiara flushed, and was suddenly angry. 'That's my business. It doesn't concern anyone else.'

'On the contrary, my dear young lady. I hope to persuade you that it is the business of everyone. The settlement, for example, would not be payable if you were to marry Faber—or, indeed, if you were to marry anyone within six months.'

'Then I don't want the settlement.'

'I shouldn't be too hasty about that, child. It's a lot of money. Besides . . .' She reached out a skinny claw and imprisoned Chiara's hand. 'Besides, you don't want to make another mistake. You've been hurt enough already. I should hate to see you wounded again. Take time, child. Enjoy yourself. You're still young. The world's full of attractive men. Kick up your heels a while. Don't tie yourself down before you've had three looks at what's offering in the marriage market. There's another thing, too . . . Even if you did want to marry Faber there might well be certain difficulties.'

'What sort of difficulties?'

She was frightened now, and they read the fear in her eyes. Perosi pressed the advantage shrewdly. 'You are both Catholics, so naturally I presume you will want to be married in the Church.'

'Of course, but . . .'

'In that case you both come immediately into conflict with canon law. You have, if I may put it bluntly, been living in sin. It is a delicate question whether in the terms of canon law this would constitute "public and notorious concubinage.".. My own view is that it might. In this case a principle applies: that a guilty person shall not be permitted to enjoy the fruits of guilt. In canon law this is called *crimen*, and it is an invalidating impediment to marriage. It would be necessary to approach the Church for a dispensation. I have to tell you that there is no certainty that it would be granted.'

The old princess added a final rejoinder. 'You don't want this kind of complication, do you? You deserve better. One mess is enough for any lifetime . . . You do see that, don't you?'

She saw it very clearly. She saw that they had her trapped and beleaguered and that they would not let her go without a struggle. She saw something else, too. Something that ashamed and excited her at once. She wanted it this way. She wanted to be rid of an attachment which had already grown stale for her. She wanted to be free to hold hands and play love games with young Pietro Antonelli while the moon shone and the mandolins played soft music in a gondola on the Grand Canal.

The day after his encounter with Theo Respighi, George Faber drove back to Naples. His self-esteem had been badly damaged—by a man with too much honour and by another with too little. He felt shaken and sordid. He could hardly bear the sight of himself in a shaving-mirror. The image of the great correspondent was still there, but behind it was an empty man who lacked the courage even to sin boldly.

He was desperate for reassurance and the forgetfulness of loving. He tried to telephone Chiara in Venice, but each time she was out, and when she did not return his call, he was filled with sour anger. His imagination ran riot as he pictured her carefree and flirtatious, while he, for her sake, was making this drab and uncomfortable journey to the hollow centre of himself.

He had one more person to see—Alicia de Nogara, authoress of Ischia. But he had to restore himself before he could confront her. He spent a day in Naples hunting for copies of her books, and finally came up with a slim, expensive volume, *The Secret Island*. He sat in the gardens trying to read it, and then gave up, discouraged by its florid prose and its coy hints of perverted love among the maidens. In the end he skimmed through it to get enough information for a conversation piece and then gave it to a ragged urchin who would pawn it for the price of a biscuit.

He went back to the hotel and put in a call to Ruth Lewin. Her maid told him she was on vacation and was not expected back for several days. He gave up in disgust, and then, in sullen reaction, he determined to divert himself. If Chiara could play so could he. He set off for a three-day bachelor jaunt to Capri. He swam in the daytime, flirted sporadically in the evening, drank twice as much as he needed, and ended with an abortive night in bed with a German widow. More disgusted with himself than ever, he packed his bag the next morning and set out for Ischia.

The villa of Alicia de Nogara was a rambling pseudo-Moorish structure set on the eastern slope of Epomeo, with a spectacular view of terraced vineyards and blue water. The door was opened to him by a pale, flat-chested girl, dressed in a gypsy shirt and silk slacks. She led him into the garden, where the great authoress was at work in a vine arbour. The first sight of her was a shock. She was dressed like a Sibyl in filmy and flowing draperies, but her face was that of a faded girl and her blue eyes were bright with humour. She was writing with a quill pen on thick, expensive paper.

When he approached she stood up and held out a slim, cool hand to be kissed.

It was all so stylized, so theatrical in character, that he almost laughed aloud. But when he looked again into her bright, intelligent eyes, he thought better of it. He introduced himself formally, sat down in the chair she offered him, and tried to marshal his thoughts. The pale girl hovered protectively beside her patron.

Faber said awkwardly, 'I've come to see you about rather a delicate matter.'

Alicia de Nogara waved an imperious dismissal. 'Go away, Paula. You can bring us some coffee in half an hour.'

The pale one wandered away disconsolately, and the Sibyl began to question her visitor:

'You're rather upset, aren't you? I can feel it. I am very sensitive to emanations. Calm yourself first. Look at the land and the sea. Look at me if you want to. I am very calm because I have learned to float with the air as it moves. This is how one should live, this is how one should love, too. Floating on the air whichever way it blows. You have been in love, haven't you? . . . Many times, I should say. Not always happily.'

'I'm in love now,' said George Faber. 'That's why I've come to see you.'

'Now there's a strange thing! Only yesterday I was saying to Paula that although my books are not widely read they still reach the understanding heart. I think you have an understanding heart. Haven't you?'

'I hope so. Yes. I understand you know a man called Corrado Calitri.'

'Corrado? Oh yes, I know him very well. A brilliant boy. A little perverted, I'm afraid, but very brilliant. People say I'm perverted, too. You've read my books, I presume. Do you think so?'

'I'm sure you're not,' said George Faber.

'There, you see. You do have an understanding heart. Perversion is something different. Perversion is the urge to destroy the thing one loves. I want to preserve, to nurture. That's why Corrado is doomed. He can never be happy. I told him that many times . . . Before he was married, after his marriage broke up.'

'That's what I wanted to talk to you about. Calitri's marriage.'

'Of course. I knew it. That's what the emanations were telling me. You're in love with his wife.'

'How did you know?'

'I'm a woman. Not an ordinary woman. Oh no! A sapphic woman they call me, but I prefer to say a full woman, a guardian of the deep mysteries of our sex . . . So you're in love with Corrado's wife.'

'I want to marry her.'

The Sibyl leaned forward, cupping her small face in her hands and fixing him with her bright blue eyes. 'Marriage. That's usually a terrible mistake. The air, remember! One must be free—to float, to rise, to fall, to be held or to be let go. Strange that men never understand these things. I was married once, a long time ago. It was a great mistake. Sometimes I think men were born defective. They lack intuition. They were born to be slaves of their own appetite!'

'I'm afraid we were,' said George Faber with a grin. 'May I tell you what I want?'

'Please, please do.'

'I want evidence for the Holy Roman Rota. For Chiara to be free, we have to prove that Corrado Calitri entered into marriage with a defective intention. We have to prove that he expressed his defective intention to a third person before the marriage took place.' He fished in his pocket and drew out a typewritten statement which he had prepared that morning. 'That, more or less, is the thing we want. Would you be prepared to sign it?'

Alicia de Nogara picked up the paper with fastidious fingers, read it and laid it down on the table. 'How crude! How terribly crude of the Church to demand this sort of indignity. Freedom again, you see! If people fail in love, let them be free to begin again. The Church tries to close up the soul in a bottle as if it were a foetus preserved in formaldehyde . . . So very vulgar and medieval . . . Tell me, does Corrado know that you've come to me?'

'No, he doesn't. For a reason I can't understand he wants to hold on to Chiara . . . Not to live with her, of course, but to hold her like a piece of land or an apartment.'

'I know, I know. I told you he was perverse, didn't I? This is how it shows. He likes to torment people. He tried to torment me even though I wanted nothing from him. All I wanted to do was teach him how to give and return love. I thought I had succeeded, too. He seemed very happy with me. Then he went away, back to his boys, back to his little game of promises and refusals. I wonder if he's as happy now as he was with me.'

'I doubt it.'

'Do you want to hurt him?'

'No. I just want Chiara to be free and to have the chance of making her happy.'

'But if I sign this it will hurt him, won't it?'

'It will hurt his pride, probably.'

'Good! That's where he needs to be hurt. When one loves one must be humble. When you commit yourself to the air, you have to be humble. Are you humble, Faber?'

'I guess I have to be,' said Faber ruefully. 'I haven't very much pride left. Are you prepared to sign that document? I shouldn't say this, but I was prepared to pay for the evidence.'

'Pay?' She was dramatically insulted. 'My dear man, you are desperate, aren't you? In love one must never pay. One must give, give, give! Freely, and from the full heart. Tell me something. Do you think you could love me?'

He had to swallow hard to get the thought down, but he did it. He twisted his mouth into what he hoped was a smile and answered elaborately, 'It would be my good fortune if I could. I'm afraid I shouldn't deserve it.'

She reached out and patted his cheek with a cool, dry hand. 'There, there, I'm not going to seduce you, though I think you would seduce very easily. I'm not sure I should let you throw away your life in marriage, but you have to learn in your own way, I suppose . . . Very well, I'll sign it.'

She picked up the quill and subscribed the document with a flourish. 'There now. Is that all?'

'I think we should have a witness.'

'Paula!', The pale girl came hurrying to her cry. She set her signature at the foot of the paper, and George Faber folded it and put it into his pocket. The thing was done. He had soiled himself to do it, but it was done. He let them lead him through the rituals of coffee and endless, endless talk. He exerted himself to be gentle with them. He laughed at their pathetic jokes and bent like a courtier over the hand of the Sibyl to say goodbye.

As the taxi drove him down the crowded port, as he leaned against the rail of the lake steamer that took him back to Naples, he felt the document crackling and burning against his breast. *Finita la commédia!* The shabby farce was over, and he could begin to be a man again.

When he got back to Rome, he found Chiara's letter telling him that her husband had agreed to co-operate in her petition and that she had fallen in love with another man. *Finita la commédia!* He tore the paper into a hundred shreds, and then proceeded, savagely and systematically, to get himself drunk.

EXTRACT FROM THE SECRET MEMORIALS OF KIRIL I PONT. MAX.

I have had a wonderful holiday, the first in more than twenty years. I feel rested and renewed. I am comforted by a friendship which grows in depth and warmth each day. I never had a brother, and my only sister died in childhood. So my brotherhood with Jean Télémond has become very precious to me. Our lives are full of contrasts. I sit at the summit of the Church; he lies under the rigid obedience of his Order. I spent seventeen years in prison; he has had twenty years of wandering in the far corners of the earth. Yet we understand each other perfectly. We communicate swiftly and intuitively. We are both caught up in this shining hope of unity and common growth toward God, the Beginning, the Centre, and the End . . .

We have talked much these last few days in the grains of truth that underlie even the most divergent errors. For Islam God is one, and this is already a leap from paganism to the idea of a single spiritual creator. It is the beginning of a God-centred universe. Buddhism has degenerated into a series of sterile formulae, but the Buddhist code, although it makes a few moral demands, conduces to co-operation, to non-violence, and to a polite converse among many people. Communism has abrogated a personal god, but there is implicit in its thesis an idea of the brotherhood of man . . .

My immediate predecessor encouraged the growth of the Ecumenical spirit in Christendom—the exploration and the confirmation of common grounds of belief and action. Jean Télémond and I have talked much about the possibility of the Christian idea beginning to infuse the great non-Christian religions. Can we, for example, make any penetration of Islam, which is spreading so quickly through the new nations of Africa and Indonesia? A dream, perhaps, but perhaps, also, an opportunity for another bold experiment like that of the White Fathers.

The grand gesture! The action that changes the course of history! I wonder if I shall ever have the opportunity to make it . . . The gesture of a Gregory the Great, or a Pius V. Who knows? It is a question of historic circumstance and the readiness of a man to co-operate with God and in the moment . . .

Ever since the visit of Georg Wilhelm Forster, I have been trying to think myself into the minds of Kamenev and the President of the United States. It is true, I think, that all men who arrive at authority have certain attitudes in common. They are not always the right attitudes, but at least they provide a ground of understanding. The man in power begins to see more largely. If he has not been corrupted, his private passions tend to diminish with age and responsibility. He looks, if not to permanence, at least for a peaceful development of the system he has helped to create. On the other hand, he is vulnerable to the temptations of pride. On the other, he cannot fail to be humbled by the magnitude and complexity of the human problem . . . He understands the meaning of contingency and mutual dependence . . .

It is well, I think, that the Papacy has been slowly stripped of its temporal power. It gives the Church the opportunity to speak more freely, and with less suspicion of material interest, than in other ages. I must continue to build this moral authority, which has its analogies in the political influence of small nations like Sweden and Switzerland and even Israel.

I have given instructions to the Secretariat of State to encourage the visit of representatives of all nations and all faiths to the Vatican. At the lowest they constitute a useful diplomatic courtesy; at their best they may be the beginning of a fruitful friendship and understanding . . .

This week I had Cardinal Rinaldi to lunch. I like this man. I talked with him about the possible reform of the Roman Rota, and he gave me valuable information about its methods and its personalities. In his quiet fashion, he administered a reproof as well. He told me that Cardinal Leone felt that I did not repose enough trust in him. He pointed out that, for all his vigour, he was an old man who had deserved well of the Church, and that I should perhaps bestow on him a mark of favour and acknowledgement. I find it hard to like Leone; he is so very much a Roman. But I agree with Rinaldi. I have written a gentle letter to Leone thanking him for his work and asking him to wait on me as soon as I return to Rome. I have also asked for his private advice on the appointment of a new Cardinal to take the place of the Englishman, Brandon, who died two days ago. Brandon was one of those who voted against me in the conclave, and our relations were always rather formal and distant. Yet he was an apostolic man, and one always regrets deeply the passing of a labourer from the vineyard. I said a special Mass yesterday morning for the repose of his soul . . .

News from Hungary and Poland is bad. The new taxation laws have already put several more schools and seminaries out of existence. Potocki is ill in Warsaw. My information is that he will recover. But the illness is serious, and we shall have to think of appointing a new man to help him and later to take over his office as Primate of Poland. Potocki is a man of political genius and deep spiritual life. We shall not easily find another to match him . . .

Jean Télémond's first volume, *The Progress of Man*, is now ready for publication. This is the crucial part of his work, upon which all the rest depends. He is anxious to have it assessed by the Holy Office as soon as possible. For his sake I am anxious too. I have asked Cardinal Leone to appoint commissioners to scrutinize it and report to me as quickly as may be. I have suggested that these commissioners be different men from those who made the first examination. We shall then have two sets of opinions and there will be no question of a carry-over from earlier, and far less complete, works. I am glad to say that Jean is very calm about it. He seems to be well, although I notice that he tires easily and is sometimes out of breath after a small exertion. I have ordered him to submit to an examination by the Vatican physician as soon as we go back to Rome . . .

I want to keep him by me, but he is afraid of doing me a disservice. The hierarchy and the Curia are suspicious and uncomfortable about a Grey Eminence in the Vatican. Cardinal Rinaldi repeated his invitation to let

Jean work at his villa. Jean likes the idea, so I suppose I shall have to let him go. At least we shall not be far from each other, and I shall have the pleasure of his company at dinner on Sundays. Now that I have found him, I am loath to let him go . . .

I learned so much with him during our journeys through the Italian countryside. The thing that impressed me most vividly was the contrast between entrenched wealth and the grinding poverty in which so many of the people still live. This is the reason for the strength and attraction of communism in Italy. It will take a long time—longer than I have at my disposal—to redress the balance. However, I have thought of a gesture which may become a symbol of what is needed.

The Congregation of Rites has informed me that they are ready to proceed to the beatification of two new servants of God. Beatification is a long and expensive process, and the ceremonies which conclude it are also very expensive. I am informed that the total cost may well be as much as fifty thousand American dollars. It could be that I shall be accused of diminishing the splendour of liturgical life of the Church; but I have decided to reduce the ceremony to a simple formality and to devote whatever funds are available to the establishment of local works of charity. I shall take steps to see that my reasons are published as widely as possible so that people will understand that the service of the servants of God is much more important than their glorification.

Oddly enough I am reminded at this moment of the woman, Ruth Lewin, and the work which she and others like her are doing, without encouragement and without apparent spiritual help in various places in the world. I am reminded too of the saying of the Master that even a cup of water given to His name is a gift made to Him. A thousand candles in St Peter's mean nothing beside a poor man grateful to God because he is grateful to one of his fellows . . .

Wherever I turn, I find myself being drawn irresistibly to the primitive thought of the Church, and I cannot believe that I am being drawn into error. I have no private inspiration. I am in the Church and of the Church, and if my heart beats in tune with its pulse, I cannot be too far wrong. 'Judge me, O God, and distinguish my cause from that of the unholy.'

9

Summer was in decline. The first colours of autumn were showing across the land. There was a pinch in the air, and soon the cold winds would begin to blow from the steppes down along the Alpine ridges. But the Sunday crowds in the Villa Borghese were still jealous of the warmth, and they paraded themselves cheerfully among the sellers of sweetmeats and the pedlars of novelties, while their children stood gaping at the antics of Pulcinella.

Ruth Lewin was among them, playing nursemaid to a child—a tiny spastic creature with bobbing head and slobbering mouth—whom she had brought out from the slums for an airing. They were sitting on a bench, watching a fiddler with a dancing monkey while the child crammed himself with candy and bobbed a grotesque balloon in happy ignorance of his misfortune.

For all the pathos of her mission, Ruth Lewin felt calm and content. Her illness was over. She had come back from her holiday refreshed. She had made, at long last, a landfall. After the years of confusion her mind was clear. She knew what she was and what she had a right to be. It was not a conversion but an arrival. If she was not fulfilled, at least she was no longer in flight. If she was not satisfied, at least she could rest in hope of a betterment.

She was a Jew. She had inherited a race and a history. She was prepared to accept them both, not as a burden, but as an enrichment. She understood now that she had never really rejected them, but had been forced into flight from them by the circumstance of childhood. The flight was not a guilt, but an affliction, and she had survived it, as her ancestors had survived the captivities and the dispersions and the obloquy of the European ghettoes. By the simple fact of this survival, by the half-conscious act of accepting, she had earned the right to be what she wanted to be, to believe what she needed to believe to grow to whatever shape her nature dictated.

She understood something else: that joy was a gift which one accepted gratefully and should not try to pay for, any more than one tried to pay for sunlight and birdsong. One held out grateful hands to take the gift, and then held up the gift for a sharing. Payment was too gross a word to describe a disbursal like this. Flowers grew out of the eyes of the dead, but because one picked the flowers one should not carry a corpse on one's back for all the days of living. Children were born maimed and misshapen, but to deny them beauty and love by way of personal penance was a monstrous paradox. Doubt was a burden on all questing spirits, but when the doubt was resolved one should not cling to it in the luxury of self-torment.

She had no doubts now. She had entered into the Christian faith in childhood. She had made it a refuge and then launched herself out of it into terror and confusion. Now it was no longer a refuge but an ambience in which she wanted to live and to grow. Like the sunlight, the birdsong and the flower, it was free. She had no right to it but she had no cause to refuse it either. Everyone had a claim to sleep on his own pillow, hard or soft, because without sleep one died; and dying paid no debts but only cancelled them.

So, quite simply, on this Sunday morning she found herself at home.

To the traveller tossing on a windy ocean, homecoming always presented itself as a drama, a moment of revelation or of conquest. But the moment, when it came, was usually very trite. There were no banners and no trumpets. One was there, walking down a familiar street, seeing familiar faces in the doorways, wondering if the passage of time, the cavalcade of events, were not an illusion after all.

The child tugged at her arm with sticky fingers, begging to be taken to the toilet. She laughed aloud at the irony. This was the true shape of life at last—a succession of simplicities, snotty noses and soiled linen, bacon and eggs for breakfast, some laughter, some tears, and, hanging over it all, the majesty of mere existence. She took the child's hand and led him stumbling and crowing across the grass to unbutton his breeches . . .

When she reached home it was already dusk and the chill autumn was settling down on the city. She bathed and changed, and then, because her maid was out, she made her own supper, put a stack of records on the radio-player, and settled down to a comfortable evening.

Time was, not so long ago, when the prospect of a solitary night would have driven her to desperation. Now, at peace with herself, she was glad of it. She was not sufficient to herself, but life, with its small services and its occasional piquant encounters, might now be sufficient to her. She was no longer an alien. She had her domain of giving and sooner or later there might be a time of receiving too. She could commune with herself because she had discovered herself. She was one, she was real. She was Ruth Lewin, widow, Jew by birth, Christian by adoption. She was old enough to understand, and still young enough to love if love were offered. For one day and one new woman it was more than enough.

Then the bell rang, and when she opened it she found George Faber, drunk and mumbling, at the top of the stairs. His shirt was limp. His clothes were stained, his hair was in disorder, and he had not shaved for days.

It took her nearly an hour to sober him with black coffee and make sense out of his story. Ever since Chiara had left him he had been drinking steadily. He had done no work at all. His bureau was being kept open by a stringer and by the kindness of his colleagues, who filed stories for him, answered his cables, and kept him out of trouble with New York.

For a man so urbane and precise, it was a sorry downfall. For one so prominent in Rome, the tragedy could quickly develop beyond remedy. Yet George Faber seemed to have no heart left to help himself. He despised himself utterly. He poured out the story of his affronted manhood. He abandoned himself to maudlin tears. Ambition had deserted him, and he seemed to have no foothold left from which to grope his way back to dignity.

He submitted like a child when she ordered him to take a bath and then tucked him into her bed to sleep off the rest of the drink. While he slept, muttering and restless, she emptied his pockets, bundled up his soiled clothes, and then set off to his apartment to find a new suit, clean linen, and a razor. He was still sleeping when she returned, and she settled down to another vigil and a critical examination of her own role in the drama of George Faber.

It would be all too easy now to present herself as Our Lady of Succour, ready with salve and sticking-plaster to patch up his wounded pride. It would be dangerously simple to wrap up her love in a candy-box and offer it as solace for the lost one. For her own sake and for his, she must not do it. Love was less than half the answer when the pillars of a man's self-respect were shaken and the rooftrees came tumbling round his ears. Sooner or later he had to walk out of the wreckage on his own two feet, and the truest recipe of love was to let him do it.

When he came down to breakfast, haggard but tidy, she told him so, bluntly:

'This has got to stop, George—here and now! You've made a fool of yourself over a woman. You're not the first. You won't be the last. But you can't destroy yourself for Chiara or for anyone else.'

'Destroy myself!' He made a gesture of defeat. 'Don't you understand? That's what I found out! There's nothing to destroy. There's no me at all. There's just a bundle of good manners and journalist's habits . . . Chiara was shrewd enough to see it. That's why she got out.'

'For my money, Chiara is a selfish little bitch. You're lucky to be rid of her.'

He was still stubborn in self-pity. He shook his head. 'Campeggio was right. I'm too soft. One push and I fell apart.'

'Comes a time when we all fall apart, George. The real test is when we have to put ourselves together again.'

'And what do you expect me to do? Dust myself off, stick a flower in my buttonhole, and walk back into business as if nothing happened?'

'Just that, George!'

'Schmalz!' He threw the word at her in angry derision. 'Yiddisher schmalz! Straight out of Brooklyn and *Marjorie Morningstar*! Rome is laughing its head off about Chiara and me. You think I can sit up and let them throw coconuts at me just for laughs!'

'I think you must.'

'I won't do it.'

'Fine! So what's the alternative? Drink yourself silly every day? On money that other men are earning for you?'

'Why the hell should I care what I do?'

It was on the tip of her tongue to say, 'I love you', but she bit back the words and gave him a more brutal answer. 'I don't care, George! You came to me! I didn't go to you! I've cleaned you up and made you look like a man again! But if you don't want to be a man, then it's your own affair!'

'But I'm not a man, sweetheart! Chiara proved it to me. Two weeks away and she's playing kiss-me-quick on the Lido with someone else. I risked everything for her and then she put the horns on me. So I'm a man already?'

'Are you more of a man because you drink like a pig?'

She had silenced him at last, and now she began to plead with him. 'Look, George, a man's life is his own business. I'd like to make you my business, but I'm not going to unless you tell me clearly and soberly that you want it like that. I'm not going to pity you, because I can't afford it. You've made a fool of yourself. Admit it! At least you'll wear it with more dignity than the horns. You think I haven't felt the way you do? I have, and for much longer. In the end I grew up. I'm grown up now, George. It's late in the day but I'm grown up. You've got to grow up too.'

'I'm so damn lonely,' said George Faber pathetically.

'So am I. I've made the round of the bars, too, George. If I didn't have a weak stomach I'd be a lush three times over. It's no answer, believe me.'

'What is the answer?'

'A clean shirt and a flower in the buttonhole.'

'Nothing else?'

'Oh yes! But that's for afterwards. Please give it a try.'

'Will you help me?'

'How?'

'I don't quite know. Maybe—' for the first time he smiled ruefully –'maybe, let me wear you in my buttonhole.'

'If it's for pride, George. Yes.'

'What do you mean?'

'I'm half a Roman too, you know. You lose one woman, you have to find another. It's the only way to get rid of the horns.'

'I didn't mean that.'

'I know you didn't, darling; but I do. The moment you can tell yourself that I'm trying to mother you, or make myself another Chiara, then I'm no good to you. You're up and away, and on the bottle again. So, let's make me a buttonhole. Wear me to show the town that George Faber is back on the job. Is it a bargain?'

'It's a bargain ... Thanks, Ruth.'

'*Prego*, Signore.' She poured him a fresh cup of coffee and then asked him quietly, 'What else is on your mind, George?'

He hesitated a moment and then told her. 'I'm afraid of Calitri.'

'You think he knows what you did?'

'I think he could know. There was a man at Positano who threatened to tell him. If there were money in it he would have told him by now.'

'But you haven't heard from Calitri.'

'No. But he could be biding his time.'

'For what?'

'Revenge.'

'What sort of revenge?'

'I don't know. But I'm in a ticklish position. I've committed a criminal act. If Calitri wanted to, he could bring me to law.'

She answered him resolutely. 'You'll wear that too, George, if it happens.'

'I'll have to . . . Meantime I think I should tell Campeggio.'

'Is he involved in this?'

'Not openly, but he lent me money. He makes no secret of his enmity for Calitri. And Calitri could easily guess at a connection between us. As a servant of the Vatican, Campeggio is even more vulnerable than I am.'

'Then you must tell him . . . But, George . . .'

'Yes?'

'Whatever happens, remember the clean shirt and the flower in the buttonhole!'

He gave her a long searching look and then said softly, 'You do care, don't you?'

'Very much.'

'Why?'

'Ask me in a month and I'll tell you . . . Now you get yourself down to the bureau and start work . . . Leave me your key and I'll clean up your apartment. The place is like a barnyard.'

When they parted he kissed her on the cheek, and she watched him striding down the street to his first encounter with reality. It was too early to tell whether he would be able to restore his own dignity, but she had kept hers, and the knowledge was a strength. She went upstairs, dressed herself in a new frock, and half an hour later was kneeling in the confessional in the apse of St Peter's Basilica.

'He has beaten us,' said Orlando Campeggio. 'At our own game—and with nothing but profit to himself.'

'I still don't understand what made him do it,' said George Faber.

They were sitting together in the same restaurant where they had made their first conspiracy. Campeggio was drawing the same pattern on the tablecloth, and George Faber, grim and perplexed, was trying to fit the jigsaw together.

Campeggio stopped his tracing and looked up. He said evenly, 'I hear you've been out of circulation for a while.'

'I went on a bender.'

'Then you've missed the beginning of a good story. Calitri is being groomed to lead the country after the next election. The Princess Maria Poliziano is handling the campaign below stairs.'

'My God!' said George Faber. 'As simple as that.'

'As simple and as complicated. Calitri needs the favour of the Church. His return to the confessional has been discreetly publicized. The next and most obvious step is to regularize his marriage.'

'And you think he'll bring it off?'

'I'm sure he will. The Rota, like any other court, can only deal with the evidence presented to it. It can make no judgements in the internal forum of conscience.'

'The clever bastard,' said George Faber with feeling.

'As you say, a clever bastard. He's been clever with me too. My son has been promoted. He thinks the sun, moon and stars shine out of Calitri's backside.'

'I'm sorry.'

Campeggio shrugged. 'You have your own problem.'

'I'll survive it–I hope! I'm expecting Calitri to move against me at any moment. I'm trying to figure out what he may do.'

'At worst,' said Campeggio thoughtfully, 'he could have you tried on a criminal charge and then expelled from the country. Personally I don't think he'll do it. He has too much to lose if there is a public scandal over his marriage case. At best–and it's not a very good best, I admit–he could make things so uncomfortable for you that you would have to go anyway. You can't function as a correspondent if you are not on reasonable terms with the men who make the news. Also he could embarrass you with a whole lot of minor legalities.'

'Those are my thoughts too. But there is a chance that Calitri hasn't heard of my activities. Our drunken friend in Positano may have been bluffing.'

'That's true. You won't know, of course, until the verdict has been handed down from the Holy Roman Rota. Whether Calitri knows or not, he won't make any move until after the case is over.'

'So I sit pat.'

'May I ask you a question, Faber?'

'Sure.'

'Have you ever mentioned my connection with you to anybody else?'

'Well, yes. To Chiara and to another friend. Why do you ask?'

'Because in that case I'm afraid I can't sit pat. I have to make a move.'

'For God's sake! What sort of move?'

'I have to resign from the *Osservatore*. I told you I was a man of confidence at the Vatican. I could not compromise myself or my employers by continuing to work under a constant threat of exposure.'

'But there may be no exposure.'

Campeggio smiled and shook his head. 'Even so, I find that I cannot come to terms with an uneasy conscience. I am no longer a man of confidence because I can no longer trust myself. I must resign. The only question is how I shall do it . . . On the basis of full disclosure to the Pontiff, or on a plea of age and infirmity.'

'If you make a disclosure,' said George Faber, 'you ruin me more quickly than Calitri can do it. The Vatican is my beat as much as the Quirinale.'

'I know that. You have problems enough without me. So this is what I propose to do. I shall wait until after a decision on the Calitri case is handed down from the Rota. If Calitri does not move against you, then I shall go to the Holy Father and offer him my resignation, telling him simply that I am acting under doctor's orders. If, on the other hand, Calitri moves against you, then I shall make a full disclosure. That way we may both salvage a little from the wreckage.' He was silent a moment and then in a more friendly tone he added, 'I'm sorry, Faber, more sorry than I can say. You've lost your Chiara, I've lost my son. We have both lost something more important.'

'I know,' said Faber moodily. 'I should do what you're doing. Pack up quietly and head back home. But I've been here fifteen years. I hate the thought of being uprooted by a son-of-a-bitch like Calitri.'

Campeggio waved an expressive hand and quoted gently, '"*Che l'uomo il suo destin fugge di raro . . .*" It's a rare man who dodges his destiny. And you and I were born for a troubled one. Don't fight it too long. One should always save a little dignity for the exit.'

In his office at No. 5 Borgo Santo Spirito, Rudolf Semmering, Father General of the Jesuits, talked with his subject, Jean Télémond. There were letters under his hand which contained the reports of the Vatican physicians. He held them out to Télémond. 'You know what these say, Father?'

'I do.'

'Your cardiographs show that you have already suffered one and possibly two heart attacks.'

'That's right. I had a mild seizure in India the year before last, and another while I was in the Celebes last January. I understand I may expect another at any time.'

'Why didn't you write and tell me you had been so ill?'

'It seemed of small consequence. There was nothing anyone could do about it.'

'We should have given you an easier way of life.'

'I was happy in my work. I wanted to go on doing it.'

The Father General frowned and said firmly, 'It was a matter of rule and obedience, Father. You should have told me.'

'I'm sorry. I did not look at it like that. I should have known better.'

The stern features of the Father General relaxed, and he went on more mildly. 'You know what this means, Father? You're a man in the shadow of death. You may be called without warning at any time.'

'I've known that for months.'

'Are you ready for it?'

Jean Télémond said nothing and the Father General went on quietly. 'You understand, Father, that this is the essential meaning of my office—a care of the souls entrusted to me by the Society and by the Church. Rightly or wrongly I have laid heavy burdens on you. Now I want to be as much help to you as I can.'

'I am very grateful, Father,' Jean Télémond. 'I'm not sure how I should answer your question. Is any man ever truly ready for death? I doubt it. The best I can say is this: I have tried to live a logical life as a man and a priest. I have tried to develop my talents to make them serviceable to the world and to God. I have tried to be a good minister of the Word, and of the Grace of the Sacraments. I have not always succeeded, but I think my failures have been honest ones. I am not afraid to go . . . I do not think God wants any of us to fall out of His hands.'

Semmering's lined face puckered into a smile of genuine affection. 'Good. I am very happy for you, Father . . . I hope we shall have you with us a long time yet. I want to tell you that I was deeply impressed by your address at the Gregoriana. I am not sure that I can agree with all of it. There were certain propositions which troubled me and still do. But of you I am sure. Tell me something else. How firmly do you hold to what you propounded then, and in your other works.'

Télémond considered the question carefully, and then answered. 'From a scientific point of view, Father, I should explain it this way. Experiment and discovery bring one by a certain line to a certain point of arrival. Up to that point, one is scientifically certain because the discoveries have been documented and the logic has been proven by experiment . . . Beyond the arrival point, the line projects itself infinitely further. One follows it by hypothesis and by strides of speculation . . . One believes that the logic will continue to prove itself as it has done before. One cannot be certain, of course, until the logic of speculation has proved itself against the logic of discovery . . . So–again as a scientist–one has to preserve an open mind. I think I have done that . . . As a philosopher I am perhaps less well equipped, but I believe that knowledge does not contradict itself. It develops on to successive planes so that we see first as a symbol may enlarge itself on another plane into a reality which to our unfamiliar eyes is different. Again, one tried to keep the mind open to new modes of thought and knowledge . . . One understands that language is at best a limited instrument to express our expanding concepts. As a theologian I am committed to the validity of reason as an instrument for attaining to a limited knowledge of the Creator. I am committed also by an Act of Faith to the validity of divine revelation, expressed in the Deposit of Faith . . . Of one thing I am sure–as I am sure of my own existence–that there is no possible conflict between any knowledge at any plane, once the knowledge is wholly apprehended . . . I remember the old Spanish proverb, "God writes straight with crooked lines", but the final vector is an arrow which leads straight to the Almighty. This is the reason why I have tried to live fully in and with the world, and not in separation from it. The redemptive act is barren without the co-operation of man . . . but man as he is, in the world in which he lives . . .' He broke off and gave a little shrug of deprecation. 'Forgive me, Father, I didn't mean to read lectures.'

'It's a very good lecture, Father,' said Rudolf Semmering. 'But I want you to add something else to it. By your vow you are a child of obedience, an obedience of formal act, of submissive will, and humble intellect. Have you conformed the terms of your vow with the terms of your personal search?'

'I don't know,' said Jean Télémond softly. 'I am not sure that I can know until I am put to a final test. Cardinal Rinaldi expressed it very clearly when he said that this was the cross I was born to bear. I admit that often its weight oppresses me. Of this, however, I am sure, that there cannot be in the ultimate any conflict between what I seek and what I believe. I wish I could put it more clearly.'

'Is there any way in which I can help you now, Father?'

Télémond shook his head. 'I don't think so. If there were, believe me I should ask it. I think at this moment I am more afraid of this dilemma than I am of dying.'

'You do not think you have been reckless?'

'No, I do not. I have had to dare much because all exploration is a risk. But reckless? No. Confronted with the mystery of an orderly universe one cannot be anything but humble. Confronted by death as I am, one cannot be anything but truthful . . .' A new thought seemed to strike him. He paused a moment to weigh it and then said bluntly, 'There is a problem, though, in one's relations with the Church–not with the faith, you understand, but with the human body of the Church. The problem is this. There are some believers who are as ignorant of the real world as certain unbelievers are ignorant of the world of faith. "God is great and terrible," they say. But the world also is great and terrible and wonderful, and we are heretics if we ignore or deny it. We are like the old Manichees who affirm that matter is evil and the flesh is corrupt. This is not true. It is not the world which is corrupt or the flesh. It is the will of man, which is torn between God and the self. This is the whole meaning of the Fall.'

'One of the things which bothered me in your address is that you did not mention the Fall. I know it will bother the Holy Office as well.'

'I did not mention it,' said Jean Télémond stoutly, 'because I do not believe that it has any place in the phenomenal order, but only in the moral and spiritual one.'

'They will say,' persisted Rudolf Semmering, 'that you have confused the two.'

'There has never been any confusion in my mind. There may be some in my expression.'

'It is on your expression that they will judge you.'

'On that ground I am amenable to judgement.'

'You will be judged, and soon. I hope you will find patience to support the verdict.'

'I hope so too,' said Jean Télémond fervently. 'I get so very tired sometimes.'

'I am not afraid of you,' said Rudolf Semmering with a smile. 'And His Holiness speaks very warmly of you. You know he wants to keep you at the Vatican.'

'I know that. I should like to be with him. He is a great man and a loving one, but until I am tested I should not want to compromise him. Cardinal Rinaldi has invited me to work at his villa while the Holy Office is examining my work. Have I your permission to do that?'

'Of course. I want you to be as free and comfortable as possible. I think you deserve that.'

Jean Télémond's eyes were misty. He clasped his hands together to stop their trembling. 'I am very grateful, Father–to you and to the Society.'

'And we are grateful to you.' Semmering stood up, walked round his desk, and laid a friendly hand on the shoulder of his subject. 'It's a strange brotherhood, this of the faith and of the Society. We are many minds and many tempers. But we talk a common road, and we have much need of a common charity.'

Jean Télémond seemed suddenly withdrawn into a private world of his own. He said absently, 'We are living in a new world. But we do not know it. Deep ideas are fermenting in the human mass. Man for all his frailness is being subjected to monstrous tensions, political, economic, mechanical. Knowledge is reaching like a rocket toward the galaxies. I have seen machines that make calculations beyond the mind of Einstein . . . There are those who fear that we are exploding ourselves into a new chaos. I dare not contemplate it. I do not believe it. I think, I know, that this is only a time of preparation of something infinitely wonderful in God's design for His creatures. I wish–I wish so much–I could stay to see it.'

'Why wait?' said Rudolf Semmering with rare gentleness. 'When you go you will go to God. In Him and through Him you will see the fulfilment. Wait in peace, Father.'

'On the judgement?' asked Jean Télémond wryly.

'On God,' said Rudolf Semmering. 'You will not fall out of His hands.'

Immediately after his return from Castel Gandolfo, Kiril the Pontiff was caught in a press of new and varied business.

The Institute for Works of Religion had prepared its annual survey of the financial resources of the Papacy. It was a long and complex document, and Kiril had to study it with care and concentration. His reactions were mixed. On the one hand he had to commend the industry and acumen of those who had built the Papal State and the Vatican Bank into stable and solvent institutions, with operations stretching all over the world. This was the nature of their stewardship. Five Cardinals and a staff of highly competent financiers administered the temporal goods of the Church. They bought and sold in the stock markets of the world. They invested in real estate and hotels and public utilities, and on their efforts depended the stability of the Holy See as a temporal institution, whose members had to be fed, clothed, housed, and hospitalized, so that they might be free to work with reference to eternity.

But Kiril was too much an ironist not to see the disparity between the efficiency of a financial operation and the doubt that hung over so many works for the salvation of human souls. It cost money to train a priest and maintain a nursing sister. It cost money to build schools and orphanages and homes for the aged. But all the money in the world could not buy a willing spirit or fill a slothful one with the love of God.

By the time he had finished the document and the financial conferences, he had come to a resolution. His stewards had done well. He would leave them be, but he himself must concentrate all his time and all his energy on the prime function of the Church: the leading of men to a knowledge of their relationship with their Creator. A God-centred man could sit barefoot under a tree and set the world afire. A huckster with a million in gold, and scrip stacked up to the roof, would leave the planet unmourned and unremembered.

There was trouble in Spain. The younger clergy were in revolt against what they considered the archaic and obscurantist attitudes of certain senior prelates. There were two sides to the question. Pastoral authority had to be maintained, and at the same time the vivid and apostolic spirit of the younger Spaniards had to be preserved. Some of the older men had become too closely identified with the dictatorial system. The new ones, identified with the people and their hopes of reform, found themselves repressed and inhibited in their work. A violent reaction was beginning to make itself felt against the semi-secret work of Opus Dei, which was on the face of it an institute for lay action within the Spanish Church, but which many claimed was being controlled by reactionary elements in Church and State. This was the climate in which schism, and rebellion were born, yet the climate could not be reversed overnight.

After a week of discussions with his advisers, he decided on a double step; a secret letter to the Primate and the bishops of Spain, urging them to accommodate themselves with more liberality and more charity to the changing times, and an open letter to the clergy and the laity approving the good work done, but urging upon them the duty of obedience to local ordinaries. It was at best a compromise, and he knew it. But the Church was a human society as well as a divine one, and its development was the result of checks and balances, of conflicts and retreats, of disagreements and slow enlightenment.

In England there was the question of naming a new cardinal to succeeed Brandon. The appointment posed a neat alternative! A politician or a missionary? A man of stature and reputation who would uphold the dignity of the Church–and the place it had regained in the established order? Or a rugged evangelist who understood the ferment of a crowded industrial country, and the disillusion of a once imperial society, and its fading confidence in a social and humanitarian religion?

At first blush the choice was simple. Yet given the temper of the English, their historic mistrust of Rome, their odd reaction toward revivalism, it was not half as simple as it looked.

Cardinal Leone summed it up for him nearly. 'Parker in Liverpool is the true missionary bishop. His work among the labouring classes and the Irish immigrants has been quite spectacular. On the other hand he is often very outspoken, and he has been accused of being a political firebrand. I do not believe that. He is an urgent man. Perhaps too urgent for the phlegmatic English. Ellison, in Wales, is in a very good standing with the establishment. He's urbane, intelligent, and understands the art of the possible. His advantage to us is that he can prepare a situation in which more apostolic men can work with some freedom.'

'How long do we have?' asked Kiril, 'before a new appointment is necessary?'

'Two months, I should say, three at the outside, England needs a red hat.'

'If it were left to Your Eminence, whom would you choose? Parker or Ellison?'

'I should choose Ellison.'

'I'm inclined to agree with you. Let's do this. We shall defer a decision for one month. During that time I should like you to make another canvass of opinion among the Curia, and among the English hierarchy. After that we shall decide.'

Then there were the reports from Poland. Cardinal Potocki had pneumonia and was critically ill. If he died there would be two immediate problems. He was deeply loved by his people, and deeply feared by the government against whom he had held out stubbornly for sixteen years. His funeral might well be the occasion for spontaneous demonstrations, which the government could use for provocative action against the Catholic population. Equally important was the question of his successor. He had to be named and in readiness to take office immediately the old fighter died. He had to know of his appointment, yet it had to be kept secret lest the authorities moved against him, before Potocki's death. A secret emissary had to get from the Vatican to Warsaw and present the papal rescript of succession.

So one by one the countries of the world came under review, and the memory of a summer holiday faded further and further into the background. Finally, toward the end of September, came a letter from Cardinal Morand in Paris.

> ... A suggestion was made to Your Holiness's Illustrious Predecessor that a papal visit to the shrine of Our Lady of Lourdes might have a spectacular effect

upon the life of the Church in France. There were at that time several obstacles to the project–the health of the Holy Father, the war in Algeria, and the political climate in metropolitan France.

Now these obstacles do not exist. I am informed that the French government would look with great favour on a papal visit, and would be delighted to welcome your Holiness to Paris after the visit to Lourdes.

I need not say how delighted the clergy and faithful would be to have the Vicar of Christ on the soil of France after so long a time.

If Your Holiness were prepared to entertain the idea, I should like to suggest that the most appropriate time would be the feast of Our Lady of Lourdes on February 11, next year. The French government concurs heartily with this timing.

May I beg Your Holiness most humbly to consider our request, and the good which might come from it, not only for Catholic France, but for the whole world. It would make a historic occasion–the first journey of a Pope into this land for more than a century. The eyes of all the world would be focused on the person of Your Holiness and there would be for a while a public and universal pulpit available. . . .

The letter excited him. Here was the historic gesture ready to be made. After his first exit from Rome others would follow almost inevitably. In the convergent world of the twentieth century, the apostolic mission of the Pontiff might be reaffirmed in a startling style.

Immediately, and without consultation, he wrote a reply to Moran in his own hand:

... We are delighted by Your Eminence's suggestion of a visit to France in February of next year. We have no doubt that there will be certain voices in the Church raised against it, but We Ourselves are most favourably disposed. We shall discuss the matter at the earliest opportunity with Cardinal Goldoni and later with members of the Curia.

Meantime, Your Eminence may accept this letter as Our personal authority to initiate preliminary discussions with the French authorities concerned. We suggest that no public announcement be made until all the formalities are concluded.

To Your Eminence and Our Brother Bishops, to the clergy and all the people of France, we send from a full heart Our apostolic benediction.

He smiled as he sealed the letter, and sent it out for posting. Goldoni and the Curia would be full of doubts and consequential fears. They would invoke history and protocol, and logistics and political side-effects. But Kiril the Pontiff was a man elected to rule in God's name, and in the name of God he would rule. If doors were open to him he would walk through them, and not wait to be led through them by the hand like a petty princeling . . .

The idea of a peripatetic Pope had, with the passage of time, become strange in the Church. There were those who saw in it a succession of dangers–to dignity, since a man who packed his bags and went flying round the world might look too human; to authority, since he would be required to speak *ex tempore* on many subjects without study and without advice; to order and discipline, since the Vatican Court needed at all times a firm hand to hold it together; to stability, since modern air travel entailed a constant risk, and to lose one Pontiff and elect another was an expensive, not to say perilous, business. Besides, the world was full of fanatics who might affront the august personage of Christ's Vicar, and even threaten his life.

But history was not made by those who shied away from risks. Always

the Gospel had been preached by men who took death for a daily companion . . . More than all, Kiril Lakota was an opportunist with a restless
heart. If a journey were possible, he would make it, discounting all but the
profit in souls . . .

From Kamenev, holidaying by the Black Sea, came a letter delivered
by the ubiquitous Georg Wilhelm Forster. It was longer and more relaxed
than the others, and it carried the first clear expression of his thoughts on
the approaching crisis:

> . . . At least I am in private conversation with the other side of the Atlantic. I am
> more grateful than I can say for your good offices.
>
> I have been resting for a while, thinking out the programme for the coming
> year and asking myself, at the same time, where I stand at this moment of my
> public and private life. My career is an apogee. I can go no higher. I have
> perhaps five more years of full authority and activity; after that the inevitable
> decline will begin, and I must be prepared to accept it.
>
> I know I have done well for this country. I should like to do better. For this
> betterment, peace is necessary. I am prepared to go far to maintain it, yet you
> must understand that I want to go farther than I shall be permitted by the Party
> and the Praesidium.
>
> First, therefore, let me show you the position as I see it. You can trace my
> thesis on a child's map of the world. China is in a bad way. That means six
> hundred million people are in a bad way. This year's harvests have been
> dangerously light. There is real starvation in many areas. There have been
> reports, hard to confirm because of rigid censorship, that bubonic plague has
> broken out in some coastal towns. We have taken a serious view of this, and we
> have imposed a sanitary cordon at all frontier posts along our borders with
> China.
>
> Her industrial development is slow. We have deliberately made it somewhat
> slower by withdrawing many of our construction teams and experts, because we
> do not want China to grow too quickly under the present régime.
>
> The present leaders are old men. They are subject to increasing pressures
> from their juniors. If the economic crisis gets any worse, they will be forced into
> action, and they will inevitably mount military moves in the direction of South
> Korea, and Burma, and the north-east frontier of India. At the same time they
> will ask us to provide a diversionary front by renewing our pressure on Berlin
> and by pressing for a solution to the East German question, even to the point of
> armed intervention.
>
> Once these moves are made, America must set herself in battle order against
> us.
>
> Is there any remedy for this hair-trigger situation? I believe there is. But we
> must not be naïve about its efficacy. Let us get a breathing space first, so that we
> may proceed with a little more confidence to a long-term solution.
>
> The first and most obvious remedy is nuclear disarmament. We have been
> debating this for years now, and we are no nearer to agreement. I think it is still
> out of the question, because public and Party opinion can be so swiftly excited
> by the issue. I know I could not risk a decisive move, and neither can my
> opposite number. So we must discount it for a while.
>
> The second remedy might appear to be the admission of China to the United
> Nations. This again is complicated by the fiction of the two Chinas and the
> existence of a rump government-in-arms on Formosa. Again we are involved in
> a highly political situation, too easily complicated by catchwords and prepared
> attitudes.
>
> It is my view that, with some preparation and a minimum of good will, a
> remedy may be found elsewhere. If the miseries of China were fully exposed to
> the world, not as a political, but as a human spectacle, and if an offer were made

by America and the nations of the West to resume normal trade relations with the Chinese, by exporting food to her, by allowing the free passage of vital commodities, then we might at least defer the crisis. Of course, China would have to be prepared to accept the gesture—and to get her to do it is a delicate problem. We, on our part, would have to put our weight behind the Western offer, and we should have to make some kind of proposal of our own.

How far can we go? More properly, how far can I go with any hope of support from the Party and the country? I must be honest with you. I must not promise more than I can hope to fulfill.

Here I think is my limit. We would put no further pressure on Berlin, and leave the East German question in abeyance, while we reach for a less rigid form of settlement. We would discontinue nuclear tests in return for an assurance that the United States would also discontinue. We would reopen immediately—with a more practical compromise formula—the question of nuclear disarmament, and I would add my own personal authority to any effort to achieve a settlement within a reasonable time limit.

I do not know whether the Americans will find this enough, but it is the best I could assure in any negotiations. Even so, both we and the United States will need a very favourable climate to bring off a settlement. There is not too much time to prepare it.

I can almost hear you ask yourself how far you can trust me now. I cannot swear an oath, because I have nothing to swear by, but what I have written here is the truth. How I comport myself in the public view, how I behave during the negotiation, is another matter. Politics is more than half theatre, as you know. But this is the bargain I propose, and even if the Americans hedge it a little, we can do business and give the world what it desperately needs at this moment, a breathing space to measure the current value of peace against what may happen if we lose it.

I hope your health is good. Mine is fairly robust, but sometimes I am reminded sharply of the passing of the years. My son has finished his training and has now been admitted as a bomber pilot in our air force. If war comes he will be one of the first victims. This is a cold thought that haunts me while I sleep. This, I think, is what saves me from the ultimate corruption of power. What do I want for him? In olden times kings murdered their sons lest they prove rivals—and when they got lonely they could always breed other ones. It is different now. There are those who say we have simply grown softer—I like to think we are growing at least a little wiser.

I am reminded of your request to ease some of the burdens of your flock in Hungary, Poland and the Baltic areas. Here again I must be honest, and not promise more than I can perform. I cannot issue a direct command, nor can I reverse abruptly a traditional Party policy, to which, moreover, I am personally committed. However, there will be a meeting of Premiers of the fringe countries in Moscow next week. I shall put it to them as a proposal to prepare the atmosphere for what I hope will be a discussion of the Chinese question between ourselves and America.

I am hoping your Cardinal Potocki will recover. He is a danger to us, but as things are I should rather have him alive than dead. I admire him almost as much as I admire you.

One more point, perhaps the most important of them all. If we are to negotiate along the lines I have suggested, we shall need to reach a settlement before the middle of March next year. If the Chinese begin a military build-up it will be early in April. Once they start we are in real trouble.

I read a copy of your letter to the Church on education. I thought it excellent and at times moving, but we have been doing so much better than the Church for forty years. One would think that you had less to lose than we have. Forgive the irony. It is hard to lose bad habits. Help us if you can. Greetings.

Kamenev

Kiril the Pontiff sat a long time pondering over the letter. Then he went into his private chapel and knelt in prayer for nearly an hour. That same evening after supper, he summoned Goldoni from the Secretariat of State and was closeted with him until after midnight.

'You are an embarrassment to me, Mr Faber,' said Corrado Calitri gently. 'I imagine you are an embarrassment to Chiara as well. She is very young. Now that the Holy Roman Rota has pronounced her free to marry, I imagine she will quickly find a new husband. The presence of an elderly lover could make things very difficult for her.'

He was sitting in a high carved chair behind a buhl desk, slim, pale and dangerous as a medieval prince. His lips were smiling, but his eyes were cold. He waited for George Faber to say something; and when he did not answer, he went on, in the same silken tone. 'You understand, Mr Faber, that under the terms of the Concordat the decision of the Holy Roman Rota takes effect in civil law as well.'

'Yes, I understand that.'

'Legally, therefore, your attempt to suborn a witness is a criminal offence under the laws of the Republic.'

'It would be very difficult to prove subornation. No money was passed. There were no witnesses. Theo Respighi is a somewhat disreputable character.'

'Don't you think his testimony would make you look disreputable too, Mr Faber?'

'It might. But you wouldn't come out of the affair very well either.'

'I know that, Mr Faber.'

'So it's a stalemate. I can't touch you. You can't touch me.'

Calitri selected a cigarette from an alabaster box, lit it and leaned back in his chair, watching the smoke rings curl upwards toward the coffered ceiling of his office. His dark eyes were lit with malicious amusement. 'A stalemate? I rather think it is a checkmate. I have to win, you see. No government, and certainly no political party, can support a situation where a correspondent for the foreign press can determine the career of one of its ministers.'

In spite of himself Faber laughed dryly. 'Do you think that's likely to happen?'

'After what you have done, Mr Faber, anything is likely to happen. I certainly do not trust you. I doubt whether you will ever be able to trust yourself again. Hardly an edifying sight, was it? The dean of the press corps offering a bribe to a broken-down actor to pervert the law—and all because he wanted to go to bed legally with a girl! You're discredited, my friend! I have only to say a word and you will never again be received in any government office, or any of the Vatican congregations. Your name will be dropped from every guest list in Italy. You see, I've never made any pretence of what I am. People have accepted me on my own terms, just as the country will accept me again at the next election . . . So, it is checkmate. The game is over. You should pack up and go home.'

'You mean I'm expelled from the country?'

'Not quite. Expulsion is an official act of the administration. So far we are speaking . . . unofficially. I am simply advising you to leave.'

'How long do I have?'

'How long would you need to make other arrangements with your paper?'

'I don't know. A month, two months.'

Calitri smiled. 'Two months then. Sixty days from this date.' He laughed lightly. 'You will note, Mr Faber, that I am much more generous with you than you would have been with me.'

'May I go now?'

'In a moment. You interest me very much. Tell me, were you in love with Chiara?'

'Yes.'

'Were you unhappy when she left you?'

'Yes.'

'Strange,' said Calitri with sardonic humour. 'I have always thought that Chiara would make a better mistress than a wife. You were too old for her, of course. Not potent enough, perhaps. Or were you too much the Puritan? That's the answer, I think. One has to be bold in love, Faber. In whatever kind of loving one elects . . . By the way, is Campeggio a friend of yours?'

'He's a colleague,' said Faber evenly. 'Nothing more.'

'Have you ever lent him money?'

'No.'

'Borrowed from him?'

'No.'

'That's curious. A cheque in the amount of six hundred thousand lire–one thousand American dollars–was drawn by Campeggio and paid into your bank account.'

'That was a business transaction. How the hell did you know about it.'

'I'm a director of the bank, Mr Faber. I like to do my work thoroughly . . . You have two months. Why don't you take a real holiday and enjoy our lovely country? . . . You may go now.'

Sick with anger and humiliation, George Faber walked out into the thin autumn sunshine. He turned into a telephone booth and called Orlando Campeggio. Then he hailed a taxi and had himself driven to Ruth Lewin's apartment.

She fed him brandy and black coffee, and listened without comment while he rehearsed his short and ignominious interview with Corrado Calitri. When he had finished she sat silent for a moment and then asked quietly, 'What now, George? Where do you go from here?'

'Back home, I suppose. Although, after fifteen years in Rome, it's hard to think of New York as home.'

'Will you have any trouble with the paper?'

'I don't think so. They'll accept any explanation I care to give them. They'll give me a senior job in the home office.'

'So your career isn't really finished, is it?'

'Not my career. Just a way of life that I liked and wanted.'

'But it's not really the end of the world.'

He gave her an odd, searching look. 'No. But it is the end of George Faber.'

'Why?'

'Because he doesn't exist any more. He's just a name and a suit of clothes.'

'Is that the way you feel, George?'

'It's what I am, sweetheart. I knew it as soon as I sat down in Calitri's office this morning. I was nothing–a straw man. I didn't believe anything, I didn't want anything, I had nothing to fight with, I had nothing to fight for. The wonder is that I feel quite calm about it.'

'I know that calm, George,' she told him gravely. 'It's the danger signal.

The quiet time before the big storm. Next, you start hating yourself and despising yourself, and feeling empty and alone and inadequate. Then you start to run, and you keep running until you hit a brick wall, or fall over a cliff, or end up in the gutter with your head in your hands. I know. I've been there.'

'Then you mustn't be around when it happens to me.'

'It mustn't happen, George. I'm not going to let it happen.'

'Buy out, girl!' he told her with sudden harshness. 'Buy out and stay out! You've had your storms. You deserve better now. I've made a bloody fool of myself, I'm the one who has to pay.'

'No, George!' She reached out urgent hands and forced him to turn to her. 'That's the other thing I've learned. You can never pay for anything you've done, because you can't change the consequences. They go on and on. The bill keeps mounting up by compound interest until, in the end, you're crushed and bankrupt. It isn't payment we need, George. It's forgiving . . . And we have to forgive ourselves, too . . . You're a straw man, you say. So be it! You can either burn the straw man and destroy him. Or you can live with him and—who knows?—in the end you may get to like him. I've always liked him, George. In fact I've learned to love him.'

'I wish the hell I could,' said George Faber sombrely. 'I think he's a pompous, windy, gutless snob!'

'I still love him.'

'But you can't live with him for the next twenty years and then come to despise him as he despises himself.'

'He hasn't asked me to live with him yet.'

'And he's not going to ask.'

'Then I'll ask him: he's a straw man, I'm a straw woman. I don't have any pride, George. I don't have any pity, either. I'm just so damn glad to be alive . . . It's not leap year but I'm still asking you to marry me. I'm not a bad catch, as widows go. I don't have any children. I still have some looks. I do have money . . . What do you say, George?'

'I'd like to say yes but I daren't.'

'So what does that mean, George? A fight or a surrender?'

For a moment he was the old uneasy George, running his hands through his grey hair, half-mocking, half-pitying himself. Then he said soberly, 'It's the wrong thing for a man to say; but could you wait a while? Could you give me time to get into training for the fight?'

'How, George?'

He did not answer her directly, but explained himself haltingly. 'It's a thing hard to explain . . . I—I don't want to lose you . . . I don't want to lean on you too much, either. With Chiara I was trying to hold on to youth, and I didn't have enough of it left. I don't want to come to you as empty as I am now. I want to have something to give as well . . . If we could be friends for a while . . . Hold hands. Walk in the Villa Borghese. Drink and dance a little, and come back here when we're tired. With you I don't want to be what I'm not, but I'm still not sure what I am. These next two months are going to be strange. All the town will be laughing up its sleeve. I'm going to have to rake up some dignity.'

'And then, George?'

'Then maybe we can go home together. Can you give me that long?'

'It may take longer, George,' she warned him gently. 'Don't be too anxious.'

'What do you mean?'

But even when she had explained, she was not sure that he had understood.

...Today has been long and troublesome. Early this morning Orlando Campeggio, editor of the *Osservatore*, waited upon me to offer his resignation. He told me an involved and sordid story of a conspiracy to introduce suborned evidence into the marital case of Corrado Calitri, which has just been decided by the Holy Roman Rota. Campeggio told me that he himself had been a party to the conspiracy.

The attempt was unsuccessful; but I was deeply shocked by this revelation of the tangled lives of people who are old enough and educated enough to do better. I had no alternative but to accept Campeggio's resignation. I had, however, to commend his honesty, and I told him that his pension arrangements would not be disturbed. I understand very well the motives which led him to this breach of trust, but I cannot for that reason condone the act.

When Campeggio left me, I called immediately for the file on the Calitri case, and went over it carefully with an official of the Rota. There is no doubt in my mind that, on the evidence presented, the Rota acted rightly in issuing a decree of nullity. There was another side to the picture, however; Corrado Calitri, a man of power and influence in Italy, has been living for a long time in moral danger of his soul. I have little doubt that his sincerity in this case is suspect, but the Holy Roman Rota can give judgement only in the external forum. A man's soul can only be judged in the tribunal of the confessional.

So, I am brought to a curious position. As a Minister of the Republic, Corrado Calitri is not amenable to my authority. Our relationship in the temporal order is defined by treaty and limited by diplomacy. If we quarrel I may do much harm to the Church and Italy, especially as I am not an Italian. In the spiritual order, however, Calitri is subject to me. As Bishop of Rome, I am his pastor. And I am not only authorized, but obliged if I can, to intervene in the affairs of his soul. I have, therefore, asked him to wait upon me at a suitable time, and I hope that I may be able to offer him a pastoral service in the regulation of his conscience.

I have had a short but cheerful letter from Ruth Lewin. She tells me that she has finally resolved her position, and has decided to return to the practice of the Catholic faith. She was kind enough to say that she was indebted to me for the enlightenment and the courage to make the step. I know that this is only half the truth, and that I am at best an instrument for the working of the Divine Grace. I am consoled, however, that having stepped outside the rigid confines of my office, I was permitted to make contact with her and to co-operate in re-establishing her peace of soul . . .

Once more I have been brought to see vividly that the real battleground of the Church is not in politics or in diplomacy or finance or material extension. It is the secret landscape of the individual spirit. To enter into this hidden place, the pastor needs tact and understanding, and the very particular grace bestowed by the Sacrament of Holy Orders. If I am not to fail Corrado Calitri—and it is very easy to fail those who are framed differently from other men—then I must pray and consider carefully before I meet him. If I do fail, if he leaves me in enmity, then I shall have created a new problem since I shall have to deal with him in public matters for a long time.

The President of the United States has received Kamenev's letter and my commentary on it. His reply is before me as I write:

> ... On the face of it, Kamenev does seem to offer a feasible basis for a short-term solution to our problem. I think we must get a better bargain than the one he offers. He is too good a horse-trader to offer everything at once. I am not prepared to say how much more we need without submitting the project to study and taking the advice of my counsellors.
>
> However, you may tell Kamenev that I am prepared to open negotiations at this point, but that in my view they should now be initiated at diplomatic level. And he must be the one to begin them. If he is prepared to co-operate in this fashion, then, like Your Holiness, I believe we may make progress.
>
> I too am very concerned about the political climate in which these negotiations are begun. One always expects a certain amount of skirmishing and propaganda. We have to use it as much as the Russians. However, it must not be allowed to go beyond a safe limit. We shall need an atmosphere of moderation and good will, not only in our own negotiations but in our talks with members of the European bloc and with the representatives of uncommitted nations. In a deal like this there are so many limiting factors that it is difficult enough to maintain patience and restraint without calculated provocation.
>
> I agree in the main with Kamenev's estimate of the political and military situation. It is broadly confirmed by my own advisers. They agree also that if the situation still remains unsettled at the end of next March, the crisis will already be upon us.
>
> I note with lively interest the fact that Your Holiness is considering a journey to France early next February. This would be a very notable event, and I ask myself—as I ask Your Holiness—whether it might not be possible to use it to good purpose for the whole world.
>
> I understand very clearly that the Holy See cannot, and does not wish, to enter directly or indirectly into a political negotiation between the great powers. But if, on this occasion, Your Holiness could sum up the hopes of all men, for peace and a negotiated settlement of our differences, then at one stroke we might have the climate we need.
>
> I know that it will not be easy to do. The Holy See may well have to speak for those countries where she has suffered the greatest injustice, but a historic occasion calls for a historic magnanimity. I wonder whether something like this was not in Kamenev's mind when he wrote to you first. I know that it is now in mine.
>
> With all respect I should like to make a suggestion. The churches of Christendom are still, unhappily, divided. However, there have been signs for a long time of a growing desire for reunion. If it were possible to associate other Christian bodies with Your Holiness's plea for peace, then it would be an even greater advantage.
>
> I understand that a decision has not yet been made. I understand the weight and prudent reasons for the delay. I can only say that I wish and hope that Your Holiness will finally decide to go to Lourdes ...

Goldoni has seen the letter, and I know that he is torn between the excitement of the project and a prudent wish to consider all the possible consequences before a decision is made.

He suggested, diffidently, that I might care to discuss the matter with members of the Curia. I am inclined to agree with him. My authority is absolute, but common sense dictates that in so large and consequential a matter I should get the best advice available to me. I think also that I should call Cardinal Pallenberg from Germany and Morand from Paris to take part in the discussion. We have decided finally to name Archbishop Ellison, Cardinal Archbishop of Westminster. This might be a suitable occasion to call him also to Rome and offer him the red hat . . .

Jean Télémond came yesterday to have dinner with me. He looks thinner and rather tired. He tells me, however, that he is feeling well, and working steadily. He is very happy with Cardinal Rinaldi, and the two of them have become good friends. I am a little jealous of Rinaldi's good fortune, because I miss my Jean, and in all this press of business I could use a little of his wondering vision of the world. Rinaldi sent me a short note by his hand, thanking me for my kindness to Leone. I have to admit that it was not so much a kindness as a calculated gesture. However, it did not go unnoticed and I am glad.

I know that Jean is still worried about the verdict of the Holy Office on his first volume. However, it is impossible to hurry an examination like this, and I have urged him to be patient. Cardinal Leone had promised to let me have an interim opinion by the end of October. I notice that he is treating the matter with extreme moderation, and is displaying personally a careful good will toward Jean Télémond. However, he is most emphatic that we should not appoint him to any office of preaching or teaching until the conclusions of the Holy Office are known.

I cannot disagree with him, but I still wish I could learn to like him. I have a free and easy commerce with other members of the Curia, but between Leone and myself there is always a kind of inhibition and uneasiness. It is my defect as much as his. I am still resentful of his Roman rigidity . . .

Georg Wilhelm Forster has been to see me, and I have passed on to him the reply of the President of the United States. Forster is a strange little man who lives a dangerous life in apparently untroubled good humour. When I asked him about himself, he told me that his mother was a Lett and his father a Georgian. He studied in Leipzig and Moscow, and borrowed his German name for professional purposes. He is still a practising member of the Russian Orthodox Church. When I asked him how he squared his conscience with the service of a Godless state, he turned the question very neatly:

'Is not this what you are trying to do, Holiness? Serve Mother Russia in the best fashion available to you? Systems pass, but the land is always there, and we are bound to it as if by a navel cord . . . Kamenev understands me. I understand him. Neither demands too much of the other . . . And God understands us all, better than we do ourselves.'

The thought has remained with me all day, mixed up with thoughts of the coming crisis, and Jean Télémond, and the pilgrimage to Lourdes, and the strange bargain of Corrado Calitri. My own understanding stumbles often. But if God understands, then we are still in hopeful case . . . When the poet writes, the pen needs not to understand the verse. Whether the pot be whole or broken, it still stands witness to the skill of the potter . . .

10

In the last week of October, Cardinal Leone, in private audience with the Pontiff, presented the judgement of the Holy Office on Jean Télémond's book. Leone seemed embarrassed by the occasion. He took pains to explain the nature and form of the document:

'There has been a question of time, Holiness, and a question of the special circumstances of the life of Father Jean Télémond, and the private relationship which he enjoys with Your Holiness. With reference to the time factor, the Fathers of the Sacred Congregation of the Holy Office have preferred to issue an interim opinion on the work in question, rather than a formal judgement. Their opinion is brief, but it is accompanied by a commentary setting down certain propositions which are basic to the whole thesis. With respect to the person of Jean Télémond, the commissioners make a special note of the evident spirituality of the man and his submissive spirit as a son of the Church and as a regular cleric. They attach no censure to him and advise no canonical process.'

Kiril nodded and said quietly, 'I should be grateful if Your Eminence would read me this interim opinion.'

Leone looked up sharply, but the Pontiff's eyes were hooded and his scarred face was as impassive as a mask. Leone read carefully from the Latin text:

'The most Eminent and most Reverend Fathers of the Supreme Sacred Congregation of the Holy Office, acting under instructions from His Holiness, Kiril I, Supreme Pontiff, transmitted through the Secretary of the said Sacred Congregation, have made a diligent examination of a manuscript work written by the Reverend Father Jean Télémond of the Society of Jesus and entitled *The Progress of Man.* They take note of the fact that this work was submitted voluntarily and in a spirit of religious obedience by its author, and they recommend that so long as he continues in this spirit, no censure should attach to him, nor any process be instituted against him under the canons. They recognize the honest intention of the author and the contribution he has made to scientific research, particularly in the field of palaeontology. It is their opinion, however, that the above-named work presents ambiguities and even grave errors in philosophical and theological matters which offend Catholic doctrine. A full schedule of objectionable propositions is annexed to this opinion in the form of extracts from the author's work, and commentaries by the most Eminent and Reverend Fathers of the Sacred Congregation of the Holy Office. The major grounds of objection are as follows:

'1. The author's attempt to apply the terms and concepts of evolutionary theory to the fields of metaphysics and theology is improper.

'2. The concept of creative union expressed in the said work would seem to make the divine creation a completion of absolute being, rather than an effect of efficient causality. Some of the expressions used by the author lead the reader to think the believed creation to be in some manner a necessary action in contrast with the classical theological concept of creation as an act of God's perfect and absolute freedom.

'3. The concept of unity, of unifying action, strictly tied to Télémond's evolutionary theory, is more than once extended and applied even to the supernatural order. As a consequence, there seems to be attributed to Christ a third nature, neither human nor divine, but cosmic.

'4. In the author's thesis the distinction and difference between the natural and the supernatural order are not clear, and it is difficult to see how he can logically save the gratuitous nature of the supernatural order, and thus of grace.

'The most Reverend Fathers have not desired to take, letter for letter, what the author has written on these points; for otherwise they would be forced to consider some of the author's conclusions as a true and real heresy. They are very well aware of the semantic difficulties involved in expressing a new and original thought, and they wish to concede that the thought of the author may still remain in a problematic phase.

'It is, however, their considered opinion that the Reverend Father Jean Télémond be required to re-examine this work, and those later ones which may depend on it, to bring them into conformity with the traditional doctrine of the Church. In the meantime, he should be prohibited from preaching, teaching, publishing, or disseminating in any other fashion the dubious opinions noted by the Fathers of the Sacred Congregation.

'Given at Rome this twentieth day of October in the first year of the pontificate of His Holiness Kiril I, Gloriously Reigning.'

Leone finished his reading, laid the document on Kiril's desk, and waited in silence.

'Twenty years,' said Kiril softly. 'Twenty years demolished in one stroke. I wonder how he will take it.'

'I'm sorry, Holiness. There was nothing else we could do. I myself had no part in this. The commissioners were appointed at Your Holiness's direction.'

'We know that.' Kiril's address was studiously formal. 'You have our thanks, Eminence. You may carry our thanks and our appreciation also to the Reverend Fathers of the Sacred Congregation.'

'I shall do that, Holiness. Meantime, how is this news to be conveyed to Father Télémond?'

'We shall tell him ourselves. Your Eminence has our leave to go.'

The old lion stood his ground, stubborn and unafraid. 'This is a grief to Your Holiness. I know it, I wish I could share it. But neither my colleagues nor I could have returned a different verdict. Your Holiness must know that.'

'We do know it. Our grief is private to ourselves. Now we should like to be alone.'

He knew it was brutal but he could not help himself. He watched the old Cardinal walk, proud and erect, out of the chamber, and then sat down heavily at the desk, staring at the document.

They were caught now, Jean Télémond and himself. At one stride they had come together to the point of decision. For himself the issue was clear. As custodian of the Deposit of Faith, he could not accept error or even risk its dissemination. If Jean Télémond broke under the weight of judgement, he had to stand by and see him destroyed rather than permit one single deviation from the truth transmitted from Christ to His Apostles, and from the Apostles to the living Church.

For Jean Télémond, he knew, the problem was far greater. He would submit to judgement, yes. He would bend his will obediently to the Faith. But what of his intellect, that fine-tempered, far-ranging instrument that had grappled so long with a cosmic mystery? How would it bear the immense strain laid upon it? And its tenement, the weakened body with its fluttering, uncertain heart. How would it tolerate the battle soon to be waged within it?

Kiril the Pontiff bent his head on his hands and prayed an instant, desperately, for himself and the man who had become a brother to him. Then he lifted the telephone and asked to be connected with Cardinal Rinaldi at his villa.

The old man came on almost immediately.

Kiril asked him, 'Where is Father Télémond?'

'In the garden, Holiness. Do you want to talk with him?'

'No. With yourself, Eminence . . . How is he today?'

'Not too well, I think. He had a bad night. He looks tired. Is something wrong?'

'I have just had the verdict from the Holy Office.'

'Oh! . . . Good or bad?'

'Not good. They have gone as far as they can to minimize their objections, but their objections are still there.'

'Are they valid, Holiness?'

'Most of them, I think.'

'Does Your Holiness want me to tell Jean?'

'No. I should like to tell him myself. Can you put him in a car and send him to the Vatican?'

'Of course . . . I think perhaps I should prepare him a little.'

'If you can I shall be grateful.'

'How do you feel, Holiness?'

'Worried for Jean.'

'Try not to worry too much. He is better prepared than he knows.'

'I hope so. When he returns take care of him.'

'I shall, Holiness. I have a great affection for him.'

'I know. And I am grateful to Your Eminence.'

'Who delivered the verdict, Holiness?'

'Leone.'

'Was he distressed?'

'A little, I think. I have never been able to read him very well.'

'Would you like me to telephone him?'

'If you wish . . . How long will it take Jean to get here?'

'An hour, I should say.'

'Tell him to come to the Angelic Gate. I shall leave orders that he is to be brought straight to my room.'

'I shall do that, Holiness . . . Believe me, I am deeply sorry.'

When Jean Télémond came in, pale of visage but straight and soldierly, Kiril went forward to greet him with outstretched hands. When he went to kiss the ring of the Fisherman, Kiril drew him erect and led him to the chair by his desk. He said affectionately,

'I'm afraid I have bad news for you, Jean.'

'The verdict?'

'Yes.'

'I thought so. May I see it, please?'

Kiril handed the paper across the desk and watched him intently as he read it. His fine face seemed to crumple under the shock, and small beads of sweat broke out on his forehead and on his lips. When he had finished, he laid the document on the desk and looked at the Pontiff with eyes full of pain and perplexity. He said unsteadily, 'It's worse than I thought . . . They've tried to be kind, but it's very bad.'

'It's not final, Jean, you know that. Some of it seems to be a matter of semantics. For the rest there is no censure. They simply ask for a re-examination.'

Télémond seemed to shrink back into himself. His hands trembled. He shook his head. 'There isn't time . . . Twenty years' work depends on that volume. It's the keystone of the structure. Without it, the rest falls apart.'

Kiril went to him swiftly, laying his hands on his trembling shoulders. 'It isn't all wrong, Jean. They don't say that. They simply challenge certain propositions. These are the only things you have to clarify . . .'

'There isn't time . . . At night I hear the knocking on the gate. I am being summoned, Holiness, and suddenly the work is undone. What am I to do?'

'You know what you have to do, Jean. This is the moment you were afraid of. I am here with you. I am your friend–your brother. But the moment is yours.'

'You want me to submit?'

'You must, Jean, you know that.'

Through his own fingertips, Kiril could feel the struggle that racked him in body and spirit. He felt the tremor of nerve and muscle, the dampness of sweat. He smelt the odour of a man in mortal torment. Then the tremor subsided.

Slowly Jean Télémond lifted a pain-racked face. In a voice that seemed to be wrenched out of him, he said at last, 'Very well. I submit . . . What now? I submit, but I see no light. I am deaf to all the harmony I used to hear. Where has it gone? I'm lost, left . . . I submit, but where do I go?'

'Stay here with me, Jean. Let me share the darkness with you. We're friends–brothers. This is the time of gall and vinegar. Let me drink it with you.'

For a moment it seemed that he would consent. Then with a great effort he took possession of himself again. He heaved himself out of his chair and stood facing the Pontiff, ravaged, shaken, but still a whole man. 'No, Holiness! I'm grateful, but no! Everyone has to drink the gall and vinegar by himself. I should like to go now.'

'I shall come and see you tomorrow, Jean.'

'I may need more time, Holiness.'

'Will you telephone me?'

'Only when I am ready, Holiness . . . Only when I see light. Everything is dark to me now. I feel abandoned in a desert. Twenty years down the drain!'

'Not all of it, Jean. Hold to that, I beg of you. Not all of it.'

'Perhaps it doesn't matter.'

'Everything matters, Jean. The right and the wrong as well. Everything matters. Take courage.'

'Courage? You know all I have at this moment? A small pulse inside me that flickers and beats and tells me tomorrow I may be dead . . . I have said it, Holiness. I submit. Please let me go now.'

'I love you, Jean,' said Kiril the Pontiff. 'I love you as I have never loved another person in my whole life. If I could take this pain from you I would do it gladly.'

'I know it,' said Jean Télémond simply. 'I am more grateful than I can say. But even with loving, a man must die alone. And this, I have always known, would be ten times worse than dying.'

When the door closed behind him, Kiril the Pontiff slammed his fists down on the desk, and cried aloud in anger at his own impotence.

The next day and the next, and the day after, he had no word of Jean Télémond. He could only guess at what he must be suffering. For all his authority as Supreme Pastor, this was one drama, one very intimate dialogue, in which he dared not intervene.

Besides, he himself was besieged with business, from the Secretariat of State, from the Congregation for the Affairs of the Eastern Church, from the Congregation of Rites . . . Every tribunal and commission in Rome seemed to demand his attention at once. He had to drive himself through the days with a relentless discipline, and at night his desk was still piled high with papers, and his soul cried out for the refreshment of prayer and solitude.

Still he could not put Télémond out of his mind, and on the morning of the fourth day–a day taken up with private and semi-private audiences–he called Cardinal Rinaldi at the villa.

Rinaldi's report was less than comforting:

'He is suffering greatly, Holiness. There is no doubt about his submission, but I cannot begin to count what it is costing him.'

'How is his health?'

'Indifferent. I have had the doctor to him twice. His blood pressure is dangerously high, but this, of course, is the result of tension and fatigue. There is little to be done for it.'

'Is he still happy with you?'

'Happier here than anywhere else, I think. We understand each other. He is as private as he needs to be, and, strangely enough, I think the children are good for him.'

'What does he do with himself?'

'In the morning he says Mass, and then walks for a while in the country. At midday he goes to our parish church and reads his office alone. He rests after lunch, although I do not think he sleeps. In the afternoon he walks in the garden. He talks with the children when they come home. At night we play a game of chess together.'

'He's not working?'

'No. He is in deep perplexity . . . Yesterday Semmering came to see him. They talked together for a long time. Afterwards Jean seemed a little calmer.'

'Would he like me to visit him?'

Rinaldi hesitated a moment. 'I don't think so, Holiness. He has a deep affection for you. He talks of you very much with gentleness and gratitude. But he feels, I think, that he must not ask you to bend yourself, or your office, to his personal problem. He is very brave you know, very noble.'

'Does he know that I love him?'

'He knows. He has told me. But the only way he can return the love is by maintaining his own dignity. Your Holiness must understand that.'

'I do. And, Valerio . . .' It was the first time he had used the Cardinal's first name. 'I am very grateful to you.'

'And I to you, Holiness. You have given me peace and the opportunity to share my life with a great man.'

'If he gets really ill, you will call me immediately?'

'Immediately, I promise.'

'God bless you, Valerio.'

He put down the receiver and sat for a while collecting his energies for the formalities of the morning. He did not belong to himself any more. He could spend no more than a part of himself even on Jean Télémond. He belonged to God, then through God to the Church. No man's purse was deep enough to stand such a constant expense of body and spirit. Yet he had to go on spending, trusting in the Almighty for a renewal of the funds.

The audience list was on his desk. When he picked it up he saw that the first name was that of Corrado Calitri. He pressed the bell. The door of the audience chamber opened, and the Maestro di Camera led the Minister of the Republic into his presence.

When the first formalities were over, Kiril dismissed the Maestro di Camera and asked Calitri to sit down. He noted the containment of the man, the intelligent eyes, the ease with which he moved in an ambience of authority. This was one born to eminence. He had to be dealt with honestly. His pride had to be respected, his intelligence also. Kiril sat down and addressed himself quietly to his visitor:

'I am anchored to this place, my friend. I am not so free to move as others, so I have to ask you to come to see me.'

'I am honoured, Holiness,' said Calitri formally.

'I shall have to ask you to be patient with me, and not resent me too much. Later I believe you will sit on the Quirinal Hill; I shall sit here in the Vatican; and between us we shall rule Rome.'

'There is a long way to go before then, Holiness,' said Calitri with a thin smile. 'Politics is a risky business.'

'So this morning,' said Kiril gently, 'let us ignore politics. I am a priest and your bishop. I want to talk to you about yourself.'

He saw Calitri stiffen under the shock, and the swift flush that mounted to his pale cheeks. He hurried on. 'The editor of the *Osservatore Romano* resigned a few days ago. I think you know why.'

'I do.'

'I was sufficiently concerned to call for the file on your case from the Holy Roman Rota. I examined it very carefully. I have to tell you that the record of the proceedings is completely in order, and that the decree of nullity handed down was fully justified by the evidence.'

Calitri's relief was evident. 'I'm glad to hear that, Holiness. I did a great wrong in attempting marriage. I'm not very proud of myself, but I'm glad to see justice done at last.'

Kiril the Pontiff said evenly, 'There was something else in the record which interested me more than the legal process. It was the evidence of a deep spiritual dilemma in your own soul.' Calitri opened his mouth to speak, but the Pontiff stayed him with an uplifted hand. 'No, please! Let me finish. I did not ask you here to accuse you. You are my son in Christ, I want to help you. You have a special and very difficult problem. I should like to help you to solve it.'

Calitri flushed again and then gave an ironic shrug. 'We are what we are, Holiness . . . We have to make the best terms we can with life. The record shows, I think, that I have tried to improve the terms.'

'But the problem is still there, is it not?'

'Yes. One tries to make substitutions, sublimations. Some of them work, some of them don't. Not all of us are ready for a life-long crucifixion, Holiness. Perhaps we should be but we are not.' He gave a small, dry chuckle. 'Just as well, perhaps; otherwise you might find half the world in monasteries, and the other half jumping off a cliff.'

To his surprise Kiril acknowledged the irony with a smile of good humour. 'Strange as it may sound, I don't disagree with you. Somehow or other, we all have to come to terms with ourselves as we are, and with the world as it is. I have never believed that we have to do it by destroying ourselves . . . Or, even more importantly, by destroying others. May I ask you a question, my son?'

'I may not be able to answer it, Holiness.'

'This problem of yours. This thing that drives you. How do you define it for yourself?'

To his surprise Calitri did not balk the question. He answered it bluntly. 'I defined it a long time ago, Holiness. It is a question of love. There are many varieties of love and–I am not ashamed to say it–I am susceptible to, and capable of, one special variety.' He hurried on urgently. 'Some people love children, others find them little monsters. We don't blame them, we accept them for what they are! Most men can love women–but even then not all women. I am drawn to men. Why should I be ashamed of that?'

'You should not be ashamed,' said Kiril the Pontiff. 'Only when your love becomes destructive–as it has done in the past, as it may do with Campeggio's son. A man who is promiscuous is not a true lover. He is too centred upon himself. He has a long way yet to grow to maturity. Do you understand what I am trying to say?'

'I understand it. I understand also that one does not arrive at maturity in one leap. I think I am beginning to arrive there.'

'Sincerely?'

'Which of us is wholly sincere with himself, Holiness? That too takes a lifetime of practice. Let us say that perhaps I am beginning to be sincere. But politics is not the best training ground, nor is the world.'

'Are you angry with me, my friend?' asked Kiril the Pontiff with a smile.

'No, Holiness. I am not angry. But you must not expect me to surrender to you like a schoolgirl at first confession.'

'I don't expect that, but sooner or later you will have to surrender. Not to me, but to God.'

'That too takes time.'

'Which of us can promise himself time? Is your span so certain? Or mine?'

Calitri was silent.

'Will you think about what I have said?'

'I will think about it.'

'And not resent me?'

'I will try not to resent you, Holiness.'

'Thank you. Before you go I should like to tell you that here, in this place three nights ago, I stood and suffered with a man who is as dear to me as life.

I love him. I love him in the spirit and in the flesh. I am not ashamed of it because love is the noblest emotion of humankind . . . Do you ever read the New Testament?'

'I haven't read it for a long time.'

'Then you should read the description of the Last Supper, where John the Apostle sat on the right hand of the Master, and leaned his head on His breast so that all the others looked and wondered and said, "See how he loves Him."' He stood up and said briskly, 'You are a busy man. I have taken up too much of your time. Please forgive me.'

Calitri too stood up and felt himself dwarfed by the tall, commanding figure of the Pontiff. He said, not without humour, 'Your Holiness took a great risk calling me here.'

'This is a risky office,' said Kiril evenly. 'But very few people understand it–besides, your own risk is much greater. Don't, I beg of you, underrate it.'

He pressed the bell and handed his visitor back into the practised hands of the Maestro di Camera.

When Corrado Calitri walked out of the bronze gate and into the pale sunshine of St Peter's Square, the Princess Maria-Rina was waiting for him in the car. She questioned him shrewdly and eagerly. 'Well, boy, how did it go? No problems, I hope? You got along well together? Did he talk about the verdict? About politics? This sort of thing is most important, you know. You are going to live with this man for a long time.'

'For Christ's sake, Aunt,' said Corrado Calitri irritably. 'Will you shut up and let me think!'

At eleven o'clock the same evening, the telephone rang in Kiril's private apartment. Cardinal Rinaldi was on the line. He was in deep distress. Jean Télémond had suffered a heart attack, and the doctors expected another at any moment. There was no hope for his life. Rinaldi had already administered the last rites and summoned the Father General of the Jesuits. Kiril slammed down the phone and ordered his car to be ready in five minutes with an escort of Italian police.

As he dressed hurriedly for the road, childish, simple prayers leapt to his lips. It must not be. It could not be. God must be kinder to Jean Télémond, who had risked so much for so long. 'Please, please hold him a little longer! Hold him at least till I get there and can set him at peace. I love him! I need him! Don't take him so abruptly!'

As the big car roared out through the night-time city, with the Vatican pennant fluttering and the police sirens clearing the traffic, Kiril the Pontiff closed his eyes and fingered the beads of his rosary, concentrating all the resources of his spirit in a single petition for the life and the soul of Jean Télémond.

He offered himself as a hostage–a victim, if necessary–in his place. And even as he prayed, he wrestled with the guilty resentment that, thus incontinently, the man he loved should be snatched away from him. The darkness that Jean Télémond had endured seemed now to come down on him, so that even while he wrenched his will into submission, his heart cried out bitterly for a stay of judgement.

But when Rinaldi met him at the door of the villa, grey-faced and shaken, he knew that his petition had been refused. Jean Télémond, the restless traveller, was already embarked on his last voyage.

'He's sinking, Holiness,' said Valerio Rinaldi. 'The doctor's with him. He will not last the night.'

He led the Pontiff into the antique room where the doctor stood, with the Father General of the Jesuits, looking down on Télémond, and the candles burned for a last light to the departing spirit. Télémond lay, slack and unconscious, his hands at rest on the white coverlet, his face shrunken, his eyes closed deep in their sockets.

Kiril knelt by the bedside and tried to summon him back into consciousness. 'Jean! Can you hear me? It's I, Kiril. I came as soon as I could. I'm here with you, holding your hand. Jean, my brother, please speak to me if you can!'

There was no sign from Jean Télémond. His hands were still slack, his eyelids closed against the light of the candles. From his cyanosed lips there issued only the shallow, rattling breath of the dying.

Kiril the Pontiff leaned his head on the breast of his friend and wept as he had not wept since his nights of madness in the bunker. Rinaldi and Semmering stood watching him, moved, but helpless, and Semmering, unconscious of the trick of memory, whispered the Gospel words, 'See how he loved Him.'

Then when the weeping had spent itself, Rinaldi laid his old hand on the sacred shoulder of the Pontiff and summoned him gently. 'Let him go, Holiness! He is at peace. It is the best we can wish him. Let him go!'

Early the next morning, Cardinal Leone presented himself unannounced in the papal apartment. He was kept waiting for twenty minutes and then was shown into the Pontiff's study. Kiril was sitting behind his desk, lean, withdrawn, weary of mouth and eye after the night-long vigil. His manner was strained and distant. It seemed an effort for him to speak.

'We had asked to be left alone. Is there something special we can do for Your Eminence?'

Leone's craggy face tightened at the snub, but he controlled himself and said quietly, 'I came to offer my sympathy to Your Holiness, on the death of Father Télémond. I heard the news from my friend Rinaldi. I thought Your Holiness would like to know that I offered a Mass this morning for the repose of his soul.'

Kiril's eyes softened a little, but he still held to the formality of speech. 'We are grateful to Your Eminence. This is a great personal loss to us.'

'I feel guilty about it,' said Leone. 'As if in some way I were responsible for his death.'

'You have no cause to feel that, Eminence. Father Télémond had been ailing for some time, and the Holy Office verdict was a shock to him. But neither you nor the Eminent Fathers could have acted differently. You should dismiss the matter from your mind.'

'I cannot dismiss it, Holiness,' said Leone in his strong fashion. 'I have a confession to make.'

'Then you should make it to your confessor.'

Leone shook his white mane and lifted his old head in answer to the challenge. 'You are a priest, Holiness. I am a soul in distress. I elect to make my confession to you. Do you refuse me?'

For a moment it seemed as if the Pontiff would explode into anger. Then slowly his taut features relaxed, and his mouth turned upwards into a tired smile. 'You have me there, Eminence. What is your confession?'

'I was jealous of Jean Télémond, Holiness. I did what was right, but my intention was not right while I did it.'

Kiril the Pontiff looked at the old man with puzzled eyes. 'Why were you jealous of him?'

'Because of you, Holiness. Because I need but could not have what you gave him at a first meeting—intimacy, trust, affection, a place in your private counsels. I am an old man. I have served the Church a long time. I felt I had deserved better. I was wrong. None of us deserves anything, but the promised wage for a worker in the vineyard . . . I'm sorry. Now will Your Holiness absolve me?'

As the Pontiff moved toward him, he went down stiffly on his knees and bent his white head under the words of absolution. When they were finished he asked, 'And the penance, Holiness?'

'Tomorrow you will say a Mass for one who has lost a friend, and is still only half resigned to God's will.'

'I will do that.'

Kiril's strong hands reached down and drew him to his feet, so that they stood facing each other, priest and penitent, Pope and Cardinal, caught in the momentary wonder of understanding.

'I too have sinned, Eminence,' said Kiril. 'I kept you at a distance from me because I could not tolerate your opposition in my projects. I was at fault with Jean Télémond, too, I think, because I clung to him too strongly; and when the moment came to let him go into the hands of God, I could not do it without bitterness. I am empty today, and very troubled. I am glad you came.'

'May I tell you something, Holiness?'

'Of course.'

'I have seen three men sit in this room, you are the last I shall see. Each of them came in his turn to the moment where you stand now—the moment of solitude. I have to tell you that there is no remedy for it, and no escape. You cannot retire from this place as Rinaldi has done, as I hope you will let me do very soon. You are here until the day you die. The longer you live, the more lonely you will become. You will use this man and that for the work of the Church, but when the work is done, or when the man has proved unequal to it, then you will let him go and find another. You want love. You need it as I do, even though I am old. You may have it for a while, but then you will lose it because a noble man cannot commit himself to an unequal affection. And a gross man will not satisfy you. Like it or not, you are condemned to a solitary pilgrimage, from the day of your election until the day of your death. This is a Calvary, Holiness, and you have just begun the climb. Only God can walk with you all the way, because He took on flesh to make the same climb Himself . . . I wish I could tell you differently. I cannot.'

'I know it,' said Kiril sombrely. 'I know it in the marrow of my bones. I think I have shrunk from it every day since my election. When Jean Télémond died last night a part of me died with him.'

'If we die to ourselves,' said the old lion, 'in the end we come to live in God. But it is a long, slow dying. Believe me, I know! You are a young man. You have yet to learn what it is to be old.' He paused a moment, recovering himself, and then asked, 'Now that we are at one, Holiness, may I ask you a favour?'

'What is it, Eminence?'

'I should like you to let me retire, like Rinaldi.'

Kiril the Pontiff pondered on it for a moment and then shook his head. 'No. I cannot let you go yet.'

'You ask a great deal, Holiness.'

'I hope you will be generous with me. You were not made to rusticate or wither away in a convent garden . . . There are lions abroad in the streets and we need lions to fight them. Stay with me a while longer.'

'I can only stay in trust, Holiness.'

'In trust, I promise you.'

'You must not flatter me, Holiness.'

'I do not flatter you, Eminence,' said Kiril gravely. 'You have much courage. I want to borrow it for a while . . . Just now, you see, I am very much afraid.'

The fear was tangible, familiar, and mightily threatening. It was the same which he had endured in the hands of Kamenev and he had been brought to it by the same process: months of self-questioning; recurrent crises of pain; sudden and spectacular revelations of the complexities of existence, beside which the simple propositions of faith seemed pitifully inadequate.

If the pressure was kept on long enough, the delicate mechanism of reflection and decision seized up like an overdriven motor. All the processes of the personality seemed to fall into syncope so that one was left confused and irresolute–even grateful to be swayed by a stronger will.

Every day during these first months of his pontificate, he had been forced to question his motives and his capacities. He had been forced to measure his private convictions against the accumulated experience of the bureaucracy and the hierarchy. He felt like a man pushing a stone uphill only to have it roll back upon him at every third step.

Then, just when the progress seemed easier, he had been faced with a deep and long-hidden weakness in himself: the need for love that had driven him to cling so urgently to the friendship of Jean Télémond that his detachment as a religious man had been almost wholly destroyed. The foundations of his confidence had been weakened still further by his indulgence of resentment against Leone. It was not he who had made the first step to reconciliation, but the old Cardinal. It was not he who had helped Jean Télémond to the conformity in which he needed to die, but Rinaldi and Rudolf Semmering.

If he had failed so dismally in these simple relationships, how could he trust himself and his convictions under the complex demands of leadership in the universal Church?

So, even after seventeen years of endurance for the faith, everything was called in question again, and he saw how easy it would be to shift the burden of action. He had only to relax, to let the system of the Church take over. He did not have to decide anything. He had simply to propose and suggest, and work according to the opinions tendered to him by the Secretariat of State, by the Sacred Congregations, and by all the administrative bodies, little and great, within the Church.

It was a legitimate method of government. It was a safe one, too. It rested itself firmly upon the collective wisdom of the Church and could be justified as an act of humility on the part of a leader who had found himself wanting. It would preserve the integrity of the Church, and the dignity of his office, against the consequences of his own incapacity. Yet, deep inside him–deep as the roots of life itself–was the conviction that the work to which he had been called was far other. He had to show forth in himself the faculty for renewal which was one of the marks of the living Church. The problem now was that he could no longer reason out the conviction. The fear was now that he was living an illusion of self-love, and self-deception, and destructive pride.

Daily the evidence was mounting up against him. The question of his visit to France and of his involvement in the political discussion of the nations was already being canvassed among the Cardinals and Primates of the Church. Daily their opinions were being brought to his desk and he was troubled by the extent to which they differed from his own.

Cardinal Carlin wrote from New York: 'So far the President of the United States has professed himself happy with what Your Holiness has done to assist the opening of negotiations with the Soviet Union. However, now that the talks have begun at diplomatic level, there is a fear that the Holy See may try to colour them by using its influence in the European bloc of nations, whose interests diverge at certain important points from those of America. Under this aspect, Your Holiness's proposed visit to France may wear a far different look from that which is intended.'

From Archbishop Ellison, who had not yet received the red hat, came the cool comment: 'Your Holiness must be aware that the republic of France was the bitterest opponent of the participation of Britain in the European community of nations. If Your Holiness goes to France, inevitably you will be invited to Belgium and to Germany as well. It might seem to many Englishmen that France is trying to use the Holy See, as she used her before, to strengthen her own position in Europe at the cost of ours.'

Platino, the 'Red Pope', had another point of view. 'I am convinced, as is Your Holiness, that sooner or later the Vicar of Christ must take advantage of modern travel to present himself in person to the churches throughout the world. I ask myself, however, whether the first gesture should not be one which is free from historic association. Might it not be better to plan much further ahead for a visit, say, to South America or to the Philippines, so that the missionary work of the Church would receive an impetus which it so badly needs at this moment? . . .'

From Poland, where Potocki was dying and where his successor had already been secretly named, came a warning even more blunt. It was delivered by word of mouth from the emissary who had carried the papal appointment to the new incumbent:

'There is a feeling strongly expressed that Kamenev, who is known as a subtle and ruthless politician, may be trying to create a situation in which the Holy See can be named as a co-operator with the Kremlin. The effect of this among Catholics behind the Iron Curtain could well be disastrous . . .'

On the other hand, there was Kamenev's last letter, which, if it meant anything at all, meant a startling change in the rigid Marxist thought, and a deeper change working in the man himself. Man was not a static animal. Society was not static, nor the Church either. Whether in the sense of Jean Télémond or in another, they were evolving, shedding historic accretions, developing new attitudes and new potentials, groping consciously or instinctively toward the promise of more light and fuller life. They all needed time—time and the leaven of divinity working in the human lump. Every moment saved was a deferment of chaos. Every hint of good was an evidence of God's fervent in His own creation.

... So, thanks to your good offices, we are enabled to begin at diplomatic level a negotiation with the United States which has at least some hope of success. There will be rough words and hard bargaining, but time is running out and of this at least we are all convinced.

I am interested in your plan for a visit to France in the first part of February. I agree–though the Party would have my head if they heard it–that you may do much toward preparing a suitable climate for our discussions.

I shall be more than interested to read what you will say. Inevitably you must discuss the question of rights and duties between nations. How will you treat the rights of Russia, where you have suffered so much and whence your Church has been extirpated? How will you treat the rights of China, where your bishops and priests are in prison?

Forgive me. I am an incurable joker, but this time the joke is against myself. If any man could convince me that there is a God, you, Kiril Lakota, would be the one to do it. But for me there is still an empty heaven and I must plot and plan, and lie and bargain, and close my eyes on terror and violence, so that my son and a million other sons may grow and breed without a canker in the guts or a monster in the cradle because of atomic radiation.

The irony is that all I do may be proved a folly and a precipitant for what I am trying to avoid. You are more fortunate. You believe you rest in the providence of God. Sometimes I wish–how very much I wish–that I could believe with you. But a man carries his destiny written on the palm of his hand, and mine is written differently from yours. I am often ashamed of what I did to you–I should like to prove to you that you have some reason to be proud of what you have done for me. If we have peace for only a year, you will have earned a great part of it.·

Think of me gently sometimes.

Yours, Kamenev

They were all separate voices. Yet in their diverse accents they expressed a common hope that man, living under the shadow of the mushroom cloud, might yet survive in peace to fulfil a divine plan in his regard.

He had to listen to them all. He might hope that in the end the conflict of their opinions would resolve itself into a harmony. Yet, for all his fears he knew that this hope was an illusion.

He could not, without a grim risk, step outside the field of action set down for him by divine commission. But inside that field of action he was supreme. The government was upon his shoulders and upon no other's. In the end he must decide . . . Yet knowing his own infirmities he shrank away from the decision.

Only two things were guaranteed to him by divine promise–that standing in the shoes of the Fisherman he would not err in doctrine and that, whatever folly he might commit, the Church would survive . . . In all else he was left to his own devices. He might augment the Church, gloriously, or inflict upon it a terrible diminishment. And this was the prospect that terrified him.

He was free to act but he had no promise of the consequences of his action. He was ordered to pray, but he had to pray in darkness and could not demand to know the form in which the answer might come . . .

He was still wrestling with the dilemma when the Father General of the Jesuits telephoned and requested an audience with him. He had, he said, a mass of business to discuss with the Pontiff, but this could wait until the day set for normal audiences. This time he wanted to convey to the Holy Father the substance of his last talk with Jean Télémond.

'When I went to see him, Holiness, I found him in deep confusion. I have never known a man so shocked. It took me a long time to calm him. But of this I am convinced. The submission he had made to Your Holiness was firm and true, and when he died he was at peace . . .'

'I am glad to hear it, Father. I knew what he was suffering. I wanted so much to share it, but he felt he had to withdraw from me.'

'He did not withdraw, Holiness,' said Semmering earnestly. 'The thought in his mind was that he had to carry his own cross and work out his own salvation. He gave me a message for you.'

'What message?'

'He said that he did not believe he could have made this final and necessary Act of Faith without you. He said that when the moment came it presented itself to him as the greatest risk of his life. A risk of his integrity and of reason itself. It was almost—and I use his own words—as if he might be launching himself into insanity. He said that the only thing that gave him courage to make the leap was that Your Holiness had already made it before him, and that you had not shirked a single risk of speculation or of authority . . . I wish I could convey to Your Holiness the intensity with which he expressed himself.' He gave a grim, restrained smile. 'I have learned to be very sceptical, Holiness, of displays of fervour and religious emotion, but I am convinced that in this struggle of Father Télémond I was witnessing the very real battle of a soul with itself and with the powers of darkness. I felt myself ennobled by the victory.'

Kiril was moved. 'I am grateful, Father, that you have told me. I am myself facing a crisis. I am sure Jean'would have understood it. I hope he is interceding for me now with the Almighty.'

'I am sure he is, Holiness. In a way his death was a kind of martyrdom. He met it very bravely . . .' He hesitated a moment and then continued, 'There is another thing, Holiness. Before he died Father Télémond told me that you had promised that his work would not be lost or suppressed. This was, of course, before the Holy Office issued its opinion. All Father Télémond's manuscripts have now come into my possession. I should like an indication of how Your Holiness would prefer us to deal with them.'

Kiril nodded thoughtfully. 'I've been thinking of that too. I have to agree with the option of the Holy Office that Jean's opinions require re-examination. Speaking privately, I believe that there is much of value in them. It would be my thought to submit them to new study, and possibly to publish them later with annotation and commentary. I should think the Society of Jesus admirably equipped to carry out this work.'

'We should be happy to undertake it, Holiness.'

'Good. Now I should like to ask you a question . . . You are a theologian and a religious superior. How far was Jean Télémond justified in taking the risks he did?'

'I have thought about that a long time, Holiness,' said Rudolf Semmering. 'It is a question I have had to ask myself many times, not only with Father Télémond, but with many other brilliant men inside the Society.'

'And your conclusion, Father?'

'If a man is centred upon himself, the smallest risk is too great for him, because both success and failure can destroy him. If he is centred upon God, then no risk is too great because success is already guaranteed—the successful union of Creator and creature beside which everything else is meaningless.'

'I agree with you, Father,' said Kiril the Pontiff. 'But you ignore one risk—the one which I am facing now—that at any moment up to the moment of death man can separate himself from God. Even I who am His Vicar.'

'What do you want me to say, Holiness?' asked Rudolf Semmering. 'I have to admit it. From the day we begin to reason until the day we die, we are at risk of damnation. All of us. This is the price of existence. Your Holiness has to pay it like the rest of us. I could judge Jean Télémond because he was my subject. But you I cannot judge, Holiness . . .'

'Then pray, Father—and have all your brethren pray—for the Pope on a tightrope.'

The meeting of the Roman Curia, which Kiril had called to discuss the international situation and his proposed visit to France, was set down for the first week in November. It was preceded by a week of private discussions in which each of the Cardinals was invited to explore with the Pontiff his private opinions.

He did not attempt to sway them, but only to expose to them his thinking and to give them the confidence which they deserved as his counsellors. They were still divided. There were the few who agreed, the many who doubted, those who were openly hostile. His own fears were no less, and he still hoped that when the Curia came together in assembly, they would find a common voice to counsel him.

To assist them in their deliberations he had called Cardinal Morand from Paris, Pallenberg from Germany, Ellison from London, Charles Corbet Carlin from New York. Cardinal Ragambwe was there by accident because he had flown from Africa to confer with the Congregation of Rites on the new liturgical proposals.

The place of their meeting was to be the Sistine Chapel. He had chosen it because it was luminous with memories of his own election and all the others which had taken place there. He himself spent the night of the vigil in prayer, hoping to prepare himself to interpret his thoughts to the Curia and to receive from them some clear and concerted expression of the mind of the Church.

He was no longer confused, but he was still afraid, knowing how much might hang upon the outcome. The proposition which Semmering had presented to him was devastatingly simple—that a man centred in God had nothing to fear. But he was still troubled by the knowledge that he had been all too easily separated from this centre and led astray into egotism. It was not the enormity of the act that troubled him, but the knowledge that the small lapses might be symptomatic of greater and undiscovered weaknesses in himself.

So, when the Cardinal Camerlengo led him into the Chapel and he knelt to intone the invocation to the Holy Spirit, he found himself praying with a vivid intensity that the moment would not find him wanting. When the prayer was done, he stood to address the Cardinals:

'We have called you here, our brethren and our counsellors, to share with you a moment of decision in the life of the Church. You are all aware that in the spring of next year there may well be a political crisis which will bring the world closer to war than it has been since 1939. We want to show you the shape of the crisis. We want to show you also certain proposals that have been made to us which may help to minimize it.

'We are not so naïve as to believe that anything we may do in the material order will effectively change the dangerous military and political situation which exists today. The temporal domain of the Holy See has been reduced to a small plot of ground in Rome, and we believe that this is a good thing because we shall not be tempted to use man-made instruments of intervention, when we should be using those provided us by God Himself.

'We do believe, however, and believe with firmest faith, that it is our commission to change the course of history by establishing the kingdom of Christ in the hearts of men, so that they may establish for themselves a temporal order based firmly upon truth, justice, charity, and the moral law.

'This is our charge from Christ. We cannot abrogate it. We must not shrink from a single one of its consequences. We dare not neglect any, even the most dangerous, opportunity to fulfil it.

'First let us show you the shape of the crisis.'

With swift, decisive strokes he sketched it for them—the world embattled as it looked to one man sitting on a pinnacle with the nations spread below, and the atomic threat hanging above. None of them disagreed with him. How could they? Each from his own vantage point had seen the same situation.

He read them Kamenev's letters and those from the President of the United States. He read them his own commentaries and his own assessment of the characters and the dispositions of both men. Then he went on:

'It may seem to you, my brethren, that in the intervention we have already made, there is a great element of risk. We admit it. It is clearly defined even in the letters from Kamenev and the President of the United States. We as Supreme Pontiff recognize the risk, but we had to accept it or let slip out of our hands a possible opportunity to serve the cause of peace in this dangerous time.

'We are aware, as each of you is aware, that we cannot count wholly on the sincerity or the protestations of friendship of any man who holds public office, even if he be a member of the Church. Such men are always subject to the pressure of influence, and opinion, and the actions of others over whom they have no control. But so long as a light of hope flickers, we must try to keep it alight and shield it from the harsh winds of circumstance.

'We have always believed, as a matter of private conviction, that our connection with the Premier of Russia, which dates back seventeen years to the time of our first imprisonment for the faith, had in it an element of Divine Providence which might one day be used by God for Kamenev's good or ours, or for the good of the world. In spite of all risks and doubts this is still our conviction.

'You are all aware that we have received an invitation from the Cardinal Archbishop of Paris to visit the shrine of Our Lady of Lourdes on her feast day, February 11 next year. An invitation has also been added from the government of France to make a State visit to Paris afterwards. We do not have to tell you the risks of one kind or another which such an historic step would entail. Nevertheless, we are disposed to make it. Immediately we do so other invitations will no doubt be issued, to visit other countries of the world. We should be disposed to accept these also as time and circumstances permitted. We are still young enough, thank God, and transport is now swift enough to permit us to do so without too great or too disastrous an interruption to the work of the Holy See.

'We have said we are disposed to do it. Before making a final decision, we are anxious to have your opinion as our brothers and counsellors. We point out that if we decide to make the visit an immense amount of work will have to be done in a short time to prepare the public mind and to secure, so far as is possible, a friendly attitude from our brethren of other communions in Christendom. We do not wish to make a barren spectacle of our office. We do not want to raise historic animosities. We wish to go forth in charity to show ourselves as a pastor and to proclaim the brotherhood of all men, without exception of nation, race or creed, in the Fatherhood of one God.

'If we do decide to go out thus into the world–this new world which is so different from the old–then we do not wish to insist on niceties of protocol and ceremony. These are affairs of court, and if we are a prince by protocol, we are still a priest and a pastor by the anointing and the laying-on of hands.

'What more can we say to you? These first months of our pontificate have been full of labour and full of problems. We have learned much more than we should ever have believed possible, about the nature of our office, the problems of our Holy Mother Church and Her constant battle to make Her human body a fit vessel for the Divine Life which infuses Her. We have made mistakes. We shall no doubt make many others, but we ask you, our brethren in the pastoral office, to forgive us and pray for us. Last week we suffered a grievous personal loss by the death of our dear friend, Father Jean Télémond of the Society of Jesus. We beg you to pray for him, and we beg you to pray for us also, who stand on this stormy eminence between God and man.

'The question is before you, dear brethren. Shall we go out from Rome and travel like the first Apostles to confront the twentieth century, or shall we stay at home here in Rome and let our brother bishops take care of their own vineyards in their own fashion? Shall we let the world look after its own affairs, or shall we, a Supreme Pontiff, risk our worldly dignity to step down into the market-place and proclaim the Unknown God . . .?

'*Quid vobis videtur?* How does it seem to you?'

He sat down on the throne prepared for him and waited. Silence hung over the assembly like a cloud. He saw the old men looking one at the other, as if they were exchanging a thought that they had already discussed in private. Then slowly, Cardinal Leone, senior among the seniors of the Church, stood up and confronted the assembly:

'. . . I will not rehearse for you, brethren, the hundred and one reasons for or against this project. His Holiness knows them as well as we. I will not recount the risks because they are as vividly present in the mind of the Pontiff as they are in ours. There are those among us–and I say frankly that I am one of them–who have grave doubts about the wisdom of a papal visit to France or anywhere else, for that matter. There are others, I know, who see such a visit as a gesture both timely and efficacious. Who is right and who is wrong? Only God can decide the outcome, and history pass a verdict on it. I do not think that any of us here would wish to increase the burden of His Holiness by attempting to sway him this way or that.

'The position is very simple. The authority of the Holy Father is supreme in the matter. Now or later he must decide on what is to be done. Whether our votes are for or against, *he* must decide . . .'

For a brief moment he stood doughty and challenging and then flung the last words down like a gage in front of the Curia:

'*Placetne fratres?* What you say, my brothers? Does that please you or not?'

There was a moment of hesitation and then one after the other the red caps came off, and the murmur of assent ran round the assembly:

'*Placet* . . . It pleases us. We are agreed.'

This was something Kiril had not expected. It was more than a formality. It was a vote of confidence. It was a gesture, prepared by Leone and the Curia to affirm their loyalty and to comfort him in his trial.

It was more yet—an irony like the handful of flax burned under his nose before they crowned him, so that he would always remember his mortality. It was a committal of the Church, not to him, but to the Holy Spirit who, even in spite of him, would keep Her whole and alive until Judgement Day.

Now everything that he had inherited, everything that he had secretly demanded in his office, was in his hands: authority, dignity, freedom of decision, the power to loose and bind . . . And he had to begin paying for it . . . So there was nothing to do but say the ritual words of dismissal, and let his counsellors go.

One by one the Cardinals came and knelt before him and kissed his ring in token of fealty. One by one they left. And when the door closed upon the last of them, he rose from his throne and knelt on the altar step before the tabernacle.

Above him was the towering splendour of Michelangelo's 'Judgement'. In front of him was the small golden door, behind which dwelt the Hidden God. The weight of the Cross was on his shoulders. The long Calvary was about to begin. He was left, as he would be left henceforward for all the days of his life.

EXTRACT FROM THE SECRET MEMORIALS OF KIRIL I PONT. MAX.

. . . I am calm now because the moment of decision has come and passed, and I cannot rescind the choice I have made. But the calm is at best a truce: uncertain, embattled, dangerous to him who rests in it too confidently.

The next day or the next, the clash of arms will begin again: the battle of myself with myself, of man with his ambient world—and with his God, whose call to love is always and most strangely a call to bloody conflict.

The mystery of evil is the deepest one of all. It is the mystery of the primal creative act, when God called into existence the human soul, made in His own image, and presented it with the terrifying choice, to centre itself upon itself, or to centre itself upon Him without whom it could not subsist at all . . . The mystery renews itself daily in me, as it does in every man born of woman.

Where do I go? Where do I turn? I am called like Moses to the mountain-tip to intercede for my people. I cannot go down until they carry me down dead. I cannot go up until God elects to call me to Himself. The most I can expect of my brothers in the Church is that they will hold up my arms when I grow weary of this lifelong intercession . . . And here is the shape of another mystery: that I who am called to spend so much find myself so poor in the things that are of God . . .

'Forgive us our trespasses as we forgive those who trespass against us. And lead us not into temptation but deliver us from evil. Amen.'